Andy Adams

The Log of the Cowboy and Other Trail Tales – 5 Western Novels in One Volume

e-artnow 2019

Andy Adams

The Log of the Cowboy and Other Trail Tales – 5 Western Novels in One Volume

Exciting Life-Narratives and Adventure Tales of Brave Texas Cowboys

e-artnow, 2019
Contact: info@e-artnow.org

ISBN 978-80-273-3288-5

Contents

The Log of a Cowboy: A Narrative of the Old Trail Days	15
CHAPTER I UP THE TRAIL	17
CHAPTER II RECEIVING	20
CHAPTER III THE START	26
CHAPTER IV THE ATASCOSA	30
CHAPTER V A DRY DRIVE	35
CHAPTER VI A REMINISCENT NIGHT	40
CHAPTER VII THE COLORADO	45
CHAPTER VIII ON THE BRAZOS AND WICHITA	51
CHAPTER IX DOAN'S CROSSING	57
CHAPTER X "NO MAN'S LAND"	62
CHAPTER XI A BOGGY FORD	69
CHAPTER XII THE NORTH FORK	75
CHAPTER XIII DODGE	79
CHAPTER XIV SLAUGHTER'S BRIDGE	86
CHAPTER XV THE BEAVER	93
CHAPTER XVI THE REPUBLICAN	96
CHAPTER XVII OGALALLA	102
CHAPTER XVIII THE NORTH PLATTE	108
CHAPTER XIX FORTY ISLANDS FORD	113
CHAPTER XX A MOONLIGHT DRIVE	119
CHAPTER XXI THE YELLOWSTONE	125
CHAPTER XXII OUR LAST CAMP-FIRE	132
CHAPTER XXIII DELIVERY	137
CHAPTER XXIV BACK TO TEXAS	143
A Texas Matchmaker	147
CHAPTER I LANCE LOVELACE	148
CHAPTER II SHEPHERD'S FERRY	152
CHAPTER III LAS PALOMAS	158
CHAPTER IV CHRISTMAS	164
CHAPTER V A PIGEON HUNT	169
CHAPTER VI SPRING OF '76	176
CHAPTER VII SAN JACINTO DAY	182
CHAPTER VIII A CAT HUNT ON THE FRIO	188
CHAPTER IX THE ROSE AND ITS THORN	192
CHAPTER X AFTERMATH	196
CHAPTER XI A TURKEY BAKE	202
CHAPTER XII SUMMER OF '77	206

CHAPTER XIII HIDE HUNTING	213
CHAPTER XIV A TWO YEARS' DROUTH	219
CHAPTER XV IN COMMEMORATION	226
CHAPTER XVI MATCHMAKING	231
CHAPTER XVII WINTER AT LAS PALOMAS	237
CHAPTER XVIII AN INDIAN SCARE	242
CHAPTER XIX HORSE BRANDS	247
CHAPTER XX SHADOWS	252
CHAPTER XXI INTERLOCUTORY PROCEEDINGS	258
CHAPTER XXII SUNSET	264
The Outlet	269
PREFACE	270
CHAPTER I OPENING THE CAMPAIGN	272
CHAPTER II ORGANIZING THE FORCES	276
CHAPTER III RECEIVING AT LOS LOBOS	282
CHAPTER IV MINGLING WITH THE EXODUS	288
CHAPTER V RED RIVER STATION	294
CHAPTER VI CAMP SUPPLY	299
CHAPTER VII WHEN GREEK MEETS GREEK	304
CHAPTER VIII EN PASSANT	309
CHAPTER IX AT SHERIFF'S CREEK	315
CHAPTER X A FAMILY REUNION	320
CHAPTER XI ALL IN THE DAY'S WORK	325
CHAPTER XII MARSHALING THE FORCES	329
CHAPTER XIII JUSTICE IN THE SADDLE	333
CHAPTER XIV TURNING THE TABLES	338
CHAPTER XV TOLLESTON BUTTS IN	342
CHAPTER XVI CROSSING THE NIOBRARA	347
CHAPTER XVII WATER-BOUND	352
CHAPTER XVIII THE LITTLE MISSOURI	358
CHAPTER XIX IN QUARANTINE	363
CHAPTER XX ON THE JUST AND THE UNJUST	369
CHAPTER XXI FORT BUFORD	374
CHAPTER XXII A SOLDIER'S HONOR	380
CHAPTER XXIII KANGAROOED	385
CHAPTER XXIV THE WINTER OF OUR DISCONTENT	390
Reed Anthony, Cowman: An Autobiography	395
CHAPTER I IN RETROSPECT	396
CHAPTER II MY APPRENTICESHIP	401
CHAPTER III A SECOND TRIP TO FORT SUMNER	407

CHAPTER IV A FATAL TRIP	412
CHAPTER V SUMMER OF '68	417
CHAPTER VI SOWING WILD OATS	422
CHAPTER VII "THE ANGEL"	428
CHAPTER VIII THE "LAZY L"	433
CHAPTER IX THE SCHOOL OF EXPERIENCE	438
CHAPTER X THE PANIC OF '73	443
CHAPTER XI A PROSPEROUS YEAR	448
CHAPTER XII CLEAR FORK AND SHENANDOAH	454
CHAPTER XIII THE CENTENNIAL YEAR	459
CHAPTER XIV ESTABLISHING A NEW RANCH	465
CHAPTER XV HARVEST HOME	470
CHAPTER XVI AN ACTIVE SUMMER	476
CHAPTER XVII FORESHADOWS	482
CHAPTER XVIII THE BEGINNING OF THE BOOM	488
CHAPTER XIX THE CHEYENNE AND ARAPAHOE CATTLE COMPANY	494
CHAPTER XX HOLDING THE FORT	499
CHAPTER XXI THE FRUITS OF CONSPIRACY	504
CHAPTER XXII IN CONCLUSION	510
The Wells Brothers: The Young Cattle Kings	517
CHAPTER I WAIFS OF THE PLAIN	518
CHAPTER II THE HOSPITAL ON THE BEAVER	523
CHAPTER III THE BOTTOM RUNG	528
CHAPTER IV THE BROTHERS CLAIM A RANGE	533
CHAPTER V A FALL OF CRUMBS	538
CHAPTER VI SUNSHINE AND SHADOW	542
CHAPTER VII ALL IN THE DAY'S WORK	547
CHAPTER VIII THE LINES OF INTRENCHMENT	551
CHAPTER IX A WINTRY CRUCIBLE	556
CHAPTER X GOOD FIGHTING	561
CHAPTER XI HOLDING THE FORT	566
CHAPTER XII A WINTER DRIFT	571
CHAPTER XIII A WELCOME GUEST	576
CHAPTER XIV AN ILL WIND	580
CHAPTER XV WATER! WATER!	585
CHAPTER XVI A PROTECTED CREDIT	590
CHAPTER XVII "THE WAGON"	595
CHAPTER XVIII AN OPEN WINTER	599
CHAPTER XIX AN INDIAN SCARE	604
CHAPTER XX HARVEST ON THE RANGE	608

CHAPTER XXI LIVING IN THE SADDLE	614
CHAPTER XXII INDEPENDENCE	619

The Log of a Cowboy: A Narrative of the Old Trail Days

"Our cattle also shall go with us." — *Exodus* iv. 26.

CHAPTER I
UP THE TRAIL

Just why my father moved, at the close of the civil war, from Georgia to Texas, is to this good hour a mystery to me. While we did not exactly belong to the poor whites, we classed with them in poverty, being renters; but I am inclined to think my parents were intellectually superior to that common type of the South. Both were foreign born, my mother being Scotch and my father a north of Ireland man, — as I remember him, now, impulsive, hasty in action, and slow to confess a fault. It was his impulsiveness that led him to volunteer and serve four years in the Confederate army, — trying years to my mother, with a brood of seven children to feed, garb, and house. The war brought me my initiation as a cowboy, of which I have now, after the long lapse of years, the greater portion of which were spent with cattle, a distinct recollection. Sherman's army, in its march to the sea, passed through our county, devastating that section for miles in its passing.

Foraging parties scoured the country on either side of its path. My mother had warning in time and set her house in order. Our work stock consisted of two yoke of oxen, while our cattle numbered three cows, and for saving them from the foragers credit must be given to my mother's generalship. There was a wild canebrake, in which the cattle fed, several hundred acres in extent, about a mile from our little farm, and it was necessary to bell them in order to locate them when wanted. But the cows were in the habit of coming up to be milked, and a soldier can hear a bell as well as any one. I was a lad of eight at the time, and while my two older brothers worked our few fields, I was sent into the canebrake to herd the cattle. We had removed the bells from the oxen and cows, but one ox was belled after darkness each evening, to be unbelled again at daybreak. I always carried the bell with me, stuffed with grass, in order to have it at hand when wanted.

During the first few days of the raid, a number of mounted foraging parties passed our house, but its poverty was all too apparent, and nothing was molested. Several of these parties were driving herds of cattle and work stock of every description, while by day and by night gins and plantation houses were being given to the flames. Our one-roomed log cabin was spared, due to the ingenious tale told by my mother as to the whereabouts of my father; and yet she taught her children to fear God and tell the truth. My vigil was trying to one of my years, for the days seemed like weeks, but the importance of hiding our cattle was thoroughly impressed upon my mind. Food was secretly brought to me, and under cover of darkness, my mother and eldest brother would come and milk the cows, when we would all return home together. Then, before daybreak, we would be in the cane listening for the first tinkle, to find the cattle and remove the bell. And my day's work commenced anew.

Only once did I come near betraying my trust. About the middle of the third day I grew very hungry, and as the cattle were lying down, I crept to the edge of the canebrake to see if my dinner was not forthcoming. Soldiers were in sight, which explained everything. Concealed in the rank cane I stood and watched them. Suddenly a squad of five or six turned a point of the brake and rode within fifty feet of me. I stood like a stone statue, my concealment being perfect. After they had passed, I took a step forward, the better to watch them as they rode away, when the grass dropped out of the bell and it clattered. A red-whiskered soldier heard the tinkle, and wheeling his horse, rode back. I grasped the clapper and lay flat on the ground, my heart beating like a trip-hammer. He rode within twenty feet of me, peering into the thicket of cane, and not seeing anything unusual, turned and galloped away after his companions. Then the lesson, taught me by my mother, of being "faithful over a few things," flashed through my mind, and though our cattle were spared to us, I felt very guilty.

Another vivid recollection of those boyhood days in Georgia was the return of my father from the army. The news of Lee's surrender had reached us, and all of us watched for his coming. Though he was long delayed, when at last he did come riding home on a swallow-marked brown mule, he was a conquering hero to us children. We had never owned a horse, and he assured us that the animal was his own, and by turns set us on the tired mule's back. He explained to mother and us children how, though he was an infantryman, he came into possession of the animal. Now, however, with my mature years and knowledge of brands, I regret to state that the mule had not been condemned and was in the "U.S." brand. A story which Priest, "The Rebel," once told me throws some light on the matter; he asserted that all good soldiers would steal. "Can you take the city of St. Louis?" was asked of General Price. "I don't know as I can take it," replied the general to his consulting superiors, "but if you will give me Louisiana troops, I'll agree to steal it."

Though my father had lost nothing by the war, he was impatient to go to a new country. Many of his former comrades were going to Texas, and, as our worldly possessions were movable, to Texas we started. Our four oxen were yoked to the wagon, in which our few household effects were loaded and in which mother and the smaller children rode, and with the cows, dogs, and elder boys bringing up the rear, our caravan started, my father riding the mule and driving the oxen. It was an entire summer's trip, full of incident, privation, and hardship. The stock fared well, but several times we were compelled to halt and secure work in order to supply our limited larder. Through certain sections, however, fish and game were abundant. I remember the enthusiasm we all felt when we reached the Sabine River, and for the first time viewed the promised land. It was at a ferry, and the sluggish river was deep. When my father informed the ferryman that he had no money with which to pay the ferriage, the latter turned on him remarking, sarcastically: "What, no money? My dear sir, it certainly can't make much difference to a man which side of the river he's on, when he has no money."

Nothing daunted by this rebuff, my father argued the point at some length, when the ferryman relented so far as to inform him that ten miles higher up, the river was fordable. We arrived at the ford the next day. My father rode across and back, testing the stage of the water and the river's bottom before driving the wagon in. Then taking one of the older boys behind him on the mule in order to lighten the wagon, he drove the oxen into the river. Near the middle the water was deep enough to reach the wagon box, but with shoutings and a free application of the gad, we hurried through in safety. One of the wheel oxen, a black steer which we called "Pop-eye," could be ridden, and I straddled him in fording, laving my sunburned feet in the cool water. The cows were driven over next, the dogs swimming, and at last, bag and baggage, we were in Texas.

We reached the Colorado River early in the fall, where we stopped and picked cotton for several months, making quite a bit of money, and near Christmas reached our final destination on the San Antonio River, where we took up land and built a house. That was a happy home; the country was new and supplied our simple wants; we had milk and honey, and, though the fig tree was absent, along the river grew endless quantities of mustang grapes. At that time the San Antonio valley was principally a cattle country, and as the boys of our family grew old enough the fascination of a horse and saddle was too strong to be resisted. My two older brothers went first, but my father and mother made strenuous efforts to keep me at home, and did so until I was sixteen. I suppose it is natural for every country boy to be fascinated with some other occupation than the one to which he is bred. In my early teens, I always thought I should like either to drive six horses to a stage or clerk in a store, and if I could have attained either of those lofty heights, at that age, I would have asked no more. So my father, rather than see me follow in the footsteps of my older brothers, secured me a situation in a village store some twenty miles distant. The storekeeper was a fellow countryman of my father — from the same county in Ireland, in fact — and I was duly elated on getting away from home to the life of the village.

But my elation was short-lived. I was to receive no wages for the first six months. My father counseled the merchant to work me hard, and, if possible, cure me of the "foolish notion," as he termed it. The storekeeper cured me. The first week I was with him he kept me in a back warehouse shelling corn. The second week started out no better. I was given a shovel and put on the street to work out the poll-tax, not only of the merchant but of two other clerks in the store. Here was two weeks' work in sight, but the third morning I took breakfast at home. My mercantile career had ended, and forthwith I took to the range as a preacher's son takes to vice. By the time I was twenty there was no better cow-hand in the entire country. I could, besides, speak Spanish and play the fiddle, and thought nothing of riding thirty miles to a dance. The vagabond temperament of the range I easily assimilated.

Christmas in the South is always a season of festivity, and the magnet of mother and home yearly drew us to the family hearthstone. There we brothers met and exchanged stories of our experiences. But one year both my brothers brought home a new experience. They had been up the trail, and the wondrous stories they told about the northern country set my blood on fire. Until then I thought I had had adventures, but mine paled into insignificance beside theirs. The following summer, my eldest brother, Robert, himself was to boss a herd up the trail, and I pleaded with him to give me a berth, but he refused me, saying: "No, Tommy; the trail is one place where a foreman can have no favorites. Hardship and privation must be met, and the men must throw themselves equally into the collar. I don't doubt but you're a good hand; still the fact that you're my brother might cause other boys to think I would favor you. A trail outfit has to work as a unit, and dissensions would be ruinous." I had seen favoritism shown on ranches, and understood his position to be right. Still I felt that I must make that trip if it were possible. Finally Robert, seeing that I was overanxious to go, came to me and said: "I've been thinking that if I recommended you to Jim Flood, my old foreman, he might take you with him next year. He is to have a herd that will take five months from start to delivery, and that will be the chance of your life. I'll see him next week and make a strong talk for you."

True to his word, he bespoke me a job with Flood the next time he met him, and a week later a letter from Flood reached me, terse and pointed, engaging my services as a trail hand for the coming summer. The outfit would pass near our home on its way to receive the cattle which were to make up the trail herd. Time and place were appointed where I was to meet them in the middle of March, and I felt as if I were made. I remember my mother and sisters twitted me about the swagger that came into my walk, after the receipt of Flood's letter, and even asserted that I sat my horse as straight as a poker. Possibly! but wasn't I going up the trail with Jim Flood, the boss foreman of Don Lovell, the cowman and drover?

Our little ranch was near Cibollo Ford on the river, and as the outfit passed down the country, they crossed at that ford and picked me up. Flood was not with them, which was a disappointment to me, "Quince" Forrest acting as *segundo* at the time. They had four mules to the "chuck" wagon under Barney McCann as cook, while the *remuda*, under Billy Honeyman as horse wrangler, numbered a hundred and forty-two, ten horses to the man, with two extra for the foreman. Then, for the first time, I learned that we were going down to the mouth of the Rio Grande to receive the herd from across the river in Old Mexico; and that they were contracted for delivery on the Blackfoot Indian Reservation in the northwest corner of Montana. Lovell had several contracts with the Indian Department of the government that year, and had been granted the privilege of bringing in, free of duty, any cattle to be used in filling Indian contracts.

My worst trouble was getting away from home on the morning of starting. Mother and my sisters, of course, shed a few tears; but my father, stern and unbending in his manner, gave me his benediction in these words: "Thomas Moore, you're the third son to leave our roof, but your father's blessing goes with you. I left my own home beyond the sea before I was your age." And as they all stood at the gate, I climbed into my saddle and rode away, with a lump in my throat which left me speechless to reply.

CHAPTER II
RECEIVING

It was a nice ten days' trip from the San Antonio to the Rio Grande River. We made twenty-five to thirty miles a day, giving the saddle horses all the advantage of grazing on the way. Rather than hobble, Forrest night-herded them, using five guards, two men to the watch of two hours each. "As I have little hope of ever rising to the dignity of foreman," said our *segundo*, while arranging the guards, "I'll take this occasion to show you varmints what an iron will I possess. With the amount of help I have, I don't propose to even catch a night horse; and I'll give the cook orders to bring me a cup of coffee and a cigarette before I arise in the morning. I've been up the trail before and realize that this authority is short-lived, so I propose to make the most of it while it lasts. Now you all know your places, and see you don't incur your foreman's displeasure."

The outfit reached Brownsville on March 25th, where we picked up Flood and Lovell, and dropping down the river about six miles below Fort Brown, went into camp at a cattle ford known as Paso Ganado. The Rio Grande was two hundred yards wide at this point, and at its then stage was almost swimming from bank to bank. It had very little current, and when winds were favorable the tide from the Gulf ran in above the ford. Flood had spent the past two weeks across the river, receiving and road-branding the herd, so when the cattle should reach the river on the Mexican side we were in honor bound to accept everything bearing the "circle dot" the left hip. The contract called for a thousand she cattle, three and four years of age, and two thousand four and five year old beeves, estimated as sufficient to fill a million-pound beef contract. For fear of losses on the trail, our foreman had accepted fifty extra head of each class, and our herd at starting would number thirty-one hundred head. They were coming up from ranches in the interior, and we expected to cross them the first favorable day after their arrival. A number of different rancheros had turned in cattle in making up the herd, and Flood reported them in good, strong condition.

Lovell and Flood were a good team of cowmen. The former, as a youth, had carried a musket in the ranks of the Union army, and at the end of that struggle, cast his fortune with Texas, where others had seen nothing but the desolation of war, Lovell saw opportunities of business, and had yearly forged ahead as a drover and beef contractor. He was well calculated to manage the cattle business, but was irritable and inclined to borrow trouble, therefore unqualified personally to oversee the actual management of a cow herd. In repose, Don Lovell was slow, almost dull, but in an emergency was astonishingly quick-witted and alert. He never insisted on temperance among his men, and though usually of a placid temperament, when out of tobacco — Lord!

Jim Flood, on the other hand, was in a hundred respects the antithesis of his employer. Born to the soil of Texas, he knew nothing but cattle, but he knew them thoroughly. Yet in their calling, the pair were a harmonious unit. He never crossed a bridge till he reached it, was indulgent with his men, and would overlook any fault, so long as they rendered faithful service. Priest told me this incident: Flood had hired a man at Red River the year before, when a self-appointed guardian present called Flood to one side and said, — "Don't you know that that man you've just hired is the worst drunkard in this country?"

"No, I didn't know it," replied Flood, "but I'm glad to hear he is. I don't want to ruin an innocent man, and a trail outfit is not supposed to have any morals. Just so the herd don't count out shy on the day of delivery, I don't mind how many drinks the outfit takes."

The next morning after going into camp, the first thing was the allotment of our mounts for the trip. Flood had the first pick, and cut twelve bays and browns. His preference for solid colors, though they were not the largest in the *remuda*, showed his practical sense of horses. When it came the boys' turn to cut, we were only allowed to cut one at a time by turns, even casting lots for first choice. We had ridden the horses enough to have a fair idea as to their merits, and every lad was his own judge. There were, as it happened, only three pinto horses in the entire saddle stock, and these three were the last left of the entire bunch. Now a little boy or girl, and many an older person, thinks that a spotted horse is the real thing, but practical cattle men know that this freak of color in range-bred horses is the result of in-and-in breeding, with consequent physical and mental deterioration. It was my good fortune that morning to get a good mount of horses, — three sorrels, two grays, two coyotes, a black, a brown, and a *grulla*. The black was my second pick, and though the color is not a hardy one, his "bread-basket" indicated that he could carry food for a long ride, and ought to be a good swimmer. My judgment of him was confirmed throughout the trip, as I used him for my night horse and when we had swimming rivers to ford. I gave this black the name of "Nigger Boy."

For the trip each man was expected to furnish his own accoutrements. In saddles, we had the ordinary Texas make, the housings of which covered our mounts from withers to hips, and would weigh from thirty to forty pounds, bedecked with the latest in the way of trimmings and trappings.

Our bridles were in keeping with the saddles, the reins as long as plough lines, while the bit was frequently ornamental and costly. The indispensable slicker, a greatcoat of oiled canvas, was ever at hand, securely tied to our cantle strings. Spurs were a matter of taste. If a rider carried a quirt, he usually dispensed with spurs, though, when used, those with large, dull rowels were the make commonly chosen. In the matter of leggings, not over half our outfit had any, as a trail herd always kept in the open, and except for night herding they were too warm in summer. Our craft never used a cattle whip, but if emergency required, the loose end of a rope served instead, and was more humane.

Either Flood or Lovell went into town every afternoon with some of the boys, expecting to hear from the cattle. On one trip they took along the wagon, laying in a month's supplies. The rest of us amused ourselves in various ways. One afternoon when the tide was in, we tried our swimming horses in the river, stripping to our underclothing, and, with nothing but a bridle on our horses, plunged into tidewater. My Nigger Boy swam from bank to bank like a duck. On the return I slid off behind, and taking his tail, let him tow me to our own side, where he arrived snorting like a tugboat.

One evening, on their return from Brownsville, Flood brought word that the herd would camp that night within fifteen miles of the river. At daybreak Lovell and the foreman, with "Fox" Quarternight and myself, started to meet the herd. The nearest ferry was at Brownsville, and it was eleven o'clock when we reached the cattle. Flood had dispensed with an interpreter and had taken Quarternight and me along to do the interpreting. The cattle were well shed and in good flesh for such an early season of the year, and in receiving, our foreman had been careful and had accepted only such as had strength for a long voyage. They were the long-legged, long-horned Southern cattle, pale-colored as a rule, possessed the running powers of a deer, and in an ordinary walk could travel with a horse. They had about thirty vaqueros under a corporal driving the herd, and the cattle were strung out in regular trailing manner. We rode with them until the noon hour, when, with the understanding that they were to bring the herd to Paso Ganado by ten o'clock the following day, we rode for Matamoros. Lovell had other herds to start on the trail that year, and was very anxious to cross the cattle the following day, so as to get the weekly steamer — the only mode of travel — which left Point Isabel for Galveston on the first of April.

The next morning was bright and clear, with an east wind, which insured a flood tide in the river. On first sighting the herd that morning, we made ready to cross them as soon as they reached the river. The wagon was moved up within a hundred yards of the ford, and a substantial corral of ropes was stretched. Then the entire saddle stock was driven in, so as to be at hand in case a hasty change of mounts was required. By this time Honeyman knew the horses of each man's mount, so all we had to do was to sing out our horse, and Billy would have a rope on one and have him at hand before you could unsaddle a tired one. On account of our linguistic accomplishments, Quarternight and I were to be sent across the river to put the cattle in and otherwise assume control. On the Mexican side there was a single string of high brush fence on the lower side of the ford, commencing well out in the water and running back about two hundred yards, thus giving us a half chute in forcing the cattle to take swimming water. This ford had been in use for years in crossing cattle, but I believe this was the first herd ever crossed that was intended for the trail, or for beyond the bounds of Texas.

When the herd was within a mile of the river, Fox and I shed our saddles, boots, and surplus clothing and started to meet it. The water was chilly, but we struck it with a shout, and with the cheers of our outfit behind us, swam like smugglers. A swimming horse needs freedom, and we scarcely touched the reins, but with one hand buried in a mane hold, and giving gentle slaps on the neck with the other, we guided our horses for the other shore. I was proving out my black, Fox had a gray of equal barrel displacement, — both good swimmers; and on reaching the Mexican shore, we dismounted and allowed them to roll in the warm sand.

Flood had given us general instructions, and we halted the herd about half a mile from the river. The Mexican corporal was only too glad to have us assume charge, and assured us that he and his outfit were ours to command. I at once proclaimed Fox Quarternight, whose years and experience outranked mine, the *gringo* corporal for the day, at which the vaqueros smiled, but I noticed they never used the word. On Fox's suggestion the Mexican corporal brought up his wagon and corralled his horses as we had done, when his cook, to our delight, invited all to have coffee before starting. That cook won our everlasting regards, for his coffee was delicious. We praised it highly, whereupon the corporal ordered the cook to have it at hand for the men in the intervals between crossing the different bunches of cattle. A March day on the Rio Grande with wet clothing is not summer, and the vaqueros hesitated a bit before following the example of Quarternight and myself and dispensing with saddles and boots. Five men were then detailed to hold the herd as compact as possible, and the remainder, twenty-seven all told, cut off about three hundred head and started for the river. I took the lead, for though cattle are less gregarious by nature than other animals, under pressure of excitement they will follow a leader. It was about noon and the herd were thirsty, so when we reached the brush chute, all hands started them on a run for the water. When the cattle were once inside the wing we went rapidly, four vaqueros riding outside the fence to keep the cattle from turning the chute on reaching swimming water. The leaders were crowding me close when Nigger breasted the water, and closely followed by several lead cattle, I struck straight for the American shore. The vaqueros forced every hoof into the river, following and shouting as far as the midstream, when they were swimming so nicely, Quarternight called off the men and all turned their horses back to the Mexican side. On landing opposite the exit from the ford, our men held the cattle as they came out, in order to bait the next bunch.

I rested my horse only a few minutes before taking the water again, but Lovell urged me to take an extra horse across, so as to have a change in case my black became fagged in swimming. Quarternight was a harsh *segundo*, for no sooner had I reached the other bank than he cut off the second bunch of about four hundred and started them. Turning Nigger Boy loose behind the brush fence, so as to be out of the way, I galloped out on my second horse, and meeting the cattle, turned and again took the lead for the river. My substitute did not swim with the freedom and ease of the black, and several times cattle swam so near me that I could lay my hand on their backs. When about halfway over, I heard shoutings behind me in English, and on looking back saw Nigger Boy swimming after us. A number of vaqueros attempted to catch him, but he outswam them and came out with the cattle; the excitement was too much for him to miss.

Each trip was a repetition of the former, with varying incident. Every hoof was over in less than two hours. On the last trip, in which there were about seven hundred head, the horse of one of the Mexican vaqueros took cramps, it was supposed, at about the middle of the river, and sank without a moment's warning. A number of us heard the man's terrified cry, only in time to see horse and rider sink. Every man within reach turned to the rescue, and a moment later the man rose to the surface. Fox caught him by the shirt, and, shaking the water out of him, turned him over to one of the other vaqueros, who towed him back to their own side. Strange as it may appear, the horse never came to the surface again, which supported the supposition of cramps.

After a change of clothes for Quarternight and myself, and rather late dinner for all hands, there yet remained the counting of the herd. The Mexican corporal and two of his men had come over for the purpose, and though Lovell and several wealthy rancheros, the sellers of the cattle, were present, it remained for Flood and the corporal to make the final count, as between buyer and seller. There was also present a river guard, — sent out by the United States Custom House, as a matter of form in the entry papers, — who also insisted on counting. In order to have a second count on the herd, Lovell ordered The Rebel to count opposite the government's man. We strung the cattle out, now logy with water, and after making quite a circle, brought the herd around where there was quite a bluff bank of the river. The herd handled well, and for a quarter of an hour we lined them between our four mounted counters. The only difference in the manner of counting between Flood and the Mexican corporal was that the American used a tally string tied to the pommel of his saddle, on which were ten knots, keeping count by slipping a knot on each even hundred, while the Mexican used ten small pebbles, shifting a pebble from one hand to the other on hundreds. "Just a mere difference in nationality," Lovell had me interpret to the selling dons.

When the count ended only two of the men agreed on numbers, The Rebel and the corporal making the same thirty-one hundred and five, — Flood being one under and the Custom House man one over. Lovell at once accepted the count of Priest and the corporal; and the delivery, which, as I learned during the interpreting that followed, was to be sealed with a supper that night in Brownsville, was consummated. Lovell was compelled to leave us, to make the final payment for the herd, and we would not see him again for some time. They were all seated in the vehicle ready to start for town, when the cowman said to his foreman, —

"Now, Jim, I can't give you any pointers on handling a herd, but you have until the 10th day of September to reach the Blackfoot Agency. An average of fifteen miles a day will put you there on time, so don't hurry. I'll try and see you at Dodge and Ogalalla on the way. Now, live well, for I like your outfit of men. Your credit letter is good anywhere you need supplies, and if you want more horses on the trail, buy them and draft on me through your letter of credit. If any of your men meet with accident or get sick, look out for them the same as you would for yourself, and I'll honor all bills. And don't be stingy over your expense account, for if that herd don't make money, you and I had better quit cows."

I had been detained to do any interpreting needful, and at parting Lovell beckoned to me. When I rode alongside the carriage, he gave me his hand and said, —

"Flood tells me to-day that you're a brother of Bob Quirk. Bob is to be foreman of my herd that I'm putting up in Nueces County. I'm glad you're here with Jim, though, for it's a longer trip. Yes, you'll get all the circus there is, and stay for the concert besides. They say God is good to the poor and the Irish; and if that's so, you'll pull through all right. Good-by, son." And as he gave me a hearty, ringing grip of the hand, I couldn't help feeling friendly toward him, Yankee that he was.

After Lovell and the dons had gone, Flood ordered McCann to move his wagon back from the river about a mile. It was now too late in the day to start the herd, and we wanted to graze them well, as it was our first night with them. About half our outfit grazed them around on a large circle, preparatory to bringing them up to the bed ground as it grew dusk. In the untrammeled freedom of the native range, a cow or steer will pick old dry grass on which to lie down, and if it is summer, will prefer an elevation sufficient to catch any passing breeze. Flood was familiar with the habits of cattle, and selected a nice elevation on which the old dry grass of the previous summer's growth lay matted like a carpet.

Our saddle horses by this time were fairly well broken to camp life, and, with the cattle on hand, night herding them had to be abandoned. Billy Honeyman, however, had noticed several horses that were inclined to stray on day herd, and these few leaders were so well marked in his memory that, as a matter of precaution, he insisted on putting a rope hobble on them. At every noon and night camp we strung a rope from the hind wheel of our wagon and another from the end of the wagon tongue back to stakes driven in the ground or held by a man, forming a triangular corral. Thus in a few minutes, under any conditions, we could construct a temporary corral for catching a change of mounts, or for the wrangler to hobble untrustworthy horses. On the trail all horses are free at night, except the regular night ones, which are used constantly during the entire trip, and under ordinary conditions keep strong and improve in flesh.

Before the herd was brought in for the night, and during the supper hour, Flood announced the guards for the trip. As the men usually bunked in pairs, the foreman chose them as they slept, but was under the necessity of splitting two berths of bedfellows. "Rod" Wheat, Joe Stallings, and Ash Borrowstone were assigned to the first guard, from eight to ten thirty P.M. Bob Blades, "Bull" Durham, and Fox Quarternight were given second guard, from ten thirty to one. Paul Priest, John Officer, and myself made up the third watch, from one to three thirty. The Rebel and I were bunkies, and this choice of guards, while not ideal, was much better than splitting bedfellows and having them annoy each other by going out and returning from guard separately. The only fault I ever found with Priest was that he could use the poorest judgment in selecting a bed ground for our blankets, and always talked and told stories to me until I fell asleep. He was a light sleeper himself, while I, being much younger, was the reverse. The fourth and last guard, from three thirty until relieved after daybreak, fell to Wyatt Roundtree, Quince Forrest, and "Moss" Strayhorn. Thus the only men in the outfit not on night duty were Honeyman, our horse wrangler, Barney McCann, our cook, and Flood, the foreman. The latter, however, made up by riding almost double as much as any man in his outfit. He never left the herd until it was bedded down for the night, and we could always hear him quietly arousing the cook and horse wrangler an hour before daybreak. He always kept a horse on picket for the night, and often took the herd as it left the bed ground at clear dawn.

A half hour before dark, Flood and all the herd men turned out to bed down the cattle for our first night. They had been well grazed after counting, and as they came up to the bed ground there was not a hungry or thirsty animal in the lot. All seemed anxious to lie down, and by circling around slowly, while gradually closing in, in the course of half an hour all were bedded nicely on possibly five or six acres. I remember there were a number of muleys among the cattle, and these would not venture into the compact herd until the others had lain down. Being hornless, instinct taught them to be on the defensive, and it was noticeable that they were the first to arise in the morning, in advance of their horned kin. When all had lain down, Flood and the first guard remained, the others returning to the wagon.

The guards ride in a circle about four rods outside the sleeping cattle, and by riding in opposite directions make it impossible for any animal to make its escape without being noticed by the riders. The guards usually sing or whistle continuously, so that the sleeping herd may know that a friend and not an enemy is keeping vigil over their dreams. A sleeping herd of cattle make a pretty picture on a clear moonlight night, chewing their cuds and grunting and blowing over contented stomachs. The night horses soon learn their duty, and a rider may fall asleep or doze along in the saddle, but the horses will maintain their distance in their leisurely, sentinel rounds.

On returning to the wagon, Priest and I picketed our horses, saddled, where we could easily find them in the darkness, and unrolled our bed. We had two pairs of blankets each, which, with an ordinary wagon sheet doubled for a tarpaulin, and coats and boots for pillows, completed our couch. We slept otherwise in our clothing worn during the day, and if smooth, sandy ground was available on which to spread our bed, we had no trouble in sleeping the sleep that long hours in the saddle were certain to bring. With all his pardonable faults, The Rebel was a good bunkie and a hail companion, this being his sixth trip over the trail. He had been with Lovell over a year before the two made the discovery that they had been on opposite sides during the "late unpleasantness." On making this discovery, Lovell at once rechristened Priest "The Rebel," and that name he always bore. He was fifteen years my senior at this time, a wonderfully complex nature, hardened by unusual experiences into a character the gamut of whose moods ran from that of a good-natured fellow to a man of unrelenting severity in anger.

We were sleeping a nine knot gale when Fox Quarternight of the second guard called us on our watch. It was a clear, starry night, and our guard soon passed, the cattle sleeping like tired soldiers. When the last relief came on guard and we had returned to our blankets, I remember Priest telling me this little incident as I fell asleep.

"I was at a dance once in Live Oak County, and there was a stuttering fellow there by the name of Lem Todhunter. The girls, it seems, didn't care to dance with him, and pretended they couldn't understand him. He had asked every girl at the party, and received the same answer from each — they couldn't understand him. 'W-w-w-ell, g-g-g-go to hell, then. C-c-c-can y-y-you understand that?' he said to the last girl, and her brother threatened to mangle him horribly if he didn't apologize, to which he finally agreed. He went back into the house and said to the girl, 'Y-y-you n-n-n-needn't g-g-g-go to hell; y-y-your b-b-b-brother and I have m-m-made other 'r-r-r-rangements.'"

CHAPTER III
THE START

On the morning of April 1, 1882, our Circle Dot herd started on its long tramp to the Blackfoot Agency in Montana. With six men on each side, and the herd strung out for three quarters of a mile, it could only be compared to some mythical serpent or Chinese dragon, as it moved forward on its sinuous, snail-like course. Two riders, known as point men, rode out and well back from the lead cattle, and by riding forward and closing in as occasion required, directed the course of the herd. The main body of the herd trailed along behind the leaders like an army in loose marching order, guarded by outriders, known as swing men, who rode well out from the advancing column, warding off range cattle and seeing that none of the herd wandered away or dropped out. There was no driving to do; the cattle moved of their own free will as in ordinary travel. Flood seldom gave orders; but, as a number of us had never worked on the trail before, at breakfast on the morning of our start he gave in substance these general directions: —

"Boys, the secret of trailing cattle is never to let your herd know that they are under restraint. Let everything that is done be done voluntarily by the cattle. From the moment you let them off the bed ground in the morning until they are bedded at night, never let a cow take a step, except in the direction of its destination. In this manner you can loaf away the day, and cover from fifteen to twenty miles, and the herd in the mean time will enjoy all the freedom of an open range. Of course, it's long, tiresome hours to the men; but the condition of the herd and saddle stock demands sacrifices on our part, if any have to be made. And I want to caution you younger boys about your horses; there is such a thing as having ten horses in your string, and at the same time being afoot. You are all well mounted, and on the condition of the *remuda* depends the success and safety of the herd. Accidents will happen to horses, but don't let it be your fault; keep your saddle blankets dry and clean, for no better word can be spoken of a man than that he is careful of his horses. Ordinarily a man might get along with six or eight horses, but in such emergencies as we are liable to meet, we have not a horse to spare, and a man afoot is useless."

And as all of us younger boys learned afterward, there was plenty of good, solid, horse-sense in Flood's advice; for before the trip ended there were men in our outfit who were as good as afoot, while others had their original mounts, every one fit for the saddle. Flood had insisted on a good mount of horses, and Lovell was cowman enough to know that what the mule is to the army the cow-horse is to the herd.

The first and second day out there was no incident worth mentioning. We traveled slowly, hardly making an average day's drive. The third morning Flood left us, to look out a crossing on the Arroyo Colorado. On coming down to receive the herd, we had crossed this sluggish bayou about thirty-six miles north of Brownsville. It was a deceptive-looking stream, being over fifty feet deep and between bluff banks. We ferried our wagon and saddle horses over, swimming the loose ones. But the herd was keeping near the coast line for the sake of open country, and it was a question if there was a ford for the wagon as near the coast as our course was carrying us. The murmurings of the Gulf had often reached our ears the day before, and herds had been known, in former years, to cross from the mainland over to Padre Island, the intervening Laguna Madre being fordable.

We were nooning when Flood returned with the news that it would be impossible to cross our wagon at any point on the bayou, and that we would have to ford around the mouth of the stream. Where the fresh and salt water met in the laguna, there had formed a delta, or shallow bar; and by following its contour we would not have over twelve to fourteen inches of water, though the half circle was nearly two miles in length. As we would barely have time to cross that day, the herd was at once started, veering for the mouth of the Arroyo Colorado. On reaching it, about the middle of the afternoon, the foreman led the way, having crossed in the morning and learned the ford. The wagon followed, the saddle horses came next, while the herd brought up the rear. It proved good footing on the sandbar, but the water in the laguna was too salty for the cattle, though the loose horses lay down and wallowed in it. We were about an hour in crossing, and on reaching the mainland met a vaquero, who directed us to a large fresh-water lake a few miles inland, where we camped for the night.

It proved an ideal camp, with wood, water, and grass in abundance, and very little range stock to annoy us. We had watered the herd just before noon, and before throwing them upon the bed ground for the night, watered them a second time. We had a splendid camp-fire that night, of dry live oak logs, and after supper was over and the first guard had taken the herd, smoking and story telling were the order of the evening. The camp-fire is to all outdoor life what the evening fireside is to domestic life. After the labors of the day are over, the men gather around the fire, and the social hour of the day is spent in yarning. The stories told may run from the sublime to the ridiculous, from a true incident to a base fabrication, or from a touching bit of pathos to the most vulgar vulgarity.

"Have I ever told this outfit my experience with the vigilantes when I was a kid?" inquired Bull Durham. There was a general negative response, and he proceeded. "Well, our folks were living on the Frio at the time, and there was a man in our neighborhood who had an outfit of four men out beyond Nueces Cañon hunting wild cattle for their hides. It was necessary to take them out supplies about every so often, and on one trip he begged my folks to let me go along for company. I was a slim slip of a colt about fourteen at the time, and as this man was a friend of ours, my folks consented to let me go along. We each had a good saddle horse, and two pack mules with provisions and ammunition for the hunting camp. The first night we made camp, a boy overtook us with the news that the brother of my companion had been accidentally killed by a horse, and of course he would have to return. Well, we were twenty miles on our way, and as it would take some little time to go back and return with the loaded mules, I volunteered, like a fool kid, to go on and take the packs through.

"The only question was, could I pack and unpack. I had helped him at this work, double-handed, but now that I was to try it alone, he showed me what he called a squaw hitch, with which you can lash a pack single-handed. After putting me through it once or twice, and satisfying himself that I could do the packing, he consented to let me go on, he and the messenger returning home during the night. The next morning I packed without any trouble and started on my way. It would take me two days yet, poking along with heavy packs, to reach the hunters. Well, I hadn't made over eight or ten miles the first morning, when, as I rounded a turn in the trail, a man stepped out from behind a rock, threw a gun in my face, and ordered me to hold up my hands. Then another appeared from the opposite side with his gun leveled on me. Inside of half a minute a dozen men galloped up from every quarter, all armed to the teeth. The man on leaving had given me his gun for company, one of these old smoke-pole, cap-and-ball six-shooters, but I must have forgotten what guns were for, for I elevated my little hands nicely. The leader of the party questioned me as to who I was, and what I was doing there, and what I had in those packs. That once, at least, I told the truth. Every mother's son of them was cursing and cross-questioning me in the same breath. They ordered me off my horse, took my gun, and proceeded to verify my tale by unpacking the mules. So much ammunition aroused their suspicions, but my story was as good as it was true, and they never shook me from the truth of it. I soon learned that robbery was not their motive, and the leader explained the situation.

"A vigilance committee had been in force in that county for some time, trying to rid the country of lawless characters. But lawlessness got into the saddle, and had bench warrants issued and served on every member of this vigilance committee. As the vigilantes numbered several hundred, there was no jail large enough to hold such a number, so they were released on parole for appearance at court. When court met, every man served with a capias" —

"Hold on! hold your horses just a minute," interrupted Quince Forrest, "I want to get that word. I want to make a memorandum of it, for I may want to use it myself sometime. Capias? Now I have it; go ahead."

"When court met, every man served with a bench warrant from the judge presiding was present, and as soon as court was called to order, a squad of men arose in the court room, and the next moment the judge fell riddled with lead. Then the factions scattered to fight it out, and I was passing through the county while matters were active.

"They confiscated my gun and all the ammunition in the packs, but helped me to repack and started me on my way. A happy thought struck one of the men to give me a letter, which would carry me through without further trouble, but the leader stopped him, saying, 'Let the boy alone. Your letter would hang him as sure as hell's hot, before he went ten miles farther.' I declined the letter. Even then I didn't have sense enough to turn back, and inside of two hours I was rounded up by the other faction. I had learned my story perfectly by this time, but those packs had to come off again for everything to be examined. There was nothing in them now but flour and salt and such things — nothing that they might consider suspicious. One fellow in this second party took a fancy to my horse, and offered to help hang me on general principles, but kinder counsels prevailed. They also helped me to repack, and I started on once more. Before I reached my destination the following evening, I was held up seven different times. I got so used to it that I was happily disappointed every shelter I passed, if some man did not step out and throw a gun in my face.

"I had trouble to convince the cattle hunters of my experiences, but the absence of any ammunition, which they needed worst, at last led them to give credit to my tale. I was expected home within a week, as I was to go down on the Nueces on a cow hunt which was making up, and I only rested one day at the hunters' camp. On their advice, I took a different route on my way home, leaving the mules behind me. I never saw a man the next day returning, and was feeling quite gala on my good fortune. When evening came on, I sighted a little ranch house some distance off the trail, and concluded to ride to it and stay overnight. As I approached, I saw that some one lived there, as there were chickens and dogs about, but not a person in sight. I dismounted and knocked on the door, when, without a word, the door was thrown wide open and a half dozen guns were poked into my face. I was ordered into the house and given a chance to tell my story again. Whether my story was true or not, they took no chances on me, but kept me all night. One of the men took my horse to the stable and cared for him, and I was well fed and given a place to sleep, but not a man offered a word of explanation, from which I took it they did not belong to the vigilance faction. When it came time to go to bed, one man said to me, 'Now, sonny, don't make any attempt to get away, and don't move out of your bed without warning us, for you'll be shot as sure as you do. We won't harm a hair on your head if you're telling us the truth; only do as you're told, for we'll watch you.'

"By this time I had learned to obey orders while in that county, and got a fair night's sleep, though there were men going and coming all night. The next morning I was given my breakfast; my horse, well cuffed and saddled, was brought to the door, and with this parting advice I was given permission to go: 'Son, if you've told us the truth, don't look back when you ride away. You'll be watched for the first ten miles after leaving here, and if you've lied to us it will go hard with you. Now, remember, don't look back, for these are times when no one cares to be identified.' I never questioned that man's advice; it was 'die dog or eat the hatchet' with me. I mounted my horse, waved the usual parting courtesies, and rode away. As I turned into the trail about a quarter mile from the house, I noticed two men ride out from behind the stable and follow me. I remembered the story about Lot's wife looking back, though it was lead and not miracles that I was afraid of that morning.

"For the first hour I could hear the men talking and the hoofbeats of their horses, as they rode along always the same distance behind me. After about two hours of this one-sided joke, as I rode over a little hill, I looked out of the corner of my eye back at my escort, still about a quarter of a mile behind me. One of them noticed me and raised his gun, but I instantly changed my view, and the moment the hill hid me, put spurs to my horse, so that when they reached the brow of the hill, I was half a mile in the lead, burning the earth like a canned dog. They threw lead close around me, but my horse lengthened the distance between us for the next five miles, when they dropped entirely out of sight. By noon I came into the old stage road, and by the middle of the afternoon reached home after over sixty miles in the saddle without a halt."

Just at the conclusion of Bull's story, Flood rode in from the herd, and after picketing his horse, joined the circle. In reply to an inquiry from one of the boys as to how the cattle were resting, he replied, —

"This herd is breaking into trail life nicely. If we'll just be careful with them now for the first month, and no bad storms strike us in the night, we may never have a run the entire trip. That last drink of water they had this evening gave them a night-cap that'll last them until morning. No, there's no danger of any trouble to-night."

For fully an hour after the return of our foreman, we lounged around the fire, during which there was a full and free discussion of stampedes. But finally, Flood, suiting the action to the word by arising, suggested that all hands hunt their blankets and turn in for the night. A quiet wink from Bull to several of the boys held us for the time being, and innocently turning to Forrest, Durham inquired, —

"Where was — when was — was it you that was telling some one about a run you were in last summer? I never heard you tell it. Where was it?"

"You mean on the Cimarron last year when we mixed two herds," said Quince, who had taken the bait like a bass and was now fully embarked on a yarn. "We were in rather close quarters, herds ahead and behind us, when one night here came a cow herd like a cyclone and swept right through our camp. We tumbled out of our blankets and ran for our horses, but before we could bridle" —

Bull had given us the wink, and every man in the outfit fell back, and the snoring that checked the storyteller was like a chorus of rip saws running through pine knots. Forrest took in the situation at a glance, and as he arose to leave, looked back and remarked, —

"You must all think that's smart."

Before he was out of hearing, Durham said to the rest of us, —

"A few doses like that will cure him of sucking eggs and acting smart, interrupting folks."

CHAPTER IV
THE ATASCOSA

For the next few days we paralleled the coast, except when forced inland by various arms of the Laguna Madre. When about a week out from the Arroyo Colorado, we encountered the Salt Lagoon, which threw us at least fifty miles in from the coast. Here we had our last view of salt water, and the murmurings of the Gulf were heard no more. Our route now led northward through what were then the two largest ranches in Texas, the "Running W" and Laurel Leaf, which sent more cattle up the trail, bred in their own brand, than any other four ranches in the Lone Star State. We were nearly a week passing through their ranges, and on reaching Santa Gertruda ranch learned that three trail herds, of over three thousand head each, had already started in these two brands, while four more were to follow.

So far we had been having splendid luck in securing water for the herd, once a day at least, and often twice and three times. Our herd was becoming well trail-broken by this time, and for range cattle had quieted down and were docile and easy to handle. Flood's years of experience on the trail made him a believer in the theory that stampedes were generally due to negligence in not having the herd full of grass and water on reaching the bed ground at night. Barring accidents, which will happen, his view is the correct one, if care has been used for the first few weeks in properly breaking the herd to the trail. But though hunger and thirst are probably responsible for more stampedes than all other causes combined, it is the unexpected which cannot be guarded against. A stampede is the natural result of fear, and at night or in an uncertain light, this timidity might be imparted to an entire herd by a flash of lightning or a peal of thunder, while the stumbling of a night horse, or the scent of some wild animal, would in a moment's time, from frightening a few head, so infect a herd as to throw them into the wildest panic. Amongst the thousands of herds like ours which were driven over the trail during its brief existence, none ever made the trip without encountering more or less trouble from runs. Frequently a herd became so spoiled in this manner that it grew into a mania with them, so that they would stampede on the slightest provocation, — or no provocation at all.

A few days after leaving Santa Gertruda Ranch, we crossed the Nueces River, which we followed up for several days, keeping in touch with it for water for the herd. But the Nueces, after passing Oakville, makes an abrupt turn, doubling back to the southwest; and the Atascosa, one of its tributaries, became our source of water supply. We were beginning to feel a degree of overconfidence in the good behavior of our herd, when one night during the third week out, an incident occurred in which they displayed their running qualities to our complete satisfaction.

It occurred during our guard, and about two o'clock in the morning. The night was an unusually dark one and the atmosphere was very humid. After we had been on guard possibly an hour, John Officer and I riding in one direction on opposite sides of the herd, and The Rebel circling in the opposite, Officer's horse suddenly struck a gopher burrow with his front feet, and in a moment horse and rider were sprawling on the ground. The accident happened but a few rods from the sleeping herd, which instantly came to their feet as one steer, and were off like a flash. I was riding my Nigger Boy, and as the cattle headed toward me, away from the cause of their fright, I had to use both quirt and rowel to keep clear of the onrush. Fortunately we had a clear country near the bed ground, and while the terrified cattle pressed me close, my horse kept the lead. In the rumbling which ensued, all sounds were submerged by the general din; and I was only brought to the consciousness that I was not alone by seeing several distinct flashes from six-shooters on my left, and, realizing that I also had a gun, fired several times in the air in reply. I was soon joined by Priest and Officer, the latter having lost no time in regaining his seat in the saddle, and the three of us held together some little distance, for it would have been useless to attempt to check or turn this onslaught of cattle in their first mad rush.

The wagon was camped about two hundred yards from the bed ground, and the herd had given ample warning to the boys asleep, so that if we three could hold our position in the lead, help would come to us as soon as the men in camp could reach their horses. Realizing the wide front of the running cattle, Priest sent Officer to the left and myself to the right, to point in the leaders in order to keep the herd from splitting or scattering, while he remained in the centre and led the herd. I soon gained the outside of the leaders, and by dropping back and coming up the line, pointed them in to the best of my ability. I had repeated this a number of times, even quirting some cattle along the outside, or burning a little powder in the face of some obstinate leader, when across the herd and to the rear I saw a succession of flashes like fireflies, which told me the boys were coming to our assistance.

Running is not a natural gait with cattle, and if we could only hold them together and prevent splitting up, in time they would tire, while the rear cattle could be depended on to follow the leaders. All we could hope to do was to force them to run straight, and in this respect we were succeeding splendidly, though to a certain extent it was a guess in the dark. When they had run possibly a mile, I noticed a horseman overtake Priest. After they had ridden together a moment, one of them came over to my point, and the next minute our foreman was racing along by my side. In his impatience to check the run, he took me with him, and circling the leaders we reached the left point, by which time the remainder of the outfit had come up. Now massing our numbers, we fell on the left point, and amid the flash of guns deflected their course for a few moments. A dozen men, however, can cover but a small space, and we soon realized that we had turned only a few hundred head, for the momentum of the main body bore steadily ahead. Abandoning what few cattle we had turned, which, owing to their running ability, soon resumed their places in the lead, we attempted to turn them to the left. Stretching out our line until there was a man about every twenty feet, we threw our force against the right point and lead in the hope of gradually deviating their course. For a few minutes the attempt promised to be successful, but our cordon was too weak and the cattle went through between the riders, and we soon found a portion of our forces on either side of the herd, while a few of the boys were riding out of the rush in the lead.

On finding our forces thus divided, the five or six of us who remained on the right contented ourselves by pointing in the leaders, for the cattle, so far as we could tell, were running compactly. Our foreman, however, was determined to turn the run, and after a few minutes' time rejoined us on the right, when under his leadership we circled the front of the herd and collected on the left point, when, for a third time, we repeated the same tactics in our efforts to turn the stampede. But in this, which was our final effort, we were attempting to turn them slowly and on a much larger circle, and with a promise of success. Suddenly in the dark we encountered a mesquite thicket into which the lead cattle tore with a crashing of brush and a rattle of horns that sent a chill up and down my spine. But there was no time to hesitate, for our horses were in the thicket, and with the herd closing in on us there was no alternative but to go through it, every man for himself. I gave Nigger a free rein, shutting my eyes and clutching both cantle and pommel to hold my seat; the black responded to the rowel and tore through the thicket, in places higher than my head, and came out in an open space considerably in the lead of the cattle.

This thicket must have been eight or ten rods wide, and checked the run to a slight extent; but as they emerged from it, they came out in scattering flies and resumed their running. Being alone, and not knowing which way to turn, I rode to the right and front and soon found myself in the lead of quite a string of cattle. Nigger and I were piloting them where they listed, when Joe Stallings, hatless himself and his horse heaving, overtook me, and the two of us gave those lead cattle all the trouble we knew how. But we did not attempt to turn them, for they had caught their wind in forcing the thicket, and were running an easy stroke. Several times we worried the leaders into a trot, but as other cattle in the rear came up, we were compelled to loosen out and allow them to resume their running, or they would have scattered on us like partridges. At this stage of the run, we had no idea where the rest of the outfit were, but both of us were satisfied the herd had scattered on leaving the mesquite thicket, and were possibly then running in half a dozen bunches like the one we were with.

Stallings's horse was badly winded, and on my suggestion, he dropped out on one side to try to get some idea how many cattle we were leading. He was gone some little time, and as

Nigger cantered along easily in the lead, I managed to eject the shells from my six-shooter and refill the cylinder. On Joe's overtaking me again, he reported that there was a slender column of cattle, half a mile in length, following. As one man could easily lead this string of the herd until daybreak, I left Stallings with them and rode out to the left nearly a quarter of a mile, listening to hear if there were any cattle running to the left of those we were leading. It took me but a few minutes to satisfy myself that ours was the outside band on the left, and after I rejoined Joe, we made an effort to check our holding.

There were about fifty or sixty big steers in the lead of our bunch, and after worrying them into a trot, we opened in their front with our six-shooters, shooting into the ground in their very faces, and were rewarded by having them turn tail and head the other way. Taking advantage of the moment, we jumped our horses on the retreating leaders, and as fast as the rear cattle forged forward, easily turned them. Leaving Joe to turn the rear as they came up, I rode to the lead, unfastening my slicker as I went, and on reaching the turned leaders, who were running on an angle from their former course, flaunted my "fish" in their faces until they reentered the rear guard of our string, and we soon had a mill going which kept them busy, and rested our horses. Once we had them milling, our trouble, as far as running was concerned, was over, for all two of us could hope to do was to let them exhaust themselves in this endless circle.

It then lacked an hour of daybreak, and all we could do was to ride around and wait for daylight. In the darkness preceding dawn, we had no idea of the number of our bunch, except as we could judge from the size and compactness of the milling cattle, which must have covered an acre or more. The humidity of the atmosphere, which had prevailed during the night, by dawn had changed until a heavy fog, cutting off our view on every hand, left us as much at sea as we had been previously. But with the break of day we rode through our holding a number of times, splitting and scattering the milling cattle, and as the light of day brightened, we saw them quiet down and go to grazing as though they had just arisen from the bed ground. It was over an hour before the fog lifted sufficiently to give us any idea as to our whereabouts, and during the interim both Stallings and myself rode to the nearest elevation, firing a number of shots in the hope of getting an answer from the outfit, but we had no response.

When the sun was sufficiently high to scatter the mists which hung in clouds, there was not an object in sight by which we could determine our location. Whether we had run east, west, or south during the night neither of us knew, though both Stallings and myself were satisfied that we had never crossed the trail, and all we did know for a certainty was that we had between six and seven hundred head of cattle. Stallings had lost his hat, and I had one sleeve missing and both outside pockets torn out of my coat, while the mesquite thorns had left their marks on the faces of both of us, one particularly ugly cut marking Joe's right temple. "I've worn leggins for the last ten years," said Stallings to me, as we took an inventory of our disfigurements, "and for about ten seconds in forcing that mesquite thicket was the only time I ever drew interest on my investment. They're a heap like a six-shooter — wear them all your life and never have any use for them."

With a cigarette for breakfast, I left Joe to look after our bunch, and after riding several miles to the right, cut the trail of quite a band of cattle. In following up this trail I could easily see that some one was in their lead, as they failed to hold their course in any one direction for any distance, as free cattle would. After following this trail about three miles, I sighted the band of cattle, and on overtaking them, found two of our boys holding about half as many as Stallings had. They reported that The Rebel and Bob Blades had been with them until daybreak, but having the freshest horses had left them with the dawn and ridden away to the right, where it was supposed the main body of the herd had run. As Stallings's bunch was some three or four miles to the rear and left of this band, Wyatt Roundtree suggested that he go and pilot in Joe's cattle, as he felt positive that the main body were somewhere to our right. On getting directions from me as to where he would find our holding, he rode away, and I again rode off to the right, leaving Rod Wheat with their catch.

The sun was now several hours high, and as my black's strength was standing the test bravely, I cross-cut the country and was soon on another trail of our stampeded cattle. But in following this trail, I soon noticed two other horsemen preceding me. Knowing that my services would be too late, I only followed far enough to satisfy myself of the fact. The signs left by the running cattle were as easy to follow as a public road, and in places where the ground was sandy, the sod was cut up as if a regiment of cavalry had charged across it. On again bearing off to the right, I rode for an elevation which ought to give me a good view of the country. Slight as this elevation was, on reaching it, I made out a large band of cattle under herd, and as I was on the point of riding to them, saw our wagon and saddle horses heave in sight from a northwest quarter. Supposing they were following up the largest trail, I rode for the herd, where Flood and two of the boys had about twelve hundred cattle. From a comparison of notes, our foreman was able to account for all the men with the exception of two, and as these proved to be Blades and Priest, I could give him a satisfactory explanation as to their probable whereabouts. On my report of having sighted the wagon and *remuda*, Flood at once ordered me to meet and hurry them in, as not only he, but Strayhorn and Officer, were badly in need of a change of mounts.

I learned from McCann, who was doing the trailing from the wagon, that the regular trail was to the west, the herd having crossed it within a quarter of a mile after leaving the bed ground. Joining Honeyman, I took the first horse which came within reach of my rope, and with a fresh mount under me, we rushed the saddle horses past the wagon and shortly came up with our foreman. There we rounded in the horses as best we could without the aid of the wagon, and before McCann arrived, all had fresh mounts and were ready for orders. This was my first trip on the trail, and I was hungry and thirsty enough to hope something would be said about eating, but that seemed to be the last idea in our foreman's mind. Instead, he ordered me to take the two other boys with me, and after putting them on the trail of the bunch which The Rebel and Blades were following, to drift in what cattle we had held on our left. But as we went, we managed to encounter the wagon and get a drink and a canteen of water from McCann before we galloped away on our mission. After riding a mile or so together, we separated, and on my arrival at the nearest bunch, I found Roundtree and Stallings coming up with the larger holding. Throwing the two hunches together, we drifted them a free clip towards camp. We soon sighted the main herd, and saw across to our right and about five miles distant two of our men bringing in another hunch. As soon as we turned our cattle into the herd, Flood ordered me, on account of my light weight, to meet this bunch, find out where the last cattle were, and go to their assistance.

With a hungry look in the direction of our wagon, I obeyed, and on meeting Durham and Borrowstone, learned that the outside bunch on the right, which had got into the regular trail, had not been checked until daybreak. All they knew about their location was that the up stage from Oakville had seen two men with Circle Dot cattle about five miles below, and had sent up word by the driver that they had something like four hundred head. With this meagre information, I rode away in the direction where one would naturally expect to find our absent men, and after scouring the country for an hour, sighted a single horseman on an elevation, whom from the gray mount I knew for Quince Forrest. He was evidently on the lookout for some one to pilot them in. They had been drifting like lost sheep ever since dawn, but we soon had their cattle pointed in the right direction, and Forrest taking the lead, Quarternight and I put the necessary push behind them. Both of them cursed me roundly for not bringing them a canteen of water, though they were well aware that in an emergency like the present, our foreman would never give a thought to anything but the recovery of the herd. Our comfort was nothing; men were cheap, but cattle cost money.

We reached the camp about two o'clock, and found the outfit cutting out range cattle which had been absorbed into the herd during the run. Throwing in our contingent, we joined in the work, and though Forrest and Quarternight were as good as afoot, there were no orders for a change of mounts, to say nothing of food and drink. Several hundred mixed cattle were in the herd, and after they had been cut out, we lined our cattle out for a count. In the absence of

Priest, Flood and John Officer did the counting, and as the hour of the day made the cattle sluggish, they lined through between the counters as though they had never done anything but walk in their lives. The count showed sixteen short of twenty-eight hundred, which left us yet over three hundred out. But good men were on their trail, and leaving two men on herd, the rest of us obeyed the most welcome orders of the day when Flood intimated that we would "eat a bite and go after the rest."

As we had been in our saddles since one or two o'clock the morning before, it is needless to add that our appetites were equal to the spread which our cook had waiting for us. Our foreman, as though fearful of the loss of a moment's time, sent Honeyman to rustle in the horses before we had finished our dinners. Once the *remuda* was corralled, under the rush of a tireless foreman, dinner was quickly over, and fresh horses became the order of the moment. The Atascosa, our nearest water, lay beyond the regular trail to the west, and leaving orders for the outfit to drift the herd into it and water, Flood and myself started in search of our absent men, not forgetting to take along two extra horses as a remount for Blades and Priest. The leading of these extra horses fell to me, but with the loose end of a rope in Jim Flood's hand as he followed, it took fast riding to keep clear of them.

After reaching the trail of the missing cattle, our foreman set a pace for five or six miles which would have carried us across the Nueces by nightfall, and we were only checked by Moss Strayhorn riding in on an angle and intercepting us in our headlong gait. The missing cattle were within a mile of us to the right, and we turned and rode to them. Strayhorn explained to us that the cattle had struck some recent fencing on their course, and after following down the fence several miles had encountered an offset, and the angle had held the squad until The Rebel and Blades overtook them. When Officer and he reached them, they were unable to make any accurate count, because of the range cattle amongst them, and they had considered it advisable to save horseflesh, and not cut them until more help was available. When we came up with the cattle, my bunkie and Blades looked wistfully at our saddles, and anticipating their want, I untied my slicker, well remembering the reproof of Quarternight and Forrest, and produced a full canteen of water, — warm of course, but no less welcome.

No sooner were saddles shifted than we held up the bunch, cut out the range cattle, counted, and found we had some three hundred and thirty odd Circle Dots, — our number more than complete. With nothing now missing, Flood took the loose horses and two of the boys with him and returned to the herd, leaving three of us behind to bring in this last contingent of our stampeded cattle. This squad were nearly all large steers, and had run fully twenty miles, before, thanks to an angle in a fence, they had been checked. As our foreman galloped away, leaving us behind, Bob Blades said, —

"Hasn't the boss got a wiggle on himself today! If he'd made this old world, he'd have made it in half a day, and gone fishing in the afternoon — if his horses had held out."

We reached the Atascosa shortly after the arrival of the herd, and after holding the cattle on the water for an hour, grazed them the remainder of the evening, for if there was any virtue in their having full stomachs, we wanted to benefit from it. While grazing that evening, we recrossed the trail on an angle, and camped in the most open country we could find, about ten miles below our camp of the night before. Every precaution was taken to prevent a repetition of the run; our best horses were chosen for night duty, as our regular ones were too exhausted; every advantage of elevation for a bed ground was secured, and thus fortified against accident, we went into camp for the night. But the expected never happens on the trail, and the sun arose the next morning over our herd grazing in peace and contentment on the flowery prairies which border on the Atascosa.

CHAPTER V
A DRY DRIVE

Our cattle quieted down nicely after this run, and the next few weeks brought not an incident worth recording. There was no regular trail through the lower counties, so we simply kept to the open country. Spring had advanced until the prairies were swarded with grass and flowers, while water, though scarcer, was to be had at least once daily. We passed to the west of San Antonio — an outfitting point which all herds touched in passing northward — and Flood and our cook took the wagon and went in for supplies. But the outfit with the herd kept on, now launched on a broad, well-defined trail, in places seventy-five yards wide, where all local trails blent into the one common pathway, known in those days as the Old Western Trail. It is not in the province of this narrative to deal with the cause or origin of this cattle trail, though it marked the passage of many hundred thousand cattle which preceded our Circle Dots, and was destined to afford an outlet to several millions more to follow. The trail proper consisted of many scores of irregular cow paths, united into one broad passageway, narrowing and widening as conditions permitted, yet ever leading northward. After a few years of continued use, it became as well defined as the course of a river.

Several herds which had started farther up country were ahead of ours, and this we considered an advantage, for wherever one herd could go, it was reasonable that others could follow. Flood knew the trail as well as any of the other foremen, but there was one thing he had not taken into consideration: the drouth of the preceding summer. True, there had been local spring showers, sufficient to start the grass nicely, but water in such quantities as we needed was growing daily more difficult to find. The first week after leaving San Antonio, our foreman scouted in quest of water a full day in advance of the herd. One evening he returned to us with the news that we were in for a dry drive, for after passing the next chain of lakes it was sixty miles to the next water, and reports regarding the water supply even after crossing this arid stretch were very conflicting.

"While I know every foot of this trail through here," said the foreman, "there's several things that look scaly. There are only five herds ahead of us, and the first three went through the old route, but the last two, after passing Indian Lakes, for some reason or other turned and went westward. These last herds may be stock cattle, pushing out west to new ranges; but I don't like the outlook. It would take me two days to ride across and back, and by that time we could be two thirds of the way through. I've made this drive before without a drop of water on the way, and wouldn't dread it now, if there was any certainty of water at the other end. I reckon there's nothing to do but tackle her; but isn't this a hell of a country? I've ridden fifty miles to-day and never saw a soul."

The Indian Lakes, some seven in number, were natural reservoirs with rocky bottoms, and about a mile apart. We watered at ten o'clock the next day, and by night camped fifteen miles on our way. There was plenty of good grazing for the cattle and horses, and no trouble was experienced the first night. McCann had filled an extra twenty gallon keg for this trip. Water was too precious an article to be lavish with, so we shook the dust from our clothing and went unwashed. This was no serious deprivation, and no one could be critical of another, for we were all equally dusty and dirty.

The next morning by daybreak the cattle were thrown off the bed ground and started grazing before the sun could dry out what little moisture the grass had absorbed during the night. The heat of the past week had been very oppressive, and in order to avoid it as much as possible, we made late and early drives. Before the wagon passed the herd during the morning drive, what few canteens we had were filled with water for the men. The *remuda* was kept with the herd, and four changes of mounts were made during the day, in order not to exhaust any one horse. Several times for an hour or more, the herd was allowed to lie down and rest; but by the middle of the afternoon thirst made them impatient and restless, and the point men were compelled to ride steadily in the lead in order to hold the cattle to a walk. A number of times during the afternoon we attempted to graze them, but not until the twilight of evening was it possible.

After the fourth change of horses was made, Honeyman pushed on ahead with the saddle stock and overtook the wagon. Under Flood's orders he was to tie up all the night horses, for if the cattle could be induced to graze, we would not bed them down before ten that night, and all hands would be required with the herd. McCann had instructions to make camp on the divide, which was known to be twenty-five miles from our camp of the night before, or forty miles from the Indian Lakes. As we expected, the cattle grazed willingly after nightfall, and with a fair moon, we allowed them to scatter freely while grazing forward. The beacon of McCann's fire on the divide was in sight over an hour before the herd grazed up to camp, all hands remaining to bed the thirsty cattle. The herd was given triple the amount of space usually required for bedding, and even then for nearly an hour scarcely half of them lay down.

We were handling the cattle as humanely as possible under the circumstances. The guards for the night were doubled, six men on the first half and the same on the latter, Bob Blades being detailed to assist Honeyman in night-herding the saddle horses. If any of us got more than an hour's sleep that night, he was lucky. Flood, McCann, and the horse wranglers did not even try to rest. To those of us who could find time to eat, our cook kept open house. Our foreman knew that a well-fed man can stand an incredible amount of hardship, and appreciated the fact that on the trail a good cook is a valuable asset. Our outfit therefore was cheerful to a man, and jokes and songs helped to while away the weary hours of the night.

The second guard, under Flood, pushed the cattle off their beds an hour before dawn, and before they were relieved had urged the herd more than five miles on the third day's drive over this waterless mesa. In spite of our economy of water, after breakfast on this third morning there was scarcely enough left to fill the canteens for the day. In view of this, we could promise ourselves no midday meal — except a can of tomatoes to the man; so the wagon was ordered to drive through to the expected water ahead, while the saddle horses were held available as on the day before for frequent changing of mounts. The day turned out to be one of torrid heat, and before the middle of the forenoon, the cattle lolled their tongues in despair, while their sullen lowing surged through from rear to lead and back again in piteous yet ominous appeal. The only relief we could offer was to travel them slowly, as they spurned every opportunity offered them either to graze or to lie down.

It was nearly noon when we reached the last divide, and sighted the scattering timber of the expected watercourse. The enforced order of the day before — to hold the herd in a walk and prevent exertion and heating — now required four men in the lead, while the rear followed over a mile behind, dogged and sullen. Near the middle of the afternoon, McCann returned on one of his mules with the word that it was a question if there was water enough to water even the horse stock. The preceding outfit, so he reported, had dug a shallow well in the bed of the creek, from which he had filled his kegs, but the stock water was a mere loblolly. On receipt of this news, we changed mounts for the fifth time that day; and Flood, taking Forrest, the cook, and the horse wrangler, pushed on ahead with the *remuda* to the waterless stream.

The outlook was anything but encouraging. Flood and Forrest scouted the creek up and down for ten miles in a fruitless search for water. The outfit held the herd back until the twilight of evening, when Flood returned and confirmed McCann's report. It was twenty miles yet to the next water ahead, and if the horse stock could only be watered thoroughly, Flood was determined to make the attempt to nurse the herd through to water. McCann was digging an extra well, and he expressed the belief that by hollowing out a number of holes, enough water could be secured for the saddle stock. Honeyman had corralled the horses and was letting only a few go to the water at a time, while the night horses were being thoroughly watered as fast as the water rose in the well.

Holding the herd this third night required all hands. Only a few men at a time were allowed to go into camp and eat, for the herd refused even to lie down. What few cattle attempted to rest were prevented by the more restless ones. By spells they would mill, until riders were sent through the herd at a break-neck pace to break up the groups. During these milling efforts of the herd, we drifted over a mile from camp; but by the light of moon and stars and the number of riders, scattering was prevented. As the horses were loose for the night, we could not start them on the trail until daybreak gave us a change of mounts, so we lost the early start of the morning before.

Good cloudy weather would have saved us, but in its stead was a sultry morning without a breath of air, which bespoke another day of sizzling heat. We had not been on the trail over two hours before the heat became almost unbearable to man and beast. Had it not been for the condition of the herd, all might yet have gone well; but over three days had now elapsed without water for the cattle, and they became feverish and ungovernable. The lead cattle turned back several times, wandering aimlessly in any direction, and it was with considerable difficulty that the herd could be held on the trail. The rear overtook the lead, and the cattle gradually lost all semblance of a trail herd. Our horses were fresh, however, and after about two hours' work, we once more got the herd strung out in trailing fashion; but before a mile had been covered, the leaders again turned, and the cattle congregated into a mass of unmanageable animals, milling and lowing in their fever and thirst. The milling only intensified their sufferings from the heat, and the outfit split and quartered them again and again, in the hope that this unfortunate outbreak might be checked. No sooner was the milling stopped than they would surge hither and yon, sometimes half a mile, as ungovernable as the waves of an ocean. After wasting several hours in this manner, they finally turned back over the trail, and the utmost efforts of every man in the outfit failed to check them. We threw our ropes in their faces, and when this failed, we resorted to shooting; but in defiance of the fusillade and the smoke they walked sullenly through the line of horsemen across their front. Six-shooters were discharged so close to the leaders' faces as to singe their hair, yet, under a noonday sun, they disregarded this and every other device to turn them, and passed wholly out of our control. In a number of instances wild steers deliberately walked against our horses, and then for the first time a fact dawned on us that chilled the marrow in our bones, — *the herd was going blind.*

The bones of men and animals that lie bleaching along the trails abundantly testify that this was not the first instance in which the plain had baffled the determination of man. It was now evident that nothing short of water would stop the herd, and we rode aside and let them pass. As the outfit turned back to the wagon, our foreman seemed dazed by the sudden and unexpected turn of affairs, but rallied and met the emergency.

"There's but one thing left to do," said he, as we rode along, "and that is to hurry the outfit back to Indian Lakes. The herd will travel day and night, and instinct can be depended on to carry them to the only water they know. It's too late to be of any use now, but it's plain why those last two herds turned off at the lakes; some one had gone back and warned them of the very thing we've met. We must beat them to the lakes, for water is the only thing that will check them now. It's a good thing that they are strong, and five or six days without water will hardly kill any. It was no vague statement of the man who said if he owned hell and Texas, he'd rent Texas and live in hell, for if this isn't Billy hell, I'd like to know what you call it."

We spent an hour watering the horses from the wells of our camp of the night before, and about two o'clock started back over the trail for Indian Lakes. We overtook the abandoned herd during the afternoon. They were strung out nearly five miles in length, and were walking about a three-mile gait. Four men were given two extra horses apiece and left to throw in the stragglers in the rear, with instructions to follow them well into the night, and again in the morning as long as their canteens lasted. The remainder of the outfit pushed on without a halt, except to change mounts, and reached the lakes shortly after midnight. There we secured the first good sleep of any consequence for three days.

It was fortunate for us that there were no range cattle at these lakes, and we had only to cover a front of about six miles to catch the drifting herd. It was nearly noon the next day before the cattle began to arrive at the water holes in squads of from twenty to fifty. Pitiful objects as they were, it was a novelty to see them reach the water and slack their thirst. Wading out into the lakes until their sides were half covered, they would stand and low in a soft moaning voice, often for half an hour before attempting to drink. Contrary to our expectation, they drank very little at first, but stood in the water for hours. After coming out, they would lie down and rest for hours longer, and then drink again before attempting to graze, their thirst overpowering hunger. That they were blind there was no question, but with the causes that produced it once removed, it was probable their eyesight would gradually return.

By early evening, the rear guard of our outfit returned and reported the tail end of the herd some twenty miles behind when they left them. During the day not over a thousand head reached the lakes, and towards evening we put these under herd and easily held them during the night. All four of the men who constituted the rear guard were sent back the next morning to prod up the rear again, and during the night at least a thousand more came into the lakes, which held them better than a hundred men. With the recovery of the cattle our hopes grew, and with the gradual accessions to the herd, confidence was again completely restored. Our saddle stock, not having suffered as had the cattle, were in a serviceable condition, and while a few men were all that were necessary to hold the herd, the others scoured the country for miles in search of any possible stragglers which might have missed the water.

During the forenoon of the third day at the lakes, Nat Straw, the foreman of Ellison's first herd on the trail, rode up to our camp. He was scouting for water for his herd, and, when our situation was explained and he had been interrogated regarding loose cattle, gave us the good news that no stragglers in our road brand had been met by their outfit. This was welcome news, for we had made no count yet, and feared some of them, in their locoed condition, might have passed the water during the night. Our misfortune was an ill wind by which Straw profited, for he had fully expected to keep on by the old route, but with our disaster staring him in the face, a similar experience was to be avoided. His herd reached the lakes during the middle of the afternoon, and after watering, turned and went westward over the new route taken by the two herds which preceded us. He had a herd of about three thousand steers, and was driving to the Dodge market. After the experience we had just gone through, his herd and outfit were a welcome sight. Flood made inquiries after Lovell's second herd, under my brother Bob as foreman, but Straw had seen or heard nothing of them, having come from Goliad County with his cattle.

After the Ellison herd had passed on and out of sight, our squad which had been working the country to the northward, over the route by which the abandoned herd had returned, came in with the information that that section was clear of cattle, and that they had only found three head dead from thirst. On the fourth morning, as the herd left the bed ground, a count was ordered, and to our surprise we counted out twenty-six head more than we had received on the banks of the Rio Grande a month before. As there had been but one previous occasion to count, the number of strays absorbed into our herd was easily accounted for by Priest: "If a steer herd could increase on the trail, why shouldn't ours, that had over a thousand cows in it?" The observation was hardly borne out when the ages of our herd were taken into consideration. But 1882 in Texas was a liberal day and generation, and "cattle stealing" was too drastic a term to use for the chance gain of a few cattle, when the foundations of princely fortunes were being laid with a rope and a branding iron.

In order to give the Ellison herd a good start of us, we only moved our wagon to the farthest lake and went into camp for the day. The herd had recovered its normal condition by this time, and of the troubles of the past week not a trace remained. Instead, our herd grazed in leisurely content over a thousand acres, while with the exception of a few men on herd, the outfit lounged around the wagon and beguiled the time with cards.

We had undergone an experience which my bunkie, The Rebel, termed "an interesting incident in his checkered career," but which not even he would have cared to repeat. That night while on night herd together — the cattle resting in all contentment — we rode one round together, and as he rolled a cigarette he gave me an old war story: —

"They used to tell the story in the army, that during one of the winter retreats, a cavalryman, riding along in the wake of the column at night, saw a hat apparently floating in the mud and water. In the hope that it might be a better hat than the one he was wearing, he dismounted to get it. Feeling his way carefully through the ooze until he reached the hat, he was surprised to find a man underneath and wearing it. 'Hello, comrade,' he sang out, 'can I lend you a hand?'

"'No, no,' replied the fellow, 'I'm all right; I've got a good mule yet under me.'"

CHAPTER VI
A REMINISCENT NIGHT

On the ninth morning we made our second start from the Indian Lakes. An amusing incident occurred during the last night of our camp at these water holes. Coyotes had been hanging around our camp for several days, and during the quiet hours of the night these scavengers of the plain had often ventured in near the wagon in search of scraps of meat or anything edible. Rod Wheat and Ash Borrowstone had made their beds down some distance from the wagon; the coyotes as they circled round the camp came near their bed, and in sniffing about awoke Borrowstone. There was no more danger of attack from these cowards than from field mice, but their presence annoyed Ash, and as he dared not shoot, he threw his boots at the varmints. Imagine his chagrin the next morning to find that one boot had landed among the banked embers of the camp-fire, and was burned to a crisp. It was looked upon as a capital joke by the outfit, as there was no telling when we would reach a store where he could secure another pair.

The new trail, after bearing to the westward for several days, turned northward, paralleling the old one, and a week later we came into the old trail over a hundred miles north of the Indian Lakes. With the exception of one thirty-mile drive without water, no fault could be found with the new trail. A few days after coming into the old trail, we passed Mason, a point where trail herds usually put in for supplies. As we passed during the middle of the afternoon, the wagon and a number of the boys went into the burg. Quince Forrest and Billy Honeyman were the only two in the outfit for whom there were any letters, with the exception of a letter from Lovell, which was common property. Never having been over the trail before, and not even knowing that it was possible to hear from home, I wasn't expecting any letter; but I felt a little twinge of homesickness that night when Honeyman read us certain portions of his letter, which was from his sister. Forrest's letter was from a sweetheart, and after reading it a few times, he burnt it, and that was all we ever knew of its contents, for he was too foxy to say anything, even if it had not been unfavorable. Borrowstone swaggered around camp that evening in a new pair of boots, which had the Lone Star set in filigree-work in their red tops.

At our last camp at the lakes, The Rebel and I, as partners, had been shamefully beaten in a game of seven-up by Bull Durham and John Officer, and had demanded satisfaction in another trial around the fire that night. We borrowed McCann's lantern, and by the aid of it and the camp-fire had an abundance of light for our game. In the absence of a table, we unrolled a bed and sat down Indian fashion over a game of cards in which all friendship ceased.

The outfit, with the exception of myself, had come from the same neighborhood, and an item in Honeyman's letter causing considerable comment was a wedding which had occurred since the outfit had left. It seemed that a number of the boys had sparked the bride in times past, and now that she was married, their minds naturally became reminiscent over old sweethearts.

"The way I make it out," said Honeyman, in commenting on the news, "is that the girl had met this fellow over in the next county while visiting her cousins the year before. My sister gives it as a horseback opinion that she'd been engaged to this fellow nearly eight months; girls, you know, sabe each other that way. Well, it won't affect my appetite any if all the girls I know get married while I'm gone."

"You certainly have never experienced the tender passion," said Fox Quarternight to our horse wrangler, as he lighted his pipe with a brand from the fire. "Now I have. That's the reason why I sympathize with these old beaus of the bride. Of course I was too old to stand any show on her string, and I reckon the fellow who got her ain't so powerful much, except his veneering and being a stranger, which was a big advantage. To be sure, if she took a smile to this stranger, no other fellow could check her with a three-quarter rope and a snubbing post. I've seen girls walk right by a dozen good fellows and fawn over some scrub. My experience teaches me that when there's a woman in it, it's haphazard pot luck with no telling which way the cat will hop. You can't play any system, and merit cuts little figure in general results."

"Fox," said Durham, while Officer was shuffling the cards, "your auger seems well oiled and working keen to-night. Suppose you give us that little experience of yours in love affairs. It will be a treat to those of us who have never been in love, and won't interrupt the game a particle. Cut loose, won't you?"

"It's a long time back," said Quarternight, meditatively, "and the scars have all healed, so I don't mind telling it. I was born and raised on the border of the Blue Grass Region in Kentucky. I had the misfortune to be born of poor but honest parents, as they do in stories; no hero ever had the advantage of me in that respect. In love affairs, however, it's a high card in your hand to be born rich. The country around my old home had good schools, so we had the advantage of a good education. When I was about nineteen, I went away from home one winter to teach school — a little country school about fifteen miles from home. But in the old States fifteen miles from home makes you a dead rank stranger. The trustee of the township was shucking corn when I went to apply for the school. I simply whipped out my peg and helped him shuck out a shock or two while we talked over school matters. The dinner bell rang, and he insisted on my staying for dinner with him. Well, he gave me a better school than I had asked for — better neighborhood, he said — and told me to board with a certain family who had no children; he gave his reasons, but that's immaterial. They were friends of his, so I learned afterwards. They proved to be fine people. The woman was one of those kindly souls who never know where to stop. She planned and schemed to marry me off in spite of myself. The first month that I was with them she told me all about the girls in that immediate neighborhood. In fact, she rather got me unduly excited, being a youth and somewhat verdant. She dwelt powerful heavy on a girl who lived in a big brick house which stood back of the road some distance. This girl had gone to school at a seminary for young ladies near Lexington, — studied music and painting and was 'way up on everything. She described her to me as black-eyed with raven tresses, just like you read about in novels.

"Things were rocking along nicely, when a few days before Christmas a little girl who belonged to the family who lived in the brick house brought me a note one morning. It was an invitation to take supper with them the following evening. The note was written in a pretty hand, and the name signed to it — I'm satisfied now it was a forgery. My landlady agreed with me on that point; in fact, she may have mentioned it first. I never ought to have taken her into my confidence like I did. But I wanted to consult her, showed her the invitation, and asked her advice. She was in the seventh heaven of delight; had me answer it at once, accept the invitation with pleasure and a lot of stuff that I never used before — she had been young once herself. I used up five or six sheets of paper in writing the answer, spoilt one after another, and the one I did send was a flat failure compared to the one I received. Well, the next evening when it was time to start, I was nervous and uneasy. It was nearly dark when I reached the house, but I wanted it that way. Say, but when I knocked on the front door of that house it was with fear and trembling. 'Is this Mr. Quarternight?' inquired a very affable lady who received me. I knew I was one of old man Quarternight's seven boys, and admitted that that was my name, though it was the first time any one had ever called me *mister*. I was welcomed, ushered in, and introduced all around. There were a few small children whom I knew, so I managed to talk to them. The girl whom I was being braced against was not a particle overrated, but sustained the Kentucky reputation for beauty. She made herself so pleasant and agreeable that my fears soon subsided. When the man of the house came in I was cured entirely. He was gruff and hearty, opened his mouth and laughed deep. I built right up to him. We talked about cattle and horses until supper was announced. He was really sorry I hadn't come earlier, so as to look at a three year old colt that he set a heap of store by. He showed him to me after supper with a lantern. Fine colt, too. I don't remember much about the supper, except that it was fine and I came near spilling my coffee several times, my hands were so large and my coat sleeves so short. When we returned from looking at the colt, we went into the parlor. Say, fellows, it was a little the nicest thing that ever I went against. Carpet that made you think you were going to bog down every step, springy like marsh land, and I was glad I came. Then the younger children were ordered to retire, and shortly afterward the man and his wife followed suit.

"When I heard the old man throw his heavy boots on the floor in the next room, I realized that I was left all alone with their charming daughter. All my fears of the early part of the evening tried to crowd on me again, but were calmed by the girl, who sang and played on the piano with no audience but me. Then she interested me by telling her school experiences, and how glad she was that they were over. Finally she lugged out a great big family album, and sat down aside of me on one of these horsehair sofas. That album had a clasp on it, a buckle of pure silver, same as these eighteen dollar bridles. While we were looking at the pictures — some of the old varmints had fought in the Revolutionary war, so she said — I noticed how close we were sitting together. Then we sat farther apart after we had gone through the album, one on each end of the sofa, and talked about the neighborhood, until I suddenly remembered that I had to go. While she was getting my hat and I was getting away, somehow she had me promise to take dinner with them on Christmas.

"For the next two or three months it was hard to tell if I lived at my boarding house or at the brick. If I failed to go, my landlady would hatch up some errand and send me over. If she hadn't been such a good woman, I'd never forgive her for leading me to the sacrifice like she did. Well, about two weeks before school was out, I went home over Saturday and Sunday. Those were fatal days in my life. When I returned on Monday morning, there was a letter waiting for me. It was from the girl's mamma. There had been a quilting in the neighborhood on Saturday, and at this meet of the local gossips, some one had hinted that there was liable to be a wedding as soon as school was out. Mamma was present, and neither admitted nor denied the charge. But there was a woman at this quilting who had once lived over in our neighborhood and felt it her duty to enlighten the company as to who I was. I got all this later from my landlady. 'Law me,' said this woman, 'folks round here in this section think our teacher is the son of that big farmer who raises so many cattle and horses. Why, I've known both families of those Quarternights for nigh on to thirty year. Our teacher is one of old John Fox's boys, the Irish Quarternights, who live up near the salt licks on Doe Run. They were always so poor that the children never had enough to eat and hardly half enough to wear.'

"This plain statement of facts fell like a bombshell on mamma. She started a private investigation of her own, and her verdict was in that letter. It was a centre shot. That evening when I locked the schoolhouse door it was for the last time, for I never unlocked it again. My landlady, dear old womanly soul, tried hard to have me teach the school out at least, but I didn't see it that way. The cause of education in Kentucky might have gone straight to eternal hell, before I'd have stayed another day in that neighborhood. I had money enough to get to Texas with, and here I am. When a fellow gets it burnt into him like a brand that way once, it lasts him quite a while. He'll feel his way next time."

"That was rather a raw deal to give a fellow," said Officer, who had been listening while playing cards. "Didn't you never see the girl again?"

"No, nor you wouldn't want to either if that letter had been written to you. And some folks claim that seven is a lucky number; there were seven boys in our family and nary one ever married."

"That experience of Fox's," remarked Honeyman, after a short silence, "is almost similar to one I had. Before Lovell and Flood adopted me, I worked for a horse man down on the Nueces. Every year he drove up the trail a large herd of horse stock. We drove to the same point on the trail each year, and I happened to get acquainted up there with a family that had several girls in it. The youngest girl in the family and I seemed to understand each other fairly well. I had to stay at the horse camp most of the time, and in one way and another did not get to see her as much as I would have liked. When we sold out the herd, I hung around for a week or so, and spent a month's wages showing her the cloud with the silver lining. She stood it all easy, too. When the outfit went home, of course I went with them. I was banking plenty strong, however, that next year, if there was a good market in horses, I'd take her home with me. I had saved my wages and rustled around, and when we started up the trail next year, I had forty horses of my own in the herd. I had figured they would bring me a thousand dollars, and there was my wages besides.

"When we reached this place, we held the herd out twenty miles, so it was some time before I got into town to see the girl. But the first time I did get to see her I learned that an older sister of hers, who had run away with some renegade from Texas a year or so before, had drifted back home lately with tears in her eyes and a big fat baby boy in her arms. She warned me to keep away from the house, for men from Texas were at a slight discount right then in that family. The girl seemed to regret it and talked reasonable, and I thought I could see encouragement. I didn't crowd matters, nor did her folks forget me when they heard that Byler had come in with a horse herd from the Nueces. I met the girl away from home several times during the summer, and learned that they kept hot water on tap to scald me if I ever dared to show up. One son-in-law from Texas had simply surfeited that family — there was no other vacancy. About the time we closed out and were again ready to go home, there was a cattleman's ball given in this little trail town. We stayed over several days to take in this ball, as I had some plans of my own. My girl was at the ball all easy enough, but she warned me that her brother was watching me. I paid no attention to him, and danced with her right along, begging her to run away with me. It was obviously the only play to make. But the more I'd 'suade her the more she'd 'fuse. The family was on the prod bigger than a wolf, and there was no use reasoning with them. After I had had every dance with her for an hour or so, her brother coolly stepped in and took her home. The next morning he felt it his duty, as his sister's protector, to hunt me up and inform me that if I even spoke to his sister again, he'd shoot me like a dog.

"'Is that a bluff, or do you mean it for a real play?' I inquired, politely.

"'You'll find that it will be real enough,' he answered, angrily.

"'Well, now, that's too bad,' I answered; 'I'm really sorry that I can't promise to respect your request. But this much I can assure you: any time that you have the leisure and want to shoot me, just cut loose your dog. But remember this one thing — that it will be my second shot.'"

"Are you sure you wasn't running a blazer yourself, or is the wind merely rising?" inquired Durham, while I was shuffling the cards for the next deal.

"Well, if I was, I hung up my gentle honk before his eyes and ears and gave him free license to call it. The truth is, I didn't pay any more attention to him than I would to an empty bottle. I reckon the girl was all right, but the family were these razor-backed, barnyard savages. It makes me hot under the collar yet when I think of it. They'd have lawed me if I had, but I ought to have shot him and checked the breed."

"Why didn't you run off with her?" inquired Fox, dryly.

"Well, of course a man of your nerve is always capable of advising others. But you see, I'm strong on the breed. Now a girl can't show her true colors like the girl's brother did, but get her in the harness once, and then she'll show you the white of her eye, balk, and possibly kick over the wagon tongue. No, I believe in the breed — blood'll tell."

"I worked for a cowman once," said Bull, irrelevantly, "and they told it on him that he lost twenty thousand dollars the night he was married."

"How, gambling?" I inquired.

"No. The woman he married claimed to be worth twenty thousand dollars and she never had a cent. Spades trump?"

"No; hearts," replied The Rebel. "I used to know a foreman up in DeWitt County, — 'Honest' John Glen they called him. He claimed the only chance he ever had to marry was a widow, and the reason he didn't marry her was, he was too honest to take advantage of a dead man."

While we paid little attention to wind or weather, this was an ideal night, and we were laggard in seeking our blankets. Yarn followed yarn; for nearly every one of us, either from observation or from practical experience, had a slight acquaintance with the great mastering passion. But the poetical had not been developed in us to an appreciative degree, so we discussed the topic under consideration much as we would have done horses or cattle.

Finally the game ended. A general yawn went the round of the loungers about the fire. The second guard had gone on, and when the first rode in, Joe Stallings, halting his horse in passing the fire, called out sociably, "That muley steer, the white four year old, didn't like to bed down amongst the others, so I let him come out and lay down by himself. You'll find him over on the far side of the herd. You all remember how wild he was when we first started? Well, you can ride within three feet of him to-night, and he'll grunt and act sociable and never offer to get up. I promised him that he might sleep alone as long as he was good; I just love a good steer. Make down our bed, pardner; I'll be back as soon as I picket my horse."

CHAPTER VII
THE COLORADO

The month of May found our Circle Dot herd, in spite of all drawbacks, nearly five hundred miles on its way. For the past week we had been traveling over that immense tableland which skirts the arid portion of western Texas. A few days before, while passing the blue mountains which stand as a southern sentinel in the chain marking the headwaters of the Concho River, we had our first glimpse of the hills. In its almost primitive condition, the country was generous, supplying every want for sustenance of horses and cattle. The grass at this stage of the season was well matured, the herd taking on flesh in a very gratifying manner, and, while we had crossed some rocky country, lame and sore-footed cattle had as yet caused us no serious trouble.

One morning when within one day's drive of the Colorado River, as our herd was leaving the bed ground, the last guard encountered a bunch of cattle drifting back down the trail. There were nearly fifty head of the stragglers; and as one of our men on guard turned them to throw them away from our herd, the road brand caught his eye, and he recognized the strays as belonging to the Ellison herd which had passed us at the Indian Lakes some ten days before. Flood's attention once drawn to the brand, he ordered them thrown into our herd. It was evident that some trouble had occurred with the Ellison cattle, possibly a stampede; and it was but a neighborly act to lend any assistance in our power. As soon as the outfit could breakfast, mount, and take the herd, Flood sent Priest and me to scout the country to the westward of the trail, while Bob Blades and Ash Borrowstone started on a similar errand to the eastward, with orders to throw in any drifting cattle in the Ellison road brand. Within an hour after starting, the herd encountered several straggling bands, and as Priest and I were on the point of returning to the herd, we almost overrode a bunch of eighty odd head lying down in some broken country. They were gaunt and tired, and The Rebel at once pronounced their stiffened movements the result of a stampede.

We were drifting them back towards the trail, when Nat Straw and two of his men rode out from our herd and met us. "I always did claim that it was better to be born lucky than handsome," said Straw as he rode up. "One week Flood saves me from a dry drive, and the very next one, he's just the right distance behind to catch my drift from a nasty stampede. Not only that, but my peelers and I are riding Circle Dot horses, as well as reaching the wagon in time for breakfast and lining our flues with Lovell's good chuck. It's too good luck to last, I'm afraid.

"I'm not hankering for the dramatic in life, but we had a run last night that would curl your hair. Just about midnight a bunch of range cattle ran into us, and before you could say Jack Robinson, our dogies had vamoosed the ranch and were running in half a dozen different directions. We rounded them up the best we could in the dark, and then I took a couple of men and came back down the trail about twenty miles to catch any drift when day dawned. But you see there's nothing like being lucky and having good neighbors, — cattle caught, fresh horses, and a warm breakfast all waiting for you. I'm such a lucky dog, it's a wonder some one didn't steal me when I was little. I can't help it, but some day I'll marry a banker's daughter, or fall heir to a ranch as big as old McCulloch County."

Before meeting us, Straw had confided to our foreman that he could assign no other plausible excuse for the stampede than that it was the work of cattle rustlers. He claimed to know the country along the Colorado, and unless it had changed recently, those hills to the westward harbored a good many of the worst rustlers in the State. He admitted it might have been wolves chasing the range cattle, but thought it had the earmarks of being done by human wolves. He maintained that few herds had ever passed that river without loss of cattle, unless the rustlers were too busy elsewhere to give the passing herd their attention. Straw had ordered his herd to drop back down the trail about ten miles from their camp of the night previous, and about noon the two herds met on a branch of Brady Creek. By that time our herd had nearly three hundred head of the Ellison cattle, so we held it up and cut theirs out. Straw urged our foreman, whatever he did, not to make camp in the Colorado bottoms or anywhere near the river, if he didn't want a repetition of his experience. After starting our herd in the afternoon, about half a dozen of us turned back and lent a hand in counting Straw's herd, which proved to be over a hundred head short, and nearly half his outfit were still out hunting cattle. Acting on Straw's advice, we camped that night some five or six miles back from the river on the last divide. From the time the second guard went on until the third was relieved, we took the precaution of keeping a scout outriding from a half to three quarters of a mile distant from the herd, Flood and Honeyman serving in that capacity. Every precaution was taken to prevent a surprise; and in case anything did happen, our night horses tied to the wagon wheels stood ready saddled and bridled for any emergency. But the night passed without incident.

An hour or two after the herd had started the next morning, four well mounted, strange men rode up from the westward, and representing themselves as trail cutters, asked for our foreman. Flood met them, in his usual quiet manner, and after admitting that we had been troubled more or less with range cattle, assured our callers that if there was anything in the herd in the brands they represented, he would gladly hold it up and give them every opportunity to cut their cattle out. As he was anxious to cross the river before noon, he invited the visitors to stay for dinner, assuring them that before starting the herd in the afternoon, he would throw the cattle together for their inspection. Flood made himself very agreeable, inquiring into cattle and range matters in general as well as the stage of water in the river ahead. The spokesman of the trail cutters met Flood's invitation to dinner with excuses about the pressing demands on his time, and urged, if it did not seriously interfere with our plans, that he be allowed to inspect the herd before crossing the river. His reasons seemed trivial and our foreman was not convinced.

"You see, gentlemen," he said, "in handling these southern cattle, we must take advantage of occasions. We have timed our morning's drive so as to reach the river during the warmest hour of the day, or as near noon as possible. You can hardly imagine what a difference there is, in fording this herd, between a cool, cloudy day and a clear, hot one. You see the herd is strung out nearly a mile in length now, and to hold them up and waste an hour or more for your inspection would seriously disturb our plans. And then our wagon and *remuda* have gone on with orders to noon at the first good camp beyond the river. I perfectly understand your reasons, and you equally understand mine; but I will send a man or two back to help you recross any cattle you may find in our herd. Now, if a couple of you gentlemen will ride around on the far side with me, and the others will ride up near the lead, we will trail the cattle across when we reach the river without cutting the herd into blocks."

Flood's affability, coupled with the fact that the lead cattle were nearly up to the river, won his point. Our visitors could only yield, and rode forward with our lead swing men to assist in forcing the lead cattle into the river. It was swift water, but otherwise an easy crossing, and we allowed the herd, after coming out on the farther side, to spread out and graze forward at its pleasure. The wagon and saddle stock were in sight about a mile ahead, and leaving two men on herd to drift the cattle in the right direction, the rest of us rode leisurely on to the wagon, where dinner was waiting. Flood treated our callers with marked courtesy during dinner, and casually inquired if any of their number had seen any cattle that day or the day previous in the Ellison road brand. They had not, they said, explaining that their range lay on both sides of the Concho, and that during the trail season they kept all their cattle between that river and the main Colorado. Their work had kept them on their own range recently, except when trail herds were passing and needed to be looked through for strays. It sounded as though our trail cutters could also use diplomacy on occasion.

When dinner was over and we had caught horses for the afternoon and were ready to mount, Flood asked our guests for their credentials as duly authorized trail cutters. They replied that they had none, but offered in explanation the statement that they were merely cutting in the interest of the immediate locality, which required no written authority.

Then the previous affability of our foreman turned to iron. "Well, men," said he, "if you have no authority to cut this trail, then you don't cut this herd. I must have inspection papers before I can move a brand out of the county in which it is bred, and I'll certainly let no other man, local or duly appointed, cut an animal out of this herd without written and certified authority. You know that without being told, or ought to. I respect the rights of every man posted on a trail to cut it. If you want to see my inspection papers, you have a right to demand them, and in turn I demand of you your credentials, showing who you work for and the list of brands you represent; otherwise no harm's done; nor do you cut any herd that I'm driving."

"Well," said one of the men, "I saw a couple of head in my own individual brand as we rode up the herd. I'd like to see the man who says that I haven't the right to claim my own brand, anywhere I find it."

"If there's anything in our herd in your individual brand," said Flood, "all you have to do is to give me the brand, and I'll cut it for you. What's your brand?"

"The 'Window Sash.'"

"Have any of you boys seen such a brand in our herd?" inquired Flood, turning to us as we all stood by our horses ready to start.

"I didn't recognize it by that name," replied Quince Forrest, who rode in the swing on the branded side of the cattle and belonged to the last guard, "but I remember seeing such a brand, though I would have given it a different name. Yes, come to think, I'm sure I saw it, and I'll tell you where: yesterday morning when I rode out to throw those drifting cattle away from our herd, I saw that brand among the Ellison cattle which had stampeded the night before. When Straw's outfit cut theirs out yesterday, they must have left the 'Window Sash' cattle with us; those were the range cattle which stampeded his herd. It looked to me a little blotched, but if I'd been called on to name it, I'd called it a thief's brand. If these gentlemen claim them, though, it'll only take a minute to cut them out."

"This outfit needn't get personal and fling out their insults," retorted the claimant of the "Window Sash" brand, "for I'll claim my own if there were a hundred of you. And you can depend that any animal I claim, I'll take, if I have to go back to the ranch and bring twenty men to help me do it."

"You won't need any help to get all that's coming to you," replied our foreman, as he mounted his horse. "Let's throw the herd together, boys, and cut these 'Window Sash' cattle out. We don't want any cattle in our herd that stampede on an open range at midnight; they must certainly be terrible wild."

As we rode out together, our trail cutters dropped behind and kept a respectable distance from the herd while we threw the cattle together. When the herd had closed to the required compactness, Flood called our trail cutters up and said, "Now, men, each one of you can take one of my outfit with you and inspect this herd to your satisfaction. If you see anything there you claim, we'll cut it out for you, but don't attempt to cut anything yourselves."

We rode in by pairs, a man of ours with each stranger, and after riding leisurely through the herd for half an hour, cut out three head in the blotched brand called the "Window Sash." Before leaving the herd, one of the strangers laid claim to a red cow, but Fox Quarternight refused to cut the animal.

When the pair rode out the stranger accosted Flood. "I notice a cow of mine in there," said he, "not in your road brand, which I claim. Your man here refuses to cut her for me, so I appeal to you."

"What's her brand, Fox?" asked Flood.

"She's a 'Q' cow, but the colonel here thinks it's an 'O.' I happen to know the cow and the brand both; she came into the herd four hundred miles south of here while we were watering the herd in the Nueces River. The 'Q' is a little dim, but it's plenty plain to hold her for the present."

"If she's a 'Q' cow I have no claim on her," protested the stranger, "but if the brand is an 'O,' then I claim her as a stray from our range, and I don't care if she came into your herd when you were watering in the San Fernando River in Old Mexico, I'll claim her just the same. I'm going to ask you to throw her."

"I'll throw her for you," coolly replied Fox, "and bet you my saddle and six-shooter on the side that it isn't an 'O,' and even if it was, you and all the thieves on the Concho can't take her. I know a few of the simple principles of rustling myself. Do you want her thrown?"

"That's what I asked for."

"Throw her, then," said Flood, "and don't let's parley."

Fox rode back in to the herd, and after some little delay, located the cow and worked her out to the edge of the cattle. Dropping his rope, he cut her out clear of the herd, and as she circled around in an endeavor to reenter, he rode close and made an easy cast of the rope about her horns. As he threw his horse back to check the cow, I rode to his assistance, my rope in hand, and as the cow turned ends, I heeled her. A number of the outfit rode up and dismounted, and one of the boys taking her by the tail, we threw the animal as humanely as possible. In order to get at the brand, which was on the side, we turned the cow over, when Flood took out his knife and cut the hair away, leaving the brand easily traceable.

"What is she, Jim?" inquired Fox, as he sat his horse holding the rope taut.

"I'll let this man who claims her answer that question," replied Flood, as her claimant critically examined the brand to his satisfaction.

"I claim her as an 'O' cow," said the stranger, facing Flood.

"Well, you claim more than you'll ever get," replied our foreman.
"Turn her loose, boys."

The cow was freed and turned back into the herd, but the claimant tried to argue the matter with Flood, claiming the branding iron had simply slipped, giving it the appearance of a "Q" instead of an "O" as it was intended to be. Our foreman paid little attention to the stranger, but when his persistence became annoying checked his argument by saying, —

"My Christian friend, there's no use arguing this matter. You asked to have the cow thrown, and we threw her. You might as well try to tell me that the cow is white as to claim her in any other brand than a 'Q.' You may read brands as well as I do, but you're wasting time arguing against the facts. You'd better take your 'Window Sash' cattle and ride on, for you've cut all you're going to cut here to-day. But before you go, for fear I may never see you again, I'll take this occasion to say that I think you're common cow thieves."

By his straight talk, our foreman stood several inches higher in our estimation as we sat our horses, grinning at the discomfiture of the trail cutters, while a dozen six-shooters slouched languidly at our hips to give emphasis to his words.

"Before going, I'll take this occasion to say to you that you will see me again," replied the leader, riding up and confronting Flood. "You haven't got near enough men to bluff me. As to calling me a cow thief, that's altogether too common a name to offend any one; and from what I can gather, the name wouldn't miss you or your outfit over a thousand miles. Now in taking my leave, I want to tell you that you'll see me before another day passes, and what's more, I'll bring an outfit with me and we'll cut your herd clean to your road brand, if for no better reasons, just to learn you not to be so insolent."

After hanging up this threat, Flood said to him as he turned to ride away, "Well, now, my young friend, you're bargaining for a whole lot of fun. I notice you carry a gun and quite naturally suppose you shoot a little as occasion requires. Suppose when you and your outfit come back, you come a-shooting, so we'll know who you are; for I'll promise you there's liable to be some powder burnt when you cut this herd."

Amid jeers of derision from our outfit, the trail cutters drove off their three lonely "Window Sash" cattle. We had gained the point we wanted, and now in case of any trouble, during inspection or at night, we had the river behind us to catch our herd. We paid little attention to the threat of our disappointed callers, but several times Straw's remarks as to the character of the residents of those hills to the westward recurred to my mind. I was young, but knew enough, instead of asking foolish questions, to keep mum, though my eyes and ears drank in everything. Before we had been on the trail over an hour, we met two men riding down the trail towards the river. Meeting us, they turned and rode along with our foreman, some distance apart from the herd, for nearly an hour, and curiosity ran freely among us boys around the herd as to who they might be. Finally Flood rode forward to the point men and gave the order to throw off the trail and make a short drive that afternoon. Then in company with the two strangers, he rode forward to overtake our wagon, and we saw nothing more of him until we reached camp that evening. This much, however, our point man was able to get from our foreman: that the two men were members of a detachment of Rangers who had been sent as a result of information given by the first herd over the trail that year. This herd, which had passed some twenty days ahead of us, had met with a stampede below the river, and on reaching Abilene had reported the presence of rustlers preying on through herds at the crossing of the Colorado.

On reaching camp that evening with the herd, we found ten of the Rangers as our guests for the night. The detachment was under a corporal named Joe Hames, who had detailed the two men we had met during the afternoon to scout this crossing. Upon the information afforded by our foreman about the would-be trail cutters, these scouts, accompanied by Flood, had turned back to advise the Ranger squad, encamped in a secluded spot about ten miles northeast of the Colorado crossing. They had only arrived late the day before, and this was their first meeting with any trail herd to secure any definite information.

Hames at once assumed charge of the herd, Flood gladly rendering every assistance possible. We night herded as usual, but during the two middle guards, Hames sent out four of his Rangers to scout the immediate outlying country, though, as we expected, they met with no adventure. At daybreak the Rangers threw their packs into our wagon and their loose stock into our *remuda*, and riding up the trail a mile or more, left us, keeping well out of sight. We were all hopeful now that the trail cutters of the day before would make good their word and return. In this hope we killed time for several hours that morning, grazing the cattle and holding the wagon in the rear. Sending the wagon ahead of the herd had been agreed on as the signal between our foreman and the Ranger corporal, at first sight of any posse behind us. We were beginning to despair of their coming, when a dust cloud appeared several miles back down the trail. We at once hurried the wagon and *remuda* ahead to warn the Rangers, and allowed the cattle to string out nearly a mile in length.

A fortunate rise in the trail gave us a glimpse of the cavalcade in our rear, which was entirely too large to be any portion of Straw's outfit; and shortly we were overtaken by our trail cutters of the day before, now increased to twenty-two mounted men. Flood was intentionally in the lead of the herd, and the entire outfit galloped forward to stop the cattle. When they had nearly reached the lead, Flood turned back and met the rustlers.

"Well, I'm as good as my word," said the leader, "and I'm here to trim your herd as I promised you I would. Throw off and hold up your cattle, or I'll do it for you."

Several of our outfit rode up at this juncture in time to hear Flood's reply: "If you think you're equal to the occasion, hold them up yourself. If I had as big an outfit *as* you have, I wouldn't ask any man to help me. I want to watch a Colorado River outfit work a herd, — I might learn something. My outfit will take a rest, or perhaps hold the cut or otherwise clerk for you. But be careful and don't claim anything that you are not certain is your own, for I reserve the right to look over your cut before you drive it away."

The rustlers rode in a body to the lead, and when they had thrown the herd off the trail, about half of them rode back and drifted forward the rear cattle. Flood called our outfit to one side and gave us our instructions, the herd being entirely turned over to the rustlers. After they began cutting, we rode around and pretended to assist in holding the cut as the strays in our herd were being cut out. When the red "Q" cow came out, Fox cut her back, which nearly precipitated a row, for she was promptly recut to the strays by the man who claimed her the day before. Not a man of us even cast a glance up the trail, or in the direction of the Rangers; but when the work was over, Flood protested with the leader of the rustlers over some five or six head of dim-branded cattle which actually belonged to our herd. But he was exultant and would listen to no protests, and attempted to drive away the cut, now numbering nearly fifty head. Then we rode across their front and stopped them.

In the parley which ensued, harsh words were passing, when one of our outfit blurted out in well feigned surprise, —

"Hello, who's that, coming over there?"

A squad of men were riding leisurely through our abandoned herd, coming over to where the two outfits were disputing.

"What's the trouble here, gents?" inquired Hames as he rode up.

"Who are you and what might be your business, may I ask?" inquired the leader of the rustlers.

"Personally I'm nobody, but officially I'm Corporal in Company B, Texas Rangers — well, if there isn't smiling Ed Winters, the biggest cattle thief ever born in Medina County. Why, I've got papers for you; for altering the brands on over fifty head of 'C' cattle into a 'G' brand. Come here, dear, and give me that gun of yours. Come on, and no false moves or funny work or I'll shoot the white out of your eye. Surround this layout, lads, and let's examine them more closely."

At this command, every man in our outfit whipped out his six-shooter, the Rangers leveled their carbines on the rustlers, and in less than a minute's time they were disarmed and as crestfallen a group of men as ever walked into a trap of their own setting. Hames got out a "black book," and after looking the crowd over concluded to hold the entire covey, as the descriptions of the "wanted" seemed to include most of them. Some of the rustlers attempted to explain their presence, but Hames decided to hold the entire party, "just to learn them to be more careful of their company the next time," as he put it.

The cut had drifted away into the herd again during the arrest, and about half our outfit took the cattle on to where the wagon camped for noon. McCann had anticipated an extra crowd for dinner and was prepared for the emergency. When dinner was over and the Rangers had packed and were ready to leave, Hames said to Flood, —

"Well, Flood, I'm powerful glad I met you and your outfit. This has been one of the biggest round-ups for me in a long time. You don't know how proud I am over this bunch of beauties. Why, there's liable to be enough rewards out for this crowd to buy my girl a new pair of shoes. And say, when your wagon comes into Abilene, if I ain't there, just drive around to the sheriff's office and leave those captured guns. I'm sorry to load your wagon down that way, but I'm short on pack mules and it will be a great favor to me; besides, these fellows are not liable to need any guns for some little time. I like your company and your chuck, Flood, but you see how it is; the best of friends must part; and then I have an invitation to take dinner in Abilene by to-morrow noon, so I must be a-riding. Adios, everybody."

CHAPTER VIII
ON THE BRAZOS AND WICHITA

As we neared Buffalo Gap a few days later, a deputy sheriff of Taylor County, who resided at the Gap, rode out and met us. He brought an urgent request from Hames to Flood to appear as a witness against the rustlers, who were to be given a preliminary trial at Abilene the following day. Much as he regretted to leave the herd for even a single night, our foreman finally consented to go. To further his convenience we made a long evening drive, camping for the night well above Buffalo Gap, which at that time was little more than a landmark on the trail. The next day we made an easy drive and passed Abilene early in the afternoon, where Flood rejoined us, but refused any one permission to go into town, with the exception of McCann with the wagon, which was a matter of necessity. It was probably for the best, for this cow town had the reputation of setting a pace that left the wayfarer purseless and breathless, to say nothing about headaches. Though our foreman had not reached those mature years in life when the pleasures and frivolities of dissipation no longer allure, yet it was but natural that he should wish to keep his men from the temptation of the cup that cheers and the wiles of the siren. But when the wagon returned that evening, it was evident that our foreman was human, for with a box of cigars which were promised us were several bottles of Old Crow.

After crossing the Clear Fork of the Brazos a few days later, we entered a well-watered, open country, through which the herd made splendid progress. At Abilene, we were surprised to learn that our herd was the twentieth that had passed that point. The weather so far on our trip had been exceptionally good; only a few showers had fallen, and those during the daytime. But we were now nearing a country in which rain was more frequent, and the swollen condition of several small streams which have their headwaters in the Staked Plains was an intimation to us of recent rains to the westward of our route. Before reaching the main Brazos, we passed two other herds of yearling cattle, and were warned of the impassable condition of that river for the past week. Nothing daunted, we made our usual drive; and when the herd camped that night, Flood, after scouting ahead to the river, returned with the word that the Brazos had been unfordable for over a week, five herds being waterbound.

As we were then nearly twenty miles south of the river, the next morning we threw off the trail and turned the herd to the northeast, hoping to strike the Brazos a few miles above Round Timber ferry. Once the herd was started and their course for the day outlined to our point men by definite landmarks, Flood and Quince Forrest set out to locate the ferry and look up a crossing. Had it not been for our wagon, we would have kept the trail, but as there was no ferry on the Brazos at the crossing of the western trail, it was a question either of waiting or of making this detour. Then all the grazing for several miles about the crossing was already taken by the waterbound herds, and to crowd up and trespass on range already occupied would have been a violation of an unwritten law. Again, no herd took kindly to another attempting to pass them when in traveling condition the herds were on an equality. Our foreman had conceived the scheme of getting past these waterbound herds, if possible, which would give us a clear field until the next large watercourse was reached.

Flood and Forrest returned during the noon hour, the former having found, by swimming, a passable ford near the mouth of Monday Creek, while the latter reported the ferry in "apple-pie order." No sooner, then, was dinner over than the wagon set out for the ferry under Forrest as pilot, though we were to return to the herd once the ferry was sighted. The mouth of Monday Creek was not over ten miles below the regular trail crossing on the Brazos, and much nearer our noon camp than the regular one; but the wagon was compelled to make a direct elbow, first turning to the eastward, then doubling back after the river was crossed. We held the cattle off water during the day, so as to have them thirsty when they reached the river. Flood had swum it during the morning, and warned us to be prepared for fifty or sixty yards of swimming water in crossing. When within a mile, we held up the herd and changed horses, every man picking out one with a tested ability to swim. Those of us who were expected to take the water as the herd entered the river divested ourselves of boots and clothing, which we intrusted to riders in the rear. The approach to crossing was gradual, but the opposite bank was abrupt, with only a narrow passageway leading out from the channel. As the current was certain to carry the swimming cattle downstream, we must, to make due allowance, take the water nearly a hundred yards above the outlet on the other shore. All this was planned out in advance by our foreman, who now took the position of point man on the right hand or down the riverside; and with our saddle horses in the immediate lead, we breasted the angry Brazos.

The water was shallow as we entered, and we reached nearly the middle of the river before the loose saddle horses struck swimming water. Honeyman was on their lee, and with the cattle crowding in their rear, there was no alternative but to swim. A loose horse swims easily, however, and our *remuda* readily faced the current, though it was swift enough to carry them below the passageway on the opposite side. By this time the lead cattle were adrift, and half a dozen of us were on their lower side, for the footing under the cutbank was narrow, and should the cattle become congested on landing, some were likely to drown. For a quarter of an hour it required cool heads to keep the trail of cattle moving into the water and the passageway clear on the opposite landing. While they were crossing, the herd represented a large letter "U," caused by the force of the current drifting the cattle downstream, or until a foothold was secured on the farther side. Those of us fortunate enough to have good swimming horses swam the river a dozen times, and then after the herd was safely over, swam back to get our clothing. It was a thrilling experience to us younger lads of the outfit, and rather attractive; but the elder and more experienced men always dreaded swimming rivers. Their reasons were made clear enough when, a fortnight later, we crossed Red River, where a newly made grave was pointed out to us, amongst others of men who had lost their lives while swimming cattle.

Once the bulk of the cattle were safely over, with no danger of congestion on the farther bank, they were allowed to loiter along under the cutbank and drink to their hearts' content. Quite a number strayed above the passageway, and in order to rout them out, Bob Blades, Moss Strayhorn, and I rode out through the outlet and up the river, where we found some of them in a passageway down a dry arroyo. The steers had found a soft, damp place in the bank, and were so busy horning the waxy, red mud, that they hardly noticed our approach until we were within a rod of them. We halted our horses and watched their antics. The kneeling cattle were cutting the bank viciously with their horns and matting their heads with the red mud, but on discovering our presence, they curved their tails and stampeded out as playfully as young lambs on a hillside.

"Can you sabe where the fun comes in to a steer, to get down on his knees in the mud and dirt, and horn the bank and muss up his curls and enjoy it like that?" inquired Strayhorn of Blades and me.

"Because it's healthy and funny besides," replied Bob, giving me a cautious wink. "Did you never hear of people taking mud baths? You've seen dogs eat grass, haven't you? Well, it's something on the same order. Now, if I was a student of the nature of animals, like you are, I'd get off my horse and imagine I had horns, and scar and otherwise mangle that mud bank shamefully. I'll hold your horse if you want to try it — some of the secrets of the humor of cattle might be revealed to you."

The banter, though given in jest, was too much for this member of a craft that can always be depended on to do foolish things; and when we rejoined the outfit, Strayhorn presented a sight no sane man save a member of our tribe ever would have conceived of.

The herd had scattered over several thousand acres after leaving the river, grazing freely, and so remained during the rest of the evening. Forrest changed horses and set out down the river to find the wagon and pilot it in, for with the long distance that McCann had to cover, it was a question if he would reach us before dark. Flood selected a bed ground and camp about a mile out from the river, and those of the outfit not on herd dragged up an abundance of wood for the night, and built a roaring fire as a beacon to our absent commissary. Darkness soon settled over camp, and the prospect of a supperless night was confronting us; the first guard had taken the herd, and yet there was no sign of the wagon. Several of us youngsters then mounted our night horses and rode down the river a mile or over in the hope of meeting McCann. We came to a steep bank, caused by the shifting of the first bottom of the river across to the north bank, rode up this bluff some little distance, dismounted, and fired several shots; then with our ears to the earth patiently awaited a response. It did not come, and we rode back again. "Hell's fire and little fishes!" said Joe Stallings, as we clambered into our saddles to return, "it's not supper or breakfast that's troubling me, but will we get any dinner to-morrow? That's a more pregnant question."

It must have been after midnight when I was awakened by the braying of mules and the rattle of the wagon, to hear the voices of Forrest and McCann, mingled with the rattle of chains as they unharnessed, condemning to eternal perdition the broken country on the north side of the Brazos, between Round Timber ferry and the mouth of Monday Creek.

"I think that when the Almighty made this country on the north side of the Brazos," said McCann the next morning at breakfast, "the Creator must have grown careless or else made it out of odds and ends. There's just a hundred and one of these dry arroyos that you can't see until you are right onto them. They wouldn't bother a man on horseback, but with a loaded wagon it's different. And I'll promise you all right now that if Forrest hadn't come out and piloted me in, you might have tightened up your belts for breakfast and drank out of cow tracks and smoked cigarettes for nourishment. Well, it'll do you good; this high living was liable to spoil some of you, but I notice that you are all on your feed this morning. The black strap? Honeyman, get that molasses jug out of the wagon — it sits right in front of the chuck box. It does me good to see this outfit's tastes once more going back to the good old staples of life."

We made our usual early start, keeping well out from the river on a course almost due northward. The next river on our way was the Wichita, still several days' drive from the mouth of Monday Creek. Flood's intention was to parallel the old trail until near the river, when, if its stage of water was not fordable, we would again seek a lower crossing in the hope of avoiding any waterbound herds on that watercourse. The second day out from the Brazos it rained heavily during the day and drizzled during the entire night. Not a hoof would bed down, requiring the guards to be doubled into two watches for the night. The next morning, as was usual when off the trail, Flood scouted in advance, and near the middle of the afternoon's drive we came into the old trail. The weather in the mean time had faired off, which revived life and spirit in the outfit, for in trail work there is nothing that depresses the spirits of men like falling weather. On coming into the trail, we noticed that no herds had passed since the rain began. Shortly afterward our rear guard was overtaken by a horseman who belonged to a mixed herd which was encamped some four or five miles below the point where we came into the old trail. He reported the Wichita as having been unfordable for the past week, but at that time falling; and said that if the rain of the past few days had not extended as far west as the Staked Plains, the river would be fordable in a day or two.

Before the stranger left us, Flood returned and confirmed this information, and reported further that there were two herds lying over at the Wichita ford expecting to cross the following day. With this outlook, we grazed our herd up to within five miles of the river and camped for the night, and our visitor returned to his outfit with Flood's report of our expectation of crossing on the morrow. But with the fair weather and the prospects of an easy night, we encamped entirely too close to the trail, as we experienced to our sorrow. The grazing was good everywhere, the recent rains having washed away the dust, and we should have camped farther away. We were all sleepy that night, and no sooner was supper over than every mother's son of us was in his blankets. We slept so soundly that the guards were compelled to dismount when calling the relief, and shake the next guards on duty out of their slumber and see that they got up, for men would unconsciously answer in their sleep. The cattle were likewise tired, and slept as willingly as the men.

About midnight, however, Fox Quarternight dashed into camp, firing his six-shooter and yelling like a demon. We tumbled out of our blankets in a dazed condition to hear that one of the herds camped near the river had stampeded, the heavy rumbling of the running herd and the shooting of their outfit now being distinctly audible. We lost no time getting our horses, and in less than a minute were riding for our cattle, which had already got up and were timidly listening to the approaching noise. Although we were a good quarter mile from the trail, before we could drift our herd to a point of safety, the stampeding cattle swept down the trail like a cyclone and our herd was absorbed into the maelstrom of the onrush like leaves in a whirlwind. It was then that our long-legged Mexican steers set us a pace that required a good horse to equal, for they easily took the lead, the other herd having run between three and four miles before striking us, and being already well winded. The other herd were Central Texas cattle, and numbered over thirty-five hundred, but in running capacity were never any match for ours.

Before they had run a mile past our camp, our outfit, bunched well together on the left point, made the first effort to throw them out and off the trail, and try to turn them. But the waves of an angry ocean could as easily have been brought under subjection as our terrorized herd during this first mad dash. Once we turned a few hundred of the leaders, and about the time we thought success was in reach, another contingent of double the number had taken the lead; then we had to abandon what few we had, and again ride to the front. When we reached the lead, there, within half a mile ahead, burned the camp-fire of the herd of mixed cattle which had moved up the trail that evening. They had had ample warning of impending trouble, just as we had; and before the running cattle reached them about half a dozen of their outfit rode to our assistance, when we made another effort to turn or hold the herds from mixing. None of the outfit of the first herd had kept in the lead with us, their horses fagging, and when the foreman of this mixed herd met us, not knowing that we were as innocent of the trouble as himself, he made some slighting remarks about our outfit and cattle. But it was no time to be sensitive, and with his outfit to help we threw our whole weight against the left point a second time, but only turned a few hundred; and before we could get into the lead again their campfire had been passed and their herd of over three thousand cattle more were in the run. As cows and calves predominated in this mixed herd, our own southerners were still leaders in the stampede.

It is questionable if we would have turned this stampede before daybreak, had not the nature of the country come to our assistance. Something over two miles below the camp of the last herd was a deep creek, the banks of which were steep and the passages few and narrow. Here we succeeded in turning the leaders, and about half the outfit of the mixed herd remained, guarding the crossing and turning the lagging cattle in the run as they came up. With the leaders once turned and no chance for the others to take a new lead, we had the entire run of cattle turned back within an hour and safely under control. The first outfit joined us during the interim, and when day broke we had over forty men drifting about ten thousand cattle back up the trail. The different outfits were unfortunately at loggerheads, no one being willing to assume any blame. Flood hunted up the foreman of the mixed herd and demanded an apology for his remarks on our abrupt meeting with him the night before; and while it was granted, it was plain that it was begrudged. The first herd disclaimed all responsibility, holding that the stampede was due to an unavoidable accident, their cattle having grown restless during their enforced lay-over. The indifferent attitude of their foreman, whose name was Wilson, won the friendly regard of our outfit, and before the wagon of the mixed cattle was reached, there was a compact, at least tacit, between their outfit and ours. Our foreman was not blameless, for had we taken the usual precaution and camped at least a mile off the trail, which was our custom when in close proximity to other herds, we might and probably would have missed this mix-up, for our herd was inclined to be very tractable. Flood, with all his experience, well knew that if stampeded cattle ever got into a known trail, they were certain to turn backward over their course; and we were now paying the fiddler for lack of proper precaution.

Within an hour after daybreak, and before the cattle had reached the camp of the mixed herd, our saddle horses were sighted coming over a slight divide about two miles up the trail, and a minute later McCann's mules hove in sight, bringing up the rear. They had made a start with the first dawn, rightly reasoning, as there was no time to leave orders on our departure, that it was advisable for Mahomet to go to the mountain. Flood complimented our cook and horse wrangler on their foresight, for the wagon was our base of sustenance; and there was little loss of time before Barney McCann was calling us to a hastily prepared breakfast. Flood asked Wilson to bring his outfit to our wagon for breakfast, and as fast as they were relieved from herd, they also did ample justice to McCann's cooking. During breakfast, I remember Wilson explaining to Flood what he believed was the cause of the stampede. It seems that there were a few remaining buffalo ranging north of the Wichita, and at night when they came into the river to drink they had scented the cattle on the south side. The bellowing of buffalo bulls had been distinctly heard by his men on night herd for several nights past. The foreman stated it as his belief that a number of bulls had swum the river and had by stealth approached near the sleeping cattle, — then, on discovering the presence of the herders, had themselves stampeded, throwing his herd into a panic.

We had got a change of mounts during the breakfast hour, and when all was ready Flood and Wilson rode over to the wagon of the mixed herd, the two outfits following, when Flood inquired of their foreman, —

"Have you any suggestions to make in the cutting of these herds?"

"No suggestions," was the reply, "but I intend to cut mine first and cut them northward on the trail."

"You intend to cut them northward, you mean, provided there are no objections, which I'm positive there will be," said Flood. "It takes me some little time to size a man up, and the more I see of you during our brief acquaintance, the more I think there's two or three things that you might learn to your advantage. I'll not enumerate them now, but when these herds are separated, if you insist, it will cost you nothing but the asking for my opinion of you. This much you can depend on: when the cutting's over, you'll occupy the same position on the trail that you did before this accident happened. Wilson, here, has nothing but jaded horses, and his outfit will hold the herd while yours and mine cut their cattle. And instead of you cutting north, you can either cut south where you belong on the trail or sulk in your camp, your own will and pleasure to govern. But if you are a cowman, willing to do your part, you'll have your outfit ready to work by the time we throw the cattle together."

Not waiting for any reply, Flood turned away, and the double outfit circled around the grazing herd and began throwing the sea of cattle into a compact body ready to work. Rod Wheat and Ash Borrowstone were detailed to hold our cut, and the remainder of us, including Honeyman, entered the herd and began cutting. Shortly after we had commenced the work, the mixed outfit, finding themselves in a lonesome minority, joined us and began cutting out their cattle to the westward. When we had worked about half an hour, Flood called us out, and with the larger portion of Wilson's men, we rode over and drifted the mixed cut around to the southward, where they belonged. The mixed outfit pretended they meant no harm, and were politely informed that if they were sincere, they could show it more plainly. For nearly three hours we sent a steady stream of cattle out of the main herd into our cut, while our horses dripped with sweat. With our advantage in the start, as well as that of having the smallest herd, we finished our work first. While the mixed outfit were finishing their cutting, we changed mounts, and then were ready to work the separated herds. Wilson took about half his outfit, and after giving our herd a trimming, during which he recut about twenty, the mixed outfit were given a similar chance, and found about half a dozen of their brand. These cattle of Wilson's and the other herd amongst ours were not to be wondered at, for we cut by a liberal rule. Often we would find a number of ours on the outside of the main herd, when two men would cut the squad in a bunch, and if there was a wrong brand amongst them, it was no matter, — we knew our herd would have to be retrimmed anyhow, and the other outfits might be disappointed if they found none of their cattle amongst ours.

The mixed outfit were yet working our herd when Wilson's wagon and saddle horses arrived, and while they were changing mounts, we cut the mixed herd of our brand and picked up a number of strays which we had been nursing along, though when we first entered the main herd, strays had received our attention, being well known to us by ranch brands as well as flesh marks. In gathering up this very natural flotsam of the trail, we cut nothing but what our herd had absorbed in its travels, showing due regard to a similar right of the other herds. Our work was finished first, and after Wilson had recut the mixed herd, we gave his herd one more looking over in a farewell parting. Flood asked him if he wanted the lead, but Wilson waived his right in his open, frank manner, saying, "If I had as long-legged cattle as you have, I wouldn't ask no man for the privilege of passing. Why, you ought to out-travel horses. I'm glad to have met you and your outfit, personally, but regret the incident which has given you so much trouble. As I don't expect to go farther than Dodge or Ogalalla at the most, you are more than welcome to the lead. And if you or any of these rascals in your outfit are ever in Coryell County, hunt up Frank Wilson of the Block Bar Ranch, and I'll promise you a drink of milk or something stronger if possible."

We crossed the Wichita late that afternoon, there being not over fifty feet of swimming water for the cattle. Our wagon gave us the only trouble, for the load could not well be lightened, and it was an imperative necessity to cross it the same day. Once the cattle were safely over and a few men left to graze them forward, the remainder of the outfit collected all the ropes and went back after the wagon. As mules are always unreliable in the water, Flood concluded to swim them loose. We lashed the wagon box securely to the gearing with ropes, arranged our bedding in the wagon where it would be on top, and ran the wagon by hand into the water as far as we dared without flooding the wagon box. Two men, with guy ropes fore and aft, were then left to swim with the wagon in order to keep it from toppling over, while the remainder of us recrossed to the farther side of the swimming channel, and fastened our lariats to two long ropes from the end of the tongue. We took a wrap on the pommels of our saddles with the loose end, and when the word was given our eight horses furnished abundant motive power, and the wagon floated across, landing high and dry amid the shoutings of the outfit.

CHAPTER IX
DOAN'S CROSSING

It was a nice open country between the Wichita and Pease rivers. On reaching the latter, we found an easy stage of water for crossing, though there was every evidence that the river had been on a recent rise, the débris of a late freshet littering the cutbank, while high-water mark could be easily noticed on the trees along the river bottom. Summer had advanced until the June freshets were to be expected, and for the next month we should be fortunate if our advance was not checked by floods and falling weather. The fortunate stage of the Pease encouraged us, however, to hope that possibly Red River, two days' drive ahead, would be fordable. The day on which we expected to reach it, Flood set out early to look up the ford which had then been in use but a few years, and which in later days was known as Doan's Crossing on Red River. Our foreman returned before noon and reported a favorable stage of water for the herd, and a new ferry that had been established for wagons. With this good news, we were determined to put that river behind us in as few hours as possible, for it was a common occurrence that a river which was fordable at night was the reverse by daybreak. McCann was sent ahead with the wagon, but we held the saddle horses with us to serve as leaders in taking the water at the ford.

The cattle were strung out in trailing manner nearly a mile, and on reaching the river near the middle of the afternoon, we took the water without a halt or even a change of horses. This boundary river on the northern border of Texas was a terror to trail drovers, but on our reaching it, it had shallowed down, the flow of water following several small channels. One of these was swimming, with shallow bars intervening between the channels. But the majestic grandeur of the river was apparent on every hand, — with its red, bluff banks, the sediment of its red waters marking the timber along its course, while the driftwood, lodged in trees and high on the banks, indicated what might be expected when she became sportive or angry. That she was merciless was evident, for although this crossing had been in use only a year or two when we forded, yet five graves, one of which was less than ten days made, attested her disregard for human life. It can safely be asserted that at this and lower trail crossings on Red River, the lives of more trail men were lost by drowning than on all other rivers together. Just as we were nearing the river, an unknown horseman from the south overtook our herd. It was evident that he belonged to some through herd and was looking out the crossing. He made himself useful by lending a hand while our herd was fording, and in a brief conversation with Flood, informed him that he was one of the hands with a "Running W" herd, gave the name of Bill Mann as their foreman, the number of cattle they were driving, and reported the herd as due to reach the river the next morning. He wasted little time with us, but recrossed the river, returning to his herd, while we grazed out four or five miles and camped for the night.

I shall never forget the impression left in my mind of that first morning after we crossed Red River into the Indian lands. The country was as primitive as in the first day of its creation. The trail led up a divide between the Salt and North forks of Red River. To the eastward of the latter stream lay the reservation of the Apaches, Kiowas, and Comanches, the latter having been a terror to the inhabitants of western Texas. They were a warlike tribe, as the records of the Texas Rangers and government troops will verify, but their last effective dressing down was given them in a fight at Adobe Walls by a party of buffalo hunters whom they hoped to surprise. As we wormed our way up this narrow divide, there was revealed to us a panorama of green-swarded plain and timber-fringed watercourse, with not a visible evidence that it had ever been invaded by civilized man, save cattlemen with their herds. Antelope came up in bands and gratified their curiosity as to who these invaders might be, while old solitary buffalo bulls turned tail at our approach and lumbered away to points of safety. Very few herds had ever passed over this route, but buffalo trails leading downstream, deep worn by generations of travel, were to be seen by hundreds on every hand. We were not there for a change of scenery or for our health, so we may have overlooked some of the beauties of the landscape. But we had a keen eye for the things of our craft. We could see almost back to the river, and several times that morning noticed clouds of dust on the horizon. Flood noticed them first. After some little time the dust clouds arose clear and distinct, and we were satisfied that the "Running W" herd had forded and were behind us, not more than ten or twelve miles away.

At dinner that noon, Flood said he had a notion to go back and pay Mann a visit. "Why, I've not seen 'Little-foot' Bill Mann," said our foreman, as he helped himself to a third piece of "fried chicken" (bacon), "since we separated two years ago up at Ogalalla on the Platte. I'd just like the best in the world to drop back and sleep in his blankets one night and complain of his chuck. Then I'd like to tell him how we had passed them, starting ten days' drive farther south. He must have been amongst those herds laying over on the Brazos."

"Why don't you go, then?" said Fox Quarternight. "Half the outfit could hold the cattle now with the grass and water we're in at present."

"I'll go you one for luck," said our foreman. "Wrangler, rustle in your horses the minute you're through eating. I'm going visiting."

We all knew what horse he would ride, and when he dropped his rope on "Alazanito," he had not only picked his own mount of twelve, but the top horse of the entire *remuda*, — a chestnut sorrel, fifteen hands and an inch in height, that drew his first breath on the prairies of Texas. No man who sat him once could ever forget him. Now, when the trail is a lost occupation, and reverie and reminiscence carry the mind back to that day, there are friends and faces that may he forgotten, but there are horses that never will be. There were emergencies in which the horse was everything, his rider merely the accessory. But together, man and horse, they were the force that made it possible to move the millions of cattle which passed up and over the various trails of the West.

When we had caught our horses for the afternoon, and Flood had saddled and was ready to start, he said to us, "You fellows just mosey along up the trail. I'll not be gone long, but when I get back I shall expect to find everything running smooth. An outfit that can't run itself without a boss ought to stay at home and do the milking. So long, fellows!"

The country was well watered, and when rounded the cattle into the bed ground that night, they were actually suffering from stomachs gorged with grass and water. They went down and to sleep like tired children; one man could have held them that night. We all felt good, and McCann got up an extra spread for supper. We even had dried apples for dessert. McCann had talked the storekeeper at Doan's, where we got our last supplies, out of some extras as a *pelon*. Among them was a can of jam. He sprung this on us as a surprise. Bob Blades toyed with the empty can in mingled admiration and disgust over a picture on the paper label. It was a supper scene, every figure wearing full dress. "Now, that's General Grant," said he, pointing with his finger, "and this is Tom Ochiltree. I can't quite make out this other duck, but I reckon he's some big auger — a senator or governor, maybe. Them old girls have got their gall with them. That style of dress is what you call *lo* and *behold*. The whole passel ought to be ashamed. And they seem to be enjoying themselves, too."

Though it was a lovely summer night, we had a fire, and supper over, the conversation ranged wide and free. As the wagon on the trail is home, naturally the fire is the hearthstone, so we gathered and lounged around it.

"The only way to enjoy such a fine night as this," remarked Ash, "is to sit up smoking until you fall asleep with your boots on. Between too much sleep and just enough, there's a happy medium which suits me."

"Officer," inquired Wyatt Roundtree, trailing into the conversation very innocently, "why is it that people who live up among those Yankees always say 'be' the remainder of their lives?"

"What's the matter with the word?" countered Officer.

"Oh, nothing, I reckon, only it sounds a little odd, and there's a tale to it."

"A story, you mean," said Officer, reprovingly.

"Well, I'll tell it to you," said Roundtree, "and then you can call it to suit yourself. It was out in New Mexico where this happened. There was a fellow drifted into the ranch where I was working, dead broke. To make matters worse, he could do nothing; he wouldn't fit anywhere.

Still, he was a nice fellow and we all liked him. Must have had a good education, for he had good letters from people up North. He had worked in stores and had once clerked in a bank, at least the letters said so. Well, we put up a job to get him a place in a little town out on the railroad. You all know how clannish Kentuckians are. Let two meet who never saw each other before, and inside of half an hour they'll be chewing tobacco from the same plug and trying to loan each other money."

"That's just like them," interposed Fox Quarternight.

"Well, there was an old man lived in this town, who was the genuine blend of bluegrass and Bourbon. If another Kentuckian came within twenty miles of him, and he found it out, he'd hunt him up and they'd hold a two-handed reunion. We put up the job that this young man should play that he was a Kentuckian, hoping that the old man would take him to his bosom and give him something to do. So we took him into town one day, coached and fully posted how to act and play his part. We met the old man in front of his place of business, and, after the usual comment on the news over our way, weather, and other small talk, we were on the point of passing on, when one of our own crowd turned back and inquired, 'Uncle Henry, have you met the young Kentuckian who's in the country?'

"'No,' said the old man, brightening with interest, 'who is he and where is he?'

"'He's in town somewhere,' volunteered one of the boys. We pretended to survey the street from where we stood, when one of the boys blurted out, 'Yonder he stands now. That fellow in front of the drug store over there, with the hard-boiled hat on.'

"The old man started for him, angling across the street, in disregard of sidewalks. We watched the meeting, thinking it was working all right. We were mistaken. We saw them shake hands, when the old man turned and walked away very haughtily. Something had gone wrong. He took the sidewalk on his return, and when he came near enough to us, we could see that he was angry and on the prod. When he came near enough to speak, he said, 'You think you're smart, don't you? He's a Kentuckian, is he? Hell's full of such Kentuckians!' And as he passed beyond hearing he was muttering imprecations on us. The young fellow joined us a minute later with the question, 'What kind of a crank is that you ran me up against?'

"'He's as nice a man as there is in this country,' said one of the crowd. 'What did you say to him?'

"'Nothing'; he came up to me, extended his hand, saying, "My young friend, I understand that you're from Kentucky." "I be, sir," I replied, when he looked me in the eye and said, "You're a G — — d — — liar," and turned and walked away. Why, he must have wanted to insult me. And then we all knew why our little scheme had failed. There was food and raiment in it for him, but he would use that little word 'be.'"

"Did any of you notice my saddle horse lie down just after we crossed this last creek this afternoon?" inquired Rod Wheat.

"No; what made him lie down?" asked several of the boys.

"Oh, he just found a gopher hole and stuck his forefeet into it one at a time, and then tried to pull them both out at once, and when he couldn't do it, he simply shut his eyes like a dying sheep and lay down."

"Then you've seen sheep die," said the horse wrangler.

"Of course I have; a sheep can die any time he makes up his mind to by simply shutting both eyes — then he's a goner."

Quince Forrest, who had brought in his horse to go out with the second watch, he and Bob Blades having taken advantage of the foreman's absence to change places on guard for the night, had been listening to the latter part of Wyatt's yarn very attentively. We all hoped that he would mount and ride out to the herd, for though he was a good story-teller and meaty with personal experiences, where he thought they would pass muster he was inclined to overcolor his statements. We usually gave him respectful attention, but were frequently compelled to regard him as a cheerful, harmless liar. So when he showed no disposition to go, we knew we were in for one from him.

"When I was boss bull-whacker," he began, "for a big army sutler at Fort Concho, I used to make two round trips a month with my train. It was a hundred miles to wagon from the freight point where we got our supplies. I had ten teams, six and seven yoke to the team, and trail wagons to each. I was furnished a night herder and a cook, saddle horses for both night herder and myself. You hear me, it was a slam up fine layout. We could handle three or four tons to the team, and with the whole train we could chamber two car loads of anything. One day we were nearing the fort with a mixed cargo of freight, when a messenger came out and met us with an order from the sutler. He wanted us to make the fort that night and unload. The mail buckboard had reported us to the sutler as camped out back on a little creek about ten miles. We were always entitled to a day to unload and drive back to camp, which gave us good grass for the oxen, but under the orders the whips popped merrily that afternoon, and when they all got well strung out, I rode in ahead, to see what was up. Well, it seems that four companies of infantry from Fort McKavett, which were out for field practice, were going to be brought into this post to be paid three months' wages. This, with the troops stationed at Concho, would turn loose quite a wad of money. The sutler called me into his office when I reached the fort, and when he had produced a black bottle used for cutting the alkali in your drinking water, he said, 'Jack,' — he called me Jack; my full name is John Quincy Forrest, — 'Jack, can you make the round trip, and bring in two cars of bottled beer that will be on the track waiting for you, and get back by pay day, the 10th?'

"I figured the time in my mind; it was twelve days.

"'There's five extra in it for each man for the trip, and I'll make it right with you,' he added, as he noticed my hesitation, though I was only making a mental calculation.

"'Why, certainly, Captain,' I said. 'What's that fable about the jack rabbit and the land tarrapin?' He didn't know and I didn't either, so I said to illustrate the point: 'Put your freight on a bull train, and it always goes through on time. A race horse can't beat an ox on a hundred miles and repeat to a freight wagon.' Well, we unloaded before night, and it was pitch dark before we made camp. I explained the situation to the men. We planned to go in empty in five days, which would give us seven to come back loaded. We made every camp on time like clockwork. The fifth morning we were anxious to get a daybreak start, so we could load at night. The night herder had his orders to bring in the oxen the first sign of day, and I called the cook an hour before light. When the oxen were brought in, the men were up and ready to go to yoking. But the nigh wheeler in Joe Jenk's team, a big brindle, muley ox, a regular pet steer, was missing. I saw him myself, Joe saw him, and the night herder swore he came in with the rest. Well, we looked high and low for that Mr. Ox, but he had vanished. While the men were eating their breakfast, I got on my horse and the night herder and I scoured and circled that country for miles around, but no ox. The country was so bare and level that a jack rabbit needed to carry a fly for shade. I was worried, for we needed every ox and every moment of time. I ordered Joe to tie his mate behind the trail wagon and pull out one ox shy.

"Well, fellows, that thing worried me powerful. Half the teamsters, good, honest, truthful men as ever popped a whip, swore they saw that ox when they came in. Well, it served a strong argument that a man can be positive and yet be mistaken. We nooned ten miles from our night camp that day. Jerry Wilkens happened to mention it at dinner that he believed his trail needed greasing. 'Why,' said Jerry, 'you'd think that I was loaded, the way my team kept their chains taut.' I noticed Joe get up from dinner before he had finished, as if an idea had struck him. He went over and opened the sheet in Jerry's trail wagon, and a smile spread over his countenance. 'Come here, fellows,' was all he said.

"We ran over to the wagon and there" —

The boys turned their backs with indistinct mutterings of disgust.

"You all don't need to believe this if you don't want to, but there was the missing ox, coiled up and sleeping like a bear in the wagon. He even had Jerry's roll of bedding for a pillow. You see, the wagon sheet was open in front, and he had hopped up on the trail tongue and crept in there to steal a ride. Joe climbed into the wagon, and gave him a few swift kicks in the short ribs, when he opened his eyes, yawned, got up, and jumped out."

Bull was rolling a cigarette before starting, while Fox's night horse was hard to bridle, which hindered them. With this slight delay, Forrest turned his horse back and continued: "That same ox on the next trip, one night when we had the wagons parked into a corral, got away from the herder, tip-toed over the men's beds in the gate, stood on his hind legs long enough to eat four fifty-pound sacks of flour out of the rear end of a wagon, got down on his side, and wormed his way under the wagon back into the herd, without being detected or waking a man."

As they rode away to relieve the first guard, McCann said, "Isn't he a muzzle-loading daisy? If I loved a liar I'd hug that man to death."

The absence of our foreman made no difference. We all knew our places on guard. Experience told us there would be no trouble that night. After Wyatt Roundtree and Moss Strayhorn had made down their bed and got into it, Wyatt remarked, —

"Did you ever notice, old sidey, how hard this ground is?"

"Oh, yes," said Moss, as he turned over, hunting for a soft spot, "it is hard, but we'll forget all that when this trip ends. Brother, dear, just think of those long slings with red cherries floating around in them that we'll be drinking, and picture us smoking cigars in a blaze. That thought alone ought to make a hard bed both soft and warm. Then to think we'll ride all the way home on the cars."

McCann banked his fire, and the first guard, Wheat, Stallings, and Borrowstone, rode in from the herd, all singing an old chorus that had been composed, with little regard for music or sense, about a hotel where they had stopped the year before: —

> "Sure it's one cent for coffee and two cents for bread,
>   Three for a steak and five for a bed,
>   Sea breeze from the gutter wafts a salt water smell,
>   To the festive cowboy in the Southwestern hotel."

CHAPTER X
"NO MAN'S LAND"

Flood overtook us the next morning, and as a number of us gathered round him to hear the news, told us of a letter that Mann had got at Doan's, stating that the first herd to pass Camp Supply had been harassed by Indians. The "Running W" people, Mann's employers, had a representative at Dodge, who was authority for the statement. Flood had read the letter, which intimated that an appeal would be made to the government to send troops from either Camp Supply or Fort Sill to give trail herds a safe escort in passing the western border of this Indian reservation. The letter, therefore, admonished Mann, if he thought the Indians would give any trouble, to go up the south side of Red River as far as the Pan-handle of Texas, and then turn north to the government trail at Fort Elliot.

"I told Mann," said our foreman, "that before I'd take one step backward, or go off on a wild goose chase through that Pan-handle country, I'd go back home and start over next year on the Chisholm trail. It's the easiest thing in the world for some big auger to sit in a hotel somewhere and direct the management of a herd. I don't look for no soldiers to furnish an escort; it would take the government six months to get a move on her, even in an emergency. I left Billy Mann in a quandary; he doesn't know what to do. That big auger at Dodge is troubling him, for if he don't act on his advice, and loses cattle as the result — well, he'll never boss any more herds for King and Kennedy. So, boys, if we're ever to see the Blackfoot Agency, there's but one course for us to take, and that's straight ahead. As old Oliver Loving, the first Texas cowman that ever drove a herd, used to say, 'Never borrow trouble, or cross a river before you reach it.' So when the cattle are through grazing, let them hit the trail north. It's entirely too late for us to veer away from any Indians."

We were following the regular trail, which had been slightly used for a year or two, though none of our outfit had ever been over it, when late on the third afternoon, about forty miles out from Doan's, about a hundred mounted bucks and squaws sighted our herd and crossed the North Fork from their encampment. They did not ride direct to the herd, but came into the trail nearly a mile above the cattle, so it was some little time from our first sighting them before we met. We did not check the herd or turn out of the trail, but when the lead came within a few hundred yards of the Indians, one buck, evidently the chief of the band, rode forward a few rods and held up one hand, as if commanding a halt. At the sight of this gaudily bedecked apparition, the cattle turned out of the trail, and Flood and I rode up to the chief, extending our hands in friendly greeting. The chief could not speak a word of English, but made signs with his hands; when I turned loose on him in Spanish, however, he instantly turned his horse and signed back to his band. Two young bucks rode forward and greeted Flood and myself in good Spanish.

On thus opening up an intelligible conversation, I called Fox Quarternight, who spoke Spanish, and he rode up from his position of third man in the swing and joined in the council. The two young Indians through whom we carried on the conversation were Apaches, no doubt renegades of that tribe, and while we understood each other in Spanish, they spoke in a heavy guttural peculiar to the Indian. Flood opened the powwow by demanding to know the meaning of this visit. When the question had been properly interpreted to the chief, the latter dropped his blanket from his shoulders and dismounted from his horse. He was a fine specimen of the Plains Indian, fully six feet in height, perfectly proportioned, and in years well past middle life. He looked every inch a chief, and was a natural born orator. There was a certain easy grace to his gestures, only to be seen in people who use the sign language, and often when he was speaking to the Apache interpreters, I could anticipate his requests before they were translated to us, although I did not know a word of Comanche.

Before the powwow had progressed far it was evident that begging was its object. In his prelude, the chief laid claim to all the country in sight as the hunting grounds of the Comanche tribe, — an intimation that we were intruders. He spoke of the great slaughter of the buffalo by the white hide-hunters, and the consequent hunger and poverty amongst his people. He dwelt on the fact that he had ever counseled peace with the whites, until now his band numbered but a few squaws and papooses, the younger men having deserted him for other chiefs of the tribe who advocated war on the palefaces. When he had fully stated his position, he offered to allow us to pass through his country in consideration of ten beeves. On receiving this proposition, all of us dismounted, including the two Apaches, the latter seating themselves in their own fashion, while we whites lounged on the ground in truly American laziness, rolling cigarettes. In dealing with people who know not the value of time, the civilized man is taken at a disadvantage, and unless he can show an equal composure in wasting time, results will be against him. Flood had had years of experience in dealing with Mexicans in the land of *mañana*, where all maxims regarding the value of time are religiously discarded. So in dealing with this Indian chief he showed no desire to hasten matters, and carefully avoided all reference to the demand for beeves.

His first question, instead, was to know the distance to Fort Sill and Fort Elliot. The next was how many days it would take for cavalry to reach him. He then had us narrate the fact that when the first herd of cattle passed through the country less than a month before, some bad Indians had shown a very unfriendly spirit. They had taken many of the cattle and had killed and eaten them, and now the great white man's chief at Washington was very much displeased. If another single ox were taken and killed by bad Indians, he would send his soldiers from the forts to protect the cattle, even though their owners drove the herds through the reservation of the Indians — over the grass where their ponies grazed. He had us inform the chief that our entire herd was intended by the great white man's chief at Washington as a present to the Blackfeet Indians who lived in Montana, because they were good Indians, and welcomed priests and teachers amongst them to teach them the ways of the white man. At our foreman's request we then informed the chief that he was under no obligation to give him even a single beef for any privilege of passing through his country, but as the squaws and little papooses were hungry, he would give him two beeves.

The old chief seemed not the least disconcerted, but begged for five beeves, as many of the squaws were in the encampment across the North Fork, those present being not quite half of his village. It was now getting late in the day and the band seemed to be getting tired of the parleying, a number of squaws having already set out on their return to the village. After some further talk, Flood agreed to add another beef, on condition they be taken to the encampment before being killed. This was accepted, and at once the entire band set up a chattering in view of the coming feast. The cattle had in the mean time grazed off nearly a mile, the outfit, however, holding them under a close herd during the powwowing. All the bucks in the band, numbering about forty, now joined us, and we rode away to the herd. I noticed, by the way, that quite a number of the younger braves had arms, and no doubt they would have made a display of force had Flood's diplomacy been of a more warlike character. While drifting the herd back to the trail we cut out a big lame steer and two stray cows for the Indians, who now left us and followed the beeves which were being driven to their village.

Flood had instructed Quarternight and me to invite the two Apaches to our camp for the night, on the promise of sugar, coffee, and tobacco. They consulted with the old chief, and gaining his consent came with us. We extended the hospitality of our wagon to our guests, and when supper was over, promised them an extra beef if they would give us particulars of the trail until it crossed the North Fork, after that river turned west towards the Pan-handle. It was evident that they were familiar with the country, for one of them accepted our offer, and with his finger sketched a rude map on the ground where there had formerly been a campfire. He outlined the two rivers between which we were then encamped, and traced the trail until it crossed the North Fork or beyond the Indian reservation. We discussed the outline of the trail in detail for an hour, asking hundreds of unimportant questions, but occasionally getting in a leading one, always resulting in the information wanted. We learned that the big summer encampment of the Comanches and Kiowas was one day's ride for a pony or two days' with cattle up the trail, at the point where the divide between Salt and North Fork narrows to about ten miles in width. We leeched out of them very cautiously the information that the encampment was a large one, and that all herds this year had given up cattle, some as many as twenty-five head.

Having secured the information we wanted, Flood gave to each Apache a package of Arbuckle coffee, a small sack of sugar, and both smoking and chewing tobacco. Quarternight informed them that as the cattle were bedded for the night, they had better remain until morning, when he would pick them out a nice fat beef. On their consenting, Fox stripped the wagon sheet off the wagon and made them a good bed, in which, with their body blankets, they were as comfortable as any of us. Neither of them was armed, so we felt no fear of them, and after they had lain down on their couch, Flood called Quarternight and me, and we strolled out into the darkness and reviewed the information. We agreed that the topography of the country they had given was most likely correct, because we could verify much of it by maps in our possession. Another thing on which we agreed was, that there was some means of communication between this small and seemingly peaceable band and the main encampment of the tribe; and that more than likely our approach would be known in the large encampment before sunrise. In spite of the good opinion we entertained of our guests, we were also satisfied they had lied to us when they denied they had been in the large camp since the trail herds began to pass. This was the last question we had asked, and the artful manner in which they had parried it showed our guests to be no mean diplomats themselves.

Our camp was astir by daybreak, and after breakfast, as we were catching our mounts for the day, one of the Apaches offered to take a certain pinto horse in our *remuda* in lieu of the promised beef, but Flood declined the offer. On overtaking the herd after breakfast, Quarternight cut out a fat two year old stray heifer, and he and I assisted our guests to drive their beef several miles toward their village. Finally bidding them farewell, we returned to the herd, when the outfit informed us that Flood and The Rebel had ridden on ahead to look out a crossing on the Salt Fork. From this move it was evident that if a passable ford could be found, our foreman intended to abandon the established route and avoid the big Indian encampment.

On the return of Priest and Flood about noon, they reported having found an easy ford of the Salt Fork, which, from the indications of their old trails centring from every quarter at this crossing, must have been used by buffalo for generations. After dinner we put our wagon in the lead, and following close at hand with the cattle, turned off the trail about a mile above our noon camp and struck to the westward for the crossing. This we reached and crossed early that evening, camping out nearly five miles to the west of the river. Rain was always to be dreaded in trail work, and when bedding down the herd that night, we had one of the heaviest downpours which we had experienced since leaving the Rio Grande. It lasted several hours, but we stood it uncomplainingly, for this fortunate drenching had obliterated every trace left by our wagon and herd since abandoning the trail, as well as the sign left at the old buffalo crossing on the Salt Fork. The rain ceased about ten o'clock, when the cattle bedded down easily, and the second guard took them for their watch. Wood was too scarce to afford a fire, and while our slickers had partially protected us from the rain, many of us went to bed in wet clothing that night. After another half day's drive to the west, we turned northward and traveled in that direction through a nice country, more or less broken with small hills, but well watered. On the morning of the first day after turning north, Honeyman reported a number of our saddle horses had strayed from camp. This gave Flood some little uneasiness, and a number of us got on our night horses without loss of time and turned out to look up the missing saddle stock. The Rebel and I set out together to the southward, while others of the outfit set off to the other points of the compass.

I was always a good trailer, was in fact acknowledged to be one of the best, with the exception of my brother Zack, on the San Antonio River, where we grew up as boys. In circling about that morning, I struck the trail of about twenty horses — the missing number — and at once signaled to Priest, who was about a mile distant, to join me. The ground was fortunately fresh from the recent rain and left an easy trail. We galloped along it easily for some little distance, when the trail suddenly turned and we could see that the horses had been running, having evidently received a sudden scare. On following up the trail nearly a mile, we noticed where they had quieted down and had evidently grazed for several hours, but in looking up the trail by which they had left these parts, Priest made the discovery of signs of cattle. We located the trail of the horses soon, and were again surprised to find that they had been running as before, though the trail was much fresher, having possibly been made about dawn. We ran the trail out until it passed over a slight divide, when there before us stood the missing horses. They never noticed us, but were standing at attention, cautiously sniffing the early morning air, on which was borne to them the scent of something they feared. On reaching them, their fear seemed not the least appeased, and my partner and I had our curiosity sufficiently aroused to ride forward to the cause of their alarm. As we rounded the spur of the hill, there in plain view grazed a band of about twenty buffalo. We were almost as excited as the horses over the discovery. By dropping back and keeping the hill between us and them, then dismounting and leaving our horses, we thought we could reach the apex of the hill. It was but a small elevation, and from its summit we secured a splendid view of the animals, now less than three hundred yards distant. Flattening ourselves out, we spent several minutes watching the shaggy animals as they grazed leisurely forward, while several calves in the bunch gamboled around their mothers. A buffalo calf, I had always heard, made delicious veal, and as we had had no fresh meat since we had started, I proposed to Priest that we get one. He suggested trying our ropes, for if we could ever get within effective six-shooter range, a rope was much the surest. Certainly such cumbrous, awkward looking animals, he said, could be no match for our Texas horses. We accordingly dropped back off the hill to our saddle stock, when Priest said that if he only had a certain horse of his out of the band we had been trailing he would promise me buffalo veal if he had to follow them to the Pan-handle. It took us but a few minutes to return to our horses, round them in, and secure the particular horse he wanted. I was riding my Nigger Boy, my regular night horse, and as only one of my mount was in this bunch, — a good horse, but sluggish, — I concluded to give my black a trial, not depending on his speed so much as his staying qualities. It took but a minute for The Rebel to shift his saddle from one horse to another, when he started around to the south, while I turned to the north, so as to approach the buffalo simultaneously. I came in sight of the band first, my partner having a farther ride to make, but had only a few moments to wait, before I noticed the quarry take alarm, and the next instant Priest dashed out from behind a spur of the hill and was after them, I following suit. They turned westward, and when The Rebel and I came together on the angle of their course, we were several hundred yards in their rear. My bunkie had the best horse in speed by all odds, and was soon crowding the band so close that they began to scatter, and though I passed several old bulls and cows, it was all I could do to keep in sight of the calves. After the chase had continued over a mile, the staying qualities of my horse began to shine, but while I was nearing the lead, The Rebel tied to the largest calf in the bunch. The calf he had on his rope was a beauty, and on overtaking him, I reined in my horse, for to have killed a second one would have been sheer waste. Priest wanted me to shoot the calf, but I refused, so he shifted the rope to the pommel of my saddle, and, dismounting, dropped the calf at the first shot. We skinned him, cut off his head, and after disemboweling him, lashed the carcass across my saddle. Then both of us mounted Priest's horse, and started on our return.

On reaching the horse stock, we succeeded in catching a sleepy old horse belonging to Rod Wheat's mount, and I rode him bridleless and bareback to camp. We received an ovation on our arrival, the recovery of the saddle horses being a secondary matter compared to the buffalo veal. "So it was buffalo that scared our horses, was it, and ran them out of camp?" said McCann, as he helped to unlash the calf. "Well, it's an ill wind that blows nobody good." There was no particular loss of time, for the herd had grazed away on our course several miles, and after changing our mounts we overtook the herd with the news that not only the horses had been found, but that there was fresh meat in camp — and buffalo veal at that! The other men out horse hunting, seeing the cattle strung out in traveling shape, soon returned to their places beside the trailing herd.

We held a due northward course, which we figured ought to carry us past and at least thirty miles to the westward of the big Indian encampment. The worst thing with which we had now to contend was the weather, it having rained more or less during the past day and night, or ever since we had crossed the Salt Fork. The weather had thrown the outfit into such a gloomy mood that they would scarcely speak to or answer each other. This gloomy feeling had been growing on us for several days, and it was even believed secretly that our foreman didn't know where he was; that the outfit was drifting and as good as lost. About noon of the third day, the weather continuing wet with cold nights, and with no abatement of the general gloom, our men on point noticed smoke arising directly ahead on our course, in a little valley through which ran a nice stream of water. When Flood's attention was directed to the smoke, he rode forward to ascertain the cause, and returned worse baffled than I ever saw him.

It was an Indian camp, and had evidently been abandoned only that morning, for the fires were still smouldering. Ordering the wagon to camp on the creek and the cattle to graze forward till noon, Flood returned to the Indian camp, taking two of the boys and myself with him. It had not been a permanent camp, yet showed evidence of having been occupied several days at least, and had contained nearly a hundred lean-tos, wickyups, and tepees — altogether too large an encampment to suit our tastes. The foreman had us hunt up the trail leaving, and once we had found it, all four of us ran it out five or six miles, when, from the freshness of it, fearing that we might be seen, we turned back. The Indians had many ponies and possibly some cattle, though the sign of the latter was hard to distinguish from buffalo. Before quitting their trail, we concluded they were from one of the reservations, and were heading for their old stamping ground, the Pan-handle country, — peaceable probably; but whether peaceable or not, we had no desire to meet with them. We lost little time, then, in returning to the herd and making late and early drives until we were out of that section.

But one cannot foresee impending trouble on the cattle trail, any more than elsewhere, and although we encamped that night a long distance to the north of the abandoned Indian camp, the next morning we came near having a stampede. It happened just at dawn. Flood had called the cook an hour before daybreak, and he had started out with Honeyman to drive in the *remuda*, which had scattered badly the morning before. They had the horses rounded up and were driving them towards camp when, about half a mile from the wagon, four old buffalo bulls ran quartering past the horses. This was tinder among stubble, and in their panic the horses outstripped the wranglers and came thundering for camp. Luckily we had been called to breakfast, and those of us who could see what was up ran and secured our night horses. Before half of the horses were thus secured, however, one hundred and thirty loose saddle stock dashed through camp, and every horse on picket went with them, saddles and all, and dragging the picket ropes. Then the cattle jumped from the bed ground and were off like a shot, the fourth guard, who had them in charge, with them. Just for the time being it was an open question which way to ride, our saddle horses going in one direction and the herd in another. Priest was an early riser and had hustled me out early, so fortunately we reached our horses, though over half the outfit in camp could only look on and curse their luck at being left afoot. The Rebel was first in the saddle, and turned after the horses, but I rode for the herd. The cattle were not badly scared, and as the morning grew clearer, five of us quieted them down before they had run more than a short mile.

The horses, however, gave us a long, hard run, and since a horse has a splendid memory, the effects of this scare were noticeable for nearly a month after. Honeyman at once urged our foreman to hobble at night, but Flood knew the importance of keeping the *remuda* strong, and refused. But his decision was forced, for just as it was growing dusk that evening, we heard the horses running, and all hands had to turn out, to surround them and bring them into camp. We hobbled every horse and side-lined certain leaders, and for fully a week following, one scare or another seemed to hold our saddle stock in constant terror. During this week we turned out our night horses, and taking the worst of the leaders in their stead, tied them solidly to the wagon wheels all night, not being willing to trust to picket ropes. They would even run from a mounted man during the twilight of evening or early dawn, or from any object not distinguishable in uncertain light; but the wrangler now never went near them until after sunrise, and their nervousness gradually subsided. Trouble never comes singly, however, and when we struck the Salt Fork, we found it raging, and impassable nearly from bank to bank. But get across we must. The swimming of it was nothing, but it was necessary to get our wagon over, and there came the rub. We swam the cattle in twenty minutes' time, but it took us a full half day to get the wagon over. The river was at least a hundred yards wide, three quarters of which was swimming to a horse. But we hunted up and down the river until we found an eddy, where the banks had a gradual approach to deep water, and started to raft the wagon over — a thing none of the outfit had ever seen done, though we had often heard of it around camp-fires in Texas. The first thing was to get the necessary timber to make the raft. We scouted along the Salt Fork for a mile either way before we found sufficient dry, dead cottonwood to form our raft. Then we set about cutting it, but we had only one axe, and were the poorest set of axemen that were ever called upon to perform a similar task; when we cut a tree it looked as though a beaver had gnawed it down. On horseback the Texan shines at the head of his class, but in any occupation which must be performed on foot he is never a competitor. There was scarcely a man in our outfit who could not swing a rope and tie down a steer in a given space of time, but when it came to swinging an axe to cut logs for the raft, our lustre faded. "Cutting these logs," said Joe Stallings, as he mopped the sweat from his brow, "reminds me of what the Tennessee girl who married a Texan wrote home to her sister. 'Texas,' so she wrote, 'is a good place for men and dogs, but it's hell on women and oxen.'"

Dragging the logs up to the place selected for the ford was an easy matter. They were light, and we did it with ropes from the pommels of our saddles, two to four horses being sufficient to handle any of the trees. When everything was ready, we ran the wagon out into two-foot water and built the raft under it. We had cut the dry logs from eighteen to twenty feet long, and now ran a tier of these under the wagon between the wheels. These we lashed securely to the axle, and even lashed one large log on the underside of the hub on the outside of the wheel. Then we cross-timbered under these, lashing everything securely to this outside guard log. Before we had finished the cross-timbering, it was necessary to take an anchor rope ashore for fear our wagon would float away. By the time we had succeeded in getting twenty-five dry cottonwood logs under our wagon, it was afloat. Half a dozen of us then swam the river on our horses, taking across the heaviest rope we had for a tow line. We threw the wagon tongue back and lashed it, and making fast to the wagon with one end of the tow rope, fastened our lariats to the other. With the remainder of our unused rope, we took a guy line from the wagon and snubbed it to a tree on the south bank. Everything being in readiness, the word was given, and as those on the south bank eased away, those on horseback on the other side gave the rowel to their horses, and our commissary floated across. The wagon floated so easily that McCann was ordered on to the raft to trim the weight when it struck the current. The current carried it slightly downstream, and when it lodged on the other side, those on the south bank fastened lariats to the guy rope; and with them pulling from that side and us from ours, it was soon brought opposite the landing and hauled into shallow water. Once the raft timber was unlashed and removed, the tongue was lowered, and from the pommels of six saddles the wagon was set high and dry on the north bank. There now only remained to bring up the cattle and swim them, which was an easy task and soon accomplished.

After putting the Salt Fork behind us, our spirits were again dampened, for it rained all the latter part of the night and until noon the next day. It was with considerable difficulty that McCann could keep his fire from drowning out while he was getting breakfast, and several of the outfit refused to eat at all. Flood knew it was useless to rally the boys, for a wet, hungry man is not to be jollied or reasoned with. Five days had now elapsed since we turned off the established trail, and half the time rain had been falling. Besides, our doubt as to where we were had been growing, so before we started that morning, Bull Durham very good-naturedly asked Flood if he had any idea where he was.

"No, I haven't. No more than you have," replied our foreman. "But this much I do know, or will just as soon as the sun comes out: I know north from south. We have been traveling north by a little west, and if we hold that course we're bound to strike the North Fork, and within a day or two afterwards we will come into the government trail, running from Fort Elliot to Camp Supply, which will lead us into our own trail. Or if we were certain that we had cleared the Indian reservation, we could bear to our right, and in time we would reënter the trail that way. I can't help the weather, boys, and as long as I have chuck, I'd as lief be lost as found."

If there was any recovery in the feelings of the outfit after this talk of Flood's, it was not noticeable, and it is safe to say that two thirds of the boys believed we were in the Pan-handle of Texas. One man's opinion is as good as another's in a strange country, and while there wasn't a man in the outfit who cared to suggest it, I know the majority of us would have indorsed turning northeast. But the fates smiled on us at last. About the middle of the forenoon, on the following day, we cut an Indian trail, about three days old, of probably fifty horses. A number of us followed the trail several miles on its westward course, and among other things discovered that they had been driving a small bunch of cattle, evidently making for the sand hills which we could see about twenty miles to our left. How they had come by the cattle was a mystery, — perhaps by forced levy, perhaps from a stampede. One thing was certain: the trail must have contributed them, for there were none but trail cattle in the country. This was reassuring and gave some hint of guidance. We were all tickled, therefore, after nooning that day and on starting the herd in the afternoon, to hear our foreman give orders to point the herd a little east of north. The next few days we made long drives, our saddle horses recovered from their scare, and the outfit fast regained its spirits.

On the morning of the tenth day after leaving the trail, we loitered up a long slope to a divide in our lead from which we sighted timber to the north. This we supposed from its size must be the North Fork. Our route lay up this divide some distance, and before we left it, some one in the rear sighted a dust cloud to the right and far behind us. As dust would hardly rise on a still morning without a cause, we turned the herd off the divide and pushed on, for we suspected Indians. Flood and Priest hung back on the divide, watching the dust signals, and after the herd had left them several miles in the rear, they turned and rode towards it, — a move which the outfit could hardly make out. It was nearly noon when we saw them returning in a long lope, and when they came in sight of the herd, Priest waved his hat in the air and gave the long yell. When he explained that there was a herd of cattle on the trail in the rear and to our right, the yell went around the herd, and was reechoed by our wrangler and cook in the rear. The spirits of the outfit instantly rose. We halted the herd and camped for noon, and McCann set out his best in celebrating the occasion. It was the most enjoyable meal we had had in the past ten days. After a good noonday rest, we set out, and having entered the trail during the afternoon, crossed the North Fork late that evening. As we were going into camp, we noticed a horseman coming up the trail, who turned out to be smiling Nat Straw, whom we had left on the Colorado River. "Well, girls," said Nat, dismounting, "I didn't know who you were, but I just thought I'd ride ahead and overtake whoever it was and stay all night. Indians? Yes; I wouldn't drive on a trail that hadn't any excitement on it. I gave the last big encampment ten strays, and won them all back and four ponies besides on a horse race. Oh, yes, got some running stock with us. How soon will supper be ready, cusi? Get up something extra, for you've got company."

CHAPTER XI
A BOGGY FORD

That night we learned from Straw our location on the trail. We were far above the Indian reservation, and instead of having been astray our foreman had held a due northward course, and we were probably as far on the trail as if we had followed the regular route. So in spite of all our good maxims, we had been borrowing trouble; we were never over thirty miles to the westward of what was then the new Western Cattle Trail. We concluded that the "Running W" herd had turned back, as Straw brought the report that some herd had recrossed Red River the day before his arrival, giving for reasons the wet season and the danger of getting waterbound.

About noon of the second day after leaving the North Fork of Red River, we crossed the Washita, a deep stream, the slippery banks of which gave every indication of a recent rise. We had no trouble in crossing either wagon or herd, it being hardly a check in our onward course. The abandonment of the regular trail the past ten days had been a noticeable benefit to our herd, for the cattle had had an abundance of fresh country to graze over as well as plenty of rest. But now that we were back on the trail, we gave them their freedom and frequently covered twenty miles a day, until we reached the South Canadian, which proved to be the most delusive stream we had yet encountered. It also showed, like the Washita, every evidence of having been on a recent rampage. On our arrival there was no volume of water to interfere, but it had a quicksand bottom that would bog a saddle blanket. Our foreman had been on ahead and examined the regular crossing, and when he returned, freely expressed his opinion that we would be unable to trail the herd across, but might hope to effect it by cutting it into small bunches. When we came, therefore, within three miles of the river, we turned off the trail to a near-by creek and thoroughly watered the herd. This was contrary to our practice, for we usually wanted the herd thirsty when reaching a large river. But any cow brute that halted in fording the Canadian that day was doomed to sink into quicksands from which escape was doubtful.

We held the wagon and saddle horses in the rear, and when we were half a mile away from the trail ford, cut off about two hundred head of the leaders and started for the crossing, leaving only the horse wrangler and one man with the herd. On reaching the river we gave them an extra push, and the cattle plunged into the muddy water. Before the cattle had advanced fifty feet, instinct earned them of the treacherous footing, and the leaders tried to turn back; but by that time we had the entire bunch in the water and were urging them forward. They had halted but a moment and begun milling, when several heavy steers sank; then we gave way and allowed the rest to come back. We did not realize fully the treachery of this river until we saw that twenty cattle were caught in the merciless grasp of the quicksand. They sank slowly to the level of their bodies, which gave sufficient resistance to support their weight, but they were hopelessly bogged. We allowed the free cattle to return to the herd, and immediately turned our attention to those that were bogged, some of whom were nearly submerged by water. We dispatched some of the boys to the wagon for our heavy corral ropes and a bundle of horse-hobbles; and the remainder of us, stripped to the belt, waded out and surveyed the situation at close quarters. We were all experienced in handling bogged cattle, though this quicksand was the most deceptive that I, at least, had ever witnessed. The bottom of the river as we waded through it was solid under our feet, and as long as we kept moving it felt so, but the moment we stopped we sank as in a quagmire. The "pull" of this quicksand was so strong that four of us were unable to lift a steer's tail out, once it was imbedded in the sand. And when we had released a tail by burrowing around it to arm's length and freed it, it would sink of its own weight in a minute's time until it would have to be burrowed out again. To avoid this we had to coil up the tails and tie them with a soft rope hobble.

Fortunately none of the cattle were over forty feet from the bank, and when our heavy rope arrived we divided into two gangs and began the work of rescue. We first took a heavy rope from the animal's horns to solid footing on the river bank, and tied to this five or six of our lariats. Meanwhile others rolled a steer over as far as possible and began burrowing with their hands down alongside a fore and hind leg simultaneously until they could pass a small rope around the pastern above the cloof, or better yet through the cloven in the hoof, when the leg could be readily lifted by two men. We could not stop burrowing, however, for a moment, or the space would fill and solidify. Once a leg was freed, we doubled it back short and securely tied it with a hobble, and when the fore and hind leg were thus secured, we turned the animal over on that side and released the other legs in a similar manner. Then we hastened out of the water and into our saddles, and wrapped the loose end of our ropes to the pommels, having already tied the lariats to the heavy corral rope from the animal's horns. When the word was given, we took a good swinging start, and unless something gave way there was one steer less in the hog. After we had landed the animal high and dry on the bank, it was but a minute's work to free the rope and untie the hobbles. Then it was advisable to get into the saddle with little loss of time and give him a wide berth, for he generally arose angry and sullen.

It was dark before we got the last of the bogged cattle out and retraced our way to camp from the first river on the trip that had turned us. But we were not the least discouraged, for we felt certain there was a ford that had a bottom somewhere within a few miles, and we could hunt it up on the morrow. The next one, however, we would try before we put the cattle in. There was no question that the treacherous condition of the river was due to the recent freshet, which had brought down new deposits of sediment and had agitated the old, even to changing the channel of the river, so that it had not as yet had sufficient time to settle and solidify.

The next morning after breakfast, Flood and two or three of the boys set out up the river, while an equal number of us started, under the leadership of The Rebel, down the river on a similar errand, — to prospect for a crossing. Our party scouted for about five miles, and the only safe footing we could find was a swift, narrow channel between the bank and an island in the river, while beyond the island was a much wider channel with water deep enough in several places to swim our saddle horses. The footing seemed quite secure to our horses, but the cattle were much heavier; and if an animal ever bogged in the river, there was water enough to drown him before help could be rendered. We stopped our horses a number of times, however, to try the footing, and in none of our experiments was there any indication of quicksand, so we counted the crossing safe. On our return we found the herd already in motion, headed up the river where our foreman had located a crossing. As it was then useless to make any mention of the island crossing which we had located, at least until a trial had been given to the upper ford, we said nothing. When we came within half a mile of the new ford, we held up the herd and allowed them to graze, and brought up the *remuda* and crossed and recrossed them without bogging a single horse. Encouraged at this, we cut off about a hundred head of heavy lead cattle and started for the ford. We had a good push on them when we struck the water, for there were ten riders around them and Flood was in the lead. We called to him several times that the cattle were bogging, but he never halted until he pulled out on the opposite bank, leaving twelve of the heaviest steers in the quicksand.

"Well, in all my experience in trail work," said Flood, as he gazed back at the dozen animals struggling in the quicksand, "I never saw as deceptive a bottom in any river. We used to fear the Cimarron and Platte, but the old South Canadian is the girl that can lay it over them both. Still, there ain't any use crying over spilt milk, and we haven't got men enough to hold two herds, so surround them, boys, and we'll recross them if we leave twenty-four more in the river. Take them back a good quarter, fellows, and bring them up on a run, and I'll take the lead when they strike the water; and give them no show to halt until they get across."

As the little bunch of cattle had already grazed out nearly a quarter, we rounded them into a compact body and started for the river to recross them. The nearer we came to the river, the faster we went, till we struck the water. In several places where there were channels, we could neither force the cattle nor ride ourselves faster than a walk on account of the depth of the water, but when we struck the shallows, which were the really dangerous places, we forced the cattle with horse and quirt. Near the middle of the river, in shoal water, Rod Wheat was quirting up the cattle, when a big dun steer, trying to get out of his reach, sank in the quicksand, and

Rod's horse stumbled across the animal and was thrown. He floundered in attempting to rise, and his hind feet sank to the haunches. His ineffectual struggles caused him to sink farther to the flanks in the loblolly which the tramping of the cattle had caused, and there horse and steer lay, side by side, like two in a bed. Wheat loosened the cinches of the saddle on either side, and stripping the bridle off, brought up the rear, carrying saddle, bridle, and blankets on his back. The river was at least three hundred yards wide, and when we got to the farther bank, our horses were so exhausted that we dismounted and let them blow. A survey showed we had left a total of fifteen cattle and the horse in the quicksands. But we congratulated ourselves that we had bogged down only three head in recrossing. Getting these cattle out was a much harder task than the twenty head gave us the day before, for many of these were bogged more than a hundred yards from the bank. But no time was to be lost; the wagon was brought up in a hurry, fresh horses were caught, and we stripped for the fray. While McCann got dinner we got out the horse, even saving the cinches that were abandoned in freeing him of the saddle.

During the afternoon we were compelled to adopt a new mode of procedure, for with the limited amount of rope at hand, we could only use one rope for drawing the cattle out to solid footing, after they were freed from the quagmire. But we had four good mules to our chuck wagon, and instead of dragging the cattle ashore from the pommels of saddles, we tied one end of the rope to the hind axle and used the mules in snaking the cattle out. This worked splendidly, but every time we freed a steer we had to drive the wagon well out of reach, for fear he might charge the wagon and team. But with three crews working in the water, tying up tails and legs, the work progressed more rapidly than it had done the day before, and two hours before sunset the last animal had been freed. We had several exciting incidents during the operation, for several steers showed fight, and when released went on the prod for the first thing in sight. The herd was grazing nearly a mile away during the afternoon, and as fast as a steer was pulled out, some one would take a horse and give the freed animal a start for the herd. One big black steer turned on Flood, who generally attended to this, and gave him a spirited chase. In getting out of the angry steer's way, he passed near the wagon, when the maddened beef turned from Flood and charged the commissary. McCann was riding the nigh wheel mule, and when he saw the steer coming, he poured the whip into the mules and circled around like a battery in field practice, trying to get out of the way. Flood made several attempts to cut off the steer from the wagon, but he followed it like a mover's dog, until a number of us, fearing our mules would be gored, ran out of the water, mounted our horses, and joined in the chase. When we came up with the circus, our foreman called to us to rope the beef, and Fox Quarternight, getting in the first cast, caught him by the two front feet and threw him heavily. Before he could rise, several of us had dismounted and were sitting on him like buzzards on carrion. McCann then drove the team around behind a sand dune, out of sight; we released the beef, and he was glad to return to the herd, quite sobered by the throwing.

Another incident occurred near the middle of the afternoon. From some cause or other, the hind leg of a steer, after having been tied up, became loosened. No one noticed this; but when, after several successive trials, during which Barney McCann exhausted a large vocabulary of profanity, the mule team was unable to move the steer, six of us fastened our lariats to the main rope, and dragged the beef ashore with great *éclat*. But when one of the boys dismounted to unloose the hobbles and rope, a sight met our eyes that sent a sickening sensation through us, for the steer had left one hind leg in the river, neatly disjointed at the knee. Then we knew why the mules had failed to move him, having previously supposed his size was the difficulty, for he was one of the largest steers in the herd. No doubt the steer's leg had been unjointed in swinging him around, but it had taken six extra horses to sever the ligaments and skin, while the merciless quicksands of the Canadian held the limb. A friendly shot ended the steer's sufferings, and before we finished our work for the day, a flight of buzzards were circling around in anticipation of the coming feast.

Another day had been lost, and still the South Canadian defied us. We drifted the cattle back to the previous night camp, using the same bed ground for our herd. It was then that

The Rebel broached the subject of a crossing at the island which we had examined that morning, and offered to show it to our foreman by daybreak. We put two extra horses on picket that night, and the next morning, before the sun was half an hour high, the foreman and The Rebel had returned from the island down the river with word that we were to give the ford a trial, though we could not cross the wagon there. Accordingly we grazed the herd down the river and came opposite the island near the middle of the forenoon. As usual, we cut off about one hundred of the lead cattle, the leaders naturally being the heaviest, and started them into the water. We reached the island and scaled the farther bank without a single animal losing his footing. We brought up a second bunch of double, and a third of triple the number of the first, and crossed them with safety, but as yet the Canadian was dallying with us. As we crossed each successive bunch, the tramping of the cattle increasingly agitated the sands, and when we had the herd about half over, we bogged our first steer on the farther landing. As the water was so shallow that drowning was out of the question, we went back and trailed in the remainder of the herd, knowing the bogged steer would be there when we were ready for him, The island was about two hundred yards long by twenty wide, lying up and down the river, and in leaving it for the farther bank, we always pushed off at the upper end. But now, in trailing the remainder of the cattle over, we attempted to force them into the water at the lower end, as the footing at that point of this middle ground had not, as yet, been trampled up as had the upper end. Everything worked nicely until the rear guard of the last five or six hundred congested on the island, the outfit being scattered on both sides of the river as well as in the middle, leaving a scarcity of men at all points. When the final rear guard had reached the river the cattle were striking out for the farther shore from every quarter of the island at their own sweet will, stopping to drink and loitering on the farther side, for there was no one to hustle them out.

All were over at last, and we were on the point of congratulating ourselves, — for, although the herd had scattered badly, we had less than a dozen bogged cattle, and those near the shore, — when suddenly up the river over a mile, there began a rapid shooting. Satisfied that it was by our own men, we separated, and, circling right and left, began to throw the herd together. Some of us rode up the river bank and soon located the trouble. We had not ridden a quarter of a mile before we passed a number of our herd bogged, these having reëntered the river for their noonday drink, and on coming up with the men who had done the shooting, we found them throwing the herd out from the water. They reported that a large number of cattle were bogged farther up the river.

All hands rounded in the herd, and drifting them out nearly a mile from the river, left them under two herders, when the remainder of us returned to the bogged cattle. There were by actual count, including those down at the crossing, over eighty bogged cattle that required our attention, extending over a space of a mile or more above the island ford.

The outlook was anything but pleasing. Flood was almost speechless over the situation, for it might have been guarded against. But realizing the task before us, we recrossed the river for dinner, well knowing the inner man needed fortifying for the work before us. No sooner had we disposed of the meal and secured a change of mounts all round, than we sent two men to relieve the men on herd. When they were off, Flood divided up our forces for the afternoon work.

"It will never do," said he, "to get separated from our commissary. So, Priest, you take the wagon and *remuda* and go back up to the regular crossing and get our wagon over somehow. There will be the cook and wrangler besides yourself, and you may have two other men. You will have to lighten your load; and don't attempt to cross those mules hitched to the wagon; rely on your saddle horses for getting the wagon over. Forrest, you and Bull, with the two men on herd, take the cattle to the nearest creek and water them well. After watering, drift them back, so they will be within a mile of these bogged cattle. Then leave two men with them and return to the river. I'll take the remainder of the outfit and begin at the ford and work up the river. Get the ropes and hobbles, boys, and come on."

John Officer and I were left with The Rebel to get the wagon across, and while waiting for the men on herd to get in, we hooked up the mules. Honeyman had the *remuda* in hand to start the minute our herders returned, their change of mounts being already tied to the wagon wheels. The need of haste was very imperative, for the river might rise without an hour's notice, and a two-foot rise would drown every hoof in the river as well as cut us off from our wagon. The South Canadian has its source in the Staked Plains and the mountains of New Mexico, and freshets there would cause a rise here, local conditions never affecting a river of such width. Several of us had seen these Plains rivers, — when the mountain was sportive and dallying with the plain, — under a clear sky and without any warning of falling weather, rise with a rush of water like a tidal wave or the stream from a broken dam. So when our men from herd galloped in, we stripped their saddles from tired horses and cinched them to fresh ones, while they, that there might be no loss of time, bolted their dinners. It took us less than an hour to reach the ford, where we unloaded the wagon of everything but the chuck-box, which was ironed fast. We had an extra saddle in the wagon, and McCann was mounted on a good horse, for he could ride as well as cook. Priest and I rode the river, selecting a route; and on our return, all five of us tied our lariats to the tongue and sides of the wagon. We took a running start, and until we struck the farther bank we gave the wagon no time to sink, but pulled it out of the river with a shout, our horses' flanks heaving. Then recrossing the river, we lashed all the bedding to four gentle saddle horses and led them over. But to get our provisions across was no easy matter, for we were heavily loaded, having taken on a supply at Doan's sufficient to last us until we reached Dodge, a good month's journey. Yet over it must go, and we kept a string of horsemen crossing and recrossing for an hour, carrying everything from pots and pans to axle grease, as well as the staples of life. When we had got the contents of the wagon finally over and reloaded, there remained nothing but crossing the saddle stock.

The wagon mules had been turned loose, harnessed, while we were crossing the wagon and other effects; and when we drove the *remuda* into the river, one of the wheel mules turned back, and in spite of every man, reached the bank again. Part of the boys hurried the others across, but McCann and I turned back after our wheeler. We caught him without any trouble, but our attempt to lead him across failed. In spite of all the profanity addressed personally to him, he proved a credit to his sire, and we lost ground in trying to force him into the river. The boys across the river watched a few minutes, when all recrossed to our assistance.

"Time's too valuable to monkey with a mule to-day," said Priest, as he rode up; "skin off that harness."

It was off at once, and we blindfolded and backed him up to the river bank; then taking a rope around his forelegs, we threw him, hog-tied him, and rolled him into the water. With a rope around his forelegs and through the ring in the bridle bit, we asked no further favors, but snaked him ignominiously over to the farther side and reharnessed him into the team.

The afternoon was more than half spent when we reached the first bogged cattle, and by the time the wagon overtook us we had several tied up and ready for the mule team to give us a lift. The herd had been watered in the mean time and was grazing about in sight of the river, and as we occasionally drifted a freed animal out to the herd, we saw others being turned in down the river. About an hour before sunset, Flood rode up to us and reported having cleared the island ford, while a middle outfit under Forrest was working down towards it. During the twilight hours of evening, the wagon and saddle horses moved out to the herd and made ready to camp, but we remained until dark, and with but three horses released a number of light cows. We were the last outfit to reach the wagon, and as Honeyman had tied up our night horses, there was nothing for us to do but eat and go to bed, to which we required no coaxing, for we all knew that early morning would find us once more working with bogged cattle.

The night passed without incident, and the next morning in the division of the forces, Priest was again allowed the wagon to do the snaking out with, but only four men, counting McCann. The remainder of the outfit was divided into several gangs, working near enough each other to lend a hand in case an extra horse was needed on a pull. The third animal we struck in the river that morning was the black steer that had showed fight the day before. Knowing his temper would not be improved by soaking in the quicksand overnight, we changed our tactics.

While we were tying up the steer's tail and legs, McCann secreted his team at a safe distance. Then he took a lariat, lashed the tongue of the wagon to a cottonwood tree, and jacking up a hind wheel, used it as a windlass. When all was ready, we tied the loose end of our cable rope to a spoke, and allowing the rope to coil on the hub, manned the windlass and drew him ashore. When the steer was freed, McCann, having no horse at hand, climbed into the wagon, while the rest of us sought safety in our saddles, and gave him a wide berth. When he came to his feet he was sullen with rage and refused to move out of his tracks. Priest rode out and baited him at a distance, and McCann, from his safe position, attempted to give him a scare, when he savagely charged the wagon. McCann reached down, and securing a handful of flour, dashed it into his eyes, which made him back away; and, kneeling, he fell to cutting the sand with his horns. Rising, he charged the wagon a second time, and catching the wagon sheet with his horns, tore two slits in it like slashes of a razor. By this time The Rebel ventured a little nearer, and attracted the steer's attention. He started for Priest, who gave the quirt to his horse, and for the first quarter mile had a close race. The steer, however, weakened by the severe treatment he had been subjected to, soon fell to the rear, and gave up the chase and continued on his way to the herd.

After this incident we worked down the river until the outfits met. We finished the work before noon, having lost three full days by the quicksands of the Canadian. As we pulled into the trail that afternoon near the first divide and looked back to take a parting glance at the river, we saw a dust cloud across the Canadian which we knew must be the Ellison herd under Nat Straw. Quince Forrest, noticing it at the same time as I did, rode forward and said to me, "Well, old Nat will get it in the neck this time, if that old girl dallies with him as she did with us. I don't wish him any bad luck, but I do hope he'll bog enough cattle to keep his hand in practice. It will be just about his luck, though, to find it settled and solid enough to cross." And the next morning we saw his signal in the sky about the same distance behind us, and knew he had forded without any serious trouble.

CHAPTER XII
THE NORTH FORK

There was never very much love lost between government soldiers and our tribe, so we swept past Camp Supply in contempt a few days later, and crossed the North Fork of the Canadian to camp for the night. Flood and McCann went into the post, as our supply of flour and navy beans was running rather low, and our foreman had hopes that he might be able to get enough of these staples from the sutler to last until we reached Dodge. He also hoped to receive some word from Lovell.

The rest of us had no lack of occupation, as a result of a chance find of mine that morning. Honeyman had stood my guard the night before, and in return, I had got up when he was called to help rustle the horses. We had every horse under hand before the sun peeped over the eastern horizon, and when returning to camp with the *remuda*, as I rode through a bunch of sumach bush, I found a wild turkey's nest with sixteen fresh eggs in it. Honeyman rode up, when I dismounted, and putting them in my hat, handed them up to Billy until I could mount, for they were beauties and as precious to us as gold. There was an egg for each man in the outfit and one over, and McCann threw a heap of swagger into the inquiry, "Gentlemen, how will you have your eggs this morning?" just as though it was an everyday affair. They were issued to us fried, and I naturally felt that the odd egg, by rights, ought to fall to me, but the opposing majority was formidable, — fourteen to one, — so I yielded. A number of ways were suggested to allot the odd egg, but the gambling fever in us being rabid, raffling or playing cards for it seemed to be the proper caper. Raffling had few advocates.

"It reflects on any man's raising," said Quince Forrest, contemptuously, "to suggest the idea of raffling, when we've got cards and all night to play for that egg. The very idea of raffling for it! I'd like to see myself pulling straws or drawing numbers from a hat, like some giggling girl at a church fair. Poker is a science; the highest court in Texas has said so, and I want some little show for my interest in that speckled egg. What have I spent twenty years learning the game for, will some of you tell me? Why, it lets me out if you raffle it." The argument remained unanswered, and the play for it gave interest to that night.

As soon as supper was over and the first guard had taken the herd, the poker game opened, each man being given ten beans for chips. We had only one deck of cards, so one game was all that could be run at a time, but there were six players, and when one was frozen out another sat in and took his place. As wood was plentiful, we had a good fire, and this with the aid of the cook's lantern gave an abundance of light. We unrolled a bed to serve as a table, sat down on it Indian fashion, and as fast as one seat was vacated there was a man ready to fill it, for we were impatient for our turns in the game. The talk turned on an accident which had happened that afternoon. While we were crossing the North Fork of the Canadian, Bob Blades attempted to ride out of the river below the crossing, when his horse bogged down. He instantly dismounted, and his horse after floundering around scrambled out and up the bank, but with a broken leg. Our foreman had ridden up and ordered the horse unsaddled and shot, to put him out of his suffering.

While waiting our turns, the accident to the horse was referred to several times, and finally Blades, who was sitting in the game, turned to us who were lounging around the fire, and asked, "Did you all notice that look he gave me as I was uncinching the saddle? If he had been human, he might have told what that look meant. Good thing he was a horse and couldn't realize."

From then on, the yarning and conversation was strictly *horse*.

"It was always a mystery to me," said Billy Honeyman, "how a Mexican or Indian knows so much more about a horse than any of us. I have seen them trail a horse across a country for miles, riding in a long lope, with not a trace or sign visible to me. I was helping a horseman once to drive a herd of horses to San Antonio from the lower Rio Grande country. We were driving them to market, and as there were no railroads south then, we had to take along saddle horses to ride home on after disposing of the herd. We always took favorite horses which we didn't wish to sell, generally two apiece for that purpose. This time, when we were at least a hundred miles from the ranch, a Mexican, who had brought along a pet horse to ride home, thought he wouldn't hobble this pet one night, fancying the animal wouldn't leave the others. Well, next morning his pet was missing. We scoured the country around and the trail we had come over for ten miles, but no horse. As the country was all open, we felt positive he would go back to the ranch.

"Two days later and about forty miles higher up the road, the Mexican was riding in the lead of the herd, when suddenly he reined in his horse, throwing him back on his haunches, and waved for some of us to come to him, never taking his eyes off what he saw in the road. The owner was riding on one point of the herd and I on the other. We hurried around to him and both rode up at the same time, when the vaquero blurted out, 'There's my horse's track.'

"'What horse?' asked the owner.

"'My own; the horse we lost two days ago,' replied the Mexican.

"'How do you know it's your horse's track from the thousands of others that fill the road?' demanded his employer.

"'Don Tomas,' said the Aztec, lifting his hat, 'how do I know your step or voice from a thousand others?'

"We laughed at him. He had been a peon, and that made him respect our opinions — at least he avoided differing with us. But as we drove on that afternoon, we could see him in the lead, watching for that horse's track. Several times he turned in his saddle and looked back, pointed to some track in the road, and lifted his hat to us. At camp that night we tried to draw him out, but he was silent.

"But when we were nearing San Antonio, we overtook a number of wagons loaded with wool, lying over, as it was Sunday, and there among their horses and mules was our Mexican's missing horse. The owner of the wagons explained how he came to have the horse. The animal had come to his camp one morning, back about twenty miles from where we had lost him, while he was feeding grain to his work stock, and being a pet insisted on being fed. Since then, I have always had a lot of respect for a Greaser's opinion regarding a horse."

"Turkey eggs is too rich for my blood," said Bob Blades, rising from the game. "I don't care a continental who wins the egg now, for whenever I get three queens pat beat by a four card draw, I have misgivings about the deal. And old Quince thinks he can stack cards. He couldn't stack hay."

"Speaking about Mexicans and Indians," said Wyatt Roundtree, "I've got more use for a good horse than I have for either of those grades of humanity. I had a little experience over east here, on the cut off from the Chisholm trail, a few years ago, that gave me all the Injun I want for some time to come. A band of renegade Cheyennes had hung along the trail for several years, scaring or begging passing herds into giving them a beef. Of course all the cattle herds had more or less strays among them, so it was easier to cut out one of these than to argue the matter. There was plenty of herds on the trail then, so this band of Indians got bolder than bandits. In the year I'm speaking of, I went up with a herd of horses belonging to a Texas man, who was in charge with us. When we came along with our horses — only six men all told — the chief of the band, called Running Bull Sheep, got on the bluff bigger than a wolf and demanded six horses. Well, that Texan wasn't looking for any particular Injun that day to give six of his own dear horses to. So we just drove on, paying no attention to Mr. Bull Sheep. About half a mile farther up the trail, the chief overtook us with all his bucks, and they were an ugly looking lot. Well, this time he held up four fingers, meaning that four horses would be acceptable. But the Texan wasn't recognizing the Indian levy of taxation that year. When he refused them, the Indians never parleyed a moment, but set up a 'ki yi' and began circling round the herd on their ponies, Bull Sheep in the lead.

"As the chief passed the owner, his horse on a run, he gave a special shrill 'ki yi,' whipped a short carbine out of its scabbard, and shot twice into the rear of the herd. Never for a moment considering consequences, the Texan brought his six-shooter into action. It was a long, purty shot, and Mr. Bull Sheep threw his hands in the air and came off his horse backward, hard hit. This shooting in the rear of the horses gave them such a scare that we never checked them short of a mile. While the other Indians were holding a little powwow over their chief, we were making good time in the other direction, considering that we had over eight hundred loose horses. Fortunately our wagon and saddle horses had gone ahead that morning, but in the run we overtook them. As soon as we checked the herd from its scare, we turned them up the trail, stretched ropes from the wheels of the wagon, ran the saddle horses in, and changed mounts just a little quicker than I ever saw it done before or since. The cook had a saddle in the wagon, so we caught him up a horse, clapped leather on him, and tied him behind the wagon in case of an emergency. And you can just bet we changed to our best horses. When we overtook the herd, we were at least a mile and a half from where the shooting occurred, and there was no Indian in sight, but we felt that they hadn't given it up. We hadn't long to wait, though we would have waited willingly, before we heard their yells and saw the dust rising in clouds behind us. We quit the herd and wagon right there and rode for a swell of ground ahead that would give us a rear view of the scenery. The first view we caught of them was not very encouraging. They were riding after us like fiends and kicking up a dust like a wind storm. We had nothing but six-shooters, no good for long range. The owner of the horses admitted that it was useless to try to save the herd now, and if our scalps were worth saving it was high time to make ourselves scarce.

"Cantonment was a government post about twenty-five miles away, so we rode for it. Our horses were good Spanish stock, and the Indians' little bench-legged ponies were no match for them. But not satisfied with the wagon and herd falling into their hands, they followed us until we were within sight of the post. As hard luck would have it, the cavalry stationed at this post were off on some escort duty, and the infantry were useless in this case. When the cavalry returned a few days later, they tried to round up those Indians, and the Indian agent used his influence, but the horses were so divided up and scattered that they were never recovered."

"And did the man lose his horses entirely?" asked Flood, who had anteed up his last bean and joined us.

"He did. There was, I remember, a tin horn lawyer up about Dodge who thought he could recover their value, as these were agency Indians and the government owed them money. But all I got for three months' wages due me was the horse I got away on."

McCann had been frozen out during Roundtree's yarn, and had joined the crowd of storytellers on the other side of the fire. Forrest was feeling quite gala, and took a special delight in taunting the vanquished as they dropped out.

"Is McCann there?" inquired he, well knowing he was. "I just wanted to ask, would it be any trouble to poach that egg for my breakfast and serve it with a bit of toast; I'm feeling a little bit dainty. You'll poach it for me, won't you, please?"

McCann never moved a muscle as he replied, "Will you please go to hell?"

The story-telling continued for some time, and while Fox Quarternight was regaling us with the history of a little black mare that a neighbor of theirs in Kentucky owned, a dispute arose in the card game regarding the rules of discard and draw.

"I'm too old a girl," said The Rebel, angrily, to Forrest, "to allow a pullet like you to teach me this game. When it's my deal, I'll discard just when I please, and it's none of your business so long as I keep within the rules of the game;" which sounded final, and the game continued.

Quarternight picked up the broken thread of his narrative, and the first warning we had of the lateness of the hour was Bull Durham calling to us from the game, "One of you fellows can have my place, just as soon as we play this jack pot. I've got to saddle my horse and get ready for our guard. Oh, I'm on velvet, anyhow, and before this game ends, I'll make old Quince curl his tail; I've got him going south now."

It took me only a few minutes to lose my chance at the turkey egg, and I sought my blankets. At one A.M., when our guard was called, the beans were almost equally divided among Priest, Stallings, and Durham; and in view of the fact that Forrest, whom we all wanted to see beaten, had met defeat, they agreed to cut the cards for the egg, Stallings winning. We mounted our horses and rode out into the night, and the second guard rode back to our camp-fire, singing: —

"Two little niggers upstairs in bed,
　One turned ober to de oder an' said,
　'How 'bout dat short'nin' bread,
　How 'bout dat short'nin' bread?'"

CHAPTER XIII
DODGE

At Camp Supply, Flood received a letter from Lovell, requesting him to come on into Dodge ahead of the cattle. So after the first night's camp above the Cimarron, Flood caught up a favorite horse, informed the outfit that he was going to quit us for a few days, and designated Quince Forrest as the *segundo* during his absence.

"You have a wide, open country from here into Dodge," said he, when ready to start, "and I'll make inquiry for you daily from men coming in, or from the buckboard which carries the mail to Supply. I'll try to meet you at Mulberry Creek, which is about ten miles south of Dodge. I'll make that town to-night, and you ought to make the Mulberry in two days. You will see the smoke of passing trains to the north of the Arkansaw, from the first divide south of Mulberry. When you reach that creek, in case I don't meet you, hold the herd there and three or four of you can come on into town. But I'm almost certain to meet you," he called back as he rode away.

"Priest," said Quince, when our foreman had gone, "I reckon you didn't handle your herd to suit the old man when he left us that time at Buffalo Gap. But I think he used rare judgment this time in selecting a *segundo*. The only thing that frets me is, I'm afraid he'll meet us before we reach the Mulberry, and that won't give me any chance to go in ahead like a sure enough foreman. Fact is I have business there; I deposited a few months' wages at the Long Branch gambling house last year when I was in Dodge, and failed to take a receipt. I just want to drop in and make inquiry if they gave me credit, and if the account is drawing interest. I think it's all right, for the man I deposited it with was a clever fellow and asked me to have a drink with him just as I was leaving. Still, I'd like to step in and see him again."

Early in the afternoon of the second day after our foreman left us, we sighted the smoke of passing trains, though they were at least fifteen miles distant, and long before we reached the Mulberry, a livery rig came down the trail to meet us. To Forrest's chagrin, Flood, all dressed up and with a white collar on, was the driver, while on a back seat sat Don Lovell and another cowman by the name of McNulta. Every rascal of us gave old man Don the glad hand as they drove around the herd, while he, liberal and delighted as a bridegroom, passed out the cigars by the handful. The cattle were looking fine, which put the old man in high spirits, and he inquired of each of us if our health was good and if Flood had fed us well. They loitered around the herd the rest of the evening, until we threw off the trail to graze and camp for the night, when Lovell declared his intention of staying all night with the outfit.

While we were catching horses during the evening, Lovell came up to me where I was saddling my night horse, and recognizing me gave me news of my brother Bob. "I had a letter yesterday from him," he said, "written from Red Fork, which is just north of the Cimarron River over on the Chisholm route. He reports everything going along nicely, and I'm expecting him to show up here within a week. His herd are all beef steers, and are contracted for delivery at the Crow Indian Agency. He's not driving as fast as Flood, but we've got to have our beef for that delivery in better condition, as they have a new agent there this year, and he may be one of these knowing fellows. Sorry you couldn't see your brother, but if you have any word to send him, I'll deliver it."

I thanked him for the interest he had taken in me, and assured him that I had no news for Robert; but took advantage of the opportunity to inquire if our middle brother, Zack Quirk, was on the trail with any of his herds. Lovell knew him, but felt positive he was not with any of his outfits.

We had an easy night with the cattle. Lovell insisted on standing a guard, so he took Rod Wheat's horse and stood the first watch, and after returning to the wagon, he and McNulta, to our great interest, argued the merits of the different trails until near midnight. McNulta had two herds coming in on the Chisholm trail, while Lovell had two herds on the Western and only one on the Chisholm.

The next morning Forrest, who was again in charge, received orders to cross the Arkansaw River shortly after noon, and then let half the outfit come into town. The old trail crossed the river about a mile above the present town of Dodge City, Kansas, so when we changed horses at noon, the first and second guards caught up their top horses, ransacked their war bags, and donned their best toggery. We crossed the river about one o'clock in order to give the boys a good holiday, the stage of water making the river easily fordable. McCann, after dinner was over, drove down on the south side for the benefit of a bridge which spanned the river opposite the town. It was the first bridge he had been able to take advantage of in over a thousand miles of travel, and to-day he spurned the cattle ford as though he had never crossed at one. Once safely over the river, and with the understanding that the herd would camp for the night about six miles north on Duck Creek, six of our men quit us and rode for the town in a long gallop. Before the rig left us in the morning, McNulta, who was thoroughly familiar with Dodge, and an older man than Lovell, in a friendly and fatherly spirit, seeing that many of us were youngsters, had given us an earnest talk and plenty of good advice.

"I've been in Dodge every summer since '77," said the old cowman, "and I can give you boys some points. Dodge is one town where the average bad man of the West not only finds his equal, but finds himself badly handicapped. The buffalo hunters and range men have protested against the iron rule of Dodge's peace officers, and nearly every protest has cost human life. Don't ever get the impression that you can ride your horses into a saloon, or shoot out the lights in Dodge; it may go somewhere else, but it don't go there. So I want to warn you to behave yourselves. You can wear your six-shooters into town, but you'd better leave them at the first place you stop, hotel, livery, or business house. And when you leave town, call for your pistols, but don't ride out shooting; omit that. Most cowboys think it's an infringement on their rights to give up shooting in town, and if it is, it stands, for your six-shooters are no match for Winchesters and buckshot; and Dodge's officers are as game a set of men as ever faced danger."

Nearly a generation has passed since McNulta, the Texan cattle drover, gave our outfit this advice one June morning on the Mulberry, and in setting down this record, I have only to scan the roster of the peace officials of Dodge City to admit its correctness. Among the names that graced the official roster, during the brief span of the trail days, were the brothers Ed, Jim, and "Bat" Masterson, Wyatt Earp, Jack Bridges, "Doc" Holliday, Charles Bassett, William Tillman, "Shotgun" Collins, Joshua Webb, Mayor A.B. Webster, and "Mysterious" Dave Mather. The puppets of no romance ever written can compare with these officers in fearlessness. And let it be understood, there were plenty to protest against their rule; almost daily during the range season some equally fearless individual defied them.

"Throw up your hands and surrender," said an officer to a Texas cowboy, who had spurred an excitable horse until it was rearing and plunging in the street, leveling meanwhile a double-barreled shotgun at the horseman.

"Not to you, you white-livered s — — of a b — — ," was the instant reply, accompanied by a shot.

The officer staggered back mortally wounded, but recovered himself, and the next instant the cowboy reeled from his saddle, a load of buckshot through his breast.

After the boys left us for town, the remainder of us, belonging to the third and fourth guard, grazed the cattle forward leisurely during the afternoon. Through cattle herds were in sight both up and down the river on either side, and on crossing the Mulberry the day before, we learned that several herds were holding out as far south as that stream, while McNulta had reported over forty herds as having already passed northward on the trail. Dodge was the meeting point for buyers from every quarter. Often herds would sell at Dodge whose destination for delivery was beyond the Yellowstone in Montana. Herds frequently changed owners when the buyer never saw the cattle. A yearling was a yearling and a two year old was a two year old, and the seller's word, that they were "as good or better than the string I sold you last year," was sufficient. Cattle were classified as northern, central, and southern animals, and, except in case of severe drouth in the preceding years, were pretty nearly uniform in size throughout each section. The prairie section of the State left its indelible imprint on the cattle bred in the open country, while the coast, as well as the piney woods and black-jack sections, did the same, thus making classification easy.

McCann overtook us early in the evening, and, being an obliging fellow, was induced by Forrest to stand the first guard with Honeyman so as to make up the proper number of watches, though with only two men on guard at a time, for it was hardly possible that any of the others would return before daybreak. There was much to be seen in Dodge, and as losing a night's sleep on duty was considered nothing, in hilarious recreation sleep would be entirely forgotten. McCann had not forgotten us, but had smuggled out a quart bottle to cut the alkali in our drinking water. But a quart amongst eight of us was not dangerous, so the night passed without incident, though we felt a growing impatience to get into town. As we expected, about sunrise the next morning our men off on holiday rode into camp, having never closed an eye during the entire night. They brought word from Flood that the herd would only graze over to Saw Log Creek that day, so as to let the remainder of us have a day and night in town. Lovell would only advance half a month's wages — twenty-five dollars — to the man. It was ample for any personal needs, though we had nearly three months' wages due, and no one protested, for the old man was generally right in his decisions. According to their report the boys had had a hog-killing time, old man Don having been out with them all night. It seems that McNulta stood in well with a class of practical jokers which included the officials of the town, and whenever there was anything on the tapis, he always got the word for himself and friends. During breakfast Fox Quarternight told this incident of the evening.

"Some professor, a professor in the occult sciences I think he called himself, had written to the mayor to know what kind of a point Dodge would be for a lecture. The lecture was to be free, but he also intimated that he had a card or two on the side up his sleeve, by which he expected to graft onto some of the coin of the realm from the wayfaring man as well as the citizen. The mayor turned the letter over to Bat Masterson, the city marshal, who answered it, and invited the professor to come on, assuring him that he was deeply interested in the occult sciences, personally, and would take pleasure in securing him a hall and a date, besides announcing his coming through the papers.

"Well, he was billed to deliver his lecture last night. Those old long horns, McNulta and Lovell, got us in with the crowd, and while they didn't know exactly what was coming, they assured us that we couldn't afford to miss it. Well, at the appointed hour in the evening, the hall was packed, not over half being able to find seats. It is safe to say there were over five hundred men present, as it was announced for 'men only.' Every gambler in town was there, with a fair sprinkling of cowmen and our tribe. At the appointed hour, Masterson, as chairman, rapped for order, and in a neat little speech announced the object of the meeting. Bat mentioned the lack of interest in the West in the higher arts and sciences, and bespoke our careful attention to the subject under consideration for the evening. He said he felt it hardly necessary to urge the importance of good order, but if any one had come out of idle curiosity or bent on mischief, as chairman of the meeting and a peace officer of the city, he would certainly brook no interruption. After a few other appropriate remarks, he introduced the speaker as Dr. J. Graves-Brown, the noted scientist.

"The professor was an oily-tongued fellow, and led off on the prelude to his lecture, while the audience was as quiet as mice and as grave as owls. After he had spoken about five minutes and was getting warmed up to his subject, he made an assertion which sounded a little fishy, and some one back in the audience blurted out, 'That's a damned lie.' The speaker halted in his discourse and looked at Masterson, who arose, and, drawing two six-shooters, looked the audience over as if trying to locate the offender. Laying the guns down on the table, he informed the meeting that another interruption would cost the offender his life, if he had to follow him to the Rio Grande or the British possessions. He then asked the professor, as there would be no further interruptions, to proceed with his lecture. The professor hesitated about going on, when Masterson assured him that it was evident that his audience, with the exception of one skulking coyote, was deeply interested in the subject, but that no one man could interfere with the freedom of speech in Dodge as long as it was a free country and he was city marshal. After this little talk, the speaker braced up and launched out again on his lecture. When he was once more under good headway, he had occasion to relate an exhibition which he had witnessed while studying his profession in India. The incident related was a trifle rank for any one to swallow raw, when the same party who had interrupted before sang out, 'That's another damn lie.'

"Masterson came to his feet like a flash, a gun in each hand, saying, 'Stand up, you measly skunk, so I can see you.' Half a dozen men rose in different parts of the house and cut loose at him, and as they did so the lights went out and the room filled with smoke. Masterson was blazing away with two guns, which so lighted up the rostrum that we could see the professor crouching under the table. Of course they were using blank cartridges, but the audience raised the long yell and poured out through the windows and doors, and the lecture was over. A couple of police came in later, so McNulta said, escorted the professor to his room in the hotel, and quietly advised him that Dodge was hardly capable of appreciating anything so advanced as a lecture on the occult sciences."

Breakfast over, Honeyman ran in the *remuda*, and we caught the best horses in our mounts, on which to pay our respects to Dodge. Forrest detailed Rod Wheat to wrangle the horses, for we intended to take Honeyman with us. As it was only about six miles over to the Saw Log, Quince advised that they graze along Duck Creek until after dinner, and then graze over to the former stream during the afternoon. Before leaving, we rode over and looked out the trail after it left Duck, for it was quite possible that we might return during the night; and we requested McCann to hang out the lantern, elevated on the end of the wagon tongue, as a beacon. After taking our bearings, we reined southward over the divide to Dodge.

"The very first thing I do," said Quince Forrest, as we rode leisurely along, "after I get a shave and hair-cut and buy what few tricks I need, is to hunt up that gambler in the Long Branch, and ask him to take a drink with me — I took the parting one on him. Then I'll simply set in and win back every dollar I lost there last year. There's something in this northern air that I breathe in this morning that tells me that this is my lucky day. You other kids had better let the games alone and save your money to buy red silk handkerchiefs and soda water and such harmless jimcracks." The fact that The Rebel was ten years his senior never entered his mind as he gave us this fatherly advice, though to be sure the majority of us were his juniors in years.

On reaching Dodge, we rode up to the Wright House, where Flood met us and directed our cavalcade across the railroad to a livery stable, the proprietor of which was a friend of Lovell's. We unsaddled and turned our horses into a large corral, and while we were in the office of the livery, surrendering our artillery, Flood came in and handed each of us twenty-five dollars in gold, warning us that when that was gone no more would be advanced. On receipt of the money, we scattered like partridges before a gunner. Within an hour or two, we began to return to the stable by ones and twos, and were stowing into our saddle pockets our purchases, which ran from needles and thread to .45 cartridges, every mother's son reflecting the art of the barber, while John Officer had his blond mustaches blackened, waxed, and curled like a French dancing master. "If some of you boys will hold him," said Moss Strayhorn, commenting on Officer's appearance, "I'd like to take a good smell of him, just to see if he took oil up there where the end of his neck's haired over." As Officer already had several drinks comfortably stowed away under his belt, and stood up strong six feet two, none of us volunteered.

After packing away our plunder, we sauntered around town, drinking moderately, and visiting the various saloons and gambling houses. I clung to my bunkie, The Rebel, during the rounds, for I had learned to like him, and had confidence he would lead me into no indiscretions. At the Long Branch, we found Quince Forrest and Wyatt Roundtree playing the faro bank, the former keeping cases. They never recognized us, but were answering a great many questions, asked by the dealer and lookout, regarding the possible volume of the cattle drive that year. Down at another gambling house, The Rebel met Ben Thompson, a faro dealer not on duty and an old cavalry comrade, and the two cronied around for over an hour like long lost brothers, pledging anew their friendship over several social glasses, in which I was always included. There was no telling how long this reunion would have lasted, but happily for my sake, Lovell — who had been asleep all the morning — started out to round us up for dinner with him at the Wright House, which was at that day a famous hostelry, patronized almost exclusively by the Texas cowmen and cattle buyers.

We made the rounds of the gambling houses, looking for our crowd. We ran across three of the boys piking at a monte game, who came with us reluctantly; then, guided by Lovell, we started for the Long Branch, where we felt certain we would find Forrest and Roundtree, if they had any money left. Forrest was broke, which made him ready to come, and Roundtree, though quite a winner, out of deference to our employer's wishes, cashed in and joined us. Old man Don could hardly do enough for us; and before we could reach the Wright House, had lined us up against three different bars; and while I had confidence in my navigable capacity, I found they were coming just a little too fast and free, seeing I had scarcely drunk anything in three months but branch water. As we lined up at the Wright House bar for the final before dinner, The Rebel, who was standing next to me, entered a waiver and took a cigar, which I understood to be a hint, and I did likewise.

We had a splendid dinner. Our outfit, with McNulta, occupied a ten-chair table, while on the opposite side of the room was another large table, occupied principally by drovers who were waiting for their herds to arrive. Among those at the latter table, whom I now remember, was "Uncle" Henry Stevens, Jesse Ellison, "Lum" Slaughter, John Blocker, Ike Pryor, "Dun" Houston, and last but not least, Colonel "Shanghai" Pierce. The latter was possibly the most widely known cowman between the Rio Grande and the British possessions. He stood six feet four in his stockings, was gaunt and raw-boned, and the possessor of a voice which, even in ordinary conversation, could be distinctly heard across the street.

"No, I'll not ship any more cattle to your town," said Pierce to a cattle solicitor during the dinner, his voice in righteous indignation resounding like a foghorn through the dining-room, "until you adjust your yardage charges. Listen! I can go right up into the heart of your city and get a room for myself, with a nice clean bed in it, plenty of soap, water, and towels, and I can occupy that room for twenty-four hours for two bits. And your stockyards, away out in the suburbs, want to charge me twenty cents a head and let my steer stand out in the weather."

After dinner, all the boys, with the exception of Priest and myself, returned to the gambling houses as though anxious to work overtime. Before leaving the hotel, Forrest effected the loan of ten from Roundtree, and the two returned to the Long Branch, while the others as eagerly sought out a monte game. But I was fascinated with the conversation of these old cowmen, and sat around for several hours listening to their yarns and cattle talk.

"I was selling a thousand beef steers one time to some Yankee army contractors," Pierce was narrating to a circle of listeners, "and I got the idea that they were not up to snuff in receiving cattle out on the prairie. I was holding a herd of about three thousand, and they had agreed to take a running cut, which showed that they had the receiving agent fixed. Well, my foreman and I were counting the cattle as they came between us. But the steers were wild, long-legged coasters, and came through between us like scared wolves. I had lost the count several times, but guessed at them and started over, the cattle still coming like a whirlwind; and when I thought about nine hundred had passed us, I cut them off and sang out, 'Here they come and there they go; just an even thousand, by gatlins! What do you make it, Bill?'

"'Just an even thousand, Colonel,' replied my foreman. Of course the contractors were counting at the same time, and I suppose didn't like to admit they couldn't count a thousand cattle where anybody else could, and never asked for a recount, but accepted and paid for them. They had hired an outfit, and held the cattle outside that night, but the next day, when they cut them into car lots and shipped them, they were a hundred and eighteen short. They wanted to come back on me to make them good, but, shucks! I wasn't responsible if their Jim Crow outfit lost the cattle."

Along early in the evening, Flood advised us boys to return to the herd with him, but all the crowd wanted to stay in town and see the sights. Lovell interceded in our behalf, and promised to see that we left town in good time to be in camp before the herd was ready to move the next morning. On this assurance, Flood saddled up and started for the Saw Log, having ample time to make the ride before dark. By this time most of the boys had worn off the wire edge for gambling and were comparing notes. Three of them were broke, but Quince Forrest had turned the tables and was over a clean hundred winner for the day. Those who had no money fortunately had good credit with those of us who had, for there was yet much to be seen, and in Dodge in '82 it took money to see the elephant. There were several variety theatres, a number of dance halls, and other resorts which, like the wicked, flourish best under darkness. After supper, just about dusk, we went over to the stable, caught our horses, saddled them, and tied them up for the night. We fully expected to leave town by ten o'clock, for it was a good twelve mile ride to the Saw Log. In making the rounds of the variety theatres and dance halls, we hung together. Lovell excused himself early in the evening, and at parting we assured him that the outfit would leave for camp before midnight. We were enjoying ourselves immensely over at the Lone Star dance hall, when an incident occurred in which we entirely neglected the good advice of McNulta, and had the sensation of hearing lead whistle and cry around our ears before we got away from town.

Quince Forrest was spending his winnings as well as drinking freely, and at the end of a quadrille gave vent to his hilarity in an old-fashioned Comanche yell. The bouncer of the dance hall of course had his eye on our crowd, and at the end of a change, took Quince to task. He was a surly brute, and instead of couching his request in appropriate language, threatened to throw him out of the house. Forrest stood like one absent-minded and took the abuse, for physically he was no match for the bouncer, who was armed, moreover, and wore an officer's star. I was dancing in the same set with a red-headed, freckled-faced girl, who clutched my arm and wished to know if my friend was armed. I assured her that he was not, or we would have had notice of it before the bouncer's invective was ended. At the conclusion of the dance, Quince and The Rebel passed out, giving the rest of us the word to remain as though nothing was wrong. In the course of half an hour, Priest returned and asked us to take our leave one at a time without attracting any attention, and meet at the stable. I remained until the last, and noticed The Rebel and the bouncer taking a drink together at the bar, — the former apparently in a most amiable mood. We passed out together shortly afterward, and found the other boys mounted and awaiting our return, it being now about midnight. It took but a moment to secure our guns, and once in the saddle, we rode through the town in the direction of the herd. On the outskirts of the town, we halted. "I'm going back to that dance hall," said Forrest, "and have one round at least with that whore-herder. No man who walks this old earth can insult me, as he did, not if he has a hundred stars on him. If any of you don't want to go along, ride right on to camp, but I'd like to have you all go. And when I take his measure, it will be the signal to the rest of you to put out the lights. All that's going, come on." There were no dissenters to the programme. I saw at a glance that my bunkie was heart and soul in the play, and took my cue and kept my mouth shut. We circled round the town to a vacant lot within a block of the rear of the dance hall. Honeyman was left to hold the horses; then, taking off our belts and hanging them on the pommels of our saddles, we secreted our six-shooters inside the waistbands of our trousers. The hall was still crowded with the revelers when we entered, a few at a time, Forrest and Priest being the last to arrive. Forrest had changed hats with The Rebel, who always wore a black one, and as the bouncer circulated around, Quince stepped squarely in front of him. There was no waste of words, but a gun-barrel flashed in the lamplight, and the bouncer, struck with the six-shooter, fell like a beef. Before the bewildered spectators could raise a hand, five six-shooters were turned into the ceiling. The lights went out at the first fire, and amidst the rush of men and the screaming of women, we reached the outside, and within a minute were in our saddles. All would have gone well had we returned by the same route and avoided the town; but after crossing the railroad track, anger and pride having not been properly satisfied, we must ride through the town.

On entering the main street, leading north and opposite the bridge on the river, somebody of our party in the rear turned his gun loose into the air. The Rebel and I were riding in the lead, and at the clattering of hoofs and shooting behind us, our horses started on the run, the shooting by this time having become general. At the second street crossing, I noticed a rope of fire belching from a Winchester in the doorway of a store building. There was no doubt in my mind but we were the object of the manipulator of that carbine, and as we reached the next cross street, a man kneeling in the shadow of a building opened fire on us with a six-shooter. Priest reined in his horse, and not having wasted cartridges in the open-air shooting, returned the compliment until he emptied his gun. By this time every officer in the town was throwing lead after us, some of which cried a little too close for comfort. When there was no longer any shooting on our flanks, we turned into a cross street and soon left the lead behind us. At the outskirts of the town we slowed up our horses and took it leisurely for a mile or so, when Quince Forrest halted us and said, "I'm going to drop out here and see if any one follows us. I want to be alone, so that if any officers try to follow us up, I can have it out with them."

As there was no time to lose in parleying, and as he had a good horse, we rode away and left him. On reaching camp, we secured a few hours' sleep, but the next morning, to our surprise, Forrest failed to appear. We explained the situation to Flood, who said if he did not show up by noon, he would go back and look for him. We all felt positive that he would not dare to go back to town; and if he was lost, as soon as the sun arose he would be able to get his bearings. While we were nooning about seven miles north of the Saw Log, some one noticed a buggy coming up the trail. As it came nearer we saw that there were two other occupants of the rig besides the driver. When it drew up old Quince, still wearing The Rebel's hat, stepped out of the rig, dragged out his saddle from under the seat, and invited his companions to dinner. They both declined, when Forrest, taking out his purse, handed a twenty-dollar gold piece to the driver with an oath. He then asked the other man what he owed him, but the latter very haughtily declined any recompense, and the conveyance drove away.

"I suppose you fellows don't know what all this means," said Quince, as he filled a plate and sat down in the shade of the wagon. "Well, that horse of mine got a bullet plugged into him last night as we were leaving town, and before I could get him to Duck Creek, he died on me. I carried my saddle and blankets until daylight, when I hid in a draw and waited for something to turn up. I thought some of you would come back and look for me sometime, for I knew you wouldn't understand it, when all of a sudden here comes this livery rig along with that drummer — going out to Jetmore, I believe he said. I explained what I wanted, but he decided that his business was more important than mine, and refused me. I referred the matter to Judge Colt, and the judge decided that it was more important that I overtake this herd. I'd have made him take pay, too, only he acted so mean about it."

After dinner, fearing arrest, Forrest took a horse and rode on ahead to the Solomon River. We were a glum outfit that afternoon, but after a good night's rest were again as fresh as daisies. When McCann started to get breakfast, he hung his coat on the end of the wagon rod, while he went for a bucket of water. During his absence, John Officer was noticed slipping something into Barney's coat pocket, and after breakfast when our cook went to his coat for his tobacco, he unearthed a lady's cambric handkerchief, nicely embroidered, and a silver mounted garter. He looked at the articles a moment, and, grasping the situation at a glance, ran his eye over the outfit for the culprit. But there was not a word or a smile. He walked over and threw the articles into the fire, remarking, "Good whiskey and bad women will be the ruin of you varmints yet."

CHAPTER XIV
SLAUGHTER'S BRIDGE

Herds bound for points beyond the Yellowstone, in Montana, always considered Dodge as the halfway landmark on the trail, though we had hardly covered half the distance to the destination of our Circle Dots. But with Dodge in our rear, all felt that the backbone of the drive was broken, and it was only the middle of June. In order to divide the night work more equitably, for the remainder of the trip the first and fourth guards changed, the second and third remaining as they were. We had begun to feel the scarcity of wood for cooking purposes some time past, and while crossing the plains of western Kansas, we were frequently forced to resort to the old bed grounds of a year or two previous for cattle chips. These chips were a poor substitute, and we swung a cowskin under the reach of the wagon, so that when we encountered wood on creeks and rivers we could lay in a supply. Whenever our wagon was in the rear, the riders on either side of the herd were always on the skirmish for fuel, which they left alongside the wagon track, and our cook was sure to stow it away underneath on the cowskin.

In spite of any effort on our part, the length of the days made long drives the rule. The cattle could be depended on to leave the bed ground at dawn, and before the outfit could breakfast, secure mounts, and overtake the herd, they would often have grazed forward two or three miles. Often we never threw them on the trail at all, yet when it came time to bed them at night, we had covered twenty miles. They were long, monotonous days; for we were always sixteen to eighteen hours in the saddle, while in emergencies we got the benefit of the limit. We frequently saw mirages, though we were never led astray by shady groves of timber or tempting lakes of water, but always kept within a mile or two of the trail. The evening of the third day after Forrest left us, he returned as we were bedding down the cattle at dusk, and on being assured that no officers had followed us, resumed his place with the herd. He had not even reached the Solomon River, but had stopped with a herd of Millet's on Big Boggy. This creek he reported as bottomless, and the Millet herd as having lost between forty and fifty head of cattle in attempting to force it at the regular crossing the day before his arrival. They had scouted the creek both up and down since without finding a safe crossing. It seemed that there had been unusually heavy June rains through that section, which accounted for Boggy being in its dangerous condition. Millet's foreman had not considered it necessary to test such an insignificant stream until he got a couple of hundred head of cattle floundering in the mire. They had saved the greater portion of the mired cattle, but quite a number were trampled to death by the others, and now the regular crossing was not approachable for the stench of dead cattle. Flood knew the stream, and so did a number of our outfit, but none of them had any idea that it could get into such an impassable condition as Forrest reported.

The next morning Flood started to the east and Priest to the west to look out a crossing, for we were then within half a day's drive of the creek. Big Boggy paralleled the Solomon River in our front, the two not being more than five miles apart. The confluence was far below in some settlements, and we must keep to the westward of all immigration, on account of the growing crops in the fertile valley of the Solomon. On the westward, had a favorable crossing been found, we would almost have had to turn our herd backward, for we were already within the half circle which this creek described in our front. So after the two men left us, we allowed the herd to graze forward, keeping several miles to the westward of the trail in order to get the benefit of the best grazing. Our herd, when left to itself, would graze from a mile to a mile and a half an hour, and by the middle of the forenoon the timber on Big Boggy and the Solomon beyond was sighted. On reaching this last divide, some one sighted a herd about five or six miles to the eastward and nearly parallel with us. As they were three or four miles beyond the trail, we could easily see that they were grazing along like ourselves, and Forrest was appealed to to know if it was the Millet herd. He said not, and pointed out to the northeast about the location of the Millet cattle, probably five miles in advance of the stranger on our right. When we overtook our wagon at noon, McCann, who had never left the trail, reported having seen the herd. They looked to him like heavy beef cattle, and had two yoke of oxen to their chuck wagon, which served further to proclaim them as strangers.

Neither Priest nor Flood returned during the noon hour, and when the herd refused to lie down and rest longer, we grazed them forward till the fringe of timber which grew along the stream loomed up not a mile distant in our front. From the course we were traveling, we would strike the creek several miles above the regular crossing, and as Forrest reported that Millet was holding below the old crossing on a small rivulet, all we could do was to hold our wagon in the rear, and await the return of our men out on scout for a ford. Priest was the first to return, with word that he had ridden the creek out for twenty-five miles and had found no crossing that would be safe for a mud turtle. On hearing this, we left two men with the herd, and the rest of the outfit took the wagon, went on to Boggy, and made camp. It was a deceptive-looking stream, not over fifty or sixty feet wide. In places the current barely moved, shallowing and deepening, from a few inches in places to several feet in others, with an occasional pool that would swim a horse. We probed it with poles until we were satisfied that we were up against a proposition different from anything we had yet encountered. While we were discussing the situation, a stranger rode up on a fine roan horse, and inquired for our foreman. Forrest informed him that our boss was away looking for a crossing, but we were expecting his return at any time; and invited the stranger to dismount. He did so, and threw himself down in the shade of our wagon. He was a small, boyish-looking fellow, of sandy complexion, not much, if any, over twenty years old, and smiled continuously.

"My name is Pete Slaughter," said he, by way of introduction, "and I've got a herd of twenty-eight hundred beef steers, beyond the trail and a few miles back. I've been riding since daybreak down the creek, and I'm prepared to state that the chance of crossing is as good right here as anywhere. I wanted to see your foreman, and if he'll help, we'll bridge her. I've been down to see this other outfit, but they ridicule the idea, though I think they'll come around all right. I borrowed their axe, and to-morrow morning you'll see me with my outfit cutting timber to bridge Big Boggy. That's right, boys; it's the only thing to do. The trouble is I've only got eight men all told. I don't aim to travel over eight or ten miles a day, so I don't need a big outfit. You say your foreman's name is Flood? Well, if he don't return before I go, some of you tell him that he's wasting good time looking for a ford, for there ain't none."

In the conversation which followed, we learned that Slaughter was driving for his brother Lum, a widely known cowman and drover, whom we had seen in Dodge. He had started with the grass from north Texas, and by the time he reached the Platte, many of his herd would be fit to ship to market, and what were not would be in good demand as feeders in the corn belt of eastern Nebraska. He asked if we had seen his herd during the morning, and on hearing we had, got up and asked McCann to let him see our axe. This he gave a critical examination, before he mounted his horse to go, and on leaving said, —

"If your foreman don't want to help build a bridge, I want to borrow that axe of yours. But you fellows talk to him. If any of you boys has ever been over on the Chisholm trail, you will remember the bridge on Rush Creek, south of the Washita River. I built that bridge in a day with an outfit of ten men. Why, shucks! if these outfits would pull together, we could cross to-morrow evening. Lots of these old foremen don't like to listen to a cub like me, but, holy snakes! I've been over the trail oftener than any of them. Why, when I wasn't big enough to make a hand with the herd, — only ten years old, — in the days when we drove to Abilene, they used to send me in the lead with an old cylinder gun to shoot at the buffalo and scare them off the trail. And I've made the trip every year since. So you tell Flood when he comes in, that Pete Slaughter was here, and that he's going to build a bridge, and would like to have him and his outfit help."

Had it not been for his youth and perpetual smile, we might have taken young Slaughter more seriously, for both Quince Forrest and The Rebel remembered the bridge on Rush Creek over on the Chisholm. Still there was an air of confident assurance in the young fellow; and the fact that he was the trusted foreman of Lum Slaughter, in charge of a valuable herd of cattle, carried weight with those who knew that drover. The most unwelcome thought in the project was that it required the swinging of an axe to fell trees and to cut them into the necessary lengths, and, as I have said before, the Texan never took kindly to manual labor. But Priest looked favorably on the suggestion, and so enlisted my support, and even pointed out a spot where timber was most abundant as a suitable place to build the bridge.

"Hell's fire," said Joe Stallings, with infinite contempt, "there's thousands of places to build a bridge, and the timber's there, but the idea is to cut it." And his sentiments found a hearty approval in the majority of the outfit.

Flood returned late that evening, having ridden as far down the creek as the first settlement. The Rebel, somewhat antagonized by the attitude of the majority, reported the visit and message left for him by young Slaughter. Our foreman knew him by general reputation amongst trail bosses, and when Priest vouched for him as the builder of the Rush Creek bridge on the Chisholm trail, Flood said, "Why, I crossed my herd four years ago on that Rush Creek bridge within a week after it was built, and wondered who it could be that had the nerve to undertake that task. Rush isn't over half as wide a bayou as Boggy, but she's a true little sister to this miry slough. So he's going to build a bridge anyhow, is he?"

The next morning young Slaughter was at our camp before sunrise, and never once mentioning his business or waiting for the formality of an invitation, proceeded to pour out a tin cup of coffee and otherwise provide himself with a substantial breakfast. There was something amusing in the audacity of the fellow which all of us liked, though he was fifteen years the junior of our foreman. McCann pointed out Flood to him, and taking his well-loaded plate, he went over and sat down by our foreman, and while he ate talked rapidly, to enlist our outfit in the building of the bridge. During breakfast, the outfit listened to the two bosses as they discussed the feasibility of the project, — Slaughter enthusiastic, Flood reserved, and asking all sorts of questions as to the mode of procedure. Young Pete met every question with promptness, and assured our foreman that the building of bridges was his long suit. After breakfast, the two foremen rode off down the creek together, and within half an hour Slaughter's wagon and *remuda* pulled up within sight of the regular crossing, and shortly afterwards our foreman returned, and ordered our wagon to pull down to a clump of cotton woods which grew about half a mile below our camp. Two men were detailed to look after our herd during the day, and the remainder of us returned with our foreman to the site selected for the bridge. On our arrival three axes were swinging against as many cottonwoods, and there was no doubt in any one's mind that we were going to be under a new foreman for that day at least. Slaughter had a big negro cook who swung an axe in a manner which bespoke him a job for the day, and McCann was instructed to provide dinner for the extra outfit.

The site chosen for the bridge was a miry bottom over which oozed three or four inches of water, where the width of the stream was about sixty feet, with solid banks on either side. To get a good foundation was the most important matter, but the brush from the trees would supply the material for that; and within an hour, brush began to arrive, dragged from the pommels of saddles, and was piled into the stream. About this time a call went out for a volunteer who could drive oxen, for the darky was too good an axeman to be recalled. As I had driven oxen as a boy, I was going to offer my services, when Joe Stallings eagerly volunteered in order to avoid using an axe. Slaughter had some extra chain, and our four mules were pressed into service as an extra team in snaking logs. As McCann was to provide for the inner man, the mule team fell to me; and putting my saddle on the nigh wheeler, I rode jauntily past Mr. Stallings as he trudged alongside his two yoke of oxen.

About ten o'clock in the morning, George Jacklin, the foreman of the Millet herd, rode up with several of his men, and seeing the bridge taking shape, turned in and assisted in dragging brush for the foundation. By the time all hands knocked off for dinner, we had a foundation of brush twenty feet wide and four feet high, to say nothing about what had sunk in the mire. The logs were cut about fourteen feet long, and old Joe and I had snaked them up as fast as the axemen could get them ready. Jacklin returned to his wagon for dinner and a change of horses, though Slaughter, with plenty of assurance, had invited him to eat with us, and when he declined had remarked, with no less confidence, "Well, then, you'll be back right after dinner. And say, bring all the men you can spare; and if you've got any gunny sacks or old tarpaulins, bring them; and by all means don't forget your spade."

Pete Slaughter was a harsh master, considering he was working volunteer labor; but then we all felt a common interest in the bridge, for if Slaughter's beeves could cross, ours could, and so could Millet's. All the men dragging brush changed horses during dinner, for there was to be no pause in piling in a good foundation as long as the material was at hand. Jacklin and his outfit returned, ten strong, and with thirty men at work, the bridge grew. They began laying the logs on the brush after dinner, and the work of sodding the bridge went forward at the same time. The bridge stood about two feet above the water in the creek, but when near the middle of the stream was reached, the foundation gave way, and for an hour ten horses were kept busy dragging brush to fill that sink hole until it would bear the weight of the logs. We had used all the acceptable timber on our side of the stream for half a mile either way, and yet there were not enough logs to complete the bridge. When we lacked only some ten or twelve logs, Slaughter had the boys sod a narrow strip across the remaining brush, and the horsemen led their mounts across to the farther side. Then the axemen crossed, felled the nearest trees, and the last logs were dragged up from the pommels of our saddles.

It now only remained to sod over and dirt the bridge thoroughly. With only three spades the work was slow, but we cut sod with axes, and after several hours' work had it finished. The two yoke of oxen were driven across and back for a test, and the bridge stood it nobly. Slaughter then brought up his *remuda*, and while the work of dirting the bridge was still going on, crossed and recrossed his band of saddle horses twenty times. When the bridge looked completed to every one else, young Pete advised laying stringers across on either side; so a number of small trees were felled and guard rails strung across the ends of the logs and staked. Then more dirt was carried in on tarpaulins and in gunny sacks, and every chink and crevice filled with sod and dirt. It was now getting rather late in the afternoon, but during the finishing touches, young Slaughter had dispatched his outfit to bring up his herd; and at the same time Flood had sent a number of our outfit to bring up our cattle. Now Slaughter and the rest of us took the oxen, which we had unyoked, and went out about a quarter of a mile to meet his herd coming up. Turning the oxen in the lead, young Pete took one point and Flood the other, and pointed in the lead cattle for the bridge. On reaching it the cattle hesitated for a moment, and it looked as though they were going to balk, but finally one of the oxen took the lead, and they began to cross in almost Indian file. They were big four and five year old beeves, and too many of them on the bridge at one time might have sunk it, but Slaughter rode back down the line of cattle and called to the men to hold them back.

"Don't crowd the cattle," he shouted. "Give them all the time they want. We're in no hurry now; there's lots of time."

They were a full half hour in crossing, the chain of cattle taking the bridge never for a moment being broken. Once all were over, his men rode to the lead and turned the herd up Boggy, in order to have it well out of the way of ours, which were then looming up in sight. Slaughter asked Flood if he wanted the oxen; and as our cattle had never seen a bridge in their lives, the foreman decided to use them; so we brought them back and met the herd, now strung out nearly a mile. Our cattle were naturally wild, but we turned the oxen in the lead, and the two bosses again taking the points, moved the herd up to the bridge. The oxen were again slow to lead out in crossing, and several hundred head of cattle had congested in front of the new bridge, making us all rather nervous, when a big white ox led off, his mate following, and the herd began timidly to follow. Our cattle required careful handling, and not a word was spoken as we nursed them forward, or rode through them to scatter large bunches. A number of times we cut the train of cattle off entirely, as they were congesting at the bridge entrance, and, in crossing, shied and crowded so that several were forced off the bridge into the mire. Our herd crossed in considerably less time than did Slaughter's beeves, but we had five head to pull out;

this, however, was considered nothing, as they were light, and the mire was as thin as soup. Our wagon and saddle horses crossed while we were pulling out the bogged cattle, and about half the outfit, taking the herd, drifted them forward towards the Solomon. Since Millet intended crossing that evening, herds were likely to be too thick for safety at night. The sun was hardly an hour high when the last herd came up to cross. The oxen were put in the lead, as with ours, and all four of the oxen took the bridge, but when the cattle reached the bridge, they made a decided balk and refused to follow the oxen. Not a hoof of the herd would even set foot on the bridge. The oxen were brought back several times, but in spite of all coaxing and nursing, and our best endeavors and devices, they would not risk it. We worked with them until dusk, when all three of the foremen decided it was useless to try longer, but both Slaughter and Flood promised to bring back part of their outfits in the morning and make another effort.

McCann's camp-fire piloted us to our wagon, at least three miles from the bridge, for he had laid in a good supply of wood during the day; and on our arrival our night horses were tied up, and everything made ready for the night. The next morning we started the herd, but Flood took four of us with him and went back to Big Boggy. The Millet herd was nearly two miles back from the bridge, where we found Slaughter at Jacklin's wagon; and several more of his men were, we learned, coming over with the oxen at about ten o'clock. That hour was considered soon enough by the bosses, as the heat of the day would be on the herd by that time, which would make them lazy. When the oxen arrived at the bridge, we rode out twenty strong and lined the cattle up for another trial. They had grazed until they were full and sleepy, but the memory of some of them was too vivid of the hours they had spent in the slimy ooze of Big Boggy once on a time, and they began milling on sight of the stream. We took them back and brought them up a second time with the same results. We then brought them around in a circle a mile in diameter, and as the rear end of the herd was passing, we turned the last hundred, and throwing the oxen into their lead, started them for the bridge; but they too sulked and would have none of it. It was now high noon, so we turned the herd and allowed them to graze back while we went to dinner. Millet's foreman was rather discouraged with the outlook, but Slaughter said they must be crossed if he had to lay over a week and help. After dinner, Jacklin asked us if we wanted a change of horses, and as we could see a twenty mile ride ahead of us in overtaking our herd, Flood accepted.

When all was ready to start, Slaughter made a suggestion. "Let's go out," he said, "and bring them up slowly in a solid body, and when we get them opposite the bridge, round them in gradually as if we were going to bed them down. I'll take a long lariat to my white wheeler, and when they have quieted down perfectly, I'll lead old Blanco through them and across the bridge, and possibly they'll follow. There's no use crowding them, for that only excites them, and if you ever start them milling, the jig's up. They're nice, gentle cattle, but they've been balked once and they haven't forgotten it."

What we needed right then was a leader, for we were all ready to catch at a straw, and Slaughter's suggestion was welcome, for he had established himself in our good graces until we preferred him to either of the other foremen as a leader. Riding out to the herd, which were lying down, we roused and started them back towards Boggy. While drifting them back, we covered a front a quarter of a mile in width, and as we neared the bridge we gave them perfect freedom. Slaughter had caught out his white ox, and we gradually worked them into a body, covering perhaps ten acres, in front of the bridge. Several small bunches attempted to mill, but some of us rode in and split them up, and after about half an hour's wait, they quieted down. Then Slaughter rode in whistling and leading his white ox at the end of a thirty-five foot lariat, and as he rode through them they were so logy that he had to quirt them out of the way. When he came to the bridge, he stopped the white wheeler until everything had quieted down; then he led old Blanco on again, but giving him all the time he needed and stopping every few feet. We held our breath, as one or two of the herd started to follow him, but they shied and turned back, and our hopes of the moment were crushed. Slaughter detained the ox on the bridge for several minutes, but seeing it was useless, he dismounted and drove him back into the herd. Again and again he tried the same ruse, but it was of no avail. Then we threw the herd back about half a mile, and on Flood's suggestion cut off possibly two hundred head, a bunch which with our numbers we ought to handle readily in spite of their will, and by putting their *remuda* of over a hundred saddle horses in the immediate lead, made the experiment of forcing them. We took the saddle horses down and crossed and recrossed the bridge several times with them, and as the cattle came up turned the horses into the lead and headed for the bridge. With a cordon of twenty riders around them, no animal could turn back, and the horses crossed the bridge on a trot, but the cattle turned tail and positively refused to have anything to do with it. We held them like a block in a vise, so compactly that they could not even mill, but they would not cross the bridge.

When it became evident that it was a fruitless effort, Jacklin, usually a very quiet man, gave vent to a fit of profanity which would have put the army in Flanders to shame. Slaughter, somewhat to our amusement, reproved him: "Don't fret, man; this is nothing, — I balked a herd once in crossing a railroad track, and after trying for two days to cross them, had to drive ten miles and put them under a culvert. You want to cultivate patience, young fellow, when you're handling dumb brutes."

If Slaughter's darky cook had been thereabouts then, and suggested a means of getting that herd to take the bridge, his suggestion would have been welcomed, for the bosses were at their wits' ends. Jacklin swore that he would bed that herd at the entrance, and hold them there until they starved to death or crossed, before he would let an animal turn back. But cooler heads were present, and The Rebel mentioned a certain adage, to the effect that when a bird or a girl, he didn't know which, could sing and wouldn't, she or it ought to be made to sing. He suggested that we hold the four oxen on the bridge, cut off fifteen head of cattle, and give them such a running start, they wouldn't know which end their heads were on when they reached the bridge. Millet's foreman approved of the idea, for he was nursing his wrath. The four oxen were accordingly cut out, and Slaughter and one of his men, taking them, started for the bridge with instructions to hold them on the middle. The rest of us took about a dozen head of light cattle, brought them within a hundred yards of the bridge, then with a yell started them on a run from which they could not turn back. They struck the entrance squarely, and we had our first cattle on the bridge. Two men held the entrance, and we brought up another bunch in the same manner, which filled the bridge. Now, we thought, if the herd could be brought up slowly, and this bridgeful let off in their lead, they might follow. To June a herd of cattle across in this manner would have been shameful, and the foreman of the herd knew it as well as any one present; but no one protested, so we left men to hold the entrance securely and went back after the herd. When we got them within a quarter of a mile of the creek, we cut off about two hundred head of the leaders and brought them around to the rear, for amongst these leaders were certain to be the ones which had been bogged, and we wanted to have new leaders in this trial. Slaughter was on the farther end of the bridge, and could be depended on to let the oxen lead off at the opportune moment. We brought them up cautiously, and when the herd came within a few rods of the creek the cattle on the bridge lowed to their mates in the herd, and Slaughter, considering the time favorable, opened out and allowed them to leave the bridge on the farther side. As soon as the cattle started leaving on the farther side, we dropped back, and the leaders of the herd to the number of a dozen, after smelling the fresh dirt and seeing the others crossing, walked cautiously up on the bridge. It was a moment of extreme anxiety. None of us spoke a word, but the cattle crowding off the bridge at the farther end set it vibrating. That was enough: they turned as if panic-stricken and rushed back to the body of the herd. I was almost afraid to look at Jacklin. He could scarcely speak, but he rode over to me, ashen with rage, and kept repeating, "Well, wouldn't that beat hell!"

Slaughter rode back across the bridge, and the men came up and gathered around Jacklin. We seemed to have run the full length of our rope. No one even had a suggestion to offer, and if any one had had, it needed to be a plausible one to find approval, for hope seemed to have vanished. While discussing the situation, a one-eyed, pox-marked fellow belonging to

Slaughter's outfit galloped up from the rear, and said almost breathlessly, "Say, fellows, I see a cow and calf in the herd. Let's rope the calf, and the cow is sure to follow. Get the rope around the calf's neck, and when it chokes him, he's liable to bellow, and that will call the steers. And if you never let up on the choking till you get on the other side of the bridge, I think it'll work. Let's try it, anyhow."

We all approved, for we knew that next to the smell of blood, nothing will stir range cattle like the bellowing of a calf. At the mere suggestion, Jacklin's men scattered into the herd, and within a few minutes we had a rope round the neck of the calf. As the roper came through the herd leading the calf, the frantic mother followed, with a train of excited steers at her heels. And as the calf was dragged bellowing across the bridge, it was followed by excited, struggling steers who never knew whether they were walking on a bridge or on *terra firma*. The excitement spread through the herd, and they thickened around the entrance until it was necessary to hold them back, and only let enough pass to keep the chain unbroken.

They were nearly a half hour in crossing, for it was fully as large a herd as ours; and when the last animal had crossed, Pete Slaughter stood up in his stirrups and led the long yell. The sun went down that day on nobody's wrath, for Jacklin was so tickled that he offered to kill the fattest beef in his herd if we would stay overnight with him. All three of the herds were now over, but had not this herd balked on us the evening before, over nine thousand cattle would have crossed Slaughter's bridge the day it was built.

It was now late in the evening, and as we had to wait some little time to get our own horses, we stayed for supper. It was dark before we set out to overtake the herd, but the trail was plain, and letting our horses take their own time, we jollied along until after midnight. We might have missed the camp, but, by the merest chance, Priest sighted our camp-fire a mile off the trail, though it had burned to embers. On reaching camp, we changed saddles to our night horses, and, calling Officer, were ready for our watch. We were expecting the men on guard to call us any minute, and while Priest was explaining to Officer the trouble we had had in crossing the Millet herd, I dozed off to sleep there as I sat by the rekindled embers. In that minute's sleep my mind wandered in a dream to my home on the San Antonio River, but the next moment I was aroused to the demands of the hour by The Rebel shaking me and saying, — "Wake up, Tom, and take a new hold. They're calling us on guard. If you expect to follow the trail, son, you must learn to do your sleeping in the winter."

CHAPTER XV
THE BEAVER

After leaving the country tributary to the Solomon River, we crossed a wide tableland for nearly a hundred miles, and with the exception of the Kansas Pacific Railroad, without a landmark worthy of a name. Western Kansas was then classified, worthily too, as belonging to the Great American Desert, and most of the country for the last five hundred miles of our course was entitled to a similar description. Once the freshness of spring had passed, the plain took on her natural sunburnt color, and day after day, as far as the eye could reach, the monotony was unbroken, save by the variations of the mirages on every hand. Except at morning and evening, we were never out of sight of these optical illusions, sometimes miles away, and then again close up, when an antelope standing half a mile distant looked as tall as a giraffe. Frequently the lead of the herd would be in eclipse from these illusions, when to the men in the rear the horsemen and cattle in the lead would appear like giants in an old fairy story. If the monotony of the sea can be charged with dulling men's sensibilities until they become pirates, surely this desolate, arid plain might be equally charged with the wrongdoing of not a few of our craft.

On crossing the railroad at Grinnell, our foreman received a letter from Lovell, directing him to go to Culbertson, Nebraska, and there meet a man who was buying horses for a Montana ranch. Our employer had his business eye open for a possible purchaser for our *remuda*, and if the horses could be sold for delivery after the herd had reached its destination, the opportunity was not to be overlooked. Accordingly, on reaching Beaver Creek, where we encamped, Flood left us to ride through to the Republican River during the night. The trail crossed this river about twenty miles west of Culbertson, and if the Montana horse buyer were yet there, it would be no trouble to come up to the trail crossing and look at our horses.

So after supper, and while we were catching up our night horses, Flood said to us, "Now, boys, I'm going to leave the outfit and herd under Joe Stallings as *segundo*. It's hardly necessary to leave you under any one as foreman, for you all know your places. But some one must be made responsible, and one bad boss will do less harm than half a dozen that mightn't agree. So you can put Honeyman on guard in your place at night, Joe, if you don't want to stand your own watch. Now behave yourselves, and when I meet you on the Republican, I'll bring out a box of cigars and have it charged up as axle grease when we get supplies at Ogalalla. And don't sit up all night telling fool stories."

"Now, that's what I call a good cow boss," said Joe Stallings, as our foreman rode away in the twilight; "besides, he used passable good judgment in selecting a *segundo*. Now, Honeyman, you heard what he said. Billy dear, I won't rob you of this chance to stand a guard. McCann, have you got on your next list of supplies any jam and jelly for Sundays? You have? That's right, son — that saves you from standing a guard tonight. Officer, when you come off guard at 3.30 in the morning, build the cook up a good fire. Let me see; yes, and I'll detail young Tom Quirk and The Rebel to grease the wagon and harness your mules before starting in the morning. I want to impress it on your mind, McCann, that I can appreciate a thoughtful cook. What's that, Honeyman? No, indeed, you can't ride my night horse. Love me, love my dog; my horse shares this snap. Now, I don't want to be under the necessity of speaking to any of you first guard, but flop into your saddles ready to take the herd. My turnip says it's eight o'clock now."

"Why, you've missed your calling — you'd make a fine second mate on a river steamboat, driving niggers," called back Quince Forrest, as the first guard rode away.

When our guard returned, Officer intentionally walked across Stallings's bed, and catching his spur in the tarpaulin, fell heavily across our *segundo*.

"Excuse me," said John, rising, "but I was just nosing around looking for the foreman. Oh, it's you, is it? I just wanted to ask if 4.30 wouldn't be plenty early to build up the fire. Wood's a little scarce, but I'll burn the prairies if you say so. That's all I wanted to know; you may lay down now and go to sleep."

Our camp-fire that night was a good one, and in the absence of Flood, no one felt like going to bed until drowsiness compelled us. So we lounged around the fire smoking the hours away, and in spite of the admonition of our foreman, told stories far into the night. During the early portion of the evening, dog stories occupied the boards. As the evening wore on, the subject of revisiting the old States came up for discussion.

"You all talk about going back to the old States," said Joe Stallings, "but I don't take very friendly to the idea. I felt that way once and went home to Tennessee; but I want to tell you that after you live a few years in the sunny Southwest and get onto her ways, you can't stand it back there like you think you can. Now, when I went back, and I reckon my relations will average up pretty well, — fought in the Confederate army, vote the Democratic ticket, and belong to the Methodist church, — they all seemed to be rapidly getting locoed. Why, my uncles, when they think of planting the old buck field or the widow's acre into any crop, they first go projecting around in the soil, and, as they say, analyze it, to see what kind of a fertilizer it will require to produce the best results. Back there if one man raises ten acres of corn and his neighbor raises twelve, the one raising twelve is sure to look upon the other as though he lacked enterprise or had modest ambitions. Now, up around that old cow town, Abilene, Kansas, it's a common sight to see the cornfields stretch out like an ocean.

"And then their stock — they are all locoed about that. Why, I know people who will pay a hundred dollars for siring a colt, and if there's one drop of mongrel blood in that sire's veins for ten generations back on either side of his ancestral tree, it condemns him, though he may be a good horse otherwise. They are strong on standard bred horses; but as for me, my mount is all right. I wouldn't trade with any man in this outfit, without it would be Flood, and there's none of them standard bred either. Why, shucks! if you had the pick of all the standard bred horses in Tennessee, you couldn't handle a herd of cattle like ours with them, without carrying a commissary with you to feed them. No; they would never fit here — it takes a range-raised horse to run cattle; one that can rustle and live on grass."

"Another thing about those people back in those old States: Not one in ten, I'll gamble, knows the teacher he sends his children to school to. But when he has a promising colt to be shod, the owner goes to the blacksmith shop himself, and he and the smith will sit on the back sill of the shop, and they will discuss how to shoe that filly so as to give her certain knee action which she seems to need. Probably, says one, a little weight on her toe would give her reach. And there they will sit and powwow and make medicine for an hour or two. And while the blacksmith is shoeing her, the owner will tell him in confidence what a wonderful burst of speed she developed yesterday, while he was speeding her on the back stretch. And then just as he turned her into the home stretch, she threw a shoe and he had to check her in; but if there'd been any one to catch her time, he was certain it was better than a two-ten clip. And that same colt, you couldn't cut a lame cow out of the shade of a tree on her. A man back there — he's rich, too, though his father made it — gave a thousand dollars for a pair of dogs before they were born. The terms were one half cash and the balance when they were old enough to ship to him. And for fear they were not the proper mustard, he had that dog man sue him in court for the balance, so as to make him prove the pedigree. Now Bob, there, thinks that old hound of his is the real stuff, but he wouldn't do now; almost every year the style changes in dogs back in the old States. One year maybe it's a little white dog with red eyes, and the very next it's a long bench-legged, black dog with a Dutch name that right now I disremember. Common old pot hounds and everyday yellow dogs have gone out of style entirely. No, you can all go back that want to, but as long as I can hold a job with Lovell and Flood, I'll try and worry along in my own way."

On finishing his little yarn, Stallings arose, saying, "I must take a listen to my men on herd. It always frets me for fear my men will ride too near the cattle."

A minute later he called us, and when several of us walked out to where he was listening, we recognized Roundtree's voice, singing: —

> "Little black bull came down the hillside,
>   Down the hillside, down the hillside,
>   Little black bull came down the hillside,
>   Long time ago."

"Whenever my men sing that song on guard, it tells me that everything is amply serene," remarked our *segundo*, with the air of a field-marshal, as we walked back to the fire.

The evening had passed so rapidly it was now almost time for the second guard to be called, and when the lateness of the hour was announced, we skurried to our blankets like rabbits to their warrens. The second guard usually got an hour or two of sleep before being called, but in the absence of our regular foreman, the mice would play. When our guard was called at one o'clock, as usual, Officer delayed us several minutes looking for his spurs, and I took the chance to ask The Rebel why it was that he never wore spurs.

"It's because I'm superstitious, son," he answered. "I own a fine pair of silver-plated spurs that have a history, and if you're ever at Lovell's ranch I'll show them to you. They were given to me by a mortally wounded Federal officer the day the battle of Lookout Mountain was fought. I was an orderly, carrying dispatches, and in passing through a wood from which the Union army had been recently driven, this officer was sitting at the root of a tree, fatally wounded. He motioned me to him, and when I dismounted, he said, 'Johnny Reb, please give a dying man a drink.' I gave him my canteen, and after drinking from it he continued, 'I want you to have my spurs. Take them off. Listen to their history: as you have taken them off me to-day, so I took them off a Mexican general the day the American army entered the capital of Mexico.'"

CHAPTER XVI
THE REPUBLICAN

The outfit were awakened out of sleep the next morning by shouts of "Whoa, *mula*! Whoa, you mongrel outcasts! Catch them blankety blank mules!" accompanied by a rattle of chain harness, and Quince Forrest dashed across our *segundo's* bed, shaking a harness in each hand. We kicked the blankets off, and came to our feet in time to see the offender disappear behind the wagon, while Stallings sat up and yawningly inquired "what other locoed fool had got funny." But the camp was awake, for the cattle were leisurely leaving the bed ground, while Honeyman, who had been excused from the herd with the first sign of dawn, was rustling up the horses in the valley of the Beaver below camp. With the understanding that the Republican River was a short three days' drive from our present camp, the herd trailed out the first day with not an incident to break the monotony of eating and sleeping, grazing and guarding. But near noon of the second day, we were overtaken by an old, long-whiskered man and a boy of possibly fifteen. They were riding in a light, rickety vehicle, drawn by a small Spanish mule and a rough but clean-limbed bay mare. The strangers appealed to our sympathy, for they were guileless in appearance, and asked so many questions, indicating that ours might have been the first herd of trail cattle they had ever seen. The old man was a free talker, and innocently allowed us to inveigle it out of him that he had been down on the North Beaver, looking up land to homestead, and was then on his way up to take a look at the lands along the Republican. We invited him and the boy to remain for dinner, for in that monotonous waste, we would have been only too glad to entertain a bandit, or an angel for that matter, provided he would talk about something else than cattle. In our guest, however, we found a good conversationalist, meaty with stories not eligible to the retired list; and in return, the hospitality of our wagon was his and welcome. The travel-stained old rascal proved to be a good mixer, and before dinner was over he had won us to a man, though Stallings, in the capacity of foreman, felt it incumbent on him to act the host in behalf of the outfit. In the course of conversation, the old man managed to unearth the fact that our acting foreman was a native of Tennessee, and when he had got it down to town and county, claimed acquaintanceship with a family of men in that locality who were famed as breeders of racehorses. Our guest admitted that he himself was a native of that State, and in his younger days had been a devotee of the racecourse, with the name of every horseman in that commonwealth as well as the bluegrass regions of Kentucky on his tongue's end. But adversity had come upon him, and now he was looking out a new country in which to begin life over again.

After dinner, when our *remuda* was corralled to catch fresh mounts, our guest bubbled over with admiration of our horses, and pointed out several as promising speed and action. We took his praise of our horseflesh as quite a compliment, never suspecting flattery at the hands of this nomadic patriarch. He innocently inquired which was considered the fastest horse in the *remuda*, when Stallings pointed out a brown, belonging to Flood's mount, as the best quarter horse in the band. He gave him a critical examination, and confessed he would never have picked him for a horse possessing speed, though he admitted that he was unfamiliar with range-raised horses, this being his first visit in the West. Stallings offered to loan him a horse out of his mount, and as the old man had no saddle, our *segundo* prevailed on McCann to loan his for the afternoon. I am inclined to think there was a little jealousy amongst us that afternoon, as to who was best entitled to entertain our company; and while he showed no partiality, Stallings seemed to monopolize his countryman to our disadvantage. The two jollied along from point to rear and back again, and as they passed us riders in the swing, Stallings ignored us entirely, though the old man always had a pleasant word as he rode by.

"If we don't do something to wean our *segundo* from that old man," said Fox Quarternight, as he rode up and overtook me, "he's liable to quit the herd and follow that old fossil back to Tennessee or some other port. Just look at the two now, will you? Old Joe's putting on as much dog as though he was asking the Colonel for his daughter. Between me and you and the gatepost, Quirk, I'm a little dubious about the old varmint — he talks too much."

But I had warmed up to our guest, and gave Fox's criticism very little weight, well knowing if any one of us had been left in charge, he would have shown the old man similar courtesies. In this view I was correct, for when Stallings had ridden on ahead to look up water that afternoon, the very man that entirely monopolized our guest for an hour was Mr. John Fox Quarternight. Nor did he jar loose until we reached water, when Stallings cut him off by sending all the men on the right of the herd to hold the cattle from grazing away until every hoof had had ample time to drink. During this rest, the old man circulated around, asking questions as usual, and when I informed him that, with a half mile of water front, it would take a full hour to water the herd properly, he expressed an innocent amazement which seemed as simple as sincere. When the wagon and *remuda* came up, I noticed the boy had tied his team behind our wagon, and was riding one of Honeyman's horses bareback, assisting the wrangler in driving the saddle stock. After the wagon had crossed the creek, and the kegs had been filled and the teams watered, Stallings took the old man with him and the two rode away in the lead of the wagon and *remuda* to select a camp and a bed ground for the night. The rest of us grazed the cattle, now thoroughly watered, forward until the wagon was sighted, when, leaving two men as usual to nurse them up to bed, the remainder of us struck out for camp. As I rode in, I sought out my bunkie to get his opinion regarding our guest. But The Rebel was reticent, as usual, of his opinions of people, so my inquiries remained unanswered, which only served to increase my confidence in the old man.

On arriving at camp we found Stallings and Honeyman entertaining our visitor in a little game of freeze-out for a dollar a corner, while McCann looked wistfully on, as if regretting that his culinary duties prevented his joining in. Our arrival should have been the signal to our wrangler for rounding in the *remuda* for night horses, but Stallings was too absorbed in the game even to notice the lateness of the hour and order in the saddle stock. Quarternight, however, had a few dollars burning holes in his pocket, and he called our horse rustler's attention to the approaching twilight; not that he was in any hurry, but if Honeyman vacated, he saw an opportunity to get into the game. The foreman gave the necessary order, and Quarternight at once bargained for the wrangler's remaining beans, and sat into the game. While we were catching up our night horses, Honeyman told us that the old man had been joking Stallings about the speed of Flood's brown, even going so far as to intimate that he didn't believe that the gelding could outrun that old bay harness mare which he was driving. He had confessed that he was too hard up to wager much on it, but he would risk a few dollars on his judgment on a running horse any day. He also said that Stallings had come back at him, more in earnest than in jest, that if he really thought his harness mare could outrun the brown, he could win every dollar the outfit had. They had codded one another until Joe had shown some spirit, when the old man suggested they play a little game of cards for fun, but Stallings had insisted on stakes to make it interesting, and on the old homesteader pleading poverty, they had agreed to make it for a dollar on the corner. After supper our *segundo* wanted to renew the game; the old man protested that he was too unlucky and could not afford to lose, but was finally persuaded to play one more game, "just to pass away the evening." Well, the evening passed, and within the short space of two hours, there also passed to the supposed lean purse of our guest some twenty dollars from the feverish pockets of the outfit. Then the old man felt too sleepy to play any longer, but loitered around some time, and casually inquired of his boy if he had picketed their mare where she would get a good bait of grass. This naturally brought up the proposed race for discussion.

"If you really think that that old bay palfrey of yours can outrun any horse in our *remuda*," said Stallings, tauntingly, "you're missing the chance of your life not to pick up a few honest dollars as you journey along. You stay with us to-morrow, and when we meet our foreman at the Republican, if he'll loan me the horse, I'll give you a race for any sum you name, just to show you that I've got a few drops of sporting blood in me. And if your mare can outrun a cow, you stand an easy chance to win some money."

Our visitor met Joe's bantering in a timid manner. Before turning in, however, he informed us that he appreciated our hospitality, but that he expected to make an early drive in the morning to the Republican, where he might camp several days. With this the old man and the boy unrolled their blankets, and both were soon sound asleep. Then our *segundo* quietly took Fox Quarternight off to one side, and I heard the latter agree to call him when the third guard was aroused. Having notified Honeyman that he would stand his own watch that night, Stallings, with the rest of the outfit, soon joined the old man in the land of dreams. Instead of the rough shaking which was customary on arousing a guard, when we of the third watch were called, we were awakened in a manner so cautious as to betoken something unusual in the air. The atmosphere of mystery soon cleared after reaching the herd, when Bob Blades informed us that it was the intention of Stallings and Quarternight to steal the old man's harness mare off the picket rope, and run her against their night horses in a trial race. Like love and war, everything is fair in horse racing, but the audacity of this proposition almost passed belief. Both Blades and Durham remained on guard with us, and before we had circled the herd half a dozen times, the two conspirators came riding up to the bed ground, leading the bay mare. There was a good moon that night; Quarternight exchanged mounts with John Officer, as the latter had a splendid night horse that had outstripped the outfit in every stampede so far, and our *segundo* and the second guard rode out of hearing of both herd and camp to try out the horses.

After an hour, the quartette returned, and under solemn pledges of secrecy Stallings said, "Why, that old bay harness mare can't run fast enough to keep up with a funeral. I rode her myself, and if she's got any run in her, rowel and quirt won't bring it out. That chestnut of John's ran away from her as if she was hobbled and side-lined, while this coyote of mine threw dust in her face every jump in the road from the word 'go.' If the old man isn't bluffing and will hack his mare, we'll get back our freeze-out money with good interest. Mind you, now, we must keep it a dead secret from Flood — that we've tried the mare; he might get funny and tip the old man."

We all swore great oaths that Flood should never hear a breath of it. The conspirators and their accomplices rode into camp, and we resumed our sentinel rounds. I had some money, and figured that betting in a cinch like this would be like finding money in the road.

But The Rebel, when we were returning from guard, said, "Tom, you keep out of this race the boys are trying to jump up. I've met a good many innocent men in my life, and there's something about this old man that reminds me of people who have an axe to grind. Let the other fellows run on the rope if they want to, but you keep your money in your pocket. Take an older man's advice this once. And I'm going to round up John in the morning, and try and beat a little sense into his head, for he thinks it's a dead immortal cinch."

I had made it a rule, during our brief acquaintance, never to argue matters with my bunkie, well knowing that his years and experience in the ways of the world entitled his advice to my earnest consideration. So I kept silent, though secretly wishing he had not taken the trouble to throw cold water on my hopes, for I had built several air castles with the money which seemed within my grasp. We had been out then over four months, and I, like many of the other boys, was getting ragged, and with Ogalalla within a week's drive, a town which it took money to see properly, I thought it a burning shame to let this opportunity pass. When I awoke the next morning the camp was astir, and my first look was in the direction of the harness mare, grazing peacefully on the picket rope where she had been tethered the night before.

Breakfast over, our venerable visitor harnessed in his team, preparatory to starting. Stallings had made it a point to return to the herd for a parting word.

"Well, if you must go on ahead," said Joe to the old man, as the latter was ready to depart, "remember that you can get action on your money, if you still think that your bay mare can outrun that brown cow horse which I pointed out to you yesterday. You needn't let your poverty interfere, for we'll run you to suit your purse, light or heavy. The herd will reach the river by the middle of the afternoon, or a little later, and you be sure and stay overnight there, — stay with us if you want to, — and we'll make up a little race for any sum you say, from marbles and chalk to a hundred dollars. I may be as badly deceived in your mare as I think you are in my horse; but if you're a Tennesseean, here's your chance."

But beyond giving Stallings his word that he would see him again during the afternoon or evening, the old man would make no definite proposition, and drove away. There was a difference of opinion amongst the outfit, some asserting that we would never see him again, while the larger portion of us were at least hopeful that we would. After our guest was well out of sight, and before the wagon started, Stallings corralled the *remuda* a second time, and taking out Flood's brown and Officer's chestnut, tried the two horses for a short dash of about a hundred yards. The trial confirmed the general opinion of the outfit, for the brown outran the chestnut over four lengths, starting half a neck in the rear. A general canvass of the outfit was taken, and to my surprise there was over three hundred dollars amongst us. I had over forty dollars, but I only promised to loan mine if it was needed, while Priest refused flat-footed either to lend or bet his. I wanted to bet, and it would grieve me to the quick if there was any chance and I didn't take it — but I was young then.

Flood met us at noon about seven miles out from the Republican with the superintendent of a cattle company in Montana, and, before we started the herd after dinner, had sold our *remuda*, wagon, and mules for delivery at the nearest railroad point to the Blackfoot Agency sometime during September. This cattle company, so we afterwards learned from Flood, had headquarters at Helena, while their ranges were somewhere on the headwaters of the Missouri. But the sale of the horses seemed to us an insignificant matter, compared with the race which was on the tapis; and when Stallings had made the ablest talk of his life for the loan of the brown, Flood asked the new owner, a Texan himself, if he had any objections.

"Certainly not," said he; "let the boys have a little fun. I'm glad to know that the *remuda* has fast horses in it. Why didn't you tell me, Flood? — I might have paid you extra if I had known I was buying racehorses. Be sure and have the race come off this evening, for I want to see it."

And he was not only good enough to give his consent, but added a word of advice. "There's a deadfall down here on the river," said he, "that robs a man going and coming. They've got booze to sell you that would make a pet rabbit fight a wolf. And if you can't stand the whiskey, why, they have skin games running to fleece you as fast as you can get your money to the centre. Be sure, lads, and let both their whiskey and cards alone."

While changing mounts after dinner, Stallings caught out the brown horse and tied him behind the wagon, while Flood and the horse buyer returned to the river in the conveyance, our foreman having left his horse at the ford. When we reached the Republican with the herd about two hours before sundown, and while we were crossing and watering, who should ride up on the Spanish mule but our Tennessee friend. If anything, he was a trifle more talkative and boastful than before, which was easily accounted for, as it was evident that he was drinking; and producing a large bottle which had but a few drinks left in it, insisted on every one taking a drink with him. He said he was encamped half a mile down the river, and that he would race his mare against our horse for fifty dollars; that if we were in earnest, and would go back with him and post our money at the tent, he would cover it. Then Stallings in turn became crafty and diplomatic, and after asking a number of unimportant questions regarding conditions, returned to the joint with the old man, taking Fox Quarternight. To the rest of us it looked as though there was going to be no chance to bet a dollar even. But after the herd had been watered and we had grazed out some distance from the river, the two worthies returned. They had posted their money, and all the conditions were agreed upon; the race was to take place at sundown over at the saloon and gambling joint. In reply to an earnest inquiry by Bob Blades, the outfit were informed that we might get some side bets with the gamblers, but the money already posted was theirs, win or lose. This selfishness was not looked upon very favorably, and some harsh comments were made, but Stallings and Quarternight were immovable.

We had an early supper, and pressing in McCann to assist The Rebel in grazing the herd until our return, the cavalcade set out, Flood and the horse buyer with us. My bunkie urged me to let him keep my money, but under the pretense of some of the outfit wanting to borrow it, I took it with me. The race was to be catch weights, and as Rod Wheat was the lightest in our outfit, the riding fell to him. On the way over I worked Bull Durham out to one side, and after explaining the jacketing I had got from Priest, and the partial promise I had made not to bet, gave him my forty dollars to wager for me if he got a chance. Bull and I were good friends, and on the understanding that it was to be a secret, I intimated that some of the velvet would line his purse. On reaching the tent, we found about half a dozen men loitering around, among them the old man, who promptly invited us all to have a drink with him. A number of us accepted and took a chance against the vintage of this canvas roadhouse, though the warnings of the Montana horse buyer were fully justified by the quality of the goods dispensed. While taking the drink, the old man was lamenting his poverty, which kept him from betting more money, and after we had gone outside, the saloonkeeper came and said to him, in a burst of generous feeling, —

"Old sport, you're a stranger to me, but I can see at a glance that you're a dead game man. Now, if you need any more money, just give me a bill of sale of your mare and mule, and I'll advance you a hundred. Of course I know nothing about the merits of the two horses, but I noticed your team as you drove up to-day, and if you can use any more money, just ask for it."

The old man jumped at the proposition in delighted surprise; the two reëntered the tent, and after killing considerable time in writing out a bill of sale, the old graybeard came out shaking a roll of bills at us. He was promptly accommodated, Bull Durham making the first bet of fifty; and as I caught his eye, I walked away, shaking hands with myself over my crafty scheme. When the old man's money was all taken, the hangers-on of the place became enthusiastic over the betting, and took every bet while there was a dollar in sight amongst our crowd, the horse buyer even making a wager. When we were out of money they offered to bet against our saddles, six-shooters, and watches. Flood warned us not to bet our saddles, but Quarternight and Stallings had already wagered theirs, and were stripping them from their horses to turn them over to the saloonkeeper as stakeholder. I managed to get a ten-dollar bet on my six-shooter, though it was worth double the money, and a similar amount on my watch. When the betting ended, every watch and six-shooter in the outfit was in the hands of the stakeholder, and had it not been for Flood our saddles would have been in the same hands.

It was to be a three hundred yard race, with an ask and answer start between the riders. Stallings and the old man stepped off the course parallel with the river, and laid a rope on the ground to mark the start and the finish. The sun had already set and twilight was deepening when the old man signaled to his boy in the distance to bring up the mare. Wheat was slowly walking the brown horse over the course, when the boy came up, cantering the mare, blanketed with an old government blanket, over the imaginary track also. These preliminaries thrilled us like the tuning of a fiddle for a dance. Stallings and the old homesteader went out to the starting point to give the riders the terms of the race, while the remainder of us congregated at the finish. It was getting dusk when the blanket was stripped from the mare and the riders began jockeying for a start. In that twilight stillness we could hear the question, "Are you ready?" and the answer "No," as the two jockeys came up to the starting rope. But finally there was an affirmative answer, and the two horses were coming through like arrows in their flight. My heart stood still for the time being, and when the bay mare crossed the rope at the outcome an easy winner, I was speechless. Such a crestfallen-looking lot of men as we were would be hard to conceive. We had been beaten, and not only felt it but looked it. Flood brought us to our senses by calling our attention to the approaching darkness, and setting off in a gallop toward the herd. The rest of us trailed along silently after him in threes and fours. After the herd had been bedded and we had gone in to the wagon my spirits were slightly lightened at the sight of the two arch conspirators, Stallings and Quarternight, meekly riding in bareback. I enjoyed the laughter of The Rebel and McCann at their plight; but when my bunkie noticed my six-shooter missing, and I admitted having bet it, he turned the laugh on me.

"That's right, son," he said; "don't you take anybody's advice. You're young yet, but you'll learn. And when you learn it for yourself, you'll remember it that much better."

That night when we were on guard together, I eased my conscience by making a clean breast of the whole affair to my bunkie, which resulted in his loaning me ten dollars with which to redeem, my six-shooter in the morning. But the other boys, with the exception of Officer, had no banker to call on as we had, and when Quaternight and Stallings asked the foreman what they were to do for saddles, the latter suggested that one of them could use the cook's, while the other could take it bareback or ride in the wagon. But the Montana man interceded in their behalf, and Flood finally gave in and advanced them enough to redeem their saddles. Our foreman had no great amount of money with him, but McCann and the horse buyer came to the rescue for what they had, and the guns were redeemed; not that they were needed, but we would have been so lonesome without them. I had worn one so long I didn't trim well without it, but toppled forward and couldn't maintain my balance. But the most cruel exposure of the whole affair occurred when Nat Straw, riding in ahead of his herd, overtook us one day out from Ogalalla.

"I met old 'Says I' Littlefield," said Nat, "back at the ford of the Republican, and he tells me that they won over five hundred dollars off this Circle Dot outfit on a horse race. He showed me a whole basketful of your watches. I used to meet old 'Says I' over on the Chisholm trail, and he's a foxy old innocent. He told me that he put tar on his harness mare's back to see if you fellows had stolen the nag off the picket rope at night, and when he found you had, he robbed you to a finish. He knew you fool Texans would bet your last dollar on such a cinch. That's one of his tricks. You see the mare you tried wasn't the one you ran the race against. I've seen them both, and they look as much alike as two pint bottles. My, but you fellows are easy fish!"

And then Jim Flood lay down on the grass and laughed until the tears came into his eyes, and we understood that there were tricks in other trades than ours.

CHAPTER XVII
OGALALLA

From the head of Stinking Water to the South Platte was a waterless stretch of forty miles. But by watering the herd about the middle of one forenoon, after grazing, we could get to water again the following evening. With the exception of the meeting with Nat Straw, the drive was featureless, but the night that Nat stayed with us, he regaled us with his experiences, in which he was as lucky as ever. Where we had lost three days on the Canadian with bogged cattle, he had crossed it within fifteen minutes after reaching it. His herd was sold before reaching Dodge, so that he lost no time there, and on reaching Slaughter's bridge, he was only two days behind our herd. His cattle were then en route for delivery on the Crazy Woman in Wyoming, and, as he put it, "any herd was liable to travel faster when it had a new owner."

Flood had heard from our employer at Culbertson, learning that he would not meet us at Ogalalla, as his last herd was due in Dodge about that time. My brother Bob's herd had crossed the Arkansaw a week behind us, and was then possibly a hundred and fifty miles in our rear.

We all regretted not being able to see old man Don, for he believed that nothing was too good for his men, and we all remembered the good time he had shown us in Dodge. The smoke of passing trains hung for hours in signal clouds in our front, during the afternoon of the second day's dry drive, but we finally scaled the last divide, and there, below us in the valley of the South Platte, nestled Ogalalla, the Gomorrah of the cattle trail. From amongst its half hundred buildings, no church spire pointed upward, but instead three fourths of its business houses were dance halls, gambling houses, and saloons. We all knew the town by reputation, while the larger part of our outfit had been in it before. It was there that Joel Collins and his outfit rendezvoused when they robbed the Union Pacific train in October, '77. Collins had driven a herd of cattle for his father and brother, and after selling them in the Black Hills, gambled away the proceeds. Some five or six of his outfit returned to Ogalalla with him, and being moneyless, concluded to recoup their losses at the expense of the railway company. Going eighteen miles up the river to Big Springs, seven of them robbed the express and passengers, the former yielding sixty thousand dollars in gold. The next morning they were in Ogalalla, paying debts, and getting their horses shod. In Collins's outfit was Sam Bass, and under his leadership, until he met his death the following spring at the hands of Texas Rangers, the course of the outfit southward was marked by a series of daring bank and train robberies.

We reached the river late that evening, and after watering, grazed until dark and camped for the night. But it was not to be a night of rest and sleep, for the lights were twinkling across the river in town; and cook, horse wrangler, and all, with the exception of the first guard, rode across the river after the herd had been bedded. Flood had quit us while we were watering the herd and gone in ahead to get a draft cashed, for he was as moneyless as the rest of us. But his letter of credit was good anywhere on the trail where money was to be had, and on reaching town, he took us into a general outfitting store and paid us twenty-five dollars apiece. After warning us to be on hand at the wagon to stand our watches, he left us, and we scattered like lost sheep. Officer and I paid our loans to The Rebel, and the three of us wandered around for several hours in company with Nat Straw. When we were in Dodge, my bunkie had shown no inclination to gamble, but now he was the first one to suggest that we make up a "cow," and let him try his luck at monte. Straw and Officer were both willing, and though in rags, I willingly consented and contributed my five to the general fund.

Every gambling house ran from two to three monte layouts, as it was a favorite game of cowmen, especially when they were from the far southern country. Priest soon found a game to his liking, and after watching his play through several deals, Officer and I left him with the understanding that he would start for camp promptly at midnight. There was much to be seen, though it was a small place, for the ends of the earth's iniquity had gathered in Ogalalla. We wandered through the various gambling houses, drinking moderately, meeting an occasional acquaintance from Texas, and in the course of our rounds landed in the Dew-Drop-In dance hall. Here might be seen the frailty of women in every grade and condition. From girls in their teens, launching out on a life of shame, to the adventuress who had once had youth and beauty in her favor, but was now discarded and ready for the final dose of opium and the coroner's verdict, — all were there in tinsel and paint, practicing a careless exposure of their charms. In a town which has no night, the hours pass rapidly; and before we were aware, midnight was upon us. Returning to the gambling house where we had left Priest, we found him over a hundred dollars winner, and, calling his attention to the hour, persuaded him to cash in and join us. We felt positively rich, as he counted out to each partner his share of the winnings! Straw was missing to receive his, but we knew he could be found on the morrow, and after a round of drinks, we forded the river. As we rode along, my bunkie said, — "I'm superstitious, and I can't help it. But I've felt for a day or so that I was in luck, and I wanted you lads in with me if my warning was true. I never was afraid to go into battle but once, and just as we were ordered into action, a shell killed my horse under me and I was left behind. I've had lots of such warnings, good and bad, and I'm influenced by them. If we get off to-morrow, and I'm in the mood, I'll go back there and make some monte bank look sick."

We reached the wagon in good time to be called on our guard, and after it was over secured a few hours' sleep before the foreman aroused us in the morning. With herds above and below us, we would either have to graze contrary to our course or cross the river. The South Platte was a wide, sandy river with numerous channels, and as easily crossed as an alkali flat of equal width, so far as water was concerned. The sun was not an hour high when we crossed, passing within two hundred yards of the business section of the town, which lay under a hill. The valley on the north side of the river, and beyond the railroad, was not over half a mile wide, and as we angled across it, the town seemed as dead as those that slept in the graveyard on the first hill beside the trail.

Finding good grass about a mile farther on, we threw the herd off the trail, and leaving orders to graze until noon, the foreman with the first and second guard returned to town. It was only about ten miles over to the North Platte, where water was certain; and in the hope that we would be permitted to revisit the village during the afternoon, we who were on guard threw riders in the lead of the grazing cattle, in order not to be too far away should permission be granted us. That was a long morning for us of the third and fourth guards, with nothing to do but let the cattle feed, while easy money itched in our pockets. Behind us lay Ogalalla — and our craft did dearly love to break the monotony of our work by getting into town. But by the middle of the forenoon, the wagon and saddle horses overtook us, and ordering McCann into camp a scant mile in our lead, we allowed the cattle to lie down, they having grazed to contentment. Leaving two men on guard, the remainder of us rode in to the wagon, and lightened with an hour's sleep in its shade the time which hung heavy on our hands. We were aroused by our horse wrangler, who had sighted a cavalcade down the trail, which, from the color of their horses, he knew to be our outfit returning. As they came nearer and their numbers could be made out, it was evident that our foreman was not with them, and our hopes rose. On coming up, they informed us that we were to have a half holiday, while they would take the herd over to the North River during the afternoon. Then emergency orders rang out to Honeyman and McCann, and as soon as a change of mounts could be secured, our dinners bolted, and the herders relieved, we were ready to go. Two of the six who returned had shed their rags and swaggered about in new, cheap suits; the rest, although they had money, simply had not had the time to buy clothes in a place with so many attractions.

When the herders came in deft hands transferred their saddles to waiting mounts while they swallowed a hasty dinner, and we set out for Ogalalla, happy as city urchins in an orchard. We were less than five miles from the burg, and struck a free gait in riding in, where we found several hundred of our craft holding high jinks. A number of herds had paid off their outfits and were sending them home, while from the herds for sale, holding along the river, every man not on day herd was paying his respects to the town. We had not been there five minutes when a horse race was run through the main street, Nat Straw and Jim Flood acting as judges on

103

the outcome. The officers of Ogalalla were a different crowd from what we had encountered at Dodge, and everything went. The place suited us. Straw had entirely forgotten our "cow" of the night before, and when The Rebel handed him his share of the winnings, he tucked it away in the watch pocket of his trousers without counting. But he had arranged a fiddling match between a darky cook of one of the returning outfits and a locoed white man, a mendicant of the place, and invited us to be present. Straw knew the foreman of the outfit to which the darky belonged, and the two had fixed it up to pit the two in a contest, under the pretense that a large wager had been made on which was the better fiddler. The contest was to take place at once in the corral of the Lone Star livery stable, and promised to be humorous if nothing more. So after the race was over, the next number on the programme was the fiddling match, and we followed the crowd. The Rebel had given us the slip during the race, though none of us cared, as we knew he was hungering for a monte game. It was a motley crowd which had gathered in the corral, and all seemed to know of the farce to be enacted, though the Texas outfit to which the darky belonged were flashing their money on their dusky cook, "as the best fiddler that ever crossed Red River with a cow herd."

"Oh, I don't know that your man is such an Ole Bull as all that," said Nat Straw. "I just got a hundred posted which says he can't even play a decent second to my man. And if we can get a competent set of judges to decide the contest, I'll wager a little more on the white against the black, though I know your man is a cracker-jack."

A canvass of the crowd was made for judges, but as nearly every one claimed to be interested in the result, having made wagers, or was incompetent to sit in judgment on a musical contest, there was some little delay. Finally, Joe Stallings went to Nat Straw and told him that I was a fiddler, whereupon he instantly appointed me as judge, and the other side selected a redheaded fellow belonging to one of Dillard Fant's herds. Between the two of us we selected as the third judge a bartender whom I had met the night before. The conditions governing the contest were given us, and two chuck wagons were drawn up alongside each other, in one of which were seated the contestants and in the other the judges. The gravity of the crowd was only broken as some enthusiast cheered his favorite or defiantly offered to wager on the man of his choice. Numerous sham bets were being made, when the redheaded judge arose and announced the conditions, and urged the crowd to remain quiet, that the contestants might have equal justice. Each fiddler selected his own piece. The first number was a waltz, on the conclusion of which partisanship ran high, each faction cheering its favorite to the echo. The second number was a jig, and as the darky drew his bow several times across the strings tentatively, his foreman, who stood six inches taller than any man in a crowd of tall men, tapped himself on the breast with one forefinger, and with the other pointed at his dusky champion, saying, "Keep your eye on me, Price. We're going home together, remember. You black rascal, you can make a mocking bird ashamed of itself if you try. You know I've swore by you through thick and thin; now win this money. Pay no attention to any one else. Keep your eye on me."

Straw, not to be outdone in encouragement, cheered his man with promises of reward, and his faction of supporters raised such a din that Fant's man arose, and demanded quiet so the contest could proceed. Though boisterous, the crowd was good-tempered, and after the second number was disposed of, the final test was announced, which was to be in sacred music. On this announcement, the tall foreman waded through the crowd, and drawing the darky to him, whispered something in his ear, and then fell back to his former position. The dusky artist's countenance brightened, and with a few preliminaries he struck into "The Arkansaw Traveler," throwing so many contortions into its execution that it seemed as if life and liberty depended on his exertions. The usual applause greeted him on its conclusion, when Nat Straw climbed up on the wagon wheel, and likewise whispered something to his champion. The little, old, weazened mendicant took his cue, and cut into "The Irish Washerwoman" with a great flourish, and in the refrain chanted an unintelligible gibberish like the yelping of a coyote, which the audience so cheered that he repeated it several times. The crowd now gathered around the wagons and clamored for the decision, and after consulting among ourselves some little time, and knowing that a neutral or indefinite verdict was desired, we delegated the bartender to announce our conclusions. Taking off his hat, he arose, and after requesting quietness, pretended to read our decision.

"Gentlemen," he began, "your judges feel a delicacy in passing on the merits of such distinguished artists, but in the first number the decision is unanimously in favor of the darky, while the second is clearly in favor of the white contestant. In regard to the last test, your judges cannot reach any decision, as the selections rendered fail to qualify under the head of" —

But two shots rang out in rapid succession across the street, and the crowd, including the judges and fiddlers, rushed away to witness the new excitement. The shooting had occurred in a restaurant, and quite a mob gathered around the door, when the sheriff emerged from the building.

"It's nothing," said he; "just a couple of punchers, who had been drinking a little, were eating a snack, and one of them asked for a second dish of prunes, when the waiter got gay and told him that he couldn't have them, — 'that he was full of prunes now.' So the lad took a couple of shots at him, just to learn him to be more courteous to strangers. There was no harm done, as the puncher was too unsteady."

As the crowd dispersed from the restaurant, I returned to the livery stable, where Straw and several of our outfit were explaining to the old mendicant that he had simply outplayed his opponent, and it was too bad that they were not better posted in sacred music. Under Straw's leadership, a purse was being made up amongst them, and the old man's eyes brightened as he received several crisp bills and a handful of silver. Straw was urging the old fiddler to post himself in regard to sacred music, and he would get up another match for the next day, when Rod Wheat came up and breathlessly informed Officer and myself that The Rebel wanted us over at the Black Elephant gambling hall. As we turned to accompany him, we eagerly inquired if there were any trouble. Wheat informed us there was not, but that Priest was playing in one of the biggest streaks of luck that ever happened. "Why, the old man is just wallowing in velvet," said Rod, as we hurried along, "and the dealer has lowered the limit from a hundred to fifty, for old Paul is playing them as high as a cat's tack. He isn't drinking a drop, and is as cool as a cucumber. I don't know what he wants with you fellows, but he begged me to hunt you up and send you to him."

The Black Elephant was about a block from the livery, and as we entered, a large crowd of bystanders were watching the playing around one of the three monte games which were running. Elbowing our way through the crowd, we reached my bunkie, whom Officer slapped on the back and inquired what he wanted.

"Why, I want you and Quirk to bet a little money for me," he replied. "My luck is with me to-day, and when I try to crowd it, this layout gets foxy and pinches the limit down to fifty. Here, take this money and cover both those other games. Call out as they fall the layouts, and I'll pick the card to bet the money on. And bet her carelessly, boys, for she's velvet."

As he spoke he gave Officer and myself each a handful of uncounted money, and we proceeded to carry out his instructions. I knew the game perfectly, having spent several years' earnings on my tuition, and was past master in the technical Spanish terms of the game, while Officer was equally informed. John took the table to the right, while I took the one on the left, and waiting for a new deal, called the cards as they fell. I inquired the limit of the dealer, and was politely informed that it was fifty to-day. At first our director ordered a number of small bets made, as though feeling his way, for cards will turn; but as he found the old luck was still with him, he gradually increased them to the limit. After the first few deals, I caught on to his favorite cards, which were the queen and seven, and on these we bet the limit. Aces and a "face against an ace" were also favorite bets of The Rebel's, but for a smaller sum. During the first hour of my playing — to show the luck of cards — the queen won five consecutive times, once against a favorite at the conclusion of a deal. My judgment was to take up this bet, but Priest ordered otherwise, for it was one of his principles never to doubt a card as long as it won for you.

The play had run along some time, and as I was absorbed with watching, some one behind me laid a friendly hand on my shoulder. Having every card in the layout covered with a bet at the time, and supposing it to be some of our outfit, I never looked around, when there came a slap on my back which nearly loosened my teeth. Turning to see who was making so free with me when I was absorbed, my eye fell on my brother Zack, but I had not time even to shake hands with him, for two cards won in succession and the dealer was paying me, while the queen and seven were covered to the limit and were yet to be drawn for. When the deal ended and while the dealer was shuffling, I managed to get a few words with my brother, and learned that he had come through with a herd belonging to one-armed Jim Reed, and that they were holding about ten miles up the river. He had met Flood, who told him that I was in town; but as he was working on first guard with their herd, it was high time he was riding. The dealer was waiting for me to cut the cards, and stopping only to wring Zack's hand in farewell, I turned again to the monte layout.

Officer was not so fortunate as I was, partly by reason of delays, the dealer in his game changing decks on almost every deal, and under Priest's orders, we counted the cards with every change of the deck. A gambler would rather burn money than lose to a citizen, and every hoodoo which the superstition of the craft could invoke to turn the run of the cards was used to check us. Several hours passed and the lamps were lighted, but we constantly added to the good — to the discomfiture of the owners of the games. Dealers changed, but our vigilance never relaxed for a moment. Suddenly an altercation sprang up between Officer and the dealer of his game. The seven had proved the most lucky card to John, which fact was as plain to dealer as to player, but the dealer, by slipping one seven out of the pack after it had been counted, which was possible in the hands of an adept in spite of all vigilance, threw the percentage against the favorite card and in favor of the bank. Officer had suspected something wrong, for the seven had been loser during several deals, when with a seven-king layout, and two cards of each class yet in the pack, the dealer drew down until there were less than a dozen cards left, when the king came, which lost a fifty dollar bet on the seven. Officer laid his hand on the money, and, as was his privilege, said to the dealer, "Let me look over the remainder of those cards. If there's two sevens there, you have won. If there isn't, don't offer to touch this bet."

But the gambler declined the request, and Officer repeated his demand, laying a blue-barreled six-shooter across the bet with the remark, "Well, if you expect to rake in this bet you have my terms."

Evidently the demand would not have stood the test, for the dealer bunched the deck among the passed cards, and Officer quietly raked in the money. "When I want a skin game," said John, as he arose, "I'll come back and see you. You saw me take this money, did you? Well, if you've got anything to say, now's your time to spit it out."

But his calling had made the gambler discreet, and he deigned no reply to the lank Texan, who, chafing under the attempt to cheat him, slowly returned his six-shooter to its holster. Although holding my own in my game, I was anxious to have it come to a close, but neither of us cared to suggest it to The Rebel; it was his money. But Officer passed outside the house shortly afterward, and soon returned with Jim Flood and Nat Straw.

As our foreman approached the table at which Priest was playing, he laid his hand on The Rebel's shoulder and said, "Come on, Paul, we're all ready to go to camp. Where's Quirk?"

Priest looked up in innocent amazement, — as though he had been awakened out of a deep sleep, for, in the absorption of the game, he had taken no note of the passing hours and did not know that the lamps were burning. My bunkie obeyed as promptly as though the orders had been given by Don Lovell in person, and, delighted with the turn of affairs, I withdrew with him. Once in the street, Nat Straw threw an arm around The Rebel's neck and said to him, "My dear sir, the secret of successful gambling is to quit when you're winner, and before luck turns. You may think this is a low down trick, but we're your friends, and when we heard that you were a big winner, we were determined to get you out of there if we had to rope and drag you out. How much are you winner?"

Before the question could be correctly answered, we sat down on the sidewalk and the three of us disgorged our winnings, so that Flood and Straw could count. Priest was the largest winner, Officer the smallest, while I never will know the amount of mine, as I had no idea what I started with. But the tellers' report showed over fourteen hundred dollars among the three of us. My bunkie consented to allow Flood to keep it for him, and the latter attempted to hurrah us off to camp, but John Officer protested.

"Hold on a minute, Jim," said Officer. "We're in rags; we need some clothes. We've been in town long enough, and we've got the price, but it's been such a busy afternoon with us that we simply haven't had the time."

Straw took our part, and Flood giving in, we entered a general outfitting store, from which we emerged within a quarter of an hour, wearing cheap new suits, the color of which we never knew until the next day. Then bidding Straw a hearty farewell, we rode for the North Platte, on which the herd would encamp. As we scaled the bluffs, we halted for our last glimpse of the lights of Ogalalla, and The Rebel remarked, "Boys, I've traveled some in my life, but that little hole back there could give Natchez-under-the-hill cards and spades, and then outhold her as a tough town."

CHAPTER XVIII
THE NORTH PLATTE

It was now July. We had taken on new supplies at Ogalalla, and a week afterwards the herd was snailing along the North Platte on its way to the land of the Blackfeet. It was always hard to get a herd past a supply point. We had the same trouble when we passed Dodge. Our long hours in the saddle, coupled with the monotony of our work, made these supply points of such interest to us that they were like oases in desert lands to devotees on pilgrimage to some consecrated shrine. We could have spent a week in Ogalalla and enjoyed our visit every blessed moment of the time. But now, a week later, most of the headaches had disappeared and we had settled down to our daily work.

At Horse Creek, the last stream of water before entering Wyoming, a lad who cut the trail at that point for some cattle companies, after trimming us up, rode along for half a day through their range, and told us of an accident which happened about a week before. The horse of some peeler, working with one of Shanghai Pierce's herds, acted up one morning, and fell backward with him so that his gun accidentally discharged. The outfit lay over a day and gave him as decent a burial as they could. We would find the new-made grave ahead on Squaw Creek, beyond the crossing, to the right hand side in a clump of cottonwoods. The next day, while watering the herd at this creek, we all rode over and looked at the grave. The outfit had fixed things up quite nicely. They had built a square pen of rough cottonwood logs around the grave, and had marked the head and foot with a big flat stone, edged up, heaping up quite a mound of stones to keep the animals away. In a tree his name was cut — sounded natural, too, though none of us knew him, as Pierce always drove from the east coast country. There was nothing different about this grave from the hundreds of others which made landmarks on the Old Western Trail, except it was the latest.

That night around the camp-fire some of the boys were moved to tell their experiences. This accident might happen to any of us, and it seemed rather short notice to a man enjoying life, even though his calling was rough.

"As for myself," said Rod Wheat, "I'm not going to fret. You can't avoid it when it comes, and every now and then you miss it by a hair. I had an uncle who served four years in the Confederate army, went through thirty engagements, was wounded half a dozen times, and came home well and sound. Within a month after his return, a plough handle kicked him in the side and we buried him within a week."

"Oh, well," said Fox, commenting on the sudden call of the man whose grave we had seen, "it won't make much difference to this fellow back here when the horn toots and the graves give up their dead. He might just as well start from there as anywhere. I don't envy him none, though; but if I had any pity to offer now, it would be for a mother or sister who might wish that he slept nearer home."

This last remark carried our minds far away from their present surroundings to other graves which were not on the trail. There was a long silence. We lay around the camp-fire and gazed into its depths, while its flickering light threw our shadows out beyond the circle. Our reverie was finally broken by Ash Borrowstone, who was by all odds the most impressionable and emotional one in the outfit, a man who always argued the moral side of every question, yet could not be credited with possessing an iota of moral stamina. Gloomy as we were, he added to our depression by relating a pathetic incident which occurred at a child's funeral, when Flood reproved him, saying, —

"Well, neither that one you mention, nor this one of Pierce's man is any of our funeral. We're on the trail with Lovell's cattle. You should keep nearer the earth."

There was a long silence after this reproof of the foreman. It was evident there was a gloom settling over the outfit. Our thoughts were ranging wide. At last Rod Wheat spoke up and said that in order to get the benefit of all the variations, the blues were not a bad thing to have.

But the depression of our spirits was not so easily dismissed. In order to avoid listening to the gloomy tales that were being narrated around the camp-fire, a number of us got up and went out as if to look up the night horses on picket. The Rebel and I pulled our picket pins and changed our horses to fresh grazing, and after lying down among the horses, out of hearing of the camp, for over an hour, returned to the wagon expecting to retire. A number of the boys were making down their beds, as it was already late; but on our arrival at the fire one of the boys had just concluded a story, as gloomy as the others which had preceded it.

"These stories you are all telling to-night," said Flood, "remind me of what Lige Link said to the book agent when he was shearing sheep. 'I reckon,' said Lige, 'that book of yours has a heap sight more poetry in it than there is in shearing sheep.' I wish I had gone on guard to-night, so I could have missed these stories."

> At this juncture the first guard rode in, having been relieved, and
> John Officer, who had exchanged places on guard that night with Moss
> Strayhorn, remarked that the cattle were uneasy.

"This outfit," said he, "didn't half water the herd to-day. One third of them hasn't bedded down yet, and they don't act as if they aim to, either. There's no excuse for it in a well-watered country like this. I'll leave the saddle on my horse, anyhow."

"Now that's the result," said our foreman, "of the hour we spent around that grave to-day, when we ought to have been tending to our job. This outfit," he continued, when Officer returned from picketing his horse, "have been trying to hold funeral services over that Pierce man's grave back there. You'd think so, anyway, from the tales they've been telling. I hope you won't get the sniffles and tell any."

"This letting yourself get gloomy," said Officer, "reminds me of a time we once had at the 'J.H.' camp in the Cherokee Strip. It was near Christmas, and the work was all done up. The boys had blowed in their summer's wages and were feeling glum all over. One or two of the boys were lamenting that they hadn't gone home to see the old folks. This gloomy feeling kept spreading until they actually wouldn't speak to each other. One of them would go out and sit on the wood pile for hours, all by himself, and make a new set of good resolutions. Another would go out and sit on the ground, on the sunny side of the corrals, and dig holes in the frozen earth with his knife. They wouldn't come to meals when the cook called them.

"Now, Miller, the foreman, didn't have any sympathy for them; in fact he delighted to see them in that condition. He hadn't any use for a man who wasn't dead tough under any condition. I've known him to camp his outfit on alkali water, so the men would get out in the morning, and every rascal beg leave to ride on the outside circle on the morning roundup.

"Well, three days before Christmas, just when things were looking gloomiest, there drifted up from the Cheyenne country one of the old timers. None of them had seen him in four years, though he had worked on that range before, and with the exception of myself, they all knew him. He was riding the chuckline all right, but Miller gave him a welcome, as he was the real thing. He had been working out in the Pan-handle country, New Mexico, and the devil knows where, since he had left that range. He was meaty with news and scarey stories. The boys would sit around and listen to him yarn, and now and then a smile would come on their faces. Miller was delighted with his guest. He had shown no signs of letting up at eleven o'clock the first night, when he happened to mention where he was the Christmas before.

"'There was a little woman at the ranch,' said he, 'wife of the owner, and I was helping her get up dinner, as we had quite a number of folks at the ranch. She asked me to make the bear sign — doughnuts, she called them — and I did, though she had to show me how some little. Well, fellows, you ought to have seen them — just sweet enough, browned to a turn, and enough to last a week. All the folks at dinner that day praised them. Since then, I've had a chance to try my hand several times, and you may not tumble to the diversity of all my accomplishments, but I'm an artist on bear sign.'

"Miller arose, took him by the hand, and said, 'That's straight, now, is it?'

"'That's straight. Making bear sign is my long suit.'

"'Mouse,' said Miller to one of the boys, 'go out and bring in his saddle from the stable and put it under my bed. Throw his horse in the big pasture in the morning. He stays here until spring; and the first spear of green grass I see, his name goes on the pay roll. This outfit is shy on men who can make bear sign. Now, I was thinking that you could spread down your blankets on the hearth, but you can sleep with me to-night. You go to work on this specialty of yours right after breakfast in the morning, and show us what you can do in that line.'

"They talked quite a while longer, and then turned in for the night. The next morning after breakfast was over, he got the needed articles together and went to work. But there was a surprise in store for him. There was nearly a dozen men lying around, all able eaters. By ten o'clock he began to turn them out as he said he could. When the regular cook had to have the stove to get dinner, the taste which we had had made us ravenous for more. Dinner over, he went at them again in earnest. A boy riding towards the railroad with an important letter dropped in, and as he claimed he could only stop for a moment, we stood aside until he had had a taste, though he filled himself like a poisoned pup. After eating a solid hour, he filled his pockets and rode away. One of our regular men called after him, 'Don't tell anybody what we got.'

"We didn't get any supper that night. Not a man could have eaten a bite. Miller made him knock off along in the shank of the evening, as he had done enough for any one day. The next morning after breakfast he fell to at the bear sign once more. Miller rolled a barrel of flour into the kitchen from the storehouse, and told him to fly at them. 'About how many do you think you'll want?' asked our bear sign man.

"'That big tub full won't be any too many,' answered Miller. 'Some of these fellows haven't had any of this kind of truck since they were little boys. If this gets out, I look for men from other camps.'

"The fellow fell to his work like a thoroughbred, which he surely was. About ten o'clock two men rode up from a camp to the north, which the boy had passed the day before with the letter. They never went near the dug-out, but straight to the kitchen. That movement showed that they were on to the racket. An hour later old Tom Cave rode in, his horse all in a lather, all the way from Garretson's camp, twenty-five miles to the east. The old sinner said that he had been on the frontier some little time, and that there were the best bear sign he had tasted in forty years. He refused to take a stool and sit down like civilized folks, but stood up by the tub and picked out the ones which were a pale brown.

"After dinner our man threw off his overshirt, unbuttoned his red undershirt and turned it in until you could see the hair on his breast. Rolling up his sleeves, he flew at his job once more. He was getting his work reduced to a science by this time. He rolled his dough, cut his dough, and turned out the fine brown bear sign to the satisfaction of all.

"His capacity, however, was limited. About two o'clock Doc Langford and two of his peelers were seen riding up. When he came into the kitchen, Doc swore by all that was good and holy that he hadn't heard that our artist had come back to that country. But any one that was noticing could see him edge around to the tub. It was easy to see that he was lying. This luck of ours was circulating faster than a secret amongst women. Our man, though, stood at his post like the boy on the burning deck. When night came on, he hadn't covered the bottom of the tub. When he knocked off, Doc Langford and his men gobbled up what was left. We gave them a mean look as they rode off, but they came back the next day, five strong. Our regular men around camp didn't like it, the way things were going. They tried to act polite to" —

"Calling bear sign doughnuts," interrupted Quince Forrest, "reminds me what" —

"Will you kindly hobble your lip," said Officer; "I have the floor at present. As I was saying, they tried to act polite to company that way, but we hadn't got a smell the second day. Our man showed no signs of fatigue, and told several good stories that night. He was tough. The next day was Christmas, but he had no respect for a holiday, and made up a large batch of dough before breakfast. It was a good thing he did, for early that morning 'Original' John Smith and four of his peelers rode in from the west, their horses all covered with frost. They must have started at daybreak — it was a good twenty-two mile ride. They wanted us to believe that they had simply come over to spend Christmas with us. Company that way, you can't say anything. But the easy manner in which they gravitated around that tub — not even waiting to be invited — told a different tale. They were not nearly satisfied by noon.

"Then who should come drifting in as we were sitting down to dinner, but Billy Dunlap and Jim Hale from Quinlin's camp, thirty miles south on the Cimarron. Dunlap always holed up like a bear in the winter, and several of the boys spilled their coffee at sight of him. He put up a thin excuse just like the rest. Any one could see through it. But there it was again — he was company. Lots of us had eaten at his camp and complained of his chuck; therefore, we were nice to him. Miller called our man out behind the kitchen and told him to knock off if he wanted to. But he wouldn't do it. He was clean strain — I'm not talking. Dunlap ate hardly any dinner, we noticed, and the very first batch of bear sign turned out, he loads up a tin plate and goes out and sits behind the storehouse in the sun, all alone in his glory. He satisfied himself out of the tub after that.

"He and Hale stayed all night, and Dunlap kept every one awake with the nightmare. Yes, kept fighting the demons all night. The next morning Miller told him that he was surprised that an old gray-haired man like him didn't know when he had enough, but must gorge himself like some silly kid. Miller told him that he was welcome to stay a week if he wanted to, but he would have to sleep in the stable. It was cruel to the horses, but the men were entitled to a little sleep, at least in the winter. Miller tempered his remarks with all kindness, and Dunlap acted as if he was sorry, and as good as admitted that his years were telling on him. That day our man filled his tub. He was simply an artist on bear sign."

"Calling bear sign doughnuts," cut in Quince Forrest again, as soon as he saw an opening, "reminds me what the little boy said who went" —

But there came a rumbling of many hoofs from the bed ground. "There's hell for you," said half a dozen men in a chorus, and every man in camp ran for his horse but the cook, and he climbed into the wagon. The roar of the running cattle was like approaching thunder, but the flash from the six-shooters of the men on guard indicated they were quartering by camp, heading out towards the hills. Horses became so excited they were difficult to bridle. There was plenty of earnest and sincere swearing done that night. All the fine sentiment and melancholy of the hour previous vanished in a moment, as the men threw themselves into their saddles, riding deep, for it was uncertain footing to horses.

Within two minutes from the time the herd left the bed ground, fourteen of us rode on their left point and across their front, firing our six-shooters in their faces. By the time the herd had covered a scant mile, we had thrown them into a mill. They had run so compactly that there were no stragglers, so we loosened out and gave them room; but it was a long time before they relaxed any, but continued going round and round like a water wheel or an endless chain. The foreman ordered three men on the heaviest horses to split them. The men rode out a short distance to get the required momentum, wheeled their horses, and, wedge-shaped, struck this sea of cattle and entered, but it instantly closed in their wake as though it had been water. For an hour they rode through the herd, back and forth, now from this quarter, now from that, and finally the mill was broken. After midnight, as luck would have it, heavy dark clouds banked in the northwest, and lightning flashed, and before a single animal had lain down, a drizzling rain set in. That settled it; it was an all-night job now. We drifted about hither and yon. Horses, men, and cattle turned their backs to the wind and rain and waited for morning. We were so familiar with the signs of coming day that we turned them loose half an hour before dawn, leaving herders, and rode for camp.

As we groped our way in that dark hour before dawn, hungry, drenched, and bedraggled, there was nothing gleeful about us, while Bob Blades expressed his disgust over our occupation. "If ever I get home again," said he, and the tones of his voice were an able second to his remarks, "you all can go up the trail that want to, but here's one chicken that won't. There isn't a cowman in Texas who has money enough to hire me again."

"Ah, hell, now," said Bull, "you oughtn't to let a little rain ruffle your feathers that way. Cheer up, sonny; you may be rich some day yet and walk on brussels and velvet."

CHAPTER XIX
FORTY ISLANDS FORD

After securing a count on the herd that morning and finding nothing short, we trailed out up the North Platte River. It was an easy country in which to handle a herd; the trail in places would run back from the river as far as ten miles, and again follow close in near the river bottoms. There was an abundance of small creeks putting into this fork of the Platte from the south, which afforded water for the herd and good camp grounds at night. Only twice after leaving Ogalalla had we been compelled to go to the river for water for the herd, and with the exception of thunderstorms and occasional summer rains, the weather had been all one could wish. For the past week as we trailed up the North Platte, some one of us visited the river daily to note its stage of water, for we were due to cross at Forty Islands, about twelve miles south of old Fort Laramie. The North Platte was very similar to the South Canadian, — a wide sandy stream without banks; and our experience with the latter was fresh in our memories. The stage of water had not been favorable, for this river also had its source in the mountains, and as now midsummer was upon us, the season of heavy rainfall in the mountains, augmented by the melting snows, the prospect of finding a fordable stage of water at Forty Islands was not very encouraging.

We reached this well-known crossing late in the afternoon the third day after leaving the Wyoming line, and found one of the Prairie Cattle Company's herds water-bound. This herd had been wintered on one of that company's ranges on the Arkansaw River in southern Colorado, and their destination was in the Bad Lands near the mouth of the Yellowstone, where the same company had a northern range. Flood knew the foreman, Wade Scholar, who reported having been waterbound over a week already with no prospect of crossing without swimming. Scholar knew the country thoroughly, and had decided to lie over until the river was fordable at Forty Islands, as it was much the easiest crossing on the North Platte, though there was a wagon ferry at Fort Laramie. He returned with Flood to our camp, and the two talked over the prospect of swimming it on the morrow.

"Let's send the wagons up to the ferry in the morning," said Flood, "and swim the herds. If you wait until this river falls, you are liable to have an experience like we had on the South Canadian, — lost three days and bogged over a hundred cattle. When one of these sandy rivers has had a big freshet, look out for quicksands; but you know that as well as I do. Why, we've swum over half a dozen rivers already, and I'd much rather swim this one than attempt to ford it just after it has fallen. We can double our outfits and be safely across before noon. I've got nearly a thousand miles yet to make, and have just *got* to get over. Think it over to-night, and have your wagon ready to start with ours."

Scholar rode away without giving our foreman any definite answer as to what he would do, though earlier in the evening he had offered to throw his herd well out of the way at the ford, and lend us any assistance at his command. But when it came to the question of crossing his own herd, he seemed to dread the idea of swimming the river, and could not be induced to say what he would do, but said that we were welcome to the lead. The next morning Flood and I accompanied our wagon up to his camp, when it was plainly evident that he did not intend to send his wagon with ours, and McCann started on alone, though our foreman renewed his efforts to convince Scholar of the feasibility of swimming the herds. Their cattle were thrown well away from the ford, and Scholar assured us that his outfit would be on hand whenever we were ready to cross, and even invited all hands of us to come to his wagon for dinner. When returning to our herd, Flood told me that Scholar was considered one of the best foremen on the trail, and why he should refuse to swim his cattle was unexplainable. He must have time to burn, but that didn't seem reasonable, for the earlier through cattle were turned loose on their winter range the better. We were in no hurry to cross, as our wagon would be gone all day, and it was nearly high noon when we trailed up to the ford.

With the addition to our force of Scholar and nine or ten of his men, we had an abundance of help, and put the cattle into the water opposite two islands, our saddle horses in the lead as usual. There was no swimming water between the south shore and the first island, though it wet our saddle skirts for some considerable distance, this channel being nearly two hundred yards wide. Most of our outfit took the water, while Scholar's men fed our herd in from the south bank, a number of their men coming over as far as the first island. The second island lay down the stream some little distance; and as we pushed the cattle off the first one we were in swimming water in no time, but the saddle horses were already landing on the second island, and our lead cattle struck out, and, breasting the water, swam as proudly as swans. The middle channel was nearly a hundred yards wide, the greater portion of which was swimming, though the last channel was much wider. But our saddle horses had already taken it, and when within fifty yards of the farther shore, struck solid footing. With our own outfit we crowded the leaders to keep the chain of cattle unbroken, and before Honeyman could hustle his horses out of the river, our lead cattle had caught a foothold, were heading up stream and edging out for the farther shore.

I had one of the best swimming horses in our outfit, and Flood put me in the lead on the point. As my horse came out on the farther bank, I am certain I never have seen a herd of cattle, before or since, which presented a prettier sight when swimming than ours did that day. There was fully four hundred yards of water on the angle by which we crossed, nearly half of which was swimming, but with the two islands which gave them a breathing spell, our Circle Dots were taking the water as steadily as a herd leaving their bed ground. Scholar and his men were feeding them in, while half a dozen of our men on each island were keeping them moving. Honeyman and I pointed them out of the river; and as they grazed away from the shore, they spread out fan-like, many of them kicking up their heels after they left the water in healthy enjoyment of their bath. Long before they were half over, the usual shouting had ceased, and we simply sat in our saddles and waited for the long train of cattle to come up and cross. Within less than half an hour from the time our saddle horses entered the North Platte, the tail end of our herd had landed safely on the farther bank.

As Honeyman and I were the only ones of our outfit on the north side of the river during the passage, Flood called to us from across the last channel to graze the herd until relieved, when the remainder of the outfit returned to the south side to recover their discarded effects and to get dinner with Scholar's wagon. I had imitated Honeyman, and tied my boots to my cantle strings, so that my effects were on the right side of the river; and as far as dinner was concerned, — well, I'd much rather miss it than swim the Platte twice in its then stage of water. There is a difference in daring in one's duty and in daring out of pure venturesomeness, and if we missed our dinners it would not be the first time, so we were quite willing to make the sacrifice. If the Quirk family never achieve fame for daring by field and flood, until this one of the old man's boys brings the family name into prominence, it will be hopelessly lost to posterity.

We allowed the cattle to graze of their own free will, and merely turned in the sides and rear, but on reaching the second bottom of the river, where they caught a good breeze, they lay down for their noonday siesta, which relieved us of all work but keeping watch over them. The saddle horses were grazing about in plain view on the first bottom, so Honeyman and I dismounted on a little elevation overlooking our charges. We were expecting the outfit to return promptly after dinner was over, for it was early enough in the day to have trailed eight or ten miles farther. It would have been no trouble to send some one up the river to meet our wagon and pilot McCann to the herd, for the trail left on a line due north from the river. We had been lounging about for an hour while the cattle were resting, when our attention was attracted by our saddle horses in the bottom. They were looking at the ford, to which we supposed their attention had been attracted by the swimming of the outfit, but instead only two of the boys showed up, and on sighting us nearly a mile away, they rode forward very leisurely. Before their arrival we recognized them by their horses as Ash Borrowstone and Rod Wheat, and on their riding up the latter said as he dismounted, —

"Well, they're going to cross the other herd, and they want you to come back and point the cattle with that famous swimming horse of yours. You'll learn after a while not to blow so much about your mount, and your cutting horses, and your night horses, and your swimming horses. I wish every horse of mine had a nigger brand on him, and I had to ride in the wagon, when it comes to swimming these rivers. And I'm not the only one that has a distaste for a wet proposition, for I wouldn't have to guess twice as to what's the matter with Scholar. But Flood has pounded him on the back ever since he met him yesterday evening to swim his cattle, until it's either swim or say he's afraid to, — it's 'Shoot, Luke, or give up the gun' with him. Scholar's a nice fellow, but I'll bet my interest in goose heaven that I know what's the matter with him. And I'm not blaming him, either; but I can't understand why our boss should take such an interest in having him swim. It's none of his business if he swims now, or fords a month hence, or waits until the river freezes over in the winter and crosses on the ice. But let the big augers wrangle it out; you noticed, Ash, that ne'er one of Scholar's outfit ever said a word one way or the other, but Flood poured it into him until he consented to swim. So fork that swimming horse of yours and wet your big toe again in the North Platte."

As the orders had come from the foreman, there was nothing to do but obey. Honeyman rode as far as the river with me, where after shedding my boots and surplus clothing and secreting them, I rode up above the island and plunged in. I was riding the gray which I had tried in the Rio Grande the day we received the herd, and now that I understood handling him better, I preferred him to Nigger Boy, my night horse. We took the first and second islands with but a blowing spell between, and when I reached the farther shore, I turned in my saddle and saw Honeyman wave his hat to me in congratulation. On reaching their wagon, I found the herd was swinging around about a mile out from the river, in order to get a straight shoot for the entrance at the ford. I hurriedly swallowed my dinner, and as we rode out to meet the herd, asked Flood if Scholar were not going to send his wagon up to the ferry to cross, for there was as yet no indication of it. Flood replied that Scholar expected to go with the wagon, as he needed some supplies which he thought he could get from the sutler at Fort Laramie.

Flood ordered me to take the lower point again, and I rode across the trail and took my place when the herd came within a quarter of a mile of the river, while the remainder of the outfit took positions near the lead on the lower side. It was a slightly larger herd than ours, — all steers, three-year-olds that reflected in their glossy coats the benefits of a northern winter. As we came up to the water's edge, it required two of their men to force their *remuda* into the water, though it was much smaller than ours, — six horses to the man, but better ones than ours, being northern wintered. The cattle were well trail-broken, and followed the leadership of the saddle horses nicely to the first island, but they would have balked at this second channel, had it not been for the amount of help at hand. We lined them out, however, and they breasted the current, and landed on the second island. The saddle horses gave some little trouble on leaving for the farther shore, and before they were got off, several hundred head of cattle had landed on the island. But they handled obediently and were soon trailing out upon terra firma, the herd following across without a broken link in the chain. There was nothing now to do but keep the train moving into the water on the south bank, see that they did not congest on the islands, and that they left the river on reaching the farther shore. When the saddle horses reached the farther bank, they were thrown up the river and turned loose, so that the two men would be available to hold the herd after it left the water. I had crossed with the first lead cattle to the farther shore, and was turning them up the river as fast as they struck solid footing on that side. But several times I was compelled to swim back to the nearest island, and return with large bunches which had hesitated to take the last channel.

The two outfits were working promiscuously together, and I never knew who was the directing spirit in the work; but when the last two or three hundred of the tail-enders were leaving the first island for the second, and the men working in the rear started to swim the channel, amid the general hilarity I recognized a shout that was born of fear and terror. A hushed silence fell over the riotous riders in the river, and I saw those on the sand bar nearest my side rush down the narrow island and plunge back into the middle channel. Then it dawned on my mind in a flash that some one had lost his seat, and that terrified cry was for help. I plunged my gray into the river and swam to the first bar, and from thence to the scene of the trouble. Horses and men were drifting with the current down the channel, and as I appealed to the men I could get no answer but their blanched faces, though it was plain in every countenance that one of our number was under water if not drowned. There were not less than twenty horsemen drifting in the middle channel in the hope that whoever it was would come to the surface, and a hand could be stretched out in succor.

About two hundred yards down the river was an island near the middle of the stream. The current carried us near it, and, on landing, I learned that the unfortunate man was none other than Wade Scholar, the foreman of the herd. We scattered up and down this middle island and watched every ripple and floating bit of flotsam in the hope that he would come to the surface, but nothing but his hat was seen. In the disorder into which the outfits were thrown by this accident, Flood first regained his thinking faculties, and ordered a few of us to cross to either bank, and ride down the river and take up positions on the other islands, from which that part of the river took its name. A hundred conjectures were offered as to how it occurred; but no one saw either horse or rider after sinking. A free horse would be hard to drown, and on the nonappearance of Scholar's mount it was concluded that he must have become entangled in the reins or that Scholar had clutched them in his death grip, and horse and man thus met death together. It was believed by his own outfit that Scholar had no intention until the last moment to risk swimming the river, but when he saw all the others plunge into the channel, his better judgment was overcome, and rather than remain behind and cause comment, he had followed and lost his life.

We patrolled the river until darkness without result, the two herds in the mean time having been so neglected that they had mixed. Our wagon returned along the north bank early in the evening, and Flood ordered Priest to go in and make up a guard from the two outfits and hold the herd for the night. Some one of Scholar's outfit went back and moved their wagon up to the crossing, within hailing distance of ours. It was a night of muffled conversation, and every voice of the night or cry of waterfowl in the river sent creepy sensations over us. The long night passed, however, and the sun rose in Sabbath benediction, for it was Sunday, and found groups of men huddled around two wagons in silent contemplation of what the day before had brought. A more broken and disconsolate set of men than Scholar's would be hard to imagine.

Flood inquired of their outfit if there was any sub-foreman, or *segundo* as they were generally called. It seemed there was not, but their outfit was unanimous that the leadership should fall to a boyhood acquaintance of Scholar's by the name of Campbell, who was generally addressed as "Black" Jim. Flood at once advised Campbell to send their wagon up to Laramie and cross it, promising that we would lie over that day and make an effort to recover the body of the drowned foreman. Campbell accordingly started his wagon up to the ferry, and all the remainder of the outfits, with the exception of a few men on herd, started out in search of the drowned man. Within a mile and a half below the ford, there were located over thirty of the forty islands, and at the lower end of this chain of sand bars we began and searched both shores, while three or four men swam to each island and made a vigorous search.

The water in the river was not very clear, which called for a close inspection; but with a force of twenty-five men in the hunt, we covered island and shore rapidly in our search. It was about eight in the morning, and we had already searched half of the islands, when Joe Stallings and two of Scholar's men swam to an island in the river which had a growth of small cottonwoods covering it, while on the upper end was a heavy lodgment of driftwood. John Officer, The Rebel, and I had taken the next island above, and as we were riding the shallows surrounding it we heard a shot in our rear that told us the body had been found. As we turned in the direction of the signal, Stallings was standing on a large driftwood log, and signaling. We started back to him, partly wading and partly swimming, while from both sides of the river men were swimming their horses for the brushy island. Our squad, on nearing the lower bar, was compelled to swim around the driftwood, and some twelve or fifteen men from either shore reached the scene before us. The body was lying face upward, in about eighteen inches of eddy water. Flood and Campbell waded out, and taking a lariat, fastened it around his chest under the arms. Then Flood, noticing I was riding my black, asked me to tow the body ashore. Forcing a passage through the driftwood, I took the loose end of the lariat and started for the north bank, the double outfit following. On reaching the shore, the body was carried out of the water by willing hands, and one of our outfit was sent to the wagon for a tarpaulin to be used as a stretcher.

Meanwhile, Campbell took possession of the drowned foreman's watch, six-shooter, purse, and papers. The watch was as good as ruined, but the leather holster had shrunk and securely held the gun from being lost in the river. On the arrival of the tarpaulin, the body was laid upon it, and four mounted men, taking the four corners of the sheet, wrapped them on the pommels of their saddles and started for our wagon. When the corpse had been lowered to the ground at our camp, a look of inquiry passed from face to face which seemed to ask, "What next?" But the inquiry was answered a moment later by Black Jim Campbell, the friend of the dead man. Memory may have dimmed the lesser details of that Sunday morning on the North Platte, for over two decades have since gone, but his words and manliness have lived, not only in my mind, but in the memory of every other survivor of those present. "This accident," said he in perfect composure, as he gazed into the calm, still face of his dead friend, "will impose on me a very sad duty. I expect to meet his mother some day. She will want to know everything. I must tell her the truth, and I'd hate to tell her we buried him like a dog, for she's a Christian woman. And what makes it all the harder, I know that this is the third boy she has lost by drowning. Some of you may not have understood him, but among those papers which you saw me take from his pockets was a letter from his mother, in which she warned him to guard against just what has happened. Situated as we are, I'm going to ask you all to help me give him the best burial we can. No doubt it will be crude, but it will be some solace to her to know we did the best we could."

Every one of us was eager to lend his assistance. Within five minutes Priest was galloping up the north bank of the river to intercept the wagon at the ferry, a well-filled purse in his pocket with which to secure a coffin at Fort Laramie. Flood and Campbell selected a burial place, and with our wagon spade a grave was being dug on a near-by grassy mound, where there were two other graves.

There was not a man among us who was hypocrite enough to attempt to conduct a Christian burial service, but when the subject came up, McCann said as he came down the river the evening before he noticed an emigrant train of about thirty wagons going into camp at a grove about five miles up the river. In a conversation which he had had with one of the party, he learned that they expected to rest over Sunday. Their respect for the Sabbath day caused Campbell to suggest that there might be some one in the emigrant camp who could conduct a Christian burial, and he at once mounted his horse and rode away to learn.

In preparing the body for its last resting-place we were badly handicapped, but by tearing a new wagon sheet into strips about a foot in width and wrapping the body, we gave it a humble bier in the shade of our wagon, pending the arrival of the coffin. The features were so ashened by having been submerged in the river for over eighteen hours, that we wrapped the face also, as we preferred to remember him as we had seen him the day before, strong, healthy, and buoyant. During the interim, awaiting the return of Campbell from the emigrant camp and of the wagon, we sat around in groups and discussed the incident. There was a sense of guilt expressed by a number of our outfit over their hasty decision regarding the courage of the dead man. When we understood that two of his brothers had met a similar fate in Red River within the past five years, every guilty thought or hasty word spoken came back to us with tenfold weight. Priest and Campbell returned together; the former reported having secured a coffin which would arrive within an hour, while the latter had met in the emigrant camp a superannuated minister who gladly volunteered his services. He had given the old minister such data as he had, and two of the minister's granddaughters had expressed a willingness to assist by singing at the burial services. Campbell had set the hour for four, and several conveyances would be down from the emigrant camp. The wagon arriving shortly afterward, we had barely time to lay the corpse in the coffin before the emigrants drove up. The minister was a tall, homely man, with a flowing beard, which the frosts of many a winter had whitened, and as he mingled amongst us in the final preparations, he had a kind word for every one. There were ten in his party; and when the coffin had been carried out to the grave, the two granddaughters of the old man opened the simple service by singing very impressively the first three verses of the Portuguese Hymn. I had heard the old hymn sung often before, but the impression of the last verse rang in my ears for days afterward.

> "When through the deep waters I call thee to go,
> The rivers of sorrow shall not overflow;
> For I will be with thee thy troubles to bless,
> And sanctify to thee thy deepest distress."

As the notes of the hymn died away, there was for a few moments profound stillness, and not a move was made by any one. The touching words of the old hymn expressed quite vividly the disaster of the previous day, and awakened in us many memories of home. For a time we were silent, while eyes unused to weeping filled with tears. I do not know how long we remained so. It may have been only for a moment, it probably was; but I do know the silence was not broken till the aged minister, who stood at the head of the coffin, began his discourse. We stood with uncovered heads during the service, and when the old minister addressed us he spoke as though he might have been holding family worship and we had been his children. He invoked Heaven to comfort and sustain the mother when the news of her son's death reached her, as she would need more than human aid in that hour; he prayed that her faith might not falter and that she might again meet and be with her loved ones forever in the great beyond. He then took up the subject of life, — spoke of its brevity, its many hopes that are never realized, and the disappointments from which no prudence or foresight can shield us. He dwelt at some length on the strange mingling of sunshine and shadow that seemed to belong to every life; on the mystery everywhere, and nowhere more impressively than in ourselves. With his long bony finger he pointed to the cold, mute form that lay in the coffin before us, and said, "But this, my friends, is the mystery of all mysteries." The fact that life terminated in death, he said, only emphasized its reality; that the death of our companion was not an accident, though it was sudden and unexpected; that the difficulties of life are such that it would be worse than folly in us to try to meet them in our own strength. Death, he said, might change, but it did not destroy; that the soul still lived and would live forever; that death was simply the gateway out of time into eternity; and if we were to realize the high aim of our being, we could do so by casting our burdens on Him who was able and willing to carry them for us. He spoke feelingly of the Great Teacher, the lowly Nazarene, who also suffered and died, and he concluded with an eloquent description of the blessed life, the immortality of the soul, and the resurrection of the body. After the discourse was ended and a brief and earnest prayer was covered, the two young girls sang the hymn, "Shall we meet beyond the river?" The services being at an end, the coffin was lowered into the grave.

Campbell thanked the old minister and his two granddaughters on their taking leave, for their presence and assistance; and a number of us boys also shook hands with the old man at parting.

CHAPTER XX
A MOONLIGHT DRIVE

The two herds were held together a second night, but after they had grazed a few hours the next morning, the cattle were thrown together, and the work of cutting out ours commenced. With a double outfit of men available, about twenty men were turned into the herd to do the cutting, the remainder holding the main herd and looking after the cut. The morning was cool, every one worked with a vim, and in about two hours the herds were again separated and ready for the final trimming. Campbell did not expect to move out until he could communicate with the head office of the company, and would go up to Fort Laramie for that purpose during the day, hoping to be able to get a message over the military wire. When his outfit had finished retrimming our herd, and we had looked over his cattle for the last time, the two outfits bade each other farewell, and our herd started on its journey.

The unfortunate accident at the ford had depressed our feelings to such an extent that there was an entire absence of hilarity by the way. This morning the farewell songs generally used in parting with a river which had defied us were omitted. The herd trailed out like an immense serpent, and was guided and controlled by our men as if by mutes. Long before the noon hour, we passed out of sight of Forty Islands, and in the next few days, with the change of scene, the gloom gradually lifted. We were bearing almost due north, and passing through a delightful country. To our left ran a range of mountains, while on the other hand sloped off the apparently limitless plain. The scarcity of water was beginning to be felt, for the streams which had not a source in the mountains on our left had dried up weeks before our arrival. There was a gradual change of air noticeable too, for we were rapidly gaining altitude, the heat of summer being now confined to a few hours at noonday, while the nights were almost too cool for our comfort.

When about three days out from the North Platte, the mountains disappeared on our left, while on the other hand appeared a rugged-looking country, which we knew must be the approaches of the Black Hills. Another day's drive brought us into the main stage road connecting the railroad on the south with the mining camps which nestled somewhere in those rocky hills to our right. The stage road followed the trail some ten or fifteen miles before we parted company with it on a dry fork of the Big Cheyenne River. There was a road house and stage stand where these two thoroughfares separated, the one to the mining camp of Deadwood, while ours of the Montana cattle trail bore off for the Powder River to the northwest. At this stage stand we learned that some twenty herds had already passed by to the northern ranges, and that after passing the next fork of the Big Cheyenne we should find no water until we struck the Powder River, — a stretch of eighty miles. The keeper of the road house, a genial host, informed us that this drouthy stretch in our front was something unusual, this being one of the dryest summers that he had experienced since the discovery of gold in the Black Hills.

Here was a new situation to be met, an eighty-mile dry drive; and with our experience of a few months before at Indian Lakes fresh in our memories, we set our house in order for the undertaking before us. It was yet fifteen miles to the next and last water from the stage stand. There were several dry forks of the Cheyenne beyond, but as they had their source in the tablelands of Wyoming, we could not hope for water in their dry bottoms. The situation was serious, with only this encouragement: other herds had crossed this arid belt since the streams had dried up, and our Circle Dots could walk with any herd that ever left Texas. The wisdom of mounting us well for just such an emergency reflected the good cow sense of our employer; and we felt easy in regard to our mounts, though there was not a horse or a man too many. In summing up the situation, Flood said, "We've got this advantage over the Indian Lake drive: there is a good moon, and the days are cool. We'll make twenty-five miles a day covering this stretch, as this herd has never been put to a test yet to see how far they could walk in a day. They'll have to do their sleeping at noon; at least cut it into two shifts, and if we get any sleep we'll have to do the same. Let her come as she will; every day's drive is a day nearer the Blackfoot agency."

We made a dry camp that night on the divide between the road house and the last water, and the next forenoon reached the South Fork of the Big Cheyenne. The water was not even running in it, but there were several long pools, and we held the cattle around them for over an hour, until every hoof had been thoroughly watered. McCann had filled every keg and canteen in advance of the arrival of the herd, and Flood had exercised sufficient caution, in view of what lay before us, to buy an extra keg and a bull's-eye lantern at the road house. After watering, we trailed out some four or five miles and camped for noon, but the herd were allowed to graze forward until they lay down for their noonday rest. As the herd passed opposite the wagon, we cut a fat two-year-old stray heifer and killed her for beef, for the inner man must be fortified for the journey before us. After a two hours' siesta, we threw the herd on the trail and started on our way. The wagon and saddle horses were held in our immediate rear, for there was no telling when or where we would make our next halt of any consequence. We trailed and grazed the herd alternately until near evening, when the wagon was sent on ahead about three miles to get supper, while half the outfit went along to change mounts and catch up horses for those remaining behind with the herd. A half hour before the usual bedding time, the relieved men returned and took the grazing herd, and the others rode in to the wagon for supper and a change of mounts. While we shifted our saddles, we smelled the savory odor of fresh beef frying.

"Listen to that good old beef talking, will you?" said Joe Stallings, as he was bridling his horse. "McCann, I'll take my *carne fresco* a trifle rare to-night, garnished with a sprig of parsley and a wee bit of lemon."

Before we had finished supper, Honeyman had rehooked the mules to the wagon, while the *remuda* was at hand to follow. Before we left the wagon, a full moon was rising on the eastern horizon, and as we were starting out Flood gave us these general directions: "I'm going to take the lead with the cook's lantern, and one of you rear men take the new bull's-eye. We'll throw the herd on the trail; and between the lead and rear light, you swing men want to ride well outside, and you point men want to hold the lead cattle so the rear will never be more than a half a mile behind. I'll admit that this is somewhat of an experiment with me, but I don't see any good reason why she won't work. After the moon gets another hour high we can see a quarter of a mile, and the cattle are so well trail broke they'll never try to scatter. If it works all right, we'll never bed them short of midnight, and that will put us ten miles farther. Let's ride, lads."

By the time the herd was eased back on the trail, our evening camp-fire had been passed, while the cattle led out as if walking on a wager. After the first mile on the trail, the men on the point were compelled to ride in the lead if we were to hold them within the desired half mile. The men on the other side, or the swing, were gradually widening, until the herd must have reached fully a mile in length; yet we swing riders were never out of sight of each other, and it would have been impossible for any cattle to leave the herd unnoticed. In that moonlight the trail was as plain as day, and after an hour, Flood turned his lantern over to one of the point men, and rode back around the herd to the rear. From my position that first night near the middle of the swing, the lanterns both rear and forward being always in sight, I was as much at sea as any one as to the length of the herd, knowing the deceitfulness of distance of campfires and other lights by night. The foreman appealed to me as he rode down the column, to know the length of the herd, but I could give him no more than a simple guess. I could assure him, however, that the cattle had made no effort to drop out and leave the trail. But a short time after he passed me I noticed a horseman galloping up the column on the opposite side of the herd, and knew it must be the foreman. Within a short time, some one in the lead wig-wagged his lantern; it was answered by the light in the rear, and the next minute the old rear song, —

> "Ip-e-la-ago, go 'long little doggie,
> You 'll make a beef-steer by-and-by," —

reached us riders in the swing, and we knew the rear guard of cattle was being pushed forward. The distance between the swing men gradually narrowed in our lead, from which we could tell the leaders were being held in, until several times cattle grazed out from the herd, due to the checking in front. At this juncture Flood galloped around the herd a second time, and as he passed us riding along our side, I appealed to him to let them go in front, as it now required constant riding to keep the cattle from leaving the trail to graze. When he passed up the opposite side, I could distinctly hear the men on that flank making a similar appeal, and shortly afterwards the herd loosened out and we struck our old gait for several hours.

Trailing by moonlight was a novelty to all of us, and in the stillness of those splendid July nights we could hear the point men chatting across the lead in front, while well in the rear, the rattling of our heavily loaded wagon and the whistling of the horse wrangler to his charges reached our ears. The swing men were scattered so far apart there was no chance for conversation amongst us, but every once in a while a song would be started, and as it surged up and down the line, every voice, good, bad, and indifferent, joined in. Singing is supposed to have a soothing effect on cattle, though I will vouch for the fact that none of our Circle Dots stopped that night to listen to our vocal efforts. The herd was traveling so nicely that our foreman hardly noticed the passing hours, but along about midnight the singing ceased, and we were nodding in our saddles and wondering if they in the lead were never going to throw off the trail, when a great wig-wagging occurred in front, and presently we overtook The Rebel, holding the lantern and turning the herd out of the trail. It was then after midnight, and within another half hour we had the cattle bedded down within a few hundred yards of the trail. One-hour guards was the order of the night, and as soon as our wagon and saddle horses came up, we stretched ropes and caught out our night horses. These we either tied to the wagon wheels or picketed near at hand, and then we sought our blankets for a few hours' sleep. It was half past three in the morning when our guard was called, and before the hour passed, the first signs of day were visible in the east. But even before our watch had ended, Flood and the last guard came to our relief, and we pushed the sleeping cattle off the bed ground and started them grazing forward.

Cattle will not graze freely in a heavy dew or too early in the morning, and before the sun was high enough to dry the grass, we had put several miles behind us. When the sun was about an hour high, the remainder of the outfit overtook us, and shortly afterward the wagon and saddle horses passed on up the trail, from which it was evident that "breakfast would be served in the dining car ahead," as the traveled Priest aptly put it. After the sun was well up, the cattle grazed freely for several hours; but when we sighted the *remuda* and our commissary some two miles in our lead, Flood ordered the herd lined up for a count. The Rebel was always a reliable counter, and he and the foreman now rode forward and selected the crossing of a dry wash for the counting. On receiving their signal to come on, we allowed the herd to graze slowly forward, but gradually pointed them into an immense "V," and as the point of the herd crossed the dry arroyo, we compelled them to pass in a narrow file between the two counters, when they again spread out fan-like and continued their feeding.

The count confirmed the success of our driving by night, and on its completion all but two men rode to the wagon for breakfast. By the time the morning meal was disposed of, the herd had come up parallel with the wagon but a mile to the westward, and as fast as fresh mounts could be saddled, we rode away in small squads to relieve the herders and to turn the cattle into the trail. It was but a little after eight o'clock in the morning when the herd was again trailing out on the Powder River trail, and we had already put over thirty miles of the dry drive behind us, while so far neither horses nor cattle had been put to any extra exertion. The wagon followed as usual, and for over three hours we held the trail without a break, when sighting a divide in our front, the foreman went back and sent the wagon around the herd with instructions to make the noon camp well up on the divide. We threw the herd off the trail, within a mile of this stopping place, and allowed them to graze, while two thirds of the outfit galloped away to the wagon.

We allowed the cattle to lie down and rest to their complete satisfaction until the middle of the afternoon; meanwhile all hands, with the exception of two men on herd, also lay down and slept in the shade of the wagon. When the cattle had had several hours' sleep, the want of water made them restless, and they began to rise and graze away. Then all hands were aroused and we threw them upon the trail. The heat of the day was already over, and until the twilight of the evening, we trailed a three-mile clip, and again threw the herd off to graze. By our traveling and grazing gaits, we could form an approximate idea as to the distance we had covered, and the consensus of opinion of all was that we had already killed over half the distance. The herd was beginning to show the want of water by evening, but amongst our saddle horses the lack of water was more noticeable, as a horse subsisting on grass alone weakens easily; and riding them made them all the more gaunt. When we caught up our mounts that evening, we had used eight horses to the man since we had left the South Fork, and another one would be required at midnight, or whenever we halted.

We made our drive the second night with more confidence than the one before, but there were times when the train of cattle must have been nearly two miles in length, yet there was never a halt as long as the man with the lead light could see the one in the rear. We bedded the herd about midnight; and at the first break of day, the fourth guard with the foreman joined us on our watch and we started the cattle again. There was a light dew the second night, and the cattle, hungered by their night walk, went to grazing at once on the damp grass, which would allay their thirst slightly. We allowed them to scatter over several thousand acres, for we were anxious to graze them well before the sun absorbed the moisture, but at the same time every step they took was one less to the coveted Powder River.

When we had grazed the herd forward several miles, and the sun was nearly an hour high, the wagon failed to come up, which caused our foreman some slight uneasiness. Nearly another hour passed, and still the wagon did not come up nor did the outfit put in an appearance. Soon afterwards, however, Moss Strayhorn overtook us, and reported that over forty of our saddle horses were missing, while the work mules had been overtaken nearly five miles back on the trail. On account of my ability as a trailer, Flood at once dispatched me to assist Honeyman in recovering the missing horses, instructing some one else to take the *remuda*, and the wagon and horses to follow up the herd. By the time I arrived, most of the boys at camp had secured a change of horses, and I caught up my *grulla*, that I was saving for the last hard ride, for the horse hunt which confronted us. McCann, having no fire built, gave Honeyman and myself an impromptu breakfast and two canteens of water; but before we let the wagon get away, we rustled a couple of cans of tomatoes and buried them in a cache near the camp-ground, where we would have no trouble in finding them on our return. As the wagon pulled out, we mounted our horses and rode back down the trail.

Billy Honeyman understood horses, and at once volunteered the belief that we would have a long ride overtaking the missing saddle stock. The absent horses, he said, were principally the ones which had been under saddle the day before, and as we both knew, a tired, thirsty horse will go miles for water. He recalled, also, that while we were asleep at noon the day before, twenty miles back on the trail, the horses had found quite a patch of wild sorrel plant, and were foolish over leaving it. Both of us being satisfied that this would hold them for several hours at least, we struck a free gait for it. After we passed the point where the mules had been overtaken, the trail of the horses was distinct enough for us to follow in an easy canter. We saw frequent signs that they left the trail, no doubt to graze, but only for short distances, when they would enter it again, and keep it for miles. Shortly before noon, as we gained the divide above our noon camp of the day before, there about two miles distant we saw our missing horses, feeding over an alkali flat on which grew wild sorrel and other species of sour plants. We rounded them up, and finding none missing, we first secured a change of mounts. The only two horses of my mount in this portion of the *remuda* had both been under saddle the afternoon and night before, and were as gaunt as rails, and Honeyman had one unused horse of his mount in the hand. So when, taking down our ropes, we halted the horses and began riding slowly around them, forcing them into a compact body, I had my eye on a brown horse of Flood's that had not had a saddle on in a week, and told Billy to fasten to him if he got a chance. This was in violation of all custom, but if the foreman kicked, I had a good excuse to offer.

Honeyman was left-handed and threw a rope splendidly; and as we circled around the horses on opposite sides, on a signal from him we whirled our lariats and made casts simultaneously. The wrangler fastened to the brown I wanted, and my loop settled around the neck of his unridden horse. As the band broke away from our swinging ropes, a number of them ran afoul of my rope; but I gave the rowel to my *grulla*, and we shook them off. When I returned to Honeyman, and we had exchanged horses and were shifting our saddles, I complimented him on the long throw he had made in catching the brown, and incidentally mentioned that I had read of vaqueros in California who used a sixty-five foot lariat. "Hell," said Billy, in ridicule of the idea, "there wasn't a man ever born who could throw a sixty-five foot rope its full length — without he threw it down a well."

The sun was straight overhead when we started back to overtake the herd. We struck into a little better than a five-mile gait on the return trip, and about two o'clock sighted a band of saddle horses and a wagon camped perhaps a mile forward and to the side of the trail. On coming near enough, we saw at a glance it was a cow outfit, and after driving our loose horses a good push beyond their camp, turned and rode back to their wagon.

"We'll give them a chance to ask us to eat," said Billy to me, "and if they don't, why, they'll miss a hell of a good chance to entertain hungry men."

But the foreman with the stranger wagon proved to be a Bee County Texan, and our doubts did him an injustice, for, although dinner was over, he invited us to dismount and ordered his cook to set out something to eat. They had met our wagon, and McCann had insisted on their taking a quarter of our beef, so we fared well. The outfit was from a ranch near Miles City, Montana, and were going down to receive a herd of cattle at Cheyenne, Wyoming. The cattle had been bought at Ogalalla for delivery at the former point, and this wagon was going down with their ranch outfit to take the herd on its arrival. They had brought along about seventy-five saddle horses from the ranch, though in buying the herd they had taken its *remuda* of over a hundred saddle horses. The foreman informed us that they had met our cattle about the middle of the forenoon, nearly twenty-five miles out from Powder River. After we had satisfied the inner man, we lost no time getting off, as we could see a long ride ahead of us; but we had occasion as we rode away to go through their *remuda* to cut out a few of our horses which had mixed, and I found I knew over a dozen of their horses by the ranch brands, while Honeyman also recognized quite a few. Though we felt a pride in our mounts, we had to admit that theirs were better; for the effect of climate had transformed horses that we had once ridden on ranches in southern Texas. It does seem incredible, but it is a fact nevertheless, that a horse, having reached the years of maturity in a southern climate, will grow half a hand taller and carry two hundred pounds more flesh, when he has undergone the rigors of several northern winters.

We halted at our night camp to change horses and to unearth our cached tomatoes, and again set out. By then it was so late in the day that the sun had lost its force, and on this last leg in overtaking the herd we increased our gait steadily until the sun was scarcely an hour high, and yet we never sighted a dust-cloud in our front. About sundown we called a few minutes' halt, and after eating our tomatoes and drinking the last of our water, again pushed on. Twilight had faded into dusk before we reached a divide which we had had in sight for several hours, and which we had hoped to gain in time to sight the timber on Powder River before dark. But as we put mile after mile behind us, that divide seemed to move away like a mirage, and the evening star had been shining for an hour before we finally reached it, and sighted, instead of Powder's timber, the campfire of our outfit about five miles ahead. We fired several shots on seeing the light, in the hope that they might hear us in camp and wait; otherwise we knew they would start the herd with the rising of the moon.

When we finally reached camp, about nine o'clock at night, everything was in readiness to start, the moon having risen sufficiently. Our shooting, however, had been heard, and horses for a change were tied to the wagon wheels, while the remainder of the *remuda* was under herd in charge of Rod Wheat. The runaways were thrown into the horse herd while we bolted our suppers. Meantime McCann informed us that Flood had ridden that afternoon to the Powder

River, in order to get the lay of the land. He had found it to be ten or twelve miles distant from the present camp, and the water in the river barely knee deep to a saddle horse. Beyond it was a fine valley. Before we started, Flood rode in from the herd, and said to Honeyman, "I'm going to send the horses and wagon ahead to-night, and you and McCann want to camp on this side of the river, under the hill and just a few hundred yards below the ford. Throw your saddle horses across the river, and build a fire before you go to sleep, so we will have a beacon light to pilot us in, in case the cattle break into a run on scenting the water. The herd will get in a little after midnight, and after crossing, we'll turn her loose just for luck."

It did me good to hear the foreman say the herd was to be turned loose, for I had been in the saddle since three that morning, had ridden over eighty miles, and had now ten more in sight, while Honeyman would complete the day with over a hundred to his credit. We let the *remuda* take the lead in pulling out, so that the wagon mules could be spurred to their utmost in keeping up with the loose horses. Once they were clear of the herd, we let the cattle into the trail. They had refused to bed down, for they were uneasy with thirst, but the cool weather had saved them any serious suffering. We all felt gala as the herd strung out on the trail. Before we halted again there would be water for our dumb brutes and rest for ourselves. There was lots of singing that night. "There's One more River to cross," and "Roll, Powder, roll," were wafted out on the night air to the coyotes that howled on our flanks, or to the prairie dogs as they peeped from their burrows at this weird caravan of the night, and the lights which flickered in our front and rear must have been real Jack-o'-lanterns or Will-o'-the-wisps to these occupants of the plain. Before we had covered half the distance, the herd was strung-out over two miles, and as Flood rode back to the rear every half hour or so, he showed no inclination to check the lead and give the sore-footed rear guard a chance to close up the column; but about an hour before midnight we saw a light low down in our front, which gradually increased until the treetops were distinctly visible, and we knew that our wagon had reached the river. On sighting this beacon, the long yell went up and down the column, and the herd walked as only long-legged, thirsty Texas cattle can walk when they scent water. Flood called all the swing men to the rear, and we threw out a half-circle skirmish line covering a mile in width, so far back that only an occasional glimmer of the lead light could be seen. The trail struck the Powder on an angle, and when within a mile of the river, the swing cattle left the deep-trodden paths and started for the nearest water.

The left flank of our skirmish line encountered the cattle as they reached the river, and prevented them from drifting up the stream. The point men abandoned the leaders when within a few hundred yards of the river. Then the rear guard of cripples and sore-footed cattle came up, and the two flanks of horsemen pushed them all across the river until they met, when we turned and galloped into camp, making the night hideous with our yelling. The longest dry drive of the trip had been successfully made, and we all felt jubilant. We stripped bridles and saddles from our tired horses, and unrolling our beds, were soon lost in well-earned sleep.

The stars may have twinkled overhead, and sundry voices of the night may have whispered to us as we lay down to sleep, but we were too tired for poetry or sentiment that night.

CHAPTER XXI
THE YELLOWSTONE

The tramping of our *remuda* as they came trotting up to the wagon the next morning, and Honeyman's calling, "Horses, horses," brought us to the realization that another day had dawned with its duty. McCann had stretched the ropes of our corral, for Flood was as dead to the world as any of us were, but the tramping of over a hundred and forty horses and mules, as they crowded inside the ropes, brought him into action as well as the rest of us. We had had a good five hours' sleep, while our mounts had been transformed from gaunt animals to round-barreled saddle horses, — that fought and struggled amongst themselves or artfully dodged the lariat loops which were being cast after them. Honeyman reported the herd quietly grazing across the river, and after securing our mounts for the morning, we breakfasted before looking after the cattle. It took us less than an hour to round up and count the cattle, and turn them loose again under herd to graze. Those of us not on herd returned to the wagon, and our foreman instructed McCann to make a two hours' drive down the river and camp for noon, as he proposed only to graze the herd that morning. After seeing the wagon safely beyond the rocky crossing, we hunted up a good bathing pool and disported ourselves for half an hour, taking a much needed bath. There were trails on either side of the Powder, and as our course was henceforth to the northwest, we remained on the west side and grazed or trailed down it. It was a beautiful stream of water, having its source in the Big Horn Mountains, frequently visible on our left. For the next four or five days we had easy work. There were range cattle through that section, but fearful of Texas fever, their owners gave the Powder River a wide berth. With the exception of holding the herd at night, our duties were light. We caught fish and killed grouse; and the respite seemed like a holiday after our experience of the past few days. During the evening of the second day after reaching the Powder, we crossed the Crazy Woman, a clear mountainous fork of the former river, and nearly as large as the parent stream. Once or twice we encountered range riders, and learned that the Crazy Woman was a stock country, a number of beef ranches being located on it, stocked with Texas cattle.

Somewhere near or about the Montana line, we took a left-hand trail. Flood had ridden it out until he had satisfied himself that it led over to the Tongue River and the country beyond. While large trails followed on down the Powder, their direction was wrong for us, as they led towards the Bad Lands and the lower Yellowstone country. On the second day out, after taking the left-hand trail, we encountered some rough country in passing across a saddle in a range of hills forming the divide between the Powder and Tongue rivers. We were nearly a whole day crossing it, but had a well-used trail to follow, and down in the foothills made camp that night on a creek which emptied into the Tongue. The roughness of the trail was well compensated for, however, as it was a paradise of grass and water. We reached the Tongue River the next afternoon, and found it a similar stream to the Powder, — clear as crystal, swift, and with a rocky bottom. As these were but minor rivers, we encountered no trouble in crossing them, the greatest danger being to our wagon. On the Tongue we met range riders again, and from them we learned that this trail, which crossed the Yellowstone at Frenchman's Ford, was the one in use by herds bound for the Musselshell and remoter points on the upper Missouri. From one rider we learned that the first herd of the present season which went through on this route were cattle wintered on the Niobrara in western Nebraska, whose destination was Alberta in the British possessions. This herd outclassed us in penetrating northward, though in distance they had not traveled half as far as our Circle Dots.

After following the Tongue River several days and coming out on that immense plain tributary to the Yellowstone, the trail turned to the northwest, gave us a short day's drive to the Rosebud River, and after following it a few miles, bore off again on the same quarter. In our rear hung the mountains with their sentinel peaks, while in our front stretched the valley tributary to the Yellowstone, in extent, itself, an inland empire. The month was August, and, with the exception of cool nights, no complaint could be made, for that rarefied atmosphere was a tonic to man and beast, and there was pleasure in the primitive freshness of the country which rolled away on every hand. On leaving the Rosebud, two days' travel brought us to the east fork of Sweet Grass, an insignificant stream, with a swift current and rocky crossings. In the first two hours after reaching it, we must have crossed it half a dozen times, following the grassy bottoms, which shifted from one bank to the other. When we were full forty miles distant from Frenchman's Ford on the Yellowstone, the wagon, in crossing Sweet Grass, went down a sidling bank into the bottom of the creek, the left hind wheel collided with a boulder in the water, dishing it, and every spoke in the wheel snapped off at the shoulder in the felloe. McCann never noticed it, but poured the whip into the mules, and when he pulled out on the opposite bank left the felloe of his wheel in the creek behind. The herd was in the lead at the time, and when Honeyman overtook us and reported the accident, we threw the herd off to graze, and over half the outfit returned to the wagon.

When we reached the scene, McCann had recovered the felloe, but every spoke in the hub was hopelessly ruined. Flood took in the situation at a glance. He ordered the wagon unloaded and the reach lengthened, took the axe, and, with The Rebel, went back about a mile to a thicket of lodge poles which we had passed higher up the creek. While the rest of us unloaded the wagon, McCann, who was swearing by both note and rhyme, unearthed his saddle from amongst the other plunder and cinched it on his nigh wheeler. We had the wagon unloaded and had reloaded some of the heaviest of the plunder in the front end of the wagon box, by the time our foreman and Priest returned, dragging from their pommels a thirty-foot pole as perfect as the mast of a yacht. We knocked off all the spokes not already broken at the hub of the ruined wheel, and after jacking up the hind axle, attached the "crutch." By cutting a half notch in the larger end of the pole, so that it fitted over the front axle, lashing it there securely, and allowing the other end to trail behind on the ground, we devised a support on which the hub of the broken wheel rested, almost at its normal height. There was sufficient spring to the pole to obviate any jolt or jar, while the rearrangement we had effected in distributing the load would relieve it of any serious burden. We took a rope from the coupling pole of the wagon and loosely noosed it over the crutch, which allowed leeway in turning, but prevented the hub from slipping off the support on a short turn to the left. Then we lashed the tire and felloe to the front end of the wagon, and with the loss of but a couple of hours our commissary was again on the move.

The trail followed the Sweet Grass down to the Yellowstone; and until we reached it, whenever there were creeks to ford or extra pulls on hills, half a dozen of us would drop back and lend a hand from our saddle pommels. The gradual decline of the country to the river was in our favor at present, and we should reach the ford in two days at the farthest, where we hoped to find a wheelwright. In case we did not, our foreman thought he could effect a trade for a serviceable wagon, as ours was a new one and the best make in the market. The next day Flood rode on ahead to Frenchman's Ford, and late in the day returned with the information that the Ford was quite a pretentious frontier village of the squatter type. There was a blacksmith and a wheelwright shop in the town, but the prospect of an exchange was discouraging, as the wagons there were of the heavy freighting type, while ours was a wide tread — a serious objection, as wagons manufactured for southern trade were eight inches wider than those in use in the north, and therefore would not track on the same road. The wheelwright had assured Flood that the wheel could be filled in a day, with the exception of painting, and as paint was not important, he had decided to move up within three or four miles of the Ford and lie over a day for repairing the wagon, and at the same time have our mules reshod. Accordingly we moved up the next morning, and after unloading the wagon, both box and contents, over half the outfit — the first and second guards — accompanied the wagon into the Ford. They were to return by noon, when the remainder of us were to have our turn in seeing the sights of Frenchman's Ford. The horse wrangler remained behind with us, to accompany the other half of the outfit in the afternoon. The herd was no trouble to hold, and after watering about the middle of the forenoon, three of us went into camp and got dinner. As this was the first time since starting that our cook was absent, we rather enjoyed the opportunity to practice our culinary skill. Pride in our ability to cook was a weakness in our craft. The work was divided up between Joe Stallings, John Officer, and myself, Honeyman being excused on agreeing to rustle the wood and water. Stallings prided himself on being an artist in making coffee, and while hunting for the coffee mill, found a bag of dried peaches.

"Say, fellows," said Joe, "I'll bet McCann has hauled this fruit a thousand miles and never knew he had it amongst all this plunder. I'm going to stew a saucepan full of it, just to show his royal nibs that he's been thoughtless of his boarders."

Officer volunteered to cut and fry the meat, for we were eating stray beef now with great regularity; and the making of the biscuits fell to me. Honeyman soon had a fire so big that you could not have got near it without a wet blanket on; and when my biscuits were ready for the Dutch oven, Officer threw a bucket of water on the fire, remarking: "Honeyman, if you was *cusi segundo* under me, and built up such a big fire for the chef, there would be trouble in camp. You may be a good enough horse wrangler for a through Texas outfit, but when it comes to playing second fiddle to a cook of my accomplishments — well, you simply don't know salt from wild honey. A man might as well try to cook on a burning haystack as on a fire of your building."

When the fire had burned down sufficiently, the cooks got their respective utensils upon the fire; I had an ample supply of live coals for the Dutch oven, and dinner was shortly afterwards announced as ready. After dinner, Officer and I relieved the men on herd, but over an hour passed before we caught sight of the first and second guards returning from the Ford. They were men who could stay in town all day and enjoy themselves; but, as Flood had reminded them, there were others who were entitled to a holiday. When Bob Blades and Fox Quarternight came to our relief on herd, they attempted to detain us with a description of Frenchman's Ford, but we cut all conversation short by riding away to camp.

"We'll just save them the trouble, and go in and see it for ourselves," said Officer to me, as we galloped along. We had left word with Honeyman what horses we wanted to ride that afternoon, and lost little time in changing mounts; then we all set out to pay our respects to the mushroom village on the Yellowstone. Most of us had money; and those of the outfit who had returned were clean shaven and brought the report that a shave was two-bits and a drink the same price. The town struck me as something new and novel, two thirds of the habitations being of canvas. Immense quantities of buffalo hides were drying or already baled, and waiting transportation as we afterward learned to navigable points on the Missouri. Large bull trains were encamped on the outskirts of the village, while many such outfits were in town, receiving cargoes or discharging freight. The drivers of these ox trains lounged in the streets and thronged the saloons and gambling resorts. The population was extremely mixed, and almost every language could be heard spoken on the streets. The men were fine types of the pioneer, — buffalo hunters, freighters, and other plainsmen, though hardly as picturesque in figure and costume as a modern artist would paint them. For native coloring, there were typical specimens of northern Indians, grunting their jargon amid the babel of other tongues; and groups of squaws wandered through the irregular streets in gaudy blankets and red calico. The only civilizing element to be seen was the camp of engineers, running the survey of the Northern Pacific railroad.

Tying our horses in a group to a hitch-rack in the rear of a saloon called The Buffalo Bull, we entered by a rear door and lined up at the bar for our first drink since leaving Ogalalla. Games of chance were running in the rear for those who felt inclined to try their luck, while in front of the bar, against the farther wall, were a number of small tables, around which were seated the patrons of the place, playing for the drinks. One couldn't help being impressed with the unrestrained freedom of the village, whose sole product seemed to be buffalo hides. Every man in the place wore the regulation six-shooter in his belt, and quite a number wore two. The primitive law of nature known as self-preservation, was very evident in August of '82 at Frenchman's Ford. It reminded me of the early days at home in Texas, where, on arising in the morning, one buckled on his six-shooter as though it were part of his dress. After a second round of drinks, we strolled out into the front street to look up Flood and McCann, and incidentally get a shave. We soon located McCann, who had a hunk of dried buffalo meat, and was chipping it off and feeding it to some Indian children whose acquaintance he seemed to be cultivating. On sighting us, he gave the children the remainder of the jerked buffalo, and at once placed himself at our disposal as guide to Frenchman's Ford. He had been all over the town that morning; knew the name of every saloon and those of several barkeepers as well; pointed out the bullet holes in a log building where the last shooting scrape occurred, and otherwise showed us the sights in the village which we might have overlooked. A barber shop? Why, certainly; and he led the way, informing us that the wagon wheel would be filled by evening, that the mules were already shod, and that Flood had ridden down to the crossing to look at the ford.

Two barbers turned us out rapidly, and as we left we continued to take in the town, strolling by pairs and drinking moderately as we went. Flood had returned in the mean time, and seemed rather convivial and quite willing to enjoy the enforced lay-over with us. While taking a drink in Yellowstone Bob's place, the foreman took occasion to call the attention of The Rebel to a cheap lithograph of General Grant which hung behind the bar. The two discussed the merits of the picture, and Priest, who was an admirer of the magnanimity as well as the military genius of Grant, spoke in reserved yet favorable terms of the general, when Flood flippantly chided him on his eulogistic remarks over an officer to whom he had once been surrendered. The Rebel took the chaffing in all good humor, and when our glasses were filled, Flood suggested to Priest that since he was such an admirer of Grant, possibly he wished to propose a toast to the general's health.

"You're young, Jim," said The Rebel, "and if you'd gone through what I have, your views of things might be different. My admiration for the generals on our side survived wounds, prisons, and changes of fortune; but time has tempered my views on some things, and now I don't enthuse over generals when the men of the ranks who made them famous are forgotten. Through the fortunes of war, I saluted Grant when we were surrendered, but I wouldn't propose a toast or take off my hat now to any man that lives."

During the comments of The Rebel, a stranger, who evidently overheard them, rose from one of the tables in the place and sauntered over to the end of the bar, an attentive listener to the succeeding conversation. He was a younger man than Priest, — with a head of heavy black hair reaching his shoulders, while his dress was largely of buckskin, profusely ornamented with beadwork and fringes. He was armed, as was every one else, and from his languid demeanor as well as from his smart appearance, one would classify him at a passing glance as a frontier gambler. As we turned away from the bar to an unoccupied table, Priest waited for his change, when the stranger accosted him with an inquiry as to where he was from. In the conversation that ensued, the stranger, who had noticed the good-humored manner in which The Rebel had taken the chiding of our foreman, pretending to take him to task for some of his remarks. But in this he made a mistake. What his friends might safely say to Priest would be treated as an insult from a stranger. Seeing that he would not stand his chiding, the other attempted to mollify him by proposing they have a drink together and part friendly, to which The Rebel assented. I was pleased with the favorable turn of affairs, for my bunkie had used some rather severe language in resenting the remarks of the stranger, which now had the promise of being dropped amicably.

I knew the temper of Priest, and so did Flood and Honeyman, and we were all anxious to get him away from the stranger. So I asked our foreman as soon as they had drunk together, to go over and tell Priest we were waiting for him to make up a game of cards. The two were standing at the bar in a most friendly attitude, but as they raised their glasses to drink, the stranger, holding his at arm's length, said: "Here's a toast for you: To General Grant, the ablest" —

But the toast was never finished, for Priest dashed the contents of his glass in the stranger's face, and calmly replacing the glass on the bar, backed across the room towards us. When half-across, a sudden movement on the part of the stranger caused him to halt. But it seemed the picturesque gentleman beside the bar was only searching his pockets for a handkerchief.

"Don't get your hand on that gun you wear," said The Rebel, whose blood was up, "unless you intend to use it. But you can't shoot a minute too quick to suit me. What do you wear a gun for, anyhow? Let's see how straight you can shoot."

As the stranger made no reply, Priest continued, "The next time you have anything to rub in, pick your man better. The man who insults me'll get all that's due him for his trouble." Still eliciting no response, The Rebel taunted him further, saying, "Go on and finish your toast, you patriotic beauty. I'll give you another: Jeff Davis and the Southern Confederacy."

We all rose from the table, and Flood, going over to Priest, said, "Come along, Paul we don't want to have any trouble here. Let's go across the street and have a game of California Jack."

But The Rebel stood like a chiseled statue, ignoring the friendly counsel of our foreman, while the stranger, after wiping the liquor from his face and person, walked across the room and seated himself at the table from which he had risen. A stillness as of death pervaded the room, which was only broken by our foreman repeating his request to Priest to come away, but the latter replied, "No; when I leave this place it will not be done in fear of any one. When any man goes out of his way to insult me he must take the consequences, and he can always find me if he wants satisfaction. We'll take another drink before we go. Everybody in the house, come up and take a drink with Paul Priest."

The inmates of the place, to the number of possibly twenty, who had been witness to what had occurred, accepted the invitation, quitting their games and gathering around the bar. Priest took a position at the end of the bar, where he could notice any movement on the part of his adversary as well as the faces of his guests, and smiling on them, said in true hospitality, "What will you have, gentlemen?" There was a forced effort on the part of the drinkers to appear indifferent to the situation, but with the stranger sitting sullenly in their rear and an iron-gray man standing at the farther end of the line, hungering for an opportunity to settle differences with six-shooters, their indifference was an empty mockery. Some of the players returned to their games, while others sauntered into the street, yet Priest showed no disposition to go. After a while the stranger walked over to the bar and called for a glass of whiskey.

The Rebel stood at the end of the bar, calmly rolling a cigarette, and as the stranger seemed not to notice him, Priest attracted his attention and said, "I'm just passing through here, and shall only be in town this afternoon; so if there's anything between us that demands settlement, don't hesitate to ask for it."

The stranger drained his glass at a single gulp, and with admirable composure replied, "If there's anything between us, we'll settle it in due time, and as men usually settle such differences in this country. I have a friend or two in town, and as soon as I see them, you will receive notice, or you may consider the matter dropped. That's all I care to say at present."

He walked away to the rear of the room, Priest joined us, and we strolled out of the place. In the street, a grizzled, gray-bearded man, who had drunk with him inside, approached my bunkie and said, "You want to watch that fellow. He claims to be from the Gallatin country, but he isn't, for I live there. There's a pal with him, and they've got some good horses, but I know every brand on the headwaters of the Missouri, and their horses were never bred on any of its three forks. Don't give him any the best of you. Keep an eye on him, comrade." After this warning, the old man turned into the first open door, and we crossed over to the wheelwright's shop; and as the wheel would not be finished for several hours yet, we continued our survey of the town, and our next landing was at The Buffalo Bull. On entering we found four of our men in a game of cards at the very first table, while Officer was reported as being in the gambling room in the rear. The only vacant table in the bar-room was the last one in the far corner, and calling for a deck of cards, we occupied it. I sat with my back to the log wall of the low one-story room, while on my left and fronting the door, Priest took a seat with Flood for his pardner, while Honeyman fell to me. After playing a few hands, Flood suggested that Billy go forward and exchange seats with some of our outfit, so as to be near the door, where he could see any one that entered, while from his position the rear door would be similarly guarded. Under this change, Rod Wheat came back to our table and took Honeyman's place. We had been playing along for an hour, with people passing in and out of the gambling room, and expected shortly to start for camp, when Priest's long-haired adversary came in at the front door, and, walking through the room, passed into the gambling department.

John Officer, after winning a few dollars in the card room, was standing alongside watching our game; and as the stranger passed by, Priest gave him the wink, on which Officer followed the stranger and a heavy-set companion who was with him into the rear room. We had played only a few hands when the heavy-set man came back to the bar, took a drink, and walked over to watch a game of cards at the second table from the front door. Officer came back shortly afterward, and whispered to us that there were four of them to look out for, as he had seen them conferring together. Priest seemed the least concerned of any of us, but I noticed he eased the holster on his belt forward, where it would be ready to his hand. We had called for a round of drinks, Officer taking one with us, when two men came out of the gambling hell, and halting at the bar, pretended to divide some money which they wished to have it appear they had won in the card room. Their conversation was loud and intended to attract attention, but Officer gave us the wink, and their ruse was perfectly understood. After taking a drink and attracting as much attention as possible over the division of the money, they separated, but remained in the room.

I was dealing the cards a few minutes later, when the long-haired man emerged from the gambling hell, and imitating the maudlin, sauntered up to the bar and asked for a drink. After being served, he walked about halfway to the door, then whirling suddenly, stepped to the end of the bar, placed his hands upon it, sprang up and stood upright on it. He whipped out two six-shooters, let loose a yell which caused a commotion throughout the room, and walked very deliberately the length of the counter, his attention centred upon the occupants of our table. Not attracting the notice he expected in our quarter, he turned, and slowly repaced the bar, hurling anathemas on Texas and Texans in general.

I saw The Rebel's eyes, steeled to intensity, meet Flood's across the table, and in that glance of our foreman he evidently read approval, for he rose rigidly with the stealth of a tiger, and for the first time that day his hand went to the handle of his six-shooter. One of the two pretended winners at cards saw the movement in our quarter, and sang out as a warning, "Cuidado, mucho." The man on the bar whirled on the word of warning, and blazed away with his two guns into our corner. I had risen at the word and was pinned against the wall, where on the first fire a rain of dirt fell from the chinking in the wall over my head. As soon as the others sprang away from the table, I kicked it over in clearing myself, and came to my feet just as The Rebel fired his second shot. I had the satisfaction of seeing his long-haired adversary reel backwards, firing his guns into the ceiling as he went, and in falling crash heavily into the glassware on the back bar.

The smoke which filled the room left nothing visible for a few moments. Meantime Priest, satisfied that his aim had gone true, turned, passed through the rear room, gained his horse, and was galloping away to the herd before any semblance of order was restored. As the smoke cleared away and we passed forward through the room, John Officer had one of the three pardners standing with his hands to the wall, while his six-shooter lay on the floor under Officer's foot. He had made but one shot into our corner, when the muzzle of a gun was pushed against his ear with an imperative order to drop his arms, which he had promptly done. The two others, who had been under the surveillance of our men at the forward table, never made a move or offered to bring a gun into action, and after the killing of their picturesque pardner passed together out of the house. There had been five or six shots fired into our corner, but the first double shot, fired when three of us were still sitting, went too high for effect, while the remainder were scattering, though Rod Wheat got a bullet through his coat, close enough to burn the skin on his shoulder.

The dead man was laid out on the floor of the saloon; and through curiosity, for it could hardly have been much of a novelty to the inhabitants of Frenchman's Ford, hundreds came to gaze on the corpse and examine the wounds, one above the other through his vitals, either of which would have been fatal. Officer's prisoner admitted that the dead man was his pardner, and offered to remove the corpse if released. On turning his six-shooter over to the proprietor of the place, he was given his freedom to depart and look up his friends.

As it was after sundown, and our wheel was refilled and ready, we set out for camp, where we found that Priest had taken a fresh horse and started back over the trail. No one felt any uneasiness over his absence, for he had demonstrated his ability to protect himself; and truth compels me to say that the outfit to a man was proud of him. Honeyman was substituted on our guard in The Rebel's place, sleeping with me that night, and after we were in bed, Billy said in his enthusiasm: "If that horse thief had not relied on pot shooting, and had been modest and only used one gun, he might have hurt some of you fellows. But when I saw old Paul raising his gun to a level as he shot, I knew he was cool and steady, and I'd rather died right there than see him fail to get his man."

CHAPTER XXII
OUR LAST CAMP-FIRE

By early dawn the next morning we were astir at our last camp on Sweet Grass, and before the horses were brought in, we had put on the wagon box and reloaded our effects. The rainy season having ended in the mountain regions, the stage of water in the Yellowstone would present no difficulties in fording, and our foreman was anxious to make a long drive that day so as to make up for our enforced lay-over. We had breakfasted by the time the horses were corralled, and when we overtook the grazing herd, the cattle were within a mile of the river. Flood had looked over the ford the day before, and took one point of the herd as we went down into the crossing. The water was quite chilly to the cattle, though the horses in the lead paid little attention to it, the water in no place being over three feet deep. A number of spectators had come up from Frenchman's to watch the herd ford, the crossing being about half a mile above the village. No one made any inquiry for Priest, though ample opportunity was given them to see that the gray-haired man was missing. After the herd had crossed, a number of us lent a rope in assisting the wagon over, and when we reached the farther bank, we waved our hats to the group on the south side in farewell to them and to Frenchman's Ford.

The trail on leaving the river led up Many Berries, one of the tributaries of the Yellowstone putting in from the north side; and we paralleled it mile after mile. It was with difficulty that riders could be kept on the right hand side of the herd, for along it grew endless quantities of a species of upland huckleberry, and, breaking off branches, we feasted as we rode along. The grade up this creek was quite pronounced, for before night the channel of the creek had narrowed to several yards in width. On the second day out the wild fruit disappeared early in the morning, and after a continued gradual climb, we made camp that night on the summit of the divide within plain sight of the Musselshell River. From this divide there was a splendid view of the surrounding country as far as eye could see. To our right, as we neared the summit, we could see in that rarefied atmosphere the buttes, like sentinels on duty, as they dotted the immense tableland between the Yellowstone and the mother Missouri, while on our left lay a thousand hills, untenanted save by the deer, elk, and a remnant of buffalo. Another half day's drive brought us to the shoals on the Musselshell, about twelve miles above the entrance of Flatwillow Creek. It was one of the easiest crossings we had encountered in many a day, considering the size of the river and the flow of water. Long before the advent of the white man, these shoals had been in use for generations by the immense herds of buffalo and elk migrating back and forth between their summer ranges and winter pasturage, as the converging game trails on either side indicated. It was also an old Indian ford. After crossing and resuming our afternoon drive, the cattle trail ran within a mile of the river, and had it not been for the herd of northern wintered cattle, and possibly others, which had passed along a month or more in advance of us, it would have been hard to determine which were cattle and which were game trails, the country being literally cut up with these pathways.

When within a few miles of the Flatwillow, the trail bore off to the northwest, and we camped that night some distance below the junction of the former creek with the Big Box Elder. Before our watch had been on guard twenty minutes that night, we heard some one whistling in the distance; and as whoever it was refused to come any nearer the herd, a thought struck me, and I rode out into the darkness and hailed him.

"Is that you, Tom?" came the question to my challenge, and the next minute I was wringing the hand of my old bunkie, The Rebel. I assured him that the coast was clear, and that no inquiry had been even made for him the following morning, when crossing the Yellowstone, by any of the inhabitants of Frenchman's Ford. He returned with me to the bed ground, and meeting Honeyman as he circled around, was almost unhorsed by the latter's warmth of reception, and Officer's delight on meeting my bunkie was none the less demonstrative. For nearly half an hour he rode around with one or the other of us, and as we knew he had had little if any sleep for the last three nights, all of us begged him to go on into camp and go to sleep. But the old rascal loafed around with us on guard, seemingly delighted with our company and reluctant to leave. Finally Honeyman and I prevailed on him to go to the wagon, but before leaving us he said, "Why, I've been in sight of the herd for the last day and night, but I'm getting a little tired of lying out with the dry cattle these cool nights, and living on huckleberries and grouse, so I thought I'd just ride in and get a fresh horse and a square meal once more. But if Flood says stay, you'll see me at my old place on the point to-morrow."

Had the owner of the herd suddenly appeared in camp, he could not have received such an ovation as was extended Priest the next morning when his presence became known. From the cook to the foreman, they gathered around our bed, where The Rebel sat up in the blankets and held an informal reception; and two hours afterward he was riding on the right point of the herd as if nothing had happened. We had a fair trail up Big Box Elder, and for the following few days, or until the source of that creek was reached, met nothing to check our course. Our foreman had been riding in advance of the herd, and after returning to us at noon one day, reported that the trail turned a due northward course towards the Missouri, and all herds had seemingly taken it. As we had to touch at Fort Benton, which was almost due westward, he had concluded to quit the trail and try to intercept the military road running from Fort Maginnis to Benton. Maginnis lay to the south of us, and our foreman hoped to strike the military road at an angle on as near a westward course as possible.

Accordingly after dinner he set out to look out the country, and took me with him. We bore off toward the Missouri, and within half an hour's ride after leaving the trail we saw some loose horses about three miles distant, down in a little valley through which flowed a creek towards the Musselshell. We reined in and watched the horses several minutes, when we both agreed from their movements that they were hobbled. We scouted out some five or six miles, finding the country somewhat rough, but passable for a herd and wagon. Flood was anxious to investigate those hobbled horses, for it bespoke the camp of some one in the immediate vicinity. On our return, the horses were still in view, and with no little difficulty, we descended from the mesa into the valley and reached them. To our agreeable surprise, one of them was wearing a bell, while nearly half of them were hobbled, there being twelve head, the greater portion of which looked like pack horses. Supposing the camp, if there was one, must be up in the hills, we followed a bridle path up stream in search of it, and soon came upon four men, placer mining on the banks of the creek.

When we made our errand known, one of these placer miners, an elderly man who seemed familiar with the country, expressed some doubts about our leaving the trail, though he said there was a bridle path with which he was acquainted across to the military road. Flood at once offered to pay him well if he would pilot us across to the road, or near enough so that we could find our way. The old placerman hesitated, and after consulting among his partners, asked how we were fixed for provision, explaining that they wished to remain a month or so longer, and that game had been scared away from the immediate vicinity, until it had become hard to secure meat. But he found Flood ready in that quarter, for he immediately offered to kill a beef and load down any two pack horses they had, if he would consent to pilot us over to within striking distance of the Fort Benton road. The offer was immediately accepted, and I was dispatched to drive in their horses. Two of the placer miners accompanied us back to the trail, both riding good saddle horses and leading two others under pack saddles. We overtook the herd within a mile of the point where the trail was to be abandoned, and after sending the wagon ahead, our foreman asked our guests to pick out any cow or steer in the herd. When they declined, he cut out a fat stray cow which had come into the herd down on the North Platte, had her driven in after the wagon, killed and quartered. When we had laid the quarters on convenient rocks to cool and harden during the night, our future pilot timidly inquired what we proposed to do with the hide, and on being informed that he was welcome to it, seemed delighted, remarking, as I helped him to stake it out where it would dry, that "rawhide was mighty handy repairing pack saddles."

Our visitors interested us, for it is probable that not a man in our outfit had ever seen a miner before, though we had read of the life and were deeply interested in everything they did or said. They were very plain men and of simple manners, but we had great difficulty in getting them to talk. After supper, while idling away a couple of hours around our camp-fire, the outfit told stories, in the hope that our guests would become reminiscent and give us some insight into their experiences, Bob Blades leading off.

"I was in a cow town once up on the head of the Chisholm trail at a time when a church fair was being pulled off. There were lots of old long-horn cowmen living in the town, who owned cattle in that Cherokee Strip that Officer is always talking about. Well, there's lots of folks up there that think a nigger is as good as anybody else, and when you find such people set in their ways, it's best not to argue matters with them, but lay low and let on you think that way too. That's the way those old Texas cowmen acted about it.

"Well, at this church fair there was to be voted a prize of a nice baby wagon, which had been donated by some merchant, to the prettiest baby under a year old. Colonel Bob Zellers was in town at the time, stopping at a hotel where the darky cook was a man who had once worked for him on the trail. 'Frog,' the darky, had married when he quit the colonel's service, and at the time of this fair there was a pickaninny in his family about a year old, and nearly the color of a new saddle. A few of these old cowmen got funny and thought it would be a good joke to have Frog enter his baby at the fair, and Colonel Bob being the leader in the movement, he had no trouble convincing the darky that that baby wagon was his, if he would only enter his youngster. Frog thought the world of the old Colonel, and the latter assured him that he would vote for his baby while he had a dollar or a cow left. The result was, Frog gave his enthusiastic consent, and the Colonel agreed to enter the pickaninny in the contest.

"Well, the Colonel attended to the entering of the baby's name, and then on the dead quiet went around and rustled up every cowman and puncher in town, and had them promise to be on hand, to vote for the prettiest baby at ten cents a throw. The fair was being held in the largest hall in town, and at the appointed hour we were all on hand, as well as Frog and his wife and baby. There were about a dozen entries, and only one blackbird in the covey. The list of contestants was read by the minister, and as each name was announced, there was a vigorous clapping of hands all over the house by the friends of each baby. But when the name of Miss Precilla June Jones was announced, the Texas contingent made their presence known by such a deafening outburst of applause that old Frog grinned from ear to ear — he saw himself right then pushing that baby wagon.

"Well, on the first heat we voted sparingly, and as the vote was read out about every quarter hour, Precilla June Jones on the first turn was fourth in the race. On the second report, our favorite had moved up to third place, after which the weaker ones were deserted, and all the voting blood was centered on the two white leaders, with our blackbird a close third. We were behaving ourselves nicely, and our money was welcome if we weren't. When the third vote was announced, Frog's pickaninny was second in the race, with her nose lapped on the flank of the leader. Then those who thought a darky was as good as any one else got on the prod in a mild form, and you could hear them voicing their opinions all over the hall. We heard it all, but sat as nice as pie and never said a word.

"When the final vote was called for, we knew it was the home stretch, and every rascal of us got his weasel skin out and sweetened the voting on Miss Precilla June Jones. Some of those old long-horns didn't think any more of a twenty-dollar gold piece than I do of a white chip, especially when there was a chance to give those good people a dose of their own medicine. I don't know how many votes we cast on the last whirl, but we swamped all opposition, and our favorite cantered under the wire an easy winner. Then you should have heard the kicking, but we kept still and inwardly chuckled. The minister announced the winner, and some of those good people didn't have any better manners than to hiss and cut up ugly. We stayed until Frog got the new baby wagon in his clutches, when we dropped out casually and met at the

Ranch saloon, where Colonel Zellers had taken possession behind the bar and was dispensing hospitality in proper celebration of his victory."

Much to our disappointment, our guests remained silent and showed no disposition to talk, except to answer civil questions which Flood asked regarding the trail crossing on the Missouri, and what that river was like in the vicinity of old Fort Benton. When the questions had been answered, they again relapsed into silence. The fire was replenished, and after the conversation had touched on several subjects, Joe Stallings took his turn with a yarn.

"When my folks first came to Texas," said Joe, "they settled in Ellis County, near Waxahachie. My father was one of the pioneers in that county at a time when his nearest neighbor lived ten miles from his front gate. But after the war, when the country had settled up, these old pioneers naturally hung together and visited and chummed with one another in preference to the new settlers. One spring when I was about fifteen years old, one of those old pioneer neighbors of ours died, and my father decided that he would go to the funeral or burst a hame string. If any of you know anything about that black-waxy, hog-wallow land in Ellis County, you know that when it gets muddy in the spring a wagon wheel will fill solid with waxy mud. So at the time of this funeral it was impossible to go on the road with any kind of a vehicle, and my father had to go on horseback. He was an old man at the time and didn't like the idea, but it was either go on horseback or stay at home, and go he would.

"They raise good horses in Ellis County, and my father had raised some of the best of them — brought the stock from Tennessee. He liked good blood in a horse, and was always opposed to racing, but he raised some boys who weren't. I had a number of brothers older than myself, and they took a special pride in trying every colt we raised, to see what he amounted to in speed. Of course this had to be done away from home; but that was easy, for these older brothers thought nothing of riding twenty miles to a tournament, barbecue, or round-up, and when away from home they always tried their horses with the best in the country. At the time of this funeral, we had a crackerjack five year old chestnut sorrel gelding that could show his heels to any horse in the country. He was a peach, — you could turn him on a saddle blanket and jump him fifteen feet, and that cow never lived that he couldn't cut.

"So the day of the funeral my father was in a quandary as to which horse to ride, but when he appealed to his boys, they recommended the best on the ranch, which was the chestnut gelding. My old man had some doubts as to his ability to ride the horse, for he hadn't been on a horse's back for years; but my brothers assured him that the chestnut was as obedient as a kitten, and that before he had been on the road an hour the mud would take all the frisk and frolic out of him. There was nearly fifteen miles to go, and they assured him that he would never get there if he rode any other horse. Well, at last he consented to ride the gelding, and the horse was made ready, properly groomed, his tail tied up, and saddled and led up to the block. It took every member of the family to get my father rigged to start, but at last he announced himself as ready. Two of my brothers held the horse until he found the off stirrup, and then they turned him loose. The chestnut danced off a few rods, and settled down into a steady clip that was good for five or six miles an hour.

"My father reached the house in good time for the funeral services, but when the procession started for the burial ground, the horse was somewhat restless and impatient from the cold. There was quite a string of wagons and other vehicles from the immediate neighborhood which had braved the mud, and the line was nearly half a mile in length between the house and the graveyard. There were also possibly a hundred men on horseback bringing up the rear of the procession; and the chestnut, not understanding the solemnity of the occasion, was right on his mettle. Surrounded as he was by other horses, he kept his weather eye open for a race, for in coming home from dances and picnics with my brothers, he had often been tried in short dashes of half a mile or so. In order to get him out of the crowd of horses, my father dropped back with another pioneer to the extreme rear of the funeral line.

"When the procession was nearing the cemetery, a number of horsemen, who were late, galloped up in the rear. The chestnut, supposing a race was on, took the bit in his teeth and tore down past the procession as though it was a free-for-all Texas sweepstakes, the old man's white beard whipping the breeze in his endeavor to hold in the horse. Nor did he check him until the head of the procession had been passed. When my father returned home that night, there was a family round-up, for he was smoking under the collar. Of course, my brothers denied having ever run the horse, and my mother took their part; but the old gent knew a thing or two about horses, and shortly afterwards he got even with his boys by selling the chestnut, which broke their hearts properly."

The elder of the two placer miners, a long-whiskered, pock-marked man, arose, and after walking out from the fire some distance returned and called our attention to signs in the sky, which he assured us were a sure indication of a change in the weather. But we were more anxious that he should talk about something else, for we were in the habit of taking the weather just as it came. When neither one showed any disposition to talk, Flood said to them, —

"It's bedtime with us, and one of you can sleep with me, while I 've fixed up an extra bed for the other. I generally get out about daybreak, but if that's too early for you, don't let my getting up disturb you. And you fourth guard men, let the cattle off the bed ground on a due westerly course and point them up the divide. Now get to bed, everybody, for we want to make a big drive tomorrow."

CHAPTER XXIII
DELIVERY

I shall never forget the next morning, — August 26, 1882. As we of the third guard were relieved, about two hours before dawn, the wind veered around to the northwest, and a mist which had been falling during the fore part of our watch changed to soft flakes of snow. As soon as we were relieved, we skurried back to our blankets, drew the tarpaulin over our heads, and slept until dawn, when on being awakened by the foreman, we found a wet, slushy snow some two inches in depth on the ground. Several of the boys in the outfit declared it was the first snowfall they had ever seen, and I had but a slight recollection of having witnessed one in early boyhood in our old Georgia home. We gathered around the fire like a lot of frozen children, and our only solace was that our drive was nearing an end. The two placermen paid little heed to the raw morning, and our pilot assured us that this was but the squaw winter which always preceded Indian summer.

We made our customary early start, and while saddling up that morning, Flood and the two placer miners packed the beef on their two pack horses, first cutting off enough to last us several days. The cattle, when we overtook them, presented a sorry spectacle, apparently being as cold as we were, although we had our last stitch of clothing on, including our slickers, belted with a horse hobble. But when Flood and our guide rode past the herd, I noticed our pilot's coat was not even buttoned, nor was the thin cotton shirt which he wore, but his chest was exposed to that raw morning air which chilled the very marrow in our bones. Our foreman and guide kept in sight in the lead, the herd traveling briskly up the long mountain divide, and about the middle of the forenoon the sun came out warm and the snow began to melt. Within an hour after starting that morning, Quince Forrest, who was riding in front of me in the swing, dismounted, and picking out of the snow a brave little flower which looked something like a pansy, dropped back to me and said, "My weather gauge says it's eighty-eight degrees below freezo. But I want you to smell this posy, Quirk, and tell me on the dead thieving, do you ever expect to see your sunny southern home again? And did you notice the pock-marked colonel, baring his brisket to the morning breeze?"

Two hours after the sun came out, the snow had disappeared, and the cattle fell to and grazed until long after the noon hour. Our pilot led us up the divide between the Missouri and the headwaters of the Musselshell during the afternoon, weaving in and out around the heads of creeks putting into either river; and towards evening we crossed quite a creek running towards the Missouri, where we secured ample water for the herd. We made a late camp that night, and our guide assured us that another half day's drive would put us on the Judith River, where we would intercept the Fort Benton road.

The following morning our guide led us for several hours up a gradual ascent to the plateau, till we reached the tableland, when he left us to return to his own camp. Flood again took the lead, and within a mile we turned on our regular course, which by early noon had descended into the valley of the Judith River, and entered the Fort Maginnis and Benton military road. Our route was now clearly defined, and about noon on the last day of the month we sighted, beyond the Missouri River, the flag floating over Fort Benton. We made a crossing that afternoon below the Fort, and Flood went into the post, expecting either to meet Lovell or to receive our final instructions regarding the delivery.

After crossing the Missouri, we grazed the herd over to the Teton River, a stream which paralleled the former watercourse, — the military post being located between the two. We had encamped for the night when Flood returned with word of a letter he had received from our employer and an interview he had had with the commanding officer of Fort Benton, who, it seemed, was to have a hand in the delivery of the herd. Lovell had been detained in the final settlement of my brother Bob's herd at the Crow Agency by some differences regarding weights. Under our present instructions, we were to proceed slowly to the Blackfoot Agency, and immediately on the arrival of Lovell at Benton, he and the commandant would follow by ambulance and overtake us. The distance from Fort Benton to the agency was variously reported to be from one hundred and twenty to one hundred and thirty miles, six or seven days' travel for the herd at the farthest, and then good-by, Circle Dots!

A number of officers and troopers from the post overtook us the next morning and spent several hours with us as the herd trailed out up the Teton. They were riding fine horses, which made our through saddle stock look insignificant in comparison, though had they covered twenty-four hundred miles and lived on grass as had our mounts, some of the lustre of their glossy coats would have been absent. They looked well, but it would have been impossible to use them or any domestic bred horses in trail work like ours, unless a supply of grain could be carried with us. The range country produced a horse suitable to range needs, hardy and a good forager, which, when not overworked under the saddle, met every requirement of his calling, as well as being self-sustaining. Our horses, in fact, were in better flesh when we crossed the Missouri than they were the day we received the herd on the Rio Grande. The spectators from the fort quitted us near the middle of the forenoon, and we snailed on westward at our leisurely gait.

There was a fair road up the Teton, which we followed for several days without incident, to the forks of that river, where we turned up Muddy Creek, the north fork of the Teton. That noon, while catching saddle horses, dinner not being quite ready, we noticed a flurry amongst the cattle, then almost a mile in our rear. Two men were on herd with them as usual, grazing them forward up the creek and watering as they came, when suddenly the cattle in the lead came tearing out of the creek, and on reaching open ground turned at bay. After several bunches had seemingly taken fright at the same object, we noticed Bull Durham, who was on herd, ride through the cattle to the scene of disturbance. We saw him, on nearing the spot, lie down on the neck of his horse, watch intently for several minutes, then quietly drop back to the rear, circle the herd, and ride for the wagon. We had been observing the proceedings closely, though from a distance, for some time. Daylight was evidently all that saved us from a stampede, and as Bull Durham galloped up he was almost breathless. He informed us that an old cinnamon bear and two cubs were berrying along the creek, and had taken the right of way. Then there was a hustling and borrowing of cartridges, while saddles were cinched on to horses as though human life depended on alacrity. We were all feeling quite gala anyhow, and this looked like a chance for some sport. It was hard to hold the impulsive ones in check until the others were ready. The cattle pointed us to the location of the quarry as we rode forward. When within a quarter of a mile, we separated into two squads, in order to gain the rear of the bears, cut them off from the creek, and force them into the open. The cattle held the attention of the bears until we had gained their rear, and as we came up between them and the creek, the old one reared up on her haunches and took a most astonished and innocent look at us.

A single "woof" brought one of the cubs to her side, and she dropped on all fours and lumbered off, a half dozen shots hastening her pace in an effort to circle the horsemen who were gradually closing in. In making this circle to gain the protection of some thickets which skirted the creek, she was compelled to cross quite an open space, and before she had covered the distance of fifty yards, a rain of ropes came down on her, and she was thrown backward with no less than four lariats fastened over her neck and fore parts. Then ensued a lively scene, for the horses snorted and in spite of rowels refused to face the bear. But ropes securely snubbed to pommels held them to the quarry. Two minor circuses were meantime in progress with the two cubs, but pressure of duty held those of us who had fastened on to the old cinnamon. The ropes were taut and several of them were about her throat; the horses were pulling in as many different directions, yet the strain of all the lariats failed to choke her as we expected. At this juncture, four of the loose men came to our rescue, and proposed shooting the brute. We were willing enough, for though we had better than a tail hold, we were very ready to let go. But while there were plenty of good shots among us, our horses had now become wary, and could not, when free from ropes, be induced to approach within twenty yards of the bear, and they were so fidgety that accurate aim was impossible. We who had ropes on the old bear begged the boys to get down and take it afoot, but they were not disposed to listen to our reasons, and blazed away from rearing horses, not one shot in ten taking effect. There was no telling how long this random shooting would have lasted; but one shot cut my rope two feet from the noose, and with one rope less on her the old bear made some ugly surges, and had not Joe Stallings had a wheeler of a horse on the rope, she would have done somebody damage.

The Rebel was on the opposite side from Stallings and myself, and as soon as I was freed, he called me around to him, and shifting his rope to me, borrowed my six-shooter and joined those who were shooting. Dismounting, he gave the reins of his horse to Flood, walked up to within fifteen steps of mother bruin, and kneeling, emptied both six-shooters with telling accuracy. The old bear winced at nearly every shot, and once she made an ugly surge on the ropes, but the three guy lines held her up to Priest's deliberate aim. The vitality of that cinnamon almost staggers belief, for after both six-shooters had been emptied into her body, she floundered on the ropes with all her former strength, although the blood was dripping and gushing from her numerous wounds. Borrowing a third gun, Priest returned to the fight, and as we slacked the ropes slightly, the old bear reared, facing her antagonist. The Rebel emptied his third gun into her before she sank, choked, bleeding, and exhausted, to the ground; and even then no one dared to approach her, for she struck out wildly with all fours as she slowly succumbed to the inevitable.

One of the cubs had been roped and afterwards shot at close quarters, while the other had reached the creek and climbed a sapling which grew on the bank, when a few shots brought him to the ground. The two cubs were about the size of a small black bear, though the mother was a large specimen of her species. The cubs had nice coats of soft fur, and their hides were taken as trophies of the fight, but the robe of the mother was a summer one and worthless. While we were skinning the cubs, the foreman called our attention to the fact that the herd had drifted up the creek nearly opposite the wagon. During the encounter with the bears he was the most excited one in the outfit, and was the man who cut my rope with his random shooting from horseback. But now the herd recovered his attention, and he dispatched some of us to ride around the cattle. When we met at the wagon for dinner, the excitement was still on us, and the hunt was unanimously voted the most exciting bit of sport and powder burning we had experienced on our trip.

Late that afternoon a forage wagon from Fort Benton passed us with four loose ambulance mules in charge of five troopers, who were going on ahead to establish a relay station in anticipation of the trip of the post commandant to the Blackfoot Agency. There were to be two relay stations between the post and the agency, and this detachment expected to go into camp that night within forty miles of our destination, there to await the arrival of the commanding officer and the owner of the herd at Benton. These soldiers were out two days from the post when they passed us, and they assured us that the ambulance would go through from Benton to Blackfoot without a halt, except for the changing of relay teams. The next forenoon we passed the last relay camp, well up the Muddy, and shortly afterwards the road left that creek, turning north by a little west, and we entered on the last tack of our long drive. On the evening of the 6th of September, as we were going into camp on Two Medicine Creek, within ten miles of the agency, the ambulance overtook us, under escort of the troopers whom we had passed at the last relay station. We had not seen Don Lovell since June, when we passed Dodge, and it goes without saying that we were glad to meet him again. On the arrival of the party, the cattle had not yet been bedded, so Lovell borrowed a horse, and with Flood took a look over the herd before darkness set in, having previously prevailed on the commanding officer to rest an hour and have supper before proceeding to the agency.

When they returned from inspecting the cattle, the commandant and Lovell agreed to make the final delivery on the 8th, if it were agreeable to the agent, and with this understanding continued their journey. The next morning Flood rode into the agency, borrowing McCann's saddle and taking an extra horse with him, having left us instructions to graze the herd all day and have them in good shape with grass and water, in case they were inspected that evening on their condition. Near the middle of the afternoon quite a cavalcade rode out from the agency, including part of a company of cavalry temporarily encamped there. The Indian agent and the commanding officer from Benton were the authorized representatives of the government, it seemed, as Lovell took extra pains in showing them over the herd, frequently consulting the contract which he held, regarding sex, age, and flesh of the cattle.

The only hitch in the inspection was over a number of sore-footed cattle, which was unavoidable after such a long journey. But the condition of these tender-footed animals being otherwise satisfactory, Lovell urged the agent and commandant to call up the men for explanations. The agent was no doubt a very nice man, and there may have been other things that he understood better than cattle, for he did ask a great many simple, innocent questions. Our replies, however, might have been condensed into a few simple statements. We had, we related, been over five months on the trail; after the first month, tender-footed cattle began to appear from time to time in the herd, as stony or gravelly portions of the trail were encountered, — the number so affected at any one time varying from ten to forty head. Frequently well-known lead cattle became tender in their feet and would drop back to the rear, and on striking soft or sandy footing recover and resume their position in the lead; that since starting, it was safe to say, fully ten per cent of the entire herd had been so affected, yet we had not lost a single head from this cause; that the general health of the animal was never affected, and that during enforced layovers nearly all so affected recovered. As there were not over twenty-five sore-footed animals in the herd on our arrival, our explanation was sufficient and the herd was accepted. There yet remained the counting and classification, but as this would require time, it went over until the following day. The cows had been contracted for by the head, while the steers went on their estimated weight in dressed beef, the contract calling for a million pounds with a ten per cent leeway over that amount.

I was amongst the first to be interviewed by the Indian agent, and on being excused, I made the acquaintance of one of two priests who were with the party. He was a rosy-cheeked, well-fed old padre, who informed me that he had been stationed among the Blackfeet for over twenty years, and that he had labored long with the government to assist these Indians. The cows in our herd, which were to be distributed amongst the Indian families for domestic purposes, were there at his earnest solicitation. I asked him if these cows would not perish during the long winter — my recollection was still vivid of the touch of squaw winter we had experienced some two weeks previous. But he assured me that the winters were dry, if cold, and his people had made some progress in the ways of civilization, and had provided shelter and forage against the wintry weather. He informed me that previous to his labors amongst the Blackfeet their ponies wintered without loss on the native grasses, though he had since taught them to make hay, and in anticipation of receiving these cows, such families as were entitled to share in the division had amply provided for the animals' sustenance.

Lovell returned with the party to the agency, and we were to bring up the herd for classification early in the morning. Flood informed us that a beef pasture had been built that summer for the steers, while the cows would be held under herd by the military, pending their distribution. We spent our last night with the herd singing songs, until the first guard called the relief, when realizing the lateness of the hour, we burrowed into our blankets.

"I don't know how you fellows feel about it," said Quince Forrest, when the first guard were relieved and they had returned to camp, "but I bade those cows good-by on their beds to-night without a regret or a tear. The novelty of night-herding loses its charm with me when it's drawn out over five months. I might be fool enough to make another such trip, but I'd rather be the Indian and let the other fellow drive the cows to me — there's a heap more comfort in it."

The next morning, before we reached the agency, a number of gaudily bedecked bucks and squaws rode out to meet us. The arrival of the herd had been expected for several weeks, and our approach was a delight to the Indians, who were flocking to the agency from the nearest villages. Physically, they were fine specimens of the aborigines. But our Spanish, which Quarternight and I tried on them, was as unintelligible to them as their guttural gibberish was to us.

Lovell and the agent, with a detachment of the cavalry, met us about a mile from the agency buildings, and we were ordered to cut out the cows. The herd had been grazed to contentment, and were accordingly rounded in, and the task begun at once. Our entire outfit were turned into the herd to do the work, while an abundance of troopers held the herd and looked after the cut. It took about an hour and a half, during which time we worked like Trojans. Cavalrymen several times attempted to assist us, but their horses were no match for ours in the work. A cow can turn on much less space than a cavalry horse, and except for the amusement they afforded, the military were of very little effect.

After we had retrimmed the cut, the beeves were started for their pasture, and nothing now remained but the counting to complete the receiving. Four of us remained behind with the cows, but for over two hours the steers were in plain sight, while the two parties were endeavoring to make a count. How many times they recounted them before agreeing on the numbers I do not know, for the four of us left with the cows became occupied by a controversy over the sex of a young Indian — a Blackfoot — riding a cream-colored pony. The controversy originated between Fox Quarternight and Bob Blades, who had discovered this swell among a band who had just ridden in from the west, and John Officer and myself were appealed to for our opinions. The Indian was pointed out to us across the herd, easily distinguished by beads and beaver fur trimmings in the hair, so we rode around to pass our judgment as experts on the beauty. The young Indian was not over sixteen years of age, with remarkable features, from which every trace of the aborigine seemed to be eliminated. Officer and myself were in a quandary, for we felt perfectly competent when appealed to for our opinions on such a delicate subject, and we made every endeavor to open a conversation by signs and speech. But the young Blackfoot paid no attention to us, being intent upon watching the cows. The neatly moccasined feet and the shapely hand, however, indicated the feminine, and when Blades and Quarter-night rode up, we rendered our decision accordingly. Blades took exception to the decision and rode alongside the young Indian, pretending to admire the long plaits of hair, toyed with the beads, pinched and patted the young Blackfoot, and finally, although the rest of us, for fear the Indian might take offense and raise trouble, pleaded with him to desist, he called the youth his "squaw," when the young blood, evidently understanding the appellation, relaxed into a broad smile, and in fair English said, "Me buck."

Blades burst into a loud laugh at his success, at which the Indian smiled but accepted a cigarette, and the two cronied together, while we rode away to look after our cows. The outfit returned shortly afterward, when The Rebel rode up to me and expressed himself rather profanely at the inability of the government's representatives to count cattle in Texas fashion. On the arrival of the agent and others, the cows were brought around; and these being much more gentle, and being under Lovell's instruction fed between the counters in the narrowest file possible, a satisfactory count was agreed upon at the first trial. The troopers took charge of the cows after counting, and, our work over, we galloped away to the wagon, hilarious and care free.

McCann had camped on the nearest water to the agency, and after dinner we caught out the top horses, and, dressed in our best, rode into the agency proper. There was quite a group of houses for the attachés, one large general warehouse, and several school and chapel buildings. I again met the old padre, who showed us over the place. One could not help being favorably impressed with the general neatness and cleanliness of the place. In answer to our questions, the priest informed us that he had mastered the Indian language early in his work, and had adopted it in his ministry, the better to effect the object of his mission. There was something touching in the zeal of this devoted padre in his work amongst the tribe, and the recognition of the government had come as a fitting climax to his work and devotion.

As we rode away from the agency, the cows being in sight under herd of a dozen soldiers, several of us rode out to them, and learned that they intended to corral the cows at night, and within a week distribute them to Indian families, when the troop expected to return to Fort Benton. Lovell and Flood appeared at the camp about dusk — Lovell in high spirits. This, he said, was the easiest delivery of the three herds which he had driven that year. He was justified in feeling well over the year's drive, for he had in his possession a voucher for our Circle Dots which would crowd six figures closely. It was a gay night with us, for man and horse were free, and as we made down our beds, old man Don insisted that Flood and he should make theirs down alongside ours. He and The Rebel had been joking each other during the evening, and as we went to bed were taking an occasional fling at one another as opportunity offered.

"It's a strange thing to me," said Lovell, as he was pulling off his boots, "that this herd counted out a hundred and twelve head more than we started with, while Bob Quirk's herd was only eighty-one long at the final count;"

"Well, you see," replied The Rebel, "Quirk's was a steer herd, while ours had over a thousand cows in it, and you must make allowance for some of them to calve on the way. That ought to be easy figuring for a foxy, long-headed Yank like you."

CHAPTER XXIV
BACK TO TEXAS

The nearest railroad point from the Blackfoot Agency was Silver Bow, about a hundred and seventy-five miles due south, and at that time the terminal of the Utah Northern Railroad. Everything connected with the delivery having been completed the previous day, our camp was astir with the dawn in preparation for departure on our last ride together. As we expected to make not less than forty miles a day on the way to the railroad, our wagon was lightened to the least possible weight. The chuck-box, water kegs, and such superfluities were dropped, and the supplies reduced to one week's allowance, while beds were overhauled and extra wearing apparel of the outfit was discarded. Who cared if we did sleep cold and hadn't a change to our backs? We were going home and would have money in our pockets.

"The first thing I do when we strike that town of Silver Bow," said Bull Durham, as he was putting on his last shirt, "is to discard to the skin and get me new togs to a finish. I'll commence on my little pattering feet, which will require fifteen-dollar moccasins, and then about a six-dollar checked cottonade suit, and top off with a seven-dollar brown Stetson. Then with a few drinks under my belt and a rim-fire cigar in my mouth, I'd admire to meet the governor of Montana if convenient."

Before the sun was an hour high, we bade farewell to the Blackfoot Agency and were doubling back over the trail, with Lovell in our company. Our first night's camp was on the Muddy and the second on the Sun River. We were sweeping across the tablelands adjoining the main divide of the Rocky Mountains like the chinook winds which sweep that majestic range on its western slope. We were a free outfit; even the cook and wrangler were relieved; their little duties were divided among the crowd and almost disappeared. There was a keen rivalry over driving the wagon, and McCann was transferred to the hurricane deck of a cow horse, which he sat with ease and grace, having served an apprenticeship in the saddle in other days. There were always half a dozen wranglers available in the morning, and we traveled as if under forced marching orders. The third night we camped in the narrows between the Missouri River and the Rocky Mountains, and on the evening of the fourth day camped several miles to the eastward of Helena, the capital of the territory.

Don Lovell had taken the stage for the capital the night before; and on making camp that evening, Flood took a fresh horse and rode into town. The next morning he and Lovell returned with the superintendent of the cattle company which had contracted for our horses and outfit on the Republican. We corralled the horses for him, and after roping out about a dozen which, as having sore backs or being lame, he proposed to treat as damaged and take at half price, the *remuda* was counted out, a hundred and forty saddle horses, four mules, and a wagon constituting the transfer. Even with the loss of two horses and the concessions on a dozen others, there was a nice profit on the entire outfit over its cost in the lower country, due to the foresight of Don Lovell in mounting us well. Two of our fellows who had borrowed from the superintendent money to redeem their six-shooters after the horse race on the Republican, authorized Lovell to return him the loans and thanked him for the favor. Everything being satisfactory between buyer and seller, they returned to town together for a settlement, while we moved on south towards Silver Bow, where the outfit was to be delivered.

Another day's easy travel brought us to within a mile of the railroad terminus; but it also brought us to one of the hardest experiences of our trip, for each of us knew, as we unsaddled our horses, that we were doing it for the last time. Although we were in the best of spirits over the successful conclusion of the drive; although we were glad to be free from herd duty and looked forward eagerly to the journey home, there was still a feeling of regret in our hearts which we could not dispel. In the days of my boyhood I have shed tears when a favorite horse was sold from our little ranch on the San Antonio, and have frequently witnessed Mexican children unable to hide their grief when need of bread had compelled the sale of some favorite horse to a passing drover. But at no time in my life, before or since, have I felt so keenly the parting between man and horse as I did that September evening in Montana. For on the trail an affection springs up between a man and his mount which is almost human. Every privation which he endures his horse endures with him, — carrying him through falling weather, swimming rivers by day and riding in the lead of stampedes by night, always faithful, always willing, and always patiently enduring every hardship, from exhausting hours under saddle to the sufferings of a dry drive. And on this drive, covering nearly three thousand miles, all the ties which can exist between man and beast had not only become cemented, but our *remuda* as a whole had won the affection of both men and employer for carrying without serious mishap a valuable herd all the way from the Rio Grande to the Blackfoot Agency. Their hones may be bleaching in some coulee by now, but the men who knew them then can never forget them or the part they played in that long drive.

Three men from the ranch rode into our camp that evening, and the next morning we counted over our horses to them and they passed into strangers' hands. That there might he no delay, Flood had ridden into town the evening before and secured a wagon and gunny bags in which to sack our saddles; for while we willingly discarded all other effects, our saddles were of sufficient value to return and could be checked home as baggage. Our foreman reported that Lovell had arrived by stage and was awaiting us in town, having already arranged for our transportation as far as Omaha, and would accompany us to that city, where other transportation would have to be secured to our destination. In our impatience to get into town, we were trudging in by twos and threes before the wagon arrived for our saddles, and had not Flood remained behind to look after them, they might have been abandoned.

There was something about Silver Bow that reminded me of Frenchman's Ford on the Yellowstone. Being the terminal of the first railroad into Montana, it became the distributing point for all the western portion of that territory, and immense ox trains were in sight for the transportation of goods to remoter points in the north and west. The population too was very much the same as at Frenchman's, though the town in general was an improvement over the former, there being some stability to its buildings. As we were to leave on an eleven o'clock train, we had little opportunity to see the town, and for the short time at our disposal, barber shops and clothing stores claimed our first attention. Most of us had some remnants of money, while my bunkie was positively rich, and Lovell advanced us fifty dollars apiece, pending a final settlement on reaching our destination.

Within an hour after receiving the money, we blossomed out in new suits from head to heel. Our guard hung together as if we were still on night herd, and in the selection of clothing the opinion of the trio was equal to a purchase. The Rebel was very easily pleased in his selection, but John Officer and myself were rather fastidious. Officer was so tall it was with some little difficulty that a suit could be found to fit him, and when he had stuffed his pants in his boots and thrown away the vest, for he never wore either vest or suspenders, he emerged looking like an Alpine tourist, with his new pink shirt and nappy brown beaver slouch hat jauntily cocked over one ear. As we sauntered out into the street, Priest was dressed as became his years and mature good sense, while my costume rivaled Officer's in gaudiness, and it is safe to assert two thirds of our outlay had gone for boots and hats.

Flood overtook us in the street, and warned us to be on hand at the depot at least half an hour in advance of train time, informing us that he had checked our saddles and didn't want any of us to get left at the final moment. We all took a drink together, and Officer assured our foreman that he would be responsible for our appearance at the proper time, "sober and sorry for it." So we sauntered about the straggling village, drinking occasionally, and on the suggestion of The Rebel, made a cow by putting in five apiece and had Officer play it on faro, he claiming to be an expert on the game. Taking the purse thus made up, John sat into a game, while Priest and myself, after watching the play some minutes, strolled out again and met others of our outfit in the street, scarcely recognizable in their killing rigs. The Rebel was itching for a monte game, but this not being a cow town there was none, and we strolled next into a saloon, where a piano was being played by a venerable-looking individual, — who proved quite amiable, taking a drink with us and favoring us with a number of selections of our choosing. We were enjoying this musical treat when our foreman came in and asked us to get the boys together. Priest and I at once started for Officer, whom we found quite a winner, but succeeded in choking him off on our employer's order, and after the checks had been cashed, took a parting drink, which made us the last in reaching the depot. When we were all assembled, our employer informed us that he only wished to keep us together until embarking, and invited us to accompany him across the street to Tom Robbins's saloon.

On entering the saloon, Lovell inquired of the young fellow behind the bar, "Son, what will you take for the privilege of my entertaining this outfit for fifteen minutes?"

"The ranch is yours, sir, and you can name your own figures," smilingly and somewhat shrewdly replied the young fellow, and promptly vacated his position.

"Now, two or three of you rascals get in behind there," said old man Don, as a quartet of the boys picked him up and set him on one end of the bar, "and let's see what this ranch has in the way of refreshment."

McCann, Quarternight, and myself obeyed the order, but the fastidious tastes of the line in front soon compelled us to call to our assistance both Robbins and the young man who had just vacated the bar in our favor.

"That's right, fellows," roared Lovell from his commanding position, as he jingled a handful of gold coins, "turn to and help wait on these thirsty Texans; and remember that nothing's too rich for our blood to-day. This outfit has made one of the longest cattle drives on record, and the best is none too good for them. So set out your best, for they can't cut much hole in the profits in the short time we have to stay. The train leaves in twenty minutes, and see that every rascal is provided with an extra bottle for the journey. And drop down this way when you get time, as I want a couple of boxes of your best cigars to smoke on the way. Montana has treated us well, and we want to leave some of our coin with you."

A Texas Matchmaker

CHAPTER I
LANCE LOVELACE

When I first found employment with Lance Lovelace, a Texas cowman, I had not yet attained my majority, while he was over sixty. Though not a native of Texas, "Uncle Lance" was entitled to be classed among its pioneers, his parents having emigrated from Tennessee along with a party of Stephen F. Austin's colonists in 1821. The colony with which his people reached the state landed at Quintana, at the mouth of the Brazos River, and shared the various hardships that befell all the early Texan settlers, moving inland later to a more healthy locality. Thus the education of young Lovelace was one of privation. Like other boys in pioneer families, he became in turn a hewer of wood or drawer of water, as the necessities of the household required, in reclaiming the wilderness. When Austin hoisted the new-born Lone Star flag, and called upon the sturdy pioneers to defend it, the adventurous settlers came from every quarter of the territory, and among the first who responded to the call to arms was young Lance Lovelace. After San Jacinto, when the fighting was over and the victory won, he laid down his arms, and returned to ranching with the same zeal and energy. The first legislature assembled voted to those who had borne arms in behalf of the new republic, lands in payment for their services. With this land scrip for his pay, young Lovelace, in company with others, set out for the territory lying south of the Nueces. They were a band of daring spirits. The country was primitive and fascinated them, and they remained. Some settled on the Frio River, though the majority crossed the Nueces, many going as far south as the Rio Grande. The country was as large as the men were daring, and there was elbow room for all and to spare. Lance Lovelace located a ranch a few miles south of the Nueces River, and, from the cooing of the doves in the encinal, named it Las Palomas.

"When I first settled here in 1838," said Uncle Lance to me one morning, as we rode out across the range, "my nearest neighbor lived forty miles up the river at Fort Ewell. Of course there were some Mexican families nearer, north on the Frio, but they don't count. Say, Tom, but she was a purty country then! Why, from those hills yonder, any morning you could see a thousand antelope in a band going into the river to drink. And wild turkeys? Well, the first few years we lived here, whole flocks roosted every night in that farther point of the encinal. And in the winter these prairies were just flooded with geese and brant. If you wanted venison, all you had to do was to ride through those mesquite thickets north of the river to jump a hundred deer in a morning's ride. Oh, I tell you she was a land of plenty."

The pioneers of Texas belong to a day and generation which has almost gone. If strong arms and daring spirits were required to conquer the wilderness, Nature seemed generous in the supply; for nearly all were stalwart types of the inland viking. Lance Lovelace, when I first met him, would have passed for a man in middle life. Over six feet in height, with a rugged constitution, he little felt his threescore years, having spent his entire lifetime in the outdoor occupation of a ranchman. Living on the wild game of the country, sleeping on the ground by a camp-fire when his work required it, as much at home in the saddle as by his ranch fireside, he was a romantic type of the strenuous pioneer.

He was a man of simple tastes, true as tested steel in his friendships, with a simple honest mind which followed truth and right as unerringly as gravitation. In his domestic affairs, however, he was unfortunate. The year after locating at Las Palomas, he had returned to his former home on the Colorado River, where he had married Mary Bryan, also of the family of Austin's colonists. Hopeful and happy they returned to their new home on the Nueces, but before the first anniversary of their wedding day arrived, she, with her first born, were laid in the same grave. But grief does not kill, and the young husband bore his loss as brave men do in living out their allotted day. But to the hour of his death the memory of Mary Bryan mellowed him into a child, and, when unoccupied, with every recurring thought of her or the mere mention of her name, he would fall into deep reverie, lasting sometimes for hours. And although he contracted two marriages afterward, they were simply marriages of convenience, to which, after their termination, he frequently referred flippantly, sometimes with irreverence, for they were unhappy alliances.

On my arrival at Las Palomas, the only white woman on the ranch was "Miss Jean," a spinster sister of its owner, and twenty years his junior. After his third bitter experience in the lottery of matrimony, evidently he gave up hope, and induced his sister to come out and preside as the mistress of Las Palomas. She was not tall like her brother, but rather plump for her forty years. She had large gray eyes, with long black eyelashes, and she had a trick of looking out from under them which was both provoking and disconcerting, and no doubt many an admirer had been deceived by those same roguish, laughing eyes. Every man, Mexican and child on the ranch was the devoted courtier of Miss Jean, for she was a lovable woman; and in spite of her isolated life and the constant plaguings of her brother on being a spinster, she fitted neatly into our pastoral life. It was these teasings of her brother that gave me my first inkling that the old ranchero was a wily matchmaker, though he religiously denied every such accusation. With a remarkable complacency, Jean Lovelace met and parried her tormentor, but her brother never tired of his hobby while there was a third person to listen.

Though an unlettered man, Lance Lovelace had been a close observer of humanity. The big book of Life had been open always before him, and he had profited from its pages. With my advent at Las Palomas, there were less than half a dozen books on the ranch, among them a copy of Bret Harte's poems and a large Bible.

"That book alone," said he to several of us one chilly evening, as we sat around the open fireplace, "is the greatest treatise on humanity ever written. Go with me to-day to any city in any country in Christendom, and I'll show you a man walk up the steps of his church on Sunday who thanks God that he's better than his neighbor. But you needn't go so far if you don't want to. I reckon if I could see myself, I might show symptoms of it occasionally. Sis here thanks God daily that she is better than that Barnes girl who cut her out of Amos Alexander. Now, don't you deny it, for you know it's gospel truth! And that book is reliable on lots of other things. Take marriage, for instance. It is just as natural for men and women to mate at the proper time, as it is for steers to shed in the spring. But there's no necessity of making all this fuss about it. The Bible way discounts all these modern methods. 'He took unto himself a wife' is the way it describes such events. But now such an occurrence has to be announced, months in advance. And after the wedding is over, in less than a year sometimes, they are glad to sneak off and get the bond dissolved in some divorce court, like I did with my second wife."

All of us about the ranch, including Miss Jean, knew that the old ranchero's views on matrimony could be obtained by leading up to the question, or differing, as occasion required. So, just to hear him talk on his favorite theme, I said: "Uncle Lance, you must recollect this is a different generation. Now, I've read books" —

"So have I. But it's different in real life. Now, in those novels you have read, the poor devil is nearly worried to death for fear he'll not get her. There's a hundred things happens; he's thrown off the scent one day and cuts it again the next, and one evening he's in a heaven of bliss and before the dance ends a rival looms up and there's hell to pay, — excuse me, Sis, — but he gets her in the end. And that's the way it goes in the books. But getting down to actual cases — when the money's on the table and the game's rolling — it's as simple as picking a sire and a dam to raise a race horse. When they're both willing, it don't require any expert to see it — a one-eyed or a blind man can tell the symptoms. Now, when any of you boys get into that fix, get it over with as soon as possible."

"From the drift of your remarks," said June Deweese very innocently, "why wouldn't it be a good idea to go back to the old method of letting the parents make the matches?"

"Yes; it would be a good idea. How in the name of common sense could you expect young sap-heads like you boys to understand anything about a woman? I know what I'm talking about. A single woman never shows her true colors, but conceals her imperfections. The average man is not to be blamed if he fails to see through her smiles and Sunday humor. Now, I was forty when I married the second time, and forty-five the last whirl. Looks like I'd-had some little sense, now, don't it? But I didn't. No, I didn't have any more show than a snowball in — Sis, hadn't you better retire. You're not interested in my talk to these boys. — Well, if ever any of you want to get married you have my consent. But you'd better get my opinion on her dimples when you do. Now, with my sixty odd years, I'm worth listening to. I can take a cool, dispassionate view of a woman now, and pick every good point about her, just as if she was a cow horse that I was buying for my own saddle."

Miss Jean, who had a ready tongue for repartee, took advantage of the first opportunity to remark: "Do you know, brother, matrimony is a subject that I always enjoy hearing discussed by such an oracle as yourself. But did it never occur to you what an unjust thing it was of Providence to reveal so much to your wisdom and conceal the same from us babes?"

It took some little time for the gentle reproof to take effect, but Uncle Lance had an easy faculty of evading a question when it was contrary to his own views. "Speaking of the wisdom of babes," said he, "reminds me of what Felix York, an old '36 comrade of mine, once said. He had caught the gold fever in '49, and nothing would do but he and some others must go to California. The party went up to Independence, Missouri, where they got into an overland emigrant train, bound for the land of gold. But it seems before starting, Senator Benton had made a speech in that town, in which he made the prophecy that one day there would be a railroad connecting the Missouri River with the Pacific Ocean. Felix told me this only a few years ago. But he said that all the teamsters made the prediction a byword. When, crossing some of the mountain ranges, the train halted to let the oxen blow, one bull-whacker would say to another: 'Well, I'd like to see old Tom Benton get his railroad over *this* mountain.' When Felix told me this he said — 'There's a railroad to-day crosses those same mountain passes over which we forty-niners whacked our bulls. And to think I was a grown man and had no more sense or foresight than a little baby blinkin' its eyes in the sun.'"

With years at Las Palomas, I learned to like the old ranchero. There was something of the strong, primitive man about him which compelled a youth of my years to listen to his counsel. His confidence in me was a compliment which I appreciate to this day. When I had been in his employ hardly two years, an incident occurred which, though only one of many similar acts cementing our long friendship, tested his trust.

One morning just as he was on the point of starting on horseback to the county seat to pay his taxes, a Mexican arrived at the ranch and announced that he had seen a large band of *javalina* on the border of the chaparral up the river. Uncle Lance had promised his taxes by a certain date, but he was a true sportsman and owned a fine pack of hounds; moreover, the peccary is a migratory animal and does not wait upon the pleasure of the hunter. As I rode out from the corrals to learn what had brought the vaquero with such haste, the old ranchero cried, "Here, Tom, you'll have to go to the county seat. Buckle this money belt under your shirt, and if you lack enough gold to cover the taxes, you'll find silver here in my saddle-bags. Blow the horn, boys, and get the guns. Lead the way, Pancho. And say, Tom, better leave the road after crossing the Sordo, and strike through that mesquite country," he called back as he swung into the saddle and started, leaving me a sixty-mile ride in his stead. His warning to leave the road after crossing the creek was timely, for a ranchman had been robbed by bandits on that road the month before. But I made the ride in safety before sunset, paying the taxes, amounting to over a thousand dollars.

During all our acquaintance, extending over a period of twenty years, Lance Lovelace was a constant revelation to me, for he was original in all things. Knowing no precedent, he recognized none which had not the approval of his own conscience. Where others were content to follow, he blazed his own pathways — immaterial to him whether they were followed by others or even noticed. In his business relations and in his own way, he was exact himself and likewise exacting of others. Some there are who might criticise him for an episode which occurred about four years after my advent at Las Palomas.

Mr. Whitley Booth, a younger man and a brother-in-law of the old ranchero by his first wife, rode into the ranch one evening, evidently on important business. He was not a frequent caller, for he was also a ranchman, living about forty miles north and west on the Frio River, but was in the habit of bringing his family down to the Nueces about twice a year for a visit of from ten days to two weeks' duration. But this time, though we had been expecting the family for some little time, he came alone, remained over night, and at breakfast ordered his horse, as if expecting to return at once. The two ranchmen were holding a conference in the sitting-room when a Mexican boy came to me at the corrals and said I was wanted in the house. On my presenting myself, my employer said: "Tom, I want you as a witness to a business transaction. I'm lending Whit, here, a thousand dollars, and as we have never taken any notes between us, I merely want you as a witness. Go into my room, please, and bring out, from under my bed, one of those largest bags of silver."

The door was unlocked, and there, under the ranchero's bed, dust-covered, were possibly a dozen sacks of silver. Finding one tagged with the required amount, I brought it out and laid it on the table between the two men. But on my return I noticed Uncle Lance had turned his chair from the table and was gazing out of the window, apparently absorbed in thought. I saw at a glance that he was gazing into the past, for I had become used to these reveries on his part. I had not been excused, and an embarrassing silence ensued, which was only broken as he looked over his shoulder and said: "There it is, Whit; count it if you want to."

But Mr. Booth, knowing the oddities of Uncle Lance, hesitated. "Well — why — Look here, Lance. If you have any reason for not wanting to loan me this amount, why, say so."

"There's the money, Whit; take it if you want to. It'll pay for the hundred cows you are figuring on buying. But I was just thinking: can two men at our time of life, who have always been friends, afford to take the risk of letting a business transaction like this possibly make us enemies? You know I started poor here, and what I have made and saved is the work of my lifetime. You are welcome to the money, but if anything should happen that you didn't repay me, you know I wouldn't feel right towards you. It's probably my years that does it, but — now, I always look forward to the visits of your family, and Jean and I always enjoy our visits at your ranch. I think we'd be two old fools to allow anything to break up those pleasant relations." Uncle Lance turned in his chair, and, looking into the downcast countenance of Mr. Booth, continued: "Do you know, Whit, that youngest girl of yours reminds me of her aunt, my own Mary, in a hundred ways. I just love to have your girls tear around this old ranch — they seem to give me back certain glimpses of my youth that are priceless to an old man."

"That'll do, Lance," said Mr. Booth, rising and extending his hand. "I don't want the money now. Your view of the matter is right, and our friendship is worth more than a thousand cattle to me. Lizzie and the girls were anxious to come with me, and I'll go right back and send them down."

CHAPTER II
SHEPHERD'S FERRY

Within a few months after my arrival at Las Palomas, there was a dance at Shepherd's Ferry. There was no necessity for an invitation to such local meets; old and young alike were expected and welcome, and a dance naturally drained the sparsely settled community of its inhabitants from forty to fifty miles in every direction. On the Nueces in 1875, the amusements of the countryside were extremely limited; barbecues, tournaments, and dancing covered the social side of ranch life, and whether given up or down our home river, or north on the Frio, so they were within a day's ride, the white element of Las Palomas could always be depended on to be present, Uncle Lance in the lead.

Shepherd's Ferry is somewhat of a misnomer, for the water in the river was never over knee-deep to a horse, except during freshets. There may have been a ferry there once; but from my advent on the river there was nothing but a store, the keeper of which also conducted a road-house for the accommodation of travelers. There was a fine grove for picnic purposes within easy reach, which was also frequently used for camp-meeting purposes. Gnarly old live-oaks spread their branches like a canopy over everything, while the sea-green moss hung from every limb and twig, excluding the light and lazily waving with every vagrant breeze. The fact that these grounds were also used for camp-meetings only proved the broad toleration of the people. On this occasion I distinctly remember that Miss Jean introduced a lady to me, who was the wife of an Episcopal minister, then visiting on a ranch near Oakville, and I danced several times with her and found her very amiable.

On receipt of the news of the approaching dance at the ferry, we set the ranch in order. Fortunately, under seasonable conditions work on a cattle range is never pressing. A programme of work outlined for a certain week could easily be postponed a week or a fortnight for that matter; for this was the land of "la mañana," and the white element on Las Palomas easily adopted the easy-going methods of their Mexican neighbors. So on the day everything was in readiness. The ranch was a trifle over thirty miles from Shepherd's, which was a fair half day's ride, but as Miss Jean always traveled by ambulance, it was necessary to give her an early start. Las Palomas raised fine horses and mules, and the ambulance team for the ranch consisted of four mealy-muzzled brown mules, which, being range bred, made up in activity what they lacked in size.

Tiburcio, a trusty Mexican, for years in the employ of Uncle Lance, was the driver of the ambulance, and at an early morning hour he and his mules were on their mettle and impatient to start. But Miss Jean had a hundred petty things to look after. The lunch — enough for a round-up — was prepared, and was safely stored under the driver's seat. Then there were her own personal effects and the necessary dressing and tidying, with Uncle Lance dogging her at every turn.

"Now, Sis," said he, "I want you to rig yourself out in something sumptuous, because I expect to make a killing with you at this dance. I'm almost sure that that Louisiana mule-drover will be there. You know you made quite an impression on him when he was through here two years ago. Well, I'll take a hand in the game this time, and if there's any marry in him, he'll have to lead trumps. I'm getting tired of having my dear sister trifled with by every passing drover. Yes, I am! The next one that hangs around Las Palomas, basking in your smiles, has got to declare his intentions whether he buys mules or not. Oh, you've got a brother, Sis, that'll look out for you. But you must play your part. Now, if that mule-buyer's there, shall I" —

"Why, certainly, brother, invite him to the ranch," replied Miss Jean, as she busied herself with the preparations. "It's so kind of you to look after me. I was listening to every word you said, and I've got my best bib and tucker in that hand box. And just you watch me dazzle that Mr. Mule-buyer. Strange you didn't tell me sooner about his being in the country. Here, take these boxes out to the ambulance. And, say, I put in the middle-sized coffee pot, and do you think two packages of ground coffee will be enough? All right, then. Now, where's my gloves?"

We were all dancing attendance in getting the ambulance off, but Uncle Lance never relaxed his tormenting, "Come, now, hurry up," said he, as Jean and himself led the way to the gate where the conveyance stood waiting; "for I want you to look your best this evening, and you'll be all tired out if you don't get a good rest before the dance begins. Now, in case the mule-buyer don't show up, how about Sim Oliver? You see, I can put in a good word there just as easily as not. Of course, he's a widower like myself, but you're no spring pullet — you wouldn't class among the buds — besides Sim branded eleven hundred calves last year. And the very last time I was talking to him, he allowed he'd crowd thirteen hundred close this year — big calf crop, you see. Now, just why he should go to the trouble to tell me all this, unless he had his eye on you, is one too many for me. But if you want me to cut him out of your string of eligibles, say the word, and I'll chouse him out. You just bet, little girl, whoever wins you has got to score right. Great Scott! but you have good taste in selecting perfumery. Um-ee! it makes me half drunk to walk alongside of you. Be sure and put some of that ointment on your kerchief when you get there."

"Really," said Miss Jean, as they reached the ambulance, "I wish you had made a little memorandum of what I'm expected to do — I'm all in a flutter this morning. You see, without your help my case is hopeless. But I think I'll try for the mule-buyer. I'm getting tired looking at these slab-sided cowmen. Now, just look at those mules — haven't had a harness on in a month. And Tiburcio can't hold four of them, nohow. Lance, it looks like you'd send one of the boys to drive me down to the ferry."

"Why, Lord love you, girl, those mules are as gentle as kittens; and you don't suppose I'm going to put some gringo over a veteran like Tiburcio. Why, that old boy used to drive for Santa Anna during the invasion in '36. Besides, I'm sending Theodore and Glenn on horseback as a bodyguard. Las Palomas is putting her best foot forward this morning in giving you a stylish turnout, with outriders in their Sunday livery. And those two boys are the best ropers on the ranch, so if the mules run off just give one of your long, keen screams, and the boys will rope and hog-tie every mule in the team. Get in now and don't make any faces about it."

It was pettishness and not timidity that ailed Jean Lovelace, for a pioneer woman like herself had of course no fear of horse-flesh. But the team was acting in a manner to unnerve an ordinary woman. With me clinging to the bits of the leaders, and a man each holding the wheelers, as they pawed the ground and surged about in their creaking harness, they were anything but gentle; but Miss Jean proudly took her seat; Tiburcio fingered the reins in placid contentment; there was a parting volley of admonitions from brother and sister — the latter was telling us where we would find our white shirts — when Uncle Lance signaled to us; and we sprang away from the team. The ambulance gave a lurch, forward, as the mules started on a run, but Tiburcio dexterously threw them on to a heavy bed of sand, poured the whip into them as they labored through it; they crossed the sand bed, Glenn Gallup and Theodore Quayle, riding, at their heads, pointed the team into the road, and they were off.

The rest of us busied ourselves getting up saddle horses and dressing for the occasion. In the latter we had no little trouble, for dress occasions like this were rare with us. Miss Jean had been thoughtful enough to lay our clothes out, but there was a busy borrowing of collars and collar buttons, and a blacking of boots which made the sweat stand out on our foreheads in beads. After we were dressed and ready to start, Uncle Lance could not be induced to depart from his usual custom, and wear his trousers outside his boots. Then we had to pull the boots off and polish them clear up to the ears in order to make him presentable. But we were in no particular hurry about starting, as we expected to out across the country and would overtake the ambulance at the mouth of the Arroyo Seco in time for the noonday lunch. There were six in our party, consisting of Dan Happersett, Aaron Scales, John Cotton, June Deweese, Uncle Lance, and myself. With the exception of Deweese, who was nearly twenty-five years old, the remainder of the boys on the ranch were young fellows, several of whom besides myself had not yet attained their majority. On ranch work, in the absence of our employer, June was recognized as the *segundo* of Los Palomas, owing to his age and his long employment on the ranch. He was a trustworthy man, and we younger lads entertained no envy towards him.

It was about nine o'clock when we mounted our horses and started. We jollied along in a party, or separated into pairs in cross-country riding, covering about seven miles an hour. "I remember," said Uncle Lance, as we were riding in a group, "the first time I was ever at Shepherd's Ferry. We had been down the river on a cow hunt for about three weeks and had run out of bacon. We had been eating beef, and venison, and antelope for a week until it didn't taste right any longer, so I sent the outfit on ahead and rode down to the store in the hope of getting a piece of bacon. Shepherd had just established the place at the time, and when I asked him if he had any bacon, he said he had, 'But is it good?' I inquired, and before he could reply an eight-year-old boy of his stepped between us, and throwing back his tow head, looked up into my face and said: 'Mister, it's a little the best I ever tasted.'"

"Now, June," said Uncle Lance, as we rode along, "I want you to let Henry Annear's wife strictly alone to-night. You know what a stink it raised all along the river, just because you danced with her once, last San Jacinto day. Of course, Henry made a fool of himself by trying to borrow a six-shooter and otherwise getting on the prod. And I'll admit that it don't take the best of eyesight to see that his wife to-day thinks more of your old boot than she does of Annear's wedding suit, yet her husband will be the last man to know it. No man can figure to a certainty on a woman. Three guesses is not enough, for she will and she won't, and she'll straddle the question or take the fence, and when you put a copper on her to win, she loses. God made them just that way, and I don't want to criticise His handiwork. But if my name is Lance Lovelace, and I'm sixty-odd years old, and this a chestnut horse that I'm riding, then Henry Annear's wife is an unhappy woman. But that fact, son, don't give you any license to stir up trouble between man and wife. Now, remember, I've warned you not to dance, speak to, or even notice her on this occasion. The chances are that that locoed fool will come heeled this time, and if you give him any excuse, he may burn a little powder."

June promised to keep on his good behavior, saying: "That's just what I've made up my mind to do. But look'ee here: Suppose he goes on the war path, you can't expect me to show the white feather, nor let him run any sandys over me. I loved his wife once and am not ashamed of it, and he knows it. And much as I want to obey you, Uncle Lance, if he attempts to stand up a bluff on me, just as sure as hell's hot there'll be a strange face or two in heaven."

I was a new man on the ranch and unacquainted with the facts, so shortly afterwards I managed to drop to the rear with Dan Happersett, and got the particulars. It seems that June and Mrs. Annear had not only been sweethearts, but that they had been engaged, and that the engagement had been broken within a month of the day set for their wedding, and that she had married Annear on a three weeks' acquaintance. Little wonder Uncle Lance took occasion to read the riot act to his *segundo* in the interests of peace. This was all news to me, but secretly I wished June courage and a good aim if it ever came to a show-down between them.

We reached the Arroyo Seco by high noon, and found the ambulance in camp and the coffee pot boiling. Under the direction of Miss Jean, Tiburcio had removed the seats from the conveyance, so as to afford seating capacity for over half our number. The lunch was spread under an old live-oak on the bank of the Nueces, making a cosy camp. Miss Jean had the happy knack of a good hostess, our twenty-mile ride had whetted our appetites, and we did ample justice to her tempting spread. After luncheon was over and while the team was being harnessed in, I noticed Miss Jean enticing Deweese off on one side, where the two held a whispered conversation, seated on an old fallen tree. As they returned, June was promising something which she had asked of him. And if there was ever a woman lived who could exact a promise that would be respected, Jean Lovelace was that woman; for she was like an elder sister to us all.

In starting, the ambulance took the lead as before, and near the middle of the afternoon we reached the ferry. The merry-makers were assembling from every quarter, and on our arrival possibly a hundred had come, which number was doubled by the time the festivities began.

We turned our saddle and work stock into a small pasture, and gave ourselves over to the fast-gathering crowd. I was delighted to see that Miss Jean and Uncle Lance were accorded a warm welcome by every one, for I was somewhat of a stray on this new range. But when it became known that I was a recent addition to Las Palomas, the welcome was extended to me, which I duly appreciated.

The store and hostelry did a rushing business during the evening hours, for the dance did not begin until seven. A Mexican orchestra, consisting of a violin, an Italian harp, and two guitars, had come up from Oakville to furnish the music for the occasion. Just before the dance commenced, I noticed Uncle Lance greet a late arrival, and on my inquiring of June who he might be, I learned that the man was Captain Frank Byler from Lagarto, the drover Uncle Lance had been teasing Miss Jean about in the morning, and a man, as I learned later, who drove herds of horses north on the trail during the summer and during the winter drove mules and horses to Louisiana, for sale among the planters. Captain Byler was a good-looking, middle-aged fellow, and I made up my mind at once that he was due to rank as the lion of the evening among the ladies.

It is useless to describe this night of innocent revelry. It was a rustic community, and the people assembled were, with few exceptions, purely pastoral. There may have been earnest vows spoken under those spreading oaks — who knows? But if there were, the retentive ear which listened, and the cautious tongue which spake the vows, had no intention of having their confidences profaned on this page. Yet it was a night long to be remembered. Timid lovers sat apart, oblivious to the gaze of the merry revelers. Matrons and maidens vied with each other in affability to the sterner sex. I had a most enjoyable time.

I spoke Spanish well, and made it a point to cultivate the acquaintance of the leader of the orchestra. On his learning that I also played the violin, he promptly invited me to play a certain new waltz which he was desirous of learning. But I had no sooner taken the violin in my hand than the lazy rascal lighted a cigarette and strolled away, absenting himself for nearly an hour. But I was familiar with the simple dance music of the country, and played everything that was called for. My talent was quite a revelation to the boys of our ranch, and especially to the owner and mistress of Las Palomas. The latter had me play several old Colorado River favorites of hers, and I noticed that when she had the dashing Captain Byler for her partner, my waltzes seemed never long enough to suit her.

After I had been relieved, Miss Jean introduced me to a number of nice girls, and for the remainder of the evening I had no lack of partners. But there was one girl there whom I had not been introduced to, who always avoided my glance when I looked at her, but who, when we were in the same set and I squeezed her hand, had blushed just too lovely. When that dance was over, I went to Miss Jean for an introduction, but she did not know her, so I appealed to Uncle Lance, for I knew he could give the birth date of every girl present. We took a stroll through the crowd, and when I described her by her big eyes, he said in a voice so loud that I felt sure she must hear: "Why, certainly, I know her. That's Esther McLeod. I've trotted her on my knee a hundred times. She's the youngest girl of old man Donald McLeod who used to ranch over on the mouth of the San Miguel, north on the Frio. Yes, I'll give you an interslaption." Then in a subdued tone: "And if you can drop your rope on her, son, tie her good and fast, for she's good stock."

I was made acquainted as his latest adopted son, and inferred the old ranchero's approbation by many a poke in the ribs from him in the intervals between dances; for Esther and I danced every dance together until dawn. No one could charge me with neglect or inattention, for I close-herded her like a hired hand. She mellowed nicely towards me after the ice was broken, and with the limited time at my disposal, I made hay. When the dance broke up with the first signs of day, I saddled her horse and assisted her to mount, when I received the cutest little invitation, 'if ever I happened over on the Sau Miguel, to try and call.' Instead of beating about the bush, I assured her bluntly that if she ever saw me on Miguel Creek, it would be intentional; for I should have made the ride purely to see her. She blushed again in a way which sent a thrill through me. But on the Nueces in '75, if a fellow took a fancy to a girl there was no harm in showing it or telling her so.

I had been so absorbed during the latter part of the night that I had paid little attention to the rest of the Las Palomas outfit, though I occasionally caught sight of Miss Jean and the drover, generally dancing, sometimes promenading, and once had a glimpse of them tête-à-tête on a rustic settee in a secluded corner. Our employer seldom danced, but kept his eye on June Deweese in the interests of peace, for Annear and his wife were both present. Once while Esther and I were missing a dance over some light refreshment, I had occasion to watch June as he and Annear danced in the same set. I thought the latter acted rather surly, though Deweese was the acme of geniality, and was apparently having the time of his life as he tripped through the mazes of the dance. Had I not known of the deadly enmity existing between them, I could never have suspected anything but friendship, he was acting the part so perfectly. But then I knew he had given his plighted word to the master and mistress, and nothing but an insult or indignity could tempt him to break it.

On the return trip, we got the ambulance off before sunrise, expecting to halt and breakfast again at the Arroyo Seco. Aaron Scales and Dan Happersett acted as couriers to Miss Jean's conveyance, while the rest dallied behind, for there was quite a cavalcade of young folks going a distance our way. This gave Uncle Lance a splendid chance to quiz the girls in the party. I was riding with a Miss Wilson from Ramirena, who had come up to make a visit at a near-by ranch and incidentally attend the dance at Shepherd's. I admit that I was a little too much absorbed over another girl to be very entertaining, but Uncle Lance helped out by joining us. "Nice morning overhead, Miss Wilson," said he, on riding up. "Say, I've waited just as long as I'm going to for that invitation to your wedding which you promised me last summer. Now, I don't know so much about the young men down about Ramirena, but when I was a youngster back on the Colorado, when a boy loved a girl he married her, whether it was Friday or Monday, rain or shine. I'm getting tired of being put off with promises. Why, actually, I haven't been to a wedding in three years. What are we coming to?"

On reaching the road where Miss Wilson and her party separated from us, Uncle Lance returned to the charge: "Now, no matter how busy I am when I get your invitation, I don't care if the irons are in the fire and the cattle in the corral, I'll drown the fire and turn the cows out. And if Las Palomas has a horse that'll carry me, I'll merely touch the high places in coming. And when I get there I'm willing to do anything, — give the bride away, say grace, or carve the turkey. And what's more, I never kissed a bride in my life that didn't have good luck. Tell your pa you saw me. Good-by, dear."

On overtaking the ambulance in camp, our party included about twenty, several of whom were young ladies; but Miss Jean insisted that every one remain for breakfast, assuring them that she had abundance for all. After the impromptu meal was disposed of, we bade our adieus and separated to the four quarters. Before we had gone far, Uncle Lance rode alongside of me and said: "Tom, why didn't you tell me you was a fiddler? God knows you're lazy enough to be a good one, and you ought to be good on a bee course. But what made me warm to you last night was the way you built to Esther McLeod. Son, you set her cush about right. If you can hold sight on a herd of beeves on a bad night like you did her, you'll be a foreman some day. And she's not only good blood herself, but she's got cattle and land. Old man Donald, her father, was killed in the Confederate army. He was an honest Scotchman who kept Sunday and everything else he could lay his hands on. In all my travels I never met a man who could offer a longer prayer or take a bigger drink of whiskey. I remember the first time I ever saw him. He was serving on the grand jury, and I was a witness in a cattle-stealing case. He was a stranger to me, and we had just sat down at the same table at a hotel for dinner. We were on the point of helping ourselves, when the old Scot arose and struck the table a blow that made the dishes rattle. 'You heathens,' said he, 'will you partake of the bounty of your Heavenly Father without returning thanks?' We laid down our knives and forks like boys caught in a watermelon patch, and the old man asked a blessing. I've been at his house often. He was a good man, but

Secession caught him and he never came back. So, Quirk, you see, a son-in-law will be a handy man in the family, and with the start you made last night I hope for good results." The other boys seemed to enjoy my embarrassment, but I said nothing in reply, being a new man with the outfit. We reached the ranch an hour before noon, two hours in advance of the ambulance; and the sleeping we did until sunrise the next morning required no lullaby.

CHAPTER III
LAS PALOMAS

There is something about those large ranches of southern Texas that reminds one of the old feudal system. The pathetic attachment to the soil of those born to certain Spanish land grants can only be compared to the European immigrant when for the last time he looks on the land of his birth before sailing. Of all this Las Palomas was typical. In the course of time several such grants had been absorbed into its baronial acres. But it had always been the policy of Uncle Lance never to disturb the Mexican population; rather he encouraged them to remain in his service. Thus had sprung up around Las Palomas ranch a little Mexican community numbering about a dozen families, who lived in *jacals* close to the main ranch buildings. They were simple people, and rendered their new master a feudal loyalty. There were also several small *ranchites* located on the land, where, under the Mexican régime, there had been pretentious adobe buildings. A number of families still resided at these deserted ranches, content in cultivating small fields or looking after flocks of goats and a few head of cattle, paying no rental save a service tenure to the new owner.

The customs of these Mexican people were simple and primitive. They blindly accepted the religious teachings imposed with fire and sword by the Spanish conquerors upon their ancestors. A padre visited them yearly, christening the babes, marrying the youth, shriving the penitent, and saying masses for the repose of the souls of the departed. Their social customs were in many respects unique. For instance, in courtship a young man was never allowed in the presence of his inamorata, unless in company of others, or under the eye of a chaperon. Proposals, even among the nearest of neighbors or most intimate of friends, were always made in writing, usually by the father of the young man to the parents of the girl, but in the absence of such, by a godfather or *padrino*. Fifteen days was the term allowed for a reply, and no matter how desirable the match might be, it was not accounted good taste to answer before the last day. The owner of Las Palomas was frequently called upon to act as *padrino* for his people, and so successful had he always been that the vaqueros on his ranch preferred his services to those of their own fathers. There was scarcely a vaquero at the home ranch but, in time past, had invoked his good offices in this matter, and he had come to be looked on as their patron saint.

The month of September was usually the beginning of the branding season at Las Palomas. In conducting this work, Uncle Lance was the leader, and with the white element already enumerated, there were twelve to fifteen vaqueros included in the branding outfit. The dance at Shepherd's had delayed the beginning of active operations, and a large calf crop, to say nothing of horse and mule colts, now demanded our attention and promised several months' work. The year before, Las Palomas had branded over four thousand calves, and the range was now dotted with the crop, awaiting the iron stamp of ownership.

The range was an open one at the time, compelling us to work far beyond the limits of our employer's land. Fortified with our own commissary, and with six to eight horses apiece in our mount, we scoured the country for a radius of fifty miles. When approaching another range, it was our custom to send a courier in advance to inquire of the ranchero when it would be convenient for him to give us a rodeo. A day would be set, when our outfit and the vaqueros of that range rounded up all the cattle watering at given points. Then we cut out the Las Palomas brand, and held them under herd or started them for the home ranch, where the calves were to be branded. In this manner we visited all the adjoining ranches, taking over a month to make the circuit of the ranges.

In making the tour, the first range we worked was that of rancho Santa Maria, south of our range and on the head of Tarancalous Creek. On approaching the ranch, as was customary, we prepared to encamp and ask for a rodeo. But in the choice of a vaquero to be dispatched on this mission, a spirited rivalry sprang up. When Uncle Lance learned that the rivalry amongst the vaqueros was meant to embarrass Enrique Lopez, who was *oso* to Anita, the pretty daughter of the corporal of Santa Maria, his matchmaking instincts came to the fore. Calling Enrique to one side, he made the vaquero confess that he had been playing for the favor of the señorita at Santa Maria. Then he dispatched Enrique on the mission, bidding him carry the choicest compliments of Las Palomas to every Don and Doña of Santa Maria. And Enrique was quite capable of adding a few embellishments to the old matchmaker's extravagant flatteries.

Enrique was in camp next morning, but at what hour of the night he had returned is unknown. The rodeo had been granted for the following day; there was a pressing invitation to Don Lance — unless he was willing to offend — to spend the idle day as the guest of Don Mateo. Enrique elaborated the invitation with a thousand adornments. But the owner of Las Palomas had lived nearly forty years among the Spanish-American people on the Nueces, and knew how to make allowances for the exuberance of the Latin tongue. There was no telling to what extent Enrique could have kept on delivering messages, but to his employer he was avoiding the issue.

"But did you get to see Anita?" interrupted Uncle Lance. Yes, he had seen her, but that was about all. Did not Don Lance know the customs among the Castilians? There was her mother ever present, or if she must absent herself, there was a bevy of *tias comadres* surrounding her, until the Doña Anita dare not even raise her eyes to meet his. "To perdition with such customs, no?" The freedom of a cow camp is a splendid opportunity to relieve one's mind upon prevailing injustices.

"Don't fret your cattle so early in the morning, son," admonished the wary matchmaker. "I've handled worse cases than this before. You Mexicans are sticklers on customs, and we must deal with our neighbors carefully. Before I show my hand in this, there's just one thing I want to know — is the girl willing? Whenever you can satisfy me on that point, Enrique, just call on the old man. But before that I won't stir a step. You remember what a time I had over Tiburcio's Juan — that's so, you were too young then. Well, June here remembers it. Why, the girl just cut up shamefully. Called Juan an Indian peon, and bragged about her Castilian family until you'd have supposed she was a princess of the blood royal. Why, it took her parents and myself a whole day to bring the girl around to take a sensible view of matters. On my soul, except that I didn't want to acknowledge defeat, I felt a dozen times like telling her to go straight up. And when she did marry you, she was as happy as a lark — wasn't she, Juan? But I like to have the thing over with in — well, say half an hour's time. Then we can have refreshments, and smoke, and discuss the prospects of the young couple."

Uncle Lance's question was hard to answer. Enrique had known the girl for several years, had danced with her on many a feast day, and never lost an opportunity to whisper the old, old story in her willing ear. Others had done the like, but the dark-eyed señorita is an adept in the art of coquetry, and there you are. But Enrique swore a great oath he would know. Yes, he would. He would lay siege to her as he had never done before. He would become *un oso grande*. Just wait until the branding was over and the fiestas of the Christmas season were on, and watch him dog her every step until he received her signal of surrender. Witness, all the saints, this row of Enrique Lopez, that the Doña Anita should have no peace of mind, no, not for one little minute, until she had made a complete capitulation. Then Don Lance, the *padrino* of Las Palomas, would at once write the letter which would command the hand of the corporal's daughter. Who could refuse such a request, and what was a daughter of Santa Maria compared to a son of Las Palomas?

Tarancalous Creek ran almost due east, and rancho Santa Maria was located near its source, depending more on its wells for water supply than on the stream which only flowed for a few months during the year. Where the watering facilities were so limited the rodeo was an easy matter. A number of small round-ups at each established watering point, a swift cutting out of everything bearing the Las Palomas brand, and we moved on to the next rodeo, for we had an abundance of help at Santa Maria. The work was finished by the middle of the afternoon. After sending, under five or six men, our cut of several hundred cattle westward on our course, our outfit rode into rancho Santa Maria proper to pay our respects. Our wagon had provided an abundant dinner for our assistants and ourselves; but it would have been, in Mexican etiquette, extremely rude on our part not to visit the rancho and partake of a cup of coffee and a cigarette, thanking the ranchero on parting for his kindness in granting us the rodeo.

So when the last round-up was reached, Don Mateo and Uncle Lance turned the work over to their corporals, and in advance rode up to Santa Maria. The vaqueros of our ranch were anxious to visit the rancho, so it devolved on the white element to take charge of the cut. Being a stranger to Santa Maria, I was allowed to accompany our *segundo*, June Deweese, on an introductory visit. On arriving at the rancho, the vaqueros scattered among the *jacals* of their *amigos*, while June and myself were welcomed at the *casa primero*. There we found Uncle Lance partaking of refreshment, and smoking a cigarette as though he had been born a Señor Don of some ruling hacienda. June and I were seated at another table, where we were served with coffee, wafers, and home-made cigarettes. This was perfectly in order, but I could hardly control myself over the extravagant Spanish our employer was using in expressing the amity existing between Santa Maria and Las Palomas. In ordinary conversation, such as cattle and ranch affairs, Uncle Lance had a good command of Spanish; but on social and delicate topics some of his efforts were ridiculous in the extreme. He was well aware of his shortcomings, and frequently appealed to me to assist him. As a boy my playmates had been Mexican children, so that I not only spoke Spanish fluently but could also readily read and write it. So it was no surprise to me that, before taking our departure, my employer should command my services as an interpreter in driving an entering wedge. He was particular to have me assure our host and hostess of his high regard for them, and his hope that in the future even more friendly relations might exist between the two ranches. Had Santa Maria no young cavalier for the hand of some daughter of Las Palomas? Ah! there was the true bond for future friendships. Well, well, if the soil of this rancho was so impoverished, then the sons of Las Palomas must take the bit in their teeth and come courting to Santa Maria. And let Doña Gregoria look well to her daughters, for the young men of Las Palomas, true to their race, were not only handsome fellows but ardent lovers, and would be hard to refuse.

After taking our leave and catching up with the cattle, we pushed westward for the Ganso, our next stream of water. This creek was a tributary to the Nueces, and we worked down it several days, or until we had nearly a thousand cattle and were within thirty miles of home. Turning this cut over to June Deweese and a few vaqueros to take in to the ranch and brand, the rest of us turned westward and struck the Nueces at least fifty miles above Las Palomas. For the next few days our dragnet took in both sides of the Nueces, and when, on reaching the mouth of the Ganso, we were met by Deweese and the vaqueros we had another bunch of nearly a thousand ready. Dan Happersett was dispatched with the second bunch for branding, when we swung north to Mr. Booth's ranch on the Frio, where we rested a day. But there is little recreation on a cow hunt, and we were soon under full headway again. By the time we had worked down the Frio, opposite headquarters, we had too large a herd to carry conveniently, and I was sent in home with them, never rejoining the outfit until they reached Shepherd's Ferry. This was a disappointment to me, for I had hopes that when the outfit worked the range around the mouth of San Miguel, I might find some excuse to visit the McLeod ranch and see Esther. But after turning back up the home river to within twenty miles of the ranch, we again turned southward, covering the intervening ranches rapidly until we struck the Tarancalous about twenty-five miles east of Santa Maria.

We had spent over thirty days in making this circle, gathering over five thousand cattle, about one third of which were cows with calves by their sides. On the remaining gap in the circle we lost two days in waiting for rodeos, or gathering independently along the Tarancalous, and, on nearing the Santa Maria range, we had nearly fifteen hundred cattle. Our herd passed within plain view of the rancho, but we did not turn aside, preferring to make a dry camp for the night, some five or six miles further on our homeward course. But since we had used the majority of our *remuda* very hard that day, Uncle Lance dispatched Enrique and myself, with our wagon and saddle horses, by way of Santa Maria, to water our saddle stock and refill our kegs for camping purposes. Of course, the compliments of our employer to the ranchero of Santa Maria went with the *remuda* and wagon.

I delivered the compliments and regrets to Don Mateo, and asked the permission to water our saddle stock, which was readily granted. This required some time, for we had about a hundred and twenty-five loose horses with us, and the water had to be raised by rope and pulley from the pommel of a saddle horse. After watering the team we refilled our kegs, and the cook pulled out to overtake the herd, Enrique and I staying to water the *remuda*. Enrique, who was riding the saddle horse, while I emptied the buckets as they were hoisted to the surface, was evidently killing time. By his dilatory tactics, I knew the young rascal was delaying in the hope of getting a word with the Doña Anita. But it was getting late, and at the rate we were hoisting darkness would overtake us before we could reach the herd. So I ordered Enrique to the bucket, while I took my own horse and furnished the hoisting power. We were making some headway with the work, when a party of women, among them the Doña Anita, came down to the well to fill vessels for house use.

This may have been all chance — and then again it may not. But the gallant Enrique now outdid himself, filling jar after jar and lifting them to the shoulder of the bearer with the utmost zeal and amid a profusion of compliments. I was annoyed at the interruption in our work, but I could see that Enrique was now in the highest heaven of delight. The Doña Anita's mother was present, and made it her duty to notice that only commonplace formalities passed between her daughter and the ardent vaquero. After the jars were all filled, the bevy of women started on their return; but Doña Anita managed to drop a few feet to the rear of the procession, and, looking back, quietly took up one corner of her mantilla, and with a little movement, apparently all innocence, flashed a message back to the entranced Enrique. I was aware of the flirtation, but before I had made more of it Enrique sprang down from the abutment of the well, dragged me from my horse, and in an ecstasy of joy, crouching behind the abutments, cried: Had I seen the sign? Had I not noticed her token? Was my brain then so befuddled? Did I not understand the ways of the señoritas among his people? — that they always answered by a wave of the handkerchief, or the mantilla? Ave Maria, Tomas! Such stupidity! Why, to be sure, they could talk all day with their eyes.

A setting sun finally ended his confidences, and the watering was soon finished, for Enrique lowered the bucket in a gallop. On our reaching the herd and while we were catching our night horses, Uncle Lance strode out to the rope corral, with the inquiry, what had delayed us. "Nothing particular," I replied, and looked at Enrique, who shrugged his shoulders and repeated my answer. "Now, look here, you young liars," said the old ranchero; "the wagon has been in camp over an hour, and, admitting it did start before you, you had plenty of time to water the saddle stock and overtake it before it could possibly reach the herd. I can tell a lie myself, but a good one always has some plausibility. You rascals were up to some mischief, I'll warrant."

I had caught out my night horse, and as I led him away to saddle up, Uncle Lance, not content with my evasive answer, followed me. "Go to Enrique," I whispered; "he'll just bubble over at a good chance to tell you. Yes; it was the Doña Anita who caused the delay." A smothered chuckling shook the old man's frame, as he sauntered over to where Enrique was saddling. As the two led off the horse to picket in the gathering dusk, the ranchero had his arm around the vaquero's neck, and I felt that the old matchmaker would soon be in possession of the facts. A hilarious guffaw that reached me as I was picketing my horse announced that the story was out, and as the two returned to the fire Uncle Lance was slapping Enrique on the back at every step and calling him a lucky dog. The news spread through the camp like wild-fire, even to the vaqueros on night herd, who instantly began chanting an old love song. While Enrique and I were eating our supper, our employer paced backward and forward in meditation like a sentinel on picket, and when we had finished our meal, he joined us around the fire, inquiring of Enrique how soon the demand should be made for the corporal's daughter, and was assured that it could not be done too soon. "The padre only came once a year," he concluded, "and they must be ready."

"Well, now, this is a pretty pickle," said the old matchmaker, as he pulled his gray mustaches; "there isn't pen or paper in the outfit. And then we'll be busy branding on the home range for a month, and I can't spare a vaquero a day to carry a letter to Santa Maria. And besides, I might not be at home when the reply came. I think I'll just take the bull by the horns; ride back in the morning and set these old precedents at defiance, by arranging the match verbally. I can make the talk that this country is Texas now, and that under the new regime American customs are in order. That's what I'll do — and I'll take Tom Quirk with me for fear I bog down in my Spanish."

But several vaqueros, who understood some English, advised Enrique of what the old matchmaker proposed to do, when the vaquero threw his hands in the air and began sputtering Spanish in terrified disapproval. Did not Don Lance know that the marriage usages among his people were their most cherished customs? "Oh, yes, son," languidly replied Uncle Lance. "I'm some strong on the cherish myself, but not when it interferes with my plans. It strikes me that less than a month ago I heard you condemning to perdition certain customs of your people. Now, don't get on too high a horse — just leave it to Tom and me. We may stay a week, but when we come back we'll bring your betrothal with us in our vest pockets. There was never a Mexican born who can outhold me on palaver; and we'll eat every chicken on Santa Maria unless they surrender."

As soon as the herd had started for home the next morning, Uncle Lance and I returned to Santa Maria. We were extended a cordial reception by Don Mateo, and after the chronicle of happenings since the two rancheros last met had been reviewed, the motive of our sudden return was mentioned. By combining the vocabularies of my employer and myself, we mentioned our errand as delicately as possible, pleading guilty and craving every one's pardon for our rudeness in verbally conducting the negotiations. To our surprise, — for to Mexicans customs are as rooted as Faith, — Don Mateo took no offense and summoned Doña Gregoria. I was playing a close second to the diplomat of our side of the house, and when his Spanish failed him and he had recourse to English, it is needless to say I handled matters to the best of my ability. The Spanish is a musical, passionate language and well suited to love making, and though this was my first use of it for that purpose, within half an hour we had won the ranchero and his wife to our side of the question.

Then, at Don Mateo's orders, the parents of the girl were summoned. This involved some little delay, which permitted coffee being served, and discussion, over the cigarettes, of the commonplace matters of the country. There was beginning to be a slight demand for cattle to drive to the far north on the trails, some thought it was the sign of a big development, but neither of the rancheros put much confidence in the movement, etc., etc. The corporal and his wife suddenly made their appearance, dressed in their best, which accounted for the delay, and all cattle conversation instantly ceased. Uncle Lance arose and greeted the husky corporal and his timid wife with warm cordiality. I extended my greetings to the Mexican foreman, whom I had met at the rodeo about a month before. We then resumed our seats, but the corporal and his wife remained standing, and with an elegant command of his native tongue Don Mateo informed the couple of our mission. They looked at each other in bewilderment. Tears came into the wife's eyes. For a moment I pitied her. Indeed, the pathetic was not lacking. But the hearty corporal reminded his better half that her parents, in his interests, had once been asked for her hand under similar circumstances, and the tears disappeared. Tears are womanly; and I have since seen them shed, under less provocation, by fairer-skinned women than this simple, swarthy daughter of Mexico.

It was but natural that the parents of the girl should feign surprise and reluctance if they did not feel it. The Doña Anita's mother offered several trivial objections. Her daughter had never taken her into her confidence over any suitor. And did Anita really love Enrique Lopez of Las Palomas? Even if she did, could he support her, being but a vaquero? This brought Uncle Lance to the front. He had known Enrique since the day of his birth. As a five-year-old, and naked as the day he was born, had he not ridden a colt at branding time, twice around the big corral without being thrown? At ten, had he not thrown himself across a gateway and allowed a *caballada* of over two hundred wild range horses to jump over his prostrate body as they passed in a headlong rush through the gate? Only the year before at branding, when an infuriated bull had driven every vaquero out of the corrals, did not Enrique mount his horse, and, after baiting the bull out into the open, play with him like a kitten with a mouse? And when the bull, tiring, attempted to make his escape, who but Enrique had lassoed the animal by the fore feet, breaking his neck in the throw? The diplomat of Las Palomas dejectedly admitted that the bull was a prize animal, but could not deny that he himself had joined in the plaudits to the daring vaquero. But if there were a possible doubt that the Doña Anita did not love this son of Las Palomas, then Lance Lovelace himself would oppose the union. This was an important matter. Would Don Mateo be so kind as to summon the señorita?

The señorita came in response to the summons. She was a girl of possibly seventeen summers, several inches taller than her mother, possessing a beautiful complexion with large lustrous eyes. There was something fawnlike in her timidity as she gazed at those about the table. Doña Gregoria broke the news, informing her that the ranchero of Las Palomas had asked her hand in marriage for Enrique, one of his vaqueros. Did she love the man and was she willing to marry him? For reply the girl hid her face in the mantilla of her mother. With commendable tact Doña Gregoria led the mother and daughter into another room, from which the two elder women soon returned with a favorable reply. Uncle Lance arose and assured the corporal and his wife that their daughter would receive his special care and protection; that as long as water ran and grass grew, Las Palomas would care for her own children.

We accepted an invitation to remain for dinner, as several hours had elapsed since our arrival. In company with the corporal, I attended to our horses, leaving the two rancheros absorbed in a discussion of Texas fever, rumors of which were then attracting widespread attention in the north along the cattle trails. After dinner we took our leave of host and hostess, promising to send Enrique to Santa Maria at the earliest opportunity.

It was a long ride across country to Las Palomas, but striking a free gait, unencumbered as we were, we covered the country rapidly. I had somewhat doubted the old matchmaker's sincerity in making this match, but as we rode along he told me of his own marriage to Mary Bryan, and the one happy year of life which it brought him, mellowing into a mood of seriousness which dispelled all doubts. It was almost sunset when we sighted in the distance the ranch buildings at Las Palomas, and half an hour later as we galloped up to assist the herd which was nearing the corrals, the old man stood in his stirrups and, waving his hat, shouted to his outfit: "Hurrah for Enrique and the Doña Anita!" And as the last of the cattle entered the corral, a rain of lassos settled over the smiling rascal and his horse, and we led him in triumph to the house for Miss Jean's blessing.

CHAPTER IV
CHRISTMAS

The branding on the home range was an easy matter. The cattle were compelled to water from the Nueces, so that their range was never over five or six miles from the river. There was no occasion even to take out the wagon, though we made a one-night camp at the mouth of the Ganso, and another about midway between the home ranch and Shepherd's Ferry, pack mules serving instead of the wagon. On the home range, in gathering to brand, we never disturbed the mixed cattle, cutting out only the cows and calves. On the round-up below the Ganso, we had over three thousand cattle in one rodeo, finding less than five hundred calves belonging to Las Palomas, the bulk on this particular occasion being steer cattle. There had been little demand for steers for several seasons and they had accumulated until many of them were fine beeves, five and six years old.

When the branding proper was concluded, our tally showed nearly fifty-one hundred calves branded that season, indicating about twenty thousand cattle in the Las Palomas brand. After a week's rest, with fresh horses, we re-rode the home range in squads of two, and branded any calves we found with a running iron. This added nearly a hundred more to our original number. On an open range like ours, it was not expected that everything would be branded; but on quitting, it is safe to say we had missed less than one per cent of our calf crop.

The cattle finished, we turned our attention to the branding of the horse stock. The Christmas season was approaching, and we wanted to get the work well in hand for the usual holiday festivities. There were some fifty *manadas* of mares belonging to Las Palomas, about one fourth of which were used for the rearing of mules, the others growing our saddle horses for ranch use. These bands numbered twenty to twenty-five brood mares each, and ranged mostly within twenty miles of the home ranch. They were never disturbed except to brand the colts, market surplus stock, or cut out the mature geldings to be broken for saddle use. Each *manada* had its own range, never trespassing on others, but when they were brought together in the corral there was many a battle royal among the stallions.

I was anxious to get the work over in good season, for I intended to ask for a two weeks' leave of absence. My parents lived near Cibollo Ford on the San Antonio River, and I made it a rule to spend Christmas with my own people. This year, in particular, I had a double motive in going home; for the mouth of San Miguel and the McLeod ranch lay directly on my route. I had figured matters down to a fraction; I would have a good excuse for staying one night going and another returning. And it would be my fault if I did not reach the ranch at an hour when an invitation to remain over night would be simply imperative under the canons of Texas hospitality. I had done enough hard work since the dance at Shepherd's to drive every thought of Esther McLeod out of my mind if that were possible, but as the time drew nearer her invitation to call was ever uppermost in my thoughts.

So when the last of the horse stock was branded and the work was drawing to a close, as we sat around the fireplace one night and the question came up where each of us expected to spend Christmas, I broached my plan. The master and mistress were expected at the Booth ranch on the Frio. Nearly all the boys, who had homes within two or three days' ride, hoped to improve the chance to make a short visit to their people. When, among the others, I also made my application for leave of absence, Uncle Lance turned in his chair with apparent surprise. "What's that? You want to go home? Well, now, that's a new one on me. Why, Tom, I never knew you had any folks; I got the idea, somehow, that you was won on a horse race. Here I had everything figured out to send you down to Santa Maria with Enrique. But I reckon with the ice broken, he'll have to swim out or drown. Where do your folks live?" I explained that they lived on the San Antonio River, northeast about one hundred and fifty miles. At this I saw my employer's face brighten. "Yes, yes, I see," said he musingly; "that will carry you past the widow McLeod's. You can go, son, and good luck to you."

I timed my departure from Las Palomas, allowing three days for the trip, so as to reach home on Christmas eve. By making a slight deviation, there was a country store which I could pass on the last day, where I expected to buy some presents for my mother and sisters. But I was in a pickle as to what to give Esther, and on consulting Miss Jean, I found that motherly elder sister had everything thought out in advance. There was an old Mexican woman, a pure Aztec Indian, at a ranchita belonging to Las Palomas, who was an expert in Mexican drawn work. The mistress of the home ranch had been a good patron of this old woman, and the next morning we drove over to the ranchita, where I secured half a dozen ladies' handkerchiefs, inexpensive but very rare.

I owned a private horse, which had run idle all summer, and naturally expected to ride him on this trip. But Uncle Lance evidently wanted me to make a good impression on the widow McLeod, and brushed my plans aside, by asking me as a favor to ride a certain black horse belonging to his private string. "Quirk," said he, the evening before my departure, "I wish you would ride Wolf, that black six-year-old in my mount. When that rascal of an Enrique saddle-broke him for me, he always mounted him with a free head and on the move, and now when I use him he's always on the fidget. So you just ride him over to the San Antonio and back, and see if you can't cure him of that restlessness. It may be my years, but I just despise a horse that's always dancing a jig when I want to mount him."

Glenn Gallup's people lived in Victoria County, about as far from Las Palomas as mine, and the next morning we set out down the river. Our course together only led a short distance, but we jogged along until noon, when we rested an hour and parted, Glenn going on down the river for Oakville, while I turned almost due north across country for the mouth of San Miguel. The black carried me that afternoon as though the saddle was empty. I was constrained to hold him in, in view of the long journey before us, so as not to reach the McLeod ranch too early. Whenever we struck cattle on our course, I rode through them to pass away the time, and just about sunset I cantered up to the McLeod ranch with a dash. I did not know a soul on the place, but put on a bold front and asked for Miss Esther. On catching sight of me, she gave a little start, blushed modestly, and greeted me cordially.

Texas hospitality of an early day is too well known to need comment; I was at once introduced to the McLeod household. It was rather a pretentious ranch, somewhat dilapidated in appearance — appearances are as deceitful on a cattle ranch as in the cut of a man's coat. Tony Hunter, a son-in-law of the widow, was foreman on the ranch, and during the course of the evening in the discussion of cattle matters, I innocently drew out the fact that their branded calf crop of that season amounted to nearly three thousand calves. When a similar question was asked me, I reluctantly admitted that the Las Palomas crop was quite a disappointment this year, only branding sixty-five hundred calves, but that our mule and horse colts ran nearly a thousand head without equals in the Nueces valley.

I knew there was no one there who could dispute my figures, though Mrs. McLeod expressed surprise at them. "Ye dinna say," said my hostess, looking directly at me over her spectacles, "that Las Palomas branded that mony calves thi' year? Why, durin' ma gudeman's life we alway branded mair calves than did Mr. Lovelace. But then my husband would join the army, and I had tae depend on greasers tae do ma work, and oor kye grew up mavericks." I said nothing in reply, knowing it to be quite natural for a woman or inexperienced person to feel always the prey of the fortunate and far-seeing.

The next morning before leaving, I managed to have a nice private talk with Miss Esther, and thought I read my title clear, when she surprised me with the information that her mother contemplated sending her off to San Antonio to a private school for young ladies. Her two elder sisters had married against her mother's wishes, it seemed, and Mrs. McLeod was determined to give her youngest daughter an education and fit her for something better than being the wife of a common cow hand. This was the inference from the conversation which passed between us at the gate. But when Esther thanked me for the Christmas remembrance I had brought her, I felt that I would take a chance on her, win or lose. Assuring her that I would make it a point to call on my return, I gave the black a free rein and galloped out of sight.

I reached home late on Christmas eve. My two elder brothers, who also followed cattle work, had arrived the day before, and the Quirk family were once more united, for the first time in two years. Within an hour after my arrival, I learned from my brothers that there was to be a dance that night at a settlement about fifteen miles up the river. They were going, and it required no urging on their part to insure the presence of Quirk's three boys. Supper over, a fresh horse was furnished me, and we set out for the dance, covering the distance in less than two hours. I knew nearly every one in the settlement, and got a cordial welcome. I played the fiddle, danced with my former sweethearts, and, ere the sun rose in the morning, rode home in time for breakfast. During that night's revelry, I contrasted my former girl friends on the San Antonio with another maiden, a slip of the old Scotch stock, transplanted and nurtured in the sunshine and soil of the San Miguel. The comparison stood all tests applied, and in my secret heart I knew who held the whip hand over the passions within me.

As I expected to return to Las Palomas for the New Year, my time was limited to a four days' visit at home. But a great deal can be said in four days; and at the end I was ready to saddle my black, bid my adieus, and ride for the southwest. During my visit I was careful not to betray that I had even a passing thought of a sweetheart, and what parents would suspect that a rollicking, carefree young fellow of twenty could have any serious intentions toward a girl? With brothers too indifferent, and sisters too young, the secret was my own, though Wolf, my mount, as he put mile after mile behind us, seemed conscious that his mission to reach the San Miguel without loss of time was of more than ordinary moment. And a better horse never carried knight in the days of chivalry.

On reaching the McLeod ranch during the afternoon of the second day, I found Esther expectant; but the welcome of her mother was of a frigid order. Having a Scotch mother myself, I knew something of arbitrary natures, and met Mrs. McLeod's coolness with a fund of talk and stories; yet I could see all too plainly that she was determinedly on the defensive. I had my favorite fiddle with me which I was taking back to Las Palomas, and during the evening I played all the old Scotch ballads I knew and love songs of the highlands, hoping to soften her from the decided stand she had taken against me and my intentions. But her heritage of obstinacy was large, and her opposition strong, as several well-directed thrusts which reached me in vulnerable places made me aware, but I smiled as if they were flattering compliments. Several times I mentally framed replies only to smother them, for I was the stranger within her gates, and if she saw fit to offend a guest she was still within her rights.

But the next morning as I tarried beyond the reasonable hour for my departure, her wrath broke out in a torrent. "If ye dinna ken the way hame, Mr. Quirk, I'll show it ye," she said as she joined Esther and me at the hitch-rack, where we had been loitering for an hour. "And I dinna care muckle whaur ye gang, so ye get oot o' ma sight, and stay oot o' it. I thocht ye waur a ceevil stranger when ye bided wi' us last week, but noo I ken ye are something mair, ridin' your fine horses an' makin' presents tae ma lassie. That's a' the guid that comes o' lettin' her rin tae every dance at Shepherd's Ferry. Gang ben the house tae your wark, ye jade, an' let me attend tae this fine gentleman. Noo, sir, gin ye ony business onywhaur else, ye 'd aye better be ridin' tae it, for ye are no wanted here, ye ken."

"Why, Mrs. McLeod," I broke in politely. "You hardly know anything about me."

"No, an' I dinna wish it. You are frae Las Palomas, an' that's aye enough for me. I ken auld Lance Lovelace, an' those that bide wi' him. Sma' wonder he brands sae mony calves and sells mair kye than a' the ither ranchmen in the country. Ay, man, I ken him well."

I saw that I had a tartar to deal with, but if I could switch her invective on some one absent, it would assist me in controlling myself. So I said to the old lady: "Why, I've known Mr. Lovelace now almost a year, and over on the Nueces he is well liked, and considered a cowman whose word is as good as gold. What have you got against him?"

"Ower much, ma young freend. I kent him afore ye were born. I'm sorry tae say that while ma gudeman was alive, he was a frequent visitor at oor place. But we dinna see him ony mair. He aye keeps awa' frae here, and camps wi' his wagons when he's ower on the San Miguel to gather cattle. He was no content merely wi' what kye drifted doon on the Nueces, but warked a big outfit the year around, e'en comin' ower on the Frio an' San Miguel maverick huntin'. That's why he brands twice the calves that onybody else does, and owns a forty-mile front o' land on both sides o' the river. Ye see, I ken him weel."

"Well, isn't that the way most cowmen got their start?" I innocently inquired, well knowing it was. "And do you blame him for running his brand on the unowned cattle that roamed the range? I expect if Mr. Lovelace was my father instead of my employer, you wouldn't be talking in the same key," and with that I led my horse out to mount.

"Ye think a great deal o' yersel', because ye're frae Las Palomas. Aweel, no vaquero of auld Lance Lovelace can come sparkin' wi' ma lass. I've heard o' auld Lovelace's matchmaking. I'm told he mak's matches and then laughs at the silly gowks. I've twa worthless sons-in-law the noo, are here an' anither a stage-driver. Aye, they 're capital husbands for Donald McLeod's lassies, are they no? Afore I let Esther marry the first scamp that comes simperin' aroond here, I'll put her in a convent, an' mak' a nun o' the bairn. I gave the ither lassies their way, an' look at the reward. I tell ye I'm goin' to bar the door on the last one, an' the man that marries her will be worthy o' her. He winna be a vaquero frae Las Palomas either!"

I had mounted my horse to start, well knowing it was useless to argue with an angry woman. Esther had obediently retreated to the safety of the house, aware that her mother had a tongue and evidently willing to be spared its invective in my presence. My horse was fidgeting about, impatient to be off, but I gave him the rowel and rode up to the gate, determined, if possible, to pour oil on the troubled waters. "Mrs. McLeod," said I, in humble tones, "possibly you take the correct view of this matter. Miss Esther and I have only been acquainted a few months, and will soon forget each other. Please take me in the house and let me tell her good-by."

"No, sir. Dinna set foot inside o' this gate. I hope ye know ye're no wanted here. There's your road, the one leadin' south, an' ye'd better be goin', I'm thinkin'."

I held in the black and rode off in a walk. This was the first clean knock-out I had ever met. Heretofore I had been egotistical enough to hold my head rather high, but this morning it drooped. Wolf seemed to notice it, and after the first mile dropped into an easy volunteer walk. I never noticed the passing of time until we reached the river, and the black stopped to drink. Here I unsaddled for several hours; then went on again in no cheerful mood. Before I came within sight of Las Palomas near evening, my horse turned his head and nickered, and in a few minutes Uncle Lance and June Deweese galloped up and overtook me. I had figured out several very plausible versions of my adventure, but this sudden meeting threw me off my guard — and Lance Lovelace was a hard man to tell an undetected, white-faced lie. I put on a bold front, but his salutation penetrated it at a glance.

"What's the matter, Tom; any of your folks dead?"

"No."

"Sick?"

"No."

"Girl gone back on you?"

"I don't think."

"It's the old woman, then?"

"How do you know?"

"Because I know that old dame. I used to go over there occasionally when old man Donald was living, but the old lady — excuse me! I ought to have posted you, Tom, but I don't suppose it would have done any good. Brought your fiddle with you, I see. That's good. I expect the old lady read my title clear to you."

My brain must have been under a haze, for I repeated every charge she had made against him, not even sparing the accusation that he had remained out of the army and added to his brand by mavericking cattle.

"Did she say that?" inquired Uncle Lance, laughing. "Why, the old hellion! She must have been feeling in fine fettle!"

CHAPTER V
A PIGEON HUNT

The new year dawned on Las Palomas rich in promise of future content. Uncle Lance and I had had a long talk the evening before, and under the reasoning of the old optimist the gloom gradually lifted from my spirits. I was glad I had been so brutally blunt that evening, regarding what Mrs. McLeod had said about him; for it had a tendency to increase the rancher's aggressiveness in my behalf. "Hell, Tom," said the old man, as we walked from the corrals to the house, "don't let a little thing like this disturb you. Of course she'll four-flush and bluff you if she can, but you don't want to pay any more attention to the old lady than if she was some *pelado*. To be sure, it would be better to have her consent, but then" —

Glenn Gallup also arrived at the ranch on New Year's eve. He brought the report that wild pigeons were again roosting at the big bend of the river. It was a well-known pigeon roost, but the birds went to other winter feeding grounds, except during years when there was a plentiful sweet mast. This bend was about midway between the ranch and Shepherd's, contained about two thousand acres, and was heavily timbered with ash, pecan, and hackberry. The feeding grounds lay distant, extending from the encinal ridges on the Las Palomas lands to live-oak groves a hundred miles to the southward. But however far the pigeons might go for food, they always returned to the roosting place at night.

"That means pigeon pie," said Uncle Lance, on receiving Glenn's report. "Everybody and the cook can go. We only have a sweet mast about every three or four years in the encinal, but it always brings the wild pigeons. We'll take a couple of pack mules and the little and the big pot and the two biggest Dutch ovens on the ranch. Oh, you got to parboil a pigeon if you want a tender pie. Next to a fish fry, a good pigeon pie makes the finest eating going. I've made many a one, and I give notice right now that the making of the pie falls to me or I won't play. And another thing, not a bird shall be killed more than we can use. Of course we'll bring home a mess, and a few apiece for the Mexicans."

We had got up our horses during the forenoon, and as soon as dinner was over the white contingent saddled up and started for the roost. Tiburcio and Enrique accompanied us, and, riding leisurely, we reached the bend several hours before the return of the birds. The roost had been in use but a short time, but as we scouted through the timber there was abundant evidence of an immense flight of pigeons. The ground was literally covered with feathers; broken limbs hung from nearly every tree, while in one instance a forked hackberry had split from the weight of the birds.

We made camp on the outskirts of the timber, and at early dusk great flocks of pigeons began to arrive at their roosting place. We only had four shotguns, and, dividing into pairs, we entered the roost shortly after dark. Glenn Gallup fell to me as my pardner. I carried the gunny sack for the birds, not caring for a gun in such unfair shooting. The flights continued to arrive for fully an hour after we entered the roost, and in half a dozen shots we bagged over fifty birds. Remembering the admonition of Uncle Lance, Gallup refused to kill more, and we sat down and listened to the rumbling noises of the grove. There was a constant chattering of the pigeons, and as they settled in great flights in the trees overhead, whipping the branches with their wings in search of footing, they frequently fell to the ground at our feet.

Gallup and I returned to camp early. Before we had skinned our kill the others had all come in, disgusted with the ease with which they had filled their bags. We soon had two pots filled and on the fire parboiling, while Tiburcio lined two ovens with pastry, all ready for the baking. In a short time two horsemen, attracted by our fire, crossed the river below our camp and rode up.

"Hello, Uncle Lance," lustily shouted one of them, as he dismounted. "It's you, is it, that's shooting my pigeons? All right, sir, I'll stay all night and help you eat them. I had figured on riding back to the Frio to-night, but I've changed my mind. Got any horse hobbles here?" The two men, George Nathan and Hugh Trotter, were accommodated with hobbles, and after an exchange of commonplace news of the country, we settled down to story-telling. Trotter was a convivial acquaintance of Aaron Scales, quite a vagabond and consequently a story-teller. After Trotter had narrated a late dream, Scales unlimbered and told one of his own.

"I remember a dream I had several years ago, and the only way I can account for it was, I had been drinking more or less during the day. I dreamt I was making a long ride across a dreary desert, and towards night it threatened a bad storm. I began to look around for some shelter. I could just see the tops of a clump of trees beyond a hill, and rode hard to get to them, thinking that there might be a house amongst them. How I did ride! But I certainly must have had a poor horse, for I never seemed to get any nearer that timber. I rode and rode, but all this time, hours and hours it seemed, and the storm gathering and scattering raindrops falling, the timber seemed scarcely any nearer.

"At last I managed to reach the crest of the hill. Well, sir, there wasn't a tree in sight, only, under the brow of the hill, a deserted adobe *jacal*, and I rode for that, picketed my horse and went in. The *jacal* had a thatched roof with several large holes in it, and in the fireplace burned a roaring fire. That was some strange, but I didn't mind it and I was warming my hands before the fire and congratulating myself on my good luck, when a large black cat sprang from the outside into an open window, and said: 'Pardner, it looks like a bad night outside.'

"I eyed him a little suspiciously; but, for all that, if he hadn't spoken, I wouldn't have thought anything about it, for I like cats. He walked backward and forward on the window sill, his spine and tail nicely arched, and rubbed himself on either window jamb. I watched him some little time, and finally concluded to make friends with him. Going over to the window, I put out my hand to stroke his glossy back, when a gust of rain came through the window and the cat vanished into the darkness.

"I went back to the fire, pitying the cat out there in the night's storm, and was really sorry I had disturbed him. I didn't give the matter overmuch attention but sat before the fire, wondering who could have built it and listening to the rain outside, when all of a sudden Mr. Cat walked between my legs, rubbing himself against my boots, purring and singing. Once or twice I thought of stroking his fur, but checked myself on remembering he had spoken to me on the window sill. He would walk over and rub himself against the jambs of the fireplace, and then come back and rub himself against my boots friendly like. I saw him just as clear as I see those pots on the fire or these saddles lying around here. I was noting every move of his as he meandered around, when presently he cocked up an eye at me and remarked: 'Old sport, this is a fine fire we have here.'

"I was beginning to feel a little creepy, for I'd seen mad dogs and skunks, and they say a cat gets locoed likewise, and the cuss was talking so cleverly that I began to lose my regard for him. After a little while I concluded to pet him, for he didn't seem a bit afraid; but as I put out my hand to catch him, he nimbly hopped into the roaring fire and vanished. Then I did feel foolish. I had a good six-shooter, and made up my mind if he showed up again I'd plug him one for luck. I was growing sleepy, and it was getting late, so I concluded to spread down my saddle blankets and slicker before the fire and go to sleep. While I was making down my bed, I happened to look towards the fire, when there was my black cat, with not even a hair singed. I drew my gun quietly and cracked away at him, when he let out the funniest little laugh, saying: 'You've been drinking, Aaron; you're nervous; you couldn't hit a flock of barns.'

"I was getting excited by this time, and cut loose on him rapidly, but he dodged every shot, jumping from the hearth to the mantel, from the mantel to an old table, from there to a niche in the wall, and from the niche clear across the room and out of the window. About then I was some nervous, and after a while lay down before the fire and tried to go to sleep.

"It was a terrible night outside — one of those nights when you can hear things; and with the vivid imagination I was enjoying then, I was almost afraid to try to sleep. But just as I was going into a doze, I raised up my head, and there was my cat walking up and down my frame, his back arched and his tail flirting with the slow sinuous movement of a snake. I reached for my gun, and as it clicked in cocking, he began raking my legs, sharpening his claws and growling like a tiger. I gave a yell and kicked him off, when he sprang up on the old table and I could see his eyes glaring at me. I emptied my gun at him a second time, and at every shot he crouched lower and crept forward as if getting ready to spring. When I had fired the last shot I jumped up and ran out into the rain, and hadn't gone more than a hundred yards before I fell into a dry wash. When I crawled out there was that d — — d cat rubbing himself against my boot leg. I stood breathless for a minute, thinking what next to do, and the cat remarked: 'Wasn't that a peach of a race we just had!'

"I made one or two vicious kicks at him and he again vanished. Well, fellows, in that dream I walked around that old *jacal* all night in my shirt sleeves, and it raining pitchforks. A number of times I peeped in through the window or door, and there sat the cat on the hearth, in full possession of the shack, and me out in the weather. Once when I looked in he was missing, but while I was watching he sprang through a hole in the roof, alighting in the fire, from which he walked out gingerly, shaking his feet as if he had just been out in the wet. I shot away every cartridge I had at him, but in the middle of the shooting he would just coil up before the fire and snooze away.

"That night was an eternity of torment to me, and I was relieved when some one knocked on the door, and I awoke to find myself in a good bed and pounding my ear on a goose-hair pillow in a hotel in Oakville. Why, I wouldn't have another dream like that for a half interest in the Las Palomas brand. No, honest, if I thought drinking gave me that hideous dream, here would be one lad ripe for reform."

"It strikes me," said Uncle Lance, rising and lifting a pot lid, "that these birds are parboiled by this time. Bring me a fork, Enrique. Well, I should say they were. I hope hell ain't any hotter than that fire. Now, Tiburcio, if you have everything ready, we'll put them in the oven, and bake them a couple of hours."

Several of us assisted in fixing the fire and properly coaling the ovens. When this had been attended to, and we had again resumed our easy positions around the fire, Trotter remarked: "Aaron, you ought to cut drinking out of your amusements; you haven't the constitution to stand it. Now with me it's different. I can drink a week and never sleep; that's the kind of a build to have if you expect to travel and meet all comers. Last year I was working for a Kansas City man on the trail, and after the cattle were delivered about a hundred miles beyond, — Ellsworth, up in Kansas, — he sent us home by way of Kansas City. In fact, that was about the only route we could take. Well, it was a successful trip, and as this man was plum white, anyhow, he concluded to show us the sights around his burg. He was interested in a commission firm out at the stockyards, and the night we reached there all the office men, including the old man himself, turned themselves loose to show us a good time.

"We had been drinking alkali water all summer, and along about midnight they began to drop out until there was no one left to face the music except a little cattle salesman and myself. After all the others quit us, we went into a feed trough on a back street, and had a good supper. I had been drinking everything like a good fellow, and at several places there was no salt to put in the beer. The idea struck me that I would buy a sack of salt from this eating ranch and take it with me. The landlord gave me a funny look, but after some little parley went to the rear and brought out a five-pound sack of table salt.

"It was just what I wanted, and after paying for it the salesman and I started out to make a night of it. This yard man was a short, fat Dutchman, and we made a team for your whiskers. I carried the sack of salt under my arm, and the quantity of beer we killed before daylight was a caution. About daybreak, the salesman wanted me to go to our hotel and go to bed, but as I never drink and sleep at the same time, I declined. Finally he explained to me that he would have to be at the yards at eight o'clock, and begged me to excuse him. By this time he was several sheets in the wind, while I could walk a chalk line without a waver. Somehow we drifted around to the hotel where the outfit were supposed to be stopping, and lined up at the bar for a final drink. It was just daybreak, and between that Dutch cattle salesman and the barkeeper and myself, it would have taken a bookkeeper to have kept a check on the drinks we consumed — every one the last.

"Then the Dutchman gave me the slip and was gone, and I wandered into the office of the hotel. A newsboy sold me a paper, and the next minute a bootblack wanted to give me a shine. Well, I took a seat for a shine, and for two hours I sat there as full as a tick, and as dignified as a judge on the bench. All the newsboys and bootblacks caught on, and before any of the outfit showed up that morning to rescue me, I had bought a dozen papers and had my boots shined for the tenth time. If I'd been foxy enough to have got rid of that sack of salt, no one could have told I was off the reservation; but there it was under my arm. If ever I make another trip over the trail, and touch at Kansas City returning, I'll hunt up that cattle salesman, for he's the only man I ever met that can pace in my class."

"Did you hear that tree break a few minutes ago?" inquired Mr. Nathan. "There goes another one. It hardly looks possible that enough pigeons could settle on a tree to break it down. Honestly, I'd give a purty to know how many birds are in that roost to-night. More than there are cattle in Texas, I'll bet. Why, Hugh killed, with both barrels, twenty-two at one shot."

We had brought blankets along, but it was early and no one thought of sleeping for an hour yet. Mr. Nathan was quite a sportsman, and after he and Uncle Lance had discussed the safest method of hunting *javalina*, it again devolved on the boys to entertain the party with stories.

"I was working on a ranch once," said Glenn Gallup, "out on the Concho River. It was a stag outfit, there being few women then out Concho way. One day two of the boys were riding in home when an accident occurred. They had been shooting more or less during the morning, and one of them, named Bill Cook, had carelessly left the hammer of his six-shooter on a cartridge. As Bill jumped his horse over a dry *arroyo*, his pistol was thrown from its holster, and, falling on the hard ground, was discharged. The bullet struck him in the ankle, ranged upward, shattering the large bone in his leg into fragments, and finally lodged in the saddle.

"They were about five miles from camp when the accident happened. After they realized how bad he was hurt, Bill remounted his horse and rode nearly a mile; but the wound bled so then that the fellow with him insisted on his getting off and lying on the ground while he went into the ranch for a wagon. Well, it's to be supposed that he lost no time riding in, and I was sent to San Angelo for a doctor. It was just noon when I got off. I had to ride thirty miles. Talk about your good horses — I had one that day. I took a free gait from the start, but the last ten miles was the fastest, for I covered the entire distance in less than three hours. There was a doctor in the town who'd been on the frontier all of his life, and was used to such calls. Well, before dark that evening we drove into the ranch.

"They had got the lad into the ranch, had checked the flow of blood and eased the pain by standing on a chair and pouring water on the wound from a height. But Bill looked pale as a ghost from the loss of blood. The doctor gave the leg a single look, and, turning to us, said: 'Boys, she has to come off.'

"The doctor talked to Bill freely and frankly, telling him that it was the only chance for his life. He readily consented to the operation, and while the doctor was getting him under the influence of opiates we fixed up an operating table. When all was ready, the doctor took the leg off below the knee, cursing us generally for being so sensitive to cutting and the sight of blood. There was quite a number of boys at the ranch, but it affected them all alike. It was interesting to watch him cut and tie arteries and saw the bones, and I think I stood it better than any of them. When the operation was over, we gave the fellow the best bed the ranch afforded and fixed him up comfortable. The doctor took the bloody stump and wrapped it up in an old newspaper, saying he would take it home with him.

"After supper the surgeon took a sleep, saying we would start back to town by two o'clock, so as to be there by daylight. He gave instructions to call him in case Bill awoke, but he hoped the boy would take a good sleep. As I had left my horse in town, I was expected to go back with him. Shortly after midnight the fellow awoke, so we aroused the doctor, who reported him doing well. The old Doc sat by his bed for an hour and told him all kinds of stories. He had been a surgeon in the Confederate army, and from the drift of his talk you'd think it was impossible to kill a man without cutting off his head.

"'Now take a young fellow like you,' said the doctor to his patient, 'if he was all shot to pieces, just so the parts would hang together, I could fix him up and he would get well. You have no idea, son, how much lead a young man can carry.' We had coffee and lunch before starting, the doctor promising to send me back at once with necessary medicines.

"We had a very pleasant trip driving back to town that night. The stories he could tell were like a song with ninety verses, no two alike. It was hardly daybreak when we reached San Angelo, rustled out a sleepy hostler at the livery stable where the team belonged, and had the horses cared for; and as we left the stable the doctor gave me his instrument case, while he carried the amputated leg in the paper. We both felt the need of a bracer after our night's ride, so we looked around to see if any saloons were open. There was only one that showed any signs of life, and we headed for that. The doctor was in the lead as we entered, and we both knew the barkeeper well. This barkeeper was a practical joker himself, and he and the doctor were great hunting companions. We walked up to the bar together, when the doctor laid the package on the counter and asked: 'Is this good for two drinks?' The barkeeper, with a look of expectation in his face as if the package might contain half a dozen quail or some fresh fish, broke the string and unrolled it. Without a word he walked straight from behind the bar and out of the house. If he had been shot himself he couldn't have looked whiter.

"The doctor went behind the bar and said: 'Glenn, what are you going to take?' 'Let her come straight, doctor,' was my reply, and we both took the same. We had the house all to ourselves, and after a second round of drinks took our leave. As we left by the front door, we saw the barkeeper leaning against a hitching post half a block below. The doctor called to him as we were leaving: 'Billy, if the drinks ain't on you, charge them to me.'"

The moon was just rising, and at Uncle Lance's suggestion we each carried in a turn of wood. Piling a portion of it on the fire, the blaze soon lighted up the camp, throwing shafts of light far into the recesses of the woods around us. "In another hour," said Uncle Lance, recoaling the oven lids, "that smaller pie will be all ready to serve, but we'll keep the big one for breakfast. So, boys, if you want to sit up awhile longer, we'll have a midnight lunch, and then all turn in for about forty winks." As the oven lid was removed from time to time to take note of the baking, savory odors of the pie were wafted to our anxious nostrils. On the intimation that one oven would be ready in an hour, not a man suggested blankets, and, taking advantage of the lull, Theodore Quayle claimed attention.

"Another fellow and myself," said Quayle, "were knocking around Fort Worth one time seeing the sights. We had drunk until it didn't taste right any longer. This chum of mine was queer in his drinking. If he ever got enough once, he didn't want any more for several days: you could cure him by offering him plenty. But with just the right amount on board, he was a hail fellow. He was a big, ambling, awkward cuss, who could be led into anything on a hint or suggestion. We had been knocking around the town for a week, until there was nothing new to be seen.

"Several times as we passed a millinery shop, kept by a little blonde, we had seen her standing at the door. Something — it might have been his ambling walk, but, anyway, something — about my chum amused her, for she smiled and watched him as we passed. He never could walk along beside you for any distance, but would trail behind and look into the windows. He could not be hurried — not in town. I mentioned to him that he had made a mash on the little blond milliner, and he at once insisted that I should show her to him. We passed down on the opposite side of the street and I pointed out the place. Then we walked by several times, and finally passed when she was standing in the doorway talking to some customers. As we came up he straightened himself, caught her eye, and tipped his hat with the politeness of a dancing master. She blushed to the roots of her hair, and he walked on very erect some little distance, then we turned a corner and held a confab. He was for playing the whole string, discount or no discount, anyway.

"An excuse to go in was wanting, but we thought we could invent one; however, he needed a drink or two to facilitate his thinking and loosen his tongue. To get them was easier than the excuse; but with the drinks the motive was born. 'You wait here,' said he to me, 'until I go round to the livery stable and get my coat off my saddle.' He never encumbered himself with extra clothing. We had not seen our horses, saddles, or any of our belongings during the week of our visit. When he returned he inquired, 'Do I need a shave?'

"'Oh, no,' I said, 'you need no shave. You may have a drink too many, or lack one of having enough. It's hard to make a close calculation on you.'

"'Then I'm all ready,' said he, 'for I've just the right gauge of steam.' He led the way as we entered. It was getting dark and the shop was empty of customers. Where he ever got the manners, heaven only knows. Once inside the door we halted, and she kept a counter between us as she approached. She ought to have called the police and had us run in. She was probably scared, but her voice was fairly steady as she spoke. 'Gentlemen, what can I do for you?'

"'My friend here,' said he, with a bow and a wave of the hand, 'was unfortunate enough to lose a wager made between us. The terms of the bet were that the loser was to buy a new hat for one of the dining-room girls at our hotel. As we are leaving town to-morrow, we have just dropped in to see if you have anything suitable. We are both totally incompetent to decide on such a delicate matter, but we will trust entirely to your judgment in the selection.' The milliner was quite collected by this time, as she asked: 'Any particular style? — and about what price?'

"'The price is immaterial,' said he disdainfully. 'Any man who will wager on the average weight of a train-load of cattle, his own cattle, mind you, and miss them twenty pounds, ought to pay for his lack of judgment. Don't you think so, Miss — er — er. Excuse me for being unable to call your name — but — but — ' 'De Ment is my name,' said she with some little embarrassment.

"'Livingstone is mine,' said he with a profound bow,' and this gentleman is Mr. Ochiltree, youngest brother of Congressman Tom. Now regarding the style, we will depend entirely upon your selection. But possibly the loser is entitled to some choice in the matter. Mr. Ochiltree, have you any preference in regard to style?'

"'Why, no, I can generally tell whether a hat becomes a lady or not, but as to selecting one I am at sea. We had better depend on Miss De Ment's judgment. Still, I always like an abundance of flowers on a lady's hat. Whenever a girl walks down the street ahead of me, I like to watch the posies, grass, and buds on her hat wave and nod with the motion of her walk. Miss De Ment, don't you agree with me that an abundance of flowers becomes a young lady? And this girl can't be over twenty.'

"'Well, now,' said she, going into matters in earnest, 'I can scarcely advise you. Is the young lady a brunette or blonde?'

"'What difference does that make?' he innocently asked.

"'Oh,' said she, smiling, 'we must harmonize colors. What would suit one complexion would not become another. What color is her hair?'

"'Nearly the color of yours,' said he. 'Not so heavy and lacks the natural wave which yours has — but she's all right. She can ride a string of my horses until they all have sore backs. I tell you she is a cute trick. But, say, Miss De Ment, what do you think of a green hat, broad brimmed, turned up behind and on one side, long black feathers run round and turned up behind, with a blue bird on the other side swooping down like a pigeon hawk, long tail feathers and an arrow in its beak? That strikes me as about the mustard. What do you think of that kind of a hat, dear?'

"'Why, sir, the colors don't harmonize,' she replied, blushing.

"'Theodore, do you know anything about this harmony of colors? Excuse me, madam, — and I crave your pardon, Mr. Ochiltree, for using your given name, — but really this harmony of colors is all French to me.'

"'Well, if the young lady is in town, why can't you have her drop in and make her own selection?' suggested the blond milliner. He studied a moment, and then awoke as if from a trance. 'Just as easy as not; this very evening or in the morning. Strange we didn't think of that sooner. Yes; the landlady of the hotel can join us, and we can count on your assistance in selecting the hat.' With a number of comments on her attractive place, inquiries regarding trade, and a flattering compliment on having made such a charming acquaintance, we edged towards the door. 'This evening then, or in the morning at the farthest, you may expect another call, when my friend must pay the penalty of his folly by settling the bill. Put it on heavy.' And he gave her a parting wink.

"Together we bowed ourselves out, and once safe in the street he said: 'Didn't she help us out of that easy? If she wasn't a blonde, I'd go back and buy her two hats for suggesting it as she did.'

"'Rather good looking too,' I remarked.

"'Oh, well, that's a matter of taste. I like people with red blood in them. Now if you was to saw her arm off, it wouldn't bleed; just a little white water might ooze out, possibly. The best-looking girl I ever saw was down in the lower Rio Grande country, and she was milking a goat. Theodore, my dear fellow, when I'm led blushingly to the altar, you'll be proud of my choice. I'm a judge of beauty.'"

It was after midnight when we disposed of the first oven of pigeon pot-pie, and, wrapping ourselves in blankets, lay down around the fire. With the first sign of dawn, we were aroused by Mr. Nathan and Uncle Lance to witness the return flight of the birds to their feeding grounds. Hurrying to the nearest opening, we saw the immense flight of pigeons blackening the sky overhead. Stiffened by their night's rest, they flew low; but the beauty and immensity of the flight overawed us, and we stood in mute admiration, no one firing a shot. For fully a half-hour the flight continued, ending in a few scattering birds.

CHAPTER VI
SPRING OF '76

The spring of '76 was eventful at Las Palomas. After the pigeon hunt, Uncle Lance went to San Antonio to sell cattle for spring delivery. Meanwhile, Father Norquin visited the ranch and spent a few days among his parishioners, Miss Jean acting the hostess in behalf of Las Palomas. The priest proved a congenial fellow of the cloth, and among us, with Miss Jean's countenance, it was decided not to delay Enrique's marriage; for there was no telling when Uncle Lance would return. All the arrangements were made by the padre and Miss Jean, the groom-to-be apparently playing a minor part in the preliminaries. Though none of the white element of the ranch were communicants of his church, the priest apparently enjoyed the visit. At parting, the mistress pressed a gold piece into his chubby palm as the marriage fee for Enrique; and, after naming a day for the ceremony, the padre mounted his horse and left us for the Tarancalous, showering his blessings on Las Palomas and its people.

During the intervening days before the wedding, we overhauled an unused *jacal* and made it habitable for the bride and groom. The *jacal* is a crude structure of this semi-tropical country, containing but a single room with a shady, protecting stoop. It is constructed by standing palisades on end in a trench. These constitute the walls. The floor is earthen, while the roof is thatched with the wild grass which grows rank in the overflow portions of the river valley. It forms a serviceable shelter for a warm country, the peculiar roofing equally defying rain and the sun's heat. Under the leadership of the mistress of the ranch, assisted by the Mexican women, the *jacal* was transformed into a rustic bower; for Enrique was not only a favorite among the whites, but also among his own people. A few gaudy pictures of Saints and the Madonna ornamented the side walls, while in the rear hung the necessary crucifix. At the time of its building the *jacal* had been blessed, as was customary before occupancy, and to Enrique's reasoning the potency of the former sprinkling still held good.

Weddings were momentous occasions among the Mexican population at Las Palomas. In outfitting the party to attend Enrique's wedding at Santa Maria, the ranch came to a standstill. Not only the regular ambulance but a second conveyance was required to transport the numerous female relatives of the groom, while the men, all in gala attire, were mounted on the best horses on the ranch. As none of the whites attended, Deweese charged Tiburcio with humanity to the stock, while the mistress admonished every one to be on his good behavior. With greetings to Santa Maria, the wedding party set out. They were expected to return the following evening, and the ranch was set in order to give the bride a rousing reception on her arrival at Las Palomas. The largest place on the ranch was a warehouse, and we shifted its contents in such a manner as to have quite a commodious ball-room. The most notable decoration of the room was an immense heart-shaped figure, in which was worked in live-oak leaves the names of the two ranches, flanked on either side with the American and Mexican flags. Numerous other decorations, expressing welcome to the bride, were in evidence on every hand. Tallow was plentiful at Las Palomas, and candles were fastened at every possible projection.

The mounted members of the wedding party returned near the middle of the afternoon. According to reports, Santa Maria had treated them most hospitably. The marriage was simple, but the festivities following had lasted until dawn. The returning guests sought their *jacals* to snatch a few hours' sleep before the revelry would be resumed at Las Palomas. An hour before sunset the four-mule ambulance bearing the bride and groom drove into Las Palomas with a flourish. Before leaving the bridal couple at their own *jacal*, Tiburcio halted the ambulance in front of the ranch-house for the formal welcome. In the absence of her brother, Miss Jean officiated in behalf of Las Palomas, tenderly caressing the bride. The boys monopolized her with their congratulations and welcome, which delighted Enrique. As for the bride, she seemed at home from the first, soon recognizing me as the *padrino segundo* at the time of her betrothal.

Quite a delegation of the bride's friends from Santa Maria accompanied the party on their return, from whom were chosen part of the musicians for the evening — violins and guitars in the hands of the native element of the two ranches making up a pastoral orchestra. I volunteered my services; but so much of the music was new to me that I frequently excused myself for a dance with the senoritas. In the absence of Uncle Lance, our *segundo*, June Deweese, claimed the first dance of the evening with the bride. Miss Jean lent only the approval of her presence, not participating, and withdrawing at an early hour. As all the American element present spoke Spanish slightly, that became the language of the evening. But, further than to countenance with our presence the festivities, we were out of place, and, ere midnight, all had excused themselves with the exception of Aaron Scales and myself. On the pleadings of Enrique, I remained an hour or two longer, dancing with his bride, or playing some favorite selection for the delighted groom.

Several days after the wedding Uncle Lance returned. He had been successful in contracting a trail herd of thirty-five hundred cattle, and a *remuda* of one hundred and twenty-five saddle horses with which to handle them. The contract called for two thousand two-year-old steers and fifteen hundred threes. There was a difference of four dollars a head in favor of the older cattle, and it was the ranchero's intention to fill the latter class entirely from the Las Palomas brand. As to the younger cattle, neighboring ranches would be invited to deliver twos in filling the contract, and if any were lacking, the home ranch would supply the deficiency. Having ample range, the difference in price was an inducement to hold the younger cattle. To keep a steer another year cost nothing, while the ranchero returned convinced that the trail might soon furnish an outlet for all surplus cattle. In the matter of the horses, too, rather than reduce our supply of saddle stock below the actual needs of the ranch, Uncle Lance concluded to buy fifty head in making up the *remuda*. There were several hundred geldings on the ranch old enough for saddle purposes, but they would be as good as useless in handling cattle the first year after breaking.

As this would be the first trail herd from Las Palomas, we naturally felt no small pride in the transaction. According to contract, everything was to be ready for final delivery on the twenty-fifth of March. The contractors, Camp & Dupree, of Fort Worth, Texas, were to send their foreman two weeks in advance to receive, classify, and pass upon the cattle and saddle stock. They were exacting in their demands, yet humane and reasonable. In making up the herd no cattle were to be corralled at night, and no animal would be received which had been roped. The saddle horses were to be treated likewise. These conditions would put into the saddle every available man on the ranch as well as on the ranchitas. But we looked eagerly forward to the putting up of the herd. Letters were written and dispatched to a dozen ranches within striking distance, inviting them to turn in two-year-old steers at the full contract price. June Deweese was sent out to buy fifty saddle horses, which would fill the required standard, "fourteen hands or better, serviceable and gentle broken." I was dispatched to Santa Maria, to invite Don Mateo Gonzales to participate in the contract. The range of every saddle horse on the ranch was located, so that we could gather them, when wanted, in a day. Less than a month's time now remained before the delivery day, though we did not expect to go into camp for actual gathering until the arrival of the trail foreman.

In going and returning from San Antonio my employer had traveled by stage. As it happened, the driver of the up-stage out of Oakville was Jack Martin, the son-in-law of Mrs. McLeod. He and Uncle Lance being acquainted, the old ranchero's matchmaking instincts had, during the day's travel, again forged to the front. By roundabout inquiries he had elicited the information that Mrs. McLeod had, immediately after the holidays, taken Esther to San Antonio and placed her in school. By innocent artful suggestions of his interest in the welfare of the family, he learned the name of the private school of which Esther was a pupil. Furthermore, he cultivated the good will of the driver in various ways over good cigars, and at parting assured him on returning he would take the stage so as to have the pleasure of his company on the return trip — the highest compliment that could be paid a stage-driver.

From several sources I had learned that Esther had left the ranch for the city, but on Uncle Lance's return I got the full particulars. As a neighboring ranchman, and bearing self-invented messages from the family, he had the assurance to call at the school. His honest countenance was a passport anywhere, and he not only saw Esther but prevailed on her teachers to give the girl, some time during his visit in the city, a half holiday. The interest he manifested in the girl won his request, and the two had spent an afternoon visiting the parks and other points of interest. It is needless to add that he made hay in my behalf during this half holiday. But the most encouraging fact that he unearthed was that Esther was disgusted with her school life and was homesick. She had declared that if she ever got away from school, no power on earth could force her back again.

"Shucks, Tom," said he, the next morning after his return, as we were sitting in the shade of the corrals waiting for the *remuda* to come in, "that poor little country girl might as well be in a penitentiary as in that school. She belongs on these prairies, and you can't make anything else out of her. I can read between the lines, and any one can see that her education is finished. When she told me how rudely her mother had treated you, her heart was an open book and easily read. Don't you lose any sleep on how you stand in her affections — that's all serene. She'll he home on a spring vacation, and that'll be your chance. If I was your age, I'd make it a point to see that she didn't go back to school. She'll run off with you rather than that. In the game of matrimony, son, you want to play your cards boldly and never hesitate to lead trumps."

To further matters, when returning by stage my employer had ingratiated himself into the favor of the driver in many ways, and urged him to send word to Mrs. McLeod to turn in her two-year-olds on his contract. A few days later her foreman and son-in-law, Tony Hunter, rode down to Las Palomas, anxious for the chance to turn in cattle. There had been little opportunity for several years to sell steers, and when a chance like this came, there would have been no trouble to fill half a dozen contracts, as supply far exceeded demand.

Uncle Lance let Mrs. McLeod's foreman feel that in allotting her five hundred of the younger cattle, he was actuated by old-time friendship for the family. As a mark of special consideration he promised to send the trail foreman to the San Miguel to pass on the cattle on their home range, but advised the foreman to gather at least seven hundred steers, allowing for two hundred to be culled or cut back. Hunter remained over night, departing the next morning, delighted over his allowance of cattle and the liberal terms of the contract.

It was understood that, in advance of his outfit, the trail foreman would come down by stage, and I was sent into Oakville with an extra saddle horse to meet him. He had arrived the day previous, and we lost no time in starting for Las Palomas. This trail foreman was about thirty years of age, a quiet red-headed fellow, giving the name of Frank Nancrede, and before we had covered half the distance to the ranch I was satisfied that he was a cowman. I always prided myself on possessing a good eye for brands, but he outclassed me, reading strange brands at over a hundred yards, and distinguishing cattle from horse stock at a distance of three miles.'

We got fairly well acquainted before reaching the ranch, but it was impossible to start him on any subject save cattle. I was able to give him a very good idea of the *remuda*, which was then under herd and waiting his approval, and I saw the man brighten into a smile for the first time on my offering to help him pick out a good mount for his own saddle. I had a vague idea of what the trail was like, and felt the usual boyish attraction for it; but when I tried to draw him out in regard to it, he advised me, if I had a regular job on a ranch, to let trail work alone.

We reached the ranch late in the evening and I introduced Nancrede to Uncle Lance, who took charge of him. We had established a horse camp for the trail *remuda*, north of the river, and the next morning the trail foreman, my employer, and June Deweese, rode over to pass on the saddle stock. The *remuda* pleased him, being fully up to the contract standard, and he accepted it with but a single exception. This exception tickled Uncle Lance, as it gave him an opportunity to annoy his sister about Nancrede, as he did about every other cowman or drover who visited the ranch. That evening, as I was chatting with Miss Jean, who was superintending the Mexican help milking at the cow pen, Uncle Lance joined us.

"Say, Sis," said he, "our man Nancrede is a cowman all right. I tried to ring in a 'hipped' horse on him this morning, — one hip knocked down just the least little bit, — but he noticed it and refused to accept him. Oh, he's got an eye in his head all right. So if you say so, I'll give him the best horse on the ranch in old Hippy's place. You're always making fun of slab-sided cowmen; he's pony-built enough to suit you, and I kind o' like the color of his hair myself. Did you notice his neck? — he'll never tie it if it gets broken. I like a short man; if he stubs his toe and falls down he doesn't reach halfway home. Now, if he has as good cow sense in receiving the herd as he had on the *remuda*, I'd kind o' like to have him for a brother-in-law. I'm getting a little too old for active work and would like to retire, but June, the durn fool, won't get married, and about the only show I've got is to get a husband for you. I'd as lief live in Hades as on a ranch without a woman on it. What do you think of him?"

"Why, I think he's an awful nice fellow, but he won't talk. And besides, I'm not baiting my hook for small fish like trail foremen; I was aiming to keep my smiles for the contractors. Aren't they coming down?"

"Well, they might come to look the herd over before it starts out. Now, Dupree is a good cowman, but he's got a wife already. And Camp, the financial man of the firm, made his money peddling Yankee clocks. Now, you don't suppose for a moment I'd let you marry him and carry you away from Las Palomas. Marry an old clock peddler? — not if he had a million! The idea! If they come down here and I catch you smiling on old Camp, I'll set the hounds on you. What you want to do is to set your cap for Nancrede. Of course, you're ten years the elder, but that needn't cut any figure. So just burn a few smiles on the red-headed trail foreman! You know you can count on your loving brother to help all he can."

The conversation was interrupted by our *segundo* and the trail foreman riding up to the cow pen. The two had been up the river during the afternoon, looking over the cattle on the range, for as yet we had not commenced gathering. Nancrede was very reticent, discovering a conspicuous lack of words to express his opinion of what cattle Deweese had shown him.

The second day after the arrival of the trail foreman, we divided our forces into two squads and started out to gather our three-year-olds. By the ranch records, there were over two thousand steers of that age in the Las Palomas brand. Deweese took ten men and half of the ranch saddle horses and went up above the mouth of the Ganso to begin gathering. Uncle Lance took the remainder of the men and horses and went down the river nearly to Shepherd's, leaving Dan Happersett and three Mexicans to hold and night-herd the trail *remuda*. Nancrede declined to stay at the ranch and so joined our outfit on the down-river trip. We had postponed the gathering until the last hour, for every day improved the growing grass on which our mounts must depend for subsistence, and once we started, there would be little rest for men or horses.

The younger cattle for the herd were made up within a week after the invitations were sent to the neighboring ranches. Naturally they would be the last cattle to be received and would come in for delivery between the twentieth and the last of the month. With the plans thus outlined, we started our gathering. Counting Nancrede, we had twelve men in the saddle in our down-river outfit. Taking nothing but three-year-olds, we did not accumulate cattle fast; but it was continuous work, every man, with the exception of Uncle Lance, standing a guard on night-herd. The first two days we only gathered about five hundred steers. This number was increased by about three hundred on the third day, and that evening Dan Happersett with a vaquero rode into camp and reported that Nancrede's outfit had arrived from San Antonio. He had turned the *remuda* over to them on their arrival, sending the other two Mexicans to join Deweese above on the river.

The fourth day finished the gathering. Nancrede remained with us to the last, making a hand which left no doubt in any one's mind that he was a cowman from the ground up. The last round-up on the afternoon of the fourth day, our outriders sighted the vaqueros from Deweese's outfit, circling and drifting in the cattle on their half of the circle. The next morning the two camps were thrown together on the river opposite the ranch. Deweese had fully as many cattle as we had, and when the two cuts had been united and counted, we lacked but five head of nineteen hundred. Several of Nancrede's men joined us that morning, and within an hour, under the trail foreman's directions, we cut back the overplus, and the cattle were accepted.

Under the contract we were to road-brand them, though Nancrede ordered his men to assist us in the work. Under ordinary circumstances we should also have vented the ranch brand, but owing to the fact that this herd was to be trailed to Abilene, Kansas, and possibly sold beyond that point, it was unnecessary and therefore omitted. We had a branding chute on the ranch for grown cattle, and the following morning the herd was corralled and the road-branding commenced. The cattle were uniform in size, and the stamping of the figure '4' over the holding "Lazy L" of Las Palomas, moved like clockwork. With a daybreak start and an abundance of help the last animal was ironed up before sundown. As a favor to Nancrede's outfit, their camp being nearly five miles distant, we held them the first night after branding.

No sooner had the trail foreman accepted our three-year-olds than he and Glen Gallup set out for the McLeod ranch on the San Miguel. The day our branding was finished, the two returned near midnight, reported the San Miguel cattle accepted and due the next evening at Las Palomas. By dawn Nancrede and myself started for Santa Maria, the former being deficient in Spanish, the only weak point, if it was one, in his make-up as a cowman. We were slightly disappointed in not finding the cattle ready to pass upon at Santa Maria. That ranch was to deliver seven hundred, and on our arrival they had not even that number under herd. Don Mateo, an easy-going ranchero, could not understand the necessity of such haste. What did it matter if the cattle were delivered on the twenty-fifth or twenty-seventh? But I explained as delicately as I could that this was a trail man, whose vocabulary did not contain *mañana*. In interpreting for Nancrede, I learned something of the trail myself: that a herd should start with the grass and move with it, keeping the freshness of spring, day after day and week after week, as they trailed northward. The trail foreman assured Don Mateo that had his employers known that this was to be such an early spring, the herd would have started a week sooner.

By impressing on the ranchero the importance of not delaying this trail man, we got him to inject a little action into his corporal. We asked Don Mateo for horses and, joining his outfit, made three rodeos that afternoon, turning into the cattle under herd nearly two hundred and fifty head by dark that evening. Nancrede spent a restless night, and at dawn, as the cattle were leaving the bed ground, he and I got an easy count on them and culled them down to the required number before breakfasting. We had some little trouble explaining to Don Mateo the necessity of giving the bill of sale to my employer, who, in turn, would reconvey the stock to the contractors. Once the matter was made clear, the accepted cattle were started for Las Palomas. When we overtook them an hour afterward, I instructed the corporal, at the instance of the red-headed foreman, to take a day and a half in reaching the ranch; that tardiness in gathering must not be made up by a hasty drive to the point of delivery; that the animals must be treated humanely.

On reaching the ranch we found that Mr. Booth and some of his neighbors had arrived from the Frio with their contingent. They had been allotted six hundred head, and had brought down about two hundred extra cattle in order to allow some choice in accepting. These were the only mixed brands that came in on the delivery, and after they had been culled down and accepted, my employer appointed Aaron Scales as clerk. There were some five or six owners, and Scales must catch the brands as they were freed from the branding chute. Several of the owners kept a private tally, but not once did they have occasion to check up the Marylander's decisions. Before the branding of this bunch was finished, Wilson, from Ramirena, rode into the ranch and announced his cattle within five miles of Las Palomas. As these were the last two hundred to be passed upon, Nancrede asked to have them in sight of the ranch by sun-up in the morning.

On the arrival of the trail outfit from San Antonio, they brought a letter from the contractors, asking that a conveyance meet them at Oakville, as they wished to see the herd before it started. Tiburcio went in with the ambulance to meet them, and they reached the ranch late at night. On their arrival twenty-six hundred of the cattle had already been passed upon, branded, and were then being held by Nancrede's outfit across the river at their camp. Dupree, being a practical cowman, understood the situation; but Camp was restless and uneasy as if he expected to find the cattle in the corrals at the ranch. Camp was years the older of the two, a pudgy man with a florid complexion and nasal twang, and kept the junior member busy answering his questions. Uncle Lance enjoyed the situation, jollying his sister about the elder contractor and quietly inquiring of the red-haired foreman how and where Dupree had picked him up.

The contractors had brought no saddles with them, so the ambulance was the only mode of travel. As we rode out to receive the Wilson cattle the next morning, Uncle Lance took advantage of the occasion to jolly Nancrede further about the senior member of the firm, the foreman smiling appreciatively. "The way your old man talked last night," said he, "you'd think he expected to find the herd in the front yard. Too bad to disappoint him; for then he could have looked them over with a lantern from the gallery of the house. Now, if they had been Yankee clocks instead of cattle, why, he'd been right at home, and could have taken them in the house and handled them easily. It certainly beats the dickens why some men want to break into the cattle business. It won't surprise me if he asks you to trail the herd past the ranch so he can see them. Well, you and Dupree will have to make him some *dinero* this summer or you will lose him for a partner. I can see that sticking out."

We received and branded the two hundred Wilson cattle that forenoon, sending them to the main herd across the river. Mr. Wilson and Uncle Lance were great cronies, and as the latter was feeling in fine fettle over the successful fulfillment of his contract, he was tempted also to jolly his neighbor ranchero over his cattle, which, by the way, were fine. "Nate," said he to Mr. Wilson, "it looks like you'd quit breeding goats and rear cattle instead. Honest, if I didn't know your brand, I'd swear some Mexican raised this bunch. These Fort Worth cowmen are an easy lot, or yours would never have passed under the classification."

An hour before noon, Tomas Martines, the corporal of Santa Maria, rode up to inquire what time we wished his cattle at the corrals. They were back several miles, and he could deliver them on an hour's notice. One o'clock was agreed upon, and, never dismounting, the corporal galloped away to his herd. "Quirk," said Nancrede to me, noticing the Mexican's unaccustomed air of enterprise, "if we had that fellow under us awhile we'd make a cow-hand out of him. See the wiggle he gets on himself now, will you?" Promptly at the hour, the herd were counted and corralled, Don Mateo Gonzales not troubling to appear, which was mystifying to the North Texas men, but Uncle Lance explained that a mere incident like selling seven hundred cattle was not sufficient occasion to arouse the ranchero of Santa Maria when his corporal could attend to the business.

That evening saw the last of the cattle branded. The herd was completed and ready to start the following morning. The two contractors were driven across the river during the afternoon to look over the herd and *remuda*. At the instance of my employer, I wrote a letter of congratulation to Don Mateo, handing it to his corporal, informing him that in the course of ten days a check would he sent him in payment. Uncle Lance had fully investigated the financial standing of the contractors, but it was necessary for him to return with them to San Antonio for a final settlement.

The ambulance made an early start for Oakville on the morning of the twenty-sixth, carrying the contractors and my employer, and the rest of us rode away to witness the start of the herd. Nancrede's outfit numbered fifteen, — a cook, a horse wrangler, himself, and twelve outriders. They comprised an odd mixture of men, several barely my age, while others were gray-haired and looked like veteran cow-hands. On leaving the Nueces valley, the herd was strung out a mile in length, and after riding with them until they reached the first hills, we bade them good-by. As we started to return Frank Nancrede made a remark to June Deweese which I have often recalled: "You fellows may think this is a snap; but if I had a job on as good a ranch as Las Palomas, you'd never catch me on a cattle trail."

CHAPTER VII
SAN JACINTO DAY

A few days later, when Uncle Lance returned from San Antonio, we had a confidential talk, and he decided not to send me with the McLeod check to the San Miguel. He had reasons of his own, and I was dispatched to the Frio instead, while to Enrique fell the pleasant task of a similar errand to Santa Maria. In order to grind an axe, Glenn Gallup was sent down to Wilson's with the settlement for the Ramirena cattle, which Uncle Lance made the occasion of a jovial expression of his theory of love-making. "Don't waste any words with old man Nate," said he, as he handed Glenn the check; "but build right up to Miss Jule. Holy snakes, boy, if I was your age I would make her dizzy with a big talk. Tell her you're thinking of quitting Las Palomas and driving a trail herd yourself next year. Tell it big and scary. Make her eyes fairly bulge out, and when you can't think of anything else, tell her she's pretty."

I spent a day or two at the Booth ranch, and on my return found the Las Palomas outfit in the saddle working our horse stock. Yearly we made up new *manadas* from the two-year-old fillies. There were enough young mares to form twelve bands of about twenty-five head each. In selecting these we were governed by standard colors, bays, browns, grays, blacks, and sorrels forming separate *manadas,* while all mongrel colors went into two bands by themselves. In the latter class there was a tendency for the colors of the old Spanish stock, — coyotes, and other hybrid mixtures, — after being dormant for generations, to crop out again. In breaking these fillies into new bands, we added a stallion a year or two older and of acceptable color, and they were placed in charge of a trusty vaquero, whose duty was to herd them for the first month after being formed. The Mexican in charge usually took the band round the circuit of the various ranchitas, corralling his charge at night, drifting at will, so that by the end of the month old associations would be severed, and from that time the stallion could be depended on as herdsman.

In gathering the fillies, we also cut out all the geldings three years old and upward to break for saddle purposes. There were fully two hundred of these, and the month of April was spent in saddle-breaking this number. They were a fine lot of young horses, and under the master eye of two perfect horsemen, our *segundo* and employer, every horse was broken with intelligence and humanity. Since the day of their branding as colts these geldings had never felt the touch of a human hand; and it required more than ordinary patience to overcome their fear, bring them to a condition of submission, and make serviceable ranch horses out of them. The most difficult matter was in overcoming their fear. It was also necessary to show the mastery of man over the animal, though this process was tempered with humanity. We had several circular, sandy corrals into which the horse to be broken was admitted for the first saddling. As he ran round, a lasso skillfully thrown encircled his front feet and he came down on his side. One fore foot was strapped up, a hackamore or bitless bridle was adjusted in place, and he was allowed to arise. After this, all depended on the patience and firmness of the handler. Some horses yielded to kind advances and accepted the saddle within half an hour, not even offering to pitch, while others repelled every kindness and fought for hours. But in handling the gelding of spirit, we could always count on the help of an extra saddler.

While this work was being done, the herd of geldings was held close at hand. After the first riding, four horses were the daily allowance of each rider. With the amount of help available, this allowed twelve to fifteen horses to the man, so that every animal was ridden once in three or four days. Rather than corral, we night-herded, penning them by dawn and riding our first horse before sun-up. As they gradually yielded, we increased our number to six a day and finally before the breaking was over to eight. When the work was finally over they were cut into *remudas* of fifty horses each, furnished a gentle bell mare, when possible with a young colt by her side, and were turned over to a similar treatment as was given the fillies in forming *manadas.* Thus the different *remudas* at Las Palomas always took the name of the bell mare, and when we were at work, it was only necessary for us to hobble the princess at night to insure the presence of her band in the morning.

When this month's work was two thirds over, we enjoyed a holiday. All good Texans, whether by birth or adoption, celebrate the twenty-first of April, — San Jacinto Day. National holidays may not always be observed in sparsely settled communities, but this event will remain a great anniversary until the sons and daughters of the Lone Star State lose their patriotism or forget the blessings of liberty. As Shepherd's Ferry was centrally located, it became by common consent the meeting-point for our local celebration. Residents from the Frio and San Miguel and as far south on the home river as Lagarto, including the villagers of Oakville, usually lent their presence on this occasion. The white element of Las Palomas was present without an exception. As usual, Miss Jean went by ambulance, starting the afternoon before and spending the night at a ranch above the ferry. Those remaining made a daybreak start, reaching Shepherd's by ten in the morning.

While on the way from the ranch to the ferry, I was visited with some misgivings as to whether Esther McLeod had yet returned from San Antonio. At the delivery of San Miguel's cattle at Las Palomas, Miss Jean had been very attentive to Tony Hunter, Esther's brother-in-law, and through him she learned that Esther's school closed for the summer vacation on the fifteenth of April, and that within a week afterward she was expected at home. Shortly after our reaching the ferry, a number of vehicles drove in from Oakville. One of these conveyances was an elaborate six-horse stage, owned by Bethel & Oxenford, star route mail contractors between San Antonio and Brownsville, Texas. Seated by young Oxenford's side in the driver's box sat Esther McLeod, while inside the coach was her sister, Mrs. Martin, with the senior member of the firm, his wife, and several other invited guests. I had heard something of the gallantry of young Jack Oxenford, who was the nephew of a carpet-bag member of Congress, and prided himself on being the best whip in the country. In the latter field I would gladly have yielded him all honors, but his attentions to Esther were altogether too marked to please either me or my employer. I am free to admit that I was troubled by this turn of affairs. The junior mail contractor made up in egotism what he lacked in appearance, and no doubt had money to burn, as star route mail contracting was profitable those days, while I had nothing but my monthly wages. To make matters more embarrassing, a blind man could have read Mrs. Martin's approval of young Oxenford.

The programme for the forenoon was brief — a few patriotic songs and an oration by a young lawyer who had come up from Corpus Christi for the occasion. After listening to the opening song, my employer and I took a stroll down by the river, as we were too absorbed in the new complications to pay proper attention to the young orator.

"Tom," said Uncle Lance, as we strolled away from the grove, "we are up against the real thing now. I know young Oxenford, and he's a dangerous fellow to have for a rival, if he really is one. You can't tell much about a Yankee, though, for he's usually egotistical enough to think that every girl in the country is breaking her neck to win him. The worst of it is, this young fellow is rich — he's got dead oodles of money and he's making more every hour out of his mail contracts. One good thing is, we understand the situation, and all's fair in love and war. You can see, though, that Mrs. Martin has dealt herself a hand in the game. By the dough on her fingers she proposes to have a fist in the pie. Well, now, son, we'll give them a run for their money or break a tug in the effort. Tom, just you play to my lead to-day and we'll see who holds the high cards or knows best how to play them. If I can cut him off, that'll be your chance to sail in and do a little close-herding yourself."

We loitered along the river bank until the oration was concluded, my employer giving me quite an interesting account of my rival. It seems that young Oxenford belonged to a family then notoriously prominent in politics. He had inherited quite a sum of money, and, through the influence of his congressional uncle, had been fortunate enough to form a partnership with Bethel, a man who knew all the ropes in mail contracting. The senior member of the firm knew how to shake the tree, while the financial resources of the junior member and the political influence of his uncle made him a valuable man in gathering the plums on their large field of star route contracts. Had not exposure interrupted, they were due to have made a large fortune out of the government.

On our return to the picnic grounds, the assembly was dispersing for luncheon. Miss Jean had ably provided for the occasion, and on reaching our ambulance on the outer edge of the grove, Tiburcio had coffee all ready and the boys from the home ranch began to straggle in for dinner. Miss Jean had prevailed on Tony Hunter and his wife, who had come down on horseback from the San Miguel, to take luncheon with us, and from the hearty greetings which Uncle Lance extended to the guests of his sister, I could see that the owner and mistress of Las Palomas were diplomatically dividing the house of McLeod. I followed suit, making myself agreeable to Mrs. Hunter, who was but very few years the elder of Esther. Having spent a couple of nights at their ranch, and feeling a certain comradeship with her husband, I decided before dinner was over that I had a friend and ally in Tony's wife. There was something romantic about the young matron, as any one could see, and since the sisters favored each other in many ways, I had hopes that Esther might not overvalue Jack Oxenford's money.

After luncheon, as we were on our way to the dancing arbor, we met the Oakville party with Esther in tow. I was introduced to Mrs. Martin, who, in turn, made me acquainted with her friends, including her sister, perfectly unconscious that we were already more than mere acquaintances. From the demure manner of Esther, who accepted the introduction as a matter of course, I surmised she was concealing our acquaintance from her sister and my rival. We had hardly reached the arbor before Uncle Lance created a diversion and interested the mail contractors with a glowing yarn about a fine lot of young mules he had at the ranch, large enough for stage purposes. There was some doubt expressed by the stage men as to their size and weight, when my employer invited them to the outskirts of the grove, where he would show them a sample in our ambulance team. So he led them away, and I saw that the time had come to play to my employer's lead. The music striking up, I claimed Esther for the first dance, leaving Mrs. Martin, for the time being, in charge of her sister and Miss Jean. Before the first waltz ended I caught sight of all three of the ladies mingling in the dance. It was a source of no small satisfaction to me to see my two best friends, Deweese and Gallup, dancing with the married sisters, while Miss Jean was giving her whole attention to her partner, Tony Hunter. With the entire Las Palomas crowd pulling strings in my interest, and Father, in the absence of Oxenford, becoming extremely gracious, I grew bold and threw out my chest like the brisket on a beef steer.

I permitted no one to separate me from Esther. We started the second dance together, but no sooner did I see her sister, Mrs. Martin, whirl by us in the polka with Dan Happersett, than I suggested that we drop out and take a stroll. She consented, and we were soon out of sight, wandering in a labyrinth of lover's lanes which abounded throughout this live-oak grove. On reaching the outskirts of the picnic grounds, we came to an extensive opening in which our saddle horses were picketed. At a glance Esther recognized Wolf, the horse I had ridden the Christmas before when passing their ranch. Being a favorite saddle horse of the old ranchero, he was reserved for special occasions, and Uncle Lance had ridden him down to Shepherd's on this holiday. Like a bird freed from a cage, the ranch girl took to the horses and insisted on a little ride. Since her proposal alone prevented my making a similar suggestion, I allowed myself to be won over, but came near getting caught in protesting. "But you told me at the ranch that Wolf was one of ten in your Las Palomas mount," she poutingly protested.

"He is," I insisted, "but I have loaned him to Uncle Lance for the day."

"Throw the saddle on him then — I'll tell Mr. Lovelace when we return that I borrowed his horse when he wasn't looking."

Had she killed the horse, I felt sure that the apology would have been accepted; so, throwing saddles on the black and my own mount, we were soon scampering down the river. The inconvenience of a man's saddle, or the total absence of any, was a negligible incident to this daughter of the plains. A mile down the river, we halted and watered the horses. Then, crossing the stream, we spent about an hour circling slowly about on the surrounding uplands, never being over a mile from the picnic grounds. It was late for the first flora of the season, but there was still an abundance of blue bonnets. Dismounting, we gathered and wove wreaths for our horses' necks, and wandered picking the Mexican strawberries which grew plentifully on every hand.

But this was all preliminary to the main question. When it came up for discussion, this one of Quirk's boys made the talk of his life in behalf of Thomas Moore. Nor was it in vain. When Esther apologized for the rudeness her mother had shown me at her home, that afforded me the opening for which I was longing. We were sitting on a grassy hummock, weaving garlands, when I replied to the apology by declaring my intention of marrying her, with or without her mother's consent. Unconventional as the declaration was, to my surprise she showed neither offense nor wonderment. Dropping the flowers with which we were working, she avoided my gaze, and, turning slightly from me, began watching our horses, which had strayed away some distance. But I gave her little time for meditation, and when I aroused her from her reverie, she rose, saying, "We'd better go back — they'll miss us if we stay too long."

Before complying with her wish, I urged an answer; but she, artfully avoiding my question, insisted on our immediate return. Being in a quandary as to what to say or do, I went after the horses, which was a simple proposition. On my return, while we were adjusting the garlands about the necks of our mounts, I again urged her for an answer, but in vain. We stood for a moment between the two horses, and as I lowered my hand on my knee to afford her a stepping-stone in mounting, I thought she did not offer to mount with the same alacrity as she had done before. Something flashed through my addled mind, and, withdrawing the hand proffered as a mounting block, I clasped the demure maiden closely in my arms. What transpired has no witnesses save two saddle horses, and as Wolf usually kept an eye on his rider in mounting, I dropped the reins and gave him his freedom rather than endure his scrutiny. When we were finally aroused from this delicious trance, the horses had strayed away fully fifty yards, but I had received a favorable answer, breathed in a voice so low and tender that it haunts me yet.

As we rode along, returning to the grove, Esther requested that our betrothal be kept a profound secret. No doubt she had good reasons, and it was quite possible that there then existed some complications which she wished to conceal, though I avoided all mention of any possible rival. Since she was not due to return to her school before September, there seemed ample time to carry out our intentions of marrying. But as we jogged along, she informed me that after spending a few weeks with her sister in Oakville, it was her intention to return to the San Miguel for the summer. To allay her mother's distrust, it would be better for me not to call at the ranch. But this was easily compensated for when she suggested making several visits during the season with the Vaux girls, chums of hers, who lived on the Frio about thirty miles due north of Las Palomas. This was fortunate, since the Vaux ranch and ours were on the most friendly terms.

We returned by the route by which we had left the grounds. I repicketed the horses and we were soon mingling again with the revelers, having been absent little over an hour. No one seemed to have taken any notice of our absence. Mrs. Martin, I rejoiced to see, was still in tow of her sister and Miss Jean, and from the circle of Las Palomas courtiers who surrounded the ladies, I felt sure they had given her no opportunity even to miss her younger sister. Uncle Lance was the only member of our company absent, but I gave myself no uneasiness about him, since the mail contractors were both likewise missing. Rejoining our friends and assuming a nonchalant air, I flattered myself that my disguise was perfect.

During the remainder of the afternoon, in view of the possibility that Esther might take her sister, Mrs. Martin, into our secret and win her as an ally, I cultivated that lady's acquaintance, dancing with her and leaving nothing undone to foster her friendship. Near the middle of the afternoon, as the three sisters, Miss Jean, and I were indulging in light refreshment at a booth some distance from the dancing arbor, I sighted my employer, Dan Happersett, and the two stage men returning from the store. They passed near, not observing us, and from the defiant tones of Uncle Lance's voice, I knew they had been tampering with the 'private stock' of the merchant at Shepherd's. "Why, gentlemen," said he, "that ambulance team is no exception to the quality of mules I'm raising at Las Palomas. Drive up some time and spend a few days and take a look at the stock we're breeding. If you will, and I don't show you fifty mules fourteen and a half hands or better, I'll round up five hundred head and let you pick fifty as a pelon for your time and trouble. Why, gentlemen, Las Palomas has sold mules to the government."

On the return of our party to the arbor, Happersett claimed a dance with Esther, thus freeing me. Uncle Lance was standing some little distance away, still entertaining the mail contractors, and I edged near enough to notice Oxenford's florid face and leery eye. But on my employer's catching sight of me, he excused himself to the stage men, and taking my arm led me off. Together we promenaded out of sight of the crowd. "How do you like my style of a man herder?" inquired the old matchmaker, once we were out of hearing. "Why, Tom, I'd have held those mail thieves until dark, if Dan hadn't drifted in and given me the wink. Shepherd kicked like a bay steer on letting me have a second quart bottle, but it took that to put the right glaze in the young Yank's eye. Oh, I had him going south all right! But tell me, how did you and Esther make it?"

We had reached a secluded spot, and, seating ourselves on an old fallen tree trunk, I told of my success, even to the using of his horse. Never before or since did I see Uncle Lance give way to such a fit of hilarity as he indulged in over the perfect working out of our plans. With his hat he whipped me, the ground, the log on which we sat, while his peals of laughter rang out like the reports of a rifle. In his fit of ecstasy, tears of joy streaming from his eyes, he kept repeating again and again, "Oh, sister, run quick and tell pa to come!"

As we neared the grounds returning, he stopped me and we had a further brief confidential talk together. I was young and egotistical enough to think that I could defy all the rivals in existence, but he cautioned me, saying: "Hold on, Tom. You're young yet; you know nothing about the weaker sex, absolutely nothing. It's not your fault, but due to your mere raw youth. Now, listen to me, son: Don't underestimate any rival, particularly if he has gall and money, most of all, money. Humanity is the same the world over, and while you may not have seen it here among the ranches, it is natural for a woman to rave over a man with money, even if he is only a pimply excuse for a creature. Still, I don't see that we have very much to fear. We can cut old lady McLeod out of the matter entirely. But then there's the girl's sister, Mrs. Martin, and I look for her to cut up shameful when she smells the rat, which she's sure to do. And then there's her husband to figure on. If the ox knows his master's crib, it's only reasonable to suppose that Jack Martin knows where his bread and butter comes from. These stage men will stick up for each other like thieves. Now, don't you be too crack sure. Be just a trifle leary of every one, except, of course, the Las Palomas outfit."

I admit that I did not see clearly the reasoning behind much of this lecture, but I knew better than reject the advice of the old matchmaker with his sixty odd years of experience. I was still meditating over his remarks when we rejoined the crowd and were soon separated among the dancers. Several urged me to play the violin; but I was too busy looking after my own fences, and declined the invitation. Casting about for the Vaux girls, I found the eldest, with whom I had a slight acquaintance, being monopolized by Theodore Quayle and John Cotton, friendly rivals and favorites of the young lady. On my imploring the favor of a dance, she excused herself, and joined me on a promenade about the grounds, missing one dance entirely. In arranging matters with her to send me word on the arrival of Esther at their ranch, I attempted to make her show some preference between my two comrades, under the pretense of knowing which one to bring along, but she only smiled and maintained an admirable neutrality.

After a dance I returned the elder Miss Vaux to the tender care of John Cotton, and caught sight of my employer leaving the arbor for the refreshment booth with a party of women, including Mrs. Martin and Esther McLeod, to whom he was paying the most devoted attention. Witnessing the tireless energy of the old matchmaker, and in a quarter where he had little hope of an ally, brought me to thinking that there might be good cause for alarm in his warnings not to be overconfident. Miss Jean, whom I had not seen since luncheon, aroused me from my reverie, and on her wishing to know my motive for cultivating the acquaintance of Miss Vaux and neglecting my own sweetheart, I told her the simple truth. "Good idea, Tom," she assented. "I think I'll just ask Miss Frances home with me to spend Sunday. Then you can take her across to the Frio on horseback, so as not to offend either John or Theodore. What do you think?"

I thought it was a good idea, and said so. At least the taking of the young lady home would be a pleasanter task for me than breaking horses. But as I expressed myself so, I could not help thinking, seeing Miss Jean's zeal in the matter, that the matchmaking instinct was equally well developed on both sides of the Lovelace family.

The afternoon was drawing to a close. The festivities would conclude by early sundown. Miss Jean would spend the night again at the halfway ranch, returning to Las Palomas the next morning; we would start on our return with the close of the amusements. Many who lived at a distance had already started home. It lacked but a few minutes of the closing hour when I sought out Esther for the "Home, Sweet Home" waltz, finding her in company of Oxenford, chaperoned by Mrs. Martin, of which there was need. My sweetheart excused herself with a poise that made my heart leap, and as we whirled away in the mazes of the final dance, rivals and all else passed into oblivion. Before we could realize the change in the music, the orchestra had stopped, and struck into "My Country, 'tis of Thee," in which the voice of every patriotic Texan present swelled the chorus until it echoed throughout the grove, befittingly closing San Jacinto Day.

CHAPTER VIII
A CAT HUNT ON THE FRIO

The return of Miss Jean the next forenoon, accompanied by Frances Vaux, was an occasion of more than ordinary moment at Las Palomas. The Vaux family were of creole extraction, but had settled on the Frio River nearly a generation before. Under the climatic change, from the swamps of Louisiana to the mesas of Texas, the girls grew up fine physical specimens of rustic Southern beauty. To a close observer, certain traces of the French were distinctly discernible in Miss Frances, notably in the large, lustrous eyes, the swarthy complexion, and early maturity of womanhood. Small wonder then that our guest should have played havoc among the young men of the countryside, adding to her train of gallants the devoted Quayle and Cotton of Las Palomas.

Aside from her charming personality, that Miss Vaux should receive a cordial welcome at Las Palomas goes without saying, since there were many reasons why she should. The old ranchero and his sister chaperoned the young lady, while I, betrothed to another, became her most obedient slave. It is needless to add that there was a fair field and no favor shown by her hosts, as between John and Theodore. The prize was worthy of any effort. The best man was welcome to win, while the blessings of master and mistress seemed impatient to descend on the favored one.

In the work in hand, I was forced to act as a rival to my friends, for I could not afford to lower my reputation for horsemanship before Miss Frances, when my betrothed was shortly to be her guest. So it was not to be wondered at that Quayle and Cotton should abandon the *medeno* in mounting their unbroken geldings, and I had to follow suit or suffer by comparison. The other rascals, equal if not superior to our trio in horsemanship, including Enrique, born with just sense enough to be a fearless vaquero, took to the heavy sand in mounting vicious geldings; but we three jauntily gave the wildest horses their heads and even encouraged them to buck whenever our guest was sighted on the gallery. What gave special vim to our work was the fact that Miss Frances was a horsewoman herself, and it was with difficulty that she could be kept away from the corrals. Several times a day our guest prevailed on Uncle Lance to take her out to witness the roping. From a safe vantage place on the palisades, the old ranchero and his protégé would watch us catching, saddling, and mounting the geldings. Under those bright eyes, lariats encircled the feet of the horse to be ridden deftly indeed, and he was laid on his side in the sand as daintily as a mother would lay her babe in its crib. Outside of the trio, the work of the gang was bunglesome, calling for many a protest from Uncle Lance, — they had no lady's glance to spur them on, — while ours merited the enthusiastic plaudits of Miss Frances.

Then came Sunday and we observed the commandment. Miss Jean had planned a picnic for the day on the river. We excused Tiburcio, and pressed the ambulance team into service to convey the party of six for the day's outing among the fine groves of elm that bordered the river in several places, and afforded ample shade from the sun. The day was delightfully spent. The chaperons were negligent and dilatory. Uncle Lance even fell asleep for several hours. But when we returned at twilight, the ambulance mules were garlanded as if for a wedding party.

The next morning our guest was to depart, and to me fell the pleasant task of acting as her escort. Uncle Lance prevailed on Miss Frances to ride a spirited chestnut horse from his mount, while I rode a *grulla* from my own. We made an early start, the old ranchero riding with us as far as the river. As he held the hand of Miss Vaux in parting, he cautioned her not to detain me at their ranch, as he had use for me at Las Palomas. "Of course," said he, "I don't mean that you shall hurry him right off to-day or even to-morrow. But these lazy rascals of mine will hang around a girl a week, if she'll allow it. Had John or Theodore taken you home, I shouldn't expect to see either of them in a fortnight. Now, if they don't treat you right at home, come back and live with us. I'll adopt you as my daughter. And tell your pa that the first general rain that falls, I'm coming over with my hounds for a cat hunt with him. Good-by, sweetheart."

It was a delightful ride across to the Frio. Mounted on two splendid horses, we put the Nueces behind us as the hours passed. Frequently we met large strings of cattle drifting in towards the river for their daily drink, and Miss Frances insisted on riding through the cows, noticing every brand as keenly as a vaquero on the lookout for strays from her father's ranch. The young calves scampered out of our way, but their sedate mothers permitted us to ride near enough to read the brands as we met and passed. Once we rode a mile out of our way to look at a *manada*. The stallion met us as we approached as if to challenge all intruders on his domain, but we met him defiantly and he turned aside and permitted us to examine his harem and its frolicsome colts.

But when cattle and horses no longer served as a subject, and the wide expanse of flowery mesa, studded here and there with Spanish daggers whose creamy flowers nodded to us as we passed, ceased to interest us, we turned to the ever interesting subject of sweethearts. But try as I might, I could never wring any confession from her which even suggested a preference among her string of admirers. On the other hand, when she twitted me about Esther, I proudly plead guilty of a Platonic friendship which some day I hoped would ripen into something more permanent, fully realizing that the very first time these two chums met there would be an interchange of confidences. And in the full knowledge that during these whispered admissions the truth would be revealed, I stoutly denied that Esther and I were even betrothed.

But during that morning's ride I made a friend and ally of Frances Vaux. There was some talk of a tournament to be held during the summer at Campbellton on the Atascosa. She promised that she would detain Esther for it and find a way to send me word, and we would make up a party and attend it together. I had never been present at any of these pastoral tourneys and was hopeful that one would be held within reach of our ranch, for I had heard a great deal about them and was anxious to see one. But this was only one of several social outings which she outlined as on her summer programme, to all of which I was cordially invited as a member of her party. There was to be a dance on St. John's Day at the Mission, a barbecue in June on the San Miguel, and other local meets for the summer and early fall. By the time we reached the ranch, I was just beginning to realize that, socially, Shepherd's Ferry and the Nueces was a poky place.

The next morning I returned to Las Palomas. The horse-breaking was nearing an end. During the month of May we went into camp on a new tract of land which had been recently acquired, to build a tank on a dry *arroyo* which crossed this last landed addition to the ranch. It was a commercial peculiarity of Uncle Lance to acquire land but never to part with it under any consideration. To a certain extent, cows and land had become his religion, and whenever either, adjoining Las Palomas, was for sale, they were looked upon as a safe bank of deposit for any surplus funds. The last tract thus secured was dry, but by damming the *arroyo* we could store water in this tank or reservoir to tide over the dry spells. All the Mexican help on the ranch was put to work with wheelbarrows, while six mule teams ploughed, scraped, and hauled rock, one four-mule team being constantly employed in hauling water over ten miles for camp and stock purposes. This dry stream ran water, when conditions were favorable, several months in the year, and by building the tank our cattle capacity would be largely increased.

One evening, late in the month, when the water wagon returned, Tiburcio brought a request from Miss Jean, asking me to come into the ranch that night. Responding to the summons, I was rewarded by finding a letter awaiting me from Frances Vaux, left by a vaquero passing from the Frio to Santa Maria. It was a dainty missive, informing me that Esther was her guest; that the tournament would not take place, but to be sure and come over on Sunday. Personally the note was satisfactory, but that I was to bring any one along was artfully omitted. Being thus forced to read between the lines, on my return to camp the next morning by dawn, without a word of explanation, I submitted the matter to John and Theodore. Uncle Lance, of course, had to know what had called me in to the ranch, and, taking the letter from Quayle, read it himself.

"That's plain enough," said he, on the first reading. "John will go with you Sunday, and if it rains next month, I'll take Theodore with me when I go over for a cat hunt with old man Pierre. I'll let him act as master of the horse, — no, of the hounds, — and give him a chance to toot his own horn with Frances. Honest, boys, I'm getting disgusted with the white element of Las Palomas. We raise most everything here but white babies. Even Enrique, the rascal, has to live in camp now to hold down his breakfast. But you young whites — with the country just full of young women — well, it's certainly discouraging. I do all I can, and Sis helps a little, but what does it amount to — what are the results? That poem that Jean reads to us occasionally must be right. I reckon the Caucasian is played out."

Before the sun was an hour high, John Cotton and myself rode into the Vaux ranch on Sunday morning. The girls gave us a cheerful welcome. While we were breakfasting, several other lads and lasses rode up, and we were informed that a little picnic for the day had been arranged. As this was to our liking, John and I readily acquiesced, and shortly afterward a mounted party of about a dozen young folks set out for a hackberry grove, up the river several miles. Lunch baskets were taken along, but no chaperons. The girls were all dressed in cambric and muslin and as light in heart as the fabrics and ribbons they flaunted. I was gratified with the boldness of Cotton, as he cantered away with Frances, and with the day before him there was every reason to believe that his cause would he advanced. As to myself, with Esther by my side the livelong day, I could not have asked the world to widen an inch.

It was midnight when we reached Las Palomas returning. As we rode along that night, John confessed to me that Frances was a tantalizing enigma. Up to a certain point, she offered every encouragement, but beyond that there seemed to be a dead line over which she allowed no sentiment to pass. It was plain to be seen that he was discouraged, but I told him I had gone through worse ordeals.

Throughout southern Texas and the country tributary to the Nueces River, we always looked for our heaviest rainfall during the month of June. This year in particular, we were anxious to see a regular downpour to start the *arroyo* and test our new tank. Besides, we had sold for delivery in July, twelve hundred beef steers for shipment at Rockport on the coast. If only a soaking rain would fall, making water plentiful, we could make the drive in little over a hundred miles, while a dry season would compel; us to follow the river nearly double the distance.

We were riding our range thoroughly, locating our fattest beeves, when one evening as June Deweese and I were on the way back from the Ganso, a regular equinoctial struck us, accompanied by a downpour of rain and hail. Our horses turned their backs to the storm, but we drew slickers over our heads, and defied the elements. Instead of letting up as darkness set in, the storm seemed to increase in fury and we were forced to seek shelter. We were at least fifteen miles from the ranch, and it was simply impossible to force a horse against that sheeting rain. So turning to catch the storm in our backs, we rode for a ranchita belonging to Las Palomas. By the aid of flashes of lightning and the course of the storm, we reached the little ranch and found a haven. A steady rain fell all night, continuing the next day, but we saddled early and rode for our new reservoir on the *arroyo*. Imagine our surprise on sighting the embankment to see two horsemen ride up from the opposite direction and halt at the dam. Giving rein to our horses and galloping up, we found they were Uncle Lance and Theodore Quayle. Above the dam the *arroyo* was running like a mill-tail. The water in the reservoir covered several acres and had backed up stream nearly a quarter mile, the deepest point in the tank reaching my saddle skirts. The embankment had settled solidly, holding the gathering water to our satisfaction, and after several hours' inspection we rode for home.

With this splendid rain, Las Palomas ranch took on an air of activity. The old ranchero paced the gallery for hours in great glee, watching the downpour. It was too soon yet by a week to gather the beeves. But under the glowing prospect, we could not remain inert. The next morning the *segunão* took all the teams and returned to the tank to watch the dam and haul rock to rip-rap the flanks of the embankment. Taking extra saddle horses with us, Uncle Lance, Dan Happersett, Quayle, and myself took the hounds and struck across for the Frio. On reaching the Vaux ranch, as showers were still falling and the underbrush reeking with moisture, wetting any one to the skin who dared to invade it, we did not hunt that afternoon. Pierre Vaux was enthusiastic over the rain, while his daughters were equally so over the prospects of riding to the hounds, there being now nearly forty dogs in the double pack.

At the first opportunity, Frances confided to me that Mrs. McLeod had forbidden Esther visiting them again, since some busybody had carried the news of our picnic to her ears. But she promised me that if I could direct the hunt on the morrow within a few miles of the McLeod ranch, she would entice my sweetheart out and give me a chance to meet her. There was a roguish look in Miss Frances's eye during this disclosure which I was unable to fathom, but I promised during the few days' hunt to find some means to direct the chase within striking distance of the ranch on the San Miguel.

I promptly gave this bit of news in confidence to Uncle Lance, and was told to lie low and leave matters to him. That evening, amid clouds of tobacco smoke, the two old rancheros discussed the best hunting in the country, while we youngsters danced on the gallery to the strains of a fiddle. I heard Mr. Vaux narrating a fight with a cougar which killed two of his best dogs during the winter just passed, and before we retired it was understood that we would give the haunts of this same old cougar our first attention.

CHAPTER IX
THE ROSE AND ITS THORN

Dawn found the ranch astir and a heavy fog hanging over the Frio valley. Don Pierre had a *remuda* corralled before sun-up, and insisted on our riding his horses, an invitation which my employer alone declined. For the first hour or two the pack scouted the river bottoms with no success, and Uncle Lance's verdict was that the valley was too soggy for any animal belonging to the cat family, so we turned back to the divide between the Frio and San Miguel. Here there grew among the hills many Guajio thickets, and from the first one we beat, the hounds opened on a hot trail in splendid chorus. The pack led us through thickets for over a mile, when they suddenly turned down a ravine, heading for the river. With the ground ill splendid condition for trailing, the dogs in full cry, the quarry sought every shelter possible; but within an hour of striking the scent, the pack came to bay in the encinal. On coming up with the hounds, we found the animal was a large catamount. A single shot brought him from his perch in a scraggy oak, and the first chase of the day was over. The pelt was worthless and was not taken.

It was nearly noon when the kill was made, and Don Pierre insisted that we return to the ranch. Uncle Lance protested against wasting the remainder of the day, but the courteous Creole urged that the ground would be in fine condition for hunting at least a week longer; this hunt he declared was merely preliminary — to break the pack together and give them a taste of the chase before attacking the cougar. "Ah," said Don Pierre, with a deprecating shrug of the shoulders, "you have nothing to hurry you home. I come by your rancho an' stay one hol' week. You come by mine, al' time hurry. Sacré! Let de li'l dogs rest, an' in de mornin', mebbe we hunt de cougar. Ah, Meester Lance, we must haff de pack fresh for him. By Gar, he was one dam' wil' fellow. Mek one two pass, so. Biff! two dog dead."

Uncle Lance yielded, and we rode back to the ranch. The next morning our party included the three daughters of our host. Don Pierre led the way on a roan stallion, and after two hours' riding we crossed the San Miguel to the north of his ranch. A few miles beyond we entered some chalky hills, interspersed with white chaparral thickets which were just bursting into bloom, with a fragrance that was almost intoxicating. Under the direction of our host, we started to beat a long chain of these thickets, and were shortly rewarded by hearing the pack give mouth. The quarry kept to the cover of the thickets for several miles, impeding the chase until the last covert in the chain was reached, where a fight occurred with the lead hound. Don Pierre was the first to reach the scene, and caught several glimpses of a monster puma as he slunk away through the Brazil brush, leaving one of the Don's favorite hounds lacerated to the bone. But the pack passed on, and, lifting the wounded dog to a vaquero's saddle, we followed, lustily shouting to the hounds.

The spoor now turned down the San Miguel, and the pace was such that it took hard riding to keep within hearing. Mr. Vaux and Uncle Lance usually held the lead, the remainder of the party, including the girls, bringing up the rear. The chase continued down stream for fully an hour, until we encountered some heavy timber on the main Frio, our course having carried us several miles to the north of the McLeod ranch. Some distance below the juncture with the San Miguel the river made a large horseshoe, embracing nearly a thousand acres, which was covered with a dense growth of ash, pecan, and cypress. The trail led into this jungle, circling it several times before leading away. We were fortunately able to keep track of the chase from the baying of the hounds without entering the timber, and were watching its course, when suddenly it changed; the pack followed the scent across a bridge of driftwood on the Frio, and started up the river in full cry.

As the chase down the San Miguel passed beyond the mouth of the creek, Theodore Quayle and Frances Vaux dropped out and rode for the McLeod ranch. It was still early in the day, and understanding their motive, I knew they would rejoin us if their mission was successful. By the sudden turn of the chase, we were likely to pass several miles south of the home of my sweetheart, but our location could be easily followed by the music of the pack. Within an hour after leaving us, Theodore and Frances rejoined the chase, adding Tony Hunter and Esther to our numbers. With this addition, I lost interest in the hunt, as the course carried us straightaway five miles up the stream. The quarry was cunning and delayed the pack at every thicket or large body of timber encountered. Several times he craftily attempted to throw the hounds off the scent by climbing leaning trees, only to spring down again. But the pack were running wide and the ruse was only tiring the hunted. The scent at times left the river and circled through outlying mesquite groves, always keeping well under cover. On these occasions we rested our horses, for the hunt was certain to return to the river.

From the scattering order in which we rode, I was afforded a good opportunity for free conversation with Esther. But the information I obtained was not very encouraging. Her mother's authority had grown so severe that existence under the same roof was a mere armistice between mother and daughter, while this day's sport was likely to break the already strained relations. The thought that her suffering was largely on my account, nerved me to resolution.

The kill was made late in the day, in a bend of the river, about fifteen miles above the Vaux ranch, forming a jungle of several thousand acres. In this thickety covert the fugitive made his final stand, taking refuge in an immense old live-oak, the mossy festoons of which partially screened him from view. The larger portion of the cavalcade remained in the open, but the rest of us, under the leadership of the two rancheros, forced our horses through the underbrush and reached the hounds. The pack were as good as exhausted by the long run, and, lest the animal should spring out of the tree and escape, we circled it at a distance. On catching a fair view of the quarry, Uncle Lance called for a carbine. Two shots through the shoulders served to loosen the puma's footing, when he came down by easy stages from limb to limb, spitting and hissing defiance into the upturned faces of the pack. As he fell, we dashed in to beat off the dogs as a matter of precaution, but the bullets had done their work, and the pack mouthed the fallen feline with entire impunity.

Dan Happersett dragged the dead puma out with a rope over the neck for the inspection of the girls, while our horses, which had had no less than a fifty-mile ride, were unsaddled and allowed a roll and a half hour's graze before starting back. As we were watering our mounts, I caught my employer's ear long enough to repeat what I had learned about Esther's home difficulties. After picketing our horses, we strolled away from the remainder of the party, when Uncle Lance remarked: "Tom, your chance has come where you must play your hand and play it boldly. I'll keep Tony at the Vaux ranch, and if Esther has to go home to-night, why, of course, you'll have to take her. There's your chance to run off and marry. Now, Tom, you've never failed me yet; and this thing has gone far enough. We'll give old lady McLeod good cause to hate us from now on. I've got some money with me, and I'll rob the other boys, and to-night you make a spoon or spoil a horn. Sabe?"

I understood and approved. As we jogged along homeward, Esther and I fell to the rear, and I outlined my programme. Nor did she protest when I suggested that to-night was the accepted time. Before we reached the Vaux ranch every little detail was arranged. There was a splendid moon, and after supper she plead the necessity of returning home. Meanwhile every cent my friends possessed had been given me, and the two best horses of Las Palomas were under saddle for the start. Uncle Lance was arranging a big hunt for the morrow with Tony Hunter and Don Pierre, when Esther took leave of her friends, only a few of whom were cognizant of our intended elopement.

With fresh mounts under us, we soon covered the intervening distance between the two ranches. I would gladly have waived touching at the McLeod ranch, but Esther had torn her dress during the day and insisted on a change, and I, of necessity, yielded. The corrals were at some distance from the main buildings, and, halting at a saddle shed adjoining, Esther left me and entered the house. Fortunately her mother had retired, and after making a hasty change of apparel, she returned unobserved to the corrals. As we quietly rode out from the inclosure, my spirits soared to the moon above us. The night was an ideal one. Crossing the Frio, we followed the divide some distance, keeping in the open, and an hour before midnight forded the Nueces at Shepherd's. A flood of recollections crossed my mind, as our steaming horses bent their heads to drink at the ferry. Less than a year before, in this very grove, I had met her; it was but two months since, on those hills beyond, we had gathered flowers, plighted our troth, and exchanged our first rapturous kiss. And the thought that she was renouncing home and all for my sake, softened my heart and nerved me to every exertion.

Our intention was to intercept the south-bound stage at the first road house south of Oakville. I knew the hour it was due to leave the station, and by steady riding we could connect with it at the first stage stand some fifteen miles below. Lighthearted and happy, we set out on this last lap of our ride. Our horses seemed to understand the emergency, as they put the miles behind them, thrilling us with their energy and vigor. Never for a moment in our flight did my sweetheart discover a single qualm over her decision, while in my case all scruples were buried in the hope of victory. Recrossing the Nueces and entering the stage road, we followed it down several miles, sighting the stage stand about two o'clock in the morning. I was saddle weary from the hunt, together with this fifty-mile ride, and rejoiced in reaching our temporary destination. Esther, however, seemed little the worse for the long ride.

The welcome extended by the keeper of this relay station was gruff enough. But his tone and manner moderated when he learned we were passengers for Corpus Christi. When I made arrangements with him to look after our horses for a week or ten days at a handsome figure, he became amiable, invited us to a cup of coffee, and politely informed us that the stage was due in half an hour. But on its arrival, promptly on time, our hearts sank within us. On the driver's box sat an express guard holding across his knees a sawed-off, double-barreled shotgun. As it halted, two other guards stepped out of the coach, similarly armed. The stage was carrying an unusual amount of treasure, we were informed, and no passengers could be accepted, as an attempted robbery was expected between this and the next station.

Our situation became embarrassing. For the first time during our ride, Esther showed the timidity of her sex. The chosen destination of our honeymoon, nearly a hundred miles to the south, was now out of the question. To return to Oakville, where a sister and friends of my sweetheart resided, seemed the only avenue open. I had misgivings that it was unsafe, but Esther urged it, declaring that Mrs. Martin would offer no opposition, and even if she did, nothing now could come that would ever separate us. We learned from the keeper that Jack Martin was due to drive the north-bound stage out of Oakville that morning, and was expected to pass this relay station about daybreak. This was favorable, and we decided to wait and allow the stage to pass north before resuming our journey.

On the arrival of the stage, we learned that the down coach had been attacked, but the robbers, finding it guarded, had fled after an exchange of shots in the darkness. This had a further depressing effect on my betrothed, and only my encouragement to be brave and face the dilemma confronting us kept her up. Bred on the frontier, this little ranch girl was no weakling; but the sudden overturn of our well-laid plans had chilled my own spirits as well as hers. Giving the up stage a good start of us, we resaddled and started for Oakville, slightly crestfallen but still confident. In the open air Esther's fears gradually subsided, and, invigorated by the morning and the gallop, we reached our destination after our night's adventure with hopes buoyant and colors flying.

Mrs. Martin looked a trifle dumfounded at her early callers, but I lost no time in informing her that our mission was an elopement, and asked her approval and blessing. Surprised as she was, she welcomed us to breakfast, inquiring of our plans and showing alarm over our experience. Since Oakville was a county seat where a license could be secured, for fear of pursuit I urged an immediate marriage, but Mrs. Martin could see no necessity for haste. There was, she said, no one there whom she would allow to solemnize a wedding of her sister, and, to my chagrin, Esther agreed with her.

This was just what I had dreaded; but Mrs. Martin, with apparent enthusiasm over our union, took the reins in her own hands, and decided that we should wait until Jack's return, when we would all take the stage to Pleasanton, where an Episcopal minister lived. My heart sank at this, for it meant a delay of two days, and I stood up and stoutly protested. But now that the excitement of our flight had abated, my own Esther innocently sided with her sister, and I was at my wit's end. To all my appeals, the sisters replied with the argument that there was no hurry — that while the hunt lasted at the Vaux ranch Tony Hunter could be depended upon to follow the hounds; Esther would never be missed until his return; her mother would suppose she was with the Vaux girls, and would be busy preparing a lecture against her return.

Of course the argument of the sisters won the hour. Though dreading some unforeseen danger, I temporarily yielded. I knew the motive of the hunt well enough to know that the moment we had an ample start it would be abandoned, and the Las Palomas contingent would return to the ranch. Yet I dare not tell, even my betrothed, that there were ulterior motives in my employer's hunting on the Frio, one of which was to afford an opportunity for our elopement. Full of apprehension and alarm, I took a room at the village hostelry, for I had our horses to look after, and secured a much-needed sleep during the afternoon. That evening I returned to the Martin cottage, to urge again that we carry out our original programme by taking the south-bound stage at midnight. But all I could say was of no avail. Mrs. Martin was equal to every suggestion. She had all the plans outlined, and there was no occasion for me to do any thinking at all. Corpus Christi was not to be considered for a single moment, compared to Pleasanton and an Episcopalian service. What could I do?

At an early hour Mrs. Martin withdrew. The reaction from our escapade had left a pallor on my sweetheart's countenance, almost alarming. Noticing this, I took my leave early, hoping that a good night's rest would restore her color and her spirits. Returning to the hostelry, I resignedly sought my room, since there was nothing I could do but wait. Tossing and pitching on my bed, I upbraided myself for having returned to Oakville, where any interference with our plans could possibly develop.

The next morning at breakfast, I noticed that I was the object of particular attention, and of no very kindly sort. No one even gave me a friendly nod, while several avoided my glances. Supposing that some rumor of our elopement might be abroad, I hurriedly finished my meal and started for the Martins'. On reaching the door, I was met by its mistress, who, I had need to remind myself, was the sister of my betrothed. To my friendly salutation, she gave me a scornful, withering look.

"You're too late, young man," she said. "Shortly after you left last night, Esther and Jack Oxenford took a private conveyance for Beeville, and are married before this. You Las Palomas people are slow. Old Lance Lovelace thought he was playing it cute San Jacinto Day, but I saw through his little game. Somebody must have told him he was a matchmaker. Well, just give him my regards, and tell him he don't know the first principles of that little game. Tell him to drop in some time when he's passing; I may be able to give him some pointers that I'm not using at the moment. I hope your sorrow will not exceed my happiness. Good-morning, sir."

CHAPTER X
AFTERMATH

My memory of what happened immediately after Mrs. Martin's contemptuous treatment of me is as vague and indefinite as the vaporings of a fevered dream. I have a faint recollection of several friendly people offering their sympathy. The old stableman, who looked after the horses, cautioned me not to start out alone; but I have since learned that I cursed him and all the rest, and rode away as one in a trance. But I must have had some little caution left, for I remember giving Shepherd's a wide berth, passing several miles to the south.

The horses, taking their own way, were wandering home. Any exercise of control or guidance over them on my part was inspired by an instinct to avoid being seen. Of conscious direction there was none. Somewhere between the ferry and the ranch I remember being awakened from my torpor by the horse which I was leading showing an inclination to graze. Then I noticed their gaunted condition, and in sympathy for the poor brutes unsaddled and picketed them in a secluded spot. What happened at this halt has slipped from my memory. But I must have slept a long time; for I awoke to find the moon high overhead, and my watch, through neglect, run down and stopped. I now realized the better my predicament, and reasoned with myself whether I should return to Las Palomas or not. But there was no place else to go, and the horses did not belong to me. If I could only reach the ranch and secure my own horse, I felt that no power on earth could chain me to the scenes of my humiliation.

The horses decided me to return. Resaddling at an unknown hour, I rode for the ranch. The animals were refreshed and made good time. As I rode along I tried to convince myself that I could slip into the ranch, secure my own saddle horse, and meet no one except the Mexicans. There was a possibility that Deweese might still be in camp at the new reservoir, and I was hopeful that my employer might not yet be returned from the hunt on the Frio. After a number of hours' riding, the horse under saddle nickered. Halting him, I listened and heard the roosters crowing in a chorus at the ranch. Clouds had obscured the moon, and so by making a detour around the home buildings I was able to reach the Mexican quarters unobserved. I rode up to the house of Enrique, and quietly aroused him; told him my misfortune and asked him to hide me until he could get up my horse. We turned the animals loose, and, taking my saddle inside the *jacal*, held a whispered conversation. Deweese was yet at the tank. If the hunting party had returned, they had done so during the night. The distant range of my horse made it impossible to get him before the middle of the forenoon, but Enrique and Doña Anita assured me that my slightest wish was law to them. Furnishing me with a blanket and pillow, they made me a couch on a dry cowskin on the dirt floor at the foot of their bed, and before day broke I had fallen asleep.

On awakening, I found the sun had already risen. Enrique and his wife were missing from the room, but a peep through a crevice in the palisade wall revealed Doña Anita in the kitchen adjoining. She had detected my awakening, and soon brought me a cup of splendid coffee, which I drank with relish. She urged on me also some dainty dishes, which had always been favorites with me in Mexican cookery, but my appetite was gone. Throwing myself back on the cowskin, I asked Doña Anita how long Enrique had been gone in quest of my horse, and was informed that he left before dawn, not even waiting for his customary cup of coffee. With the kindness of a sister, the girl wife urged me to take their bed; but I assured her that comfort was the least of my concerns, complete effacement being my consuming thought.

Doña Anita withdrew, and as I lay pondering over the several possible routes of escape, I heard a commotion in the ranch. I was in the act of rising when Doña Anita burst into the *jacal* to tell me that Don Lance had been sighted returning. I was on my feet in an instant, heard the long-drawn notes of the horn calling in the hounds, and, peering through the largest crack, saw the cavalcade. As they approached, driving their loose mounts in front of them, I felt that my ill luck still hung over me; for among the unsaddled horses were the two which I had turned free but a few hours before. The hunters had met the gaunted animals between the ranch and the river, and were bringing them in to return them to their own *remuda*. But at the same time the horses were evidence that I was in the ranch. From the position of Uncle Lance, in advance, I could see that he was riding direct to the house, and my absence there would surely cause surprise. At best it was but a question of time until I was discovered.

In the face of this new development, I gave up. There was no escaping fate. Enrique might not return for two hours yet, and if he came, driving in my horse, it would only prove my presence. I begged Doña Anita to throw open the door and conceal nothing. But she was still ready to aid in my concealment until night, offering to deny my presence. But how could I conceal myself in a single room, and what was so simple a device to a worldly man of sixty years' experience? To me the case looked hopeless. Even before we had concluded our discussion, I saw Uncle Lance and the boys coming towards the Mexican quarters, followed by Miss Jean and the household contingent. The fact that the door of Enrique's *jacal* was closed, made it a shining mark for investigation. Opening the inner door, I started to meet the visitors; but Doña Anita planted herself at the outer entrance of the stoop, met the visitors, and within my hearing and without being asked stoutly denied my presence. "Hush up, you little liar," said a voice, and I heard a step and clanking spurs which I recognized. I had sat down on the edge of the bed, and was rolling a cigarette as the crowd filed into the *jacal*. A fortunate flush of anger came over me which served to steady my voice; but I met their staring, after all, much as if I had been a culprit and they a vigilance committee.

"Well, young fellow, explain your presence here," demanded Uncle Lance. Had it not been for the presence of Miss Jean, I had on my tongue's end a reply, relative to the eleventh commandment, emphasized with sulphurous adjectives. But out of deference to the mistress of the ranch, I controlled my anger, and, taking out of my pocket a flint, a steel, and, a bit of *yesca,* struck fire and leisurely lighted my cigarette. Throwing myself back on the bed, as my employer repeated his demand, I replied, "Ask Anita." The girl understood, and, nothing abashed, told the story in her native tongue, continually referring to me as *pobre Tomas.* When her disconnected narrative was concluded, Uncle Lance turned on me, saying: —

"And this is the result of all our plans. You went into Oakville, did you? Tom, you haven't, got as much sense as a candy frog. Walked right into a trap with your head up and sassy. That's right — don't you listen to any one. Didn't I tell you that stage people would stick by each other like thieves? And you forgot all my warnings and deliberately" —

"Hold on," I interrupted. "You must recollect that the horses had had a fifty-mile forced ride, were jaded, and on the point of collapse. With the down stage refusing to carry us, and the girl on the point of hysteria, where else could I go?"

"Go to jail if necessary. Go anywhere but the place you went. The horses were jaded on a fifty-mile ride, were they? Either one of them was good for a hundred without unsaddling, and you know it. Haven't I told you that this ranch would raise horses when we were all dead and gone? Suppose you had killed a couple of horses? What would that have been, compared to your sneaking into the ranch this way, like a whipped cur with your tail between your legs? Now, the countryside will laugh at us both."

"The country may laugh," I answered, "but I'll not be here to hear it. Enrique has gone after my horse, and as soon as he gets in I'm leaving you for good."

"You'll do nothing of the kind. You think you're all shot to pieces, don't you? Well, you'll stay right here until all your wounds heal. I've taken all these degrees myself, and have lived to laugh at them afterward. And I have had lessons that I hope you'll never have to learn. When I found out that my third wife had known a gambler before she married me, I found out what the Bible means by rottenness of the bones with which it says an evil woman uncrowns her husband. I'll tell you about it some day. But you've not been scarred in this little side-play. You're not even powder burnt. Why, in less than a month you'll be just as happy again as if you had good sense."

Miss Jean now interrupted. "Clear right out of here," she said to her brother and the rest. "Yes, the whole pack of you. I want to talk with Tom alone. Yes, you too — you've said too much already. Run along out."

As they filed out, I noticed Uncle Lance pick up my saddle and throw it across his shoulder, while Theodore gathered up the rancid blankets and my fancy bridle, taking everything with them to the house. Waiting until she saw that her orders were obeyed, Miss Jean came over and sat down beside me on the bed. Anita stood like a fawn near the door, likewise fearing banishment, but on a sign from her mistress she spread a goatskin on the floor and sat down at our feet. Between two languages and two women, I was as helpless as an ironed prisoner. Not that Anita had any influence over me, but the mistress of the ranch had. In her hands I was as helpless as a baby. I had come to the ranch a stranger only a little over a year before, but had I been born there her interest could have been no stronger. Jean Lovelace relinquished no one, any more than a mother would one of her boys. I wanted to escape, to get away from observation; I even plead for a month's leave of absence. But my reasons were of no avail, and after arguing pro and con for over an hour, I went with her to the house. If the Almighty ever made a good woman and placed her among men for their betterment, then the presence of Jean Lovelace at Las Palomas savored of divine appointment.

On reaching the yard, we rested a long time on a settee under a group of china trees. The boys had dispersed, and after quite a friendly chat together, we saw Uncle Lance sauntering out of the house, smiling as he approached. "Tom's going to stay," said Miss Jean to her brother, as the latter seated himself beside us; "but this abuse and blame you're heaping on him must stop. He did what he thought was best under the circumstances, and you don't know what they were. He has given me his promise to stay, and I have given him mine that talk about this matter will be dropped. Now that your anger has cooled, and I have you both together, I want your word."

"Tom," said my employer, throwing his long bony arm around me, "I was disappointed, terribly put out, and I showed it in freeing my mind. But I feel better now — towards you, at least. I understand just how you felt when your plans were thwarted by an unforeseen incident. If I don't know everything, then, since the milk is spilt, I'm not asking for further particulars. If you did what you thought was best under the circumstances, why, that's all we ever ask of any one at Las Palomas. A mistake is nothing; my whole life is a series of errors. I've been trying, and expect to keep right on trying, to give you youngsters the benefit of my years; but if you insist on learning it for yourselves, well enough. When I was your age, I took no one's advice; but look how I've paid the fiddler. Possibly it was ordained otherwise, but it looks to me like a shame that I can't give you boys the benefit of my dearly bought experience. But whether you take my advice or not, we're going to be just as good friends as ever. I need young fellows like you on this ranch. I've sent Dan out after Deweese, and to-morrow we're going to commence gathering beeves. A few weeks' good hard work will do you worlds of good. In less than a year, you'll look back at this as a splendid lesson. Shucks! boy, a man is a narrow, calloused creature until he has been shook up a few times by love affairs. They develop him into the man he was intended to be. Come on into the house, Tom, and Jean will make us a couple of mint juleps."

What a blessed panacea for mental trouble is work! We were in the saddle by daybreak the next morning, rounding up *remudas*. Every available vaquero at the outlying ranchitas had been summoned. Dividing the outfit and horses, Uncle Lance took twelve men and struck west for the Ganso. With an equal number of men, Deweese pushed north for the Frio, which he was to work down below Shepherd's, thence back along the home river. From the ranch books, we knew there were fully two thousand beeves over five years old in our brand. These cattle had never known an hour's restraint since the day they were branded, and caution and cool judgment would be required in handling them. Since the contract only required twelve hundred, we expected to make an extra clean gathering, using the oldest and naturally the largest beeves.

During the week spent in gathering, I got the full benefit of every possible hour in the saddle. We reached the Ganso about an hour before sundown. The weather had settled; water was plentiful, and every one realized that the work in hand would require wider riding than under dry conditions. By the time we had caught up fresh horses, the sun had gone down. "Boys," said Uncle Lance, "we want to make a big rodeo on the head of this creek in the morning. Tom, you take two vaqueros and lay off to the southwest about ten miles, and make a dry camp to-night. Glenn may have the same help to the southeast; and every rascal of you be in your saddles by daybreak. There are a lot of big *ladino* beeves in those brushy hills to the south and west. Be sure and be in your saddles early enough to catch *all* wild cattle out on the prairies. If you want to, you can take a lunch in your pocket for breakfast. No; you need no blankets — you'll get up earlier if you sleep cold."

Taking José Pena and Pasquale Arispe with me, I struck off on our course in the gathering twilight. The first twitter of a bird in the morning brought me to my feet; I roused the others, and we saddled and were riding with the first sign of dawn in the east. Taking the outside circle myself, I gave every bunch of cattle met on my course a good start for the centre of the round-up. Pasquale and Jose followed several miles to my rear on inner circles, drifting on the cattle which I had started inward. As the sun arose, dispelling the morning mists, I could see other cattle coming down in long strings out of the hills to the eastward. Within an hour after starting, Gallup and I met. Our half circle to the southward was perfect, and each turning back, we rode our appointed divisions until the vaqueros from the wagon were sighted, throwing in cattle and closing up the northern portion of the circle. Before the sun was two hours high, the first rodeo of the day was together, numbering about three thousand mixed cattle. In the few hours since dawn, we had concentrated all animals in a territory at least fifteen miles in diameter.

Uncle Lance was in his element. Detailing two vaqueros to hold the beef cut within reach and a half dozen to keep the main herd compact, he ordered the remainder of us to enter and begin the selecting of beeves. There were a number of big wild steers in the round-up, but we left those until the cut numbered over two hundred. When every hoof over five years of age was separated, we had a nucleus for our beef herd numbering about two hundred and forty steers. They were in fine condition for grass cattle, and, turning the main herd free, we started our cut for the wagon, being compelled to ride wide of them as we drifted down stream towards camp, as there were a number of old beeves which showed impatience at the restraint. But by letting them scatter well, by the time they reached the wagon it required but two vaqueros to hold them.

The afternoon was but a repetition of the morning. Everything on the south side of the Nueces between the river and the wagon was thrown together on the second round-up of the day, which yielded less than two hundred cattle for our beef herd. But when we went into camp, dividing into squads for night-herding, the day's work was satisfactory to the ranchero. Dan Happersett was given five vaqueros and stood the first watch or until one A.M. Glenn Gallup and myself took the remainder of the men and stood guard until morning. When Happersett called our guard an hour after midnight, he said to Gallup and me as we were pulling on our boots: "About a dozen big steers haven't laid down. There's only one of them that has given any trouble. He's a pinto that we cut in the first round-up in the morning. He has made two breaks already to get away, and if you don't watch him close, he'll surely give you the slip."

While riding to the relief, Glenn and I posted our vaqueros to be on the lookout for the pinto beef. The cattle were intentionally bedded loose; but even in the starlight and waning moon, every man easily spotted the *ladino* beef, uneasily stalking back and forth like a caged tiger across the bed ground. A half hour before dawn, he made a final effort to escape, charging out between Gallup and the vaquero following up on the same side. From the other side of the bed ground, I heard the commotion, but dare not leave the herd to assist. There was a mile of open country surrounding our camp, and if two men could not turn the beef on that space, it was useless for others to offer assistance. In the stillness of the morning hour, we could hear the running and see the flashes from six-shooters, marking the course of the outlaw. After making a half circle, we heard them coming direct for the herd. For fear of a stampede, we raised a great commotion around the sleeping cattle; but in spite of our precaution, as the *ladino* beef reëntered the herd, over half the beeves jumped to their feet and began milling. But we held them until dawn, and after scattering them over several hundred acres, left them grazing contentedly, when, leaving two vaqueros with the feeding herd, we went back to the wagon. The camp had been astir some time, and when Glenn reported the incident of our watch, Uncle Lance said: "I thought I heard some shooting while I was cat-napping at daylight. Well, we can use a little fresh beef in this very camp. We'll kill him at noon. The wagon will move down near the river this morning, so we can make three rodeos from it without moving camp, and to-night we'll have a side of Pinto's ribs barbecued. My mouth is watering this very minute for a rib roast."

That morning after a big rodeo on the Nueces, well above the Ganso, we returned to camp. Throwing into our herd the cut of less than a hundred secured on the morning round-up, Uncle Lance, who had preceded us, rode out from the wagon with a carbine. Allowing the beeves to scatter, the old ranchero met and rode zigzagging through them until he came face to face with the pinto *ladino*. On noticing the intruding horseman, the outlaw threw up his head. There was a carbine report and the big fellow went down in his tracks. By the time the herd had grazed away, Tiburcio, who was cooking with our wagon, brought out all the knives, and the beef was bled, dressed, and quartered.

"You can afford to be extravagant with this beef," said Uncle Lance to the old cook, when the quarters had been carried in to the wagon. "I've been ranching on this river nearly forty years, and I've always made it a rule, where cattle cannot be safely handled, to beef them then and there. I've sat up many a night barbecuing the ribs of a *ladino*. If you have plenty of salt, Tiburcio, you can make a brine and jerk those hind quarters. It will make fine chewing for the boys on night herd when once we start for the coast."

Following down the home river, we made ten other rodeos before we met Deweese. We had something over a thousand beeves while he had less than eight hundred. Throwing the two cuts together, we made a count, and cut back all the younger and smaller cattle until the herd was reduced to the required number. Before my advent at Las Palomas, about the only outlet for beef cattle had been the canneries at Rockport and Fulton. But these cattle were for shipment by boat to New Orleans and other coast cities. The route to the coast was well known to my employer, and detailing twelve men for the herd, a horse wrangler and cook extra, we started for it, barely touching at the ranch on our course. It was a nice ten days' trip. After the first night, we used three guards of four men each. Grazing contentedly, the cattle quieted down until on our arrival half our numbers could have handled them. The herd was counted and received on the outlying prairies, and as no steamer was due for a few days, another outfit took charge of them.

Uncle Lance was never much of a man for towns, and soon after settlement the next morning we were ready to start home. But the payment, amounting to thirty thousand dollars, presented a problem, as the bulk of it came to us in silver. There was scarcely a merchant in the place who would assume the responsibility of receiving it even on deposit, and in the absence of a bank, there was no alternative but to take it home. The agent for the steamship company solicited the money for transportation to New Orleans, mentioning the danger of robbery, and referring to the recent attempt of bandits to hold up the San Antonio and Corpus Christi stage. I had good cause to remember that incident, and was wondering what my employer would do under the circumstances, when he turned from the agent, saying: —

"Well, we'll take it home just the same. I have no use for money in New Orleans. Nor do I care if every bandit in Texas knows we've got the money in the wagon. I want to buy a few new guns, anyhow. If robbers tackle us, we'll promise them a warm reception — and I never knew a thief who didn't think more of his own carcass than of another man's money."

The silver was loaded into the wagon in sacks, and we started on our return. It was rather a risky trip, but we never concealed the fact that we had every dollar of the money in the wagon. It would have been dangerous to make an attempt on us, for we were all well armed. We reached the ranch in safety, rested a day, and then took the ambulance and went on to San Antonio. Three of us, besides Tiburcio, accompanied our employer, each taking a saddle horse, and stopping by night at ranches where we were known. On the third day we reached the city in good time to bank the money, much to my relief.

As there was no work pressing at home, we spent a week in the city, thoroughly enjoying ourselves. Uncle Lance was negotiating for the purchase of a large Spanish land grant, which adjoined our range on the west, taking in the Ganso and several miles' frontage on both sides of the home river. This required his attention for a few days, during which time Deweese met two men on the lookout for stock cattle with which to start a new ranch on the Devil's River in Valverde County. They were in the market for three thousand cows, to be delivered that fall or the following spring. Our *segundo* promptly invited them to meet his employer that evening at our hotel. As the ranges in eastern Texas became of value for agriculture, the cowman moved westward, disposing of his cattle or taking them with him. It was men of this class whom Deweese had met during the day, and on filling their appointment in the evening, our employer and the buyers soon came to an agreement. References were exchanged, and the next afternoon a contract was entered into whereby we were to deliver, May first, at Las Palomas ranch, three thousand cows between the ages of two and four years.

There was some delay in perfecting the title to the land grant. "We'll start home in the morning, boys," said Uncle Lance, the evening after the contract was drawn. "You simply can't hurry a land deal. I'll get that tract in time, but there's over a hundred heirs now of the original Don. I'd just like to know what the grandee did for his king to get that grant. Tickled his royal nibs, I reckon, with some cock and bull story, and here I have to give up nearly forty thousand dollars of good honest money. Twenty years ago I was offered this same grant for ten cents an acre, and now I'm paying four bits. But I didn't have the money then, and I'm not sure I'd have bought it if I had. But I need it now, and I need it bad, and that's why I'm letting them hold me up for such a figure."

Stopping at the "last chance" road house on the outskirts of the city the next morning, for a final drink as we were leaving, Uncle Lance said to us over the cattle contract: "There's money in it — good money, too. But we're not going to fill it out of our home brand. Not in this year of our Lord. I think too much of my cows to part with a single animal. Boys, cows made Las Palomas what she is, and as long as they win for me, I intend — to swear by them through thick and thin, in good and bad repute, fair weather or foul. So, June, just as soon as the fall branding is over, you can take Tom with you for an interpreter and start for Mexico to contract these cows. Las Palomas is going to branch out and spread herself. As a ranchman, I can bring the cows across for breeding purposes free of duty, and I know of no good reason why I can't change my mind and sell them. Dan, take Tiburcio out a cigar."

CHAPTER XI
A TURKEY BAKE

Deweese and I came back from Mexico during Christmas week. On reaching Las Palomas, we found Frank Nancrede and Add Tully, the latter being also a trail foreman, at the ranch. They were wintering in San Antonio, and were spending a few weeks at our ranch, incidentally on the lookout for several hundred saddle horses for trail purposes the coming spring. We had no horses for sale, but nevertheless Uncle Lance had prevailed on them to make Las Palomas headquarters during their stay in the country.

The first night at the ranch, Miss Jean and I talked until nearly midnight. There had been so many happenings during my absence that it required a whole evening to tell them all. From the naming of Anita's baby to the rivalry between John and Theodore for the favor of Frances Vaux, all the latest social news of the countryside was discussed. Miss Jean had attended the dance at Shepherd's during the fall, and had heard it whispered that Oxenford and Esther were anything but happy. The latest word from the Vaux ranch said that the couple had separated; at least there was some trouble, for when Oxenford had attempted to force her to return to Oakville, and had made some disparaging remarks, Tony Hunter had crimped a six-shooter over his head. I pretended not to be interested in this, but secretly had I learned that Hunter had killed Oxenford, I should have had no very serious regrets.

Uncle Lance had promised Tully and Nancrede a turkey hunt during the holidays, so on our unexpected return it was decided to have it at once. There had been a heavy mast that year, and in the encinal ridges to the east wild turkeys were reported plentiful. Accordingly we set out the next afternoon for a camp hunt in some oak cross timbers which grew on the eastern border of our ranch lands. Taking two pack mules and Tiburcio as cook, a party of eight of us rode away, expecting to remain overnight. Uncle Lance knew of a fine camping spot about ten miles from the ranch. When within a few miles of the place, Tiburcio was sent on ahead with the pack mules to make camp. "Boys, we'll divide up here," said Uncle Lance, "and take a little scout through these cross timbers and try and locate some roosts. The camp will be in those narrows ahead yonder where that burnt timber is to your right. Keep an eye open for *javalina* signs; they used to be plentiful through here when there was good mast. Now, scatter out in pairs, and if you can knock down a gobbler or two we'll have a turkey bake to-night."

Dan Happersett knew the camping spot, so I went with him, and together we took a big circle through the encinal, keeping alert for game signs. Before we had gone far, evidence became plentiful, not only of turkeys, but of peccary and deer. Where the turkeys had recently been scratching, many times we dismounted and led our horses — but either the turkeys were too wary for us, or else we had been deceived as to the freshness of the sign. Several successive shots on our right caused us to hurry out of the timber in the direction of the reports. Halting in the edge of the timber, we watched the strip of prairie between us and the next cover to the south. Soon a flock of fully a hundred wild turkeys came running out of the encinal on the opposite side and started across to our ridge. Keeping under cover, we rode to intercept them, never losing sight of the covey. They were running fast; but when they were nearly halfway across the opening, there was another shot and they took flight, sailing into cover ahead of us, well out of range. But one gobbler was so fat that he was unable to fly over a hundred yards and was still in the open. We rode to cut him off. On sighting us, he attempted to rise; but his pounds were against him, and when we crossed his course he was so winded that our horses ran all around him. After we had both shot a few times, missing him, he squatted in some tall grass and stuck his head under a tuft. Dismounting, Dan sprang on to him like a fox, and he was ours. We wrung his neck, and agreed to report that we had shot him through the head, thus concealing, in the absence of bullet wounds, our poor marksmanship.

When we reached the camp shortly before dark, we found the others had already arrived, ours making the sixth turkey in the evening's bag. We had drawn ours on killing it, as had the others, and after supper Uncle Lance superintended the stuffing of the two largest birds.

While this was in progress, others made a stiff mortar, and we coated each turkey with about three inches of the waxy play, feathers and all. Opening our camp-fire, we placed the turkeys together, covered them with ashes and built a heaping fire over and around them. A number of haunts had been located by the others, but as we expected to make an early hunt in the morning, we decided not to visit any of the roosts that night. After Uncle Lance had regaled us with hunting stories of an early day, the discussion innocently turned to my recent elopement. By this time the scars had healed fairly well, and I took the chaffing in all good humor. Tully told a personal experience, which, if it was the truth, argued that in time I might become as indifferent to my recent mishap as any one could wish.

"My prospects of marrying a few years ago," said Tully, lying full stretch before the fire, "were a whole lot better than yours, Quirk. But my ambition those days was to boss a herd up the trail and get top-notch wages. She was a Texas girl, just like yours, bred up in Van Zandt County. She could ride a horse like an Indian. Bad horses seemed afraid of her. Why, I saw her once when she was about sixteen, take a black stallion out of his stable, — lead him out with but a rope about his neck, — throw a half hitch about his nose, and mount him as though he was her pet. Bareback and without a bridle she rode him ten miles for a doctor. There wasn't a mile of the distance either but he felt the quirt burning in his flank and knew he was being ridden by a master. Her father scolded her at the time, and boasted about it later.

"She had dozens of admirers, and the first impression I ever made on her was when she was about twenty. There was a big tournament being given, and all the young bloods in many counties came in to contest for the prizes. I was a double winner in the games and contests — won a roping prize and was the only lad that came inside the time limit as a lancer, though several beat me on rings. Of course the tournament ended with a ball. Having won the lance prize, it was my privilege of crowning the 'queen' of the ball. Of course I wasn't going to throw away such a chance, for there was no end of rivalry amongst the girls over it. The crown was made of flowers, or if there were none in season, of live-oak leaves. Well, at the ball after the tournament I crowned Miss Kate with a crown of oak leaves. After that I felt bold enough to crowd matters, and things came my way. We were to be married during Easter week, but her mother up and died, so we put it off awhile for the sake of appearances.

"The next spring I got a chance to boss a herd up the trail for Jesse Ellison. It was the chance of my life and I couldn't think of refusing. The girl put up quite a mouth about it, and I explained to her that a hundred a month wasn't offered to every man. She finally gave in, but still you could see she wasn't pleased. Girls that way don't sabe cattle matters a little bit. She promised to write me at several points which I told her the herd would pass. When I bade her good-by, tears stood in her eyes, though she tried to hide them. I'd have gambled my life on her that morning.

"Well, we had a nice trip, good outfit and strong cattle. Uncle Jess mounted us ten horses to the man, every one fourteen hands or better, for we were contracted for delivery in Nebraska. It was a five months' drive with scarcely an incident on the way. Just a run or two and a dry drive or so. I had lots of time to think about Kate. When we reached the Chisholm crossing on Red River, I felt certain that I would find a letter, but I didn't. I wrote her from there, but when we reached Caldwell, nary a letter either. The same luck at Abilene. Try as I might, I couldn't make it out. Something was wrong, but what it was, was anybody's guess.

"At this last place we got our orders to deliver the cattle at the junction of the middle and lower Loup. It was a terror of a long drive, but that wasn't a circumstance compared to not hearing from Kate. I kept all this to myself, mind you. When our herd reached its destination, which it did on time, as hard luck would have it there was a hitch in the payment. The herd was turned loose and all the outfit but myself sent home. I stayed there two months longer at a little place called Broken Bow. I held the bill of sale for the herd, and would turn it over, transferring the cattle from one owner to another, on the word from my employer. At last I received a letter from Uncle Jesse saying that the payment in full had been made, so I surrendered the final document and came home. Those trains seemed to run awful slow. But I got home all too soon, for she had then been married three months.

"You see an agent for eight-day clocks came along, and being a stranger took her eye. He was one of those nice, dapper fellows, wore a red necktie, and could talk all day to a woman. He worked by the rule of three, — tickle, talk, and flatter, with a few cutes thrown in for a pelon; that gets nearly any of them. They live in town now. He's a windmill agent. I never went near them."

Meanwhile the fire kept pace with the talk, thanks to Uncle Lance's watchful eye. "That's right, Tiburcio, carry up plenty of good lena," he kept saying. "Bring in all the black-jack oak that you can find; it makes fine coals. These are both big gobblers, and to bake them until they fall to pieces like a watermelon will require a steady fire till morning. Pile up a lot of wood, and if I wake up during the night, trust to me to look after the fire. I've baked so many turkeys this way that I'm an expert at the business."

"A girl's argument," remarked Dan Happersett in a lull of talk, "don't have to be very weighty to fit any case. Anything she does is justifiable. That's one reason why I always kept shy of women. I admit that I've toyed around with some of them; have tossed my tug on one or two just to see if they would run on the rope. But now generally I keep a wire fence between them and myself if they show any symptoms of being on the marry. Maybe so I was in earnest once, back on the Trinity. But it seems that every time that I made a pass, my loop would foul or fail to open or there was brush in the way."

"Just because you have a few gray hairs in your head you think you're awful foxy, don't you?" said Uncle Lance to Dan. "I've seen lots of independent fellows like you. If I had a little widow who knew her cards, and just let her kitten up to you and act coltish, inside a week you would be following her around like a pet lamb."

"I knew a fellow," said Nancrede, lighting his pipe with a firebrand, "that when the clerk asked him, when he went for a license to marry, if he would swear that the young lady — his intended — was over twenty-one, said: 'Yes, by G — , I'll swear that she's over thirty-one.'"

At the next pause in the yarning, I inquired why a wild turkey always deceived itself by hiding its head and leaving the body exposed. "That it's a fact, we all know," volunteered Uncle Lance, "but the why and wherefore is too deep for me. I take it that it's due to running to neck too much in their construction. Now an ostrich is the same way, all neck with not a lick of sense. And the same applies to the human family. You take one of these long-necked cowmen and what does he know outside of cattle. Nine times out of ten, I can tell a sensible girl by merely looking at her neck. Now snicker, you dratted young fools, just as if I wasn't talking horse sense to you. Some of you boys haven't got much more sabe than a fat old gobbler."

"When I first came to this State," said June Deweese, who had been quietly and attentively listening to the stories, "I stopped over on the Neches River near a place called Shot-a-buck Crossing. I had an uncle living there with whom I made my home the first few years that I lived in Texas. There are more or less cattle there, but it is principally a cotton country. There was an old cuss living over there on that river who was land poor, but had a powerful purty girl. Her old man owned any number of plantations on the river — generally had lots of nigger renters to look after. Miss Sallie, the daughter, was the belle of the neighborhood. She had all the graces with a fair mixture of the weaknesses of her sex. The trouble was, there was no young man in the whole country fit to hold her horse. At least she and her folks entertained that idea. There was a storekeeper and a young doctor at the county seat, who it seems took turns calling on her. It looked like it was going to be a close race. Outside of these two there wasn't a one of us who could touch her with a twenty-four-foot fish-pole. We simply took the side of the road when she passed by.

"About this time there drifted in from out west near Fort McKavett, a young fellow named Curly Thorn. He had relatives living in that neighborhood. Out at the fort he was a common foreman on a ranch. Talk about your graceful riders, he sat a horse in a manner that left nothing to be desired. Well, Curly made himself very agreeable with all the girls on the range, but played no special favorites. He stayed in the country, visiting among cousins, until camp meeting began over at the Alabama Camp Ground. During this meeting Curly proved himself quite a gallant by carrying first one young lady and the next evening some other to camp meeting. During these two weeks of the meeting, some one introduced him to Miss Sallie. Now, remember, he didn't play her for a favorite no more than any other. That's what miffed her. She thought he ought to.

"One Sunday afternoon she intimated to him, like a girl sometimes will, that she was going home, and was sorry that she had no companion for the ride. This was sufficient for the gallant Curly to offer himself to her as an escort. She simply thought she was stealing a beau from some other girl, and he never dreamt he was dallying with Neches River royalty. But the only inequality in that couple as they rode away from the ground was an erroneous idea in her and her folks' minds. And that difference was in the fact that her old dad had more land than he could pay taxes on. Well, Curly not only saw her home, but stayed for tea — that's the name the girls have for supper over on the Neches — and that night carried her back to the evening service. From that day till the close of the session he was devotedly hers. A month afterward when he left, it was the talk of the country that they were to be married during the coming holidays.

"But then there were the young doctor and the storekeeper still in the game. Curly was off the scene temporarily, but the other two were riding their best horses to a shadow. Miss Sallie's folks were pulling like bay steers for the merchant, who had some money, while the young doctor had nothing but empty pill bags and a saddle horse or two. The doctor was the better looking, and, before meeting Curly Thorn, Miss Sallie had favored him. Knowing ones said they were engaged. But near the close of the race there was sufficient home influence used for the storekeeper to take the lead and hold it until the show down came. Her folks announced the wedding, and the merchant received the best wishes of his friends, while the young doctor took a trip for his health. Well, it developed afterwards that she was engaged to both the storekeeper and the doctor at the same time. But that's nothing. My experience tells me that a girl don't need broad shoulders to carry three or four engagements at the same time.

"Well, within a week of the wedding, who should drift in to spend Christmas but Curly Thorn. His cousins, of course, lost no time in giving him the lay of the land. But Curly acted indifferent, and never even offered to call on Miss Sallie. Us fellows joked him about his girl going to marry another fellow, and he didn't seem a little bit put out. In fact, he seemed to enjoy the sudden turn as a good joke on himself. But one morning, two days before the wedding was to take place, Miss Sallie was missing from her home, as was likewise Curly Thorn from the neighborhood. Yes, Thorn had eloped with her and they were married the next morning in Nacogdoches. And the funny thing about it was, Curly never met her after his return until the night they eloped. But he had a girl cousin who had a finger in the pie. She and Miss Sallie were as thick as three in a bed, and Curly didn't have anything to do but play the hand that was dealt him.

"Before I came to Las Palomas, I was over round Fort McKavett and met Curly. We knew each other, and he took me home and had me stay overnight with him. They had been married then four years. She had a baby on each knee and another in her arms. There was so much reality in life that she had no time to become a dreamer. Matrimony in that case was a good leveler of imaginary rank. I always admired Curly for the indifferent hand he played all through the various stages of the courtship. He never knew there was such a thing as difference. He simply coppered the play to win, and the cards came his way."

"Bully for Curly!" said Uncle Lance, arising and fixing the fire, as the rest of us unrolled our blankets. "If some of my rascals could make a ten strike like that it would break a streak of bad luck which has overshadowed Las Palomas for over thirty years. Great Scott! — but those gobblers smell good. I can hear them blubbering and sizzling in their shells. It will surely take an axe to crack that clay in the morning. But get under your blankets, lads, for I'll call you for a turkey breakfast about dawn."

CHAPTER XII
SUMMER OF '77

During our trip into Mexico the fall before, Deweese contracted for three thousand cows at two haciendas on the Rio San Juan. Early in the spring June and I returned to receive the cattle. The ranch outfit under Uncle Lance was to follow some three weeks later and camp on the American side at Roma, Texas. We made arrangements as we crossed into Mexico with a mercantile house in Mier to act as our bankers, depositing our own drafts and taking letters of credit to the interior. In buying the cows we had designated Mier, which was just opposite Roma, as the place for settlement and Uncle Lance on his arrival brought drafts to cover our purchases, depositing them with the same merchant. On receiving, we used a tally mark which served as a road brand, thus preventing a second branding, and throughout — much to the disgust of the Mexican vaqueros — Deweese enforced every humane idea which Nancrede had practiced the spring before in accepting the trail herd at Las Palomas. There were endless quantities of stock cattle to select from on the two haciendas, and when ready to start, under the specifications, a finer lot of cows would have been hard to find. The worst drawback was that they were constantly dropping calves on the road, and before we reached the river we had a calf-wagon in regular use. On arriving at the Rio Grande, the then stage of water was fortunately low and we crossed the herd without a halt, the import papers having been attended to in advance.

Uncle Lance believed in plenty of help, and had brought down from Las Palomas an ample outfit of men and horses. He had also anticipated the dropping of calves and had rigged up a carrier, the box of which was open framework. Thus until a calf was strong enough to follow, the mother, as she trailed along beside the wagon, could keep an eye on her offspring. We made good drives the first two or three days; but after clearing the first bottoms of the Rio Grande and on reaching the tablelands, we made easy stages of ten to twelve miles a day. When near enough to calculate on our arrival at Las Palomas, the old ranchero quit us and went on into the ranch. Several days later a vaquero met the herd about thirty miles south of Santa Maria, and brought the information that the Valverde outfit was at the ranch, and instructions to veer westward and drive down the Ganso on approaching the Nueces. By these orders the delivery on the home river would occur at least twenty miles west of the ranch headquarters.

As we were passing to the westward of Santa Maria, our employer and one of the buyers rode out from that ranch and met the herd. They had decided not to brand until arriving at their destination on the Devil's River, which would take them at least a month longer. While this deviation was nothing to us, it was a gain to them. The purchaser was delighted with the cattle and our handling of them, there being fully a thousand young calves, and on reaching their camp on the Ganso, the delivery was completed — four days in advance of the specified time. For fear of losses, we had received a few head extra, and, on counting them over, found we had not lost a single hoof. The buyers received the extra cattle, and the delivery was satisfactorily concluded. One of the partners returned with us to Las Palomas for the final settlement, while the other, taking charge of the herd, turned them up the Nueces. The receiving outfit had fourteen men and some hundred and odd horses. Aside from their commissary, they also had a calf-wagon, drawn by two yoke of oxen and driven by a strapping big negro. In view of the big calf crop, the partners concluded that an extra conveyance would not be amiss, and on Uncle Lance making them a reasonable figure on our calf-wagon and the four mules drawing it, they never changed a word but took the outfit. As it was late in the day when the delivery was made, the double outfit remained in the same camp that night, and with the best wishes, bade each other farewell in the morning. Nearly a month had passed since Deweese and I had left Las Palomas for the Rio San Juan, and, returning with the herd, had met our own outfit at the Rio Grande. During the interim, before the ranch outfit had started, the long-talked-of tournament on the Nueces had finally been arranged. The date had been set for the fifth of June, and of all the home news which the outfit brought down to the Rio Grande, none was as welcome as this. According to the programme, the contests were to include riding, roping, relay races, and handling the lance. Several of us had never witnessed a tournament; but as far as roping and riding were concerned, we all considered ourselves past masters of the arts. The relay races were simple enough, and Dan Happersett volunteered this explanation of a lance contest to those of us who were uninitiated: —

"Well," said Dan, while we were riding home from the Ganso, "a straight track is laid off about two hundred yards long. About every forty yards there is a post set up along the line with an arm reaching out over the track. From this there is suspended an iron ring about two inches in diameter. The contestant is armed with a wooden lance of regulation length, and as he rides down this track at full speed and within a time limit, he is to impale as many of these rings as possible. Each contestant is entitled to three trials and the one impaling the most rings is declared the victor. That's about all there is to it, except the award. The festivities, of course, close with a dance, in which the winner crowns the Queen of the ball. That's the reason the girls always take such an interest in the lancing, because the winner has the choosing of his Queen. I won it once, over on the Trinity, and chose a little cripple girl. Had to do it or leave the country, for it was looked upon as an engagement to marry. Oh, I tell you, if a girl is sweet on a fellow, it's a mighty strong card to play."

Before starting for the Rio Grande, the old ranchero had worked our horse stock, forming fourteen new *manadas*, so that on our return about the only work which could command our attention was the breaking of more saddle horses. We had gentled two hundred the spring before, and breaking a hundred and fifty now, together with the old *remudas*, would give Las Palomas fully five hundred saddle horses. The ranch had the geldings, the men had time, and there was no good excuse for not gentling more horses. So after a few days' rest the oldest and heaviest geldings were gathered and we then settled down to routine horse work. But not even this exciting employment could keep the coming tournament from our minds. Within a week after returning to the ranch, we laid off a lancing course, and during every spare hour the knights of Las Palomas might be seen galloping over the course, practicing. I tried using the lance several times, only to find that it was not as easy as it looked, and I finally gave up the idea of lancing honors, and turned my attention to the relay races.

Miss Jean had been the only representative of our ranch at Shepherd's on San Jacinto Day. But she had had her eyes open on that occasion, and on our return had a message for nearly every one of us. I was not expecting any, still the mistress of Las Palomas had met my old sweetheart and her sister, Mrs. Hunter, at the ferry, and the three had talked the matter over and mingled their tears in mutual sympathy. I made a blustering talk which was to cover my real feelings and to show that I had grown indifferent toward Esther, but that tactful woman had not lived in vain, and read me aright.

"Tom," said she, "I was a young woman when you were a baby. There's lots of things in which you might deceive me, but Esther McLeod is not one of them. You loved her once, and you can't tell me that in less than a year you have forgotten her. I won't say that men forget easier than women, but you have never suffered one tenth the heartaches over Esther McLeod that she has over you. You can afford to be generous with her, Tom. True, she allowed an older sister to browbeat and bully her into marrying another man, but she was an inexperienced girl then. If you were honest, you would admit that Esther of her own accord would never have married Jack Oxenford. Then why punish the innocent? Oh, Tom, if you could only see her now! Sorrow and suffering have developed the woman in her, and she is no longer the girl you knew and loved."

Miss Jean was hewing too close to the line for my comfort. Her observations were so near the truth that they touched me in a vulnerable spot. Yet as I paced the room, I expressed myself emphatically as never wishing to meet Esther McLeod again. I really felt that way. But I had not reckoned on the mistress of Las Palomas, nor considered that her strong sympathy for my former sweetheart had moved her to more than ordinary endeavor.

The month of May passed. Uncle Lance spent several weeks at the Booth ranch on the Frio. At the home ranch practice for the contests went forward with vigor. By the first of June we had sifted the candidates down until we had determined on our best men for each entry. The old ranchero and our *segundo*, together with Dan Happersett, made up a good set of judges on our special fitness for the different contests, and we were finally picked in this order: Enrique Lopez was to rope; Pasquale Arispe was to ride; to Theodore Quayle fell the chance of handling the lance, while I, being young and nimble on my feet, was decided on as the rider in the ten-mile relay race.

In this contest I was fortunate in having the pick of over three hundred and fifty saddle horses. They were the accumulation of years of the best that Las Palomas bred, and it was almost bewildering to make the final selection. But in this I had the benefit of the home judges, and when the latter differed on the speed of a horse, a trial usually settled the point. June Deweese proved to be the best judge of the ranch horses, yet Uncle Lance never yielded his opinion without a test of speed. When the horses were finally decided on, we staked off a half-mile circular track on the first bottom of the river, and every evening the horses were sent over the course. Under the conditions, a contestant was entitled to use as many horses as he wished, but must change mounts at least twenty times in riding the ten miles, and must finish under a time limit of twenty-five minutes. Out of our abundance we decided to use ten mounts, thus allotting each horse two dashes of a half mile with a rest between.

The horse-breaking ended a few days before the appointed time. Las Palomas stood on the tiptoe of expectancy over the coming tourney. Even Miss Jean rode — having a gentle saddle horse caught up for her use, and taking daily rides about the ranch, to witness the practice, for she was as deeply interested as any of us in the forthcoming contests. Born to the soil of Texas, she was a horsewoman of no ordinary ability, and rode like a veteran. On the appointed day, Las Palomas was abandoned; even the Mexican contingent joining in the exodus for Shepherd's, and only a few old servants remaining at the ranch. As usual, Miss Jean started by ambulance the afternoon before, taking along a horse for her own saddle. The white element and the vaqueros made an early start, driving a *remuda* of thirty loose horses, several of which were outlaws, and a bell mare. They were the picked horses of the ranch — those which we expected to use in the contests, and a change of mounts for the entire outfit on reaching the martial field. We had herded the horses the night before, and the vaqueros were halfway to the ferry when we overtook them. Uncle Lance was with us and in the height of his glory, in one breath bragging on Enrique and Pasquale, and admonishing and cautioning Theodore and myself in the next.

On nearing Shepherd's, Uncle Lance preceded us, to hunt up the committee and enter a man from Las Palomas for each of the contests. The ground had been well chosen, — a large open bottom on the north side of the river and about a mile above the ferry. The lancing course was laid off; temporary corrals had been built, to hold about thirty range cattle for the roping, and an equal number of outlaw horses for the riding contests; at the upper end of the valley a half-mile circular racecourse had been staked off. Throwing our outlaws into the corral, and leaving the *remuda* in charge of two vaqueros, we galloped into Shepherd's with the gathering crowd. From all indications this would be a red-letter day at the ferry, for the attendance drained a section of country fully a hundred miles in diameter. On the north from Campbellton on the Atascosa to San Patricio on the home river to the south, and from the Blanco on the east to well up the Frio and San Miguel on the west, horsemen were flocking by platoons. I did not know one man in twenty, but Deweese greeted them all as if they were near neighbors. Later in the morning, conveyances began to arrive from Oakville and near-by points, and the presence of women lent variety to the scene.

Under the rules, all entries were to be made before ten o'clock. The contests were due to begin half an hour later, and each contestant was expected to be ready to compete in the order of his application. There were eight entries in the relay race all told, mine being the seventh, which gave me a good opportunity to study the riding of those who preceded me. There were ten or twelve entries each in the roping and riding contests, while the knights of the lance numbered an even thirty. On account of the large number of entries the contests would require a full day, running the three classes simultaneously, allowing a slight intermission for lunch. The selection of disinterested judges for each class slightly delayed the commencement. After changing horses on reaching the field, the contests with the lance opened with a lad from Ramirena, who galloped over the course and got but a single ring. From the lateness of our entries, none of us would be called until afternoon, and we wandered at will from one section of the field to another. "Red" Earnest, from Waugh's ranch on the Frio, was the first entry in the relay race. He had a good mount of eight Spanish horses which he rode bareback, making many of his changes in less than fifteen seconds apiece, and finishing full three minutes under the time limit. The feat was cheered to the echo, I joining with the rest, and numerous friendly bets were made that the time would not be lowered that day. Two other riders rode before the noon recess, only one of whom came under the time limit, and his time was a minute over Earnest's record.

Miss Jean had camped the ambulance in sight of the field, and kept open house to all comers. Suspecting that she would have Mrs. Hunter and Esther for lunch, if they were present, I avoided our party and took dinner with Mrs. Booth. Meanwhile Uncle Lance detailed Deweese and Happersett to handle my horses, allowing us five vaqueros, and distributing the other men as assistants to our other three contestants. The day was an ideal one for the contests, rather warm during the morning, but tempered later by a fine afternoon breeze. It was after four o'clock when I was called, with Waugh's man still in the lead. Forming a small circle at the starting-point, each of our vaqueros led a pair of horses, in bridles only, around a ring, — constantly having in hand eight of my mount of ten. As handlers, I had two good men in our *segundo* and Dan Happersett. I crossed the line amid the usual shouting with a running start, determined, if possible, to lower the record of Red Earnest. In making the changes, all I asked was a good grip on the mane, and I found my seat as the horse shot away. The horses had broken into an easy sweat before the race began, and having stripped to the lowest possible ounce of clothing, I felt that I was getting out of them every fraction of speed they possessed. The ninth horse in my mount, a roan, for some unknown reason sulked at starting, then bolted out on the prairie, but got away with the loss of only about ten seconds, running the half mile like a scared wolf. Until it came the roan's turn to go again, no untoward incident happened, friendly timekeepers posting me at every change of mounts. But when this bolter's turn came again, he reared and plunged away stiff-legged, crossed the inward furrow, and before I could turn him again to the track, cut inside the course for two stakes or possibly fifty yards. By this time I was beyond recall, but as I came round and passed the starting-point, the judges attempted to stop me, and I well knew my chances were over. Uncle Lance promptly waived all rights to the award, and I was allowed to finish the race, lowering Earnest's time over twenty seconds. The eighth contestant, so I learned later, barely came under the time limit.

The vaqueros took charge of the relay mounts, and, reinvesting myself in my discarded clothing, I mounted my horse to leave the field, when who should gallop up and extend sympathy and congratulations but Miss Jean and my old sweetheart. There was no avoiding them, and discourtesy to the mistress of Las Palomas being out of the question, I greeted Esther with an affected warmth and cordiality. As I released her hand I could not help noticing how she had saddened into a serious woman, while the gentleness in her voice condemned me for my attitude toward her. But Miss Jean artfully gave us little time for embarrassment, inviting me to show them the unconcluded programme. From contest to contest, we rode the field until the sun went down, and the trials ended.

It was my first tournament and nothing escaped my notice. There were fully one hundred and fifty women and girls, and possibly double that number of men, old and young, every one mounted and galloping from one point of the field to another. Blushing maidens and their swains dropped out of the throng, and from shady vantage points watched the crowd surge back and forth across the field of action. We were sorry to miss Enrique's roping; for having snapped his saddle horn with the first cast, he recovered his rope, fastened it to the fork of his saddletree, and tied his steer in fifty-four seconds, or within ten of the winner's record. When he apologized to Miss Jean for his bad luck, hat in hand and his eyes as big as saucers, one would have supposed he had brought lasting disgrace on Las Palomas.

We were more fortunate in witnessing Pasquale's riding. For this contest outlaws and spoilt horses had been collected from every quarter. Riders drew their mounts by lot, and Pasquale drew a cinnamon-colored coyote from the ranch of "Uncle Nate" Wilson of Ramirena. Uncle Nate was feeling in fine fettle, and when he learned that his contribution to the outlaw horses had been drawn by a Las Palomas man, he hunted up the ranchero. "I'll bet you a new five-dollar hat that that cinnamon horse throws your vaquero so high that the birds build nests in his crotch before he hits the ground." Uncle Lance took the bet, and disdainfully ran his eye up and down his old friend, finally remarking, "Nate, you ought to keep perfectly sober on an occasion like this — you're liable to lose all your money."

Pasquale was a shallow-brained, clownish fellow, and after saddling up, as he led the coyote into the open to mount, he imitated a drunken vaquero. Tipsily admonishing the horse in Spanish to behave himself, he vaulted into the saddle and clouted his mount over the head with his hat. The coyote resorted to every ruse known to a bucking horse to unseat his rider, in the midst of which Pasquale, languidly lolling in his saddle, took a small bottle from his pocket, and, drinking its contents, tossed it backward over his head. "Look at that, Nate," said Uncle Lance, slapping Mr. Wilson with his hat; "that's one of the Las Palomas vaqueros, bred with just sense enough to ride anything that wears hair. We'll look at those new hats this evening."

In the fancy riding which followed, Pasquale did a number of stunts. He picked up hat and handkerchief from the ground at full speed, and likewise gathered up silver dollars from alternate sides of his horse as the animal sped over a short course. Stripping off his saddle and bridle, he rode the naked horse with the grace of an Indian, and but for his clownish indifference and the apparent ease with which he did things, the judges might have taken his work more seriously. As it was, our outfit and those friendly to our ranch were proud of his performance, but among outsiders, and even the judges, it was generally believed that he was tipsy, which was an injustice to him.

On the conclusion of the contest with the lance, among the thirty participants, four were tied on honors, one of whom was Theodore Quayle. The other contests being over, the crowd gathered round the lancing course, excitement being at its highest pitch. A lad from the Blanco was the first called for on the finals, and after three efforts failed to make good his former trial. Quayle was the next called, and as he sped down the course my heart stood still for a moment; but as he returned, holding high his lance, five rings were impaled upon it. He was entitled to two more trials, but rested on his record until it was tied or beaten, and the next man was called. Forcing her way through the crowded field, Miss Jean warmly congratulated Theodore, leaving Esther to my tender care. But at this juncture, my old sweetheart caught sight of Frances Vaux and some gallant approaching from the river's shade, and together we galloped out to meet them. Miss Vaux's escort was a neighbor lad from the Frio, but both he and I for the time being were relegated to oblivion, in the prospects of a Las Palomas man by the name of Quayle winning the lancing contest. Miss Frances, with a shrug, was for denying all interest in the result, but Esther and I doubled on her, forcing her to admit "that it would be real nice if Teddy should win." I never was so aggravated over the indifference of a girl in my life, and my regard for my former sweetheart, on account of her enthusiasm for a Las Palomas lad, kindled anew within me.

But as the third man sped over the course, we hastily returned to watch the final results. After a last trial the man threw down his lance, and, riding up, congratulated Quayle. The last contestant was a red-headed fellow from the Atascosa above Oakville, and seemed to have a host of friends. On his first trial over the course, he stripped four rings, but on neither subsequent effort did he equal his first attempt. Imitating the former contestant, the red-headed fellow broke his lance and congratulated the winner.

The tourney was over. Esther and I urged Miss Frances to ride over with us and congratulate Quayle. She demurred; but as the crowd scattered I caught Theodore's eye and, signaling to him, he rode out of the crowd and joined us. The compliments of Miss Vaux to the winner were insipid and lifeless, while Esther, as if to atone for her friend's lack of interest, beamed with happiness over Quayle's good luck. Poor Teddy hardly knew which way to turn, and, nice girl as she was, I almost hated Miss Frances for her indifferent attitude. A plain, blunt fellow though he was, Quayle had noticed the coolness in the greeting of the young lady whom he no doubt had had in mind for months, in case he should win the privilege, to crown as Queen of the ball. Piqued and unsettled in his mind, he excused himself on some trivial pretense and withdrew. Every one was scattering to the picnic grounds for supper, and under the pretense of escorting Esther to the Vaux conveyance, I accompanied the young ladies. Managing to fall to the rear of Miss Frances and her gallant for the day, I bluntly asked my old sweetheart if she understood the attitude of her friend. For reply she gave me a pitying glance, saying, "Oh, you boys know so little about a girl! You see that Teddy chooses Frances for his Queen to-night, and leave the rest to me."

On reaching their picnic camp, I excused myself, promising to meet them later at the dance, and rode for our ambulance. Tiburcio had supper all ready, and after it was over I called Theodore to one side and repeated Esther's message. Quayle was still doubtful, and I called Miss Jean to my assistance, hoping to convince him that Miss Vaux was not unfriendly towards him. "You always want to judge a woman by contraries," said Miss Jean, seating herself on the log beside us. "When it comes to acting her part, always depend on a girl to conceal her true feelings, especially if she has tact. Now, from what you boys say, my judgment is that she'd cry her eyes out if any other girl was chosen Queen."

Uncle Lance had promised Mr. Wilson to take supper with his family, and as we were all sprucing up for the dance, he returned. He had not been present at the finals of the lancing contest, but from guests of the Wilsons' had learned that one of his boys had won the honors. So on riding into camp, as the finishing touches were being added to our rustic toilets, he accosted Quayle and said: "Well, Theo, they tell me that you won the elephant. Great Scott, boy, that's the best luck that has struck Las Palomas since the big rain a year ago this month! Of course, we all understand that you're to choose the oldest Vaux girl. What's that? You don't know? Well, I do. I've had that all planned out, in case you won, ever since we decided that you was to contest as the representative of Las Palomas. And now you want to balk, do you?"

Uncle Lance was showing some spirit, but his sister checked him with this explanation: "Just because Miss Frances didn't show any enthusiasm over Theo winning, he and Tom somehow have got the idea in their minds that she don't care a rap to be chosen Queen. I've tried to explain it to them, but the boys don't understand girls, that's all. Why, if Theo was to choose any other girl, she'd set the river afire."

"That's it, is it?" snorted Uncle Lance, pulling his gray mustaches. "Well, I've known for some time that Tom didn't have good sense, but I have always given you, Theo, credit for having a little. I'll gamble my all that what Jean says is Bible truth. Didn't I have my eye on you and that girl for nearly a week during the hunt a year ago, and haven't you been riding my horses over to the Frio once or twice a month ever since? You can read a brand as far as I can, but I can see that you're as blind as a bat about a girl. Now, young fellow, listen to me: when the master of ceremonies announces the winners of the day, and your name is called, throw out your brisket, stand straight on those bow-legs of yours, step forward and claim your privilege. When the wreath is tendered you, accept it, carry it to the lady of your choice, and kneeling before her, if she bids you arise, place the crown on her brow and lead the grand march. I'd gladly give Las Palomas and every hoof on it for your years and chance."

The festivities began with falling darkness. The master of ceremonies, a school teacher from Oakville, read out the successful contestants and the prizes to which they were entitled. The name of Theodore Quayle was the last to be called, and excusing himself to Miss Jean, who had him in tow, he walked forward with a military air, executing every movement in the ceremony like an actor. As the music struck up, he and the blushing Frances Vaux, rare in rustic beauty and crowned with a wreath of live-oak leaves, led the opening march. Hundreds of hands clapped in approval, and as the applause quieted down, I turned to look for a partner, only to meet Miss Jean and my former sweetheart. Both were in a seventh heaven of delight, and promptly took occasion to remind me of my lack of foresight, repeating in chorus, "Didn't I tell you?" But the music had broken into a waltz, which precluded any argument, and on the mistress remarking "You young folks are missing a fine dance," involuntarily my arm encircled my old sweetheart, and we drifted away into elysian fields.

The night after the first tournament at Shepherd's on the Nueces in June, '77, lingers as a pleasant memory. Veiled in hazy retrospect, attempting to recall it is like inviting the return of childish dreams when one has reached the years of maturity. If I danced that night with any other girl than poor Esther McLeod, the fact has certainly escaped me. But somewhere in the archives of memory there is an indelible picture of a stroll through dimly lighted picnic grounds; of sitting on a rustic settee, built round the base of a patriarchal live-oak, and listening to a broken-hearted woman lay bare the sorrows which less than a year had brought her. I distinctly recall that my eyes, though unused to weeping, filled with tears, when Esther in words of deepest sorrow and contrition begged me to forgive her heedless and reckless act. Could I harbor resentment in the face of such entreaty? The impulsiveness of youth refused to believe that true happiness had gone out of her life. She was again to me as she had been before her unfortunate marriage, and must be released from the hateful bonds that bound her. Firm in this resolve, dawn stole upon us, still sitting at the root of the old oak, oblivious and happy in each other's presence, having pledged anew our troth for time and eternity.

With the breaking of day the revelers dispersed. Quite a large contingent from those present rode several miles up the river with our party. The *remuda* had been sent home the evening before with the returning vaqueros, while the impatience of the ambulance mules frequently carried them in advance of the cavalcade. The mistress of Las Palomas had as her guest returning, Miss Jule Wilson, and the first time they passed us, some four or five miles above the ferry, I noticed Uncle Lance ride up, swaggering in his saddle, and poke Glenn Gallup in the ribs, with a wink and nod towards the conveyance as the mules dashed past. The pace we were traveling would carry us home by the middle of the forenoon, and once we were reduced to the home crowd, the old matchmaker broke out enthusiastically: —

"This tourney was what I call a success. I don't care a tinker's darn for the prizes, but the way you boys built up to the girls last night warmed the sluggish blood in my old veins. Even if Cotton did claim a dance or two with the oldest Vaux girl, if Theo and her don't make the riffle now — well, they simply can't help it, having gone so far. And did any of you notice Scales and old June and Dan cutting the pigeon wing like colts? I reckon Quirk will have to make some new resolutions this morning. Oh, I heard about your declaring that you never wanted to see Esther McLeod again. That's all right, son, but hereafter remember that a resolve about a woman is only good for the day it is made, or until you meet her. And notice, will you, ahead yonder, that sister of mine playing second fiddle as a matchmaker. Glenn, if I was you, the next time Miss Jule looks back this way, I'd play sick, and maybe they'd let you ride in the ambulance. I can see at a glance that she's being poorly entertained."

CHAPTER XIII
HIDE HUNTING

During the month of June only two showers fell, which revived the grass but added not a drop of water to our tank supply or to the river. When the coast winds which followed set in, all hope for rain passed for another year. During the residence of the old ranchero at Las Palomas, the Nueces valley had suffered several severe drouths as disastrous in their effects as a pestilence. There were places in its miles of meanderings across our range where the river was paved with the bones of cattle which had perished with thirst. Realizing that such disasters repeat themselves, the ranch was set in order. That fall we branded the calf crop with unusual care. In every possible quarter, we prepared for the worst. A dozen wells were sunk over the tract and equipped with windmills. There was sufficient water in the river and tanks during the summer and fall, but by Christmas the range was eaten off until the cattle, ranging far, came in only every other day to slake their thirst.

The social gayeties of the countryside received a check from the threatened drouth. At Las Palomas we observed only the usual Christmas festivities. Miss Jean always made it a point to have something extra for the holiday season, not only in her own household, but also among the Mexican families at headquarters and the outlying ranchites. Among a number of delicacies brought up this time from Shepherd's was a box of Florida oranges, and in assisting Miss Jean to fill the baskets for each *jacal*, Aaron Scales opened this box of oranges and found a letter, evidently placed there by some mischievous girl in the packery from which the oranges were shipped. There was not only a letter but a visiting card and a small photograph of the writer. This could only be accepted by the discoverer as a challenge, for the sender surely knew this particular box was intended for shipment to Texas, and banteringly invited the recipient to reply. The missive certainly fell upon fertile soil, and Scales, by right of discovery, delegated to himself the pleasure of answering.

Scales was the black sheep of Las Palomas. Born of a rich, aristocratic family in Maryland, he had early developed into a good-natured but reckless spendthrift, and his disreputable associates had contributed no small part in forcing him to the refuge of a cattle ranch. He had been offered every opportunity to secure a good education, but during his last year in college had been expelled, and rather than face parental reproach had taken passage in a coast schooner for Galveston, Texas. Then by easy stages he drifted westward, and at last, to his liking, found a home at Las Palomas. He made himself a useful man on the ranch, but, not having been bred to the occupation and with a tendency to waywardness, gave a rather free rein to the vagabond spirit which possessed him. He was a good rider, even for a country where every one was a born horseman, but the use of the rope was an art he never attempted to master.

With the conclusion of the holiday festivities and on the return of the absentees, a feature, new to me in cattle life, presented itself — hide hunting. Freighters who brought merchandise from the coast towns to the merchants of the interior were offering very liberal terms for return cargoes. About the only local product was flint hides, and of these there were very few, but the merchant at Shepherd's Ferry offered so generous inducements that Uncle Lance investigated the matter; the result was his determination to rid his range of the old, logy, worthless bulls. Heretofore they had been allowed to die of old age, but ten cents a pound for flint hides was an encouragement to remove these cumberers of the range, and turn them to some profit. So we were ordered to kill every bull on the ranch over seven years old.

In our round-up for branding, we had driven to the home range all outside cattle indiscriminately. They were still ranging near, so that at the commencement of this work nearly all the bulls in our brand were watering from the Nueces. These old residenter bulls never ranged over a mile away from water, and during the middle of the day they could be found along the river bank. Many of them were ten to twelve years old, and were as useless on the range as drones in autumn to a colony of honey-bees. Las Palomas boasted quite an arsenal of firearms, of every make and pattern, from a musket to a repeater. The outfit was divided into two squads, one going down nearly to Shepherd's, and the other beginning operations considerably above the Ganso. June Deweese took the down-river end, while Uncle Lance took some ten of us with one wagon on the up-river trip. To me this had all the appearance of a picnic. But the work proved to be anything but a picnic. To make the kill was most difficult. Not willing to leave the carcasses near the river, we usually sought the bulls coming in to water; but an ordinary charge of powder and lead, even when well directed at the forehead, rarely killed and tended rather to aggravate the creature. Besides, as we were compelled in nearly every instance to shoot from horseback, it was almost impossible to deliver an effective shot from in front. After one or more unsuccessful shots, the bull usually started for the nearest thicket, or the river; then our ropes came into use. The work was very slow; for though we operated in pairs, the first week we did not average a hide a day to the man; after killing, there was the animal to skin, the hide to be dragged from a saddle pommel into a hide yard and pegged out to dry.

Until we had accumulated a load of hides, Tiburcio Leal, our teamster, fell to me as partner. We had with us an abundance of our best horses, and those who were reliable with the rope had first choice of the *remuda*. Tiburcio was well mounted, but, on account of his years, was timid about using a rope; and well he might be, for frequently we found ourselves in a humorous predicament, and sometimes in one so grave that hilarity was not even a remote possibility.

The second morning of the hunt, Tiburcio and I singled out a big black bull about a mile from the river. I had not yet been convinced that I could not make an effective shot from in front, and, dismounting, attracted the bull's attention and fired. The shot did not even stagger him and he charged us; our horses avoided his rush, and he started for the river. Sheathing my carbine, I took down my rope and caught him before he had gone a hundred yards. As I threw my horse on his haunches to receive the shock, the weight and momentum of the bull dragged my double-cinched saddle over my horse's head and sent me sprawling on the ground. In wrapping the loose end of the rope around the pommel of the saddle, I had given it a half hitch, and as I came to my feet my saddle and carbine were bumping merrily along after Toro. Regaining my horse, I soon overtook Tiburcio, who was attempting to turn the animal back from the river, and urged him to "tie on," but he hesitated, offering me his horse instead. As there was no time to waste, we changed horses like relay riders. I soon overtook the animal and made a successful cast, catching the bull by the front feet. I threw Tiburcio's horse, like a wheeler, back on his haunches, and, on bringing the rope taut, fetched Toro to his knees; but with the strain the half-inch manila rope snapped at the pommel like a twine string. Then we were at our wit's end, the bull lumbering away with the second rope noosed over one fore foot, and leaving my saddle far in the rear. But after a moment's hesitation my partner and I doubled on him, to make trial of our guns, Tiburcio having a favorite old musket while I had only my six-shooter. Tiburcio, on my stripped horse, overtook the bull first, and attempted to turn him, but El Toro was not to be stopped. On coming up myself, I tried the same tactics, firing several shots into the ground in front of him but without deflecting the enraged bull from his course. Then I unloosed a Mexican blanket from Tiburcio's saddle, and flaunting it in his face, led him like a matador inviting a charge. This held his attention until Tiburcio, gaining courage, dashed past him from the rear and planted a musket ball behind the base of his ear, and the patriarch succumbed.

After the first few days' work, we found that the most vulnerable spot was where the spinal cord connects with the base of the brain. A well-directed shot at this point, even from a six-shooter, never failed to bring Toro to grass; and some of us became so expert that we could deliver this favorite shot from a running horse. The trouble was to get the bull to run evenly. That was one thing he objected to, and yet unless he did we could not advantageously attack him with a six-shooter. Many of these old bulls were surly in disposition, and even when they did run, there was no telling what moment they would sulk, stop without an instant's notice, and attempt to gore a passing horse.

We usually camped two or three days at a place, taking in both sides of the river, and after the work was once well under way we kept our wagon busy hauling the dry hides to a common yard on the river opposite Las Palomas. Without apology, it can be admitted that we did not confine our killing to the Las Palomas brand alone, but all cumberers on our range met the same fate. There were numerous stray bulls belonging to distant ranches which had taken up their abode on the Nueces, all of which were fish to our net. We kept a brand tally of every bull thus killed; for the primary motive was not one of profit, but to rid the range of these drones.

When we had been at work some two weeks, we had an exciting chase one afternoon in which Enrique Lopez figured as the hero. In coming in to dinner that day, Uncle Lance told of the chase after a young *ladino* bull with which we were all familiar. The old ranchero's hatred to wild cattle had caused him that morning to risk a long shot at this outlaw, wounding him. Juan Leal and Enrique Lopez, who were there, had both tried their marksmanship and their ropes on him in vain. Dragging down horses and snapping ropes, the bull made his escape into a chaparral thicket. He must have been exceedingly nimble; for I have seen Uncle Lance kill a running deer at a hundred yards with a rifle. At any rate, the entire squad turned out after dinner to renew the attack. We saddled the best horses in our *remuda* for the occasion, and sallied forth to the lair of the *ladino* bull, like a procession of professional bull-fighters.

The chaparral thicket in which the outlaw had taken refuge lay about a mile and a half back from the river and contained about two acres. On reaching the edge of the thicket, Uncle Lance called for volunteers to beat the brush and rout out the bull. As this must be done on foot, responses were not numerous. But our employer relieved the embarrassment by assigning vaqueros to the duty, also directing Enrique to take one point of the thicket and me the other, with instructions to use our ropes should the outlaw quit the thicket for the river. Detailing Tiburcio, who was with us that afternoon, to assist him in leading the loose saddle horses, he divided the six other men into two squads under Theodore Quayle and Dan Happersett. When all was ready, Enrique and myself took up our positions, hiding in the outlying mesquite brush; leaving the loose horses under saddle in the cover at a distance. The thicket was oval in form, lying with a point towards the river, and we all felt confident if the bull were started he would make for the timber on the river. With a whoop and hurrah and a free discharge of firearms, the beaters entered the chaparral. From my position I could see Enrique lying along the neck of his horse about fifty yards distant; and I had fully made up my mind to give that bucolic vaquero the first chance. During the past two weeks my enthusiasm for roping stray bulls had undergone a change; I was now quite willing that all honors of the afternoon should fall to Enrique. The beaters approached without giving any warning that the bull had been sighted, and so great was the strain and tension that I could feel the beating of my horse's heart beneath me. The suspense was finally broken by one or two shots in rapid succession, and as the sound died away, the voice of Juan Leal rang out distinctly: "Cuidado por el toro!" and the next moment there was a cracking of brush and a pale dun bull broke cover.

For a moment he halted on the border of the thicket: then, as the din of the beaters increased, struck boldly across the prairie for the river. Enrique and I were after him without loss of time. Enrique made a successful cast for his horns, and reined in his horse; but when the slack of the rope was taken up the rear cinch broke, the saddle was jerked forward on the horse's withers, and Enrique was compelled to free the rope or have his horse dragged down. I saw the mishap, and, giving my horse the rowel, rode at the bull and threw my rope. The loop neatly encircled his front feet, and when the shock came between horse and bull, it fetched the toro a somersault in the air, but unhappily took off the pommel of my saddle. The bull was on his feet in a jiffy, and before I could recover my rope, Enrique, who had reset his saddle, passed me, followed by the entire squad. Uncle Lance had been a witness to both mishaps, and on overtaking us urged me to tie on to the bull again. For answer I could only point to my missing pommel; but every man in the squad had loosened his rope, and it looked as if they would all fasten on to the *ladino*, for they were all good ropers. Man after man threw his loop on him; but the dun outlaw snapped the ropes as if they had been cotton strings, dragging down two horses with their riders and leaving them in the rear. I rode up alongside Enrique and offered him my rope, but he refused it, knowing it would be useless to try again with only a single cinch on his saddle. The young rascal had a daring idea in mind. We were within a quarter mile of the river, and escape of the outlaw seemed probable, when Enrique rode down on the bull, took up his tail, and, wrapping the brush on the pommel of his saddle, turned his horse abruptly to the left, rolling the bull over like a hoop, and of course dismounting himself in the act. Then before the dazed animal could rise, with the agility of a panther the vaquero sprang astride his loins, and as he floundered, others leaped from their horses. Toro was pinioned, and dispatched with a shot.

Then we loosened cinches to allow our heaving horses to breathe, and threw ourselves on the ground for a moment's rest. "That's the best kill we'll make on this trip," said Uncle Lance as we mounted, leaving two vaqueros to take the hide. "I despise wild cattle, and I've been hungering to get a shot at that fellow for the last three years. Enrique, the day the baby is born, I'll buy it a new cradle, and Tom shall have a new saddle and we'll charge it to Las Palomas — she's the girl that pays the bills."

Scarcely a day passed but similar experiences were related around the camp-fire. In fact, as the end of the work came in view, they became commonplace with us. Finally the two outfits were united at the general hide yard near the home ranch. Coils of small rope were brought from headquarters, and a detail of men remained in camp, baling the flint hides, while the remainder scoured the immediate country. A crude press was arranged, and by the aid of a long lever the hides were compressed into convenient space for handling by the freighters.

When we had nearly finished the killing and baling, an unlooked-for incident occurred. While Deweese was working down near Shepherd's Ferry, report of our work circulated around the country, and his camp had been frequently visited by cattlemen. Having nothing to conceal, he had showed his list of outside brands killed, which was perfectly satisfactory in most instances. As was customary in selling cattle, we expected to make report of every outside hide taken, and settle for them, deducting the necessary expense. But in every community there are those who oppose prevailing customs, and some who can always see sinister motives. One forenoon, when the baling was nearly finished, a delegation of men, representing brands of the Frio and San Miguel, rode up to our hide yard. They were all well-known cowmen, and Uncle Lance, being present, saluted them in his usual hearty manner. In response to an inquiry — "what he thought he was doing" — Uncle Lance jocularly replied: —

"Well, you see, you fellows allow your old bulls to drift down on my range, expecting Las Palomas to pension them the remainder of their days. But that's where you get fooled. Ten cents a pound for flint hides beats letting these old stagers die of old age. And this being an idle season with nothing much to do, we wanted to have a little fun. And we've had it. But laying all jokes aside, fellows, it's a good idea to get rid of these old varmints. Hereafter, I'm going to make a killing off every two or three years. The boys have kept a list of all stray brands killed, and you can look them over and see how many of yours we got. We have baled all the stray hides separate, so they can be looked over. But it's nearly noon, and you'd better all ride up to the ranch for dinner — they feed better up there than we do in camp."

Rather than make a three-mile ride to the house, the visitors took dinner with the wagon, and about one o'clock Deweese and a vaquero came in, dragging a hide between them. June cordially greeted the callers, including Henry Annear, who represented the Las Norias ranch, though I suppose it was well known to every one present that there was no love lost between them. Uncle Lance asked our foreman for his list of outside brands, explaining that these men wished to look them over. Everything seemed perfectly satisfactory to all parties concerned, and after remaining in camp over an hour, Deweese and the vaquero saddled fresh horses and rode away. The visitors seemed in no hurry to go, so Uncle Lance sat around camp entertaining them, while the rest of us proceeded with our work of baling. Before leaving, however, the entire party in company of our employer took a stroll about the hide yard, which was some distance from camp. During this tour of inspection, Annear asked which were the bales of outside hides taken in Deweese's division, claiming he represented a number of brands outside of Las Norias. The bales were pointed out and some dozen unbaled hides looked over. On a count the baled and unbaled hides were found to tally exactly with the list submitted. But unfortunately Annear took occasion to insinuate that the list of brands rendered had been "doctored." Uncle Lance paid little attention, though he heard, but the other visitors remonstrated with Annear. This only seemed to make him more contentious. Finally matters came to an open rupture when Annear demanded that the cordage be cut on certain bales to allow him to inspect them. Possibly he was within his rights, but on the Nueces during the seventies, to question a man's word was equivalent to calling him a liar; and *liar* was a fighting word all over the cattle range.

"Well, Henry," said Uncle Lance, rather firmly, "if you are not satisfied, I suppose I'll have to open the bales for you, but before I do, I'm going to send after June. Neither you nor any one else can cast any reflections on a man in my employ. No unjust act can be charged in my presence against an absent man. The vaqueros tell me that my foreman is only around the bend of the river, and I'm going to ask all you gentlemen to remain until I can send for him."

John Cotton was dispatched after Deweese. Conversation meanwhile became polite and changed to other subjects. Those of us at work baling hides went ahead as if nothing unusual was on the tapis. The visitors were all armed, which was nothing unusual, for the wearing of six-shooters was as common as the wearing of boots. During the interim, several level-headed visitors took Henry Annear to one side, evidently to reason with him and urge an apology, for they could readily see that Uncle Lance was justly offended. But it seemed that Annear would listen to no one, and while they were yet conversing among themselves, John Cotton and our foreman galloped around the bend of the river and rode up to the yard. No doubt Cotton had explained the situation, but as they dismounted Uncle Lance stepped between his foreman and Annear, saying: —

"June, Henry, here, questions the honesty of your list of strays killed, and insists on our cutting the bales for his inspection." Turning to Annear, Uncle Lance inquired, "Do you still insist on opening the bales?"

"Yes, sir, I do."

Deweese stepped to one side of his employer, saying to Annear: "You offer to cut a bale here to-day, and I'll cut your heart out. Behind my back, you questioned my word. Question it to my face, you dirty sneak."

Annear sprang backward and to one side, drawing a six-shooter in the movement, while June was equally active. Like a flash, two shots rang out. Following the reports, Henry turned halfway round, while Deweese staggered a step backward. Taking advantage of the instant, Uncle Lance sprang like a panther on to June and bore him to the ground, while the visitors fell on Annear and disarmed him in a flash. They were dragged struggling farther apart, and after some semblance of sanity had returned, we stripped our foreman and found an ugly flesh wound crossing his side under the armpit, the bullet having been deflected by a rib. Annear had fared worse, and was spitting blood freely, and the marks of exit and entrance of the bullet indicated that the point of one lung had been slightly chipped.

"I suppose this outcome is what you might call the *amende honorable*" smilingly said George Nathan, one of the visitors, later to Uncle Lance. "I always knew there was a little bad blood existing between the boys, but I had no idea that it would flash in the pan so suddenly or I'd have stayed at home. Shooting always lets me out. But the question now is, How are we going to get our man home?"

Uncle Lance at once offered them horses and a wagon, in case Annear would not go into Las Palomas. This he objected to, so a wagon was fitted up, and, promising to return it the next day, our visitors departed with the best of feelings, save between the two belligerents. We sent June into the ranch and a man to Oakville after a surgeon, and resumed our work in the hide yard as if nothing had happened. Somewhere I have seen the statement that the climate of California was especially conducive to the healing of gunshot wounds. The same claim might be made in behalf of the Nueces valley, for within a month both the combatants were again in their saddles.

Within a week after this incident, we concluded our work and the hides were ready for the freighters. We had spent over a month and had taken fully seven hundred hides, many of which, when dry, would weigh one hundred pounds, the total having a value of between five and six thousand dollars. Like their predecessors the buffalo, the remains of the ladinos were left to enrich the soil; but there was no danger of the extinction of the species, for at Las Palomas it was the custom to allow every tenth male calf to grow up a bull.

CHAPTER XIV
A TWO YEARS' DROUTH

The spring of '78 was an early one, but the drouth continued, and after the hide hunting was over we rode our range almost night and day. Thousands of cattle had drifted down from the Frio River country, which section was suffering from drouth as badly as the Nueces. The new wells were furnishing a limited supply of water, but we rigged pulleys on the best of them, and when the wind failed we had recourse to buckets and a rope worked from the pommel of a saddle. A breeze usually arose about ten in the morning and fell about midnight. During the lull the buckets rose and fell incessantly at eight wells, with no lack of suffering cattle in attendance to consume it as fast as it was hoisted. Many thirsty animals gorged themselves, and died in sight of the well; weak ones being frequently trampled to death by the stronger, while flint hides were corded at every watering point. The river had quit flowing, and with the first warmth of spring the pools became rancid and stagnant. In sandy and subirrigated sections, under a March sun, the grass made a sickly effort to spring; but it lacked substance, and so far from furnishing food for the cattle, it only weakened them.

This was my first experience with a serious drouth. Uncle Lance, however, met the emergency as though it were part of the day's work, riding continually with the rest of us. During the latter part of March, Aaron Scales, two vaqueros, and myself came in one night from the Ganso and announced not over a month's supply of water in that creek. We also reported to our employer that during our two days' ride, we had skinned some ten cattle, four of which were in our own brand.

"That's not as bad as it might be," said the old ranchero, philosophically. "You see, boys, I've been through three drouths since I began ranching on this river. The second one, in '51, was the worst; cattle skulls were as thick along the Nueces that year as sunflowers in August. In '66 it was nearly as bad, there being more cattle; but it didn't hurt me very much, as mavericking had been good for some time before and for several years following, and I soon recovered my losses. The first one lasted three years, and had there been as many cattle as there are now, half of them would have died. The spring before the second drouth, I acted as *padrino* for Tiburcio and his wife, who was at that time a mere slip of a girl living at the Mission. Before they had time to get married, the dry spell set in and they put the wedding off until it should rain. I ridiculed the idea, but they were both superstitious and stuck it out. And honest, boys, there wasn't enough rain fell in two years to wet your shirt. In my forty years on the Nueces, I've seen hard times, but that drouth was the toughest of them all. Game and birds left the country, and the cattle were too poor to eat. Whenever our provisions ran low, I sent Tiburcio to the coast with a load of hides, using six yoke of oxen to handle a cargo of about a ton. The oxen were so poor that they had to stand twice in one place to make a shadow, and we wouldn't take gold for our flint hides but insisted on the staples of life. At one point on the road, Tiburcio had to give a quart of flour for watering his team both going and coming. They say that when the Jews quit a country, it's time for the gentiles to leave. But we old timers are just like a horse that chooses a new range and will stay with it until he starves or dies with old age."

I could see nothing reassuring in the outlook. Near the wells and along the river the stock had trampled out the grass until the ground was as bare as a city street. Miles distant from the water the old dry grass, with only an occasional green blade, was the only grazing for the cattle. The black, waxy soil on the first bottom of the river, on which the mesquite grass had flourished, was as bare now as a ploughed field, while the ground had cracked open in places to an incredible depth, so that without exercising caution it was dangerous to ride across. This was the condition of the range at the approach of April. Our horse stock, to be sure, fared better, ranging farther and not requiring anything like the amount of water needed by the cattle. It was nothing unusual to meet a Las Palomas *manada* from ten to twelve miles from the river, and coming in only every second or third night to quench their thirst. We were fortunate in having an abundance of saddle horses, which, whether under saddle or not, were always given the preference in the matter of water. They were the motive power of the ranch, and during this crisis, though worked hard, must be favored in every possible manner.

Early that spring the old ranchero sent Deweese to Lagarto in an attempt to sell Captain Byler a herd of horse stock for the trail. The mission was a failure, though our *segundo* offered to sell a thousand, in the straight Las Palomas brand, at seven dollars a head on a year's credit. Even this was no inducement to the trail drover, and on Deweese's return my employer tried San Antonio and other points in Texas in the hope of finding a market. From several places favorable replies were received, particularly from places north of the Colorado River; for the drouth was local and was chiefly confined to the southern portion of the state. There was enough encouragement in the letters to justify the old ranchero's attempt to reduce the demand on the ranch's water supply, by sending a herd of horse stock north on sale. Under ordinary conditions, every ranchman preferred to sell his surplus stock at the ranch, and Las Palomas was no exception, being generally congested with marketable animals. San Antonio was, however, beginning to be a local horse and mule market of some moment, and before my advent several small selected bunches of mares, mules, and saddle horses had been sent there, and had found a ready and profitable sale.

But this was an emergency year, and it was decided to send a herd of stock horses up the country. Accordingly, before April, we worked every *manada* which we expected to keep, cutting out all the two-year-old fillies. To these were added every mongrel-colored band to the number of twenty odd, and when ready to start the herd numbered a few over twelve hundred of all ages from yearlings up. A *remuda* of fifty saddle horses, broken in the spring of '76, were allotted to our use, and our *segundo*, myself, and five Mexican vaqueros were detailed to drive the herd. We were allowed two pack mules for our commissary, which was driven with the *remuda*. With instructions to sell and hurry home, we left our horse camp on the river, and started on the morning of the last day of March.

Live-stock commission firms in San Antonio were notified of our coming, and with six men to the herd and the seventh driving the *remuda*, we put twenty miles behind us the first day. With the exception of water for saddle stock, which we hoisted from a well, there was no hope of watering the herd before reaching Mr. Booth's ranch on the Frio. He had been husbanding his water supply, and early the second evening we watered the herd to its contentment from a single shaded pool. From the Frio we could not follow any road, but were compelled to direct our course wherever there was a prospect of water. By hobbling the bell mare of the *remuda* at evening, and making two watches of the night-herding, we easily systematized our work. Until we reached the San Antonio River, about twenty miles below the city, not over two days passed without water for all the stock, though, on account of the variations from our course, we were over a week in reaching San Antonio. Having moved the herd up near some old missions within five or six miles of the city, with an abundance of water and some grass, Deweese went into town, visiting the commission firms and looking for a buyer. Fortunately a firm, which was expecting our arrival, had a prospective purchaser from Fort Worth for about our number. Making a date with the firm to show our horses the next morning, our *segundo* returned to the herd, elated over the prospect of a sale.

On their arrival the next morning, we had the horses already watered and were grazing them along an abrupt slope between the first and second bottoms of the river. The salesman understood his business, and drove the conveyance back and forth on the down hill side, below the herd, and the rise in the ground made our range stock look as big as American horses. After looking at the animals for an hour, from a buckboard, the prospective buyer insisted on looking at the *remuda*. But as these were gentle, he gave them a more critical examination, insisting on their being penned in a rope corral at our temporary camp, and had every horse that was then being ridden unsaddled to inspect their backs. The *remuda* was young, gentle, and sound, many of them submitting to be caught without a rope. The buyer was pleased with them, and when the price came up for discussion Deweese artfully set a high figure on the saddle stock, and, to make his bluff good, offered to reserve them and take them back to the ranch. But

Tuttle would not consider the herd without the *remuda*, and sparring between them continued until all three returned to town.

It was a day of expectancy to the vaqueros and myself. In examining the saddle horses, the buyer acted like a cowman; but as regarding the range stock, it was evident to me that his armor was vulnerable, and if he got any the best of our *segundo* he was welcome to it. Deweese returned shortly after dark, coming directly to the herd where I and two vaqueros were on guard, to inform us that he had sold lock, stock, and barrel, including the two pack mules. I felt like shouting over the good news, when June threw a damper on my enthusiasm by the news that he had sold for delivery at Fort Worth.

"You see," said Deweese, by way of explanation, "the buyer is foreman of a cattle company out on the forks of the Brazos in Young County. He don't sabe range horses as well as he does cows, and when we had agreed on the saddle stock, and there were only two bits between us on the herd, he offered me six bits a head all round, over and above his offer, if I would put them in Fort Worth, and I took him up so quick that I nearly bit my tongue doing it. Captain Redman tells me that it's only about three hundred miles, and grass and water is reported good. I intended to take him up at his offer, anyhow, and seventy-five cents a head extra will make the old man nearly a thousand dollars, which is worth picking up. We'll put them there easy in three weeks, learn the trail and see the country besides. Uncle Lance can't have any kick coming, for I offered them to Captain Byler for seven dollars, and here I'm getting ten six-bits — nearly four thousand dollars' advance, and we won't be gone five weeks. Any money down? Well, I should remark! Five thousand deposited with Smith & Redman, and I was particular to have it inserted in the contract between us that every saddle horse, mare, mule, gelding, and filly was to be in the straight 'horse hoof' brand. There is a possibility that when Tuttle sees them again at Fort Worth, they won't look as large as they did on that hillside this morning."

We made an early start from San Antonio the next morning, passing to the westward of the then straggling city. The vaqueros were disturbed over the journey, for Fort Worth was as foreign to them as a European seaport, but I jollied them into believing it was but a little *pasear*. Though I had never ridden on a train myself, I pictured to them the luxuriant ease with which we would return, as well as the trip by stage to Oakville. I threw enough enthusiasm into my description of the good time we were going to have, coupled with their confidence in Deweese, to convince them in spite of their forebodings. Our *segundo* humored them in various ways, and after a week on the trail, water getting plentiful, using two guards, we only herded until midnight, turning the herd loose from then until daybreak. It usually took us less than an hour to gather and count them in the morning, and encouraged by their contentment, a few days later, we loose-herded until darkness and then turned them free. From then on it was a picnic as far as work was concerned, and our saddle horses and herd improved every day.

After crossing the Colorado River, at every available chance en route we mailed a letter to the buyer, notifying him of our progress as we swept northward. When within a day's drive of the Brazos, we mailed our last letter, giving notice that we would deliver within three days of date. On reaching that river, we found it swimming for between thirty and forty yards; but by tying up the pack mules and cutting the herd into four bunches, we swam the Brazos with less than an hour's delay. Overhauling and transferring the packs to horses, throwing away everything but the barest necessities, we crossed the lightened commissary, the freed mules swimming with the *remuda*. On the morning of the twentieth day out from San Antonio, our *segundo* rode into the fort ahead of the herd. We followed at our regular gait, and near the middle of the forenoon were met by Deweese and Tuttle, who piloted us to a pasture west of the city, where an outfit was encamped to receive the herd. They numbered fifteen men, and looked at our insignificant crowd with contempt; but the count which followed showed we had not lost a hoof since we left the Nueces, although for the last ten nights the stock had had the fullest freedom.

The receiving outfit looked the brands over carefully. The splendid grass and water of the past two weeks had transformed the famishing herd of a month before, and they were received without a question. Rounding in our *remuda* for fresh mounts before starting to town, the vaqueros and I did some fancy roping in catching out the horses, partially from sheer lightness of heart because we were at our journey's end, and partially to show this north Texas outfit that we were like the proverbial singed cat — better than we looked. Two of Turtle's men rode into town with us that evening to lead back our mounts, the outfit having come in purposely to receive the horse herd and drive it to their ranch in Young County. While riding in, they thawed nicely towards us, but kept me busy interpreting for them with our Mexicans. Tuttle and Deweese rode together in the lead, and on nearing town one of the strangers bantered Pasquale to sell him a nice maguey rope which the vaquero carried. When I interpreted the other's wish to him, Pasquale loosened the lasso and made a present of it to Tuttle's man. I had almost as good a rope of the same material, which I presented to the other lad with us, and the drinks we afterward consumed over this slight testimony of the amicable relations existing between a northern and southern Texas outfit over the delivery and receiving of a horse herd, showed no evidence of a drouth. The following morning I made inquiry for Frank Nancrede and the drovers who had driven a trail herd of cattle from Las Palomas two seasons before. They were all well known about the fort, but were absent at the time, having put up two trail herds that spring in Uvalde County. Deweese did not waste an hour more than was necessary in that town, and while waiting for the banks to open, arranged for our transportation to San Antonio. We were all ready to start back before noon. Fort Worth was a frontier town at the time, bustling and alert with live-stock interests; but we were anxious to get home, and promptly boarded a train for the south. After entering the train, our *segundo* gave each of the vaqueros and myself some spending money, the greater portion of which went to the "butcher" for fruits. He was an enterprising fellow and took a marked interest in our comfort and welfare. But on nearing San Antonio after midnight, he attempted to sell us our choice of three books, between the leaves of one of which he had placed a five-dollar bill and in another a ten, and offered us our choice for two dollars, and June Deweese became suddenly interested. Coming over to where we were sitting, he knocked the books on the floor, kicked them under a seat, and threatened to bend a gun over the butcher's head unless he made himself very scarce. Then reminding us that "there were tricks in all trades but ours," he kept an eye over us until we reached the city.

We were delayed another day in San Antonio, settling with the commission firm and banking the money. The next morning we took stage for Oakville, where we arrived late at night. When a short distance out of San Antonio I inquired of our driver who would relieve him beyond Pleasanton, and was gratified to hear that his name was not Jack Martin. Not that I had anything particular against Martin, but I had no love for his wife, and had no desire to press the acquaintance any further with her or her husband. On reaching Oakville, we were within forty miles of Las Palomas. We had our saddles with us, and early the next morning tried to hire horses; but as the stage company domineered the village we were unable to hire saddle stock, and on appealing to the only livery in town we were informed that Bethel & Oxenford had the first claim on their conveyances. Accordingly Deweese and I visited the offices of the stage company, where, to our surprise, we came face to face with Jack Oxenford. I do not think he knew us, though we both knew him at a glance. Deweese made known his wants, but only asked for a conveyance as far as Shepherd's. Yankeelike, Oxenford had to know who we were, where we had been, and where we were going. Our *segundo* gave him rather a short answer, but finally admitted that we belonged at Las Palomas. Then the junior member of the mail contractors became arrogant, claiming that the only conveyance capable of carrying our party was being held for a sheriff with some witnesses. On second thought he offered to send us to the ferry by two lighter vehicles in consideration of five dollars apiece, insolently remarking that we could either pay it or walk. I will not repeat Deweese's reply, which I silently endorsed.

With the soil of the Nueces valley once more under our feet we felt independent. On returning to the vaqueros, we found a stranger among them, Bernabe Cruze by name, who was a *muy amigo* of Santiago Ortez, one of our Mexicans. He belonged at the Mission, and when he learned of our predicament offered to lend us his horse, as he expected to be in town a few days. The offer was gratefully accepted, and within a quarter of an hour Manuel Flores had started for Shepherd's with an order to the merchant to send in seven horses for us. It was less than a two hours' ride to the ferry, and with the early start we expected Manuel to return before noon. Making ourselves at home in a coffeehouse conducted by a Mexican, Deweese ordered a few bottles of wine to celebrate properly our drive and to entertain Cruze and our vaqueros. Before the horses arrived, those of us who had any money left spent it in the *cantina*, not wishing to carry it home, where it would be useless. The result was that on the return of Flores with mounts we were all about three sheets in the wind, reckless and defiant.

After saddling up, I suggested to June that we ride by the stage office and show Mr. Oxenford that we were independent of him. The stage stand and office were on the outskirts of the scattered village, and while we could have avoided it, our *segundo* willingly led the way, and called for the junior member of the firm. A hostler came to the door and informed us that Mr. Oxenford was not in.

"Then I'll just leave my card," said Deweese, dismounting. Taking a brown cigarette paper from his pocket, he wrote his name on it; then pulling a tack from a notice pasted beside the office door, he drew his six-shooter, and with it deftly tacked the cigarette paper against the office door jamb. Remounting his horse, and perfectly conscious that Oxenford was within hearing, he remarked to the hostler: "When your boss returns, please tell him that those fellows from Las Palomas will neither walk with him nor ride with him. We thought he might fret as to how we were to get home, and we have just ridden by to tell him that he need feel no uneasiness. Since I have never had the pleasure of an introduction to him, I've put my name on that cigarette paper. Good-day, sir."

Arriving at Shepherd's, we rested several hours, and on the suggestion of the merchant changed horses before starting home. At the ferry we learned that there had been no serious loss of cattle so far, but that nearly all the stock from the Frio and San Miguel had drifted across to the Nueces. We also learned that the attendance on San Jacinto Day had been extremely light, not a person from Las Palomas being present, while the tournament for that year had been abandoned. During our ride up the river before darkness fell, we passed a strange medley of brands, many of which Deweese assured me were owned from fifty to a hundred miles to the north and west. Riding leisurely, it was nearly midnight when we sighted the ranch and found it astir. An extra breeze had been blowing, and the vaqueros were starting to their work at the wells in order to be on hand the moment the wind slackened. Around the two wells at headquarters were over a thousand cattle, whose constant moaning reached our ears over a mile from the ranch.

Our return was like entering a house of mourning. Miss Jean barely greeted Deweese and myself, while Uncle Lance paced the gallery without making a single inquiry as to what had become of the horse herd. On the mistress's orders, servants set out a cold luncheon, and disappeared, as if in the presence of death, without a word of greeting. Ever thoughtful, Miss Jean added several little delicacies to our plain meal, and, seating herself at the table with us, gave us a clear outline of the situation. In seventy odd miles of the meanderings of the river across our range, there was not a pool to the mile with water enough for a hundred cattle. The wells were gradually becoming weaker, yielding less water every week, while of four new ones which were commenced before our departure, two were dry and worthless. The vaqueros were then skinning on an average forty dead cattle a day, fully a half of which were in the Las Palomas brand. Sympathetically as a sister could, she accounted for her brother's lack of interest in our return by his anxiety and years, and she cautioned us to let no evil report reach his ears, as this drouth had unnerved him.

Deweese at once resumed his position on the ranch, and the next morning the ranchero held a short council with him, authorizing him to spare no expense to save the cattle. Deweese returned the borrowed horses by Enrique, and sent a letter to the merchant at the ferry, directing him to secure and send at least twenty men to Las Palomas. The first day after our return, we rode the mills and the river. Convinced that to sink other wells on the mesas would be fruitless, the foreman decided to dig a number of shallow ones in the bed of the river, in the hope of catching seepage water. Accordingly the next morning, I was sent with a commissary wagon and seven men to the mouth of the Ganso, with instructions to begin sinking wells about two miles apart. Taking with us such tools as we needed, we commenced our first well at the confluence of the Ganso with the Nueces, and a second one above. From timber along the river we cut the necessary temporary curbing, and put it in place as the wells were sunk. On the third day both wells became so wet as to impede our work, and on our foreman riding by, he ordered them curbed to the bottom and a tripod set up over them on which to rig a rope and pulley. The next morning troughs and rigging, with a *remuda* of horses and a watering crew of four strange vaqueros, arrived. The wells were only about twenty feet deep; but by drawing the water as fast as the seepage accumulated, each was capable of watering several hundred head of cattle daily. By this time Deweese had secured ample help, and started a second crew of well diggers opposite the ranch, who worked down the river while my crew followed some fifteen miles above. By the end of the month of May, we had some twenty temporary wells in operation, and these, in addition to what water the pools afforded, relieved the situation to some extent, though the ravages of death by thirst went on apace among the weaker cattle.

With the beginning of June, we were operating nearly thirty wells. In some cases two vaqueros could hoist all the water that accumulated in three wells. We had a string of camps along the river, and at every windmill on the mesas men were stationed night and day. Among the cattle, the death rate was increasing all over the range. Frequently we took over a hundred skins in a single day, while at every camp cords of fallen flint hides were accumulating. The heat of summer was upon us, the wind arose daily, sand storms and dust clouds swept across the country, until our once prosperous range looked like a desert, withered and accursed. Young cows forsook their offspring in the hour of their birth. Motherless calves wandered about the range, hollow-eyed, their piteous appeals unheeded, until some lurking wolf sucked their blood and spread a feast to the vultures, constantly wheeling in great flights overhead. The prickly pear, an extremely arid plant, affording both food and drink to herds during drouths, had turned white, blistered by the torrid sun until it had fallen down, lifeless. The chaparral was destitute of foliage, and on the divides and higher mesas, had died. The native women stripped their *jacals* of every sacred picture, and hung them on the withered trees about their doors, where they hourly prayed to their patron saints. In the humblest homes on Las Palomas, candles burned both night and day to appease the frowning Deity.

The white element on the ranch worked almost unceasingly, stirring the Mexicans to the greatest effort. The middle of June passed without a drop of rain, but on the morning of the twentieth, after working all night, as Pasquale Arispe and I were drawing water from a well on the border of the encinal I felt a breeze spring up, that started the windmill. Casting my eyes upward, I noticed that the wind had veered to a quarter directly opposite to that of the customary coast breeze. Not being able to read aright the portent of the change in the wind, I had to learn from that native-born son of the soil: "Tomas," he cried, riding up excitedly, "in three days it will rain! Listen to me: Pasquale Arispe says that in three days the *arroyos* on the hacienda of Don Lancelot will run like a mill-race. See, *companero*, the wind has changed. The breeze is from the northwest this morning. Before three days it will rain! Madre de Dios!"

The wind from the northwest continued steadily for two days, relieving us from work. On the morning of the third day the signs in sky and air were plain for falling weather. Cattle, tottering with weakness, came into the well, and after drinking, playfully kicked up their heels on leaving. Before noon the storm struck us like a cloud-burst. Pasquale and I took refuge under the wagon to avoid the hailstones. In spite of the parched ground drinking to its contentment, water flooded under the wagon, driving us out. But we laughed at the violence of the deluge, and after making everything secure, saddled our horses and set out for home, taking our relay mounts with us. It was fifteen miles to the ranch and in the eye of the storm; but the loose horses faced the rain as if they enjoyed it, while those under saddle followed the free ones as a hound does a scent. Within two hours after leaving the well, we reined in at the gate, and I saw Uncle Lance and a number of the boys promenading the gallery. But the old ranchero leisurely walked down the pathway to the gate, and amid the downpour shouted to us: "Turn those horses loose; this ranch is going to take a month's holiday."

CHAPTER XV
IN COMMEMORATION

A heavy rainfall continued the greater portion of two days. None of us ventured away from the house until the weather settled, and meantime I played the fiddle almost continuously. Night work and coarse living in camps had prepared us to enjoy the comforts of a house, as well as to do justice to the well-laden table. Miss Jean prided herself, on special occasions and when the ranch had company, on good dinners; but in commemoration of the breaking of this drouth, with none but us boys to share it, she spread a continual feast. The Mexican contingent were not forgotten by master or mistress, and the ranch supplies in the warehouse were drawn upon, delicacies as well as staples, not only for the *jacals* about headquarters but also for the outlying ranchitas. The native element had worked faithfully during the two years in which no rain to speak of had fallen, until the breaking hour, and were not forgotten in the hour of deliverance. Even the stranger vaqueros were compelled to share the hospitality of Las Palomas like invited guests.

While the rain continued falling, Uncle Lance paced the gallery almost night and day. Fearful lest the downpour might stop, he stood guard, noting every change in the rainfall, barely taking time to eat or catch an hour's sleep. But when the grateful rain had continued until the evening of the second day, assuring a bountiful supply of water all over our range, he joined us at supper, exultant as a youth of twenty. "Boys," said he, "this has been a grand rain. If our tanks hold, we will be independent for the next eighteen months, and if not another drop falls, the river ought to flow for a year. I have seen worse drouths since I lived here, but what hurt us now was the amount of cattle and the heavy drift which flooded down on us from up the river and north on the Frio. The loss is nothing; we won't notice it in another year. I have kept a close tally of the hides taken, and our brand will be short about two thousand, or less than ten per cent of our total numbers. They were principally old cows and will not be missed. The calf crop this fall will be short, but taking it up one side and down the other, we got off lucky."

The third day after the rain began the sun rose bright and clear. Not a hoof of cattle or horses was in sight, and though it was midsummer, the freshness of earth and air was like that of a spring morning. Every one felt like riding. While awaiting the arrival of saddle horses, the extra help hired during the drouth was called in and settled with. Two brothers, Fidel and Carlos Trujillo, begged for permanent employment. They were promising young fellows, born on the Aransas River, and after consulting with Deweese Uncle Lance took both into permanent service on the ranch. A room in an outbuilding was allotted them, and they were instructed to get their meals in the kitchen. The *remudas* had wandered far, but one was finally brought in by a vaquero, and by pairs we mounted and rode away. On starting, the tanks demanded our first attention, and finding all four of them safe, we threw out of gear all the windmills. Theodore Quayle and I were partners during the day's ride to the south, and on coming in at evening fell in with Uncle Lance and our *segundo*, who had been as far west as the Ganso. Quayle and I had discussed during the day the prospect of a hunt at the Vaux ranch, and on meeting our employer, artfully interested the old ranchero regarding the amount of cat sign seen that day along the Arroyo Sordo.

"It's hard luck, boys," said he, "to find ourselves afoot, and the hunting so promising. But we haven't a horse on the ranch that could carry a man ten miles in a straightaway dash after the hounds. It will be a month yet before the grass has substance enough in it to strengthen our *remudas*. Oh, if it hadn't been for the condition of saddle stock, Don Pierre would have come right through the rain yesterday. But when Las Palomas can't follow the hounds for lack of mounts, you can depend on it that other ranches can't either. It just makes me sick to think of this good hunting, but what can we do for a month but fold our hands and sit down? But if you boys are itching for an excuse to get over on the Frio, why, I'll make you a good one. This drouth has knocked all the sociability out of the country; but now the ordeal is past, Theodore is in honor bound to go over to the Vaux ranch. I don't suppose you boys have seen the girls on the Frio and San Miguel in six months. Time? That's about all we have got right now. Time? — we've got time to burn."

Our feeler had borne fruit. An excuse or permission to go to the Frio was what Quayle and I were after, though no doubt the old matchmaker was equally anxious to have us go. In expressing our thanks for the promised vacation, we included several provisos — in case there was nothing to do, or if we concluded to go — when Uncle Lance turned in his saddle and gave us a withering look. "I've often wondered," said he, "if the blood in you fellows is really red, or if it's white like a fish's. Now, when I was your age, I had to steal chances to go to see my girl. But I never gave her any show to forget me, and worried her to a fare-ye-well. And if my observation and years go for anything, that's just the way girls like to have a fellow act. Of course they'll bluff and let on they must be wooed and all that, just like Frances did at the tournament a year ago. I contend that with a clear field the only way to make any progress in sparking a girl, is to get one arm around her waist, and with the other hand keep her from scratching you. That's the very way they like to be courted."

Theodore and I dropped behind after this lecture, and before we reached the ranch had agreed to ride over to the Frio the next morning. During our absence that day, there had arrived at Las Palomas from the Mission, a *padrino* in the person of Don Alejandro Travino. Juana Leal, only daughter of Tiburcio, had been sought in marriage by a nephew of Don Alejandro, and the latter, dignified as a Castilian noble, was then at the house negotiating for the girl's hand. Juana was nearly eighteen, had been born at the ranch, and after reaching years of usefulness had been adopted into Miss Jean's household. To ask for her hand required audacity, for to master and mistress of Las Palomas it was like asking for a daughter of the house. Miss Jean was agitated and all in a flutter; Tiburcio and his wife were struck dumb; for Juana was the baby and only unmarried one of their children, and to take her from Las Palomas — they could never consent to that. But Uncle Lance had gone through such experiences before, and met the emergency with promptness.

"That's all right, little sister," said the old matchmaker to Miss Jean, who had come out to the gate where we were unsaddling. "Don't you borrow any trouble in this matter — leave things to me. I've handled trifles like this among these natives for nearly forty years now, and I don't see any occasion to try and make out a funeral right after the drouth's been broken by a fine rain. Shucks, girl, this is a time for rejoicing! You go back in the house and entertain Don Alejandro with your best smiles till I come in. I want to have a talk with Tiburcio and his wife before I meet the *padrino*. There's several families of those Travinos over around the Mission and I want to locate which tribe this *oso* comes from. Some of them are good people and some of them need a rope around their necks, and in a case of keeps like getting married, it's always safe to know what's what and who's who. Now, Sis, go on back in the house and entertain the Don. Come with me, Tom."

I saw our plans for the morrow vanish into thin air. On arriving at the jacal, we were admitted, but a gloom like the pall of death seemed to envelop the old Mexican couple. When we had taken seats around a small table, Tia Inez handed the ranchero the formal written request. As it was penned in Spanish, it was passed to me to read, and after running through it hastily, I read it aloud, several times stopping to interpret to Uncle Lance certain extravagant phrases. The salutatory was in the usual form; the esteem which each family had always entertained for the other was dwelt upon at length, and choicer language was never used than the *padrino* penned in asking for the hand of Doña Juana. This dainty missive was signed by the godfather of the swain, Don Alejandro Travino, whose rubric riotously ran back and forth entirely across the delicately tinted sheet. On the conclusion of the reading, Uncle Lance brushed the letter aside as of no moment, and, turning to the old couple, demanded to know to which branch of the Travino family young Don Blas belonged.

The account of Tiburcio and his wife was definite and clear. The father of the swain conducted a small country store at the Mission, and besides had landed and cattle interests. He was a younger brother of Don Alejandro, who was the owner of a large land grant, had cattle

227

in abundance, and was a representative man among the Spanish element. No better credentials could have been asked. But when their patron rallied them as to the cause of their gloom, Tia Inez burst into tears, admitting the match was satisfactory, but her baby would be carried away from Las Palomas and she might never see her again. Her two sons who lived at the ranch, allowed no day to pass without coming to see their mother, and the one who lived at a distant ranchita came at every opportunity. But if her little girl was carried away to a distant ranch — ah! that made it impossible! Let Don Lance, worthy patron of his people, forbid the match, and win the gratitude of an anguished mother. Invoking the saints to guide her aright, Doña Inez threw herself on the bed in hysterical lamentation. Realizing it is useless to argue with a woman in tears, the old matchmaker suggested to Tiburcio that we delay the answer the customary fortnight.

Promising to do nothing further without consulting them, we withdrew from the *jacal*. On returning to the house, we found Miss Jean entertaining the Don to the best of her ability, and, commanding my presence, the old matchmaker advanced to meet the *padrino*, with whom he had a slight acquaintance. Bidding his guest welcome to the ranch, he listened to the Don's apology for being such a stranger to Las Palomas until a matter of a delicate nature had brought him hither.

Don Alejandro was a distinguished-looking man, and spoke his native tongue in a manner which put my efforts as an interpreter to shame. The conversation was allowed to drift at will, from the damages of the recent drouth to the prospect of a market for beeves that fall, until supper was announced. After the evening repast was over we retired to the gallery, and Uncle Lance reopened the matchmaking by inquiring of Don Alejandro if his nephew proposed taking his bride to the Mission. The Don was all attention. Fortunately, anticipating that the question might arise, he had discussed that very feature with his nephew. At present the young man was assisting his father at the Mission, and in time, no doubt, would succeed to the business. However, realizing that her living fifty miles distant might be an objection to the girl's parents, he was not for insisting on that point, as no doubt Las Palomas offered equally good advantages for business. He simply mentioned this by way of suggestion, and invited the opinion of his host.

"Well, now, Don Alejandro," said the old matchmaker, in flutelike tones, "we are a very simple people here at Las Palomas. Breeding a few horses and mules for home purposes, and the rearing of cattle has been our occupation. As to merchandising here at the ranch, I could not countenance it, as I refused that privilege to the stage company when they offered to run past Las Palomas. At present our few wants are supplied by a merchant at Shepherd's Ferry. True, it's thirty miles, but I sometimes wish it was farther, as it is quite a temptation to my boys to ride down there on various pretexts. We send down every week for our mail and such little necessities as the ranch may need. If there was a store here, it would attract loafers and destroy the peace and contentment which we now enjoy. I would object to it; 'one man to his trade and another to his merchandise.'"

The *padrino*, with good diplomacy, heartily agreed that a store was a disturbing feature on a ranch, and instantly went off on a tangent on the splendid business possibilities of the Mission. The matchmaker in return agreed as heartily with him, and grew reminiscent. "In the spring of '51," said he, "I made the match between Tiburcio and Doña Inez, father and mother of Juana. Tiburcio was a vaquero of mine at the time, Inez being a Mission girl, and I have taken a great interest in the couple ever since. All their children were born here and still live on the ranch. Understand, Don Alejandro, I have no personal feeling in the matter, beyond the wishes of the parents of the girl. My sister has taken a great interest in Juana, having had the girl under her charge for the past eight years. Of course, I feel a pride in Juana, and she is a fine girl. If your nephew wins her, I shall tell the lucky rascal when he comes to claim her that he has won the pride of Las Palomas. I take it, Don Alejandro, that your visit and request was rather unexpected here, though I am aware that Juana has visited among cousins at the Mission several times the past few years. But that she had lost her heart to some of your gallants comes as a surprise to me, and from what I learn, to her parents also. Under the circumstances, if I were you, I would not urge an immediate reply, but give them the customary period to think it over. Our vaqueros will not be very busy for some time to come, and it will not inconvenience us to send a reply by messenger to the Mission. And tell Don Blas, even should the reply be unfavorable, not to be discouraged. Women, you know, are peculiar. Ah, Don Alejandro, when you and I were young and went courting, would we have been discouraged by a first refusal?"

Señor Travino appreciated the compliment, and, with a genial smile, slapped his host on the back, while the old matchmaker gave vent to a vociferous guffaw. The conversation thereafter took several tacks, but always reverted to the proposed match. As the hour grew late, the host apologized to his guest, as no doubt he was tired by his long ride, and offered to show him his room. The *padrino* denied all weariness, maintaining that the enjoyable evening had rested him, but reluctantly allowed himself to be shown to his apartment. No sooner were the good-nights spoken, than the old ranchero returned, and, snapping his fingers for attention, motioned me to follow. By a circuitous route we reached the *jacal* of Tiburcio. The old couple had not yet retired, and Juana blushingly admitted us. Uncle Lance jollied the old people like a robust, healthy son amusing his elders. We took seats as before around the small table, and Uncle Lance scattered the gloom of the *jacal* with his gayety.

"Las Palomas forever!" said he, striking the table with his bony fist. "This *padrino* from the Mission is a very fine gentleman but a poor matchmaker. Just because young Don Blas is the son of a Travino, the keeper of a picayune *tienda* at the Mission, was that any reason to presume for the hand of a daughter of Las Palomas? Was he any better than a vaquero just because he doled out *frijoles* by the quart, and never saw a piece of money larger than a *media real*? Why, a Las Palomas vaquero was a prince compared to a fawning attendant in a Mission store. Let Tia Inez stop fretting herself about losing Juana — it would not be yet awhile. Just leave matters to him, and he'd send Don Alejandro home, pleased with his visit and hopeful over the match, even if it never took place. And none of those frowns from the young lady!"

As we all arose at parting, the old matchmaker went over to Juana and, shaking his finger at her, said: "Now, look here, my little girl, your mistress, your parents, and myself are all interested in you, and don't think we won't act for your best interests. You've seen this young fellow ride by on a horse several times, haven't you? Danced with him a few times under the eyes of a chaperon at the last *fiesta*, haven't you? And that's all you care to know, and are ready to marry him. Well, well, it's fortunate that the marriage customs of the Mexicans protect such innocents as you. Now, if young Don Blas had worked under me for a year as a vaquero, I might be as ready to the match as you are; for then I'd know whether he was worthy of you. What does a girl of your age know about a man? But when you have as many gray hairs in your head as your mother has, you'll thank me for cautioning every one to proceed slowly in this match. Now dry those tears and go to your mother."

The next morning Don Alejandro proposed returning to the Mission. But the old ranchero hooted the idea, and informed his guest that he had ordered the ambulance, as he intended showing him the recent improvements made on Las Palomas. When the guest protested against a longer absence from home, the host artfully intimated that by remaining another day a favorable reply might possibly go with him. Don Alejandro finally consented. I was pressed in as driver and interpreter, and our team tore away from the ranch with a flourish. To put it mildly, I was disgusted at having my plans for the day knocked in the head, yet knew better than protest. As we drove along, myriads of grass-blades were peeping up since the rain, giving every view a greenish cast. Nearly every windmill on the ranch on our circuit was pointed out, and we passed three of our four tanks, one of which was over half a mile in length. After stopping at an outlying ranchita for refreshment, we spent the afternoon in a similar manner. From a swell of the prairie some ten miles to the westward of the ranch, we could distinctly see an outline of the Ganso. Halting the ambulance, the old ranchero pointed out to his guest the meanderings of that creek from its confluence with the parent stream until it became lost in the hills to the southward.

"That tract of ground," said he, "is my last landed addition to Las Palomas. It lies north and south, giving me six miles' frontage on the Nueces. and extending north of the river about four miles, Don Alejandro, when I note the great change which has come over this valley since I settled here, it convinces me that if one wishes to follow ranching he had better acquire title to what range he needs. Land has advanced in price from a few cents an acre to four bits, and now they say the next generation will see it worth a dollar. This Ganso grant contains a hundred and fourteen sections, and I have my eye on one or two other adjoining tracts. My generation will not need it, but the one who succeeds me may. Now, as we drive home, I'll try to show you the northern boundary of our range; it's fairly well outlined by the divide between the Nueces and the Frio rivers."

From the conversation which followed until we reached headquarters, I readily understood that the old matchmaker was showing the rose and concealing its thorn. His motive was not always clear to me, for one would have supposed from his almost boastful claims regarding its extent and carrying capacity for cattle, he was showing the ranch to a prospective buyer. But as we neared home, the conversation innocently drifted to the Mexican element and their love for the land to which they were born. Then I understood why I was driving four mules instead of basking in the smiles of my own sweetheart on the San Miguel. Nor did this boasting cease during the evening, but alternated from lands and cattle to the native people, and finally centred about a Mexican girl who had been so fortunate as to have been born to the soil of Las Palomas.

When Don Alejandro asked for his horse the following morning on leaving, Uncle Lance, Quayle, and myself formed a guard of honor to escort our guest a distance on his way. He took leave of the mistress of Las Palomas in an obeisance worthy of an old-time cavalier. Once we were off, Uncle Lance pretended to have had a final interview with the parents, in which they had insisted on the customary time in which to consider the proposal. The *padrino* graciously accepted the situation, thanking his host for his interest in behalf of his nephew. On reaching the river, where our ways separated, all halted for a few minutes at parting.

"Well, Don Alejandro," said the old ranchero, "this is my limit of escort to guests of the ranch. Now, the only hope I have in parting is, in case the reply should he unfavorable, that Don Blas will not be discouraged and that we may see you again at Las Palomas. Tender my congratulations to your nephew, and tell him that a welcome always awaits him in case he finds time and inclination to visit us. I take some little interest in matches. These boys of mine are going north to the Frio on a courting errand to-day. But our marriage customs are inferior to yours, and our young people, left to themselves, don't seem to marry. Don Alejandro, if you and I had the making of the matches, there'd be a cradle rocking in every *jacal*." Both smiled, said their "Adios, amigos," and he was gone.

As our guest cantered away, down the river road, Quayle and I began looking for a ford. The river had been on a rampage, and while we were seeking out a crossing our employer had time for a few comments. "The Don's tickled with his prospects. He thinks he's got a half inch rope on Juana right now; but if I thought your prospects were no better than I know his are, you wouldn't tire any horse-flesh of mine by riding to the Frio and the San Miguel. But go right on, and stay as long as you want to, for I'm in no hurry to see your faces again. Tom, with the ice broken as it is, as soon as Esther can remove her disabilities — well, you won't have to run off the next time. And Theodore, remember what I told you the other day about sparking a girl. You're too timid and backward for a young fellow. I don't care if you come home with one eye scratched out, just so you and Frances have come to an understanding and named the day."

CHAPTER XVI
MATCHMAKING

After our return to the Frio, my first duty was writing, relative to the proposed match, an unfavorable reply to Don Alejandro Travino.

On resuming work, we spent six weeks baling hides, thus occupying our time until the beginning of the branding season. A general round-up of the Nueces valley, commencing on the coast at Corpus Christi Bay, had been agreed upon among the cowmen of the country. In pursuance of the plan four well-mounted men were sent from our ranch with Wilson's wagon to the coast, our *segundo* following a week later with the wagon, *remuda* and twelve men, to meet the rodeo at San Patricio as they worked up the river. Our cattle had drifted in every direction during the drouth and though many of them had returned since the range had again become good, they were still widely scattered. So Uncle Lance took the rest of us and started for the Frio, working down that river and along the Nueces, until we met the round-up coming up from below. During this cow hunt, I carried my fiddle with me in the wagon, and at nearly every ranch we passed we stopped and had a dance. Not over once a week did we send in cattle to the ranch to brand, and on meeting the rodeo from below, Deweese had over three thousand of our cattle. After taking these in and branding the calves, we worked over our home range until near the holidays.

On our return to the ranch, we learned that young Blas Travino from the Mission had passed Las Palomas some days before. He had stopped in passing; but, finding the ranchero absent, plead a matter of business at Santa Maria, promising to call on his return. He was then at the ranch on the Tarancalous, and hourly expecting his reappearance, the women of the household were in an agitated state of mind. Since the formal answer had been sent, no word had come from Don Blas and a rival had meanwhile sprung up in the person of Fidel Trujillo. Within a month after his employment I noticed the new vaquero casting shy glances at Juana, but until the cow hunt on the Frio I did not recognize the fine handwriting of the old matchmaker. Though my services were never called for as interpreter between Uncle Lance and the new man, any one could see there was an understanding between them. That the old ranchero was pushing Fidel forward was evident during the fall cow hunting by his sending that Mexican into Las Palomas with every bunch of cattle gathered.

That evening Don Blas rode into the ranch, accompanied by Father Norquin. The priest belonged at the Mission, and their meeting at Santa Maria might, of course, have been accidental. None of the padre's parishioners at headquarters were expecting him, however, for several months, and padres are able *padrinos*, — sometimes, among their own faith, even despotic. Taking account, as it appeared, of the ulterior motive, Uncle Lance welcomed the arrivals with a hearty hospitality, which to a stranger seemed so genuine as to dispel any suspicion. Not in many a day had a visitor at Las Palomas received more courteous consideration than did Father Norquin. The choicest mint which grew in the inclosures about the wells was none too good for the juleps which were concocted by Miss Jean. Had the master and mistress of the ranch been communicants of his church, the rosy-cheeked padre could have received no more marked attention.

The conversation touched lightly on various topics, until Santa Maria ranch was mentioned, when Uncle Lance asked the padre if Don Mateo had yet built him a chapel. The priest shrugged his shoulders deprecatingly and answered the question with another, — when Las Palomas proposed building a place of worship.

"Well, Father, I'm glad you've brought the matter up again," replied the host. "That I should have lived here over forty years and never done anything for your church or my people who belong to your faith, is certainly saying little in my behalf. I never had the matter brought home to me so clearly as during last summer's drouth. Do you remember that old maxim regarding when the devil was sick? Well, I was good and sick. If you had happened in then and had asked for a chapel, — not that I have any confidence in your teaching, — you could have got a church with a steeple on it. I was in such sore straits that the women were kept busy making candles, and we burnt them in every *jacal* until the hour of deliverance."

Helping himself from the proffered snuffbox of the padre, the host turned to his guest, and in all sincerity continued: "Yes, Father, I ought to build you a nice place of worship. We could quarry the rock during idle time, and burn our own lime right here on the ranch. While you are here, give me some plans, and we'll show you that the white element of Las Palomas are not such hopeless heretics as you suppose. Now, if we build the chapel, I'm just going to ask one favor in return: I expect to die and be buried on this ranch. You're a younger man by twenty years and will outlive me, and on the day of my burial I want you to lay aside your creed and preach my funeral in this little chapel which you and I are going to build. I have been a witness to the self-sacrifice of you and other priests ever since I lived here. Father, I like an honest man, and the earnestness of your cloth for the betterment of my people no one can question. And my covenant is, that you are to preach a simple sermon, merely commemorating the fact that here lived a man named Lovelace, who died and would be seen among his fellow men no more. These being facts, you can mention them; but beyond that, for fear our faiths might differ, the less said the better. Won't you have another mint julep before supper? No? You will, won't you, Don Blas?"

That the old ranchero was in earnest about building a chapel on Las Palomas there was no doubt. In fact, the credit should be given to Miss Jean, for she had been urging the matter ever since my coming to the ranch. At headquarters and outlying ranchitas on the land, there were nearly twenty families, or over a hundred persons of all ages. But that the old matchmaker was going to make the most out of his opportunity by erecting the building at an opportune time, there was not the shadow of a question.

The evening passed without mention of the real errand of our guests. The conversation was allowed to wander at will, during which several times it drifted into gentle repartee between host and padre, both artfully avoiding the rock of matchmaking. But the next morning, as if anxious to begin the day's work early, Father Norquin, on arising, inquired for his host, strutted out to the corrals, and, on meeting him, promptly inquired why, during the previous summer, Don Alejandro Travino's mission to obtain the hand of Juana Leal had failed.

"That's so," assented Uncle Lance, very affably, "Don Alejandro was here as godfather to his nephew. And this young man with you is Don Blas, the bear? Well, why did we waste so much time last night talking about chapels and death when we might have made a match in less time? You priests have everything in your favor as *padrinos*, but you are so slow that a rival might appear and win the girl while you were drumming up your courage. I don't write Spanish myself, but I have boys here on the ranch who do. One of them, if I remember rightly, wrote the answer at the request of Juana's mother. If my memory hasn't failed me entirely, the parents objected to being separated from their only daughter. You know how that is among your people; and I never like to interfere in family matters. But from what I hear Don Blas has a rival now. Yes; young Travino failed to press his suit, and a girl will stand for nearly anything but neglect. But that's one thing they won't stand for, not when there's a handsome fellow at hand to play the bear. Then the old lover is easily forgotten for the new. Eh, Father?"

"Ah, Don Lance, I know your reputation as a matchmaker," replied Father Norquin, in a rich French accent. "Report says had you not had a hand in it the match would have been successful. The supposition is that it only lacked your approval. The daughter of a vaquero refusing a Travino? Tut, tut, man!"

A hearty guffaw greeted these aspersions. "And so you've heard I was a matchmaker, have you? Of course, you believed it just like any other old granny. Now, of course, when I'm asked by any of my people to act as *padrino*, I never refuse any more than you do. I've made many a match and hope to be spared to make several more. But come; they're calling us to breakfast, and after that we'll take a walk over to the ranch burying ground. It's less than a half mile — in that point of encinal yonder. I want to show you what I think would be a nice spot for our chapel."

The conversation during breakfast was artfully directed by the host to avoid the dangerous shoals, though the padre constantly kept an eye on Juana as she passed back and forth. As we arose from the table and were passing to the gallery, Uncle Lance nudged the priest, and, poking Don Blas in the ribs, said: "Isn't Juana a stunning fine cook? Got up that breakfast herself. There isn't an eighteen-year-old girl in Texas who can make as fine biscuits as she does. But Las Palomas raises just as fine girls as she does horses and cattle. The rascal who gets her for a wife can thank his lucky stars. Don Blas, you ought to have me for *padrino*. Your uncle and the padre here are too poky. Why, if I was making a match for as fine a girl as Juana is, I'd set the river afire before I'd let an unfavorable answer discourage me. Now, the padre and I are going for a short walk, and we'll leave you here at the house to work out your own salvation. Don't pay any attention to the mistress, and I want to tell you right now, if you expect to win Juana, never depend on old fogy *padrinos* like your uncle and Father Norquin. Do a little hustling for yourself."

The old ranchero and the priest were gone nearly an hour, and on their return looked at another site in the rear of the Mexican quarters. It was a pretty knoll, and as the two joined us where we were repairing a windmill at the corrals, Father Norquin, in an ecstasy of delight, said: "Well, my children, the chapel is assured at Las Palomas. Don Lance wanted to build it over in the encinal, with twice as nice a site right here in the rancho. We may need the building for a school some day, and if we should, we don't want it a mile away. The very idea! And the master tells me that a chapel has been the wish of his sister for years. Poor woman — to have such a brother. I must hasten to the house and thank her."

No sooner had the padre started than I was called aside by my employer. "Tom," said he, "you slip around to Tia Inez's *jacal* and tell her that I'm going to send Father Norquin over to see her. Tell her to stand firm on not letting Juana leave the ranch for the Mission. Tell her that I've promised the padre a chapel for Las Palomas, and rather than miss it, the priest would consign the whole Travino family to endless perdition. Tell her to laugh at his scoldings and inform him that Juana can get a husband without going so far. And that you heard me say that I was going to give Fidel, the day he married her daughter, the same number of heifers that all her brothers got. Impress it on Tia Inez's mind that it means something to be born to Las Palomas."

I set out on my errand and he hastened away to overtake the padre before the latter reached the house. Tia Inez welcomed me, no doubt anticipating that I was the bearer of some message. When I gave her the message her eyes beamed with gratitude and she devoutly crossed her breast invoking the blessing of the saints upon the master. I added a few words of encouragement of my own — that I understood that when we quarried the rock for the chapel, there was to be enough extra cut to build a stone cottage for Juana and Fidel. This was pure invention on my part, but I felt a very friendly interest in Las Palomas, for I expected to bring my bride to it as soon as possible. Therefore, if I could help the present match forward by the use of a little fiction, why not?

Father Norquin's time was limited at Las Palomas, as he was under appointment to return to Santa Maria that evening. Therefore it became an active morning about the ranch. Long before we had finished the repairs on the windmill, a *mozo* from the house came out to the corrals to say I was wanted by the master. Returning with the servant, I found Uncle Lance and the mistress of the ranch entertaining their company before a cheerful fire in the sitting-room. On my entrance, my employer said: —

"Tom, I have sent for you because I want you to go over with the padre to the *jacal* of Juana's parents. Father Norquin here is such an old granny that he believes I interfered, or the reply of last summer would have been favorable. Now, Tom, you're not to open your mouth one way or the other. The padre will state his errand, and the old couple will answer him in your presence. Don Blas will remain here, and whatever the answer is, he and I must abide by it. Really, as I have said, I have no interest in the match, except the welfare of the girl. Go on now, Father, and let's see what you can do as a *padrino*."

As we arose to go, Miss Jean interposed and suggested that, out of deference to Father Norquin, the old couple be sent for, but her brother objected. He wanted the parents to make their own answer beneath their own roof, unembarrassed by any influence. As we left the room, the old matchmaker accompanied us as far as the gate, where he halted and said to the padre: —

"Father Norquin, in a case like the present, you will not mind my saying that your wish is not absolute, and I am sending a witness with you to see that you issue no peremptory orders on this ranch. And remember, that this old couple have been over thirty years in my employ, and temper your words to them as you would to your own parents, were they living. Juana was born here, which means a great deal, and with the approval of her parents, she'll marry the man of her choice, and no *padrino*, let him be priest or layman, can crack his whip on the soil of Las Palomas to the contrary. As my guest, you must excuse me for talking so plain, but my people are as dear to me as your church is to you."

As my employer turned and leisurely walked back to the house, Father Norquin stood stock-still. I was slightly embarrassed myself, but it was easily to be seen that the padre's plans had received a severe shock. I made several starts toward the Mexican quarters before the priest shook away his hesitations and joined me. That the old ranchero's words had agitated him was very evident in his voice and manner. Several times he stopped me and demanded explanations, finally raising the question of a rival. I told him all I knew about the matter; that Fidel, a new vaquero on the ranch, had found favor in Juana's eyes, that he was a favorite man with master and mistress, but what view the girl's parents took of the matter I was unable to say. This cleared up the situation wonderfully, and the padre brightened as we neared the *jacal*.

Tiburcio was absent, and while awaiting his return, the priest became amiable and delivered a number of messages from friends and relatives at the Mission. Tia Inez was somewhat embarrassed at first, but gradually grew composed, and before the return of her husband all three of us were chatting like cronies. On the appearance of Tio Tiburcio, coffee was ordered and the padre told several good stories, over which we all laughed heartily. Cigarettes were next, and in due time Father Norquin very good naturedly inquired why an unfavorable answer, regarding the marriage of their daughter with young Blas Travino, had been returned the previous summer. The old couple looked at each other a moment, when the husband turned in his chair, and with a shrug of his shoulders and a jerk of his head, referred the priest to his wife. Tia Inez met the padre's gaze, and in a clear, concise manner, and in her native tongue, gave her reasons. Father Norquin explained the prominence of the Travino family and their disappointment over the refusal, and asked if the decision was final, to which he received an affirmative reply. Instead of showing any displeasure, he rose to take his departure, turning in the doorway to say to the old couple: —

"My children, peace and happiness in this life is a priceless blessing. I should be untrue to my trust did I counsel a marriage that would give a parent a moment of unhappiness. My blessing upon this house and its dwellers, and upon its sons and daughters as they go forth to homes of their own." While he lifted his hand in benediction, the old couple and myself bowed our heads for a moment, after which the padre and I passed outside.

I was as solemn as an owl, yet inwardly delighted at the turn of affairs. But Father Norquin had nothing to conceal, while delight was wreathed all over his rosy countenance. Again and again he stopped me to make inquiries about Fidel, the new vaquero. That lucky rascal was a good-looking native, a much larger youth than the aspiring Don Blas, and I pictured him to the padre as an Adonis. To the question if he was in the ranch at present, fortune favored me, as Fidel and nearly all the regular vaqueros were cutting timbers in the encinal that day with which to build new corrals at one of the outlying tanks. As he would not return before dark, and I knew the padre was due at Santa Maria that evening, my description of him made Don Blas a mere pigmy in comparison. But we finally reached the house, and on our reëntering the sitting-room, young Travino very courteously arose and stood until Father Norquin should be seated. But the latter faced his parishioner, saying: —

"You young simpleton, what did you drag me up here for on a fool's errand? I was led to believe that our generous host was the instigator of the unfavorable answer to your uncle's negotiations last summer. Now I have the same answer repeated from the lips of the girl's parents. Consider the predicament in which you have placed a servant of the Church. Every law of hospitality has been outraged through your imbecility. And to complete my humiliation, I have received only kindness on every hand. The chapel which I have desired for years is now a certainty, thanks to the master and mistress of Las Palomas. What apology can I offer for your" —

"Hold on there, Father," interrupted Uncle Lance. "If you owe this ranch any apology, save your breath for a more important occasion. Don Blas is all right; any suitor who would not be jealous over a girl like Juana is not welcome at Las Palomas. Why, when I was his age I was suspicious of my sweetheart's own father, and you should make allowance for this young man's years and impetuosity. Sit down, Father, and let's have a talk about this chapel — that's what interests me most right now. You see, within a few days my boys will have all the palisades cut for the new corrals, and then we can turn our attention to getting out the rock for the chapel. We have a quarry of nice soft stone all opened up, and I'll put a dozen vaqueros to blocking out the rock in a few days. We always have a big stock of *zacahuiste* grass on hand for thatching *jacals*, plenty of limestone to burn for the lime, sand in abundance, and all we lack is the masons. You'll have to send them out from the Mission, but I'll pay them. Oh, I reckon the good Lord loves Las Palomas, for you see He's placed everything convenient with which to build the chapel."

Father Norquin could not remain seated, but paced the room enumerating the many little adornments which the mother church would be glad to supply. Enthusiastic as a child over a promised toy, no other thought entered the simple padre's mind, until dinner was announced. And all during the meal, the object of our guest's mission was entirely lost sight of, in contemplation of the coming chapel. The padre seemed as anxious to avoid the subject of matchmaking as his host, while poor Don Blas sat like a willing sacrifice, unable to say a word. I sympathized with him, for I knew what it was to meet disappointment. At the conclusion of the mid-day repast, Father Norquin flew into a great bustle in preparing to start for Santa Maria, and I was dispatched for the horses. Our guests and my employer were waiting at the stile when I led up their mounts, and at final parting the old matchmaker said to the priest: —

"Now, remember, I expect you to have this chapel completed by Easter Sunday, when I want you to come out and spend at least two weeks with us and see that it is finished to suit you, and arrange for the dedication. Las Palomas will build the chapel, but when our work is done yours commences. And I want to tell you right now, there's liable to be several weddings in it before the mortar gets good and dry. I have it on pretty good authority that one of my boys and Pierre Vaux's eldest girl are just about ready to have you pronounce them man and wife. No, he's not of any faith, but she's a good Catholic. Now, look here, Father Norquin, if I have to proselyte you to my way of thinking, it'll never hurt you any. I was never afraid to do what was right, and when at Las Palomas you needn't be afraid either, even if we have to start a new creed. Well, good-by to both of you."

We had a windmill to repair that afternoon, some five miles from the ranch, so that I did not return to the house until evening; but when all gathered around the supper table that night, Uncle Lance was throwing bouquets at himself for the crafty manner in which he had switched the padre from his mission, and yet sent him away delighted. He admitted that he was scared on the appearance of Father Norquin as a *padrino*, on account of the fact that a priest was usually supreme among his own people. That he had early come to the conclusion if there was to be any coercion used in this case, he was determined to get in his bluff first. But Miss Jean ridiculed the idea that there was any serious danger.

"Goodness me, Lance," said she, "I could have told you there was no cause for alarm. In this case between Fidel and Juana, I've been a very liberal chaperon. Oh, well, now, never mind about the particulars. Once, to try his nerve, I gave him a chance, and I happen to know the rascal kissed her the moment my back was turned. Oh, I think Juana will stay at Las Palomas."

CHAPTER XVII
WINTER AT LAS PALOMAS

The winter succeeding the drouth was an unusually mild one, frost and sleet being unseen at Las Palomas. After the holidays several warm rains fell, affording fine hunting and assuring enough moisture in the soil to insure an early spring. The preceding winter had been gloomy, but this proved to be the most social one since my advent, for within fifty miles of the ranch no less than two weddings occurred during Christmas week. As to little neighborhood happenings, we could hear of half a dozen every time we went to Shepherd's after the mail.

When the native help on the ranch was started at blocking out the stone for the chapel, Uncle Lance took the hounds and with two of the boys went down to Wilson's ranch for a hunt. Gallup went, of course, but just why he took Scales along, unless with the design of making a match between one of the younger daughters of this neighboring ranchman and the Marylander, was not entirely clear. When he wanted to, Scales could make himself very agreeable, and had it not been for his profligate disposition, his being taken along on the hunt would have been no mystery. Every one on the ranch, including the master and mistress, were cognizant of the fact that for the past year he had maintained a correspondence with a girl in Florida — the one whose letter and photograph had been found in the box of oranges. He hardly deserved the confidence of the roguish girl, for he showed her letters to any one who cared to read them. I had read every line of the whole correspondence, and it was plain that Scales had deceived the girl into believing that he was a prominent ranchman, when in reality the best that could be said of him was that he was a lovable vagabond. From the last letter, it was clear that he had promised to marry the girl during the Christmas week just past, but he had asked for a postponement on the ground that the drouth had prevented him from selling his beeves.

When Uncle Lance made the discovery, during a cow hunt the fall before, of the correspondence between Scales and the Florida girl, he said to us around the camp-fire that night: "Well, all I've got to say is that that girl down in Florida is hard up. Why, it's entirely contrary to a girl's nature to want to be wooed by letter. Until the leopard changes his spots, the good old way, of putting your arm around the girl and whispering that you love her, will continue to be popular. If I was to hazard an opinion about that girl, Aaron, I'd say that she was ambitious to rise above her surroundings. The chances are that she wants to get away from home, and possibly she's as much displeased with the young men in the orange country as I sometimes get with you dodrotted cow hands. Now, I'm not one of those people who're always harping about the youth of his day and generation being so much better than the present. That's all humbug. But what does get me is, that you youngsters don't profit more by the experience of an old man like me who's been married three times. Line upon line and precept upon precept, I have preached this thing to my boys for the last ten years, and what has it amounted to? Not a single white bride has ever been brought to Las Palomas. They can call me a matchmaker if they want to, but the evidence is to the contrary." This was on the night after we passed Shepherd's, where Scales had received a letter from the Florida girl. But why he should accompany the hunt now to Remirena, unless the old ranchero proposed reforming him, was too deep a problem for me.

On leaving for Wilson's, there was the usual bustle; hounds responding to the horn and horses under saddle champing their bits. I had hoped that permission to go over to the Frio and San Miguel would be given John and myself, but my employer's mind was too absorbed in something else, and we were overlooked in the hurry to get away. Since the quarrying of the rock had commenced, my work had been overseeing the native help, of which we had some fifteen cutting and hauling. In numerous places within a mile of headquarters, a soft porous rock cropped out. By using a crowbar with a tempered chisel point, the Mexicans easily channeled the rock into blocks, eighteen by thirty inches, splitting each stone a foot in thickness, so that when hauled to the place of use, each piece was ready to lay up in the wall. The ranch house at headquarters was built out of this rock, and where permanency was required, it was the best material available, whitening and apparently becoming firmer with time and exposure.

I had not seen my sweetheart in nearly a month, but there I was, chained to a rock quarry and mule teams. The very idea of Gallup and the profligate Scales riding to hounds and basking in the society of charming girls nettled me. The remainder of the ranch outfit was under Deweese, building the new corrals, so that I never heard my own tongue spoken except at meals and about the house. My orders included the cutting of a few hundred rock extra above the needs of the chapel, and when this got noised among the help, I had to explain that there was some talk of building a stone cottage, and intimated that it was for Juana and Fidel. But that lucky rascal was one of the crew cutting rock, and from some source or other he had learned that I was liable to need a cottage at Las Palomas in the near future. The fact that I was acting *segundo* over the quarrying outfit, was taken advantage of by Fidel to clear his skirts and charge the extra rock to my matrimonial expectations. He was a fast workman, and on every stone he split from the mother ledge, he sang out, "Otro piedra por Don Tomas!" And within a few minutes' time some one else would cry out, "Otro cillar por Fidel y Juana," or "Otro piedra por padre Norquin."

A week passed and there was no return of the hunters. We had so systematized our work at the quarry that my presence was hardly needed, so every evening I urged Cotton to sound the mistress for permission to visit our sweethearts. John was a good-natured fellow who could be easily led or pushed forward, and I had come to look upon Miss Jean as a ready supporter of any of her brother's projects. For that reason her permission was as good as the master's; but she parried all Cotton's hints, pleading the neglect of our work in the absence of her brother. I was disgusted with the monotony of quarry work, and likewise was John over building corrals, as no cow hand ever enthuses over manual labor, when an incident occurred which afforded the opportunity desired. The mistress needed some small article from the store at Shepherd's, and a Mexican boy had been sent down on this errand and also to get the mail of the past two weeks. On the boy's return, he brought a message from the merchant, saying that Henry Annear had been accidentally killed by a horse that day, and that the burial would take place at ten o'clock the next morning.

The news threw the mistress of Las Palomas into a flutter. Her brother was absent, and she felt a delicacy in consulting Deweese, and very naturally turned to me for advice. Funerals in the Nueces valley were so very rare that I advised going, even if the unfortunate man had stood none too high in our estimation. Annear lived on the divide between Shepherd's and the Frio at a ranch called Las Norias. As this ranch was not over ten miles from the mouth of the San Miguel, the astute mind can readily see the gleam of my ax in attending. Funerals were such events that I knew to a certainty that all the countryside within reach would attend, and the Vaux ranch was not over fifteen miles distant from Las Norias. Acting on my advice, the mistress ordered the ambulance to be ready to start by three o'clock the next morning, and gave every one on the ranch who cared, permission to go along. All of us took advantage of the offer, except Deweese, who, when out of hearing of the mistress, excused himself rather profanely.

The boy had returned late in the day, but we lost no time in acting on Miss Jean's orders. Fortunately the ambulance teams were in hand hauling rock, but we rushed out several vaqueros to bring in the *remuda* which contained our best saddle horses. It was after dark when they returned with the mounts wanted, and warning Tiburcio that we would call him at an early hour, every one retired for a few hours' rest. I would resent the charge that I am selfish or unsympathetic, yet before falling asleep that night the deplorable accident was entirely overlooked in the anticipated pleasure of seeing Esther.

As it was fully a thirty-five-mile drive we started at daybreak, and to encourage the mules Quayle and Happersett rode in the lead until sun-up, when they dropped to the rear with Cotton and myself. We did not go by way of Shepherd's, but crossed the river several miles above the ferry, following an old cotton road made during the war, from the interior of the state to Matamoras, Mexico. It was some time before the hour named for the burial when we sighted Las Norias on the divide, and spurred up the ambulance team, to reach the ranch in time for the funeral. The services were conducted by a strange minister who happened to be visiting in Oakville, but what impressed me in particular was the solicitude of Miss Jean for the widow. She had been frequently entertained at Las Palomas by its mistress, as the sweetheart of June Deweese, though since her marriage to Annear a decided coolness had existed between the two women. But in the present hour of trouble, the past was forgotten and they mingled their tears like sisters.

On our return, which was to be by way of the Vauxes', I joined those from the McLeod ranch, while Happersett and Cotton accompanied the ambulance to the Vaux home. Nearly every one going our way was on horseback, and when the cavalcade was some distance from Las Norias, my sweetheart dropped to the rear for a confidential chat and told me that a lawyer from Corpus Christi, an old friend of the family, had come up for the purpose of taking the preliminary steps for securing her freedom, and that she expected to be relieved of the odious tie which bound her to Oxenford at the May term of court. This was pleasant news to me, for there would then be no reason for delaying our marriage.

Happersett rode down to the San Miguel the next morning to inform Quayle and myself that the mistress was then on the way to spend the night with the widow Annear, and that the rest of us were to report at home the following evening. She had apparently inspected the lines on the Frio, and, finding everything favorable, turned to other fields. I was disappointed, for Esther and I had planned to go up to the Vaux ranch during the visit. Dan suggested that we ride home together by way of the Vauxes'. But Quayle bitterly refused even to go near the ranch. He felt very sore and revengeful over being jilted by Frances after she had let him crown her Queen of the ball at the tournament dance. So, agreeing to meet on the divide the next day for the ride back to Las Palomas, we parted.

The next afternoon, on reaching the divide between the Frio and the home river, Theodore and I scanned the horizon in vain for any horsemen. We dismounted, and after waiting nearly an hour, descried two specks to the northward which we knew must be our men. On coming up they also threw themselves on the ground, and we indulged in a cigarette while we compared notes. I had nothing to conceal, and frankly confessed that Esther and I expected to marry during the latter part of May. Cotton, though, seemed reticent, and though Theodore cross-questioned him rather severely, was non-committal and dumb as an oyster; but before we recrossed the Nueces that evening, John and I having fallen far to the rear of the other two, he admitted to me that his wedding would occur within a month after Lent. It was to be a confidence between us, but I advised him to take Uncle Lance into the secret at once.

But on reaching the ranch we learned that the hunting party had not returned, nor had the mistress. The next morning we resumed our work, Quayle and Cotton at corral building and I at the rock quarry. The work had progressed during my absence, and the number of pieces desired was nearing completion, and with but one team hauling the work-shop was already congested with cut building stone. By noon the quarry was so cluttered with blocks that I ordered half the help to take axes and go to the encinal to cut dry oak wood for burning the lime. With the remainder of my outfit we cleaned out and sealed off the walls of an old lime kiln, which had served ever since the first rock buildings rose on Las Palomas. The oven was cut in the same porous formation, the interior resembling an immense jug, possibly twelve feet in diameter and fifteen feet in height to the surface of the ledge. By locating the kiln near the abrupt wall of an abandoned quarry, ventilation was given from below by a connecting tunnel some twenty feet in length. Layers of wood and limestone were placed within until the interior was filled, when it was fired, and after burning for a few hours the draft was cut off below and above, and the heat retained until the limestone was properly burned.

Near the middle of the afternoon, the drivers hauling the blocks drove near the kiln and shouted that the hunters had returned. Scaling off the burnt rock in the interior and removing the debris made it late before our job was finished; then one of the vaqueros working on the outside told us that the ambulance had crossed the river over an hour before, and was then in the ranch. This was good news, and mounting our horses we galloped into headquarters and found the corral outfit already there. Miss Jean soon had our *segundo* an unwilling prisoner in a corner, and from his impatient manner and her low tones it was plain to be seen that her two days' visit with Mrs. Annear had resulted in some word for Deweese. Not wishing to intrude, I avoided them in search of my employer, finding him and Gallup at an outhouse holding a hound while Scales was taking a few stitches in an ugly cut which the dog had received from a *javeline*. Paying no attention to the two boys, I gave him the news, and bluntly informed him that Esther and I expected to marry in May.

"Bully for you, Tom," said he. "Here, hold this fore foot, and look out he don't bite you. So she'll get her divorce at the May term, and then all outdoors can't stand in your way the next time. Now, that means that you'll have to get out fully two hundred more of those building rock, for your cottage will need three rooms. Take another stitch, knot your thread well, and be quick about it. I tell you the *javeline* were pretty fierce; this is the fifth dog we've doctored since we returned."

On freeing the poor hound, we both looked the pack over carefully, and as no others needed attention, Aaron and Glenn were excused. No sooner were they out of hearing than I suggested that the order be made for five hundred stone, as no doubt John Cotton would also need a cottage shortly after Lent. The old matchmaker beamed with smiles. "Is that right, Tom?" he inquired. "Of course, you boys tell each other what you would hardly tell me. And so they have made the riffle at last? Why, of course they shall have a cottage, and have it so near that I can hear the baby when it cries. Bully for tow-headed John. Oh, I reckon Las Palomas is coming to the front this year. Three new cottages and three new brides is not to be sneezed at! Does your mistress know all this good news?"

I informed him that I had not seen Miss Jean to speak to since the funeral, and that Cotton wished his intentions kept a secret. "Of course," he said; "that's just like a sap-headed youth, as if getting married was anything to be ashamed of. Why, when I was the age of you boys I'd have felt proud over the fact. Wants it kept a secret, does he? Well, I'll tell everybody I meet, and I'll send word to the ferry and to every ranch within a hundred miles, that our John Cotton and Frank Vaux are going to get married in the spring. There's nothing disgraceful in matrimony, and I'll publish this so wide that neither of them will dare back out. I've had my eye on that girl for years, and now when there's a prospect of her becoming the wife of one of my boys, he wants it kept a secret? Well, I don't think it'll keep."

After that I felt more comfortable over my own confession. Before we were called to supper every one in the house, including the Mexicans about headquarters, knew that Cotton and I were soon to be married. And all during the evening the same subject was revived at every lull in the conversation, though Deweese kept constantly intruding the corral building and making inquiries after the hunt. "What difference does it make if we hunted or not?" replied Uncle Lance to his foreman with some little feeling. "Suppose we did only hunt every third or fourth day? Those Wilson folks have a way of entertaining friends which makes riding after hounds seem commonplace. Why, the girls had Glenn and Aaron on the go until old man Nate and myself could hardly get them out on a hunt at all. And when they did, provided the girls were along, they managed to get separated, and along about dusk they'd come slouching in by pairs, looking as innocent as turtle-doves. Not that those Wilson girls can't ride, for I never saw a better horsewoman than Susie — the one who took such a shine to Scales."

I noticed Miss Jean cast a reproving glance at her brother on his connecting the name of Susie Wilson with that of his vagabond employee. The mistress was a puritan in morals. That Scales fell far below her ideal there was no doubt, and the brother knew too well not to differ with her on this subject. When all the boys had retired except Cotton and me, the brother and sister became frank with each other.

"Well, now, you must not blame me if Miss Susie was attentive to Aaron," said the old matchmaker, in conciliation, pacing the room. "He was from Las Palomas and their guest, and I see no harm in the girls being courteous and polite. Susie was just as nice as pie to me, and I hope you don't think I don't entertain the highest regard for Nate Wilson's family. Suppose one of the girls did smile a little too much on Aaron, was that my fault? Now, mind you, I never said a word one way or the other, but I'll bet every cow on Las Palomas that Aaron Scales, vagabond that he is, can get Susie Wilson for the asking. I know your standard of morals, but you must make allowance for others who look upon things differently from you and me. You remember Katharine Vedder who married Carey Troup at the close of the war. There's a similar case for you. Katharine married Troup just because he was so wicked, at least that was the reason she gave, and she and you were old run-togethers. And you remember too that getting married was the turning-point in Carey Troup's life. Who knows but Aaron might sober down if he was to marry? Just because a man has sown a few wild oats in his youth, does that condemn him for all time? You want to be more liberal. Give me the man who has stood the fire tests of life in preference to one who has never been tempted."

"Now, Lance, you know you had a motive in taking Aaron down to Wilson's," said the sister, reprovingly. "Don't get the idea that I can't read you like an open book. Your argument is as good as an admission of your object in going to Ramirena. Ever since Scales got up that flirtation with Suzanne Vaux last summer, it was easy to see that Aaron was a favorite with you. Why don't you take Happersett around and introduce him to some nice girls? Honest, Lance, I wouldn't give poor old Dan for the big beef corral full of rascals like Scales. Look how he trifled with that silly girl in Florida."

Instead of continuing the argument, the wily ranchero changed the subject.

"The trouble with Dan is he's too old. When a fellow begins to get a little gray around the edges, he gets so foxy that you couldn't bait him into a matrimonial trap with sweet grapes. But, Sis, what's the matter with your keeping an eye open for a girl for Dan, if he's such a favorite with you? If I had half the interest in him that you profess, I certainly wouldn't ask any one to help. It wouldn't surprise me if the boys take to marrying freely after John and Tom bring their brides to Las Palomas. Now that Mrs. Annear is a widow, there's the same old chance for June. If Glenn don't make the riffle with Miss Jule, he ought to be shot on general principles. And I don't know, little sister, if you and I were both to oppose it, that we could prevent that rascal of an Aaron from marrying into the Wilson family. You have no idea what a case Susie and Scales scared up during our ten days' hunt. That only leaves Dan and Theodore. But what's the use of counting the chickens so soon? You go to bed, for I'm going to send to the Mission to-morrow after the masons. There's no use in my turning in, for I won't sleep a wink to-night, thinking all this over."

CHAPTER XVIII
AN INDIAN SCARE

Near the close of January, '79, the Nueces valley was stirred by an Indian scare. I had a distinct recollection of two similar scares in my boyhood on the San Antonio River, in which I never caught a glimpse of the noble red man. But whether the rumors were groundless or not, Las Palomas set her house in order. The worst thing we had to fear was the loss of our saddle stock, as they were gentle and could be easily run off and corralled on the range by stretching lariats. At this time the ranch had some ten *remudas* including nearly five hundred saddle horses, some of them ranging ten or fifteen miles from the ranch, and on receipt of the first rumor, every *remuda* was brought in home and put under a general herd, night and day.

"These Indian scares," said Uncle Lance, "are just about as regular as drouths. When I first settled here, the Indians hunted up and down this valley every few years, but they never molested anything. Why, I got well acquainted with several bucks, and used to swap rawhide with them for buckskin. Game was so abundant then that there was no temptation to kill cattle or steal horses. But the rascals seem to be getting worse ever since. The last scare was just ten years ago next month, and kept us all guessing. The renegades were Kickapoos and came down the Frio from out west. One Sunday morning they surprised two of Waugh's vaqueros while the latter were dressing a wild hog which they had killed. The Mexicans had only one horse and one gun between them. One of them took the horse and the other took the carbine. Not daring to follow the one with the gun for fear of ambuscade, the Indians gave chase to the vaquero on horseback, whom they easily captured. After stripping him of all his clothing, they tied his hands with thongs, and pinned the poor devil to a tree with spear thrusts through the back.

"The other Mexican made his escape in the chaparral, and got back to the ranch. As it happened, there was only a man or two at Waugh's place at the time, and no attempt was made to follow the Indians, who, after killing the vaquero, went on west to Altita Creek — the one which puts into the Nueces from the north, just about twenty miles above the Ganso. Waugh had a sheep camp on the head of Altito, and there the Kickapoos killed two of his *pastors* and robbed the camp. From that creek on westward, their course was marked with murders and horse stealing, but the country was so sparsely settled that little or no resistance could be offered, and the redskins escaped without punishment. At that time they were armed with bow and arrow and spears, but I have it on good authority that all these western tribes now have firearms. The very name of Indians scares women and children, and if they should come down this river, we must keep in the open and avoid ambush, as that is an Indian's forte."

All the women and children at the outlying ranchitas were brought into headquarters, the men being left to look after the houses and their stock and flocks. In the interim, Father Norquin and the masons had arrived and the chapel was daily taking shape. But the rumors of the Indian raid thickened. Reports came in of shepherds shot with their flocks over near Espontos Lake and along the Leona River, and Las Palomas took on the air of an armed camp. Though we never ceased to ride the range wherever duty called, we went always in squads of four or five.

The first abatement of the scare took place when one evening a cavalcade of Texas Rangers reached our ranch from DeWitt County. They consisted of fifteen mounted men under Lieutenant Frank Barr, with a commissary of four pack mules. The detachment was from one of the crack companies of the state, and had with them several half-blood trailers, though every man in the squad was more or less of an expert in that line. They were traveling light, and had covered over a hundred miles during the day and a half preceding their arrival at headquarters. The hospitality of Las Palomas was theirs to command, and as their most urgent need was mounts, they were made welcome to the pick of every horse under herd. Sunrise saw our ranger guests on their way, leaving the high tension relaxed and every one on the ranch breathing easier. But the Indian scare did not prove an ill wind to the plans of Father Norquin. With the concentration of people from the ranchitas and those belonging at the home ranch, the chapel building went on by leaps and bounds. A native carpenter had been secured from Santa Maria, and the enthusiastic padre, laying aside his vestments, worked with his hands as a common laborer. The energy with which he inspired the natives made him a valuable overseer. From assisting the carpenter in hewing the rafters, to advising the masons in laying a keystone, or with his own hands mixing the mortar and tamping the earth to give firm foundation to the cement floor, he was the directing spirit. Very little lumber was used in the construction of buildings at Las Palomas. The houses were thatched with a coarse salt grass, called by the natives *zacahuiste*. Every year in the overflowed portions of the valley, great quantities of this material were cut by the native help and stored against its need. The grass sometimes grew two feet in height, and at cutting was wrapped tightly and tied in "hands" about two inches in diameter. For fastening to the roofing lath, green blades of the Spanish dagger were used, which, after being roasted over a fire to toughen the fibre, were split into thongs and bound the hands securely in a solid mass, layer upon layer like shingles. Crude as it may appear, this was a most serviceable roof, being both rain proof and impervious to heat, while, owing to its compactness, a live coal of fire laid upon it would smoulder but not ignite.

No sooner had the masons finished the plastering of the inner walls and cementing the floor, than they began on a two-roomed cottage. As its white walls arose conjecture was rife as to who was to occupy it. I made no bones of the fact that I expected to occupy a *jacal* in the near future, but denied that this was to be mine, as I had been promised one with three rooms. Out of hearing of our employer, John Cotton also religiously denied that the tiny house was for his use. Fidel, however, took the chaffing without a denial, the padre and Uncle Lance being his two worst tormentors.

During the previous visit of the padre, when the chapel was decided on, the order for the finishing material for the building had been placed with the merchant at Shepherd's, and was brought up from Corpus Christi through his freighters. We now had notice from the merchant that his teamsters had returned, and two four-mule teams went down to the ferry for the lumber, glassware, sash and doors. Miss Jean had been importuning the padre daily to know when the dedication would take place, as she was planning to invite the countryside.

"Ah, my daughter," replied the priest, "we must learn to cultivate patience. All things that abide are of slow but steady growth, and my work is for eternity. Therefore I must be an earnest servant, so that when my life's duty ends, it can be said in truth, 'Well done, thou good and faithful servant.' But I am as anxious to consecrate this building to the Master's service as any one. My good woman, if I only had a few parishioners like you, we would work wonders among these natives."

On the return of the mule teams, the completion of the building could be determined, and the padre announced the twenty-first of February as the date of dedication. On reaching this decision, the ranch was set in order for an occasion of more than ordinary moment. Fidel and Juana were impatient to be married, and the master and mistress had decided that the ceremony should be performed the day after the dedication, and all the guests of the ranch should remain for the festivities. The padre, still in command, dispatched a vaquero to the Mission, announcing the completion of the chapel, and asking for a brother priest to bring out certain vestments and assist in the dedicatory exercises. The Indian scare was subsiding, and as no word had come from the rangers confidence grew that the worst was over, so we scattered in every direction inviting guests. From the Booths on the Frio to the Wilsons of Ramirena, and along the home river as far as Lagarto, our friends were bidden in the name of the master and mistress of Las Palomas.

On my return from taking the invitations to the ranches north, the chapel was just receiving the finishing touches. The cross crowning the front glistened in fresh paint, while on the interior walls shone cheap lithographs of the Madonna and Christ. The old padre, proud and jealous as a bridegroom over his bride, directed the young friar here and there, himself standing aloof and studying with an artist's eye every effect in color and drapery. The only discordant note in the interior was the rough benches, in the building of which Father Norquin himself had worked, thus following, as he repeatedly admonished us, in the footsteps of his Master, the carpenter of Galilee.

The ceremony of dedication was to be followed by mass at high noon. Don Mateo Gonzales of Santa Maria sent his regrets, as did likewise Don Alejandro Travino of the Mission, but the other invited guests came early and stayed late. The women and children of the outlying ranchitas had not yet returned to their homes, and with our invited guests made an assembly of nearly a hundred and fifty persons. Unexpectedly, and within two hours of the appointed time for the service to commence, a cavalcade was sighted approaching the ranch from the west. As they turned in towards headquarters, some one recognized the horses, and a shout of welcome greeted our ranger guests of over two weeks before. Uncle Lance met them as if they had been expected, and invited the lieutenant and his men to dismount and remain a few days as guests of Las Palomas. When they urged the importance of continuing on their journey to report to the governor, the host replied: —

"Lieutenant Barr, that don't go here. Fall out of your saddles and borrow all the razors and white shirts on the ranch, for we need you for the dedication of a chapel to-day, and for a wedding and infare for to-morrow. We don't see you along this river as often as we'd like to, and when you do happen along in time for a peaceful duty, you can't get away so easily. If you have any special report to make to your superiors, why, write her out, and I'll send a vaquero with it to Oakville this afternoon, and it'll go north on the stage to-morrow. But, lieutenant, you mustn't think you can ride right past Las Palomas when you're not under emergency orders. Now, fall off those horses and spruce up a little, for I intend to introduce you to some as nice girls as you ever met. You may want to quit rangering some day, and I may need a man about your size, and I'm getting tired of single ones."

Lieutenant Barr surrendered. Saddles were stripped from horses, packs were unlashed from mules, and every animal was sent to our *remudas* under herd. The accoutrements were stacked inside the gate like haycocks, with slickers thrown over them; the carbines were thrown on the gallery, and from every nail, peg, or hook on the wall belts and six-shooters hung in groups. These rangers were just ordinary looking men, and might have been mistaken for an outfit of cow hands. In age they ranged from a smiling youth of twenty to grizzled men of forty, yet in every countenance was written a resolute determination. All the razors on the ranch were brought into immediate use, while every presentable shirt, collar, and tie in the house was unearthed and placed at their disposal. While arranging hasty toilets, the men informed us that when they reached Espontos Lake the redskins had left, and that they had trailed them south until the Indians had crossed the Rio Grande into Mexico several days in advance of their arrival. The usual number of isolated sheepherders killed, and of horses stolen, were the features of the raid.

The guests had been arriving all morning. The Booths had reached the ranch the night before, and the last to put in an appearance was the contingent from the Frio and San Miguel. Before the appearance of the rangers, they had been sighted across the river, and they rode up with Pierre Vaux, like a captain of the Old Guard, in the lead.

"Ah, Don Lance," he cried, "vat you tink? Dey say Don Pierre no ride fas' goin' to church. Dese youngsters laff all time and say I never get here unless de dogs is 'long. Sacré! Act all time lak I vas von ol' man. *Humbre*, keep away from dis horse; he allow nobody but me to lay von han' on him — keep away, I tol' you!"

I helped the girls to dismount, Miss Jean kissing them right and left, and bustling them off into the house to tidy up as fast as possible; for the hour was almost at hand. On catching sight of Mrs. Annear, fresh and charming in her widow's weeds, Uncle Lance brushed Don Pierre aside and cordially greeted her. Vaqueros took the horses, and as I strolled up the pathway with Esther, I noticed an upper window full of ranger faces peering down on the girls. Before this last contingent had had time to spruce up, Pasquale's eldest boy rode around all the *jacals*, ringing a small handbell to summon the population to the dedication. Outside of our home crowd, we had forty white guests, not including the two Booth children and the priests. As fast as the rangers were made presentable, the master and mistress introduced them to all the girls present. Of course, there were a few who could not be enticed near a woman, but Quayle and Happersett, like kindred spirits, took the backward ones under their wing, and the procession started for the chapel.

The audience was typical of the Texas frontier at the close of the '70's. Two priests of European birth conducted the services. Pioneer cowmen of various nationalities and their families intermingled and occupied central seats. By the side of his host, a veteran of '36, when Mexican rule was driven from the land, sat Lieutenant Barr, then engaged in accomplishing a second redemption of the state from crime and lawlessless. Lovable and esteemed men were present, who had followed the fortunes of war until the Southern flag, to which they had rallied, went down in defeat. The younger generation of men were stalwart in physique, while the girls were modest in their rustic beauty. Sitting on the cement floor on three sides of us were the natives of the ranch, civilized but with little improvement over their Aztec ancestors.

The dedicatory exercises were brief and simple. Every one was invited to remain for the celebration of the first mass in the newly consecrated building. Many who were not communicants accepted, but noticing the mistress and my sweetheart taking their leave, I joined them and assisted in arranging the tables so that all our guests could be seated at two sittings. At the conclusion of the services, dinner was waiting, and Father Norquin and Mr. Nate Wilson were asked to carve at one table, while the young friar and Lieutenant Barr, in a similar capacity, officiated at the other. There was so much volunteer help in the kitchen that I was soon excused, and joined the younger people on the gallery. As to whom Cotton and Gallup were monopolizing there was no doubt, but I had a curiosity to notice what Scales would do when placed between two fires. But not for nothing had he cultivated the acquaintance of a sandy-mustached young ranger, who was at that moment entertaining Suzanne Vaux in an alcove at the farther end of the veranda. Aaron, when returning from the chapel with Susie Wilson, had succeeded in getting no nearer the house than a clump of oak trees which sheltered an old rustic settee. And when the young folks were called in to dinner, the vagabond Scales and Miss Wilson of Ramirena had to be called the second time.

In seating the younger generation, Miss Jean showed her finesse. Nearly all the rangers had dined at the first tables, but the widow Annear waited for the second one — why, only a privileged few of us could guess. Artfully and with seeming unconsciousness on the part of every one, Deweese was placed beside the charming widow, though I had a suspicion that June was the only innocent party in the company. Captain Byler and I were carving at the same table at which our foreman and the widow were seated, and, being in the secret, I noted step by step the progress of the widow, and the signs of gradual surrender of the corporal *segundo*. I had a distinct recollection of having once smashed some earnest resolves, and of having capitulated under similar circumstances, and now being happily in love, I secretly wished success to the little god Cupid in the case in hand. And all during the afternoon and evening, it was clearly apparent to any one who cared to notice that success was very likely.

The evening was a memorable one at Las Palomas. Never before in my knowledge had the ranch had so many and such amiable guests. The rangers took kindly to our hospitality, and Father Norquin waddled about, God-blessing every one, old and young, frivolous and sedate. Owing to the nature of the services of the day, the evening was spent in conversation among the elders, while the younger element promenaded the spacious gallery, or occupied alcoves, nooks, and corners about the grounds. On retiring for the night, the men yielded the house to the women guests, sleeping on the upper and lower verandas, while the ranger contingent, scorning beds or shelter, unrolled their blankets under the spreading live-oaks in the yard.

But the real interest centred in the marriage of Fidel and Juana, which took place at six o'clock the following evening. Every one, including the native element, repaired to the new chapel to attend the wedding. Uncle Lance and his sister had rivaled each other as to whether man or maid should have the better outfit. Fidel was physically far above the average of the natives, slightly bow-legged, stolid, and the coolest person in the church. The bride was in quite a flutter, but having been coached and rehearsed daily by her mistress, managed to get through the ordeal. The young priest performed the ceremony, using his own native tongue, the rich, silvery accents of Spanish. At the conclusion of the service, every one congratulated the happy couple, the women and girls in tears, the sterner sex without demonstration of feeling. When we were outside the chapel, and waiting for our sweethearts to dry their tears and join us, Uncle Lance came swaggering' over to John Cotton and me, and, slapping us both on the back, said: —

"Boys, that rascal of a Fidel has a splendid nerve. Did you notice how he faced the guns without a tremor; never batted an eye but took his medicine like a little man. I hope both of you boys will show equally good nerve when your turn comes. Why, I doubt if there was a ranger in the whole squad, unless it was that red-headed rascal who kissed the bride, who would have stood the test like that vaquero — without a shiver. And it's something you can't get used to. Now, as you all know, I've been married three times. The first two times I was as cool as most, but the third whirl I trembled all over. Quavers ran through me, my tongue was palsied, my teeth chattered, my knees knocked together, and I felt like a man that was sent for and couldn't go. Now, mind you, it was the third time and I was only forty-five."

What a night that was! The contents of the warehouse had been shifted, native musicians had come up from Santa Maria, and every one about the home ranch who could strum a guitar was pressed into service. The storeroom was given over to the natives, and after honoring the occasion with their presence as patrons, the master and mistress, after the opening dance, withdrew in company with their guests. The night had then barely commenced. Claiming two guitarists, we soon had our guests waltzing on veranda, hall, and spacious dining-room to the music of my fiddle. Several of the rangers could play, and by taking turns every one had a joyous time, including the two priests. Among the Mexicans the dancing continued until daybreak. Shortly after midnight our guests retired, and the next morning found all, including the priests, preparing to take their departure. As was customary, we rode a short distance with our guests, bidding them again to Las Palomas and receiving similar invitations in return. With the exception of Captain Byler, the rangers were the last to take their leave. When the mules were packed and their mounts saddled, the old ranchero extended them a welcome whenever they came that way again.

"Well, now, Mr. Lovelace," said Lieutenant Barr, "you had better not press that invitation too far. The good time we have had with you discounts rangering for the State of Texas. Rest assured, sir, that we will not soon forget the hospitality of Las Palomas, nor its ability to entertain. Push on with the packs, boys, and I'll take leave of the mistress in behalf of you all, and overtake the squad before it reaches the river."

CHAPTER XIX
HORSE BRANDS

Before gathering the fillies and mares that spring, and while riding the range, locating our horse stock, Pasquale brought in word late one evening that a *ladino* stallion had killed the regular one, and was then in possession of the *manada*. The fight between the outlaw and the ranch stallion had evidently occurred above the mouth of the Ganso and several miles to the north of the home river, for he had accidentally found the carcass of the dead horse at a small lake and, recognizing the animal by his color, had immediately scoured the country in search of the band. He had finally located the *manada*, many miles off their range; but at sight of the vaquero the *ladino* usurper had deserted the mares, halting, however, out of gunshot, yet following at a safe distance as Pasquale drifted them back. Leaving the *manada* on their former range, Pasquale had ridden into the ranch and reported. It was then too late in the day to start against the interloper, as the range was fully twenty-five miles away, and we were delayed the next morning in getting up speedy saddle horses from distant and various *remudas*, and did not get away from the ranch until after dinner. But then we started, taking the usual pack mules, and provisioned for a week's outing.

Included in the party was Captain Frank Byler, the regular home crowd, and three Mexicans. With an extra saddle horse for each, we rode away merrily to declare war on the *ladino* stallion. "This is the third time since I've teen ranching here," said Uncle Lance to Captain Frank, as we rode along, "that I've had stallions killed. There always have been bands of wild horses, west here between the Leona and Nueces rivers and around Espontos Lake. Now that country is settling up, the people walk down the bands and the stallions escape, and in drifting about find our range. They're wiry rascals, and our old stallions don't stand any more show with them than a fat hog would with a *javaline*. That's why I take as much pride in killing one as I do a rattlesnake."

We made camp early that evening on the home river, opposite the range of the *manada*. Sending out Pasquale to locate the band and watch them until dark, Uncle Lance outlined his idea of circling the band and bagging the outlaw in the uncertain light of dawn. Pasquale reported on his return after dark that the *manada* were contentedly feeding on their accustomed range within three miles of camp. Pasquale had watched the band for an hour, and described the *ladino* stallion as a cinnamon-colored coyote, splendidly proportioned and unusually large for a mustang.

Naturally, in expectation of the coming sport, the horses became the topic around the campfire that night. Every man present was a born horseman, and there was a generous rivalry for the honor in telling horse stories. Aaron Scales joined the group at a fortunate time to introduce an incident from his own experience, and, raking out a coal of fire for his pipe, began: —

"The first ranch I ever worked on," said he, "was located on the Navidad in Lavaca County. It was quite a new country then, rather broken and timbered in places and full of bear and wolves. Our outfit was working some cattle before the general round-up in the spring. We wanted to move one brand to another range as soon as the grass would permit, and we were gathering them for that purpose. We had some ninety saddle horses with us to do the work, — sufficient to mount fifteen men. One night we camped in a favorite spot, and as we had no cattle to hold that night, all the horses were thrown loose, with the usual precaution of hobbling, except two or three on picket. All but about ten head wore the bracelets, and those ten were pals, their pardners wearing the hemp. Early in the evening, probably nine o'clock, with a bright fire burning, and the boys spreading down their beds for the night, suddenly the horses were heard running, and the next moment they hobbled into camp like a school of porpoise, trampling over the beds and crowding up to the fire and the wagon. They almost knocked down some of the boys, so sudden was their entrance. Then they set up a terrible nickering for mates. The boys went amongst them, and horses that were timid and shy almost caressed their riders, trembling in limb and muscle the while through fear, like a leaf. We concluded a bear had scented the camp, and in approaching it had circled round, and run amuck our saddle horses. Every horse by instinct is afraid of a bear, but more particularly a range-raised one. It's the same instinct that makes it impossible to ride or drive a range-raised horse over a rattlesnake. Well, after the boys had petted their mounts and quieted their fears, they were still reluctant to leave camp, but stood around for several hours, evidently feeling more secure in our presence. Now and then one of the free ones would graze out a little distance, cautiously sniff the air, then trot back to the others. We built up a big fire to scare away any bear or wolves that might be in the vicinity, but the horses stayed like invited guests, perfectly contented as long as we would pet them and talk to them. Some of the boys crawled under the wagon, hoping to get a little sleep, rather than spread their bed where a horse could stampede over it. Near midnight we took ropes and saddle blankets and drove them several hundred yards from camp. The rest of the night we slept with one eye open, expecting every moment to hear them take fright and return. They didn't, but at daylight every horse was within five hundred yards of the wagon, and when we unhobbled them and broke camp that morning, we had to throw riders in the lead to hold them back."

On the conclusion of Scales's experience, there was no lack of volunteers to take up the thread, though an unwritten law forbade interruptions. Our employer was among the group, and out of deference to our guest, the boys remained silent. Uncle Lance finally regaled us with an account of a fight between range stallions which he had once witnessed, and on its conclusion Theodore Quayle took his turn.

"The man I was working for once moved nearly a thousand head of mixed range stock, of which about three hundred were young mules, from the San Saba to the Concho River. It was a dry country and we were compelled to follow the McKavett and Fort Chadbourne trail. We had timed our drives so that we reached creeks once a day at least, sometimes oftener. It was the latter part of summer, and was unusually hot and drouthy. There was one drive of twenty-five miles ahead that the owner knew of without water, and we had planned this drive so as to reach it at noon, drive halfway, make a dry camp over night, and reach the pools by noon the next day. Imagine our chagrin on reaching the watering place to find the stream dry. We lost several hours riding up and down the *arroyo* in the hope of finding relief for the men, if not for the stock. It had been dusty for weeks. The cook had a little water in his keg, but only enough for drinking purposes. It was twenty miles yet to the Concho, and make it before night we must. Turning back was farther than going ahead, and the afternoon was fearfully hot. The heat waves looked like a sea of fire. The first part of the afternoon drive was a gradual ascent for fifteen miles, and then came a narrow plateau of a divide. As we reached this mesa, a sorrier-looking lot of men, horses, and mules can hardly be imagined. We had already traveled over forty miles without water for the stock, and five more lay between us and the coveted river.

"The heat was oppressive to the men, but the herd suffered most from the fine alkali dust which enveloped them. Their eyebrows and nostrils were whitened with this fine powder, while all colors merged into one. On reaching this divide, we could see the cotton-woods that outlined the stream ahead. Before we had fully crossed this watershed and begun the descent, the mules would trot along beside the riders in the lead, even permitting us to lay our hands on their backs. It was getting late in the day before the first friendly breeze of the afternoon blew softly in our faces. Then, Great Scott! what a change came over man and herd. The mules in front threw up their heads and broke into a grand chorus. Those that were strung out took up the refrain and trotted forward. The horses set up a rival concert in a higher key. They had scented the water five miles off.

"All hands except one man on each side now rode in the lead. Every once in a while, some enthusiastic mule would break through the line of horsemen, and would have to be brought back. Every time we came to an elevation where we could catch the breeze, the grand horse and mule concert would break out anew. At the last elevation between us and the water, several mules broke through, and before they could be brought back the whole herd had broken into a run which was impossible to check. We opened out then and let them go.

"The Concho was barely running, but had long, deep pools here and there, into which horses and mules plunged, dropped down, rolled over, and then got up to nicker and bray. The young mules did everything but drink, while the horses were crazy with delight. When the wagon came up we went into camp and left them to play out their hands. There was no herding to do that night, as the water would hold them as readily as a hundred men."

"Well, I'm going to hunt my blankets," said Uncle Lance, rising. "You understand, Captain, that you are to sleep with me to-night. Davy Crockett once said that the politest man he ever met in Washington simply set out the decanter and glasses, and then walked over and looked out of the window while he took a drink. Now I want to be equally polite and don't want to hurry you to sleep, but whenever you get tired of yarning, you'll find the bed with me in it to the windward of that live-oak tree top over yonder."

Captain Frank showed no inclination to accept the invitation just then, but assured his host that he would join him later. An hour or two passed by.

"Haven't you fellows gone to bed yet?" came an inquiry from out of a fallen tree top beyond the fire in a voice which we all recognized. "All right, boys, sit up all night and tell fool stories if you want to. But remember, I'll have the last rascal of you in the saddle an hour before daybreak. I have little sympathy for a man who won't sleep when he has a good chance. So if you don't turn in at all it will be all right, but you'll be routed out at three in the morning, and the man who requires a second calling will get a bucket of water in his face."

Captain Frank and several of us rose expecting to take the hint of our employer, when our good intentions were arrested by a query from Dan Happersett, "Did any of you ever walk down a wild horse?" None of us had, and we turned back and reseated ourselves in the group.

"I had a little whirl of it once when I was a youngster," said Dan, "except we didn't walk. It was well known that there were several bands of wild horses ranging in the southwest corner of Tom Green County. Those who had seen them described one band as numbering forty to fifty head with a fine chestnut stallion as a leader. Their range was well located when water was plentiful, but during certain months of the year the shallow lagoons where they watered dried up, and they were compelled to leave. It was when they were forced to go to other waters that glimpses of them were to be had, and then only at a distance of one or two miles. There was an outfit made up one spring to go out to their range and walk these horses down. This season of the year was selected, as the lagoons would be full of water and the horses would be naturally reduced in flesh and strength after the winter, as well as weak and thin blooded from their first taste of grass. We took along two wagons, one loaded with grain for our mounts. These saddle horses had been eating grain for months before we started and their flesh was firm and solid.

"We headed for the lagoons, which were known to a few of our party, and when we came within ten miles of the water holes, we saw fresh signs of a band — places where they had apparently grazed within a week. But it was the second day before we caught sight of the wild horses, and too late in the day to give them chase. They were watering at a large lake south of our camp, and we did not disturb them. We watched them until nightfall, and that night we planned to give them chase at daybreak. Four of us were to do the riding by turns, and imaginary stations were allotted to the four quarters of our camp. If they refused to leave their range and circled, we could send them at least a hundred and fifty miles the first day, ourselves riding possibly a hundred, and this riding would be divided among four horses, with plenty of fresh ones at camp for a change.

"Being the lightest rider in the party, it was decided that I was to give them the first chase. We had a crafty plainsman for our captain, and long before daylight he and I rode out and waited for the first peep of day. Before the sun had risen, we sighted the wild herd within a mile of the place where darkness had settled over them the night previous. With a few parting instructions from our captain, I rode leisurely between them and the lake where they had watered the evening before. At first sight of me they took fright and ran to a slight elevation. There they halted a moment, craning their necks and sniffing the air. This was my first fair view of the chestnut stallion. He refused to break into a gallop, and even stopped before the rest, turning defiantly on this intruder of his domain. From the course I was riding, every moment I was expecting them to catch the wind of me. Suddenly they scented me, knew me for an enemy, and with the stallion in the lead they were off to the south.

"It was an exciting ride that morning. Without a halt they ran twenty miles to the south, then turned to the left and there halted on an elevation; but a shot in the air told them that all was not well and they moved on. For an hour and a half they kept their course to the east, and at last turned to the north. This was, as we had calculated, about their range. In another hour at the farthest, a new rider with a fresh horse would take up the running. My horse was still fresh and enjoying the chase, when on a swell of the plain I made out the rider who was to relieve me; and though it was early yet in the day the mustangs had covered sixty miles to my forty. When I saw my relief locate the band, I turned and rode leisurely to camp. When the last two riders came into camp that night, they reported having left the herd at a new lake, to which the mustang had led them, some fifteen miles from our camp to the westward.

"Each day for the following week was a repetition of the first with varying incident. But each day it was plain to be seen that they were fagging fast. Toward the evening of the eighth day, the rider dared not crowd them for fear of their splitting into small bands, a thing to be avoided. On the ninth day two riders took them at a time, pushing them unmercifully but preventing them from splitting, and in the evening of this day they could be turned at the will of the riders. It was then agreed that after a half day's chase on the morrow, they could be handled with ease. By noon next day, we had driven them within a mile of our camp.

"They were tired out and we turned them into an impromptu corral made of wagons and ropes. All but the chestnut stallion. At the last he escaped us; he stopped on a little knoll and took a farewell look at his band.

"There were four old United States cavalry horses among our captive band of mustangs, gray with age and worthless — no telling where they came from. We clamped a mule shoe over the pasterns of the younger horses, tied toggles to the others, and the next morning set out on our return to the settlements."

Under his promise the old ranchero had the camp astir over an hour before dawn. Horses were brought in from picket ropes, and divided into two squads, Pasquale leading off to the windward of where the band was located at dusk previous. The rest of the men followed Uncle Lance to complete the leeward side of the circle. The location of the *manada*, had been described as between a small hill covered with Spanish bayonet on one hand, and a *zacahuiste* flat nearly a mile distant on the other, both well-known landmarks. As we rode out and approached the location, we dropped a man every half mile until the hill and adjoining salt flat had been surrounded. We had divided what rifles the ranch owned between the two squads, so that each side of the circle was armed with four guns. I had a carbine, and had been stationed about midway of the leeward half-circle. At the first sign of dawn, the signal agreed upon, a turkey call, sounded back down the line, and we advanced. The circle was fully two miles in diameter, and on receiving the signal I rode slowly forward, halting at every sound. It was a cloudy morning and dawn came late for clear vision. Several times I dismounted and in approaching objects at a distance drove my horse before me, only to find that, as light increased, I was mistaken.

When both the flat and the dagger crowned hill came into view, not a living object was in sight. I had made the calculation that, had the *manada* grazed during the night, we should be far to the leeward of the band, for it was reasonable to expect that they would feed against the wind. But there was also the possibility that the outlaw might have herded the band several miles distant during the night, and while I was meditating on this theory, a shot rang out about a mile distant and behind the hill. Giving my horse the rowel, I rode in the direction of the report; but before I reached the hill the *manada* tore around it, almost running into me. The coyote mustang was leading the band; but as I halted for a shot, he turned inward, and, the mares intervening, cut off my opportunity. But the warning shot had reached every rider on the circle, and as I plied rowel and quirt to turn the band, Tio Tiburcio cut in before me and headed them backward. As the band whirled away from us the stallion forged to the front and, by biting and a free use of his heels, attempted to turn the *manada* on their former course. But it mattered little which way they turned now, for our cordon was closing round them, the windward line then being less than a mile distant.

As the band struck the eastward or windward line of horsemen, the mares, except for the control of the stallion, would have yielded, but now, under his leadership, they recoiled like a band of *ladinos*. But every time they approached the line of the closing circle they were checked, and as the cordon closed to less than half a mile in diameter, in spite of the outlaw's lashings, the *manada* quieted down and halted. Then we unslung our carbines and rifles and slowly closed in upon the quarry. Several times the mustang stallion came to the outskirts of the band, uttering a single piercing snort, but never exposed himself for a shot. Little by little as we edged in he grew impatient, and finally trotted out boldly as if determined to forsake his harem and rush the line. But the moment he cleared the band Uncle Lance dismounted, and as he knelt the stallion stopped like a statue, gave a single challenging snort, which was answered by a rifle report, and he fell in his tracks.

CHAPTER XX
SHADOWS

Spring was now at hand after an unusually mild winter. With the breaking of the drouth of the summer before there had sprung up all through the encinal and sandy lands an immense crop of weeds, called by the natives *margoso*, fallow-weed. This plant had thriven all winter, and the cattle had forsaken the best mesquite grazing in the river bottoms to forage on it. The results showed that their instinct was true; for with very rare exceptions every beef on the ranch was fit for the butcher's block. Truly it was a year of fatness succeeding a lean one. Never during my acquaintance with Las Palomas had I seen the cattle come through a winter in such splendid condition. But now there was no market. Faint rumors reached us of trail herds being put up in near-by counties, and it was known that several large ranches in Nueces County were going to try the experiment of sending their own cattle up the trail. Lack of demand was discouraging to most ranchmen, and our range was glutted with heavy steer cattle.

The first spring work of any importance was gathering the horses to fill a contract we had with Captain Byler. Previous to the herd which Deweese had sold and delivered at Fort Worth the year before, our horse stock had amounted to about four thousand head. With the present sale the ranch holdings would be much reduced, and it was our intention to retain all *manadas* used in the breeding of mules. When we commenced gathering we worked over every one of our sixty odd bands, cutting out all the fillies and barren mares. In disposing of whole *manadas* we kept only the geldings and yearlings, throwing in the old stallions for good measure, as they would be worthless to us when separated from their harems. In less than a week's time we had made up the herd, and as they were all in the straight 'horse hoof' we did not road-brand them. While gathering them we put them under day and night herd, throwing in five *remudas* as we had agreed, but keeping back the bell mares, as they were gentle and would be useful in forming new bands of saddle horses. The day before the appointed time for the delivery, the drover brought up saddle horses and enough picked mares to make his herd number fifteen hundred.

The only unpleasant episode of the sale was a difference between Theodore Quayle and my employer. Quayle had cultivated the friendship of the drover until the latter had partially promised him a job with the herd, in case there was no objection. But when Uncle Lance learned that Theodore expected to accompany the horses, he took Captain Frank to task for attempting to entice away his men. The drover entered a strong disclaimer, maintaining that he had promised Quayle a place only in case it was satisfactory to all concerned; further, that in trail work with horses he preferred Mexican vaqueros, and had only made the conditional promise as a favor to the young man. Uncle Lance accepted the explanation and apologized to the drover, but fell on Theodore Quayle and cruelly upbraided him for forsaking the ranch without cause or reason. Theodore was speechless with humiliation, but no sooner were the hasty words spoken than my employer saw that he had grievously hurt another's feelings, and humbly craved Quayle's pardon.

The incident passed and was apparently forgotten. The herd started north on the trail on the twenty-fifth of March, Quayle stayed on at Las Palomas, and we resumed our regular spring work on the ranch. While gathering the mares and fillies, we had cut out all the geldings four years old and upward to the number of nearly two hundred, and now our usual routine of horse breaking commenced. The masons had completed their work on all three of the cottages and returned to the Mission, but the carpenter yet remained to finish up the woodwork. Fidel and Juana had begun housekeeping in their little home, and the cosy warmth which radiated from it made me impatient to see my cottage finished. Through the mistress, arrangements had been made for the front rooms in both John's cottage and mine to be floored instead of cemented.

Some two weeks before Easter Sunday, Cotton returned from the Frio, where he had been making a call on his intended. Uncle Lance at once questioned him to know if they had set the day, and was informed that the marriage would occur within ten days after Lent, and that he expected first to make a hurried trip to San Antonio for a wedding outfit.

"That's all right, John," said the old ranchero approvingly, "and I expect Quirk might as well go with you. You can both draw every cent due you, and take your time, as wages will go right on the same as if you were working. There will not be much to do except the usual horse breaking and a little repairing about the ranch. It's quite likely I shan't be able to spare Tom in the early summer, for if no cattle buyers come along soon, I'm going to send June to the coast and let him sniff around for one. I'd like the best in the world to sell about three thousand beeves, and we never had fatter ones than we have to-day. If we can make a sale, it'll keep us busy all the fore part of the summer. So both you fellows knock off any day you want to and go up to the city. And go horseback, for this ranch don't give Bethel & Oxenford's stages any more of its money."

With this encouragement, we decided to start for the city the next morning. But that evening I concluded to give a certain roan gelding a final ride before turning him over to the vaqueros. He was a vicious rascal, and after trying a hundred manoeuvres to unhorse me, reared and fell backward, and before I could free my foot from the stirrup, caught my left ankle, fracturing several of the small bones in the joint. That settled my going anywhere on horseback for a month, as the next morning I could not touch my foot to the ground. John did not like to go alone, and the mistress insisted that Theodore was well entitled to a vacation. The master consented, each was paid the wages due him, and catching up their own private horses, the old cronies started off to San Antonio. They expected to make Mr. Booth's ranch in a little over half a day, and from there a sixty-mile ride would put them in the city.

After the departure of the boys the dull routine of ranch work went heavily forward. The horse breaking continued, vaqueros rode the range looking after the calf crop, while I had to content myself with nursing a crippled foot and hobbling about on crutches. Had I been able to ride a horse, it is quite possible that a ranch on the San Miguel would have had me as its guest; but I must needs content myself with lying around the house, visiting with Juana, or watching the carpenter finishing the cottages. I tried several times to interest my mistress in a scheme to invite my sweetheart over for a week or two, but she put me off on one pretext and another until I was vexed at her lack of enthusiasm. But truth compels me to do that good woman justice, and I am now satisfied that my vexation was due to my own peevishness over my condition and not to neglect on her part. And just then she was taking such an absorbing interest in June and the widow, and likewise so sisterly a concern for Dan Happersett, that it was little wonder she could give me no special attention when I was soon to be married. It was the bird in the bush that charmed Miss Jean.

Towards the close of March a number of showers fell, and we had a week of damp, cloudy weather. This was unfortunate, as it called nearly every man from the horse breaking to ride the range and look after the young calves. One of the worst enemies of a newly born calf is screw worms, which flourish in wet weather, and prove fatal unless removed; for no young calf withstands the pest over a few days. Clear dry weather was the best preventive against screw worms, but until the present damp spell abated every man in the ranch was in the saddle from sunrise to sunset.

In the midst of this emergency work a beef buyer by the name of Wayne Orahood reached the ranch. He was representing the lessees of a steamship company plying between New Orleans and Texas coast points. The merchant at the ferry had advised Orahood to visit Las Palomas, but on his arrival about noon there was not a white man on the ranch to show him the cattle. I knew the anxiety of my employer to dispose of his matured beeves, and as the buyer was impatient there was nothing to do but get up horses and ride the range with him. Miss Jean was anxious to have the stock shown, and in spite of my lameness I ordered saddle horses for both of us. Unable to wear a boot and still hobbling on crutches, I managed to Indian mount an old horse, my left foot still too inflamed to rest in the stirrup. From the ranch we rode for the encinal ridges and sandy lands to the southeast, where the fallow-weed still throve in rank profusion, and where our heaviest steers were liable to range. By riding far from the watering points we encountered the older cattle, and within an hour after leaving the ranch I was showing some of the largest beeves on Las Palomas.

How that beef buyer did ride! Scarcely giving the cattle a passing look, he kept me leading the way from place to place where our salable stock was to be encountered. Avoiding the ranchitos and wells, where the cows and younger cattle were to be found, we circled the extreme outskirts of our range, only occasionally halting, and then but for a single glance over some prime beeves. We turned westward from the encinal at a gallop, passing about midway between Santa Maria and the home ranch. Thence we pushed on for the hills around the head of the Ganso. Not once in the entire ride did we encounter any one but a Mexican vaquero, and there was no relief for my foot in meeting him! Several times I had an inclination to ask Mr. Orahood to remember my sore ankle, and on striking the broken country I suggested we ride slower, as many of our oldest beeves ranged through these hills. This suggestion enabled me to ease up and to show our best cattle to advantage until the sun set. We were then twenty-five miles from the ranch. But neither distance nor approaching darkness checked Wayne Orahood's enthusiasm. A dozen times he remarked, "We'll look at a few more cattle, son, and then ride in home." We did finally turn homeward, and at a leisurely gait, but not until it was too dark to see cattle, and it was several hours after darkness when we sighted the lamps at headquarters, and finished the last lap in our afternoon's sixty-mile ride.

My employer and Mr. Orahood had met before, and greeted each other with a rugged cordiality common among cowmen. The others had eaten their supper; but while the buyer and I satisfied the inner man, Uncle Lance sat with us at the table and sparred with Orahood in repartee, or asked regarding mutual friends, artfully avoiding any mention of cattle. But after we had finished Mr. Orahood spoke of his mission, admitted deprecatingly that he had taken a little ride south and west that afternoon, and if it was not too much trouble he would like to look over our beeves on the north of the Nueces in the morning. He showed no enthusiasm, but acknowledged that he was buying for shipment, and thought that another month's good grass ought to put our steers in fair condition. I noticed Uncle Lance clouding up over the buyer's lack of appreciation, but he controlled himself, and when Mr. Orahood expressed a wish to retire, my employer said to his guest, as with candle in hand the two stood in parting: —

"Well, now, Wayne, that's too bad about the cattle being so thin. I've been working my horse stock lately, and didn't get any chance to ride the range until this wet spell. But since the screw worms got so bad, being short-handed, I had to get out and rustle myself or we'd lost a lot of calves. Of course, I have noticed a steer now and then, and have been sorry to find them so spring-poor. Actually, Wayne, if we were expecting company, we'd have to send to the ferry and get a piece of bacon, as I haven't seen a hoof fit to kill. That roast beef which you had for supper — well, that was sent us by a neighbor who has fat cows. About a year ago now, water was awful scarce with us, and a few old cows died up and down this valley. I suppose you didn't hear of it, living so far away. Heretofore, every time we had a drouth there was such a volunteer growth of fallow-weed that the cattle got mud fat following every dry spell. Still I'll show you a few cattle among the guajio brush and sand hills on the divide in the morning and see what you think of them. But of course, if they lack flesh, in case you are buying for shipment I shan't expect you to bid on them."

The old ranchero and the buyer rode away early the next morning, and did not return until near the middle of the afternoon, having already agreed on a sale. I was asked to write in duplicate the terms and conditions. In substance, Las Palomas ranch agreed to deliver at Rockport on the coast, on the twentieth of May, and for each of the following three months, twelve hundred and fifty beeves, four years old and upward. The consideration was $27.50 per head, payable on delivery. I knew my employer had oversold his holdings, but there would be no trouble in making up the five thousand head, as all our neighbors would gladly turn in cattle to fill the contract. The buyer was working on commission, and the larger the quantity he could contract for, the better he was suited. After the agreement had been signed in duplicate, Mr. Orahood smilingly admitted that ours were the best beeves he had bought that spring.

"I knew it," said Uncle Lance; "you don't suppose I've been ranching in this valley over forty years without knowing a fat steer when I see one. Tom, send a *muchacho* after a bundle of mint. Wayne, you haven't got a lick of sense in riding — I'm as tired as a dog."

The buyer returned to Shepherd's the next morning. The horse breaking was almost completed, except allotting them into *remudas*, assigning bell mares, and putting each band under herd for a week or ten days. The weather was fairing off, relieving the strain of riding the range, and the ranch once more relaxed into its languid existence. By a peculiar coincidence, Easter Sunday occurred on April the 13th that year, it being also the sixty-sixth birthday of the ranchero. Miss Jean usually gave a little home dinner on her brother's birthday, and had planned one for this occasion, which was but a few days distant. In the mail which had been sent for on Saturday before Easter, a letter had come from John Cotton to his employer, saying he would start home in a few days, and wanted Father Norquin sent for, as the wedding would take place on the nineteenth of the month. He also mentioned the fact that Theodore expected to spend a day or two with the Booths returning, but he would ride directly down to the Vaux ranch, and possibly the two would reach home about the same time.

I doubt if Uncle Lance ever enjoyed a happier birthday than this one. There was every reason why he should enjoy it. For a man of his age, his years rested lightly. The ranch had never been more prosperous. Even the drouth of the year before had not proved an ill wind; for the damage then sustained had been made up by conditions resulting in one of the largest sales of cattle in the history of the ranch. A chapel and three new cottages had been built without loss of time and at very little expense. A number of children had been born to the soil, while the natives were as loyal to their master as subjects in the days of feudalism. There was but one thing lacking to fill the cup to overflowing — the ranchero was childless. Possessed with a love of the land so deep as to be almost his religion, he felt the need of an heir.

"Birthdays to a man of my years," said Uncle Lance, over Easter dinner, "are food for reflection. When one nears the limit of his allotted days, and looks back over his career, there is little that satisfies. Financial success is a poor equivalent for other things. But here I am preaching when I ought to be rejoicing. Some one get John's letter and read it again. Let's see, the nineteenth falls on Saturday. Lucky day for Las Palomas! Well, we'll have the padre here, and if he says barbecue a beef, down goes the fattest one on the ranch. This is the year in which we expect to press our luck. I begin to feel it in my old bones that the turning-point has come. When Father Norquin arrives, I think I'll have him preach us a sermon on the evils of single life. But then it's hardly necessary, for most of you boys have got your eye on some girl right now. Well, hasten the day, every rascal of you, and you'll find a cottage ready at a month's notice."

The morning following Easter opened bright and clear, while on every hand were the signs of spring. A vaquero was dispatched to the Mission to summon the padre, carrying both a letter and the compliments of the ranch. Among the jobs outlined for the week was the repairing of a well, the walls of which had caved in, choking a valuable water supply with débris. This morning Deweese took a few men and went to the well, to raise the piping and make the necessary repairs, curbing being the most important. But while the foreman and Santiago Ortez were standing on a temporary platform some thirty feet down, a sudden and unexpected cave-in occurred above them. Deweese saw the danger, called to his companion, and, in a flash laid hold of a rope with which materials were being lowered. The foreman's warning to his companion reached the helpers above, and Deweese was hastily windlassed to the surface, but the unfortunate vaquero was caught by the falling debris, he and the platform being carried down into the water beneath. The body of Ortez was recovered late that evening, a coffin was made during the night, and the next morning the unfortunate man was laid in his narrow home.

The accident threw a gloom over the ranch. Yet no one dreamt that a second disaster was at hand. But the middle of the week passed without the return of either of the absent boys. Foul play began to be suspected, and meanwhile Father Norquin arrived, fully expecting to solemnize within a few days the marriage of one of the missing men. Aaron Scales was dispatched to the Vaux ranch, and returned the next morning by daybreak with the information that neither Quayle nor Cotton had been seen on the Frio recently. A vaquero was sent to the Booth ranch, who brought back the intelligence that neither of the missing boys had been seen since they passed northward some two weeks before. Father Norquin, as deeply affected as any one, returned to the Mission, unable to offer a word of consolation. Several days passed without tidings. As the days lengthened into a week, the master, as deeply mortified over the incident as if the two had been his own sons, let his suspicion fall on Quayle. And at last when light was thrown on the mystery, the old ranchero's intuition proved correct.

My injured foot improved slowly, and before I was able to resume my duties on the ranch, I rode over one day to the San Miguel for a short visit. Tony Hunter had been down to Oakville a few days before my arrival, and while there had met Clint Dansdale, who was well acquainted with Quayle and Cotton. Clint, it appeared, had been in San Antonio and met our missing men, and the three had spent a week in the city chumming together. As Dansdale was also on horseback, the trio agreed to start home the same time, traveling in company until their ways separated. Cotton had told Dansdale what business had brought him to the city, and received the latter's congratulations. The boys had decided to leave for home on the ninth, and on the morning of the day set forth, moneyless but rich in trinkets and toggery. But some where about forty miles south of San Antonio they met a trail herd of cattle from the Aransas River. Some trouble had occurred between the foreman and his men the day before, and that morning several of the latter had taken French leave. On meeting the travelers, the trail boss, being short-handed, had offered all three of them a berth. Quayle had accepted without a question. The other two had stayed all night with the herd, Dansdale attempting to dissuade Cotton, and Quayle, on the other hand, persuading him to go with the cattle. In the end Quayle's persuasions won. Dansdale admitted that the opportunity appealed strongly to him, but he refused the trail foreman's blandishments and returned to his ranch, while the two Las Palomas lads accompanied the herd, neither one knowing or caring where they were going.

When I returned home and reported this to my employer, he was visibly affected. "So that explains all," said he, "and my surmises regarding Theodore were correct. I have no particular right to charge him with ingratitude, and yet this ranch was as much his home as mine. He had the same to eat, drink, and wear as I had, with none of the concern, and yet he deserted me. I never spoke harshly to him but once, and now I wish I had let him go with Captain Byler. That would have saved me Cotton and the present disgrace to Las Palomas. I ought to have known that a good honest boy like John would be putty in the hands of a fellow like Theodore. But it's just like a fool boy to throw away his chances in life. They still sell their birthright for a mess of pottage. And there stands the empty cottage to remind me that I have something to learn. Old as I am, my temper will sometimes get away from me. Tom, you are my next hope, and I am almost afraid some unseen obstacle will arise as this one did. Does Frances know the facts?" I answered that Hunter had kept the facts to himself, not even acquainting his own people with them, so that aside from myself he was the first to know the particulars. After pacing the room for a time in meditation, Uncle Lance finally halted and asked me if Scales would be a capable messenger to carry the news to the Vaux family. I admitted that he was the most tactful man on the ranch. Aaron was summoned, given the particulars, and commanded to use the best diplomacy at his command in transmitting the facts, and to withhold nothing; to express to the ranchman and his family the deep humiliation every one at Las Palomas felt over the actions of John Cotton.

Years afterward I met Quayle at a trail town in the north. In the limited time at our command, the old days we spent together in the Nueces valley occupied most of our conversation. Unmentioned by me, his desertion of Las Palomas was introduced by himself, and in attempting to apologize for his actions, he said: —

"Quirk, that was the only dirty act I was ever guilty of. I never want to meet the people the trick was practiced on. Leaving Las Palomas was as much my privilege as going there was. But I was unfortunate enough to incur a few debts while living there that nothing but personal revenge could ever repay. Had it been any other man than Lance Lovelace, he or I would have died the morning Captain Byler's horse herd started from the Nueces River. But he was an old man, and my hand was held and my tongue was silent. You know the tricks of a certain girl who, with her foot on my neck, stretched forth a welcoming hand to a rival. Tom, I have lived to pay her my last obligation in a revenge so sweet that if I die an outcast on the roadside, all accounts are square."

CHAPTER XXI
INTERLOCUTORY PROCEEDINGS

A big summer's work lay before us. When Uncle Lance realized the permanent loss of three men from the working force of Las Palomas, he rallied to the situation. The ranch would have to run a double outfit the greater portion of the summer, and men would have to be secured to fill our ranks. White men who were willing to isolate themselves on a frontier ranch were scarce; but the natives, when properly treated, were serviceable and, where bred to the occupation and inclined to domesticity, made ideal vaqueros. My injured foot improved slowly, and as soon as I was able to ride, it fell to me to secure the extra help needed. The desertion of Quayle and Cotton had shaken my employer's confidence to a noticeable degree, and in giving me my orders to secure vaqueros, he said: —

"Tom, you take a good horse and go down the Tarancalous and engage five vaqueros. Satisfy yourself that the men are fit for the work, and hire every one by the year. If any of them are in debt, a hundred dollars is my limit of advance money to free them. And hire no man who has not a family, for I'm losing confidence every minute in single ones, especially if they are white. We have a few empty *jacals*, and the more children that I see running naked about the ranch, the better it suits me. I'll never get my money back in building that Cotton cottage until I see a mother, even though she is a Mexican, standing in the door with a baby in her arms. The older I get, the more I see my mistake in depending on the white element."

I was gone some three days in securing the needed help. It was a delicate errand, for no ranchero liked to see people leave his lands, and it was only where I found men unemployed that I applied for and secured them. We sent wagons from Las Palomas after their few effects, and had all the families contentedly housed, either about headquarters or at the outlying ranchitas, before the first contingent of beeves was gathered. But the attempt to induce any of the new families to occupy the stone cottage proved futile, as they were superstitious. There was a belief among the natives, which no persuasion could remove, regarding houses that were built for others and never occupied. The new building was tendered to Tio Tiburcio and his wife, instead of their own palisaded *jacal*, but it remained tenantless — an eyesore to its builder.

Near the latter end of April, a contract was let for two new tanks on the Ganso grant of land. Had it not been for the sale of beef, which would require our time the greater portion of the summer, it was my employer's intention to have built these reservoirs with the ranch help. But with the amount of work we had in sight, it was decided to let the contract to parties who made it their business and were outfitted for the purpose. Accordingly in company with the contractor, Uncle Lance and myself spent the last few days of the month laying off and planning the reservoir sites on two small tributaries which formed the Ganso. We were planning to locate these tanks several miles above the juncture of the small rivulets, and as far apart as possible. Then the first rainfall which would make running water, would assure us a year's supply on the extreme southwestern portion of our range. The contractor had a big outfit of oxen and mules, and the conditions called for one of the reservoirs to be completed before June 15th. Thus, if rains fell when they were expected, one receptacle at least would be in readiness.

When returning one evening from starting the work, we found Tony Hunter a guest of the ranch. He had come over for the special purpose of seeing me, but as the matter was not entirely under my control, my employer was brought into the consultation. In the docket for the May term of court, the divorce proceedings between Esther and Jack Oxenford would come up for a hearing at Oakville on the seventh of the month. Hunter was anxious, if possible, to have all his friends present at the trial. But dates were getting a little close, for our first contingent of beeves was due on the coast on the twentieth, and to gather and drive them would require not less than ten days. A cross-bill had been filed by Oxenford's attorney at the last hour, and a fight was going to be made to prevent the decree from issuing. The judge was a hold-over from the reconstruction régime, having secured his appointment through the influence of congressional friends, one of whom was the uncle of the junior stage man. Unless the statutory grounds were clear, there was a doubt expressed by Esther's attorney whether the court would grant the decree. But that was the least of Hunter's fears, for in his eyes the man who would willfully abuse a woman had no rights, in court or out. Tony, however, had enemies; for he and Oxenford had had a personal altercation, and since the separation the Martin family had taken the side of Jack's employer and severed all connections with the ranch. That the mail contractors had the village of Oakville under their control, all agreed, as we had tested that on our return from Fort Worth the spring before. In all the circumstances, though Hunter had no misgivings as to the ultimate result, yet being a witness and accused of being the main instigator in the case, he felt that he ought, as a matter of precaution, to have a friend or two with him.

"Well, now, Tony," said my employer, "this is crowding the mourners just a trifle, but Las Palomas was never called on in a good cause but she could lend a man or two, even if they had to get up from the dinner table and go hungry. I don't suppose the trial will last over a day or two at the furthest, and even if it did, the boys could ride home in the night. In our first bunch and in half a day, we'll gather every beef in two rodeos and start that evening. Steamships won't wait, and if we were a day behind time, they might want to hold out demurrage on us. If it wasn't for that, the boys could stay a week and you would be welcome to them. Of course, Tom will want to go, and about the next best man I could suggest would be June. I'd like the best in the world to go myself, but you see how I'm situated, getting these cattle off and a new tank building at the same time. Now, you boys make your own arrangements among yourselves, and this ranch stands ready to back up anything you say or do."

Tony remained overnight, and we made arrangements to meet him, either at Shepherd's the evening before or in Oakville on the morning of the trial. Owing to the behavior of Quayle and Cotton, none of us had attended the celebration of San Jacinto Day at the ferry. Nor had any one from the Vaux or McLeod ranches, for while they did not understand the situation, it was obvious that something was wrong, and they had remained away as did Las Palomas. But several of Hunter's friends from the San Miguel had been present, as likewise had Oxenford, and reports came back to the ranch of the latter's conduct and of certain threats he had made when he found there was no one present to resent them. The next morning, before starting home, Tony said to our *segundo* and myself; —

"Then I'll depend on you two, and I may have a few other friends who will want to attend. I don't need very many for a coward like Jack Oxenford. He is perfectly capable of abusing an unprotected woman, or an old man if he had a crowd of friends behind to sick him on. Oh, he's a cur all right; for when I told him that he was whelped under a house, he never resented it. He loves me all right, or has good cause to. Why, I bent the cylinder pin of a new six-shooter over his head when he had a gun on him, and he forgot to use it. I don't expect any trouble, but if you don't look a sneaking cur right in the eye, he may slip up behind and bite you."

After making arrangements to turn in two hundred beeves on our second contingent, and send a man with them to the coast, Hunter returned home. There was no special programme for the interim until gathering the beeves commenced, yet on a big ranch like Las Palomas there is always work. While Deweese finished curbing the well in which Ortez lost his life, I sawed off and cut new threads on all the rods and piping belonging to that particular windmill. With a tireless energy for one of his years, Uncle Lance rode the range, until he could have told at a distance one half his holdings of cattle by flesh marks alone. A few days before the date set for the trial, Enrique brought in word one evening that an outfit of strange men were encamped north of the river on the Ganso Tract. The vaquero was unable to make out their business, but was satisfied they were not there for pleasure, so my employer and I made an early start the next morning to see who the campers were. On the extreme northwestern corner of our range, fully twenty-five miles from headquarters, we met them and found they were a corps of engineers, running a preliminary survey for a railroad. They were in the employ of the International and Great Northern Company, which was then contemplating extending their line to some point on the Rio Grande. While there was nothing definite in this prior survey, it sounded a note of warning; for the course they were running would carry the line up the Ganso on the south side of the river, passing between the new tanks, and leaving our range through a sag in the hills on the south end of the grant. The engineer in charge very courteously informed my employer that he was under instructions to run, from San Antonio to different points on the river, three separate lines during the present summer. He also informed us that the other two preliminary surveys would be run farther west, and there was a possibility that the Las Palomas lands would be missed entirely, a prospect that was very gratifying to Uncle Lance.

"Tom," said he, as we rode away, "I've been dreading this very thing for years. It was my wish that I would never live to see the necessity of fencing our lands, and to-day a railroad survey is being run across Las Palomas. I had hoped that when I died, this valley would be an open range and as primitive as the day of my coming to it. Here a railroad threatens our peace, and the signs are on every hand that we'll have to fence to protect ourselves. But let it come, for we can't stop it. If I'm spared, within the next year, I'll secure every tract of land for sale adjoining the ranch if it costs me a dollar an acre. Then if it comes to the pinch, Las Palomas will have, for all time, land and to spare. You haven't noticed the changes in the country, but nearly all this chaparral has grown up, and the timber is twice as heavy along the river as when I first settled here. I hate the sight even of a necessity like a windmill, and God knows we have no need of a railroad. To a ranch that doesn't sell fat beeves over once in ten years, transportation is the least of its troubles."

About dusk on the evening of the day preceding the trial, June Deweese and I rode into Shepherd's, expecting to remain overnight. Shortly after our arrival, Tony Hunter hastily came in and informed us that he had been unable to get hotel accommodations for his wife and Esther in Oakville, and had it not been that they had old friends in the village, all of them would have had to return to the ferry for the night. These friends of the McLeod family told Hunter that the stage people had coerced the two hotels into refusing them, and had otherwise prejudiced the community in Oxenford's favor. Hunter had learned also that the junior member of the stage firm had collected a crowd of hangers-on, and being liberal in the use of money, had convinced the rabble of the village that he was an innocent and injured party. The attorney for Esther had arrived, and had cautioned every one interested on their side of the case to be reserved and careful under every circumstance, as they had a bitter fight on their hands.

The next morning all three of us rode into the village. Court had been in session over a week, and the sheriff had sworn in several deputies to preserve the peace, as there was considerable bitterness between litigants outside the divorce case. These under-sheriffs made it a point to see that every one put aside his arms on reaching the town, and tried as far as lay in their power to maintain the peace. During the early days of the reconstruction regime, before opening the term the presiding judge had frequently called on the state for a company of Texas Rangers to preserve order and enforce the mandates of the court. But in '79 there seemed little occasion for such a display of force, and a few fearless officers were considered sufficient. On reaching the village, we rode to the house where the women were awaiting us. Fortunately there was ample corral room at the stable, so we were independent of hostelries and liveries. Mrs. Hunter was the very reverse of her husband, being a timid woman, while poor Esther was very nervous under the dread of the coming trial. But we cheered them with our presence, and by the time court opened, they had recovered their composure.

Our party numbered four women and five men. Esther lacked several summers of being as old as her sister, while I was by five years the youngest of the men, and naturally looked to my elders for leadership. Having left our arms at the house, we entered the court-room in as decorous and well-behaved a manner as if it had been a house of worship and this a Sabbath morning. A peculiar stillness pervaded the room, which could have been mistaken as an omen of peace, or the tension similar to the lull before a battle. Personally I was composed, but as I allowed my eyes from time to time to rest upon Esther, she had never seemed so near and dear to me as in that opening hour of court. She looked very pale, and moved by the subtle power of love, I vowed that should any harm come to or any insulting word be spoken of her, my vengeance would be sure and swift.

Court convened, and the case was called. As might have been expected, the judge held that under the pleadings it was not a jury case. The panel was accordingly excused for the day, and joined those curiously inclined in the main body of the room. The complaining witnesses were called, and under direct examination the essential facts were brought forth, laying the foundation for a legal separation. The plaintiff was the last witness to testify. As she told her simple story, a hushed silence fell over the room, every spectator, from the judge on the bench to the sheriff, being eager to catch every syllable of the recital. But as in duty bound to a client, the attorney for the defendant, a young man who had come from San Antonio to conduct the case, opened a sharp cross-questioning. As the examination proceeded, an altercation between the attorneys was prevented only by the presence of the sheriff and deputies. Before the inquiry progressed, the attorney for the plaintiff apologized to the court, pleading extenuating circumstances in the offense offered to his client. Under his teachings, he informed the court, the purity of womanhood was above suspicion, and no man who wished to be acknowledged as a gentleman among his equals would impugn or question the statement of a lady. The witness on the stand was more to him than an ordinary client, as her father and himself had been young men together, had volunteered under the same flag, his friend offering up his life in its defense, and he spared to carry home the news of an unmarked grave on a Southern battle-field. It was a privilege to him to offer his assistance and counsel to-day to a daughter of an old comrade, and any one who had the temerity to offer an affront to this witness would be held to a personal account for his conduct.

The first day was consumed in taking testimony. The defense introduced much evidence in rebuttal. Without regard to the truth or their oaths, a line of witnesses were introduced who contradicted every essential point of the plaintiff's case. When the credibility of their testimony was attacked, they sought refuge in the technicalities of the law, and were supported by rulings of the presiding judge. When Oxenford took the stand in his own behalf, there were not a dozen persons present who believed the perjured statements which fell from his lips. Yet when his testimony was subjected to a rigid cross-questioning, every attempt to reach the truth precipitated a controversy between attorneys as bitter as it was personal. That the defendant at the bar had escaped prosecution for swindling the government out of large sums of money for a mail service never performed was well known to every one present, including the judge, yet he was allowed to testify against the character of a woman pure as a child, while his own past was protected from exposure by rulings from the bench.

When the evidence was all in, court adjourned until the following day. That evening our trio, after escorting the women to the home of their friend, visited every drinking resort, hotel, and public house in the village, meeting groups of Oxenford's witnesses, even himself as he dispensed good cheer to his henchmen. But no one dared to say a discourteous word, and after amusing ourselves by a few games of billiards, we mounted our horses and returned to Shepherd's for the night. As we rode along leisurely, all three of us admitted misgivings as to the result, for it was clear that the court had favored the defense. Yet we had a belief that the statutory grounds were sufficient, and on that our hopes hung.

The next morning found our party in court at the opening hour. The entire forenoon was occupied by the attorney for the plaintiff in reviewing the evidence, analyzing and weighing every particle, showing an insight into human motives which proved him a master in his profession. After the noon recess, the young lawyer from the city addressed the court for two hours, his remarks running from bombast to flights of oratory, and from eulogies upon his client to praise of the unimpeachable credibility of the witnesses for the defense. In concluding, the older lawyer prefaced his remarks by alluding to the divine intent in the institution of marriage, and contending that of the two, women were morally the better. In showing the influence of the stronger upon the weaker sex, he asserted that it was in the power of the man to lift the woman or to sink her into despair. In his peroration he rose to the occasion, and amid breathless silence, facing the court, who quailed before him, demanded whether this was a temple of justice. Replying to his own interrogatory, he dipped his brush in the sunshine of life, and sketched a throne with womanhood enshrined upon it. While chivalry existed among men, it mattered little, he said, as to the decrees of courts, for in that higher tribunal, human hearts, woman would remain forever in control. At his conclusion, women were hysterical, and men were aroused from their usual languor by the eloquence of the speaker. Had the judge rendered an adverse decision at that moment, he would have needed protection; for to the men of the South it was innate to be chivalrous to womanhood. But the court was cautious, and after announcing that he would take the case under advisement until morning, adjourned for the day.

All during the evening men stood about in small groups and discussed the trial. The consensus of opinion was favorable to the plaintiff. But in order to offset public opinion, Oxenford and a squad of followers made the rounds of the public places, offering to wager any sum of money that the decree would not be granted. Since feeling was running rather high, our little party avoided the other faction, and as we were under the necessity of riding out to the ferry for accommodation, concluded to start earlier than the evening before. After saddling, we rode around the square, and at the invitation of Deweese dismounted before a public house for a drink and a cigar before starting. We were aware that the town was against us, and to maintain a bold front was a matter of necessity. Unbuckling our belts in compliance with the sheriff's orders, we hung our six-shooters on the pommels of our saddles and entered the bar-room. Other customers were being waited on, and several minutes passed before we were served. The place was rather crowded, and as we were being waited on, a rabble of roughs surged through a rear door, led by Jack Oxenford. He walked up to within two feet of me where I stood at the counter, and apparently addressing the barkeeper, as we were charging our glasses, said in a defiant tone: —

"I'll bet a thousand dollars Judge Thornton refuses to grant a separation between my wife and me."

The words flashed through me like an electric shock, and understanding the motive, I turned on the speaker and with the palm of my hand dealt him a slap in the face that sent him staggering back into the arms of his friends. Never before or since have I felt the desire to take human life which possessed me at that instant. With no means of defense in my possession but a penknife, I backed away from him, he doing the like, and both keeping close to the bar, which was about twenty feet long. In one hand I gripped the open-bladed pocket knife, and, with the other behind my back, retreated to my end of the counter as did Oxenford to his, never taking our eyes off each other. On reaching his end of the bar, I noticed the barkeeper going through motions that looked like passing him a gun, and in the same instant some friend behind me laid the butt of a pistol in my hand behind my back. Dropping the knife, I shifted the six-shooter to my right hand, and, advancing on the object of my hate, fired in such rapid succession that I was unable to tell even whether my fire was being returned. When my gun was empty, the intervening clouds of smoke prevented any view of my adversary; but my lust for his life was only intensified when, on turning to my friends, I saw Deweese supporting Hunter in his arms. Knowing that one or the other had given me the pistol, I begged them for another to finish my work. But at that moment the smoke arose sufficiently to reveal my enemy crippling down at the farther end of the bar, a smoking pistol in his hand. As Oxenford sank to the floor, several of his friends ran to his side, and Deweese, noticing the movement, rallied the wounded man in his arms. Shaking him until his eyes opened, June, exultingly as a savage, cried, "Tony, for God's sake stand up just a moment longer. Yonder he lies. Let me carry you over so you can watch the cur die." Turning to me he continued: "Tom, you've got your man. Run for your life; don't let them get you."

Passing out of the house during the excitement, I was in my saddle in an instant, riding like a fiend for Shepherd's. The sun was nearly an hour high, and with a good horse under me, I covered the ten miles to the ferry in less than an hour. Portions of the route were sheltered by timber along the river, but once as I crossed a rise opposite a large bend, I sighted a posse in pursuit several miles to the rear. On reaching Shepherd's, fortunately for me a single horse stood at the hitch-rack. The merchant and owner of the horse came to the door as I dashed up, and never offering a word of explanation, I changed horses. Luckily the owner of the horse was Red Earnest, a friend of mine, and feeling that they would not have long to wait for explanations, I shook out the reins and gave him the rowel. I knew the country, and soon left the river road, taking an air-line course for Las Palomas, which I reached within two hours after nightfall. In few and profane words, I explained the situation to my employer, and asked for a horse that would put the Rio Grande behind me before morning. A number were on picket near by, and several of the boys ran for the best mounts available. A purse was forced into my pocket, well filled with gold. Meanwhile I had in my possession an extra six-shooter, and now that I had a moment's time to notice it, recognized the gun as belonging to Tony Hunter. Filling the empty chambers, and waving a farewell to my friends, I passed out by the rear and reached the saddle shed, where a well-known horse was being saddled by dexterous hands. Once on his back, I soon passed the eighty miles between me and the Rio Grande, which I swam on my horse the next morning within an hour after sunrise.

CHAPTER XXII
SUNSET

Of my exile of over two years in Mexico, little need be said. By easy stages, I reached the haciendas on the Rio San Juan where we had received the cows in the summer of '77. The reception extended me was all one could ask, but cooled when it appeared that my errand was one of refuge and not of business. I concealed my offense, and was given employment as corporal *segundo* over a squad of vaqueros. But while the hacienda to which I was attached was larger than Las Palomas, with greater holdings in live-stock, yet my life there was one of penal servitude. I strove to blot out past memories in the innocent pleasures of my associates, mingling in all the social festivities, dancing with the dark-eyed señoritas and gambling at every *fiesta*. Yet in the midst of the dissipation, there was ever present to my mind the thought of a girl, likewise living a life of loneliness at the mouth of the San Miguel.

During my banishment, but twice did any word or message reach me from the Nueces valley. Within a few months after my locating on the Rio San Juan, Enrique Lopez, a trusted vaquero from Las Palomas, came to the hacienda, apparently seeking employment. Recognizing me at a glance, at the first opportunity he slipped me a letter unsigned and in an unknown hand. After reading it I breathed easier, for both Hunter and Oxenford had recovered, the former having been shot through the upper lobe of a lung, while the latter had sustained three wounds, one of which resulted in the loss of an arm. The judge had reserved his decision until the recovery of both men was assured, but before the final adjournment of court, refused the decree. I had had misgivings that this would be the result, and the message warned me to remain away, as the stage company was still offering a reward for my arrest. Enrique loitered around the camp several days, and on being refused employment, made inquiry for a ranch in the south and rode away in the darkness of evening. But we had had several little chats together, in which the rascal delivered many oral messages, one of which he swore by all the saints had been intrusted to him by my own sweetheart while visiting at the ranch. But Enrique was capable of enriching any oral message, and I was compelled to read between the lines; yet I hope the saints, to whom he daily prayed, will blot out any untruthful embellishments.

The second message was given me by Frank Nancrede, early in January, '81. As was his custom, he was buying saddle horses at Las Palomas during the winter for trail purposes, when he learned of my whereabouts in Mexico. Deweese had given him directions where I could be found, and as the Rio San Juan country was noted for good horses, Nancrede and a companion rode directly from the Nueces valley to the hacienda where I was employed. They were on the lookout for a thousand saddle horses, and after buying two hundred from the ranch where I was employed, secured my services as interpreter in buying the remainder. We were less than a month in securing the number wanted, and I accompanied the herd to the Rio Grande on its way to Texas. Nancrede offered me every encouragement to leave Mexico, assuring me that Bethel & Oxenford had lost their mail contract between San Antonio and Brownsville, and were now operating in other sections of the state. He was unable to give me the particulars, but frauds had been discovered in Star Route lines, and the government had revoked nearly all the mail contracts in southern Texas. The trail boss promised me a job with any of their herds, and assured me that a cow hand of my abilities would never want a situation in the north. I was anxious to go with him, and would have done so, but felt a compunction which I did not care to broach to him, for I was satisfied he would not understand.

The summer passed, during which I made it a point to meet other drovers from Texas who were buying horses and cattle. From several sources the report of Nancrede, that the stage line south from San Antonio was now in new hands, was confirmed. One drover assured me that a national scandal had grown out of the Star Route contracts, and several officials in high authority had been arraigned for conspiracy to defraud. He further asserted that the new contractor was now carrying the mail for ten per cent, of what was formerly allowed to Bethel & Oxenford, and making money at the reduced rate. This news was encouraging, and after an exile of over two years and a half, I recrossed the Rio Grande on the same horse on which I had entered. Carefully avoiding ranches where I was known, two short rides put me in Las Palomas, reaching headquarters after nightfall, where, in seclusion, I spent a restless day and night.

A few new faces were about the ranch, but the old friends bade me a welcome and assured me that my fears were groundless. During the brief time at my disposal, Miss Jean entertained me with numerous disclosures regarding my old sweetheart. The one that both pleased and interested me was that she was contented and happy, and that her resignation was due to religious faith. According to my hostess's story, a camp meeting had been held at Shepherd's during the fall after my banishment, by a sect calling themselves Predestinarians. I have since learned that a belief in a predetermined state is entertained by a great many good people, and I admit it seems as if fate had ordained that Esther McLeod and I should never wed. But it was a great satisfaction to know that she felt resigned and could draw solace from a spiritual source, even though the same was denied to me. During the last meeting between Esther and Miss Jean, but a few weeks before, the former had confessed that there was now no hope of our ever marrying.

As I had not seen my parents for several years, I continued my journey to my old home on the San Antonio River. Leaving Las Palomas after nightfall, I passed the McLeod ranch after midnight. Halting my horse to rest, I reviewed the past, and the best reasoning at my command showed nothing encouraging on the horizon. That Esther had sought consolation from a spiritual source did not discourage me; for, under my observation, where it had been put to the test, the love of man and wife overrode it. But to expect this contented girl to renounce her faith and become my wife, was expecting her to share with me nothing, unless it was the chance of a felon's cell, and I remounted my horse and rode away under a starry sky, somewhat of a fatalist myself. But I derived contentment from my decision, and on reaching home no one could have told that I had loved and lost. My parents were delighted to see me after my extended absence, my sisters were growing fast into womanhood, and I was bidden the welcome of a prodigal son. During this visit a new avenue in life opened before me, and through the influence of my eldest brother I secured a situation with a drover and followed the cattle trail until the occupation became a lost one. My last visit to Las Palomas was during the winter of 1894-95. It lacked but a few months of twenty years since my advent in the Nueces valley. After the death of Oxenford by small-pox, I had been a frequent visitor at the ranch, business of one nature and another calling me there. But in this last visit, the wonderful changes which two decades had wrought in the country visibly impressed me, and I detected a note of decay in the old ranch. A railroad had been built, passing within ten miles of the western boundary line of the Ganso grant. The Las Palomas range had been fenced, several large tracts of land being added after my severing active connections with the ranch. Even the cattle, in spite of all the efforts made for their improvement, were not so good as in the old days of the open range, or before there was a strand of wire between the Nueces and Rio Grande rivers. But the alterations in the country were nothing compared to the changes in my old master and mistress. Uncle Lance was nearing his eighty-second birthday, physically feeble, but mentally as active as the first morning of our long acquaintance. Miss Jean, over twenty years the junior of the ranchero, had mellowed into a ripeness consistent with her days, and in all my aimless wanderings I never saw a brother and sister of their ages more devoted to, or dependent on each other.

On the occasion of this past visit, I was in the employ of a live-stock commission firm. A member of our house expected to attend the cattle convention at Forth Worth in the near future, and I had been sent into the range sections to note the conditions of stock and solicit for my employers. The spring before, our firm had placed sixty thousand cattle for customers. Demand continued, and the house had inquiry sufficient to justify them in sending me out to secure, of all ages, not less than a hundred thousand steer cattle. And thus once more I found myself a guest of Las Palomos.

"Don't talk cattle to me," said Uncle Lance, when I mentioned my business; "go to June — he'll give you the ages and numbers. And whatever you do, Tom, don't oversell us, for wire fences have cut us off, until it seems like old friends don't want to neighbor any more. In the days of the open range, I used to sell every hoof I had a chance to, but since then things have changed. Why, only last year a jury indicted a young man below here on the river for mavericking a yearling, and sent him to Huntsville for five years. That's a fair sample of these modern days. There isn't a cowman in Texas to-day who amounts to a pinch of snuff, but got his start the same way, but if a poor fellow looks out of the corner of his eye now at a critter, they imagine he wants to steal it. Oh, I know them; and the bigger rustlers they were themselves on the open range, the bitterer their persecution of the man who follows their example."

June Deweese was then the active manager of the ranch, and after securing a classification of their salable stock, I made out a memorandum and secured authority in writing, to sell their holdings at prevailing prices for Nueces river cattle. The remainder of the day was spent with my old friends in a social visit, and as we delved into the musty past, the old man's love of the land and his matchmaking instincts constantly cropped out.

"Tom," said he, in answer to a remark of mine, "I was an awful fool to think my experience could be of any use to you boys. Every last rascal of you went off on the trail and left me here with a big ranch to handle. Gallup was no better than the rest, for he kept Jule Wilson waiting until now she's an old maid. Sis, here, always called Scales a vagabond, but I still believe something could have been made of him with a little encouragement. But when the exodus of the cattle to the north was at its height, he went off with a trail herd just like the rest of you. Then he followed the trail towns as a gambler, saved money, and after the cattle driving ended, married an adventuress, and that's the end of him. The lack of a market was one of the great drawbacks to ranching, but when the trail took every hoof we could breed and every horse we could spare, it also took my boys. Tom, when you get old, you'll understand that all is vanity and vexation of spirit. But I am perfectly resigned now. In my will, Las Palomas and everything I have goes to Jean. She can dispose of it as she sees fit, and if I knew she was going to leave it to Father Norquin or his successor, my finger wouldn't be raised to stop it. I spent a lifetime of hard work acquiring this land, and now that there is no one to care for the old ranch, I wash my hands of it."

Knowing the lifetime of self-sacrifice in securing the land of Las Palomas, I sympathized with the old ranchero in his despondency.

"I never blamed you much, Tom," he resumed after a silence; "but there's something about cattle life which I can't explain. It seems to disqualify a man for ever making a good citizen afterward. He roams and runs around, wasting his youth, and gets so foxy he never marries."

"But June and the widow made the riffle finally," I protested.

"Yes, they did, and that's something to the good, but they never had any children. Waited ten years after Annear was killed, and then got married. That was one of Jean's matches. Tom, you must go over and see Juana before you go. There was a match that I made. Just think of it, they have eight children, and Fidel is prouder over them than I ever was of this ranch. The natives have never disappointed me, but the Caucasian seems to be played out."

I remained overnight at the ranch. After supper, sitting in his chair before a cheerful fire, Uncle Lance dozed off to sleep, leaving his sister and myself to entertain each other. I had little to say of my past, and the future was not encouraging, except there was always work to do. But Miss Jean unfolded like the pages of an absorbing chronicle, and gave me the history of my old acquaintances in the valley. Only a few of the girls had married. Frances Vaux, after flirting away her youth, had taken the veil in one of the orders in her church. My old sweetheart was contentedly living a life of seclusion on the ranch on which she was born, apparently happy, but still interested in any word of me in my wanderings. The young men of my acquaintance, except where married, were scattered wide, the whereabouts of nearly all of them unknown. Tony Hunter had held the McLeod estate together, and it had prospered exceedingly under his management. My old friend, Red Earnest, who outrode me in the relay race at the tournament in June, '77, was married and serving in the Customs Service on the Rio Grande as a mounted river guard.

The next morning, I made the round of the Mexican quarters, greeting my old friends, before taking my leave and starting for the railroad. The cottage which had been built for Esther and me stood vacant and windowless, being used only for a storehouse for *zacahuiste*. As I rode away, the sight oppressed me; it brought back the June time of my youth, even the hour and instant in which our paths separated. On reaching the last swell of ground, several miles from the ranch, which would give me a glimpse of headquarters, I halted my horse in a farewell view. The sleepy old ranch cosily nestled among the encinal oaks revived a hundred memories, some sad, some happy, many of which have returned in retrospect during lonely hours since.

The Outlet

PREFACE

At the close of the civil war the need for a market for the surplus cattle of Texas was as urgent as it was general. There had been numerous experiments in seeking an outlet, and there is authority for the statement that in 1857 Texas cattle were driven to Illinois. Eleven years later forty thousand head were sent to the mouth of Red River in Louisiana, shipped by boat to Cairo, Illinois, and thence inland by rail. Fever resulted, and the experiment was never repeated. To the west of Texas stretched a forbidding desert, while on the other hand, nearly every drive to Louisiana resulted in financial disaster to the drover. The republic of Mexico, on the south, afforded no relief, as it was likewise overrun with a surplus of its own breeding. Immediately before and just after the war, a slight trade had sprung up in cattle between eastern points on Red River and Baxter Springs, in the southeast corner of Kansas. The route was perfectly feasible, being short and entirely within the reservations of the Choctaws and Cherokees, civilized Indians. This was the only route to the north; for farther to the westward was the home of the buffalo and the unconquered, nomadic tribes. A writer on that day, Mr. Emerson Hough, an acceptable authority, says: "The civil war stopped almost all plans to market the range cattle, and the close of that war found the vast grazing lands of Texas fairly covered with millions of cattle which had no actual or determinate value. They were sorted and branded and herded after a fashion, but neither they nor their increase could be converted into anything but more cattle. The demand for a market became imperative."

This was the situation at the close of the '50's and meanwhile there had been no cessation in trying to find an outlet for the constantly increasing herds. Civilization was sweeping westward by leaps and bounds, and during the latter part of the '60's and early '70's, a market for a very small percentage of the surplus was established at Abilene, Ellsworth, and Wichita, being confined almost exclusively to the state of Kansas. But this outlet, slight as it was, developed the fact that the transplanted Texas steer, after a winter in the north, took on flesh like a native, and by being double-wintered became a marketable beef. It should be understood in this connection that Texas, owing to climatic conditions, did not mature an animal into marketable form, ready for the butcher's block. Yet it was an exceptional country for breeding, the percentage of increase in good years reaching the phenomenal figures of ninety-five calves to the hundred cows. At this time all eyes were turned to the new Northwest, which was then looked upon as the country that would at last afford the proper market. Railroads were pushing into the domain of the buffalo and Indian; the rush of emigration was westward, and the Texan was clamoring for an outlet for his cattle. It was written in the stars that the Indian and buffalo would have to stand aside.

Philanthropists may deplore the destruction of the American bison, yet it was inevitable. Possibly it is not commonly known that the general government had under consideration the sending of its own troops to destroy the buffalo. Yet it is a fact, for the army in the West fully realized the futility of subjugating the Indians while they could draw subsistence from the bison. The well-mounted aborigines hung on the flanks of the great buffalo herds, migrating with them, spurning all treaty obligations, and when opportunity offered murdering the advance guard of civilization with the fiendish atrocity of carnivorous animals. But while the government hesitated, the hide-hunters and the railroads solved the problem, and the Indian's base of supplies was destroyed.

Then began the great exodus of Texas cattle. The red men were easily confined on reservations, and the vacated country in the Northwest became cattle ranges. The government was in the market for large quantities of beef with which to feed its army and Indian wards. The maximum year's drive was reached in 1884, when nearly eight hundred thousand cattle, in something over three hundred herds, bound for the new Northwest, crossed Red River, the northern boundary of Texas. Some slight idea of this exodus can be gained when one considers that in the above year about four thousand men and over thirty thousand horses were required on the trail, while the value of the drive ran into millions. The history of the world can show no pastoral movement in comparison. The Northwest had furnished the market — the outlet for Texas.

CHAPTER I
OPENING THE CAMPAIGN

"Well, gentlemen, if that is the best rate you can offer us, then we'll drive the cattle. My boys have all been over the trail before, and your figures are no inducement to ship as far as Red River. We are fully aware of the nature of the country, but we can deliver the herds at their destination for less than you ask us for shipping them one third of the distance. No; we'll drive all the way."

The speaker was Don Lovell, a trail drover, and the parties addressed were the general freight agents of three railroad lines operating in Texas. A conference had been agreed upon, and we had come in by train from the ranch in Medina County to attend the meeting in San Antonio. The railroad representatives were shrewd, affable gentlemen, and presented an array of facts hard to overcome. They were well aware of the obstacles to be encountered in the arid, western portion of the state, and magnified every possibility into a stern reality. Unrolling a large state map upon the table, around which the principals were sitting, the agent of the Denver and Fort Worth traced the trail from Buffalo Gap to Doan's Crossing on Red River. Producing what was declared to be a report of the immigration agent of his line, he showed by statistics that whole counties through which the old trail ran had recently been settled up by Scandinavian immigrants. The representative of the Missouri, Kansas, and Texas, when opportunity offered, enumerated every disaster which had happened to any herd to the westward of his line in the past five years. The factor of the International was equally well posted.

"Now, Mr. Lovell," said he, dumping a bundle of papers on the table, "if you will kindly glance over these documents, I think I can convince you that it is only a question of a few years until all trail cattle will ship the greater portion of the way. Here is a tabulated statement up to and including the year '83. From twenty counties tributary to our line and south of this city, you will notice that in '80 we practically handled no cattle intended for the trail. Passing on to the next season's drive, you see we secured a little over ten per cent. of the cattle and nearly thirty per cent. of the horse stock. Last year, or for '83, drovers took advantage of our low rates for Red River points, and the percentage ran up to twenty-four and a fraction, or practically speaking, one fourth of the total drive. We are able to offer the same low rates this year, and all arrangements are completed with our connecting lines to give live-stock trains carrying trail cattle a passenger schedule. Now, if you care to look over this correspondence, you will notice that we have inquiries which will tax our carrying capacity to its utmost. The 'Laurel Leaf' and 'Running W' people alone have asked for a rate on thirty thousand head."

But the drover brushed the correspondence aside, and asked for the possible feed bills. A blanket rate had been given on the entire shipment from that city, or any point south, to Wichita Falls, with one rest and feed. Making a memorandum of the items, Lovell arose from the table and came over to where Jim Flood and I were searching for Fort Buford on a large wall map. We were both laboring under the impression that it was in Montana, but after our employer pointed it out to us at the mouth of the Yellowstone in Dakota, all three of us adjourned to an ante-room. Flood was the best posted trail foreman in Don Lovell's employ, and taking seats at the table, we soon reduced the proposed shipping expense to a pro-rata sum per head. The result was not to be considered, and on returning to the main office, our employer, as already expressed, declined the proffered rate.

Then the freight men doubled on him, asking if he had taken into consideration a saving in wages. In a two days' run they would lay down the cattle farther on their way than we could possibly drive in six weeks, even if the country was open, not to say anything about the wear and tear of horseflesh. But Don Lovell had not been a trail drover for nearly fifteen years without understanding his business as well as the freight agents did theirs. After going over a large lot of other important data, our employer arose to take his leave, when the agent of the local line expressed a hope that Mr. Lovell would reconsider his decision before spring opened, and send his drive a portion of the way by rail.

"Well, I'm glad I met you, gentlemen," said the cowman at parting, "but this is purely a business proposition, and you and I look at it from different viewpoints. At the rate you offer, it will cost me one dollar and seventy-five cents to lay a steer down on Red River. Hold on; mine are all large beeves; and I must mount my men just the same as if they trailed all the way. Saddle horses were worth nothing in the North last year, and I kept mine and bought enough others around Dodge to make up a thousand head, and sent them back over the trail to my ranch. Now, it will take six carloads of horses for each herd, and I propose to charge the freight on them against the cattle. I may have to winter my remudas in the North, or drive them home again, and if I put two dollars a head freight in them, they won't bring a cent more on that account. With the cattle it's different; they are all under contract, but the horses must be charged as general expense, and if nothing is realized out of them, the herd must pay the fiddler. My largest delivery is a sub-contract for Fort Buford, calling for five million pounds of beef on foot. It will take three herds or ten thousand cattle to fill it. I was anxious to give those Buford beeves an early start, and that was the main reason in my consenting to this conference. I have three other earlier deliveries at Indian agencies, but they are not as far north by several hundred miles, and it's immaterial whether we ship or not. But the Buford contract sets the day of delivery for September 15, and it's going to take close figuring to make a cent. The main contractors are all right, but I'm the one that's got to scratch his head and figure close and see that there's no leakages. Your freight bill alone would be a nice profit. It may cost us a little for water getting out of Texas, but with the present outlet for cattle, it's bad policy to harass the herds. Water is about the best crop some of those settlers along the trail have to sell, and they ought to treat us right."

After the conference was over, we scattered about the city, on various errands, expecting to take the night train home. It was then the middle of February, and five of the six herds were already purchased. In spite of the large numbers of cattle which the trail had absorbed in previous years, there was still an abundance of all ages, anxious for a market. The demand in the North had constantly been for young cattle, leaving the matured steers at home. Had Mr. Lovell's contracts that year called for forty thousand five and six year old beeves, instead of twenty, there would have been the same inexhaustible supply from which to pick and choose. But with only one herd yet to secure, and ample offerings on every hand, there was no necessity for a hurry. Many of the herds driven the year before found no sale, and were compelled to winter in the North at the drover's risk. In the early spring of '84, there was a decided lull over the enthusiasm of the two previous years, during the former of which the trail afforded an outlet for nearly seven hundred thousand Texas cattle.

In regard to horses we were well outfitted. During the summer of '83, Don Lovell had driven four herds, two on Indian contract and two of younger cattle on speculation. Of the latter, one was sold in Dodge for delivery on the Purgatory River in southern Colorado, while the other went to Ogalalla, and was disposed of and received at that point. In both cases there was no chance to sell the saddle horses, and they returned to Dodge and were sent to pasture down the river in the settlements. My brother, Bob Quirk, had driven one of the other herds to an agency in the Indian Territory. After making the delivery, early in August, on his employer's orders, he had brought his remuda and outfit into Dodge, the horses being also sent to pasture and the men home to Texas. I had made the trip that year to the Pine Ridge Agency in Dakota with thirty-five hundred beeves, under Flood as foreman. Don Lovell was present at the delivery, and as there was no hope of effecting a sale of the saddle stock among the Indians, after delivering the outfit at the nearest railroad, I was given two men and the cook, and started back over the trail for Dodge with the remuda. The wagon was a drawback, but on reaching Ogalalla, an emigrant outfit offered me a fair price for the mules and commissary, and I sold them. Lashing our rations and blankets on two pack-horses, we turned our backs on the Platte and crossed the Arkansaw at Dodge on the seventh day.

But instead of the remainder of the trip home by rail, as we fondly expected, the programme had changed. Lovell and Flood had arrived in Dodge some ten days before, and looking over the situation, had come to the conclusion it was useless even to offer our remudas. As remnants of that year's drive, there had concentrated in and around that market something like ten thousand saddle horses. Many of these were from central and north Texas, larger and better stock than ours, even though care had been used in selecting the latter. So on their arrival, instead of making any effort to dispose of our own, the drover and his foreman had sized up the congested condition of the market, and turned buyers. They had bought two whole remudas, and picked over five or six others until their purchases amounted to over five hundred head. Consequently on our reaching Dodge with the Pine Ridge horses, I was informed that they were going to send all the saddle stock back over the trail to the ranch and that I was to have charge of the herd. Had the trip been in the spring and the other way, I certainly would have felt elated over my promotion. Our beef herd that year had been put up in Dimmit County, and from there to the Pine Ridge Agency and back to the ranch would certainly be a summer's work to gratify an ordinary ambition.

In the mean time and before our arrival, Flood had brought up all the stock and wagons from the settlement, and established a camp on Mulberry Creek, south of Dodge on the trail. He had picked up two Texans who were anxious to see their homes once more, and the next day at noon we started. The herd numbered a thousand and sixty head, twenty of which were work-mules. The commissary which was to accompany us was laden principally with harness; and waving Flood farewell, we turned homeward, leaving behind unsold of that year's drive only two wagons. Lovell had instructed us never to ride the same horse twice, and wherever good grass and water were encountered, to kill as much time as possible. My employer was enthusiastic over the idea, and well he might be, for a finer lot of saddle horses were not in the possession of any trail drover, while those purchased in Dodge could have been resold in San Antonio at a nice profit. Many of the horses had run idle several months and were in fine condition. With the allowance of four men and a cook, a draft-book for personal expenses, and over a thousand horses from which to choose a mount, I felt like an embryo foreman, even if it was a back track and the drag end of the season. Turning everything scot free at night, we reached the ranch in old Medina in six weeks, actually traveling about forty days.

But now, with the opening of the trail season almost at hand, the trials of past years were forgotten in the enthusiasm of the present. I had a distinct recollection of numerous resolves made on rainy nights, while holding a drifting herd, that this was positively my last trip over the trail. Now, however, after a winter of idleness, my worst fear was that I might be left at home with the ranch work, and thus miss the season's outing entirely. There were new charms in the Buford contract which thrilled me, — its numerical requirements, the sight of the Yellowstone again, and more, to be present at the largest delivery of the year to the government. Rather than have missed the trip, I would have gladly cooked or wrangled the horses for one of the outfits.

On separating, Lovell urged his foreman and myself to be at the depot in good time to catch our train. That our employer's contracts for the year would require financial assistance, both of us were fully aware. The credit of Don Lovell was gilt edge, not that he was a wealthy cowman, but the banks and moneyed men of the city recognized his business ability. Nearly every year since he began driving cattle, assistance had been extended him, but the promptness with which he had always met his obligations made his patronage desirable.

Flood and I had a number of errands to look after for the boys on the ranch and ourselves, and, like countrymen, reached the depot fully an hour before the train was due. Not possessed of enough gumption to inquire if the westbound was on time, we loitered around until some other passengers informed us that it was late. Just as we were on the point of starting back to town, Lovell drove up in a hack, and the three of us paced the platform until the arrival of the belated train.

"Well, boys, everything looks serene," said our employer, when we had walked to the farther end of the depot. "I can get all the money I need, even if we shipped part way, which I don't intend to do. The banks admit that cattle are a slow sale and a shade lower this spring, and are not as free with their money as a year or two ago. My bankers detained me over an hour until they could send for a customer who claimed to have a very fine lot of beeves for sale in Lasalle County. That he is anxious to sell there is no doubt, for he offered them to me on my own time, and agrees to meet any one's prices. I half promised to come back next week and go down with him to Lasalle and look his cattle over. If they show up right, there will be no trouble in buying them, which will complete our purchases. It is my intention, Jim, to give you the herd to fill our earliest delivery. Our next two occur so near together that you will have to represent me at one of them. The Buford cattle, being the last by a few weeks, we will both go up there and see it over with. There are about half a dozen trail foremen anxious for the two other herds, and while they are good men, I don't know of any good reason for not pushing my own boys forward. I have already decided to give Dave Sponsilier and Quince Forrest two of the Buford herds, and I reckon, Tom, the last one will fall to you."

The darkness in which we were standing shielded my egotism from public view. But I am conscious that I threw out my brisket several inches and stood straight on my bow-legs as I thanked old man Don for the foremanship of his sixth herd. Flood was amused, and told me afterward that my language was extravagant. There is an old superstition that if a man ever drinks out of the Rio Grande, it matters not where he roams afterward, he is certain to come back to her banks again. I had watered my horse in the Yellowstone in '82, and ever afterward felt an itching to see her again. And here the opportunity opened before me, not as a common cow-hand, but as a trail boss and one of three in filling a five million pound government beef contract! But it was dark and I was afoot, and if I was a trifle "chesty," there had suddenly come new colorings to my narrow world.

On the arrival of the train, several other westward-bound cowmen boarded it. We all took seats in the smoker, it being but a two hours' run to our destination. Flood and I were sitting well forward in the car, the former almost as elated over my good fortune as myself. "Well, won't old Quince be all puffed up," said Jim to me, "when the old man tells him he's to have a herd. Now, I've never said a word in favor of either one of you. Of course, when Mr. Lovell asked me if I knew certain trail foremen who were liable to be idle this year, I intimated that he had plenty of material in his employ to make a few of his own. The old man may be a trifle slow on reaching a decision, but once he makes up his mind, he's there till the cows come home. Now, all you and Quince need to do is to make good, for you couldn't ask for a better man behind you. In making up your outfit, you want to know every man you hire, and give a preference to gray hairs, for they're not so liable to admire their shadow in sunny or get homesick in falling weather. Tom, where you made a ten-strike with the old man was in accepting that horse herd at Dodge last fall. Had you made a whine or whimper then, the chances are you wouldn't be bossing a herd this year. Lovell is a cowman who likes to see a fellow take his medicine with a smile."

CHAPTER II
ORGANIZING THE FORCES

Don Lovell and Jim Flood returned from Lasalle County on the last day of February. They had spent a week along the Upper Nueces, and before returning to the ranch closed a trade on thirty-four hundred five and six year old beeves. According to their report, the cattle along the river had wintered in fine condition, and the grass had already started in the valley. This last purchase concluded the buying for trail purposes, and all absent foremen were notified to be on hand at the ranch on March 10, for the beginning of active operations. Only some ten of us had wintered at headquarters in Medina County, and as about ninety men would be required for the season's work, they would have to be secured elsewhere. All the old foremen expected to use the greater portion of the men who were in their employ the year before, and could summon them on a few days' notice. But Forrest and myself were compelled to hire entirely new outfits, and it was high time we were looking up our help.

One of Flood's regular outfit had married during the winter, and with Forrest's and my promotion, he had only to secure three new men. He had dozens of applications from good cow-hands, and after selecting for himself offered the others to Quince and me. But my brother Bob arrived at the ranch, from our home in Karnes County, two days later, having also a surplus of men at his command. Although he did not show any enthusiasm over my promotion, he offered to help me get up a good outfit of boys. I had about half a dozen good fellows in view, and on Bob's approval of them, he selected from his overplus six more as first choice and four as second. It would take me a week of constant riding to see all these men, and as Flood and Forrest had made up an outfit for the latter from the former's available list, Quince and I saddled up and rode away to hire outfits. Forrest was well acquainted in Wilson, where Lovell had put up several trail herds, and as it joined my home county, we bore each other company the first day.

A long ride brought us to the Atascosa, where we stayed all night. The next morning we separated, Quince bearing due east for Floresville, while I continued southeast towards my home near Cibollo Ford on the San Antonio River. It had been over a year since I had seen the family, and on reaching the ranch, my father gruffly noticed me, but my mother and sisters received me with open arms. I was a mature man of twenty-eight at the time, mustached, and stood six feet to a plumb-line. The family were cognizant of my checkered past, and although never mentioning it, it seemed as if my misfortunes had elevated me in the estimation of my sisters, while to my mother I had become doubly dear.

During the time spent in that vicinity, I managed to reach home at night as often as possible. Constantly using fresh horses, I covered a wide circle of country, making one ride down the river into Goliad County of over fifty miles, returning the next day. Within a week I had made up my outfit, including the horse-wrangler and cook. Some of the men were ten years my senior, while only a few were younger, but I knew that these latter had made the trip before and were as reliable as their elders. The wages promised that year were fifty dollars a month, the men to furnish only their own saddles and blankets, and at that figure I picked two pastoral counties, every man bred to the occupation. The trip promised six months' work with return passage, and I urged every one employed to make his appearance at headquarters, in Medina, on or before the 15th of the month. There was no railroad communication through Karnes and Goliad counties at that time, and all the boys were assured that their private horses would have good pasturage at the home ranch while they were away, and I advised them all to come on horseback. By this method they would have a fresh horse awaiting them on their return from the North with which to continue their homeward journey. All the men engaged were unmarried, and taken as a whole, I flattered myself on having secured a crack outfit.

I was in a hurry to get back to the ranch. There had been nothing said about the remudas before leaving, and while we had an abundance of horses, no one knew them better than I did. For that reason I wanted to be present when their allotment was made, for I knew that every foreman would try to get the best mounts, and I did not propose to stand behind the door and take the culls. Many of the horses had not had a saddle on them in eight months, while all of them had run idle during the winter in a large mesquite pasture and were in fine condition with the opening of spring. So bidding my folks farewell, I saddled at noon and took a cross-country course for the ranch, covering the hundred and odd miles in a day and a half. Reaching headquarters late at night, I found that active preparations had been going on during my absence. There were new wagons to rig, harness to oil, and a carpenter was then at work building chuck-boxes for each of the six commissaries. A wholesale house in the city had shipped out a stock of staple supplies, almost large enough to start a store. There were whole coils of new rope of various sizes, from lariats to corral cables, and a sufficient amount of the largest size to make a stack of hobbles as large as a haycock. Four new branding-irons to the wagon, the regulation "Circle Dot," completed the main essentials.

All the foremen had reported at the ranch, with the exception of Forrest, who came in the next evening with three men. The division of the horses had not even come up for discussion, but several of the boys about headquarters who were friendly to my interests posted me that the older foremen were going to claim first choice. Archie Tolleston, next to Jim Flood in seniority in Lovell's employ, had spent every day riding among the horses, and had even boasted that he expected to claim fifteen of the best for his own saddle. Flood was not so particular, as his destination was in southern Dakota, but my brother Bob was again ticketed for the Crow Agency in Montana, and would naturally expect a good remuda. Tolleston was going to western Wyoming, while the Fort Buford cattle were a two-weeks' later delivery and fully five hundred miles farther travel. On my return Lovell was in the city, but I felt positive that if he took a hand in the division, Tolleston would only run on the rope once.

A few days before the appointed time, the men began thronging into headquarters. Down to the minutest detail about the wagons and mule teams, everything was shipshape. The commissary department was stocked for a month, and everything was ready to harness in and move. Lovell's headquarters was a stag ranch, and as fast as the engaged cooks reported, they were assigned to wagons, and kept open house in relieving the home cocinero. In the absence of our employer, Flood was virtually at the head of affairs, and artfully postponed the division of horses until the last moment. My outfit had all come in in good time, and we were simply resting on our oars until the return of old man Don from San Antonio. The men were jubilant and light-hearted as a lot of school-boys, and with the exception of a feeling of jealousy among the foremen over the remudas, we were a gay crowd, turning night into day. But on the return of our employer, all frivolity ceased, and the ranch stood at attention. The only unfinished work was the division of the horses, and but a single day remained before the agreed time for starting. Jim Flood had met his employer at the station the night before, and while returning to the ranch, the two discussed the apportionment of the saddle stock. The next morning all the foremen were called together, when the drover said to his trail bosses:

"Boys, I suppose you are all anxious to get a good remuda for this summer's trip. Well, I've got them for you. The only question is, how can we distribute them equitably so that all interests will be protected. One herd may not have near the distance to travel that the others have. It would look unjust to give it the best horses, and yet it may have the most trouble. Our remudas last year were all picked animals. They had an easy year's work. With the exception of a few head, we have the same mounts and in much better condition than last year. This is about my idea of equalizing things. You four old foremen will use your remudas of last year. Then each of you six bosses select twenty-five head each of the Dodge horses, — turn and turn about. Add those to your old remudas, and cull back your surplus, allowing ten to the man, twelve to the foreman, and five extra to each herd in case of cripples or of galled backs. By this method, each herd will have two dozen prime saddlers, the pick of a thousand picked ones, and fit for any man who was ever in my employ. I'm breaking in two new foremen this year, and they shall have no excuse for not being mounted, and will divide the remainder. Now, take four men apiece and round up the saddle stock, and have everything in shape to go into camp to-night. I'll be present at the division, and I warn you all that I want no clashing."

A ranch remuda was driven in, and we saddled. There were about thirty thousand acres in the pasture, and by eleven o'clock everything was thrown together. The private horses of all the boys had been turned into a separate inclosure, and before the cutting out commenced, every mother's son, including Don Lovell, arrived at the round-up. There were no corrals on the ranch which would accommodate such a body of animals, and thus the work had to be done in the open; but with the force at hand we threw a cordon around them, equal to a corral, and the cutting out to the four quarters commenced.

The horses were gentle and handled easily. Forrest and I turned to and helped our old foreman cut out his remuda of the year before. There were several horses in my old mount that I would have liked to have again, but I knew it was useless to try and trade Jim out of them, as he knew their qualities and would have robbed me in demanding their equivalent. When the old remudas were again separated, they were counted and carefully looked over by both foremen and men, and were open to the inspection of all who cared to look. Everything was passing very pleasantly, and the cutting of the extra twenty-five began. Then my selfishness was weighed in the balance and found to be full weight. I had ridden over a hundred of the best of them, but when any one appealed to me, even my own dear brother, I was as dumb as an oyster about a horse. Tolleston, especially, cursed, raved, and importuned me to help him get a good private mount, but I was as innocent as I was immovable. The trip home from Dodge was no pleasure jaunt, and now I was determined to draw extra pay in getting the cream of that horse herd. There were other features governing my actions: Flood was indifferent; Forrest, at times, was cruel to horses, and had I helped my brother, I might have been charged with favoritism. Dave Sponsilier was a good horseman, as his selections proved, and I was not wasting any love and affection on Archie Tolleston that day, anyhow.

That no undue advantage should be taken, Lovell kept tally of every horse cut out, and once each foreman had taken his number, he was waved out of the herd. I did the selecting of my own, and with the assistance of one man, was constantly waiting my turn. With all the help he could use, Tolleston was over half an hour making his selections, and took the only blind horse in the entire herd. He was a showy animal, a dapple gray, fully fifteen hands high, bred in north Texas, and belonged to one of the whole remudas bought in Dodge. At the time of his purchase, neither Lovell nor Flood detected anything wrong, and no one could see anything in the eyeball which would indicate he was moon-eyed. Yet any horseman need only notice him closely to be satisfied of his defect, as he was constantly shying from other horses and objects and smelled everything which came within his reach. There were probably half a dozen present who knew of his blindness, but not a word was said until all the extras were chosen and the culling out of the overplus of the various remudas began. It started in snickers, and before the cutting back was over developed into peals of laughter, as man after man learned that the dapple gray in Tolleston's remuda was blind.

Among the very last to become acquainted with the fact was the trail foreman himself. After watching the horse long enough to see his mistake, Tolleston culled the gray back and rode into the herd to claim another. But the drover promptly summoned his foreman out, and, as they met, Lovell said to his trail boss, "Arch, you're no better than anybody else. I bought that gray and paid my good money for him. No doubt but the man who sold him has laughed about it often since, and if ever we meet, I'll take my hat off and compliment him on being the only person who ever sold me a moon-eyed horse. I'm still paying my tuition, and you needn't flare up when the laugh's on you. You have a good remuda without him, and the only way you can get another horse out of that herd is with the permission of Quince Forrest and Tom Quirk."

"Well, if the permission of those new foremen is all I lack, then I'll cut all the horses I want," retorted Tolleston, and galloped back towards the herd. But Quince and I were after him like a flash, followed leisurely by Lovell. As he slacked his mount to enter the mass of animals, I passed him, jerking the bridle reins from his hand. Throwing my horse on his haunches, I turned just as Forrest slapped Tolleston on the back, and said: "Look-ee here, Arch; just because you're a little hot under the collar, don't do anything brash, for fear you may regret it afterward. I'm due to take a little pasear myself this summer, and I always did like to be well mounted. Now, don't get your back up or attempt to stand up any bluffs, for I can whip you in any sized circle you can name. You never saw me burn powder, did you? Well, just you keep on acting the d — — fool if you want a little smoke thrown in your face. Just fool with me and I'll fog you till you look like an angel in the clouds."

But old man Don reached us, and raised his hand. I threw the reins back over the horse's head. Tolleston was white with rage, but before he could speak our employer waved us aside and said, "Tom, you and Quince clear right out of here and I'll settle this matter. Arch, there's your remuda. Take it and go about your business or say you don't want to. Now, we know each other, and I'll not mince or repeat any words with you. Go on."

"Not an inch will I move until I get another horse," hissed Tolleston between gasps. "If it lies between you and me, then I'll have one in place of that gray, or you'll get another foreman. Now, you have my terms and ticket."

"Very well then, Archie; that changes the programme entirely," replied Lovell, firmly. "You'll find your private horse in the small pasture, and we'll excuse you for the summer. Whenever a man in my employ gets the impression that I can't get along without him, that moment he becomes useless to me. It seems that you are bloated with that idea, and a season's rest and quiet may cool you down and make a useful man of you again. Remember that you're always welcome at my ranch, and don't let this make us strangers," he called back as he turned away.

Riding over with us to where a group were sitting on their horses, our employer scanned the crowd without saying a word. Turning halfway in his saddle, he looked over towards Flood's remuda and said: "One of you boys please ride over and tell Paul I want him." During the rather embarrassing interim, the conversation instantly changed, and we borrowed tobacco and rolled cigarettes to kill time.

Priest was rather slow in making his appearance, riding leisurely, but on coming up innocently inquired of his employer, "Did you want to see me?"

"Yes. Paul, I've just lost one of my foremen. I need a good reliable man to take a herd to Fort Washakie. It's an Indian agency on the head waters of the North Platte in Wyoming. Will you tackle the job?"

"A good soldier is always subject to orders," replied The Rebel with a military salute. "If you have a herd for delivery in Wyoming, give me the men and horses, and I'll put the cattle there if possible. You are the commandant in the field, and I am subject to instructions."

"There's your remuda and outfit, then," said Lovell, pointing to the one intended for Tolleston, "and you'll get a commissary at the ranch and go into camp this evening. You'll get your herd in Nueces County, and Jim will assist in the receiving. Any other little details will all be arranged before you get away."

Calling for all the men in Tolleston's outfit, the two rode away for that remuda. Shortly before the trouble arose, our employer instructed those with the Buford cattle to take ten extra horses for each herd. There were now over a hundred and forty head to be culled back, and Sponsilier was entitled to ten of them. In order to be sure of our numbers, we counted the remaining band, and Forrest and I trimmed them down to two hundred and fifty-four head. As this number was too small to be handled easily in the open, we decided to take them into the corrals for the final division. After the culling back was over, and everything had started for the ranch, to oblige Sponsilier, I remained behind and helped him to retrim his remuda. Unless one knew the horses personally, it was embarrassing even to try and pick ten of the best ones from the overplus. But I knew many of them at first hand, and at Dave's request, after picking out the extra ones, continued selecting others in exchange for horses in his old band. We spent nearly an hour cutting back and forth, or until we were both satisfied that his saddle stock could not be improved from the material at hand.

The ranch headquarters were fully six miles from the round-up. Leaving Sponsilier delighted with the change in his remuda, I rode to overtake the undivided band which were heading for the ranch corrals. On coming up with them, Forrest proposed that we divide the horses by a running cut in squads of ten, and toss for choice. Once they were in the corrals, this could have been easily done by simply opening a gate and allowing blocks of ten to pass alternately from the main into smaller inclosures. But I was expecting something like this from Quince, and had entirely different plans of my own. Forrest and I were good friends, but he was a foxy rascal, and I had never wavered in my determination to get the pick of that horse herd. Had I accepted his proposal, the chance of a spinning coin might have given him a decided advantage, and I declined his proposition. I had a remuda in sight that my very being had hungered for, and now I would take no chance of losing it. But on the other hand, I proposed to Forrest that he might have the assistance of two men in Flood's outfit who had accompanied the horse herd home from Dodge. In the selecting of Jim's extra twenty-five, the opinion of these two lads, as the chosen horses proved, was a decided help to their foreman. But Quince stood firm, and arguing the matter, we reached the corrals and penned the band.

The two top bunches were held separate and were left a mile back on the prairie, under herd. The other remudas were all in sight of the ranch, while a majority of the men were eating a late dinner. Still contending for his point, Forrest sent a lad to the house to ask our employer to come over to the corrals. On his appearance, accompanied by Flood, each of us stated our proposition.

"Well, the way I size this up," said old man Don, "one of you wants to rely on his own judgment and the other don't. It looks to me, Quince, you want a gambler's chance where you can't lose. Tom's willing to bank on his own judgment, but you ain't. Now, I like a man who does his own thinking, and to give you a good lesson in that line, why, divide them, horse and horse, turn about. Now, I'll spin this coin for first pick, and while it's in the air, Jim will call the turn.... Tom wins first choice."

"That's all right, Mr. Lovell," said Quince, smilingly. "I just got the idea that you wanted the remudas for the Buford herds to be equally good. How can you expect it when Tom knows every horse and I never saddled one of them. Give me the same chance, and I might know them as well as the little boy knew his pap."

"You had the same chance," I put in, "but didn't want it. You were offered the Pine Ridge horses last year to take back to Dodge, and you kicked like a bay steer. But I swallowed their dust to the Arkansaw, and from there home we lived in clouds of alkali. You went home drunk and dressed up, with a cigar in your mouth and your feet through the car window, claiming you was a brother-in-law to Jay Gould, and simply out on a tour of inspection. Now you expect me to give you the benefit of my experience and rob myself. Not this summer, John Quincy."

But rather than let Forrest feel that he was being taken advantage of, I repeated my former proposition. Accepting it as a last resort, the two boys were sent for and the dividing commenced. Remounting our horses, we entered the large corral, and as fast as they were selected the different outfits were either roped or driven singly through a guarded gate. It took over an hour of dusty work to make the division, but when it was finished I had a remuda of a hundred and fifty-two saddle horses that would make a man willing to work for his board and the privilege of riding them. Turning out of the corrals, Priest and I accompanied the horses out on the prairie where our toppy ones were being grazed. Paul was tickled over my outfit of saddle stock, but gave me several hints that he was entitled to another picked mount. I attempted to explain that he had a good remuda, but he still insisted, and I promised him if he would be at my wagon the next morning when we corralled, he should have a good one. I could well afford to be generous with my old bunkie.

There now only remained the apportionment of the work-stock. Four mules were allowed to the wagon, and in order to have them in good condition they had been grain-fed for the past month. In their allotment the Buford herds were given the best teams, and when mine was pointed out by my employer, the outfit assisted the cook to harness in. Giving him instructions to go into camp on a creek three miles south of headquarters, my wagon was the second one to get away. Some of the teams bolted at the start, and only for timely assistance Sponsilier's commissary would have been overturned in the sand. Two of the wagons headed west for Uvalde, while my brother Bob's started southeast for Bee County. The other two belonging to Flood and The Rebel would camp on the same creek as mine, their herds being also south. Once the wagons were off, the saddle stock was brought in and corralled for our first mounts. The final allotment of horses to the men would not take place until the herds were ready to be received, and until then, they would be ridden uniformly but promiscuously. With instructions from our employer to return to the ranch after making camp, the remudas were started after the wagons.

On our return after darkness, the ranch was as deserted as a school-house on Saturday. A Mexican cook and a few regular ranch hands were all that were left. Archie Tolleston had secured his horse and quit headquarters before any one had even returned from the round-up. When the last of the foremen came in, our employer delivered his final messages. "Boys," said he, "I'll only detain you a few minutes. I'm going west in the morning to Uvalde County, and will be present at the receiving of Quince and Dave's herds. After they start, I'll come back to the city and take stage to Oakville. But you go right ahead and receive your cattle, Bob, for we don't know what may turn up. Flood will help Tom first, and then Paul, to receive their cattle. That will give the Buford herds the first start, and I'll be waiting for you at Abilene when you reach there. And above all else, boys, remember that I've strained my credit in this drive, and that the cattle must be A 1, and that we must deliver them on the spot in prime condition. Now, that's all, but you'd better be riding so as to get an early start in the morning."

Our employer walked with us to the outer gate where our horses stood at the hitch-rack. That he was reticent in his business matters was well known among all his old foremen, including Forrest and myself. If he had a confidant among his men, Jim Flood was the man — and there were a few things he did not know. As we mounted our horses to return to our respective camps, old man Don quietly took my bridle reins in hand and allowed the others to ride away. "I want a parting word with you, Tom," said he a moment later. "Something has happened to-day which will require the driving of the Buford herds in some road brand other than the 'Circle Dot.' The first blacksmith shop you pass, have your irons altered into 'Open A's,' and I'll do the same with Quince and Dave's brands. Of the why or wherefore of this, say nothing to any one, as no one but myself knows. Don't breathe a word even to Flood, for he don't know any more than he should. When the time comes, if it ever does, you'll know all that is necessary — or nothing. That's all."

CHAPTER III
RECEIVING AT LOS LOBOS

The trip to Lasalle County was mere pastime. All three of the outfits kept in touch with each other, camping far enough apart to avoid any conflict in night-herding the remudas. The only incident to mar the pleasure of the outing was the discovery of ticks in many of our horses' ears. The pasture in which they had wintered was somewhat brushy, and as there had been no frost to kill insect life, myriads of seed-ticks had dropped from the mesquite thickets upon the animals when rubbing against or passing underneath them. As the inner side of a horse's ear is both warm and tender, that organ was frequently infested with this pest, whose ravages often undermined the supporting cartilages and produced the drooping or "gotch" ear. In my remuda over one half the horses were afflicted with ticks, and many of them it was impossible to bridle, owing to the inflamed condition of their ears. Fortunately we had with us some standard preparations for blistering, so, diluting this in axle-grease, we threw every animal thus affected and thoroughly swabbed his ears. On reaching the Nueces River, near the western boundary of Lasalle County, the other two outfits continued on down that stream for their destination in the lower country. Flood remained behind with me, and going into camp on the river with my outfit, the two of us rode over to Los Lobos Ranch and announced ourselves as ready to receive the cattle. Dr. Beaver, the seller of the herd, was expecting us, and sending word of our arrival to neighboring cowmen, we looked over the corrals before returning to camp. They had built a new branding-chute and otherwise improved their facilities for handling cattle. The main inclosure had been built of heavy palisades in an early day, but recently several of smaller sized lumber had been added, making the most complete corrals I had ever seen. An abundance of wood was at hand for heating the branding-irons, and every little detail to facilitate the work had been provided for. Giving notice that we would receive every morning on the open prairie only, we declined an invitation to remain at the ranch and returned to my wagon.

In the valley the grass was well forward. We had traveled only some twenty miles a day coming down, and our horses had fared well. But as soon as we received any cattle, night-herding the remuda would cease, and we must either hobble or resort to other measures. John Levering was my horse-wrangler. He had made two trips over the trail with Fant's herds in the same capacity, was careful, humane, and an all-round horseman. In employing a cook, I had given the berth to Neal Parent, an old boyhood chum of mine. He never amounted to much as a cow-hand, but was a lighthearted, happy fool; and as cooking did not require much sense, I gave him the chance to make his first trip. Like a court jester, he kept the outfit in fine spirits and was the butt of all jokes. In entertaining company he was in a class by himself, and spoke with marked familiarity of all the prominent cowmen in southern Texas. To a stranger the inference might be easily drawn that Lovell was in his employ.

As we were expecting to receive cattle on the third day, the next morning the allotment of horses was made. The usual custom of giving the foreman first choice was claimed, and I cut twelve of solid colors but not the largest ones. Taking turns, the outfit roped out horse after horse until only the ten extra ones were left. In order that these should bear a fair share in the work, I took one of them for a night-horse and allotted the others to the second, third, and last guard in a similar capacity. This gave the last three watches two horses apiece for night work, but with the distinct understanding that in case of accident or injury to any horse in the remuda, they could be recalled. There was little doubt that before the summer ended, they would be claimed to fill vacancies in the regular mounts. Flood had kept behind only two horses with which to overtake the other outfits, and during his stay with us would ride these extras and loans from my mount.

The entire morning was spent working with the remuda. Once a man knew his mount, extra attention was shown each horse. There were witches' bridles to be removed from their manes, extra long tails were thinned out to the proper length, and all hoofs trimmed short. The horses were fast shedding their winter coats, matting the saddle blankets with falling hair, and unless carefully watched, galled backs would result. The branding-irons had been altered en route, and about noon a vaquero came down the river and reported that the second round-up of the day would meet just over the county line in Dimmit. He belonged at Los Lobos, and reported the morning rodeo as containing over five hundred beeves, which would be ready for delivery at our pleasure. We made him remain for dinner, after which Flood and I saddled up and returned with him. We reached the round-up just as the cutting-out finished. They were a fine lot of big rangy beeves, and Jim suggested that we pass upon them at once. The seller agreed to hold them overnight, and Flood and I culled back about one hundred and twenty which were under age or too light. The round-up outfit strung the cattle out and counted them, reporting a few over seven hundred head. This count was merely informal and for the information of the seller; but in the morning the final one would be made, in which we could take a hand.

After the cut had started in for the ranch, we loitered along, looking them over, and I noticed several that might have been thrown out. "Well, now," said Flood, "if you are going to be so very choice as all that, I might as well ride on. You can't use me if that bunch needs any more trimming. I call them a fine lot of beeves. It's all right for Don to rib the boys up and make them think that the cattle have to be top-notchers. I've watched him receive too often; he's about the easiest man I know to ring in short ages on. Just so a steer looks nice, it's hard for the old man to turn one back. I've seen him receiving three-year-olds, when one fourth of the cattle passed on were short twos. And if you call his attention to one, he'll just smile that little smile of his, and say, 'yes, he may be shy a few months, but he'll grow.' But then that's just old man Don's weakness for cattle; he can't look a steer in the face without falling in love with him. Now, I've received before when by throwing out one half the stock offered, you couldn't get as uniform a bunch of beeves as those are. But you go right ahead, Tom, and be sure that every hoof you accept will dress five hundred pounds at Fort Buford. I'll simply sit around and clerk and help you count and give you a good chance to make a reputation."

Los Lobos was still an open range. They claimed to have over ten thousand mixed cattle in the straight ranch brand. There had been no demand for matured beeves for several years, and now on effecting this sale they were anxious to deliver all their grown steers. Dr. Beaver informed us that, previous to our arrival, his foreman had been throwing everything in on the home range, and that he hoped to deliver to us over two thousand head from his own personal holdings. But he was liberal with his neighbors, for in the contingent just passed upon, there must have been over a hundred head in various ranch brands. Assuring him that we would be on hand in the morning to take possession of the cattle, and requesting him to have a fire burning, on coming opposite the camp, we turned off and rode for our wagon. It meant a big day's work to road-brand this first contingent, and with the first sign of dawn, my outfit were riding for Los Lobos. We were encamped about three miles from the corrals, and leaving orders for the cook to follow up, the camp was abandoned with the exception of the remuda. It was barely sun-up when we counted and took possession of the beeves. On being relieved, the foreman of Los Lobos took the ranch outfit and started off to renew the gathering. We penned the cattle without any trouble, and as soon as the irons were ready, a chuteful were run in and the branding commenced. This branding-chute was long enough to chamber eight beeves. It was built about a foot wide at the bottom and flared upward just enough to prevent an animal from turning round. A heavy gate closed the exit, while bull-bars at the rear prevented the occupant from backing out. A high platform ran along either side of the branding-chute, on which the men stood while handling the irons.

Two men did the branding. "Runt" Pickett attended the fire, passing up the heated irons, and dodging the cold branding-steel. A single iron was often good for several animals, and sometimes a chuteful was branded with two irons. It was necessary that the work should be well done; not that a five months' trip required it, but the unforeseen must be guarded against. Many trail herds had met disaster and been scattered to the four winds with nothing but a road brand to identify them afterward. The cattle were changing owners, and custom decreed that an abstract of title should be indelibly seared on their sides. The first guard, Jake Blair, Morg

Tussler, and Clay Zilligan, were detailed to cut and drive the squads into the chute. These three were the only mounted men, the others being placed so as to facilitate the work. Cattle are as innocent as they are strong, and in this necessary work everything was done quietly, care being taken to prevent them from becoming excited. As fast as they were released from the chute, Dr. Beaver took a list of the ranch brands, in order to bill of sale them to Lovell and settle with his neighbors.

The work moved with alacrity. As one chuteful was being freed the next one was entering. Gates closed in their faces and the bull-bars at the rear locked them as in a vice. We were averaging a hundred an hour, but the smoke from the burning hair was offensive to the lungs. During the forenoon Burl Van Vedder and Vick Wolf "spelled" Flood and myself for half an hour at a time, or until we could recover from the nauseous fumes. When the cook called us to dinner, we had turned out nearly five hundred branded cattle. No sooner was the midday meal bolted than the cook was ordered back to camp with his wagon, the branded contingent of cattle following in charge of the first guard. Less than half an hour was lost in refreshing the inner man, and ordering "G — G" Cederdall, Tim Stanley, and Jack Splann of the second guard into their saddles to take the place of the relieved men, we resumed our task. The dust of the corrals settled on us unheeded, the smoke of the fire mingled with that of the singeing hair and its offensive odors, bringing tears to our eyes, but the work never abated until the last steer had passed the chute and bore the "Open A."

The work over, a pretense was made at washing the dust and grime from our faces. It was still early in the day, and starting the cattle for camp, I instructed the boys to water and graze them as long as they would stand up. The men all knew their places on guard, this having been previously arranged; and joining Dr. Beaver, Jim and I rode for the ranch about a mile distant. The doctor was a genial host, and prescribed a series of mint-juleps, after which he proposed that we ride out and meet the cattle gathered during the day. The outfit had been working a section of country around some lagoons, south of the ranch, and it was fully six o'clock when we met them, heading homeward. The cattle were fully up to the standard of the first bunch, and halting the herd we trimmed them down and passed on them. After Flood rode out of this second contingent, I culled back about a dozen light weights. On finishing, Jim gave me a quiet wink, and said something to Dr. Beaver about a new broom. But I paid no attention to these remarks; in a country simply teeming with prime beeves, I was determined to get a herd to my liking. Dr. Beaver had assured Lovell that he and his neighbors would throw together over four thousand beeves in making up the herd, and now I was perfectly willing that they should. It would take two days longer to gather the cattle on the Los Lobos range, and then there were the outside offerings, which were supposed to number fully two thousand. There was no excuse for not being choice.

On returning to Los Lobos about dusk, rather than offend its owner, Flood consented to remain at the ranch overnight, but I rode for camp. Darkness had fallen on my reaching the wagon, the herd had been bedded down, and Levering felt so confident that the remuda was contented that he had concluded to night-herd them himself until midnight, and then turn them loose until dawn. He had belled a couple of the leaders, and assured me that he would have them in hand before sun-up. The cook was urging me to supper, but before unsaddling, I rode around both herd and remuda. The cattle were sleeping nicely, and the boys assured me that they had got a splendid fill on them before bedding down. That was the only safe thing to do, and after circling the saddle stock on the opposite side of camp, I returned to find that a stranger had arrived during my brief absence. Parent had fully enlightened him as to who he was, who the outfit were, the destination of the herd, the names of both buyer and seller, and, on my riding in, was delivering a voluble dissertation on the tariff and the possible effect on the state of putting hides on the free list. And although in cow-camps a soldier's introduction is usually sufficient, the cook inquired the stranger's name and presented me to our guest with due formality. Supper being waiting, the stranger was invited to take pot-luck with us, and before the meal was over recognized me. He was a deputy cattle inspector for Dimmit County, and had issued the certificate for Flood's herd the year before. He had an eye for the main chance, and informed me that fully one half the cattle making up our herd belonged to Dimmit; that the county line was only a mile up the river, and that if I would allow the herd to drift over into his territory, he would shade the legal rate. The law compelling the inspection of herds before they could be moved out of the county, like the rain, fell upon the just and the unjust. It was not the intent of the law to impose a burden on an honest drover. Yet he was classed with the rustler, and must have in his possession a certificate of inspection before he could move out a purchased herd, or be subject to arrest. A list of brands was recorded, at the county seat, of every herd leaving, and if occasion required could be referred to in future years. No railroad would receive any consignment of hides or live stock, unless accompanied by a certificate from the county inspector. The legal rate was ten cents on the first hundred, and three cents on all over that number, frequently making the office a lucrative one.

Once the object of his call was made clear, I warmed to our guest. If the rate allowed by law was enforced, it meant an expense of over a hundred dollars for a certificate of inspection covering both herd and saddle stock. We did not take out certificates in Medina on the remudas as a matter of economy. By waiting until the herd was ready, the two would be inspected as one, and the lower rate apply. So I urged the deputy to make himself at home and share my blankets. Pretending that I remembered him well, I made numerous inquiries about the ranch where we received our herd the year before, and by the time to turn in, we were on the most friendly terms. The next morning I offered him a horse from our extras, assuring him that Flood would be delighted to renew his acquaintance, and invited him to go with us for the day. Turning his horse among ours, he accepted and rode away with us. The cattle passed on the evening before had camped out several miles from the corrals and were grazing in when we met them. Flood and the Doctor joined us shortly afterward, and I had a quiet word with Jim before he and the inspector met. After the count was over, Flood made a great ado over my guest and gave him the glad hand as if he had been a long-lost brother. We were a trifle short-handed the second day, and on my guest volunteering to help, I assigned him to Runt Pickett's place at the fire, where he shortly developed a healthy sweat. As we did not have a large bunch of beeves to brand that day, the wagon did not come over and we branded them at a single shift. It was nearly one o'clock when we finished, and instead of going in to Los Lobos, we left the third guard, Wayne Outcault, "Dorg" Seay, and Owen Ubery, to graze the cattle over to our camp.

The remainder of the afternoon was spent in idleness and in the entertainment of our guest. Official-like, he pretended he could hardly spare the time to remain another night, but was finally prevailed on and did so. After dark, I took him some distance from camp, and the two of us had a confidential chat. I assured him if there was any object in doing so, we could move camp right to or over the county line, and frankly asked him what inducement he would offer. At first he thought that throwing off everything over a hundred dollars would be about right. But I assured him that there were whole families of inspectors in Lasalle County who would discount that figure, and kindly advised him, if he really wanted the fee, to meet competition at least. We discussed the matter at length, and before returning to camp, he offered to make out the certificate, covering everything, for fifty dollars. As it was certain to be several days yet before we would start, and there was a prospect of a falling market in certificates of inspection, I would make no definite promises. The next morning I insisted that he remain at some near-by ranch in his own territory, and, if convenient, ride down every few days and note the progress of the herd.

We were promised a large contingent of cattle for that day. The ranch outfit were to make three rodeos down the river the day before, where the bulk of their beeves ranged. Flood was anxious to overtake the other outfits before they reached the lower country, and as he assured me I had no further use for him, we agreed that after receiving that morning he might leave us. Giving orders at camp to graze the received beeves within a mile of the corrals by noon, and the wagon to follow, we made an early start, Flood taking his own horses with him. We met the cattle coming up the river a thousand strong. It was late when the last round-up of the day before had finished, and they had camped for the night fully five miles from the corrals. It took less than an hour to cull back and count, excuse the ranch outfit, and start this contingent for the branding-pens in charge of my boys. Flood was in a hurry, and riding a short distance with him, I asked that he pass or send word to the county seat, informing the inspector of hides and animals that a trail herd would leave Los Lobos within a week. Jim knew my motive in getting competition on the inspection, and wishing me luck on my trip, I wrung his hand in farewell until we should meet again in the upper country.

The sun was setting that night when we finished road-branding the last of the beeves received in the morning. After dinner, when the wagon returned to camp, I instructed Parent to move up the river fully a mile. We needed the change, anyhow, and even if it was farther, the next morning we would have the Los Lobos outfit to assist in the branding, as that day would finish their gathering. The outside cattle were beginning to report in small bunches, from three hundred upward. Knowing that Dr. Beaver was anxious to turn in as many as possible of his own, we delayed receiving from the neighboring ranches for another day. But the next morning, as we were ironing-up the last contingent of some four hundred Los Lobos beeves, a deputy inspector for Lasalle arrived from the county seat. He was likewise officious, and professed disappointment that the herd was not ready to pass upon. On his arrival, I was handling the irons, and paid no attention to him until the branding was over for the morning. When he introduced himself, I cordially greeted him, but at the first intimation of disappointment from his lips, I checked him.

Using the best diplomacy at my command, I said, "Well, I'm sorry to cause you this long ride when it might have been avoided. You see, we are receiving cattle from both this and Dimmit County. In fact, we are holding our herd across the line just at present. On starting, we expect to go up the river to the first creek, and north on it to the Leona River. I have partially promised the work to an inspector from Dimmit. He inspected our herd last year, and being a personal friend that way, you couldn't meet his figures. Very sorry to disappoint you, but won't you come over to the wagon and stay all night?"

But Dr. Beaver, who understood my motive, claimed the privilege of entertaining the deputy at Los Lobos, and I yielded. We now had a few over twenty-four hundred beeves, of which nineteen hundred were in the Los Lobos brand, the others being mixed. There was a possibility of fully a hundred more coming in with the neighboring cattle, and Dr. Beaver was delighted over the ranch delivery. The outside contingents were in four bunches, then encamped in different directions and within from three to five miles of the ranch. Taking Vick Wolf with me for the afternoon, I looked over the separate herds and found them numbering more than fifteen hundred. They were the same uniform Nueces Valley cattle, and as we lacked only a few over a thousand, the offerings were extremely liberal. Making arrangements with three of the four herds to receive the next day, Vick and I reached our camp on the county line about sunset. The change was a decided advantage; wood, water, and grass were plentiful, and not over a mile farther from the branding-pens.

The next morning found us in our saddles at the usual early hour. We were anxious to receive and brand every animal possible that day, so that with a few hours' work the next forenoon the herd would be ready to start. After we had passed on the first contingent of the outside cattle, and as we were nearing the corrals, Dr. Beaver overtook us. Calling me aside, he said: "Quirk, if you play your cards right, you'll get a certificate of inspection for nothing and a chromo as a pelon. I've bolstered up the Lasalle man that he's better entitled to the work than the Dimmit inspector, and he'll wait until the herd is ready to start. Now, you handle the one, and I'll keep the other as my guest. We must keep them apart and let them buck each other to their hearts' content. Every hoof in your herd will be in a ranch brand of record; but still the law demands inspection and you must comply with it. I'll give you a duplicate list of the brands, so that neither inspector need see the herd, and if we don't save your employer a hundred dollars, then we are amateurs."

Everything was pointing to an auspicious start. The last cattle on the delivery were equal to the first, if not better. The sky clouded over, and before noon a light shower fell, settling the dust in the corrals. Help increased as the various bunches were accepted, and at the end of the day only a few over two hundred remained to complete our numbers. The last contingent were fully up to the standard; and rather than disappoint the sellers, I accepted fifty head extra, making my herd at starting thirty-four hundred and fifty. When the last beef had passed the branding-chute, there was nothing remaining but to give a receipt to the seller for the number of head received, in behalf of my employer, pending a later settlement between them.

Meanwhile competition in the matter of inspection had been carefully nursed. Conscious of each other's presence, and both equally anxious for the fee, the one deputy was entertained at my camp and the other at Los Lobos. They were treated courteously, but given to understand that in the present instance money talked. With but a small bunch of beeves to brand on the starting day, the direction in which the herd was allowed to leave the bed-ground would be the final answer. If west, Dimmit had underbid Lasalle; if the contrary, then the departure of this herd would be a matter of record in the latter county. Dr. Beaver enjoyed the situation hugely, acting the intermediary in behalf of his guest. Personally I was unconcerned, but was neutral and had little to say.

My outfit understood the situation perfectly. Before retiring on the night of our last camp on the county line, and in the presence of the Dimmit inspector, the last relief received instructions, in the absence of contrary orders, to allow the herd to drift back into Lasalle in the morning. Matters were being conducted in pantomime, and the players understood their parts. Our guest had made himself useful in various ways, and I naturally felt friendly towards him. He had stood several guards for the boys, and Burl Van Vedder, of the last watch, had secret instructions to call him for that guard.

The next morning the camp was not astir as early as usual. On the cook's arousing us, in the uncertain light of dawn, the herd was slowly rising, and from the position of a group of four horsemen, it was plainly evident that our guest had shaded all competition. Our camp was in plain view of Los Lobos, and only some five or six miles distant. With the rising of the sun, and from the top of a windmill derrick, by the aid of a field-glass, the Lasalle inspector had read his answer; and after the work in the morning was over, and the final papers had been exchanged, Dr. Beaver insisted that, in commiseration of his departed guest, just one more mint-julep should be drunk standing.

When Don Lovell glanced over my expense account on our arrival at Abilene, he said: "Look here, Tom, is this straight? — twenty dollars for inspection? — the hell you say! Corrupted them, did you? Well, that's the cheapest inspection I ever paid, with one exception. Dave Sponsilier once got a certificate for his herd for five dollars and a few drinks. But he paid for it a month in advance of the starting of the herd. It was dated ahead, properly sealed, and all ready for filling in the brands and numbers. The herd was put up within a mile of where four counties cornered, and that inspector was a believer in the maxim of the early bird. The office is a red-tape one, anyhow, and little harm in taking all the advantage you can. — This item marked 'sundries' was DRY goods, I suppose? All right, Quirk; I reckon rattlesnakes were rather rabid this spring."

CHAPTER IV
MINGLING WITH THE EXODUS

By noon the herd had grazed out five miles on its way. The boys were so anxious to get off that on my return the camp was deserted with the exception of the cook and the horse-wrangler, none even returning for dinner. Before leaving I had lunched at Los Lobos with its owner, and on reaching the wagon, Levering and I assisted the cook to harness in and start the commissary. The general course of the Nueces River was southeast by northwest, and as our route lay on the latter angle, the herd would follow up the valley for the first day. Once outside the boundaries of our camp of the past week, the grass matted the ground with its rank young growth. As far as the eye could see, the mesas, clothed in the verdure of spring, rolled in long swells away to the divides. Along the river and in the first bottom, the timber and mesquite thickets were in leaf and blossom, while on the outlying prairies the only objects which dotted this sea of green were range cattle and an occasional band of horses.

The start was made on the 27th of March. By easy drives and within a week, we crossed the "Sunset" Railway, about thirty miles to the westward of the ranch in Medina. On reaching the divide between the Leona and Frio rivers, we sighted our first herd of trail cattle, heading northward. We learned that some six herds had already passed upward on the main Frio, while a number of others were reported as having taken the east fork of that river. The latter stream almost paralleled the line between Medina and Uvalde counties, and as we expected some word from headquarters, we crossed over to the east fork. When westward of and opposite the ranch, Runt Pickett was sent in for any necessary orders that might be waiting. By leaving us early in the evening he could reach headquarters that night and overtake us before noon the next day. We grazed leisurely forward the next morning, killing as much time as possible, and Pickett overtook us before the wagon had even gone into camp for dinner. Lovell had not stopped on his return from the west, but had left with the depot agent at the home station a letter for the ranch. From its contents we learned that the other two Buford herds had started from Uvalde, Sponsilier in the lead, one on the 24th and the other the following day. Local rumors were encouraging in regard to grass and water to the westward, and the intimation was clear that if favorable reports continued, the two Uvalde herds would intersect an old trail running from the head of Nueces Canon to the Llano River. Should they follow this route there was little hope of their coming into the main western trail before reaching the Colorado River. Sponsilier was a daring fellow, and if there was a possible chance to get through beyond the borders of any settlement, he was certain to risk it.

The letter contained no personal advice. Years of experience in trail matters had taught my employer that explicit orders were often harmful. The emergencies to be met were of such a varied nature that the best method was to trust to an outfit worming its way out of any situation which confronted it. From the information disclosed, it was evident that the other Buford herds were then somewhere to the northwest, and possibly over a hundred miles distant. Thus freed from any restraint, we held a due northward course for several days, or until we encountered some rocky country. Water was plentiful and grass fairly good, but those flinty hills must be avoided or sorefooted beeves would be the result. I had seen trails of blood left by cattle from sandy countries on encountering rock, and now the feet of ours were a second consideration to their stomachs. But long before the herd reached this menace, Morg Tussler and myself, scouting two full days in advance, located a safe route to the westward. Had we turned to the other hand, we should have been forced into the main trail below Fredericksburg, and we preferred the sea-room of the boundless plain. From every indication and report, this promised to be the banner year in the exodus of cattle from the South to the then new Northwest. This latter section was affording the long-looked-for outlet, by absorbing the offerings of cattle which came up from Texas over the trail, and marking an epoch barely covering a single decade.

Turning on a western angle, a week's drive brought us out on a high tableland. Veering again to the north, we snailed along through a delightful country, rich in flora and the freshness of the season. From every possible elevation, we scanned the west in the hope of sighting some of the herd which had followed up the main Frio, but in vain. Sweeping northward at a leisurely gait, the third week out we sighted the Blue Mountains, the first familiar landmark on our course. As the main western trail skirted its base on the eastward, our position was easily established.

So far the cattle were well behaved, not a run, and only a single incident occurring worth mention. About half an hour before dawn one morning, the cook aroused the camp with the report that the herd was missing. The beeves had been bedded within two hundred yards of the wagon, and the last watch usually hailed the rekindling of the cook's fire as the first harbinger of day. But on this occasion the absence of the usual salutations from the bed-ground aroused Parent's suspicion. He rushed into camp, and laboring under the impression that the cattle had stampeded, trampled over our beds, yelling at the top of his lungs. Aroused in the darkness from heavy sleep, bewildered by a bright fire burning and a crazy man shouting, "The beeves have stampeded! the herd's gone! Get up, everybody!" we were almost thrown into a panic. Many of the boys ran for their night-horses, but Clay Zilligan and I fell on the cook and shook the statement out of him that the cattle had left their beds. This simplified the situation, but before I could recall the men, several of them had reached the bed-ground. As fast as horses could be secured, others dashed through the lighted circle and faded into the darkness. From the flickering of matches it was evident that the boys were dismounting and looking for some sign of trouble. Zilligan was swearing like a pirate, looking for his horse in the murky night; but instead of any alarm, oaths and derision greeted our ears as the men returned to camp. Halting their horses within the circle of the fire, Dorg Seay said to the cook:

"Neal, the next time you find a mare's nest, keep the secret to yourself. I don't begrudge losing thirty minutes' beauty sleep, but I hate to be scared out of a year's growth. Haven't you got cow-sense enough to know that if those beeves had run, they'd have shook the earth? If they had stampeded, that alarm clock of yours wouldn't be a circumstance to the barking of the boys' guns. Why, the cattle haven't been gone thirty minutes. You can see where they got up and then quietly walked away. The ground where they lay is still steaming and warm. They were watered a little too soon yesterday and naturally got up early this morning. The boys on guard didn't want to alarm the outfit, and just allowed the beeves to graze off on their course. When day breaks, you'll see they ain't far away, and in the right direction. Parent, if I didn't sabe cows better than you do, I'd confine my attention to a cotton patch."

Seay had read the sign aright. When day dawned the cattle were in plain view about a mile distant. On the return of the last guard to camp, Vick Wolf explained the situation in a few words. During their watch the herd had grown restless, many of the cattle arising; and knowing that dawn was near at hand, the boys had pushed the sleepy ones off their beds and started them feeding. The incident had little effect on the irrepressible Parent, who seemed born to blunder, yet gifted with a sunny disposition which atoned for his numerous mistakes.

With the Blue Mountains as our guiding star, we kept to the westward of that landmark, crossing the Llano River opposite some Indian mounds. On reaching the divide between this and the next water, we sighted two dust-clouds to the westward. They were ten to fifteen miles distant, but I was anxious to hear any word of Sponsilier or Forrest, and sent Jake Blair to make a social call. He did not return until the next day, and reported the first herd as from the mouth of the Pecos, and the more distant one as belonging to Jesse Presnall. Blair had stayed all night with the latter, and while its foreman was able to locate at least a dozen trail herds in close proximity, our two from Uvalde had neither been seen nor heard of. Baffled again, necessity compelled us to turn within touch of some outfitting point. The staples of life were running low in our commissary, no opportunity having presented itself to obtain a new supply since we left the ranch in Medina over a month before. Consequently, after crossing the San Saba, we made our first tack to the eastward.

Brady City was an outfitting point for herds on the old western trail. On coming opposite that frontier village, Parent and I took the wagon and went in after supplies, leaving the herd on its course, paralleling the former route. They had instructions to camp on Brady Creek that night. On reaching the supply point, there was a question if we could secure the simple staples needed. The drive that year had outstripped all calculations, some half-dozen chuck-wagons being in waiting for the arrival of a freight outfit which was due that morning. The nearest railroad was nearly a hundred miles to the eastward, and all supplies must be freighted in by mule and ox teams. While waiting for the freight wagons, which were in sight several miles distant, I made inquiry of the two outfitting stores if our Buford herds had passed. If they had, no dealings had taken place on the credit of Don Lovell, though both merchants knew him well. Before the freight outfit arrived, some one took Abb Blocker, a trail foreman for his brother John, to task for having an odd ox in his wheel team. The animal was a raw, unbroken "7L" bull, surly and chafing under the yoke, and attracted general attention. When several friends of Blocker, noticing the brand, began joking him, he made this explanation: "No, I don't claim him; but he came into my herd the other night and got to hossing my steers around. We couldn't keep him out, and I thought if he would just go along, why we'd put him under the yoke and let him hoss that chuck-wagon to amuse himself. One of my wheelers was getting a little tenderfooted, anyhow."

On the arrival of the freight outfit, short shift was made in transferring a portion of the cargo to the waiting chuck-wagons. As we expected to reach Abilene, a railroad point, within a week, we took on only a small stock of staple supplies. Having helped ourselves, the only delay was in getting a clerk to look over our appropriation, make out an itemized bill, and receive a draft on my employer. When finally the merchant in person climbed into our wagon and took a list of the articles, Parent started back to overtake the herd. I remained behind several hours, chatting with the other foremen.

None of the other trail bosses had seen anything of Lovell's other herds, though they all knew him personally or by reputation, and inquired if he was driving again in the same road brand. By general agreement, in case of trouble, we would pick up each other's cattle; and from half a cent to a cent a head was considered ample remuneration in buying water in Texas. Owing to the fact that many drovers had shipped to Red River, it was generally believed that there would be no congestion of cattle south of that point. All herds were then keeping well to the westward, some even declaring their intention to go through the Panhandle until the Canadian was reached.

Two days later we came into the main trail at the crossing of the Colorado River. Before we reached it, several ominous dust-clouds hung on our right for hours, while beyond the river were others, indicating the presence of herds. Summer weather had already set in, and during the middle of the day the glare of heat-waves and mirages obstructed our view of other wayfarers like ourselves, but morning and evening we were never out of sight of their signals. The banks of the river at the ford were trampled to the level of the water, while at both approach and exit the ground was cut into dust. On our arrival, the stage of water was favorable, and we crossed without a halt of herd, horses, or commissary. But there was little inducement to follow the old trail. Washed into ruts by the seasons, the grass on either side eaten away for miles, there was a look of desolation like that to be seen in the wake of an army. As we felt under obligations to touch at Abilene within a few days, there was a constant skirmish for grass within a reasonable distance of the trail; and we were early, fully two thirds of the drive being in our rear. One sultry morning south of Buffalo Gap, as we were grazing past the foot of Table Mountain, several of us rode to the summit of that butte. From a single point of observation we counted twelve herds within a space of thirty miles both south and north, all moving in the latter direction.

When about midway between the Gap and the railroad we were met at noon one day by Don Lovell. This was his first glimpse of my herd, and his experienced eye took in everything from a broken harness to the peeling and legibility of the road brand. With me the condition of the cattle was the first requisite, but the minor details as well as the more important claimed my employer's attention. When at last, after riding with the herd for an hour, he spoke a few words of approbation on the condition, weight, and uniformity of the beeves, I felt a load lifted from my shoulders. That the old man was in a bad humor on meeting us was evident; but as he rode along beside the cattle, lazy and large as oxen, the cockles of his heart warmed and he grew sociable. Near the middle of the afternoon, as we were in the rear, looking over the drag steers, he complimented me on having the fewest tender-footed animals of any herd that had passed Abilene since his arrival. Encouraged, I ventured the double question as to how this one would average with the other Buford herds, and did he know their whereabouts. As I recall his reply, it was that all Nueces Valley cattle were uniform, and if there was any difference it was due to carelessness in receiving. In regard to the locality of the other herds, it was easily to be seen that he was provoked about something.

"Yes, I know where they are," said he, snappishly, "but that's all the good it does me. They crossed the railroad, west, at Sweetwater, about a week ago. I don't blame Quince, for he's just trailing along, half a day behind Dave's herd. But Sponsilier, knowing that I wanted to see him, had the nerve to write me a postal card with just ten words on it, saying that all was well and to meet him in Dodge. Tom, you don't know what a satisfaction it is to me to spend a day or so with each of the herds. But those rascals didn't pay any more attention to me than if I was an old woman. There was some reason for it — sore-footed cattle, or else they have skinned up their remudas and didn't want me to see them. If I drive a hundred herds hereafter, Dave Sponsilier will stay at home as far as I'm concerned. He may think it's funny to slip past, but this court isn't indulging in any levity just at present. I fail to see the humor in having two outfits with sixty-seven hundred cattle somewhere between the Staked Plain and No-Man's-Land, and unable to communicate with them. And while my herds are all contracted, mature beeves have broke from three to five dollars a head in price since these started, and it won't do to shout before we're out of the woods. Those fool boys don't know that, and I can't get near enough to tell them."

I knew better than to ask further questions or offer any apologies for others. My employer was naturally irritable, and his abuse or praise of a foreman was to be expected. Previously and under the smile of prosperity, I had heard him laud Sponsilier, and under an imaginary shadow abuse Jim Flood, the most experienced man in his employ. Feeling it was useless to pour oil on the present troubled waters, I excused myself, rode back, and ordered the wagon to make camp ahead about four miles on Elm Creek. We watered late in the afternoon, grazing thence until time to bed the herd. When the first and second guards were relieved to go in and catch night-horses and get their supper, my employer remained behind with the cattle. While feeding during the evening, we allowed the herd to scatter over a thousand acres. Taking advantage of the loose order of the beeves, the old man rode back and forth through them until approaching darkness compelled us to throw them together on the bedground. Even after the first guard took charge, the drover loitered behind, reluctant to leave until the last steer had lain down; and all during the night, sharing my blankets, he awoke on every change of guards, inquiring of the returning watch how the cattle were sleeping.

As we should easily pass Abilene before noon, I asked him as a favor that he take the wagon in and get us sufficient supplies to last until Red River was reached. But he preferred to remain behind with the herd, and I went instead. This suited me, as his presence overawed my outfit, who were delirious to see the town. There was no telling how long he would have stayed with us, but my brother Bob's herd was expected at any time. Remaining with us a second night, something, possibly the placidness of the cattle, mellowed the old man and he grew amiable with the outfit, and myself in particular. At breakfast the next morning, when I asked him if he was in a position to recommend any special route, he replied:

"No, Tom, that rests with you. One thing's certain; herds are going to be dangerously close together on the regular trail which crosses Red River at Doan's. The season is early yet, but over fifty herds have already crossed the Texas Pacific Railway. Allowing one half the herds to start north of that line, it gives you a fair idea what to expect. When seven hundred thousand cattle left Texas two years ago, it was considered the banner year, yet it won't be a marker to this one. The way prices are tumbling shows that the Northwest was bluffing when they offered to mature all the cattle that Texas could breed for the next fifty years. That's the kind of talk that suits me, but last year there were some forty herds unsold, which were compelled to winter in the North. Not over half the saddle horses that came up the trail last summer were absorbed by these Northern cowmen. Talk's cheap, but it takes money to buy whiskey. Lots of these men are new ones at the business and may lose fortunes. The banks are getting afraid of cattle paper, and conditions are tightening. With the increased drive this year, if the summer passes without a slaughter in prices, the Texas drovers can thank their lucky stars. I'm not half as bright as I might be, but this is one year that I'm smooth enough not to have unsold cattle on the trail."

The herd had started an hour before, and when the wagon was ready to move, I rode a short distance with my employer. It was possible that he had something to say of a confidential nature, for it was seldom that he acted so discouraged when his every interest seemed protected by contracts. But at the final parting, when we both had dismounted and sat on the ground for an hour, he had disclosed nothing. On the contrary, he even admitted that possibly it was for the best that the other Buford herds had held a westward course and thus avoided the crush on the main routes. The only intimation which escaped him was when we had remounted and each started our way, he called me back and said, "Tom, no doubt but you've noticed that I'm worried. Well, I am. I'd tell you in a minute, but I may be wrong in the matter. But I'll know before you reach Dodge, and then, if it's necessary, you shall know all. It's nothing about the handling of the herds, for my foremen have always considered my interests first. Keep this to yourself, for it may prove a nightmare. But if it should prove true, then we must stand together. Now, that's all; mum's the word until we meet. Drop me a line if you get a chance, and don't let my troubles worry you."

While overtaking the herd, I mused over my employer's last words. But my brain was too muddy even to attempt to solve the riddle. The most plausible theory that I could advance was that some friendly cowmen were playing a joke on him, and that the old man had taken things too seriously. Within a week the matter was entirely forgotten, crowded out of mind by the demands of the hour. The next night, on the Clear Fork of the Brazos, a stranger, attracted by our camp-fire, rode up to the wagon. Returning from the herd shortly after his arrival, I recognized in our guest John Blocker, a prominent drover. He informed us that he and his associates had fifty-two thousand cattle on the trail, and that he was just returning from overtaking two of their five lead herds. Knowing that he was a well-posted cowman on routes and sustenance, having grown up on the trail, I gave him the best our camp afforded, and in return I received valuable information in regard to the country between our present location and Doan's Crossing. He reported the country for a hundred miles south of Red River as having had a dry, backward spring, scanty of grass, and with long dry drives; and further, that in many instances water for the herds would have to be bought from those in control.

The outlook was not to my liking. The next morning when I inquired of our guest what he would advise me to do, his answer clearly covered the ground. "Well, I'm not advising any one," said he, "but you can draw your own conclusions. The two herds of mine, which I overtook, have orders to turn northeast and cross into the Nations at Red River Station. My other cattle, still below, will all be routed by way of Fort Griffin. Once across Red River, you will have the Chisholm Trail, running through civilized tribes, and free from all annoyance of blanket Indians. South of the river the grass is bound to be better than on the western route, and if we have to buy water, we'll have the advantage of competition."

With this summary of the situation, a decision was easily reached. The Chisholm Trail was good enough for me. Following up the north side of the Clear Fork, we passed about twenty miles to the west of Fort Griffin. Constantly bearing east by north, a few days later we crossed the main Brazos at a low stage of water. But from there to Red River was a trial not to be repeated. Wire fences halted us at every turn. Owners of pastures refused permission to pass through. Lanes ran in the wrong direction, and open country for pasturage was scarce. What we dreaded most, lack of drink for the herd, was the least of our troubles, necessity requiring its purchase only three or four times. And like a climax to a week of sore trials, when we were in sight of Red River a sand and dust storm struck us, blinding both men and herd for hours.

The beeves fared best, for with lowered heads they turned their backs to the howling gale, while the horsemen caught it on every side. The cattle drifted at will in an uncontrollable mass. The air was so filled with sifting sand and eddying dust that it was impossible to see a mounted man at a distance of fifty yards. The wind blew a hurricane, making it impossible to dismount in the face of it. Our horses trembled with fear, unsteady on their feet. The very sky overhead darkened as if night was falling. Two thirds of the men threw themselves in the lead of the beeves, firing six-shooters to check them, which could not even be heard by the ones on the flank and in the rear. Once the herd drifted against a wire fence, leveled it down and moved on, sullen but irresistible. Towards evening the storm abated, and half the outfit was sent out in search of the wagon, which was finally found about dark some four miles distant.

That night Owen Ubery, as he bathed his bloodshot eyes in a pail of water, said to the rest of us: "Fellows, if ever I have a boy, and tell him how his pa suffered this afternoon, and he don't cry, I'll cut a switch and whip him until he does."

CHAPTER V
RED RIVER STATION

When the spirit of a man is once broken, he becomes useless. On the trail it is necessary to have some diversion from hard work, long hours, and exposure to the elements. With man and beast, from the Brazos to Red River was a fire test of physical endurance. But after crossing into the Chickasaw Nation, a comparatively new country would open before us. When the strain of the past week was sorest, in buoying up the spirits of my outfit, I had promised them rest and recreation at the first possible opportunity.

Fortunately we had an easy ford. There was not even an indication that there had been a freshet on the river that spring. This was tempering the wind, for we were crippled, three of the boys being unable to resume their places around the herd on account of inflamed eyes. The cook had weathered the sand-storm better than any of us. Sheltering his team, and fastening his wagon-sheet securely, he took refuge under it until the gale had passed. Pressing him into the service the next morning, and assigning him to the drag end of the herd, I left the blind to lead the blind in driving the wagon. On reaching the river about the middle of the forenoon, we trailed the cattle across in a long chain, not an animal being compelled to swim. The wagon was carried over on a ferryboat, as it was heavily loaded, a six weeks' supply of provisions having been taken on before crossing. Once the trail left the breaks, on the north side of the river, we drew off several miles to the left and went into camp for the remainder of the day. Still keeping clear of the trail, daily we moved forward the wagon from three to five miles, allowing the cattle to graze and rest to contentment. The herd recuperated rapidly, and by the evening of the fourth day after crossing, the inflammation was so reduced in those whose eyes were inflamed, that we decided to start in earnest the next morning.

The cook was ordered to set out the best the wagon afforded, several outside delicacies were added, and a feast was in sight. G — G Cederdall had recrossed the river that day to mail a letter, and on his return proudly carried a basket of eggs on his arm. Three of the others had joined a fishing party from the Texas side, and had come in earlier in the day with a fine string of fish. Parent won new laurels in the supper to which he invited us about sundown. The cattle came in to their beds groaning and satiated, and dropped down as if ordered. When the first watch had taken them, there was nothing to do but sit around and tell stories. Since crossing Red River, we had slept almost night and day, but in that balmy May evening sleep was banished. The fact that we were in the Indian country, civilized though the Indians were, called forth many an incident. The raids of the Comanches into the Panhandle country during the buffalo days was a favorite topic. Vick Wolf, however, had had an Indian experience in the North with which he regaled us at the first opportunity.

"There isn't any trouble nowadays," said he, lighting a cigarette, "with these blanket Indians on the reservations. I had an experience once on a reservation where the Indians could have got me easy enough if they had been on the war-path. It was the first winter I ever spent on a Northern range, having gone up to the Cherokee Strip to avoid — well, no matter. I got a job in the Strip, not riding, but as a kind of an all-round rustler. This was long before the country was fenced, and they rode lines to keep the cattle on their ranges. One evening about nightfall in December, the worst kind of a blizzard struck us that the country had ever seen. The next day it was just as bad, and BLOODY cold. A fellow could not see any distance, and to venture away from the dugout meant to get lost. The third day she broke and the sun came out clear in the early evening. The next day we managed to gather the saddle horses, as they had not drifted like the cattle.

"Well, we were three days overtaking the lead of that cattle drift, and then found them in the heart of the Cheyenne country, at least on that reservation. They had drifted a good hundred miles before the storm broke. Every outfit in the Strip had gone south after their cattle. Instead of drifting them back together, the different ranches rustled for their own. Some of the foremen paid the Indians so much per head to gather for them, but ours didn't. The braves weren't very much struck on us on that account. I was cooking for the outfit, which suited me in winter weather. We had a permanent camp on a small well-wooded creek, from which we worked all the country round.

"One afternoon when I was in camp all alone, I noticed an Indian approaching me from out of the timber. There was a Winchester standing against the wagon wheel, but as the bucks were making no trouble, I gave the matter no attention. Mr. Injun came up to the fire and professed to be very friendly, shook hands, and spoke quite a number of words in English. After he got good and warm, he looked all over the wagon, and noticing that I had no sixshooter on, he picked up the carbine and walked out about a hundred yards to a little knoll, threw his arms in the air, and made signs.

"Instantly, out of the cover of some timber on the creek a quarter above, came about twenty young bucks, mounted, and yelling like demons. When they came up, they began circling around the fire and wagon. I was sitting on an empty corn-crate by the fire. One young buck, seeing that I was not scaring to suit him, unslung a carbine as he rode, and shot into the fire before me. The bullet threw fire and ashes all over me, and I jumped about ten feet, which suited them better. They circled around for several minutes, every one uncovering a carbine, and they must have fired a hundred and fifty shots into the fire. In fact they almost shot it out, scattering the fire around so that it came near burning up the bedding of our outfit. I was scared thoroughly by this time. If it was possible for me to have had fits, I'd have had one sure. The air seemed full of coals of fire and ashes. I got good practical insight into what hell's like. I was rustling the rolls of bedding out of the circle of fire, expecting every moment would be my last. It's a wonder I wasn't killed. Were they throwing lead? Well, I should remark! You see the ground was not frozen around the fire, and the bullets buried themselves in the soft soil.

"After they had had as much fun as they wanted, the leader gave a yell and they all circled the other way once, and struck back into the timber. Some of them had brought up the decoy Indian's horse when they made the dash at first, and he suddenly turned as wild as a Cheyenne generally gets. When the others were several hundred yards away, he turned his horse, rode back some little distance, and attracted my attention by holding out the Winchester. From his horse he laid it carefully down on the ground, whirled his pony, and rode like a scared wolf after the others. I could hear their yells for miles, as they made for their encampment over on the North Fork. As soon as I got the fire under control, I went out and got the carbine. It was empty; the Indian had used its magazine in the general hilarity. That may be an Indian's style of fun, but I failed to see where there was any in it for me."

The cook threw a handful of oily fish-bones on the fire, causing it to flame up for a brief moment. With the exception of Wayne Outcault, who was lying prone on the ground, the men were smoking and sitting Indian fashion around the fire. After rolling awhile uneasily, Outcault sat up and remarked, "I feel about half sick. Eat too much? Don't you think it. Why, I only ate seven or eight of those fish, and that oughtn't to hurt a baby. There was only half a dozen hard-boiled eggs to the man, and I don't remember of any of you being so generous as to share yours with me. Those few plates of prunes that I ate for dessert wouldn't hurt nobody — they're medicine to some folks. Unroll our bed, pardner, and I'll thrash around on it awhile."

Several trail stories of more or less interest were told, when Runt Pickett, in order to avoid the smoke, came over and sat down between Burl Van Vedder and me. He had had an experience, and instantly opened on us at short range. "Speaking of stampedes," said Runt, "reminds me of a run I was in, and over which I was paid by my employer a very high compliment. My first trip over the trail, as far north as Dodge, was in '78. The herd sold next day after reaching there, and as I had an old uncle and aunt living in middle Kansas, I concluded to run down and pay them a short visit. So I threw away all my trail togs — well, they were worn out, anyway — and bought me a new outfit complete. Yes, I even bought button shoes. After visiting a couple of weeks with my folks, I drifted back to Dodge in the hope of getting in with some herd bound farther north — I was perfectly useless on a farm. On my return to Dodge, the only thing about me that indicated a cow-hand was my Texas saddle and outfit, but in toggery, in my visiting harness, I looked like a rank tenderfoot.

"Well, boys, the first day I struck town I met a through man looking for hands. His herd had just come in over the Chisholm Trail, crossing to the western somewhere above. He was disgusted with his outfit, and was discharging men right and left and hiring new ones to take their places. I apologized for my appearance, showed him my outfit, and got a job cow-punching with this through man. He expected to hold on sale a week or two, when if unsold he would drift north to the Platte. The first week that I worked, a wet stormy night struck us, and before ten o'clock we lost every hoof of cattle. I was riding wild after little squads of cattle here and there, guided by flashes of lightning, when the storm finally broke. Well, there it was midnight, and I didn't have a HOOF OF CATTLE to hold and no one to help me if I had. The truth is, I was lost. Common horse-sense told me that; but where the outfit or wagon was was anybody's guess. The horses in my mount were as good as worthless; worn out, and if you gave one free rein he lacked the energy to carry you back to camp. I ploughed around in the darkness for over an hour, but finally came to a sudden stop on the banks of the muddy Arkansaw. Right there I held a council of war with myself, the decision of which was that it was at least five miles to the wagon.

"After I'd prowled around some little time, a bright flash of lightning revealed to me an old deserted cabin a few rods below. To this shelter I turned without even a bid, unsaddled my horse and picketed him, and turned into the cabin for the night. Early the next morning I was out and saddled my horse, and the question was, Which way is camp? As soon as the sun rose clearly, I got my bearings. By my reasoning, if the river yesterday was south of camp, this morning the wagon must be north of the river, so I headed in that direction. Somehow or other I stopped my horse on the first little knoll, and looking back towards the bottom, I saw in a horseshoe which the river made a large bunch of cattle. Of course I knew that all herds near about were through cattle and under herd, and the absence of any men in sight aroused my curiosity. I concluded to investigate it, and riding back found over five hundred head of the cattle we had lost the night before. 'Here's a chance to make a record with my new boss,' I said to myself, and circling in behind, began drifting them out of the bottoms towards the uplands. By ten o'clock I had got them to the first divide, when who should ride up but the owner, the old cowman himself — the sure enough big auger.

"'Well, son,' said my boss, 'you held some of them, didn't you?' 'Yes,' I replied, surly as I could, giving him a mean look, 'I've nearly ridden this horse to death, holding this bunch all night. If I had only had a good man or two with me, we could have caught twice as many. What kind of an outfit are you working, anyhow, Captain?' And at dinner that day, the boss pointed me out to the others and said, 'That little fellow standing over there with the button shoes on is the only man in my outfit that is worth a — — — — .'"

The cook had finished his work, and now joined the circle. Parent began regaling us with personal experiences, in which it was evident that he would prove the hero. Fortunately, however, we were spared listening to his self-laudation. Dorg Seay and Tim Stanley, bunkies, engaged in a friendly scuffle, each trying to make the other get a firebrand for his pipe. In the tussle which followed, we were all compelled to give way or get trampled underfoot. When both had exhausted themselves in vain, we resumed our places around the fire. Parent, who was disgusted over the interruption, on resuming his seat refused to continue his story at the request of the offenders, replying, "The more I see of you two varmints the more you remind me of mule colts."

Once the cook refused to pick up the broken thread of his story, John Levering, our horse-wrangler, preempted the vacated post. "I was over in Louisiana a few winters ago with a horse herd," said John, "and had a few experiences. Of all the simple people that I ever met, the 'Cajin' takes the bakery. You'll meet darkies over there that can't speak a word of anything but French. It's nothing to see a cow and mule harnessed together to a cart. One day on the road, I met a man, old enough to be my father, and inquired of him how far it was to the parish centre, a large town. He didn't know, except it was a long, long ways. He had never been there, but his older brother, once when he was a young man, had been there as a witness at court. The brother was dead now, but if he was living and present, it was quite possible that he would remember the distance. The best information was that it was a very long ways off. I rode it in the mud in less than two hours; just about ten miles.

"But that wasn't a circumstance to other experiences. We had driven about three hundred horses and mules, and after disposing of over two thirds of them, my employer was compelled to return home, leaving me to dispose of the remainder. I was a fair salesman, and rather than carry the remnant of the herd with me, made headquarters with a man who owned a large cane-brake pasture. It was a convenient stopping-place, and the stock did well on the young cane. Every week I would drive to some distant town eighteen or twenty head, or as many as I could handle alone. Sometimes I would sell out in a few days, and then again it would take me longer. But when possible I always made it a rule to get back to my headquarters to spend Sunday. The owner of the cane-brake and his wife were a simple couple, and just a shade or two above the Arcadians. But they had a daughter who could pass muster, and she took quite a shine to the 'Texas-Hoss-Man,' as they called me. I reckon you understand now why I made that headquarters? — there were other reasons besides the good pasturage.

"Well, the girl and her mother both could read, but I have some doubt about the old man on that score. They took no papers, and the nearest approach to a book in the house was an almanac three years old. The women folks were ravenous for something to read, and each time on my return after selling out, I'd bring them a whole bundle of illustrated papers and magazines. About my fourth return after more horses, — I was mighty near one of the family by that time, — when we were all seated around the fire one night, the women poring over the papers and admiring the pictures, the old man inquired what the news was over in the parish where I had recently been. The only thing that I could remember was the suicide of a prominent man. After explaining the circumstances, I went on to say that some little bitterness arose over his burial. Owing to his prominence it was thought permission would be given to bury him in the churchyard. But it seems there was some superstition about permitting a self-murderer to be buried in the same field as decent folks. It was none of my funeral, and I didn't pay overmuch attention to the matter, but the authorities refused, and they buried him just outside the grounds, in the woods.

"My host and I discussed the matter at some length. He contended that if the man was not of sound mind, he should have been given his little six feet of earth among the others. A horse salesman has to be a good second-rate talker, and being anxious to show off before the girl, I differed with her father. The argument grew spirited yet friendly, and I appealed to the women in supporting my view. My hostess was absorbed at the time in reading a sensational account of a woman shooting her betrayer. The illustrations covered a whole page, and the girl was simply burning, at short range, the shirt from off her seducer. The old lady was bogged to the saddle skirts in the story, when I interrupted her and inquired, 'Mother, what do you think ought to be done with a man who commits suicide?' She lowered the paper just for an instant, and looking over her spectacles at me replied, 'Well, I think any man who would do THAT ought to be made to support the child.'"

No comment was offered. Our wrangler arose and strolled away from the fire under the pretense of repicketing his horse. It was nearly time for the guards to change, and giving the last watch orders to point the herd, as they left the bed-ground in the morning, back on an angle towards the trail, I prepared to turn in. While I was pulling off my boots in the act of retiring, Clay Zilligan rode in from the herd to call the relief. The second guard were bridling their horses, and as Zilligan dismounted, he said to the circle of listeners, "Didn't I tell you fellows that there was another herd just ahead of us? I don't care if they didn't pass up the trail since we've been laying over, they are there just the same. Of course you can't see their camp-fire from here, but it's in plain view from the bed-ground, and not over four or five miles away. If I remember rightly, there's a local trail comes in from the south of the Wichita River, and joins the Chisholm just ahead. And what's more, that herd was there at nine o'clock this morning, and they haven't moved a peg since. Well, there's two lads out there waiting to be relieved, and you second guard know where the cattle are bedded."

CHAPTER VI
CAMP SUPPLY

In gala spirits we broke camp the next morning. The herd had left the bed-ground at dawn, and as the outfit rode away to relieve the last guard, every mother's son was singing. The cattle were a refreshing sight as they grazed forward, their ragged front covering half a mile in width. The rest of the past few days had been a boon to the few tender-footed ones. The lay-over had rejuvenated both man and beast. From maps in our possession we knew we were somewhere near the western border of the Chickasaw Nation, while on our left was the reservation of three blanket tribes of Indians. But as far as signs of occupancy were concerned, the country was unmarked by any evidence of civilization. The Chisholm Cattle Trail, which ran from Red River to the Kansas line, had almost fallen into disuse, owing to encroachments of settlements south of the former and westward on the latter. With the advancement of immigration, Abilene and Ellsworth as trail terminals yielded to the tide, and the leading cattle trace of the '70's was relegated to local use in '84.

The first guard was on the qui vive for the outfit whose camp-fire they had sighted the night before. I was riding with Clay Zilligan on the left point, when he sighted what we supposed was a small bunch of cattle lying down several miles distant. When we reached the first rise of ground, a band of saddle horses came in view, and while we were trying to locate their camp, Jack Splann from the opposite point attracted our attention and pointed straight ahead. There a large band of cattle under herd greeted our view, compelling us to veer to the right and intersect the trail sooner than we intended. Keeping a clear half-mile between us, we passed them within an hour and exchanged the compliments of the trail. They proved to be "Laurel Leaf" and "Running W" cattle, the very ones for which the International Railway agent at the meeting in February had so boastfully shown my employer the application for cars. The foreman was cursing like a stranded pirate over the predicament in which he found himself. He had left Santo Gertrudo Ranch over a month before with a herd of three thousand straight two-year-old steers. But in the shipment of some thirty-three thousand cattle from the two ranches to Wichita Falls, six trains had been wrecked, two of which were his own. Instead of being hundreds of miles ahead in the lead of the year's drive, as he expected, he now found himself in charge of a camp of cripples. What few trains belonging to his herd had escaped the ditch were used in filling up other unfortunate ones, the injured cattle from the other wrecks forming his present holdings.

"Our people were anxious to get their cattle on to the market early this year," said he, "and put their foot into it up to the knee. Shipping to Red River was an experiment with them, and I hope they've got their belly full. We've got dead and dying cattle in every pasture from the falls to the river, while these in sight aren't able to keep out of the stench of those that croaked between here and the ford. Oh, this shipping is a fine thing — for the railroads. Here I've got to rot all summer with these cattle, just because two of my trains went into the ditch while no other foreman had over one wrecked. And mind you, they paid the freight in advance, and now King and Kennedy have brought suit for damages amounting to double the shipping expense. They'll get it all right — in pork. I'd rather have a claim against a nigger than a railroad company. Look at your beeves, slick as weasels, and from the Nueces River. Have to hold them in, I reckon, to keep from making twenty miles a day. And here I am — Oh, hell, I'd rather be on a rock-pile with a ball and chain to my foot! Do you see those objects across yonder about two miles — in that old grass? That's where we bedded night before last and forty odd died. We only lost twenty-two last night. Oh, we're getting in shape fast. If you think you can hold your breakfast down, just take a ride through mine. No, excuse me — I've seen them too often already."

Several of the boys and myself rode into the herd some little distance, but the sight was enough to turn a copper-lined stomach. Scarcely an animal had escaped without more or less injury. Fully one half were minus one or both horns, leaving instead bloody stumps. Broken

299

bones and open sores greeted us on every hand; myriads of flies added to the misery of the cattle, while in many instances there was evidence of maggots at work on the living animal. Turning from the herd in disgust, we went back to our own, thankful that the rate offered us had been prohibitory. The trials and vexations of the road were mere nothings to be endured, compared to the sights we were then leaving. Even what we first supposed were cattle lying down, were only bed-grounds, the occupants having been humanely relieved by unwaking sleep. Powerless to render any assistance, we trailed away, glad to blot from our sight and memory such scenes of misery and death.

Until reaching the Washita River, we passed through a delightful country. There were numerous local trails coming into the main one, all of which showed recent use. Abandoned camp-fires and bed-grounds were to be seen on every hand, silent witnesses of an exodus which was to mark the maximum year in the history of the cattle movement from Texas. Several times we saw some evidence of settlement by the natives, but as to the freedom of the country, we were monarchs of all we surveyed. On arriving at the Washita, we encountered a number of herds, laboring under the impression that they were water-bound. Immediate entrance at the ford was held by a large herd of young cattle in charge of a negro outfit. Their stock were scattered over several thousand acres, and when I asked for the boss, a middle-aged darky of herculean figure was pointed out as in charge. To my inquiry why he was holding the ford, his answer was that until to-day the river had been swimming, and now he was waiting for the banks to dry. Ridiculing his flimsy excuse, I kindly yet firmly asked him either to cross or vacate the ford by three o'clock that afternoon. Receiving no definite reply, I returned to our herd, which was some five miles in the rear. Beyond the river's steep, slippery banks and cold water, there was nothing to check a herd.

After the noonday halt, the wrangler and myself took our remuda and went on ahead to the river. Crossing and recrossing our saddle stock a number of times, we trampled the banks down to a firm footing. While we were doing this work, the negro foreman and a number of his men rode up and sullenly watched us. Leaving our horses on the north bank, Levering and I returned, and ignoring the presence of the darky spectators, started back to meet the herd, which was just then looming up in sight. But before we had ridden any distance, the dusky foreman overtook us and politely said, "Look-ee here, Cap'n; ain't you-all afraid of losin' some of your cattle among ours?" Never halting, I replied, "Not a particle; if we lose any, you eat them, and we'll do the same if our herd absorbs any of yours. But it strikes me that you had better have those lazy niggers throw your cattle to one side," I called back, as he halted his horse. We did not look backward until we reached the herd; then as we turned, one on each side to support the points, it was evident that a clear field would await us on reaching the river. Every horseman in the black outfit was pushing cattle with might and main, to give us a clean cloth at the crossing.

The herd forded the Washita without incident. I remained on the south bank while the cattle were crossing, and when they were about half over some half-dozen of the darkies rode up and stopped apart, conversing among themselves. When the drag cattle passed safely out on the farther bank, I turned to the dusky group, only to find their foreman absent. Making a few inquiries as to the ownership of their herd, its destination, and other matters of interest, I asked the group to express my thanks to their foreman for moving his cattle aside. Our commissary crossed shortly afterward, and the Washita was in our rear. But that night, as some of my outfit returned from the river, where they had been fishing, they reported the negro outfit as having crossed and encamped several miles in our rear.

"All they needed was a good example," said Dorg Seay. "Under a white foreman, I'll bet that's a good lot of darkies. They were just about the right shade — old shiny black. As good cowhands as ever I saw were nigs, but they need a white man to blow and brag on them. But it always ruins one to give him any authority."

Without effort we traveled fifteen miles a day. In the absence of any wet weather to gall their backs, there was not a horse in our remuda unfit for the saddle. In fact, after reaching the

Indian Territory, they took on flesh and played like lambs. With the exception of long hours and night-herding, the days passed in seeming indolence as we swept northward, crossing rivers without a halt which in previous years had defied the moving herds. On arriving at the Cimarron River, in reply to a letter written to my employer on leaving Texas behind us, an answer was found awaiting me at Red Fork. The latter was an Indian trading-post, located on the mail route to Fort Reno, and only a few miles north of the Chisholm Crossing. The letter was characteristic of my employer. It contained but one imperative order, — that I should touch, either with or without the herd, at Camp Supply. For some unexplained reason he would make that post his headquarters until after the Buford herds had passed that point. The letter concluded with the injunction, in case we met any one, to conceal the ownership of the herd and its destination.

The mystery was thickening. But having previously declined to borrow trouble, I brushed this aside as unimportant, though I gave my outfit instructions to report the herd to every one as belonging to Omaha men, and on its way to Nebraska to be corn-fed. Fortunately I had ridden ahead of the herd after crossing the Cimarron, and had posted the outfit before they reached the trading-station. I did not allow one of my boys near the store, and the herd passed by as in contempt of such a wayside place. As the Dodge cut-off left the Chisholm Trail some ten miles above the Indian trading-post, the next morning we waved good-bye to the old cattle trace and turned on a northwest angle. Our route now lay up the Cimarron, which we crossed and recrossed at our pleasure, for the sake of grazing or to avoid several large alkali flats. There was evidence of herds in our advance, and had we not hurried past Red Fork, I might have learned something to our advantage. But disdaining all inquiry of the cut-off, fearful lest our identity be discovered, we deliberately walked into the first real danger of the trip.

At low water the Cimarron was a brackish stream. But numerous tributaries put in from either side, and by keeping above the river's ebb, an abundance of fresh water was daily secured from the river's affluents. The fifth day out from Red Rock was an excessively sultry one, and suffering would have resulted to the herd had we not been following a divide where we caught an occasional breeze. The river lay some ten miles to our right, while before us a tributary could be distinctly outlined by the cottonwoods which grew along it. Since early morning we had been paralleling the creek, having nooned within sight of its confluence with the mother stream, and consequently I had considered it unnecessary to ride ahead and look up the water. When possible, we always preferred watering the herd between three and four o'clock in the afternoon. But by holding our course, we were certain to intersect the creek at about the usual hour for the cattle's daily drink, and besides, as the creek neared the river, it ran through an alkali flat for some distance. But before the time arrived to intersect the creek on our course, the herd turned out of the trail, determined to go to the creek and quench their thirst. The entire outfit, however, massed on the right flank, and against their will we held them on their course. As their thirst increased with travel, they made repeated attempts to break through our cordon, requiring every man to keep on the alert. But we held them true to the divide, and as we came to the brow of a small hill within a quarter-mile of the water, a stench struck us until we turned in our saddles, gasping for breath. I was riding third man in the swing from the point, and noticing something wrong in front, galloped to the brow of the hill. The smell was sickening and almost unendurable, and there before us in plain view lay hundreds of dead cattle, bloated and decaying in the summer sun.

I was dazed by the awful scene. A pretty, greenswarded little valley lay before me, groups of cottonwoods fringed the stream here and there, around the roots of which were both shade and water. The reeking stench that filled the air stupefied me for the instant, and I turned my horse from the view, gasping for a mouthful of God's pure ozone. But our beeves had been scenting the creek for hours, and now a few of the leaders started forward in a trot for it. Like a flash it came to me that death lurked in that water, and summoning every man within hearing, I dashed to the lead of our cattle to turn them back over the hill. Jack Splann was on the point, and we turned the leaders when within two hundred yards of the creek, frequently jumping our horses over the putrid carcasses of dead cattle. The main body of the herd were trailing for three quarters of a mile in our rear, and none of the men dared leave their places. Untying our slickers, Splann and I fell upon the leaders and beat them back to the brow of the hill, when an unfortunate breeze was wafted through that polluted atmosphere from the creek to the cattle's nostrils. Turning upon us and now augmented to several hundred head, they sullenly started forward. But in the few minutes' interim, two other lads had come to our support, and dismounting we rushed them, whipping our slickers into ribbons over their heads. The mastery of man again triumphed over brutes in their thirst, for we drove them in a rout back over the divide.

Our success, however, was only temporary. Recovering our horses we beat the cattle back, seemingly inch by inch, until the rear came up, when we rounded them into a compact body. They quieted down for a short while, affording us a breathing spell, for the suddenness of this danger had not only unnerved me but every one of the outfit who had caught a glimpse of that field of death. The wagon came up, and those who needed them secured a change of horses. Leaving the outfit holding the herd, Splann and I took fresh mounts, and circling around, came in on the windward side of the creek. As we crossed it half a mile above the scene of disaster, each of us dipped a hand in the water and tasted it. The alkali was strong as concentrated lye, blistering our mouths in the experiment. The creek was not even running, but stood in long, deep pools, clear as crystal and as inviting to the thirsty as a mountain spring. As we neared the dead cattle, Splann called my attention to the attitude of the animals when death relieved them, the heads of fully two thirds being thrown back on their sides. Many, when stricken, were unable to reach the bank, and died in the bed of the stream. Making a complete circle of the ghastly scene, we returned to our own, agreeing that between five and six hundred cattle had met their fate in those death-dealing pools.

We were not yet out of the woods. On our return, many of the cattle were lying down, while in the west thunder-clouds were appearing. The North Fork of the Canadian lay on our left, which was now our only hope for water, yet beyond our reach for the day. Keeping the slight divide between us and the creek, we started the herd forward. Since it was impossible to graze them in their thirsty condition, I was determined to move them as far as possible before darkness overtook us. But within an hour we crossed a country trail over which herds had passed on their way northwest, having left the Chisholm after crossing the North Fork. At the first elevation which would give me a view of the creek, another scene of death and desolation greeted my vision, only a few miles above the first one. Yet from this same hill I could easily trace the meanderings of the creek for miles as it made a half circle in our front, both inviting and defying us. Turning the herd due south, we traveled until darkness fell, going into camp on a high, flat mesa of several thousand acres. But those evening breezes wafted an invitation to come and drink, and our thirsty herd refused to bed down. To add to our predicament, a storm thickened in the west. Realizing that we were confronting the most dangerous night in all my cattle experience, I ordered every man into the saddle. The remuda and team were taken in charge by the wrangler and cook, and going from man to man, I warned them what the consequences would be if we lost the herd during the night, and the cattle reached the creek.

The cattle surged and drifted almost at will, for we were compelled to hold them loose to avoid milling. Before ten o'clock the lightning was flickering overhead and around us, revealing acres of big beeves, which in an instant might take fright, and then, God help us. But in that night of trial a mercy was extended to the dumb brutes in charge. A warm rain began falling, first in a drizzle, increasing after the first hour, and by midnight we could hear the water slushing under our horses' feet. By the almost constant flashes of lightning we could see the cattle standing as if asleep, in grateful enjoyment of the sheeting downpour. As the night wore on, our fears of a stampede abated, for the buffalo wallows on the mesa filled, and water was on every hand. The rain ceased before dawn, but owing to the saturated condition underfoot, not a hoof lay down during the night, and when the gray of morning streaked the east, what a sense of relief it brought us. The danger had passed.

Near noon that day, and within a few miles of the North Fork, we rounded an alkaline plain in which this deadly creek had its source. Under the influence of the season, alkali had oozed up out of the soil until it looked like an immense lake under snow. The presence of range cattle in close proximity to this creek, for we were in the Cherokee Strip, baffled my reasoning; but the next day we met a range-rider who explained that the present condition of the stream was unheard of before, and that native cattle had instinct enough to avoid it. He accounted for its condition as due to the dry season, there being no general rains sufficient to flood the alkaline plain and thoroughly flush the creek. In reply to an inquiry as to the ownership of the unfortunate herds, he informed me that there were three, one belonging to Bob Houston, another to Major Corouthers, and the third to a man named Murphy, the total loss amounting to about two thousand cattle.

From this same range-man we also learned our location. Camp Supply lay up the North Fork some sixty miles, while a plain trail followed up the first bottom of the river. Wishing to avoid, if possible, intersecting the western trail south of Dodge, the next morning I left the herd to follow up, and rode into Camp Supply before noon. Lovell had sighted me a mile distant, and after a drink at the sutler's bar, we strolled aside for a few minutes' chat. Once I had informed him of the locality of the herd and their condition, he cautioned me not to let my business be known while in the post. After refreshing the inner man, my employer secured a horse and started with me on my return. As soon as the flag over Supply faded out of sight in our rear, we turned to the friendly shade of the timber on the North Fork and dismounted. I felt that the precaution exercised by the drover was premonitory of some revelation, and before we arose from the cottonwood log on which we took seats, the scales had fallen from my eyes and the atmosphere of mystery cleared.

"Tom," said my employer, "I am up against a bad proposition. I am driving these Buford cattle, you understand, on a sub-contract. I was the second lowest bidder with the government, and no sooner was the award made to The Western Supply Company than they sent an agent who gave me no peace until they sublet their contract. Unfortunately for me, when the papers were drawn, my regular attorney was out of town, and I was compelled to depend on a stranger. After the articles were executed, I submitted the matter to my old lawyer; he shook his head, arguing that a loophole had been left open, and that I should have secured an assignment of the original contract. After studying the matter over, we opened negotiations to secure a complete relinquishment of the award. But when I offered the company a thousand dollars over and above what they admitted was their margin, and they refused it, I opened my eyes to the true situation. If cattle went up, I was responsible and would have to fill my contract; if they went down, the company would buy in the cattle and I could go to hell in a hand-basket for all they cared. Their bond to the government does me no good, and beyond that they are irresponsible. Beeves have broken from four to five dollars a head, and unless I can deliver these Buford herds on my contract, they will lose me fifty thousand dollars."

"Have you any intimation that they expect to buy in other cattle?" I inquired.

"Yes. I have had a detective in my employ ever since my suspicions were aroused. There are two parties in Dodge this very minute with the original contract, properly assigned, and they are looking for cattle to fill it. That's why I'm stopping here and lying low. I couldn't explain it to you sooner, but you understand now why I drove those Buford herds in different road brands. Tom, we're up against it, and we've got to fight the devil with fire. Henceforth your name will be Tom McIndoo, your herd will be the property of the Marshall estate, and their agent, my detective, will be known as Charles Siringo. Any money or supplies you may need in Dodge, get in the usual form through the firm of Wright, Beverly & Co. — they understand. Hold your herd out south on Mulberry, and Siringo will have notice and be looking for you, or you can find him at the Dodge House. I've sent a courier to Fort Elliott to meet Dave and Quince, and once I see them, I'll run up to Ogalalla and wait for you. Now, until further orders, remember you never knew a man by the name of Don Lovell, and by all means don't forget to use what wits Nature gave you."

CHAPTER VII
WHEN GREEK MEETS GREEK

It was late that night when I reached the herd. Before I parted with my employer we had carefully reviewed the situation in its minutest details. Since the future could not be foreseen, we could only watch and wait. The Texan may have his shortcomings, but lack of fidelity to a trust is not one of them, and relying on the metal of my outfit, I at once put them in possession of the facts. At first their simple minds could hardly grasp the enormity of the injustice to our employer, but once the land lay clear, they would gladly have led a forlorn hope in Don Lovell's interests. Agitation over the matter was maintained at white heat for several days, as we again angled back towards the Cimarron. Around the camp-fires at night, the chicanery of The Western Supply Company gave place to the best stories at our command. "There ought to be a law," said Runt Pickett, in wrathy indignation, "making it legal to kill some people, same as rattlesnakes. Now, you take a square gambler and I don't think anything of losing my money against his game, but one of these sneaking, under-dealing, top-and-bottom-business pimps, I do despise. You can find them in every honest calling, same as vultures hover round when cattle are dying. Honest, fellows, I'd just dearly love to pull on a rope and watch one of the varmints make his last kick."

Several days of showery weather followed. Crossing the Cimarron, we followed up its north slope to within thirty miles of the regular western trail. Not wishing to intercept it until necessity compelled us, when near the Kansas line we made our last tack for Dodge. The rains had freshened the country and flushed the creeks, making our work easy, and early in the month of June we reached the Mulberry. Traveling at random, we struck that creek about twenty miles below the trail, and moved up the stream to within a short distance of the old crossing. The presence of a dozen other herds holding along it forced us into a permanent camp a short half-day's ride from the town. The horse-wrangler was pressed into service in making up the first guard that night, and taking Morg Tussler with me, I struck out for Dodge in the falling darkness. On reaching the first divide, we halted long enough to locate the camp-fires along the Mulberry to our rear, while above and below and beyond the river, fires flickered like an Indian encampment. The lights of Dodge were inviting us, and after making a rough estimate of the camps in sight, we rode for town, arriving there between ten and eleven o'clock. The Dodge House was a popular hostelry for trail men and cattle buyers, and on our making inquiry of the night clerk if a Mr. Siringo was stopping there, we were informed that he was, but had retired. I put up a trivial excuse for seeing him, the clerk gave me the number of his room, and Tussler and I were soon closeted with him. The detective was a medium-sized, ordinary man, badly pock-marked, with a soft, musical voice, and apparently as innocent as a boy. In a brief preliminary conversation, he proved to be a Texan, knowing every in and out of cattle, having been bred to the occupation. Our relations to each other were easily established. Reviewing the situation thoroughly, he informed me that he had cultivated the acquaintance of the parties holding the assignment of the Buford award. He had represented to them that he was the fiscal agent of some six herds on the trail that year, three of which were heavy beeves, and they had agreed to look them over, provided they arrived before the 15th of the month. He further assured me that the parties were mere figureheads of The Supply Company; that they were exceedingly bearish on the market, gloating over the recent depreciation in prices, and perfectly willing to fatten on the wreck and ruin of others.

It was long after midnight when the consultation ended. Appointing an hour for showing the herd the next day, or that one rather, Tussler and I withdrew, agreeing to be out of town before daybreak. But the blaze of gambling and the blare of dance-halls held us as in a siren's embrace until the lights dimmed with the breaking of dawn. Mounting our horses, we forded the river east of town and avoided the herds, which were just arising from their bed-grounds. On the divide we halted. Within the horizon before us, it is safe to assert that one hundred thousand cattle grazed in lazy contentment, all feeding against the morning breeze. Save for the freshness of early summer, with its background of green and the rarified atmosphere of the elevated plain, the scene before us might be compared to a winter drift of buffalo, ten years previous. Riding down the farther slope, we reached our camp in time for a late breakfast, the fifteen-mile ride having whetted our appetites. Three men were on herd, and sending two more with instructions to water the cattle an hour before noon, Tussler and I sought the shade of the wagon and fell asleep. It was some time after midday when, on sighting the expected conveyance approaching our camp, the cook aroused us. Performing a rather hasty ablution, I met the vehicle, freshened, and with my wits on tap. I nearly dragged the detective from the livery rig, addressing him as "Charley," and we made a rough ado over each other. Several of the other boys came forward and, shaking hands, greeted him with equal familiarity. As two strangers alighted on the opposite side, the detective took me around and they were introduced as Mr. Field and Mr. Radcliff, prospective beef buyers. The boys had stretched a tarpaulin, affording ample shade, and Parent invited every one to dinner. The two strangers were rather testy, but Siringo ate ravenously, repeatedly asking for things which were usually kept in a well-stocked chuck-wagon, meanwhile talking with great familiarity with Tussler and me.

The strangers said little, but were amused at the lightness of our dinner chat. I could see at a glance that they were not cowmen. They were impatient to see the cattle; and when dinner was over, I explained to them that the men on herd would be relieved for dinner by those in camp, and orders would be given, if it was their wish, to throw the cattle compactly together. To this Siringo objected. "No, Mac," said he, "that isn't the right way to show beeves. Here, Morg, listen to me; I'm foreman for the time being. When you relieve the other lads, edge in your cattle from an ordinary loose herd until you have them on two or three hundred acres. Then we can slowly drive through them for an hour or so, or until these gentlemen are satisfied. They're not wild, are they, Mac?"

I assured every one that the cattle were unusually gentle; that we had not had a run so far, but urged caution in approaching them with a conveyance. As soon as the relief started, I brought in the livery team off picket, watered, and harnessed them into the vehicle. It was my intention to accompany them on horseback, but Siringo hooted at the idea, and Mr. Radcliff and I occupied the back seat, puffing splendid cigars. We met the relieved men coming in, who informed us that the herd was just over the hill on the south side of the creek. On reaching the gentle rise, there below us grazed the logy, lazy beeves, while the boys quietly rode round, silently moving them together as instructed. Siringo drove to their lead, and halting, we allowed the cattle to loiter past us on either side of the conveyance. It was an easy herd to show, for the pounds avoirdupois were there. Numerous big steers, out of pure curiosity, came up near the vehicle and innocently looked at us as if expecting a dole or sweetmeat. A snap of the finger would turn them, showing their rounded buttocks, and they would rejoin the guard of honor. If eyes could speak, the invitation was timidly extended, "Look at me, Mr. Buyer." We allowed the herd to pass by us, then slowly circled entirely around them, and finally drove back and forth through them for nearly two hours, when the prospective buyers expressed themselves as satisfied.

But the fiscal agent was not. Calling two of the boys, he asked for the loan of their horses and insisted that the buyers ride the cattle over and thoroughly satisfy themselves on the brands. The boys gladly yielded, and as Mr. Field and Mr. Radcliff mounted to ride away, the detective halted them long enough to say: "Now, gentlemen, I wish to call your attention to the fact that over one half the herd are in the single Marshall ranch brand. There are also some five hundred head in the '8=8,' that being an outside ranch, but belonging to the estate. I am informed that the remainder of nearly a thousand were turned in by neighboring ranchmen in making up the herd, and you'll find those in various mixed brands. If there's a hoof among them not in the 'Open A' road, we'll cut them out for fear of trouble to the buyer. I never sold a man cattle in my life who wasn't my customer ever afterward. You gentlemen are strangers to me; and for that reason I conceal nothing. Now look them over carefully, and keep a sharp lookout for strays — cattle not in the road brand."

I knew there were about twenty strays in the herd, and informed Siringo to that effect, but the cattle buyers noticed only two, a red and a roan, which again classed them as inexperienced men among cattle. We returned to camp, not a word being said about trading, when the buyers suggested returning to town. Siringo looked at his watch, asked if there was anything further they wished to see or know, and expressed himself like a true Texan, "that there was ample time." I was the only one who had alighted, and as they started to drive away, I said to Siringo: "Charley, let me talk to you a minute first. You see how I'm situated here — too many neighbors. I'm going to ride north of town to-morrow, and if I can find a good camp on Saw Log, why I'll move over. We are nearly out of supplies, anyhow, and the wagon can go by town and load up. There's liable to be a mix-up here some night on the Mulberry, and I'd rather be excused than present."

"That's all right, Mac; that's just what I want you to do. If we trade, we'll make the deal within a day or two, and if not you can start right on for Ogalalla. I've been selling cattle the last few years to the biggest feeders in Nebraska, and I'm not a little bit afraid of placing those 'Open A's.' About four months full feed on corn will fit those steers to go to any market. Drop into town on your way back from the Saw Log to-morrow."

That evening my brother Bob rode into camp. He had seen our employer at Supply, and accordingly understood the situation. The courier had returned from Fort Elliott and reported his mission successful; he had met both Forrest and Sponsilier. The latter had had a slight run in the Panhandle during a storm, losing a few cattle, which he recovered the next day. For fear of a repetition, Forrest had taken the lead thereafter, and was due at Supply within a day or two. Flood and Priest had passed Abilene, Texas, in safety, but no word had reached our employer since, and it was believed that they had turned eastward and would come up the Chisholm Trail. Bob reported the country between Abilene and Doan's Crossing as cut into dust and barren of sustenance, many weak cattle having died in crossing the dry belt. But the most startling news, seriously disturbing us both, was that Archie Tolleston was stationed at Doan's Crossing on Red River as a trail-cutter. He had come up from the south to Wichita Falls by train with trail cattle, and finding no opening as a foreman, had accepted the position of inspector for some Panhandle cattle companies. He and Bob had had a friendly chat, and Archie admitted that it was purely his own hot-headedness which prevented his being one of Lovell's foremen on the present drive. The disturbing feature was, that after leaving headquarters in Medina County, he had gone into San Antonio, where he met a couple of strangers who partially promised him a job as trail boss, in case he presented himself in Dodge about June 15. They had intimated to him that it was possible they would need a foreman or two who knew the trail from the Arkansaw to the Yellowstone and Missouri River country. Putting this and that together, the presence of Archie Tolleston in Dodge was not at all favorable to the working out of our plans. "And Arch isn't the man to forget a humiliation," concluded Bob, to which I agreed.

The next morning I rode across to the Saw Log, and up that creek beyond all the herds. The best prospect for a camp was nearly due north opposite us, as the outfit lowest down the stream expected to start for the Platte the next morning. Having fully made up my mind to move camp, I rode for town, taking dinner on Duck Creek, which was also littered with cattle and outfits. I reached town early in the afternoon, and after searching all the hotels, located the fiscal agent in company with the buyers at the Lone Star saloon. They were seated around a table, and Mr. Field, noticing my entrance, beckoned me over and offered a chair. As I took the proffered seat, both strangers turned on me, and Mr. Radcliff said: "McIndoo, this agent of yours is the hardest man I ever tried to trade with. Here we've wasted the whole morning dickering, and are no nearer together than when we started. The only concession which Mr. Siringo seems willing to admit is that cattle are off from three to five dollars a head, while we contend that heavy beeves are off seven dollars."

"Excuse me for interrupting," said the fiscal agent, "but since you have used the words HEAVY BEEVES, either one of you ask Mac, here, what those 'Open A's' will dress to-day, and what they ought to gain in the next three months on good grass and water. There he sits; ask him."

Mr. Field explained that they had also differed as to what the herd would dress out, and invited my opinion. "Those beeves will dress off from forty-five to fifty per cent.," I replied. "The Texan being a gaunt animal does not shrink like a domestic beef. Take that 'Open A' herd straight through and they will dress from four fifty to six hundred pounds, or average better than five hundred all round. In three months, under favorable conditions, those steers ought to easily put on a hundred pounds of tallow apiece. Mr. Radcliff, do you remember pointing out a black muley yesterday and saying that he looked like a native animal? I'll just bet either one of you a hundred dollars that he'll dress out over five hundred pounds; and I'll kill him in your presence and you can weigh his quarters with a steelyard."

They laughed at me, Siringo joining in, and Mr. Field ordered the drinks. "Mac," said the detective, "these gentlemen are all right, and you shouldn't take any offense, for I don't blame them for driving a hard bargain. I'd probably do the same thing if I was the buyer instead of the seller. And remember, Mac, if the deal goes through, you are to drive the herd at the seller's risk, and deliver it at any point the buyer designates, they accepting without expense or reserve the cattle only. It means over three months' further expense, with a remuda thrown back on your hands; and all these incidentals run into money fast. Gentlemen, unless you increase the advance cash payment, I don't see how you can expect me to shade my offer. What's your hurry, Mac?"

As it was growing late, I had arisen, and saying that I expected to move camp to-morrow, invited the party to join me at the bar. I informed the buyers, during the few minutes' interim, that if they wished to look the cattle over again, the herd would cross the river below old Fort Dodge about noon the next day. They thanked me for the information, saying it was quite possible that they might drive down, and discussing the matter we all passed into the street. With the understanding that the prospect of making a deal was not hopeless, Siringo excused himself, and we strolled away together. No sooner was the coast clear than I informed the detective of the arrival of my brother, putting him in possession of every fact regarding Archie Tolleston. He readily agreed with me that the recent break between the latter and his former employer was a dangerous factor, and even went so far as to say that Tolleston's posing as a trail-cutter at Doan's Crossing was more than likely a ruse. I was giving the detective a detailed description of Archie, when he stopped me and asked what his special weaknesses were, if he had any. "Whiskey and women," I replied. "That's good," said he, "and I want you to send me in one of your best men in the morning — I mean one who will drink and carouse. He can watch the trains, and if this fellow shows up, we'll keep him soaked and let him enjoy himself. Send me one that's good for a ten days' protracted drunk. You think the other herds will be here within a few days? That's all I want to know."

I reached camp a little before dark, and learned that Bob's herd had dropped in just below us on the Mulberry. He expected to lie over a few days in passing Dodge, and I lost no time in preparing to visit his camp. While riding out that evening, I had made up my mind to send in Dorg Seay, as he was a heady fellow, and in drinking had an oak-tan stomach. Taking him with me, I rode down the Mulberry and reached the lower camp just as my brother and his outfit were returning from bedding-down the cattle. Bob readily agreed that the detective's plans were perfectly feasible, and offered to play a close second to Seay if it was necessary. And if his own brother does say so, Bob Quirk never met the man who could drink him under the table.

My herd started early for the Saw Log, and the wagon for town. Bob had agreed to go into Dodge in the morning, so Dorg stayed with our outfit and was to go in with me after crossing the river. We threaded our way through the other herds, and shortly before noon made an easy ford about a mile below old Fort Dodge. As we came down to the river, a carriage was seen on the farther bank, and I dropped from the point back to the drag end. Sure enough, as we trailed out, the fiscal agent and the buyers were awaiting me. "Well, Mac, I sold your herd last night after you left," said Siringo, dejectedly. "It was a kind of compromise trade; they raised the cash payment to thirty thousand dollars, and I split the difference in price. The herd goes at $29 a head all round. So from now on, Mac, you're subject to these gentlemen's orders."

Mr. Field, the elder of the two buyers, suggested that if a convenient camp could be found, we should lie over a few days, when final instructions would be given me. He made a memorandum of the number of head that I claimed in our road brand, and asked me if we could hold up the herd for a closer inspection. The lead cattle were then nearly a mile away, and galloping off to overtake the point, I left the party watching the saddle horses, which were then fording in our rear. But no sooner had I reached the lead and held up the herd, than I noticed Siringo on the wrangler's horse, coming up on the opposite side of the column of cattle from the vehicle. Supposing he had something of a private nature to communicate, I leisurely rode down the line and met him.

"Did you send that man in this morning?" he sternly demanded. I explained that my brother had done, properly coached, and that Seay would go in with me in the course of an hour.

"Give him any money you have and send him at once," commanded the detective. "Tolleston was due on the ten o'clock train, but it was an hour late. Those buyers wanted me to wait for it, so he could come along, but I urged the importance of catching you at the ford. Now, send your man Seay at once, get Tolleston beastly drunk, and quarter him in some crib until night."

Unobserved by the buyers, I signaled Seay, and gave him the particulars and what money I had. He rode back through the saddle stock, recrossed the river, and after rounding the bend, galloped away. Siringo continued: "You see, after we traded, they inquired if you were a safe man, saying if you didn't know the Yellowstone country, they had a man in sight who did. That was last night, and it seems that this morning they got a letter from Tolleston, saying he would be there on the next train. They're either struck on him, or else he's in their employ. Mark my words."

When we had showed the herd to the satisfaction of the purchasers, they expressed themselves as anxious to return to town; but the fiscal agent of the Marshall estate wished to look over the saddle horses first. Since they were unsold, and amounted to quite an item, he begged for just a few minutes' time to look them over carefully. Who could refuse such a reasonable request? The herd had started on for the Saw Log, while the remuda had wandered down the river about half a mile, and it took us nearly an hour to give them a thorough inspection. Once by ourselves, the detective said, with a chuckle: "All I was playing for was to get as large a cash payment as possible. Those mixed brands were my excuse for the money; the Marshall estate might wait for theirs, but the small ranchmen would insist on an immediate settlement the moment the cattle were reported sold. If it wasn't for this fellow Tolleston, I'd sell the other two Buford herds the day they arrive, and then we could give The Western Supply Company the laugh. And say, when they drew me a draft for thirty thousand dollars on a Washington City bank, I never let the ink dry on it until I took it around to Wright, Beverly & Co., and had them wire its acceptance. We'll give Seay plenty of time, and I think there'll be an answer on the check when we get back to town."

CHAPTER VIII
EN PASSANT

It was intentionally late in the day when we reached Dodge. My horse, which I was leading, gave considerable trouble while returning, compelling us to drive slow. The buyers repeatedly complained that dinner would be over at their hotel, but the detective knew of a good restaurant and promised all of us a feast. On reaching town, we drove to the stable where the rig belonged, and once free of the horses, Siringo led the way to a well-known night-and-day eating-house on a back street. No sooner had we entered the place than I remembered having my wagon in town, and the necessity of its reaching camp before darkness made my excuse imperative. I hurried around to the outfitting house and found the order filled and all ready to load into the wagon. But Parent was missing, and in skirmishing about to locate him, I met my brother Bob. Tolleston had arrived, but his presence had not been discovered until after Seay reached town. Archie was fairly well "organized" and had visited the hotel where the buyers were stopping, leaving word for them of his arrival. My brother and Seay had told him that they had met, down the trail that morning, two cattle buyers by the name of Field and Radcliff; that they were inquiring for a herd belonging to Tom Coleman, which was believed to be somewhere between Dodge and the Cimarron River. The two had assured Tolleston that the buyers might not be back for a week, and suggested a few drinks in memory of old times. As Archie was then three sheets in the wind, his effacement, in the hands of two rounders like Dorg Seay and Bob Quirk, was an easy matter.

Once the wagon was loaded and started for camp, I returned to the restaurant. The dinner was in progress, and taking the vacant seat, I lifted my glass with great regularity as toast after toast was drunk. Cigars were ordered, and with our feet on the table, the fiscal agent said: "Gentlemen, this is a mere luncheon and don't count. But if I'm able to sell you my other two beef herds, why, I'll give you a blow-out right. We'll make it six-handed — the three trail foremen and ourselves — and damn the expense so long as the cattle are sold. Champagne will flow like water, and when our teeth float, we'll wash our feet in what's left."

At a late hour the dinner ended. We were all rather unsteady on our feet, but the pock-marked detective and myself formed a guard of honor in escorting the buyers to their hotel, when an officious clerk attempted to deliver Tolleston's message. But anticipating it, I interrupted his highness and informed him that we had met the party; I was a thousand times obliged to him for his kindness, and forced on him a fine cigar, which had been given me by Bob Wright of the outfitting store. While Siringo and the buyers passed upstairs, I entertained the office force below with an account of the sale of my herd, constantly referring to my new employers. The fiscal agent returned shortly, bought some cigars at the counter, asked if he could get a room for the night, in case he was detained in town, and then we passed out of the hotel. This afforded me the first opportunity to notify Siringo of the presence of Tolleston, and I withheld nothing which was to his interest to know. But he was impatient to learn if the draft had been accepted, and asking me to bring my brother to his room within half an hour, he left me.

It was growing late in the day. The sun had already set when I found my brother, who was anxious to return to his camp for the night. But I urged his seeing Siringo first, and after waiting in the latter's room some time, he burst in upon us with a merry chuckle. "Well, the draft was paid all right," said he; "and this is Bob Quirk. Boys, things are coming nicely. This fellow Tolleston is the only cloud in the sky. If we can keep him down for a week, and the other herds come in shortly, I see nothing to thwart our plans. Where have you picketed Tolleston?" "Around in Dutch Jake's crib," replied Bob.

"That's good," continued the fiscal agent, "and I'll just drop in to-night and see the madam. A little money will go a long way with her, and in a case like this, the devil himself would be a welcome ally. You boys stay in town as much as you can and keep Tolleston snowed deep, and I'll take the buyers down the trail in the morning and meet the herds coming up."

My brother returned to his camp, and Siringo and I separated for the time being. In '84 Dodge, the Port Said of the plains, was in the full flower of her wickedness. Literally speaking, night was turned into day in the old trail town, for with the falling of darkness, the streets filled with people. Restaurants were crowded with women of the half-world, bar-rooms thronged with the wayfaring man, while in gambling and dance halls the range men congregated as if on special invitation. The familiar bark of the six-shooter was a matter of almost nightly occurrence; a dispute at the gaming table, a discourteous word spoken, or the rivalry for the smile of a wanton was provocation for the sacrifice of human life. Here the man of the plains reverted to and gave utterance to the savagery of his nature, or, on the other hand, was as chivalrous as in the days of heraldry.

I knew the town well, this being my third trip over the trail, and mingled with the gathering throng. Near midnight, and when in the Lady Gay dance-hall, I was accosted by Dorg Seay and the detective. They had just left Dutch Jake's, and reported all quiet on the Potomac. Seay had not only proved himself artful, but a good fellow, and had unearthed the fact that Tolleston had been in the employ of Field and Radcliff for the past three months. "You see," said Dorg, "Archie never knew me except the few days that I was about headquarters in Medina before we started. He fully believes that I've been discharged — and with three months' pay in my hip-pocket. The play now is that he's to first help me spend my wages, and then I'm to have a job under him with beeves which he expects to drive to the Yellowstone. He has intimated that he might be able to give me a herd. So, Tom, if I come out there and take possession of your cattle, don't be surprised. There's only one thing to beat our game — I can't get him so full but what he's over-anxious to see his employers. But if you fellows furnish the money, I'll try and pickle him until he forgets them."

The next morning Siringo and the buyers started south on the trail, and I rode for my camp on the Saw Log. Before riding many miles I sighted my outfit coming in a long lope for town. They reported everything serene at camp, and as many of the boys were moneyless, I turned back with them. An enjoyable day was before us; some drank to their hearts' content, while all gambled with more or less success. I was anxious that the outfit should have a good carouse, and showed the lights and shadows of the town with a pride worthy of one of its founders. Acting the host, I paid for our dinners; and as we sauntered into the street, puffing vile cigars, we nearly ran amuck of Dorg Seay and Archie Tolleston, trundling a child's wagon between them up the street. We watched them, keeping a judicious distance, as they visited saloon after saloon, the toy wagon always in possession of one or the other.

While we were amusing ourselves at the antics of these two, my attention was attracted by a four-mule wagon pulling across the bridge from the south. On reaching the railroad tracks, I recognized the team, and also the driver, as Quince Forrest's. Here was news, and accordingly I accosted him. Fortunately he was looking for me or my brother, as his foreman could not come in with the wagon, and some one was wanted to vouch for him in getting the needed supplies. They had reached the Mulberry the evening before, but several herds had mixed in a run during the night, though their cattle had escaped. Forrest was determined not to risk a second night on that stream, and had started his herd with the dawn, expecting to camp with his cattle that night west on Duck Creek. The herd was then somewhere between the latter and the main Arkansaw, and the cook was anxious to secure the supplies and reach the outfit before darkness overtook him. Sponsilier was reported as two days behind Forrest when the latter crossed the Cimarron, since when there had been no word from his cattle. They had met the buyers near the middle of the forenoon, and when Forrest admitted having the widow Timberlake's beef herd, they turned back and were spending the day with the cattle.

The situation demanded instant action. Taking Forrest's cook around to our outfitting store, I introduced and vouched for him. Hurrying back, I sent Wayne Outcault, as he was a stranger to Tolleston, to mix with the two rascals and send Seay to me at once. Some little time was consumed in engaging Archie in a game of pool, but when Dorg presented himself I lost no time in explaining the situation. He declared that it was no longer possible to interest Tolleston at Dutch Jake's crib during the day, and that other means of amusement must be resorted to, as Archie was getting clamorous to find his employers. To my suggestion to get a livery rig and take him for a ride, Dorg agreed. "Take him down the river to Spearville," I urged, "and try and break into the calaboose if you can. Paint the town red while you're about it, and if you both land in the lock-up, all the better. If the rascal insists on coming back to Dodge, start after night, get lost, and land somewhere farther down the river. Keep him away from this town for a week, and I'll gamble that you boss a herd for old man Don next year."

The afternoon was waning. The buyers might return at any moment, as Forrest's herd had no doubt crossed the river but a few miles above town.

I was impatiently watching the boys, as Dorg and Wayne cautiously herded Tolleston around to a livery stable, when my brother Bob rode up. He informed me that he had moved his camp that day across to the Saw Log; that he had done so to accommodate Jim Flood and The Rebel with a camp; their herds were due on the Mulberry that evening. The former had stayed all night at Bob's wagon, and reported his cattle, considering the dry season, in good condition. As my brother expected to remain in town overnight, I proposed starting for my camp as soon as Seay and his ward drove out of sight. They parleyed enough before going to unnerve a saint, but finally, with the little toy wagon on Tolleston's knee and the other driving, they started. Hurrahing my lads to saddle up, we rode past the stable where Seay had secured the conveyance; and while I was posting the stable-keeper not to be uneasy if the rig was gone a week, Siringo and the buyers drove past the barn with a flourish. Taking a back street, we avoided meeting them, and just as darkness was falling, rode into our camp some twelve miles distant.

My brother Bob's camp was just above us on the creek, and a few miles nearer town. As his wagon expected to go in after supplies the next morning, a cavalcade of fifteen men from the two outfits preceded it. My horse-wrangler had made arrangements with the cook to look after his charges, and in anticipation of the day before him, had our mounts corralled before sun-up. Bob's wrangler was also with us, and he and Levering quarreled all the way in about the respective merits of each one's remuda. A match was arranged between the two horses which they were riding, and on reaching a straight piece of road, my man won it and also considerable money. But no matter how much we differed among ourselves, when the interests of our employer were at stake, we were a unit. On reaching town, our numbers were augmented by fully twenty more from the other Lovell outfits, including the three foremen. My old bunkie, The Rebel, nearly dragged me from my horse, while Forrest and I forgot past differences over a social glass. And then there was Flood, my first foreman, under whom I served my apprenticeship on the trail, the same quiet, languid old Jim. The various foremen and their outfits were aware of the impending trouble over the Buford delivery, and quietly expressed their contempt for such underhand dealings. Quince Forrest had spent the evening before in town, and about midnight his herd of "Drooping T's" were sold at about the same figures as mine, except five thousand more earnest-money, and the privilege of the buyers placing their own foreman in charge thereafter. Forrest further reported that the fiscal agent and the strangers had started to meet Sponsilier early that morning, and that the probability of all the herds moving out in a few days was good.

Seay and his charge were still absent, and the programme, as outlined, was working out nicely. With the exception of Forrest and myself, the other foremen were busy looking after their outfits, while Bob Quirk had his wagon to load and start on its return. Quince confided to me that though he had stayed on Duck Creek the night before, his herd would noon that day on Saw Log, and camp that evening on the next creek north. When pressed for his reasons, he shrugged his shoulders, and with a quiet wink, said: "If this new outfit put a man over me, just the minute we get out of the jurisdiction of this county, off his horse he goes and walks back. If it's Tolleston, the moment he sees me and recognizes my outfit as belonging to Lovell, he'll raise the long yell and let the cat out. When that happens, I want to be in an unorganized country where a six-shooter is the highest authority." The idea was a new one to me, and I saw the advantage of it, but could not move without Siringo's permission, which

Forrest had. Accordingly about noon, Quince summoned his men together, and they rode out of town. Looking up a map of Ford County, I was delighted to find that my camp on Saw Log was but a few miles below the north line.

Among the boys the day passed in riotousness. The carousing was a necessary stimulant after the long, monotonous drive and exposure to the elements. Near the middle of the forenoon, Flood and The Rebel rounded up their outfits and started south for the Mulberry, while Bob Quirk gathered his own and my lads preparatory to leaving for the Saw Log. I had agreed to remain on guard for that night, for with the erratic turn on Tolleston's part, we were doubly cautious. But when my outfit was ready to start, Runt Pickett, the feisty little rascal, had about twenty dollars in his possession which he insisted on gambling away before leaving town. Runt was comfortably drunk, and as Bob urged humoring him, I gave my consent, provided he would place it all at one bet, to which Pickett agreed. Leaving the greater part of the boys holding the horses, some half-dozen of us entered the nearest gambling-house, and Runt bet nineteen dollars "Alce" on the first card which fell in a monte lay-out. To my chagrin, he won. My brother was delighted over the little rascal's luck, and urged him to double his bet, but Pickett refused and invited us all to have a drink. Leaving this place, we entered the next gaming-hall, when our man again bet nineteen dollars alce on the first card. Again he won, and we went the length of the street, Runt wagering nineteen dollars alce on the first card for ten consecutive times without losing a bet. In his groggy condition, the prospect of losing Pickett's money was hopeless, and my brother and I promised him that he might come back the next morning and try to get rid of his winnings.

Two whole days passed with no report from either Seay or the buyers. Meanwhile Flood and The Rebel threaded their way through the other herds, crossing the Arkansaw above town, their wagons touching at Dodge for new supplies, never halting except temporarily until they reached the creek on which Forrest was encamped. The absence of Siringo and the buyers, to my thinking, was favorable, for no doubt when they came in, a deal would have been effected on the last of the Buford herds. They returned some time during the night of the third day out, and I failed to see the detective before sunrise the next morning. When I did meet him, everything seemed so serene that I felt jubilant over the outlook. Sponsilier's beeves had firmly caught the fancy of the buyers, and the delay in closing the trade was only temporary. "I can close the deal any minute I want to," said Siringo to me, "but we mustn't appear too anxious. Old man Don's idea was to get about one hundred thousand dollars earnest-money in hand, but if I can get five or ten more, it might help tide us all over a hard winter. My last proposition to the buyers was that if they would advance forty-five thousand dollars on the 'Apple' beeves — Sponsilier's cattle — they might appoint, at the seller's expense, their own foreman from Dodge to the point of delivery. They have agreed to give me an answer this morning, and after sleeping over it, I look for no trouble in closing the trade."

The buyers were also astir early. I met Mr. Field in the post-office, where he was waiting for it to open. To his general inquiries I reported everything quiet, but suggested we move camp soon or the cattle would become restless. He listened very attentively, and promised that within a few days permission would be given to move out for our final destination. The morning were the quiet hours of the town, and when the buyers had received and gone over their large and accumulated mail, the partners came over to the Dodge House, looking for the fiscal agent, as I supposed, to close the trade on Sponsilier's cattle. Siringo was the acme of indifference, but listened to a different tale. A trusted man, in whom they had placed a great deal of confidence, had failed to materialize. He was then overdue some four or five days, and foul play was suspected. The wily detective poured oil on the troubled waters, assuring them if their man failed to appear within a day or two, he would gladly render every assistance in looking him up. Another matter of considerable moment would be the arrival that morning of a silent partner, the financial man of the firm from Washington, D.C. He was due to arrive on the "Cannon Ball" at eight o'clock, and we all sauntered down to meet the train from the East. On its arrival, Siringo and I stood back among the crowd, but the buyers pushed forward, looking for their friend. The first man to alight from the day coach, coatless and with both eyes blackened, was Archie Tolleston; he almost fell into the arms of our cattle buyers. I recognized Archie at a glance, and dragging the detective inside the waiting-room, posted him as to the arrival with the wild look and blood-shot optics. Siringo cautioned me to go to his room and stay there, promising to report as the day advanced.

Sponsilier had camped the night before on the main river, and as I crossed to the hotel, his commissary pulled up in front of Wright, Beverly & Co.'s outfitting store. Taking the chances of being seen, I interviewed Dave's cook, and learned that his foreman had given him an order for the supplies, and that Sponsilier would not come in until after the herd had passed the Saw Log. As I turned away, my attention was attracted by the deference being shown the financial man of the cattle firm, as the party wended their way around to the Wright House. The silent member of the firm was a portly fellow, and there was no one in the group but did him honor, even the detective carrying a light grip, while Tolleston lumbered along with a heavy one.

My effacement was only temporary, as Siringo appeared at his room shortly afterward. "Well, Quirk," said he, with a smile, "I reckon my work is all done. Field and Radcliff didn't feel like talking business this morning, at least until they had shown the financial member their purchases, both real and prospective. Yes, they took the fat Colonel and Tolleston with them and started for your camp with a two-seated rig. From yours they expect to drive to Forrest's camp, and then meet Sponsilier on the way coming back. No; I declined a very pressing invitation to go along — you see my mixed herds might come in any minute. And say, that man Tolleston was there in a hundred places with the big conversation; he claims to have been kidnapped, and was locked up for the last four days. He says he whipped your man Seay, but couldn't convince the authorities of his innocence until last night, when they set him free. According to his report, Seay's in jail yet at a little town down the road called Kinsley. Now, I'm going to take a conveyance to Spearville, and catch the first train out of there East. Settle my bill with this hotel, and say that I may be out of town for a few days, meeting a herd which I'm expecting. When Tolleston recognizes all three of those outfits as belonging to Don Lovell — well, won't there be hell to pay? Yes, my work is all done."

I fully agreed with the detective that Archie would recognize the remudas and outfits as Lovell's, even though the cattle were road-branded out of the usual "Circle Dot." Siringo further informed me that north of Ford County was all an unorganized country until the Platte River was reached at Ogalalla, and advised me to ignore any legal process served outside those bounds. He was impatient to get away, and when he had put me in possession of everything to our advantage, we wrung each other's hands in farewell. As the drive outlined by the cattle buyers would absorb the day, I felt no necessity of being in a hurry. The absence of Dorg Seay was annoying, and the fellow had done us such valiant service, I felt in honor bound to secure his release. Accordingly I wired the city marshal at Kinsley, and received a reply that Seay had been released early that morning, and had started overland for Dodge. This was fortunate, and after settling all bills, I offered to pay the liveryman in advance for the rig in Seay's possession, assuring him by the telegram that it would return that evening. He refused to make any settlement until the condition of both the animal and the conveyance had been passed upon, and fearful lest Dorg should come back moneyless, I had nothing to do but await his return. I was growing impatient to reach camp, there being no opportunity to send word to my outfit, and the passing hours seemed days, when late in the afternoon Dorg Seay drove down the main street of Dodge as big as a government beef buyer. The liveryman was pleased and accepted the regular rate, and Dorg and I were soon galloping out of town. As we neared the first divide, we dropped our horses into a walk to afford them a breathing spell, and in reply to my fund of information, Seay said:

"So Tolleston's telling that he licked me. Well, that's a good one on this one of old man Seay's boys. Archie must have been crazy with the heat. The fact is that he had been trying to quit me for several days. We had exhausted every line of dissipation, and when I decided that it was no longer possible to hold him, I insulted and provoked him into a quarrel, and we were both arrested. Licked me, did he? He couldn't lick his upper lip."

CHAPTER IX
AT SHERIFF'S CREEK

The sun had nearly set when we galloped into Bob Quirk's camp. Halting only long enough to advise my brother of the escape of Tolleston and his joining the common enemy, I asked him to throw any pursuit off our trail, as I proposed breaking camp that evening. Seay and myself put behind us the few miles between the two wagons, and dashed up to mine just as the outfit were corralling the remuda for night-horses. Orders rang out, and instead of catching our regular guard mounts, the boys picked the best horses in their strings. The cattle were then nearly a mile north of camp, coming in slowly towards the bed-ground, but a half-dozen of us rushed away to relieve the men on herd and turn the beeves back. The work-mules were harnessed in, and as soon as the relieved herders secured mounts, our camp of the past few days was abandoned. The twilight of evening was upon us, and to the rattling of the heavily loaded wagon and the shouting of the wrangler in our rear were added the old herd songs. The cattle, without trail or trace to follow, and fit ransom for a dozen kings in pagan ages, moved north as if imbued with the spirit of the occasion.

A fair moon favored us. The night was an ideal one for work, and about twelve o'clock we bedded down the herd and waited for dawn. As we expected to move again with the first sign of day, no one cared to sleep; our nerves were under a high tension with expectation of what the coming day might bring forth. Our location was an unknown quantity. All agreed that we were fully ten miles north of the Saw Log, and, with the best reasoning at my command, outside the jurisdiction of Ford County. The regular trail leading north was some six or eight miles to the west, and fearful that we had not reached unorganized territory, I was determined to push farther on our course before veering to the left. The night halt, however, afforded us an opportunity to compare notes and arrive at some definite understanding as to the programme of the forthcoming day. "Quirk, you missed the sight of your life," said Jake Blair, as we dismounted around the wagon, after bedding the cattle, "by not being there when the discovery was made that these 'Open A's' were Don Lovell's cattle. Tolleston, of course, made the discovery; but I think he must have smelt the rat in advance. Archie and the buyers arrived for a late dinner, and several times Tolleston ran his eye over one of the boys and asked, 'Haven't I met you somewhere?' but none of them could recall the meeting. Then he got to nosing around the wagon and noticing every horse about camp. The road-brand on the cattle threw him off the scent just for a second, but when he began reading the ranch-brands, he took a new hold. As he looked over the remuda, the scent seemed to get stronger, and when he noticed the 'Circle Dot' on those work-mules, he opened up and bayed as if he had treed something. And sure enough he had; for you know, Tom, those calico lead mules belonged in his team last year, and he swore he'd know them in hell, brand or no brand. When Archie announced the outfit, lock, stock, and barrel, as belonging to Don Lovell, the old buyers turned pale as ghosts, and the fat one took off his hat and fanned himself. That act alone was worth the price of admission. But when we boys were appealed to, we were innocent and likewise ignorant, claiming that we always understood that the herd belonged to the Marshall estate, but then we were just common hands and not supposed to know the facts in the case. Tolleston argued one way, and we all pulled the other, so they drove away, looking as if they hoped it wasn't true. But it was the sight of your life to see that fat fellow fan himself as he kept repeating, 'I thought you boys hurried too much in buying these cattle.'"

The guards changed hourly. No fire was allowed, but Parent set out all the cold food available, and supplementing this with canned goods, we had a midnight lunch. Dorg Seay regaled the outfit with his recent experience, concealing nothing, and regretfully admitting that his charge had escaped before the work was finished. A programme was outlined for the morrow, the main feature of which was that, in case of pursuit, we would all tell the same story. Dawn came between three and four on those June mornings, and with the first streak of gray in the east we divided the outfit and mounted our horses, part riding to push the cattle off their beds and the others to round in the remuda. Before the herd had grazed out a half-mile, we were overtaken by half the outfit on fresh mounts, who at once took charge of the herd. When the relieved men had secured horses, I remained behind and assisted in harnessing in the team and gathering the saddle stock, a number of which were missed for lack of proper light. With the wagon once started, Levering and myself soon had the full remuda in hand and were bringing up the rear in a long, swinging trot. Before the sun peeped over the eastern horizon, we passed the herd and overtook the wagon, which was bumping along over the uneven prairie. Ordering the cook to have breakfast awaiting us beyond a divide which crossed our front, I turned back to the herd, now strung out in regular trailing form. The halt ahead would put us full fifteen miles north of our camp on the Saw Log. An hour later, as we were scaling the divide, one of the point-men sighted a posse in our rear, coming after us like fiends. I was riding in the swing at the time, the herd being strung out fully a mile, and on catching first sight of the pursuers, turned and hurried to the rear. To my agreeable surprise, instead of a sheriff's posse, my brother and five of his men galloped up and overtook us.

"Well, Tom, it's a good thing you moved last night," said Bob, as he reined in his reeking horse. "A deputy sheriff and posse of six men had me under arrest all night, thinking I was the Quirk who had charge of Don Lovell's 'Open A' herd. Yes, they came to my camp about midnight, and I admitted that my name was Quirk and that we were holding Lovell's cattle. They guarded me until morning, — I slept like an innocent babe myself, — when the discovery was made that my herd was in a 'Circle Dot' road-brand instead of an 'Open A,' which their warrant called for. Besides, I proved by fourteen competent witnesses, who had known me for years, that my name was Robert Burns Quirk. My outfit told the posse that the herd they were looking for were camped three miles below, but had left during the afternoon before, and no doubt were then beyond their bailiwick. I gave the posse the horse-laugh, but they all went down the creek, swearing they would trail down that herd of Lovell's. My cattle are going to follow up this morning, so I thought I'd ride on ahead and be your guest in case there is any fun to-day."

The auxiliary was welcomed. The beeves moved on up the divide like veterans assaulting an intrenchment. On reaching a narrow mesa on the summit, a northwest breeze met the leaders, and facing it full in the eye, the herd was allowed to tack westward as they went down the farther slope. This watershed afforded a fine view of the surrounding country, and from its apex I scanned our rear for miles without detecting any sign of animate life. From our elevation, the plain dipped away in every direction. Far to the east, the depression seemed as real as a trough in the ocean when seen from the deck of a ship. The meanderings of this divide were as crooked as a river, and as we surveyed its course one of Bob's men sighted with the naked eye two specks fully five miles distant to the northwest, and evidently in the vicinity of the old trail. The wagon was in plain view, and leaving three of my boys to drift the cattle forward, we rode away with ravenous appetites to interview the cook. Parent maintained his reputation as host, and with a lofty conversation reviewed the legal aspect of the situation confronting us. A hasty breakfast over, my brother asked for mounts for himself and men; and as we were corralling our remuda, one of the three lads on herd signaled to us from the mesa's summit. Catching the nearest horses at hand, and taking our wrangler with us, we cantered up the slope to our waiting sentinel.

"You can't see them now," said Burl Van Vedder, our outlook; "but wait a few minutes and they'll come up on higher ground. Here, here, you are looking a mile too far to the right — they're not following the cattle, but the wagon's trail. Keep your eyes to the left of that shale outcropping, and on a line with that lone tree on the Saw Log. Hold your horses a minute; I've been watching them for half an hour before I called you; be patient, and they'll rise like a trout. There! there comes one on a gray horse. See those two others just behind him. Now, there come the others — six all told." Sure enough, there came the sleuths of deputy sheriffs, trailing up our wagon. They were not over three miles away, and after patiently waiting nearly an hour, we rode to the brink of the slope, and I ordered one of the boys to fire his pistol to attract their attention. On hearing the report, they halted, and taking off my hat I waved them forward. Feeling that we were on safe territory, I was determined to get in the first bluff, and as they rode up, I saluted the leader and said:

"Good-morning, Mr. Sheriff. What are you fooling along on our wagon track for, when you could have trailed the herd in a long lope? Here we've wasted a whole hour waiting for you to come up, just because the sheriff's office of Ford County employs as deputies 'nesters' instead of plainsmen. But now since you are here, let us proceed to business, or would you like to breakfast first? Our wagon is just over the other slope, and you-all look pale around the gills this morning after your long ride and sleepless night. Which shall it be, business or breakfast?"

Haughtily ignoring my irony, the leader of the posse drew from his pocket several papers, and first clearing his throat, said in an imperious tone, "I have a warrant here for the arrest of Tom Quirk, alias McIndoo, and a distress warrant for a herd of 'Open A' — "

"Old sport, you're in the right church, but the wrong pew," I interrupted. "This may be the state of Kansas, but at present we are outside the bailiwick of Ford County, and those papers of yours are useless. Let me take those warrants and I'll indorse them for you, so as to dazzle your superiors on their return without the man or property. I was deputized once by a constable in Texas to assist in recovering some cattle, but just like the present case they got out of our jurisdiction before we overtook them. The constable was a lofty, arrogant fellow like yourself, but had sense enough to keep within his rights. But when it came to indorsing the warrant for return, we were all up a stump, and rode twenty miles out of our way so as to pass Squire Little's ranch and get his advice on the matter. The squire had been a justice in Tennessee before coming to our state, and knew just what to say. Now let me take those papers, and I'll indorse them 'Non est inventus,' which is Latin for SCOOTED, BY GOSH! Ain't you going to let me have them?"

"Now, look here, young man," scornfully replied the chief deputy, "I'll — "

"No, you won't," I again interrupted. "Let me read you a warrant from a higher court. In the name of law, you are willing to prostitute your office to assist a gang of thieves who have taken advantage of an opportunity to ruin my employer, an honest trail drover. The warrant I'm serving was issued by Judge Colt, and it says he is supreme in unorganized territory; that your official authority ceases the moment you step outside your jurisdiction, and you know the Ford County line is behind us. Now, as a citizen, I'll treat you right, but as an official, I won't even listen to you. And what's more, you can't arrest me or any man in my outfit; not that your hair's the wrong color, but because you lack authority. I'm the man you're looking for, and these are Don Lovell's cattle, but you can't touch a hoof of them, not even a stray. Now, if you want to dispute the authority which I've sighted, all you need to do is pull your guns and open your game."

"Mr. Quirk," said the deputy, "you are a fugitive from justice, and I can legally take you wherever I find you. If you resist arrest, all the worse, as it classes you an outlaw. Now, my advice is — "

But the sentence was never finished, for coming down the divide like a hurricane was a band of horsemen, who, on sighting us, raised the long yell, and the next minute Dave Sponsilier and seven of his men dashed up. The boys opened out to avoid the momentum of the onslaught, but the deputies sat firm; and as Sponsilier and his lads threw their horses back on their haunches in halting, Dave stood in his stirrups, and waving his hat shouted, "Hurrah for Don Lovell, and to hell with the sheriff and deputies of Ford County!" Sponsilier and I were great friends, as were likewise our outfits, and we nearly unhorsed each other in our rough but hearty greetings. When quiet was once more restored, Dave continued: "I was in Dodge last night, and Bob Wright put me next that the sheriff was going to take possession of two of old man Don's herds this morning. You can bet your moccasins that the grass didn't grow very much while I was getting back to camp. Flood and The Rebel took fifteen men and went to Quince's support, and I have been scouting since dawn trying to locate you. Yes, the sheriff himself and five deputies passed up the trail before daybreak to arrest Forrest and take possession of his herd — I don't think. I suppose these strangers are deputy sheriffs? If it was me, do you know what I'd do with them?"

The query was half a command. It required no order, for in an instant the deputies were surrounded, and had it not been for the cool judgment of Bob Quirk, violence would have resulted. The primitive mind is slow to resent an affront, and while the chief deputy had couched his last remarks in well-chosen language, his intimation that I was a fugitive from justice, and an outlaw in resisting arrest, was tinder to stubble. Knowing the metal of my outfit, I curbed the tempest within me, and relying on a brother whom I would gladly follow to death if need be, I waved hands off to my boys. "Now, men," said Bob to the deputies, "the easiest way out of this matter is the best. No one here has committed any crime subjecting him to arrest, neither can you take possession of any cattle belonging to Don Lovell. I'll renew the invitation for you to go down to the wagon and breakfast, or I'll give you the best directions at my command to reach Dodge. Instead of trying to attempt to accomplish your object you had better go back to the chaparral — you're spelled down. Take your choice, men."

Bob's words had a soothing effect. He was thirty-three years old and a natural born leader among rough men. His advice carried the steely ring of sincerity, and for the first time since the meeting, the deputies wilted. The chief one called his men aside, and after a brief consultation my brother was invited to join them, which he did. I afterwards learned that Bob went into detail in defining our position in the premises, and the posse, once they heard the other side of the question, took an entirely different view of the matter. While the consultation was in progress, we all dismounted; cigarettes were rolled, and while the smoke arose in clouds, we reviewed the interim since we parted in March in old Medina. The sheriff's posse accompanied my brother to the wagon, and after refreshing themselves, remounted their horses. Bob escorted them back across the summit of the mesa, and the olive branch waved in peace on the divide.

The morning was not far advanced. After a brief consultation, the two older foremen urged that we ride to the relief of Forrest. A hint was sufficient, and including five of my best-mounted men, a posse of twenty of us rode away. We held the divide for some distance on our course, and before we left it, a dust-cloud, indicating the presence of Bob's herd, was sighted on the southern slope, while on the opposite one my cattle were beginning to move forward. Sponsilier knew the probable whereabouts of Forrest, and under his lead we swung into a free gallop as we dropped down the northern slope from the mesa. The pace was carrying us across country at a rate of ten miles an hour, scarcely a word being spoken, as we shook out kink after kink in our horses or reined them in to recover their wind. Our objective point was a slight elevation on the plain, from which we expected to sight the trail if not the herds of Flood, Forrest, and The Rebel. On reaching this gentle swell, we reined in and halted our horses, which were then fuming with healthy sweat. Both creek and trail were clearly outlined before us, but with the heat-waves and mirages beyond, our view was naturally restricted. Sponsilier felt confident that Forrest was north of the creek and beyond the trail, and again shaking out our horses, we silently put the intervening miles behind us. Our mounts were all fresh and strong, and in crossing the creek we allowed them a few swallows of water before continuing our ride. We halted again in crossing the trail, but it was so worn by recent use that it afforded no clue to guide us in our quest. But from the next vantage-point which afforded us a view, a sea of cattle greeted our vision, all of which seemed under herd. Wagon sheets were next sighted, and finally a horseman loomed up and signaled to us. He proved to be one of Flood's men, and under his direction Forrest's camp and cattle were soon located. The lad assured us that a pow-wow had been in session since daybreak, and we hurried away to add our numbers to its council. When we sighted Forrest's wagon among some cottonwoods, a number of men were just mounting to ride away, and before we reached camp, they crossed the creek heading south. A moment later, Forrest walked out, and greeting us, said:

"Hello, fellows. Get down and let your horses blow and enjoy yourselves. You're just a minute late to meet some very nice people. Yes, we had the sheriff from Dodge and a posse of men for breakfast. No — no particular trouble, except John Johns, the d — fool, threw the loop of his rope over the neck of the sheriff's horse, and one of the party offered to unsling a carbine. But about a dozen six-shooters clicked within hearing, and he acted on my advice and cut gun-plays out. No trouble at all except a big medicine talk, and a heap of legal phrases that I don't sabe very clear. Turn your horses loose, I tell you, for I'm going to kill a nice fat stray, and towards evening, when the other herds come up, we'll have a round-up of Don Lovell's outfits. I'll make a little speech, and on account of the bloodless battle this morning, this stream will be rechristened Sheriff's Creek."

CHAPTER X
A FAMILY REUNION

The hospitality of a trail wagon was aptly expressed in the invitation to enjoy ourselves. Some one had exercised good judgment in selecting a camp, for every convenience was at hand, including running water and ample shade from a clump of cottonwoods. Turning our steaming horses free, we threw ourselves, in complete abandonment and relaxation, down in the nearest shade. Unmistakable hints were given our host of certain refreshments which would be acceptable, and in reply Forrest pointed to a bucket of creek water near the wagon wheel, and urged us not to be at all backward.

Every one was well fortified with brown cigarette papers and smoking tobacco, and singly and in groups we were soon smoking like hired hands and reviewing the incidents of the morning. Forrest's cook, a tall, red-headed fellow, in anticipation of the number of guests his wagon would entertain for the day, put on the little and the big pot. As it only lacked an hour of noon on our arrival, the promised fresh beef would not be available in time for dinner; but we were not like guests who had to hurry home — we would be right there when supper was ready.

The loss of a night's sleep on my outfit was a good excuse for an after-dinner siesta. Untying our slickers, we strolled out of hearing of the camp, and for several hours obliterated time. About three o'clock Bob Quirk aroused and informed us that he had ordered our horses, and that the signal of Sponsilier's cattle had been seen south on the trail. Dave was impatient to intercept his herd and camp them well down the creek, at least below the regular crossing. This would throw Bob's and my cattle still farther down the stream; and we were all determined to honor Forrest with our presence for supper and the evening hours. Quince's wrangler rustled in the horses, and as we rejoined the camp the quarters of a beef hung low on a cottonwood, while a smudge beneath them warned away all insect life. Leaving word that we would return during the evening, the eleventh-hour guests rode away in the rough, uneven order in which we had arrived. Sponsilier and his men veered off to the south, Bob Quirk and his lads soon following, while the rest of us continued on down the creek. My cattle were watering when we overtook them, occupying fully a mile of the stream, and nearly an hour's ride below the trail crossing. It takes a long time to water a big herd thoroughly, and we repeatedly turned them back and forth across the creek, but finally allowed them to graze away with a broad, fan-like front. As ours left the stream, Bob's cattle were coming in over a mile above, and in anticipation of a dry camp that night, Parent had been advised to fill his kegs and supply himself with wood.

Detailing the third and fourth guard to wrangle the remuda, I sent Levering up the creek with my brother's horses and to recover our loaned saddle stock; even Bob Quirk was just thoughtless enough to construe a neighborly act into a horse trade. About two miles out from the creek and an equal distance from the trail, I found the best bed-ground of the trip. It sloped to the northwest, was covered with old dry grass, and would catch any vagrant breeze except an eastern one. The wagon was ordered into camp, and the first and second guards were relieved just long enough to secure their night-horses. Nearly all of these two watches had been with me during the day, and on the return of Levering with the horses, we borrowed a number of empty flour-sacks for beef, and cantered away, leaving behind only the cook and the first two guards.

What an evening and night that was! As we passed up the creek, we sighted in the gathering twilight the camp-fires of Sponsilier and my brother, several miles apart and south of the stream. When we reached Forrest's wagon the clans were gathering, The Rebel and his crowd being the last to come in from above. Groups of saddle horses were tied among the trees, while around two fires were circles of men broiling beef over live coals. The red-headed cook had anticipated forty guests outside of his own outfit, and was pouring coffee into tin cups and shying biscuit right and left on request. The supper was a success, not on account of the spread or our superior table manners, but we graced the occasion with appetites which required the staples of life to satisfy. Then we smoked, falling into groups when the yarning began. All the fresh-beef stories of our lives, and they were legion, were told, no one group paying any attention to another.

"Every time I run a-foul of fresh beef," said The Rebel, as he settled back comfortably between the roots of a cottonwood, with his back to its trunk, "it reminds me of the time I was a prisoner among the Yankees. It was the last year of the war, and I had got over my first desire to personally whip the whole North. There were about five thousand of us held as prisoners of war for eleven months on a peninsula in the Chesapeake Bay. The fighting spirit of the soldier was broken in the majority of us, especially among the older men and those who had families. But we youngsters accepted the fortunes of war and were glad that we were alive, even if we were prisoners. In my mess in prison there were fifteen, all having been captured at the same time, and many of us comrades of three years' standing.

"I remember the day we were taken off the train and marched through the town for the prison, a Yankee band in our front playing national airs and favorites of their army, and the people along the route jeering us and asking how we liked the music. Our mess held together during the march, and some of the boys answered them back as well as they could. Once inside the prison stockade, we went into quarters and our mess still held together. Before we had been there long, one day there was a call among the prisoners for volunteers to form a roustabout crew. Well, I enlisted as a roustabout. We had to report to an officer twice a day, and then were put under guard and set to work. The kind of labor I liked best was unloading the supplies for the prison, which were landed on a near-by wharf. This roustabout crew had all the unloading to do, and the reason I liked it was it gave us some chance to steal. Whenever there was anything extra, intended for the officers, to be unloaded, look out for accidents. Broken crates were common, and some of the contents was certain to reach our pockets or stomachs, in spite of the guard.

"I was a willing worker and stood well with the guards. They never searched me, and when they took us outside the stockade, the captain of the guard gave me permission, after our work was over, to patronize the sutler's store and buy knick-knacks from the booths. There was always some little money amongst soldiers, even in prison, and I was occasionally furnished money by my messmates to buy bread from a baker's wagon which was outside the walls. Well, after I had traded a few times with the baker's boy, I succeeded in corrupting him. Yes, had him stealing from his employer and selling to me at a discount. I was a good customer, and being a prisoner, there was no danger of my meeting his employer. You see the loaves were counted out to him, and he had to return the equivalent or the bread. At first the bread cost me ten cents for a small loaf, but when I got my scheme working, it didn't cost me five cents for the largest loaves the boy could steal from the bakery. I worked that racket for several months, and if we hadn't been exchanged, I'd have broke that baker, sure.

"But the most successful scheme I worked was stealing the kidneys out of beef while we were handling it. It was some distance from the wharf to the warehouse, and when I'd get a hind quarter of beef on my shoulder, it was an easy trick to burrow my hand through the tallow and get a good grip on the kidney. Then when I'd throw the quarter down in the warehouse, it would be minus a kidney, which secretly found lodgment in a large pocket in the inside of my shirt. I was satisfied with one or two kidneys a day when I first worked the trick, but my mess caught on, and then I had to steal by wholesale to satisfy them. Some days, when the guards were too watchful, I couldn't get very many, and then again when things were lax, 'Elijah's Raven' would get a kidney for each man in our mess. With the regular allowance of rations and what I could steal, when the Texas troops were exchanged, our mess was ragged enough, but pig-fat, and slick as weasels. Lord love you, but we were a great mess of thieves."

Nearly all of Flood's old men were with him again, several of whom were then in Forrest's camp. A fight occurred among a group of saddle horses tied to the front wheel of the wagon, among them being the mount of John Officer. After the belligerents had been quieted, and Officer had removed and tied his horse to a convenient tree, he came over and joined our group, among which were the six trail bosses. Throwing himself down among us, and using Sponsilier for a pillow and myself for footstool, he observed:

"All you foremen who have been over the Chisholm Trail remember the stage-stand called Bull Foot, but possibly some of the boys haven't. Well, no matter, it's just about midway between Little Turkey Creek and Buffalo Springs on that trail, where it runs through the Cherokee Strip. I worked one year in that northern country — lots of Texas boys there too. It was just about the time they began to stock that country with Texas steers, and we rode lines to keep our cattle on their range. You bet, there was riding to do in that country then. The first few months that these Southern steers are turned loose on a new range, Lord! but they do love to drift against a breeze. In any kind of a rain-storm, they'll travel farther in a night than a whole outfit can turn them back in a day.

"Our camp was on the Salt Fork of the Cimarron, and late in the fall when all the beeves had been shipped, the outfit were riding lines and loose-herding a lot of Texas yearlings, and mixed cattle, natives to that range. Up in that country they have Indian summer and Squaw winter, both occurring in the fall. They have lots of funny weather up there. Well, late one evening that fall there came an early squall of Squaw winter, sleeted and spit snow wickedly. The next morning there wasn't a hoof in sight, and shortly after daybreak we were riding deep in our saddles to catch the lead drift of our cattle. After a hard day's ride, we found that we were out several hundred head, principally yearlings of the through Texas stock. You all know how locoed a bunch of dogies can get — we hunted for three days and for fifty miles in every direction, and neither hide, hair, nor hoof could we find. It was while we were hunting these cattle that my yarn commences.

"The big augers of the outfit lived in Wichita, Kansas. Their foreman, Bibleback Hunt, and myself were returning from hunting this missing bunch of yearlings when night overtook us, fully twenty-five miles from camp. Then this Bull Foot stage came to mind, and we turned our horses and rode to it. It was nearly dark when we reached it, and Bibleback said for me to go in and make the talk. I'll never forget that nice little woman who met me at the door of that sod shack. I told her our situation, and she seemed awfully gracious in granting us food and shelter for the night. She told us we could either picket our horses or put them in the corral and feed them hay and grain from the stage-company's supply. Now, old Bibleback was what you might call shy of women, and steered clear of the house until she sent her little boy out and asked us to come in. Well, we sat around in the room, owly-like, and to save my soul from the wrath to come, I couldn't think of a word that was proper to say to the little woman, busy getting supper. Bibleback was worse off than I was; he couldn't do anything but look at the pictures on the wall. What was worrying me was, had she a husband? Or what was she doing away out there in that lonesome country? Then a man old enough to be her grandfather put in an appearance. He was friendly and quite talkative, and I built right up to him. And then we had a supper that I distinctly remember yet. Well, I should say I do — it takes a woman to get a good supper, and cheer it with her presence, sitting at the head of the table and pouring the coffee.

"This old man was a retired stage-driver, and was doing the wrangling act for the stage-horses. After supper I went out to the corral and wormed the information out of him that the woman was a widow; that her husband had died before she came there, and that she was from Michigan. Amongst other things that I learned from the old man was that she had only been there a few months, and was a poor but deserving woman. I told Bibleback all this after we had gone to bed, and we found that our finances amounted to only four dollars, which she was more than welcome to. So the next morning after breakfast, when I asked her what I owed her for our trouble, she replied so graciously: 'Why, gentlemen, I couldn't think of taking advantage of your necessity to charge you for a favor that I'm only too happy to grant.' 'Oh,' said I, 'take this, anyhow,' laying the silver on the corner of the table and starting for the door, when she stopped me. 'One moment, sir; I can't think of accepting this. Be kind enough to grant my request,' and returned the money. We mumbled out some thanks, bade her good-day, and started for the corral, feeling like two sheep thieves. While we were saddling up — will you believe it? — her little boy came out to the corral and gave each one of us as fine a cigar as ever I buttoned my lip over. Well, fellows, we had had it put all over us by this little Michigan woman, till we couldn't look each other in the face. We were accustomed to hardship and neglect, but here was genuine kindness enough to kill a cat.

"Until we got within five miles of our camp that morning, old Bibleback wouldn't speak to me as we rode along. Then he turned halfway in his saddle and said: 'What kind of folks are those?' 'I don't know,' I replied, 'what kind of people they are, but I know they are good ones.' 'Well, I'll get even with that little woman if it takes every sou in my war-bags,' said Hunt.

"When within a mile of camp, Bibleback turned again in his saddle and asked, 'When is Christmas?' 'In about five weeks,' I answered. 'Do you know where that big Wyoming stray ranges?' he next asked. I trailed onto his game in a second. 'Of course I do.' 'Well,' says he, 'let's kill him for Christmas and give that little widow every ounce of the meat. It'll be a good one on her, won't it? We'll fool her a plenty. Say nothing to the others,' he added; and giving our horses the rein we rode into camp on a gallop.

"Three days before Christmas we drove up this Wyoming stray and beefed him. We hung the beef up overnight to harden in the frost, and the next morning bright and early, we started for the stage-stand with a good pair of ponies to a light wagon. We reached the widow's place about eleven o'clock, and against her protests that she had no use for so much, we hung up eight hundred pounds of as fine beef as you ever set your peepers on. We wished her a merry Christmas, jumped into the wagon, clucked to the ponies, and merely hit the high places getting away. When we got well out of sight of the house — well, I've seen mule colts play and kid goats cut up their antics; I've seen children that was frolicsome; but for a man with gray hair on his head, old Bibleback Hunt that day was the happiest mortal I ever saw. He talked to the horses; he sang songs; he played Injun; and that Christmas was a merry one, for the debt was paid and our little widow had beef to throw to the dogs. I never saw her again, but wherever she is to-night, if my prayer counts, may God bless her!"

Early in the evening I had warned my boys that we would start on our return at ten o'clock. The hour was nearly at hand, and in reply to my inquiry if our portion of the beef had been secured, Jack Splann said that he had cut off half a loin, a side of ribs, and enough steak for breakfast. Splann and I tied the beef to our cantle-strings, and when we returned to the group, Sponsilier was telling of the stampede of his herd in the Panhandle about a month before. "But that run wasn't a circumstance to one in which I figured once, and in broad daylight," concluded Dave. It required no encouragement to get the story; all we had to do was to give him time to collect his thoughts.

"Yes, it was in the summer of '73," he finally continued. "It was my first trip over the trail, and I naturally fell into position at the drag end of the herd. I was a green boy of about eighteen at the time, having never before been fifty miles from the ranch where I was born. The herd belonged to Major Hood, and our destination was Ellsworth, Kansas. In those days they generally worked oxen to the chuck-wagons, as they were ready sale in the upper country, and in good demand for breaking prairie. I reckon there must have been a dozen yoke of work-steers in our herd that year, and they were more trouble to me than all the balance of the cattle, for they were slothful and sinfully lazy. My vocabulary of profanity was worn to a frazzle before we were out a week, and those oxen didn't pay any more attention to a rope or myself than to the buzzing of a gnat.

"There was one big roan ox, called Turk, which we worked to the wagon occasionally, but in crossing the Arbuckle Mountains in the Indian Territory, he got tender-footed. Another yoke was substituted, and in a few days Turk was on his feet again. But he was a cunning rascal and had learned to soldier, and while his feet were sore, I favored him with sandy trails and gave him his own time. In fact, most of my duties were driving that one ox, while the other boys handled the herd. When his feet got well — I had toadied and babied him so — he was plum ruined. I begged the foreman to put him back in the chuck team, but the cook kicked on account of his well-known laziness, so Turk and I continued to adorn the rear of the column. I reckon the foreman thought it better to have Turk and me late than no dinner. I tried a hundred different schemes to instill ambition and self-respect into that ox, but he was an old dog and contented with his evil ways.

"Several weeks passed, and Turk and I became a standing joke with the outfit. One morning I made the discovery that he was afraid of a slicker. For just about a full half day, I had the best of him, and several times he was out of sight in the main body of the herd. But he always dropped to the rear, and finally the slicker lost its charm to move him. In fact he rather enjoyed having me fan him with it — it seemed to cool him. It was the middle of the afternoon, and Turk had dropped about a quarter-mile to the rear, while I was riding along beside and throwing the slicker over him like a blanket. I was letting him carry it, and he seemed to be enjoying himself, switching his tail in appreciation, when the matted brush of his tail noosed itself over one of the riveted buttons on the slicker. The next switch brought the yellow 'fish' bumping on his heels, and emitting a blood-curdling bellow, he curved his tail and started for the herd. Just for a minute it tickled me to see old Turk getting such a wiggle on him, but the next moment my mirth turned to seriousness, and I tried to cut him off from the other cattle, but he beat me, bellowing bloody murder. The slicker was sailing like a kite, and the rear cattle took fright and began bawling as if they had struck a fresh scent of blood. The scare flashed through the herd from rear to point, and hell began popping right then and there. The air filled with dust and the earth trembled with the running cattle. Not knowing which way to turn, I stayed right where I was — in the rear. As the dust lifted, I followed up, and about a mile ahead picked up my slicker, and shortly afterward found old Turk, grazing contentedly. With every man in the saddle, that herd ran seven miles and was only turned by the Cimarron River. It was nearly dark when I and the roan ox overtook the cattle. Fortunately none of the swing-men had seen the cause of the stampede, and I attributed it to fresh blood, which the outfit believed. My verdant innocence saved my scalp that time, but years afterward I nearly lost it when I admitted to my old foreman what had caused the stampede that afternoon. But I was a trail boss then and had learned my lesson."

The Rebel, who was encamped several miles up the creek, summoned his men, and we all arose and scattered after our horses. There was quite a cavalcade going our way, and as we halted within the light of the fires for the different outfits to gather, Flood rode up, and calling Forrest, said: "In the absence of any word from old man Don, we might as well all pull out in the morning. More than likely we'll hear from him at Grinnell, and until we reach the railroad, the Buford herds had better take the lead. I'll drag along in the rear, and if there's another move made from Dodge, you will have warning. Now, that's about all, except to give your cattle plenty of time; don't hurry. S'long, fellows."

CHAPTER XI
ALL IN THE DAY'S WORK

The next morning the herds moved out like brigades of an army on dress-parade. Our front covered some six or seven miles, the Buford cattle in the lead, while those intended for Indian delivery naturally fell into position on flank and rear. My beeves had enjoyed a splendid rest during the past week, and now easily took the lead in a steady walk, every herd avoiding the trail until necessity compelled us to reenter it. The old pathway was dusty and merely pointed the way, and until rain fell to settle it, our intention was to give it a wide berth. As the morning wore on and the herds drew farther and farther apart, except for the dim dust-clouds of ten thousand trampling feet on a raw prairie, it would have been difficult for us to establish each other's location. Several times during the forenoon, when a swell of the plain afforded us a temporary westward view, we caught glimpses of Forrest's cattle as they snailed forward, fully five miles distant and barely noticeable under the low sky-line. The Indian herds had given us a good start in the morning, and towards evening as the mirages lifted, not a dust-signal was in sight, save one far in our lead.

The month of June, so far, had been exceedingly droughty. The scarcity of water on the plains between Dodge and Ogalalla was the dread of every trail drover. The grass, on the other hand, had matured from the first rank growth of early spring into a forage, rich in sustenance, from which our beeves took on flesh and rounded into beauties. Lack of water being the one drawback, long drives, not in miles but hours, became the order of the day; from four in the morning to eight at night, even at an ox's pace, leaves every landmark of the day far in the rear at nightfall. Thus for the next few days we moved forward, the monotony of existence broken only by the great variety of mirage, the glare of heat-waves, and the silent signal in the sky of other voyageurs like ourselves. On reaching Pig Boggy, nothing but pools greeted us, while the regular crossing was dry and dusty and paved with cattle bones. My curiosity was strong enough to cause me to revisit the old bridge which I had helped to build two seasons before; though unused, it was still intact, a credit to the crude engineering of Pete Slaughter. After leaving the valley of the Solomon, the next running water was Pawnee Fork, where we overtook and passed six thousand yearling heifers in two herds, sold the winter before by John Blocker for delivery in Montana. The Northwest had not yet learned that Texas was the natural breeding-ground for cattle, yet under favorable conditions in both sections, the ranchman of the South could raise one third more calves from an equal number of cows.

The weather continued hot and sultry. Several times storms hung on our left for hours which we hoped would reach us, and at night the lightning flickered in sheets, yet with the exception of cooling the air, availed us nothing. But as we encamped one night on the divide before reaching the Smoky River, a storm struck us that sent terror to our hearts. There were men in my outfit, and others in Lovell's employ, who were from ten to twenty years my senior, having spent almost their lifetime in the open, who had never before witnessed such a night. The atmosphere seemed to be overcharged with electricity, which played its pranks among us, neither man nor beast being exempt. The storm struck the divide about two hours after the cattle had been bedded, and from then until dawn every man was in the saddle, the herd drifting fully three miles during the night. Such keen flashes of lightning accompanied by instant thunder I had never before witnessed, though the rainfall, after the first dash, was light in quantity. Several times the rain ceased entirely, when the phosphorus, like a prairie fire, appeared on every hand. Great sheets of it flickered about, the cattle and saddle stock were soon covered, while every bit of metal on our accoutrements was coated and twinkling with phosphorescent light. My gauntlets were covered, and wherever I touched myself, it seemed to smear and spread and refuse to wipe out. Several times we were able to hold up and quiet the cattle, but along their backs flickered the ghostly light, while across the herd, which occupied acres, it reminded one of the burning lake in the regions infernal. As the night wore on, several showers fell, accompanied by almost incessant bolts of lightning, but the rainfall only added moisture to the ground and this acted like fuel in reviving the phosphor. Several hours before dawn, great sheets of the fiery elements chased each other across the northern sky, lighting up our surroundings until one could have read ordinary print. The cattle stood humped or took an occasional step forward, the men sat their horses, sullen and morose, forming new resolutions for the future, in which trail work was not included. But morning came at last, cool and cloudy, a slight recompense for the heat which we had endured since leaving Dodge.

With the breaking of day, the herd was turned back on its course. For an hour or more the cattle grazed freely, and as the sun broke through the clouds, they dropped down like tired infantry on a march, and we allowed them an hour's rest. We were still some three or four miles eastward of the trail, and after breakfasting and changing mounts we roused the cattle and started on an angle for the trail, expecting to intercept it before noon. There was some settlement in the Smoky River Valley which must be avoided, as in years past serious enmity had been engendered between settlers and drovers in consequence of the ravages of Texas fever among native cattle. I was riding on the left point, and when within a short distance of the trail, one of the boys called my attention to a loose herd of cattle, drifting south and fully two miles to the west of us. It was certainly something unusual, and as every man of us scanned them, a lone horseman was seen to ride across their front, and, turning them, continue on for our herd. The situation was bewildering, as the natural course of every herd was northward, but here was one apparently abandoned like a water-logged ship at sea.

The messenger was a picture of despair. He proved to be the owner of the abandoned cattle, and had come to us with an appeal for help. According to his story, he was a Northern cowman and had purchased the cattle a few days before in Dodge. He had bought the outfit complete, with the understanding that the through help would continue in his service until his range in Wyoming was reached. But it was a Mexican outfit, foreman and all, and during the storm of the night before, one of the men had been killed by lightning. The accident must have occurred near dawn, as the man was not missed until daybreak, and like ours, his cattle had drifted with the storm. Some time was lost in finding the body, and to add to the panic that had already stricken the outfit, the shirt of the unfortunate vaquero was burnt from the corpse. The horse had escaped scathless, though his rider met death, while the housings were stripped from the saddle so that it fell from the animal. The Mexican foreman and vaqueros had thrown their hands in the air; steeped in superstition, they considered the loss of their comrade a bad omen, and refused to go farther. The herd was as good as abandoned unless we could lend a hand.

The appeal was not in vain. Detailing four of my men, and leaving Jack Splann as segundo in charge of our cattle, I galloped away with the stranger. As we rode the short distance between the two herds and I mentally reviewed the situation, I could not help but think it was fortunate for the alien outfit that their employer was a Northern cowman instead of a Texan. Had the present owner been of the latter school, there would have been more than one dead Mexican before a valuable herd would have been abandoned over an unavoidable accident. I kept my thoughts to myself, however, for the man had troubles enough, and on reaching his drifting herd, we turned them back on their course. It was high noon when we reached his wagon and found the Mexican outfit still keening over their dead comrade. We pushed the cattle, a mixed herd of about twenty-five hundred, well past the camp, and riding back, dismounted among the howling vaqueros. There was not the semblance of sanity among them. The foreman, who could speak some little English, at least his employer declared he could, was carrying on like a madman, while a majority of the vaqueros were playing a close second. The dead man had been carried in and was lying under a tarpaulin in the shade of the wagon. Feeling that my boys would stand behind me, and never offering to look at the corpse, I inquired in Spanish of the vaqueros which one of the men was their corporal. A heavy-set, bearded man was pointed out, and walking up to him, with one hand I slapped him in the face and with the other relieved him of a six-shooter. He staggered back, turned ashen pale, and before he could recover from the surprise, in his own tongue I berated him as a worthless cur for deserting his employer over an accident. Following up the temporary advantage, I inquired for the cook and horse-wrangler, and intimated clearly that there would be other dead Mexicans if the men were not fed and the herd and saddle stock looked after; that they were not worthy of the name of vaqueros if they were lax in a duty with which they had been intrusted.

"But Pablo is dead," piped one of the vaqueros in defense.

"Yes, he is," said G — G Cederdall in Spanish, bristling up to the vaquero who had volunteered the reply; "and we'll bury him and a half-dozen more of you if necessary, but the cattle will not be abandoned — not for a single hour. Pablo is dead, but he was no better than a hundred other men who have lost their lives on this trail. If you are a lot of locoed sheep-herders instead of vaqueros, why didn't you stay at home with the children instead of starting out to do a man's work. Desert your employer, will you? Not in a country where there is no chance to pick up other men. Yes, Pablo is dead, and we'll bury him."

The aliens were disconcerted, and wilted. The owner picked up courage and ordered the cook to prepare dinner. We loaned our horses to the wrangler and another man, the remuda was brought in, and before we sat down to the midday meal, every vaquero had a horse under saddle, while two of them had ridden away to look after the grazing cattle. With order restored, we set about systematically to lay away the unfortunate man. A detail of vaqueros under Cederdall prepared a grave on the nearest knoll, and wrapping the corpse in a tarpaulin, we buried him like a sailor at sea. Several vaqueros were visibly affected at the graveside, and in order to pacify them, I suggested that we unload the wagon of supplies and haul up a load of rock from a near-by outcropping ledge. Pablo had fallen like a good soldier at his post, I urged, and it was befitting that his comrades should mark his last resting-place. To our agreeable surprise the corporal hurrahed his men and the wagon was unloaded in a jiffy and dispatched after a load of rock. On its return, we spent an hour in decorating the mound, during which time lament was expressed for the future of Pablo's soul. Knowing the almost universal faith of this alien race, as we stood around the finished mound, Cederdall, who was Catholic born, called for contributions to procure the absolution of the Church. The owner of the cattle was the first to respond, and with the aid of my boys and myself, augmented later by the vaqueros, a purse of over fifty dollars was raised and placed in charge of the corporal, to be expended in a private mass on their return to San Antonio. Meanwhile the herd and saddle stock had started, and reloading the wagon, we cast a last glance at the little mound which made a new landmark on the old trail.

The owner of the cattle was elated over the restoration of order. My contempt for him, however, had not decreased; the old maxim of fools rushing in where angels feared to tread had only been again exemplified. The inferior races may lack in courage and leadership, but never in cunning and craftiness. This alien outfit had detected some weakness in the armor of their new employer, and when the emergency arose, were ready to take advantage of the situation. Yet under an old patron, these same men would never dare to mutiny or assert themselves. That there were possible breakers ahead for this cowman there was no doubt; for every day that those Mexicans traveled into a strange country, their Aztec blood would yearn for their Southern home. And since the unforeseen could not be guarded against, at the first opportunity I warned the stranger that it was altogether too soon to shout. To his anxious inquiries I replied that his very presence with the herd was a menace to its successful handling by the Mexican outfit. He should throw all responsibility on the foreman, or take charge himself, which was impossible now; for an outfit which will sulk and mutiny once will do so again under less provocation. When my curtain lecture was ended, the owner authorized me to call his outfit together and give them such instructions as I saw fit.

We sighted our cattle but once during the afternoon. On locating the herd, two of my boys left us to return, hearing the message that the rest of us might not put in an appearance before morning. All during the evening, I made it a point to cultivate the acquaintance of several vaqueros, and learned the names of their master and rancho. Taking my cue from the general information gathered, when we encamped for the night and all hands, with the exception of those on herd, had finished catching horses, I attracted their attention by returning the six-shooter taken from their corporal at noontime. Commanding attention, in their mother tongue I addressed myself to the Mexican foreman.

"Felipe Esquibil," said I, looking him boldly in the face, "you were foreman of this herd from Zavalla County, Texas, to the Arkansaw River, and brought your cattle through without loss or accident.

"The herd changed owners at Dodge, but with the understanding that you and your vaqueros were to accompany the cattle to this gentleman's ranch in the upper country. An accident happens, and because you are not in full control, you shift the responsibility and play the baby act by wanting to go home. Had the death of one of your men occurred below the river, and while the herd was still the property of Don Dionisio of Rancho Los Olmus, you would have lost your own life before abandoning your cattle. Now, with the consent and approval of the new owner, you are again invested with full charge of this herd until you arrive at the Platte River. A new outfit will relieve you on reaching Ogalalla, and then you will be paid your reckoning and all go home. In your immediate rear are five herds belonging to my employer, and I have already sent warning to them of your attempted desertion. A fortnight or less will find you relieved, and the only safety in store for you is to go forward. Now your employer is going to my camp for the night, and may not see you again before this herd reaches the Platte. Remember, Don Felipe, that the opportunity is yours to regain your prestige as a corporal — and you need it after to-day's actions. What would Don Dionisio say if he knew the truth? And do you ever expect to face your friends again at Los Olmus? From a trusted corporal back to a sheep-shearer would be your reward — and justly."

Cederdall, Wolf, and myself shook hands with several vaqueros, and mounting our horses we started for my camp, taking the stranger with us. Only once did he offer any protest to going. "Very well, then," replied G — G, unable to suppress his contempt, "go right back. I'll gamble that you sheathe a knife before morning if you do. It strikes me you don't sabe Mexicans very much."

Around the camp-fire that night, the day's work was reviewed. My rather drastic treatment of the corporal was fully commented upon and approved by the outfit, yet provoked an inquiry from the irrepressible Parent. Turning to the questioner, Burl Van Vedder said in dove-like tones: "Yes, dear, slapped him just to remind the varmint that his feet were on the earth, and that pawing the air and keening didn't do any good. Remember, love, there was the living to be fed, the dead to bury, and the work in hand required every man to do his duty. Now was there anything else you'd like to know?"

CHAPTER XII
MARSHALING THE FORCES

Both herds had watered in the Smoky during the afternoon. The stranger's cattle were not compelled to go down to the crossing, but found an easy passage several miles above the regular ford. After leaving the river, both herds were grazed out during the evening, and when darkness fell we were not over three miles apart, one on either side of the trail. The Wyoming cowman spent a restless night, and early the next morning rode to the nearest elevation which would give him a view of his cattle. Within an hour after sun-up he returned, elated over the fact that his herd was far in the lead of ours, camp being already broken, while we were only breakfasting. Matters were working out just as I expected. The mixed herd under the Mexican corporal, by moving early and late, could keep the lead of our beeves, and with the abundance of time at my disposal we were in no hurry. The Kansas Pacific Railroad was but a few days' drive ahead, and I advised our guest to take the train around to Ogalalla and have a new outfit all ready to relieve the aliens immediately on their arrival. Promising to take the matter under consideration, he said nothing further for several days, his cattle in the mean time keeping a lead of from five to ten miles.

The trail crossed the railroad at a switch east of Grinnell. I was naturally expecting some word from Don Lovell, and it was my intention to send one of the boys into that station to inquire for mail. There was a hostelry at Grinnell, several stores and a livery stable, all dying an easy death from the blight of the arid plain, the town profiting little or nothing from the cattle trade. But when within a half-day's drive of the railway, on overtaking the herd after dinner, there was old man Don talking to the boys on herd. The cattle were lying down, and rather than disturb them, he patiently bided his time until they had rested and arose to resume their journey. The old man was feeling in fine spirits, something unusual, and declined my urgent invitation to go back to the wagon and have dinner. I noticed that he was using his own saddle, though riding a livery horse, and in the mutual inquiries which were exchanged, learned that he had arrived at Grinnell but a few days before. He had left Camp Supply immediately after Forrest and Sponsilier passed that point, and until Siringo came in with his report, he had spent the time about detective headquarters in Kansas City. From intimate friends in Dodge, he had obtained the full particulars of the attempted but unsuccessful move of The Western Supply Company to take possession of his two herds. In fact there was very little that I could enlighten him on, except the condition of the cattle, and they spoke for themselves, their glossy coats shining with the richness of silk. On the other hand, my employer opened like a book.

"Tom, I think we're past the worst of it," said he. "Those Dodge people are just a trifle too officious to suit me, but Ogalalla is a cow-town after my own heart. They're a law unto themselves up there, and a cowman stands some show — a good one against thieves. Ogalalla is the seat of an organized county, and the town has officers, it's true, but they've got sense enough to know which side their bread's buttered on; and a cowman who's on the square has nothing to fear in that town. Yes, the whole gang, Tolleston and all, are right up here at Ogalalla now; bought a herd this week, so I hear, and expect to take two of these away from us the moment we enter Keith County. Well, they may; I've seen bad men before take a town, but it was only a question of time until the plain citizens retook it. They may try to bluff us, but if they do, we'll meet them a little over halfway. Which one of your boys was it that licked Archie? I want to thank him until such a time as I can reward him better."

The herd was moving out, and as Seay was working in the swing on the opposite side, we allowed the cattle to trail past, and then rode round and overtook him. The two had never met before, but old man Don warmed towards Dorg, who recited his experience in such an inimitable manner that our employer rocked in his saddle in spasms of laughter. Leaving the two together, I rode on ahead to look out the water, and when the herd came up near the middle of the afternoon, they were still inseparable. The watering over, we camped for the night several miles south of the railroad, the mixed herd having crossed it about noon. My guest of the past few days had come to a point requiring a decision and was in a quandary to know what to do. But when the situation had been thoroughly reviewed between Mr. Lovell and the Wyoming man, my advice was indorsed, — to trust implicitly to his corporal, and be ready to relieve the outfit at the Platte. Saddles were accordingly shifted, and the stranger, after professing a profusion of thanks, rode away on the livery horse by which my employer had arrived. Once the man was well out of hearing, the old trail drover turned to my outfit and said:

"Boys, there goes a warning that the days of the trail are numbered. To make a success of any business, a little common sense is necessary. Nine tenths of the investing in cattle to-day in the Northwest is being done by inexperienced men. No other line of business could prosper in such incompetent hands, and it's foolish to think that cattle companies and individuals, nearly all tenderfeet at the business, can succeed. They may for a time, — there are accidents in every calling, — but when the tide turns, there won't be one man or company in ten survive. I only wish they would, as it means life and expansion for the cattle interests in Texas. As long as the boom continues, and foreigners and tenderfeet pour their money in, the business will look prosperous. Why, even the business men are selling out their stores and going into cattle. But there's a day of reckoning ahead, and there's many a cowman in this Northwest country who will never see his money again. Now the government demand is a healthy one: it needs the cattle for Indian and military purposes; but this crazy investment, especially in she stuff, I wouldn't risk a dollar in it."

During the conversation that evening, I was delighted to learn that my employer expected to accompany the herds overland to Ogalalla. There was nothing pressing elsewhere, and as all the other outfits were within a short day's ride in the rear, he could choose his abode. He was too good a cowman to interfere with the management of cattle, and the pleasure of his company, when in good humor, was to be desired. The next morning a horse was furnished him from our extras, and after seeing us safely across the railroad track, he turned back to meet Forrest or Sponsilier. This was the last we saw of him until after crossing into Nebraska. In the mean time my boys kept an eye on the Mexican outfit in our front, scarcely a day passing but what we sighted them either in person or by signal. Once they dropped back opposite us on the western side of the trail, when Cedardall, under the pretense of hunting lost horses, visited their camp, finding them contented and enjoying a lay-over. They were impatient to know the distance to the Rio Platte, and G — G assured them that within a week they would see its muddy waters and be relieved. Thus encouraged they held the lead, but several times vaqueros dropped back to make inquiries of drives and the water. The route was passable, with a short dry drive from the head of Stinking Water across to the Platte River, of which they were fully advised. Keeping them in sight, we trailed along leisurely, and as we went down the northern slope of the divide approaching the Republican River, we were overtaken at noon by Don Lovell and Dave Sponsilier.

"Quirk," said the old man, as the two dismounted, "I was just telling Dave that twenty years ago this summer I carried a musket with Sherman in his march to the sea. And here we are to-day, driving beef to feed the army in the West. But that's neither here nor there under the present programme. Jim Flood and I have talked matters over pretty thoroughly, and have decided to switch the foremen on the 'Open A' and 'Drooping T' cattle until after Ogalalla is passed. From their actions at Dodge, it is probable that they will try and arrest the foreman of those two herds as accessory under some charge or other. By shifting the foremen, even if the ones in charge are detained, we will gain time and be able to push the Buford cattle across the North Platte. The chances are that they will prefer some charges against me, and if they do, if necessary, we will all go to the lock-up together. They may have spotters ahead here on the Republican; Dave will take charge of your 'Open A's' at once, and you will drop back and follow up with his cattle. For the time being and to every stranger, you two will exchange names. The Rebel is in charge of Forrest's cattle now, and Quince will drop back with Paul's herd. Dave, here, gave me the slip on crossing the Texas Pacific in the lower country, but when we reach the Union Pacific, I want to know where he is, even if in jail. And I may be right there with him, but we'll live high, for I've got a lot of their money."

Sponsilier reported his herd on the same side of the trail and about ten miles to our rear. I had no objection to the change, for those arid plains were still to be preferred to the lock-up in Ogalalla. My only regret was in temporarily losing my mount; but as Dave's horses were nearly as good, no objection was urged, and promising, in case either landed in jail, to send flowers, I turned back, leaving my employer with the lead herd. Before starting, I learned that the "Drooping T" cattle were in advance of Sponsilier's, and as I soldiered along on my way back, rode several miles out of my way to console my old bunkie, The Rebel. He took my chaffing good-naturedly and assured me that his gray hairs were a badge of innocence which would excuse him on any charge. Turning, I rode back with him over a mile, this being my first opportunity of seeing Forrest's beeves. The steers were large and rangy, extremely uniform in ages and weight, and in general relieved me of considerable conceit that I had the best herd among the Buford cattle. With my vanity eased, I continued my journey and reached Sponsilier's beeves while they were watering. Again a surprise was in store for me, as the latter herd had, if any, the edge over the other two, while "The Apple" was by all odds the prettiest road brand I had ever seen. I asked the acting segundo, a lad named Tupps, who cut the cattle when receiving; light was thrown on the situation by his reply.

"Old man Don joined the outfit the day we reached Uvalde," said he, "and until we began receiving, he poured it into our foreman that this year the cattle had to be something extra — muy escogido, as the Mexicans say. Well, the result was that Sponsilier went to work with ideas pitched rather high. But in the first bunch received, the old man cut a pretty little four-year-old, fully a hundred pounds too light. Dave and Mr. Lovell had a set-to over the beef, the old man refusing to cut him back, but he rode out of the herd and never again offered to interfere. Forrest was present, and at dinner that day old man Don admitted that he was too easy when receiving. Sponsilier and Forrest did the trimming afterward, and that is the secret of these two herds being so uniform."

A general halt was called at the head of Stinking Water. We were then within forty miles of Ogalalla, and a day's drive would put us within the jurisdiction of Keith County. Some time was lost at this last water, waiting for the rear herds to arrive, as it was the intention to place the "Open A" and "Drooping T" cattle at the rear in crossing this dry belt. At the ford on the Republican, a number of strangers were noticed, two of whom rode a mile or more with me, and innocently asked numerous but leading questions. I frankly answered every inquiry, and truthfully, with the exception of the names of the lead foreman and my own. Direct, it was only sixty miles from the crossing on the Republican to Ogalalla, an easy night's ride, and I was conscious that our whereabouts would be known at the latter place the next morning. For several days before starting across this arid stretch, we had watered at ten o'clock in the morning, so when Flood and Forrest came up, mine being the third herd to reach the last water, I was all ready to pull out. But old man Don counseled another day's lie-over, as it would be a sore trial for the herds under a July sun, and for a full day twenty thousand beeves grazed in sight of each other on the mesas surrounding the head of Stinking Water. All the herds were aroused with the dawn, and after a few hours' sun on the cattle, the Indian beeves were turned onto the water and held until the middle of the forenoon, when the start was made for the Platte and Ogalalla.

I led out with "The Apple" cattle, throwing onto the trail for the first ten miles, which put me well in advance of Bob Quirk and Forrest, who were in my immediate rear. A well-known divide marked the halfway between the two waters, and I was determined to camp on it that night. It was fully nine o'clock when we reached it, Don Lovell in the mean time having overtaken us. This watershed was also recognized as the line of Keith County, an organized community, and the next morning expectation ran high as to what the day would bring forth. Lovell insisted on staying with the lead herd, and pressing him in as horse-wrangler, I sent him in the lead with the remuda and wagon, while Levering fell into the swing with the trailing cattle. A breakfast halt was made fully seven miles from the bed-ground, a change of mounts, and then up divide, across mesa, and down slope at the foot of which ran the Platte. Meanwhile several wayfaring men were met, but in order to avoid our dust, they took the right or unbranded side of our herd on meeting, and passed on their way without inquiry. Near noon a party of six men, driving a number of loose mounts and a pack-horse, were met, who also took the windward side. Our dragmen learned that they were on their way to Dodge to receive a herd of range horses. But when about halfway down the slope towards the river, two mounted men were seen to halt the remuda and wagon for a minute, and then continue on southward. Billy Tupps was on the left point, myself next in the swing; and as the two horsemen turned out on the branded side, their identity was suspected. In reply to some inquiry, Tupps jerked his thumb over his shoulder as much as to say, "Next man." I turned out and met the strangers, who had already noted the road brand, and politely answered every question. One of the two offered me a cigar, and after lighting it, I did remember hearing one of my boys say that among the herds lying over on the head of Stinking Water was an "Open A" and "Drooping T," but I was unable to recall the owner's or foremen's names. Complimenting me on the condition of my beeves, and assuring me that I would have time to water my herd and reach the mesa beyond Ogalalla, they passed on down the column of cattle.

I had given the cook an order on an outfitting house for new supplies, saying I would call or send a draft in the morning. A new bridge had been built across the Platte opposite the town, and when nearing the river, the commissary turned off the trail for it, but the horse-wrangler for the day gave the bridge a wide berth and crossed the stream a mile below the village. The width of the river was a decided advantage in watering a thirsty herd, as it gave the cattle room to thrash around, filling its broad bed for fully a half mile. Fortunately there were few spectators, but I kept my eye on the lookout for a certain faction, being well disguised with dust and dirt and a month's growth of beard. As we pushed out of the river and were crossing the tracks below the railroad yards, two other herds were sighted coming down to the water, their remudas having forded above and below our cattle. On scaling the bluffs, we could see the trail south of the Platte on which arose a great column of dust. Lovell was waiting with the saddle stock in the hills beyond the town, and on striking the first good grass, the cattle fell to grazing while we halted to await the arrival of the wagon. The sun was still several hours high, and while waiting for our commissary to come up, my employer and myself rode to the nearest point of observation to reconnoitre the rear. Beneath us lay the hamlet; but our eyes were concentrated beyond the narrow Platte valley on a dust-cloud which hung midway down the farther slope. As we watched, an occasional breeze wafted the dust aside, and the sinuous outline of a herd creeping forward greeted our vision. Below the town were two other herds, distinctly separate and filling the river for over a mile with a surging mass of animals, while in every direction cattle dotted the plain and valley. Turning aside from the panorama before us, my employer said:

"Tom, you will have time to graze out a few miles and camp to the left of the trail. I'll stay here and hurry your wagon forward, and wait for Bob and Quince. That lead herd beyond the river is bound to be Jim's, and he's due to camp on this mesa to-night, so these outfits must give him room. If Dave and Paul are still free to act, they'll know enough to water and camp on the south side of the Platte. I'll stay at Flood's wagon to-night, and you had better send a couple of your boys into town and let them nose around. They'll meet lads from the 'Open A' and 'Drooping T' outfits; and I'll send Jim and Bob in, and by midnight we'll have a report of what's been done. If any one but an officer takes possession of those two herds, it'll put us to the trouble of retaking them. And I think I've got men enough here to do it."

CHAPTER XIII
JUSTICE IN THE SADDLE

It was an hour after the usual time when we bedded down the cattle. The wagon had overtaken us about sunset, and the cook's fire piloted us into a camp fully two miles to the right of the trail. A change of horses was awaiting us, and after a hasty supper Tupps detailed two young fellows to visit Ogalalla. It required no urging; I outlined clearly what was expected of their mission, requesting them to return by the way of Flood's wagon, and to receive any orders which my employer might see fit to send. The horse-wrangler was pressed in to stand the guard of one of the absent lads on the second watch, and I agreed to take the other, which fell in the third. The boys had not yet returned when our guard was called, but did so shortly afterward, one of them hunting me up on night-herd.

"Well," said he, turning his horse and circling with me, "we caught onto everything that was adrift. The Rebel and Sponsilier were both in town, in charge of two deputies. Flood and your brother went in with us, and with the lads from the other outfits, including those across the river, there must have been twenty-five of Lovell's men in town. I noticed that Dave and The Rebel were still wearing their six-shooters, while among the boys the arrests were looked upon as quite a joke. The two deputies had all kinds of money, and wouldn't allow no one but themselves to spend a cent. The biggest one of the two — the one who gave you the cigar — would say to my boss: 'Sponsilier, you're a trail foreman from Texas — one of Don Lovell's boss men — but you're under arrest; your cattle are in my possession this very minute. You understand that, don't you? Very well, then; everybody come up and have a drink on the sheriff's office.' That was about the talk in every saloon and dance-hall visited. But when we proposed starting back to camp, about midnight, the big deputy said to Flood: 'I want you to tell Colonel Lovell that I hold a warrant for his arrest; urge him not to put me to the trouble of coming out after him. If he had identified himself to me this afternoon, he could have slept on a goose-hair bed to-night instead of out there on the mesa, on the cold ground. His reputation in this town would entitle him to three meals a day, even if he was under arrest. Now, we'll have one more, and tell the damned old rascal that I'll expect him in the morning.'"

We rode out the watch together. On returning to Flood's camp, they had found Don Lovell awake. The old man was pleased with the report, but sent me no special word except to exercise my own judgment. The cattle were tired after their long tramp of the day before, the outfit were saddle weary, and the first rays of the rising sun flooded the mesa before men or animals offered to arise. But the duties of another day commanded us anew, and with the cook calling us, we rose to meet them. I was favorably impressed with Tupps as a segundo, and after breakfast suggested that he graze the cattle over to the North Platte, cross it, and make a permanent camp. This was agreed to, half the men were excused for the day, and after designating, beyond the river, a clump of cottonwoods where the wagon would be found, seven of us turned and rode back for Ogalalla. With picked mounts under us, we avoided the other cattle which could be seen grazing northward, and when fully halfway to town, there before us on the brink of the mesa loomed up the lead of a herd. I soon recognized Jack Splann on the point, and taking a wide circle, dropped in behind him, the column stretching back a mile and coming up the bluffs, forty abreast like an army in loose marching order. I was proud of those "Open A's;" they were my first herd, and though in a hurry to reach town, I turned and rode back with them for fully a mile.

Splann was acting under orders from Flood, who had met him at the ford that morning. If the cattle were in the possession of any deputy sheriff, they had failed to notify Jack, and the latter had already started for the North Platte of his own accord. The "Drooping T" cattle were in the immediate rear under Forrest's segundo, and Splann urged me to accompany him that forenoon, saying: "From what the boys said this morning, Dave and Paul will not be given a hearing until two o'clock this afternoon. I can graze beyond the North Fork by that time, and

333

then we'll all go back together. Flood's right behind here with the 'Drooping T's,' and I think it's his intention to go all the way to the river. Drop back and see him."

The boys who were with me never halted, but had ridden on towards town. When the second herd began the ascent of the mesa, I left Splann and turned back, waiting on the brink for its arrival. As it would take the lead cattle some time to reach me, I dismounted, resting in the shade of my horse. But my rest was brief, for the clattering hoofs of a cavalcade of horsemen were approaching, and as I arose, Quince Forrest and Bob Quirk with a dozen or more men dashed up and halted. As their herds were intended for the Crow and Fort Washakie agencies, they would naturally follow up the south side of the North Platte, and an hour or two of grazing would put them in camp. The Buford cattle, as well as Flood's herd, were due to cross this North Fork of the mother Platte within ten miles of Ogalalla, their respective routes thenceforth being north and northeast. Forrest, like myself, was somewhat leary of entering the town, and my brother and the boys passed on shortly, leaving Quince behind. We discussed every possible phase of what might happen in case we were recognized, which was almost certain if Tolleston or the Dodge buyers were encountered. But an overweening hunger to get into Ogalalla was dominant in us, and under the excuse of settling for our supplies, after the herd passed, we remounted our horses, Flood joining us, and rode for the hamlet.

There was little external and no moral change in the town. Several new saloons had opened, and in anticipation of the large drive that year, the Dew-Drop-In dance-hall had been enlarged, and employed three shifts of bartenders. A stage had been added with the new addition, and a special importation of ladies had been brought out from Omaha for the season. I use the term LADIES advisedly, for in my presence one of the proprietors, with marked courtesy, said to an Eastern stranger, "Oh, no, you need no introduction. My wife is the only woman in town; all the balance are ladies." Beyond a shave and a hair-cut, Forrest and I fought shy of public places. But after the supplies were settled for, and some new clothing was secured, we chambered a few drinks and swaggered about with considerable ado. My bill of supplies amounted to one hundred and twenty-six dollars, and when, without a word, I drew a draft for the amount, the proprietor of the outfitting store, as a pelon, made me a present of two fine silk handkerchiefs.

Forrest was treated likewise, and having invested ourselves in white shirts, with flaming red ties, we used the new handkerchiefs to otherwise decorate our persons. We had both chosen the brightest colors, and with these knotted about our necks, dangling from pistol-pockets, or protruding from ruffled shirt fronts, our own mothers would scarcely have known us. Jim Flood, whom we met casually on a back street, stopped, and after circling us once, said, "Now if you fellows just keep perfectly sober, your disguise will be complete."

Meanwhile Don Lovell had reported at an early hour to the sheriff's office. The legal profession was represented in Ogalalla by several firms, criminal practice being their specialty; but fortunately Mike Sutton, an attorney of Dodge, had arrived in town the day before on a legal errand for another trail drover. Sutton was a frontier advocate, alike popular with the Texas element and the gambling fraternity, having achieved laurels in his home town as a criminal lawyer. Mike was born on the little green isle beyond the sea, and, gifted with the Celtic wit, was also in logic clear as the tones of a bell, while his insight into human motives was almost superhuman. Lovell had had occasion in other years to rely on Sutton's counsel, and now would listen to no refusal of his services. As it turned out, the lawyer's mission in Ogalalla was so closely in sympathy with Lovell's trouble that they naturally strengthened each other. The highest tribunal of justice in Ogalalla was the county court, the judge of which also ran the stock-yards during the shipping season, and was banker for two monte games at the Lone Star saloon. He enjoyed the reputation of being an honest, fearless jurist, and supported by a growing civic pride, his decisions gave satisfaction. A sense of crude equity governed his rulings, and as one of the citizens remarked, "Whatever the judge said, went." It should be remembered that this was in '84, but had a similar trouble occurred five years earlier, it is likely that Judge Colt would have figured in the preliminaries, and the coroner might have been called on to impanel a jury. But the rudiments of civilization were sweeping westward, and Ogalalla was nerved to the importance of the occasion; for that very afternoon a hearing was to be given for the possession of two herds of cattle, valued at over a quarter-million dollars.

The representatives of The Western Supply Company were quartered in the largest hotel in town, but seldom appeared on the streets. They had employed a firm of local attorneys, consisting of an old and a young man, both of whom evidently believed in the justice of their client's cause. All the cattle-hands in Lovell's employ were anxious to get a glimpse of Tolleston, many of them patronizing the bar and table of the same hostelry, but their efforts were futile until the hour arrived for the hearing. They probably have a new court-house in Ogalalla now, but at the date of this chronicle the building which served as a temple of justice was poorly proportioned, its height being entirely out of relation to its width. It was a two-story affair, the lower floor being used for county offices, the upper one as the court-room. A long stairway ran up the outside of the building, landing on a gallery in front, from which the sheriff announced the sitting of the honorable court of Keith County. At home in Texas, lawsuits were so rare that though I was a grown man, the novelty of this one absorbed me. Quite a large crowd had gathered in advance of the hour, and while awaiting the arrival of Judge Mulqueen, a contingent of fifteen men from the two herds in question rode up and halted in front of the court-house. Forrest and I were lying low, not caring to be seen, when the three plaintiffs, the two local attorneys, and Tolleston put in an appearance. The cavalcade had not yet dismounted, and when Dorg Seay caught sight of Tolleston, he stood up in his stirrups and sang out, "Hello there, Archibald! my old college chum, how goes it?"

Judge Mulqueen had evidently dressed for the occasion, for with the exception of the plaintiffs, he was the only man in the court-room who wore a coat. The afternoon was a sultry one; in that first bottom of the Platte there was scarcely a breath of air, and collars wilted limp as rags. Neither map nor chart graced the unplastered walls, the unpainted furniture of the room was sadly in need of repair, while a musty odor permeated the room. Outside the railing the seating capacity of the court-room was rather small, rough, bare planks serving for seats, but the spectators gladly stood along the sides and rear, eager to catch every word, as they silently mopped the sweat which oozed alike from citizen and cattleman. Forrest and I were concealed in the rear, which was packed with Lovell's boys, when the judge walked in and court opened for the hearing. Judge Mulqueen requested counsel on either side to be as brief and direct as possible, both in their pleadings and testimony, adding: "If they reach the stock-yards in time, I may have to load out a train of feeders this evening. We'll bed the cars, anyhow." Turning to the sheriff, he continued: "Frank, if you happen outside, keep an eye up the river; those Lincoln feeders made a deal yesterday for five hundred three-year-olds. — Read your complaint."

The legal document was read with great fervor and energy by the younger of the two local lawyers. In the main it reviewed the situation correctly, every point, however, being made subservient to their object, — the possession of the cattle. The plaintiffs contended that they were the innocent holders of the original contract between the government and The Western Supply Company, properly assigned; that they had purchased these two herds in question, had paid earnest-money to the amount of sixty-five thousand dollars on the same, and concluded by petitioning the court for possession. Sutton arose, counseled a moment with Lovell, and borrowing a chew of tobacco from Sponsilier, leisurely addressed the court.

"I shall not trouble your honor by reading our reply in full, but briefly state its contents," said he, in substance. "We admit that the herds in question, which have been correctly described by road brands and ages, are the property of my client. We further admit that the two trail foremen here under arrest as accessories were acting under the orders of their employer, who assumes all responsibility for their acts, and in our pleadings we ask this honorable court to discharge them from further detention. The earnest-money, said to have been paid on these herds, is correct to a cent, and we admit having the amount in our possession. But," and the little advocate's voice rose, rich in its Irish brogue, "we deny any assignment of the original contract. The Western Supply Company is a corporation name, a shield and fence of thieves. The plaintiffs here can claim no assignment, because they themselves constitute the company. It has been decided that a man cannot steal his own money, neither can he assign from himself to himself. We shall prove by a credible witness that The Western Supply Company is but another name for John C. Fields, Oliver Radcliff, and the portly gentleman who was known a year ago as 'Honest' John Griscom, one of his many aliases. If to these names you add a few moneyed confederates, you have The Western Supply Company, one and the same. We shall also prove that for years past these same gentlemen have belonged to a ring, all brokers in government contracts, and frequently finding it necessary to use assumed names, generally that of a corporation."

Scanning the document in his hand, Sutton continued: "Our motive in selling and accepting money on these herds in Dodge demands a word of explanation. The original contract calls for five million pounds of beef on foot to be delivered at Fort Buford. My client is a subcontractor under that award. There are times, your honor, when it becomes necessary to resort to questionable means to attain an end. This is one of them. Within a week after my client had given bonds for the fulfillment of his contract, he made the discovery that he was dealing with a double-faced set of scoundrels. From that day until the present moment, secret-service men have shadowed every action of the plaintiffs. My client has anticipated their every move. When beeves broke in price from five to seven dollars a head, Honest John, here, made his boasts in Washington City over a champagne supper that he and his associates would clear one hundred thousand dollars on their Buford contract. Let us reason together how this could be done. The Western Supply Company refused, even when offered a bonus, to assign their contract to my client. But they were perfectly willing to transfer it, from themselves as a corporation, to themselves as individuals, even though they had previously given Don Lovell a subcontract for the delivery of the bees. The original award was made seven months ago, and the depreciation in cattle since is the secret of why the frog eat the cabbage. My client is under the necessity of tendering his cattle on the day of delivery, and proposes to hold this earnest-money to indemnify himself in case of an adverse decision at Fort Buford. It is the only thing he can do, as The Western Supply Company is execution proof, its assets consisting of some stud-horse office furniture and a corporate seal. On the other hand, Don Lovell is rated at half a million, mostly in pasture lands; is a citizen of Medina County, Texas, and if these gentlemen have any grievance, let them go there and sue him. A judgment against my client is good. Now, your honor, you have our side of the question. To be brief, shall these old Wisinsteins come out here from Washington City and dispossess any man of his property? There is but one answer — not in the Republic of Keith."

All three of the plaintiffs took the stand, their testimony supporting the complaint, Lovell's attorney refusing even to cross-examine any one of them. When they rested their case Sutton arose, and scanning the audience for some time, inquired, "Is Jim Reed there?" In response, a tall, one-armed man worked his way from the outer gallery through the crowd and advanced to the rail. I knew Reed by sight only, my middle brother having made several trips with his trail cattle, but he was known to every one by reputation. He had lost an arm in the Confederate service, and was recognized by the gambling fraternity as the gamest man among all the trail drovers, while every cowman from the Rio Grande to the Yellowstone knew him as a poker-player. Reed was asked to take the stand, and when questioned if he knew either of the plaintiffs, said:

"Yes, I know that fat gentleman, and I'm powerful glad to meet up with him again," replied the witness, designating Honest John. "That man is so crooked that he can't sleep in a bed, and it's one of the wonders of this country that he hasn't stretched hemp before this. I made his acquaintance as manager of The Federal Supply Company, and delivered three thousand cows to him at the Washita Indian Agency last fall. In the final settlement, he drew on three different banks, and one draft of twenty-eight thousand dollars came back, indorsed, DRAWEE UNKNOWN. I had other herds on the trail to look after, and it was a month before I found out that the check was bogus, by which time Honest John had sailed for Europe. There was nothing could be done but put my claim into a judgment and lay for him. But I've got a grapevine twist on him now, for no sooner did he buy a herd here last week than Mr. Sutton transferred the judgment to this jurisdiction, and his cattle will be attached this afternoon. I've been on his trail for nearly a year, but he'll come to me now, and before he can move his beeves out of this county, the last cent must come, with interest, attorney's fees, detective bills, and remuneration for my own time and trouble. That's the reason that I'm so glad to meet him. Judge, I've gone to the trouble and expense to get his record for the last ten years. He's so snaky he sheds his name yearly, shifting for a nickname from Honest John to The Quaker. In '80 he and his associates did business under the name of The Army & Sutler Supply Company, and I know of two judgments that can be bought very reasonable against that corporation. His record would convince any one that he despises to make an honest dollar."

The older of the two attorneys for the plaintiffs asked a few questions, but the replies were so unsatisfactory to their side, that they soon passed the witness. During the cross-questioning, however, the sheriff had approached the judge and whispered something to his honor. As there were no further witnesses to be examined, the local attorneys insisted on arguing the case, but Judge Mulqueen frowned them down, saying:

"This court sees no occasion for any argument in the present case. You might spout until you were black in the face and it wouldn't change my opinion any; besides I've got twenty cars to send and a train of cattle to load out this evening. This court refuses to interfere with the herds in question, at present the property of and in possession of Don Lovell, who, together with his men, are discharged from custody. If you're in town to-night, Mr. Reed, drop into the Lone Star. Couple of nice monte games running there; hundred-dollar limit, and if you feel lucky, there's a nice bank roll behind them. Adjourn court, Mr. Sheriff."

CHAPTER XIV
TURNING THE TABLES

"Keep away from me, you common cow-hands," said Sponsilier, as a group of us waited for him at the foot of the court-house stairs. But Dave's gravity soon turned to a smile as he continued: "Did you fellows notice The Rebel and me sitting inside the rail among all the big augers? Paul, was it a dream, or did we sleep in a bed last night and have a sure-enough pillow under our heads? My memory is kind of hazy to-day, but I remember the drinks and the cigars all right, and saying to some one that this luck was too good to last. And here we are turned out in the cold world again, our fun all over, and now must go back to those measly cattle. But it's just what I expected."

The crowd dispersed quietly, though the sheriff took the precaution to accompany the plaintiffs and Tolleston back to their hotel. The absence of the two deputies whom we had met the day before was explained by the testimony of the one-armed cowman. When the two drovers came downstairs, they were talking very confidentially together, and on my employer noticing the large number of his men present, he gave orders for them to meet him at once at the White Elephant saloon. Those who had horses at hand mounted and dashed down the street, while the rest of us took it leisurely around to the appointed rendezvous, some three blocks distant. While on the way, I learned from The Rebel that the cattle on which the attachment was to be made that afternoon were then being held well up the North Fork. Sheriff Phillips joined us shortly after we entered the saloon, and informed my employer and Mr. Reed that the firm of Field, Radcliff & Co. had declared war. They had even denounced him and the sheriff's office as being in collusion against them, and had dispatched Tolleston with orders to refuse service.

"Let them get on the prod all they want to," said Don Lovell to Reed and the sheriff. "I've got ninety men here, and you fellows are welcome to half of them, even if I have to go out and stand a watch on night-herd myself. Reed, we can't afford to have our business ruined by such a set of scoundrels, and we might as well fight it out here and now. Look at the situation I'm in. A hundred thousand dollars wouldn't indemnify me in having my cattle refused as late as the middle of September at Fort Buford. And believing that I will be turned down, under my contract, so Sutton says, I must tender my beeves on the appointed day of delivery, which will absolve my bondsmen and me from all liability. A man can't trifle with the government — the cattle must be there. Now in my case, Jim, what would you do?"

"That's a hard question, Don. You see we're strangers up in this Northwest country. Now, if it was home in Texas, there would be only one thing to do. Of course I'm no longer handy with a shotgun, but you've got two good arms."

"Well, gentlemen," said the sheriff, "you must excuse me for interrupting, but if my deputies are to take possession of that herd this afternoon, I must saddle up and go to the front. If Honest John and associates try to stand up any bluffs on my office, they'll only run on the rope once. I'm much obliged to you, Mr. Lovell, for the assurance of any help I may need, for it's quite likely that I may have to call upon you. If a ring of government speculators can come out here and refuse service, or dictate to my office, then old Keith County is certainly on the verge of decadence. Now, I'll be all ready to start for the North Fork in fifteen minutes, and I'd admire to have you all go along."

Lovell and Reed both expressed a willingness to accompany the sheriff. Phillips thanked them and nodded to the force behind the mahogany, who dexterously slid the glasses up and down the bar, and politely inquired of the double row confronting them as to their tastes. As this was the third round since entering the place, I was anxious to get away, and summoning Forrest, we started for our horses. We had left them at a barn on a back street, but before reaching the livery, Quince concluded that he needed a few more cartridges. I had ordered a hundred the day before for my own personal use, but they had been sent out with the supplies and were then in camp. My own belt was filled with ammunition, but on Forrest buying fifty, I took an equal number, and after starting out of the store, both turned back and doubled our purchases. On arriving at the stable, whom should I meet but the Wyoming cowman who had left us at Grinnell. During the few minutes in which I was compelled to listen to his troubles, he informed me that on his arrival at Ogalalla, all the surplus cow-hands had been engaged by a man named Tolleston for the Yellowstone country. He had sent to his ranch, however, for an outfit who would arrive that evening, and he expected to start his herd the next morning. But without wasting any words, Forrest and I swung into our saddles, waved a farewell to the wayfaring acquaintance, and rode around to the White Elephant. The sheriff and quite a cavalcade of our boys had already started, and on reaching the street which terminated in the only road leading to the North Fork, we were halted by Flood to await the arrival of the others. Jim Reed and my employer were still behind, and some little time was lost before they came up, sufficient to give the sheriff a full half-mile start. But under the leadership of the two drovers, we shook out our horses, and the advance cavalcade were soon overtaken.

"Well, Mr. Sheriff," said old man Don, as he reined in beside Phillips, "how do you like the looks of this for a posse? I'll vouch that they're all good cow-hands, and if you want to deputize the whole works, why, just work your rabbit's foot. You might leave Reed and me out, but I think there's some forty odd without us. Jim and I are getting a little too old, but we'll hang around and run errands and do the clerking. I'm perfectly willing to waste a week, and remember that we've got the chuck and nearly a thousand saddle horses right over here on the North Fork. You can move your office out to one of my wagons if you wish, and whatever's mine is yours, just so long as Honest John and his friends pay the fiddler. If he and his associates are going to make one hundred thousand dollars on the Buford contract, one thing is certain — I'll lose plenty of money on this year's drive. If he refuses service and you take possession, your office will be perfectly justified in putting a good force of men with the herd. And at ten dollars a day for a man and horse, they'll soon get sick and Reed will get his pay. If I have to hold the sack in the end, I don't want any company."

The location of the beeves was about twelve miles from town and but a short distance above the herds of The Rebel and Bob Quirk. It was nearly four o'clock when we left the hamlet, and by striking a free gait, we covered the intervening distance in less than an hour and a half. The mesa between the two rivers was covered with through cattle, and as we neared the herd in question, we were met by the larger one of the two chief deputies. The undersheriff was on his way to town, but on sighting his superior among us, he halted and a conference ensued. Sponsilier and Priest made a great ado over the big deputy on meeting, and after a few inquiries were exchanged, the latter turned to Sheriff Phillips and said:

"Well, we served the papers and I left the other two boys in temporary possession of the cattle. It's a badly mixed-up affair. The Texas foreman is still in charge, and he seems like a reasonable fellow. The terms of the sale were to be half cash here and the balance at the point of delivery. But the buyers only paid forty thousand down, and the trail boss refuses to start until they make good their agreement. From what I could gather from the foreman, the buyers simply buffaloed the young fellow out of his beeves, and are now hanging back for more favorable terms. He accepted service all right and assured me that our men would be welcome at his wagon until further notice, so I left matters just as I found them. But as I was on the point of leaving, that segundo of the buyers arrived and tried to stir up a little trouble. We all sat down on him rather hard, and as I left he and the Texas foreman were holding quite a big pow-wow."

"That's Tolleston all right," said old man Don, "and you can depend on him stirring up a muss if there's any show. It's a mystery to me how I tolerated that fellow as long as I did. If some of you boys will corner and hold him for me, I'd enjoy reading his title to him in a few plain words. It's due him, and I want to pay everything I owe. What's the programme, Mr. Sheriff?"

"The only safe thing to do is to get full possession of the cattle," replied Phillips. "My deputies are all right, but they don't thoroughly understand the situation. Mr. Lovell, if you can lend me ten men, I'll take charge of the herd at once and move them back down the river about seven miles. They're entirely too near the west line of the county to suit me, and once they're in our custody the money will be forthcoming, or the expenses will mount up rapidly. Let's ride."

The under-sheriff turned back with us. A swell of the mesa cut off a view of the herd, but under the leadership of the deputy we rode to its summit, and there before and under us were both camp and cattle. Arriving at the wagon, Phillips very politely informed the Texas foreman that he would have to take full possession of his beeves for a few days, or until the present difficulties were adjusted. The trail boss was a young fellow of possibly thirty, and met the sheriff's demand with several questions, but, on being assured that his employer's equity in the herd would be fully protected without expense, he offered no serious objection. It developed that Reed had some slight acquaintance with the seller of the cattle, and lost no time in informing the trail boss of the record of the parties with whom his employer was dealing. The one-armed drover's language was plain, the foreman knew Reed by reputation, and when Lovell assured the young man that he would be welcome at any of his wagons, and would be perfectly at liberty to see that his herd was properly cared for, he yielded without a word. My sympathies were with the foreman, for he seemed an honest fellow, and deliberately to take his herd from him, to my impulsive reasoning looked like an injustice. But the sheriff and those two old cowmen were determined, and the young fellow probably acted for the best in making a graceful surrender.

Meanwhile the two deputies in charge failed to materialize, and on inquiry they were reported as out at the herd with Tolleston. The foreman accompanied us to the cattle, and while on the way he informed the sheriff that he wished to count the beeves over to him and take a receipt for the same. Phillips hesitated, as he was no cowman, but Reed spoke up and insisted that it was fair and just, saying: "Of course, you'll count the cattle and give him a receipt in numbers, ages, and brands. It's not this young man's fault that his herd must undergo all this trouble, and when he turns them over to an officer of the law he ought to have something to show for it. Any of Lovell's foremen here will count them to a hair for you, and Don and I will witness the receipt, which will make it good among cowmen."

Without loss of time the herd was started east. Tolleston kept well out of reach of my employer, and besought every one to know what this movement meant. But when the trail boss and Jim Flood rode out to a swell of ground ahead, and the point-men began filing the column through between the two foremen, Archie was sagacious enough to know that the count meant something serious. In the mean time Bob Quirk had favored Tolleston with his company, and when the count was nearly half over, my brother quietly informed him that the sheriff was taking possession. Once the atmosphere cleared, Archie grew uneasy and restless, and as the last few hundred beeves were passing the counters, he suddenly concluded to return to Ogalalla. But my brother urged him not to think of going until he had met his former employer, assuring Tolleston that the old man had made inquiry about and was anxious to meet him. The latter, however, could not remember anything of urgent importance between them, and pleaded the lateness of the hour and the necessity of his immediate return to town. The more urgent Bob Quirk became, the more fidgety grew Archie. The last of the cattle were passing the count as Tolleston turned away from my brother's entreaty, and giving his horse the rowel, started off on a gallop. But there was a scattering field of horsemen to pass, and before the parting guest could clear it, a half-dozen ropes circled in the air and deftly settled over his horse's neck and himself, one of which pinioned his arms. The boys were expecting something of this nature, and fully half the men in Lovell's employ galloped up and formed a circle around the captive, now livid with rage. Archie was cursing by both note and rhyme, and had managed to unearth a knife and was trying to cut the lassos which fettered himself and horse, when Dorg Seay rode in and rapped him over the knuckles with a six-shooter, saying, "Don't do that, sweetheart; those ropes cost thirty-five cents apiece."

Fortunately the knife was knocked from Tolleston's hand and his six-shooter secured, rendering him powerless to inflict injury to any one. The cattle count had ended, and escorted by a cordon of mounted men, both horse and captive were led over to where a contingent had gathered around to hear the result of the count. I was merely a delighted spectator, and as the other men turned from the cattle and met us, Lovell languidly threw one leg over his horse's neck, and, suppressing a smile, greeted his old foreman.

"Hello, Archie," said he; "it's been some little time since last we met. I've been hearing some bad reports about you, and was anxious to meet up and talk matters over. Boys, take those ropes off his horse and give him back his irons; I raised this man and made him the cow-hand he is, and there's nothing so serious between us that we should remain strangers. Now, Archie, I want you to know that you are in the employ of my enemies, who are as big a set of scoundrels as ever missed a halter. You and Flood, here, were the only two men in my employ who knew all the facts in regard to the Buford contract. And just because I wouldn't favor you over a blind horse, you must hunt up the very men who are trying to undermine me on this drive. No wonder they gave you employment, for you're a valuable man to them; but it's at a serious loss, — the loss of your honor. You can't go home to Texas and again be respected among men. This outfit you are with will promise you the earth, but the moment that they're through with you, you won't cut any more figure than a last year's bird's nest. They'll throw you aside like an old boot, and you'll fall so hard that you'll hear the clock tick in China. Now, Archie, it hurts me to see a young fellow like you go wrong, and I'm willing to forgive the past and stretch out a hand to save you. If you'll quit those people, you can have Flood's cattle from here to the Rosebud Agency, or I'll buy you a ticket home and you can help with the fall work at the ranch. You may have a day or two to think this matter over, and whatever you decide on will be final. You have shown little gratitude for the opportunities that I've given you, but we'll break the old slate and start all over with a new one. Now, that's all I wanted to say to you, except to do your own thinking. If you're going back to town, I'll ride a short distance with you."

The two rode away together, but halted within sight for a short conference, after which Lovell returned. The cattle were being drifted east by the deputies and several of our boys, the trail boss having called off his men on an agreement of the count. The herd had tallied out thirty-six hundred and ten head, but in making out the receipt, the fact was developed that there were some six hundred beeves not in the regular road brand. These had been purchased extra from another source, and had been paid for in full by the buyers, the seller of the main herd agreeing to deliver them along with his own. This was fortunate, as it increased the equity of the buyers in the cattle, and more than established a sufficient interest to satisfy the judgment and all expenses.

Darkness was approaching, which hastened our actions. Two men from each outfit present were detailed to hold the cattle that night, and were sent on ahead to Priest's camp to secure their suppers and a change of mounts. The deposed trail boss accepted an invitation to accompany us and spend the night at one of our wagons, and we rode away to overtake the drifting herd. The different outfits one by one dropped out and rode for their camps; but as mine lay east and across the river, the course of the herd was carrying me home. After passing The Rebel's wagon fully a half mile, we rounded in the herd, which soon lay down to rest on the bedground. In the gathering twilight, the camp-fires of nearly a dozen trail wagons were gleaming up and down the river, and while we speculated with Sponsilier's boys which one was ours, the guard arrived and took the bedded herd. The two old cowmen and the trail boss had dropped out opposite my brother's camp, leaving something like ten men with the attached beeves; but on being relieved by the first watch, Flood invited Sheriff Phillips and his deputies across the river to spend the night with him.

"Like to, mighty well, but can't do it," replied Phillips. "The sheriff's office is supposed to be in town, and not over on the North Fork, but I'll leave two of these deputies with you. Some of you had better ride in to-morrow, for there may be overtures made looking towards a settlement; and treat those beeves well, so that there can be no charge of damage to the cattle. Good-night, everybody."

CHAPTER XV
TOLLESTON BUTTS IN

Morning dawned on a scene of pastoral grandeur. The valley of the North Platte was dotted with cattle from hill and plain. The river, well confined within its low banks, divided an unsurveyed domain of green-swarded meadows like a boundary line between vast pastures. The exodus of cattle from Texas to the new Northwest was nearing flood-tide, and from every swell and knoll the solitary figure of the herdsman greeted the rising sun.

Sponsilier and I had agreed to rejoin our own outfits at the first opportunity. We might have exchanged places the evening before, but I had a horse and some ammunition at Dave's camp and was just contentious enough not to give up a single animal from my own mount. On the other hand, Mr. Dave Sponsilier would have traded whole remudas with me; but my love for a good horse was strong, and Fort Buford was many a weary mile distant. Hence there was no surprise shown as Sponsilier rode up to his own wagon that morning in time for breakfast. We were good friends when personal advantages did not conflict, and where our employer's interests were at stake we stood shoulder to shoulder like comrades. Yet Dave gave me a big jolly about being daffy over my horses, well knowing that there is an indescribable nearness between one of our craft and his own mount. But warding off his raillery, just the same and in due time, I cantered away on my own horse.

As I rode up the North Fork towards my outfit, the attached herd was in plain view across the river. Arriving at my own wagon, I saw a mute appeal in every face for permission to go to town, and consent was readily granted to all who had not been excused on a similar errand the day before. The cook and horse-wrangler were included, and the activities of the outfit in saddling and getting away were suggestive of a prairie fire or a stampede. I accompanied them across the river, and then turned upstream to my brother's camp, promising to join them later and make a full day of it. At Bob's wagon they had stretched a fly, and in its shade lounged half a dozen men, while an air of languid indolence pervaded the camp. Without dismounting, I announced myself as on the way to town, and invited any one who wished to accompany me. Lovell and Reed both declined; half of Bob's men had been excused and started an hour before, but my brother assured me that if I would wait until the deposed foreman returned, the latter's company could be counted on. I waited, and in the course of half an hour the trail boss came back from his cattle. During the interim, the two old cowmen reviewed Grant's siege of Vicksburg, both having been participants, but on opposite sides. While the guest was shifting his saddle to a loaned horse, I inquired if there was anything that I could attend to for any one at Ogalalla. Lovell could think of nothing; but as we mounted to start, Reed aroused himself, and coming over, rested the stub of his armless sleeve on my horse's neck, saying:

"You boys might drop into the sheriff's office as you go in and also again as you are starting back. Report the cattle as having spent a quiet night and ask Phillips if he has any word for me."

Turning to the trail boss he continued: "Young man, I would suggest that you hunt up your employer and have him stir things up. The cattle will be well taken care of, but we're just as anxious to turn them back to you as you are to receive them. Tell the seller that it would be well worth his while to see Lovell and myself before going any farther. We can put him in possession of a few facts that may save him time and trouble. I reckon that's about all. Oh, yes, I'll be at this wagon all evening."

My brother rode a short distance with us and introduced the stranger as Hugh Morris. He proved a sociable fellow, had made three trips up the trail as foreman, his first two herds having gone to the Cherokee Strip under contract. By the time we reached Ogalalla, as strong a fraternal level existed between us as though we had known each other for years. Halting for a moment at the sheriff's office, we delivered our messages, after which we left our horses at the same corral with the understanding that we would ride back together. A few drinks were indulged in before parting, then each went to attend to his own errands, but we met frequently during the day. Once my boys were provided with funds, they fell to gambling so eagerly that they required no further thought on my part until evening. Several times during the day I caught glimpses of Tolleston, always on horseback, and once surrounded by quite a cavalcade of horsemen. Morris and I took dinner at the hotel where the trio of government jobbers were stopping. They were in evidence, and amongst the jolliest of the guests, commanding and receiving the best that the hostelry afforded. Sutton was likewise present, but quiet and unpretentious, and I thought there was a false, affected note in the hilarity of the ringsters, and for effect. I was known to two of the trio, but managed to overhear any conversation which was adrift. After dinner and over fragrant cigars, they reared their feet high on an outer gallery, and the inference could be easily drawn that a contract, unless it involved millions, was beneath their notice.

Morris informed me that his employer's suspicions were aroused, and that he had that morning demanded a settlement in full or the immediate release of the herd. They had laughed the matter off as a mere incident that would right itself at the proper time, and flashed as references a list of congressmen, senators, and bankers galore. But Morris's employer had stood firm in his contentions, refusing to be overawed by flattery or empty promises. What would be the result remained to be seen, and the foreman and myself wandered aimlessly around town during the afternoon, meeting other trail bosses, nearly all of whom had heard more or less about the existing trouble. That we had the sympathy of the cattle interests on our side goes without saying, and one of them, known as "the kidgloved foreman," a man in the employ of Shanghai Pierce, invoked the powers above to witness what would happen if he were in Lovell's boots. This was my first meeting with the picturesque trail boss, though I had heard of him often and found him a trifle boastful but not a bad fellow. He distinguished himself from others of his station on the trail by always wearing white shirts, kid gloves, riding-boots, inlaid spurs, while a heavy silver chain was wound several times round a costly sombrero in lieu of a hatband. We spent an hour or more together, drinking sparingly, and at parting he begged that I would assure my employer that he sympathized with him and was at his command.

The afternoon was waning when I hunted up my outfit and started them for camp. With one or two exceptions, the boys were broke and perfectly willing to go. Morris and I joined them at the livery where they had left their horses, and together we started out of town. Ordering them to ride on to camp, and saying that I expected to return by way of Bob Quirk's wagon, Morris and myself stopped at the court-house. Sheriff Phillips was in his office and recognized us both at a glance. "Well, she's working," said he, "and I'll probably have some word for you late this evening. Yes, one of the local attorneys for your friends came in and we figured everything up. He thought that if this office would throw off a certain per cent. of its expense, and Reed would knock off the interest, his clients would consent to a settlement. I told him to go right back and tell his people that as long as they thought that way, it would only cost them one hundred and forty dollars every twenty-four hours." The lawyer was back within twenty minutes, bringing a draft, covering every item, and urged me to have it accepted by wire. The bank was closed, but I found the cashier in a poker-game and played his hand while he went over to the depot and sent the message. "The operator has orders to send a duplicate of the answer to this office, and the moment I get it, if favorable, I'll send a deputy with the news over to the North Fork. Tell Reed that I think the check's all right this time, but we'll stand pat until we know for a certainty. We'll get an answer by morning sure."

The message was hailed with delight at Bob Quirk's wagon. On nearing the river, Morris rode by way of the herd to ask the deputies in charge to turn the cattle up the river towards his camp. Several of the foreman's men were waiting at my brother's wagon, and on Morris's return he ordered his outfit to meet the beeves the next morning and be in readiness to receive them back. Our foremen were lying around temporary headquarters, and as we were starting for our respective camps for the night, Lovell suggested that we hold our outfits all ready to move out with the herds on an hour's notice. Accordingly the next morning, I refused every one leave of absence, and gave special orders to the cook and horse-wrangler to have things in hand to start on an emergency order. Jim Flood had agreed to wait for me, and we would recross the river together and hear the report from the sheriff's office. Forrest and Sponsilier rode up about the same time we arrived at his wagon, and all four of us set out for headquarters across the North Fork. The sun was several hours high when we reached the wagon, and learned that an officer had arrived during the night with a favorable answer, that the cattle had been turned over to Morris without a count, and that the deputies had started for town at daybreak.

"Well, boys," said Lovell, as we came in after picketing our horses, "Reed, here, wins out, but we're just as much at sea as ever. I've looked the situation over from a dozen different viewpoints, and the only thing to do is graze across country and tender our cattle at Fort Buford. It's my nature to look on the bright side of things, and yet I'm old enough to know that justice, in a world so full of injustice, is a rarity. By allowing the earnest-money paid at Dodge to apply, some kind of a compromise might be effected, whereby I could get rid of two of these herds, with three hundred saddle horses thrown back on my hands at the Yellowstone River. I might dispose of the third herd here and give the remuda away, but at a total loss of at least thirty thousand dollars on the Buford cattle. But then there's my bond to The Western Supply Company, and if this herd of Morris's fails to respond on the day of delivery, I know who will have to make good. An Indian uprising, or the enforcement of quarantine against Texas fever, or any one of a dozen things might tie up the herd, and September the 15th come and go and no beef offered on the contract. I've seen outfits start out and never get through with the chuck-wagon, even. Sutton's advice is good; we'll tender the cattle. There is a chance that we'll get turned down, but if we do, I have enough indemnity money in my possession to temper the wind if the day of delivery should prove a chilly one to us. I think you had all better start in the morning."

The old man's review of the situation was a rational one, in which Jim Reed and the rest of us concurred. Several of the foremen, among them myself, were anxious to start at once, but Lovell urged that we kill a beef before starting and divide it up among the six outfits. He also proposed to Flood that they go into town during the afternoon and freely announce our departure in the morning, hoping to force any issue that might be smouldering in the enemy's camp. The outlook for an early departure was hailed with delight by the older foremen, and we younger and more impulsive ones yielded. The cook had orders to get up something extra for dinner, and we played cards and otherwise lounged around until the midday meal was announced as ready. A horse had been gotten up for Lovell to ride and was on picket, all the relieved men from the attached herd were at Bob's wagon for dinner, and jokes and jollity graced the occasion. But near the middle of the noon repast, some one sighted a mounted man coming at a furious pace for the camp, and shortly the horseman dashed up and inquired for Lovell. We all arose, when the messenger dismounted and handed my employer a letter. Tearing open the missive, the old man read it and turned ashy pale. The message was from Mike Sutton, stating that a fourth member of the ring had arrived during the forenoon, accompanied by a United States marshal from the federal court at Omaha; that the officer was armed with an order of injunctive relief; that he had deputized thirty men whom Tolleston had gathered, and proposed taking possession of the two herds in question that afternoon.

"Like hell they will," said Don Lovell, as he started for his horse. His action was followed by every man present, including the one-armed guest, and within a few minutes thirty men swung into saddles, subject to orders. The camps of the two herds at issue were about four and five miles down and across the river, and no doubt Tolleston knew of their location, as they were only a little more than an hour's ride from Ogalalla. There was no time to be lost, and as we hastily gathered around the old man, he said: "Ride for your outfits, boys, and bring along every man you can spare. We'll meet north of the river about midway between Quince's and Tom's camps. Bring all the cartridges you have, and don't spare your horses going or coming."

Priest's wagon was almost on a line with mine, though south of the river. Fortunately I was mounted on one of the best horses in my string, and having the farthest to go, shook the kinks out of him as old Paul and myself tore down the mesa. After passing The Rebel's camp, I held my course as long as the footing was solid, but on encountering the first sand, crossed the river nearly opposite the appointed rendezvous. The North Platte was fordable at any point, flowing but a midsummer stage of water, with numerous wagon crossings, its shallow channel being about one hundred yards wide. I reined in my horse for the first time near the middle of the stream, as the water reached my saddle-skirts; when I came out on the other side, Priest and his boys were not a mile behind me. As I turned down the river, casting a backward glance, squads of horsemen were galloping in from several quarters and joining a larger one which was throwing up clouds of dust like a column of cavalry. In making a cut-off to reach my camp, I crossed a sand dune from which I sighted the marshal's posse less than two miles distant. My boys were gambling among themselves, not a horse under saddle, and did not notice my approach until I dashed up. Three lads were on herd, but the rest, including the wrangler, ran for their mounts on picket, while Parent and myself ransacked the wagon for ammunition. Fortunately the supply of the latter was abundant, and while saddles were being cinched on horses, the cook and I divided the ammunition and distributed it among the men. The few minutes' rest refreshed my horse, but as we dashed away, the boys yelling like Comanches, the five-mile ride had bested him and he fell slightly behind. As we turned into the open valley, it was a question if we or the marshal would reach the stream first; he had followed an old wood road and would strike the river nearly opposite Forrest's camp. The horses were excited and straining every nerve, and as we neared our crowd the posse halted on the south side and I noticed a conveyance among them in which were seated four men. There was a moment's consultation held, when the posse entered the water and began fording the stream, the vehicle and its occupants remaining on the other side. We had halted in a circle about fifty yards back from the river-bank, and as the first two men came out of the water, Don Lovell rode forward several lengths of his horse, and with his hand motioned to them to halt. The leaders stopped within easy speaking distance, the remainder of the posse halting in groups at their rear, when Lovell demanded the meaning of this demonstration.

An inquiry and answer followed identifying the speakers. "In pursuance of an order from the federal court of this jurisdiction," continued the marshal, "I am vested with authority to take into my custody two herds, numbering nearly seven thousand beeves, now in your possession, and recently sold to Field, Radcliff & Co. for government purposes. I propose to execute my orders peaceably, and any interference on your part will put you and your men in contempt of government authority. If resistance is offered, I can, if necessary, have a company of United States cavalry here from Fort Logan within forty-eight hours to enforce the mandates of the federal court. Now my advice to you would be to turn these cattle over without further controversy."

"And my advice to you," replied Lovell, "is to go back to your federal court and tell that judge that as a citizen of these United States, and one who has borne arms in her defense, I object to having snap judgment rendered against me. If the honorable court which you have the pleasure to represent is willing to dispossess me of my property in favor of a ring of government thieves, and on only hearing one side of the question, then consider me in contempt. I'll gladly go back to Omaha with you, but you can't so much as look at a hoof in my possession. Now call your troops, or take me with you for treating with scorn the orders of your court."

Meanwhile every man on our side had an eye on Archie Tolleston, who had gradually edged forward until his horse stood beside that of the marshal. Before the latter could frame a reply to Lovell's ultimatum, Tolleston said to the federal officer:

"Didn't my employers tell you that the old — — — — — — would defy you without a demonstration of soldiers at your back? Now, the laugh's on you, and —"

"No, it's on you," interrupted a voice at my back, accompanied by a pistol report. My horse jumped forward, followed by a fusillade of shots behind me, when the hireling deputies turned and plunged into the river. Tolleston had wheeled his horse, joining the retreat, and as I brought my six-shooter into action and was in the act of leveling on him, he reeled from the saddle, but clung to the neck of his mount as the animal dashed into the water. I held my fire in the hope that he would right in the saddle and afford me a shot, but he struck a swift current, released his hold, and sunk out of sight. Above the din and excitement of the moment, I heard a voice which I recognized as Reed's, shouting, "Cut loose on that team, boys! blaze away at those

345

harness horses!" Evidently the team had been burnt by random firing, for they were rearing and plunging, and as I fired my first shot at them, the occupants sprang out of the vehicle and the team ran away. A lull occurred in the shooting, to eject shells and refill cylinders, which Lovell took advantage of by ordering back a number of impulsive lads, who were determined to follow up the fleeing deputies.

"Come back here, you rascals, and stop this shooting!" shouted the old man. "Stop it, now, or you'll land me in a federal prison for life! Those horsemen may be deceived. When federal courts can be deluded with sugar-coated blandishments, ordinary men ought to be excusable."

Six-shooters were returned to their holsters. Several horses and two men on our side had received slight flesh wounds, as there had been a random return fire. The deputies halted well out of pistol range, covering the retreat of the occupants of the carriage as best they could, but leaving three dead horses in plain view. As we dropped back towards Forrest's wagon, the team in the mean time having been caught, those on foot were picked up and given seats in the conveyance. Meanwhile a remuda of horses and two chuck-wagons were sighted back on the old wood road, but a horseman met and halted them and they turned back for Ogalalla. On reaching our nearest camp, the posse south of the river had started on their return, leaving behind one of their number in the muddy waters of the North Platte.

Late that evening, as we were preparing to leave for our respective camps, Lovell said to the assembled foremen: "Quince will take Reed and me into Ogalalla about midnight. If Sutton advises it, all three of us will go down to Omaha and try and square things. I can't escape a severe fine, but what do I care as long as I have their money to pay it with? The killing of that fool boy worries me more than a dozen fines. It was uncalled for, too, but he would butt in, and you fellows were all itching for the chance to finger a trigger. Now the understanding is that you all start in the morning."

CHAPTER XVI
CROSSING THE NIOBRARA

The parting of the ways was reached. On the morning of July 12, the different outfits in charge of Lovell's drive in '84 started on three angles of the compass for their final destination. The Rosebud Agency, where Flood's herd was to be delivered on September 1, lay to the northeast in Dakota. The route was not direct, and the herd would be forced to make quite an elbow, touching on the different forks of the Loup in order to secure water. The Rebel and my brother would follow up on the south side of the North Platte until near old Fort Laramie, when their routes would separate, the latter turning north for Montana, while Priest would continue along the same watercourse to within a short distance of his destination. The Buford herds would strike due north from the first tributary putting in from above, which we would intercept the second morning out.

An early start was the order of the day. My beeves were pushed from the bed-ground with the first sign of dawn, and when the relief overtook them, they were several miles back from the river and holding a northwest course. My camp being the lowest one on the North Fork, Forrest and Sponsilier, also starting at daybreak, naturally took the lead, the latter having fully a five-mile start over my outfit. But as we left the valley and came up on the mesa, there on an angle in our front, Flood's herd snailed along like an army brigade, anxious to dispute our advance. The point-men veered our cattle slightly to the left, and as the drag-end of Flood's beeves passed before us, standing in our stirrups we waved our hats in farewell to the lads, starting on their last tack for the Rosebud Agency. Across the river were the dim outlines of two herds trailing upstream, being distinguishable from numerous others by the dust-clouds which marked the moving from the grazing cattle. The course of the North Platte was southwest, and on the direction which we were holding, we would strike the river again during the afternoon at a bend some ten or twelve miles above.

Near the middle of the forenoon we were met by Hugh Morris. He was discouraged, as it was well known now that his cattle would be tendered in competition with ours at Fort Buford. There was no comparison between the beeves, ours being much larger, more uniform in weight, and in better flesh. He looked over both Forrest's and Sponsilier's herds before meeting us, and was good enough judge of cattle to know that his stood no chance against ours, if they were to be received on their merits. We talked matters over for fully an hour, and I advised him never to leave Keith County until the last dollar in payment for his beeves was in hand. Morris thought this was quite possible, as information had reached him that the buyers had recently purchased a remuda, and now, since they had failed to take possession of two of Lovell's herds, it remained to be seen what the next move would be. He thought it quite likely, though, that a settlement could be effected whereby he would be relieved at Ogalalla. Mutually hoping that all would turn out well, we parted until our paths should cross again.

We intercepted the North Fork again during the afternoon, watering from it for the last time, and the next morning struck the Blue River, the expected tributary. Sponsilier maintained his position in the lead, but I was certain when we reached the source of the Blue, David would fall to the rear, as thenceforth there was neither trail nor trace, map nor compass. The year before, Forrest and I had been over the route to the Pine Ridge Agency, and one or the other of us must take the lead across a dry country between the present stream and tributaries of the Niobrara. The Blue possessed the attributes of a river in name only, and the third day up it, Sponsilier crossed the tributary to allow either Forrest or myself to take the lead. Quince professed a remarkable ignorance and faulty memory as to the topography of the country between the Blue and Niobrara, and threw bouquets at me regarding my ability always to find water. It is true that I had gone and returned across this arid belt the year before, but on the back trip it was late in the fall, and we were making forty miles a day with nothing but a wagon and remuda, water being the least of my troubles. But a compromise was effected whereby we would both ride out the country anew, leaving the herds to lie over on the head waters of the Blue River. There were several shallow lakes in the intervening country, and on finding the first one sufficient to our needs, the herds were brought up, and we scouted again in advance. The abundance of antelope was accepted as an assurance of water, and on recognizing certain landmarks, I agreed to take the lead thereafter, and we turned back. The seventh day out from the Blue, the Box Buttes were sighted, at the foot of which ran a creek by the same name, and an affluent of the Niobrara. Contrary to expectations, water was even more plentiful than the year before, and we grazed nearly the entire distance. The antelope were unusually tame; with six-shooters we killed quite a number by flagging, or using a gentle horse for a blind, driving the animal forward with the bridle reins, tacking frequently, and allowing him to graze up within pistol range.

The Niobrara was a fine grazing country. Since we had over two months at our disposal, after leaving the North Platte, every advantage was given the cattle to round into form. Ten miles was a day's move, and the different outfits kept in close touch with each other. We had planned a picnic for the crossing of the Niobrara, and on reaching that stream during the afternoon, Sponsilier and myself crossed, camping a mile apart, Forrest remaining on the south side. Wild raspberries had been extremely plentiful, and every wagon had gathered a quantity sufficient to make a pie for each man. The cooks had mutually agreed to meet at Sponsilier's wagon and do the baking, and every man not on herd was present in expectation of the coming banquet. One of Forrest's boys had a fiddle, and bringing it along, the festivities opened with a stag dance, the "ladies" being designated by wearing a horse-hobble loosely around their necks. While the pies were baking, a slow process with Dutch ovens, I sat on the wagon-tongue and played the violin by the hour. A rude imitation of the gentler sex, as we had witnessed in dance-halls in Dodge and Ogalalla, was reproduced with open shirt fronts, and amorous advances by the sterner one.

The dancing ceased the moment the banquet was ready. The cooks had experienced considerable trouble in restraining some of the boys from the too free exercise of what they looked upon as the inalienable right of man to eat his pie when, where, and how it best pleased him. But Sponsilier, as host, stood behind the culinary trio, and overawed the impetuous guests. The repast barely concluded in time for the wranglers and first guard from Forrest's and my outfit to reach camp, catch night-horses, bed the cattle, and excuse the herders, as supper was served only at the one wagon. The relieved ones, like eleventh-hour guests, came tearing in after darkness, and the tempting spread soon absorbed them. As the evening wore on, the loungers gathered in several circles, and the raconteur held sway. The fact that we were in a country in which game abounded suggested numerous stories. The delights of cat-hunting by night found an enthusiast in each one present. Every dog in our memory, back to early boyhood, was properly introduced and his best qualities applauded. Not only cat-hounds but coon-dogs had a respectful hearing.

"I remember a hound," said Forrest's wrangler, "which I owned when a boy back in Virginia. My folks lived in the foot-hills of the Blue Ridge Mountains in that state. We were just as poor as our poorest neighbors. But if there was any one thing that that section was rich in it was dogs, principally hounds. This dog of mine was four years old when I left home to go to Texas. Fine hound, swallow marked, and when he opened on a scent you could always tell what it was that he was running. I never allowed him to run with packs, but generally used him in treeing coon, which pestered the cornfields during roasting-ear season and in the fall. Well, after I had been out in Texas about five years, I concluded to go back on a little visit to the old folks. There were no railroads within twenty miles of my home, and I had to hoof it that distance, so I arrived after dark. Of course my return was a great surprise to my folks, and we sat up late telling stories about things out West. I had worked with cattle all the time, and had made one trip over the trail from Collin County to Abilene, Kansas.

"My folks questioned me so fast that they gave me no show to make any inquiries in return, but I finally eased one in and asked about my dog Keiser, and was tickled to hear that he was still living. I went out and called him, but he failed to show up, when mother explained his absence by saying that he often went out hunting alone now, since there was none of us boys at home to hunt with him. They told me that he was no account any longer; that he had grown old and gray, and father said he was too slow on trail to be of any use. I noticed that it was a nice damp night, and if my old dog had been there, I think I'd have taken a circle around the fields in the hope of hearing him sing once more. Well, we went back into the house, and after talking awhile longer, I climbed into the loft and went to bed. I didn't sleep very sound that night, and awakened several times. About an hour before daybreak, I awoke suddenly and imagined I heard a hound baying faintly in the distance. Finally I got up and opened the board window in the gable and listened. Say, boys, I knew that hound's baying as well as I know my own saddle. It was old Keiser, and he had something treed about a mile from the house, across a ridge over in some slashes. I slipped on my clothes, crept downstairs, and taking my old man's rifle out of the rack, started to him.

"It was as dark as a stack of black cats, but I knew every path and byway by heart. I followed the fields as far as I could, and later, taking into the timber, I had to go around a long swamp. An old beaver dam had once crossed the outlet of this marsh, and once I gained it, I gave a long yell to let the dog know that some one was coming. He answered me, and quite a little while before day broke I reached him. Did he know me? Why, he knew me as easy as the little boy knew his pap. Right now, I can't remember any simple thing in my whole life that moved me just as that little reunion of me and my dog, there in those woods that morning. Why, he howled with delight. He licked my face and hands and stood up on me with his wet feet and said just as plain as he could that he was glad to see me again. And I was glad to meet him, even though he did make me feel as mellow as a girl over a baby.

"Well, when daybreak came, I shot a nice big fat Mr. Zip Coon out of an old pin-oak, and we started for home like old pardners. Old as he was, he played like a puppy around me, and when we came in sight of the house, he ran on ahead and told the folks what he had found. Yes, you bet he told them. He came near clawing all the clothing off them in his delight. That's one reason I always like a dog and a poor man — you can't question their friendship."

A circus was in progress on the other side of the wagon. From a large rock, Jake Blair was announcing the various acts and introducing the actors and actresses. Runt Pickett, wearing a skirt made out of a blanket and belted with a hobble, won the admiration of all as the only living lady lion-tamer. Resuming comfortable positions on our side of the commissary, a lad named Waterwall, one of Sponsilier's boys, took up the broken thread where Forrest's wrangler had left off.

"The greatest dog-man I ever knew," said he, "lived on the Guadalupe River. His name was Dave Hapfinger, and he had the loveliest vagabond temperament of any man I ever saw. It mattered nothing what he was doing, all you had to do was to give old Dave a hint that you knew where there was fish to be caught, or a bee-course to hunt, and he would stop the plow and go with you for a week if necessary. He loved hounds better than any man I ever knew. You couldn't confer greater favor than to give him a promising hound pup, or, seeking the same, ask for one of his raising. And he was such a good fellow. If any one was sick in the neighborhood, Uncle Dave always had time to kill them a squirrel every day; and he could make a broth for a baby, or fry a young squirrel, in a manner that would make a sick man's mouth water.

"When I was a boy, I've laid around many a camp-fire this way and listened to old Dave tell stories. He was quite a humorist in his way, and possessed a wonderful memory. He could tell you the day of the month, thirty years before, when he went to mill one time and found a peculiar bird's nest on the way. Colonel Andrews, owner of several large plantations, didn't like Dave, and threatened to prosecute him once for cutting a bee-tree on his land. If the evidence had been strong enough, I reckon the Colonel would. No doubt Uncle Dave was guilty, but mere suspicion isn't sufficient proof.

"Colonel Andrews was a haughty old fellow, blue-blooded and proud as a peacock, and about the only way Dave could get even with him was in his own mild, humorous way. One day at dinner at a neighboring log-rolling, when all danger of prosecution for cutting the bee-tree had passed, Uncle Dave told of a recent dream of his, a pure invention. 'I dreamt,' said he, 'that Colonel Andrews died and went to heaven. There was an unusually big commotion at St.

Peter's gate on his arrival. A troop of angels greeted him, still the Colonel seemed displeased at his reception. But the welcoming hosts humored him forward, and on nearing the throne, the Almighty, recognizing the distinguished arrival, vacated the throne and came down to greet the Colonel personally. At this mark of appreciation, he relaxed a trifle, and when the Almighty insisted that he should take the throne seat, Colonel Andrews actually smiled for the first time on earth or in heaven.'

"Uncle Dave told this story so often that he actually believed it himself. But finally a wag friend of Colonel Andrews told of a dream which he had had about old Dave, which the latter hugely enjoyed. According to this second vagary, the old vagabond had also died and gone to heaven. There was some trouble at St. Peter's gate, as they refused to admit dogs, and Uncle Dave always had a troop of hounds at his heels. When he found that it was useless to argue the matter, he finally yielded the point and left the pack outside. Once inside the gate he stopped, bewildered at the scene before him. But after waiting inside some little time unnoticed, he turned and was on the point of asking the gate-keeper to let him out, when an angel approached and asked him to stay. There was some doubt in Dave's mind if he would like the place, but the messenger urged that he remain and at least look the city over. The old hunter goodnaturedly consented, and as they started up one of the golden streets Uncle Dave recognized an old friend who had once given him a hound pup. Excusing himself to the angel, he rushed over to his former earthly friend and greeted him with warmth and cordiality. The two old cronies talked and talked about the things below, and finally Uncle Dave asked if there was any hunting up there. The reply was disappointing.

"Meanwhile the angel kept urging Uncle Dave forward to salute the throne. But he loitered along, meeting former hunting acquaintances, and stopping with each for a social chat. When they finally neared the throne, the patience of the angel was nearly exhausted; and as old Dave looked up and saw Colonel Andrews occupying the throne, he rebelled and refused to salute, when the angel wrathfully led him back to the gate and kicked him out among his dogs."

Jack Splann told a yarn about the friendship of a pet lamb and dog which he owned when a boy. It was so unreasonable that he was interrupted on nearly every assertion. Long before he had finished, Sponsilier checked his narrative and informed him that if he insisted on doling out fiction he must have some consideration for his listeners, and at least tell it within reason. Splann stopped right there and refused to conclude his story, though no one but myself seemed to regret it. I had a true incident about a dog which I expected to tell, but the audience had become too critical, and I kept quiet. As it was evident that no more dog stories would be told, the conversation was allowed to drift at will. The recent shooting on the North Platte had been witnessed by nearly every one present, and was suggestive of other scenes.

"I have always contended," said Dorg Seay, "that the man who can control his temper always shoots the truest. You take one of these fellows that can smile and shoot at the same time — they are the boys that I want to stand in with. But speaking of losing the temper, did any of you ever see a woman real angry, — not merely cross, but the tigress in her raging and thirsting to tear you limb from limb? I did only once, but I have never forgotten the occasion. In supreme anger the only superior to this woman I ever witnessed was Captain Cartwright when he shot the slayer of his only son. He was as cool as a cucumber, as his only shot proved, but years afterward when he told me of the incident, he lost all control of himself, and fire flashed from his eyes like from the muzzle of a six-shooter. 'Dorg,' said he, unconsciously shaking me like a terrier does a rat, his blazing eyes not a foot from my face, 'Dorg, when I shot that cowardly — — — — — — , I didn't miss the centre of his forehead the width of my thumb nail.'

"But this woman defied a throng of men. Quite a few of the crowd had assisted the night before in lynching her husband, and this meeting occurred at the burying-ground the next afternoon. The woman's husband was a well-known horse-thief, a dissolute, dangerous character, and had been warned to leave the community. He lived in a little village, and after darkness the evening before, had crept up to a window and shot a man sitting at the supper-table with his family. The murderer had harbored a grudge against his victim, had made threats, and before he could escape, was caught red-handed with the freshly fired pistol in his hand. The evidence of guilt was beyond question, and a vigilance committee didn't waste any time in hanging him to the nearest tree.

"The burying took place the next afternoon. The murdered man was a popular citizen, and the village and country turned out to pay their last respects. But when the services were over, a number of us lingered behind, as it was understood that the slayer as well as his victim would be interred in the same grounds. A second grave had been prepared, and within an hour a wagon containing a woman, three small children, and several Mexicans drove up to the rear side of the inclosure. There was no mistaking the party, the coffin was carried in to the open grave, when every one present went over to offer friendly services. But as we neared the little group the woman picked up a shovel and charged on us like a tigress. I never saw such an expression of mingled anger and anguish in a human countenance as was pictured in that woman's face. We shrank from her as if she had been a lioness, and when at last she found her tongue, every word cut like a lash. Livid with rage, the spittle frothing from her mouth, she drove us away, saying:

"'Oh, you fiends of hell, when did I ask your help? Like the curs you are, you would lick up the blood of your victim! Had you been friends to me or mine, why did you not raise your voice in protest when they were strangling the life out of the father of my children? Away, you cowardly hounds! I've hired a few Mexicans to help me, and I want none of your sympathy in this hour. Was it your hand that cut him down from the tree this morning, and if it was not, why do I need you now? Is my shame not enough in your eyes but that you must taunt me further? Do my innocent children want to look upon the faces of those who robbed them of a father? If there is a spark of manhood left in one of you, show it by leaving me alone! And you other scum, never fear but that you will clutter hell in reward for last night's work. Begone, and leave me with my dead!'"

The circus had ended. The lateness of the hour was unobserved by any one until John Levering asked me if he should bring in my horse. It lacked less than half an hour until the guards should change, and it was high time our outfit was riding for camp. The innate modesty of my wrangler, in calling attention to the time, was not forgotten, but instead of permitting him to turn servant, I asked him to help our cook look after his utensils. On my return to the wagon, Parent was trying to quiet a nervous horse so as to allow him to carry the Dutch oven returning. But as Levering was in the act of handing up the heavy oven, one of Forrest's men, hoping to make the animal buck, attempted to place a briar stem under the horse's tail. Sponsilier detected the movement in time to stop it, and turning to the culprit, said: "None of that, my bully boy. I have no objection to killing a cheap cow-hand, but these cooks have won me, hands down. If ever I run across a girl who can make as good pies as we had for supper, she can win the affections of my young and trusting heart."

CHAPTER XVII
WATER-BOUND

Our route was carrying us to the eastward of the Black Hills. The regular trail to the Yellowstone and Montana points was by the way of the Powder River, through Wyoming; but as we were only grazing across to our destination, the most direct route was adopted. The first week after leaving the Niobrara was without incident, except the meeting with a band of Indians, who were gathering and drying the wild fruit in which the country abounded. At first sighting their camp we were uneasy, holding the herd close together; but as they proved friendly, we relaxed and shared our tobacco with the men. The women were nearly all of one stature, short, heavy, and repulsive in appearance, while the men were tall, splendid specimens of the aborigines, and as uniform in a dozen respects as the cattle we were driving. Communication was impossible, except by signs, but the chief had a letter of permission from the agent at Pine Ridge, allowing himself and band a month's absence from the reservation on a berrying expedition. The bucks rode with us for hours, silently absorbed in the beeves, and towards evening turned and galloped away for their encampment.

It must have been the latter part of July when we reached the South Fork of the Big Cheyenne River. The lead was first held by one and then the other herd, but on reaching that watercourse, we all found it more formidable than we expected. The stage of water was not only swimming, but where we struck it, the river had an abrupt cut-bank on one side or the other. Sponsilier happened to be in the lead, and Forrest and myself held back to await the decision of the veteran foreman. The river ran on a northwest angle where we encountered it, and Dave followed down it some distance looking for a crossing. The herds were only three or four miles apart, and assistance could have been rendered each other, but it was hardly to be expected that an older foreman would ask either advice or help from younger ones. Hence Quince and myself were in no hurry, nor did we intrude ourselves on David the pathfinder, but sought out a crossing up the river and on our course. A convenient riffle was soon found in the river which would admit the passage of the wagons without rafting, if a cut-bank on the south side could be overcome. There was an abrupt drop of about ten feet to the water level, and I argued that a wagon-way could be easily cut in the bank and the commissaries lowered to the river's edge with a rope to the rear axle. Forrest also favored the idea, and I was authorized to cross the wagons in case a suitable ford could be found for the cattle. My aversion to manual labor was quite pronounced, yet John Q. Forrest wheedled me into accepting the task of making a wagon-road. About a mile above the riffle, a dry wash cut a gash in the bluff bank on the opposite side, which promised the necessary passageway for the herds out of the river. The slope on the south side was gradual, affording an easy inlet to the water, the only danger being on the other bank, the dry wash not being over thirty feet wide. But we both agreed that by putting the cattle in well above the passageway, even if the current was swift, an easy and successful ford would result. Forrest volunteered to cross the cattle, and together we returned to the herds for dinner.

Quince allowed me one of his men besides the cook, and detailed Clay Zilligan to assist with the wagons. We took my remuda, the spades and axes, and started for the riffle. The commissaries had orders to follow up, and Forrest rode away with a supercilious air, as if the crossing of wagons was beneath the attention of a foreman of his standing. Several hours of hard work were spent with the implements at hand in cutting the wagon-way through the bank, after which my saddle horses were driven up and down; and when it was pronounced finished, it looked more like a beaver-slide than a roadway. But a strong stake was cut and driven into the ground, and a corral-rope taken from the axle to it; without detaching the teams, the wagons were eased down the incline and crossed in safety, the water not being over three feet deep in the shallows. I was elated over the ease and success of my task, when Zilligan called attention to the fact that the first herd had not yet crossed. The chosen ford was out of sight, but had the cattle been crossing, we could have easily seen them on the mesa opposite. "Well," said

Clay, "the wagons are over, and what's more, all the mules in the three outfits couldn't bring one of them back up that cliff."

We mounted our horses, paying no attention to Zilligan's note of warning, and started up the river. But before we came in view of the ford, a great shouting reached our ears, and giving our horses the rowel, we rounded a bend, only to be confronted with the river full of cattle which had missed the passageway out on the farther side. A glance at the situation revealed a dangerous predicament, as the swift water and the contour of the river held the animals on the farther side or under the cut-bank. In numerous places there was footing on the narrow ledges to which the beeves clung like shipwrecked sailors, constantly crowding each other off into the current and being carried downstream hundreds of yards before again catching a foothold. Above and below the chosen ford, the river made a long gradual bend, the current and deepest water naturally hugged the opposite shore, and it was impossible for the cattle to turn back, though the swimming water was not over forty yards wide. As we dashed up, the outfit succeeded in cutting the train of cattle and turning them back, though fully five hundred were in the river, while not over one fifth that number had crossed in safety. Forrest was as cool as could be expected, and exercised an elegant command of profanity in issuing his orders.

"I did allow for the swiftness of the current," said he, in reply to a criticism of mine, "but those old beeves just drifted downstream like a lot of big tubs. The horses swam it easy, and the first hundred cattle struck the mouth of the wash square in the eye, but after that they misunderstood it for a bath instead of a ford. Oh, well, it's live and learn, die and forget it. But since you're so d — — strong on the sabe, suppose you suggest a way of getting those beeves out of the river."

It was impossible to bring them back, and the only alternative was attempted. About three quarters of a mile down the river the cut-bank shifted to the south side. If the cattle could swim that distance there was an easy landing below. The beeves belonged to Forrest's herd, and I declined the proffered leadership, but plans were outlined and we started the work of rescue. Only a few men were left to look after the main herds, the remainder of us swimming the river on our horses. One man was detailed to drive the contingent which had safely forded, down to the point where the bluff bank shifted and the incline commenced on the north shore. The cattle were clinging, in small bunches, under the cut-bank like swallows to a roof for fully a quarter-mile below the mouth of the dry wash. Divesting ourselves of all clothing, a squad of six of us, by way of experiment, dropped over the bank and pushed into the river about twenty of the lowest cattle. On catching the full force of the current, which ran like a mill-race, we swept downstream at a rapid pace, sometimes clinging to a beef's tail, but generally swimming between the cattle and the bluff. The force of the stream drove them against the bank repeatedly, but we dashed water in their eyes and pushed them off again and again, and finally landed every steer.

The Big Cheyenne was a mountain stream, having numerous tributaries heading in the Black Hills. The water was none too warm, and when we came out the air chilled us; but we scaled the bluff and raced back after more cattle. Forrest was in the river on our return, but I ordered his wrangler to drive all the horses under saddle down to the landing, in order that the men could have mounts for returning. This expedited matters, and the work progressed more rapidly. Four separate squads were drifting the cattle, but in the third contingent we cut off too many beeves and came near drowning two fine ones. The animals in question were large and strong, but had stood for nearly an hour on a slippery ledge, frequently being crowded into the water, and were on the verge of collapse from nervous exhaustion. They were trembling like leaves when we pushed them off. Runt Pickett was detailed to look especially after those two, and the little rascal nursed and toyed and played with them like a circus rider. They struggled constantly for the inshore, but Runt rode their rumps alternately, the displacement lifting their heads out of the water to good advantage. When we finally landed, the two big fellows staggered out of the river and dropped down through sheer weakness, a thing which I had never seen before except in wild horses.

A number of the boys were attacked by chills, and towards evening had to be excused for fear of cramps. By six o'clock we were reduced to two squads, with about fifty cattle still remaining in the river. Forrest and I had quit the water after the fourth trip; but Quince had a man named De Manse, a Frenchman, who swam like a wharf-rat and who stayed to the finish, while I turned my crew over to Runt Pickett. The latter was raised on the coast of Texas, and when a mere boy could swim all day, with or without occasion. Dividing the remaining beeves as near equally as possible, Runt's squad pushed off slightly in advance of De Manse, the remainder of us riding along the bank with the horses and clothing, and cheering our respective crews. The Frenchman was but a moment later in taking the water, and as pretty and thrilling a race as I ever witnessed was in progress. The latter practiced a trick, when catching a favorable current, of dipping the rump of a steer, thus lifting his fore parts and rocking him forward like a porpoise. When a beef dropped to the rear, this process was resorted to, and De Manse promised to overtake Pickett. From our position on the bank, we shouted to Runt to dip his drag cattle in swift water; but amid the din and splash of the struggling swimmers our messages failed to reach his ears. De Manse was gaining slowly, when Pickett's bunch were driven inshore, a number of them catching a footing, and before they could be again pushed off, the Frenchman's cattle were at their heels. A number of De Manse's men were swimming shoreward of their charges, and succeeded in holding their beeves off the ledge, which was the last one before the landing. The remaining hundred yards was eddy water; and though Pickett fought hard, swimming among the Frenchman's lead cattle, to hold the two bunches separate, they mixed in the river. As an evidence of victory, however, when the cattle struck a foothold, Runt and each of his men mounted a beef and rode out of the water some distance. As the steers recovered and attempted to dislodge their riders, they nimbly sprang from their backs and hustled themselves into their ragged clothing.

I breathed easier after the last cattle landed, though Forrest contended there was never any danger. At least a serious predicament had been blundered into and handled, as was shown by subsequent events. At noon that day, rumblings of thunder were heard in the Black Hills country to the west, a warning to get across the river as soon as possible. So the situation at the close of the day was not a very encouraging one to either Forrest or myself. The former had his cattle split in two bunches, while I had my wagon and remuda on the other side of the river from my herd. But the emergency must be met. I sent a messenger after our wagon, it was brought back near the river, and a hasty supper was ordered. Two of my boys were sent up to the dry wash to recross the river and drift our cattle down somewhere near the wagon-crossing, thus separating the herds for the night. I have never made claim to being overbright, but that evening I did have sense or intuition enough to take our saddle horses back across the river. My few years of trail life had taught me the importance of keeping in close touch with our base of subsistence, while the cattle and the saddle stock for handling them should under no circumstances ever be separated. Yet under existing conditions it was impossible to recross our commissary, and darkness fell upon us encamped on the south side of the Big Cheyenne.

The night passed with almost constant thunder and lightning in the west. At daybreak heavy dark clouds hung low in a semicircle all around the northwest, threatening falling weather, and hasty preparations were made to move down the stream in search of a crossing. In fording the river to breakfast, my outfit agreed that there had been no perceptible change in the stage of water overnight, which quickened our desire to move at once. The two wagons were camped close together, and as usual Forrest was indifferent and unconcerned over the threatening weather; he had left his remuda all night on the north side of the river, and had actually turned loose the rescued contingent of cattle. I did not mince my words in giving Mr. Forrest my programme, when he turned on me, saying: "Quirk, you have more trouble than a married woman. What do I care if it is raining in London or the Black Hills either? Let her rain; our sugar and salt are both covered, and we can lend you some if yours gets wet. But you go right ahead and follow up Sponsilier; he may not find a crossing this side of the Belle Fourche. I can take spades and axes, and in two hours' time cut down and widen that wagon-way until the herds can cross. I wouldn't be as fidgety as you are for a large farm. You ought to take something for your nerves."

I had a mental picture of John Quincy Forrest doing any manual labor with an axe or spade. During our short acquaintance that had been put to the test too often to admit of question; but I encouraged him to fly right at the bank, assuring him that in case his tools became heated, there was always water at hand to cool them. The wrangler had rustled in the wagon-mules for our cook, and Forrest was still ridiculing my anxiety to move, when a fusillade of shots was heard across and up the river. Every man at both wagons was on his feet in an instant, not one of us even dreaming that the firing of the boys on herd was a warning, when Quince's horsewrangler galloped up and announced a flood-wave coming down the river. A rush was made for our horses, and we struck for the ford, dashing through the shallows and up the farther bank without drawing rein. With a steady rush, a body of water, less than a mile distant, greeted our vision, looking like the falls of some river, rolling forward like an immense cylinder. We sat our horses in bewilderment of the scene, though I had often heard Jim Flood describe the sudden rise of streams which had mountain tributaries. Forrest and his men crossed behind us, leaving but the cooks and a horse-wrangler on the farther side. It was easily to be seen that all the lowlands along the river would be inundated, so I sent Levering back with orders to hook up the team and strike for tall timber. Following suit, Forrest sent two men to rout the contingent of cattle out of a bend which was nearly a mile below the wagons. The wave, apparently ten to twelve feet high, moved forward slowly, great walls lopping off on the side and flooding out over the bottoms, while on the farther shore every cranny and arroyo claimed its fill from the avalanche of water. The cattle on the south side were safe, grazing well back on the uplands, so we gave the oncoming flood our undivided attention. It was traveling at the rate of eight to ten miles an hour, not at a steady pace, but sometimes almost halting when the bottoms absorbed its volume, only to catch its breath and forge ahead again in angry impetuosity. As the water passed us on the bluff bank, several waves broke over and washed around our horses' feet, filling the wagon-way, but the main volume rolled across the narrow valley on the opposite side. The wagons had pulled out to higher ground, and while every eye was strained, watching for the rescued beeves to come out of the bend below, Vick Wolf, who happened to look upstream, uttered a single shout of warning and dashed away. Turning in our saddles, we saw within five hundred feet of us a second wave about half the height of the first one. Rowels and quirts were plied with energy and will, as we tore down the river-bank, making a gradual circle until the second bottoms were reached, outriding the flood by a close margin.

The situation was anything but encouraging, as days might elapse before the water would fall. But our hopes revived as we saw the contingent of about six hundred beeves stampede out of a bend below and across the river, followed by two men who were energetically burning powder and flaunting slickers in their rear. Within a quarter of an hour, a halfmile of roaring, raging torrent, filled with floating driftwood, separated us from the wagons which contained the staples of life. But in the midst of the travail of mountain and plain, the dry humor of the men was irrepressible, one of Forrest's own boys asking him if he felt any uneasiness now about his salt and sugar.

"Oh, this is nothing," replied Quince, with a contemptuous wave of his hand. "These freshets are liable to happen at any time; rise in an hour and fall in half a day. Look there how it is clearing off in the west; the river will be fordable this evening or in the morning at the furthest. As long as everything is safe, what do we care? If it comes to a pinch, we have plenty of stray beef; berries are ripe, and I reckon if we cast around we might find some wild onions. I have lived a whole month at a time on nothing but land-terrapin; they make larruping fine eating when you are cut off from camp this way. Blankets? Never use them; sleep on your belly and cover with your back, and get up with the birds in the morning. These Lovell outfits are getting so tony that by another year or two they'll insist on bathtubs, Florida water, and towels with every wagon. I like to get down to straight beans for a few days every once in a while; it has a tendency to cure a man with a whining disposition. The only thing that's worrying me, if we get cut off, is the laugh that Sponsilier will have on us."

We all knew Forrest was bluffing. The fact that we were water-bound was too apparent to admit of question, and since the elements were beyond our control, there was no telling when relief would come. Until the weather moderated in the hills to the west, there was no hope of crossing the river; but men grew hungry and nights were chilly, and bluster and bravado brought neither food nor warmth. A third wave was noticed within an hour, raising the water-gauge over a foot. The South Fork of the Big Cheyenne almost encircled the entire Black Hills country, and with a hundred mountain affluents emptying in their tribute, the waters commanded and we obeyed. Ordering my men to kill a beef, I rode down the river in the hope of finding Sponsilier on our side, and about noon sighted his camp and cattle on the opposite bank. A group of men were dallying along the shore, but being out of hearing, I turned back without exposing myself.

On my return a general camp had been established at the nearest wood, and a stray killed. Stakes were driven to mark the rise or fall of the water, and we settled down like prisoners, waiting for an expected reprieve. Towards evening a fire was built up and the two sides of ribs were spitted over it, our only chance for supper. Night fell with no perceptible change in the situation, the weather remaining dry and clear. Forrest's outfit had been furnished horses from my remuda for guard duty, and about midnight, wrapping ourselves in slickers, we lay down in a circle with our feet to the fire like cave-dwellers. The camp-fire was kept up all night by the returning guards, even until the morning hours, when we woke up shivering at dawn and hurried away to note the stage of the water. A four-foot fall had taken place during the night, another foot was added within an hour after sun-up, brightening our hopes, when a tidal wave swept down the valley, easily establishing a new high-water mark. Then we breakfasted on broiled beefsteak, and fell back into the hills in search of the huckleberry, which abounded in that vicinity.

A second day and night passed, with the water gradually falling. The third morning a few of the best swimmers, tiring of the diet of beef and berries, took advantage of the current and swam to the other shore. On returning several hours later, they brought back word that Sponsilier had been up to the wagons the afternoon before and reported an easy crossing about five miles below. By noon the channel had narrowed to one hundred yards of swimming water, and plunging into it on our horses, we dined at the wagons and did justice to the spread. Both outfits were anxious to move, and once dinner was over, the commissaries were started down the river, while we turned up it, looking for a chance to swim back to the cattle. Forrest had secured a fresh mount of horses, and some distance above the dry wash we again took to the water, landing on the opposite side between a quarter and half mile below. Little time was lost in starting the herds, mine in the lead, while the wagons got away well in advance, accompanied by Forrest's remuda and the isolated contingent of cattle.

Sponsilier was expecting us, and on the appearance of our wagons, moved out to a new camp and gave us a clear crossing. A number of the boys came down to the river with him, and several of them swam it, meeting the cattle a mile above and piloting us into the ford. They had assured me that there might be seventy-five yards of swimming water, with a gradual entrance to the channel and a half-mile of solid footing at the outcome. The description of the crossing suited me, and putting our remuda in the lead, we struck the muddy torrent and crossed it without a halt, the chain of swimming cattle never breaking for a single moment. Forrest followed in our wake, the one herd piloting the other, and within an hour after our arrival at the lower ford, the drag-end of the "Drooping T" herd kicked up their heels on the north bank of the Big Cheyenne. Meanwhile Sponsilier had been quietly sitting his horse below the main landing, his hat pulled down over his eye, nursing the humor of the situation. As Forrest came up out of the water with the rear guard of his cattle, the opportunity was too good to be overlooked.

"Hello, Quince," said Dave; "how goes it, old sport? Do you keep stout? I was up at your wagon yesterday to ask you all down to supper. Yes, we had huckleberry pie and venison galore, but your men told me that you had quit eating with the wagon. I was pained to hear that you and Tom have both gone plum hog-wild, drinking out of cowtracks and living on wild garlic and land-terrapin, just like Injuns. Honest, boys, I hate to see good men go wrong that way."

CHAPTER XVIII
THE LITTLE MISSOURI

A week later we crossed the Belle Fourche, sometimes called the North Fork of the Big Cheyenne. Like its twin sister on the south, it was a mountain river, having numerous affluents putting in from the Black Hills, which it encircled on the north and west. Between these two branches of the mother stream were numerous tributaries, establishing it as the best watered country encountered in our long overland cruise. Besides the splendid watercourses which marked that section, numerous wagontrails, leading into the hills, were peopled with freighters. Long ox trains, moving at a snail's pace, crept over hill and plain, the common carrier between the mines and the outside world. The fascination of the primal land was there; the buttes stood like sentinels, guarding a king's domain, while the palisaded cliffs frowned down, as if erected by the hand Omnipotent to mark the boundary of nations.

Our route, after skirting the Black Hills, followed up the Belle Fourche a few days, and early in August we crossed over to the Little Missouri River. The divide between the Belle Fourche and the latter stream was a narrow one, requiring little time to graze across it, and intercepting the Little Missouri somewhere in Montana. The course of that river was almost due north, and crossing and recrossing it frequently, we kept constantly in touch with it on our last northward tack. The river led through sections of country now known as the Bad Lands, but we found an abundance of grass and an easy passage. Sponsilier held the lead all the way down the river, though I did most of the advance scouting, sometimes being as much as fifty miles in front of the herds. Near the last of the month we sighted Sentinel Butte and the smoke of railroad trains, and a few days later all three of us foremen rode into Little Missouri Station of the Northern Pacific Railway. Our arrival was expected by one man at least; for as we approached the straggling village, our employer was recognized at a distance, waving his hat, and a minute later all three of us were shaking hands with Don Lovell. Mutual inquiries followed, and when we reported the cattle fine as silk, having never known a hungry or thirsty hour after leaving the North Platte, the old man brightened and led the way to a well-known saloon.

"How did I fare at Omaha?" said old man Don, repeating Forrest's query. "Well, at first it was a question if I would be hung or shot, but we came out with colors flying. The United States marshal who attempted to take possession of the cattle on the North Platte went back on the same train with us. He was feeling sore over his defeat, but Sutton cultivated his acquaintance, and in mollifying that official, showed him how easily failure could be palmed off as a victory. In fact, I think Mike overcolored the story at my expense. He and the marshal gave it to the papers, and the next morning it appeared in the form of a sensational article. According to the report, a certain popular federal officer had gone out to Ogalalla to take possession of two herds of cattle intended for government purposes; he had met with resistance by a lot of Texas roughs, who fatally shot one of his deputies, wounding several others, and killing a number of horses during the assault; but the intrepid officer had added to his laurels by arresting the owner of the cattle and leader of the resisting mob, and had brought him back to face the charge of contempt in resisting service. The papers freely predicted that I would get the maximum fine, and one even went so far as to suggest that imprisonment might teach certain arrogant cattle kings a salutary lesson. But when the hearing came up, Sutton placed Jim Reed and me in the witness-box, taking the stand later himself, and we showed that federal court that it had been buncoed out of an order of injunctive relief, in favor of the biggest set of ringsters that ever missed stretching hemp. The result was, I walked out of that federal court scot free. And Judge Dundy, when he realized the injustice that he had inflicted, made all three of us take dinner with him, fully explaining the pressure which had been brought to bear at the time the order of relief was issued. Oh, that old judge was all right. I only hope we'll have as square a man as Judge Dundy at the final hearing at Fort Buford. Do you see that sign over there, where it says Barley Water and Bad Cigars? Well, put your horses in some corral and meet me there."

There was a great deal of news to review. Lovell had returned to Ogalalla; the body of Tolleston had been recovered and given decent burial; delivery day of the three Indian herds was at hand, bringing that branch of the season's drive to a close. But the main thing which absorbed our employer was the quarantine that the upper Yellowstone country proposed enforcing against through Texas cattle. He assured us that had we gone by way of Wyoming and down the Powder River, the chances were that the local authorities would have placed us under quarantine until after the first frost. He assured us that the year before, Texas fever had played sad havoc among the native and wintered Southern cattle, and that Miles City and Glendive, live-stock centres on the Yellowstone, were up in arms in favor of a rigid quarantine against all through cattle. If this proved true, it was certainly an ill wind to drovers on the Powder River route; yet I failed to see where we were benefited until my employer got down to details.

"That's so," said he; "I forgot to tell you boys that when Reed and I went back to Ogalalla, we found Field, Radcliff & Co. buying beeves. Yes, they had bought a remuda of horses, rigged up two wagons, and hired men to take possession of our 'Open A' and 'Drooping T' herds. But meeting with disappointment and having the outfit on their hands, they concluded to buy cattle and go ahead and make the delivery at Buford. They simply had to do it or admit that I had called their hands. But Reed and I raised such a howl around that town that we posted every man with beeves for sale until the buyers had to pony up the cash for every hoof they bought. We even hunted up young Murnane, the seller of the herd that Jim Reed ran the attachment on; and before old Jim and I got through with him, we had his promise not to move out of Keith County until the last dollar was in hand. The buyers seemed to command all kinds of money, but where they expect to make anything, even if they do deliver, beats me, as Reed and I have got a good wad of their money. Since leaving there, I have had word that they settled with Murnane, putting a new outfit with the cattle, and that they have ten thousand beef steers on the way to Fort Buford this very minute. They are coming through on the North Platte and Powder River route, and if quarantine can be enforced against them until frost falls, it will give us a clear field at Buford on the day of delivery. Now it stands us in hand to see that those herds are isolated until after the 15th day of September."

The atmosphere cleared instantly. I was well aware of the ravages of splenic fever; but two decades ago every drover from Texas denied the possibility of a through animal in perfect health giving a disease to wintered Southerners or domestic cattle, also robust and healthy. Time has demonstrated the truth, yet the manner in which the germ is transmitted between healthy animals remains a mystery to this day, although there has been no lack of theories advanced. Even the theorists differed as to the manner of germ transmission, the sporule, tick, and ship fever being the leading theories, and each having its advocates. The latter was entitled to some consideration, for if bad usage and the lack of necessary rest, food, and water will produce fever aboard emigrant steamships, the same privations might do it among animals. The overdriving of trail cattle was frequently unavoidable, dry drives and the lack of grass on arid wastes being of common occurrence. However, the presence of fever among through cattle was never noticeable to the practical man, and if it existed, it must have been very mild in form compared to its virulent nature among natives. Time has demonstrated that it is necessary for the domestic animals to walk over and occupy the same ground to contract the disease, though they may drink from the same trough or stream of water, or inhale each other's breath in play across a wire fence, without fear of contagion. A peculiar feature of Texas fever was that the very cattle which would impart it on their arrival, after wintering in the North would contract it and die the same as natives. The isolation of herds on a good range for a period of sixty days, or the falling of frost, was recognized as the only preventive against transmitting the germ. Government rewards and experiments have never demonstrated a theory that practical experience does not dispute.

The only time on this drive that our attention had been called to the fever alarm was on crossing the wagon trail running from Pierre on the Missouri River to the Black Hills. I was in the lead when a large bull train was sighted in our front, and shortly afterward the wagon-boss met me and earnestly begged that I allow his outfit to pass before we crossed the wagon-road.

I knew the usual form of ridicule of a herd foreman, but the boss bull-whacker must have anticipated my reply, for he informed me that the summer before he had lost ninety head out of two hundred yoke of oxen. The wagon-master's appeal was fortified by a sincerity which won his request, and I held up my cattle and allowed his train to pass in advance. Sponsilier's herd was out of sight in my rear, while Forrest was several miles to my left, and slightly behind me. The wagon-boss rode across and made a similar request of Forrest, but that worthy refused to recognize the right of way to a bull train at the expense of a trail herd of government beeves. Ungentlemanly remarks are said to have passed between them, when the boss bull-whacker threw down the gauntlet and galloped back to his train. Forrest pushed on, with ample time to have occupied the road in crossing, thus holding up the wagon train. My herd fell to grazing, and Sponsilier rode up to inquire the cause of my halting. I explained the request of the wagon-master, his loss the year before and present fear of fever, and called attention to the clash which was imminent between the long freight outfit in our front and Forrest's herd to the left, both anxious for the right of way. A number of us rode forward in clear view of the impending meeting. It was evident that Forrest would be the first to reach the freight road, and would naturally hold it while his cattle were crossing it. But when this also became apparent to the bull train, the lead teams drove out of the road and halted, the rear wagons passing on ahead, the two outfits being fully a mile apart. There were about twenty teams of ten yoke each, and when the first five or six halted, they unearthed old needle rifles and opened fire across Forrest's front. Once the range was found, those long-range buffalo guns threw up the dust in handfuls in the lead of the herd, and Forrest turned his cattle back, while the bull train held its way, undisputed. It was immaterial to Forrest who occupied the road first, and with the jeers of the freighters mingled the laughter of Sponsilier and my outfit, as John Quincy Forrest reluctantly turned back.

This incident served as a safety-valve, and whenever Forrest forged to the lead in coming down the Little Missouri, all that was necessary to check him was to inquire casually which held the right of way, a trail herd or a bull train.

Throughout the North, Texas fever was generally accepted as a fact, and any one who had ever come in contact with it once, dreaded it ever afterward. So when the devil was sick the devil a monk would be; and if there was any advantage in taking the contrary view to the one entertained by all drovers, so long as our herds were free, we were not like men who could not experience a change of opinion, if in doing so the wind was tempered to us. Also in this instance we were fighting an avowed enemy, and all is fair in love and war. And amid the fumes of bad cigars, Sponsilier drew out the plan of campaign.

"Now, let's see," said old man Don, "tomorrow will be the 25th day of August. I've got to be at the Crow Agency a few days before the 10th of next month, as you know we have a delivery there on that date. Flood will have to attend to matters at Rosebud on the 1st, and then hurry on west and be present at Paul's delivery at Fort Washakie. So you see I'll have to depend on two of you boys going up to Glendive and Miles and seeing that those cow-towns take the proper view of this quarantine matter. After dinner you'll fall back and bring up your herds, and after crossing the railroad here, the outfits will graze over to Buford. We'll leave four of our best saddle horses here in a pasture, so as to be independent on our return. Since things have changed so, the chances are that I'll bring Bob Quirk back with me, as I've written Flood to help The Rebel sell his remuda and take the outfit and go home. Now you boys decide among yourselves which two of you will go up the Yellowstone and promote the enforcement of the quarantine laws. Don't get the impression that you can't do this, because an all-round cowman can do anything where his interests are at stake. I'll think the programme out a little more clearly by the time you bring up the cattle."

The herds were not over fifteen miles back up the river when we left them in the morning. After honoring the village of Little Missouri with our presence for several hours, we saddled up and started to meet the cattle. There was no doubt in my mind but that Sponsilier would be one of the two to go on the proposed errand of diplomacy, as his years, experience, and good solid sense entitled him to outrank either Forrest or myself. I knew that Quince would want to go, if for no other reason than to get out of working the few days that yet remained of the drive. All three of us talked the matter of quarantine freely as we rode along, yet no one ventured any proposition looking to an agreement as to who should go on the diplomatic mission. I was the youngest and naturally took refuge behind my years, yet perfectly conscious that, in spite of the indifferent and nonchalant attitude assumed, all three of us foremen were equally anxious for the chance. Matters remained undecided; but the next day at dinner, Lovell having met us before reaching the railroad, the question arose who should go up to Miles City. Dave and Quince were also eating at my wagon, and when our employer forced an answer, Sponsilier innocently replied that he supposed that we were all willing to leave it to him. Forrest immediately approved of Dave's suggestion. I gave my assent, and old man Don didn't qualify, hedge, or mince his words in appointing the committees to represent the firm of Lovell.

"Jealous of each other, ain't you? Very well; I want these herds grazed across to Buford at the rate of four miles a day. Nothing but a Mexican pastor, or a white man as lazy as Quince Forrest can fill the bill. You're listening, are you, Quince? Well, after the sun sets to-night, you're in charge of ten thousand beeves from here to the mouth of the Yellowstone. I want to put every ounce possible on those steers for the next twenty days. We may have to make a comparison of cattle, and if we should, I want ours to lay over the opposition like a double eagle does over a lead dime. We may run up against a lot of red tape at Fort Buford, but if there is a lick of cow-sense among the government representatives, we want our beeves to speak for themselves. Fat animals do their own talking. You remember when every one was admiring the fine horse, the blind man said, 'Isn't he fat?' Now, Dave, you and Tom appoint your segundos, and we'll all catch the 10:20 train west to-night."

I dared to risk one eye on Forrest. Inwardly I was chuckling, but Quince was mincing along with his dinner, showing that languid indifference which is inborn to the Texan. Lovell continued to monopolize the conversation, blowing on the cattle and ribbing up Forrest to see that the beeves thenceforth should never know tire, hunger, or thirst. The commissaries had run low; Sponsilier's cook had been borrowing beans from us for a week past, while Parent point-blank refused to share any more of our bacon. The latter was recognized as a staple in trail-work, and it mattered not how inviting the beef or venison might be, we always fell back to bacon with avidity. When it came time to move out on the evening lap, Forrest's herd took the lead, the other two falling in behind, the wagons pulling out for town in advance of everything. Jack Splann had always acted as segundo in my absence, and as he had overheard Lovell's orders to Forrest, there was nothing further for me to add, and Splann took charge of my "Open A's."

When changing mounts at noon, I caught out two of my best saddlers and tied one behind the chuckwagon, to be left with a liveryman in town. Leaving old man Don with the cattle, all three of us foremen went into the village in order to secure a few staple supplies with which to complete the journey.

It can be taken for granted that Sponsilier and myself were feeling quite gala. The former took occasion, as we rode along, to throw several bouquets at Forrest over his preferment, when the latter turned on us, saying: "You fellows think you're d — d smart, now, don't you? You're both purty good talkers, but neither one of you can show me where the rainbow comes in in rotting along with these measly cattle. It's enough to make a man kick his own dog. But I can see where the old man was perfectly right in sending you two up to Miles City. When you fellows work your rabbit's foot, it will be Katy with those Washington City schemers — more than likely they'll not draw cards when they see that you are in the game — When it comes to the real sabe, you fellows shine like a tree full of owls. Honest, it has always been a wonder to me that Grant didn't send for both of you when he was making up his cabinet."

The herds crossed the railroad about a mile west of Little Missouri Station. The wagons secured the needed supplies, and pulled out down the river, leaving Sponsilier and myself foot-loose and free.

Lovell was riding a livery horse, and as neither of us expected him to return until it was too dark to see the cattle, we amused ourselves by looking over the town. There seemed to be a great deal of freighting to outlying points, numerous ox and mule trains coming in and also leaving for their destinations. Our employer came in about dusk, and at once went to the depot, as he was expecting a message. One had arrived during his absence, and after reading it, he came over to Dave and me, saying:

"It's from Mike Sutton. I authorized him to secure the services of the best lawyer in the West, and he has just wired me that he has retained Senator Aspgrain of Sioux City, Iowa. They will report at Fort Buford on September the 5th and will take care of any legal complications which may arise. I don't know who this senator is, but Mike has orders not to spare any expense as long as we have the other fellow's money to fight with. Well, if the Iowa lawyers are as good stuff as the Iowa troops were down in Dixie, that's all I ask. Now, we'll get our suppers and then sack our saddles — why, sure, you'll need them; every good cowman takes his saddle wherever he goes, though he may not have clothes enough with him to dust a fiddle."

CHAPTER XIX
IN QUARANTINE

We reached Miles City shortly after midnight. It was the recognized cattle centre of Montana at that time, but devoid of the high-lights which were a feature of the trail towns. The village boasted the usual number of saloons and dance-houses, and likewise an ordinance compelling such resorts to close on the stroke of twelve. Lovell had been there before, and led the way to a well-known hostelry. The house was crowded, and the best the night clerk could do was to give us a room with two beds. This was perfectly satisfactory, as it was a large apartment and fronted out on an open gallery. Old man Don suggested we take the mattresses outside, but as this was my first chance to sleep in a bed since leaving the ranch in March, I wanted all the comforts that were due me. Sponsilier likewise favored the idea of sleeping inside, and our employer yielded, taking the single bed on retiring. The night was warm, and after thrashing around for nearly an hour, supposing that Dave and I were asleep, old man Don arose and quietly dragged his mattress outside. Our bed was soft and downy, but in spite of the lateness of the hour and having been in our saddles at dawn, we tossed about, unable to sleep. After agreeing that it was the mattress, we took the covering and pillows and lay down on the floor, falling into a deep slumber almost instantly. "Well, wouldn't that jar your eccentric," said Dave to me the next morning, speaking of our inability to sleep in a bed. "I slept in one in Ogalalla, and I wasn't over-full either."

Lovell remained with us all the next day. He was well known in Miles City, having in other years sold cattle to resident cowmen. The day was spent in hunting up former acquaintances, getting the lay of the land, and feeling the public pulse on the matter of quarantine on Southern cattle. The outlook was to our liking, as heavy losses had been sustained from fever the year before, and steps had already been taken to isolate all through animals until frost fell. Report was abroad that there were already within the jurisdiction of Montana over one hundred and fifty thousand through Texas cattle, with a possibility of one third that number more being added before the close of the season. That territory had established a quarantine camp on the Wyoming line, forcing all Texas stock to follow down the eastern side of the Powder River. Fully one hundred miles on the north, a dead-line was drawn from Powderville on that watercourse eastward to a spur of the Powder River Mountains, thus setting aside a quarantine ground ample to accommodate half a million cattle. Local range-riders kept all the native and wintered Texas cattle to the westward of the river and away from the through ones, which was easily done by riding lines, the Southern herds being held under constant control and hence never straying. The first Texas herds to arrive naturally traveled north to the dead-line, and, choosing a range, went into camp until frost relieved them. It was an unwritten law that a herd was entitled to as much grazing land as it needed, and there was a report about Miles City that the quarantine ground was congested with cattle halfway from Powderville to the Wyoming line.

The outlook was encouraging. Quarantine was working a hardship to herds along the old Powder River route, yet their enforced isolation was like a tempered wind to our cause and cattle, the latter then leisurely grazing across Dakota from the Little Missouri to the mouth of the Yellowstone. Fortune favored us in many respects. About Miles City there was no concealment of our mission, resulting in an old acquaintance of Lovell's loaning us horses, while old man Don had no trouble in getting drafts cashed to the amount of two thousand dollars. What he expected to do with this amount of money was a mystery to Dave and myself, a mystery which instantly cleared when we were in the privacy of our room at the hotel.

"Here, boys," said old man Don, throwing the roll of money on the bed, "divide this wad between you. There might be such a thing as using a little here and there to sweeten matters up, and making yourselves rattling good fellows wherever you go. Now in the first place, I want you both to understand that this money is clear velvet, and don't hesitate to spend it freely. Eat and drink all you can, and gamble a little of it if that is necessary. You two will saddle up in the morning and ride to Powderville, while I will lie around here a few days and try the market for cattle next year, and then go on to Big Horn on my way to the Crow Agency. Feel your way carefully; locate the herds of Field, Radcliff & Co., and throw everything in their way to retard progress. It is impossible to foretell what may happen, and for that reason only general orders can be given. And remember, I don't want to see that money again if there is any chance to use it."

Powderville was a long day's ride from Miles City. By making an early start and resting a few hours at noon, we reached that straggling outpost shortly after nightfall. There was a road-house for the wayfaring man and a corral for his beast, a general store, opposition saloons, and the regulation blacksmith shop, constituting the business interests of Powderville. As arriving guests, a rough but cordial welcome was extended us by the keeper of the hostelry, and we mingled with the other travelers, but never once mentioning our business. I was uneasy over the money in our possession; not that I feared robbery, but my mind constantly reverted to it, and it was with difficulty that I refrained from continually feeling to see that it was safe. Sponsilier had concealed his in his boot, and as we rode along, contended that he could feel the roll chafing his ankle. I had tied two handkerchiefs together, and rolling my share in one of them, belted the amount between my overshirt and undershirt. The belt was not noticeable, but in making the ride that day, my hand involuntarily went to my side where the money lay, the action never escaping the notice of Sponsilier, who constantly twitted me over my nervousness. And although we were tired as dogs after our long ride, I awoke many times that night and felt to see if my money was safe; my partner slept like a log.

Several cowmen, ranching on the lower Powder River, had headquarters at this outpost. The next morning Sponsilier and I made their acquaintance, and during the course of the day got a clear outline of the situation. On the west the river was the recognized dead-line to the Wyoming boundary, while two camps of five men each patroled the dividing line on the north, drifting back the native stock and holding the through herds in quarantine. The nearest camp was some distance east of Powderville, and saddling up towards evening we rode out and spent the night at the first quarantine station. A wagon and two tents, a relay of saddle horses, and an arsenal of long-range firearms composed the outfit. Three of the five men on duty were Texans. Making ourselves perfectly at home, we had no trouble in locating the herds in question, they having already sounded the tocsin to clear the way, claiming government beef recognized no local quarantine. The herds were not over thirty miles to the south, and expectation ran high as to results when an attempt should be made to cross the deadline. Trouble had already occurred, where outfits respecting the quarantine were trespassed upon by three herds, making claim of being under government protection and entitled to the rights of eminent domain. Fortunately several of the herds on the immediate line had been bought at Ogalalla and were in possession of ranch outfits who owned ranges farther north, and were anxious to see quarantine enforced. These local cowmen would support the established authority, and trouble was expected. Sponsilier and I widened the breach by denouncing these intruders as the hirelings of a set of ringsters, who had no regard for the rights of any one, and volunteered our services in enforcing quarantine against them the same as others.

Our services were gratefully accepted. The next morning we were furnished fresh horses, and one of us was requested, as we were strangers, to ride down the country and reconnoitre the advance of the defiant drovers. As I was fearful that Field or Radcliff might be accompanying the herds, and recognize me, Sponsilier went instead, returning late that evening.

"Well, fellows," said Dave, as he dismounted at the quarantine camp, "I've seen the herds, and they propose to cross this dead-line of yours as easily as water goes through a gourd funnel. They'll be here by noon to-morrow, and they've got the big conversation right on tap to show that the government couldn't feed its army if it wasn't for a few big cowmen like them. There's a strange corporal over the three herds and they're working on five horses to the man. But the major-domo's the whole works; he's a windy cuss, and intimates that he has a card or two up his sleeve that will put these quarantine guards to sleep when he springs them. He's a new man to me; at least he wasn't with the gang at Ogalalla."

During the absence of my partner, I had ridden the dead-line on the north. A strip of country five miles wide was clear of cattle above the boundary, while below were massed four herds, claiming the range from the mountains to the Powder River. The leader of the quarantine guards, Fred Ullmer, had accompanied me on the ride, and on our return we visited three of the outfits, urging them to hold all their reserve forces subject to call, in case an attempt was made to force the dead-line. At each camp I took every possible chance to sow the seeds of dissension and hatred against the high-handed methods of The Western Supply Company. Defining our situation clearly, I asked each foreman, in case these herds defied local authority, who would indemnify the owners for the loss among native cattle by fever between Powderville and the mouth of the Yellowstone. Would the drovers? Would the government? Leaving these and similar thoughts for their consideration, Ullmer and I had arrived at the first quarantine station shortly before the return of my partner.

Upon the report of Sponsilier, Ullmer was appointed captain, and lost no time in taking action. After dark, a scout was sent to Camp No. 2, a meeting-place was appointed on Wolf Creek below, and orders were given to bring along every possible man from the local outfits and to meet at the rendezvous within an hour after sun-up the next morning. Ullmer changed horses and left for Powderville, assuring us that he would rally every man interested in quarantine, and have his posse below, on the creek by sunrise. The remainder of us at headquarters were under orders to bring all the arms and ammunition, and join the quarantine forces at the meeting-place some five miles from our camp. We were also to touch at and command the presence of one of the four outfits while en route. I liked the determined action of Captain Ullmer, who I learned had emigrated with his parents to Montana when a boy, and had grown into manhood on the frontier. Sponsilier was likewise pleased with the quarantine leader, and we lay awake far into the night, reviewing the situation and trying to anticipate any possible contingency that might thwart our plans. But to our best reasoning the horizon was clear, and if Field, Radcliff & Co.'s cattle reached Fort Buford on the day of delivery, well, it would be a miracle.

Fresh horses were secured at dawn, and breakfast would be secured en route with the cow outfit. There were a dozen large-calibre rifles in scabbards, and burdening ourselves with two heavy guns to the man and an abundance of ammunition, we abandoned Quarantine Station No. 1 for the time being. The camp which we were to touch at was the one nearest the river and north of Wolf Creek, and we galloped up to it before the sun had even risen. Since everything was coming our way, Sponsilier and I observed a strict neutrality, but a tow-headed Texan rallied the outfit, saying:

"Make haste, fellows, and saddle up your horses. Those three herds which raised such a rumpus up on Little Powder have sent down word that they're going to cross our dead-line to-day if they have to prize up hell and put a chunk under it. We have decided to call their bluff before they even reach the line, and make them show their hand for all this big talk. Here's half a dozen guns and cartridges galore, but hustle yourselves. Fred went into Powderville last night and will meet us above at the twin buttes this morning with every cowman in town. All the other outfits have been sent for, and we'll have enough men to make our bluff stand up, never fear. From what I learn, these herds belong to a lot of Yankee speculators, and they don't give a tinker's dam if all the cattle in Montana die from fever. They're no better than anybody else, and if we allow them to go through, they'll leave a trail of dead natives that will stink us out of this valley. Make haste, everybody."

I could see at a glance that the young Texan had touched their pride. The foreman detailed three men to look after the herd, and the balance made hasty preparations to accompany the quarantine guards. A relief was rushed away for the herders; and when the latter came in, they reported having sighted the posse from Powderville, heading across country for the twin buttes. Meanwhile a breakfast had been bolted by the guards, Sponsilier, and myself, and swinging into our saddles, we rounded a bluff bend of the creek and rode for the rendezvous, some three miles distant. I noticed by the brands that nearly every horse in that country had been born in Texas, and the short time in which we covered the intervening miles proved that the change of climate had added to their stability and bottom. Our first glimpse of the meeting-point revealed the summit of the buttes fairly covered with horsemen. From their numbers it was evident that ours was the last contingent to arrive; but before we reached the twin mounds, the posse rode down from the lookout and a courier met and turned us from our course. The lead herd had been sighted in trail formation but a few miles distant, heading north, and it was the intention to head them at the earliest moment. The messenger inquired our numbers, and reported those arrived at forty-five, making the posse when united a few over sixty men.

A juncture of forces was effected within a mile of the lead herd. It was a unique posse. Old frontiersmen, with patriarchal beards and sawed-off shotguns, chewed their tobacco complacently as they rode forward at a swinging gallop. Beardless youths, armed with the old buffalo guns of their fathers, led the way as if an Indian invasion had called them forth. Soldiers of fortune, with Southern accents, who were assisting in the conquest of a new empire, intermingled with the hurrying throng, and two men whose home was in Medina County, Texas, looked on and approved. The very horses had caught the inspiration of the moment, champing bits in their effort to forge to the front rank, while the blood-stained slaver coated many breasts or driveled from our boots. Before we met the herd a halt was called, and about a dozen men were deployed off on each flank, while the main body awaited the arrival of the cattle. The latter were checked by the point-men and turned back when within a few hundred yards of the main posse. Several horsemen from the herd rode forward, and one politely inquired the meaning of this demonstration. The question was met by a counter one from Captain Ullmer, who demanded to know the reason why these cattle should trespass on the rights of others and ignore local quarantine. The spokesman in behalf of the herd turned in his saddle and gave an order to send some certain person forward. Sponsilier whispered to me that this fellow was merely a segundo. "But wait till the 'major-domo' arrives," he added. The appearance of the posse and the halting of the herd summoned that personage from the rear to the front, and the next moment he was seen galloping up the column of cattle. With a plausible smile this high mogul, on his arrival, repeated the previous question, and on a similar demand from the captain of the posse, he broke into a jolly laugh from which he recovered with difficulty.

"Why, gentlemen," said he, every word dripping with honeyed sweetness, "this is entirely uncalled for. I assure you that it was purely an oversight on my part that I did not send you word in advance that these herds of mine are government cattle and not subject to local quarantine. My associates are the largest army contractors in the country, these cattle are due at Fort Buford on the 15th of this month, and any interference on your part would be looked upon as an insult to the government. In fact, the post commander at Fort Laramie insisted that he be permitted to send a company of cavalry to escort us across Wyoming, and assured us that a troop from Fort Keogh, if requested, would meet our cattle on the Montana line. The army is jealous over its supplies, but I declined all military protection, knowing that I had but to show my credentials to pass unmolested anywhere. Now, if you care to look over these papers, you will see that these cattle are en route to Fort Buford, on an assignment of the original contract, issued by the secretary of war to The Western Supply Company. Very sorry to put you to all this trouble, but these herds must not be interfered with. I trust that you gentlemen understand that the government is supreme."

As the papers mentioned were produced, Sponsilier kicked me on the shin, gave me a quiet wink, and nodded towards the documents then being tendered to Captain Ullmer. Groping at his idea, I rode forward, and as the papers were being returned with a mere glance on the part of the quarantine leader, I politely asked if I might see the assignment of the original contract. But a quizzical smile met my request, and shaking out the heavy parchment, he rapped it with the knuckles of his disengaged hand, remarking as he returned it to his pocket, "Sorry, but altogether too valuable to allow out of my possession." Just what I would have done with the beribboned document, except to hand it over to Sponsilier, is beyond me, yet I was vaguely conscious that its destruction was of importance to our side of the matter at issue. At the same instant in which my request was declined, the big medicine man turned to Captain Ullmer and suavely remarked, "You found everything as represented, did you?"

"Why, I heard your statement, and I have also heard it disputed from other sources. In fact I have nothing to do with you except to enforce the quarantine now established by the cattlemen of eastern Montana. If you have any papers showing that your herds were wintered north of latitude 37, you can pass, as this quarantine is only enforced against cattle from south of that degree. This territory lost half a million dollars' worth of native stock last fall from Texas fever, and this season they propose to apply the ounce of preventive. You will have ample time to reach your destination after frost falls, and your detention by quarantine will be a good excuse for your delay. Now, unless you can convince me that your herds are immune, I'll show you a good place to camp on the head of Wolf Creek. It will probably be a matter of ten to fifteen days before the quarantine is lifted, and we are enforcing it against citizens of Montana and Texas alike, and no exception can be made in your case."

"But, my dear sir, this is not a local or personal matter. Whatever you do, don't invite the frown of the government. Let me warn you not to act in haste. Now, remember — "

"You made your cracks that you would cross this quarantine line," interrupted Ullmer, bristlingly, "and I want you to find out your mistake. There is no occasion for further words, and you can either order your outfit to turn your cattle east, or I'll send men and do it myself."

The "major-domo" turned and galloped back to his men, a number of whom had congregated near at hand. The next moment he returned and haughtily threatened to surrender the cattle then and there unless he was allowed to proceed. "Give him a receipt for his beeves, Fred," quietly remarked an old cowman, gently stroking his beard, "and I'll take these boys over here on the right and start the cattle. That will be the safest way, unless the gentleman can indemnify us. I lost ten thousand dollars' worth of stock last fall, and as a citizen of Montana I have objections to leaving a trail of fever from here to the mouth of the Yellowstone. And tell him he can have a bond for his cattle," called back the old man as he rode out of hearing.

The lead herd was pointed to the east, and squads of men rode down and met the other two, veering them off on an angle to the right. Meanwhile the superintendent raved, pleaded, and threatened without avail, but finally yielded and refused the receipt and dispossession of his cattle. This was just what the quarantine captain wanted, and the dove of peace began to shake its plumage. Within an hour all three of the herds were moving out for the head of Wolf Creek, accompanied only by the quarantine guards, the remainder of the posse returning to their homes or their work. Having ample time on our hands, Sponsilier and I expected to remain at Station No. 1 until after the 10th of September, and accordingly made ourselves at home at that camp. To say that we were elated over the situation puts it mildly, and that night the two of us lost nearly a hundred dollars playing poker with the quarantine guards. A strict vigilance was maintained over the herds in question, but all reports were unanimous that they were contentedly occupying their allotted range.

But at noon on the third day of the enforced isolation, a messenger from Powderville arrived at the first station. A troop of cavalry from Fort Keogh, accompanied by a pack-train, had crossed the Powder River below the hamlet, their avowed mission being to afford an escort for certain government beef, then under detention by the local authorities. The report fell among us like a flash of lightning. Ample time had elapsed for a messenger to ride to the Yellowstone, and, returning with troops, pilot them to the camps of Field, Radcliff & Co. A consultation was immediately held, but no definite line of action had been arrived at when a horseman from one of the lower camps dashed up and informed us that the three herds were already trailing out for the dead-line, under an escort of cavalry. Saddling up, we rallied what few men were available, determined to make a protest, at least, in the interest of humanity to dumb brutes. We dispatched couriers to the nearest camps and the outer quarantine station; but before a posse of twenty men arrived, the lead herd was within a mile of the dead-line, and we rode out and met them. Fully eighty troopers, half of which rode in column formation in front, halted us as we approached. Terse and to the point were the questions and answers exchanged between the military arm of the government and the quarantine authorities of Montana. When the question arose of indemnity to citizens, in case of death to native cattle, a humane chord was touched in the young lieutenant in command, resulting in his asking several questions, to which the "major-domo" protested. Once satisfied of the justice of quarantine, the officer, in defense of his action, said:

"Gentlemen, I am under instructions to give these herds, intended for use at Fort Buford, a three days' escort beyond this quarantine line. I am very much obliged to you all for making so clear the necessity of isolating herds of Texas cattle, and that little or no hardship may attend my orders, you may have until noon to-morrow to drift all native stock west of the Powder River. When these herds encamp for the night, they will receive instructions not to move forward before twelve to-morrow. I find the situation quite different from reports; nevertheless orders are orders."

CHAPTER XX
ON THE JUST AND THE UNJUST

The quarantine guards returned to their camp. Our plans were suddenly and completely upset, and not knowing which way to turn, Sponsilier and I, slightly crestfallen, accompanied the guards. It was already late in the evening, but Captain Ullmer took advantage of the brief respite granted him to clear the east half of the valley of native cattle. Couriers were dispatched to sound the warning among the ranches down the river, while a regular round-up outfit was mustered among the camps to begin the drifting of range stock that evening. A few men were left at the two camps, as quarantine was not to be abandoned, and securing our borrowed horses, my partner and I bade our friends farewell and set out on our return for the Yellowstone. Merely touching at Powderville for a hasty supper, we held a northwest, cross-country course, far into the night, when we unsaddled to rest our horses and catch a few hours' sleep. But sunrise found us again in our saddles, and by the middle of the forenoon we were breakfasting with our friends in Miles City.

Fort Keogh was but a short distance up the river. That military interference had been secured through fraud and deception, there was not the shadow of a doubt. During the few hours which we spent in Miles, the cattle interests were duly aroused, and a committee of cowmen were appointed to call on the post commander at Keogh with a formidable protest, which would no doubt be supplemented later, on the return of the young lieutenant and his troopers. During our ride the night before, Sponsilier and I had discussed the possibility of arousing the authorities at Glendive. Since it was in the neighborhood of one hundred miles from Powderville to the former point on the railroad, the herds would consume nearly a week in reaching there. A freight train was caught that afternoon, and within twenty-four hours after leaving the quarantine camp on the Powder River, we had opened headquarters at the Stock Exchange Saloon in Glendive. On arriving, I deposited one hundred dollars with the proprietor of that bar-room, with the understanding that it was to be used in getting an expression from the public in regard to the question of Texas fever. Before noon the next day, Dave Sponsilier and Tom Quirk were not only the two most popular men in Glendive, but quarantine had been decided on with ringing resolutions.

Our standing was soon of the best. Horses were tendered us, and saddling one I crossed the Yellowstone and started down the river to arouse outlying ranches, while Sponsilier and a number of local cowmen rode south to locate a camp and a deadline. I was absent two days, having gone north as far as Wolf Island, where I recrossed the river, returning on the eastern side of the valley. At no ranch which was visited did my mission fail of meeting hearty approval, especially on the western side of the river, where severe losses from fever had been sustained the fall before. One ranch on Thirteen Mile offered, if necessary, to send every man in its employ, with their own wagon and outfit of horses, free of all charge, until quarantine was lifted. But I suggested, instead, that they send three or four men with their horses and blankets, leaving the remainder to be provided for by the local committee. In my two days' ride, over fifty volunteers were tendered, but I refused all except twenty, who were to report at Glendive not later than the morning of the 6th. On my return to the railroad, all arrangements were completed and the outlook was promising. Couriers had arrived from the south during my absence, bringing the news of the coming of the through Texas cattle, and warning the local ranches to clear the way or take the consequences. All native stock had been pushed west of the Powder and Yellowstone, as far north as Cabin Creek, which had been decided on as the second quarantine-line. Daily reports were being received of the whereabouts of the moving herds, and at the rate they were traveling, they would reach Cabin Creek about the 7th. Two wagons had been outfitted, cooks employed, and couriers dispatched to watch the daily progress of the cattle, which, if following the usual route, would strike the deadline some distance south of Glendive.

During the next few days, Sponsilier and I were social lions in that town, and so great was our popularity we could have either married or been elected to office. We limited our losses at poker to so much an evening, and what we won from the merchant class we invariably lost among the volunteer guards and cowmen, taking our luck with a sangfroid which proved us dead-game sports, and made us hosts of friends. We had contributed one hundred dollars to the general quarantine fund, and had otherwise made ourselves popular with all classes in the brief time at our command. Under the pretense that we might receive orders at any time to overtake our herds, we declined all leadership in the second campaign about to be inaugurated against Texas fever. Dave and I were both feeling rather chesty over the masterful manner in which we had aroused the popular feeling in favor of quarantine in our own interest, at the same time making it purely a local movement. We were swaggering about like ward-heelers, when on the afternoon of the 5th the unexpected again happened. The business interests of the village usually turned out to meet the daily passenger trains, even the poker-games taking a recess until the cars went past. The arrival and departure of citizens of the place were noted by every one, and strangers were looked upon with timidity, very much as in all simple communities. Not taking any interest in the passing trains, Sponsilier was writing a letter to his girl in Texas, while I was shaking dice for the cigars with the bartender of the Stock Exchange, when the Eastbound arrived. After the departure of the train, I did not take any notice of the return of the boys to the abandoned games, or the influx of patrons to the house, until some one laid a hand on my shoulder and quietly said, "Isn't your name Quirk?"

Turning to the speaker, I was confronted by Mr. Field and Mr. Radcliff, who had just arrived by train from the west. Admitting my identity, I invited them to have a cigar or liquid refreshment, inquiring whence they had come and where their cattle were. To my surprise, Fort Keogh was named as their last refuge, and the herds were reported to cross the railroad within the next few days. Similar questions were asked me, but before replying, I caught Sponsilier's eye and summoned him with a wink. On Dave's presenting himself, I innocently asked the pair if they did not remember my friend as one of the men whom they had under arrest at Dodge. They grunted an embarrassed acknowledgment, which was returned in the same coin, when I proceeded to inform them that our cattle crossed the railroad at Little Missouri ten days before, and that we were only waiting the return of Mr. Lovell from the Crow Agency before proceeding to our destination. With true Yankee inquisitiveness, other questions followed, the trend of which was to get us to admit that we had something to do with the present activities in quarantining Texas cattle. But I avoided their leading queries, and looked appealingly at Sponsilier, who came to my rescue with an answer born of the moment.

"Well, gentlemen," said Dave, seating himself on the bar and leisurely rolling a cigarette, "that town of Little Missouri is about the dullest hole that I was ever water-bound in. Honestly, I'd rather be with the cattle than loafing in it with money in my pocket. Now this town has got some get-up about it; I'll kiss a man's foot if he complains that this burg isn't sporty enough for his blood. They've given me a run here for my white alley, and I still think I know something about that game called draw-poker. But you were speaking about quarantine. Yes; there seems to have been a good many cattle lost through these parts last fall. You ought to have sent your herds up through Dakota, where there is no native stock to interfere. I'd hate to have cattle coming down the Powder River. A friend of mine passed through here yesterday; his herd was sold for delivery on the Elkhorn, north of here, and he tells me he may not be able to reach there before October. He saw your herds and tells me you are driving the guts out of them. So if there's anything in that old 'ship-fever theory,' you ought to be quarantined until it snows. There's a right smart talk around here of fixing a dead-line below somewhere, and if you get tied up before reaching the railroad, it won't surprise me a little bit. When it comes to handling the cattle, old man Don has the good hard cow-sense every time, but you shorthorns give me a pain."

"What did I tell you?" said Radcliff, the elder one, to his partner, as they turned to leave.

On nearing the door, Mr. Field halted and begrudgingly said, "See you later, Quirk."

"Not if I see you first," I replied; "you ain't my kind of cowmen."

Not even waiting for them to pass outside, Sponsilier, from his elevated position, called every one to the bar to irrigate. The boys quit their games, and as they lined up in a double row, Dave begged the bartenders to bestir themselves, and said to his guests: "Those are the kid-gloved cowmen that I've been telling you about — the owners of the Texas cattle that are coming through here. Did I hang it on them artistically, or shall I call them back and smear it on a shade deeper? They smelt a mouse all right, and when their cattle reach Cabin Creek, they'll smell the rat in earnest. Now, set out the little and big bottle and everybody have a cigar on the side. And drink hearty, lads, for to-morrow we may be drinking branch water in a quarantine camp."

The arrival of Field and Radcliff was accepted as a defiance to the local cattle interests. Popular feeling was intensified when it was learned that they were determined not to recognize any local quarantine, and were secretly inquiring for extra men to guard their herds in passing Glendive. There was always a rabble element in every frontier town, and no doubt, as strangers, they could secure assistance in quarters that the local cowmen would spurn. Matters were approaching a white heat, when late that night an expected courier arrived, and reported the cattle coming through at the rate of twenty miles a day. They were not following any particular trail, traveling almost due north, and if the present rate of travel was maintained, Cabin Creek would be reached during the forenoon of the 7th. This meant business, and the word was quietly passed around that all volunteers were to be ready to move in the morning. A cowman named Retallac, owner of a range on the Yellowstone, had previously been decided on as captain, and would have under him not less than seventy-five chosen men, which number, if necessary, could easily be increased to one hundred.

Morning dawned on a scene of active operations. The two wagons were started fully an hour in advance of the cavalcade, which was to follow, driving a remuda of over two hundred saddle horses. Sponsilier and I expected to accompany the outfit, but at the last moment our plans were changed by an incident and we remained behind, promising to overtake them later. There were a number of old buffalo hunters in town, living a precarious life, and one of their number had quietly informed Sheriff Wherry that they had been approached with an offer of five dollars a day to act as an escort to the herds while passing through. The quarantine captain looked upon that element as a valuable ally, suggesting that if it was a question of money, our side ought to be in the market for their services. Heartily agreeing with him, the company of guards started, leaving their captain behind with Sponsilier and myself. Glendive was a county seat, and with the assistance of the sheriff, we soon had every buffalo hunter in the town corralled. They were a fine lot of rough men, inclined to be convivial, and with the assistance of Sheriff Wherry, coupled with the high standing of the quarantine captain, on a soldier's introduction Dave and I made a good impression among them. Sponsilier did the treating and talking, his offer being ten dollars a day for a man and horse, which was promptly accepted, when the question naturally arose who would stand sponsor for the wages. Dave backed off some distance, and standing on his left foot, pulled off his right boot, shaking out a roll of money on the floor.

"There's the long green, boys," said he, "and you fellows can name your own banker. I'll make it up a thousand, and whoever you say goes with me. Shall it be the sheriff, or Mr. Retallac, or the proprietor of the Stock Exchange?"

Sheriff Wherry interfered, relieving the embarrassment in appointing a receiver, and vouched that these two Texans were good for any reasonable sum. The buffalo hunters approved, apologizing to Sponsilier, as he pulled on his boot, for questioning his financial standing, and swearing allegiance in every breath. An hour's time was granted in which to saddle and make ready, during which we had a long chat with Sheriff Wherry and found him a valuable ally. He had cattle interests in the country, and when the hunters appeared, fifteen strong, he mounted his horse and accompanied us several miles on the way. "Now, boys," said he, at parting, "I'll keep an eye over things around town, and if anything important happens, I'll send a courier with the news. If those shorthorns attempt to offer any opposition, I'll run a blazer on them, and if necessary I'll jug the pair. You fellows just buffalo the herds, and the sheriff's office will keep cases on any happenings around Glendive. It's understood that night or day your camp can be found on Cabin Creek, opposite the old eagle tree. Better send me word as soon as the herds arrive. Good luck to you, lads."

Neither wagons nor guards were even sighted during our three hours' ride to the appointed campground. On our arrival tents were being pitched and men were dragging up wood, while the cooks were busily preparing a late dinner, the station being fully fifteen miles south of the railroad. Scouts were thrown out during the afternoon, corrals built, and evening found the quarantine camp well established for the comfort of its ninety-odd men. The buffalo hunters were given special attention and christened the "Sponsilier Guards;" they took again to outdoor life as in the old days. The report of the scouts was satisfactory; all three of the herds had been seen and would arrive on schedule time. A hush of expectancy greeted this news, but Sponsilier and I ridiculed the idea that there would be any opposition, except a big talk and plenty of bluffing.

"Well, if that's what they rely on," said Captain Retallac, "then they're as good as in quarantine this minute. If you feel certain they can't get help from Fort Keogh a second time, those herds will be our guests until further orders. What we want to do now is to spike every possible chance for their getting any help, and the matter will pass over like a summer picnic. If you boys think there's any danger of an appeal to Fort Buford, the military authorities want to be notified that the Yellowstone Valley has quarantined against Texas fever and asks their cooperation in enforcing the same."

"I can fix that," replied Sponsilier. "We have lawyers at Buford right now, and I can wire them the situation fully in the morning. If they rely on the military, they will naturally appeal to the nearest post, and if Keogh and Buford turn them down, the next ones are on the Missouri River, and at that distance cavalry couldn't reach here within ten days. Oh, I think we've got a grapevine twist on them this time."

Sponsilier sat up half the night wording a message to our attorneys at Fort Buford. The next morning found me bright and early on the road to Glendive with the dispatch, the sending of which would deplete my cash on hand by several dollars, but what did we care for expense when we had the money and orders to spend it? I regretted my absence from the quarantine camp, as I was anxious to be present on the arrival of the herds, and again watch the "major-domo" run on the rope and fume and charge in vain. But the importance of blocking assistance was so urgent that I would gladly have ridden to Buford if necessary. In that bracing atmosphere it was a fine morning for the ride, and I was rapidly crossing the country, when a vehicle, in the dip of the plain, was sighted several miles ahead. I was following no road, but when the driver of the conveyance saw me he turned across my front and signaled. On meeting the rig, I could hardly control myself from laughing outright, for there on the rear seat sat Field and Radcliff, extremely gruff and uncongenial. Common courtesies were exchanged between the driver and myself, and I was able to answer clearly his leading questions: Yes; the herds would reach Cabin Creek before noon; the old eagle tree, which could be seen from the first swell of the plain beyond, marked the quarantine camp, and it was the intention to isolate the herds on the South Fork of Cabin. "Drive on," said a voice, and, in the absence of any gratitude expressed, I inwardly smiled in reward.

I was detained in Glendive until late in the day, waiting for an acknowledgment of the message. Sheriff Wherry informed me that the only move attempted on the part of the shorthorn drovers was the arrest of Sponsilier and myself, on the charge of being accomplices in the shooting of one of their men on the North Platte. But the sheriff had assured the gentlemen that our detention would have no effect on quarantining their cattle, and the matter was taken under advisement and dropped. It was late when I started for camp that evening. The drovers had returned, accompanied by their superintendent, and were occupying the depot, burning the wires in every direction. I was risking no chances, and cultivated the company of Sheriff Wherry until the acknowledgment arrived, when he urged me to ride one of his horses in returning to camp, and insisted on my taking a carbine. Possibly this was fortunate, for before I had ridden one third the distance to the quarantine camp, I met a cavalcade of nearly a dozen men from the isolated herds. When they halted and inquired the distance to Glendive, one of their number recognized me as having been among the quarantine guards at Powderville. I admitted that I was there, turning my horse so that the carbine fell to my hand, and politely asked if any one had any objections. It seems that no one had, and after a few commonplace inquiries were exchanged, we passed on our way.

There was great rejoicing on Cabin Creek that night. Songs were sung, and white navy beans passed current in numerous poker-games until the small hours of morning. There had been nothing dramatic in the meeting between the herds and the quarantine guards, the latter force having been augmented by visiting ranchmen and their help, until protest would have been useless. A routine of work had been outlined, much stricter than at Powderville, and a surveillance of the camps was constantly maintained. Not that there was any danger of escape, but to see that the herds occupied the country allotted to them, and did not pollute any more territory than was necessary. The Sponsilier Guards were given an easy day shift, and held a circle of admirers at night, recounting and living over again "the good old days." Visitors from either side of the Yellowstone were early callers, and during the afternoon the sheriff from Glendive arrived. I did not know until then that Mr. Wherry was a candidate for reelection that fall, but the manner in which he mixed with the boys was enough to warrant his election for life. What endeared him to Sponsilier and myself was the fund of information he had collected, and the close tab he had kept on every movement of the opposition drovers. He told us that their appeal to Fort Keogh for assistance had been refused with a stinging rebuke; that a courier had started the evening before down the river for Fort Buford, and that Mr. Radcliff had personally gone to Fort Abraham Lincoln to solicit help. The latter post was fully one hundred and fifty miles away, but that distance could be easily covered by a special train in case of government interference.

It rained on the afternoon of the 9th. The courier had returned from Fort Buford on the north, unsuccessful, as had also Mr. Radcliff from Fort Lincoln on the Missouri River to the eastward. The latter post had referred the request to Keogh, and washed its hands of intermeddling in a country not tributary to its territory. The last hope of interference was gone, and the rigors of quarantine closed in like a siege with every gun of the enemy spiked. Let it be a week or a month before the quarantine was lifted, the citizens of Montana had so willed it, and their wish was law. Evening fell, and the men drew round the fires. The guards buttoned their coats as they rode away, and the tired ones drew their blankets around them as they lay down to sleep. Scarcely a star could be seen in the sky overhead, but before my partner or myself sought our bed, a great calm had fallen, the stars were shining, and the night had grown chilly.

The old buffalo hunters predicted a change in the weather, but beyond that they were reticent. As Sponsilier and I lay down to sleep, we agreed that if three days, even two days, were spared us, those cattle in quarantine could never be tendered at Fort Buford on the appointed day of delivery. But during the early hours of morning we were aroused by the returning guards, one of whom halted his horse near our blankets and shouted, "Hey, there, you Texans; get up — a frost has fallen!"

Sure enough, it had frosted during the night, and the quarantine was lifted. When day broke, every twig and blade of grass glistened in silver sheen, and the horses on picket stood humped and shivering. The sun arose upon the herds moving, with no excuse to say them nay, and orders were issued to the guards to break camp and disperse to their homes. As we rode into Glendive that morning, sullen and defeated by a power beyond our control, in speaking of the peculiarity of the intervention, Sponsilier said: "Well, if it rains on the just and the unjust alike, why shouldn't it frost the same."

CHAPTER XXI
FORT BUFORD

We were at our rope's end. There were a few accounts to settle in Glendive, after which we would shake its dust from our feet. Very few of the quarantine guards returned to town, and with the exception of Sheriff Wherry, none of the leading cowmen, all having ridden direct for their ranches. Long before the train arrived which would carry us to Little Missouri, the opposition herds appeared and crossed the railroad west of town. Their commissaries entered the village for supplies, while the "major-domo," surrounded by a body-guard of men, rode about on his miserable palfrey. The sheriff, fearing a clash between the victorious and the vanquished, kept an eye on Sponsilier and me as we walked the streets, freely expressing our contempt of Field, Radcliff & Co., their henchmen and their methods. Dave and I were both nerved to desperation; Sheriff Wherry, anxious to prevent a conflict, councilled with the opposition drovers, resulting in their outfits leaving town, while the principals took stage across to Buford.

Meanwhile Sponsilier had wired full particulars to our employer at Big Horn. It was hardly necessary, as the frost no doubt was general all over Montana, but we were anxious to get into communication with Lovell immediately on his return to the railroad. We had written him from Miles of our failure at Powderville, and the expected second stand at Glendive, and now the elements had notified him that the opposition herds were within striking distance, and would no doubt appear at Buford on or before the day of delivery. An irritable man like our employer would neither eat nor sleep, once the delivery at the Crow Agency was over, until reaching the railroad, and our message would be awaiting him on his return to Big Horn. Our train reached Little Missouri early in the evening, and leaving word with the agent that we were expecting important messages from the west, we visited the liveryman and inquired about the welfare of our horses. The proprietor of the stable informed us that they had fared well, and that he would have them ready for us on an hour's notice. It was after dark and we were at supper when the first message came. An immediate answer was required, and arising from the table, we left our meal unfinished and hastened to the depot. From then until midnight, messages flashed back and forth, Sponsilier dictating while I wrote. As there was no train before the regular passenger the next day, the last wire requested us to have the horses ready to meet the Eastbound, saying that Bob Quirk would accompany Lovell.

That night it frosted again. Sponsilier and I slept until noon the next day without awakening. Then the horses were brought in from pasture, and preparation was made to leave that evening. It was in the neighborhood of ninety miles across to the mouth of the Yellowstone, and the chances were that we would ride it without unsaddling. The horses had had a two weeks' rest, and if our employer insisted on it, we would breakfast with the herds the next morning. I was anxious to see the cattle again and rejoin my outfit, but like a watched pot, the train was an hour late. Sponsilier and I took advantage of the delay and fortified the inner man against the night and the ride before us. This proved fortunate, as Lovell and my brother had supper en route in the dining-car. A running series of questions were asked and answered; saddles were shaken out of gunny-sacks and cinched on waiting horses as though we were starting to a prairie fire. Bob Quirk's cattle had reached the Crow Agency in splendid condition, the delivery was effected without a word, and old man Don was in possession of a letter from Flood, saying everything had passed smoothly at the Rosebud Agency.

Contrary to the expectation of Sponsilier and myself, our employer was in a good humor, fairly walking on the clouds over the success of his two first deliveries of the year. But amid the bustle and rush, in view of another frosty night, Sponsilier inquired if it would not be a good idea to fortify against the chill, by taking along a bottle of brandy. "Yes, two of them if you want to," said old man Don, in good-humored approval. "Here, Tom, fork this horse and take the pitch out of him," he continued; "I don't like the look of his eye." But before I could reach the horse, one of my own string, Bob Quirk had mounted him, when in testimony of the nutritive qualities of Dakota's grasses, he arched his spine like a true Texan and outlined a worm-fence in bucking a circle.

The start was made during the gathering dusk. Sponsilier further lifted the spirits of our employer, as we rode along, by a clear-cut description of the opposition cattle, declaring that had they ever equaled ours, the handling they had received since leaving Ogalalla, compared to his, would class them with short twos in the spring against long threes in the fall. Within an hour the stars shone out, and after following the river some ten miles, we bore directly north until Beaver Creek was reached near midnight. The pace was set at about an eight-mile, steady clip, with an occasional halt to tighten cinches or shift saddles. The horses were capable of a faster gait without tiring, but we were not sure of the route and were saving them for the finish after daybreak. Early in the night we were conscious that a frost was falling, and several times Sponsilier inquired if no one cared for a nip from his bottle. Bob Quirk started the joke on Dave by declining; old man Don uncorked the flask, and, after smelling of the contents, handed it back with his thanks. I caught onto their banter, and not wishing to spoil a good jest, also declined, leaving Sponsilier to drink alone. During the night, whenever conversation lagged, some one was certain to make reference to the remarks which are said to have passed between the governors of the Carolinas, or if that failed to provoke a rise, ask direct if no one had something to ward off the chilly air. After being refused several times, Dave had thrown the bottle away, meeting these jests with the reply that he had a private flask, but its quality was such that he was afraid of offending our cultivated tastes by asking us to join him.

Day broke about five in the morning. We had been in the saddle nearly ten hours, and were confident that sunrise would reveal some landmark to identify our location. The atmosphere was frosty and clear, and once the gray of dawn yielded to the rising sun, the outline of the Yellowstone was easily traced on our left, while the bluffs in our front shielded a view of the mother Missouri. In attempting to approach the latter we encountered some rough country and were compelled to turn towards the former, crossing it, at O'Brien's roadhouse, some seven miles above the mouth. The husbanded reserves of our horses were shaken out, and shortly afterward smoke-clouds from camp-fires, hanging low, attracted our attention. The herds were soon located as they arose and grazed away from their bed-grounds. The outfits were encamped on the eastern side of the Yellowstone; and before leaving the government road, we sighted in our front a flag ascending to greet the morning, and the location of Fort Buford was established. Turning towards the cattle, we rode for the lower wagon and were soon unsaddling at Forrest's camp. The latter had arrived two days before and visited the post; he told us that the opposition were there in force, as well as our own attorneys. The arrival of the cattle under contract for that military division was the main topic of discussion, and Forrest had even met a number of civilian employees of Fort Buford whose duties were to look after the government beeves. The foreman of these unenlisted attaches, a Texan named Sanders, had casually ridden past his camp the day before, looking over the cattle, and had pronounced them the finest lot of beeves tendered the government since his connection with that post.

"That's good news," said Lovell, as he threw his saddle astride the front wheel of the wagon; "that's the way I like to hear my cattle spoken about. Now, you boys want to make friends with all those civilians, and my attorneys and Bob and I will hobnob around with the officers, and try and win the good will of the entire post. You want to change your camp every few days and give your cattle good grazing and let them speak for themselves. Better kill a beef among the outfits, and insist on all callers staying for meals. We're strangers here, and we want to make a good impression, and show the public that we were born white, even if we do handle cattle for a living. Quince, tie up the horses for us, and after breakfast Bob and I will look over the herds and then ride into Fort Buford. — Trout for breakfast? You don't mean it!"

It was true, however, and our appetites did them justice. Forrest reported Splann as having arrived a day late, and now encamped the last herd up the valley. Taking our horses with us, Dave and I set out to look up our herds and resume our former positions. I rode through Sponsilier's cattle while en route to my own, and remembered the first impression they had made on my mind, — their uniformity in size and smoothness of build, — and now found them fatted into finished form, the herd being a credit to any drover. Continuing on my way, I intercepted my own cattle, lying down over hundreds of acres, and so contented that I refused to disturb them. Splann reported not over half a dozen sore-footed ones among them, having grazed the entire distance from Little Missouri, giving the tender cattle a good chance to recover. I held a circle of listeners for several hours, in recounting Sponsilier's and my own experiences in the quarantine camps, and our utter final failure, except that the opposition herds had been detained, which would force them to drive over twenty miles a day in order to reach Buford on time. On the other hand, an incident of more than ordinary moment had occurred with the cattle some ten days previous. The slow movement of the grazing herds allowed a great amount of freedom to the boys and was taken advantage of at every opportunity. It seems that on approaching Beaver Creek, Owen Ubery and Runt Pickett had ridden across to it for the purpose of trout-fishing. They were gone all day, having struck the creek some ten or twelve miles west of the cattle, expecting to fish down it and overtake the herds during the evening. But about noon they discovered where a wagon had been burned, years before, and near by were five human skeletons, evidently a family. It was possibly the work of Indians, or a blizzard, and to prove the discovery, Pickett had brought in one of the skulls and proposed taking it home with him as a memento of the drive. Parent objected to having the reminder in the wagon, and a row resulted between them, till Splann interfered and threw the gruesome relic away.

The next morning a dozen of us from the three herds rode into the post. Fort Buford was not only a military headquarters, but a supply depot for other posts farther west on the Missouri and Yellowstone rivers. The nearest railroad connection was Glendive, seventy-six miles up the latter stream, though steamboats took advantage of freshets in the river to transport immense supplies from lower points on the Missouri where there were rail connections. From Buford westward, transportation was effected by boats of lighter draft and the regulation wagon train. It was recognized as one of the most important supply posts in the West; as early as five years previous to this date, it had received in a single summer as many as ten thousand beeves. Its provision for cavalry was one of its boasted features, immense stacks of forage flanking those quarters, while the infantry barracks and officers' quarters were large and comfortable. A stirring little town had sprung up on the outside, affording the citizens employment in wood and hay contracts, and becoming the home of a large number of civilian employees, the post being the mainstay of the village.

After settling our quarantine bills, Sponsilier and I each had money left. Our employer refused even to look at our expense bills until after the delivery, but urged us to use freely any remaining funds in cultivating the good will of the citizens and soldiery alike. Forrest was accordingly supplied with funds, with the understanding that he was to hunt up Sanders and his outfit and show them a good time. The beef foreman was soon located in the quartermaster's office, and, having been connected with the post for several years, knew the ropes. He had come to Buford with Texas cattle, and after their delivery had accepted a situation under the acting quartermaster, easily rising to the foremanship through his superior abilities as a cowman. It was like a meeting of long-lost brothers to mingle again with a cow outfit, and the sutler's bar did a flourishing business during our stay in the post. There were ten men in Sanders's outfit, several of whom besides himself were Texans, and before we parted, every rascal had promised to visit us the next day and look over all the cattle.

The next morning Bob Quirk put in an early appearance at my wagon. He had passed the other outfits, and notified us all to have the cattle under convenient herd, properly watered in advance, as the post commandant, quartermaster, and a party of minor officers were going to ride out that afternoon and inspect our beeves. Lovell, of course, would accompany them, and Bob reported him as having made a ten-strike with the officers' mess, not being afraid to spend his money. Fortunately the present quartermaster at Buford was a former acquaintance of Lovell, the two having had business transactions. The quartermaster had been connected with frontier posts from Fort Clark, Texas, to his present position. According to report, the opposition were active and waging an aggressive campaign, but not being Western men, were at a disadvantage. Champagne had flowed freely at a dinner given the night before by our employer, during which Senator Aspgrain, in responding to a toast, had paid the army a high tribute for the part it had played in reclaiming the last of our western frontier. The quartermaster, in replying, had felicitously remarked, as a matter of his own observation, that the Californian's love for a horse was only excelled by the Texan's love for a cow, to which, amid uproarious laughter, old man Don arose and bowed his acknowledgment.

My brother changed horses and returned to Sponsilier's wagon. Dave had planned to entertain the post beef outfit for dinner, and had insisted on Bob's presence. They arrived at my herd near the middle of the forenoon, and after showing the cattle and remuda, we all returned to Sponsilier's camp. These civilian employees furnished their own mounts, and were anxious to buy a number of our best horses after the delivery was over. Not even a whisper was breathed about any uncertainty of our filling the outstanding contract, yet Sanders was given to understand that Don Lovell would rather, if he took a fancy to him, give a man a horse than sell him one. Not a word was said about any opposition to our herds; that would come later, and Sanders and his outfit were too good judges of Texas cattle to be misled by any bluster or boastful talk. Sponsilier acted the host, and after dinner unearthed a box of cigars, and we told stories and talked of our homes in the sunny South until the arrival of the military party. The herds had been well watered about noon and drifted out on the first uplands, and we intercepted the cavalcade before it reached Sponsilier's herd. They were mounted on fine cavalry horses, and the only greeting which passed, aside from a military salute, was when Lovell said: "Dave, show these officers your beeves. Answer any question they may ask to the best of your ability. Gentlemen, excuse me while you look over the cattle."

There were about a dozen military men in the party, some of them veterans of the civil war, others having spent their lifetime on our western frontier, while a few were seeing their first year's service after leaving West Point. In looking over the cattle, the post commander and quartermaster were taken under the wing of Sanders, who, as only a man could who was born to the occupation, called their attention to every fine point about the beeves. After spending fully an hour with Sponsilier's herd, the cavalcade proceeded on to mine, Lovell rejoining the party, but never once attempting to draw out an opinion, and again excusing himself on reaching my cattle. I continued with the military, answering every one's questions, from the young lieutenant's to the veteran commandant's, in which I was ably seconded by the quartermaster's foreman. My cattle had a splendid fill on them and eloquently spoke their own praises, yet Sanders lost no opportunity to enter a clincher in their favor. He pointed out beef after beef, and vouched for the pounds net they would dress, called attention to their sameness in build, ages, and general thrift, until one would have supposed that he was a salesman instead of a civilian employee.

My herd was fully ten miles from the post, and it was necessary for the military to return that evening. Don Lovell and a number of the boys had halted at a distance, and once the inspection was over, we turned and rode back to the waiting group of horsemen. On coming up, a number of the officers dismounted to shift saddles, preparatory to starting on their return, when the quartermaster halted near our employer and said:

"Colonel Lovell, let me say to you, in all sincerity, that in my twenty-five years' experience on this frontier, I never saw a finer lot of beeves tendered the government than these of yours. My position requires that I should have a fair knowledge of beef cattle, and the perquisites of my office in a post of Buford's class enable me to employ the best practical men available to perfect the service. I remember the quality of cattle which you delivered four years ago to me at Fort Randall, when it was a six-company post, yet they were not as fine a lot of beeves as these are. I have always contended that there was nothing too good in my department for the men who uphold the colors of our country, especially on the front line. You have been a soldier yourself and know that I am talking good horsesense, and I want to say to you that whatever the outcome of this dispute may be, if yours are the best cattle, you may count on my support until the drums beat tattoo. The government is liberal and insists on the best; the rank and file are worthy, and yet we don't always get what is ordered and well paid for. Now, remember, comrade, if this difference comes to an issue, I'm right behind you, and we'll stand or be turned down together."

"Thank you, Colonel," replied Mr. Lovell. "It does seem rather fortunate, my meeting up with a former business acquaintance, and at a time when I need him bad. If I am successful in delivering on this Buford award, it will round out, during my fifteen years as a drover, over a hundred thousand cattle that I have sold to the government for its Indian and army departments. There are no secrets in my business; the reason of my success is simple — my cattle were always there on the appointed day, humanely handled, and generally just a shade better than the specifications. My home country has the cattle for sale; I can tell within two bits a head what it will cost to lay them down here, and it's music to my ear to hear you insist on the best. I agree with you that the firing-line is entitled to special consideration, yet you know that there are ringsters who fatten at the expense of the rank and file. At present I haven't a word to say, but at noon to-morrow I shall tender the post commander at Ford Buford, through his quartermaster, ten thousand beeves, as a sub-contractor on the original award to The Western Supply Company." The post commander, an elderly, white-haired officer, rode over and smilingly said: "Now, look here, my Texas friend, I'm afraid you are borrowing trouble. True enough, there has been a protest made against our receiving your beeves, and I don't mince my words in saying that some hard things have been said about you. But we happen to know something about your reputation and don't give credit for all that is said. Your beeves are an eloquent argument in your favor, and if I were you I wouldn't worry. It is always a good idea in this Western country to make a proviso; and unless the unforeseen happens, the quartermaster's cattle foreman will count your beeves to-morrow afternoon; and for the sake of your company, if we keep you a day or two longer settling up, I don't want to hear you kick. Now, come on and go back with us to the post, as I promised my wife to bring you over to our house this evening. She seems to think that a man from Texas with ten thousand cattle ought to have horns, and I want to show her that she's mistaken. Come on, now, and not a damned word of protest out of you."

The military party started on their return, accompanied by Lovell. The civilian attaches followed at a respectful distance, a number of us joining them as far as Sponsilier's camp. There we halted, when Sanders insisted on an explanation of the remarks which had passed between our employer and his. Being once more among his own, he felt no delicacy in asking for information — which he would never think of doing with his superiors. My brother gave him a true version of the situation, but it remained for Dave Sponsilier to add an outline of the opposition herds and outfits.

"With humane treatment," said Dave, "the cattle would have qualified under the specifications. They were bought at Ogalalla, and any of the boys here will tell you that the first one was a good herd. The market was all shot to pieces, and they picked them up at their own price. But the owners didn't have cow-sense enough to handle the cattle, and put one of their own gang over the herds as superintendent. They left Cabin Creek, below Glendive, on the morning of the 10th, and they'll have to travel nearly twenty miles a day to reach here by noon to-morrow. Sanders, you know that gait will soon kill heavy cattle. The outfits were made up of short-card men and dance-hall ornaments, wild enough to look at, but shy on cattle sabe. Just so they showed up bad and wore a six-shooter, that was enough to win a home with Field and Radcliff. If they reach here on time, I'll gamble there ain't ten horses in the entire outfit that don't carry a nigger brand. And when it comes to the big conversation — well, they've simply got the earth faded."

It was nearly sundown when we mounted our horses and separated for the day. Bob Quirk returned to the post with the civilians, while I hastened back to my wagon. I had left orders with Splann to water the herd a second time during the evening and thus insure an easy night in holding the cattle. On my return, they were just grazing out from the river, their front a mile wide, making a pretty picture with the Yellowstone in the background. But as I sat my horse and in retrospect reviewed my connection with the cattle before me and the prospect of soon severing it, my remuda came over a near-by hill in a swinging trot for their second drink. Levering threw them into the river below the herd, and turning, galloped up to me and breathlessly asked: "Tom, did you see that dust-cloud up the river? Well, the other cattle are coming. The timber cuts off your view from here, besides the sun's gone down, but I watched their signal for half an hour from that second hill yonder. Oh, it's cattle all right; I know the sign, even if they are ten miles away."

CHAPTER XXII
A SOLDIER'S HONOR

Delivery day dawned with a heavy fog hanging over the valley of the Yellowstone. The frosts had ceased, and several showers had fallen during the night, one of which brought our beeves to their feet, but they gave no serious trouble and resumed their beds within an hour. There was an autumn feeling in the atmosphere, and when the sun arose, dispelling the mists, a glorious September day was ushered in. The foliage of the timber which skirted either river was coloring from recent frosts, while in numerous places the fallen leaves of the cottonwood were littering the ground. Enough rain had fallen to settle the dust, and the signal of the approaching herds, seen the evening before, was no longer visible.

The delay in their appearance, however, was only temporary. I rode down to Sponsilier's camp early that morning and reported the observations of my wrangler at sundown. No one at the lower wagon had noticed the dust-clouds, and some one suggested that it might be a freight outfit returning unloaded, when one of the men on herd was seen signaling the camp's notice. The attention of the day-herders, several miles distant, was centered on some object up the river; and mounting our horses, we rode for the nearest elevation, from which two herds were to be seen on the opposite side, traveling in trail formation. There was no doubting their identity; and wondering what the day would bring forth, we rode for a better point of observation, when from behind a timbered bend of the river the lead of the last herd appeared. At last the Yellowstone Valley held over twenty thousand beef cattle, in plain sight of each other, both factions equally determined on making the delivery on an award that required only half that number. Dismounting, we kept the herds in view for over an hour, or until the last one had crossed the river above O'Brien's road-house, the lead one having disappeared out of sight over on the main Missouri.

This was the situation on the morning of September 15. As we returned to Sponsilier's wagon, all the idle men about the camp joined our cavalcade, and we rode down and paid Forrest's outfit a social visit. The latter were all absent, except the cook, but shortly returned from down the river and reported the opposition herds to be crossing the Missouri, evidently going to camp at Alkali Lake.

"Well, I've been present at a good many deliveries," said Quince Forrest, as he reined in his horse, "but this one is in a class by itself. We always aimed to get within five or ten miles of a post or agency, but our friends made a worthy effort to get on the parade-ground. They did the next best thing and occupied the grazing where the cavalry horses have been herded all summer. Oh, their cattle will be hog-fat in a few days. Possibly they expect to show their cattle in town, and not trouble the quartermaster and comandante to even saddle up — they're the very kind of people who wouldn't give anybody trouble if they could help it. It wouldn't make so much difference about those old frontier officers or a common cowman, but if one of those young lieutenants was to get his feet wet, the chances are that those Washington City contractors would fret and worry for weeks. Of course, any little inconvenience that any one incurred on their account, they'd gladly come all the way back from Europe to make it right — I don't think."

While we were discussing the situation, Bob Quirk arrived at camp. He reported that Lovell, relying on the superiority of our beeves, had waived his right to deliver on the hour of high noon, and an inspection of the other cattle would be made that evening. The waiver was made at the request of the leading officers of Fort Buford, all very friendly to the best interests of the service and consequently ours, and the object was to silence all subsequent controversy. My brother admitted that some outside pressure had been brought to bear during the night, very antagonistic to the post commander, who was now more determined than ever to accept none but the best for their next year's meat supply. A well-known congressman, of unsavory reputation as a lobbyist in aiding and securing government contracts for his friends, was the latest addition to the legal forces of the opposition. He constantly mentioned his acquaintances in the War Department and maintained an air of assurance which was very disconcerting. The younger officers in the post were abashed at the effrontery of the contractors and their legal representatives, and had even gone so far as to express doubts as to the stability of their positions in case the decision favored Lovell's cattle. Opinion was current that a possible shake-up might occur at Buford after the receipt of its beef supply, and the more timorous ones were anxious to get into the right wagon, instead of being relegated to some obscure outpost.

It was now evident that the decisive issue was to occur over the delivery of the contending herds. Numerous possibilities arose in my imagination, and the various foremen advanced their views. A general belief that old man Don would fight to the last was prevalent, and amidst the discussions pro and con, I remarked that Lovell could take a final refuge behind the indemnity in hand.

"Indemnity, hell!" said Bob Quirk, giving me a withering look; "what is sixty-five thousand dollars on ten thousand beeves, within an hour of delivery and at thirty-seven and a half a head? You all know that the old man has strained his credit on this summer's drive, and he's got to have the money when he goes home. A fifteen or twenty per cent. indemnity does him no good. The Indian herds have paid out well, but if this delivery falls down, it will leave him holding the sack. On the other hand, if it goes through, he will be, financially, an independent man for life. And while he knows the danger of delay, he consented as readily as any of us would if asked for a cigarette-paper. He may come out all right, but he's just about white enough to get the worst of it. I've read these Sunday-school stories, where the good little boy always came out on top, but in real life, especially in cattle, it's quite different."

My brother's words had a magical effect. Sponsilier asked for suggestions, when Bob urged that every man available go into the post and accompany the inspection party that afternoon. Since Forrest and himself were unknown, they would take about three of the boys with them, cross the Missouri, ride through and sum up the opposition cattle. Forrest approved of the idea, and ordered his cook to bestir himself in getting up an early dinner. Meanwhile a number of my boys had ridden down to Forrest's wagon, and I immediately dispatched Clay Zilligan back to my cattle to relieve Vick Wolf and inform the day-herders that we might not return before dark. Wolf was the coolest man in my employ, had figured in several shooting scrapes, and as he was a splendid shot, I wanted to send him with Forrest and my brother. If identified as belonging to Lovell's outfits, there was a possibility that insult might be offered the boys; and knowing that it mattered not what the odds were, it would be resented, I thought it advisable to send a man who had smelt powder at short range. I felt no special uneasiness about my brother, in fact he was the logical man to go, but a little precaution would do no harm, and I saw to it that Sponsilier sent a good representative.

About one o'clock we started, thirty strong. Riding down the Yellowstone, the three detailed men, Quince Forrest, and my brother soon bore off to the left and we lost sight of them. Continuing on down the river, we forded the Missouri at the regular wagon-crossing, and within an hour after leaving Forrest's camp cantered into Fort Buford. Sanders and his outfit were waiting in front of the quartermaster's office, the hour for starting having been changed from two to three, which afforded ample time to visit the sutler's bar. Our arrival was noticed about the barracks, and evidently some complaint had been made, as old man Don joined us in time for the first round, after which he called Dave and me aside. In reply to his inquiry regarding our presence, Sponsilier informed him that we had come in to afford him an escort, in case he wished to attend the inspection of the opposition herds; that if there was any bulldozing going on he needn't stand behind the door. Dave informed him that Bob and Quince and three of the other boys would meet us at the cattle, and that he need feel no hesitancy in going if it was his wish. It was quite evident that Mr. Lovell was despondent, but he took courage and announced his willingness to go along.

"It was my intention not to go," said he, "though Mr. Aspgrain and Sutton both urged that I should. But now since you boys all feel the same way, I believe I'll go. Heaven and earth are being moved to have the other cattle accepted, but there are a couple of old war-horses at the head of this post that will fight them to the last ditch, and then some. I'm satisfied that my beeves, in any market in the West, are worth ten dollars a head more than the other ones, yet there is an effort being made to turn us down. Our claims rest on two points, — superiority of the beef tendered, and the legal impossibility of a transfer from themselves, a corporation, to themselves as individuals. If there is no outside interference, I think we will make the delivery before noon to-morrow. Now, I'll get horses for both Mr. Sutton and Senator Aspgrain, and you see that none of the boys drink too much. Sanders and his outfit are all right, and I want you lads to remind me to remember him before we leave this post. Now, we'll all go in a little party by ourselves, and I don't want a word out of a man, unless we are asked for an opinion from the officers, as our cattle must argue our cause."

A second drink, a cigar all round, and we were ready to start. As we returned to our mounts, a bustle of activity pervaded the post. Orderlies were leading forth the best horses, officers were appearing in riding-boots and gauntlets, while two conveyances from a livery in town stood waiting to convey the contractors and their legal representatives. Our employer and his counsel were on hand, awaiting the start, when the quartermaster and his outfit led off. There was some delay among the officers over the change of a horse, which had shown lameness, while the ringsters were all seated and waiting in their vehicles. Since none of us knew the trail to Alkali Lake, some one suggested that we follow up the quartermaster and allow the military and conveyances to go by the wagon-road. But Lovell objected, and ordered me forward to notice the trail and course, as the latter was a cut-off and much nearer than by road. I rode leisurely past the two vehicles, carefully scanning every face, when Mr. Field recognized and attempted to halt me, but I answered him with a contemptuous look and rode on. Instantly from the rigs came cries of "Stop that man!" "Halt that cowboy!" etc., when an orderly stepped in front of my horse and I reined in. But the shouting and my detention were seen and heard, and the next instant, led by Mike Sutton, our men dashed up, scaring the teams, overturning both of the conveyances, and spilling their occupants on the dusty ground. I admit that we were a hard-looking lot of cow-hands, our employer's grievance was our own, and just for an instant there was a blue, sulphuric tinge in the atmosphere as we accented our protest. The congressman scrambled to his feet, sputtering a complaint to the post commander, and when order was finally restored, the latter coolly said:

"Well, Mr. Y — — -, when did you assume command at Fort Buford? Any orders that you want given, while on this military reservation, please submit them to the proper authorities, and if just, they will receive attention. What right have you or any of your friends to stop a man without due process? I spent several hours with these men a few days ago and found them to my liking. I wish we could recruit the last one of them into our cavalry. But if you are afraid, I'll order out a troop of horse to protect you. Shall I?"

"I'm not at all afraid," replied Mr. Raddiff, "but feel under obligation to protect my counsel. If you please, Colonel."

"Captain O'Neill," said the commandant, turning to that officer, "order out your troop and give these conveyances ample protection from now until their return from this cattle inspection. Mr. Lovell, if you wish to be present, please ride on ahead with your men. The rest of us will proceed at once, and as soon as the escort arrives, these vehicles will bring up the rear."

As we rode away, the bugles were calling the troopers.

"That's the way to throw the gaff into them," said Sutton, when we had ridden out of hearing. "Every time they bluff, call their hand, and they'll soon get tired running blazers. I want to give notice right now that the first mark of disrespect shown me, by client or attorney, I'll slap him then and there, I don't care if he is as big as a giant. We are up against a hard crowd, and we want to meet them a little over halfway, even on a hint or insinuation. When it comes to buffaloing the opposite side, that's my long suit. The history of this case shows that the opposition has no regard for the rights of others, and it is up to us to try and teach them that a love of justice is universal. Personally, I'm nothing but a frontier lawyer from Dodge, but I'm the equal of any lobbyist that ever left Washington City."

Alkali Lake was some little distance from the post. All three of the herds were holding beyond it, a polite request having reached them to vacate the grazing-ground of the cavalry horses. Lovell still insisted that we stand aloof and give the constituted authorities a free, untrammeled hand until the inspection was over. The quartermaster and his assistants halted on approaching the first herd, and giving them a wide berth, we rode for the nearest good point of observation. The officers galloped up shortly afterward, reining in for a short conversation, but entering the first herd before the arrival of the conveyances and their escort. When the latter party arrived, the nearest one of the three herds had been passed upon, but the contractors stood on the carriage seats and attempted to look over the cordon of troopers, formed into a hollow square, which surrounded them. The troop were mounted on chestnut horses, making a pretty sight, and I think they enjoyed the folly and humor of the situation fully as much as we did. On nearing the second herd, we were met by the other boys, who had given the cattle a thorough going-over and reported finding two "Circle Dot" beeves among the opposition steers. The chances are that they had walked off a bed-ground some night while holding at Ogalalla and had been absorbed into another herd before morning. My brother announced his intention of taking them back with us, when Sponsilier taunted him with the fact that there might be objections offered.

"That'll be all right, Davy," replied Bob; "it'll take a bigger and better outfit than these pimps and tin-horns to keep me from claiming my own. You just watch and notice if those two steers don't go back with Forrest. Why, they had the nerve to question our right even to look them over. It must be a trifle dull with the GIRLS down there in Ogalalla when all these 'babies' have to turn out at work or go hungry."

Little time was lost in inspecting the last herd. The cattle were thrown entirely too close together to afford much opportunity in looking them over, and after riding through them a few times, the officers rode away for a consultation. We had kept at a distance from the convoy, perfectly contented so long as the opposition were prisoners of their own choosing. Captain O'Neill evidently understood the wishes of his superior officer, and never once were his charges allowed within hailing distance of the party of inspection. As far as exerting any influence was concerned, for that matter, all of us might have remained back at the post and received the report on the commander's return. Yet there was a tinge of uncertainty as to the result, and all concerned wanted to hear it at the earliest moment. The inspection party did not keep us long in waiting, for after a brief conference they turned and rode for the contractors under escort. We rode forward, the troop closed up in close formation about the two vehicles, and the general tension rose to that of rigidity. We halted quietly within easy hearing distance, and without noticing us the commandant addressed himself to the occupants of the conveyances, who were now standing on the seats.

"Gentlemen," said he, with military austerity, "the quality and condition of your cattle places them beyond our consideration. Beef intended for delivery at this post must arrive here with sufficient flesh to withstand the rigors of our winter. When possible to secure them, we prefer Northern wintered cattle, but if they are not available, and we are compelled to receive Southern ones, they must be of the first quality in conformation and flesh. It now becomes my duty to say to you that your beeves are rough, have been over-driven, are tender-footed and otherwise abused, and, having in view the best interests of the service, with the concurrence of my associates, I decline them."

The decision was rendered amid breathless silence. Not a word of exultation escaped one of our party, but the nervous strain rather intensified.

Mr. Y —— ——, the congressman, made the first move. Quietly alighting from the vehicle, he held a whispered conversation with his associates, very composedly turned to the commandant, and said:

"No doubt you are aware that there are higher authorities than the post commander and quartermaster of Fort Buford. This higher court to which I refer saw fit to award a contract for five million pounds of beef to be delivered at this post on foot. Any stipulations inserted or omitted in that article, the customary usages of the War Department would govern. If you will kindly look at the original contract, a copy of which is in your possession, you will notice that nothing is said about the quality of the cattle, just so the pounds avoirdupois are there. The government does not presume, when contracting for Texas cattle, that they will arrive here in perfect order; but so long as the sex, age, and weight have been complied with, there can be no evasion of the contract. My clients are sub-contractors, under an assignment of the original award, are acting in good faith in making this tender, and if your decision is against them, we will make an appeal to the War Department. I am not presuming to tell you your duty, but trust you will take this matter under full advisement before making your decision final."

"Mr. Y — , I have received cattle before without any legal advice or interference of higher authority. Although you have ignored his presence, there is another man here with a tender of beef who is entitled to more than passing consideration. He holds a sub-contract under the original award, and there is no doubt but he is also acting in good faith. My first concern as a receiving agent of this government is that the goods tendered must be of the first quality. Your cattle fall below our established standards here, while his will take rank as the finest lot of beeves ever tendered at this post, and therefore he is entitled to the award. I am not going to stand on any technicalities as to who is legally entitled to make this delivery; there have been charges and counter-charges which have reached me, the justice of which I cannot pass on, but with the cattle it is quite different. I lack but five years of being retired on my rank, the greater portion of which service has been spent on this frontier, and I feel justified in the decision made. The government buys the best, insists on its receiving agents demanding the same, and what few remaining years I serve the flag, there will be no change in my policy."

There was a hurried conference. The "major-domo" was called into the consultation, after which the congressman returned to the attack.

"Colonel, you are forcing us to make a protest to the War Department. As commander at Fort Buford, what right have you to consider the tender of any Tom, Dick, or Harry who may have cattle to sell? Armed with an assignment of the original award, we have tendered you the pounds quantity required by the existing contract, have insisted on the acceptance of the same, and if refused, our protest will be in the War Office before that sun sets. Now, my advice is — "

"I don't give a damn for you nor your advice. My reputation as a soldier is all I possess, and no man can dictate to nor intimidate me. My past record is an open book and one which I am proud of; and while I have the honor to command at Fort Buford, no threats can terrify nor cause me to deviate from my duty. Captain O'Neill, attend orders and escort these vehicles back to their quarters."

The escort loosened out, the conveyances started, and the inspection was over. We were a quiet crowd, though inwardly we all felt like shouting. We held apart from the military party, and when near the herd which held the "Circle Dot" steers, my brother and a number of the boys galloped on ahead and cut out the animals before our arrival. On entering the wagon-road near the post, the military cavalcade halted a moment for us to come up. Lovell was in the lead, and as we halted the commandant said to him: "We have decided to receive your cattle in the morning — about ten o'clock if that hour will be convenient. I may not come over, but the quartermaster's Mr. Sanders will count for us, and you cowmen ought to agree on the numbers. We have delayed you a day, and if you will put in a bill for demurrage, I will approve it. I believe that is all. We'll expect you to spend the night with us at the post. I thought it best to advise you now, so that you might give your men any final orders."

CHAPTER XXIII
KANGAROOED

Lovell and his attorneys joined the cavalcade which returned to the post, while we continued on south, fording the Missouri above Forrest's camp. The two recovered beeves were recognized by their ranch brands as belonging in Bee County, thus identifying them as having escaped from Bob Quirk's herd, though he had previously denied all knowledge of them. The cattle world was a small one, and it mattered little where an animal roamed, there was always a man near by who could identify the brand and give the bovine's past history. With the prospects bright for a new owner on the morrow, these two wayfarers found lodgment among our own for the night.

But when another day dawned, it brought new complications. Instead of the early arrival of any receiving party, the appointed hour passed, noon came, and no one appeared. I had ridden down to the lower camps about the latter hour, yet there was no one who could explain, neither had any word from the post reached Forrest's wagon. Sponsilier suggested that we ride into Buford, and accordingly all three of us foremen started. When we sighted the ford on the Missouri, a trio of horsemen were just emerging from the water, and we soon were in possession of the facts. Sanders, my brother, and Mike Sutton composed the party, and the latter explained the situation. Orders from the War Department had reached Fort Buford that morning, temporarily suspending the post commander and his quartermaster from receiving any cattle intended for that post, and giving notice that a special commissioner was then en route from Minneapolis with full authority in the premises. The order was signed by the first quartermaster and approved by the head of that department; there was no going behind it, which further showed the strength that the opposition were able to command. The little attorney was wearing his war-paint, and we all dismounted, when Sanders volunteered some valuable points on the wintering of Texas cattle in the North. Sutton made a memorandum of the data, saying if opportunity offered he would like to submit it in evidence at the final hearing. The general opinion was that a court of inquiry would be instituted, and if such was the case, our cause was not by any means hopeless.

"The chances are that the opposition will centre the fight on an assignment of the original contract which they claim to hold," said the lawyer, in conclusion. "The point was advanced yesterday that we were intruders, while, on the other hand, the government was in honor bound to recognize its outstanding obligation, no matter in whose hands it was presented, so long as it was accompanied by the proper tender. A great deal will depend on the viewpoint of this special commissioner; he may be a stickler for red tape, with no concern for the service, as were the post commander and quartermaster. Their possession of the original document will be self-evident, and it will devolve on us to show that that assignment was illegal. This may not be as easy as it seems, for the chances are that there may be a dozen men in the gang, with numerous stool-pigeons ready and willing to do their bidding. This contract may demonstrate the possibility of a ring within a ring, with everything working to the same end. The absence of Honest John Griscom at this delivery is significant as proving that his presence at Dodge and Ogalalla was a mistake. You notice, with the exception of Field and Radcliff, they are all new men. Well, another day will tell the story."

The special commissioner could not arrive before the next morning. An ambulance, with relay teams, had left the post at daybreak for Glendive, and would return that night. Since the following promised to be a decisive day, we were requested to bring every available man and report at Fort Buford at an early hour. The trio returned to the post and we foremen to our herds. My outfit received the news in anything but a cheerful mood. The monotony of the long drive had made the men restless, and the delay of a single day in being finally relieved, when looked forward to, was doubly exasperating. It had been over six months since we left the ranch in Medina, and there was a lurking suspicion among a number of the boys that the final decision would be against our cattle and that they would be thrown back on our hands. There was a general anxiety among us to go home, hastened by the recent frosty nights and a common fear of a Northern climate. I tried to stem this feeling, promising a holiday on the morrow and assuring every one that we still had a fighting chance.

We reached the post at a timely hour the next morning. Only three men were left with each herd, my wrangler and cook accompanying us for the day. Parent held forth with quite a dissertation on the legal aspects of the case, and after we forded the river, an argument arose between him and Jake Blair. "Don't talk to me about what's legal and what isn't," said the latter; "the man with the pull generally gets all that he goes after. You remember the Indian and the white man were at a loss to know how to divide the turkey and the buzzard, but in the end poor man got the buzzard. And if you'll just pay a little more attention to humanity, you may notice that the legal aspects don't cut so much figure as you thought they did. The moment that cattle declined five to seven dollars a head, The Western Supply Company didn't trouble themselves as to the legality or the right or wrong, but proceeded to take advantage of the situation at once. Neal, when you've lived about twenty-five years on the cold charity of strangers, you'll get over that blind confidence and become wary and cunning. It might be a good idea to keep your eye open to-day for your first lesson. Anyhow don't rely too strong on the right or justice of anything, but keep a good horse on picket and your powder dry."

The commissioner had arrived early that morning and would take up matters at once. Nine o'clock was set for the hearing, which would take place in the quartermaster's office. Consultations were being held among the two factions, and the only ray of light was the reported frigidity of the special officer. He was such a superior personage that ordinary mortals felt a chill radiating from his person on their slightest approach. His credentials were from the War Department and were such as to leave no doubt but that he was the autocrat of the situation, before whom all should render homage. A rigid military air prevailed about the post and grounds, quite out of the ordinary, while the officers' bar was empty and silent.

The quartermaster's office would comfortably accommodate about one hundred persons. Fort Buford had been rebuilt in 1871, the adobe buildings giving place to frame structures, and the room in which the hearing was to be held was not only commodious but furnished with good taste. Promptly on the stroke of the hour, and escorted by the post adjutant, the grand mogul made his appearance. There was nothing striking about him, except his military bearing; he was rather young and walked so erect that he actually leaned backward a trifle. There was no prelude; he ordered certain tables rearranged, seated himself at one, and called for a copy of the original contract. The post adjutant had all the papers covering the situation in hand, and the copy was placed at the disposal of the special commissioner, who merely glanced at the names of the contracting parties, amount and date, and handed the document back. Turning to the table at which Lovell and his attorneys sat, he asked for the credentials under which they were tendering beeves at Fort Buford. The sub-contract was produced, some slight memorandum was made, and it was passed back as readily as was the original. The opposition were calmly awaiting a similar request, and when it came, in offering the papers, Congressman Y — — took occasion to remark: "Our tender is not only on a sub-contract, but that agreement is fortified by an assignment of the original award, by and between the War Department and The Western Supply Company. We rely on the latter; you will find everything regular."

The customary glance was given the bulky documents. Senator Aspgrain was awaiting the opportune moment to attack the assignment. When it came, the senator arose with dignity and, addressing the commissioner, attempted to enter a protest, but was instantly stopped by that high functionary. A frozen silence pervaded the room. "There is no occasion for any remarks in this matter," austerely replied the government specialist. "Our department regularly awarded the beef contract for this post to The Western Supply Company. There was ample competition on the award, insuring the government against exorbitant prices, and the required bonds were furnished for the fulfillment of the contract. Right then and there all interest upon the part of the grantor ceased until the tender was made at this post on the appointed day of delivery. In the interim, however, it seems that for reasons purely their own, the grantees saw fit to sub-let their contract, not once but twice. Our department amply protected themselves by requiring bonds, and the sub-contractors should have done the same. That, however, is not the matter at issue, but who is entitled to deliver on the original award. Fortunately that point is beyond question; an assignment of the original has always been recognized at the War Office, and in this case the holders of the same are declared entitled to deliver. There is only one provision, — does the article of beef tendered qualify under the specifications? That is the only question before making this decision final. If there is any evidence to the contrary, I am ready to hear it."

This afforded the opportunity of using Sanders as a witness, and Sutton grasped the opportunity of calling him to testify in regard to wintering Southern cattle in the North. After stating his qualifications as a citizen and present occupation, he was asked by the commissioner regarding his experience with cattle to entitle his testimony to consideration. "I was born to the occupation in Texas," replied the witness. "Five years ago this summer I came with beef cattle from Uvalde County, that State, to this post, and after the delivery, accepted a situation under the quartermaster here in locating and holding the government's beeves. At present I am foreman and have charge of all cattle delivered at or issued from this post. I have had five years' experience in wintering Texas cattle in this vicinity, and have no hesitancy in saying that it is a matter of the utmost importance that steers should be in the best possible flesh to withstand our winters. The losses during the most favorable seasons have averaged from one to five per cent., while the same cattle in a severe season will lose from ten to twenty-five, all depending on the condition of the stock with the beginning of cold weather. Since my connection with this post we have always received good steers, and our losses have been light, but above and below this military reservation the per cent. loss has run as high as fifty among thin, weak animals."

"Now, Mr. Sanders," said the special commissioner, "as an expert, you are testifying as to the probable loss to the government in this locality in buying and holding beef on its own account. You may now state if you have seen the tender of beef made by Field, Radcliff & Co., and if so, anticipating the worst, what would be the probable loss if their cattle were accepted on this year's delivery?"

"I was present at their inspection by the officers of this post," replied the witness, "and have no hesitancy in saying that should the coming one prove as hard a winter as '82 was, there would be a loss of fully one half these cattle. At least that was my opinion as expressed to the post commander and quartermaster at the inspection, and they agreed with me. There are half a dozen other boys here whose views on wintering cattle can be had — and they're worth listening to."

This testimony was the brutal truth, and though eternal, was sadly out of place. The opposition lawyers winced; and when Sutton asked if permission would be given to hear the testimony of the post commander and quartermaster, both familiar with the quality of cattle the government had been receiving for years, the commissioner, having admitted damaging testimony, objected on the ground that they were under suspension, and military men were not considered specialists outside their own vocation. Other competent witnesses were offered and objected to, simply because they would not admit they were experts. Taking advantage of the opening, Congressman Y — — called attention to a few facts in passing. This unfortunate situation, he said, in substance, was deeply regretted by his clients and himself. The War Department was to be warmly commended for sending a special commissioner to hear the matter at issue, otherwise unjust charges might have been preferred against old and honored officers in the service. However, if specialists were to be called to testify, and their testimony considered, as to what per cent. of cattle would survive a winter, why not call on the weather prophets to testify just what the coming one would be? He ridiculed the attestations of Sanders as irrelevant, defiantly asserting that the only question at issue was, were there five million pounds of dressed beef in the tender of cattle by Field, Radcliff & Co. He insisted on the letter in the bond being observed. The government bought cattle one year with another, and assumed risks as did other people. Was there any man present to challenge his assertion that the pounds quantity had been tendered?

There was. Don Lovell arose, and addressing the special commissioner, said: "Sir, I am not giving my opinion as an expert but as a practical cowman. If the testimony of one who has delivered over ninety thousand cattle to this government, in its army and Indian departments, is of any service to you, I trust you will hear me patiently. No exception is taken to your ruling as to who is entitled to deliver on the existing award; that was expected from the first. I have been contracting beef to this government for the past fifteen years, and there may be tricks in the trade of which I am ignorant. The army has always demanded the best, while lower grades have always been acceptable to the Indian Department. But in all my experience, I have never tendered this government for its gut-eating wards as poor a lot of cattle as I am satisfied that you are going to receive at the hands of Field, Radcliff & Co. I accept the challenge that there are not five million pounds of dressed beef in their tender to-day, and what there is would be a disgrace to any commonwealth to feed its convicts. True, these cattle are not intended for immediate use, and I make the counter-assertion that this government will never kill out fifty per cent. of the weight that you accept to-day. Possibly you prefer the blandishments of a lobbyist to the opinion of a practical cowman like Sanders. That's your privilege. You refuse to allow us to show the relationship between The Western Supply Company and the present holders of its assignment, and in doing so I charge you with being in collusion with these contractors to defraud the government!"

"You're a liar!" shouted Congressman Y — — , jumping to his feet. The only reply was a chair hurled from the hand of Sutton at the head of the offender, instantly followed by a rough house. Several officers present sprang to the side of the special commissioner, but fortunately refrained from drawing revolvers. I was standing at some distance from the table, and as I made a lunge forward, old man Don was hurled backward into my arms. He could not whip a sick chicken, yet his uncontrollable anger had carried him into the general melee and he had been roughly thrown out by some of his own men. They didn't want him in the fight; they could do all that was necessary. A number of soldiers were present, and while the officers were frantically commanding them to restore order, the scrap went merrily on. Old man Don struggled with might and main, cursing me for refusing to free him, and when one of the contractors was knocked down within easy reach, I was half tempted to turn him loose. The "major-domo" had singled out Sponsilier and was trying issues with him, Bob Quirk was dropping them right and left, when the deposed commandant sprang upon a table, and in a voice like the hiss of an adder, commanded peace, and the disorder instantly ceased.

The row had lasted only a few seconds. The opposing sides stood glaring daggers at each other, when the commissioner took occasion to administer a reproof to all parties concerned, referring to Texas in not very complimentary terms. Dave Sponsilier was the only one who had the temerity to offer any reply, saying, "Mr. Yank, I'll give you one hundred dollars if you'll point me out the grave of a man, woman, or child who starved to death in that state."

A short recess was taken, after which apologies followed, and the commissioner resumed the hearing. A Western lawyer, named Lemeraux, made a very plausible plea for the immediate acceptance of the tender of Field, Radcliff & Co. He admitted that the cattle, at present, were not in as good flesh as his clients expected to offer them; that they had left the Platte River in fine condition, but had been twice quarantined en route. He was cautious in his remarks, but clearly intimated that had there been no other cattle in competition for delivery on this award, there might have been no quarantine. In his insinuations, the fact was adroitly brought out that the isolation of their herds, if not directly chargeable to Lovell and his men, had been aided and abetted by them, retarding the progress of his clients' beeves and forcing them to travel as fast as twenty-five miles a day, so that they arrived in a jaded condition. Had there been no interference, the tender of Field, Radcliff & Co. would have reached this post ten days earlier, and rest would soon have restored the cattle to their normal condition. In concluding, he boldly made the assertion that the condition of his client's tender of beef was the result of a conspiracy to injure one firm, that another drover might profit thereby; that right and justice could be conserved only by immediately making the decision final, and thus fearlessly silencing any and all imputations reflecting on the character of this government's trusted representatives.

The special commissioner assumed an air of affected dignity and announced that a conclusion had been arrived at. Turning to old man Don, he expressed the deepest regret that a civilian was beyond his power to punish, otherwise he would have cause to remember the affront offered himself; not that he personally cared, but the department of government which he had the honor to serve was jealous of its good name. Under the circumstances he could only warn him to be more guarded hereafter in choosing his language, and assured Lovell that it was in his power to escort any offender off that military reservation. Pausing a moment, he resumed a judicial air, and summed up the situation:

"There was no occasion," said he, in an amiable mood, "to refer this incident to the War Department if the authorities here had gone about their work properly. Fortunately I was in Minneapolis adjusting some flour accounts, when I was ordered here by the quartermaster-general. Instead of attempting to decide who had the best tender of cattle, the one with the legal right alone should have been considered. Our department is perfectly familiar with these petty jealousies, which usually accompany awards of this class, and generally emanate from disappointed and disgruntled competitors. The point is well taken by counsel that the government does not anticipate the unforeseen, and it matters not what the loss may be from the rigors of winter, the contractor is exempt after the day of delivery. If the cattle were delayed en route, as has been asserted, and it was necessary to make forced drives in order to reach here within the specified time, all this should be taken into consideration in arriving at a final conclusion. On his reinstatement, I shall give the quartermaster of this post instructions, in receiving these cattle, to be governed, not so much by their present condition as by what they would have been had there been no interference. Now in behalf of the War Department, I declare the award to The Western Supply Company, and assigned to Field, Radcliff, and associates, to have been fulfilled to the satisfaction of all parties concerned. This closes the incident, and if there is nothing further, the inquiry will stand adjourned without date."

"One moment, if you please," said Don Lovell, addressing the commissioner and contractors; "there is a private matter existing between Field, Radcliff & Co. and myself which demands an understanding between us. I hold a sum of money, belonging to them, as indemnity against loss in driving ten thousand cattle from Southern Texas to this post. That I will sustain a heavy loss, under your decision, is beyond question. I am indemnified to the amount of about six dollars and a half a head, and since the government is exempt from garnishment and the contractors are wholly irresponsible, I must content myself with the money in hand. To recover this amount, held as indemnity, suit has been threatened against me. Of course I can't force their hands, but I sincerely hope they will feel exultant enough over your kangaroo decision to file their action before taking their usual outing in Europe. They will have no trouble in securing my legal address, my rating can be obtained from any commercial agency, and no doubt their attorneys are aware of the statute of limitation in my state. I believe that's all, except to extend my thanks to every one about Fort Buford for the many kind attentions shown my counsel, my boys, and myself. To my enemies, I can only say that I hope to meet them on Texas soil, and will promise them a fairer hearing than was accorded me here to-day. Mr. Commissioner, I have always prided myself on being a good citizen, have borne arms in defense of my country, and in taking exception to your decision I brand you as the most despicable member of The Western Supply Company. Any man who will prostitute a trust for a money consideration — "

"That's enough!" shouted the special commissioner, rising. "Orderly, call the officer of the day, and tell him I want two companies of cavalry to furnish an escort for this man and his herds beyond the boundaries of this military reservation." Looking Lovell in the face, he said: "You have justly merited a severe punishment, and I shall report your reflections to the War and Indian departments, and you may find it more difficult to secure contracts in the future. One of you officers detail men and take charge of this man until the escort is ready. The inquiry is adjourned."

CHAPTER XXIV
THE WINTER OF OUR DISCONTENT

The inquiry was over before noon. A lieutenant detailed a few men and made a pretense of taking possession of Lovell. But once the special commissioner was out of sight, the farce was turned into an ovation, and nearly every officer in the post came forward and extended his sympathy. Old man Don was visibly affected by the generous manifestations of the military men in general, and after thanking each one personally, urged that no unnecessary demonstration should be made, begging that the order of escort beyond the boundary of the reservation be countermanded. No one present cared to suggest it, but gave assurance that it would be so modified as not in any way to interfere with the natural movement of the herds. Some little time would be required to outfit the forage-wagons to accommodate the cavalry companies, during which my brother rode up, leading Lovell's horse, permission was given to leave in advance of the escort, and we all mounted and quietly rode away.

The sudden turn of affairs had disconcerted every man in the three outfits. Just what the next move would be was conjecture with most of us, though every lad present was anxious to know. But when we were beyond the immediate grounds, Lovell turned in his saddle and asked which one of us foremen wanted to winter in the North. No one volunteered, and old man Don continued: "Anticipating the worst, I had a long talk this morning with Sanders, and he assured me that our cattle would go through any winter without serious loss. He suggested the Little Missouri as a good range, and told me of a hay ranch below the mouth of the Beaver. If it can be bought reasonably, we would have forage for our horses, and the railroad is said to be not over forty miles to the south. If the government can afford to take the risk of wintering cattle in this climate, since there is no other choice, I reckon I'll have to follow suit. Bob and I will take fresh horses and ride through to the Beaver this afternoon, and you fellows follow up leisurely with the cattle. Sanders says the winters are dry and cold, with very little if any snowfall. Well, we're simply up against it; there's no hope of selling this late in the season, and nothing is left us but to face the music of a Northern winter."

As we turned in to ford the Missouri, some one called attention to a cavalry company riding out from their quarters at the post. We halted a moment, and as the first one entered the road, the second one swung into view, followed by forage-wagons. From maps in our possession we knew the southern boundary of the Fort Buford military reservation must be under twenty miles to the south, and if necessary, we could put it behind us that afternoon. But after crossing the river, and when the two troops again came in view, they had dropped into a walk, passing entirely out of sight long before we reached Forrest's camp. Orders were left with the latter to take the lead and make a short drive that evening, at least far enough to convince observers that we were moving. The different outfits dropped out as their wagons were reached, and when my remuda was sighted, old man Don ordered it brought in for a change of horses. One of the dayherders was at camp getting dinner, and inviting themselves to join him, my employer and my brother helped themselves while their saddles were shifted to two of my well-rested mounts. Inquiry had been made of all three of the outfits if any ranch had been sighted on the Beaver while crossing that creek, but the only recollection among the forty-odd men was that of Burl Van Vedder, who contended that a dim trail, over which horses had passed that summer, ran down on the south side of the stream.

With this meagre information Lovell and my brother started. A late dinner over and the herders relieved, we all rode for the nearest eminence which would afford us a view. The cavalry were just going into camp below O'Brien's ranch, their forage-train in sight, while Forrest's cattle were well bunched and heading south. Sponsilier was evidently going to start, as his team was tied up and the saddle stock in hand, while the herd was crossing over to the eastern side of the Yellowstone. We dismounted and lay around for an hour or so, when the greater portion of the boys left to help in the watering of our herd, the remainder of us doing outpost duty. Forrest had passed out of sight, Sponsilier's wagon and remuda crossed opposite us, going up the valley, followed by his cattle in loose grazing order, and still we loitered on the hill. But towards evening I rode down to where the cavalry was encamped, and before I had conversed very long with the officers, it was clear to me that the shorter our moves the longer it would extend their outing. Before I left the soldier camp, Sanders arrived, and as we started away together, I sent him back to tell the officers to let me know any time they could use half a beef. On reaching our wagon, the boys were just corralling the saddle stock for their night-horses, when Sanders begged me to sell him two which had caught his fancy. I dared not offer them; but remembering the fellow's faithful service in our behalf, and that my employer expected to remember him, I ordered him to pick, with Don Lovell's compliments, any horse in the remuda as a present.

The proposition stunned Sanders, but I insisted that if old man Don was there, he would make him take something. He picked a good horse out of my mount and stayed until morning, when he was compelled to return, as the probabilities were that they would receive the other cattle some time during the day. After breakfast, and as he was starting to return, he said, "Well, boys, tell the old man that I don't expect ever to be able to return his kindness, though I'd ride a thousand miles for the chance. One thing sure, there isn't a man in Dakota who has money enough to tempt me to part with my pelon. If you locate down on the Little Missouri, drop me a line where you are at, and if Lovell wants four good men, I can let him have them about the first of December. You through lads are liable to be scared over the coming winter, and a few acclimated ones will put backbone in his outfit. And tell the old man that if I can ever do him a good turn just to snap his fingers and I'll quit the government — he's a few shades whiter than it, anyhow."

The herd had already left the bed-ground, headed south. About five miles above O'Brien's, we recrossed to the eastern side of the Yellowstone, and for the next three days moved short distances, the military always camped well in our rear. The fourth morning I killed a beef, a forage-wagon came forward and took half of it back to the cavalry camp with our greetings and farewell, and we parted company. Don Lovell met us about noon, elated as a boy over his purchase of the hay ranch. My brother had gone on to the railroad and thence by train to Miles City to meet his remuda and outfit. "Boys, I have bought you a new home," was the greeting of old man Don, as he dismounted at our noon camp. "There's a comfortable dugout, stabling for about ten horses, and seventy-five tons of good hay in the stack. The owner was homesick to get back to God's country, and he'll give us possession in ten days. Bob will be in Little Missouri to-day and order us a car of sacked corn from Omaha, and within a month we'll be as snug as they are down in old Medina. Bob's outfit will go home from Miles, and if he can't sell his remuda he'll bring it up here. Two of these outfits can start back in a few days, and afterward the camp will be reduced to ten men."

Two days later Forrest veered off and turned his cattle loose below the junction of the Beaver with the Little Missouri. Sponsilier crossed the former, scattering his beeves both up and down the latter, while I cut mine into a dozen bunches and likewise freed them along the creek. The range was about ten miles in length along the river, and a camp was established at either end where men would be stationed until the beeves were located. The commissaries had run low, there was a quiet rivalry as to which outfits should go home, and we all waited with bated breath for the final word. I had Dorg Seay secretly inform my employer that I had given Sanders a horse without his permission, hoping that it might displease him. But the others pointed out the fact that my outfit had far the best remuda, and that it would require well-mounted men to locate and hold that number of cattle through the winter. Old man Don listened to them all, and the next morning, as all three of us foremen were outlining certain improvements about the hay ranch with him, he turned to me and said:

"Tom, I hear you gave Sanders a horse. Well, that was all right, although it strikes me you were rather liberal in giving him the pick of a choice remuda. But it may all come right in the long run, as Bob and I have decided to leave you and your outfit to hold these cattle this winter. So divide your men and send half of them down to Quince's camp, and have your cook and wrangler come over to Dave's wagon to bring back provision and the horses, as we'll start for the railroad in the morning. I may not come back, but Bob will, and he'll see that you are well fixed for the winter before he goes home. After he leaves, I want you to write me every chance you have to send a letter to the railroad. Now, I don't want any grumbling out of you or your men; you're a disgrace to the state that raised you if you can't handle cattle anywhere that any other man can."

I felt all along it would fall to me, the youngest of six foremen; and my own dear brother consigning me to a winter in the North, while he would bask in the sunshine of our own sunny South! It was hard to face; but I remembered that the fall before it had been my lot to drive a thousand saddle horses home to the ranch, and that I had swaggered as a trail foreman afterward as the result. It had always been my luck to have to earn every little advance or promotion, while others seemed to fall into them without any effort. Bob Quirk never saw the day that he was half the all-round cowman that I was; yet he was above me and could advise, and I had to obey.

On the morning of the 25th of September, 1884, the two outfits started for the railroad, leaving the remainder of us in a country, save for the cattle, so desolate that there was no chance even to spend our wages. I committed to memory a curtain lecture for my brother, though somehow or other it escaped me and was never delivered. We rode lines between the upper and lower wagons, holding the cattle loosely on a large range. A delightful fall favored us, and before the first squall of winter came on, the beeves had contented themselves as though they had been born on the Little Missouri. Meanwhile Bob's wagon and remuda arrived, the car of corn was hauled to our headquarters, extra stabling was built, and we settled down like banished exiles. Communication had been opened with Fort Buford, and in the latter part of October the four promised men arrived, when Bob Quirk took part of my outfit and went home, leaving me ten men. Parent remained as cook, the new men assimilated easily, a fiddle was secured, and in fulfillment of the assertion of Sanders, we picked up courage. Two grain-fed horses, carefully stabled, were allowed to each man, the remainder of our large number of saddle stock running free on the range.

To that long winter on the Little Missouri a relentless memory turns in retrospect. We dressed and lived like Eskimos. The first blizzard struck us early in December, the thermometer dropped sixty degrees in twelve hours, but in the absence of wind and snow the cattle did not leave the breaks along the river. Three weeks later a second one came, and we could not catch the lead animals until near the railroad; but the storm drove them up the Little Missouri, and its sheltering banks helped us to check our worst winter drift. After the first month of wintry weather, the dread of the cold passed, and men and horses faced the work as though it was springtime in our own loved southland. The months rolled by scarcely noticed. During fine weather Sanders and some of his boys twice dropped down for a few days, but we never left camp except to send letters home.

An early spring favored us. I was able to report less than one per cent. loss on the home range, with the possibility of but few cattle having escaped us during the winter. The latter part of May we sold four hundred saddle horses to some men from the upper Yellowstone. Early in June a wagon was rigged out, extra men employed, and an outfit sent two hundred miles up the Little Missouri to attend the round-ups. They were gone a month and came in with less than five hundred beeves, which represented our winter drift. Don Lovell reached the ranch during the first week in July. One day's ride through the splendid cattle, and old man Don lost his voice, but the smile refused to come off. Everything was coming his way. Field, Radcliff & Co. had sued him, and the jury awarded him one-hundred thousand dollars. His bankers had unlimited confidence in his business ability; he had four Indian herds on the trail and three others of younger steers, intended for the Little Missouri ranch. Cattle prices in Texas had depreciated nearly one half since the spring before — "a good time for every cowman to strain his credit and enlarge his holdings," my employer assured me.

Orders were left that I was to begin shipping out the beeves early in August. It was the intention to ship them in two and three train-load lots, and I was expecting to run a double outfit, when a landslide came our way. The first train-load netted sixty dollars a head at Omaha — but they were beeves; cods like an ox's heart and waddled as they walked. We had just returned from the railroad with the intention of shipping two train-loads more, when the quartermaster and Sanders from Fort Buford rode into the ranch under an escort. The government had lost forty per cent. of the Field-Radcliff cattle during the winter just passed, and were in the market to buy the deficiency. The quartermaster wanted a thousand beeves on the first day of September and October each, and double that number for the next month. Did we care to sell that amount? A United States marshal, armed with a search-warrant, could not have found Don Lovell in a month, but they were promptly assured that our beef steers were for sale. It is easy to show prime cattle. The quartermaster, Sanders, and myself rode down the river, crossed over and came up beyond our camp, forded back and came down the Beaver, and I knew the sale was made. I priced the beeves, delivered at Buford, at sixty-five dollars a head, and the quartermaster took them.

Then we went to work in earnest. Sanders remained to receive the first contingent for Buford, which would leave our range on the 25th of each month. A single round-up and we had the beeves in hand. The next morning after Splann left for the mouth of the Yellowstone, I started south for the railroad with two train-loads of picked cattle. Professional shippers took them off our hands at the station, accompanied them en route to market, and the commission house in Omaha knew where to remit the proceeds. The beef shipping season was on with a vengeance. Our saddle stock had improved with a winter in the North, until one was equal to two Southern or trail horses. Old man Don had come on in the mean time, and was so pleased with my sale to the army post that he returned to Little Missouri Station at once and bought two herds of three-year-olds at Ogalalla by wire. This made sixteen thousand steer cattle en route from the latter point for Lovell's new ranch in Dakota.

"Tom," said old man Don, enthusiastically, "this is the making of a fine cattle ranch, and we want to get in on the flood-tide. There is always a natural wealth in a new country, and the goldmines of this one are in its grass. The instinct that taught the buffalo to choose this as their summer and winter range was unerring, and they found a grass at hand that would sustain them in any and all kinds of weather. This country to-day is just what Texas was thirty years ago. All the early settlers at home grew rich without any effort, but once the cream of the virgin land is gone, look out for a change. The early cowmen of Texas flatter themselves on being shrewd and far-seeing — just about as much as I was last fall, when I would gladly have lost twenty-five thousand dollars rather than winter these cattle. Now look where I will come out, all due to the primitive wealth of the land. From sixty to sixty-five dollars a head beats thirty-seven and a half for our time and trouble."

The first of the through cattle arrived early in September. They avoided our range for fear of fever, and dropped in about fifteen miles below our headquarters on the Little Missouri. Dorg Seay was one of the three foremen, Forrest and Sponsilier being the other two, having followed the same route as our herds of the year before. But having spent a winter in the North, we showed the through outfits a chilling contempt. I had ribbed up Parent not even to give them a pleasant word about our wagon or headquarters; and particularly if Bob Quirk came through with one of the purchased herds, he was to be given the marble heart. One outfit loose-herded the new cattle, the other two going home, and about the middle of the month, my brother and The Rebel came trailing in with the last two herds. I was delighted to meet my old bunkie, and had him remain over until the last outfit went home, when we reluctantly parted company. Not so, however, with Bob Quirk, who haughtily informed me that he came near slapping my cook for his effrontery. "So you are another one of these lousy through outfits that think we ought to make a fuss over you, are you?" I retorted. "Just you wait until we do. Every one of you except old Paul had the idea that we ought to give you a reception and ask you to sleep in our beds. I'm glad that Parent had the gumption to give you a mean look; he'll ride for me next year."

The month of October finished the shipping. There was a magic in that Northern climate that wrought wonders in an animal from the South. Little wonder that the buffalo could face the blizzard, in a country of his own choosing, and in a climate where the frost king held high revel five months out of the twelve. There was a tonic like the iron of wine in the atmosphere, absorbed alike by man and beast, and its possessor laughed at the fury of the storm. Our loss of cattle during the first winter, traceable to season, was insignificant, while we sold out over two hundred head more than the accounts called for, due to the presence of strays, which went to Buford. And when the last beef was shipped, the final delivery concluded to the army, Don Lovell was a quarter-million dollars to the good, over and above the contract price at which he failed to deliver the same cattle to the government the fall before.

As foreman of Lovell's beef ranch on the Little Missouri I spent five banner years of my life. In '89 the stock, good-will, and range were sold to a cattle syndicate, who installed a superintendent and posted rules for the observance of its employees. I do not care to say why, but in a stranger's hands it never seemed quite the same home to a few of us who were present when it was transformed into a cattle range. Late that fall, some half-dozen of us who were from Texas asked to be relieved and returned to the South. A traveler passing through that country to-day will hear the section about the mouth of the Beaver called only by the syndicate name, but old-timers will always lovingly refer to it as the Don Lovell Ranch.

Reed Anthony, Cowman: An Autobiography

CHAPTER I
IN RETROSPECT

I can truthfully say that my entire life has been spent with cattle. Even during my four years' service in the Confederate army, the greater portion was spent with the commissary department, in charge of its beef supplies. I was wounded early in the second year of the war and disabled as a soldier, but rather than remain at home I accepted a menial position under a quartermaster. Those were strenuous times. During Lee's invasion of Pennsylvania we followed in the wake of the army with over a thousand cattle, and after Gettysburg we led the retreat with double that number. Near the close of the war we frequently had no cattle to hold, and I became little more than a camp-follower.

I was born in the Shenandoah Valley, northern Virginia, May 3, 1840. My father was a thrifty planter and stockman, owned a few slaves, and as early as I can remember fed cattle every winter for the eastern markets. Grandfather Anthony, who died before I was born, was a Scotchman who had emigrated to the Old Dominion at an early day, and acquired several large tracts of land on an affluent of the Shenandoah. On my paternal side I never knew any of my ancestors, but have good cause to believe they were adventurers. My mother's maiden name was Reed; she was of a gentle family, who were able to trace their forbears beyond the colonial days, even to the gentry of England. Generations of good birth were reflected in my mother; and across a rough and eventful life I can distinctly remember the refinement of her manners, her courtesy to guests, her kindness to child and slave.

My boyhood days were happy ones. I attended a subscription school several miles from home, riding back and forth on a pony. The studies were elementary, and though I never distinguished myself in my classes, I was always ready to race my pony, and never refused to play truant when the swimming was good. Evidently my father never intended any of his boys for a professional career, though it was an earnest hope of my mother that all of us should receive a college education. My elder brother and I early developed business instincts, buying calves and accompanying our father on his trading expeditions. Once during a vacation, when we were about twelve and ten years old, both of us crossed the mountains with him into what is now West Virginia, where he bought about two hundred young steers and drove them back to our home in the valley. I must have been blessed with an unfailing memory; over fifty years have passed since that, my first trip from home, yet I remember it vividly — can recall conversations between my father and the sellers as they haggled over the cattle. I remember the money, gold and silver, with which to pay for the steers, was carried by my father in ordinary saddle-bags thrown across his saddle. As occasion demanded, frequently the funds were carried by a negro man of ours, and at night, when among acquaintances, the heavy saddle-bags were thrown into a corner, every one aware of their contents.

But the great event of my boyhood was a trip to Baltimore. There was no railroad at the time, and as that was our market for fat cattle, it was necessary to drive the entire way. My father had made the trip yearly since I could remember, the distance being nearly two hundred miles, and generally carrying as many as one hundred and fifty big beeves. They traveled slowly, pasturing or feeding grain on the way, in order that the cattle should arrive at the market in salable condition. One horse was allowed with the herd, and on another my father rode, far in advance, to engage pasture or feed and shelter for his men. When on the road a boy always led a gentle ox in the lead of the beeves; negro men walked on either flank, and the horseman brought up the rear. I used to envy the boy leading the ox, even though he was a darky. The negro boys on our plantation always pleaded with "Mars" John, my father, for the privilege; and when one of them had made the trip to Baltimore as a toll boy he easily outranked us younger whites. I must have made application for the position when I was about seven years old, for it seemed an age before my request was granted. My brother, only two years older than I, had made the trip twice, and when I was twelve the great opportunity came. My father had nearly two hundred cattle to go to market that year, and the start was made one morning early in June.

I can distinctly see my mother standing on the veranda of our home as I led the herd by with a big red ox, trembling with fear that at the final moment her permission might be withdrawn and that I should have to remain behind. But she never interfered with my father, who took great pains to teach his boys everything practical in the cattle business.

It took us twenty days to reach Baltimore. We always started early in the morning, allowing the beeves to graze and rest along the road, and securing good pastures for them at night. Several times it rained, making the road soft, but I stripped off my shoes and took it barefooted through the mud. The lead ox was a fine, big fellow, each horn tipped with a brass knob, and he and I set the pace, which was scarcely that of a snail. The days were long, I grew desperately hungry between meals, and the novelty of leading that ox soon lost its romance. But I was determined not to show that I was tired or hungry, and frequently, when my father was with us and offered to take me up behind him on his horse, I spurned his offer and trudged on till the end of the day. The mere driving of the beeves would have been monotonous, but the constant change of scene kept us in good spirits, and our darkies always crooned old songs when the road passed through woodlands. After the beeves were marketed we spent a day in the city, and my father took my brother and me to the theatre. Although the world was unfolding rather rapidly for a country boy of twelve, it was with difficulty that I was made to understand that what we had witnessed on the stage was but mimicry.

The third day after reaching the city we started on our return. The proceeds from the sale of the cattle were sent home by boat. With only two horses, each of which carried double, and walking turn about, we reached home in seven days, settling all bills on the way. That year was a type of others until I was eighteen, at which age I could guess within twenty pounds of the weight of any beef on foot, and when I bought calves and yearling steers I knew just what kind of cattle they would make at maturity. In the mean time, one summer my father had gone west as far as the State of Missouri, traveling by boat to Jefferson City, and thence inland on horseback. Several of our neighbors had accompanied him, all of them buying land, my father securing four sections. I had younger brothers growing up, and the year my oldest brother attained his majority my father outfitted him with teams, wagons, and two trusty negro men, and we started for the nearest point on the Ohio River, our destination being the new lands in the West. We embarked on the first boat, drifting down the Ohio, and up the other rivers, reaching the Ultima Thule of our hopes within a month. The land was new; I liked it; we lived on venison and wild turkeys, and when once we had built a log house and opened a few fields, we were at peace with the earth.

But this happy existence was of short duration. Rumors of war reached us in our western elysium, and I turned my face homeward, as did many another son of Virginia. My brother was sensible enough to remain behind on the new farm; but with nothing to restrain me I soon found myself in St. Louis. There I met kindred spirits, eager for the coming fray, and before attaining my majority I was bearing arms and wearing the gray of the Confederacy. My regiment saw very little service during the first year of the war, as it was stationed in the western division, but early in 1862 it was engaged in numerous actions.

I shall never forget my first glimpse of the Texas cavalry. We had moved out from Corinth, under cover of darkness, to attack Grant at Pittsburg Landing. When day broke, orders were given to open out and allow the cavalry to pass ahead and reconnoitre our front. I had always felt proud of Virginian horsemanship, but those Texans were in a class by themselves. Centaur-like they sat their horses, and for our amusement, while passing at full gallop, swung from their saddles and picked up hats and handkerchiefs. There was something about the Texans that fascinated me, and that Sunday morning I resolved, if spared, to make Texas my future home. I have good cause to remember the battle of Shiloh, for during the second day I was twice wounded, yet saved from falling into the enemy's hands.

My recovery was due to youth and a splendid constitution. Within six weeks I was invalided home, and inside a few months I was assigned to the commissary department with the army in Virginia. It was while in the latter service that I made the acquaintance of many Texans, from whom I learned a great deal about the resources of their State, — its immense herds of cattle, the cheapness of its lands, and its perpetual summer. During the last year of the war, on account of their ability to handle cattle, a number of Texans were detailed to care for the army's beef supply. From these men I received much information and a pressing invitation to accompany them home, and after the parole at Appomattox I took their address, promising to join them in the near future. On my return to the old homestead I found the place desolate, with burnt barns and fields laid waste. The Shenandoah Valley had experienced war in its dread reality, for on every hand were the charred remains of once splendid homes. I had little hope that the country would ever recover, but my father, stout-hearted as ever, had already begun anew, and after helping him that summer and fall I again drifted west to my brother's farm.

The war had developed a restless, vagabond spirit in me. I had little heart to work, was unsettled as to my future, and, to add to my other troubles, after reaching Missouri one of my wounds reopened. In the mean time my brother had married, and had a fine farm opened up. He offered me every encouragement and assistance to settle down to the life of a farmer; but I was impatient, worthless, undergoing a formative period of early manhood, even spurning the advice of father, mother, and dearest friends. If to-day, across the lapse of years, the question were asked what led me from the bondage of my discontent, it would remain unanswered. Possibly it was the advantage of good birth; surely the prayers of a mother had always followed me, and my feet were finally led into the paths of industry. Since that day of uncertainty, grandsons have sat upon my knee, clamoring for a story about Indians, the war, or cattle trails. If I were to assign a motive for thus leaving a tangible record of my life, it would be that my posterity — not the present generation, absorbed in its greed of gain, but a more distant and a saner one — should be enabled to glean a faint idea of one of their forbears. A worthy and secondary motive is to give an idea of the old West and to preserve from oblivion a rapidly vanishing type of pioneers.

My personal appearance can be of little interest to coming generations, but rather what I felt, saw, and accomplished. It was always a matter of regret to me that I was such a poor shot with a pistol. The only two exceptions worthy of mention were mere accidents. In my boyhood's home, in Virginia, my father killed yearly a large number of hogs for the household needs as well as for supplying our slave families with bacon. The hogs usually ran in the woods, feeding and thriving on the mast, but before killing time we always baited them into the fields and finished their fattening with peas and corn. It was customary to wait until the beginning of winter, or about the second cold spell, to butcher, and at the time in question there were about fifty large hogs to kill. It was a gala event with us boys, the oldest of whom were allowed to shoot one or more with a rifle. The hogs had been tolled into a small field for the killing, and towards the close of the day a number of them, having been wounded and requiring a second or third shot, became cross. These subsequent shots were usually delivered from a six-shooter, and in order to have it at hand in case of a miss I was intrusted with carrying the pistol. There was one heavy-tusked five-year-old stag among the hogs that year who refused to present his head for a target, and took refuge in a brier thicket. He was left until the last, when we all sallied out to make the final kill. There were two rifles, and had the chance come to my father, I think he would have killed him easily; but the opportunity came to a neighbor, who overshot, merely causing a slight wound. The next instant the stag charged at me from the cover of the thickety fence corner. Not having sense enough to take to the nearest protection, I turned and ran like a scared wolf across the field, the hog following me like a hound. My father risked a running shot, which missed its target. The darkies were yelling, "Run, chile! Run, Mars' Reed! Shoot! Shoot!" when it occurred to me that I had a pistol; and pointing it backward as I ran, I blazed away, killing the big fellow in his tracks.

The other occasion was years afterward, when I was a trail foreman at Abilene, Kansas. My herd had arrived at that market in bad condition, gaunted from almost constant stampedes at night, and I had gone into camp some distance from town to quiet and recuperate them. That day I was sending home about half my men, had taken them to the depot with our wagon, and intended hauling back a load of supplies to my camp. After seeing the boys off I hastened about my other business, and near the middle of the afternoon started out of town. The distance to camp was nearly twenty miles, and with a heavy load, principally salt, I knew it would be after nightfall when I reached there. About five miles out of town there was a long, gradual slope to climb, and I had to give the through team their time in pulling to its summit. Near the divide was a small box house, the only one on the road if I remember rightly, and as I was nearing it, four or five dogs ran out and scared my team. I managed to hold them in the road, but they refused to quiet down, kicking, rearing, and plunging in spite of their load; and once as they jerked me forward, I noticed there was a dog or two under the wagon, nipping at their heels. There was a six-shooter lying on the seat beside me, and reaching forward I fired it downward over the end gate of the wagon. By the merest accident I hit a dog, who raised a cry, and the last I saw of him he was spinning like a top and howling like a wolf. I quieted the team as soon as possible, and as I looked back, there was a man and woman pursuing me, the latter in the lead. I had gumption enough to know that they were the owners of the dog, and whipped up the horses in the hope of getting away from them. But the grade and the load were against me, and the next thing I knew, a big, bony woman, with fire in her eye, was reaching for me. The wagon wheel warded her off, and I leaned out of her reach to the far side, yet she kept abreast of me, constantly calling for her husband to hurry up. I was pouring the whip into the horses, fearful lest she would climb into the wagon, when the hub of the front wheel struck her on the knee, knocking her down. I was then nearing the summit of the divide, and on reaching it, I looked back and saw the big woman giving her husband the pommeling that was intended for me. She was altogether too near me yet, and I shook the lines over the horses, firing a few shots to frighten them, and we tore down the farther slope like a fire engine.

There are two events in my life that this chronicle will not fully record. One of them is my courtship and marriage, and the other my connection with a government contract with the Indian department. Otherwise my life shall be as an open book, not only for my own posterity, but that he who runs may read. It has been a matter of observation with me that a plain man like myself scarcely ever refers to his love affairs. At my time of life, now nearing my alloted span, I have little sympathy with the great mass of fiction which exploits the world-old passion. In no sense of the word am I a well-read man, yet I am conscious of the fact that during my younger days the love story interested me; but when compared with the real thing, the transcript is usually a poor one. My wife and I have now walked up and down the paths of life for over thirty-five years, and, if memory serves me right, neither one of us has ever mentioned the idea of getting a divorce. In youth we shared our crust together; children soon blessed and brightened our humble home, and to-day, surrounded by every comfort that riches can bestow, no achievement in life has given me such great pleasure, I know no music so sweet, as the prattle of my own grandchildren. Therefore that feature of my life is sacred, and will not be disclosed in these pages.

I would omit entirely mention of the Indian contract, were it not that old friends may read this, my biography, and wonder at the omission. I have no apologies to offer for my connection with the transaction, as its true nature was concealed from me in the beginning, and a scandal would have resulted had I betrayed friends. Then again, before general amnesty was proclaimed I was debarred from bidding on the many rich government contracts for cattle because I had served in the Confederate army. Smarting under this injustice at the time the Indian contract was awarded, I question if I was thoroughly *reconstructed*. Before our disabilities were removed, we ex-Confederates could do all the work, run all the risk, turn in all the cattle in filling the outstanding contracts, but the middleman got the profits. The contract in question was a blanket one, requiring about fifty thousand cows for delivery at some twenty Indian agencies. The use of my name was all that was required of me, as I was the only cowman in the entire ring. My duty was to bid on the contract; the bonds would be furnished by my partners, of which I must have had a dozen. The proposals called for sealed bids, in the usual form, to be in the hands of the Department of the Interior before noon on a certain day, marked so and so, and to be opened at high noon a week later. The contract was a large one, the competition was ample. Several other Texas drovers besides myself had submitted bids; but they stood no show — *I had been furnished the figures of every competitor.* The ramifications of the ring of which I was the mere figure-head can be readily imagined. I sublet the contract to the next lowest bidder, who delivered the cattle, and we got a rake-off of a clean hundred thousand dollars. Even then there was little in the transaction for me, as it required too many people to handle it, and none of them stood behind the door at the final "divvy." In a single year I have since cleared twenty times what my interest amounted to in that contract and have done honorably by my fellowmen. That was my first, last, and only connection with a transaction that would need deodorizing if one described the details.

But I have seen life, have been witness to its poetry and pathos, have drunk from the cup of sorrow and rejoiced as a strong man to run a race. I have danced all night where wealth and beauty mingled, and again under the stars on a battlefield I have helped carry a stretcher when the wails of the wounded on every hand were like the despairing cries of lost souls. I have seen an old demented man walking the streets of a city, picking up every scrap of paper and scanning it carefully to see if a certain ship had arrived at port — a ship which had been lost at sea over forty years before, and aboard of which were his wife and children. I was once under the necessity of making a payment of twenty-five thousand dollars in silver at an Indian village. There were no means of transportation, and I was forced to carry the specie in on eight pack mules. The distance was nearly two hundred miles, and as we neared the encampment we were under the necessity of crossing a shallow river. It was summer-time, and as we halted the tired mules to loosen the lash ropes, in order to allow them to drink, a number of Indian children of both sexes, who were bathing in the river, gathered naked on either embankment in bewilderment at such strange intruders. In the innocence of these children of the wild there was no doubt inspiration for a poet; but our mission was a commercial one, and we relashed the mules and hurried into the village with the rent money.

I have never kept a diary. One might wonder that the human mind could contain such a mass of incident and experiences as has been my portion, yet I can remember the day and date of occurrences of fifty years ago. The scoldings of my father, the kind words of an indulgent mother, when not over five years of age, are vivid in my memory as I write to-day. It may seem presumptuous, but I can give the year and date of starting, arrival, and delivery of over one hundred herds of cattle which I drove over the trail as a common hand, foreman, or owner. Yet the warnings of years — the unsteady step, easily embarrassed, love of home and dread of leaving it — bid me hasten these memoirs. Even my old wounds act as a barometer in foretelling the coming of storms, as well as the change of season, from both of which I am comfortably sheltered. But as I look into the inquiring eyes of a circle of grandchildren, all anxious to know my life story, it seems to sweeten the task, and I am encouraged to go on with the work.

CHAPTER II
MY APPRENTICESHIP

During the winter of 1865-66 I corresponded with several of my old comrades in Texas. Beyond a welcome which could not be questioned, little encouragement was, with one exception, offered me among my old friends. It was a period of uncertainty throughout the South, yet a cheerful word reached me from an old soldier crony living some distance west of Fort Worth on the Brazos River. I had great confidence in my former comrade, and he held out a hope, assuring me that if I would come, in case nothing else offered, we could take his ox teams the next winter and bring in a cargo of buffalo robes. The plains to the westward of Fort Griffin, he wrote, were swarming with buffalo, and wages could be made in killing them for their hides. This caught my fancy and I was impatient to start at once; but the healing of my reopened wound was slow, and it was March before I started. My brother gave me a good horse and saddle, twenty-five dollars in gold, and I started through a country unknown to me personally. Southern Missouri had been in sympathy with the Confederacy, and whatever I needed while traveling through that section was mine for the asking. I avoided the Indian Territory until I reached Fort Smith, where I rested several days with an old comrade, who gave me instructions and routed me across the reservation of the Choctaw Indians, and I reached Paris, Texas, without mishap.

I remember the feeling that I experienced while being ferried across Red River. That watercourse was the northern boundary of Texas, and while crossing it I realized that I was leaving home and friends and entering a country the very name of which to the outside world was a synonym for crime and outlawry. Yet some of as good men as ever it was my pleasure to know came from that State, and undaunted I held a true course for my destination. I was disappointed on seeing Fort Worth, a straggling village on the Trinity River, and, merely halting to feed my mount, passed on. I had a splendid horse and averaged thirty to forty miles a day when traveling, and early in April reached the home of my friend in Paolo Pinto County. The primitive valley of the Brazos was enchanting, and the hospitality of the Edwards ranch was typical of my own Virginia. George Edwards, my crony, was a year my junior, a native of the State, his parents having moved west from Mississippi the year after Texas won her independence from Mexico. The elder Edwards had moved to his present home some fifteen years previous, carrying with him a stock of horses and cattle, which had increased until in 1866 he was regarded as one of the substantial ranchmen in the Brazos valley. The ranch house was a stanch one, built at a time when defense was to be considered as well as comfort, and was surrounded by fine cornfields. The only drawback I could see there was that there was no market for anything, nor was there any money in the country. The consumption of such a ranch made no impression on the increase of its herds, which grew to maturity with no demand for the surplus.

I soon became impatient to do something. George Edwards had likewise lost four years in the army, and was as restless as myself. He knew the country, but the only employment in sight for us was as teamsters with outfits, freighting government supplies to Fort Griffin. I should have jumped at the chance of driving oxen, for I was anxious to stay in the country, and suggested to George that we ride up to Griffin. But the family interposed, assuring us that there was no occasion for engaging in such menial work, and we folded our arms obediently, or rode the range under the pretense of looking after the cattle. I might as well admit right here that my anxiety to get away from the Edwards ranch was fostered by the presence of several sisters of my former comrade. Miss Gertrude was only four years my junior, a very dangerous age, and in spite of all resolutions to the contrary, I felt myself constantly slipping. Nothing but my poverty and the hopelessness of it kept me from falling desperately in love.

But a temporary relief came during the latter part of May. Reports came down the river that a firm of drovers were putting up a herd of cattle for delivery at Fort Sumner, New Mexico. Their headquarters were at Belknap, a long day's ride above, on the Brazos; and immediately, on receipt of the news, George and I saddled, and started up the river. The elder Edwards was very anxious to sell his beef-cattle and a surplus of cow-horses, and we were commissioned to

401

offer them to the drovers at prevailing prices. On arriving at Belknap we met the pioneer drover of Texas, Oliver Loving, of the firm of Loving & Goodnight, but were disappointed to learn that the offerings in making up the herd were treble the drover's requirements; neither was there any chance to sell horses. But an application for work met with more favor. Mr. Loving warned us of the nature of the country, the dangers to be encountered, all of which we waived, and were accordingly employed at forty dollars a month in gold. The herd was to start early in June. George Edwards returned home to report, but I was immediately put to work, as the junior member of the firm was then out receiving cattle. They had established a camp, and at the time of our employment were gathering beef steers in Loving's brand and holding the herd as it arrived, so that I was initiated into my duties at once.

I was allowed to retain my horse, provided he did his share of the work. A mule and three range horses were also allotted to me, and I was cautioned about their care. There were a number of saddle mules in the remuda, and Mr. Loving explained that the route was through a dry country, and that experience had taught him that a mule could withstand thirst longer than a horse. I was a new man in the country, and absorbed every word and idea as a sponge does water. With the exception of roping, I made a hand from the start. The outfit treated me courteously, there was no concealment of my past occupation, and I soon had the friendship of every man in the camp. It was some little time before I met the junior partner, Charlie Goodnight, a strapping young fellow of about thirty, who had served all through the war in the frontier battalion of Texas Rangers. The Comanche Indians had been a constant menace on the western frontier of the State, and during the rebellion had allied themselves with the Federal side, and harassed the settlements along the border. It required a regiment of mounted men to patrol the frontier from Red River to the coast, as the Comanches claimed the whole western half of the State as their hunting grounds.

Early in June the herd began to assume its required numbers. George Edwards returned, and we naturally became bunkies, sharing our blankets and having the same guard on night-herd. The drovers encouraged all the men employed to bring along their firearms, and when we were ready to start the camp looked like an arsenal. I had a six-shooter, and my bunkie brought me a needle-gun from the ranch, so that I felt armed for any emergency. Each of the men had a rifle of some make or other, while a few of them had as many as four pistols, — two in their belts and two in saddle holsters. It looked to me as if this was to be a military expedition, and I began to wonder if I had not had enough war the past few years, but kept quiet. The start was made June 10, 1866, from the Brazos River, in what is now Young County, the herd numbering twenty-two hundred big beeves. A chuck-wagon, heavily loaded with supplies and drawn by six yoke of fine oxen, a remuda of eighty-five saddle horses and mules, together with seventeen men, constituted the outfit. Fort Sumner lay to the northwest, and I was mildly surprised when the herd bore off to the southwest. This was explained by young Goodnight, who was in charge of the herd, saying that the only route then open or known was on our present course to the Pecos River, and thence up that stream to our destination.

Indian sign was noticed a few days after starting. Goodnight and Loving both read it as easily as if it had been print, — the abandoned camps, the course of arrival and departure, the number of horses, indicating who and what they were, war or hunting parties — everything apparently simple and plain as an alphabet to these plainsmen. Around the camp-fire at night the chronicle of the Comanche tribe for the last thirty years was reviewed, and their overbearing and defiant attitude towards the people of Texas was discussed, not for my benefit, as it was common history. Then for the first time I learned that the Comanches had once mounted ten thousand warriors, had frequently raided the country to the coast, carrying off horses and white children, even dictating their own terms of peace to the republic of Texas. At the last council, called for the purpose of negotiating for the return of captive white children in possession of the Comanches, the assembly had witnessed a dramatic termination. The same indignity had been offered before, and borne by the whites, too weak to resist the numbers of the Comanche tribe. In this latter instance, one of the war chiefs, in spurning the remuneration offered for the return of a certain white girl, haughtily walked into the centre of the council, where an insult could be seen by all. His act, a disgusting one, was anticipated, as it was not the first time it had been witnessed, when one of the Texans present drew a six-shooter and killed the chief in the act. The hatchet of the Comanche was instantly dug up, and had not been buried at the time we were crossing a country claimed by him as his hunting ground.

Yet these drovers seemed to have no fear of an inferior race. We held our course without a halt, scarcely a day passing without seeing more or less fresh sign of Indians. After crossing the South Fork of the Brazos, we were attacked one morning just at dawn, the favorite hour of the Indian for a surprise. Four men were on herd with the cattle and one near by with the remuda, our night horses all securely tied to the wagon wheels. A feint attack was made on the commissary, but under the leadership of Goodnight a majority of us scrambled into our saddles and rode to the rescue of the remuda, the chief objective of the surprise. Two of the boys from the herd had joined the horse wrangler, and on our arrival all three were wickedly throwing lead at the circling Indians. The remuda was running at the time, and as we cut through between it and the savages we gave them the benefit of our rifles and six-shooter in passing. The shots turned the saddle stock back towards our camp and the mounted braves continued on their course, not willing to try issues with us, although they outnumbered us three to one. A few arrows had imbedded themselves in the ground around camp at the first assault, but once our rifles were able to distinguish an object clearly, the Indians kept well out of reach. The cattle made a few surges, but once the remuda was safe, there was an abundance of help in holding them, and they quieted down before sunrise. The Comanches had no use for cattle, except to kill and torture them, as they preferred the flesh of the buffalo, and once our saddle stock and the contents of the wagon were denied them, they faded into the dips of the plain.

The journey was resumed without the delay of an hour. Our first brush with the noble red man served a good purpose, as we were doubly vigilant thereafter whenever there was cause to expect an attack. There was an abundance of water, as we followed up the South Fork and its tributaries, passing through Buffalo Gap, which was afterward a well-known landmark on the Texas and Montana cattle trail. Passing over the divide between the waters of the Brazos and Concho, we struck the old Butterfield stage route, running by way of Fort Concho to El Paso, Texas, on the Rio Grande. This stage road was the original Staked Plain, surveyed and located by General John Pope in 1846. The route was originally marked by stakes, until it became a thoroughfare, from which the whole of northwest Texas afterward took its name. There was a ninety-six mile dry drive between the headwaters of the Concho and Horsehead Crossing on the Pecos, and before attempting it we rested a few days. Here Indians made a second attack on us, and although as futile as the first, one of the horse wranglers received an arrow in the shoulder. In attempting to remove it the shaft separated from the steel arrowhead, leaving the latter imbedded in the lad's shoulder. We were then one hundred and twelve miles distant from Fort Concho, the nearest point where medical relief might be expected. The drovers were alarmed for the man's welfare; it was impossible to hold the herd longer, so the young fellow volunteered to make the ride alone. He was given the best horse in the remuda, and with the falling of darkness started for Fort Concho. I had the pleasure of meeting him afterward, as happy as he was hale and hearty.

The start across the arid stretch was made at noon. Every hoof had been thoroughly watered in advance, and with the heat of summer on us it promised to be an ordeal to man and beast. But Loving had driven it before, and knew fully what was before him as we trailed out under a noonday sun. An evening halt was made for refreshing the inner man, and as soon as darkness settled over us the herd was again started. We were conscious of the presence of Indians, and deceived them by leaving our camp-fire burning, but holding our effects closely together throughout the night, the remuda even mixing with the cattle. When day broke we were fully thirty miles from our noon camp of the day before, yet with the exception of an hour's rest there was never a halt. A second day and night were spent in forging ahead, though it is doubtful if we averaged much over a mile an hour during that time. About fifteen miles out from the Pecos we were due to enter a cañon known as Castle Mountain Gap, some three or four miles long, the exit of which was in sight of the river. We were anxious to reach the entrance of this cañon before darkness on the third day, as we could then cut the cattle into bunches, the cliffs on either side forming a lane. Our horses were as good as worthless during the third day, but the saddle mules seemed to stand grief nobly, and by dint of ceaseless effort we reached the cañon and turned the cattle loose into it. This was the turning-point in the dry drive. That night two men took half the remuda and went through to Horsehead Crossing, returning with them early the next morning, and we once more had fresh mounts. The herd had been nursed through the cañon during the night, and although it was still twelve miles to the river, I have always believed that those beeves knew that water was at hand. They walked along briskly; instead of the constant moaning, their heads were erect, bawling loud and deep. The oxen drawing the wagon held their chains taut, and the commissary moved forward as if drawn by a fresh team. There was no attempt to hold the herd compactly, and within an hour after starting on our last lap the herd was strung out three miles. The rear was finally abandoned, and when half the distance was covered, the drag cattle to the number of fully five hundred turned out of the trail and struck direct for the river. They had scented the water over five miles, and as far as control was concerned the herd was as good as abandoned, except that the water would hold them.

Horsehead Crossing was named by General Pope. There is a difference of opinion as to the origin of the name, some contending that it was due to the meanderings of the river, forming a horse's head, and others that the surveying party was surprised by Indians and lost their stock. None of us had slept for three nights, and the feeling of relief on reaching the Pecos, shared alike by man and beast, is indescribable. Unless one has endured such a trial, only a faint idea of its hardships can be fully imagined — the long hours of patient travel at a snail's pace, enveloped by clouds of dust by day, and at night watching every shadow for a lurking savage. I have since slept many a time in the saddle, but in crossing that arid belt the one consuming desire to reach the water ahead benumbed every sense save watchfulness.

All the cattle reached the river before the middle of the afternoon, covering a front of five or six miles. The banks of the Pecos were abrupt, there being fully one hundred and twenty-five feet of deep water in the channel at the stage crossing. Entrance to the ford consisted of a wagon-way, cut through the banks, and the cattle crowded into the river above and below, there being but one exit on either side. Some miles above, the beeves had found several passageways down to the water, but in drifting up and down stream they missed these entrances on returning. A rally was made late that afternoon to rout the cattle out of the river-bed, one half the outfit going above, the remainder working around Horsehead, where the bulk of the herd had watered. I had gone upstream with Goodnight, but before we reached the upper end of the cattle fresh Indian sign was noticed. There was enough broken country along the river to shelter the redskins, but we kept in the open and cautiously examined every brake within gunshot of an entrance to the river. We succeeded in getting all the animals out of the water before dark, with the exception of one bunch, where the exit would require the use of a mattock before the cattle could climb it, and a few head that had bogged in the quicksand below Horsehead Crossing. There was little danger of a rise in the river, the loose contingent had a dry sand-bar on which to rest, and as the Indians had no use for them there was little danger of their being molested before morning.

We fell back about a mile from the river and camped for the night. Although we were all dead for sleep, extra caution was taken to prevent a surprise, either Goodnight or Loving remaining on guard over the outfit, seeing that the men kept awake on herd and that the guards changed promptly. Charlie Goodnight owned a horse that he contended could scent an Indian five hundred yards, and I have never questioned the statement. He had used him in the Ranger service. The horse by various means would show his uneasiness in the immediate presence of Indians, and once the following summer we moved camp at midnight on account of the warnings of that same horse. We had only a remuda with us at the time, but another outfit encamped with us refused to go, and they lost half their horses from an Indian surprise the next morning and never recovered them. I remember the ridicule which was expressed at our moving camp on the warnings of a horse. "Injun-bit," "Man-afraid-of-his-horses," were some of the terms applied to us, — yet the practical plainsman knew enough to take warning from his dumb beast. Fear, no doubt, gives horses an unusual sense of smell, and I have known them to detect the presence of a bear, on a favorable wind, at an incredible distance.

The night passed quietly, and early the next morning we rode to recover the remainder of the cattle. An effort was also made to rescue the bogged ones. On approaching the river, we found the beeves still resting quietly on the sand-bar. But we had approached them at an angle, for directly over head and across the river was a brake overgrown with thick brush, a splendid cover in which Indians might be lurking in the hope of ambushing any one who attempted to drive out the beeves. Two men were left with a single mattock to cut out and improve the exit, while the rest of us reconnoitered the thickety motte across the river. Goodnight was leery of the thicket, and suggested firing a few shots into it. We all had long-range guns, the distance from bank to bank was over two hundred yards, and a fusillade of shots was accordingly poured into the motte. To my surprise we were rewarded by seeing fully twenty Indians skulk out of the upper end of the cover. Every man raised his sights and gave them a parting volley, but a mesquite thicket, in which their horses were secreted, soon sheltered them and they fell back into the hills on the western side of the river. With the coast thus cleared, half a dozen of us rode down into the river-bed and drove out the last contingent of about three hundred cattle. Goodnight informed us that those Indians had no doubt been watching us for days, and cautioned us never to give a Comanche an advantage, advice which I never forgot.

On our return every one of the bogged cattle had been freed except two heavy beeves. These animals were mired above the ford, in rather deep water, and it was simply impossible to release them. The drovers were anxious to cross the river that afternoon, and a final effort was made to rescue the two steers. The oxen were accordingly yoked, and, with all the chain available, were driven into the river and fastened on to the nearest one. Three mounted drivers had charge of the team, and when the word was given six yoke of cattle bowed their necks and threw their weight against the yokes; but the quicksand held the steer in spite of all their efforts. The chain was freed from it, and the oxen were brought around and made fast again, at an angle and where the footing was better for the team. Again the word was given, and as the six yoke swung round, whips and ropes were plied amid a general shouting, and the team brought out the steer, but with a broken neck. There were no regrets, and our attention was at once given to the other steer. The team circled around, every available chain was brought into use, in order to afford the oxen good footing on a straight-away pull with the position in which the beef lay bogged. The word was given for an easy pull, the oxen barely stretched their chains, and were stopped. Goodnight cautioned the drivers that unless the pull was straight ahead another neck would be broken. A second trial was made; the oxen swung and weaved, the chains fairly cried, the beef's head went under water, but the team was again checked in time to keep the steer from drowning. After a breathing spell for oxen and victim, the call was made for a rush. A driver was placed over every yoke and the word given, and the oxen fell to their knees in the struggle, whips cracked over their backs, ropes were plied by every man in charge, and, amid a din of profanity applied to the struggling cattle, the team fell forward in a general collapse. At first it was thought the chain had parted, but as the latter came out of the water it held in its iron grasp the horns and a portion of the skull of the dying beef. Several of us rode out to the victim, whose brain lay bare, still throbbing and twitching with life. Rather than allow his remains to pollute the river, we made a last pull at an angle, and the dead beef was removed.

We bade Horsehead Crossing farewell that afternoon and camped for the night above Dagger Bend. Our route now lay to the northwest, or up the Pecos River. We were then out twenty-one days from Belknap, and although only half way to our destination, the worst of it was considered over. There was some travel up and down the Pecos valley, the route was even then known as the Chisum trail, and afterward extended as far north as Fort Logan in Colorado and other government posts in Wyoming. This cattle trace should never be confounded with the Chisholm trail, first opened by a half-breed named Jesse Chisholm, which ran from Red River

Station on the northern boundary of Texas to various points in Kansas. In cutting across the bends of the Rio Pecos we secured water each day for the herd, although we were frequently under the necessity of sloping down the banks with mattocks to let the cattle into the river. By this method it often took us three or four hours to water the herd. Until we neared Fort Sumner precaution never relaxed against an Indian surprise. Their sign was seen almost daily, but as there were weaker outfits than ours passing through we escaped any further molestation.

The methods of handling such a herd were a constant surprise to me, as well as the schooling of these plainsmen drovers. Goodnight had come to the plains when a boy of ten, and was a thorough master of their secrets. On one occasion, about midway between Horsehead Crossing and our destination, difficulty was encountered in finding an entrance to the river on account of its abrupt banks. It was late in the day, and in order to insure a quiet night with the cattle water became an urgent necessity. Our young foreman rode ahead and found a dry, sandy creek, its bed fully fifty yards wide, but no water, though the sand was damp. The herd was held back until sunset, when the cattle were turned into the creek bed and held as compactly as possible. The heavy beeves naturally walked back and forth, up and down, the sand just moist enough to aggravate them after a day's travel under a July sun. But the tramping soon agitated the sands, and within half an hour after the herd had entered the dry creek the water arose in pools, and the cattle drank to their hearts' content. As dew falls at night, moisture likewise rises in the earth, and with the twilight hour, the agitation of the sands, and the weight of the cattle, a spring was produced in the desert waste.

Fort Sumner was a six-company post and the agency of the Apaches and Navajos. These two tribes numbered over nine thousand people, and our herd was intended to supply the needs of the military post and these Indians. The contract was held by Patterson & Roberts, eligible by virtue of having cast their fortunes with the victor in "the late unpleasantness," and otherwise fine men. We reached the post on the 20th of July. There was a delay of several days before the cattle were accepted, but all passed the inspection with the exception of about one hundred head. These were cattle which had not recuperated from the dry drive. Some few were footsore or thin in flesh, but taken as a whole the delivery had every earmark of an honest one. Fortunately this remnant was sold a few days later to some Colorado men, and we were foot-loose and free. Even the oxen had gone in on the main delivery, and harnesses were accordingly bought, a light tongue fitted to the wagon, and we were ready to start homeward. Mules were substituted for the oxen, and we averaged forty miles a day returning, almost itching for an Indian attack, as we had supplied ourselves with ammunition from the post sutler. The trip had been a financial success (the government was paying ten cents a pound for beef on foot), friendly relations had been established with the holders of the award, and we hastened home to gather and drive another herd.

CHAPTER III
A SECOND TRIP TO FORT SUMNER

On the return trip we traveled mainly by night. The proceeds from the sale of the herd were in the wagon, and had this fact been known it would have been a tempting prize for either bandits or Indians. After leaving Horsehead Crossing we had the advantage of the dark of the moon, as it was a well-known fact that the Comanches usually choose moonlight nights for their marauding expeditions. Another thing in our favor, both going and returning, was the lightness of travel westward, it having almost ceased during the civil war, though in '66 it showed a slight prospect of resumption. Small bands of Indians were still abroad on horse-stealing forays, but the rich prizes of wagon trains bound for El Paso or Santa Fé no longer tempted the noble red man in force. This was favorable wind to our sail, but these plainsmen drovers predicted that, once traffic westward was resumed, the Comanche and his ally would be about the first ones to know it. The redskins were constantly passing back and forth, to and from their reservation in the Indian Territory, and news travels fast even among savages.

We reached the Brazos River early in August. As the second start was not to be made until the latter part of the following month, a general settlement was made with the men and all reëngaged for the next trip. I received eighty dollars in gold as my portion, it being the first money I ever earned as a citizen. The past two months were a splendid experience for one going through a formative period, and I had returned feeling that I was once more a man among men. All the uncertainty as to my future had fallen from me, and I began to look forward to the day when I also might be the owner of lands and cattle. There was no good reason why I should not, as the range was as free as it was boundless. There were any quantity of wild cattle in the country awaiting an owner, and a good mount of horses, a rope, and a branding iron were all the capital required to start a brand. I knew the success which my father had made in Virginia before the war and had seen it repeated on a smaller scale by my elder brother in Missouri, but here was a country which discounted both of those in rearing cattle without expense. Under the best reasoning at my command, I had reached the promised land, and henceforth determined to cast my fortunes with Texas.

Rather than remain idle around the Loving headquarters for a month, I returned with George Edwards to his home. Altogether too cordial a welcome was extended us, but I repaid the hospitality of the ranch by relating our experiences of trail and Indian surprise. Miss Gertrude was as charming as ever, but the trip to Sumner and back had cooled my ardor and I behaved myself as an acceptable guest should. The time passed rapidly, and on the last day of the month we returned to Belknap. Active preparations were in progress for the driving of the second herd, oxen had been secured, and a number of extra fine horses were already added to the saddle stock. The remuda had enjoyed a good month's rest and were in strong working flesh, and within a few days all the boys reported for duty. The senior member of the firm was the owner of a large number of range cattle, and it was the intention to round up and gather as many of his beeves as possible for the coming drive. We should have ample time to do this; by waiting until the latter part of the month for starting, it was believed that few Indians would be encountered, as the time was nearing for their annual buffalo hunt for robes and a supply of winter meat. This was a gala occasion with the tribes which depended on the bison for food and clothing; and as the natural hunting grounds of the Comanches and Kiowas lay south of Red River, the drovers considered that that would be an opportune time to start. The Indians would no doubt confine their operations to the first few tiers of counties in Texas, as the robes and dried meat would tax the carrying capacity of their horses returning, making it an object to kill their supplies as near their winter encampment as possible.

Some twenty days were accordingly spent in gathering beeves along the main Brazos and Clear Fork. Our herd consisted of about a thousand in the straight ranch brand, and after receiving and road-branding five hundred outside cattle we were ready to start. Sixteen men constituted our numbers, the horses were culled down until but five were left to the man, and with the previous armament the start was made. Never before or since have I enjoyed such an outing as this was until we struck the dry drive on approaching the Pecos River. The absence of the Indians was correctly anticipated, and either their presence elsewhere, preying on the immense buffalo herds, or the drift of the seasons, had driven countless numbers of that animal across our pathway. There were days and days that we were never out of sight of the feeding myriads of these shaggy brutes, and at night they became a menace to our sleeping herd. During the day, when the cattle were strung out in trail formation, we had difficulty in keeping the two species separated, but we shelled the buffalo right and left and moved forward. Frequently, when they occupied the country ahead of us, several men rode forward and scattered them on either hand until a right of way was effected for the cattle to pass. While they remained with us we killed our daily meat from their numbers, and several of the boys secured fine robes. They were very gentle, but when occasion required could give a horse a good race, bouncing along, lacking grace in flight.

Our cook was a negro. One day as we were nearing Buffalo Gap, a number of big bulls, attracted by the covered wagon, approached the commissary, the canvas sheet of which shone like a white flag. The wagon was some distance in the rear, and as the buffalo began to approach it they would scare and circle around, but constantly coming nearer the object of their curiosity. The darky finally became alarmed for fear they would gore his oxen, and unearthed an old Creedmoor rifle which he carried in the wagon. The gun could be heard for miles, and when the cook opened on the playful denizens of the plain, a number of us hurried back, supposing it was an Indian attack. When within a quarter-mile of the wagon and the situation became clear, we took it more leisurely, but the fusillade never ceased until we rode up and it dawned on the darky's mind that rescue was at hand. He had halted his team, and from a secure position in the front end of the wagon had shot down a dozen buffalo bulls. Pure curiosity and the blood of their comrades had kept them within easy range of the murderous Creedmoor; and the frenzied negro, supposing that his team might be attacked any moment, had mown down a circle of the innocent animals. We charged and drove away the remainder, after which we formed a guard of honor in escorting the commissary until its timid driver overtook the herd.

The last of the buffalo passed out of sight before we reached the headwaters of the Concho. In crossing the dry drive approaching the Pecos we were unusually fortunate. As before, we rested in advance of starting, and on the evening of the second day out several showers fell, cooling the atmosphere until the night was fairly chilly. The rainfall continued all the following day in a gentle mist, and with little or no suffering to man or beast early in the afternoon we entered the cañon known as Castle Mountain Gap, and the dry drive was virtually over. Horsehead Crossing was reached early the next morning, the size of the herd making it possible to hold it compactly, and thus preventing any scattering along that stream. There had been no freshets in the river since June, and the sandy sediment had solidified, making a safe crossing for both herd and wagon. After the usual rest of a few days, the herd trailed up the Pecos with scarcely an incident worthy of mention. Early in November we halted some distance below Fort Sumner, where we were met by Mr. Loving, — who had gone on to the post in our advance, — with the report that other cattle had just been accepted, and that there was no prospect of an immediate delivery. In fact, the outlook was anything but encouraging, unless we wintered ours and had them ready for the first delivery in the spring.

The herd was accordingly turned back to Bosque Grande on the river, and we went into permanent quarters. There was a splendid winter range all along the Pecos, and we loose-herded the beeves or rode lines in holding them in the different bends of the river, some of which were natural inclosures. There was scarcely any danger of Indian molestation during the winter months, and with the exception of a few severe "northers" which swept down the valley, the cattle did comparatively well. Tents were secured at the post; corn was purchased for our saddle mules; and except during storms little or no privation was experienced during the winter in that southern climate. Wood was plentiful in the grove in which we were encamped, and a huge fireplace was built out of clay and sticks in the end of each tent, assuring us comfort against the elements.

The monotony of existence was frequently broken by the passing of trading caravans, both up and down the river. There was a fair trade with the interior of Mexico, as well as in various settlements along the Rio Grande and towns in northern New Mexico. When other means of diversion failed we had recourse to Sumner, where a sutler's bar and gambling games flourished. But the most romantic traveler to arrive or pass during the winter was Captain Burleson, late of the Confederacy. As a sportsman the captain was a gem of the first water, carrying with him, besides a herd of nearly a thousand cattle, three race-horses, several baskets of fighting chickens, and a pack of hounds. He had a large Mexican outfit in charge of his cattle, which were in bad condition on their arrival in March, he having drifted about all winter, gambling, racing his horses, and fighting his chickens. The herd represented his winnings. As we had nothing to match, all we could offer was our hospitality. Captain Burleson went into camp below us on the river and remained our neighbor until we rounded up and broke camp in the spring. He had been as far west as El Paso during the winter, and was then drifting north in the hope of finding a market for his herd. We indulged in many hunts, and I found him the true gentleman and sportsman in every sense of the word. As I recall him now, he was a lovable vagabond, and for years afterward stories were told around Fort Sumner of his wonderful nerve as a poker player.

Early in April an opportunity occurred for a delivery of cattle to the post. Ours were the only beeves in sight, those of Captain Burleson not qualifying, and a round-up was made and the herd tendered for inspection. Only eight hundred were received, which was quite a disappointment to the drovers, as at least ninety per cent of the tender filled every qualification. The motive in receiving the few soon became apparent, when a stranger appeared and offered to buy the remaining seven hundred at a ridiculously low figure. But the drovers had grown suspicious of the contractors and receiving agent, and, declining the offer, went back and bought the herd of Captain Burleson. Then, throwing the two contingents together, and boldly announcing their determination of driving to Colorado, they started the herd out past Fort Sumner with every field-glass in the post leveled on us. The military requirements of Sumner, for its own and Indian use, were well known to the drovers, and a scarcity of beef was certain to occur at that post before other cattle could be bargained for and arrive. My employers had evidently figured out the situation to a nicety, for during the forenoon of the second day out from the fort we were overtaken by the contractors. Of course they threw on the government inspector all the blame for the few cattle received, and offered to buy five or six hundred more out of the herd. But the shoe was on the other foot now, the drovers acting as independently as the proverbial hog on ice. The herd never halted, the contractors followed up, and when we went into camp that evening a trade was closed on one thousand steers at two dollars a head advance over those which were received but a few days before. The oxen were even reserved, and after delivering the beeves at Sumner we continued on northward with the remnant, nearly all of which were the Burleson cattle.

The latter part of April we arrived at the Colorado line. There we were halted by the authorities of that territory, under some act of quarantine against Texas cattle. We went into camp on the nearest water, expecting to prove that our little herd had wintered at Fort Sumner, and were therefore immune from quarantine, when buyers arrived from Trinidad, Colorado. The steers were a mixed lot, running from a yearling to big, rough four and five year olds, and when Goodnight returned from Sumner with a certificate, attested to by every officer of that post, showing that the cattle had wintered north of latitude 34, a trade was closed at once, even the oxen going in at the phenomenal figures of one hundred and fifty dollars a yoke. We delivered the herd near Trinidad, going into that town to outfit before returning. The necessary alterations were made to the wagon, mules were harnessed in, and we started home in gala spirits. In a little over thirty days my employers had more than doubled their money on the Burleson cattle and were naturally jubilant.

The proceeds of the Trinidad sale were carried in the wagon returning, though we had not as yet collected for the second delivery at Sumner. The songs of the birds mixed with our own as we traveled homeward, and the freshness of early summer on the primitive land, as it rolled away in dips and swells, made the trip a delightful outing. Fort Sumner was reached within a week, where we halted a day and then started on, having in the wagon a trifle over fifty thousand dollars in gold and silver. At Sumner two men made application to accompany us back to Texas, and as they were well armed and mounted, and numbers were an advantage, they were made welcome. Our winter camp at Bosque Grande was passed with but a single glance as we dropped down the Pecos valley at the rate of forty miles a day. Little or no travel was encountered en route, nor was there any sign of Indians until the afternoon of our reaching Horsehead Crossing. While passing Dagger Bend, four miles above the ford, Goodnight and a number of us boys were riding several hundred yards in advance of the wagon, telling stories of old sweethearts. The road made a sudden bend around some sand-hills, and the advance guard had passed out of sight of the rear, when a fresh Indian trail was cut; and as we reined in our mounts to examine the sign, we were fired on. The rifle-shots, followed by a flight of arrows, passed over us, and we took to shelter like flushed quail. I was riding a good saddle horse and bolted off on the opposite side of the road from the shooting; but in the scattering which ensued a number of mules took down the road. One of the two men picked up at the post was a German, whose mule stampeded after his mates, and who received a galling fire from the concealed Indians, the rest of us turning to the nearest shelter. With the exception of this one man, all of us circled back through the mesquite brush and reached the wagon, which had halted. Meanwhile the shooting had attracted the men behind, who charged through the sand-dunes, flanking the Indians, who immediately decamped. Security of the remuda and wagon was a first consideration, and danger of an ambush prevented our men from following up the redskins. Order was soon restored, when we proceeded, and shortly met the young German coming back up the road, who merely remarked on meeting us, "Dem Injuns shot at me."

The Indians had evidently not been expecting us. From where they turned out and where the attack was made we back-trailed them in the road for nearly a mile. They had simply heard us coming, and, supposing that the advance guard was all there was in the party, had made the attack and were in turn themselves surprised at our numbers. But the warning was henceforth heeded, and on reaching the crossing more Indian sign was detected. Several large parties had evidently crossed the river that morning, and were no doubt at that moment watching us from the surrounding hills. The cañon of Castle Mountain Gap was well adapted for an Indian ambush; and as it was only twelve miles from the ford to its mouth, we halted within a short distance of the entrance, as if encamping for the night. All the horses under saddle were picketed fully a quarter mile from the wagon, — easy marks for poor Lo, — and the remuda was allowed to wander at will, an air of perfect carelessness prevailing in the camp. From the sign which we had seen that day, there was little doubt but there were in the neighborhood of five hundred Indians in the immediate vicinity of Horsehead Crossing, and we did everything we could to create the impression that we were tender-feet. But with the falling of darkness every horse was brought in and we harnessed up and started, leaving the fire burning to identify our supposed camp. The drovers gave our darky cook instructions, in case of an attack while passing through the Gap, never to halt his team, but push ahead for the plain. About one third of us took the immediate lead of the wagon, the remuda following closely, and the remainder of the men bringing up the rear. The moon was on the wane and would not rise until nearly midnight, and for the first few miles, or until we entered the cañon, there was scarce a sound to disturb the stillness of the night. The sandy road even muffled the noise of the wagon and the tramping of horses; but once we entered that rocky cañon, the rattling of our commissary seemed to summon every Comanche and his ally to come and rob us. There was never a halt, the reverberations of our caravan seeming to reëcho through the Gap, resounding forward and back, until our progress must have been audible at Horsehead Crossing. But the expected never happens, and within an hour we reached the summit of the plain, where the country was open and clear and an attack could have been easily repelled. Four fresh mules had been harnessed in for the night, and striking a free gait, we put twenty miles of that arid stretch behind us before the moon rose. A short halt was made after midnight, for a change of teams and saddle horses, and then we continued our hurried travel until near dawn.

Some indistinct objects in our front caused us to halt. It looked like a caravan, and we hailed it without reply. Several of us dismounted and crept forward, but the only sign of life was a dull, buzzing sound which seemed to issue from an outfit of parked wagons. The report was laid before the two drovers, who advised that we await the dawn, which was then breaking, as it was possible that the caravan had been captured and robbed by Indians. A number of us circled around to the farther side, and as we again approached the wagons in the uncertain light we hailed again and received in reply a shot, which cut off the upper lobe of one of the boys' ears. We hugged the ground for some little time, until the presence of our outfit was discovered by the lone guardian of the caravan, who welcomed us. He apologized, saying that on awakening he supposed we were Indians, not having heard our previous challenge, and fired on us under the impulse of the moment. He was a well-known trader by the name of "Honey" Allen, and was then on his way to El Paso, having pulled out on the dry stretch about twenty-five miles and sent his oxen back to water. His present cargo consisted of pecans, honey, and a large number of colonies of live bees, the latter having done the buzzing on our first reconnoitre. At his destination, so he informed us, the pecans were worth fifty cents a quart, the honey a dollar a pound, and the bees one hundred dollars a hive. After repairing the damaged ear, we hurried on, finding Allen's oxen lying around the water on our arrival. I met him several years afterward in Denver, Colorado, dressed to kill, barbered, and highly perfumed. He had just sold eighteen hundred two-year-old steers and had twenty-five thousand dollars in the bank. "Son, let me tell you something," said he, as we were taking a drink together; "that Pecos country was a dangerous region to pick up an honest living in. I'm going back to God's country, — back where there ain't no Injuns."

Yet Allen died in Texas. There was a charm in the frontier that held men captive. I always promised myself to return to Virginia to spend the declining years of my life, but the fulfillment never came. I can now realize how idle was the expectation, having seen others make the attempt and fail. I recall the experience of an old cowman, laboring under a similar delusion, who, after nearly half a century in the Southwest, concluded to return to the scenes of his boyhood. He had made a substantial fortune in cattle, and had fought his way through the vicissitudes of the frontier until success crowned his efforts. A large family had in the mean time grown up around him, and under the pretense of giving his children the advantages of an older and established community he sold his holdings and moved back to his native borough. Within six months he returned to the straggling village which he had left on the plains, bringing the family with him. Shortly afterwards I met him, and anxiously inquired the cause of his return. "Well, Reed," said he, "I can't make you understand near as well as though you had tried it yourself. You see I was a stranger in my native town. The people were all right, I reckon, but I found out that it was me who had changed. I tried to be sociable with them, but honest, Reed, I just couldn't stand it in a country where no one ever asked you to take a drink."

A week was spent in crossing the country between the Concho and Brazos rivers. Not a day passed but Indian trails were cut, all heading southward, and on a branch of the Clear Fork we nearly ran afoul of an encampment of forty teepees and lean-tos, with several hundred horses in sight. But we never varied our course a fraction, passing within a quarter mile of their camp, apparently indifferent as to whether they showed fight or allowed us to pass in peace. Our bluff had the desired effect; but we made it an object to reach Fort Griffin near midnight before camping. The Comanche and his ally were great respecters, not only of their own physical welfare, but of the Henri and Spencer rifle with which the white man killed the buffalo at the distance of twice the flight of an arrow. When every advantage was in his favor — ambush and surprise — Lo was a warrior bold; otherwise he used discretion.

CHAPTER IV
A FATAL TRIP

Before leaving Fort Sumner an agreement had been entered into between my employers and the contractors for a third herd. The delivery was set for the first week in September, and twenty-five hundred beeves were agreed upon, with a liberal leeway above and below that number in case of accident en route. Accordingly, on our return to Loving's ranch active preparations were begun for the next drive. Extra horses were purchased, several new guns of the most modern make were secured, and the gathering of cattle in Loving's brand began at once, continuing for six weeks. We combed the hills and valleys along the main Brazos, and then started west up the Clear Fork, carrying the beeves with us while gathering. The range was in prime condition, the cattle were fat and indolent, and with the exception of Indian rumors there was not a cloud in the sky.

Our last camp was made a few miles above Fort Griffin. Military protection was not expected, yet our proximity to that post was considered a security from Indian interference, as at times not over half the outfit were with the herd. We had nearly completed our numbers when, one morning early in July, the redskins struck our camp with the violence of a cyclone. The attack occurred, as usual, about half an hour before dawn, and, to add to the difficulty of the situation, the cattle stampeded with the first shot fired. I was on last guard at the time, and conscious that it was an Indian attack I unslung a new Sharp's rifle and tore away in the lead of the herd. With the rumbling of over two thousand running cattle in my ears, hearing was out of the question, while my sense of sight was rendered useless by the darkness of the morning hour. Yet I had some very distinct visions; not from the herd of frenzied beeves, thundering at my heels, but every shade and shadow in the darkness looked like a pursuing Comanche. Once I leveled my rifle at a shadow, but hesitated, when a flash from a six-shooter revealed the object to be one of our own men. I knew there were four of us with the herd when it stampeded, but if the rest were as badly bewildered as I was, it was dangerous even to approach them. But I had a king's horse under me and trusted my life to him, and he led the run until breaking dawn revealed our identity to each other.

The presence of two other men with the running herd was then discovered. We were fully five miles from camp, and giving our attention to the running cattle we soon turned the lead. The main body of the herd was strung back for a mile, but we fell on the leaders right and left, and soon had them headed back for camp. In the mean time, and with the breaking of day, our trail had been taken up by both drovers and half a dozen men, who overtook us shortly after sun-up. A count was made and we had every hoof. A determined fight had occurred over the remuda and commissary, and three of the Indians' ponies had been killed, while some thirty arrows had found lodgment in our wagon. There were no casualties in the cow outfit, and if any occurred among the redskins, the wounded or killed were carried away by their comrades before daybreak. All agreed that there were fully one hundred warriors in the attacking party, and as we slowly drifted the cattle back to camp doubt was expressed by the drovers whether it was advisable to drive the herd to its destination in midsummer with the Comanches out on their old hunting grounds.

A report of the attack was sent into Griffin that morning, and a company of cavalry took up the Indian trail, followed it until evening, and returned to the post during the night. Approaching a government station was generally looked upon as an audacious act of the redskins, but the contempt of the Comanche and his ally for citizen and soldier alike was well known on the Texas frontier and excited little comment. Several years later, in broad daylight, they raided the town of Weatherford, untied every horse from the hitching racks, and defiantly rode away with their spoil. But the prevailing spirits in our camp were not the kind to yield to an inferior race, and, true to their obligation to the contractors, they pushed forward preparations to start the herd. Within a week our numbers were completed, two extra men were secured, and on the morning of July 14, 1867, we trailed out up the Clear Fork with a few over twenty-six hundred big beeves. It was the same old route to the southwest, there was a decided lack of enthusiasm over the start, yet never a word of discouragement escaped the lips of men or employers. I have never been a superstitious man, have never had a premonition of impending danger, always rather felt an enthusiasm in my undertakings, yet that morning when the flag over Fort Griffin faded from our view, I believe there was not a man in the outfit but realized that our journey would be disputed by Indians.

Nor had we long to wait. Near the juncture of Elm Creek with the main Clear Fork we were again attacked at the usual hour in the morning. The camp was the best available, and yet not a good one for defense, as the ground was broken by shallow draws and dry washes. There were about one hundred yards of clear space on three sides of the camp, while on the exposed side, and thirty yards distant, was a slight depression of several feet. Fortunately we had a moment's warning, by several horses snorting and pawing the ground, which caused Goodnight to quietly awake the men sleeping near him, who in turn were arousing the others, when a flight of arrows buried themselves in the ground around us and the war-whoop of the Comanche sounded. Ever cautious, we had studied the situation on encamping, and had tied our horses, cavalry fashion, to a heavy rope stretched from the protected side of the wagon to a high stake driven for the purpose. With the attack the majority of the men flung themselves into their saddles and started to the rescue of the remuda, while three others and myself, detailed in anticipation, ran for the ravine and dropped into it about forty yards above the wagon. We could easily hear the exultations of the redskins just below us in the shallow gorge, and an enfilade fire was poured into them at short range. Two guns were cutting the grass from underneath the wagon, and, knowing the Indians had crept up the depression on foot, we began a rapid fire from our carbines and six-shooters, which created the impression of a dozen rifles on their flank, and they took to their heels in a headlong rout.

Once the firing ceased, we hailed our men under the wagon and returned to it. Three men were with the commissary, one of whom was a mere boy, who was wounded in the head from an arrow during the first moment of the attack, and was then raving piteously from his sufferings. The darky cook, who was one of the defenders of the wagon, was consoling the boy, so with a parting word of encouragement we swung into our saddles and rode in the direction of dim firing up the creek. The cattle were out of hearing, but the random shooting directed our course, and halting several times, we were finally piloted to the scene of activity. Our hail was met by a shout of welcome, and the next moment we dashed in among our own and reported the repulse of the Indians from the wagon. The remuda was dashing about, hither and yon, a mob of howling savages were circling about, barely within gunshot, while our men rode cautiously, checking and turning the frenzied saddle horses, and never missing a chance of judiciously throwing a little lead. There was no sign of daybreak, and, fearful for the safety of our commissary, we threw a cordon around the remuda and started for camp. Although there must have been over one hundred Indians in the general attack, we were still masters of the situation, though they followed us until the wagon was reached and the horses secured in a rope corral. A number of us again sought the protection of the ravine, and scattering above and below, we got in some telling shots at short range, when the redskins gave up the struggle and decamped. As they bore off westward on the main Clear Fork their hilarious shoutings could be distinctly heard for miles on the stillness of the morning air.

An inventory of the camp was taken at dawn. The wounded lad received the first attention. The arrowhead had buried itself below and behind the ear, but nippers were applied and the steel point was extracted. The cook washed the wound thoroughly and applied a poultice of meal, which afforded almost instant relief. While horses were being saddled to follow the cattle, I cast my eye over the camp and counted over two hundred arrows within a radius of fifty yards. Two had found lodgment in the bear-skin on which I slept. Dozens were imbedded in the running-gear and box of the wagon, while the stationary flashes from the muzzle of the cook's Creedmoor had concentrated an unusual number of arrows in and around his citadel. The darky had exercised caution and corded the six ox-yokes against the front wheel of the wagon in such a manner as to form a barrier, using the spaces between the spokes as port-holes. As he never varied his position under the wagon, the Indians had aimed at his flash, and during the rather brief fight twenty arrows had buried themselves in that barricade of ox-yokes.

The trail of the beeves was taken at dawn. This made the fifth stampede of the herd since we started, a very unfortunate thing, for stampeding easily becomes a mania with range cattle. The steers had left the bed-ground in an easterly direction, but finding that they were not pursued, the men had gradually turned them to the right, and at daybreak the herd was near Elm Creek, where it was checked. We rode the circle in a free gallop, the prairie being cut into dust and the trail as easy to follow as a highway. As the herd happened to land on our course, after the usual count the commissary was sent for, and it and the remuda were brought up. With the exception of wearing hobbles, the oxen were always given their freedom at night. This morning one of them was found in a dying condition from an arrow in his stomach. A humane shot had relieved the poor beast, and his mate trailed up to the herd, tied behind the wagon with a rope. There were several odd oxen among the cattle and the vacancy was easily filled. If I am lacking in compassion for my red brother, the lack has been heightened by his fiendish atrocities to dumb animals. I have been witness to the ruin of several wagon trains captured by Indians, have seen their ashes and irons, and even charred human remains, and was scarce moved to pity because of the completeness of the hellish work. Death is merciful and humane when compared to the hamstringing of oxen, gouging out their eyes, severing their ears, cutting deep slashes from shoulder to hip, and leaving the innocent victim to a lingering death. And when dumb animals are thus mutilated in every conceivable form of torment, as if for the amusement of the imps of the evil one, my compassion for poor Lo ceases.

It was impossible to send the wounded boy back to the settlements, so a comfortable bunk was made for him in the wagon. Late in the evening we resumed our journey, expecting to drive all night, as it was good starlight. Fair progress was made, but towards morning a rainstorm struck us, and the cattle again stampeded. In all my outdoor experience I never saw such pitchy darkness as accompanied that storm; although galloping across a prairie in a blustering rainfall, it required no strain of the imagination to see hills and mountains and forests on every hand. Fourteen men were with the herd, yet it was impossible to work in unison, and when day broke we had less than half the cattle. The lead had been maintained, but in drifting at random with the storm several contingents of beeves had cut off from the main body, supposedly from the rear. When the sun rose, men were dispatched in pairs and trios, the trail of the missing steers was picked up, and by ten o'clock every hoof was in hand or accounted for. I came in with the last contingent and found the camp in an uproar over the supposed desertion of one of the hands. Yankee Bill, a sixteen-year-old boy, and another man were left in charge of the herd when the rest of us struck out to hunt the missing cattle. An hour after sunrise the boy was seen to ride deliberately away from his charge, without cause or excuse, and had not returned. Desertion was the general supposition. Had he not been mounted on one of the firm's horses the offense might have been overlooked. But the delivery of the herd depended on the saddle stock, and two men were sent on his trail. The rain had freshened the ground, and after trailing the horse for fifteen miles the boy was overtaken while following cattle tracks towards the herd. He had simply fallen asleep in the saddle, and the horse had wandered away. Yankee Bill had made the trip to Sumner with us the fall before, and stood well with his employers, so the incident was forgiven and forgotten.

From Elm Creek to the beginning of the dry drive was one continual struggle with stampeding cattle or warding off Indians. In spite of careful handling, the herd became spoiled, and would run from the howl of a wolf or the snort of a horse. The dark hour before dawn was usually the crucial period, and until the arid belt was reached all hands were aroused at two o'clock in the morning. The start was timed so as to reach the dry drive during the full of the moon, and although it was a test of endurance for man and beast, there was relief in the desert waste — from the lurking savage — which recompensed for its severity. Three sleepless nights were borne without a murmur, and on our reaching Horsehead Crossing and watering the cattle they were turned back on the mesa and freed for the time being. The presence of Indian sign around the ford was the reason for turning loose, but at the round-up the next morning the experiment proved a costly one, as three hundred and sixty-three beeves were missing. The cattle were nervous and feverish through suffering from thirst, and had they been bedded closely, stampeding would have resulted, the foreman choosing the least of two alternatives in scattering the herd. That night we slept the sleep of exhausted men, and the next morning even awaited the sun on the cattle before throwing them together, giving the Indian thieves full ten hours the start. The stealing of cattle by the Comanches was something unusual, and there was just reason for believing that the present theft was instigated by renegade Mexicans, allies in the war of '36. Three distinct trails left the range around the Crossing, all heading south, each accompanied by fully fifty horsemen. One contingent crossed the Pecos at an Indian trail about twenty-five miles below Horsehead, another still below, while the third continued on down the left bank of the river. Yankee Bill and "Mocho" Wilson, a one-armed man, followed the latter trail, sighting them late in the evening, but keeping well in the open. When the Comanches had satisfied themselves that but two men were following them, small bands of warriors dropped out under cover of the broken country and attempted to gain the rear of our men. Wilson was an old plainsman, and once he saw the hopelessness of recovering the cattle, he and Yankee Bill began a cautious retreat. During the night and when opposite the ford where the first contingent of beeves crossed, they were waylaid, while returning, by the wily redskins. The nickering of a pony warned them of the presence of the enemy, and circling wide, they avoided an ambush, though pursued by the stealthy Comanches. Wilson was mounted on a good horse, while Yankee Bill rode a mule, and so closely were they pursued, that on reaching the first broken ground Bill turned into a coulee, while Mocho bore off on an angle, firing his six-shooter to attract the enemy after him. Yankee Bill told us afterward how he held the muzzle of his mule for an hour on dismounting, to keep the rascal from bawling after the departing horse. Wilson reached camp after midnight and reported the hopelessness of the situation; but morning came, and with it no Yankee Bill in camp. Half a dozen of us started in search of him, under the leadership of the one-armed plainsman, and an hour afterward Bill was met riding leisurely up the river. When rebuked by his comrade for not coming in under cover of darkness, he retorted, "Hell, man, I wasn't going to run my mule to death just because there were a few Comanches in the country!"

In trailing the missing cattle the day previous, I had accompanied Mr. Loving to the second Indian crossing. The country opposite the ford was broken and brushy, the trail was five or six hours old, and, fearing an ambush, the drover refused to follow them farther. With the return of Yankee Bill safe and sound to camp, all hope of recovering the beeves was abandoned, and we crossed the Pecos and turned up that river. An effort was now made to quiet the herd and bring it back to a normal condition, in order to fit it for delivery. With Indian raids, frenzy in stampeding, and an unavoidable dry drive, the cattle had gaunted like rails. But with an abundance of water and by merely grazing the remainder of the distance, it was believed that the beeves would recover their old form and be ready for inspection at the end of the month of August. Indian sign was still plentiful, but in smaller bands, and with an unceasing vigilance we wormed our way up the Pecos valley.

When within a day's ride of the post, Mr. Loving took Wilson with him and started in to Fort Sumner. The heat of August on the herd had made recovery slow, but if a two weeks' postponement could be agreed on, it was believed the beeves would qualify. The circumstances were unavoidable; the government had been lenient before; so, hopeful of accomplishing his mission, the senior member of the firm set out on his way. The two men left camp at daybreak, cautioned by Goodnight to cross the river by a well-known trail, keeping in the open, even though it was farther, as a matter of safety. They were well mounted for the trip, and no further concern was given to their welfare until the second morning, when Loving's horse came into camp, whinnying for his mates. There were blood-stains on the saddle, and the story of a man who was cautious for others and careless of himself was easily understood. Conjecture was rife.

The presence of the horse admitted of several interpretations. An Indian ambush was the most probable, and a number of men were detailed to ferret out the mystery. We were then seventy miles below Sumner, and with orders to return to the herd at night six of us immediately started. The searching party was divided into squads, one on either side of the Pecos River, but no results were obtained from the first day's hunt. The herd had moved up fifteen miles during the day, and the next morning the search was resumed, the work beginning where it had ceased the evening before. Late that afternoon and from the east bank, as Goodnight and I were scanning the opposite side of the river, a lone man, almost naked, emerged from a cave across the channel and above us. Had it not been for his missing arm it is doubtful if we should have recognized him, for he seemed demented. We rode opposite and hailed, when he skulked back into his refuge; but we were satisfied that it was Wilson. The other searchers were signaled to, and finding an entrance into the river, we swam it and rode up to the cave. A shout of welcome greeted us, and the next instant Wilson staggered out of the cavern, his eyes filled with tears.

He was in a horrible physical condition, and bewildered. We were an hour getting his story. They had been ambushed by Indians and ran for the brakes of the river, but were compelled to abandon their horses, one of which was captured, the other escaping. Loving was wounded twice, in the wrist and the side, but from the cover gained they had stood off the savages until darkness fell. During the night Loving, unable to walk, believed that he was going to die, and begged Wilson to make his escape, and if possible return to the herd. After making his employer as comfortable as possible, Wilson buried his own rifle, pistols, and knife, and started on his return to the herd. Being one-armed, he had discarded his boots and nearly all his clothing to assist him in swimming the river, which he had done any number of times, traveling by night and hiding during the day. When found in the cave, his feet were badly swollen, compelling him to travel in the river-bed to protect them from sandburs and thorns. He was taken up behind one of the boys on a horse, and we returned to camp.

Wilson firmly believed that Loving was dead, and described the scene of the fight so clearly that any one familiar with the river would have no difficulty in locating the exact spot. But the next morning as we were nearing the place we met an ambulance in the road, the driver of which reported that Loving had been brought into Sumner by a freight outfit. On receipt of this information Goodnight hurried on to the post, while the rest of us looked over the scene, recovered the buried guns of Wilson, and returned to the herd. Subsequently we learned that the next morning after Wilson left Loving had crawled to the river for a drink, and, looking upstream, saw some one a mile or more distant watering a team. By firing his pistol he attracted attention to himself and so was rescued, the Indians having decamped during the night. To his partner, Mr. Loving corroborated Wilson's story, and rejoiced to know that his comrade had also escaped. Everything that medical science could do was done by the post surgeons for the veteran cowman, but after lingering twenty-one days he died. Wilson and the wounded boy both recovered, the cattle were delivered in two installments, and early in October we started homeward, carrying the embalmed remains of the pioneer drover in a light conveyance. The trip was uneventful, the traveling was done principally by night, and on the arrival at Loving's frontier home, six hundred miles from Fort Sumner, his remains were laid at rest with Masonic honors.

Over thirty years afterward a claim was made against the government for the cattle lost at Horsehead Crossing. Wilson and I were witnesses before the commissioner sent to take evidence in the case. The hearing was held at a federal court, and after it was over, Wilson, while drinking, accused me of suspecting him of deserting his employer, — a suspicion I had, in fact, entertained at the time we discovered him at the cave. I had never breathed it to a living man, yet it was the truth, slumbering for a generation before finding expression.

CHAPTER V
SUMMER OF '68

The death of Mr. Loving ended my employment in driving cattle to Fort Sumner. The junior member of the firm was anxious to continue the trade then established, but the absence of any protection against the Indians, either state or federal, was hopeless. Texas was suffering from the internal troubles of Reconstruction, the paternal government had small concern for the welfare of a State recently in arms against the Union, and there was little or no hope for protection of life or property under existing conditions. The outfit was accordingly paid off, and I returned with George Edwards to his father's ranch. The past eighteen months had given me a strenuous schooling, but I had emerged on my feet, feeling that once more I was entitled to a place among men. The risk that had been incurred by the drovers acted like a physical stimulant, the outdoor life had hardened me like iron, and I came out of the crucible bright with the hope of youth and buoyant with health and strength.

Meanwhile there had sprung up a small trade in cattle with the North. Baxter Springs and Abilene, both in Kansas, were beginning to be mentioned as possible markets, light drives having gone to those points during the present and previous summers. The elder Edwards had been investigating the new outlet, and on the return of George and myself was rather enthusiastic over the prospects of a market. No Indian trouble had been experienced on the northern route, and although demand generally was unsatisfactory, the faith of drovers in the future was unshaken. A railroad had recently reached Abilene, stockyards had been built for the accommodation of shippers during the summer of 1861, while a firm of shrewd, far-seeing Yankees made great pretensions of having established a market and meeting-point for buyers and sellers of Texas cattle. The promoters of the scheme had a contract with the railroad, whereby they were to receive a bonus on all cattle shipped from that point, and the Texas drovers were offered every inducement to make Abilene their destination in the future. The unfriendliness of other States against Texas cattle, caused by the ravages of fever imparted by southern to domestic animals, had resulted in quarantine being enforced against all stock from the South. Matters were in an unsettled condition, and less than one per cent of the State's holdings of cattle had found an outside market during the year 1867, though ranchmen in general were hopeful.

I spent the remainder of the month of October at the Edwards ranch. We had returned in time for the fall branding, and George and I both made acceptable hands at the work. I had mastered the art of handling a rope, and while we usually corralled everything, scarcely a day passed but occasion occurred to rope wild cattle out of the brush. Anxiety to learn soon made me an expert, and before the month ended I had caught and branded for myself over one hundred mavericks. Cattle were so worthless that no one went to the trouble to brand completely; the crumbs were acceptable to me, and, since no one else cared for them and I did, the flotsam and jetsam of the range fell to my brand. Had I been ambitious, double that number could have been easily secured, but we never went off the home range in gathering calves to brand. All the hands on the Edwards ranch, darkies and Mexicans, were constantly throwing into the corrals and pointing out unclaimed cattle, while I threw and indelibly ran the figures "44" on their sides. I was partial to heifers, and when one was sighted there was no brush so thick or animal so wild that it was not "fish" to my rope. In many instances a cow of unknown brand was still followed by her two-year-old, yearling, and present calf. Under the customs of the country, any unbranded animal, one year old or over, was a maverick, and the property of any one who cared to brand the unclaimed stray. Thousands of cattle thus lived to old age, multiplied and increased, died and became food for worms, unowned.

The branding over, I soon grew impatient to be doing something. There would be no movement in cattle before the following spring, and a winter of idleness was not to my liking. Buffalo hunting had lost its charm with me, the contentious savages were jealous of any intrusion on their old hunting grounds, and, having met them on numerous occasions during the past eighteen months, I had no further desire to cultivate their acquaintance. I still owned my horse,

417

now acclimated, and had money in my purse, and one morning I announced my intention of visiting my other comrades in Texas. Protests were made against my going, and as an incentive to have me remain, the elder Edwards offered to outfit George and me the following spring with a herd of cattle and start us to Kansas. I was anxious for employment, but assuring my host that he could count on my services, I still pleaded my anxiety to see other portions of the State and renew old acquaintances. The herd could not possibly start before the middle of April, so telling my friends that I would be on hand to help gather the cattle, I saddled my horse and took leave of the hospitable ranch.

After a week of hard riding I reached the home of a former comrade on the Colorado River below Austin. A hearty welcome awaited me, but the apparent poverty of the family made my visit rather a brief one. Continuing eastward, my next stop was in Washington County, one of the oldest settled communities in the State. The blight of Reconstruction seemed to have settled over the people like a pall, the frontier having escaped it. But having reached my destination, I was determined to make the best of it. At the house of my next comrade I felt a little more at home, he having married since his return and being naturally of a cheerful disposition. For a year previous to the surrender he and I had wrangled beef for the Confederacy and had been stanch cronies. We had also been in considerable mischief together; and his wife seemed to know me by reputation as well as I knew her husband. Before the wire edge wore off my visit I was as free with the couple as though they had been my own brother and sister. The fact was all too visible that they were struggling with poverty, though lightened by cheerfulness, and to remain long a guest would have been an imposition; accordingly I began to skirmish for something to do — anything, it mattered not what. The only work in sight was with a carpet-bag dredging company, improving the lower Brazos River, under a contract from the Reconstruction government of the State. My old crony pleaded with me to have nothing to do with the job, offering to share his last crust with me; but then he had not had all the animosities of the war roughed out of him, and I had. I would work for a Federal as soon as any one else, provided he paid me the promised wage, and, giving rein to my impulse, I made application at the dredging headquarters and was put in charge of a squad of negroes.

I was to have sixty dollars a month and board. The company operated a commissary store, a regular "pluck-me" concern, and I shortly understood the incentive in offering me such good wages. All employees were encouraged and expected to draw their pay in supplies, which were sold at treble their actual value from the commissary. I had been raised among negroes, knew how to humor and handle them, the work was easy, and I drifted along with all my faculties alert. Before long I saw that the improvement of the river was the least of the company's concern, the employment of a large number of men being the chief motive, so long as they drew their wages in supplies. True, we scattered a few lodgments of driftwood; with the aid of a flat-bottomed scow we windlassed up and cut out a number of old snags, felled trees into the river to prevent erosion of its banks, and we built a large number of wind-dams to straighten or change the channel. It seemed to be a blanket contract, — a reward to the faithful, — and permitted of any number of extras which might be charged for at any figures the contractors saw fit to make. At the end of the first month I naturally looked for my wages. Various excuses were made, but I was cordially invited to draw anything needed from the commissary.

A second month passed, during which time the only currency current was in the form of land certificates. The Commonwealth of Texas, on her admission into the Union, retained the control of her lands, over half the entire area of the State being unclaimed at the close of the civil war. The carpet-bag government, then in the saddle, was prodigal to its favorites in bonuses of land to any and all kinds of public improvement. Certificates were issued in the form of scrip calling for sections of the public domain of six hundred and forty acres each, and were current at from three to five cents an acre. The owner of one or more could locate on any of the unoccupied lands of the present State by merely surveying and recording his selection at the county seat. The scrip was bandied about, no one caring for it, and on the termination of my second month I was offered four sections for my services up to date, provided I would remain longer in the company's employ. I knew the value of land in the older States, in fact, already had my eye on some splendid valleys on the Clear Fork, and accepted the offered certificates. The idea found a firm lodgment in my mind, and I traded one of my six-shooters even for a section of scrip, and won several more in card games. I had learned to play poker in the army, — knew the rudiments of the game at least, — and before the middle of March I was the possessor of certificates calling for thirty sections of land. As the time was drawing near for my return to Palo Pinto County, I severed my connection with the dredging company and returned to the home of my old comrade. I had left my horse with him, and under the pretense of paying for feeding the animal well for the return trip, had slipped my crony a small gold piece several times during the winter. He ridiculed me over my land scrip, but I was satisfied, and after spending a day with the couple I started on my return.

Evidences of spring were to be seen on every hand. My ride northward was a race with the season, but I outrode the coming grass, the budding trees, the first flowers, and the mating birds, and reached the Edwards ranch on the last day of March. Any number of cattle had already been tendered in making up the herd, over half the saddle horses necessary were in hand or promised, and they were only awaiting my return. I had no idea what the requirements of the Kansas market were, and no one else seemed to know, but it was finally decided to drive a mixed herd of twenty-five hundred by way of experiment. The promoters of the Abilene market had flooded Texas with advertising matter during the winter, urging that only choice cattle should be driven, yet the information was of little value where local customs classified all live stock. A beef was a beef, whether he weighed eight or twelve hundred pounds, a cow was a cow when over three years old, and so on to the end of the chapter. From a purely selfish motive of wanting strong cattle for the trip, I suggested that nothing under three-year-olds should be used in making up the herd, a preference to be given matured beeves. George Edwards also favored the idea, and as our experience in trailing cattle carried some little weight, orders were given to gather nothing that had not age, flesh, and strength for the journey.

I was to have fifty dollars a month and furnish my own mount. Horses were cheap, but I wanted good ones, and after skirmishing about I secured four to my liking in return for one hundred dollars in gold. I still had some money left from my wages in driving cattle to Fort Sumner, and I began looking about for oxen in which to invest the remainder. Having little, I must be very careful and make my investment in something staple; and remembering the fine prices current in Colorado the spring before for work cattle, I offered to supply the oxen for the commissary. My proposal was accepted, and accordingly I began making inquiry for wagon stock. Finally I heard of a freight outfit in the adjoining county east, the owner of which had died the winter before, the administrator offering his effects for sale. I lost no time in seeing the oxen and hunting up their custodian, who proved to be a frontier surveyor at the county seat. There were two teams of six yoke each, fine cattle, and I had hopes of being able to buy six or eight oxen. But the surveyor insisted on selling both teams, offering to credit me on any balance if I could give him security. I had never mentioned my land scrip to any one, and wishing to see if it had any value, I produced and tendered the certificates to the surveyor. He looked them over, made a computation, and informed me that they were worth in his county about five cents an acre, or nearly one thousand dollars. He also offered to accept them as security, assuring me that he could use some of them in locating lands for settlers. But it was not my idea to sell the land scrip, and a trade was easily effected on the twenty-four oxen, yokes, and chains, I paying what money I could spare and leaving the certificates for security on the balance. As I look back over an eventful life, I remember no special time in which I felt quite as rich as the evening that I drove into the Edwards ranch with twelve yoke of oxen chained together in one team. The darkies and Mexicans gathered about, even the family, to admire the big fellows, and I remember a thrill which shivered through me as Miss Gertrude passed down the column, kindly patting each near ox as though she felt a personal interest in my possessions.

We waited for good grass before beginning the gathering. Half a dozen round-ups on the home range would be all that was necessary in completing the numbers allotted to the Edwards ranch. Three other cowmen were going to turn in a thousand head and furnish and mount a man each, there being no occasion to road-brand, as every one knew the ranch, brands which would go to make up the herd. An outfit of twelve men was considered sufficient, as it was an open prairie country and through civilized tribes between Texas and Kansas. All the darkies and Mexicans from the home ranch who could be spared were to be taken along, making it necessary to hire only three outside men. The drive was looked upon as an experiment, there being no outlay of money, even the meal and bacon which went into the commissary being supplied from the Edwards household. The country contributed the horses and cattle, and if the project paid out, well and good; if not there was small loss, as they were worth nothing at home. The 20th of April was set for starting. Three days' work on the home range and we had two thousand cattle under herd, consisting of dry or barren cows and steers three years old or over, fully half the latter being heavy beeves. We culled back and trimmed our allotment down to sixteen hundred, and when the outside contingents were thrown in we had a few over twenty-eight hundred cattle in the herd. A Mexican was placed in charge of the remuda, a darky, with three yoke of oxen, looked after the commissary, and with ten mounted men around the herd we started.

Five and six horses were allotted to the man, each one had one or two six-shooters, while half a dozen rifles of different makes were carried in the wagon. The herd moved northward by easy marches, open country being followed until we reached Red River, where we had the misfortune to lose George Edwards from sickness. He was the foreman from whom all took orders. While crossing into the Chickasaw Nation it was necessary to swim the cattle. We cut them into small bunches, and in fording and refording a whole afternoon was spent in the water. Towards evening our foreman was rendered useless from a chill, followed by fever during the night. The next morning he was worse, and as it was necessary to move the herd out to open country, Edwards took an old negro with him and went back to a ranch on the Texas side. Several days afterward the darky overtook us with the word that his master would be unable to accompany the cattle, and that I was to take the herd through to Abilene. The negro remained with us, and at the first opportunity I picked up another man. Within a week we encountered a country trail, bearing slightly northwest, over which herds had recently passed. This trace led us into another, which followed up the south side of the Washita River, and two weeks after reaching the Nation we entered what afterward became famous as the Chisholm trail. The Chickasaw was one of the civilized tribes; its members had intermarried with the whites until their identity as Indians was almost lost. They owned fine homes and farms in the Washita valley, were hospitable to strangers, and where the aboriginal blood was properly diluted the women were strikingly beautiful. In this same valley, fifteen years afterward, I saw a herd of one thousand and seven head of corn-fed cattle. The grain was delivered at feed-lots at ten cents a bushel, and the beeves had then been on full feed for nine months. There were no railroads in the country and the only outlet for the surplus corn was to feed it to cattle and drive them to some shipping-point in Kansas.

Compared with the route to Fort Sumner, the northern one was a paradise. No day passed but there was an abundance of water, while the grass simply carpeted the country. We merely soldiered along, crossing what was then one of the No-man's lands and the Cherokee Outlet, never sighting another herd until after entering Kansas. We amused ourselves like urchins out for a holiday, the country was full of all kinds of game, and our darky cook was kept busy frying venison and roasting turkeys. A calf was born on the trail, the mother of which was quite gentle, and we broke her for a milk cow, while "Bull," the youngster, became a great pet. A cow-skin was slung under the wagon for carrying wood and heavy cooking utensils, and the calf was given a berth in the hammock until he was able to follow. But when Bull became older he hung around the wagon like a dog, preferring the company of the outfit to that of his own mother. He soon learned to eat cold biscuit and corn-pone, and would hang around at meal-time, ready for the scraps. We always had to notice where the calf lay down to sleep, as he was a black rascal, and the men were liable to stumble over him while changing guards during the night. He never could be prevailed on to walk with his mother, but followed the wagon or rode in his hammock, and was always happy as a lark when the recipient of the outfit's attentions. We sometimes secured as much as two gallons of milk a day from the cow, but it was pitiful to watch her futile efforts at coaxing her offspring away from the wagon.

We passed to the west of the town of Wichita and reached our destination early in June. There I found several letters awaiting me, with instructions to dispose of the herd or to report what was the prospect of effecting a sale. We camped about five miles from Abilene, and before I could post myself on cattle values half a dozen buyers had looked the herd over. Men were in the market anxious for beef cattle with which to fill army and Indian contracts, feeders from Eastern States, shippers and speculators galore, cowmen looking for she stuff with which to start new ranches, while scarcely a day passed but inquiry was made by settlers for oxen with which to break prairie. A dozen herds had arrived ahead of us, the market had fairly opened, and, once I got the drift of current prices, I was as busy as a farmer getting ready to cut his buckwheat. Every yoke of oxen was sold within a week, one ranchman took all the cows, an army contractor took one thousand of the largest beeves, feeders from Iowa took the younger steers, and within six weeks after arriving I did not have a hoof left. In the mean time I kept an account of each sale, brands and numbers, in order to render a statement to the owners of the cattle. As fast as the money was received I sent it home by drafts, except the proceeds from the oxen, which was a private matter. I bought and sold two whole remudas of horses on speculation, clearing fifteen of the best ones and three hundred dollars on the transactions.

The facilities for handling cattle at Abilene were not completed until late in the season of '67, yet twenty-five thousand cattle found a market there that summer and fall. The drive of the present year would triple that number, and every one seemed pleased with future prospects. The town took on an air of frontier prosperity; saloons and gambling and dance halls multiplied, and every legitimate line of business flourished like a green bay tree. I made the acquaintance of every drover and was generally looked upon as an extra good salesman, the secret being in our cattle, which were choice. For instance, Northern buyers could see three dollars a head difference in three-year-old steers, but with the average Texan the age classified them all alike. My boyhood knowledge of cattle had taught me the difference, but in range dealing it was impossible to apply the principle. I made many warm friends among both buyers and drovers, bringing them together and effecting sales, and it was really a matter of regret that I had to leave before the season was over. I loved the atmosphere of dicker and traffic, had made one of the largest sales of the season with our beeves, and was leaving, firm in the conviction that I had overlooked no feature of the market of future value.

After selling the oxen we broke some of our saddle stock to harness, altered the wagon tongue for horses, and started across the country for home, taking our full remuda with us. Where I had gone up the trail with five horses, I was going back with twenty; some of the oxen I had sold at treble their original cost, while none of them failed to double my money — on credit. Taking it all in all, I had never seen such good times and made money as easily. On the back track we followed the trail, but instead of going down the Washita as we had come, we followed the Chisholm trail to the Texas boundary, crossing at what was afterward known as Red River Station. From there home was an easy matter, and after an absence of four months and five days the outfit rode into the Edwards ranch with a flourish.

CHAPTER VI
SOWING WILD OATS

The results from driving cattle north were a surprise to every one. My employers were delighted with their experiment, the general expense of handling the herd not exceeding fifty cents a head. The enterprise had netted over fifty-two thousand dollars, the saddle horses had returned in good condition, while due credit was given me in the general management. From my sale accounts I made out a statement, and once my expenses were approved it was an easy matter to apportion each owner his just dues in the season's drive. This over I was free to go my way. The only incident of moment in the final settlement was the waggish contention of one of the owners, who expressed amazement that I ever remitted any funds or returned, roguishly admitting that no one expected it. Then suddenly, pretending to have discovered the governing motive, he summoned Miss Gertrude, and embarrassed her with a profusion of thanks, averring that she alone had saved him from a loss of four hundred beeves.

The next move was to redeem my land scrip. The surveyor was anxious to buy a portion of it, but I was too rich to part with even a single section. During our conversation, however, it developed that he held his commission from the State, and when I mentioned my intention of locating land, he made application to do the surveying. The fact that I expected to make my locations in another county made no difference to a free-lance official, and accordingly we came to an agreement. The apple of my eye was a valley on the Clear Fork, above its juncture with the main Brazos, and from maps in the surveyor's office I was able to point out the locality where I expected to make my locations. He proved an obliging official and gave me all the routine details, and an appointment was made with him to report a week later at the Edwards ranch. A wagon and cook would be necessary, chain carriers and flagmen must be taken along, and I began skirmishing about for an outfit. The three hired men who had been up the trail with me were still in the country, and I engaged them and secured a cook. George Edwards loaned me a wagon and two yoke of oxen, even going along himself for company. The commissary was outfitted for a month's stay, and a day in advance of the expected arrival of the surveyor the outfit was started up the Brazos. Each of the men had one or more private horses, and taking all of mine along, we had a remuda of thirty odd saddle horses. George and I remained behind, and on the arrival of the surveyor we rode by way of Palo Pinto, the county seat, to which all unorganized territory to the west was attached for legal purposes. Our chief motive in passing the town was to see if there were any lands located near the juncture of the Clear Fork with the mother stream, and thus secure an established corner from which to begin our survey. But the records showed no land taken up around the confluence of these watercourses, making it necessary to establish a corner.

Under the old customs, handed down from the Spanish to the Texans, corners were always established from natural landmarks. The union of creeks arid rivers, mounds, lagoons, outcropping of rock, in fact anything unchangeable and established by nature, were used as a point of commencement. In the locating of Spanish land grants a century and a half previous, sand-dunes were frequently used, and when these old concessions became of value and were surveyed, some of the corners had shifted a mile or more by the action of the wind and seasons on the sand-hills. Accordingly, on overtaking our outfit we headed for the juncture of the Brazos and Clear Fork, reaching our destination the second day. The first thing was to establish a corner or commencement point. Some heavy timber grew around the confluence, so, selecting an old patriarch pin oak between the two streams, we notched the tree and ran a line to low water at the juncture of the two rivers. Other witness trees were established and notched, lines were run at angles to the banks of either stream, and a hole was dug two feet deep between the roots of the pin oak, a stake set therein, and the excavation filled with charcoal and covered. A legal corner or commencement point was thus established; but as the land that I coveted lay some distance up the Clear Fork, it was necessary first to run due south six miles and establish a corner, and thence run west the same distance and locate another one.

The thirty sections of land scrip would entitle me to a block of ground five by six miles in extent, and I concluded to locate the bulk of it on the south side of the Clear Fork. A permanent camp was now established, the actual work of locating the land requiring about ten days, when the surveyor and Edwards set out on their return. They were to touch at the county seat, record the established corners and file my locations, leaving the other boys and me behind. It was my intention to build a corral and possibly a cabin on the land, having no idea that we would remain more than a few weeks longer. Timber was plentiful, and, selecting a site well out on the prairie, we began the corral. It was no easy task; palisades were cut twelve feet long and out of durable woods, and the gate-posts were fourteen inches in diameter at the small end, requiring both yoke of oxen to draw them to the chosen site. The latter were cut two feet longer than the palisades, the extra length being inserted in the ground, giving them a stability to carry the bars with which the gateway was closed. Ten days were spent in cutting and drawing timber, some of the larger palisades being split in two so as to enable five men to load them on the wagon. The digging of the narrow trench, five feet deep, in which the palisades were set upright, was a sore trial; but the ground was sandy, and by dint of perseverance it was accomplished. Instead of a few weeks, over a month was spent on the corral, but when it was finished it would hold a thousand stampeding cattle through the stormiest night that ever blew.

After finishing the corral we hunted a week. The country was alive with game of all kinds, even an occasional buffalo, while wild and unbranded cattle were seen daily. None of the men seemed anxious to leave the valley, but the commissary had to be replenished, so two of us made the trip to Belknap with a pack horse, returning the next day with meal, sugar, and coffee. A cabin was begun and completed in ten days, a crude but stable affair, with clapboard roof, clay floor, and ample fireplace. It was now late in September, and as the usual branding season was at hand, cow-hunting outfits might be expected to pass down the valley. The advantage of corrals would naturally make my place headquarters for cowmen, and we accordingly settled down until the branding season was over. But the abundance of mavericks and wild cattle was so tempting that we had three hundred under herd when the first cow-hunting outfits arrived. At one lake on what is now known as South Prairie, in a single moonlight night, we roped and tied down forty head, the next morning finding thirty of them unbranded and therefore unowned. All tame cattle would naturally water in the daytime, and anything coming in at night fell a victim to our ropes. A wooden toggle was fastened with rawhide to its neck, so it would trail between its forelegs, to prevent running, when the wild maverick was freed and allowed to enter the herd. After a week or ten days, if an animal showed any disposition to quiet down, it was again thrown, branded, and the toggle removed. We corralled the little herd every night, adding to it daily, scouting far and wide for unowned or wild cattle. But when other outfits came up or down the valley of the Clear Fork we joined forces with them, tendering our corrals for branding purposes, our rake-off being the mavericks and eligible strays. Many a fine quarter of beef was left at our cabin by passing ranchmen, and when the gathering ended we had a few over five hundred cattle for our time and trouble.

Fine weather favored us and we held the mavericks under herd until late in December. The wild ones gradually became gentle, and with constant handling these wild animals were located until they would come in of their own accord for the privilege of sleeping in a corral. But when winter approached the herd was turned free, that the cattle might protect themselves from storms, and we gathered our few effects together and started for the settlements. It was with reluctance that I left that primitive valley. Somehow or other, primal conditions possessed a charm for me which, coupled with an innate love of the land and the animals that inhabit it, seemed to influence and outline my future course of life. The pride of possession was mine; with my own hands and abilities had I earned the land, while the overflow from a thousand hills stocked my new ranch. I was now the owner of lands and cattle; my father in his palmiest days never dreamed of such possessions as were mine, while youth and opportunity encouraged me to greater exertions.

We reached the Edwards ranch a few days before Christmas. The boys were settled with and returned to their homes, and I was once more adrift. Forty odd calves had been branded as the increase of my mavericking of the year before, and, still basking in the smile of fortune, I found a letter awaiting me from Major Seth Mabry of Austin, anxious to engage my services as a trail foreman for the coming summer. I had met Major Seth the spring before at Abilene, and was instrumental in finding him a buyer for his herd, and otherwise we became fast friends. There were no outstanding obligations to my former employers, so when a protest was finally raised against my going, I had the satisfaction of vouching for George Edwards, to the manner born, and a better range cowman than I was. The same group of ranchmen expected to drive another herd the coming spring, and I made it a point to see each one personally, urging that nothing but choice cattle should be sent up the trail. My long acquaintance with the junior Edwards enabled me to speak emphatically and to the point, and I lectured him thoroughly as to the requirements of the Abilene market.

I notified Major Mabry that I would be on hand within a month. The holiday season soon passed, and leaving my horses at the Edwards ranch, I saddled the most worthless one and started south. The trip was uneventful, except that I traded horses twice, reaching my destination within a week, having seen no country en route that could compare with the valley of the Clear Fork. The capital city was a straggling village on the banks of the Colorado River, inert through political usurpation, yet the home of many fine people. Quite a number of cowmen resided there, owning ranches in outlying and adjoining counties, among them being my acquaintance of the year before and present employer. It was too early by nearly a month to begin active operations, and I contented myself about town, making the acquaintance of other cowmen and their foremen who expected to drive that year. New Orleans had previously been the only outlet for beef cattle in southern Texas, and even in the spring of '69 very few had any confidence of a market in the north. Major Mabry, however, was going to drive two herds to Abilene, one of beeves and the other of younger steers, dry cows, and thrifty two-year-old heifers, and I was to have charge of the heavy cattle. Both herds would be put up in Llano County, it being the intention to start with the grass. Mules were to be worked to the wagons, oxen being considered too slow, while both outfits were to be mounted seven horses to the man.

During my stay at Austin I frequently made inquiry for land scrip. Nearly all the merchants had more or less, the current prices being about five cents an acre. There was a clear distinction, however, in case one was a buyer or seller, the former being shown every attention. I allowed the impression to circulate that I would buy, which brought me numerous offers, and before leaving the town I secured twenty sections for five hundred dollars. I needed just that amount to cover a four-mile bend of the Clear Fork on the west end of my new ranch, — a possession which gave me ten miles of that virgin valley. My employer congratulated me on my investment, and assured me that if the people ever overthrew the Reconstruction usurpers the public domain would no longer be bartered away for chips and whetstones. I was too busy to take much interest in the political situation, and, so long as I was prosperous and employed, gave little heed to politics.

Major Mabry owned a ranch and extensive cattle interests northwest in Llano County. As we expected to start the herds as early as possible, the latter part of February found us at the ranch actively engaged in arranging for the summer's work. There were horses to buy, wagons to outfit, and hands to secure, and a busy fortnight was spent in getting ready for the drive. The spring before I had started out in debt; now, on permission being given me, I bought ten horses for my own use and invested the balance of my money in four yoke of oxen. Had I remained in Palo Pinto County the chances were that I might have enlarged my holdings in the coming drive, as in order to have me remain several offered to sell me cattle on credit. But so long as I was enlarging my experience I was content, while the wages offered me were double what I received the summer before.

We went into camp and began rounding up near the middle of March. All classes of cattle were first gathered into one herd, after which the beeves were cut separate and taken charge of by my outfit. We gathered a few over fifteen hundred of the latter, all prairie-raised cattle, four years old or over, and in the single ranch brand of my employer. Major Seth had also contracted for one thousand other beeves, and it became our duty to receive them. These outside contingents would have to be road-branded before starting, as they were in a dozen or more brands, the work being done in a chute built for that purpose. My employer and I fully agreed on the quality of cattle to be received, and when possible we both passed on each tender of beeves before accepting them. The two herds were being held separate, and a friendly rivalry existed between the outfits as to which herd would be ready to start first. It only required a few days extra to receive and road-brand the outside cattle, when all were ready to start. As Major Seth knew the most practical route, in deference to his years and experience I insisted that he should take the lead until after Red River was crossed. I had been urging the Chisholm trail in preference to more eastern ones, and with the compromise that I should take the lead after passing Fort Worth, the two herds started on the last day of March.

There was no particular trail to follow. The country was all open, and the grass was coming rapidly, while the horses and cattle were shedding their winter coats with the change of the season. Fine weather favored us, no rains at night and few storms, and within two weeks we passed Fort Worth, after which I took the lead. I remember that at the latter point I wrote a letter to the elder Edwards, inclosing my land scrip, and asking him to send a man out to my new ranch occasionally to see that the improvements were not destroyed. Several herds had already passed the fort, their destination being the same as ours, and from thence onward we had the advantage of following a trail. As we neared Red River, nearly all the herds bore off to the eastward, but we held our course, crossing into the Chickasaw Nation at the regular Chisholm ford. A few beggarly Indians, renegades from the Kiowas and Comanches on the west, annoyed us for the first week, but were easily appeased with a lame or stray beef. The two herds held rather close together as a matter of mutual protection, as in some of the encampments were fully fifty lodges with possibly as many able-bodied warriors. But after crossing the Washita River no further trouble was encountered from the natives, and we swept northward at the steady pace of an advancing army. Other herds were seen in our rear and front, and as we neared the Kansas line several long columns of cattle were sighted coming in over the safer eastern routes.

The last lap of the drive was reached. A fortnight later we went into camp within twelve miles of Abilene, having been on the trail two months and eleven days. The same week we moved north of the railroad, finding ample range within seven miles of town. Herds were coming in rapidly, and it was important to secure good grazing grounds for our cattle. Buyers were arriving from every territory in the Northwest, including California, while the usual contingent of Eastern dealers, shippers, and market-scalpers was on hand. It could hardly be said that prices had yet opened, though several contracted herds had already been delivered, while every purchaser was bearing the market and prophesying a drive of a quarter million cattle. The drovers, on the other hand, were combating every report in circulation, even offering to wager that the arrivals of stock for the entire summer would not exceed one hundred thousand head. Cowmen reported en route with ten thousand beeves came in with one fifth the number, and sellers held the whip hand, the market actually opening at better figures than the summer before. Once prices were established, I was in the thick of the fight, selling my oxen the first week to a freighter, constantly on the skirmish for a buyer, and never failing to recognize one with whom I had done business the summer before. In case Major Mabry had nothing to suit, the herd in charge of George Edwards was always shown, and I easily effected two sales, aggregating fifteen hundred head, from the latter cattle, with customers of the year previous.

But my zeal for bartering in cattle came to a sudden end near the close of June. A conservative estimate of the arrivals then in sight or known to be en route for Abilene was placed at one hundred and fifty thousand cattle. Yet instead of any weakening in prices, they seemed to strengthen with the influx of buyers from the corn regions, as the prospects of the season assured a bountiful new crop. Where States had quarantined against Texas cattle the law was easily circumvented by a statement that the cattle were immune from having wintered in the north, which satisfied the statutes — as there was no doubt but they had wintered somewhere. Steer cattle of acceptable age and smoothness of build were in demand by feeders; all classes in fact felt a stimulus. My beeves were sold for delivery north of Cheyenne, Wyoming, the buyers, who were ranchmen as well as army contractors, taking the herd complete, including the remuda and wagon. Under the terms, the cattle were to start immediately and be grazed through. I was given until the middle of September to reach my destination, and at once moved out on a northwest course. On reaching the Republican River, we followed it to the Colorado line, and then tacked north for Cheyenne. Reporting our progress to the buyers, we were met and directed to pass to the eastward of that village, where we halted a week, and seven hundred of the fattest beeves were cut out for delivery at Fort Russell. By various excuses we were detained until frost fell before we reached the ranch, and a second and a third contingent of beeves were cut out for other deliveries, making it nearly the middle of October before I was finally relieved.

With the exception of myself, a new outfit of men had been secured at Abilene. Some of them were retained at the ranch of the contractors, the remainder being discharged, all of us returning to Cheyenne together, whence we scattered to the four winds. I spent a week in Denver, meeting Charlie Goodnight, who had again fought his way up the Pecos route and delivered his cattle to the contractors at Fort Logan. Continuing homeward, I took the train for Abilene, hesitating whether to stop there or visit my brother in Missouri before returning to Texas. I had twelve hundred dollars with me, as the proceeds of my wages, horses, and oxen, and, feeling rather affluent, I decided to stop over a day at the new trail town. I knew the market was virtually over, and what evil influence ever suggested my stopping at Abilene is unexplainable. But I did stop, and found things just as I expected, — everybody sold out and gone home. A few trail foremen were still hanging around the town under the pretense of attending to unsettled business, and these welcomed me with a fraternal greeting. Two of them who had served in the Confederate army came to me and frankly admitted that they were broke, and begged me to help them out of town by redeeming their horses and saddles. Feed bills had accumulated and hotel accounts were unpaid; the appeals of the rascals would have moved a stone to pity.

The upshot of the whole matter was that I bought a span of mules and wagon and invited seven of the boys to accompany me overland to Texas. My friends insisted that we could sell the outfit in the lower country for more than cost, but before I got out of town my philanthropic venture had absorbed over half my savings. As long as I had money the purse seemed a public one, and all the boys borrowed just as freely as if they expected to repay it. I am sure they felt grateful, and had I been one of the needy no doubt any of my friends would have shared his purse with me.

It was a delightful trip across the Indian Territory, and we reached Sherman, Texas, just before the holidays. Every one had become tired of the wagon, and I was fortunate enough to sell it without loss. Those who had saddle horses excused themselves and hurried home for the Christmas festivities, leaving a quartette of us behind. But before the remainder of us proceeded to our destinations two of the boys discovered a splendid opening for a monte game, in which we could easily recoup all our expenses for the trip. I was the only dissenter to the programme, not even knowing the game; but under the pressure which was brought to bear I finally yielded, and became banker for my friends. The results are easily told. The second night there was heavy play, and before ten o'clock the monte bank closed for want of funds, it having been tapped for its last dollar. The next morning I took stage for Dallas, where I arrived with less than twenty dollars, and spent the most miserable Christmas day of my life. I had written George Edwards from Denver that I expected to go to Missouri, and asked him to take my horses and go out to the little ranch and brand my calves. There was no occasion now to contradict my advice of that letter, neither would I go near the Edwards ranch, yet I hungered for that land scrip and roundly cursed myself for being a fool. It would be two months and a half before spring work opened, and what to do in the mean time was the one absorbing question. My needs were too urgent to allow me to remain idle long, and, drifting south, working when work was to be had, at last I reached the home of my soldier crony in Washington County, walking and riding in country wagons the last hundred miles of the distance. No experience in my life ever humiliated me as that one did, yet I have laughed about it since. I may have previously heard of riches taking wings, but in this instance, now mellowed by time, no injustice will be done by simply recording it as the parting of a fool and his money.

CHAPTER VII
"THE ANGEL"

The winds of adversity were tempered by the welcome extended me by my old comrade and his wife. There was no concealment as to my financial condition, but when I explained the causes my former crony laughed at me until the tears stood in his eyes. Nor did I protest, because I so richly deserved it. Fortunately the circumstances of my friends had bettered since my previous visit, and I was accordingly relieved from any feeling of intrusion. In two short years the wheel had gone round, and I was walking heavily on my uppers and continually felt like a pauper or poor relation. To make matters more embarrassing, I could appeal to no one, and, fortified by pride from birth, I ground my teeth over resolutions that will last me till death. Any one of half a dozen friends, had they known my true condition, would have gladly come to my aid, but circumstances prevented me from making any appeal. To my brother in Missouri I had previously written of my affluence; as for friends in Palo Pinto County, — well, for the very best of reasons my condition would remain a sealed book in that quarter; and to appeal to Major Mabry might arouse his suspicions. I had handled a great deal of money for him, accounting for every cent, but had he known of my inability to take care of my own frugal earnings it might have aroused his distrust. I was sure of a position with him again as trail foreman, and not for the world would I have had him know that I could be such a fool as to squander my savings thoughtlessly.

What little correspondence I conducted that winter was by roundabout methods. I occasionally wrote my brother that I was wallowing in wealth, always inclosing a letter to Gertrude Edwards with instructions to remail, conveying the idea to her family that I was spending the winter with relatives in Missouri. As yet there was no tacit understanding between Miss Gertrude and me, but I conveyed that impression to my brother, and as I knew he had run away with his wife, I had confidence he would do my bidding. In writing my employer I reported myself as busy dealing in land scrip, and begged him not to insist on my appearance until it was absolutely necessary. He replied that I might have until the 15th of March in which to report at Austin, as my herd had been contracted for north in Williamson County. Major Mabry expected to drive three herds that spring, the one already mentioned and two from Llano County, where he had recently acquired another ranch with an extensive stock of cattle. It therefore behooved me to keep my reputation unsullied, a rather difficult thing to do when our escapade at Sherman was known to three other trail foremen. They might look upon it as a good joke, while to me it was a serious matter.

Had there been anything to do in Washington County, it was my intention to go to work. The dredging company had departed for newer fields, there was no other work in sight, and I was compelled to fold my hands and bide my time. My crony and I blotted out the days by hunting deer and turkeys, using hounds for the former and shooting the animals at game crossings. By using a turkey-call we could entice the gobblers within rifle-shot, and in several instances we were able to locate their roosts. The wild turkey of Texas was a wary bird, and although I have seen flocks of hundreds, it takes a crafty hunter to bag one. I have always loved a gun and been fond of hunting, yet the time hung heavy on my hands, and I counted the days like a prisoner until I could go to work. But my sentence finally expired, and preparations were made for my start to Austin. My friends offered their best wishes, — about all they had, — and my old comrade went so far as to take me one day on horseback to where he had an acquaintance living. There we stayed over night, which was more than half way to my destination, and the next morning we parted, he to his home with the horses, while I traveled on foot or trusted to country wagons. I arrived in Austin on the appointed day, with less than five dollars in my pocket, and registered at the best hotel in the capital. I needed a saddle, having sold mine in Wyoming the fall before, and at once reported to my employer. Fortunately my arrival was being awaited to start a remuda and wagon to Williamson County, and when I assured Major

Mabry that all I lacked was a saddle, he gave me an order on a local dealer, and we started that same evening.

At last I was saved. With the opening of work my troubles lifted like a night fog before the rising sun. Even the first view of the remuda revived my spirits, as I had been allotted one hundred fine cow-horses. They had been brought up during the winter, had run in a good pasture for some time, and with the opening of spring were in fine condition. Many trail men were short-sighted in regard to mounting their outfits, and although we had our differences, I want to say that Major Mabry and his later associates never expected a man to render an honest day's work unless he was properly supplied with horses. My allowance for the spring of 1870 was again seven horses to the man, with two extra for the foreman, which at that early day in trailing cattle was considered the maximum where Kansas was the destination. Many drovers allowed only five horses to the man, but their men were frequently seen walking with the herd, their mounts mingling with the cattle, unable to carry their riders longer.

The receiving of the herd in Williamson County was an easy matter. Four prominent ranchmen were to supply the beeves to the number of three thousand. Nearly every hoof was in the straight ranch brand of the sellers, only some two hundred being mixed brands and requiring the usual road-branding. In spite of every effort to hold the herd down to the contracted number, we received one hundred and fifty extra; but then they were cattle that no justifiable excuse could be offered in refusing. The last beeves were received on the 22d of the month, and after cutting separate all cattle of outside brands, they were sent to the chute to receive the road-mark. Major Mabry was present, and a controversy arose between the sellers and himself over our refusal to road-brand, or at least vent the ranch brands, on the great bulk of the herd. Too many brands on an animal was an objection to the shippers and feeders of the North, and we were anxious to cater to their wishes as far as possible. The sellers protested against the cattle leaving their range without some mark to indicate their change of ownership. The country was all open; in case of a stampede and loss of cattle within a few hundred miles they were certain to drift back to their home range, with nothing to distinguish them from their brothers of the same age. Flesh marks are not a good title by which to identify one's property, where those possessions consist of range cattle, and the law recognized the holding brand as the hall-mark of ownership. But a compromise was finally agreed upon, whereby we were to run the beeves through the chute and cut the brush from their tails. In a four or five year old animal this tally-mark would hold for a year, and in no wise work any hardship to the animal in warding off insect life. In case of any loss on the trail my employer agreed to pay one dollar a head for regathering any stragglers that returned within a year. The proposition was a fair one, the ranchmen yielded, and we ran the whole herd through the chute, cutting the brush within a few inches of the end of the tail-bone. By tightly wrapping the brush once around the blade of a sharp knife, it was quick work to thus vent a chuteful of cattle, both the road-branding and tally-marking being done in two days.

The herd started on the morning of the 25th. I had a good outfit of men, only four of whom were with me the year before. The spring could not be considered an early one, and therefore we traveled slow for the first few weeks, meeting with two bad runs, three days apart, but without the loss of a hoof. These panics among the cattle were unexplainable, as they were always gorged with grass and water at bedding time, the weather was favorable, no unseemly noises were heard by the men on guard, and both runs occurred within two hours of daybreak. There was a half-breed Mexican in the outfit, a very quiet man, and when the causes of the stampedes were being discussed around the camp-fire, I noticed that he shrugged his shoulders in derision of the reasons advanced. The half-breed was my horse wrangler, old in years and experience, and the idea struck me to sound him as to his version of the existing trouble among the cattle. He was inclined to be distant, but I approached him cautiously, complimented him on his handling of the remuda, rode with him several hours, and adroitly drew out his opinion of what caused our two stampedes. As he had never worked with the herd, his first question was, did we receive any blind cattle or had any gone blind since we started? He then informed me that the old Spanish rancheros would never leave a sightless animal in a corral with sound ones during the night for fear of a stampede. He cautioned me to look the herd over carefully, and if there was a blind animal found to cut it out or the trouble would be repeated in spite of all precaution. I rode back and met the herd, accosting every swing man on one side with the inquiry if any blind animal had been seen, without results until the drag end of the cattle was reached. Two men were at the rear, and when approached with the question, both admitted noticing, for the past week, a beef which acted as if he might be crazy. I had them point out the steer, and before I had watched him ten minutes was satisfied that he was stone blind. He was a fine, big fellow, in splendid flesh, but it was impossible to keep him in the column; he was always straggling out and constantly shying from imaginary objects. I had the steer roped for three or four nights and tied to a tree, and as the stampeding ceased we cut him out every evening when bedding down the herd, and allowed him to sleep alone. The poor fellow followed us, never venturing to leave either day or night, but finally fell into a deep ravine and broke his neck. His affliction had befallen him on the trail, affecting his nervous system to such an extent that he would jump from imaginary objects and thus stampede his brethren. I remember it occurred to me, then, how little I knew about cattle, and that my wrangler and I ought to exchange places. Since that day I have always been an attentive listener to the humblest of my fellowmen when interpreting the secrets of animal life.

Another incident occurred on this trip which showed the observation and insight of my half-breed wrangler. We were passing through some cross-timbers one morning in northern Texas, the remuda and wagon far in the lead. We were holding the herd as compactly as possible to prevent any straying of cattle, when our saddle horses were noticed abandoned in thick timber. It was impossible to leave the herd at the time, but on reaching the nearest opening, about two miles ahead, I turned and galloped back for fear of losing horses. I counted the remuda and found them all there, but the wrangler was missing. Thoughts of desertion flashed through my mind, the situation was unexplainable, and after calling, shooting, and circling around for over an hour, I took the remuda in hand and started after the herd, mentally preparing a lecture in case my wrangler returned. While nooning that day some six or seven miles distant, the half-breed jauntily rode into camp, leading a fine horse, saddled and bridled, with a man's coat tied to the cantle-strings. He explained to us that he had noticed the trail of a horse crossing our course at right angles. The freshness of the sign attracted his attention, and trailing it a short distance in the dewy morning he had noticed that something attached to the animal was trailing. A closer examination was made, and he decided that it was a bridle rein and not a rope that was attached to the wandering horse. From the freshness of the trail, he felt positive that he would overtake the animal shortly, but after finding him some difficulty was encountered before the horse would allow himself to be caught. He apologized for his neglect of duty, considering the incident as nothing unusual, and I had not the heart even to scold him. There were letters in the pocket of the coat, from which the owner was identified, and on arriving at Abilene the pleasure was mine of returning the horse and accoutrements and receiving a twenty-dollar gold piece for my wrangler. A stampede of trail cattle had occurred some forty miles to the northwest but a few nights before our finding the horse, during which the herd ran into some timber, and a low-hanging limb unhorsed the foreman, the animal escaping until captured by my man.

On approaching Fort Worth, still traveling slowly on account of the lateness of the spring, I decided to pay a flying visit to Palo Pinto County. It was fully eighty miles from the Fort across to the Edwards ranch, and appointing one of my old men as segundo, I saddled my best horse and set out an hour before sunset. I had made the same ride four years previously on coming to the country, a cool night favored my mount, and at daybreak I struck the Brazos River within two miles of the ranch. An eventful day followed; I reeled off innocent white-faced lies by the yard, in explaining the delightful winter I had spent with my brother in Missouri. Fortunately the elder Edwards was not driving any cattle that year, and George was absent buying oxen for a Fort Griffin freighter. Good reports of my new ranch awaited me, my cattle were increasing, and the smile of prosperity again shed its benediction over me. No one had located any lands near my little ranch, and the coveted addition on the west was still vacant and unoccupied. The silent monitor within my breast was my only accuser, but as I rode away from the Edwards ranch in the shade of evening, even it was silenced, for I held the promise of a splendid girl to become my wife. A second sleepless night passed like a pleasant dream, and early the next morning, firmly anchored in resolutions that no vagabond friends could ever shake, I overtook my herd.

After crossing Red River, the sweep across the Indian country was but a repetition of other years, with its varying monotony. Once we were waterbound for three days, severe drifts from storms at night were experienced, delaying our progress, and we did not reach Abilene until June 15. We were aware, however, of an increased drive of cattle to the north; evidences were to be seen on every hand; owners were hanging around the different fords and junctions of trails, inquiring if herds in such and such brands had been seen or spoken. While we were crossing the Nations, men were daily met hunting for lost horses or inquiring for stampeded cattle, while the regular trails were being cut into established thoroughfares from increasing use. Neither of the other Mabry herds had reached their destination on our arrival, though Major Seth put in an appearance within a week and reported the other two about one hundred miles to the rear. Cattle were arriving by the thousands, buyers from the north, east, and west were congregating, and the prospect of good prices was flattering. I was fortunate in securing my old camp-ground north of the town; a dry season had set in nearly a month before, maturing the grass, and our cattle took on flesh rapidly. Buyers looked them over daily, our prices being firm. Wintered cattle were up in the pictures, a rate war was on between all railroad lines east of the Mississippi River, cutting to the bone to secure the Western live-stock traffic. Three-year-old steers bought the fall before at twenty dollars and wintered on the Kansas prairies were netting their owners as high as sixty dollars on the Chicago market. The man with good cattle for sale could afford to be firm.

At this juncture a regrettable incident occurred, which, however, proved a boon to me. Some busybody went to the trouble of telling Major Mabry about my return to Abilene the fall before and my subsequent escapade in Texas, embellishing the details and even intimating that I had squandered funds not my own. I was thirty years old and as touchy as gunpowder, and felt the injustice of the charge like a knife-blade in my heart. There was nothing to do but ask for my release, place the facts in the hands of my employer, and court a thorough investigation. I had always entertained the highest regard for Major Mabry, and before the season ended I was fully vindicated and we were once more fast friends.

In the mean time I was not idle. By the first of July it was known that three hundred thousand cattle would be the minimum of the summer's drive to Abilene. My extensive acquaintance among buyers made my services of value to new drovers. A commission of twenty-five cents a head was offered me for effecting sales. The first week after severing my connection with Major Seth my earnings from a single trade amounted to seven hundred and fifty dollars. Thenceforth I was launched on a business of my own. Fortune smiled on me, acquaintances nicknamed me "The Angel," and instead of my foolishness reflecting on me, it made me a host of friends. Cowmen insisted on my selling their cattle, shippers consulted me, and I was constantly in demand with buyers, who wished my opinion on young steers before closing trades. I was chosen referee in a dozen disputes in classifying cattle, my decisions always giving satisfaction. Frequently, on an order, I turned buyer. Northern men seemed timid in relying on their own judgment of Texas cattle. Often, after a trade was made, the buyer paid me the regular commission for cutting and receiving, not willing to risk his judgment on range cattle. During the second week in August I sold five thousand head and bought fifteen hundred. Every man who had purchased cattle the year before had made money and was back in the market for more. Prices were easily advanced as the season wore on, whole herds were taken by three or four farmers from the corn regions, and the year closed with a flourish. In the space of four months I was instrumental in selling, buying, cutting, or receiving a few over thirty thousand head, on all of which I received a commission.

I established a camp of my own during the latter part of August. In order to avoid night-herding his cattle the summer before, some one had built a corral about ten miles northeast of Abilene. It was a temporary affair, the abrupt, bluff banks of a creek making a perfect horseshoe, requiring only four hundred feet of fence across the neck to inclose a corral of fully eight acres. The inclosure was not in use, so I hired three men and took possession of it for the time being. I had noticed in previous years that when a drover had sold all his herd but a remnant, he usually sacrificed his culls in order to reduce the expense of an outfit and return home. I had an idea that there was money in buying up these remnants and doing a small jobbing business. Frequently I had as many as seven hundred cull cattle on hand. Besides, I was constantly buying and selling whole remudas of saddle horses. So when a drover had sold all but a few hundred cattle he would come to me, and I would afford him the relief he wanted. Cripples and sore-footed animals were usually thrown in for good measure, or accepted at the price of their hides. Some buyers demanded quality and some cared only for numbers. I remember effecting a sale of one hundred culls to a settler, southeast on the Smoky River, at seven dollars a head. The terms were that I was to cut out the cattle, and as many were cripples and cost me little or nothing, they afforded a nice profit besides cleaning up my herd. When selling my own, I always priced a choice of my cattle at a reasonable figure, or offered to cull out the same number at half the price. By this method my herd was kept trimmed from both ends and the happy medium preserved.

I love to think of those good old days. Without either foresight or effort I made all kinds of money during the summer of 1870. Our best patrons that fall were small ranchmen from Kansas and Nebraska, every one of whom had coined money on their purchases of the summer before. One hundred per cent for wintering a steer and carrying him less than a year had brought every cattleman and his cousin back to Abilene to duplicate their former ventures. The little ranchman who bought five hundred steers in the fall of 1869 was in the market the present summer for a thousand head. Demand always seemed to meet supply a little over half-way. The market closed firm, with every hoof taken and at prices that were entirely satisfactory to drovers. It would seem an impossibility were I to admit my profits for that year, yet at the close of the season I started overland to Texas with fifty choice saddle horses and a snug bank account. Surely those were the golden days of the old West.

My last act before leaving Abilene that fall was to meet my enemy and force a personal settlement. Major Mabry washed his hands by firmly refusing to name my accuser, but from other sources I traced my defamer to a liveryman of the town. The fall before, on four horses and saddles, I paid a lien, in the form of a feed bill, of one hundred and twenty dollars for my stranded friends. The following day the same man presented me another bill for nearly an equal amount, claiming it had been assigned to him in a settlement with other parties. I investigated the matter, found it to be a disputed gambling account, and refused payment. An attempt was made, only for a moment, to hold the horses, resulting in my incurring the stableman's displeasure. The outcome was that on our return the next spring our patronage went to another *bran*, and the story, born in malice and falsehood, was started between employer and employee. I had made arrangements to return to Texas with the last one of Major Mabry's outfits, and the wagon and remuda had already started, when I located my traducer in a well-known saloon. I invited him to a seat at a table, determined to bring matters to an issue. He reluctantly complied, when I branded him with every vile epithet that my tongue could command, concluding by arraigning him as a coward. I was hungering for him to show some resistance, expecting to kill him, and when he refused to notice my insults, I called the barkeeper and asked for two glasses of whiskey and a pair of six-shooters. Not a word passed between us until the bartender brought the drinks and guns on a tray. "Now take your choice," said I. He replied, "I believe a little whiskey will do me good."

CHAPTER VIII
THE "LAZY L"

The homeward trip was a picnic. Counting mine, we had one hundred and fifty saddle horses. All surplus men in the employ of Major Mabry had been previously sent home until there remained at the close of the season only the drover, seven men, and myself. We averaged forty miles a day returning, sweeping down the plains like a north wind until Red River Station was reached. There our ways parted, and cutting separate my horses, we bade each other farewell, the main outfit heading for Fort Worth, while I bore to the westward for Palo Pinto. Major Seth was anxious to secure my services for another year, but I made no definite promises. We parted the best of friends. There were scattering ranches on my route, but driving fifty loose horses made traveling slow, and it was nearly a week before I reached the Edwards ranch.

The branding season was nearly over. After a few days' rest, an outfit of men was secured, and we started for my little ranch on the Clear Fork. Word was sent to the county seat, appointing a date with the surveyor, and on arriving at the new ranch I found that the corrals had been in active use by branding parties. We were soon in the thick of the fray, easily holding our own, branding every maverick on the range as well as catching wild cattle. My weakness for a good horse was the secret of much of my success in ranching during the early days, for with a remuda of seventy picked horses it was impossible for any unowned animal to escape us. Our drag-net scoured the hills and valleys, and before the arrival of the surveyor we had run the "44" on over five hundred calves, mavericks, and wild cattle. Different outfits came down the Brazos and passed up the Clear Fork, always using my corrals when working in the latter valley. We usually joined in with these cow-hunting parties, extending to them every possible courtesy, and in return many a thrifty yearling was added to my brand. Except some wild-cattle hunting which we had in view, every hoof was branded up by the time the surveyor arrived at the ranch.

The locating of twenty sections of land was an easy matter. We had established corners from which to work, and commencing on the west end of my original location, we ran off an area of country, four miles west by five south. New outside corners were established with buried charcoal and stakes, while the inner ones were indicated by half-buried rock, nothing divisional being done except to locate the land in sections. It was a beautiful tract, embracing a large bend of the Clear Fork, heavily timbered in several places, the soil being of a rich, sandy loam and covered with grass. I was proud of my landed interest, though small compared to modern ranches; and after the surveying ended, we spent a few weeks hunting out several rendezvous of wild cattle before returning to the Edwards ranch.

I married during the holidays. The new ranch was abandoned during the winter months, as the cattle readily cared for themselves, requiring no attention. I now had a good working capital, and having established myself by marriage into a respectable family of the country, I found several avenues open before me. Among the different openings for attractive investment was a brand of cattle belonging to an estate south in Comanche County. If the cattle were as good as represented they were certainly a bargain, as the brand was offered straight through at four dollars and a half a head. It was represented that nothing had been sold from the brand in a number of years, the estate was insolvent, and the trustee was anxious to sell the entire stock outright. I was impressed with the opportunity, and early in the winter George Edwards and I rode down to look the situation over. By riding around the range a few days we were able to get a good idea of the stock, and on inquiry among neighbors and men familiar with the brand, I was satisfied that the cattle were a bargain. A lawyer at the county seat was the trustee, and on opening negotiations with him it was readily to be seen that all he knew about the stock was that shown by the books and accounts. According to the branding for the past few years, it would indicate a brand of five or six thousand cattle. The only trouble in trading was to arrange the terms, my offer being half cash and the balance in six months, the cattle to be gathered early the coming spring. A bewildering list of references was given and we returned home. Within a fortnight a letter came from the trustee, accepting my offer and asking me to set a date for the gathering. I felt positive that the brand ought to run forty per cent steer cattle, and unless there was some deception, there would be in the neighborhood of two thousand head fit for the trail. I at once bought thirty more saddle horses, outfitted a wagon with oxen to draw it, besides hiring fifteen cow-hands. Early in March we started for Comanche County, having in the mean time made arrangements with the elder Edwards to supply one thousand head of trail cattle, intended for the Kansas market.

An early spring favored the work. By the 10th of the month we were actively engaged in gathering the stock. It was understood that we were to have the assistance of the ranch outfit in holding the cattle, but as they numbered only half a dozen and were miserably mounted, they were of little use except as herders. All the neighboring ranches gave us round-ups, and by the time we reached the home range of the brand I was beginning to get uneasy on account of the numbers under herd. My capital was limited, and if we gathered six thousand head it would absorb my money. I needed a little for expenses on the trail, and too many cattle would be embarrassing. There was no intention on my part to act dishonestly in the premises, even if we did drop out any number of yearlings during the last few days of the gathering. It was absolutely necessary to hold the numbers down to five thousand head, or as near that number as possible, and by keeping the ranch outfit on herd and my men out on round-ups, it was managed quietly, though we let no steer cattle two years old or over escape. When the gathering was finished, to the surprise of every one the herd counted out fifty-six hundred and odd cattle. But the numbers were still within the limits of my capital, and at the final settlement I asked the privilege of cutting out and leaving on the range one hundred head of weak, thin stock and cows heavy in calf. I offered to tally-mark and send after them during the fall branding, when the trustee begged me to make him an offer on any remnant of cattle, making me full owner of the brand. I hesitated to involve myself deeper in debt, but when he finally offered me the "Lazy L" brand outright for the sum of one thousand dollars, and on a credit, I never stuttered in accepting his proposal.

I culled back one hundred before starting, there being no occasion now to tally-mark, as I was in full possession of the brand. This amount of cattle in one herd was unwieldy to handle. The first day's drive we scarcely made ten miles, it being nearly impossible to water such an unmanageable body of animals, even from a running stream. The second noon we cut separate all the steers two years old and upward, finding a few under twenty-three hundred in the latter class. This left three thousand and odd hundred in the mixed herd, running from yearlings to old range bulls. A few extra men were secured, and some progress was made for the next few days, the steers keeping well in the lead, the two herds using the same wagon, and camping within half a mile of each other at night. It was fully ninety miles to the Edwards ranch; and when about two thirds the distance was covered, a messenger met us and reported the home cattle under herd and ready to start. It still lacked two days of the appointed time for our return, but rather than disappoint any one, I took seven men and sixty horses with the lead herd and started in to the ranch, leaving the mixed cattle to follow with the wagon. We took a day's rations on a pack horse, touched at a ranch, and on the second evening reached home. My contingent to the trail herd would have classified approximately seven hundred twos, six hundred threes, and one thousand four years old or over.

The next morning the herd started up the trail under George Edwards as foreman. It numbered a few over thirty-three hundred head and had fourteen men, all told, and ninety-odd horses, with four good mules to a new wagon. I promised to overtake them within a week, and the same evening rejoined the mixed herd some ten miles back down the country. Calves were dropping at an alarming rate, fully twenty of them were in the wagon, their advent delaying the progress of the herd. By dint of great exertion we managed to reach the ranch the next evening, where we lay over a day and rigged up a second wagon, purposely for calves. It was the intention to send the stock cattle to my new ranch on the Clear Fork, and releasing all but four men, the idle help about the home ranch were substituted. In moving cattle from one range to another, it should always be done with the coming of grass, as it gives them a full summer to locate and become attached to their new range. When possible, the coming calf crop should be born where the mothers are to be located, as it strengthens the ties between an animal and its range by making sacred the birthplace of its young. From instinctive warnings of maternity, cows will frequently return to the same retreat annually to give birth to their calves.

It was about fifty miles between the home and the new ranch. As it was important to get the cattle located as soon as possible, they were accordingly started with but the loss of a single day. Two wagons accompanied them, every calf was saved, and by nursing the herd early and late we managed to average ten miles between sunrise and sunset. The elder Edwards, anxious to see the new ranch, accompanied us, his patience with a cow being something remarkable. When we lacked but a day's drive of the Clear Fork it was considered advisable for me to return. Once the cattle reached the new range, four men would loose-herd them for a month, after which they would continue to ride the range and turn back all stragglers. The veteran cowman assumed control, and I returned to the home ranch, where a horse had been left on which to overtake the trail herd. My wife caught several glimpses of me that spring; with stocking a new ranch and starting a herd on the trail I was as busy as the proverbial cranberry-merchant. Where a year before I was moneyless, now my obligations were accepted for nearly fourteen thousand dollars.

I overtook the herd within one day's drive of Red River. Everything was moving nicely, the cattle were well trail-broken, not a run had occurred, and all was serene and lovely. We crossed into the Nations at the regular ford, nothing of importance occurring until we reached the Washita River. The Indians had been bothering us more or less, but we brushed them aside or appeased their begging with a stray beef. At the crossing of the Washita quite an encampment had congregated, demanding six cattle and threatening to dispute our entrance to the ford. Several of the boys with us pretended to understand the sign language, and this resulted in an animosity being engendered between two of the outfit over interpreting a sign made by a chief. After we had given the Indians two strays, quite a band of bucks gathered on foot at the crossing, refusing to let us pass until their demand had been fulfilled. We had a few carbines, every lad had a six-shooter or two, and, summoning every mounted man, we rode up to the ford. The braves outnumbered us about three to one, and it was easy to be seen that they had bows and arrows concealed under their blankets. I was determined to give up no more cattle, and in the powwow that followed the chief of the band became very defiant. I accused him and his band of being armed, and when he denied it one of the boys jumped a horse against the chief, knocking him down. In the mêlée, the leader's blanket was thrown from him, exposing a strung bow and quiver of arrows, and at the same instant every man brought his carbine or six-shooter to bear on the astonished braves. Not a shot was fired, nor was there any further resistance offered on the part of the Indians; but as they turned to leave the humiliated chief pointed to the sun and made a circle around his head as if to indicate a threat of scalping.

It was in interpreting this latter sign that the dispute arose between two of the outfit. One of the boys contended that I was to be scalped before the sun set, while the other interpreted the threat that we would all he scalped before the sun rose again. Neither version troubled me, but the two fellows quarreled over the matter while returning to the herd, until the lie was passed and their six-shooters began talking. Fortunately they were both mounted on horses that were gun-shy, and with the rearing and plunging the shots went wild. Every man in the outfit interfered, the two fellows were disarmed, and we started on with the cattle. No interference was offered by the Indians at the ford, the guards were doubled that night, and the incident was forgotten within a week. I simply mention this to give some idea of the men of that day, willing to back their opinions, even on trivial matters, with their lives. "I'm the quickest man on the trigger that ever came over the trail," said a cowpuncher to me one night in a saloon in Abilene. "You're a blankety blank liar," said a quiet little man, a perfect stranger to both of us, not even casting a glance our way. I wrested a six-shooter from the hand of my acquaintance and hustled him out of the house, getting roundly cursed for my interference, though no doubt I saved human life.

On reaching Stone's Store, on the Kansas line, I left the herd to follow, and arrived at Abilene in two days and a half. Only some twenty-five herds were ahead of ours, though I must have passed a dozen or more in my brief ride, staying over night with them and scarcely ever missing a meal on the road. My motive in reaching Abilene in advance of our cattle was to get in touch with the market, secure my trading-corrals again, and perfect my arrangements to do a commission business. But on arriving, instead of having the field to myself, I found the old corrals occupied by a trio of jobbers, while two new ones had been built within ten miles of town, and half a dozen firms were offering their services as salesmen. There was a lack of actual buyers, at least among my acquaintances, and the railroads had adjusted their rates, while a largely increased drive was predicted. The spring had been a wet one, the grass was washy and devoid of nutriment, and there was nothing in the outlook of an encouraging nature. Yet the majority of the drovers were very optimistic of the future, freely predicting better prices than ever before, while many declared their intention of wintering in case their hopes were not realized. By the time our herd arrived, I had grown timid of the market in general and was willing to sell out and go home. I make no pretension to having any extra foresight, probably it was my outstanding obligations in Texas that fostered my anxiety, but I was prepared to sell to the first man who talked business.

Our cattle arrived in good condition. The weather continued wet and stormy, the rank grass harbored myriads of flies and mosquitoes, and the through cattle failed to take on flesh as in former years. Rival towns were competing for the trail business, wintered cattle were lower, and a perfect chaos existed as to future prices, drovers bolstering and pretended buyers depressing them. Within a week after their arrival I sold fifteen hundred of our heaviest beeves to an army contractor from Fort Russell in Dakota. He had brought his own outfit down to receive the cattle, and as his contract called for a million and a half pounds on foot, I assisted him in buying sixteen hundred more. The contractor was a shrewd Yankee, and although I admitted having served in the Confederate army, he offered to form a partnership with me for supplying beef to the army posts along the upper Missouri River. He gave me an insight into the profits in that particular trade, and even urged the partnership, but while the opportunity was a golden one, I was distrustful of a Northern man and declined the alliance. Within a year I regretted not forming the partnership, as the government was a stable patron, and my adopted State had any quantity of beef cattle.

My brother paid me a visit during the latter part of June. We had not seen each other in five years, during which time he had developed into a prosperous stockman, feeding cattle every winter on his Missouri farm. He was anxious to interest me in corn-feeding steers, but I had my hands full at home, and within a week he went on west and bought two hundred Colorado natives, shipping them home to feed the coming winter. Meanwhile a perfect glut of cattle was arriving at Abilene, fully six hundred thousand having registered at Stone's Store on passing into Kansas, yet prices remained firm, considering the condition of the stock. Many drovers halted only a day or two, and turned westward looking for ranges on which to winter their herds. Barely half the arrivals were even offered, which afforded fair prices to those who wished to sell. Before the middle of July the last of ours was closed out at satisfactory prices, and the next day the outfit started home, leaving me behind. I was anxious to secure an extra remuda of horses, and, finding no opposition in that particular field, had traded extensively in saddle stock ever since my arrival at Abilene. Gentle horses were in good demand among shippers and ranchmen, and during my brief stay I must have handled a thousand head, buying whole remudas and retailing in quantities to suit, not failing to keep the choice ones for my own use. Within two weeks after George Edwards started home, I closed up my business, fell in with a returning outfit, and started back with one hundred and ten picked saddle horses. After crossing Red River, I hired a boy to assist me in driving the remuda, and I reached home only ten days behind the others.

I was now the proud possessor of over two hundred saddle horses which had actually cost me nothing. To use a borrowed term, they were the "velvet" of my trading operations. I hardly feel able to convey an idea of the important rôle that the horses play in the operations of a cowman. Whether on the trail or on the ranch, there is a complete helplessness when the men are not properly mounted and able to cope with any emergency that may arise. On the contrary, and especially in trail work, when men are well mounted, there is no excuse for not riding in the lead of any stampede, drifting with the herd on the stormiest night, or trailing lost cattle until overtaken. Owing to the nature of the occupation, a man may be frequently wet, cold, and hungry, and entitled to little sympathy; but once he feels that he is no longer mounted, his grievance becomes a real one. The cow-horse subsisted on the range, and if ever used to exhaustion was worthless for weeks afterward. Hence the value of a good mount in numbers, and the importance of frequent changes when the duties were arduous. The importance of good horses was first impressed on me during my trips to Fort Sumner, and I then resolved that if fortune ever favored me to reach the prominence of a cowman, the saddle stock would have my first consideration.

On my return it was too early for the fall branding. I made a trip out to the new ranch, taking along ample winter supplies, two extra lads, and the old remuda of sixty horses. The men had located the new cattle fairly well, the calf crop was abundant, and after spending a week I returned home. I had previously settled my indebtedness in Comanche County by remittances from Abilene, and early in the fall I made up an outfit to go down and gather the remnant of "Lazy L" cattle. Taking along the entire new remuda, we dropped down in advance of the branding season, visited among the neighboring ranches, and offered a dollar a head for solitary animals that had drifted any great distance from the range of the brand. A camp was established at some corrals on the original range, extra men were employed with the opening of the branding season, and after twenty days' constant riding we started home with a few over nine hundred head, not counting two hundred and odd calves. Little wonder the trustee threatened to sue me; but then it was his own proposition.

On arriving at the Edwards ranch, we halted a few days in order to gather the fruits of my first mavericking. The fall work was nearly finished, and having previously made arrangements to put my brand under herd, we received two hundred and fifty more, with seventy-five thrifty calves, before proceeding on to the new ranch on the Clear Fork. On arriving there we branded the calves, put the two brands under herd, corralling them at night and familiarizing them with their new home, and turning them loose at the end of two weeks. Moving cattle in the fall was contrary to the best results, but it was an idle time, and they were all young stuff and easily located. During the interim of loose-herding this second contingent of stock cattle, the branding had been finished on the ranch, and I was able to take an account of my year's work. The "Lazy L" was continued, and from that brand alone there was an increase of over seventeen hundred calves. With all the expenses of the trail deducted, the steer cattle alone had paid for the entire brand, besides adding over five thousand dollars to my cash capital. Who will gainsay my statement that Texas was a good country in the year 1871?

CHAPTER IX
THE SCHOOL OF EXPERIENCE

Success had made me daring. And yet I must have been wandering aimlessly, for had my ambition been well directed, there is no telling to what extent I might have amassed a fortune. Opportunity was knocking at my gate, a giant young commonwealth was struggling in the throes of political revolution, while I wandered through it all like a blind man led by a child. Precedent was of little value, as present environment controlled my actions. The best people in Texas were doubtful of ever ridding themselves of the baneful incubus of Reconstruction. Men on whose judgment I relied laughed at me for acquiring more land than a mere homestead. Stock cattle were in such disrepute that they had no cash value. Many a section of deeded land changed owners for a milk cow, while surveyors would no longer locate new lands for the customary third, but insisted on a half interest. Ranchmen were so indifferent that many never went off their home range in branding the calf crop, not considering a ten or twenty per cent loss of any importance. Yet through it all — from my Virginia rearing — there lurked a wavering belief that some day, in some manner, these lands and cattle would have a value. But my faith was neither the bold nor the assertive kind, and I drifted along, clinging to any passing straw of opinion.

The Indians were still giving trouble along the Texas frontier. A line of government posts, extending from Red River on the north to the Rio Grande on the south, made a pretense of holding the Comanches and their allies in check, while this arm of the service was ably seconded by the Texas Rangers. Yet in spite of all precaution, the redskins raided the settlements at their pleasure, stealing horses and adding rapine and murder to their category of crimes. Hence for a number of years after my marriage we lived at the Edwards ranch as a matter of precaution against Indian raids. I was absent from home so much that this arrangement suited me, and as the new ranch was distant but a day's ride, any inconvenience was more than recompensed in security. It was my intention to follow the trail and trading, at the same time running a ranch where anything unfit for market might be sent to mature or increase. As long as I could add to my working capital, I was content, while the remnants of my speculations found a refuge on the Clear Fork.

During the winter of 1871-72 very little of importance transpired. Several social letters passed between Major Mabry and myself, in one of which he casually mentioned the fact that land scrip had declined until it was offered on the streets of the capital as low as twenty dollars a section. He knew I had been dabbling in land certificates, and in a friendly spirit wanted to post me on their decline, and had incidentally mentioned the fact for my information. Some inkling of horse sense told me that I ought to secure more land, and after thinking the matter over, I wrote to a merchant in Austin, and had him buy me one hundred sections. He was very anxious to purchase a second hundred at the same figure, but it would make too serious an inroad into my trading capital, and I declined his friendly assistance. My wife was the only person whom I took into confidence in buying the scrip, and I even had her secrete it in the bottom of a trunk, with strict admonitions never to mention it unless it became of value. It was not taxable, the public domain was bountiful, and I was young enough man those days to bide my time.

The winter proved a severe one in Kansas. Nearly every drover who wintered his cattle in the north met with almost complete loss. The previous summer had been too wet for cattle to do well, and they had gone into winter thin in flesh. Instead of curing like hay, the buffalo grass had rotted from excessive rains, losing its nutritive qualities, and this resulted in serious loss among all range cattle. The result was financial ruin to many drovers, and even augured a lighter drive north the coming spring. Early in the winter I bought two brands of cattle in Erath County, paying half cash and getting six months' time on the remainder. Both brands occupied the same range, and when we gathered them in the early spring, they counted out a few over six thousand animals. These two contingents were extra good cattle, costing me five dollars a head, counting yearlings up, and from them I selected two thousand steer cattle for the trail. The mixed stuff was again sent to my Clear Fork ranch, and the steers went into a neighborhood herd intended for the Kansas market. But when the latter was all ready to start, such discouraging reports came down from the north that my friends weakened, and I bought their cattle outright.

My reputation as a good trader was my capital. I had the necessary horses, and, straining my credit, the herd started thirty-one hundred strong. The usual incidents of flood and storm, of begging Indians and caravans like ourselves, formed the chronicle of the trip. Before arriving at the Kansas line we were met by solicitors of rival towns, each urging the advantages of their respective markets for our cattle. The summer before a small business had sprung up at Newton, Kansas, it being then the terminal of the Santa Fé Railway. And although Newton lasted as a trail town but a single summer, its reputation for bloodshed and riotous disorder stands notoriously alone among its rivals. In the mean time the Santa Fé had been extended to Wichita on the Arkansas River, and its representatives were now bidding for our patronage. Abilene was abandoned, yet a rival to Wichita had sprung up at Ellsworth, some sixty-five miles west of the former market, on the Kansas Pacific Railway. The railroads were competing for the cattle traffic, each one advertising its superior advantages to drovers, shippers, and feeders. I was impartial, but as Wichita was fully one hundred miles the nearest, my cattle were turned for that point.

Wichita was a frontier village of about two thousand inhabitants. We found a convenient camp northwest of town, and went into permanent quarters to await the opening of the market. Within a few weeks a light drive was assured, and prices opened firm. Fully a quarter-million less cattle would reach the markets within the State that year, and buyers became active in securing their needed supply. Early in July I sold the last of my herd and started my outfit home, remaining behind to await the arrival of my brother. The trip was successful; the purchased cattle had afforded me a nice profit, while the steers from the two brands had more than paid for the mixed stuff left at home on the ranch. Meanwhile I renewed old acquaintances among drovers and dealers, Major Mabry among the former. In a confidential mood I confessed to him that I had bought, on the recent decline, one hundred certificates of land scrip, when he surprised me by saying that there had been a later decline to sixteen dollars a section. I was unnerved for an instant, but Major Mabry agreed with me that to a man who wanted the land the price was certainly cheap enough, — two and a half cents an acre. I pondered over the matter, and as my nerve returned I sent my merchant friend at Austin a draft and authorized him to buy me two hundred sections more of land scrip. I was actually nettled to think that my judgment was so short-sighted as to buy anything that would depreciate in value.

My brother arrived and reported splendid success in feeding Colorado cattle. He was anxious to have me join forces with him and corn-feed an increased number of beeves the coming winter on his Missouri farm. My judgment hardly approved of the venture, but when he urged a promised visit of our parents to his home, I consented and agreed to furnish the cattle. He also encouraged me to bring as many as my capital would admit of, assuring me that I would find a ready sale for any surplus among his neighbors. My brother returned to Missouri, and I took the train for Ellsworth, where I bought a carload of picked cow-horses, shipping them to Kit Carson, Colorado. From there I drifted into the Fountain valley at the base of the mountains, where I made a trade for seven hundred native steers, three and four years old. They were fine cattle, nearly all reds and roans. While I was gathering them a number of amusing incidents occurred. The round-ups carried us down on to the main Arkansas River, and in passing Pueblo we discovered a number of range cattle impounded in the town. I cannot give it as a fact, but the supposition among the cowmen was that the object of the officials was to raise some revenue by distressing the cattle. The result was that an outfit of men rode into the village during the night, tore down the pound, and turned the cattle back on the prairie. The prime movers in the raid were suspected, and the next evening when a number of us rode into town an attempt was made to arrest us, resulting in a fight, in which an officer was killed and two cowboys wounded. The citizens rallied to the support of the officers, and about thirty range men, including myself, were arrested and thrown into jail. We sent for a lawyer, and the following morning the majority of us were acquitted. Some three or four of the boys were held for trial, bonds being furnished by the best men in the town, and that night a party of cowboys reëntered the village, carried away the two wounded men and spirited them out of the country.

Pueblo at that time was a unique town. Live-stock interests were its main support, and I distinctly remember Gann's outfitting store. At night one could find anywhere from ten to thirty cowboys sleeping on the counters, the proprietor turning the keys over to them at closing time, not knowing one in ten, and sleeping at his own residence. The same custom prevailed at Gallup the saddler's, never an article being missed from either establishment, and both men amassing fortunes out of the cattle trade in subsequent years. The range man's patronage had its peculiarities; the firm of Wright, Beverly & Co. of Dodge City, Kansas, accumulated seven thousand odd vests during the trail days. When a cow-puncher bought a new suit he had no use for an unnecessary garment like a vest and left it behind. It was restored to the stock, where it can yet be found.

Early in August the herd was completed. I accepted seven hundred and twenty steers, investing every cent of spare money, reserving only sufficient to pay my expenses en route. It was my intention to drive the cattle through to Missouri, the distance being a trifle less than six hundred miles or a matter of six weeks' travel. Four men were secured, a horse was packed with provisions and blankets, and we started down the Arkansas River. For the first few days I did very little but build air castles. I pictured myself driving herds from Texas in the spring, reinvesting the proceeds in better grades of cattle and feeding them corn in the older States, selling in time to again buy and come up the trail. I even planned to send for my wife and baby, and looked forward to a happy reunion with my parents during the coming winter, with not a cloud in my roseate sky. But there were breakers ahead.

An old military trail ran southeast from Fort Larned to other posts in the Indian Territory. Over this government road had come a number of herds of Texas cattle, all of them under contract, which, in reaching their destination, had avoided the markets of Wichita and Ellsworth. I crossed their trail with my Colorado natives, — the through cattle having passed a month or more before, — never dreaming of any danger. Ten days afterward I noticed a number of my steers were ailing; their ears drooped, they refused to eat, and fell to the rear as we grazed forward. The next morning there were forty head unable to leave the bed-ground, and by noon a number of them had died. I had heard of Texas fever, but always treated it as more or less a myth, and now it held my little herd of natives in its toils. By this time we had reached some settlement on the Cottonwood, and the pioneer settlers in Kansas arose in arms and quarantined me. No one knew what the trouble was, yet the cattle began dying like sheep; I was perfectly helpless, not knowing which way to turn or what to do. Quarantine was unnecessary, as within a few days half the cattle were sick, and it was all we could do to move away from the stench of the dead ones.

A veterinary was sent for, who pronounced it Texas fever. I had previously cut open a number of dead animals, and found the contents of their stomachs and manifolds so dry that they would flash and burn like powder. The fever had dried up their very internals. In the hope of administering a purgative, I bought whole fields of green corn, and turned the sick and dying cattle into them. I bought oils by the barrel, my men and myself worked night and day, inwardly drenching affected animals, yet we were unable to stay the ravages of death. Once the cause of the trouble was located, — crossing ground over which Texas cattle had passed, — the neighbors became friendly, and sympathized with me. I gave them permission to take the fallen hides, and in return received many kindnesses where a few days before I had been confronted by shotguns. This was my first experience with Texas fever, and the lessons that I learned then and afterward make me skeptical of all theories regarding the transmission of the germ.

The story of the loss of my Colorado herd is a ghastly one. This fever is sometimes called splenic, and in the present case, where animals lingered a week or ten days, while yet alive, their skins frequently cracked along the spine until one could have laid two fingers in the opening.

The whole herd was stricken, less than half a dozen animals escaping attack, scores dying within three days, the majority lingering a week or more. In spite of our every effort to save them, as many as one hundred died in a single day. I stayed with them for six weeks, or until the fever had run through the herd, spent my last available dollar in an effort to save the dumb beasts, and, having my hopes frustrated, sold the remnant of twenty-six head for five dollars apiece. I question if they were worth the money, as three fourths of them were fever-burnt and would barely survive a winter, the only animals of value being some half dozen which had escaped the general plague. I gave each of my men two horses apiece, and divided my money with them, and they started back to Colorado, while I turned homeward a wiser but poorer man. Whereas I had left Wichita three months before with over sixteen thousand dollars clear cash, I returned with eighteen saddle horses and not as many dollars in money.

My air-castles had fallen. Troubles never come singly, and for the last two weeks, while working with the dying cattle, I had suffered with chills and fever. The summer had been an unusually wet one, vegetation had grown up rankly in the valley of the Arkansas, and after the first few frosts the very atmosphere reeked with malaria. I had been sleeping on the ground along the river for over a month, drinking impure water from the creeks, and I fell an easy victim to the prevailing miasma. Nearly all the Texas drovers had gone home, but, luckily for me, Jim Daugherty had an outfit yet at Wichita and invited me to his wagon. It might be a week or ten days before he would start homeward, as he was holding a herd of cows, sold to an Indian contractor, who was to receive the same within two weeks. In the interim of waiting, still suffering from fever and ague, I visited around among the few other cow-camps scattered up and down the river. At one of these I met a stranger, a quiet little man, who also had been under the weather from malaria, but was then recovering. He took an interest in my case and gave me some medicine to break the chills, and we visited back and forth. I soon learned that he had come down with some of his neighbors from Council Grove; that they expected to buy cattle, and that he was banker for the party. He was much interested in everything pertaining to Texas; and when I had given him an idea of the cheapness of lands and live stock in my adopted State, he expressed himself as anxious to engage in trailing cattle north. A great many Texas cattle had been matured in his home county, and he thoroughly understood the advantages of developing southern steers in a northern climate. Many of his neighbors had made small fortunes in buying young stock at Abilene, holding them a year or two, and shipping them to market as fat cattle.

The party bought six hundred two-year-old steers, and my new-found friend, the banker, invited me to assist in the receiving. My knowledge of range cattle was a decided advantage to the buyers, who no doubt were good farmers, yet were sadly handicapped when given pick and choice from a Texas herd and confined to ages. I cut, counted, and received the steers, my work giving such satisfaction that the party offered to pay me for my services. It was but a neighborly act, unworthy of recompense, yet I won the lasting regard of the banker in protecting the interests of his customers. The upshot of the acquaintance was that we met in town that evening and had a few drinks together. Neither one ever made any inquiry of the other's past or antecedents, both seeming to be satisfied with a soldier's acquaintance. At the final parting, I gave him my name and address and invited him to visit me, promising that we would buy a herd of cattle together and drive them up the trail the following spring. He accepted the invitation with a hearty grasp of the hand, and the simple promise "I'll come." Those words were the beginning of a partnership which lasted eighteen years, and a friendship that death alone will terminate.

The Indian contractor returned on time, and the next day I started home with Daugherty's outfit. And on the way, as if I were pursued by some unrelenting Nemesis, two of my horses, with others, were stolen by the Indians one night when we were encamped near Red River. We trailed them westward nearly fifty miles, but, on being satisfied they were traveling night and day, turned back and continued our journey. I reached home with sixteen horses, which for years afterwards, among my hands and neighbors, were pointed out as Anthony's thousand-dollar cow-ponies. There is no denying the fact that I keenly felt the loss of my money, as it crippled me in my business, while my ranch expenses, amounting to over one thousand dollars, were unpaid. I was rich in unsalable cattle, owned a thirty-two-thousand-acre ranch, saddle horses galore, and was in debt. My wife's trunk was half full of land scrip, and to have admitted the fact would only have invited ridicule. But my tuition was paid, and all I asked was a chance, for I knew the ropes in handling range cattle. Yet this was the second time that I had lost my money and I began to doubt myself. "You stick to cows," said Charlie Goodnight to me that winter, "and they'll bring you out on top some day. I thought I saw something in you when you first went to work for Loving and me. Reed, if you'll just imbibe a little caution with your energy, you'll make a fortune out of cattle yet."

CHAPTER X
THE PANIC OF '73

I have never forgotten those encouraging words of my first employer. Friends tided my finances over, and letters passed between my banker friend and myself, resulting in an appointment to meet him at Fort Worth early in February. There was no direct railroad at the time, the route being by St. Louis and Texarkana, with a long trip by stage to the meeting point. No definite agreement existed between us; he was simply paying me a visit, with the view of looking into the cattle trade then existing between our respective States. There was no obligation whatever, yet I had hopes of interesting him sufficiently to join issues with me in driving a herd of cattle. I wish I could describe the actual feelings of a man who has had money and lost it. Never in my life did such opportunities present themselves for investment as were tendered to me that winter. No less than half a dozen brands of cattle were offered to me at the former terms of half cash and the balance to suit my own convenience. But I lacked the means to even provision a wagon for a month's work, and I was compelled to turn my back on all bargains, many of which were duplicates of my former successes. I was humbled to the very dust; I bowed my neck to the heel of circumstances, and looked forward to the coming of my casual acquaintance.

I have read a few essays on the relation of money to a community. None of our family were ever given to theorizing, yet I know how it feels to be moneyless, my experience with Texas fever affording me a post-graduate course. Born with a restless energy, I have lived in the pit of despair for the want of money, and again, with the use of it, have bent a legislature to my will and wish. All of which is foreign to my tale, and I hasten on. During the first week in February I drove in to Fort Worth to await the arrival of my friend, Calvin Hunter, banker and stockman of Council Grove, Kansas. Several letters were awaiting me in the town, notifying me of his progress, and in due time he arrived and was welcomed. The next morning we started, driving a good span of mules to a buckboard, expecting to cover the distance to the Brazos in two days. There were several ranches at which we could touch, en route, but we loitered along, making wide detours in order to drive through cattle, not a feature of the country escaping the attention of my quiet little companion. The soil, the native grasses, the natural waters, the general topography of the country, rich in its primal beauty, furnished a panorama to the eye both pleasing and exhilarating. But the main interest centred in the cattle, thousands of which were always in sight, lingering along the watercourses or grazing at random.

We reached the Edwards ranch early the second evening. In the two days' travel, possibly twenty thousand cattle came under our immediate observation. All the country was an open range, brands intermingling, all ages and conditions, running from a sullen bull to seven-year-old beeves, or from a yearling heifer to the grandmother of younger generations. My anxiety to show the country and its cattle met a hearty second in Mr. Hunter, and abandoning the buckboard, we took horses and rode up the Brazos River as far as old Fort Belknap. All cattle were wintering strong. Turning south, we struck the Clear Fork above my range and spent a night at the ranch, where my men had built a second cabin, connecting the two by a hallway. After riding through my stock for two days, we turned back for the Brazos. My ranch hands had branded thirty-one hundred calves the fall before, and while riding over the range I was delighted to see so many young steers in my different brands. But our jaunt had only whetted the appetite of my guest to see more of the country, and without any waste of time we started south with the buckboard, going as far as Comanche County. Every day's travel brought us in contact with cattle for sale; the prices were an incentive, but we turned east and came back up the valley of the Brazos. I offered to continue our sightseeing, but my guest pleaded for a few days' time until he could hear from his banking associates. I needed a partner and needed one badly, and was determined to interest Mr. Hunter if it took a whole month. And thereby hangs a tale.

The native Texan is not distinguished for energy or ambition. His success in cattle is largely due to the fact that nearly all the work can be done on horseback. Yet in that particular field

443

he stands at the head of his class; for whether in Montana or his own sunny Texas, when it comes to handling cattle, from reading brands to cutting a trainload of beeves, he is without a peer. During the palmy days of the Cherokee Strip, a Texan invited Captain Stone, a Kansas City man, to visit his ranch in Tom Green County and put up a herd of steers to be driven to Stone's beef ranch in the Cherokee Outlet. The invitation was accepted, and on the arrival of the Kansas City man at the Texan's ranch, host and guest indulged in a friendly visit of several days' duration. It was the northern cowman's first visit to the Lone Star State, and he naturally felt impatient to see the cattle which he expected to buy. But the host made no movement to show the stock until patience ceased to be a virtue, when Captain Stone moved an adjournment of the social session and politely asked to be shown a sample of the country's cattle. The two cowmen were fast friends, and no offense was intended or taken; but the host assured his guest there was no hurry, offering to get up horses and show the stock the following day. Captain Stone yielded, and the next morning they started, but within a few miles met a neighbor, when all three dismounted in the shade of a tree. Commonplace chat of the country occupied the attention of the two Texans until hunger or some other warning caused one of them to look at his watch, when it was discovered to be three o'clock in the afternoon. It was then too late in the day to make an extensive ride, and the ranchman invited his neighbor and guest to return to the ranch for the night. Another day was wasted in entertaining the neighbor, the northern cowman, in the meantime, impatient and walking on nettles until a second start was made to see the cattle. It was a foggy morning, and they started on a different route from that previously taken, the visiting ranchman going along. Unnoticed, a pack of hounds followed the trio of horsemen, and before the fog lifted a cougar trail was struck and the dogs opened in a brilliant chorus. The two Texans put spurs to their horses in following the pack, the cattle buyer of necessity joining in, the chase leading into some hills, from which they returned after darkness, having never seen a cow during the day. One trivial incident after another interfered with seeing the cattle for ten days, when the guest took his host aside and kindly told him that he must be shown the cattle or he would go home.

"You're not in a hurry, are you, captain?" innocently asked the Texan. "All right, then; no trouble to show the cattle. Yes, they run right around home here within twenty-five miles of the ranch. Show you a sample of the stock within an hour's ride. You can just bet that old Tom Green County has got the steers! Sugar, if I'd a-known that you was in a hurry, I could have shown you the cattle the next morning after you come. Captain, you ought to know me well enough by this time to speak your little piece without any prelude. You Yankees are so restless and impatient that I seriously doubt if you get all the comfort and enjoyment out of life that's coming to you. Make haste, some of you boys, and bring in a remuda; Captain Stone and I are going to ride over on the Middle Fork this morning. Make haste, now; we're in a hurry."

In due time I suppose I drifted into the languorous ways of the Texan; but on the occasion of Mr. Hunter's first visit I was in the need of a moneyed partner, and accordingly danced attendance. Once communication was opened with his Northern associates, we made several short rides into adjoining counties, never being gone over two or three days. When we had looked at cattle to his satisfaction, he surprised me by offering to put fifty thousand dollars into young steers for the Kansas trade. I never fainted in my life, but his proposition stunned me for an instant, or until I could get my bearings. The upshot of the proposal was that we entered into an agreement whereby I was to purchase and handle the cattle, and he was to make himself useful in selling and placing the stock in his State. A silent partner was furnishing an equal portion of the means, and I was to have a third of the net profits. Within a week after this agreement was perfected, things were moving. I had the horses and wagons, men were plentiful, and two outfits were engaged. Early in March a contract was let in Parker County for thirty-one hundred two-year-old steers, and another in Young for fourteen hundred threes, the latter to be delivered at my ranch. George Edwards was to have the younger cattle, and he and Mr. Hunter received the same, after which the latter hurried west, fully ninety miles, to settle for those bought for delivery on the Clear Fork. In the mean time my ranch outfit had gathered all our steer cattle two years old and over, having nearly twenty-five hundred head under herd on my arrival to receive the three-year-olds. This amount would make an unwieldy herd, and I culled back all short-aged twos and thin steers until my individual contingent numbered even two thousand. The contracted steers came in on time, fully up to the specifications, and my herd was ready to start on the appointed day.

Every dollar of the fifty thousand was invested in cattle, save enough to provision the wagons en route. My ranch outfit, with the exception of two men and ten horses, was pressed into trail work as a matter of economy, for I was determined to make some money for my partners. Both herds were to meet and cross at Red River Station. The season was favorable, and everything augured for a prosperous summer. At the very last moment a cloud arose between Mr. Hunter and me, but happily passed without a storm. The night before the second herd started, he and I sat up until a late hour, arranging our affairs, as it was not his intention to accompany the herds overland. After all business matters were settled, lounging around a camp-fire, we grew reminiscent, when the fact developed that my quiet little partner had served in the Union army, and with the rank of major. I always enjoy a joke, even on myself, but I flashed hot and cold on this confession. What! Reed Anthony forming a partnership with a Yankee major? It seemed as though I had. Fortunately I controlled myself, and under the excuse of starting the herd at daybreak, I excused myself and sought my blankets. But not to sleep. On the one hand, in the stillness of the night and across the years, came the accusing voices of old comrades. My very wounds seemed to reopen and curse me. Did my sufferings after Pittsburg Landing mean nothing? A vision of my dear old mother in Virginia, welcoming me, the only one of her three sons who returned from the war, arraigned me sorely. And yet, on the other hand, this man was my guest. On my invitation he had eaten my salt. For mutual benefit we had entered into a partnership, and I expected to profit from the investment of his money. More important, he had not deceived me nor concealed anything; neither did he know that I had served in the Confederate army. The man was honest. I was anxious to do right. Soldiers are generous to a foe. While he lay asleep in my camp, I reviewed the situation carefully, and judged him blameless. The next morning, and ever afterward, I addressed him by his military title. Nearly a year passed before Major Hunter knew that he and his Texas partner had served in the civil war under different flags.

My partner returned to the Edwards ranch and was sent in to Fort Worth, where he took stage and train for home. The straight two-year-old herd needed road-branding, as they were accepted in a score or more brands, which delayed them in starting. Major Hunter expected to sell to farmers, to whom brands were offensive, and was therefore opposed to more branding than was absolutely necessary. In order to overcome this objection, I tally-marked all outside cattle which went into my herd by sawing from each steer about two inches from the right horn. As fast as the cattle were received this work was easily done in a chute, while in case of any loss by stampede the mark would last for years. The grass was well forward when both herds started, but on arriving at Red River no less than half a dozen herds were waterbound, one of which was George Edwards's. A delay of three days occurred, during which two other herds arrived, when the river fell, permitting us to cross. I took the lead thereafter, the second herd half a day to the rear, with the almost weekly incident of being waterbound by intervening rivers. But as we moved northward the floods seemed lighter, and on our arrival at Wichita the weather settled into well-ordered summer.

I secured my camp of the year before. Major Hunter came down by train, and within a week after our arrival my outfit was settled with and sent home. It was customary to allow a man half wages returning, my partner approving and paying the men, also taking charge of all the expense accounts. Everything was kept as straight as a bank, and with one outfit holding both herds separate, expenses were reduced to a minimum. Major Hunter was back and forth, between his home town and Wichita, and on nearly every occasion brought along buyers, effecting sales at extra good prices. Cattle paper was considered gilt-edge security among financial men, and we sold to worthy parties a great many cattle on credit, the home bank with which my partners were associated taking the notes at their face. Matters rocked along, we sold when we had an opportunity, and early in August the remnant of each herd was thrown together and half the remaining outfit sent home. A drive of fully half a million cattle had reached Kansas that year, the greater portion of which had centred at Wichita. We were persistent in selling, and, having strong local connections, had sold out all our cattle long before the financial panic of '73 even started. There was a profitable business, however, in buying herds and selling again in small quantities to farmers and stockmen. My partners were anxious to have me remain to the end of the season, doing the buying, maintaining the camp, and holding any stock on hand. In rummaging through the old musty account-books, I find that we handled nearly seven thousand head besides our own drive, fifteen hundred being the most we ever had on hand at any one time.

My active partner proved a shrewd man in business, and in spite of the past our friendship broadened and strengthened. Weeks before the financial crash reached us he knew of its coming, and our house was set in order. When the panic struck the West we did not own a hoof of cattle, while the horses on hand were mine and not for sale; and the firm of Hunter, Anthony & Co. rode the gale like a seaworthy ship. The panic reached Wichita with over half the drive of that year unsold. The local banks began calling in money advanced to drovers, buyers deserted the market, and prices went down with a crash. Shipments of the best through cattle failed to realize more than sufficient to pay commission charges and freight. Ruin stared in the face every Texan drover whose cattle were unsold. Only a few herds were under contract for fall delivery to Indian and army contractors. We had run from the approaching storm in the nick of time, even settling with and sending my outfit home before the financial cyclone reached the prairies of Kansas. My last trade before the panic struck was an individual account, my innate weakness for an abundance of saddle horses asserting itself in buying ninety head and sending them home with my men.

I now began to see the advantages of shrewd and far-seeing business associates. When the crash came, scarce a dozen drovers had sold out, while of those holding cattle at Wichita nearly every one had locally borrowed money or owed at home for their herds. When the banks, panic-stricken themselves, began calling in short-time loans, their frenzy paralyzed the market, many cattle being sacrificed at forced sale and with scarce a buyer. In the depreciation of values from the prices which prevailed in the early summer, the losses to the Texas drovers, caused by the panic, would amount to several million dollars. I came out of the general wreck and ruin untouched, though personally claiming no credit, as that must be given my partners. The year before, when every other drover went home prosperous and happy, I returned "broke," while now the situation was reversed.

I spent a week at Council Grove, visiting with my business associates. After a settlement of the year's business, I was anxious to return home, having agreed to drive cattle the next year on the same terms and conditions. My partners gave me a cash settlement, and outside of my individual cattle, I cleared over ten thousand dollars on my summer's work. Major Hunter, however, had an idea of reëntering the market, — with the first symptom of improvement in the financial horizon in the East, — and I was detained. The proposition of buying a herd of cattle and wintering them on the range had been fully discussed between us, and prices were certainly an incentive to make the venture. In an ordinary open winter, stock subsisted on the range all over western Kansas, especially when a dry fall had matured and cured the buffalo-grass like hay. The range was all one could wish, and Major Hunter and I accordingly dropped down to Wichita to look the situation over. We arrived in the midst of the panic and found matters in a deplorable condition. Drovers besought and even begged us to make an offer on their herds, while the prevailing prices of a month before had declined over half. Major Hunter and I agreed that at present figures, even if half the cattle were lost by a severe winter, there would still be money in the venture. Through financial connections East my partners knew of the first signs of improvement in the money-centres of the country. As I recall the circumstances, the panic began in the East about the middle of September, and it was the latter part of October before confidence was restored, or there was any noticeable change for the better in the monetary situation. But when this came, it found us busy buying saddle horses and cattle. The great bulk of the unsold stock consisted of cows, heifers, and young steers unfit for beef. My partners contended that a three-year-old steer ought to winter anywhere a buffalo could, provided he had the flesh and strength to withstand the rigors of the climate. I had no opinions, except what other cowmen had told me, but was willing to take the chances where there was a reasonable hope of success.

The first move was to buy an outfit of good horses. This was done by selecting from half a dozen remudas, a trail wagon was picked up, and a complement of men secured. Once it was known that we were in the market for cattle, competition was brisk, the sellers bidding against each other and fixing the prices at which we accepted the stock. None but three-year-old steers were taken, and in a single day we closed trades on five thousand head. I received the cattle, confining my selections to five road and ten single-ranch brands, as it was not our intention to rebrand so late in the season. There was nothing to do but cut, count, and accept, and on the evening of the third day the herd was all ready to start for its winter range. The wagon had been well provisioned, and we started southwest, expecting to go into winter quarters on the first good range encountered. I had taken a third interest in the herd, paying one sixth of its purchase price, the balance being carried for me by my partners. Major Hunter accompanied us, the herd being altogether too large and unwieldy to handle well, but we grazed it forward with a front a mile wide. Delightful fall weather favored the cattle, and on the tenth day we reached the Medicine River, where, by the unwritten law of squatter's rights, we preëmpted ten miles of its virgin valley. The country was fairly carpeted with well-cured buffalo-grass; on the north and west was a range of sand-dunes, while on the south the country was broken by deep coulees, affording splendid shelter in case of blizzards or wintry storms.

A dugout was built on either end of the range. Major Hunter took the wagon and team and went to the nearest settlement, returning with a load of corn, having contracted for the delivery of five hundred bushels more. Meanwhile I was busy locating the cattle, scattering them sparsely over the surrounding country, cutting them into bunches of not more than ten to twenty head. Corrals and cosy shelters were built for a few horses, comfortable quarters for the men, and we settled down for the winter with everything snug and secure. By the first of December the force was reduced to four men at each camp, all of whom were experienced in holding cattle in the winter. Lines giving ample room to our cattle were established, which were to be ridden both evening and morning in any and all weather. Two Texans, both experts as trailers, were detailed to trail down any cattle which left the boundaries of the range. The weather continued fine, and with the camps well provisioned, the major and I returned to the railroad and took train for Council Grove. I was impatient to go home, and took the most direct route then available. Railroads were just beginning to enter the West, and one had recently been completed across the eastern portion of the Indian Territory, its destination being south of Red River. With nothing but the clothes on my back and a saddle, I started home, and within twenty-four hours arrived at Denison, Texas. Connecting stages carried me to Fort Worth, where I bought a saddle horse, and the next evening I was playing with the babies at the home ranch. It had been an active summer with me, but success had amply rewarded my labors, while every cloud had disappeared and the future was rich in promise.

CHAPTER XI
A PROSPEROUS YEAR

An open winter favored the cattle on the Medicine River. My partners in Kansas wrote me encouragingly, and plans were outlined for increasing our business for the coming summer. There was no activity in live stock during the winter in Texas, and there would be no trouble in putting up herds at prevailing prices of the spring before. I spent an inactive winter, riding back and forth to my ranch, hunting with hounds, and killing an occasional deer. While visiting at Council Grove the fall before, Major Hunter explained to our silent partner the cheapness of Texas lands. Neither one of my associates cared to scatter their interests beyond the boundaries of their own State, yet both urged me to acquire every acre of cheap land that my means would permit. They both recited the history and growth in value of the lands surrounding The Grove, telling me how cheaply they could have bought the same ten years before, — at the government price of a dollar and a quarter an acre, — and that already there had been an advance of four to five hundred per cent. They urged me to buy scrip and locate land, assuring me that it was only a question of time until the people of Texas would arise in their might and throw off the yoke of Reconstruction.

At home general opinion was just the reverse. No one cared for more land than a homestead or for immediate use. No locations had been made adjoining my ranch on the Clear Fork, and it began to look as if I had more land than I needed. Yet I had confidence enough in the advice of my partners to reopen negotiations with my merchant friend at Austin for the purchase of more land scrip. The panic of the fall before had scarcely affected the frontier of Texas, and was felt in only a few towns of any prominence in the State. There had been no money in circulation since the war, and a financial stringency elsewhere made little difference among the local people. True, the Kansas cattle market had sent a little money home, but a bad winter with drovers holding cattle in the North, followed by a panic, had bankrupted nearly every cowman, many of them with heavy liabilities in Texas. There were very few banks in the State, and what little money there was among the people was generally hoarded to await the dawn of a brighter day.

My wife tells a story about her father, which shows similar conditions prevailing during the civil war. The only outlet for cotton in Texas during the rebellion was by way of Mexico. Matamoros, near the mouth of the Rio Grande, waxed opulent in its trade of contrabrand cotton, the Texas product crossing the river anywhere for hundreds of miles above and being freighted down on the Mexican side to tide-water. The town did an immense business during the blockade of coast seaports, twenty-dollar gold pieces being more plentiful then than nickels are to-day, the cotton finding a ready market at war prices and safe shipment under foreign flags. My wife's father was engaged in the trade of buying cotton at interior points, freighting it by ox trains over the Mexican frontier, and thence down the river to Matamoros. Once the staple reached neutral soil, it was palmed off as a local product, and the Federal government dared not touch it, even though they knew it to be contrabrand of war. The business was transacted in gold, and it was Mr. Edwards's custom to bury the coin on his return from each trading trip. My wife, then a mere girl and the oldest of the children at home, was taken into her father's confidence in secreting the money. The country was full of bandits, either government would have confiscated the gold had they known its whereabouts, and the only way to insure its safety was to bury it. After several years trading in cotton, Mr. Edwards accumulated considerable money, and on one occasion buried the treasure at night between two trees in an adjoining wood. Unexpectedly one day he had occasion to use some money in buying a cargo of cotton, the children were at a distant neighbor's, and he went into the woods alone to unearth the gold. But hogs, running in the timber, had rooted up the ground in search of edible roots, and Edwards was unable to locate the spot where his treasure lay buried. Fearful that possibly the money had been uprooted and stolen, he sent for the girl, who hastily returned. As my wife tells the story, great beads of perspiration were dripping from her father's brow as the two entered the woods. And although the ground was rooted up, the girl pointed out the spot, midway between two trees, and the treasure was recovered without a coin missing. Mr. Edwards lost confidence in himself, and thereafter, until peace was restored, my wife and a younger sister always buried the family treasure by night, keeping the secret to themselves, and producing the money on demand.

The merchant at Austin reported land scrip plentiful at fifteen to sixteen dollars a section. I gave him an order for two hundred certificates, and he filled the bill so promptly that I ordered another hundred, bringing my unlocated holdings up to six hundred sections. My land scrip was a standing joke between my wife and me, and I often promised her that when we built a house and moved to the Clear Fork, if the scrip was still worthless she might have the certificates to paper a room with. They were nicely lithographed, the paper was of the very best quality, and they went into my wife's trunk to await their destiny. Had it been known outside that I held such an amount of scrip, I would have been subjected to ridicule, and no doubt would have given it to some surveyor to locate on shares. Still I had a vague idea that land at two and a half cents an acre would never hurt me. Several times in the past I had needed the money tied up in scrip, and then I would regret having bought it. After the loss of my entire working capital by Texas fever, I was glad I had foresight enough to buy a quantity that summer. And thus I swung like a pendulum between personal necessities and public opinion; but when those long-headed Yankee partners of mine urged me to buy land, I felt once more that I was on the right track and recovered my grasp. I might have located fifty miles of the valley of the Clear Fork that winter, but it would have entailed some little expense, the land would then have been taxable, and I had the use of it without outlay or trouble.

An event of great importance to the people of Texas occurred during the winter of 1873-74. The election the fall before ended in dispute, both great parties claiming the victory. On the meeting of the legislature to canvass the vote, all the negro militia of the State were concentrated in and around the capitol building. The Reconstruction régime refused to vacate, and were fighting to retain control; the best element of the people were asserting in no unmistakable terms their rights and bloodshed seemed inevitable. The federal government was appealed to, but refused to interfere. The legislature was with the people, and when the latter refused to be intimidated by a display of force, those in possession yielded the reins, and Governor Coke was inaugurated January 15, 1874; and thus the prediction of my partners, uttered but a few mouths before, became history.

Major Hunter came down again about the last of February. Still unshaken in his confidence in the future of Texas, he complimented me on securing more land scrip. He had just returned from our camps on the Medicine River, and reported the cattle coming through in splendid condition. Gray wolves had harassed the herd during the early winter; but long-range rifles and poison were furnished, and our men waged a relentless war on these pirates along the Medicine. Cattle in Texas had wintered strong, which would permit of active operations beginning earlier than usual, and after riding the range for a week we were ready for business. It was well known in all the surrounding country that we would again be in the market for trail cattle, and offerings were plentiful. These tenders ran anywhere from stock cattle to heavy beeves; but the market which we were building up with farmers at Council Grove required young two and three year old steers. It again fell to my province to do the buying, and with the number of brands for sale in the country I expected, with the consent of my partners, to make a new departure. I was beginning to understand the advantages of growing cattle. My holdings of mixed stock on the Clear Fork had virtually cost me nothing, and while they may have been unsalable, yet there was a steady growth and they were a promising source of income. From the results of my mavericking and my trading operations I had been enabled to send two thousand young steers up the trail the spring before, and the proceeds from their sale had lifted me from the slough of despond and set me on a financial rock. Therefore my regard for the eternal cow was enhancing.

Home prices were again ten dollars for two-year-old steers and twelve for threes. Instead of buying outright at these figures, my proposition was to buy individually brands of stock cattle, and turn over all steers of acceptable ages at prevailing prices to the firm of Hunter, Anthony & Co. in making up trail herds. We had already agreed to drive ten thousand head that spring, and my active partner readily saw the advantages that would accrue where one had the range and outfit to take care of the remnants of mixed stock. My partners were both straining their credit at home, and since it was immaterial to them, I was given permission to go ahead. This method of buying might slightly delay the starting of herds, and rather than do so I contracted for three thousand straight threes in Erath County. This herd would start ten days in advance of any other, which would give us cattle on the market at Wichita with the opening of the season. My next purchase was two brands whose range was around the juncture of the main Brazos and Clear Fork, adjoining my ranch. These cattle were to be delivered at our corrals, as, having received the three-year-olds from both brands the spring before, I had a good idea how the stock ought to classify. A third brand was secured up the Clear Fork, adjacent to my range, supposed to number about three thousand, from which nothing had been sold in four years. This latter contingent cost me five dollars a head, but my boys knew the brand well enough to know that they would run forty per cent steer cattle. In all three cases I bought all right and title to the brand, giving them until the last day of March to gather, and anything not tendered for count on receiving, the tail went with the hide.

From these three brands I expected to make up the second herd easily. With no market for cattle, it was safe to count on a brand running one third steers or better, from which I ought to get twenty-five per cent of age for trail purposes. Long before any receiving began I bought four more brands outright in adjoining counties, setting the day for receiving on the 5th of April, everything to be delivered on my ranch on the Clear Fork. There were fully twenty-five thousand cattle in these seven brands, and as I had bought them all half cash and the balance on six months' time, it behooved me to be on the alert and protect my interests. A trusty man was accordingly sent from my ranch to assist in the gathering of each of the four outside brands, to be present at all round-ups, to see that no steer cattle were held back, and that the dropping calves were cared for and saved. This precaution was not taken around my ranch, for any animal which failed to be counted my own men would look out for by virtue of ownership of the brand. My saddle horses were all in fine condition, and were cut into remudas of ninety head each, two new wagons were fitted up, and all was ready to move.

The Erath County herd was to be delivered to us on the 20th of March. George Edwards was to have charge, and he and Major Hunter started in ample time to receive the cattle, the latter proving an apt scholar, while the former was a thorough cowman. In the mean time I had made up a second outfit, putting a man who had made a number of trips with me as foreman in charge, and we moved out to the Clear Fork. The first herd started on the 22d, Major Hunter accompanying it past the Edwards ranch and then joining us on my range. We had kept in close touch with the work then in progress along the Brazos and Clear Fork, and it was probable that we might be able to receive in advance of the appointed day. Fortunately this happened in two cases, both brands overrunning all expectations in general numbers and the quantity of steer cattle. These contingents were met, counted, and received ten miles from the ranch, nothing but the steers two years old and upward being brought in to the corrals. The third brand, from west on the Clear Fork, came in on the dot, and this also surprised me in its numbers of heavy steer cattle. From the three contingents I received over thirteen thousand head, nearly four thousand of which were steers of trail age. On the first day of April we started the second herd of thirty-five hundred twos and threes, the latter being slightly in the majority, but we classified them equally. Major Hunter was pleased with the quality of the cattle, and I was more than satisfied with results, as I had nearly five hundred heavy steers left which would easily qualify as beeves. Estimating the latter at what they ought to net me at Wichita, the remnants of stock cattle cost me about a dollar and a half a head, while I had received more cash than the amount of the half payment.

The beef steers were held under herd to await the arrival of the other contingents. If they fell short in twos and threes, I had hopes of finding an outlet for my beeves with the last herd. The young stuff and stock cattle were allowed to drift back on their own ranges, and we rested on our oars. We had warning of the approach of outside brands, several arriving in advance of appointment, and they were received at once. As before, every brand overran expectations, with no shortage in steers. My men had been wide awake, any number of mature beeves coming in with the mixed stock. As fast as they arrived we cut all steers of desirable age into our herd of beeves, sending the remnant up the river about ten miles to be put under loose herd for the first month. Fifteen-thousand cattle were tendered in the four brands, from which we cut out forty-six hundred steers of trail age. The numbers were actually embarrassing, not in stock cattle, but in steers, as our trail herd numbered now over five thousand. The outside outfits were all detained a few days for a settlement, lending their assistance, as we tally-marked all the stock cattle before sending them up the river to be put under herd. This work was done in a chute with branding irons, running a short bar over the holding-brand, the object being to distinguish animals received then from what might be gathered afterward. There were nearly one hundred men present, and with the amount of help available the third herd was ready to start on the morning of the 6th. It numbered thirty-five hundred, again nearly equal in twos and threes, my ranch foreman having charge. With the third herd started, the question arose what to do with the remnant of a few over sixteen hundred beeves. To turn them loose meant that with the first norther that blew they would go back to their own range. Major Hunter suggested that I drive an individual herd. I tried to sell him an interest in the cattle, but as their ages were unsuited to his market, he pleaded bankruptcy, yet encouraged me to fill up the herd and drive them on my own account.

Something had to be done. I bought sixty horses from the different outfits then waiting for a settlement, adding thirty of my own to the remuda, made up an outfit from the men present, rigged a wagon, and called for a general round-up of my range. Two days afterward we had fifteen hundred younger steers of my own raising in the herd, and on the 10th of the month the fourth one moved out. A day was lost in making a general settlement, after which Major Hunter and I rode through the mixed cattle under herd, finding them contentedly occupying nearly ten miles of the valley of the Clear Fork. Calves were dropping at the rate of one hundred a day, two camps of five men each held them on an ample range, riding lines well back from the valley. The next morning we turned homeward, passing my ranch and corrals, which but a few days before were scenes of activity, but now deserted even by the dogs. From the Edwards ranch we were driven in to Fort Worth, and by the middle of the month reached Wichita.

No herds were due to arrive for a month. My active partner continued on to his home at The Grove, and I started for our camps on the Medicine River. The grass was coming with a rush, the cattle were beginning to shed their winter coats, and our men assured me that the known loss amounted to less than twenty head. The boys had spent an active winter, only a few storms ever bunching the cattle, with less than half a dozen contingents crossing the established lines. Even these were followed by our trailers and brought back to their own range; and together with wolfing the time had passed pleasantly. An incident occurred at the upper camp that winter which clearly shows the difference between the cow-hand of that day and the modern bronco-buster. In baiting for wolves, many miles above our range, a supposed trail of cattle was cut by one of the boys, who immediately reported the matter to our Texas trailer at camp. They were not our cattle to a certainty, yet it was but a neighborly act to catch them, so the two men took up the trail. From appearances there were not over fifteen head in the bunch, and before following them many miles, the trailer became suspicious that they were buffalo and not cattle. He trailed them until they bedded down, when he dismounted and examined every bed. No cow ever lay down without leaving hair on its bed, so when the Texan had examined the ground where half a dozen had slept, his suspicions were confirmed. Declaring them buffalo, the two men took up the trail in a gallop, overtaking the band within ten miles and securing four fine robes. There is little or no difference in the tracks of the two animals. I simply mention this, as my patience has been sorely tried with the modern picturesque cowboy, who is merely an amateur when compared with the men of earlier days.

I spent three weeks riding the range on the Medicine. The cattle had been carefully selected, now four and five years old, and if the season was favorable they would be ready for shipment early in the fall. The lower camp was abandoned in order to enlarge the range nearly one third, and after providing for the wants of the men, I rode away to the southeast to intercept the Chisholm trail where it crossed the Kansas line south of Wichita. The town of Caldwell afterward sprang up on the border, but at this time among drovers it was known as Stone's Store, a trading-post conducted by Captain Stone, afterward a cowman, and already mentioned in these memoirs. Several herds had already passed on my arrival; I watched the trail, meeting every outfit for nearly a week, and finally George Edwards came snailing along. He reported our other cattle from seven to ten days behind, but was not aware that I had an individual herd on the trail. Edwards moved on to Wichita, and I awaited the arrival of our second outfit. A brisk rivalry existed between the solicitors for Ellsworth and Wichita, every man working faithfully for his railroad or town, and at night they generally met in social session over a poker game. I never played a card for money now, not that my morals were any too good, but I was married and had partners, and business generally absorbed me to such an extent that I neglected the game.

I met the second herd at Pond Creek, south in the Cherokee Outlet, and after spending a night with them rode through to Wichita in a day and night. We went into camp that year well up the Arkansas River, as two outfits would again hold the four herds. Our second outfit arrived at the chosen grazing grounds on time, the men were instantly relieved, and after a good carouse in town they started home. The two other herds came in without delay, the beeves arriving on the last of the month. Barely half as many cattle would arrive from Texas that summer, as many former drovers from that section were bankrupt on account of the panic of the year before. Yet the market was fairly well supplied with offerings of wintered Texans, the two classes being so distinct that there was very little competition between them. My active partner was on hand early, reporting a healthy inquiry among former customers, all of whom were more than pleased with the cattle supplied them the year before. By being in a position to extend a credit to reliable men, we were enabled to effect sales where other drovers dared not venture.

Business opened early with us. I sold fifteen hundred of my heaviest beeves to an army contractor from Wyoming. My active partner sold the straight three-year-old herd from Erath County to an ex-governor from Nebraska, and we delivered it on the Republican River in that State. Small bunches of from three to five hundred were sold to farmers, and by the first of August we had our holdings reduced to two herds in charge of one outfit. When the hipping season began with our customers at The Grove, trade became active with us at Wichita. Scarcely a week passed but Major Hunter sold a thousand or more to his neighbors, while I skirmished around in the general market. When the outfit returned from the Republican River, I took it in charge, went down on the Medicine, and cut out a thousand beeves, bringing them to the railroad and shipping them to St. Louis. I never saw fatter cattle in my life. When we got the returns from the first consignment, we shipped two trainloads every fortnight until our holding's on the Medicine were reduced to a remnant. A competent bookkeeper was employed early in the year, and in keeping our accounts at Wichita, looking after our shipments, keeping individual interests, by brands, separate from the firm's, he was about the busiest man connected with the summer's business. Aside from our drive of over thirteen thousand head, we bought three whole herds, retailing them in small quantities to our customers, all of which was profitable. I bought four whole remudas on personal account, culled out one hundred and fifty head and sold them at a sacrifice, sending home the remaining two hundred saddle horses. I found it much cheaper and more convenient to buy my supply of saddle stock at trail terminals than at home. Once railroad connections were in operation direct between Kansas and Texas, every outfit preferred to go home by rail, but I adhered to former methods for many years.

In summing up the year's business, never were three partners more surprised. With a remnant of nearly one hundred beeves unfit for shipment, the Medicine River venture had cleared us over two hundred per cent, while the horses on hand were worth ten dollars a head more than what they had cost, owing to their having wintered in the North. The ten thousand trail cattle paid splendidly, while my individual herd had sold out in a manner, leaving the stock cattle at home clear velvet. A programme was outlined for enlarging our business for the coming year, and every dollar of our profits was to be reinvested in wintering and trailing cattle from Texas. Next to the last shipment, the through outfit went home, taking the extra two hundred saddle horses with it, the final consignment being brought in to Wichita for loading out by our ranch help. The shipping ended in October. My last work of the year was the purchase of seven thousand three-year-old steers, intended for our Medicine River range. We had intentionally held George Edwards and his outfit for this purpose, and cutting the numbers into two herds, the Medicine River lads led off for winter quarters. We had bought the cattle worth the money, but not at a sacrifice like the year before, neither would we expect such profits. It takes a good nerve, but experience has taught me that in land and cattle the time of the worst depression is the time to buy. Major Hunter accompanied the herds to their winter quarters, sending Edwards with his outfit, after their arrival on the Medicine, back to Texas, while I took the train and reached home during the first week in November.

CHAPTER XII
CLEAR FORK AND SHENANDOAH

I arrived home in good time for the fall work. The first outfit relieved at Wichita had instructions to begin, immediately on reaching the ranch, a general cow-hunt for outside brands. It was possible that a few head might have escaped from the Clear Fork range and returned to their old haunts, but these would bear a tally-mark distinguishing them from any not gathered at the spring delivery. My regular ranch hands looked after the three purchased brands adjoining our home range, but an independent outfit had been working the past four months gathering strays and remnants in localities where I had previously bought brands. They went as far south as Comanche County and picked up nearly one hundred "Lazy L's," scoured the country where I had purchased the two brands in the spring of 1872, and afterward confined themselves to ranges from which the outside cattle were received that spring. They had made one delivery on the Clear Fork of seven hundred head before my return, and were then away on a second cow-hunt.

On my reaching the ranch the first contingent of gathered cattle were under herd. They were a rag-tag lot, many of them big steers, while much of the younger stuff was clear of earmark or brand until after their arrival at the home corrals. The ranch help herded them by day and penned them at night, but on the arrival of the independent outfit with another contingent of fifteen hundred the first were freed and the second put under herd. Counting both bunches, the strays numbered nearly a thousand head, and cattle bearing no tally-mark fully as many more, while the remainder were mavericks and would have paid the expenses of the outfit for the past four months. I now had over thirty thousand cattle on the Clear Fork, holding them in eleven brands, but decided thereafter to run all the increase in the original "44." This rule had gone into effect the fall previous, and I now proposed to run it on all calves branded. Never before had I felt the necessity of increasing my holdings in land, but with the number of cattle on hand it behooved me to possess a larger acreage of the Clear Fork valley. A surveyor was accordingly sent for, and while the double outfit was branding the home calf crop, I located on the west end of my range a strip of land ten miles long by five wide. At the east end of my ranch another tract was located, five by ten miles, running north and taking in all that country around the junction of the Clear Fork with the mother Brazos. This gave me one hundred and fifty sections of land, lying in the form of an immense Lazy L, and I felt that the expense was justified in securing an ample range for my stock cattle.

My calf crop that fall ran a few over seven thousand head. They were good northern Texas calves, and it would cost but a trifle to run them until they were two-year-olds; and if demand continued in the upper country, some day a trail herd of steers could easily be made up from their numbers. I was beginning to feel rather proud of my land and cattle; the former had cost me but a small outlay, while the latter were clear velvet, as I had sold thirty-five hundred from their increase during the past two years. Once the surveying and branding was over, I returned to the Edwards ranch for the winter. The general outlook in Texas was for the better; quite a mileage of railroad had been built within the State during the past year, and new and prosperous towns had sprung up along their lines. The political situation had quieted down, and it was generally admitted that a Reconstruction government could never again rear its head on Texas soil. The result was that confidence was slowly being restored among the local people, and the press of the State was making a fight for recognition, all of which augured for a brighter future. Living on the frontier and absent the greater portion of the time, I took little interest in local politics, yet could not help but feel that the restoration of self-government to the best elements of our people would in time reflect on the welfare of the State. Since my advent in Texas I had been witness to the growth of Fort Worth from a straggling village in the spring of 1866 to quite a pretentious town in the fall of 1874.

Ever since the partnership was formed I had been aware of and had fostered the political ambitions of the firm's silent member. He had been prominently identified with the State of Kansas since it was a territory, had held positions of trust, and had been a representative in Congress, and all three of us secretly hoped to see him advanced to the United States Senate. We had fully discussed the matter on various occasions, and as the fall elections had gone favorably, the present was considered the opportune time to strike. The firm mutually agreed to stand the expense of the canvass, which was estimated on a reasonable basis, and the campaign opened with a blare of trumpets. Assuming the rôle of a silent partner, I had reports furnished me regularly, and it soon developed that our estimate on the probable expense was too low. We had boldly entered the canvass, our man was worthy, and I wrote back instructing my partners to spare no expense in winning the fight. There were a number of candidates in the race and the legislature was in session, when an urgent letter reached me, urging my presence at the capital of Kansas. The race was narrowing to a close, a personal consultation was urged, and I hastened north as fast as a relay of horses and railroad trains could carry me. On my arrival at Topeka the fight had almost narrowed to a financial one, and we questioned if the game were worth the candle. Yet we were already involved in a considerable outlay, and the consultation resulted in our determination to win, which we did, but at an expense of a little over four times the original estimate, which, however, afterward proved a splendid investment.

I now had hopes that we might enlarge our operations in handling government contracts. Major Hunter saw possibilities along the same line, and our silent partner was awakened to the importance of maintaining friendly relations with the Interior and War departments, gathering all the details in contracting beef with the government for its Indian agencies and army posts in the West. Up to date this had been a lucrative field which only a few Texas drovers had ventured into, most of the contractors being Northern and Eastern men, and usually buying the cattle with which to fill the contracts near the point of delivery. I was impatient to get into this trade, as the Indian deliveries generally took cows, and the army heavy beef, two grades of cattle that at present our firm had no certain demand for. Also the market was gradually moving west from Wichita, and it was only a question of a few years until the settlements of eastern Kansas would cut us off from our established trade around The Grove. I had seen Abilene pass away as a market, Wichita was doomed by the encroachments of agriculture, and it behooved us to be alert for a new outlet.

I made up my mind to buy more land scrip. Not that there had been any perceptible improvement in wild lands, but the general outlook justified its purchase. My agent at Austin reported scrip to be had in ordinary quantities at former prices, and suggested that I supply myself fully, as the new administration was an economical one, and once the great flood of certificates issued by the last Reconstruction régime were absorbed, an advance in land scrip was anticipated. I accordingly bought three hundred sections more, hardly knowing what to do with it, yet I knew there was an empire of fine grazing country between my present home and the Pecos River. If ever the Comanches were brought under subjection there would be ranches and room for all; and our babies were principally boys.

Major Hunter came down earlier than usual. He reported a clear, cold winter on the Medicine and no serious drift of cattle, and expressed the belief that we would come through with a loss not exceeding one per cent. This was encouraging, as it meant fat cattle next fall, fit for any market in the country. It was yet too early to make any move towards putting up herds for the trail, and we took train and went down the country as far as Austin. There was always a difference in cattle prices, running from one to two dollars a head, between the northern and southern parts of the State. Both of us were anxious to acquaint ourselves with the different grades, and made stops in several intervening counties, looking at cattle on the range and pricing them. We spent a week at the capital city and met all the trail drovers living there, many of whom expected to put up herds for that year southeast on the Colorado River. "Shanghai" Pierce had for some time been a prominent figure in the markets of Abilene and Wichita, driving herds of his own from the extreme coast country. But our market required a better quality than coasters and Mexican cattle, and we turned back up the country. Before leaving the capital, Major Hunter and I had a long talk with my merchant friend over the land scrip market, and the latter urged its purchase at once, if wanted, as the issue afloat was being gradually absorbed. Already there had been a noticeable advance in the price, and my partner gave me no peace until I bought, at eighteen dollars a section, two hundred certificates more. Its purchase was making an inroad on my working capital, but the major frowned on my every protest, and I yielded out of deference to his superior judgment.

Returning, we stopped in Bell County, where we contracted for fifteen thousand two and three year old steers. They were good prairie-raised cattle, and we secured them at a dollar a head less than the prices prevailing in the first few counties south of Red River. Major Hunter remained behind, arranging his banking facilities, and I returned home after my outfits. Before leaving Bell County, I left word that we could use fifty good men for the trail, but they would have to come recommended by the ranchmen with whom we were dealing. We expected to make up five herds, and the cattle were to be ready for delivery to us between the 15th and 30th of March. I hastened home and out to the ranch, gathered our saddle stock, outfitted wagons, and engaged all my old foremen and twenty trusty men, and we started with a remuda of five hundred horses to begin the operations of the coming summer. Receiving cattle with me was an old story by this time, and frequently matters came to a standstill between the sellers and ourselves. We paid no attention to former customs of the country; all cattle had to come up full-aged or go into the younger class, while inferior or knotty stags were turned back as not wanted. Scarcely a day passed but there was more or less dispute; but we proposed paying for them, and insisted that all cattle tendered must come up to the specifications of the contract. We stood firm, and after the first two herds were received, all trouble on that score passed, and in making up the last three herds there was actually a surplus of cattle tendered. We used a road brand that year on all steers purchased, and the herds moved out from two to three days apart, the last two being made up in Coryell, the adjoining county north.

George Edwards had charge of the rear herd. There were fourteen days between the first and the last starts, a fortnight of hard work, and we frequently received from ten to thirty miles distant from the branding pens. I rode almost night and day, and Edwards likewise, while Major Hunter kept all the accounts and settled with the sellers. As fast as one herd was ready, it moved out under a foreman and fourteen men, one hundred saddle horses, and a well-stocked commissary. We did our banking at Belton, the county seat, and after the last herd started we returned to town and received quite an ovation from the business men of the village. We had invested a little over one hundred and fifty thousand dollars in cattle in that community, and a banquet was even suggested in our honor by some of the leading citizens. Most of the contracts were made with merchants, many of whom did not own a hoof of cattle, but depended on their customers to deliver the steers. The business interests of the town were anxious to have us return next year. We declined the proposed dinner, as neither Major Hunter nor myself would have made a presentable guest. A month or more had passed since I had left the ranch on the Clear Fork, the only clothes I had were on my back, and they were torn in a dozen places from running cattle in the brush. My partner had been living in cow-camps for the past three weeks, and preferred to be excused from receiving any social attentions. So we thanked our friends and started for the railroad.

Major Hunter went through to The Grove, while I stopped at Fort Worth. A buckboard from home was awaiting me, and the next morning I was at the Edwards ranch. A relay team was harnessed in, and after counting the babies I started for the Clear Fork. By early evening I was in consultation with my ranch foreman, as it was my intention to drive an individual herd if everything justified the venture. I never saw the range on the Clear Fork look better, and the books showed that we could easily gather two thousand twos and threes, while the balance of the herd could be made up of dry and barren cows. All we lacked was about thirty horses, and my ranch hands were anxious to go up the trail; but after riding the range one day I decided that it would be a pity to disturb the pastoral serenity of the valley. It was fairly dotted with my own cattle; month-old calves were playing in groups, while my horse frequently shied at new-born ones, lying like fawns in the tall grass. A round-up at that time meant the separation of mothers from their offspring and injury to cows approaching maternity, and I decided that no commercial necessity demanded the sacrifice. Then again it seemed a short-sighted policy to send half-matured steers to market, when no man could bring the same animals to a full development as cheaply as I could. Barring contagious diseases, cattle are the healthiest creatures that walk the earth, and even on an open range seldom if ever does one voluntarily forsake its birthplace.

I spent two weeks on the ranch and could have stayed the summer through, for I love cattle. Our lead herd was due on the Kansas state line early in May, so remaining at the Edwards ranch until the last possible hour, I took train and reached Wichita, where my active partner was awaiting me. He had just returned from the Medicine River, and reported everything serene. He had made arrangements to have the men attend all the country round-ups within one hundred miles of our range. Several herds had already reached Wichita, and the next day I started south on horseback to meet our cattle at Caldwell on the line, or at Pond Creek in the Cherokee Outlet. It was going to be difficult to secure range for herds within fifteen miles of Wichita, and the opinion seemed general that this would be the last year that town could hope to hold any portion of the Texas cattle trade. On arriving at Pond Creek I found that fully half the herds were turning up that stream, heading for Great Bend, Ellsworth, Ellis, and Nickerson, all markets within the State of Kansas. The year before nearly one third the drive had gone to the two first-named points, and now other towns were offering inducements and bidding for a share of the present cattle exodus.

Our lead herd arrived without an incident en route. The second one came in promptly, both passing on and picking their way through the border settlements to Wichita. I waited until the third one put in an appearance, leaving orders for it and the two rear ones to camp on some convenient creek in the Outlet near Caldwell. Arrangements were made with Captain Stone for supplying the outfits, and I hurried on to overtake the lead herds, then nearing Wichita. An ample range was found but twenty miles up the Arkansas River, and the third day all the Bell County men in the two outfits were sent home by train. The market was much the same as the year before: one herd of three thousand two-year-olds was our largest individual sale. Early in August the last herd was brought from the state line and the through help reduced to two outfits, one holding cattle at Wichita and the other bringing in shipments of beeves from the Medicine River range. The latter were splendid cattle, fatted to a finish for grass animals, and brought top prices in the different markets to which they were consigned. Omitting details, I will say it was an active year, as we bought and sold fully as many more as our drive amounted to, while I added to my stock of saddle horses an even three hundred head.

An amusing incident occurred with one of my men while holding cattle that fall at Wichita. The boys were in and out of town frequently, and one of them returned to camp one evening and informed me that he wanted to quit work, as he intended to return to Wichita and kill a man. He was a good hand and I tried to persuade him out of the idea, but he insisted that it was absolutely necessary to preserve his honor. I threatened to refuse him a horse, but seeing that menace and persuasion were useless, I ordered him to pick my holdings of saddle stock, gave him his wages due, and told him to be sure and shoot first. He bade us all good-by, and a chum of his went with him. About an hour before daybreak they returned and awoke me, when the aggrieved boy said: "Mr. Anthony, I didn't kill him. No, I didn't kill him. He's a good man. You bet he's a game one. Oh, he's a good man all right." That morning when I awoke both lads were out on herd, and I had an early appointment to meet parties in town. Major Hunter gave me the story immediately on my arrival. The boys had located the offender in a store, and he anticipated the fact that they were on his trail. As our men entered the place, the enemy stepped from behind a pile of clothing with two six-shooters leveled in their faces, and ordered a clerk to relieve the pair of their pistols, which was promptly done. Once the particulars were known at camp, it was looked upon as a good joke on the lad, and whenever he was asked what he thought of Mr. Blank, his reply invariably was, "He's a good man."

The drive that year to the different markets in Kansas amounted to about five hundred thousand cattle. One half this number were handled at Wichita, the surrounding country absorbing them to such an extent that when it came time to restock our Medicine River range I was compelled to go to Great Bend to secure the needed cattle. All saddle horses, both purchased and my own remudas, with wagons, were sent to our winter camps by the shipping crew, so that the final start for Texas would be made from the Medicine River. It was the last of October that the last six trains of beeves were brought in to the railroad for shipment, the season's work drawing to an end. Meanwhile I had closed contracts on ten thousand three-year-old steers at "The Bend," so as fast as the three outfits were relieved of their consignment of beeves they pulled out up the Arkansas River to receive the last cattle of the year. It was nearly one hundred miles from Wichita, and on the arrival of the shipping crews the herds were received and started south for their winter range. Major Hunter and I accompanied the herds to the Medicine, and within a week after reaching the range the two through outfits started home with five wagons and eight hundred saddle horses.

It was the latter part of November when we left our winter camps and returned to The Grove for the annual settlement. Our silent partner was present, and we broke the necks of a number of champagne bottles in properly celebrating the success of the year's work. The wintered cattle had cleared the Dutchman's one per cent, while every hoof in the through and purchased herds was a fine source of profit. Congress would convene within a week, and our silent partner suggested that all three of us go down to Washington and attend the opening exercises. He had already looked into the contracting of beef to the government, and was particularly anxious to have my opinion on a number of contracts to be let the coming winter. It had been ten years since I left my old home in the Shenandoah Valley, my parents were still living, and all I asked was time enough to write a letter to my wife, and buy some decent clothing. The trio started in good time for the opening of Congress, but once we sighted the Potomac River the old home hunger came on me and I left the train at Harper's Ferry. My mother knew and greeted me just as if I had left home that morning on an errand, and had now returned. My father was breaking with years, yet had a mental alertness that was remarkable and a commercial instinct that understood the value of a Texas cow or a section of land scrip. The younger members of the family gathered from their homes to meet "Texas" Anthony, and for ten continuous days I did nothing but answer questions, running from the color of the baby's eyes to why we did not drive the fifteen thousand cattle in one herd, or how big a section of country would one thousand certificates of land scrip cover. My visit was broken by the necessity of conferring with my partners, so, promising to spend Christmas with my mother, I was excused until that date.

At the War and Interior departments I made many friends. I understood cattle so thoroughly that there was no feature of a delivery to the government that embarrassed me in the least. A list of contracts to be let from each department was courteously furnished us, but not wishing to scatter our business too wide, we submitted bids for six Indian contracts and four for delivery to army posts on the upper Missouri River. Two of the latter were to be northern wintered cattle, and we had them on the Medicine River; but we also had a sure market on them, and it was a matter of indifference whether we secured them or not. The Indian contracts called for cows, and I was anxious to secure as many as possible, as it meant a market for the aging she stuff on my ranch. Heretofore this class had fulfilled their mission in perpetuating their kind, had lived their day, and the weeds grew rankly where their remains enriched the soil. The bids would not be opened until the middle of January, and we should have notice at once if fortunate in securing any of the awards. The holiday season was approaching, Major Hunter was expected at home, and the firm separated for the time being.

CHAPTER XIII
THE CENTENNIAL YEAR

I returned to Texas early in January. Quite a change had come over the situation since my leaving home the spring before. Except on the frontier, business was booming in the new towns, while a regular revolution had taken place within the past month in land values. The cheapness of wild lands had attracted outside capital, resulting in a syndicate being formed by Northern capitalists to buy up the outstanding issue of land scrip. The movement had been handled cautiously, and had possibly been in active operation for a year or more, as its methods were conducted with the utmost secrecy. Options had been taken on all scrip voted to corporations in the State and still in their possession, agents of the syndicate were stationed at all centres where any amount was afloat, and on a given day throughout the State every certificate on the market was purchased. The next morning land scrip was worth fifty dollars a section, and on my return one hundred dollars a certificate was being freely bid, while every surveyor in the State was working night and day locating lands for individual holders of scrip.

This condition of affairs was largely augmented by a boom in sheep. San Antonio was the leading wool market in the State, many clips having sold as high as forty cents a pound for several years past on the streets of that city. Free range and the high price of wool was inviting every man and his cousin to come to Texas and make his fortune. Money was feverish for investment in sheep, flock-masters were buying land on which to run their bands, and a sheepman was an envied personage. Up to this time there had been little or no occasion to own the land on which the immense flocks grazed the year round, yet under existing cheap prices of land nearly all the watercourses in the immediate country had been taken up. Personally I was dumfounded at the sudden and unexpected change of affairs, and what nettled me most was that all the land adjoining my ranch had been filed on within the past month. The Clear Fork valley all the way up to Fort Griffin had been located, while every vacant acre on the mother Brazos, as far north as Belknap, was surveyed and recorded. I was mortified to think that I had been asleep, but then the change had come like a thief in the night. My wife's trunk was half full of scrip, I had had a surveyor on the ground only a year before, and now the opportunity had passed.

But my disappointment was my wife's delight, as there was no longer any necessity for keeping secret our holdings in land scrip. The little tin trunk held a snug fortune, and next to the babies, my wife took great pride in showing visitors the beautiful lithographed certificates. My ambition was land and cattle, but now that the scrip had a cash value, my wife took as much pride in those vouchers as if the land had been surveyed, recorded, and covered with our own herds. I had met so many reverses that I was grateful for any smile of fortune, and bore my disappointment with becoming grace. My ranch had branded over eight thousand calves that fall, and as long as it remained an open range I had room for my holdings of cattle. There was no question but that the public domain was bountiful, and if it were necessary I could go farther west and locate a new ranch. But it secretly grieved me to realize that what I had so fondly hoped for had come without warning and found me unprepared. I might as well have held title to half a million acres of the Clear Fork Valley as a paltry hundred and fifty sections.

Little time was given me to lament over spilt milk. On the return from my first trip to the Clear Fork, reports from the War and Interior departments were awaiting me. Two contracts to the army and four to Indian agencies had been awarded us, all of which could be filled with through cattle. The military allotments would require six thousand heavy beeves for delivery on the upper Missouri River in Dakota, while the nation's wards would require thirteen thousand cows at four different agencies in the Indian Territory. My active partner was due in Fort Worth within a week, while bonds for the faithful fulfillment of our contracts would be executed by our silent partner at Washington, D.C. These awards meant an active year to our firm, and besides there was our established trade around The Grove, which we had no intention of abandoning. The government was a sure market, and as long as a healthy demand continued in Kansas for young cattle, the firm of Hunter, Anthony & Co. would be found actively engaged in supplying the same.

Major Hunter arrived under a high pressure of enthusiasm. By appointment we met in Fort Worth, and after carefully reviewing the situation we took train and continued on south to San Antonio. I had seen a herd of beeves, a few years before, from the upper Nueces River, and remembered them as good heavy cattle. There were two dollars a head difference, even in ages among younger stock, between the lower and upper counties in the State, and as it was pounds quantity that we wanted for the army, it was our intention to look over the cattle along the Nueces River before buying our supply of beeves. We met a number of acquaintances in San Antonio, all of whom recommended us to go west if in search of heavy cattle, and a few days later we reached Uvalde County. This was the section from which the beeves had come that impressed me so favorably; I even remembered the ranch brands, and without any difficulty we located the owners, finding them anxious to meet buyers for their mature surplus cattle. We spent a week along the Frio, Leona, and Nueces rivers, and closed contracts on sixty-one hundred five to seven year old beeves. The cattle were not as good a quality as prairie-raised north Texas stock, but the pounds avoirdupois were there, the defects being in their mongrel colors, length of legs, and breadth of horns, heritages from the original Spanish stock. Otherwise they were tall as a horse, clean-limbed as a deer, and active on their feet, and they looked like fine walkers. I estimated that two bits a head would drive them to Red River, and as we bought them at three dollars a head less than prevailing prices for the same-aged beeves north of or parallel to Fort Worth, we were well repaid for our time and trouble.

We returned to San Antonio and opened a bank account. The 15th of March was agreed on to receive. Two remudas of horses would have to be secured, wagons fitted up, and outfits engaged. Heretofore I had furnished all horses for trail work, but now, with our enlarging business, it would be necessary to buy others, which would be done at the expense of the firm. George Edwards was accordingly sent for, and met us at Waco. He was furnished a letter of credit on our San Antonio bank, and authorized to buy and equip two complete outfits for the Uvalde beeves. Edwards was a good judge of horses, there was an abundance of saddle stock in the country, and he was instructed to buy not less than one hundred and twenty-five head for each remuda, to outfit his wagons with four-mule teams, and announce us as willing to engage fourteen men to the herd. Once these details were arranged for, Major Hunter and myself bought two good horses and struck west for Coryell County, where we had put up two herds the spring before. Our return met with a flood of offerings, prices of the previous year still prevailed, and we let contracts for sixty-five hundred three-year-old steers and an equal number of dry and barren cows. We paid seven dollars a head for the latter, and in order to avoid any dispute at the final tender it was stipulated that the offerings must be in good flesh, not under five nor over eight years old, full average in weight, and showing no evidence of pregnancy. Under local customs, "a cow was a cow," and we had to be specific.

We did our banking at Waco for the Coryell herds. Hastening north, our next halt was in Hood County, where we bought thirty-three hundred two-year-old steers and three thousand and odd cows. This completed eight herds secured — three of young steers for the agricultural regions, and five intended for government delivery. We still lacked one for the Indian Bureau, and as I offered to make it up from my holdings, and on a credit, my active partner consented. I was putting in every dollar at my command, my partners were borrowing freely at home, and we were pulling together like a six-mule team to make a success of the coming summer's work. It was now the middle of February, and my active partner went to Fort Worth, where I did my banking, to complete his financial arrangements, while I returned to the ranch to organize the forces for the coming campaign. All the latter were intrusted to me, and while I had my old foremen at my beck and call, it was necessary to employ five or six new ones. With our deliveries scattered from the Indian Territory to the upper Missouri River, as well as our established trade at The Grove, two of us could not cover the field, and George Edwards had been decided on as the third and trusted man. In a practical way he was a better cowman than I was, and with my active Yankee partner for a running mate they made a team that would take care of themselves in any cow country.

A good foreman is a very important man in trail work. The drover or firm may or may not be practical cowmen, but the executive in the field must be the master of any possible situation that may arise, combining the qualities of generalship with the caution of an explorer. He must be a hail-fellow among his men, for he must command by deserving obedience; he must know the inmost thoughts of his herd, noting every sign of alarm or distress, and willingly sacrifice any personal comfort in the interest of his cattle or outfit. I had a few such men, boys who had grown up in my employ, several of whom I would rather trust in a dangerous situation with a herd than take active charge myself. No concern was given for their morals, but they must be capable, trustworthy, and honest, as they frequently handled large sums of money. All my old foremen swore by me, not one of them would accept a similar situation elsewhere, and in selecting the extra trail bosses their opinion was valued and given due consideration.

Not having driven anything from my ranch the year before, a fine herd of twos, threes, and four-year-old steers could easily be made up. It was possible that a tenth and individual herd might be sent up the country, but no movement to that effect was decided on, and my regular ranch hands had orders only to throw in on the home range and gather outside steer cattle and dry cows. I had wintered all my saddle horses on the Clear Fork, and once the foremen were decided on, they repaired to the ranch and began outfitting for the start. The Coryell herds were to be received one week later than the beef cattle, and the outfits would necessarily have to start in ample time to meet us on our return from the upper Nueces River country. The two foremen allotted to Hood County would start a week later still, so that we would really move north with the advance of the season in receiving the cattle under contract. Only a few days were required in securing the necessary foremen, a remuda was apportioned to each, and credit for the commissary supplies arranged for, the employment of the men being left entirely to the trail bosses. Taking two of my older foremen with me, I started for Fort Worth, where an agreeable surprise awaited me. We had been underbidden at the War Department on both our proposals for northern wintered beeves. The fortunate bidder on one contract was refused the award, — for some duplicity in a former transaction, I learned later, — and the Secretary of War had approached our silent partner to fill the deficiency. Six weeks had elapsed, there was no obligation outstanding, and rather than advertise and relet the contract, the head of the War Department had concluded to allot the deficiency by private award. Major Hunter had been burning the wires between Fort Worth and Washington, in order to hold the matter open until I came in for a consultation. The department had offered half a cent a pound over and above our previous bid, and we bribed an operator to reopen his office that night and send a message of acceptance. We had ten thousand cattle wintering on the Medicine River, and it would just trim them up nicely to pick out all the heavy, rough beeves for filling an army contract.

When we had got a confirmation of our message, we proceeded on south, accompanied by the two foremen, and reached Uvalde County within a week of the time set for receiving. Edwards had two good remudas in pastures, wagons and teams secured, and cooks and wranglers on hand, and it only remained to pick the men to complete the outfits. With three old trail foremen on the alert for good hands while the gathering and receiving was going on, the help would be ready in ample time to receive the herds. Gathering the beeves was in active operation on our arrival, a branding chute had been built to facilitate the work, and all five of us took to the saddle in assisting ranchmen in holding under herd, as we permitted nothing to be corralled night or day. The first herd was completed on the 14th, and the second a day later, both moving out without an hour's delay, the only instructions being to touch at Great Bend, Kansas, for final orders. The cattle more than came up to expectations, three fourths of them being six and seven years old, and as heavy as oxen. There was something about the days of the open range that left its impression on animals, as these two herds were as uniform in build as deer, and I question if the same country to-day has as heavy beeves.

Three days were lost in reaching Coryell County, where our outfits were in waiting and twenty others were at work gathering cattle. The herds were made up and started without a hitch, and we passed on to Hood County, meeting every date promptly and again finding the trail outfits awaiting us. Leaving my active partner and George Edwards to receive the two herds, I rode through to the Clear Fork in a single day. A double outfit had been at work for the past two weeks gathering outside cattle and had over a thousand under herd on my arrival. Everything had worked out so nicely in receiving the purchased herds that I finally concluded to send out my steers, and we began gathering on the home range. By making small round-ups, we disturbed the young calves as little as possible. I took charge of the extra outfit and my ranch foreman of his own, one beginning on the west end of my range, the other going north and coming down the Brazos. At the end of a week the two crews came together with nearly eight thousand cattle under herd. The next day we cut out thirty-five hundred cows and started them on the trail, turning free the remnant of she stuff, and began shaping up the steers, using only the oldest in making up thirty-two hundred head. There were fully two thousand threes, the remainder being nearly equally divided between twos and fours. No road branding was necessary; the only delay in moving out was in provisioning a wagon and securing a foreman. Failing in two or three quarters, I at last decided on a young fellow on my ranch, and he was placed in charge of the last herd. Great Bend was his destination, I instructed him where to turn off the Chisholm trail, — north of the Salt Fork in the Cherokee Outlet, — and he started like an army with banners.

I rejoined my active partner at Fort Worth. The Hood County cattle had started a week before, so taking George Edwards with us, we took train for Kansas. Major Hunter returned to his home, while Edwards and I lost no time in reaching the Medicine River. A fortnight was spent in riding our northern range, when we took horses and struck out for Pond Creek in the Outlet. The lead herds were due at this point early in May, and on our arrival a number had already passed. A road house and stage stand had previously been established, the proprietor of which kept a register of passing herds for the convenience of owners. None of ours were due, yet we looked over the "arrivals" with interest, and continued on down the trail to Red Fork. The latter was a branch of the Arkansas River, and at low water was inclined to be brackish, and hence was sometimes called the Salt Fork, with nothing to differentiate it from one of the same name sixty miles farther north. There was an old Indian trading post at Red Fork, and I lay over there while Edwards went on south to meet the cows. His work for the summer was to oversee the deliveries at the Indian agencies, Major Hunter was to look after the market at The Bend, and I was to attend to the contracts at army posts on the upper Missouri. Our first steer herd to arrive was from Hood County, and after seeing them safely on the Great Bend trail at Pond Creek, I waited for the other steer cattle from Coryell to arrive. Both herds came in within a day of each other, and I loitered along with them, finally overtaking the lead one when within fifty miles of The Bend. In fair weather it was a delightful existence to loaf along with the cattle; but once all three herds reached their destination, two outfits held them, and I took the Hood County lads and dropped back on the Medicine. Our ranch hands had everything shaped up nicely, and by working a double outfit and making round-ups at noon, when the cattle were on water, we quietly cut out three thousand head of our biggest beeves without materially disturbing our holdings on that range. These northern wintered cattle were intended for delivery at Fort Abraham Lincoln on the Missouri River in what is now North Dakota. The through heavy beeves from Uvalde County were intended for Fort Randall and intermediate posts, some of them for reissue to various Indian agencies. The reservations of half a dozen tribes were tributary to the forts along the upper Missouri, and the government was very liberal in supplying its wards with fresh beef.

The Medicine River beeves were to be grazed up the country to Fort Lincoln. We passed old Fort Larned within a week, and I left the outfit there and returned to The Bend. The outfit in charge of the wintered cattle had orders to touch at and cross the Missouri River at Fort Randall, where I would meet them again near the middle of July. The market had fairly opened at Great

Bend, and I was kept busy assisting Major Hunter until the arrival of the Uvalde beef herds. Both came through in splendid condition, were admired by every buyer in the market, and passed on north under orders to graze ten miles a day until reaching their destination. By this time the whereabouts of all the Indian herds were known, yet not a word had reached me from the foreman of my individual cattle after crossing into the Nations. It was now the middle of June, and there were several points en route from which he might have mailed a letter, as did all the other foremen. Herds, which crossed at Red River Station a week after my steers, came into The Bend and reported having spoken no "44" cattle en route. I became uneasy and sent a courier as far south as the state line, who returned with a comfortless message. Finally a foreman in the employ of Jess Evens came to me and reported having taken dinner with a "44" outfit on the South Canadian; that the herd swam the river that afternoon, after which he never hailed them again. They were my own dear cattle, and I was worrying; I was overdue at Fort Randall, and in duty bound to look after the interests of the firm. Major Hunter came to the rescue, in his usual calm manner, and expressed his confidence that all would come out right in the end; that when the mystery was unraveled the foreman would be found blameless.

I took a night train for the north, connected with a boat on the Missouri River, and by finally taking stage reached Fort Randall. The mental worry of those four days would age an ordinary man, but on my arrival at the post a message from my active partner informed me that my cattle had reached Dodge City two weeks before my leaving. Then the scales fell from my eyes, as I could understand that when inquiries were made for the Salt Fork, some wayfarer had given that name to the Red Fork; and the new Dodge trail turned to the left, from the Chisholm, at Little Turkey, the first creek crossed after leaving the river. The message was supplemented a few days later by a letter, stating that Dodge City would possibly be a better market than the Bend, and that my interests would be looked after as well as if I were present. A load was lifted from my shoulders, and when the wintered cattle passed Randall, the whole post turned out to see the beef herd on its way up to Lincoln. The government line of forts along the Missouri River had the whitest lot of officers that it was ever my good fortune to meet. I was from Texas, my tongue and colloquialisms of speech proclaimed me Southern-born, and when I admitted having served in the Confederate army, interest and attention was only heightened, while every possible kindness was simply showered on me.

The first delivery occurred at Fort Lincoln. It was a very simple affair. We cut out half a dozen average beeves, killed, dressed, and weighed them, and an honest average on the herd was thus secured. The contract called for one and a half million pounds on foot; our tender overran twelve per cent; but this surplus was accepted and paid for. The second delivery was at Fort Pierre and the last at Randall, both of which passed pleasantly, the many acquaintances among army men that summer being one of my happiest memories. Leaving Randall, we put in to the nearest railroad point returning, where thirty men were sent home, after which we swept down the country and arrived at Great Bend during the last week in September. My active partner had handled his assignment of the summer's work in a masterly manner, having wholesaled my herd at Dodge City at as good figures as our other cattle brought in retail quantities at The Bend. The former point had received three hundred and fifty thousand Texas cattle that summer, while every one conceded that Great Bend's business as a trail terminal would close with that season. The latter had handled nearly a quarter-million cattle that year, but like Abilene, Wichita, and other trail towns in eastern Kansas, it was doomed to succumb to the advance guard of pioneer settlers.

The best sale of the year fell to my active partner. Before the shipping season opened, he sold, range count, our holdings on the Medicine River, including saddle stock, improvements, and good will. The cattle might possibly have netted us more by marketing them, but it was only a question of time until the flow of immigration would demand our range, and Major Hunter had sold our squatter's rights while they had a value. A new foreman had been installed on our giving up possession, and our old one had been skirmishing the surrounding country the past month for a new range, making a favorable report on the Eagle Chief in the Outlet. By paying a trifling rental to the Cherokee Nation, permission could be secured to hold cattle on these lands, set aside as a hunting ground. George Edwards had been rotting all summer in issuing cows at Indian agencies, but on the first of October the residue of his herds would be put in pastures or turned free for the winter. Major Hunter had wound up his affairs at The Bend, and nothing remained but a general settlement of the summer's work. This took place at Council Grove, our silent partner and Edwards both being present. The profits of the year staggered us all. I was anxious to go home, the different outfits having all gone by rail or overland with the remudas, with the exception of the two from Uvalde, which were property of the firm. I had bought three hundred extra horses at The Bend, sending them home with the others, and now nothing remained but to stock the new range in the Cherokee Outlet. Edwards and my active partner volunteered for this work, it being understood that the Uvalde remudas would be retained for ranch use, and that not over ten thousand cattle were to be put on the new range for the winter. Our silent partner was rapidly awakening to the importance of his usefulness in securing future contracts with the War and Indian departments, and vaguely outlining the future, we separated to three points of the compass.

CHAPTER XIV
ESTABLISHING A NEW RANCH

I hardly knew Fort Worth on my return. The town was in the midst of a boom. The foundations of many store buildings were laid on Monday morning, and by Saturday night they were occupied and doing a land-office business. Lots that could have been bought in the spring for one hundred dollars were now commanding a thousand, while land scrip was quoted as scarce at twenty-five cents an acre. I hurried home, spoke to my wife, and engaged two surveyors to report one week later at my ranch on the Clear Fork. Big as was the State and boundless as was her public domain, I could not afford to allow this advancing prosperity to catch me asleep again, and I firmly concluded to empty that little tin trunk of its musty land scrip. True enough, the present boom was not noticeable on the frontier, yet there was a buoyant feeling in the air that betokened a brilliant future. Something enthused me, and as my creed was land and cattle, I made up my mind to plunge into both to my full capacity.

The last outfit to return from the summer's drive was detained on the Clear Fork to assist in the fall branding. Another one of fifteen men all told was chosen from the relieved lads in making up a surveying party, and taking fifty saddle horses and a well-stocked commissary with us, we started due west. I knew the country for some distance beyond Fort Griffin, and from late maps in possession of the surveyors, we knew that by holding our course, we were due to strike a fork of the mother Brazos before reaching the Staked Plain. Holding our course contrary to the needle, we crossed the Double Mountain Fork, and after a week out from the ranch the brakes which form the border between the lowlands and the Llano Estacado were sighted. Within view of the foothills which form the approach of the famous plain, the Salt and Double Mountain forks of the Brazos are not over twelve miles apart. We traveled up the divide between these two rivers, and when within thirty miles of the low-browed borderland a halt was called and we went into camp. From the view before us one could almost imagine the feelings of the discoverer of this continent when he first sighted land; for I remember the thrill which possessed our little party as we looked off into either valley or forward to the menacing Staked Plain in our front. There was something primal in the scene, — something that brought back the words, "In the beginning God created the heavens and the earth." Men who knew neither creed nor profession of faith felt themselves drawn very near to some great creative power. The surrounding view held us spellbound by its beauty and strength. It was like a rush of fern-scents, the breath of pine forests, the music of the stars, the first lovelight in a mother's eye; and now its pristine beauty was to be marred, as covetous eyes and a lust of possession moved an earth-born man to lay hands on all things created for his use.

Camp was established on the Double Mountain Fork. Many miles to the north, a spur of the Plain extended eastward, in the elbow of which it was my intention to locate the new ranch. A corner was established, a meridian line was run north beyond the Salt Fork and a random one west to the foothills. After a few days one surveyor ran the principal lines while the other did the cross-sectioning and correcting back, both working from the same camp, the wagon following up the work. Antelope were seen by the thousands, frequently buffaloes were sighted, and scarcely a day passed but our rifles added to the larder of our commissary supplies. Within a month we located four hundred sections, covering either side of the Double Mountain Fork, and embracing a country ten miles wide by forty long. Coming back to our original meridian line across to the Salt Fork, the work of surveying that valley was begun, when I was compelled to turn homeward. A list of contracts to be let by the War and Interior departments would be ready by December 1, and my partners relied on my making all the estimates. There was a noticeable advance of fully one dollar a head on steer cattle since the spring before, and I was supposed to have my finger on the pulse of supply and prices, as all government awards were let far in advance of delivery. George Edwards had returned a few days before and reported having stocked the new ranch in the Outlet with twelve thousand steers. The list of contracts to be let had arrived, and the two of us went over them carefully. The government was asking for bids on the delivery of over two hundred thousand cattle at various posts and agencies in the West, and confining ourselves to well-known territory, we submitted bids on fifteen awards, calling for forty-five thousand cattle in their fulfillment.

Our estimates were sent to Major Hunter for his approval, who in turn forwarded them to our silent partner at Washington, to be submitted to the proper departments. As the awards would not be made until the middle of January, nothing definite could be done until then, so, accompanied by George Edwards, I returned to the surveying party on the Salt Fork of the Brazos. We found them busy at their work, the only interruption having been an Indian scare, which only lasted a few days. The men still carried rifles against surprise, kept a scout on the lookout while at work, and maintained a guard over the camp and remuda at night. During my absence they had located a strip of country ten by thirty miles, covering the valley of the Salt Fork, and we still lacked three hundred sections of using up the scrip. The river, along which they were surveying, made an abrupt turn to the north, and offsetting by sections around the bend, we continued on up the valley for twenty miles or until the brakes of the Plain made the land no longer desirable. Returning to our commencement point with still one hundred certificates left, we extended the survey five miles down both rivers, using up the last acre of scrip. The new ranch was irregular in form, but it controlled the waters of fully one million acres of fine grazing land and was clothed with a carpet of nutritive grasses. This was the range of the buffalo, and the instinct of that animal could be relied on in choosing a range for its successor, the Texas cow.

The surveying over, nothing remained but the recording of the locations at the county seat to which for legal purposes this unorganized country was attached. All of us accompanied the outfit returning, and a gala week we spent, as no less than half a dozen buffalo robes were secured before reaching Fort Griffin. Deer and turkey were plentiful, and it was with difficulty that I restrained the boys from killing wantonly, as they were young fellows whose very blood yearned for the chase or any diverting excitement. We reached the ranch on the Clear Fork during the second week in January, and those of the outfit who had no regular homes were made welcome guests until work opened in the spring. My calf crop that fall had exceeded all expectations, nearly nine thousand having been branded, while the cattle were wintering in splendid condition. There was little or nothing to do, a few hunts with the hounds merely killing time until we got reports from Washington. In spite of all competition we secured eight contracts, five with the army and the remainder with the Indian Bureau.

Then the work opened in earnest. My active partner was due the first of February, and during the interim George Edwards and I rode a circle of five counties in search of brands of cattle for sale. In the course of our rounds a large number of whole stocks were offered us, but at firmer prices, yet we closed no trades, though many brands were bargains. It was my intention to stock the new ranch on the Double Mountain Fork the coming summer, and if arrangements could be agreed on with Major Hunter, I might be able to repeat my success of the summer of '74. Emigration to Texas was crowding the ranches to the frontier, many of them unwillingly, and it appealed to me strongly that the time was opportune for securing an ample holding of stock cattle. The appearance of my active partner was the beginning of active operations, and after we had outlined the programme for the summer and gone through all the details thoroughly, I asked for the privilege of supplying the cows on the Indian contracts. Never did partners stand more willingly by each other than did the firm of Hunter, Anthony & Co., and I only had to explain the opportunity of buying brands at wholesale, sending the young steers up the trail and the aging, dry, and barren cows to Indian agencies, to gain the hearty approval of the little Yankee major. He was entitled to a great deal of credit for my holdings in land, for from his first sight of Texas, day after day, line upon line, precept upon precept, he had urged upon me the importance of securing title to realty, while its equivalent in scrip was being hawked about, begging a buyer. Now we rejoiced together in the fulfillment of his prophecy, as I can lay little claim to any foresight, but am particularly anxious to give credit where credit is due.

With an asylum for any and all remnants of stock cattle, we authorized George Edwards to close trades on a number of brands. Taking with us the two foremen who had brought beef herds out of Uvalde County the spring before, the major and I started south on the lookout for beeves. The headwaters of the Nueces and its tributaries were again our destination, and the usual welcome to buyers was extended with that hospitality that only the days of the open range knew and practiced. We closed contracts with former customers without looking at their cattle. When a ranchman gave us his word to deliver us as good or better beeves than the spring before, there was no occasion to question his ability, and the cattle never deceived. There might arise petty wrangles over trifles, but the general hungering for a market among cowmen had not yet been satiated, and they offered us their best that we might come again. We placed our contracts along three rivers and over as many counties, limiting the number to ten thousand beeves of the same ages and paying one dollar a head above the previous spring. One of our foremen was provided with a letter of credit, and the two were left behind to make up three new and complete outfits for the trail.

This completed the purchase of beef cattle. Two of our contracts called for northern wintered beeves, which would be filled out of our holdings in the Cherokee Outlet. We again stopped in central Texas, but prices were too firm, and we passed on west to San Saba and Lampasas counties, where we effected trades on nine thousand five hundred three-year-old steers. My own outfits would drop down from the Clear Fork to receive these cattle, and after we had perfected our banking arrangements the major returned to San Antonio and I started homeward. George Edwards had in the mean time bargained for ten brands, running anywhere from one to five thousand head, paying straight through five to seven dollars, half cash and the balance in eight months, everything to be delivered on the Clear Fork. We intentionally made these deliveries late — during the last week in March and the first one in April — in order that Major Hunter might approve of the three herds of cows for Indian delivery. Once I had been put in possession of all necessary details, Edwards started south to join Major Hunter, as the receiving of the Nueces River beeves was set for from the 10th to the 15th of March.

I could see a busy time ahead. There was wood to haul for the branding, three complete outfits to start for the central part of the State, new wagons to equip for the trail, and others to care for the calf crop while en route to the Double Mountain Fork. There were oxen to buy in equipping teams to accompany the stock cattle to the new ranch, two yoke being allowed to each wagon, as it was strength and not speed that was desired. My old foremen rallied at a word and relieved me of the lesser details of provisioning the commissaries and engaging the help. Trusty men were sent to oversee and look out for my interests in gathering the different brands, the ranges of many of them being fifty to one hundred miles distant. The different brands were coming from six separate counties along the border, and on their arrival at my ranch we must be ready to receive, brand, and separate the herds into their respective classes, sending two grades to market and the remnant to their new home at the foot of the Staked Plain. The condition of the mules must be taken into consideration before the army can move, and in cattle life the same reliance is placed on the fitness for duty of the saddle horses. I had enough picked ones to make up a dozen remudas if necessary, and rested easy on that score. The date for receiving arrived and found us all ready and waiting.

The first herd was announced to arrive on the 25th of March. I met it ten miles from the ranch. My man assured me that the brand as gathered was intact and that it would run fifty per cent dry cows and steers over two years old. A number of mature beeves even were noticeable and younger steers were numerous, while the miscellany of the herd ran to every class and condition of the bovine race. Two other brands were expected the next day, and that evening the first one to arrive was counted and accepted. The next morning the entire herd was run through a branding chute and classified, all steers above a yearling and dry and aging cows going into one contingent and the mixed cattle into another. In order to save horseflesh, this work was easily done in the corrals. By hanging a gate at the exit of the branding chute, a man sat overhead and by swinging it a variation of two feet, as the cattle trailed through the trough in single file, the herd was cut into two classes. Those intended for the trail were put under herd, while the stock cattle were branded into the "44" and held separate. The second and third herds were treated in a similar manner, when we found ourselves with over eleven thousand cattle on hand, with two other brands due in a few days. But the evening of the fourth day saw a herd of thirty-three hundred steers on its way to Kansas, while a second one, numbering two hundred more than the first, was lopped off from the mixed stuff and started west for the Double Mountain Fork.

The situation was eased. A conveyance had been sent to the railroad to meet my partner, and before he and Edwards arrived two other brands had been received. A herd of thirty-five hundred dry cows was approved and started at once for the Indian Territory, while a second one moved out for the west, cleaning up the holdings of mixed stuff. The congestion was again relieved, and as the next few brands were expected to run light in steers, everything except cows was held under herd until all had been received. The final contingent came in from Wise County and were shaped up, and the last herd of cows, completing ten thousand five hundred, started for the Washita agency. I still had nearly sixty-five hundred steers on hand, and cutting back all of a small overplus of thin light cows, I had three brands of steers cut into one herd and four into another, both moving out for Dodge City. This left me with fully eight thousand miscellany on hand, with nothing but my ranch outfit to hold them, close-herding by day and bedding down and guarding them by night. Settlements were made with the different sellers, my outstanding obligations amounting to over one hundred thousand dollars, which the three steer herds were expected to liquidate. My active partner and George Edwards took train for the north. The only change in the programme was that Major Hunter was to look after our deliveries at army posts, while I was to meet our herds on their arrival in Dodge City. The cows were sold to the firm, and including my individual cattle, we had twelve herds on the trail, or a total of thirty-nine thousand five hundred head.

On the return of the first outfit from the west, some three weeks after leaving, the herd of stock cattle was cut in two and started. But a single man was left on the Clear Fork, my ranch foreman taking one herd, while I accompanied the other. It requires the patience of a saint to handle cows and calves, two wagons to the herd being frequently taxed to their capacity in picking up the youngsters. It was a constant sight to see some of the boys carrying a new-born calf across the saddle seat, followed by the mother, until camp or the wagon was reached. I was ashamed of my own lack of patience on that trip, while irritable men could while away the long hours, nursing along the drag end of a herd of cows and their toddling offspring. We averaged only about ten miles a day, the herds were large and unwieldy, and after twelve days out both were scattered along the Salt Fork and given their freedom. Leaving one outfit to locate the cattle on the new range, the other two hastened back to the Clear Fork and gathered two herds, numbering thirty-five hundred each, of young cows and heifers from the ranch stock. But a single day was lost in rounding-up, when they were started west, half a day apart, and I again took charge of an outfit, the trip being an easy one and made in ten days, as the calves were large enough to follow and there were no drag cattle among them. On our arrival at the new ranch, the cows and heifers were scattered among the former herds, and both outfits started back, one to look after the Clear Fork and the other to bring through the last herd in stocking my new possessions. This gave me fully twenty-five thousand mixed cattle on my new range, relieving the old ranch of a portion of its she stuff and shaping up both stocks to better advantage.

It was my intention to make my home on the Clear Fork thereafter, and the ranch outfit had orders to build a comfortable house during the summer. The frontier was rapidly moving westward, the Indian was no longer a dread, as it was only a question of time until the Comanche and his ally would imitate their red brethren and accept the dole of the superior race. I was due in Dodge City the first of June, the ranches would take care of themselves, and touching at the Edwards ranch for a day, I reached "Dodge" before any of the herds arrived. Here was a typical trail town, a winter resort for buffalo hunters, no settlement for fifty miles to the east, and an almost boundless range on which to hold through Texas cattle. The business was bound to concentrate at this place, as all other markets were abandoned within the State, while it was easily accessible to the mountain regions on the west. It was the logical meeting point for buyers and drovers; and while the town of that day has passed into history as "wicked Dodge," it had many redeeming features. The veneer of civilization may have fallen, to a certain extent, from the wayfaring man who tarried in this cow town, yet his word was a bond, and he reverenced the pure in womanhood, though to insult him invited death.

George Edwards and Major Hunter had become such great chums that I was actually jealous of being supplanted in the affections of the Yankee major. The two had been inseparable for months, visiting at The Grove, spending a fortnight together at the beef ranch in the Outlet, and finally putting in an appearance at Dodge. Headquarters for the summer were established at the latter point, our bookkeeper arrived, and we were ready for business. The market opened earlier than at more eastern points. The bulk of the sales were made to ranchmen, who used whole herds where the agricultural regions only bought cattle by the hundreds. It was more satisfactory than the retail trade; credit was out of the question, and there was no haggling over prices. Cattle companies were forming and stocking new ranges, and an influx of English and Scotch capital was seeking investment in ranches and live stock in the West, — a mere forerunner of what was to follow in later years.

Our herds began arriving, and as soon as an outfit could be freed it was started for the beef ranch under George Edwards, where a herd of wintered beeves was already made up to start for the upper Missouri River. Major Hunter followed a week later with the second relieved outfit, and our cattle were all moving for their destinations. The through beef herds from the upper Nueces River had orders to touch at old Fort Larned to the eastward, Edwards drifted on to the Indian agencies, and I bestirred myself to the task of selling six herds of young cattle at Dodge. Once more I was back in my old element, except that every feature of the latter market was on an enlarged scale. Two herds were sold to one man in Colorado, three others went under contract to the Republican River in Nebraska, and the last one was cut into blocks and found a market with feeders in Kansas. Long before deliveries were concluded to the War or Interior departments, headquarters were moved back to The Grove, my work being done. In the interim of waiting for the close of the year's business, our bookkeeper looked after two shipments of a thousand head each from the beef ranch, while I visited my brother in Missouri and surprised him by buying a carload of thoroughbred bulls. Arrangements were made for shipping them to Fort Worth during the last week in November, and promising to call for them, I returned to The Grove to meet my partners and adjust all accounts for the year.

CHAPTER XV
HARVEST HOME

The firm's profits for the summer of '77 footed up over two hundred thousand dollars. The government herds from the Cherokee Outlet paid the best, those sent to market next, while the through cattle remunerated us in the order of beeves, young steers, and lastly cows. There was a satisfactory profit even in the latter, yet the same investment in other classes paid a better per cent profit, and the banking instincts of my partners could be relied on to seek the best market for our capital. There was nothing haphazard about our business; separate accounts were kept on every herd, and at the end of the season the percentage profit on each told their own story. For instance, in the above year it cost us more to deliver a cow at an agency in the Indian Territory than a steer at Dodge City, Kansas. The herds sold in Colorado had been driven at an expense of eighty-five cents a head, those delivered on the Republican River ninety, and every cow driven that year cost us over one dollar a head in general expense. The necessity of holding the latter for a period of four months near agencies for issuing purposes added to the cost, and was charged to that particular department of our business.

George Edwards and my active partner agreed to restock our beef ranch in the Outlet, and I returned to Missouri. I make no claim of being the first cowman to improve the native cattle of Texas, yet forty years' keen observation has confirmed my original idea, — that improvement must come through the native and gradually. Climatic conditions in Texas are such that the best types of the bovine race would deteriorate if compelled to subsist the year round on the open range. The strongest point in the original Spanish cattle was their inborn ability as foragers, being inured for centuries to drouth, the heat of summer, and the northers of winter, subsisting for months on prickly pear, a species of the cactus family, or drifting like game animals to more favored localities in avoiding the natural afflictions that beset an arid country. In producing the ideal range animal it was more important to retain those rustling qualities than to gain a better color, a few pounds in weight, and a shortening of horns and legs, unless their possessor could withstand the rigors of a variable climate. Nature befriends the animal race. The buffalo of Montana could face the blizzard, while his brother on the plains of Texas sought shelter from the northers in cañons and behind sand-dunes, guided by an instinct that foretold the coming storm.

I accompanied my car of thoroughbred bulls and unloaded them at the first station north of Fort Worth. They numbered twenty-five, all two-year-olds past, and were representative of three leading beef brands of established reputation. Others had tried the experiment before me, the main trouble being in acclimation, which affects animals the same as the human family. But by wintering them at their destination, I had hopes of inuring the importation so that they would withstand the coming summer, the heat of which was a sore trial to a northern-bred animal. Accordingly I made arrangements with a farmer to feed my car of bulls during the winter, hay and grain both being plentiful. They had cost me over five thousand dollars, and rather than risk the loss of a single one by chancing them on the range, an additional outlay of a few hundred dollars was justified. Limiting the corn fed to three barrels to the animal a month, with plenty of rough feed, ought to bring them through the winter in good, healthy form. The farmer promised to report monthly on their condition, and agreeing to send for them by the first of April, I hastened on home.

My wife had taken a hand in the building of the new house on the Clear Fork. It was quite a pretentious affair, built of hewed logs, and consisted of two large rooms with a hallway between, a gallery on three sides, and a kitchen at the rear. Each of the main rooms had an ample fireplace, both hearths and chimneys built from rock, the only material foreign to the ranch being the lumber in the floors, doors, and windows. Nearly all the work was done by the ranch hands, even the clapboards were riven from oak that grew along the mother Brazos, and my wife showed me over the house as though it had been a castle that she had inherited from some feudal forbear. I was easily satisfied; the main concern was for the family, as I hardly lived at home enough to give any serious thought to the roof that sheltered me. The original buildings had been improved and enlarged for the men, and an air of prosperity pervaded the Anthony ranch consistent with the times and the success of its owner.

The two ranches reported a few over fifteen thousand calves branded that fall. A dim wagon road had been established between the ranches, by going and returning outfits during the stocking of the new ranch the spring before, and the distance could now be covered in two days by buckboard. The list of government contracts to be let was awaiting my attention, and after my estimates had been prepared, and forwarded to my active partner, it was nearly the middle of December before I found time to visit the new ranch. The hands at Double Mountain had not been idle, snug headquarters were established, and three line camps on the outskirts of the range were comfortably equipped to shelter men and horses. The cattle had located nicely, two large corrals had been built on each river, and the calves were as thrifty as weeds. Gray wolves were the worst enemy encountered, running in large bands and finding shelter in the cedar brakes in the cañons and foothills which border on the Staked Plain. My foreman on the Double Mountain ranch was using poison judiciously, all the line camps were supplied with the same, and an active winter of poisoning wolves was already inaugurated before my arrival. Long-range rifles would supplement the work, and a few years of relentless war on these pests would rid the ranch of this enemy of live stock.

Together my foreman and I planned for starting an improved herd of cattle. A cañon on the west was decided on as a range, as it was well watered from living springs, having a valley several miles wide, forming a park with ample range for two thousand cattle. The bluffs on either side were abrupt, almost an in closure, making it an easy matter for two men to loose-herd a small amount of stock, holding them adjoining my deeded range, yet separate. The survival of the fittest was adopted as the rule in beginning the herd, five hundred choice cows were to form the nucleus, to be the pick of the new ranch, thrift and formation to decide their selection. Solid colors only were to be chosen, every natural point in a cow was to be considered, with the view of reproducing the race in improved form. My foreman — an intelligent young fellow — was in complete sympathy, and promised me that he would comb the range in selecting the herd. The first appearance of grass in the spring was agreed on as the time for gathering the cows, when he would personally come to the Clear Fork and receive the importation of bulls, thus fully taking all responsibility in establishing the improved herd. By this method, unless our plans miscarried, in the course of a few years we expected to be raising quarter-bloods in the main ranch stock, and at the same time retaining all those essential qualities that distinguish the range-raised from the domestic-bred animal.

On my return to the Clear Fork, which was now my home, a letter from my active partner was waiting, informing me that he and Edwards would reach Texas about the time the list of awards would arrive. They had been unsuccessful in fully stocking our beef ranch, securing only three thousand head, as prices were against them, and the letter intimated that something must be done to provide against a repetition of this unforeseen situation. The ranch in the Outlet had paid us a higher per cent on the investment than any of our ventures, and to neglect fully stocking it was contrary to the creed of Hunter, Anthony & Co. True, we were double-wintering some four thousand head of cattle on our Cherokee range, but if a fair allowance of awards was allotted the firm, requiring northern wintered cattle in filling, it might embarrass us to supply the same when we did not have the beeves in hand; it was our business to have the beef.

At the appointed time the buckboard was sent to Fort Worth, and a few days later Major Hunter and our main segundo drove up to the Clear Fork. Omitting all preludes, atmosphere, and sunsets, we got down to business at once. If we could drive cattle to Dodge City and market them for eighty-five cents, we ought to be able to deliver them on our northern range for six bits, and the horses could be returned or sold at a profit. If any of our established trade must be sacrificed, why, drop what paid the least; but half stock our beef ranch? Never again! This was to be the slogan for the coming summer, and, on receiving the report from Washington, we were enabled to outline a programme for the year. The gradually advancing prices in cattle were alarming me, as it was now perceptible in cows, and in submitting our bids on Indian awards I had made the allowance of one dollar a head advance over the spring before. In spite of this we were allotted five contracts from the Interior Department and seven to the Army, three of the latter requiring ten thousand northern wintered beeves, — only oversold three thousand head. Major Hunter met my criticisms by taking the ground that we virtually had none of the cattle on hand, and if we could buy Southern stock to meet our requirements, why not the three thousand that we lacked in the North. Our bids had passed through his hands last; he knew our northern range was not fully stocked, and had forwarded the estimates to our silent partner at Washington, and now the firm had been assigned awards in excess of their holdings. But he was the kind of a partner I liked, and if he could see his way clear, he could depend on my backing him to the extent of my ability and credit.

The business of the firm had grown so rapidly that it was deemed advisable to divide it into three departments, — the Army, the Indian, the beef ranch and general market. Major Hunter was specially qualified to handle the first division, the second fell to Edwards, and the last was assumed by myself. We were to consult each other when convenient, but each was to act separately for the firm, my commission requiring fifteen thousand cattle for our ranch in the Outlet, and three herds for the market at Dodge City. Our banking points were limited to Fort Worth and San Antonio, so agreeing to meet at the latter point on the 1st of February for a general consultation, we separated with a view to feeling the home market. Our man Edwards dropped out in the central part of the State, my active partner wished to look into the situation on the lower Nueces River, and I returned to the headwaters of that stream. During the past two summers we had driven five herds of heavy beeves from Uvalde and adjoining counties, and while we liked the cattle of that section, it was considered advisable to look elsewhere for our beef supply. Within a week I let contracts for five herds of two and three year old steers, then dropped back to the Colorado River and bought ten thousand more in San Saba and McCulloch counties. This completed the purchases in my department, and I hastened back to San Antonio for the expected consultation. Neither my active partner nor my trusted man had arrived, nor was there a line to indicate where they were or when they might be expected, though Major Hunter had called at our hotel a few days previously for his mail. The designated day was waning, and I was worried by the non-appearance of either, when I received a wire from Austin, saying they had just sublet the Indian contracts.

The next morning my active partner and Edwards arrived. The latter had met some parties at the capital who were anxious to fill our Indian deliveries, and had wired us in the firm's name, and Major Hunter had taken the first train for Austin. Both returned wreathed in smiles, having sublet our awards at figures that netted us more than we could have realized had we bought and delivered the cattle at our own risk. It was clear money, requiring not a stroke of work, while it freed a valuable man in outfitting, receiving, and starting our other herds, as well as relieving a snug sum for reinvestment. Our capital lay idle half the year, the spring months were our harvest, and, assigning Edwards full charge of the cattle bought on the Colorado River, we instructed him to buy for the Dodge market four herds more in adjoining counties, bringing down the necessary outfits to handle them from my ranch on the Clear Fork. Previous to his return to San Antonio my active partner had closed contracts on thirteen thousand heavy beeves on the Frio River and lower Nueces, thus completing our purchases. A healthy advance was noticeable all around in steer cattle, though hardly affecting cows; but having anticipated a growing appreciation in submitting our bids, we suffered no disappointment. A week was lost in awaiting the arrival of half a dozen old foremen. On their arrival we divided them between us and intrusted them with the buying of horses and all details in making up outfits.

The trails leading out of southern Texas were purely local ones, the only established trace running from San Antonio north, touching at Fort Griffin, and crossing into the Nations at Red River Station in Montague County. All our previous herds from the Uvalde regions had turned eastward to intercept this main thoroughfare, though we had been frequently advised to try a western outlet known as the Nueces Cañon route. The latter course would bring us out on high tablelands, but before risking our herds through it, I decided to ride out the country in advance. The cañon proper was about forty miles long, through which ran the source of the Nueces River, and if the way were barely possible it looked like a feasible route. Taking a pack horse and guide with me, I rode through and out on the mesa beyond. General McKinzie had used this route during his Indian campaigns, and had even built mounds of rock on the hills to guide the wayfarer, from the exit of the cañon across to the South Llano River. The trail was a rough one, but there was grass sufficient to sustain the herds and ample bed-grounds in the valleys, and I decided to try the western outlet from Uvalde. An early, seasonable spring favored us with fine grass on which to put up and start the herds, all five moving out within a week of each other. I promised my foremen to accompany them through the cañon, knowing that the passage would be a trial to man and beast, and asked the old bosses to loiter along, so that there would be but a few hours' difference between the rear and lead herds.

I received sixteen thousand cattle, and the four days required in passing through Nueces Cañon and reaching water beyond were the supreme physical test of my life. It was a wild section, wholly unsettled, between low mountains, the river-bed constantly shifting from one flank of the valley to the other, while cliffs from three to five hundred feet high alternated from side to side. In traveling the first twenty-five miles we crossed the bed of the river twenty-one times; and besides the river there were a great number of creeks and dry arroyos putting in from the surrounding hills, so that we were constantly crossing rough ground. The beds of the streams were covered with smooth, water-worn pebbles, white as marble, and then again we encountered limestone in lava formation, honeycombed with millions of sharp, up-turned cells. Some of the descents were nearly impossible for wagons, but we locked both hind wheels and just let them slide down and bounce over the boulders at the bottom. Half-way through the cañon the water failed us, with the south fork of the Llano forty miles distant in our front. We were compelled to allow the cattle to pick their way over the rocky trail, the herds not over a mile apart, and scarcely maintaining a snail's pace. I rode from rear to front and back again a dozen times in clearing the defile, and noted that splotches of blood from tender-footed cattle marked the white pebbles at every crossing of the river-bed. On the evening of the third day, the rear herd passed the exit of the cañon, the others having turned aside to camp for the night. Two whole days had now elapsed without water for the cattle.

I had not slept a wink the two previous nights. The south fork of the Llano lay over twenty miles distant, and although it had ample water two weeks before, one of the foremen and I rode through to it that night to satisfy ourselves. The supply was found sufficient, and before daybreak we were back in camp, arousing the outfits and starting the herds. In the spring of 1878 the old military trail, with its rocky sentinels, was still dimly defined from Nueces Cañon north to the McKinzie water-hole on the South Llano. The herds moved out with the dawn. Thousands of the cattle were travel-sore, while a few hundred were actually tender-footed. The evening before, as we came out into the open country, we had seen quite a local shower of rain in our front, which had apparently crossed our course nearly ten miles distant, though it had not been noticeable during our night's ride. The herds fell in behind one another that morning like columns of cavalry, and after a few miles their stiffness passed and they led out as if they had knowledge of the water ahead. Within two hours after starting we crossed a swell of the mesa, when the lead herd caught a breeze from off the damp hills to the left where the shower had fallen the evening before. As they struck this rise, the feverish cattle raised their heads and pulled out as if that vagrant breeze had brought them a message that succor and rest lay just beyond. The point men had orders to let them go, and as fast as the rear herds came up and struck this imaginary line or air current, a single moan would surge back through the herd until it died out at the rear. By noon there was a solid column of cattle ten miles long, and two hours later the drag and point men had trouble in keeping the different herds from mixing. Without a halt, by three o'clock the lead foremen were turning their charges right and left, and shortly afterward the lead cattle were plunging into the purling waters of the South Llano.

The rear herds turned off above and below, filling the river for five miles, while the hollow-eyed animals gorged themselves until a half dozen died that evening and night.

Leaving orders with the foremen to rest their herds well and move out half a day apart, I rode night and day returning to Uvalde. Catching the first stage out, I reached San Antonio in time to overtake Major Hunter, who was awaiting the arrival of the last beef herd from the lower country, the three lead ones having already passed that point. All trail outfits from the south then touched at San Antonio to provision the wagons, and on the approach of our last herd I met it and spent half a day with it, — my first, last, and only glimpse of our heavy beeves. They were big rangy fellows many of them six and seven years old, and from the general uniformity of the herd, I felt proud of the cowman that my protégé and active partner had developed into. Major Hunter was anxious to reach home as soon as possible, in order to buy in our complement of northern wintered cattle; so, settling our business affairs in southern Texas, the day after the rear beeves passed we took train north. I stopped in the central part of the State, joining Edwards riding night and day in covering his appointments to receive cattle; and when the last trail herd moved out from the Colorado River there were no regrets.

Hastening on home, on my arrival I was assured by my ranch foreman that he could gather a trail herd in less than a week. My saddle stock now numbered over a thousand head, one hundred of which were on the Double Mountain ranch, seven remudas on the trail, leaving available over two hundred on the Clear Fork. I had the horses and cattle, and on the word being given my ranch foreman began gathering our oldest steers, while I outfitted and provisioned a commissary and secured half a dozen men. On the morning of the seventh day after my arrival, an individual herd, numbering thirty-five hundred, moved out from the Clear Fork, every animal in the straight ranch brand. An old trail foreman was given charge, Dodge City was the destination, and a finer herd of three-year-olds could not have been found in one brand within the boundaries of the State. This completed our cattle on the trail, and a breathing spell of a few weeks might now be indulged in, yet there was little rest for a cowman. Not counting the contracts to the Indian Bureau, sublet to others, and the northern wintered beeves, we had, for the firm and individually, seventeen herds, numbering fifty-four thousand five hundred cattle on the trail. In order to carry on our growing business unhampered for want of funds, the firm had borrowed on short time nearly a quarter-million dollars that spring, pledging the credit of the three partners for its repayment. We had been making money ever since the partnership was formed, and we had husbanded our profits, yet our business seemed to outgrow our means, compelling us to borrow every spring when buying trail herds.

In the mean time and while we were gathering the home cattle, my foreman and two men from the Double Mountain ranch arrived on the Clear Fork to receive the importation of bulls. The latter had not yet arrived, so pressing the boys into work, we got the trail herd away before the thoroughbreds put in an appearance. A wagon and three men from the home ranch had gone after them before my return, and they were simply loafing along, grazing five to ten miles a day, carrying corn in the wagon to feed on the grass. Their arrival found the ranch at leisure, and after resting a few days they proceeded on to their destination at a leisurely gait. The importation had wintered finely, — now all three-year-olds, — but hereafter they must subsist on the range, as corn was out of the question, and the boys had brought nothing but a pack horse from the western ranch. This was an experiment with me, but I was ably seconded by my foreman, who had personally selected every cow over a month before, and this was to make up the beginning of the improved herd. I accompanied them beyond my range and urged seven miles a day as the limit of travel. I then started for home, and within a week reached Dodge City, Kansas.

Headquarters were again established at Dodge. Fortunately a new market was being developed at Ogalalla on the Platte River in Nebraska, and fully one third the trail herds passed on to the upper point. Before my arrival Major Hunter had bought the deficiency of northern wintered beeves, and early in June three herds started from our range in the Outlet for the upper Missouri River army posts. We had wintered all horses belonging to the firm on the beef ranch, and within a fortnight after its desertion, the young steers from the upper Nueces River began arriving and were turned loose on the Eagle Chief, preempting our old range. One outfit was retained to locate the cattle, the remaining ones coming in to Dodge and returning home by train. George Edwards lent me valuable assistance in handling our affairs economically, but with the arrival of the herds at Dodge he was compelled to look after our sub-contracts at Indian agencies. The latter were delivered in our name, all money passed through our hands in settlement, so it was necessary to have a man on the ground to protect our interests. With nothing but the selling of eight herds of cattle in an active market like Dodge, I felt that the work of the summer was virtually over. One cattle company took ten thousand three-year-old steers, two herds were sold for delivery at Ogalalla, and the remaining three were placed within a month after their arrival. The occupation of the West was on with a feverish haste, and money was pouring into ranches and cattle, affording a ready market to the drover from Texas.

Nothing now remained for me but to draw the threads of our business together and await the season's settlement in the fall. I sold all the wagons and sent the remudas to our range in the Outlet, while from the first cattle sold the borrowed money was repaid. I visited Ogalalla to acquaint myself with its market, looked over our beef ranch in the Cherokee Strip during the lull, and even paid the different Indian agencies my respects to perfect my knowledge of the requirements of our business. Our firm was a strong one, enlarging its business year by year; and while we could not foresee the future, the present was a Harvest Home to Hunter, Anthony & Co.

CHAPTER XVI
AN ACTIVE SUMMER

The summer of 1878 closed with but a single cloud on the horizon. Like ourselves, a great many cattlemen had established beef ranches in the Cherokee Outlet, then a vacant country, paying a trifling rental to that tribe of civilized Indians. But a difference of opinion arose, some contending that the Cherokees held no title to the land; that the strip of country sixty miles wide by two hundred long set aside by treaty as a hunting ground, when no longer used for that purpose by the tribe, had reverted to the government. Some refused to pay the rent money, the council of the Cherokee Nation appealed to the general government, and troops were ordered in to preserve the peace. We felt no uneasiness over our holdings of cattle on the Strip, as we were paying a nominal rent, amounting to two bits a head a year, and were otherwise fortified in possession of our range. If necessary we could have secured a permit from the War Department, on the grounds of being government contractors and requiring a northern range on which to hold our cattle. But rather than do this, Major Hunter hit upon a happy solution of the difficulty by suggesting that we employ an Indian citizen as foreman, and hold the cattle in his name. The major had an old acquaintance, a half-breed Cherokee named LaFlors, who was promptly installed as owner of the range, but holding beeves for Hunter, Anthony & Co., government beef contractors.

I was unexpectedly called to Texas before the general settlement that fall. Early in the summer, at Dodge, I met a gentleman who was representing a distillery in Illinois. He was in the market for a thousand range bulls to slop-feed, and as no such cattle ever came over the trail, I offered to sell them to him delivered at Fort Worth. I showed him the sights around Dodge and we became quite friendly, but I was unable to sell him his requirements unless I could show the stock. It was easily to be seen that he was not a range cattleman, and I humored him until he took my address, saying that if he were unable to fill his wants in other Western markets he would write me later. The acquaintance resulted in several letters passing between us that autumn, and finally an appointment was made to meet in Kansas City and go down to Texas together. I had written home to have the buckboard meet us at Fort Worth on October 1, and a few days later we were riding the range on the Brazos and Clear Fork. In the past there never had been any market for this class of drones, old age and death being the only relief, and from the great number of brands that I had purchased during my ranching and trail operations, my range was simply cluttered with these old cumberers. Their hides would not have paid freighting and transportation to a market, and they had become an actual drawback to a ranch, when the opportunity occurred and I sold twelve hundred head to the Illinois distillery. The buyer informed me that they fattened well; that there was a special demand for this quality in the export trade of dressed beef, and that owing to their cheapness and consequent profit they were in demand for distillery feeding.

Fifteen dollars a head was agreed on as the price, and we earned it a second time in delivering that herd at Fort Worth. Many of the animals were ten years old, surly when irritated, and ready for a fight when their day-dreams were disturbed. There was no treating them humanely, for every effort in that direction was resented by the old rascals, individually and collectively. The first day we gathered two hundred, and the attempt to hold them under herd was a constant fight, resulting in every hoof arising on the bed-ground at midnight and escaping to their old haunts. I worked as good a ranch outfit of men as the State ever bred, I was right there in the saddle with them, yet, in spite of every effort, to say nothing of the profanity wasted, we lost the herd. The next morning every lad armed himself with a prod-pole long as a lance and tipped with a sharp steel brad, and we commenced regathering. Thereafter we corralled them at night, which always called for a free use of ropes, as a number usually broke away on approaching the pens. Often we hog-tied as many as a dozen, letting them lie outside all night and freeing them back into the herd in the morning. Even the day-herding was a constant fight, as scarcely an hour passed but some old resident would scorn the restraint imposed upon his liberties and deliberately make a break for freedom. A pair of horsemen would double on the deserter, and with a prod-pole to his ear and the pressure of a man and horse bearing their weight on the same, a circle would be covered and Toro always reëntered the day-herd. One such lesson was usually sufficient, and by reaching corrals every night and penning them, we managed, after two weeks' hard work, to land them in the stockyards at Fort Worth. The buyer remained with and accompanied us during the gathering and en route to the railroad, evidently enjoying the continuous performance. He proved a good mixer, too, and returned annually thereafter. For years following I contracted with him, and finally shipped on consignment, our business relations always pleasant and increasing in volume until his death.

Returning with the outfit, I continued on west to the new ranch, while the men began the fall branding at home. On arriving on the Double Mountain range, I found the outfit in the saddle, ironing up a big calf crop, while the improved herd was the joy and pride of my foreman. An altitude of about four thousand feet above sea-level had proved congenial to the thoroughbreds, who had acclimated nicely, the only loss being one from lightning. Two men were easily holding the isolated herd in their cañon home, the sheltering bluffs affording them ample protection from wintry weather, and there was nothing henceforth to fear in regard to the experiment. I spent a week with the outfit; my ranch foreman assured me that the brand could turn out a trail herd of three-year-old steers the following spring and a second one of twos, if it was my wish to send them to market. But it was too soon to anticipate the coming summer; and then it seemed a shame to move young steers to a northern climate to be matured, yet it was an economic necessity. Ranch headquarters looked like a trapper's cave with wolf-skins and buffalo-robes taken the winter before, and it was with reluctance that I took my leave of the cosy dugouts on the Double Mountain Fork.

On returning home I found a statement for the year and a pressing invitation awaiting me to come on to the national capital at once. The profits of the summer had exceeded the previous one, but some bills for demurrage remained to be adjusted with the War and Interior departments, and my active partner and George Edwards had already started for Washington. It was urged on me that the firm should make themselves known at the different departments, and the invitation was supplemented by a special request from our silent partner, the Senator, to spend at least a month at the capital. For years I had been promising my wife to take her on a visit to Virginia, and now when the opportunity offered, womanlike, she pleaded her nakedness in the midst of plenty. I never had but one suit at a time in my life, and often I had seen my wife dressed in the best the frontier of Texas afforded, which was all that ought to be expected. A day's notice was given her, the eldest children were sent to their grandparents, and taking the two youngest with us, we started for Fort Worth. I was anxious that my wife should make a favorable impression on my people, and in turn she was fretting about my general appearance. Out of a saddle a cowman never looks well, and every effort to improve his personal appearance only makes him the more ridiculous. Thus with each trying to make the other presentable, we started. We stopped a week at my brother's in Missouri, and finally reached the Shenandoah Valley during the last week in November. Leaving my wife to speak for herself and the remainder of the family, I hurried on to Washington and found the others quartered at a prominent hotel. A less pretentious one would have suited me, but then a United States senator must befittingly entertain his friends. New men had succeeded to the War and Interior departments, and I was properly introduced to each as the Texas partner of the firm of Hunter, Anthony & Co. Within a week, several little dinners were given at the hotel, at which from a dozen to twenty men sat down, all feverish to hear about the West and the cattle business in particular. Already several companies had been organized to engage in ranching, and the capital had been over-subscribed in every instance; and actually one would have supposed from the chat that we were holding a cattle convention in the West instead of dining with a few representatives and government officials at Washington.

I soon became the object of marked attention. Possibly it was my vocabulary, which was consistent with my vocation, together with my ungainly appearance, that differentiated me from my partners. George Edwards was neat in appearance, had a great fund of Western stories and experiences, and the two of us were constantly being importuned for incidents of a frontier nature. Both my partners, especially the Senator, were constantly introducing me and referring to me as a man who, in the course of ten years, had accumulated fifty thousand cattle and acquired title to three quarters of a million acres of land. I was willing to be a sociable fellow among my friends, but notoriety of this character was offensive, and in a private lecture I took my partners to task for unnecessary laudation. The matter was smoothed over, our estimates for the coming year were submitted, and after spending the holidays with my parents in Virginia, I returned to the capital to await the allotments for future delivery of cattle to the Army and Indian service. Pending the date of the opening of the bids a dinner was given by a senator from one of the Southern States, to which all members of our firm were invited, when the project was launched of organizing a cattle company with one million dollars capital. The many advantages that would accrue where government influence could be counted on were dwelt upon at length, the rapid occupation of the West was cited, the concentration of all Indian tribes on reservations, and the necessary requirements of beef in feeding the same was openly commented on as the opportunity of the hour. I took no hand in the general discussion, except to answer questions, but when the management of such a company was tendered me, I emphatically declined. My partners professed surprise at my refusal, but when the privacy of our rooms was reached I unburdened myself on the proposition. We had begun at the foot of the hill, and now having established ourselves in a profitable business, I was loath to give it up or share it with others. I argued that our trade was as valuable as realty or cattle in hand; that no blandishments of salary as manager could induce me to forsake legitimate channels for possibilities in other fields. "Go slow and learn to peddle," was the motto of successful merchants; I had got out on a limb before and met with failure, and had no desire to rush in where angels fear for their footing. Let others organize companies and we would sell them the necessary cattle; the more money seeking investment the better the market.

Major Hunter was Western in his sympathies and coincided with my views, the Senator was won over from the enterprise, and the project failed to materialize. The friendly relations of our firm were slightly strained over the outcome, but on the announcement of the awards we pulled together again like brothers. In the allotment for delivery during the summer and fall of 1879, some eighteen contracts fell to us, — six in the Indian Bureau and the remainder to the Army, four of the latter requiring northern wintered beeves. A single award for Fort Buford in Dakota called for five million pounds on foot and could be filled with Southern cattle. Others in the same department ran from one and a half to three million pounds, varying, as wanted for future or present use, to through or wintered beeves. The latter fattened even on the trail and were ready for the shambles on their arrival, while Southern stock required a winter and time to acclimate to reach the pink of condition. The government maintained several distributing points in the new Northwest, one of which was Fort Buford, where for many succeeding years ten thousand cattle were annually received and assigned to lesser posts. This was the market that I knew. I had felt every throb of its pulse ever since I had worked as a common hand in driving beef to Fort Sumner in 1866. The intervening years had been active ones, and I had learned the lessons of the trail, knew to a fraction the cost of delivering a herd, and could figure on a contract with any other cowman.

Leaving the arrangement of the bonds to our silent partner, the next day after the awards were announced we turned our faces to the Southwest. February 1 was agreed on for the meeting at Fort Worth, so picking up the wife and babies in Virginia, we embarked for our Texas home. My better half was disappointed in my not joining in the proposed cattle company, with its officers, its directorate, annual meeting, and other high-sounding functions. I could have turned into the company my two ranches at fifty cents an acre, could have sold my brand outright at a fancy figure, taking stock in lieu for the same, but I preferred to keep them private property. I have since known other cowmen who put their lands and cattle into companies, and after a few years' manipulation all they owned was some handsome certificates, possibly having drawn a dividend or two and held an honorary office. I did not then have even the experience of others to guide my feet, but some silent monitor warned me to stick to my trade, cows.

Leaving the family at the Edwards ranch, I returned to Fort Worth in ample time for the appointed meeting. My active partner and our segundo had become as thick as thieves, the two being inseparable at idle times, and on their arrival we got down to business at once. The remudas were the first consideration. Besides my personal holdings of saddle stock, we had sent the fall before one thousand horses belonging to the firm back to the Clear Fork to winter. Thus equipped with eighteen remudas for the trail, we were fairly independent in that line. Among the five herds driven the year before to our beef ranch in the Outlet, the books showed not over ten thousand coming four years old that spring, leaving a deficiency of northern wintered beeves to be purchased. It was decided to restock the range with straight threes, and we again divided the buying into departments, each taking the same division as the year before. The purchase of eight herds of heavy beeves would thus fall to Major Hunter. Austin and San Antonio were decided on as headquarters and banking points, and we started out on a preliminary skirmish. George Edwards had an idea that the Indian awards could again be relet to advantage, and started for the capital, while the major and I journeyed on south. Some former sellers whom we accidentally met in San Antonio complained that we had forsaken them and assured us that their county, Medina, had not less than fifty thousand mature beeves. They offered to meet any one's prices, and Major Hunter urged that I see a sample of the cattle while en route to the Uvalde country. If they came up to requirements, I was further authorized to buy in sufficient to fill our contract at Fort Buford, which would require three herds, or ten thousand head. It was an advantage to have this delivery start from the same section, hold together en route, and arrive at their destination as a unit. I was surprised at both the quality and the quantity of the beeves along the tributaries of the Frio River, and readily let a contract to a few leading cowmen for the full allotment. My active partner was notified, and I went on to the headwaters of the Nueces River. I knew the cattle of this section so well that there was no occasion even to look at them, and in a few days contracted for five herds of straight threes. While in the latter section, word reached me that Edwards had sublet four of our Indian contacts, or those intended for delivery at agencies in the Indian Territory. The remaining two were for tribes in Colorado, and notifying our segundo to hold the others open until we met, I took stage back to San Antonio. My return was awaited by both Major Hunter and Edwards, and casting up our purchases on through cattle, we found we lacked only two herds of cows and the same of beeves. I offered to make up the Indian awards from my ranches, the major had unlimited offerings from which to pick, and we turned our attention to securing young steers for the open market. Our segundo was fully relieved and ordered back to his old stamping-ground on the Colorado River to contract for six herds of young cattle. It was my intention to bring remudas down from the Clear Fork to handle the cattle from Uvalde and Medina counties, but my active partner would have to look out for his own saddle stock for the other beef herds. Hurrying home, I started eight hundred saddle horses belonging to the firm to the lower country, assigned two remudas to leave for the Double Mountain ranch, detailed the same number for the Clear Fork, and authorized the remaining six to report to Edwards on the Colorado River.

This completed the main details for moving the herds. There was an increase in prices over the preceding spring throughout the State, amounting on a general average to fully one dollar a head. We had anticipated the advance in making our contracts, there was an abundance of water everywhere, and everything promised well for an auspicious start. Only a single incident occurred to mar the otherwise pleasant relations with our ranchmen friends. In contracting for the straight threes from Uvalde County, I had stipulated that every animal tendered must be full-aged at the date of receiving; we were paying an extra price and the cattle must come up to specifications. Major Hunter had moved his herds out in time to join me in receiving the last one of the younger cattle, and I had pressed him into use as a tally clerk while receiving. Every one had been invited to turn in stock in making up the herd, but at the last moment we fell short of threes, when I offered to fill out with twos at the customary difference in price. The sellers were satisfied. We called them by ages as they were cut out, when a row threatened over a white steer. The foreman who was assisting me cut the animal in question for a two-year-old, Major Hunter repeated the age in tallying the steer, when the owner of the brand, a small ranchman, galloped up and contended that the steer was a three-year-old, though he lacked fully two months of that age. The owner swore the steer had been raised a milk calf; that he knew his age to a day; but Major Hunter firmly yet kindly told the man that he must observe the letter of the contract and that the steer must go as a two-year-old or not at all. In reply a six-shooter was thrown in the major's face, when a number of us rushed in on our horses and the pistol was struck from the man's hand. An explanation was demanded, but the only intelligent reply that could be elicited from the owner of the white steer was, "No G — — d — — Yankee can classify my cattle." One of the ranchmen with whom we were contracting took the insult off my hands and gave the man his choice, — to fight or apologize. The seller cooled down, apologies followed, and the unfortunate incident passed and was forgotten with the day's work.

A week later the herds on the Colorado River moved out. Major Hunter and I looked them over before they got away, after which he continued on north to buy in the deficiency of three thousand wintered beeves, while I returned home to start my individual cattle. The ranch outfit had been at work for ten days previous to my arrival gathering the three-year-old steers and all dry and barren cows. On my return they had about eight thousand head of mixed stock under herd and two trail outfits were in readiness, so cutting them separate and culling them down, we started them, the cows for Dodge and the steers for Ogalalla, each thirty-five hundred strong. Two outfits had left for the Double Mountain range ten days before, and driving night and day, I reached the ranch to find both herds shaped up and ready for orders. Both foremen were anxious to strike due north, several herds having crossed Red River as far west as Doan's Store the year before; but I was afraid of Indian troubles and routed them northeast for the old ford on the Chisholm trail. They would follow down the Brazos, cross over to the Wichita River, and pass about sixty miles to the north of the home ranch on the Clear Fork. I joined them for the first few days out, destinations were the same as the other private herds, and promising to meet them in Dodge, I turned homeward. The starting of these last two gave the firm and me personally twenty-three herds, numbering seventy-six thousand one hundred cattle on the trail.

An active summer followed. Each one was busy in his department. I met Major Hunter once for an hour during the spring months, and we never saw each other again until late fall. Our segundo again rendered valuable assistance in meeting outfits on their arrival at the beef ranch, as it was deemed advisable to hold the through and wintered cattle separate for fear of Texas fever. All beef herds were routed to touch at headquarters in the Outlet, and thence going north, they skirted the borders of settlement in crossing Kansas and Nebraska. Where possible, all correspondence was conducted by wire, and with the arrival of the herds at Dodge I was kept in the saddle thenceforth. The demand for cattle was growing with each succeeding year, prices were firmer, and a general advance was maintained in all grades of trail stock. On the arrival of the cattle from the Colorado River, I had them reclassed, sending three herds of threes on to Ogalalla. The upper country wanted older stock, believing that it withstood the rigors of winter better, and I trimmed my sail to catch the wind. The cows came in early and were started west for their destination, the rear herds arrived and were located, while Dodge and Ogalalla howled their advantages as rival trail towns. The three herds of two-year-olds were sold and started for the Cherokee Strip, and I took train for the west and reached the Platte River, to find our cattle safely arrived at Ogalalla. Near the middle of July a Wyoming cattle company bought all the central Texas steers for delivery a month later at Cheyenne, and we grazed them up the South Platte and counted them out to the buyers, ten thousand strong. My individual herds classed as Pan-Handle cattle, exempt from quarantine, netted one dollar a head above the others, and were sold to speculators from the corn regions on the western borders of Nebraska. One herd of cows was intended for the Southern and the other for the Uncompahgre Utes, and they had been picking their way through and across the mountains to those agencies during the summer mouths. Late in August both deliveries were made wholesale to the agents of the different tribes, and my work was at an end. All unsold remudas returned to Dodge, the outfits were sent home, and the saddle stock to our beef ranch, there to await the close of the summer's drive.

CHAPTER XVII
FORESHADOWS

I returned to Texas early in September. My foreman on the Double Mountain ranch had written me several times during the summer, promising me a surprise on the half-blood calves. There was nothing of importance in the North except the shipping of a few trainloads of beeves from our ranch in the Outlet, and as the bookkeeper could attend to that, I decided to go back. I offered other excuses for going, but home-hunger and the improved herd were the main reasons. It was a fortunate thing that I went home, for it enabled me to get into touch with the popular feeling in my adopted State over the outlook for live stock in the future. Up to this time there had been no general movement in cattle, in sympathy with other branches of industry, notably in sheep and wool, supply always far exceeding demand. There had been a gradual appreciation in marketable steers, first noticeable in 1876, and gaining thereafter about one dollar a year per head on all grades, yet so slowly as not to disturb or excite the trade. During the fall of 1879, however, there was a feeling of unrest in cattle circles in Texas, and predictions of a notable advance could be heard on every side. The trail had been established as far north as Montana, capital by the millions was seeking investment in ranching, and everything augured for a brighter future. That very summer the trail had absorbed six hundred and fifty thousand cattle, or possibly ten per cent of the home supply, which readily found a market at army posts, Indian agencies, and two little cow towns in the North. Investment in Texas steers was paying fifty to one hundred per cent annually, the whole Northwest was turning into one immense pasture, and the feeling was general that the time had come for the Lone Star State to expect a fair share in the profits of this immense industry.

Cattle associations, organized for mutual protection and the promotion of community interests, were active agencies in enlarging the Texas market. National conventions were held annually, at which every live-stock organization in the West was represented, and buyer and seller met on common ground. Two years before the Cattle Raisers' Association of Texas was formed, other States and Territories founded similar organizations, and when these met in national assembly the cattle on a thousand hills were represented. No one was more anxious than myself that a proper appreciation should follow the enlargement of our home market, yet I had hopes that it would come gradually and not excite or disturb settled conditions. In our contracts with the government, we were under the necessity of anticipating the market ten months in advance, and any sudden or unseen change in prices in the interim between submitting our estimates and buying in the cattle to fill the same would be ruinous. Therefore it was important to keep a finger on the pulse of the home market, to note the drift of straws, and to listen for every rumor afloat. Lands in Texas were advancing in value, a general wave of prosperity had followed self-government and the building of railroads, and cattle alone was the only commodity that had not proportionally risen in value.

In spite of my hopes to the contrary, I had a well-grounded belief that a revolution in cattle prices was coming. Daily meeting with men from the Northwest, at Dodge and Ogalalla, during the summer just passed, I had felt every throb of the demand that pulsated those markets. There was a general inquiry for young steers, she stuff with which to start ranches was eagerly snapped up, and it stood to reason that if this reckless Northern demand continued, its influence would soon be felt on the plains of Texas. Susceptible to all these influences, I had returned home to find both my ranches littered with a big calf crop, the brand actually increasing in numbers in spite of the drain of trail herds annually cut out. But the idol of my eye was those half-blood calves. Out of a possible five hundred, there were four hundred and fifty odd by actual count, all big as yearlings and reflecting the selection of their parents. I loafed away a week at the cañon camp, rode through them daily, and laughed at their innocent antics as they horned the bluffs or fought their mimic fights. The Double Mountain ranch was my pride, and before leaving, the foreman and I outlined some landed additions to fill and square up my holdings, in case it should ever be necessary to fence the range.

On my return to the Clear Fork, the ranch outfit had just finished gathering from my own and adjoining ranges fifteen hundred bulls for distillery feeding. The sale had been effected by correspondence with my former customer, and when the herd started the two of us drove on ahead into Fort Worth. The Illinois man was an extensive dealer in cattle and had followed the business for years in his own State, and in the week we spent together awaiting the arrival of his purchase, I learned much of value. There was a distinct difference between a range cowman and a stockman from the older Western States; but while the occupations were different, there was much in common between the two. Through my customer I learned that Western range cattle, when well fatted, were competing with grass beeves from his own State; that they dressed more to their gross weight than natives, and that the quality of their flesh was unsurpassed. As to the future, the Illinois buyer could see little to hope for in his own country, but was enthusiastic over the outlook for us ranchmen in the Southwest. All these things were but straws which foretold the course of the wind, yet neither of us looked for the cyclone which was hovering near.

I accompanied the last train of the shipment as far as Parsons, Kansas, where our ways parted, my customer going to Peoria, Illinois, while I continued on to The Grove. Both my partners and our segundo were awaiting me, the bookkeeper had all accounts in hand, and the profits of the year were enough to turn ordinary men's heads. But I sounded a note of warning, — that there were breakers ahead, — though none of them took me seriously until I called for the individual herd accounts. With all the friendly advantages shown us by the War and Interior departments, the six herds from the Colorado River, taking their chances in the open market, had cleared more money per head than had the heavy beeves requiring thirty-three per cent a larger investment. In summing up my warning, I suggested that now, while we were winners, would be a good time to drop contracting with the government and confine ourselves strictly to the open market. Instead of ten months between assuming obligations and their fulfillment, why not reduce the chances to three or four, with the hungry, clamoring West for our market?

The powwow lasted several days. Finally all agreed to sever our dealings with the Interior Department, which required cows for Indian agencies, and confine our business to the open market and supplying the Army with beef. Our partner the Senator reluctantly yielded to the opinions of Major Hunter and myself, urging our loss of prestige and its reflection on his standing at the national capital. But we countered on him, arguing that as a representative of the West the opportunity of the hour was his to insist on larger estimates for the coming year, and to secure proportionate appropriations for both the War and Interior departments, if they wished to attract responsible bidders. If only the ordinary estimates and allowances were made, it would result in a deficiency in these departments, and no one cared for vouchers, even against the government, when the funds were not available to meet the same on presentation. Major Hunter suggested to our partner that as beef contractors we be called in consultation with the head of each department, and allowed to offer our views for the general benefit of the service. The Senator saw his opportunity, promising to hasten on to Washington at once, while the rest of us agreed to hold ourselves in readiness to respond to any call.

Edwards and I returned to Texas. The former was stationed for the winter at San Antonio, under instructions to keep in touch with the market, while I loitered between Fort Worth and the home ranch. The arrival of the list of awards came promptly as usual, but beyond a random glance was neglected pending state developments. An advance of two dollars and a half a head was predicted on all grades, and buyers and superintendents of cattle companies in the North and West were quietly dropping down into Texas for the winter, inquiring for and offering to contract cattle for spring delivery at Dodge and Ogalalla. I was quietly resting on my oars at the ranch, when a special messenger arrived summoning me to Washington. The motive was easily understood, and on my reaching Fort Worth the message was supplemented by another one from Major Hunter, asking me to touch at Council Grove en route. Writing Edwards fully what would be expected of him during my absence, I reached The Grove and was joined by my partner, and we proceeded on to the national capital. Arriving fully two weeks in advance of the closing day for bids, all three of us called and paid our respects to the heads of the War and

Interior departments. On special request of the Secretaries, an appointment was made for the following day, when the Senator took Major Hunter and me under his wing and coached us in support of his suggestions to either department. There was no occasion to warn me, as I had just come from the seat of beef supply, and knew the feverish condition of affairs at home.

The appointments were kept promptly. At the Interior Department we tarried but a few minutes after informing the Secretary that we were submitting no bids that year in his division, but allowed ourselves to be drawn out as to the why and wherefore. Major Hunter was a man of moderate schooling, apt in conversation, and did nearly all the talking, though I put in a few general observations. We were cordially greeted at the War Office, good cigars were lighted, and we went over the situation fully. The reports of the year before were gone over, and we were complimented on our different deliveries to the Army. We accepted all flatteries as a matter of course, though the past is poor security for the future. When the matter of contracting for the present year was broached, we confessed our ability to handle any awards in our territory to the number of fifty to seventy-five thousand beeves, but would like some assurance that the present or forthcoming appropriations would be ample to meet all contracts. Our doubts were readily removed by the firmness of the Secretary when as we arose to leave, Major Hunter suggested, by way of friendly advice, that the government ought to look well to the bonds of contractors, saying that the beef-producing regions of the West and South had experienced an advance in prices recently, which made contracting cattle for future delivery extremely hazardous. At parting regret was expressed that the sudden change in affairs would prevent our submitting estimates only so far as we had the cattle in hand.

Three days before the limit expired, we submitted twenty bids to the War Department. Our figures were such that we felt fully protected, as we had twenty thousand cattle on our Northern range, while advice was reaching us daily from the beef regions of Texas. The opening of proposals was no surprise, only seven falling to us, and all admitting of Southern beeves. Within an hour after the result was known, a wire was sent to Edwards, authorizing him to contract immediately for twenty-two thousand heavy steer cattle and advance money liberally on every agreement. Duplicates of our estimates had been sent him the same day they were submitted at the War Office. Our segundo had triple the number of cattle in sight, and was then in a position to act intelligently. The next morning Major Hunter and I left the capital for San Antonio, taking a southern route through Virginia, sighting old battlefields where both had seen service on opposing sides, but now standing shoulder to shoulder as trail drovers and army contractors. We arrived at our destination promptly. Edwards was missing, but inquiry among our bankers developed the fact that he had been drawing heavily the past few days, and we knew that all was well. A few nights later he came in, having secured our requirements at an advance of two to three dollars a head over the prices of the preceding spring.

The live-stock interests of the State were centring in the coming cattle convention, which would be held at Fort Worth in February. At this meeting heavy trading was anticipated for present and future delivery, and any sales effected would establish prices for the coming spring. From the number of Northern buyers that were in Texas, and others expected at the convention, Edwards suggested buying, before the meeting, at least half the requirements for our beef ranch and trail cattle. Major Hunter and I both fell in with the idea of our segundo, and we scattered to our old haunts under agreement to report at Fort Worth for the meeting of the clans. I spent two weeks among my ranchmen friends on the headwaters of the Frio and Nueces rivers, and while they were fully awake to the advance in prices, I closed trades on twenty-one thousand two and three year old steers for March delivery. It was always a weakness in me to overbuy, and in receiving I could never hold a herd down to the agreed numbers, but my shortcomings in this instance proved a boon. On arriving at Fort Worth, the other two reported having combed their old stamping-grounds of half a dozen counties along the Colorado River, and having secured only fifteen thousand head. Every one was waiting until after the cattle convention, and only those who had the stock in hand could be induced to talk business or enter into agreements.

The convention was a notable affair. Men from Montana and intervening States and Territories rubbed elbows and clinked their glasses with the Texans to "Here's to a better acquaintance." The trail drovers were there to a man, the very atmosphere was tainted with cigar smoke, the only sounds were cattle talk, and the nights were wild and sleepless. "I'll sell ten thousand Pan-Handle three-year-old steers for delivery at Ogalalla," spoken in the lobby of a hotel or barroom, would instantly attract the attention of half a dozen men in fur overcoats and heavy flannel. "What are your cattle worth laid down on the Platte?" was the usual rejoinder, followed by a drink, a cigar, and a conference, sometimes ending in a deal or terminating in a friendly acquaintance. I had met many of these men at Abilene, Wichita, and Great Bend, and later at Dodge City and Ogalalla, and now they had invaded Texas, and the son of a prophet could not foretell the future. Our firm never offered a hoof, but the three days of the convention were forewarnings of the next few years to follow. I was personally interested in the general tendency of the men from the upper country to contract for heifers and young cows, and while the prices offered for Northern delivery were a distinct advance over those of the summer before, I resisted all temptations to enter into agreements. The Northern buyers and trail drovers selfishly joined issues in bearing prices in Texas; yet, in spite of their united efforts, over two hundred thousand cattle were sold during the meeting, and at figures averaging fully three dollars a head over those of the previous spring.

The convention adjourned, and those in attendance scattered to their homes and business. Between midnight and morning of the last day of the meeting, Major Hunter and I closed contracts for two trail herds of sixty-five hundred head in Erath and Comanche counties. Within a week two others of straight three-year-olds were secured, — one in my home county and the other fifty miles northwest in Throckmorton. This completed our purchases for the present, giving us a chain of cattle to receive from within one county of the Rio Grande on the south to the same distance from Red River on the north. The work was divided into divisions. One thousand extra saddle horses were needed for the beef herds and others, and men were sent south, to secure them. All private and company remudas had returned to the Clear Fork to winter, and from there would be issued wherever we had cattle to receive. A carload of wagons was bought at the Fort, teams were sent in after them, and a busy fortnight followed in organizing the forces. Edwards was assigned to assist Major Hunter in receiving the beef cattle along the lower Frio and Nueces, starting in ample time to receive the saddle stock in advance of the beeves. There was three weeks' difference in the starting of grass between northern and southern Texas, and we made our dates for receiving accordingly, mine for Medina and Uvalde counties following on the heels of the beef herds from the lower country.

From the 12th of March I was kept in the saddle ten days, receiving cattle from the headwaters of the Frio and Nueces rivers. All my old foremen rendered valuable assistance, two and three herds being in the course of formation at a time, and, as usual, we received eleven hundred over and above the contracts. The herds moved out on good grass and plenty of water, the last of the heavy beeves had passed north on my return to San Antonio, and I caught the first train out to join the others in central Texas. My buckboard had been brought down with the remudas and was awaiting me at the station, the Colorado River on the west was reached that night, and by noon the next day I was in the thick of the receiving. When three herds had started, I reported in Comanche and Erath counties, where gathering for our herds was in progress; and fixing definite dates that would allow Edwards and my partner to arrive, I drove on through to the Clear Fork. Under previous instructions, a herd of thirty-five hundred two-year-old heifers was ready to start, while nearly four thousand steers were in hand, with one outfit yet to come in from up the Brazos. We were gathering close that year, everything three years old or over must go, and the outfits were ranging far and wide. The steer herd was held down to thirty-two hundred, both it and the heifers moving out the same day, with a remnant of over a thousand three-year-old steers left over.

The herd under contract to the firm in the home county came up full in number, and was the next to get away. A courier arrived from the Double Mountain range and reported a second contingent of heifers ready, but that the steers would overrun for a wieldy herd. The next morning the overplus from the Clear Fork was started for the new ranch, with orders to make up a third steer herd and cross Red River at Doan's. This cleaned the boards on my ranches, and the next day I was in Throckmorton County, where everything was in readiness to pass upon. This last herd was of Clear Fork cattle, put up within twenty-five miles of Fort Griffin, every brand as familiar as my own, and there was little to do but count and receive. Road-branding was necessary, however; and while this work was in progress, a relay messenger arrived from the ranch, summoning me to Fort Worth posthaste. The message was from Major Hunter, and from the hurried scribbling I made out that several herds were tied up when ready to start, and that they would be thrown on the market. I hurried home, changed teams, and by night and day driving reached Fort Worth and awakened my active partner and Edwards out of their beds to get the particulars. The responsible man of a firm of drovers, with five herds on hand, had suddenly died, and the banks refused to advance the necessary funds to complete their payments. The cattle were under herd in Wise and Cook counties, both Major Hunter and our segundo had looked them over, and both pronounced the herds gilt-edged north Texas steers. It would require three hundred thousand dollars to buy and clear the herds, and all our accounts were already overdrawn, but it was decided to strain our credit. The situation was fully explained in a lengthy message to a bank in Kansas City, the wires were kept busy all day answering questions; but before the close of business we had authority to draw for the amount needed, and the herds, with remudas and outfits complete, passed into our hands and were started the next day. This gave the firm and me personally thirty-three herds, requiring four hundred and ninety-odd men and over thirty-five hundred horses, while the cattle numbered one hundred and four thousand head.

Two thirds of the herds were routed by way of Doan's Crossing in leaving Texas, while all would touch at Dodge in passing up the country. George Edwards accompanied the north Texas herds, and Major Hunter hastened on to Kansas City to protect our credit, while I hung around Doan's Store until our last cattle crossed Red River. The annual exodus from Texas to the North was on with a fury, and on my arrival at Dodge all precedents in former prices were swept aside in the eager rush to secure cattle. Herds were sold weeks before their arrival, others were met as far south as Camp Supply, and it was easily to be seen that it was a seller's market. Two thirds of the trail herds merely took on new supplies at Dodge and passed on to the Platte. Once our heavy beeves had crossed the Arkansas, my partner and I swung round to Ogalalla and met our advance herd, the foreman of which reported meeting buyers as far south as the Republican River. It was actually dangerous to price cattle for fear of being under the market; new classifications were being introduced, Pan-Handle and north Texas steers commanding as much as three dollars a head over their brethren from the coast and far south.

The boom in cattle of the early '80's was on with a vengeance. There was no trouble to sell herds that year. One morning, while I was looking for a range on the north fork of the Platte, Major Hunter sold my seven thousand heifers at twenty-five dollars around, commanding two dollars and a half a head over steers of the same age. Edwards had been left in charge at Dodge, and my active partner reluctantly tore himself away from the market at Ogalalla to attend our deliveries of beef at army posts. Within six weeks after arriving at Dodge and Ogalalla the last of our herds had changed owners, requiring another month to complete the transfers at different destinations. Many of the steers went as far north as the Yellowstone River, and Wyoming and Nebraska were liberal buyers at the upper market, while Colorado, Kansas, and the Indian Territory absorbed all offerings at the lower point. Horses were even in demand, and while we made no effort to sell our remudas, over half of them changed owners with the herds they had accompanied into the North.

The season closed with a flourish. After we had wound up our affairs, Edwards and I drifted down to the beef ranch with the unsold saddle stock, and the shipping season opened. The Santa Fé Railway had built south to Caldwell that spring, affording us a nearer shipping point, and we moved out five to ten trainloads a week of single and double wintered beeves. The through cattle for restocking the range had arrived early and were held separate until the first frost, when everything would be turned loose on the Eagle Chief. Trouble was still brewing between the Cherokee Nation and the government on the one side and those holding cattle in the Strip, and a clash occurred that fall between a lieutenant of cavalry and our half-breed foreman LaFlors. The troops had been burning hay and destroying improvements belonging to cattle outfits, and had paid our range a visit and mixed things with our foreman. The latter stood firm on his rights as a Cherokee citizen and cited his employers as government beef contractors, but the young lieutenant haughtily ignored all statements and ordered the hay, stabling, and dug-outs burned. Like a flash of light, LaFlors aimed a six-shooter at the officer's breast, and was instantly covered by a dozen carbines in the hands of troopers.

"Order them to shoot if you dare," smilingly said the Cherokee to the young lieutenant, a cocked pistol leveled at the latter's heart, "and she goes double. There isn't a man under you can pull a trigger quicker than I can." The hay was not burned, and the stabling and dug-outs housed our men and horses for several winters to come.

CHAPTER XVIII
THE BEGINNING OF THE BOOM

The great boom in cattle which began in 1880 and lasted nearly five years was the beginning of a ruinous end. The frenzy swept all over the northern and western half of the United States, extended into the British possessions in western Canada, and in the receding wave the Texan forgot the pit from which he was lifted and bowed down and worshiped the living calf. During this brief period the great breeding grounds of Texas were tested to their utmost capacity to supply the demand, the canebrakes of Arkansas and Louisiana were called upon for their knotty specimens of the bovine race, even Mexico responded, and still the insatiable maw of the early West called for more cattle. The whirlpool of speculation and investment in ranches and range stock defied the deserts on the west, sweeping across into New Mexico and Arizona, where it met a counter wave pushing inland from California to possess the new and inviting pastures. Naturally the Texan was the last to catch the enthusiasm, but when he found his herds depleted to a remnant of their former numbers, he lost his head and plunged into the vortex with the impetuosity of a gambler. Pasture lands that he had scorned at ten cents an acre but a decade before were eagerly sought at two and three dollars, and the cattle that he had bartered away he bought back at double and triple their former prices.

How I ever weathered those years without becoming bankrupt is unexplainable. No credit or foresight must be claimed, for the opinions of men and babes were on a parity; yet I am inclined to think it was my dread of debt, coupled with an innate love of land and cattle, that saved me from the almost universal fate of my fellow cowmen. Due acknowledgment must be given my partners, for while I held them in check in certain directions, the soundness of their advice saved my feet from many a stumble. Major Hunter was an unusually shrewd man, a financier of the rough and ready Western school; and while we made our mistakes, they were such as human foresight could not have avoided. Nor do I withhold a word of credit from our silent partner, the Senator, who was the keystone to the arch of Hunter, Anthony & Co., standing in the shadow in our beginning as trail drovers, backing us with his means and credit, and fighting valiantly for our mutual interests when the firm met its Waterloo.

The success of our drive for the summer of 1880 changed all plans for the future. I had learned that percentage was my ablest argument in suggesting a change of policy, and in casting up accounts for the year we found that our heavy beeves had paid the least in the general investment. The banking instincts of my partners were unerring, and in view of the open market that we had enjoyed that summer it was decided to withdraw from further contracting with the government. Our profits for the year were dazzling, and the actual growth of our beeves in the Outlet was in itself a snug fortune, while the five herds bought at the eleventh hour cleared over one hundred thousand dollars, mere pin-money. I hurried home to find that fortune favored me personally, as the Texas and Pacific Railway had built west from Fort Worth during the summer as far as Weatherford, while the survey on westward was within easy striking distance of both my ranches. My wife was dazed and delighted over the success of the summer's drive, and when I offered her the money with which to build a fine house at Fort Worth, she balked, but consented to employ a tutor at the ranch for the children.

I had a little leisure time on my hands that fall. Activity in wild lands was just beginning to be felt throughout the State, and the heavy holders of scrip were offering to locate large tracts to suit the convenience of purchasers. Several railroads held immense quantities of scrip voted to them as bonuses, all the charitable institutions of the State were endowed with liberal grants, and the great bulk of certificates issued during the Reconstruction régime for minor purposes had fallen into the hands of shrewd speculators. Among the latter was a Chicago firm, who had opened an office at Fort Worth and employed a corps of their own surveyors to locate lands for customers. They held millions of acres of scrip, and I opened negotiations with them to survey a number of additions to my Double Mountain range. Valuable water-fronts were becoming rather scarce, and the legislature had recently enacted a law setting apart every alternate section of land for the public schools, out of which grew the State's splendid system of education. After the exchange of a few letters, I went to Fort Worth and closed a contract with the Chicago firm to survey for my account three hundred thousand acres adjoining my ranch on the Salt and Double Mountain forks of the Brazos. In my own previous locations, the water-front and valley lands were all that I had coveted, the tracts not even adjoining, the one on the Salt Fork lying like a boot, while the lower one zigzagged like a stairway in following the watercourse. The prices agreed on were twenty cents an acre for arid land, forty for medium, and sixty for choice tracts, every other section to be set aside for school purposes in compliance with the law. My foreman would designate the land wanted, and the firm agreed to put an outfit of surveyors into the field at once.

My two ranches were proving a valuable source of profit. After starting five herds of seventeen thousand cattle on the trail that spring, and shipping on consignment fifteen hundred bulls to distilleries that fall, we branded nineteen thousand five hundred calves on the two ranges. In spite of the heavy drain, the brand was actually growing in numbers, and as long as it remained an open country I had ample room for my cattle even on the Clear Fork. Each stock was in splendid shape, as the culling of the aging and barren of both sexes to Indian agencies and distilleries had preserved the brand vigorous and productive. The first few years of its establishment I am satisfied that the Double Mountain ranch increased at the rate of ninety calves to the hundred cows, and once the Clear Fork range was rid of its drones, a similar ratio was easily maintained on that range. There was no such thing as counting one's holdings; the increase only was known, and these conclusions, with due allowance for their selection, were arrived at from the calf crop of the improved herd. Its numbers were known to an animal, all chosen for their vigor and thrift, the increase for the first two years averaging ninety-four per cent.

There is little rest for the wicked and none for a cowman. I was planning an enjoyable winter, hunting with my hounds, when the former proposition of organizing an immense cattle company was revived at Washington. Our silent partner was sought on every hand by capitalists eager for investment in Western enterprises, and as cattle were absorbing general attention at the time, the tendency of speculation was all one way. The same old crowd that we had turned down two winters before was behind the movement, and as certain predictions that were made at that time by Major Hunter and myself had since come true, they were all the more anxious to secure our firm as associates. Our experience and resultant profits from wintering cattle in southern Kansas and the Cherokee Strip were well known to the Senator, and, to judge from his letters and frequent conversations, he was envied by his intimate acquaintances in Congress. In the revival of the original proposition it was agreed that our firm might direct the management of the enterprise, all three of us to serve on the directorate and to have positions on the executive committee. This sounded reasonable, and as there was a movement on foot to lease the entire Cherokee Outlet from that Nation, if an adequate range could be secured, such a cattle company as suggested ought to be profitable.

Major Hunter and I were a unit in business matters, and after an exchange of views by letter, it was agreed to run down to the capital and hold a conference with the promoters of the proposed company. My parents were aging fast, and now that I was moderately wealthy it was a pleasure to drop in on them for a week and hearten their declining years. Accordingly with the expectation of combining filial duty and business, I took Edwards with me and picked up the major at his home, and the trio of us journeyed eastward. I was ten days late in reaching Washington. It was the Christmas season in the valley; every darky that our family ever owned renewed his acquaintance with Mars' Reed, and was remembered in a way befitting the season. The recess for the holidays was over on my reaching the capital, yet in the mean time a crude outline of the proposed company was under consideration. On the advice of our silent partner, who well knew that his business associates were slightly out of their element at social functions and might take alarm, all banquets were cut out, and we met in little parties at cafés and swell barrooms. In the course of a few days all the preliminaries were agreed on, and a general conference was called.

489

Neither my active partner nor myself was an orator, but we had coached the silent member of the firm to act in our behalf. The Senator was a flowery talker, and in prefacing his remarks he delved into antiquity, mentioning the Aryan myth wherein the drifting clouds were supposed to be the cows of the gods, driven to and from their feeding grounds. Coming down to a later period, he referred to cattle being figured on Egyptian monuments raised two thousand years before the Christian era, and to the important part they were made to play in Greek and Roman mythology. Referring to ancient biblical times, he dwelt upon the pastoral existence of the old patriarchs, as they peacefully led their herds from sheltered nook to pastures green. Passing down and through the cycles of change from ancient to modern times, he touched upon the relation of cattle to the food supply of the world, and finally the object of the meeting was reached. In few and concise words, an outline of the proposed company was set forth, its objects and limitations. A pound of beef, it was asserted, was as staple as a loaf of bread, the production of the one was as simple as the making of the other, and both were looked upon equally as the staff of life. Other remarks of a general nature followed. The capital was limited to one million dollars, though double the capitalization could have been readily placed at the first meeting. Satisfactory committees were appointed on organization and other preliminary steps, and books were opened for subscriptions. Deference was shown our firm, and I subscribed the same amount as my partners, except that half my subscription was made in the name of George Edwards, as I wanted him on the executive committee if the company ever got beyond its present embryo state. The trio of us taking only one hundred and fifty thousand dollars, there was a general scramble for the remainder.

The preliminary steps having been taken, nothing further could be done until a range was secured. My active partner, George Edwards, and myself were appointed on this committee, and promising to report at the earliest convenience, we made preparations for returning West. A change of administration was approaching, and before leaving the capital, Edwards, my partners, and myself called on Secretaries Schurz of the Interior Department and Ramsey of the War Department. We had done an extensive business with both departments in the past, and were anxious to learn the attitude of the government in regard to leasing lands from the civilized Indian nations. A lease for the Cherokee Outlet was pending, but for lack of precedent the retiring Secretary of the Interior, for fear of reversal by the succeeding administration, lent only a qualified approval of the same. There were six million acres of land in the Outlet, a splendid range for maturing beef, and if an adequate-sized ranch could be secured the new company could begin operations at once. The Cherokee Nation was anxious to secure a just rental, an association had offered $200,000 a year for the Strip, and all that was lacking was a single word of indorsement from the paternal government.

Hoping that the incoming administration would take favorable action permitting civilized Indian tribes to lease their surplus lands, we returned to our homes. The Cherokee Strip Cattle Association had been temporarily organized some time previous, — not being chartered, however, until March, 1883, — and was the proposed lessee of the Outlet in which our beef ranch lay. The organization was a local one, created for the purpose of removing all friction between the Cherokees and the individual holders of cattle in the Strip. The officers and directors of the association were all practical cattlemen, owners of herds and ranges in the Outlet, paying the same rental as others into the general treasury of the organization. Major Hunter was well acquainted with the officers, and volunteered to take the matter up at once, by making application in person for a large range in the Cherokee Strip. There was no intention on the part of our firm to forsake the trail, this cattle company being merely a side issue, and active preparations were begun for the coming summer.

The annual cattle convention would meet again in Fort Worth in February. With the West for our market and Texas the main source of supply, there was no occasion for any delay in placing our contracts for trail stock. The closing figures obtainable at Dodge and Ogalalla the previous summer had established a new scale of prices for Texas, and a buyer must either pay the advance or let the cattle alone. Edwards and I were in the field fully three weeks before the convention met, covering our old buying grounds and venturing into new ones, advancing money liberally on all contracts, and returning to the meeting with thirty herds secured. Major Hunter met us at the convention, and while nothing definite was accomplished in securing a range, a hopeful word had reached us in regard to the new administration. Starting the new company that spring was out of the question, and all energies were thrown into the forthcoming drive. Representatives from the Northwest again swept down on the convention, all Texas was there, and for three days and nights the cattle interests carried the keys of the city. Our firm offered nothing, but, on the other hand, bought three herds of Pan-Handle steers for acceptance early in April. Three weeks of active work were required to receive the cattle, the herds starting again with the grass. My individual contingent included ten thousand three-year-old steers, two full herds of two-year-old heifers, and seven thousand cows. The latter were driven in two herds; extra wagons with oxen attached accompanied each in order to save the calves, as a youngster was an assistance in selling an old cow. Everything was routed by Doan's Crossing, both Edwards and myself accompanying the herds, while Major Hunter returned as usual by rail. The new route, known as the Western trail, was more direct than the Chisholm though beset by Comanche and Kiowa Indians once powerful tribes, but now little more than beggars. The trip was nearly featureless, except that during a terrible storm on Big Elk, a number of Indians took shelter under and around one of our wagons and a squaw was killed by lightning. For some unaccountable reason the old dame defied the elements and had climbed up on a water barrel which was ironed to the side of the commissary wagon, when the bolt struck her and she tumbled off dead among her people. The incident created quite a commotion among the Indians, who set up a keening, and the husband of the squaw refused to be comforted until I gave him a stray cow, when he smiled and asked for a bill of sale so that he could sell the hide at the agency. I shook my head, and the cook told him in Spanish that no one but the owner could give a hill of sale, when he looked reproachfully at me and said, "Mebby so you steal him."

I caught a stage at Camp Supply and reached Dodge a week in advance of the herds. Major Hunter was awaiting me with the report that our application for an extra lease in the Cherokee Strip had been refused. Those already holding cattle in the Outlet were to retain their old grazing grounds, and as we had no more range than we needed for the firm's holding of stock, we must look elsewhere to secure one for the new company. A movement was being furthered in Washington, however, to secure a lease from the Cheyenne and Arapahoe tribes, blanket Indians, whose reservation lay just south of the Strip, near the centre of the Territory and between the Chisholm and Western trails. George Edwards knew the country, having issued cows at those agencies for several summers, and reported the country well adapted for ranging cattle. We had a number of congressmen and several distinguished senators in our company, and if there was such a thing as pulling the wires with the new administration, there was little doubt but it would be done. Kirkwood of Iowa had succeeded Schurz in the Interior Department, and our information was that he would at least approve of any lease secured. We were urged at the earliest opportunity to visit the Cheyenne and Arapahoe agency, and open negotiations with the ruling chiefs of those tribes. This was impossible just at present, for with forty herds, numbering one hundred and twenty-six thousand cattle, on the trail and for our beef ranch, a busy summer lay before us. Edwards was dispatched to meet and turn off the herds intended for our range in the Outlet, Major Hunter proceeded on to Ogalalla, while I remained at Dodge until the last cattle arrived or passed that point.

The summer of 1881 proved a splendid market for the drover. Demand far exceeded supply and prices soared upward, while she stuff commanded a premium of three to five dollars a head over steers of the same age. Pan-Handle and north Texas cattle topped the market, their quality easily classifying them above Mexican, coast, and southern breeding. Herds were sold and cleared out for their destination almost as fast as they arrived; the Old West wanted the cattle and had the range and to spare, all of which was a tempered wind to the Texas drover. I spent several months in Dodge, shaping up our herds as they arrived, and sending the majority of them on to Ogalalla. The cows were the last to arrive on the Arkansas, and they sold like pies to hungry boys, while all the remainder of my individual stock went on to the Platte and were handled by our segundo and my active partner. Near the middle of the summer I closed up our affairs at Dodge, and, taking the assistant bookkeeper with me, moved up to Ogalalla. Shortly after my arrival there, it was necessary to send a member of the firm to Miles City, on the Yellowstone River in Montana, and the mission fell to me. Major Hunter had sold twenty thousand threes for delivery at that point, and the cattle were already en route to their destination on my arrival. I took train and stage and met the herds on the Yellowstone.

On my return to Ogalalla the season was drawing to a feverish close. All our cattle were sold, the only delay being in deliveries and settlements. Several of our herds were received on the Platte, but, as it happened, nearly all our sales were effected with new cattle companies, and they had too much confidence in the ability of the Texas outfits to deliver to assume the risk themselves. Everything was fish to our net, and if a buyer had insisted on our delivering in Canada, I think Major Hunter would have met the request had the price been satisfactory. We had the outfits and horses, and our men were plainsmen and were at home as long as they could see the north star. Edwards attended a delivery on the Crazy Woman in Wyoming, Major Hunter made a trip for a similar purpose to the Niobrara in Nebraska, and various trail foremen represented the firm at minor deliveries. All trail business was closed before the middle of September, the bookkeepers made up their final statements, and we shook hands all round and broke the necks of a few bottles.

But the climax of the year's profits came from the beef ranch in the Outlet. The Eastern markets were clamoring for well-fatted Western stock, and we sent out train after train of double wintered beeves that paid one hundred per cent profit on every year we had held them. The single wintered cattle paid nearly as well, and in making ample room for the through steers we shipped out eighteen thousand head from our holdings on the Eagle Chief. The splendid profits from maturing beeves on Northern ranges naturally made us anxious to start the new company. We were doing fairly well as a firm and personally, and with our mastery of the business it was but natural that we should enlarge rather than restrict our operations. There had been no decrease of the foreign capital, principally Scotch and English, for investment in ranges and cattle in the West during the summer just past, and it was contrary to the policy of Hunter, Anthony & Co. to take a backward step. The frenzy for organizing cattle companies was on with a fury, and half-breed Indians and squaw-men, with rights on reservations, were in demand as partners in business or as managers of cattle syndicates.

An amusing situation developed during the summer of 1881 at Dodge. The Texas drovers formed a social club and rented and furnished quarters, which immediately became the rendezvous of the wayfaring mavericks. Cigars and refreshments were added, social games introduced, and in burlesque of the general craze of organizing stock companies to engage in cattle ranching, our club adopted the name of The Juan-Jinglero Cattle Company, Limited. The capital stock was placed at five million, full-paid and non-assessable, with John T. Lytle as treasurer, E.G. Head as secretary, Jess Pressnall as attorney, Captain E.G. Millet as fiscal agent for placing the stock, and a dozen leading drovers as vice-presidents, while the presidency fell to me. We used the best of printed stationery, and all the papers of Kansas City and Omaha innocently took it up and gave the new cattle company the widest publicity. The promoters of the club intended it as a joke, but the prominence of its officers fooled the outside public, and applications began to pour in to secure stock in the new company. No explanation was offered, but all applications were courteously refused, on the ground that the capital was already over-subscribed. All members were freely using the club stationery, thus daily advertising us far and wide, while no end of jokes were indulged in at the expense of the burlesque company. For instance, Major Seth Mabry left word at the club to forward his mail to Kansas City, care of Armour's Bank, as he expected to be away from Dodge for a week. No sooner had he gone than every member of the club wrote him a letter, in care of that popular bank, addressing him as first vice-president and director of The Juan-Jinglero Cattle Company. While attending to business Major Mabry was hourly honored by bankers and intimate friends desiring to secure stock in the company, to all of whom he turned a deaf ear, but kept the secret. "I told the boys," said Major Seth on his return, "that our company was a close corporation, and unless we increased the capital stock, there was no hope of them getting in on the ground floor."

In Dodge practical joking was carried to the extreme, both by citizens and cowmen. One night a tipsy foreman, who had just arrived over the trail, insisted on going the rounds with a party of us, and in order to shake him we entered a variety theatre, where my maudlin friend soon fell asleep in his seat. The rest of us left the theatre, and after seeing the sights I wandered back to the vaudeville, finding the performance over and my friend still sound asleep. I awoke him, never letting him know that I had been absent for hours, and after rubbing his eyes open, he said: "Reed, is it all over? No dance or concert? They give a good show here, don't they?"

CHAPTER XIX
THE CHEYENNE AND ARAPAHOE CATTLE COMPANY

The assassination of President Garfield temporarily checked our plans in forming the new cattle company. Kirkwood of the Interior Department was disposed to be friendly to all Western enterprises, but our advices from Washington anticipated a reorganization of the cabinet under Arthur. Senator Teller was slated to succeed Kirkwood, and as there was no question about the former being fully in sympathy with everything pertaining to the West, every one interested in the pending project lent his influence in supporting the Colorado man for the Interior portfolio. Several senators and any number of representatives were subscribers to our company, and by early fall the outlook was so encouraging that we concluded at least to open negotiations for a lease on the Cheyenne and Arapahoe reservation. A friendly acquaintance was accordingly to be cultivated with the Indian agent of these tribes. George Edwards knew him personally, and, well in advance of Major Hunter and myself, dropped down to the agency and made known his errand. There were already a number of cattle being held on the reservation by squaw-men, sutlers, contractors, and other army followers stationed at Fort Reno. The latter ignored all rights of the tribes, and even collected a rental from outside cattle for grazing on the reservation, and were naturally antagonistic to any interference with their personal plans. There had been more or less friction between the Indian agent and these usurpers of the grazing privileges, and a proposition to lease a million acres at an annual rental of fifty thousand dollars at once met with the sanction of the agent. Major Hunter and I were notified of the outlook, and at the close of the beef-shipping season we took stage for the Cheyenne and Arapahoe Agency. Our segundo had thoroughly ridden over the country, the range was a desirable one, and we soon came to terms with the agent. He was looked upon as a necessary adjunct to the success of our company, a small block of stock was set aside for his account, while his usefulness in various ways would entitle his name to grace the salary list. For the present the opposition of the army followers was to be ignored, as no one gave them credit for being able to thwart our plans.

The Indian agent called the head men of the two tribes together. The powwow was held at the summer encampment of the Cheyennes, and the principal chiefs of the Arapahoes were present. A beef was barbecued at our expense, and a great deal of good tobacco was smoked. Aside from the agent, we employed a number of interpreters; the council lasted two days, and on its conclusion we held a five years' lease, with the privilege of renewal, on a million acres of as fine grazing land as the West could boast. The agreement was signed by every chief present, and it gave us the privilege to fence our range, build shelter and stabling for our men and horses, and otherwise equip ourselves for ranching. The rental was payable semiannually in advance, to begin with the occupation of the country the following spring, and both parties to the lease were satisfied with the terms and conditions. In the territory allotted to us grazed two small stocks of cattle, one of which had comfortable winter shelters on Quartermaster Creek. Our next move was to buy both these brands and thus gain the good will of the only occupants of the range. Possession was given at once, and leaving Edwards and a few men to hold the range, the major and I returned to Kansas and reported our success to Washington.

The organization was perfected, and The Cheyenne and Arapahoe Cattle Company began operations with all the rights and privileges of an individual. One fourth of the capital stock was at once paid into the hands of the treasurer, the lease and cattle on hand were transferred to the new company, and the executive committee began operations for the future. Barbed wire by the carload was purchased sufficient to build one hundred miles of four-strand fence, and arrangements were made to have the same freighted one hundred and fifty miles inland by wagon from the railway terminal to the new ranch on Quartermaster Creek. Contracts were let to different men for cutting the posts and building the fence, and one of the old trail bosses came on from Texas and was installed as foreman of the new range. The first meeting of stockholders — for permanent organization — was awaiting the convenience of the Western contingent; and once Edwards was relieved, he and Major Hunter took my proxy and went on to the national capital. Every interest had been advanced to the farthest possible degree: surveyors would run the lines, the posts would be cut and hauled during the winter, and by the first of June the fences would be up and the range ready to receive the cattle.

I returned to Texas to find everything in a prosperous condition. The Texas and Pacific railway had built their line westward during the past summer, crossing the Colorado River sixty miles south of headquarters on the Double Mountain ranch and paralleling my Clear Fork range about half that distance below. Previous to my return, the foreman on my Western ranch shipped out four trains of sixteen hundred bulls on consignment to our regular customer in Illinois, it being the largest single shipment made from Colorado City since the railway reached that point. Thrifty little towns were springing up along the railroad, land was in demand as a result of the boom in cattle, and an air of prosperity pervaded both city and hamlet and was reflected in a general activity throughout the State. The improved herd was the pride of the Double Mountain ranch, now increased by over seven hundred half-blood heifers, while the young males were annually claimed for the improvement of the main ranch stock. For fear of in-and-in breeding, three years was the limit of use of any bulls among the improved cattle, the first importation going to the main stock, and a second consignment supplanting them at the head of the herd.

In the permanent organization of The Cheyenne and Arapahoe Cattle Company, the position of general manager fell to me. It was my wish that this place should have gone to Edwards, as he was well qualified to fill it, while I was busy looking after the firm and individual interests. Major Hunter likewise favored our segundo, but the Eastern stockholders were insistent that the management of the new company should rest in the hands of a successful cowman. The salary contingent with the position was no inducement to me, but, with the pressure brought to bear and in the interests of harmony, I was finally prevailed on to accept the management. The proposition was a simple one, — the maturing and marketing of beeves; we had made a success of the firm's beef ranch in the Cherokee Outlet, and as far as human foresight went, all things augured for a profitable future.

There was no intention on the part of the old firm to retire from the enviable position that we occupied as trail drovers. Thus enlarging the scope of our operations as cowmen simply meant that greater responsibility would rest on the shoulders of the active partners and our trusted men. Accepting the management of the new company meant, to a certain extent, a severance of my personal connection with the firm, yet my every interest was maintained in the trail and beef ranch. One of my first acts as manager of the new company was to serve a notice through our secretary-treasurer calling for the capital stock to be paid in on or before February 1, 1882. It was my intention to lay the foundation of the new company on a solid basis, and with ample capital at my command I gave the practical experiences of my life to the venture. During the winter I bought five hundred head of choice saddle horses, all bred in north Texas and the Pan-Handle, every one of which I passed on personally before accepting.

Thus outfitted, I awaited the annual cattle convention. Major Hunter and our segundo were present, and while we worked in harmony, I was as wide awake for a bargain in the interests of the new company as they were in that of the old firm. I let contracts for five herds of fifteen thousand Pan-Handle three-year-old steers for delivery on the new range in the Indian Territory, and bought nine thousand twos to be driven on company account. There was the usual whoop and hurrah at the convention, and when it closed I lacked only six thousand head of my complement for the new ranch. I was confining myself strictly to north Texas and Pan-Handle cattle, for through Montana cowmen I learned that there was an advantage, at maturity, in the northern-bred animal. Major Hunter and our segundo bought and contracted in a dozen counties from the Rio Grande to Red River during the convention, and at the close we scattered to the four winds in the interests of our respective work. In order to give my time and attention to the new organization, I assigned my individual cattle to the care of the firm, of which I was sending out ten thousand three-year-old steers and two herds of aging and dry cows. They would take their chances in the open market, though I would have dearly loved to take over the young steers for the new company rather than have bought their equivalent in numbers. I had a dislike to parting with an animal of my own breeding, and to have brought these to a ripe maturity under my own eye would have been a pleasure and a satisfaction. But such an action might have caused distrust of my management, and an honest name is a valuable asset in a cowman's capital.

My ranch foremen made up the herds and started my individual cattle on the trail. I had previously bought the two remaining herds in Archer and Clay counties, and in the five that were contracted for and would be driven at company risk and account, every animal passed and was received under my personal inspection. Three of the latter were routed by way of the Chisholm trail, and two by the Western, while the cattle under contract for delivery at the company ranch went by any route that their will and pleasure saw fit. I saw very little of my old associates during the spring months, for no sooner had I started the herds than I hastened to overtake the lead one so as to arrive with the cattle at their new range. I had kept in touch with the building of fences, and on our arrival, near the middle of May, the western and southern strings were completed. It was not my intention to inclose the entire range, only so far as to catch any possible drift of cattle to the south or west. A twenty-mile spur of fence on the east, with half that line and all the north one open, would be sufficient until further encroachments were made on our range. We would have to ride the fences daily, anyhow, and where there was no danger of drifting, an open line was as good as a fence.

As fast as the cattle arrived they were placed under loose herd for the first two weeks. Early in June the last of the contracted herds arrived and were scattered over the range, the outfits returning to Texas. I reduced my help gradually, as the cattle quieted down and became located, until by the middle of summer we were running the ranch with thirty men, which were later reduced to twenty for the winter. Line camps were established on the north and east, comfortable quarters were built for fence-riders and their horses, and aside from headquarters camp, half a dozen outposts were maintained. Hay contracts were let for sufficient forage to winter forty horses, the cattle located nicely within a month, and time rolled by without a cloud on the horizon of the new cattle company. I paid a flying visit to Dodge and Ogalalla, but, finding the season drawing to a close and the firm's cattle all sold, I contentedly returned to my accepted task. I had been buried for several months in the heart of the Indian Territory, and to get out where one could read the daily papers was a treat. During my banishment, Senator Teller had been confirmed as Secretary of the Interior, an appointment that augured well for the future of the Cheyenne and Arapahoe Cattle Company. Advices from Washington were encouraging, and while the new secretary lacked authority to sanction our lease, his tacit approval was assured.

The firm of Hunter, Anthony & Co. made a barrel of money in trailing cattle and from their beef ranch during the summer of 1882. I actually felt grieved over my portion of the season's work for while I had established a promising ranch, I had little to show, the improvement account being heavy, owing to our isolation. It was doubtful if we could have sold the ranch and cattle at a profit, yet I was complimented on my management, and given to understand that the stockholders were anxious to double the capitalization should I consent. Range was becoming valuable, and at a meeting of the directors that fall a resolution was passed, authorizing me to secure a lease adjoining our present one. Accordingly, when paying the second installment of rent money, I took the Indian agent of the two tribes with me. The leading chiefs were pleased with my punctuality in meeting the rental, and a proposition to double their income of "grass" money met with hearty grunts of approval. I made the council a little speech, — my maiden endeavor, — and when it was interpreted to the squatting circle I had won the confidence of these simple aborigines. A duplicate of our former lease in acreage and terms was drawn up and signed; and during the existence of our company the best teepee in the winter or summer encampments, of either the Cheyennes or Arapahoes, was none too good for Reed Anthony when he came with the rent money or on other business.

Our capital stock was increased to two million dollars, in the latter half of which, one hundred thousand was asked for and allotted to me. I stayed on the range until the first of December, freighting in a thousand bushels of corn for the horses and otherwise seeing that the camps were fully provisioned before returning to my home in Texas. The winter proved dry and cold, the cattle coming through in fine condition, not one per cent of loss being sustained, which is a good record for through stock. Spring came and found me on the trail, with five herds on company account and eight herds under contract, — a total of forty thousand cattle intended for the enlarged range. All these had been bought north of the quarantine line in Texas, and were turned loose with the wintered ones, fever having been unknown among our holdings of the year before. In the mean time the eastern spur of fence had been taken down and the southern line extended forty miles eastward and north the same distance. The northern line of our range was left open, the fences being merely intended to catch any possible drift from summer storms or wintry blizzards. Yet in spite of this precaution, two round-up outfits were kept in the field through the early summer, one crossing into the Chickasaw Nation and the other going as far south as Red River, gathering any possible strays from the new range.

I was giving my best services to the new company. Save for the fact that I had capable foremen on my individual ranches in Texas, my absence was felt in directing the interests of the firm and personally. Major Hunter had promoted an old foreman to a trusted man, and the firm kept up the volume of business on the trail and ranch, though I was summoned once to Dodge and twice to Ogalalla during the summer of 1883. Issues had arisen making my presence necessary, but after the last trail herd was sold I returned to my post. The boom was still on in cattle at the trail markets, and Texas was straining every energy to supply the demand, yet the cry swept down from the North for more cattle. I was branding twenty thousand calves a year on my two ranches, holding the increase down to that number by sending she stuff up the country on sale, and from half a dozen sources of income I was coining money beyond human need or necessity. I was then in the physical prime of my life and was master of a profitable business, while vistas of a brilliant future opened before me on every hand.

When the round-up outfits came in for the summer, the beef shipping began. In the first two contingents of cattle purchased in securing the good will of the original range, we now had five thousand double wintered beeves. It was my intention to ship out the best of the single wintered ones, and five separate outfits were ordered into the saddle for that purpose. With the exception of line and fence riders, — for two hundred and forty miles were ridden daily, rain or shine, summer or winter, — every man on the ranch took up his abode with the wagons. Caldwell and Hunnewell, on the Kansas state line were the nearest shipping points, requiring fifteen days' travel with beeves, and if there was no delay in cars, an outfit could easily gather the cattle and make a round trip in less than a month. Three or four trainloads, numbering from one thousand and fifty to fourteen hundred head, were cut out at a time and handled by a single outfit. I covered the country between the ranch and shipping points, riding night and day ahead in ordering cars, and dropping back to the ranch to superintend the cutting out of the next consignment of cattle. Each outfit made three trips, shipping out fifteen thousand beeves that fall, leaving sixty thousand cattle to winter on the range.

Several times that fall, when shipping beeves from Caldwell, we met up with the firm's outfits from the Eagle Chief in the Cherokee Outlet. Naturally the different shipping crews looked over each other's cattle, and an intense rivalry sprang up between the different foremen and men. The cattle of the new company outshone those of the old firm, and were outselling them in the markets, while the former's remudas were in a class by themselves, all of which was salt to open wounds and magnified the jealousy between our own outfits. The rivalry amused me, and until petty personalities were freely indulged in, I encouraged and widened the breach between the rival crews. The outfits under my direction had accumulated a large supply of saddle and sleeping blankets procured from the Indians, gaudy in color, manufactured in sizes for papoose, squaw, and buck. These goods were of the finest quality, but during the annual festivals of the tribe Lo's hunger for gambling induced him to part, for a mere song, with the blanket that the paternal government intended should shelter him during the storms of winter. Every man in my outfits owned from six to ten blankets, and the Eagle Chief lads rechristened the others, including myself, with the most odious of Indian names. In return, we refused to visit or eat at their wagons, claiming that they lived slovenly and were lousy. The latter had an educated Scotchman with them, McDougle by name, the ranch bookkeeper, who always went into town in advance to order cars. McDougle had a weakness for the cup, and on one occasion he fell into the hands of my men, who humored his failing, marching him through the streets, saloons, and hotels shouting at the top of his voice, "Hunter, Anthony & Company are going to ship!" The expression became a byword among the citizens of the town, and every reappearance of McDougle was accepted as a herald that our outfits from the Eagle Chief were coming in with cattle.

A special meeting of the stockholders was called at Washington that fall, which all the Western members attended. Reports were submitted by the secretary-treasurer and myself, the executive committee made several suggestions, the proposition, to pay a dividend was overwhelmingly voted down, and a further increase of the capital stock was urged by the Eastern contingent. I sounded a note of warning, called attention to the single cloud on the horizon, which was the enmity that we had engendered in a clique of army followers in and around Fort Reno. These men had in the past, were even then, collecting toll from every other holder of cattle on the Cheyenne and Arapahoe reservation. That this coterie of usurpers hated the new company and me personally was a well-known fact, while its influence was proving much stronger than at first anticipated, and I cheerfully admitted the same to the stockholders assembled. The Eastern mind, living under established conditions, could hardly realize the chaotic state of affairs in the West, with its vicious morals, and any attempt to levy tribute in the form of blackmail was repudiated by the stockholders in assembly. Major Hunter understood my position and delicately suggested coming to terms with the company's avowed enemies as the only feasible solution of the impending trouble. To further enlarge our holdings of cattle and leased range, he urged, would be throwing down the gauntlet in defiance of the clique of army attaches. Evidently no one took us seriously, and instead, ringing resolutions passed, enlarging the capital stock by another million, with instructions to increase our leases accordingly.

The Western contingent returned home with some misgivings as to the future. Nothing was to be feared from the tribes from whom we were leasing, nor the Comanche and his allies on the southwest, though there were renegades in both; but the danger lay in the flotsam of the superior race which infested the frontier. I felt no concern for my personal welfare, riding in and out from Fort Reno at my will and pleasure, though I well knew that my presence on the reservation was a thorn in the flesh of my enemies. There was little to fear, however, as the latter class of men never met an adversary in the open, but by secret methods sought to accomplish their objects. The breach between the Indian agent and these parasites of the army was constantly widening, and an effort had been made to have the former removed, but our friends at the national capital took a hand, and the movement was thwarted. Fuel was being constantly added to the fire, and on our taking a third lease on a million acres, the smoke gave way to flames. Our usual pacific measures were pursued, buying out any cattle in conflict, but fencing our entire range. The last addition to our pasture embraced a strip of country twenty miles wide, lying north of and parallel to the two former leases, and gave us a range on which no animal need ever feel the restriction of a fence. Ten to fifteen acres were sufficient to graze a steer the year round, but owing to the fact that we depended entirely on running water, much of the range would be valueless during the dry summer months. I readily understood the advantages of a half-stocked range, and expected in the future to allow twenty-five acres in the summer and thirty in the winter to the pasture's holdings. Everything being snug for the winter, orders were left to ride certain fences twice a day, — lines where we feared fence-cutting, — and I took my departure for home.

CHAPTER XX
HOLDING THE FORT

As in many other lines of business, there were ebb and flood tides in cattle. The opening of the trail through to the extreme Northwest gave the range live stock industry its greatest impetus. There have always been seasons of depression and advances, the cycles covering periods of ten to a dozen years, the duration of the ebb and stationary tides being double that of the flood. Outside influences have had their bearing, and the wresting of an empire from its savage possessors in the West, and its immediate occupancy by the dominant race in ranching, stimulated cattle prices far beyond what was justified by the laws of supply and demand. The boom in live stock in the Southwest which began in the early '80's stands alone in the market variations of the last half-century. And as if to rebuke the folly of man and remind him that he is but grass, Nature frowned with two successive severe winters, humbling the kings and princes of the range.

Up to and including the winter of 1883-84 the loss among range cattle was trifling. The country was new and open, and when the stock could drift freely in advance of storms, their instincts carried them to the sheltering coulees, cut banks, and broken country until the blizzard had passed. Since our firm began maturing beeves ten years before, the losses attributable to winter were never noticed, nor did they in the least affect our profits. On my ranches in Texas the primitive law of survival of the fittest prevailed, the winter-kill falling sorest among the weak and aging cows. My personal loss was always heavier than that of the firm, owing to my holdings being mixed stock, and due to the fact that an animal in the South never took on tallow enough to assist materially in resisting a winter. The cattle of the North always had the flesh to withstand the rigors of the wintry season, dry, cold, zero weather being preferable to rain, sleet, and the northers that swept across the plains of Texas. The range of the new company was intermediate between the extremes of north and south, and as we handled all steer cattle, no one entertained any fear from the climate.

I passed a comparatively idle winter at my home on the Clear Fork. Weekly reports reached me from the new ranch, several of which caused uneasiness, as our fences were several times cut on the southwest, and a prairie fire, the work of an incendiary, broke out at midnight on our range. Happily the wind fell, and by daybreak the smoke arose in columns, summoning every man on the ranch, and the fire was soon brought under control. As a precaution to such a possibility we had burned fire-guards entirely around the range by plowing furrows one hundred feet apart and burning out the middle. Taking advantage of creeks and watercourses, natural boundaries that a prairie fire could hardly jump, we had cut and quartered the pasture with fire-guards in such a manner that, unless there was a concerted action on the part of any hirelings of our enemies, it would have been impossible to have burned more than a small portion of the range at any one time. But these malicious attempts at our injury made the outfit doubly vigilant, and cutting fences and burning range would have proven unhealthful occupations had the perpetrators, red or white, fallen into the hands of the foreman and his men. I naturally looked on the bright side of the future, and in the hope that, once the entire range was fenced, we could keep trespassers out, I made preparations for the spring drive.

With the first appearance of grass, all the surplus horses were ordered down to Texas from the company ranch. There was a noticeable lull at the cattle convention that spring, and an absence of buyers from the Northwest was apparent, resulting in little or no trouble in contracting for delivery on the ranch, and in buying on company account at the prevailing prices of the spring before. Cattle were high enough as it was; in fact the market was top-heavy and wobbling on its feet, though the brightest of us cowmen naturally supposed that current values would always remain up in the pictures. As manager of the new company, I bought and contracted for fifty thousand steers, ten herds of which were to be driven on company account. All the cattle came from the Pan-Handle and north Texas, above the quarantine line, the latter precaution being necessary in order to avoid any possibility of fever, in mixing through and northern wintered stock. With the opening of spring two of my old foremen were promoted to assist in the receiving, as my contracts called for everything to be passed upon on the home range before starting the herds. Some little friction had occurred the summer before with the deliveries at the company ranch in an effort to turn in short-aged cattle. All contracts this year and the year before called for threes, and frequently several hundred long twos were found in a single herd, and I refused to accept them unless at the customary difference in price. More or less contention arose, and, for the present spring, I proposed to curb all friction at home, allotting to my assistants the receiving of the herds for company risk, and personally passing on seven under contract.

The original firm was still in the field, operating exclusively in central Texas and Pan-Handle cattle. Both my ranches sent out their usual contribution of steers and cows, consigned to the care of the firm, which was now giving more attention to quality than quantity. The absence of the men from the Northwest at the cattle convention that spring was taken as an omen that the upper country would soon be satiated, a hint that retrenchment was in order, and a better class of stock was to receive the firm's attention in its future operations. My personal contingent of steers would have passed muster in any country, and as to my consignment of cows, they were pure velvet, and could defy competition in the upper range markets. Everything moved out with the grass as usual, and when the last of the company herds had crossed Red River, I rode through to the new ranch. The north and east line of fence was nearing completion, the western string was joined to the original boundary, and, with the range fully inclosed, my ranch foreman, the men, and myself looked forward to a prosperous future.

The herds arrived and were located, the usual round-up outfits were sent out wherever there was the possibility of a stray, and we settled down in pastoral security. The ranch outfit had held their own during the winter just passed, had trailed down stolen cattle, and knew to a certainty who the thieves were and where they came from. Except what had been slaughtered, all the stock was recovered, and due notice given to offenders that Judge Lynch would preside should any one suspected of fence-cutting, starting incendiary fires, or stealing cattle be caught within the boundaries of our leases. Fortunately the other cowmen were tiring of paying tribute to the usurpers, and our determined stand heartened holders of cattle on the reservation, many of whom were now seeking leases direct from the tribes. I made it my business personally to see every other owner of live stock occupying the country, and urge upon them the securing of leases and making an organized fight for our safety. Lessees in the Cherokee Strip had fenced as a matter of convenience and protection, and I urged the same course on the Cheyenne and Arapahoe reservation, offering the free use of our line fences to any one who wished to adjoin our pastures. In the course of a month, nearly every acre of the surrounding country was taken, only one or two squaw-men holding out, and these claiming their ranges under Indian rights. The movement was made so aggressive that the usurpers were driven into obscurity, never showing their hand again until after the presidential election that fall.

During the summer a deputation of Cheyennes and Arapahoes visited me at ranch headquarters. On the last lease taken, and now inclosed in our pasture, there were a number of wild plum groves, covering thousands of acres, and the Indians wanted permission to gather the ripening fruit. Taking advantage of the opportunity, in granting the request I made it a point to fortify the friendly relations, not only with ourselves, but with all other cattlemen on the reservation. Ten days' permission was given to gather the wild plums, camps were allotted to the Indians, and when the fruit was all gathered, I barbecued five stray beeves in parting with my guests. The Indian agent and every cowman on the reservation were invited, and at the conclusion of the festival the Quaker agent made the assembled chiefs a fatherly talk. Torpid from feasting, the bucks grunted approval of the new order of things, and an Arapahoe chief, responding in behalf of his tribe, said that the rent from the grass now fed his people better than under the old buffalo days. Pledging anew the fraternal bond, and appointing the gathering of the plums as an annual festival thereafter, the tribes took up their march in returning to their encampment.

I was called to Dodge but once during the summer of 1884. My steers had gone to Ogalalla and were sold, the cows remaining at the lower market, all of which had changed owners with the exception of one thousand head. The demand had fallen off, and a dull close of the season was predicted, but I shaded prices and closed up my personal holdings before returning. Several of the firm's steer herds were unsold at Dodge, but on the approach of the shipping season I returned to my task, and we began to move out our beeves with seven outfits in the saddle. Four round trips were made to the crew, shipping out twenty thousand double and half that number of single wintered cattle. The grass had been fine that summer, and the beeves came up in prime condition, always topping the market as range cattle at the markets to which they were consigned. That branch of the work over, every energy was centred in making the ranch snug for the winter. Extra fire-guards were plowed, and the middles burned out, cutting the range into a dozen parcels, and thus, as far as possible, the winter forage was secured for our holdings of eighty thousand cattle. Hay and grain contracts had been previously let, the latter to be freighted in from southern Kansas, when the news reached us that the recent election had resulted in a political change of administration. What effect this would have on our holding cattle on Indian lands was pure conjecture, though our enemies came out of hiding, gloating over the change, and swearing vengeance on the cowmen on the Cheyenne and Arapahoe reservation.

The turn of the tide in cattle prices was noticeable at all the range markets that fall. A number of herds were unsold at Dodge, among them being one of ours, but we turned it southeast early in September and wintered it on our range in the Outlet. The largest drive in the history of the trail had taken place that summer, and the failure of the West and Northwest to absorb the entire offerings of the drovers made the old firm apprehensive of the future. There was a noticeable shrinkage in our profits from trail operations, but with the supposition that it was merely an off year, the matter was passed for the present. It was the opinion of the directors of the new company that no dividends should he declared until our range was stocked to its full capacity, or until there was a comfortable surplus. This suited me, and, returning home, I expected to spend the winter with my family, now increased to four girls and six boys.

But a cowman can promise himself little rest or pleasure. After a delightful week spent on my western ranch, I returned to the Clear Fork, and during the latter part of November a terrible norther swept down and caught me in a hunting-camp twenty-five miles from home. My two oldest boys were along, a negro cook, and a few hands, and in spite of our cosy camp, we all nearly froze to death. Nothing but a roaring fire saved us during the first night of its duration, and the next morning we saddled our horses and struck out for home, riding in the face of a sleet that froze our clothing like armor. Norther followed norther, and I was getting uneasy about the company ranch, when I received a letter from Major Hunter, stating that he was starting for our range in the Outlet and predicting a heavy loss of cattle. Headquarters in the Indian Territory were fully two hundred and fifty miles due north, and within an hour after receiving the letter, I started overland on horseback, using two of my best saddlers for the trip. To have gone by rail and stage would have taken four days, and if fair weather favored me I could nearly divide that time by half. Changing horses frequently, one day out I had left Red River in my rear, but before me lay an uninhabited country, unless I veered from my course and went through the Chickasaw Nation. For the sake of securing grain for the horses, this tack was made, following the old Chisholm trail for nearly one hundred miles. The country was in the grip of winter, sleet and snow covering the ground, with succor for man and horse far apart. Mumford Johnson's ranch on the Washita River was reached late the second night, and by daybreak the next morning I was on the trail, making Quartermaster Creek by one o'clock that day. Fortunately no storms were encountered en route, but King Winter ruled the range with an iron hand, fully six inches of snow covering the pasture, over which was a crusted sleet capable of carrying the weight of a beef. The foreman and his men were working night and day to succor the cattle. Between storms, two crews of the boys drifted everything back from the south line of fence, while others cut ice and opened the water to the perishing animals. Scarcity of food was the most serious matter; being unable to reach the grass under its coat of sleet and snow, the cattle had eaten the willows down to the ground. When a boy in Virginia I had often helped cut down basswood and maple trees in the spring for the cattle to browse upon, and, sending to the agency for new axes, I armed every man on the ranch with one, and we began felling the cottonwood and other edible timber along the creeks and rivers in the pasture. The cattle followed the axemen like sheep, eating the tender branches of the softer woods to the size of a man's wrist, the crash of a falling tree bringing them by the dozens to browse and stay their hunger. I swung an axe with the men, and never did slaves under the eye of a task-master work as faithfully or as long as we did in cutting ice and falling timber in succoring our holding of cattle. Several times the sun shone warm for a few days, melting the snow off the southern slopes, when we took to our saddles, breaking the crust with long poles, the cattle following to where the range was bared that they might get a bit of grass. Had it not been for a few such sunny days, our loss would have been double what it was; but as it was, with the general range in the clutches of sleet and snow for over fifty days, about twenty per cent, of our holdings were winter-killed, principally of through cattle.

Our saddle stock, outside of what was stabled and grain-fed, braved the winter, pawing away the snow and sleet in foraging for their subsistence. A few weeks of fine balmy weather in January and February followed the distressing season of wintry storms, the cattle taking to the short buffalo-grass and rapidly recuperating. But just when we felt that the worst was over, simultaneously half a dozen prairie fires broke out in different portions of the pasture, calling every man to a fight that lasted three days. Our enemies, not content with havoc wrought by the elements, were again in the saddle, striking in the dark and escaping before dawn, inflicting injuries on dumb animals in harassing their owners. That it was the work of hireling renegades, more likely white than red, there was little question; but the necessity of preserving the range withheld us from trailing them down and meting out a justice they so richly deserved. Dividing the ranch help into half a dozen crews, we rode to the burning grass and began counter-firing and otherwise resorting to every known method in checking the consuming flames. One of the best-known devices, in short grass and flank-fires, was the killing of a light beef, beheading and splitting it open, leaving the hide to hold the parts together. By turning the animal flesh side down and taking ropes from a front and hind foot to the pommels of two saddles, the men, by riding apart, could straddle the flames, virtually rubbing the fire out with the dragging carcass. Other men followed with wet blankets and beat out any remaining flames, the work being carried on at a gallop, with a change of horses every mile or so, and the fire was thus constantly hemmed in to a point. The variations of the wind sometimes entirely checked all effort, between midnight and morning being the hours in which most progress was accomplished. No sooner was one section of the fire brought under control than we divided the forces and hastened to lend assistance to the next nearest section, the cooks with commissaries following up the firefighters. While a single blade of grass was burning, no one thought of sleeping, and after one third of the range was consumed, the last of the incendiary fires was stamped out, when we lay down around the wagons and slept the sleep of exhaustion.

There was still enough range saved to bring the cattle safely through until spring. Leaving the entire ranch outfit to ride the fences — several lines of which were found cut by the renegades in entering and leaving the pasture — and guard the gates, I took train and stage for the Grove. Major Hunter had returned from the firm's ranch in the Strip, where heavy losses were encountered, though it then rested in perfect security from any influence except the elements. With me, the burning of the company range might be renewed at any moment, in which event we should have to cut our own fences and let the cattle drift south through an Indian country, with nothing to check them except Red River. A climax was approaching in the company's existence, and the delay of a day or week might mean inestimable loss. In cunning and craftiness our enemies were expert; they knew their control of the situation fully, and nothing but cowardice would prevent their striking the final, victorious blow. My old partner and I were a unit as to the only course to pursue, — one which meant a dishonorable compromise with our enemies, as the only hope of saving the cattle. A wire was accordingly sent East, calling a special meeting of the stockholders. We followed ourselves within an hour. On arriving at the national capital, we found that all outside shareholders had arrived in advance of ourselves, and we went into session with closed doors and the committee on entertainment and banquets inactive. In as plain words as the English language would permit, as general manager of the company, I stated the cause for calling the meeting, and bluntly suggested the only avenue of escape. Call it tribute, blackmail, or what you will, we were at the mercy of as heartless a set of scoundrels as ever missed a rope, whose mercenaries, like the willing hirelings that they were, would cheerfully do the bidding of their superiors. Major Hunter, in his remarks before the meeting, modified my rather radical statement, with the more plausible argument that this tribute money was merely insurance, and what was five or ten thousand dollars a year, where an original investment of three millions and our surplus were in jeopardy? Would any line — life, fire, or marine — carry our risk as cheaply? These men had been receiving toll from our predecessors, and were then in a position to levy tribute or wreck the company.

Notwithstanding our request for immediate action, an adjournment was taken. A wire could have been sent to a friend in Fort Reno that night, and all would have gone well for the future security of the Cheyenne and Arapahoe Cattle Company. But I lacked authority to send it, and the next morning at the meeting, the New England blood that had descended from the Puritan Fathers was again in the saddle, shouting the old slogans of no compromise while they had God and right on their side. Major Hunter and I both keenly felt the rebuke, but personal friends prevented an open rupture, while the more conservative ones saw brighter prospects in the political change of administration which was soon to assume the reins of government. A number of congressmen and senators among our stockholders were prominent in the ascendant party, and once the new régime took charge, a general shake-up of affairs in and around Fort Reno was promised. I remembered the old maxim of a new broom; yet in spite of the blandishments that were showered down in silencing my active partner and me, I could almost smell the burning range, see the horizon lighted up at night by the licking flames, hear the gloating of our enemies, in the hour of their victory, and the click of the nippers of my own men, in cutting the wire that the cattle might escape and live.

I left Washington somewhat heartened. Major Hunter, ever inclined to look on the bright side of things, believed that the crisis had passed, even bolstering up my hopes in the next administration. It was the immediate necessity that was worrying me, for it meant a summer's work to gather our cattle on Red River and in the intermediate country, and bring them back to the home range. The mysterious absence of any report from my foreman on my arrival at the Grove did not mislead me to believe that no news was good news, and I accordingly hurried on to the front. There was a marked respect shown me by the civilians located at Fort Reno, something unusual; but I hurried on to the agency, where all was quiet, and thence to ranch headquarters. There I learned that a second attempt to burn the range had been frustrated; that one of our boys had shot dead a white man in the act of cutting the east string of fence; that the same night three fires had broken out in the pasture, and that a squad of our men, in riding to the light, had run afoul of two renegade Cheyennes armed with wire-nippers, whose remains then lay in the pasture unburied. Both horses were captured and identified as not belonging to the Indians, while their owners were well known. Fortunately the wind veered shortly after the fires started, driving the flames back against the plowed guards, and the attempt to burn the range came to naught. A salutary lesson had been administered to the hirelings of the usurpers, and with a new moon approaching its full, it was believed that night marauding had ended for that winter. None of our boys recognized the white man, there being no doubt but he was imported for the purpose, and he was buried where he fell; but I notified the Indian agent, who sent for the remains of the two renegades and took possession of the horses. The season for the beginning of active operations on trail and for ranch account was fast approaching, and, leaving the boys to hold the fort during my absence, I took my private horses and turned homeward.

CHAPTER XXI
THE FRUITS OF CONSPIRACY

With a loss of fully fifteen thousand cattle staring me in the face, I began planning to recuperate the fortunes of the company. The cattle convention, which was then over, was conspicuous by the absence of all Northern buyers. George Edwards had attended the meeting, was cautious enough to make no contracts for the firm, and fully warned me of the situation. I was in a quandary; with an idle treasury of over a million, my stewardship would be subject to criticism unless I became active in the interests of my company. On the other hand, a dangerous cloud hung over the range, and until that was removed I felt like a man who was sent for and did not want to go. The falling market in Texas was an encouragement, but my experience of the previous winter had had a dampening effect, and I was simply drifting between adverse winds. But once it was known that I had returned home, my old customers approached me by letter and personally, anxious to sell and contract for immediate delivery. Trail drovers were standing aloof, afraid of the upper markets, and I could have easily bought double my requirements without leaving the ranch. The grass was peeping here and there, favorable reports came down from the reservation, and still I sat idle.

The appearance of Major Hunter acted like a stimulus. Reports about the new administration were encouraging — not from our silent partner, who was not in sympathy with the dominant party, but from other prominent stockholders who were. The original trio — the little major, our segundo, and myself — lay around under the shade of the trees several days and argued the possibilities that confronted us on trail and ranch. Edwards reproached me for my fears, referring to the time, nineteen years before, when as common hands we fought our way across the Staked Plain and delivered the cattle safely at Fort Sumner. He even taunted me with the fact that our employers then never hesitated, even if half the Comanche tribe were abroad, roving over their old hunting grounds, and that now I was afraid of a handful of army followers, contractors, and owners of bar concessions. Edwards knew that I would stand his censure and abuse as long as the truth was told, and with the major acting as peacemaker between us I was finally whipped into line. With a fortune already in hand, rounding out my forty-fifth year, I looted the treasury by contracting and buying sixty thousand cattle for my company.

The surplus horses were ordered down from above, and the spring campaign began in earnest. The old firm was to confine its operations to fine steers, handling my personal contribution as before, while I rallied my assistants, and we began receiving the contracted cattle at once. Observation had taught me that in wintering beeves in the North it was important to give the animals every possible moment of time to locate before the approach of winter. The instinct of a dumb beast is unexplainable yet unerring. The owner of a horse may choose a range that seems perfect in every appointment, but the animal will spurn the human selection and take up his abode on some flinty hills, and there thrive like a garden plant. Cattle, especially steers, locate slowly, and a good summer's rest usually fortifies them with an inward coat of tallow and an outward one of furry robe, against the wintry storms. I was anxious to get the through cattle to the new range as soon as practicable, and allowed the sellers to set their dates as early as possible, many of them agreeing to deliver on the reservation as soon as the middle of May. Ten wagons and a thousand horses came down during the last days of March, and early in April started back with thirty thousand cattle at company risk.

All animals were passed upon on the Texas range, and on their arrival at the pasture there was little to do but scatter them over the ranch to locate. I reached the reservation with the lead herd, and was glad to learn from neighboring cowmen that a suggestion of mine, made the fall before, had taken root. My proposition was to organize all the cattlemen on the Cheyenne and Arapahoe reservation into an association for mutual protection. By coöperation we could present a united front to our enemies, the usurpers, and defy them in their nefarious schemes of exacting tribute. Other ranges besides ours had suffered by fire and fence-cutters during the winter just passed, and I returned to find my fellow cowmen a unit for organization. A meeting was called at the agency, every owner of cattle on the reservation responded, and an association was perfected for our mutual interest and protection. The reservation was easily capable of carrying half a million cattle, the tribes were pleased with the new order of things, and we settled down with a feeling of security not enjoyed in many a day.

But our tranquil existence received a shock within a month, when a cowboy from a neighboring ranch, and without provocation, was shot down by Indian police in a trader's store at the agency. The young fellow was a popular Texan, and as nearly all the men employed on the reservation came from the South, it was with difficulty that our boys were restrained from retaliating. Those from Texas had little or no love for an Indian anyhow, and nothing but the plea of policy in preserving peaceful relations with the tribes held them in check. The occasional killing of cattle by Indians was overlooked, until they became so bold as to leave the hides and heads in the pasture, when an appeal was made to the agent. But the aborigine, like his white brother, has sinful ways, and the influence of one evil man can readily combat the good advice of half a dozen right-minded ones, and the Quaker agent found his task not an easy one. Cattle were being killed in remote and unfrequented places, and still we bore with it, the better class of Indians, however, lending their assistance to check the abuse. On one occasion two boys and myself detected a band of five young bucks skinning a beef in our pasture, and nothing but my presence prevented a clash between my men and the thieves. But it was near the wild-plum season, and as we were making preparations to celebrate that event, the killing of a few Indians might cause distrust, and we dropped out of sight and left them to the enjoyment of their booty. It was pure policy on my part, as we could shame or humble the Indian, and if the abuse was not abated, we could remunerate ourselves by with-holding from the rent money the value of cattle killed.

Our organization for mutual protection was accepted by our enemies as a final defiance. A pirate fights as valiantly as if his cause were just, and, through intermediaries, the gauntlet was thrown back in our faces and notice served that the conflict had reached a critical stage. I never discussed the issue direct with members of the clique, as they looked upon me as the leader in resisting their levy of tribute, but indirectly their grievances were made known. We were accused of having taken the bread out of their very mouths, which was true in a sense, but we had restored it tenfold where it was entitled to go, — among the Indians. With the exception of an occasional bottle of whiskey, none of the tribute money went to the tribes, but was divided among the usurpers. They waxed fat in their calling and were insolent and determined, while our replies to all overtures looking to peace were firm and to the point. Even at that late hour I personally knew that the clique had strength in reserve, and had I enjoyed the support of my company, would willingly have stood for a compromise. But it was out of the question to suggest it, and, trusting to the new administration, we politely told them to crack their whips.

The *fiesta* which followed the plum gathering was made a notable occasion. All the cowmen on the reservation had each contributed a beef to the barbecue, the agent saw to it that all the principal chiefs of both tribes were present, and after two days of feasting, the agent made a Quaker talk, insisting that the bond between the tribes and the cowmen must be observed to the letter. He reviewed at length the complaints that had reached him of the killing of cattle, traceable to the young and thoughtless, and pointed out the patience of the cattlemen in not retaliating, but in spreading a banquet instead to those who had wronged them. In concluding, he warned them that the patience of the white man had a limit, and, while they hoped to live in peace, unless the stealing of beef was stopped immediately, double the value of the cattle killed would be withheld from the next payment of grass money. It was in the power of the chiefs present to demand this observance of faith among their young men, if the bond to which their signatures were attached was to be respected in the future. The leading chiefs of both tribes spoke in defense, pleading their inability to hold their young men in check as long as certain evil influences were at work among their people. The love of gambling and strong drink was yearly growing among their men, making them forget their spoken word, until they were known as thieves and liars. The remedy lay in removing these evil spirits and trusting the tribes to punish their own offenders, as the red man knew no laws except his own.

The festival was well worth while and augured hopefully for the future. Clouds were hovering on the horizon, however, and, while at Ogalalla, I received a wire that a complaint had been filed against us at the national capital, and that the President had instructed the Lieutenant-General of the Army to make an investigation. Just what the inquiry was to be was a matter of conjecture; possibly to determine who was supplying the Indians with whiskey, or probably our friends at Washington were behind the movement, and the promised shake-up of army followers in and around Fort Reno was materializing. I attended to some unsettled business before returning, and, on my arrival at the reservation, a general alarm was spreading among the cattle interests, caused by the cock-sure attitude of the usurpers and a few casual remarks that had been dropped. I was appealed to by my fellow cowmen, and, in turn, wired our friends at Washington, asking that our interests be looked after and guarded. Pending a report, General P.H. Sheridan arrived with a great blare of trumpets at Fort Reno for the purpose of holding the authorized investigation. The general's brother, Michael, was the recognized leader of the clique of army followers, and was interested in the bar concessions under the sutler. Matters, therefore, took on a serious aspect. All the cowmen on the reservation came in, expecting to be called before the inquiry, as it was then clear that a fight must be made to protect our interests. No opportunity, however, was given the Indians or cattlemen to present their side of the question, and when a committee of us cowmen called on General Sheridan we were cordially received and politely informed that the investigation was private. I believe that forty years have so tempered the animosities of the Civil War that an honest opinion is entitled to expression. And with due consideration to the record of a gallant soldier, I submit the question, Were not the owners of half a million cattle on the Cheyenne and Arapahoe reservation entitled to a hearing before a report was made that resulted in an order for their removal?

I have seen more trouble at a country dance, more bloodshed in a family feud, than ever existed or was spilled on the Cheyenne and Arapahoe reservation. The Indians were pleased, the lessees were satisfied, yet by artfully concealing the true cause of any and all strife, a report, every word of which was as sweet as the notes of a flute, was made to the President, recommending the removal of the cattle. It was found that there had been a gradual encroachment on the liberties of the tribes; that the rental received from the surplus pasture lands had a bad tendency on the morals of the Indians, encouraging them in idleness; and that the present system retarded all progress in agriculture and the industrial arts. The report was superficial, religiously concealing the truth, but dealing with broad generalities. Had the report emanated from some philanthropical society, it would have passed unnoticed or been commented on as an advance in the interest of a worthy philanthropy but taken as a whole, it was a splendid specimen of the use to which words can be put in concealing the truth and cloaking dishonesty.

An order of removal by the President followed the report. Had we been subjects of a despotic government and bowed our necks like serfs, the matter would have ended in immediate compliance with the order. But we prided ourselves on our liberties as Americans, and an appeal was to be made to the first citizen of the land, the President of the United States. A committee of Western men were appointed, which would be augmented by others at the national capital, and it was proposed to lay the bare facts in the chief executive's hands and at least ask for a modification of the order. The latter was ignorant in its conception, brutal and inhuman in its intent, ending in the threat to use the military arm of the government, unless the terms and conditions were complied with within a given space of time. The Cheyenne and Arapahoe Cattle Company, alone, not to mention the other members of our association equally affected, had one hundred and twenty-five thousand head of beeves and through steers on its range, and unless some relief was granted, a wayfaring man though a fool could see ruin and death and desolation staring us in the face. Fortunately Major Hunter had the firm's trail affairs so well in hand that Edwards could close up the business, thus relieving my active partner to serve on the committee, he and four others offering to act in behalf of our association in calling on the President. I was among the latter, the only one in the delegation from Texas, and we accordingly made ready and started for Washington.

Meanwhile I had left orders to start the shipping with a vengeance. The busy season was at hand on the beef ranges, and men were scarce; but I authorized the foreman to comb the country, send to Dodge if necessary, and equip ten shipping outfits and keep a constant string of cattle moving to the markets. We had about sixty-five thousand single and double wintered beeves, the greater portion of which were in prime condition; but it was the through cattle that were worrying me, as they were unfit to ship and it was too late in the season to relocate them on a new range. But that blessed hope that springs eternal in the human breast kept us hopeful that the President had been deceived into issuing his order, and that he would right all wrongs. The more sanguine ones of the Western delegation had matters figured down to a fraction; they believed that once the chief executive understood the true cause of the friction existing on the reservation, apologies would follow, we should all be asked to remain for lunch, and in the most democratic manner imaginable everything would be righted. I had no opinions, but kept anticipating the worst; for if the order stood unmodified, go we must and in the face of winter and possibly accompanied by negro troops. To return to Texas meant to scatter the cattle to the four winds; to move north was to court death unless an open winter favored us.

On our arrival at Washington, all senators and congressmen shareholders in our company met us by appointment. It was an inactive season at the capital, and hopes were entertained that the President would grant us an audience at once; but a delay of nearly a week occurred. In the mean time several conferences were held, at which a general review of the situation was gone over, and it was decided to modify our demands, asking for nothing personally, only a modification of the order in the interest of humanity to dumb animals. Before our arrival, a congressman and two senators, political supporters of the chief executive, had casually called to pay their respects, and incidentally inquired into the pending trouble between the cattlemen and the Cheyenne and Arapahoe Indians. Reports were anything but encouraging; the well-known obstinacy of the President was admitted; it was also known that he possessed a rugged courage in pursuance of an object or purpose. Those who were not in political sympathy with the party in power characterized the President as an opinionated executive, and could see little or no hope in a personal appeal.

However, the matter was not to be dropped. The arrival of a deputation of cattlemen from the West was reported by the press, their purposes fully, set forth, and in the interim of waiting for an appointment, all of us made hay with due diligence. Major Hunter and I had a passing acquaintance at both the War and Interior departments, and taking along senators and representatives in political sympathy with the heads of those offices, we called and paid our respects. A number of old acquaintances were met, hold-overs from the former régime, and a cordial reception was accorded us. Now that the boom in cattle was over, we expressed a desire to resume our former business relations as contractors with the government. At both departments, the existent trouble on the Indian reservations was well known, and a friendly inquiry resulted, which gave us an opportunity to explain our position fully. There was a hopeful awakening to the fact that there had been a conspiracy to remove us, and the most friendly advances of assistance were proffered in setting the matter right. Public opinion is a strong factor, and with the press of the capital airing our grievances daily, sympathy and encouragement were simply showered down upon us.

Finally an audience with the President was granted. The Western delegation was increased by senators and representatives until the committee numbered an even dozen. Many of the latter were personal friends and ardent supporters of the chief executive. The rangemen were introduced, and we proceeded at once to the matter at issue. A congressman from New York stated the situation clearly, not mincing his words in condemning the means and procedure by which this order was secured, and finally asking for its revocation, or a modification that would permit the evacuation of the country without injury to the owners and their herds. Major Hunter, in replying to a question of the President, stated our position: that we were in no sense intruders, that we paid our rental in advance, with the knowledge and sanction of the two preceding Secretaries of the Interior, and only for lack of precedent was their indorsement of our leases withheld. It soon became evident that countermanding the order was out of the question, as to vacillate or waver in a purpose, right or wrong, was not a characteristic of the chief executive. Our next move was for a modification of the order, as its terms required us to evacuate that fall, and every cowman present accented the fact that to move cattle in the mouth of winter was an act that no man of experience would countenance. Every step, the why and wherefore, must be explained to the President, and at the request of the committee, I went into detail in making plain what the observations of my life had taught me of the instincts and habits of cattle, — why in the summer they took to the hills, mesas, and uplands, where the breezes were cooling and protected them from insect life; their ability to foretell a storm in winter and seek shelter in coulees and broken country. I explained that none of the cattle on the Cheyenne and Arapahoe reservation were native to that range, but were born anywhere from three to five hundred miles to the south, fully one half of them having arrived that spring; that to acquaint an animal with its new range, in cattle parlance to "locate" them, was very important; that every practical cowman moved his herds to a new range with the grass in the spring, in order that ample time should be allowed to acclimate and familiarize them with such shelters as nature provided to withstand the storms of winter. In concluding, I stated that if the existent order could be so modified as to permit all through cattle and those unfit for market to remain on their present range for the winter, we would cheerfully evacuate the country with the grass in the spring. If such relief could be consistently granted, it would no doubt save the lives of hundreds and thousands of cattle.

The President evidently was embarrassed by the justice of our prayer. He consulted with members of the committee, protesting that he should be spared from taking what would be considered a backward step, and after a stormy conference with intimate friends, lasting fully an hour, he returned and in these words refused to revoke or modify his order: "If I had known," said he, "what I know now, I never would have made the order; but having made it, I will stand by it."

Laying aside all commercial considerations, we had made our entreaty in behalf of dumb animals, and the President's answer angered a majority of the committee. I had been rebuked too often in the past by my associates easily to lose my temper, and I naturally looked at those whose conscience balked at paying tribute, while my sympathies were absorbed for the future welfare of a quarter-million cattle affected by the order. We broke into groups in taking our leave, and the only protest that escaped any one was when the York State representative refused the hand of the executive, saying, "Mr. President, I have my opinion of a man who admits he is wrong and refuses to right it." Two decades have passed since those words, rebuking wrong in high places, were uttered, and the speaker has since passed over to the silent majority. I should feel that these memoirs were incomplete did I not mention the sacrifice and loss of prestige that the utterance of these words cost, for they were the severance of a political friendship that was never renewed.

The autocratic order removing the cattle from the Cheyenne and Arapahoe reservation was born in iniquity and bore a harvest unequaled in the annals of inhumanity. With the last harbor of refuge closed against us, I hastened back and did all that was human to avert the impending doom, every man and horse available being pressed into service. Our one hope lay in a mild winter, and if that failed us the affairs of the company would be closed by the merciless elements. Once it was known that the original order had not been modified, and in anticipation of a flood of Western cattle, the markets broke, entailing a serious commercial loss. Every hoof of single and double wintered beeves that had a value in the markets was shipped regardless of price, while I besought friends in the Cherokee Strip for a refuge for those unfit and our holding of through cattle. Fortunately the depreciation in live stock and the heavy loss sustained the previous winter had interfered with stocking the Outlet to its fall capacity, and by money, prayers, and entreaty I prevailed on range owners and secured pasturage for seventy-five thousand head. Long before the shipping season ended I pressed every outfit belonging to the firm on the Eagle Chief into service, and began moving out the through cattle to their new range. Squaw winter and snow-squalls struck us on the trail, but with a time-limit hanging over our heads, and rather than see our cattle handled by nigger soldiers, we bore our burdens, if not meekly, at least in a manner consistent with our occupation. I have always deplored useless profanity, yet it was music to my ears to hear the men arraign our enemies, high and low, for our present predicament. When the last beeves were shipped, a final round-up was made, and we started out with over fifty thousand cattle in charge of twelve outfits. Storms struck us en route, but we weathered them, and finally turned the herds loose in the face of a blizzard.

The removed cattle, strangers in a strange land, drifted to the fences and were cut to the quick by the biting blasts. Early in January the worst blizzard in the history of the plains swept down from the north, and the poor wandering cattle were driven to the divides and frozen to death against the line fences. Of all the appalling sights that an ordinary lifetime on the range affords, there is nothing to compare with the suffering and death that were daily witnessed during the month of January in the winter of 1885-86. I remained on the range, and left men at winter camps on every pasture in which we had stock, yet we were powerless to relieve the drifting cattle. The morning after the great storm, with others, I rode to a south string of fence on a divide, and found thousands of our cattle huddled against it, many frozen to death, partially through and hanging on the wire. We cut the fences in order to allow them to drift on to shelter, but the legs of many of them were so badly frozen that, when they moved, the skin cracked open and their hoofs dropped off. Hundreds of young steers were wandering aimlessly around on hoofless stumps, while their tails cracked and broke like icicles. In angles and nooks of the fence, hundreds had perished against the wire, their bodies forming a scaling ladder, permitting late arrivals to walk over the dead and dying as they passed on with the fury of the storm. I had been a soldier and seen sad sights, but nothing to compare to this; the moaning of the cattle freezing to death would have melted a heart of adamant. All we could do was to cut the fences and let them drift, for to halt was to die; and when the storm abated one could have walked for miles on the bodies of dead animals. No pen could describe the harrowing details of that winter; and for years afterward, or until their remains had a commercial value, a wayfarer could have traced the south-line fences by the bleaching bones that lay in windrows, glistening in the sun like snowdrifts, to remind us of the closing chapter in the history of the Cheyenne and Arapahoe Cattle Company.

CHAPTER XXII
IN CONCLUSION

The subsequent history of the ill-fated Cheyenne and Arapahoe Cattle Company is easily told. Over ninety per cent of the cattle moved under the President's order were missing at the round-up the following spring. What few survived were pitiful objects, minus ears and tails, while their horns, both root and base, were frozen until they drooped down in unnatural positions. Compared to the previous one, the winter of 1885-86, with the exception of the great January blizzard, was the less severe of the two. On the firm's range in the Cherokee Strip our losses were much lighter than during the previous winter, owing to the fact that food was plentiful, there being little if any sleet or snow during the latter year. Had we been permitted to winter in the Cheyenne and Arapahoe country, considering our sheltered range and the cattle fully located, ten per cent would have been a conservative estimate of loss by the elements. As manager of the company I lost five valuable years and over a quarter-million dollars. Time has mollified my grievances until now only the thorn of inhumanity to dumb beasts remains. Contrasted with results, how much more humane it would have been to have ordered out negro troops from Fort Reno and shot the cattle down, or to have cut the fences ourselves, and, while our holdings were drifting back to Texas, trusted to the mercy of the Comanches.

I now understand perfectly why the business world dreads a political change in administration. Whatever may have been the policy of one political party, the reverse becomes the slogan of the other on its promotion to power. For instance, a few years ago, the general government offered a bounty on the home product of sugar, stimulating the industry in Louisiana and also in my adopted State. A change of administration followed, the bounty was removed, and had not the insurance companies promptly canceled their risks on sugar mills, the losses by fire would have been appalling. Politics had never affected my occupation seriously; in fact I profited richly through the extravagance and mismanagement of the Reconstruction régime in Texas, and again met the defeat of my life at the hands of the general government.

With the demand for trail cattle on the decline, coupled with two severe winters, the old firm of Hunter, Anthony & Co. was ripe for dissolution. We had enjoyed the cream of the trade while it lasted, but conditions were changing, making it necessary to limit and restrict our business. This was contrary to our policy, though the spring of 1886 found us on the trail with sixteen herds for the firm and four from my own ranches, one half of which were under contract. A dry summer followed, and thousands of weak cattle were lost on the trail, while ruin and bankruptcy were the portion of a majority of the drovers. We weathered the drouth on the trail, selling our unplaced cattle early, and before the beef-shipping season began, our range in the Outlet, including good will, holding of beeves, saddle horses, and general improvements, was sold to a Kansas City company, and the old firm passed out of existence. Meanwhile I had closed up the affairs of the Cheyenne and Arapahoe Company, returning a small pro rata of the original investment to shareholders, charging my loss to tuition in rounding out my education as a cowman.

The productive capacity of my ranches for years past safely tided me over all financial difficulties. With all outside connections severed, I was then enabled to give my personal attention to ranching in Texas. I was fortunate in having capable ranch foremen, for during my almost continued absence there was a steady growth, together with thorough management of my mixed cattle. The improved herd, now numbering over two thousand, was the pride of my operations in live stock, while my quarter and three-eighths blood steers were in a class by themselves. We were breeding over a thousand half and three-quarters blood bulls annually, and constantly importing the best strains to the head of the improved herd. Results were in evidence, and as long as the trail lasted, my cattle were ready sellers in the upper range markets. For the following few years I drove my own growing of steers, usually contracting them in advance. The days of the trail were numbered; 1889 saw the last herd leave Texas, many of the Northern

States having quarantined against us, and we were afterward compelled to ship by rail in filling contracts on the upper ranges.

When Kansas quarantined against Texas cattle, Dodge was abandoned as a range market. The trail moved West, first to Lakin and finally to Trail City, on the Colorado line. In attempting to pass the former point with four Pan-Handle herds in the spring of 1888, I ran afoul of a quarantine convention. The cattle were under contract in Wyoming, and it was my intention not even to halt the herds, but merely to take on supplies in passing. But a deputation met us south of the river, notifying me that the quarantine convention was in session, and requesting me not to attempt to cross the Arkansas. I explained that my cattle were from above the dead line in Texas, had heretofore gone unmolested wherever they wished, and that it was out of my way to turn west and go up through Colorado. The committee was reasonable, looked over the lead herd, and saw that I was driving graded cattle, and finally invited me in to state my case before the convention. I accompanied the men sent to warn me away, and after considerable parley I was permitted to address the assembly. In a few brief words I stated my destination, where I was from, and the quality of cattle making up my herds, and invited any doubters to accompany me across the river and look the stock over. Fortunately a number of the cattlemen in the convention knew me, and I was excused while the assembly went into executive session to consider my case. Prohibition was in effect at Lakin, and I was compelled to resort to diplomacy in order to cross the Arkansas River with my cattle. It was warm, sultry weather in the valley, and my first idea was to secure a barrel of bottled beer and send it over to the convention, but the town was dry. I ransacked all the drug stores, and the nearest approach to anything that would cheer and stimulate was Hostetter's Bitters. The prohibition laws were being rigidly enforced, but I signed a "death warrant" and ordered a case, which the druggist refused me until I explained that I had four outfits of men with me and that we had contracted malaria while sleeping on the ground. My excuse won, and taking the case of bitters on my shoulder, I bore it away to the nearest livery stable, where I wrote a note, with my compliments, and sent both by a darkey around to the rear door of the convention hall.

On adjournment for dinner, my case looked hopeless. There was a strong sentiment against admitting any cattle from Texas, all former privileges were to be set aside, and the right to quarantine against any section or state was claimed as a prerogative of a free people. The convention was patiently listening to all the oratorical talent present, and my friends held out a slender hope that once the different speakers had relieved their minds they might feel easier towards me, and possibly an exception would be made in my case. During the afternoon session I received frequent reports from the convention, and on the suggestion of a friend I began to skirmish around for a second case of bitters. There were only three drug stores in the town, and as I was ignorant of the law, I naturally went back to the druggist from whom I secured the first case. To my surprise he refused to supply my wants, and haughtily informed me that one application a day was all the law permitted him to sell to any one person. Rebuffed, I turned to another drug store, and was greeted by the proprietor, who formerly ran a saloon in Dodge. He recognized me, calling me by name; and after we had pledged our acquaintance anew behind the prescription case, I was confidentially informed that I could have his whole house and welcome, even if the State of Kansas did object and he had to go to jail. We both regretted that the good old days in the State were gone, but I sent around another case of bitters and a box of cigars, and sat down patiently to await results. With no action taken by the middle of the afternoon, I sent around a third installment of refreshments, and an hour later called in person at the door of the convention. The doorkeeper refused to admit me, but I caught his eye, which was glassy, and received a leery wink, while a bottle of bitters nestled cosily in the open bosom of his shirt. Hopeful that the signs were favorable, I apologized and withdrew, but was shortly afterwards sent for and informed that an exception had been made in my favor, and that I might cross the river at my will and pleasure. In the interim of waiting, in case I was successful, I had studied up a little speech of thanks, and as I arose to express my appreciation, a chorus of interruptions greeted me: "G' on, Reed! G' on, you d — — d old cow-thief! Git out of town or we'll hang you!"

With the trail a thing of the past, I settled down to the peaceful pursuits of a ranchman. The fencing of ranges soon became necessary, the Clear Fork tract being first inclosed, and a few years later owners of pastures adjoining the Double Mountain ranch wished to fence, and I fell in with the prevailing custom. On the latter range I hold title to a little over one million acres, while there are two hundred sections of school land included in my western pasture, on which I pay a nominal rental for its use. All my cattle are now graded, and while no effort is made to mature them, the advent of cotton-seed oil mills and other sources of demand have always afforded me an outlet for my increase. I have branded as many as twenty-five thousand calves in a year, and to this source of income alone I attribute the foundation of my present fortune. As a source of wealth the progeny of the cow in my State has proven a perennial harvest, with little or no effort on the part of the husbandman. Reversing the military rule of moving against the lines of least resistance, experience has taught me to follow those where Nature lends its greatest aid. Mine being strictly a grazing country, by preserving the native grasses and breeding only the best quality of cattle, I have always achieved success. I have brought up my boys to observe these economics of nature, and no plow shall ever mar the surface where my cows have grazed, generation after generation, to the profit and satisfaction of their owner. Where once I was a buyer in carload lots of the best strains of blood in the country, now I am a seller by hundreds and thousands of head, acclimated and native to the soil. One man to his trade and another to his merchandise, and the mistakes of my life justly rebuke me for dallying in paths remote from my legitimate calling.

There is a close relationship between a cowman and his herds. My insight into cattle character exceeds my observation of the human family. Therefore I wish to confess my great love for the cattle of the fields. When hungry or cold, sick or distressed, they express themselves intelligently to my understanding, and when dangers of night and storm and stampede threaten their peace and serenity, they instinctively turn to the refuge of a human voice. When a herd was bedded at night, and wolves howled in the distance, the boys on guard easily calmed the sleeping cattle by simply raising their voices in song. The desire of self-preservation is innate in the animal race, but as long as the human kept watch and ward, the sleeping cattle had no fear of the common enemy. An incident which I cannot explain, but was witness to, occurred during the war. While holding cattle for the Confederate army we received a consignment of beeves from Texas. One of the men who accompanied the herd through called my attention to a steer and vouchsafed the statement that the animal loved music, — that he could be lured out of the herd with singing. To prove his assertion, the man sang what he termed the steer's favorite, and to the surprise of every soldier present, a fine, big mottled beef walked out from among a thousand others and stood entranced over the simple song. In my younger days my voice was considered musical; I could sing the folk-songs of my country better than the average, and when the herdsmen left us, I was pleased to see that my vocal efforts fascinated the late arrival from Texas. Within a week I could call him out with a song, when I fell so deeply in love with the broad-horn Texan that his life was spared through my disloyalty. In the daily issue to the army we kept him back as long as possible; but when our supply was exhausted, and he would have gone to the shambles the following day, I secretly cut him out at night and drove him miles to our rear, that his life might be spared. Within a year he returned with another consignment of beef; comrades who were in the secret would not believe me; but when a quartette of us army herders sang "Rock of Ages," the steer walked out and greeted us with mute appreciation. We enjoyed his company for over a month, I could call him with a song as far as my voice reached, and when death again threatened him, we cut him to the rear and he was never spoken again. Loyal as I was to the South, I would have deserted rather than have seen that steer go to the shambles.

In bringing these reminiscences to a close, I wish to bear testimony in behalf of the men who lent their best existence that success should crown my efforts. Aside from my family, the two pleasantest recollections of my life are my old army comrades and the boys who worked with me on the range and trail. When men have roughed it together, shared their hardships in field and by camp-fire like true comrades, there is an indescribable bond between them that puts to shame any pretense of fraternal brotherhood. Among the hundreds, yes, the thousands, of men who worked for our old firm on the trail, all feel a pride in referring to former associations. I never leave home without meeting men, scattered everywhere, many of them prosperous, who come to me and say, "Of course you don't remember me, but I made a trip over the trail with your cattle, — from San Saba County in '77. Jake de Poyster was foreman. By the way, is your old partner, the little Yankee major, still living?" The acquaintance, thus renewed by chance, was always a good excuse for neglecting any business, and many a happy hour have I spent, living over again with one of my old boys the experiences of the past.

I want to say a parting word in behalf of the men of my occupation. Sterling honesty was their chief virtue. A drover with an established reputation could enter any trail town a month in advance of the arrival of his cattle, and any merchant or banker would extend him credit on his spoken word. When the trail passed and the romance of the West was over, these same men were in demand as directors of banks or custodians of trust funds. They were simple as truth itself, possessing a rugged sense of justice that seemed to guide and direct their lives. On one occasion a few years ago, I unexpectedly dropped down from my Double Mountain ranch to an old cow town on the railroad. It was our regular business point, and I kept a small bank account there for current ranch expenses. As it happened, I needed some money, but on reaching the village found the banks closed, as it was Labor Day. Casually meeting an old cowman who was a director in the bank with which I did business, I pretended to take him to task over my disappointment, and wound up my arraignment by asking, "What kind of a jim-crow bank are you running, anyhow?"

"Well, now, Reed," said he in apology, "I really don't know why the bank should close to-day, but there must be some reason for it. I don't pay much attention to those things, but there's our cashier and bookkeeper, — you know Hank and Bill, — the boys in charge of the bank. Well, they get together every once in a while and close her up for a day. I don't know why they do it, but those old boys have read history, and you can just gamble your last cow that there's good reasons for closing."

The fraternal bond between rangemen recalls the sad end of one of my old trail bosses. The foreman in question was a faithful man, working for the firm during its existence and afterwards in my employ. I would have trusted my fortune to his keeping, my family thought the world of him, and many was the time that he risked his life to protect my interests. When my wife overlooks the shortcomings of a man, it is safe to say there is something redeemable in him, even though the offense is drinking. At idle times and with convivial company, this man would drink to excess, and when he was in his cups a spirit of harmless mischief was rampant in him, alternating with uncontrollable flashes of anger. Though he was usually as innocent as a kitten, it was a deadly insult to refuse drinking with him, and one day he shot a circle of holes around a stranger's feet for declining an invitation. A complaint was lodged against him, and the sheriff, not knowing the man, thoughtlessly sent a Mexican deputy to make the arrest. Even then, had ordinary courtesy been extended, the unfortunate occurrence might have been avoided. But an undue officiousness on the part of the officer angered the old trail boss, who flashed into a rage, defying the deputy, and an exchange of shots ensued. The Mexican was killed at the first fire, and my man mounted his horse unmolested, and returned to the ranch. I was absent at the time, but my wife advised him to go in and surrender to the proper authorities, and he obeyed her like a child.

We all looked upon him as one of the family, and I employed the best of counsel. The circumstances were against him, however, and in spite of an able defense he received a sentence of ten years. No one questioned the justice of the verdict, the law must be upheld, and the poor fellow was taken to the penitentiary to serve out the sentence. My wife and I concealed the facts from the younger children, who were constantly inquiring after his return, especially my younger girls, with whom he was a great favorite. The incident was worse than a funeral; it would not die out, as never a day passed but inquiry was made after the missing man; the children dreamed about him, and awoke from their sleep to ask if he had come and if he had brought them anything. The matter finally affected my wife's nerves, the older boys knew the truth, and the younger children were becoming suspicious of the veracity of their parents. The truth was gradually leaking out, and after he had served a year in prison, I began a movement with the view of securing his pardon. My influence in state politics was always more or less courted, and appealing to my friends, I drew up a petition, which was signed by every prominent politician in that section, asking that executive clemency be extended in behalf of my old foreman. The governor was a good friend of mine, anxious to render me a service, and through his influence we managed to have the sentence so reduced that after serving two years the prisoner was freed and returned to the ranch. He was the same lovable character, tolerated by my wife and fondled by the children, and he refused to leave home for over a year. Ever cautious to remove temptation from him, both my wife and I hoped that the lesson would last him through life, but in an unguarded hour he took to drink, and shot to death his dearest friend.

For the second offense he received a life sentence. My regret over securing his pardon, and the subsequent loss of human life, affected me as no other event has ever done in my career. This man would have died for me or one of mine, and what I thought to be a generous act to a man in prison proved a curse that haunted me for many years. But all is well now between us. I make it a point to visit him at least once a year; we have talked the matter over and have come to the conclusion that the law is just and that he must remain in confinement the remainder of his days. That is now the compact, and, strange to say, both of us derive a sense of security and peace from our covenant such as we had never enjoyed during the year of his liberty. The wardens inform me that he is a model prisoner, perfectly content in his restraint; and I have promised him that on his death, whether it occurs before or after mine, his remains will be brought back to the home ranch and be given a quiet grave in some secluded spot.

For any success that I may have achieved, due acknowledgment must be given my helpmate. I was blessed with a wife such as falls to the lot of few men. Once children were born to our union and a hearthstone established, the family became the magnet of my life. It mattered not where my occupation carried me, or how long my absence from home, the lodestar of a wife and family was a sustaining help. Our first cabin, long since reduced to ashes, lives in my memory as a palace. I was absent at the time of its burning, but my wife's father always enjoyed telling the story on his daughter. The elder Edwards was branding calves some five miles distant from the home ranch, but on sighting the signal smoke of the burning house, he and his outfit turned the cattle loose, mounted their horses, and rode to the rescue at a break-neck pace. When they reached the scene our home was enveloped in flames, and there was no prospect of saving any of its contents. The house stood some distance from the other ranch buildings, and as there was no danger of the fire spreading, there was nothing that could be done and the flames held undisputed sway. The cause of the fire was unknown, my wife being at her father's house at the time; but on discovering the flames, she picked up the baby and ran to the burning cabin, entered it and rescued the little tin trunk that held her girlhood trinkets and a thousand certificates of questionable land scrip. When the men dashed up, my wife was sitting on the tin trunk, surrounded by the children, all crying piteously, fully unconscious of the fact that she had saved the foundation of my present landed holdings. The cabin had cost two weeks' labor to build, its contents were worthless, but I had no record of the numbers of the certificates, and to my wife's presence of mind or intuition in an emergency all credit is given for saving the land scrip. Many daughters have done virtuously, but thou excellest them all. The compiling of these memoirs has been a pleasant task. In this summing-up of my active life, much has been omitted; and then again, there seems to have been a hopeless repetition with the recurring years, for seedtime and harvest come to us all as the seasons roll round. Four of my boys have wandered far afield, forging out for themselves, not content to remain under the restraint of older brothers who have assumed the active management of my ranches. One bad general is still better than two good ones, and there must be a head to a ranch if it is to be made a success. I still keep an eye over things, but the rough, hard work now falls on younger shoulders, and I find myself delegated to amuse and be amused by the third generation of the Anthonys. In spite of my years, I still enjoy a good saddle horse, scarcely a day passing but I ride from ten to twenty miles. There is a range maxim that "the eyes of the boss make a fat horse," and at deliveries of cattle, rounds-ups, and branding, my mere presence makes things move with alacrity. I can still give the boys pointers in handling large bodies of cattle, and the ranch outfits seem to know that we old-time cowmen have little use for the modern picturesque cowboy, unless he is an all-round man and can deliver the goods in any emergency.

With but a few years of my allotted span yet to run, I find myself in the full enjoyment of all my faculties, ready for a romp with my grandchildren or to crack a joke with a friend. My younger girls are proving splendid comrades, always ready for a horseback ride or a trip to the city. It has always been a characteristic of the Anthony family that they could ride a horse before they could walk, and I find the third generation following in the footsteps of their elders. My grandsons were all expert with a rope before they could read, and it is one of the evidences of a merciful providence that their lives have been spared, as it is nearly impossible to keep them out of mischief and danger. To forbid one to ride a certain dangerous horse only serves to heighten his anxiety to master the outlaw, and to banish him from the branding pens means a prompt return with or without an excuse. On one occasion, on the Double Mountain ranch, with the corrals full of heavy cattle, I started down to the pens, but met two of my grandsons coming up the hill, and noticed at a glance that there had been trouble. I stopped the boys and inquired the cause of their tears, when the youngest, a barefooted, chubby little fellow, said to me between his sobs, "Grandpa, you'd — you'd — you'd better keep away from those corrals. Pa's as mad as a hornet, and — and — and he quirted us — yes, he did. If you fool around down there, he'll — he'll — he'll just about wear you out."

Should this transcript of my life ever reach the dignity of publication, the casual reader, in giving me any credit for success, should bear in mind the opportunities of my time. My lot was cast with the palmy days of the golden West, with its indefinable charm, now past and gone and never to return. In voicing this regret, I desire to add that my mistakes are now looked back to as the chastening rod, leading me to an appreciation of higher ideals, and the final testimony that life is well worth the living.

The Wells Brothers: The Young Cattle Kings

CHAPTER I
WAIFS OF THE PLAIN

The first herd of trail cattle to leave Dodge City, Kansas, for the Northwest, during the summer of 1885, was owned by the veteran drover, Don Lovell. Accidents will happen, and when about midway between the former point and Ogalalla, Nebraska, a rather serious mishap befell Quince Forrest, one of the men with the herd. He and the horse wrangler, who were bunkies, were constantly scuffling, reckless to the point of injury, the pulse of healthy manhood beating a constant alarm to rough contest.

The afternoon previous to the accident, a wayfaring man had overtaken the herd, and spent the night with the trail outfit. During the evening, a flock of sand-hill cranes was sighted, when the stranger expressed a wish to secure a specimen of the bird for its splendid plumage. On Forrest's own suggestion, his being a long-range pistol and the covey wary, the two exchanged belts. The visitor followed the flock, stealing within range a number of times, and emptying the six-shooter at every chance. On securing a fine specimen near nightfall, he returned to the herd, elated over his chance shot and beautiful trophy. However, before returning the belt, he had refilled the cylinder with six instead of five cartridges, thus resting the hammer on a loaded shell. In the enthusiasm of the moment, and ignorant of its danger, belt and pistol were returned to their owner.

Dawn found the camp astir. The sun had flooded the plain while the outfit was breakfasting, the herd was grazing forward in pastoral contentment, the horses stood under saddle for the morning's work, when the trail foreman, Paul Priest, languidly remarked: "If everybody's ready, we'll ride. Fill the canteens; it's high time we were in the saddle. Of course, that means the parting tussle between Quince and the wrangler. It would be a shame to deny those lads anything so enjoyable – they remind me so much of mule colts and half-grown dogs. Now, cut in and worry each other a spell, because you'll be separated until noon. Fly at it, or we mount."

The two addressed never cast a glance at each other, but as the men swung into their saddles, the horse wrangler, with the agility of a tiger, caught his bunkie in the act of mounting, dragging him to the ground, when the expected scuffle ensued. The outfit had barely time to turn their horses, to witness the contest, when the two crashed against the wagon wheel and Forrest's pistol was discharged. The men dismounted instantly, the wrangler eased the victim to the ground, and when the outfit gathered around, the former was smothering the burning clothing of his friend and bunkmate. A withdrawn boot, dripping with blood, was the first indication of the havoc wrought, and on stripping it was found that the bullet had ploughed an open furrow down the thigh, penetrating the calf of the leg from knee to ankle, where it was fortunately deflected outward and into the ground.

The deepest of regret was naturally expressed. The jocular remarks of the foreman, the actions of the wrangler, were instantly recalled to the surrounding group, while the negligence which caused the accident was politely suppressed. The stranger, innocently unaware of any mistake on his part, lent a valuable hand in stanching the blood and in washing and binding up the wounds. No bones were injured, and with youth and a buoyant constitution, there was every hope of recovery.

However, some disposition must be made of the wounded man. No one could recall a house or settlement nearer than the Republican River, unless down the Beaver, which was uncertain, when the visitor came to the rescue. He was positive that some two years before, an old soldier had taken a homestead five or six miles above the trail crossing on the Beaver. He was insistent, and the foreman yielded so far as to order the herd grazed forward to the Beaver, which was some ten miles distant in their front. All the blankets in the outfit were accordingly brought into use, in making a comfortable bed in the wagon, and the caravan started, carrying the wounded man with it. Taking the stranger with him, the foreman bore away in the direction of the supposed homestead, having previously sent two men on an opposite angle, in search of any settlement down the creek.

The visitor's knowledge of the surrounding country proved to be correct. About six miles above the trail crossing, the Beaver, fringed with willows, meandered through a narrow valley, in which the homestead was located. The presence of the willows was an indication of old beaver dams, which the settler had improved until the water stood in long, placid pools. In response to their hail, two boys, about fourteen and sixteen years of age, emerged from the dug-out and greeted the horsemen. On inquiry, it proved that their father had died during the previous winter, at a settlement on the Solomon River, and the boys were then confronted with the necessity of leaving the claim to avoid suffering want. It was also learned that their mother had died before their father had taken the homestead, and therefore they were left orphans to fight their own battle.

The boys gave their names as Joel and Dell Wells. Both were bright-eyed and alert, freckled from the sun, ragged and healthy. Joel was the oldest, broad-shouldered for his years, distant by nature, with a shock of auburn hair, while Dell's was red; in height, the younger was the equal of his brother, talkative, and frank in countenance. When made acquainted with the errand of the trail boss, the older boy shook his head, but Dell stepped forward: "Awful sorry," said he, with a sweep of his hand, "but our garden failed, and there won't be a dozen roasting-ears in that field of corn. If hot winds don't kill it, it might make fodder. We expect to pull out next week."

"Have you no cows?" inquired the trail foreman.

"We had two, but the funeral expenses took them, and then pa's pension was stopped. You see – "

"I see," said the trail foreman, dismounting. "Possibly we can help each other. Our wagon is well provisioned. If you'll shelter and nurse this wounded man of mine – "

"We can't winter here," said Joel, stepping forward, "and the sooner we get out and find work the better."

"Oh, I was figuring on paying you wages," countered the trail man, now aware of their necessity, "and I suppose you could use a quarter of beef."

"Oh goodness," whispered Dell to his brother; "think, fresh meat."

"And I'll give each of you twenty-five dollars a month – leave the money with my man or pay you in advance. If you say the word, I'll unload my wagon right here, and grub-stake you for two months. I can get more provision at the Republican River, and in the mean time, something may turn up."

The stranger also dismounted and took part in urging the necessity of accepting the offer. Dell brightened at every suggestion, but his brother was tactful, questioning and combating the men, and looking well to the future. A cold and unfriendly world, coupled with misfortune, had aged the elder boy beyond his years, while the younger one was sympathetic, trustful, and dependent.

"Suppose we are delayed in reaching the Solomon until fall," said Dell to his brother; "that will put us into the settlements in time for corn-shucking. If you get six-bits a day, I'm surely worth fifty cents."

"Suppose there is no corn to shuck," replied Joel. "Suppose this wounded man dies on our hands? What then? Haven't you heard pa tell how soldiers died from slight wounds? – from blood-poisoning? If we have to go, we might as well go at once."

According to his light, the boy reasoned well. But when the wayfaring man had most skillfully retold the story of the Good Samaritan, the older boy relented somewhat, while Dell beamed with enthusiasm at the opportunity of rendering every assistance.

"It isn't because we don't want to help you," protested Joel, but it's because we're so poor and have nothing to offer."

"You have health and willing hands," said the trail boss; "let me do the rest."

"But suppose he doesn't recover as soon as expected," cautiously protested Joel, "where are we to get further provision?"

"Good suggestion," assented the trail foreman. "But here: I'll leave two good horses in your care for the wounded man, and all you need to do is to ride down to the trail, hail any passing herd, and simply tell them you are harboring a crippled lad, one of Don Lovell's boys, and you can levy on them for all they have. It's high time you were getting acquainted with these trail outfits. Shelter this man of mine, and all will come out well in the end. Besides, I'll tell old man Don about you boys, and he might take you home to his ranch with him. He has no boys, and he might take a fancy to you two."

Dell's eyes moistened at the suggestion of a home. The two brothers reëntered the dug-out, and the men led their horses down to the creek for a drink. A span of poor old mules stood inside a wooden corral, a rickety wagon and a few rusty farming implements were scattered about, while over all the homestead was the blight of a merciless summer drouth.

"What a pretty little ranch this would make," said the trail boss to the stranger. "If these boys had a hundred cows, with this water and range, in a few years they would be independent men. No wonder that oldest boy is cautious. Just look around and see the reward of their father's and their own labor. Their very home denies them bread."

"Did you notice the older boy brighten," inquired the visitor, "when you suggested leaving horses in their care? It was the only argument that touched him."

"Then I'll use it," said the trail boss, brightening. "We have several cow horses in our remuda, unfit for saddle, – galled backs and the like, – and if these boys would care for them, I'll make their hungry hearts happy. Care and attention and a month's rest would make the ponies as sound as a dollar. You suggest my giving them each a saddle pony; argue the matter, and try and win me over."

The men retraced their steps, leading their horses, and when scarcely halfway from the creek to the dug-out, Dell ran down to meet them. "If you can spare us a few blankets and a pillow," earnestly said the boy, "we'll take the wounded man. He's liable to be feverish at night, and ought to have a pillow. Joel and I can sleep outside or in the stable."

"Hurrah for the Wells boys!" shouted the trail boss. "Hereafter I'll bet my money, horse and saddle, on a red-headed boy. Blankets? Why, you can have half a dozen, and as to pillows, watch me rob the outfit. I have a rubber one, there are several moss ones, and I have a lurking suspicion that there are a few genuine goose-hair pillows in the outfit, and you may pick and choose. They are all yours for the asking."

The men parleyed around some little time, offering pretexts for entering the shack, the interior of which bespoke its own poverty. When all agreements had been reviewed, the men mounted their horses, promising to fulfill their part of the covenant that afternoon or evening.

Once out of hearing, the stranger remarked: "That oldest boy is all right; it was their poverty that caused him to hesitate; he tried to shield their want. We men don't always understand boys. Hereafter, in dealing with Joel, you must use some diplomacy. The death of his parents has developed a responsibility in the older boy which the younger one doesn't feel. That's about all the difference in the two lads. You must deal gently with Joel, and never offend him or expose his needs."

"Trust me," replied the foreman, "and I'll coach Quince – that's the name of the wounded man. Within an hour, he'll be right at home with those boys. If nothing serious happens to his wound, within a week he'll have those youngsters walking on clouds."

The two men rode out of the valley, when they caught sight of a dust cloud, indicating the locality of the trailing herd, then hidden behind the last divide before reaching Beaver Creek. On every hand the undulating plain rolled away to low horizons, and the men rode forward at a leisurely pace.

"I've been thinking of those boys," suddenly said the trail foreman, arousing himself from a reverie. "They're to be pitied. This government ought to be indicted for running a gambling game, robbing children, orphan children of a soldier, at that. There's a fair sample of the skin game the government's running – bets you one hundred and sixty acres against fourteen dollars you can't hold down a homestead for five years. And big as the odds look, in nine cases out of ten, in this country, the government wins. It ought to be convicted on general principles. Men are not to be pitied, but it's a crime against women and children."

"Oh, you cowmen always rail at the settler," retorted the stranger; "you would kick if you were being hung. There's good in everything. A few years of youthful poverty, once they reach manhood, isn't going to hurt those boys. The school of experience has its advantages."

"If it's convenient, let's keep an eye on those boys the next few years," said the trail boss, catching sight of his remuda. "Now, there's the wagon. Suppose you ride down to the Beaver and select a good camp, well above the trail crossing, and I'll meet the commissary and herd. We'll have to lay over this afternoon, which will admit of watering the herd twice to-day. Try and find some shade."

The men separated, riding away on different angles. The foreman hailed his wagon, found the victim resting comfortably, and reported securing a haven for the wounded man. Instructing his cook to watch for a signal, at the hands of the stranger, indicating a camp on the creek, he turned and awaited the arrival of the lead cattle of the trailing column. Issuing orders to cover the situation, he called off half the men, first veering the herd to the nearest water, and rode to overtake his wagon and saddle horses.

Beaver Creek was barely running water, with an occasional long pool. A hedge of willows was interwoven, Indian fashion, from which a tarpaulin was stretched to the wagon bows, forming a sheltered canopy. Amid a fire of questions, the wounded man was lifted from the wagon.

"Are you sure there isn't a woman at this nester's shack," said he appealingly to the bearers of the blanket stretcher. "If there is, I ain't going. Paul, stand squarely in front of me, where I can see your eyes. After what I've been handed lately, it makes me peevish. I want to feel the walnut juice in your hand clasp. Now, tell it all over once more."

The stranger was artfully excused, to select a beef, after which the foreman sat down beside his man, giving him all the details and making valuable suggestions. He urged courteous treatment of their guest while he remained; that there was nothing to be gained, after the accident, by insult to a visitor, and concluded by praising the boys and bespeaking their protection.

The wounded man was Southern by birth and instinct, and knew that the hospitality of ranch and road and camp was one and the same. "Very well," said he, "but in this instance, remember it's my calf that's gored. Serves me right, though, kittening up to every stranger that comes along. I must be getting tired of you slatterly cow hands." He hesitated a moment. "The one thing I like," he continued, "about this nester layout is those red-headed boys. And these two are just about petting age. I can almost see them eating sugar out of my hand."

After dinner, and now that a haven was secured, the question of medical aid was considered. The couriers down the Beaver had returned and reported no habitation in that direction. Fortunately the destination of the stranger was a settlement on the Republican River, and he volunteered to ride through that afternoon and night and secure a surgeon. Frontier physicians were used to hundred-mile calls. The owner of the herd, had he been present, would have insisted on medical attention, the wounded man reluctantly consented, and the stranger, carrying a hastily written letter to Mr. Lovell, took his departure.

Early evening found the patient installed, not in the dug-out, but in a roomy tent. A quarter of beef hung on a willow, the one-room shack was bountifully provisioned, while the foreman remained to await the arrival of a physician. The day had brought forth wonders to Joel and Dell – from the dark hour of want to the dawn of plenty, while the future was a sealed book. In addition to the promised horses, Forrest's saddle hung in the sod stable, while two extra ponies aroused the wonder of the questioning boys.

"I just brought these two along," explained the foreman, "as their backs were galled during a recent rainy spell. You can see they are unfit for saddle, but with a little attention can be cured – I'll show you how. You have an abundance of water, and after I leave, wash their backs, morning and evening, and they'll be well in a month. Since you are running a trail hospital, you want to cater to man and beast. Of course, if you boys nurse this man through to health and strength, I'll make an appeal to Mr. Lovell to give you these ponies. They'll come in handy, in case you return to the Solomon, or start a little cattle ranch here."

The sun set in benediction on the little homestead. The transformation seemed magical. Even the blight of summer drouth was toned and tempered by the shadows of evening. The lesson of the day had filled empty hearts with happiness, and when darkness fell, the boys threw off all former reserve, and the bond of host and guest was firmly established. Forrest, even, cemented the tie, by dividing any needful attention between the boys.

"Do you know," said he to the foreman indifferently, in the presence of the lads, "that I was thinking of calling the oldest one Doc and the youngest one Nurse, but now I'm going to call them just plain Joel and Dell, and they can call me Mr. Quince. Honor bright, I never met a boy who can pour water on a wound, that seems to go to the right spot, like Dell Wells. One day with another, give me a red-headed boy."

CHAPTER II
THE HOSPITAL ON THE BEAVER

The patient passed a feverish night. Priest remained on watch in the tent, but on several occasions aroused the boys, as recourse to pouring water was necessary to relieve the pain. The limb had reached a swollen condition by morning, and considerable anxiety was felt over the uncertainty of a physician arriving. If summoned the previous evening, it was possible that one might arrive by noon, otherwise there was no hope before evening or during the night.

"Better post a guide on the trail," suggested Joel. "If a doctor comes from the Republican, we can pilot him across the prairie and save an hour's time. There's a dim wagon trail runs from here to the first divide, north of the trail crossing on Beaver. Pa used it when he went to Culbertson to draw his pension. It would save the doctor a six or seven mile drive."

"Now, that suggestion is to the point," cheerfully assented the trail foreman. "The herd will noon on the first divide, and we can post the boys of the cut-off. They'll surely meet the doctor this afternoon or evening. Corral the horses, and I'll shorten up the stirrup straps on Forrest's saddle. Who will we send?"

"I'll go," said Dell, jumping at the opportunity. He had admired the horses and heavy Texas saddles the evening previous, and now that a chance presented itself, his eyes danced at the prospect. "Why, I can follow a dim wagon track," he added. "Joel and I used to go halfway to the divide, to meet pa when he bought us new boots."

"I'll see who can best be spared," replied Priest. "Your patient seems to think that no one can pour water like you. Besides, there will be plenty of riding to do, and you'll get your share."

The foreman delayed shortening the stirrup straps until after the horse stood saddled, when he adjusted the lacings as an object lesson to the boys. Both rode the same length of stirrup, mounting the horse to be fitted, and when reduced to the proper length, Dell was allowed to ride past the tent for inspection.

"There's the making of a born cowman," said Forrest, as Dell halted before the open tent. "It's an absolute mistake to think that that boy was ever intended for a farmer. Notice his saddle poise, will you, Paul? Has a pretty foot, too, even if it is slightly sun-burned. We must get him some boots. With that red hair, he never ought to ride any other horse than a black stallion."

When the question arose as to which of the boys was to be sent to intercept the moving herd and await the doctor, Forrest decided the matter. "I'll have to send Joel," said he, "because I simply can't spare Dell. The swelling has benumbed this old leg of mine, and we'll have to give it an occasional rubbing to keep the circulation up. There's where Dell has the true touch; actually he reminds me of my mother. She could tie a rag around a sore toe, in a way that would make a boy forget all his trouble. Hold Joel a minute."

The sound of a moving horse had caught the ear of the wounded man, and when the older boy dismounted at the tent opening, he continued: "Now, Joel, don't let that cow outfit get funny with you. Show them the brand on that horse you're riding, and give them distinctly to understand, even if you are barefooted, that you are one of Don Lovell's men. Of course you don't know him, but with that old man, it's love me, love my dog. Get your dinner with the outfit, and watch for a dust cloud in the south. There's liable to be another herd along any day, and we'll need a cow."

Forrest was nearly forty, while Priest was fully fifty years of age; neither had ever had children of his own, and their hearts went out in manly fullness to these waifs of the plain. On the other hand, a day had brought forth promise and fulfillment, from strangers, to the boys, until the latter's confidence knew no bounds. At random, the men virtually spoke of the cattle on a thousand hills, until the boys fully believed that by merely waving a wand, the bells would tinkle and a cow walk forth. Where two horses were promised, four had appeared. Where their little store of provision was as good as exhausted, it had been multiplied many fold. Where their living quarters were threatened with intrusion, a tent, with fly, was added; all of which, as if by magic, had risen out of a dip in the plain.

There was no danger, at the hands of the trail men, of any discourtesy to Joel, but to relieve any timidity, the foreman saddled his horse and accompanied the boy a mile or more, fully reviewing the details of his errand. Left behind, and while rubbing the wounded limb, Dell regaled his patient with a scrap of family history. "Pa never let us boys go near the trail," said he. "It seemed like he was afraid of you Texas men; afraid your cattle would trample down our fields and drink up all our water. The herds were so big."

"Suppose the cattle would drink the water," replied Forrest, "the owner would pay for it, which would be better than letting it go to waste. One day's hot winds would absorb more water than the biggest herd of cattle could drink. This ain't no farming country."

"That's so," admitted Dell; "we only had one mess of peas this season, and our potatoes aren't bigger than marbles. Now, let me rub your knee, there where the bullet skipped, between the bandages."

The rubbing over, Forrest pressed home the idea of abandoning farming for cattle ranching. "What your father ought to have done," said he, "was to have made friends with the Texas drovers; given them the water, with or without price, and bought any cripples or sore-footed cattle. Nearly every herd abandons more or less cattle on these long drives, and he could have bought them for a song and sung it himself. The buffalo grass on the divides and among these sand hills is the finest winter grazing in the country. This water that you are wasting would have yearly earned you one hundred head of cripples. A month's rest on this creek and they would kick up their heels and play like calves. After one winter on this range, they would get as fat as plover. Your father missed his chance by not making friends with the Texas trail men."

"Do you think so?" earnestly said Dell.

"I know it," emphatically asserted the wounded man. "Hereafter, you and Joel want to be friendly with these drovers and their men. Cast your bread upon the waters."

"Mother used to read that to us," frankly admitted Dell. There was a marked silence, only broken by a clatter of hoofs, and the trail boss cantered up to the tent.

"That wagon track," said he, dismounting, "is little more than a dim trail. Sorry I didn't think about it sooner, but we ought to have built a smudge fire where this road intersects the cattle trail. In case the doctor doesn't reach there by noon, I sent orders to fly a flag at the junction, and Joel to return home. But if the doctor doesn't reach there until after darkness, he'll never see the flag, and couldn't follow the trail if he did. We'll have to send Joel back."

"It's my turn," said Dell. "I know how to build a smudge fire; build it in a circle, out of cattle chips, in the middle of the road."

"You're a willing boy," said Priest, handing the bridle reins to Dell, "but we'll wait until Joel returns. You may water my horse and turn him in the corral."

The day wore on, and near the middle of the afternoon Joel came riding in. He had waited fully an hour after the departure of the herd, a flag had been left unfurled at the junction, and all other instructions delivered. Both Forrest and Priest knew the distance to the ford on the Republican, and could figure to an hour, by different saddle gaits, the necessary time to cover the distance, even to Culbertson. Still there was a measure of uncertainty: the messenger might have lost his way; there might not have been any physician within call; accidents might have happened to horse or rider, – and one hour wore away, followed by another.

Against his will, Dell was held under restraint until six o'clock. "It's my intention to follow him within an hour," said the foreman, as the boy rounded a bluff and disappeared. "He can build the fire as well as any one, and we'll return before midnight. That'll give the doctor the last minute and the benefit of every doubt."

The foreman's mount stood saddled, and twilight had settled over the valley, when the occupants of the tent were startled by the neigh of a horse. "That's Rowdy," said Forrest; "he always nickers when he sights a wagon or camp. Dell's come."

Joel sprang to the open front. "It's Dell, and there's a buckboard following," he whispered. A moment later the vehicle rattled up, led by the irrepressible Dell, as if in charge of a battery of artillery. "This is the place, Doctor," said he, as if dismissing a troop from cavalry drill.

The physician proved to be a typical frontier doctor. He had left Culbertson that morning, was delayed in securing a relay team at the ford on the Republican, and still had traveled ninety miles since sunrise. "If it wasn't for six-shooters in this country," said he, as he entered the tent, "we doctors would have little to do. Your men with the herd told me how the accident happened." Then to Forrest, "Son, think it'll ever happen again?"

"Yes, unless you can cure a fool from lending his pistol," replied Forrest.

"Certainly. I've noticed that similarity in all gunshot wounds: they usually offer good excuses. It's healing in its nature," commented the doctor, as he began removing the bandages. As the examination proceeded, there was a running comment maintained, bordering on the humorous.

"If there's no extra charge," said Forrest, "I wish you would allow the boys to see the wounds. You might also deliver a short lecture on the danger of carrying the hammer of a pistol on a loaded cartridge. The boys are young and may take the lesson seriously, but you're wasting good breath on me. Call the boys – I'm an old dog."

"Gunshot wounds are the only crop in this country," continued the doctor, ignoring the request, "not affected by the drouth. There's an occasional outbreak of Texas fever among cattle, but that's not in my department. Well, that bullet surely was hungry for muscle, but fortunately it had a distaste for bone. This is just a simple case of treatment and avoiding complications. Six weeks to two months and you can buckle on your six-shooter again. Hereafter, better wear it on the other side, and if another accident occurs, it'll give you a hitch in each leg and level you up."

"But there may be no fool loafing around to borrow it," protested Forrest.

"Never fear, son; the fool's eternal," replied the doctor, with a quiet wink at the others.

The presence and unconcern of the old physician dispelled all uneasiness, and the night passed without anxiety, save between the boys. Forrest's lecture to Dell during the day, of the importance of making friends with the drovers, the value of the water, the purchase of disabled cattle, was all carefully reviewed after the boys were snugly in bed. "Were you afraid of the men with the herd to-day? – afraid of the cowboys?" inquired Dell, when the former subject was exhausted.

"Why, no," replied Joel rather scornfully, from the security of his bunk; "who would be afraid? They are just like any other folks."

Dell was skeptical. "Not like the pictures of cowboys? – not shooting and galloping their horses?"

"Why, you silly boy," said Joel, with contempt; "there wasn't a shot fired, their horses were never out of a walk, never wet a hair, and they changed to fresh ones at noon. The only difference I could see, they wore their hats at dinner. And they were surely cowboys, because they had over three thousand big beeves, and had come all the way from Texas."

"I wish I could have gone," was Dell's only comment.

"Oh, it was a great sight," continued the privileged one. "The column of cattle was a mile long, the trail twice as wide as a city street, and the cattle seemed to walk in loose marching order, of their own accord. Not a man carried a whip; no one even shouted; no one as much as looked at the cattle; the men rode away off yonder. The herd seemed so easy to handle."

"And how many men did it take?" insisted Dell.

"Only eleven with the herd. And they had such queer names for their places. Those in the lead were *point* men, those in the middle were *swing* men, and the one who brought up the rear was the *drag* man. Then there was the cook, who drove the wagon, and the wrangler, who took care of the horses – over one hundred and forty head. They call the band of saddle horses the remuda; one of the men told me it was Spanish for relay – a relay of horses."

"I'm going the next time," said Dell. "Mr. Quince said he would buy us a cow from the next herd that passed."

"These were all big beeves to-day, going to some fort on the Yellowstone River. And they had such wide, sweeping horns! And the smartest cattle! An hour before noon one of the point men gave a shrill whistle, and the whole column of beeves turned aside and began feeding. The

525

men called it 'throwing the herd off the trail to graze.' It was just like saying *halt!* to soldiers – like we saw at that reunion in Ohio."

"And you weren't afraid?" timidly queried the younger brother.

"No one else was afraid, and why should I be? I was on horseback. Stop asking foolish questions and go to sleep," concluded Joel, with pitying finality, and turned to the wall.

"But suppose those big Texas beeves had stampeded, then what?" There was challenge in Dell's voice, but the brother vouchsafed no answer. A seniority of years had given one a twelve hours' insight over the other, in range cattle, and there was no common ground between sleepy bedfellows to justify further converse. "I piloted in the doctor, anyhow," said Dell defensively. No reply rewarded his assertion.

Morning brought little or no change in the condition of the wounds. The doctor was anxious to return, but Priest urged otherwise. "Let's call it Sunday," said he, "and not work to-day. Besides, if I overtake the herd, I'll have to make a hand. Wait until to-morrow, and we'll bear each other company. If another herd shows up on the trail to-day, it may have a cow. We must make these boys comfortable."

The doctor consented to stay over, and amused himself by quarreling with his patient. During the forenoon Priest and Joel rode out to the nearest high ground, from which a grove was seen on the upper Beaver. "That's what we call Hackberry Grove," said Joel, "and where we get our wood. The creek makes a big bend, and all the bottom land has grown up with timber, some as big as a man's body. It doesn't look very far away, but it takes all day to go and come, hauling wood. There's big springs just above, and the water never fails. That's what makes the trees so thrifty."

"Too bad your father didn't start a little ranch here," said Priest, surveying the scene. "It's a natural cattle range. There are the sand hills to the south; good winter shelter and a carpet of grass."

"We were too poor," frankly admitted the boy. "Every fall we had to go to the Solomon River to hunt work. With pa's pension, and what we could earn, we held down the homestead. Last fall we proved up; pa's service in the army counted on the residence required. It doesn't matter now if we do leave it. All Dell and I have to do is to keep the taxes paid."

"You would be doing wrong to leave this range," said the trail boss in fatherly tones. "There's a fortune in this grass, if you boys only had the cattle to eat it. Try and get a hundred cows on shares, or buy young steers on a credit."

"Why, we have no money, and no one would credit boys," ruefully replied Joel.

"You have something better than either credit or money," frankly replied the cowman; "you control this range. Make that the basis of your beginning. All these cattle that are coming over the trail are hunting a market or a new owner. Convince any man that you have the range, and the cattle will be forthcoming to occupy it."

"But we only hold a quarter-section of land," replied the boy in his bewilderment.

"Good. Take possession of the range, occupy it with cattle, and every one will respect your prior right," argued the practical man. "Range is being rapidly taken up in this western country. Here's your chance. Water and grass, world without end."

Joel was evidently embarrassed. Not that he questioned the older man's advice, but the means to the end seemed totally lacking. The grind of poverty had been his constant companion, until he scarcely looked forward to any reprieve, and the castles being built and the domain surveyed at the present moment were vague and misty. "I don't doubt your advice," admitted the boy. "A man could do it, you could, but Dell and I had better return to the settlements. Mr. Quince will surely be well by fall."

"Will you make me a promise?" frankly asked the cowman.

"I will," eagerly replied the boy.

"After I leave to-morrow morning, then, tell Forrest that you are thinking of claiming Beaver Creek as a cattle range. Ask him if he knows any way to secure a few cows and yearlings with which to stock it. In the mean time, think it over yourself. Will you do that?"

"Y-e-s, I – I will," admitted Joel, as if trapped into the promise.

"Of course you will. And ask him as if life and death depended on securing the cattle. Forrest has been a trail foreman and knows all the drovers and their men. He's liable to remain with you until the season ends. Now, don't fail to ask him."

"Oh, I'll ask him," said Joel more cheerfully. "Did you say that control of a range was a basis on which to start a ranch, and that it had a value?"

"That's it. Now you're catching the idea. Lay hold and never lose sight of the fact that a range that will graze five to ten thousand cattle, the year round, is as good as money in the bank."

Joel's faculties were grappling with the idea. The two turned their horses homeward, casting an occasional glance to the southward, but were unrewarded by the sight of a dust cloud, the signal of an approaching herd. The trail foreman was satisfied that he had instilled interest and inquiry into the boy's mind, which, if carefully nurtured, might result in independence. They had ridden several miles, discussing different matters, and when within sight of the homestead, Joel reined in his horse. "Would you mind repeating," said he, "what you said awhile ago, about control of a range by prior rights?"

The trail foreman freely responded to the awakened interest. "On the range," said he, "custom becomes law. No doubt but it dates back to the first flocks and herds. Its foundations rest on a sense of equity and justice which has always existed among pastoral people. In America it dates from the first invasion of the Spanish. Among us Texans, a man's range is respected equally with his home. By merely laying claim to the grazing privileges of public domain, and occupying it with flocks or herds, the consent of custom gives a man possession. It is an asset that is bought and sold, and is only lost when abandoned. In all human migrations, this custom has followed flocks and herds. Title to land is the only condition to which the custom yields."

"And we could claim this valley, by simply occupying it with cattle, and hold possession of its grazing privileges?" repeated the boy.

"By virtue of a custom, older than any law, you surely can. It's primal range to-day. This is your epoch. The buffalo preceded you, the settler, seeking a home, will follow you. The opportunity is yours. Go in and win."

"But how can we get a start of cattle?" pondered Joel.

"Well, after I leave, you're going to ask Forrest that question. That old boy knows all the ins and outs, and he may surprise you. There's an old maxim about where there's a will there's a way. Now if you have the will, I've a strong suspicion that your Mr. Quince will find the way. Try him, anyhow."

"Oh, I will," assured Joel; "the first thing in the morning."

The leaven of interest had found lodgment. A pleasant evening was spent in the tent. Before excusing the lads for the night, Priest said to the doctor: "This is a fine cattle range, and I'd like your opinion about these boys starting a little ranch on the Beaver."

"Well," said the old physician, looking from Joel to Dell, "there are too many lawyers and doctors already. The farmers raise nothing out here, and about the only prosperous people I meet are you cowmen. You ride good horses, have means to secure your needs, and your general health is actually discouraging to my profession. Yes, I think I'll have to approve of the suggestion. A life in the open, an evening by a camp-fire, a saddle for a pillow – well, I wish I had my life to live over. It wouldn't surprise me to hear of Wells Brothers making a big success as ranchmen. They have health and youth, and there's nothing like beginning at the bottom of the ladder. In fact, the proposition has my hearty approval. Fight it out, boys; start a ranch."

"Come on, Dell," said Joel, leading the way; "these gentlemen want to make an early start. You'll have to bring in the horses while I get breakfast. Come on."

CHAPTER III
THE BOTTOM RUNG

An early start was delayed. Joel had figured without his guest, as the Texan stands in a class by himself. The peace and serenity of pastoral life affects its people, influencing their normal natures into calm and tranquil ways. Hence, instead of the expected start at sunrise, after breakfast the trail foreman languidly sauntered out to the corral, followed by the boys.

The old physician, even, grew impatient. "What on earth do you think is detaining that man?" he inquired of Forrest. "Here the sun is nearly an hour high, and not a wheel turning. And I can see him from the tent opening, sitting on a log, flicking the ground with his quirt and chatting with those boys. What do you suppose they are talking about?"

"Well, now, that's a hard question," answered Forrest. "I'll chance the subject is of no importance. Just a little social powwow with the boys, most likely. Sit down, Doctor, and take life easy – the cows will calve in the spring."

Patience had almost ceased to be a virtue when the trail boss put in an appearance at the tent. "You are in no particular hurry, are you, Doctor?" he inquired, with a friendly smile.

"Oh, no," said the physician, with delightful irony; "I was just thinking of having the team unhooked, and lay over another day. Still, I am some little distance from home, and have a family that likes to see me occasionally."

The buckboard rattled away. "Come in the tent," called Forrest to the boys. "If old Paul sees you standing out there, he's liable to think of something and come back. Honestly, when it comes to killing time, that old boy is the bell steer."

Only three were now left at the homestead. The first concern was to intercept the next passing herd. Forrest had a wide acquaintance among trail foremen, had met many of them at Dodge only ten days before, while passing that supply point, and it was a matter of waiting until a herd should appear.

There was little delay. Joel was sent at ten o'clock to the nearest swell, and Dell an hour later. The magic was working overtime; the dust cloud was there! In his haste to deliver the message, the sentinel's horse tore past the tent and was only halted at the corral. "It's there!" he shouted, returning, peering through the tent-flaps. "They're coming; another herd's coming. It's in the dip behind the first divide. Shall I go? I saw it first."

"Dismount and rest your saddle," said Forrest. "Come in and let's make a little medicine. If this herd has one, here's where we get a cow. Come in and we'll plot against the Texans."

With great misgiving, Dell dismounted. As he entered the tent, Forrest continued: "Sit on the corner of my bunk, and we'll talk the situation over. Oh, I'm going to send you, never fear. Now, the trouble is, we don't know whose herd this may be, and you must play innocent and foxy. If the herd is behind the first divide, it'll water in the Beaver about four o'clock. Now, ride down the creek and keep your eagle eye open for a lone horseman, either at the crossing or on the trail. That's the foreman, and that's the man we want to see. He may be ten miles in the lead of his herd, and you want to ride straight to him. Give him all the information you can regarding the water, and inquire if this is one of Lovell's herds. That will put you on a chatting basis, and then lead up to your errand. Tell him that you are running a trail hospital, and that you have a wounded man named Quince Forrest at your camp, and ask the foreman to come up and see him. Once you get him here, your work is over, except going back after the cow."

Dell was impatient to be off, and started for the opening. "Hold on," commanded Forrest, "or I'll put a rope on you. Now, ride slowly, let your horse set his own pace, and don't come back without your man. Make out that I'm badly wounded, and that you feel uneasy that blood poisoning may set in."

The messenger lost no time in getting away. Once out of sight of the tent, Dell could not resist the temptation to gallop his mount over level places. Carrying the weight of a boy was nothing to the horse, and before half an hour had passed, the ford and trail came in view of the anxious courier. Halting in order to survey the horizon, the haze and heat-waves of summer so obstructed his view that every object looked blurred and indistinct. Even the dust cloud was missing; and pushing on a mile farther, he reined in again. Now and then in the upper sky, an intervening cloud threw a shadow over the plain, revealing objects more distinctly. For a moment one rested over the trail crossing, and like prophecy fulfilled, there was the lone horseman at the ford!

In the waste places it is a pleasure to unexpectedly meet a fellow being. Before being observed, Dell rode within hailing distance, greeting, and man and boy were soon in friendly converse. There was water sufficient for all needs, the herd required no pilot, the summons found a ready response, and the two were soon riding up the Beaver in a jog trot.

The gait admitted of free conversation, and the new foreman soon had Dell on the defensive. "I always hate to follow a Lovell outfit," said the stranger regretfully; "they're always in trouble. Old man Don's a nice enough man, but he sure works sorry outfits on the trail. I've been expecting to hear something like this. If it isn't rebranding their saddle stock with nigger brands, it's sure to be something worse. And now that flat-headed Quince Forrest plows a fire-guard down his own leg with a six-shooter! Well, wouldn't that sour sweet milk!"

"Oh, it wasn't his fault," protested Dell; "he only loaned his pistol, and it was returned with the hammer on a cartridge."

"Of course," disgustedly assented the trail boss; "with me it's an old story. Hadn't no more sabe than to lend his gun to some prowling tenderfoot. More than likely he urged its loan on this short-horn. Yes, I know Colonel Forrest; I've known him to bet his saddle and ride bareback as the result. It shows his cow-sense. Rather shallow-brained to be allowed so far from home."

"Well," contended poor Dell, "they surely were no friends. At least Mr. Quince don't speak very highly of that man."

"That's his hindsight," said the trail foreman. "If the truth ever comes out, you'll notice his foresight was different. Colonel Quince is famous, after the horse is stolen, for locking the stable door. That other time he offered to take an oath, on a stack of Bibles, never to bet his saddle again. The trouble is the game never repeats; the play never comes up twice alike. If that old boy's gray matter ever comes to full bloom, long before his allotted time, he'll wither away."

Dell was discouraged. He realized that his defense of his friend was weak. This second foreman seemed so different from either Priest or Forrest. He spoke with such deep regret of the seeming faults of others that the boy never doubted his sincerity. He even questioned Dell with such an innocent countenance that the lad withered before his glance, and became disheartened at the success of the errand. Forced to the defense continually, on several occasions Dell nearly betrayed the object of bringing the new man to the homestead, but in each instance was saved by some fortunate turn in the conversation. Never was sight more welcome than the tent, glistening in the sun, and never was relief from duty more welcome to a courier. The only crumb of comfort left to the boy who had ridden forth so boldly was that he had not betrayed the object of his mission and had brought the range men together. Otherwise his banner was trailing in the dust.

The two rode direct to the tent. During the middle of the day, in order to provide free ventilation, the walls were tucked up, and the flaps, rear and front, thrown wide open. Stretched on his bunk, Forrest watched the opening, and when darkened by the new arrival, the wounded man's greeting was most cordial. "Well, if it isn't old Nat Straw," said he, extending his hand. "Here, I've been running over in my mind the different trail bosses who generally go north of the Platte River, but you escaped my memory. It must have gotten into my mind, somehow, that you had married and gone back to chopping cotton. Still driving for Uncle Jess Ellison, I reckon?"

"Yes, still clerking for the same drover," admitted Straw, glancing at the wounded limb. "What's this I hear about you laying off, and trying to eat some poor nester out of house and home? You must be getting doty."

"Enjoy yourself, Nat. The laugh's on me. I'm getting discouraged that I'll ever have common horse sense. Isn't it a shame to be a fool all your life!"

Straw glanced from the bunk to Dell. "I was just telling the boy, as we rode up the creek, that you needed a whole heap of fixing in your upper loft. The poor boy tried his best to defend you, but it was easy to see that he hadn't known you long."

"And of course you strung him for all he could carry," said Forrest. "Here, Dell. You were in such a hurry to get away that I overlooked warning you against these trail varmints. Right now, I can see old Nat leading you in under a wet blanket, and your colors dragging. Don't believe a word he told you, and don't even give him a pleasant look while he stays here."

The discouraged boy brightened, and Joel and Dell were excused, to water and picket the horses. "You ought to be ashamed of yourself," resumed Forrest, "brow-beating that boy. Considering my hard luck, I've fallen into angels' hands. These boys are darling fellows. Now before you leave, square yourself with that youngest one."

"A little jollying while he's young won't hurt him," replied Straw. "It's not a bad idea to learn early to believe nothing that you hear and only half of what you see. If you had been taken snipe hunting oftener when you were young, it wouldn't hurt you any now. There are just about so many knocks coming to each of us, and we've got to take them along with the croup, chicken-pox, measles, and mumps."

During the absence of the boys, Forrest informed Straw of the sad condition which confronted the lads, when accident and necessity threw him into their hands. He also repeated Priest's opinion of the valuable range, unoccupied above on the Beaver, and urged his assistance in securing some cattle with which to stock and claim it for the boys.

"There's plenty of flotsam on the trail," said he, "strays and sore-footed cattle, to occupy this valley and give these boys a start in life. I never even got thanked for a stray, and I've turned hundreds of them loose on these upper ranges, refused on the delivery of a herd. Somebody gets them, and I want these boys of mine to get a few hundred head during this summer. Here's the place to drop your cripples and stray cows. From what Paul says, there's range above here for thousands of cattle, and that's the foundation of a ranch. Without a hoof on it, it has a value in proportion to its carrying capacity, and Priest and I want these boys to secure it. They've treated me white, and I'm going to make a fight for them."

The appeal was not in vain. "Why not," commented Straw. "Let me in and we'll make it three-handed. My herd is contracted again this year to the same cattle company on the Crazy Woman, in Wyoming, as last season, and I want to fool them this trip. They got gay on my hands last summer, held me down to the straight road brand at delivery, and I'll see to it that there are no strays in my herd this year. I went hungry for fresh beef, and gave those sharks over forty good strays. They knew I'd have to leave them behind me. Watch me do it again."

"About how many have you now, and how do they run?"

"They're a hit-and-miss lot, like strays always are. Run from a good cow down to yearlings. There ought to be about twenty-five head, and I'll cut you out five or six cripples. They could never make it through, nohow."

"Any calves among the strays?"

"Two or three."

"Good enough. Give each of the boys a cow and calf, and the others to me. We'll let on that I've bought them."

That no time might be lost in friendly chat, a late dinner was eaten in the tent. Straw would have to meet his herd at the trail crossing that afternoon, which would afford an opportunity to cut out all strays and cripples. One of the boys would return with him, for the expected cow, and when volunteers were called for, Dell hesitated in offering his services. "I'll excuse you," said Straw to Joel, who had jumped at the chance. "I'm a little weak on this red-headed boy, and when a cow hand picks on me for his side partner, the choice holds until further orders. Bring in the horses off picket, son, and we'll be riding."

The latter order was addressed to Dell. No sooner had the boy departed than Straw turned to Joel. "I've fallen head over ears in love with the idea of this trail hospital. Just where it ought to be; just about midway between Dodge and Ogalalla. Of course I'm hog wild to get in on it.

I might get a man hurt any day, might get sick myself, and I want to be a stockholder in this hospital of yours. What's your favorite color in cows?"

Joel's caution caused him to hesitate. "If you have one, send me a milk-white cow *with a black face*" instantly said Forrest. "White cows are rich in cream, and I'm getting peevish, having to drink black coffee."

"A white cow for you," said Straw, nodding to Forrest, "and what color for you?" But Joel, although half convinced, made no answer.

"Send him a red one," authorized Forrest; "red steers bring a dollar a head more than mongrel colors."

"A red cow and calf for Joel, a white one for milk, and Dell can pick his own," said Straw, murmuring a memorandum. "Now, that little passel of cripples, and odds and ends," again nodding to Forrest, "that I'm sawing off on you, I'll bring them up with the cows. Yes, I'm coming back and stay all night."

Joel lost all doubts on the moment. The trail boss was coming back, was going to bring each one a cow. There was no question but that this stranger had the cattle in his possession; surely he would not trifle with his own people, with an unfortunate, wounded man. All this seemed so in keeping with the partial outline of Priest, the old gray-haired foreman, that the boy's caution gave place to firm belief. If generous princes ever walked the earth, it was just possible that liberal ones in the rough were still riding it in disguise.

Joel hastened to his brother with the news. "It's all right," said he, throwing the saddle on Straw's horse. "You go right along with this strange foreman. He gave Mr. Quince a milk cow, a white one, and you're to pick one for yourself. If I were going in your place, I'd pick a red one; red cattle are worth a dollar a head more than any other color."

There was something in Joel's voice that told Dell that his brother had not been forgotten. "And you? – don't you?" stammered the younger boy.

"Mr. Quince picked out a cow and calf for me," replied Joel, with a loftiness that two years' seniority confers on healthy boys. "I left it to him to choose mine. You'd better pick out a red one. And say, this hospital of ours is the real thing. It's the only one between Dodge and Ogalalla. This strange foreman wants to take stock in it. I wonder if that was what he meant by sawing off a little passel of cattle on Mr. Quince. Now, don't argue or ask foolish questions, but keep your eyes and ears open."

Fortified anew in courage, Dell accompanied the trail boss to meet his herd. It was a short hour's ride, and on sighting the cattle, then nearing the crossing, they gave rein to their horses and rode for the rear of the long column, where, in the rear-guard of the trailing cattle, naturally the sore and tender-footed animals were to be found. The drag men knew them to a hoof, were delighted to hear that all cripples were to be dropped, and half a dozen were cut off and started up the Beaver. "Nurse them to the nearest water," said Straw to the drag men, "and then push them up the creek until I overtake you. Here's where we drop our strays and cripples. What? No, I'm only endowing a trail hospital."

The herd numbered thirty-one hundred two-year-old steers. They filled the channel of the Beaver for a mile around the crossing, crowding into the deeper pools, and thrashing up and down the creek in slaking their thirst. Dell had never seen so many cattle, almost as uniform in size as that many marbles, and the ease with which a few men handled the herd became a nine-day wonder to the astonished boy. And when the word passed around to cut all strays up the creek, the facility with which the men culled out the alien down to one class and road brand, proved them masters in the craft. It seemed as easily done as selecting a knife from among the other trinkets in a boy's pocket.

After a change of mounts for the foreman, Dell and the trail boss drifted the strays up the creek. The latter had counted and classed them as cut out of the herd, and when thrown together with the cripples, the promised little passel numbered thirty-five cattle, not counting three calves. Straw excused his men, promising to overtake them the next morning, and man and boy drifted the nucleus of a future ranch toward the homestead.

"Barring that white cow and the red one with the speckled calf," said Straw to Dell, pointing out each, "you're entitled to pick one for yourself. Now, I'm not going to hurry you in making your choice. Any time before we sight the tent and shack, you are to pick one for your own dear cow, and stand by your choice, good or bad. Remember, it carries my compliments to you, as one of the founders of the first hospital on the Texas and Montana cattle trail."

Two miles below the homestead, the half-dozen cripples were dropped to the rear. "You can come back to-morrow morning and get these tender steers," said the foreman, "and drift them up above the improvements. You'll find them near here on the water. Now, we'll sight the tent around the next bend, and you may point out your choice."

"I'll take that red steer," said Dell with marked decision, pointing out a yearling.

A peal of laughter greeted his choice. "That's a boy," shouted Straw; "shoot at a buck and kill a fawn! Why didn't you take that black cow and calf?"

"I like red cattle the best," replied Dell, undaunted. "I've heard they bring a better price. I'll own the only red steer in the bunch."

"Yes, but when your choice is a beef, that black cow and her increase would buy two beeves. Dell, if you ever get to be a cowman, you'll have to do some of your own thinking."

Dell's mistake was in listening to others. Joel was equally guilty, as his lofty comments regarding red cattle were derived from the random remarks of Forrest. The brothers were novices in range cattle, and Dell's error was based in not relying on his own judgment.

On sighting the approaching cattle, Forrest's bunk was eased around to the tent opening, Joel holding the flaps apart, and the little herd was grazed past at a snail's pace in review. Leaving Dell to nurse the nucleus past the improvements, Straw dismounted at the tent. "Well," said he, handing the bridle reins to Joel, "that red-headed Dell is surely the making of a great cowman. All successful men begin at the bottom of the ladder, and he surely put his foot on the lowest rung. What do you suppose his choice was?"

"The bottom rung suggests a yearling," said Forrest.

"Stand up. You spelled the word correct. I'm a sheep herder, if he didn't pick out the only, little, old, red, dobe steer in the entire bunch!"

Forrest eased himself down on the bunk, unable to restrain his laughter. "Well," said he, "we all have to learn, and no one can say Dell wasn't true to his colors."

CHAPTER IV
THE BROTHERS CLAIM A RANGE

The next morning Straw dallied about until Dell brought up the crippled cattle. They were uniform in size; rest was the one thing needful, and it now would be theirs amid bountiful surroundings. They were driven up among the others, now scattered about in plain sight in the valley above, presenting a morning scene of pastoral contentment.

"Even the calves are playing this morning," said Straw to Forrest, as the former entered the tent. "A few cattle surely make this valley look good. What you want to do now is to keep on drawing more. Don't allow no outfit to pass without chipping in, at least give them the chance, and this trail hospital will be on velvet in no time. Of course, all Lovell outfits will tear their shirts boosting the endowment fund, but that needn't bar the other herds. Some outfits may have no cattle, but they can chip in a sore-back or crippled pony. My idea is to bar no one, and if they won't come in, give them a chance to say they don't want to. You ought to send word back to Dodge; any foreman going east or west from there would give you his strays."

The conception of a trail refuge had taken root. The supply points were oases for amusement, but a halfway haven for the long stretches of unsettled country, during the exodus of Texas cattle to the Northwest, was an unknown port. The monotony of from three to five months on the trail, night and day work, was tiring to men, while a glass of milk or even an hour in the shade was a distinct relief. Straw was reluctant to go, returning to make suggestions, by way of excuse, and not until forced by the advancing day did he mount and leave to overtake his herd.

Again the trio was left alone. Straw had given Forrest a list of brands and a classification of the cattle contributed, and a lesson in reading brands was given the boys. "Brands read from left to right," said Forrest to the pair of attentive listeners, "or downward. If more than one brand is on an animal, the upper one is the holding or one in which ownership is vested. Character brands are known by name, and are used because difficult to alter. There is scarcely a letter in the alphabet that a cattle thief can't change. When a cow brute leaves its home range, it's always a temptation to some rustler to alter the brand, and characters are not so easily changed."

The importance of claiming the range was pressing, and now that cattle were occupying it, the opportunity presented itself. A notice was accordingly written, laying claim to all grazing rights, from the Texas and Montana trail crossing on Beaver to the headwaters of the same, including all its tributaries, by virtue of possession and occupancy vested in the claimants, Wells Brothers. "How does that sound?" inquired Forrest, its author, giving a literal reading of the notice. "Nothing small or stingy about that, eh? When you're getting, get a-plenty."

"But where are we to get the cattle to stock such a big country?" pondered Joel. "It's twenty miles to the head of this creek."

"We might as well lay big plans as little ones. Here's where we make a spoon or spoil a horn. Saddle a horse and post this notice down at the trail crossing. Sink a stake where every one can see it, and nail your colors to the sign-board. We are the people, and must be respected."

Joel hastened away to post the important notice. Dell was detailed on sentinel duty, on lookout for another herd, but each trip he managed to find some excuse to ride among the cattle. "What's the brand on my white cow?" inquired Forrest, the object leading up to another peculiarity in color.

"I couldn't *read* it," said Dell, airing his range parlance.

"No? Well, did you ever see a white cow with a black face?" inquired the wounded man, coming direct to the matter at issue.

"Not that I remember; why?"

"Because there never lived such a colored cow. Nature has one color that she never mars. You can find any colored cow with a white face, but you'll never find a milk-white cow with a colored face. That line is drawn, and you want to remember it. You'll never shoot a wild swan with a blue wing, or see yellow snowflakes fall, or meet a pure white cow with a black face. Hereafter, if any one attempts to send you on a wild-goose chase, to hunt such a cow, tell them that no such animal ever walked this earth."

Joel returned before noon. No sign of an approaching herd was sighted by the middle of the afternoon, and the trio resigned themselves to random conversation.

"Dell," said Forrest, "it's been on my mind all day to ask you why you picked a yearling yesterday when you had a chance to take a cow. Straw laughed at you."

"Because Joel said red cattle were worth a dollar a head more than any other color."

"Young man," inquired Forrest of Joel, "what's your authority for that statement?"

"Didn't you pick me a red cow yesterday, and didn't you admit to Mr. Straw that red cattle were worth the most?" said Joel, in defense of his actions.

"And you rushed away and palmed my random talking off on Dell as original advice? You'll do. Claiming a little more than you actually know will never hurt you any. Now here's a prize for the best brand reader: The boy who brings me a correct list of brands, as furnished by Straw, gets my white cow and calf as a reward. I want the road and ranch brand on the cripples, and the only or holding brand on the others. Now, fool one another if you can. Ride through them slowly, and the one who brings me a perfect list is my bully boy."

The incentive of reward stimulated the brothers to action. They scampered away on ponies, not even waiting to saddle, and several hours were spent in copying brands. These included characters, figures, and letters, and to read them with skill was largely a matter of practice. Any novice ought to copy brands, but in this instance the amateur's list would be compared with that of an experienced trail foreman, a neutral judge from which there was no appeal.

The task occupied the entire evening. Forrest not only had them read, but looked over each copy, lending impartial assistance in reading characters that might baffle a boy. There were some half dozen of the latter in Straw's list, a *turkey track* being the most difficult to interpret, but when all characters were fully understood, Joel still had four errors to Dell's three. The cripples were found to be correct in each instance, and were exempt from further disturbance. Forrest now insisted that to classify, by enumerating each grade, would assist in locating the errors, which work would have to be postponed until morning.

The boys were thoroughly in earnest in mastering the task. Forrest regaled them with examples of the wonderful expertness of the Texans in reading brands and classifying cattle. "Down home," said he, "we have boys who read brands as easily as a girl reads a novel. I know men who can count one hundred head of mixed cattle, as they leave a corral, or trail along, and not only classify them but also give you every brand correctly. Now, that's the kind of cowmen I aim to make out of you boys, and to-morrow morning you must get these brands accurate. What was that?"

Both boys sprang to the tent opening and listened. It sounded like a shot, and within a few moments was seconded by a distant hail.

"Some one must be lost," suggested Joel. "He's down the creek."

"Lost your grandmother!" exclaimed Forrest. "We're all lost in this country. Here, fire this six-shooter in the air, and follow it up with a Comanche yell. Dell, build a little fire on the nearest knoll. It's more than likely some trail man hunting this camp."

The signal-fire was soon burning. The only answer vouchsafed was some fifteen minutes later, when the clatter of an approaching horse was distinctly heard. A lantern shone through the tent walls, and the prompt hail of the horseman proved him no stranger. "Is Quince Forrest here?" he inquired, as his horse shied at the tent.

"He is. Come in, Dorg," said Forrest, recognizing by his voice the horseman without to be Dorg Seay, one of Don Lovell's foremen. "Come in and let us feast our eyes on your handsome face."

Seay peeped within and timidly entered. "Well," said he, pulling at a straggling mustache, "evidently it isn't as bad as reported. Priest wrote back to old man Don that you had attempted suicide – unfortunate in love was the reason given – and I have orders to inquire into your health or scatter flowers on your grave. Able to sit up and take notice? – no complications, I hope?"

534

"When did you leave Dodge?" inquired Forrest, ignoring Seay's persiflage.

"About a week ago. A telegram was waiting me on the railroad, and I rode through this afternoon. If this ranch boasts anything to eat, now would be an awful nice time to mention it."

Seay's wants were looked after.

"How many herds between here and the railroad?" inquired Forrest, resuming the conversation.

"Only one ahead of mine. In fact, I'm foreman of both herds – live with the lead one and occasionally go back and see my own. It all depends on who feeds best."

"And when will your herd reach the Beaver?" continued Forrest.

"I left orders to water my lead herd in the Beaver at three o'clock to-morrow, and my own dear cattle will be at their heels. My outfit acts as rear-guard to Blocker's herd."

These men, in the employ of the same drover, had not seen each other in months, and a fire of questions followed, and were answered. The chronicle of the long drive, of accident by flood and field, led up to the prospects for a northern demand for cattle.

"The market has barely opened in Dodge," said Seay, in reply to a question. "Unless the herds are sold or contracted, very few will leave Dodge for the Platte River before the first of July. Old man Don isn't driving a hoof that isn't placed, so all his herds will pass Ogalalla before the first of the month. The bulk of the drive going north of the Platte will come next month. With the exception of scattering herds, the first of August will end the drive."

The men talked far into the night. When they were left alone in the tent, Forrest unfolded his plans for starting the boys in life.

"We found them actually on their uppers," said he; "they hadn't tasted meat in months, and were living on greens and garden truck. It's a good range, and we must get them some cattle. The first year may be a little tough, but by drawing on all of Lovell's wagons for the necessary staples, we can provision them until next spring. You must leave some flour and salt and beans and the like."

"Beans!" echoed Seay. "That will surely tickle my cook. Did you ever notice that the farther north it goes, a Texas trail outfit gets tastier? Let it start out on bacon and beans and blackstrap, and after the herd crosses the Platte, the varmints want prairie chicken and fried trout. Tasty! Why, those old boys develop an elegant taste for dainties. Nothing but good old beef ever makes them even think of home again. Yes, my cook will give you his last bean, and make a presentation speech gratis."

Forrest's wound had begun to mend, the soreness and swelling had left the knee joint, and the following morning Seay spent in making crutches. Crude and for temporary use, the wounded man tried them out, and by assistance reached the entrance, where he was eased into an old family rocking-chair in the shade of the tent.

"This has been the dream of my life," said he, "to sit like some old patriarch in my tent door and count my cattle. See that white cow yonder?" pointing with a crutch. "Well, she belongs to your uncle John Quincy. And that reminds me that she and her calf are up as a reward to complete the roll of brands. Boys, are you ready?"

The revised lists were submitted for inspection. Compared with the one rendered by Straw, there was still a difference in Dell's regarding a dun cow, while Joel's list varied on three head. Under the classification the errors were easily located, and summoning the visiting foreman, Forrest explained the situation.

"I'll have to appoint you umpire in deciding this matter. Here's the roll furnished by Nat Straw, and you'll compare it with Dell and Joel's. Of course, old Nat didn't care a whoopee about getting the list perfect, and my boy may be right on that dun cow. Joel differs on a three-year-old, a heifer, and a yearling steer. Now, get them straight, because we're expecting to receive more cattle this evening. Pass on these brands before you leave to meet your herd this afternoon. And remember, there's a cow and calf at stake for whichever one of these boys first gets the roll correct."

After dinner the three rode away for a final inspection. The cattle were lazy and logy from water, often admitting of riding within a rod, thus rendering the brands readable at a glance. Dell led the way to the dun cow, but before Seay could pass an opinion, the boy called for his list in possession of the man. "Let me take my roll a minute," said he, "and I'll make the correction. It isn't a four bar four, it's four equals four; there's two bars instead of one. The cow and calf is mine. That gives me three."

The lust of possession was in Dell's voice. The reward had been fairly earned, and turning to the other cattle in dispute, Joel's errors were easily corrected. All three were in one brand, and the mere failure to note the lines of difference between the figure eight and the letter S had resulted in repeating the mistake. Seay amused himself by pointing out different animals and calling for their brands, and an envious rivalry resulted between the brothers, in their ability to read range script.

"A good eye and a good memory," said Seay, as they rode homeward, "are gifts to a cowman. A brand once seen is hardly ever forgotten. Twenty years hence, you boys will remember all these brands. One man can read brands at twice the distance of another, and I have seen many who could distinguish cattle from horses, with the naked eye, at a distance of three miles. When a man learns to know all there is about cattle, he ought to be getting gray around the edges."

Forrest accepted the umpire's report. "I thought some novice might trip his toe on that equality sign," said he. "There's nothing like having studied your arithmetic. Dell's been to school, and it won him a cow and calf when he saw the sign used as a brand. I wonder how he is on driving mules."

"I can drive them," came the prompt reply.

"Very well. Hook up the old team. I'm sending you down to the trail crossing to levy on two commissary wagons. Take everything they give you and throw out a few hints for more. This afternoon we begin laying in a year's provisions. It may be a cold winter, followed by a late spring, and there's nothing like having enough. Relieve them of all their dried fruits, and make a strong talk for the staples of life. I may want to winter here myself, and a cow camp should make provision for more or less company."

Seay lent his approval. "Hitch up and rattle along ahead of me," said he. "The wagons may reach the crossing an hour or two ahead of the herds, and I'll be there to help you trim them down to light traveling form."

It proved an active afternoon. The wagon was started for the trail crossing, followed by Seay within half an hour. Joel was in a quandary, between duty and desire, as he was anxious to see the passing herds, yet a bond of obligation to the wounded man required his obedience. Forrest had noticed the horse under saddle, the impatience of the boy, but tactfully removed all uneasiness.

"I have been trying to figure out," said he, "how I could spare you this afternoon, as no doubt you would like to see the herds, but we have so much to do at home. Now that I can hobble out, you must get me four poles, and we will strip this fly off the tent and make a sunshade out of it – make an arbor in front of our quarters. Have the props ready, and in the morning Seay will show you how to stretch a tarpaulin for a sunshade. And then along towards evening, you must drift our little bunch of cattle at least a mile up the creek. I'm expecting more this evening, and until we learn the brands on this second contingent, they must be kept separate. And then, since we've claimed it, we want to make a showing of occupying the range, by scattering the cattle over it. Within a month, our cows must rest in the shade of Hackberry Grove and be watering out of those upper springs. When you take a country, the next thing is to hold it."

Something to do was a relief to Joel. Willow stays, for the arbor, were cut, the bark peeled off, and the poles laid ready at hand. When the cattle arose, of their own accord, from the noonday rest, the impatient lad was allowed to graze them around the bend of the creek. There was hardly enough work to keep an active boy employed, and a social hour ensued. "Things are coming our way," said Forrest. "This man Seay will just about rob Blocker's outfit. When it comes to making a poor mouth, that boy Dorg is in a class by himself. Dell will just about have a wagon load. You boys will have to sleep in the tent hereafter."

It proved so. The team returned an hour before sunset, loaded to the carrying capacity of the wagon. Not only were there remnants in the staples of life, but kegs of molasses and bags of flour and beans, while a good saddle, coils of rope, and a pair of new boots which, after a wetting, had proven too small for the owner, were among the assets. It was a motley assortment of odds and ends, a free discard of two trail outfits, all of which found an acceptable lodgment at the new ranch.

"They're coming up to supper," announced Dell to Forrest. "Mr. Blocker's foreman knows you, and sent word to get up a spread. He says that when he goes visiting, he expects his friends to not only put on the little and big pot, but kill a chicken and churn. He's such a funny fellow. He made me try on those boots, and when he saw they would fit, he ordered their owner, one of Mr. Seay's men, to give them to me or he would fight him at sunrise."

"Had them robbing each other for us, eh?" said Forrest, smiling. "Well, that's the kind of friend to have when settling up a new country. This ranch is like a fairy story. Here I sit and wave my crutch for a wand, and everything we need seems to just bob up out of the plain. Cattle coming along to stock a ranch, old chum coming to supper, in fact, everything coming our way. Dell, get up a banquet – who cares for expense!"

It was barely dusk when the second contingent of cattle passed above the homestead and were turned loose for the night. As before, the cripples had been dropped midway, and would be nursed up the next morning. With the assistance of crutches, Forrest managed to reach the opening, and by clinging to the tent-pole, waved a welcome to the approaching trail men.

Blocker's foreman, disdaining an invitation to dismount, saluted his host. "There's some question in my mind," said he, "as to what kind of a dead-fall you're running up here, but if it's on the square, there goes my contribution to your hospital. Of course, the gift carries the compliments of my employer, Captain John. That red-headed boy delivered my messages, I reckon? Well, now, make out that I'm somebody that's come a long way, and that you're tickled to death to see me, and order the fatted calf killed. Otherwise, I won't even dismount."

CHAPTER V
A FALL OF CRUMBS

An active day followed. The two trail foremen left early to overtake their herds, and the trio at the homestead was fully employed. The cripples were brought up, brands were copied, and the commissary stores assorted and arranged. Before leaving, the men had stretched the sunshade, and the wounded magician sat in state before his own tent door.

The second contingent numbered forty cattle. Like the first, they were a mixed lot, with the exception of a gentle cow. Occasionally a trail foreman would provide his outfit with a milk cow before starting, or gentle one en route, and Seay had willingly given his cow to the hospital on the Beaver.

A fine rain fell during the night. It began falling during the twilight of evening, gathering in force as the hours passed, and only ceased near the middle of the following forenoon. The creek filled to its banks, the field and garden freshened in a day, and the new ranch threw off the blight of summer drouth.

"This will bring the herds," said Forrest, as the sun burst forth at noon. "It's a general rain, and every one in Dodge, now that water is sure, will pull out for the Platte River. It will cool the weather and freshen the grass, and every drover with herds on the trail will push forward for Ogalalla. We'll have to patrol the crossing on the Beaver, as the rain will lay the dust for a week and rob us of our signal."

The crippled man's words proved prophetic. One of the boys was daily detailed to ride to the first divide south, from which a herd, if timing its march to reach the Beaver within a day, could be sighted. On a primal trace, like the Texas and Montana cattle trail, every benefit to the herd was sought, and the freshened range and running water were a welcome breeze to the drover's sail.

The first week after the rain only three herds reached the Beaver. Each foreman paid his respects to Forrest at the homestead, but the herds were heavy beef cattle, purchased at Dodge for delivery on army contracts, and were outfitted anew on a change of owners. The usual flotsam of crippled and stray cattle, of galled and lame saddle stock, and of useless commissary supplies, was missing, and only the well wishes of the wayfaring were left to hearten man and boy at the new ranch.

The second week brought better results. Four of Don Lovell's herds passed within two days, and the nucleus of cattle increased to one hundred and forty odd, seven crippled horses were left, while the commissary stores fairly showered, a second wagon load being necessary to bring up the cache from the trail crossing. In all, during the week, fifteen herds passed, only three of which refused the invitation to call, while one was merely drifting along in search of a range to take up and locate with a herd of cattle. Its owners, new men in the occupation, were scouting wide, and when one of them discovered Hackberry Grove above the homestead, his delight was unbounded, as the range met every requirement for establishing a ranch.

The tyro's exultation was brief. On satisfying himself on the source of the water, the splendid shade and abundance of fuel, he rode down the creek to intercept the trail, and on rounding a bend of the Beaver, was surprised to sight a bunch of cattle. Knowing the value of the range, Forrest had urged the boys to nurse the first contingent of strays up the creek, farther and farther, until they were then ranging within a mile of the grove. The newcomer could hardly control his chagrin, and as he rode along, scarcely a mile was passed but more cattle were encountered, and finally the tent and homestead loomed in sight.

"Well, I'm glad to have such near neighbors," affably said the stranger, as he dismounted before the tent. "Holding down a homestead, I suppose?"

Only Joel and Forrest were at home. "Not exactly," replied the latter; "this is headquarters ranch of Wells Brothers; range from the trail crossing on Beaver to the headwaters of the same. On the trail with cattle, I reckon?"

"Just grazing along until a range can be secured," replied the man. "I've found a splendid one only a few miles up the creek – fine grove of timber and living springs. If the range suits my partner, we'll move in within a few days and take possession."

"Notice any cattle as you came down the creek?" politely inquired Forrest.

"Just a few here and there. They look like strays; must have escaped from some trail herd. If we decide to locate above, I'll have them all rounded up and pushed down the creek."

Joel scented danger as a cub wolf scents blood. He crossed the arbor and took up a position behind Forrest's chair. The latter was a picture of contentment, smiling at the assurance of his caller, and qualifying his remarks with rare irony.

"Well, since you expect to be our neighbor, better unsaddle and stay for dinner," urged Forrest. "Let's get acquainted – at least, come to some friendly understanding."

"No, thank you. My partner is waiting my return to the herd, and will be anxious for my report on the range above. If possible, we don't care to locate any farther north."

"You ought to have secured your range before you bought your cattle. You seem to have the cart before the horse," observed the wounded man.

"Oh," said the novice, with a sweeping gesture, "there's plenty of unclaimed range. There's ample grass and water on this creek to graze five thousand cattle."

"Wells Brothers estimate that the range, tributary to the Beaver, will carry ten thousand head the year round," replied Forrest, languidly indifferent.

"Who are Wells Brothers?" inquired the newcomer.

Forrest turned to the stranger as if informing a child. "You have the name correct," said he. "The brothers took this range some time ago, and those cattle that you met up the creek are theirs. Before you round up any cattle and drive them out, you had better look into the situation thoroughly. You surely know and respect range customs."

"Well," said the stranger explosively, – they mustn't expect to hold the whole country with a handful of cattle."

"They only took the range recently, and are acquiring cattle as fast as possible," politely replied Forrest.

"They can't hold any more country than they can occupy," authoritatively asserted the novice. "All we want is a range for a thousand cows, and I've decided on that hackberry grove as headquarters."

"Your hearing seems defective," remarked Forrest in flute-like tones. "Let me repeat: This is headquarters for Wells Brothers. Their range runs from the trail crossing, six miles below, to the headwaters of Beaver, including all its tributaries. Since you can't stay for dinner, you'll have time to ride down to the crossing of the Texas and Montana trail on this creek. There you'll find the posted notice, so that he who runs may read, that Wells Brothers have already claimed this range. I'll furnish you a pencil and scrap of paper, and you can make a copy of the formal notice and show it to your partner. Then, if you feel strong enough to outrage all range customs, move in and throw down your glove. I've met an accident recently, leaving me a cripple, but I'll agree to get in the saddle and pick up the gauntlet."

The novice led his horse aside as if to mount. "I fail to see the object in claiming more range than one can occupy. It raises a legal question," said he, mounting.

"Custom is the law of the range," replied Forrest. "The increase of a herd must be provided for, and a year or two's experience of beginners like you usually throws cattle on the market. Abundance of range is a good asset. Joel, get the gentleman a pencil and sheet of paper."

"Not at all necessary," remarked the amateur cowman, reining away. "I suppose the range is for sale?" he called out, without halting.

"Yes, but folks who prefer to intrude are usually poor buyers," shouted the crippled Texan.

Joel was alarmed and plied Forrest with a score of questions. The boy had tasted the thrill of ownership of cattle and possession of a range, and now the envy of others had threatened his interests.

"Don't be alarmed," soothingly said the wounded man. "This is like a page from life, only twice as natural. It proves two things: that you took your range in good time, and that it has a value. This very afternoon you must push at least one hundred cattle up to those springs above Hackberry Grove. Let them track and trample around the water and noon in the shade of the motte. That's possession, and possession is nine points, and the other fellow can have the tenth. If any one wants to dispute your rights or encroach on them, I'll mount a horse and go to the trail for help. The Texans are the boys to insist on range customs being respected. It's time I was riding a little, anyhow."

Dell returned from scouting the trail, and reported two herds due to reach the Beaver that evening. "I spent an hour with one of the foremen around the ford," said he to Forrest; "and he says if you want to see him, you had better come down to the crossing. He knows you, and makes out you ain't much hurt. He says if you come down, he'll give you a quarter of beef and a speckled heifer. He's one of Jess Pressnell's bosses."

"That's the word I'm waiting for," laughed Forrest. "Corral the horses and fix up some kind of a mounting block. It'll take a scaffold to get me on a horse, but I can fall off. Make haste, because hereafter we must almost live on horseback."

The words proved true. Forrest and Dell, the latter bareback, returned to the trail, while Joel rode to drift their cattle up the Beaver, in order to be in possession of Hackberry Grove and its living springs. The plains of the West were a lawless country, and if its pioneers would not respect its age-old pastoral customs, then the consequences must be met or borne.

Three weeks had passed since the accident to Forrest, the herds were coming with a vengeance, and the scene of activity changed from the homestead to the trail crossing. Forrest did not return for a week, foraging on the wagons, camping with the herds, and never failing to levy, to the extent of his ability to plead, on cattle, horses, and needful supplies. As many as five and six herds arrived in a single day, none of which were allowed to pass without an appeal: if strangers, in behalf of a hospital; if among friends, the simple facts were sufficient. Dell was kept on the move with bunches of cattle, or freighting the caches to the homestead, while Joel received the different contingents and scouted the threatened range.

Among old acquaintances there was no denying Forrest, and Dell fell heir to the first extra saddle found among the effects of a trail outfit. The galled horses had recovered serviceable form, affording each of the boys a mount, and even the threatened cloud against the range lifted. The herd of a thousand cows crossed the Beaver, and Forrest took particular pains to inform its owners of the whereabouts of unclaimed range the year before. Evidently the embryo cowmen had taken heed and inquired into range customs, and were accordingly profuse with disclaimers of any wrong intent.

The first three weeks of July saw the bulk of the herds north of the Beaver. Water and range had been taken advantage of in the trailing of cattle to the Northwest, fully three hundred thousand head having crossed from Dodge to Ogalalla. The exodus afforded the boys an insight into pastoral life, brought them in close contact with the men of the open, drove false ideas from their immature minds, and assisted in the laying of those early foundations on which their future manhood must rest.

Dell spent every chance hour with the trail men. He and Forrest slept with the wagons, met the herds, and piloted them in to the best water. The fact that only experienced men were employed on the trail made the red-headed boy a welcome guest with every herd, while the wide acquaintance of his crippled sponsor assured the lad every courtesy of camp and road. Dell soon learned that the position of point man usually fell to a veteran of the range, and one whose acquaintance was worthy of cultivation, both in the saddle and around the camp-fire.

"I'm going to be a point man," Dell confided to Forrest, on one of their trips up to the homestead. "He don't seem to have much to do, and nearly always rides with one leg across his horse's neck."

"That's the idea," assented Forrest. "Aim high. Of course, you'll have to begin as a drag man, then a few trips to Montana in the swing, and after that you have a right to expect a place on the point. The trouble is, you are liable to slip back a notch or two at any time. Here I've been a foreman in other years, and this trip I was glad to make a hand. There's so many slips, and we can't be all point men and bosses. Cooks and horse wranglers are also useful men."

The first serious cloud to hover over the new ranch appeared early during the last week in July. Forrest's wounds had nearly healed, and he was wondering if his employer would make a further claim on his services during that summer, which was probable at the hands of a drover with such extensive interests. He and Dell were still patrolling the ford on Beaver, when one evening a conveyance from the railroad to the south drove up to the crossing. It brought a telegram from Don Lovell, requesting the presence of Forrest in Dodge City, and the messenger, a liveryman from Buffalo, further assured him that transportation was awaiting him at that station. There were no grounds on which to refuse the summons, indefinite and devoid of detail as it was, and preparations were immediately made to return with the liveryman. What few cattle had been secured during that trip were drifted up the creek, when all returned to the homestead for the night.

To Dell and Joel the situation looked serious. The crippled man, helpless as he was at first, had proven their rock of refuge, and now that he was leaving them, a tenderness of unnoticed growth was revealed. As an enforced guest, he had come to them at a moment when their poverty had protested at receiving him, his unselfishness in their behalf had proven his friendship and gratitude beyond question, and the lesson was not lost on the parentless waifs.

On the other hand, Forrest lightened all depression of spirits. "Don't worry," said he to the boys. "Just as sure as water runs and grass grows, I'll come over this trail again. So far in life, I've never done any good for myself, and I'm going to play this hand out and see if you lads land on your feet. Now, don't get the idea that I've done any great feat in rustling you boys a few cows. It's one of the laws of life, that often we can do for others what we can't do for ourselves. That sounds like preaching, but it isn't. Actually, I'm ashamed of myself, that I didn't get you double the number of cattle. What we did skirmish together was merely the flotsam of the trail, the crumbs that fall from the supper table, and all obligations to me are overpaid. If I could have had just a few tears on tap, with that hospital talk, and you boys being poor and orphans – shucks! I must be getting doty – that plea was good for a thousand strays and cripples!"

The brothers took courage. So far their chief asset was a fine range. Nearly three hundred and fifty cattle, imperfect as the titles to many of them were, had been secured and were occupying the valley. A round dozen cow ponies, worthless for the present, but which in time would round into form, were added to the new ranch. Every passing commissary had laughed at the chance to discard its plunder and useless staples, and only the departure of the man behind the venture, standing in the shadow as it were, threw a depression over the outlook.

Funds, with which to pay his reckoning, had been left with Forrest. The boys had forgotten the original agreement, and it was only with tact and diplomacy that a snug sum, against his protest and embarrassment, was forced on Joel. "It don't come off me," said the departing man, "and it may come handy with you. There's a long winter ahead, and the fight ain't near won yet. The first year in starting a ranch is always the hardest. But if you boys can only hold these cattle until grass comes again, it's the making of you. You know the boy is father to the man, and if you are true-blue seed corn – well, I'll bet on two ears to the stock."

Forrest's enthusiasm tempered the parting. The start for the railroad was made at daybreak, and in taking leave, each boy held a hand, shaking it heartily from time to time, as if to ratify the general advice. "I'll make Dodge in two days," said the departing guest, "and then I'll know the meaning of this wire. It means something – that's sure. In the mean time, sit square in your saddles, ride your range, and let the idea run riot that you are cowmen. Plan, scheme, and devise for the future. That's all until you hear from me or see my sign in the sky. Adios, señors."

CHAPTER VI
SUNSHINE AND SHADOW

An entire week passed, during which the boys were alone. A few herds were still coming over the trail, but for lack of an advocate to plead, all hope of securing more cattle must be foregone. Forrest had only taken his saddle, abandoning for the present all fixtures contributed for his comfort on arriving at the homestead, including the horses of his employers. The lads were therefore left an abundance of mounts, all cattle were drifted above the ranch, and plans for the future considered.

Winter must be met and confronted. "We must have forage for our saddle horses," said Joel to his brother, the evening after Forrest's departure. "The rain has helped our corn until it will make fodder, but that isn't enough. Pa cut hay in this valley, and I know where I can mow a ton any morning. Mr. Quince said we'd have to stable a saddle horse apiece this winter, and those mules will have to be fed. The grass has greened up since the rain, and it will be no trick at all to make ten to fifteen tons of hay. Help me grind the scythe, and we'll put in every spare hour haying. While you ride around the cattle every morning, I can mow."

A farm training proved an advantage to the boys. Before coming West, their father had owned a mowing machine, but primitive methods prevailed on the frontier, and he had been compelled to use a scythe in his haying operations. Joel swung the blade like a veteran, scattering his swath to cure in the sun, and with whetstone on steel, beat a frequent tattoo. The raking into windrows and shocking at evening was an easy task for the brothers, no day passing but the cured store was added to, until sufficient was accumulated to build a stack. That was a task which tried their mettle, but once met and overcome, it fortified their courage to meet other ordeals.

"I wish Mr. Quince could see that stack of hay," admiringly said Dell, on the completion of the first effort. "There must be five tons in it. And it's as round as an apple. I can't remember when I've worked so hard and been so hungry. No wonder the Texan despises any work he can't do on horseback. But just the same, they're dear, good fellows. I wish Mr. Quince could live with us always. He's surely a good forager."

The demand for range was accented anew. One evening two strangers rode up the creek and asked for a night's lodging. They were made welcome, and proved to be Texas cowmen, father and son, in search of pasturage for a herd of through cattle. There was an open frankness about the wayfarers that disarmed every suspicion of wrong intent, and the brothers met their inquiries with equal candor.

"And you lads are Wells Brothers?" commented the father, in kindly greeting. "We saw your notice, claiming this range, at the trail crossing, and followed your wagon track up the creek. Unless the market improves, we must secure range for three thousand two-year-old steers. Well, we'll get acquainted, anyhow."

The boys naturally lacked commercial experience in their new occupation. The absence of Forrest was sorely felt, and only the innate kindness of the guests allayed all feeling of insecurity. As the evening wore on, the old sense of dependence brought the lads in closer touch with the strangers, the conversation running over the mutual field of range and cattle matters.

"What is the reason," inquired Joel, "that so many cattle are leaving your State for the upper country?"

"The reasons are numerous and valid," replied the older cowman. "It's the natural outgrowth or expansion of the pastoral interests of our State. Before the opening of the trail, for years and years, Texas clamored for an outlet for its cattle. Our water supply was limited, the State is subject to severe drouth, the cattle were congesting on our ranges, with neither market inquiry or demand. The subjection of the Indian was followed by a sudden development of the West, the Texas and Montana cattle trail opened, and the pastoral resources of our State surprised the world. Last year we sent eight hundred thousand cattle over the trail, and they were not missed at home. That's the reason I'm your guest to-night; range has suddenly become valuable in Texas."

"There is also an economic reason for the present exodus of cattle," added the young man. "Our State is a natural breeding ground, but we can't mature into marketable beef. Nearly twenty years' experience has proven that a northern climate is necessary to fatten and bring our Texas cattle to perfect maturity. Two winters in the North will insure a gain of from three to four hundred pounds' extra weight more per head than if allowed to reach maturity on their native heath. This gain fully doubles the value of every hoof, and is a further motive why we are your guests to-night; we are looking for a northern range on which to mature our steer cattle."

The boys were grasping the fact that in their range they had an asset of value. Less than two months before, they were on the point of abandoning their home as worthless, not capable of sustaining life, the stone which the builders rejected, and now it promised a firm foundation to their future hopes. The threatened encroachment of a few weeks previous, and the causes of demand, as explained by their guests, threw a new light on range values and made the boys doubly cautious. Was there a possible tide in the primitive range, which taken at its flood would lead these waifs to fortune?

The next morning the guests insisted on looking over the upper valley of the Beaver.

"In the first place," said the elder Texan, "let it be understood that we respect your rights to this range. If we can reach some mutual agreement, by purchase or rental, good enough, but not by any form of intrusion. We might pool our interests for a period of years, and the rental would give you lads a good schooling. There are many advantages that might accrue by pooling our cattle. At least, there is no harm in looking over the range."

"They can ride with me as far as Hackberry Grove," said Dell. "None of our cattle range over a mile above the springs, and from there I can nearly point out the limits of our ranch."

"You are welcome to look over the range," assentingly said Joel, "but only on condition that any agreement reached must be made with Mr. Quince Forrest, now at Dodge."

"That will be perfectly agreeable," said the older cowman. "No one must take any advantage of you boys."

The trio rode away, with Dell pointing out around the homestead the different beaver dams in the meanderings of the creek. Joel resumed his mowing, and near noon sighted a cavalcade of horses coming down the dim road which his father used in going to Culbertson. A wagon followed, and from its general outlines the boy recognized it to be a cow outfit, heading for their improvements. Hastening homeward, he found Paul Priest, the gray-haired foreman, who had passed northward nearly two months before, sitting under the sunshade before the tent.

"Howdy, bud," said Priest languidly in greeting. "Now, let me think – Howdy, Joel!"

No prince could have been more welcome. The men behind the boys had been sadly missed, and the unexpected appearance of Priest filled every want. "Sit down," said the latter. "First, don't bother about getting any dinner; my outfit will make camp on the creek, and we'll have a little spread. Yes, I know; Forrest's in Dodge; old man Don told me he needed him. Where's your brother?"

"Dell's gone up the creek with some cowmen from Texas," admitted Joel. "They're looking for a range. I told them any agreement reached must be made with Mr. Quince. But now that you are here, you will do just as well. They'll be in soon."

"I'm liable to tell them to ride on," said the gray-haired foreman. "I'm jealous, and I want it distinctly understood that I'm a silent partner in this ranch. How many cattle have you?"

"Nearly three hundred and fifty, not counting the calves."

"Forrest only rustled you three hundred and fifty cattle? The lazy wretch – he ought to be hung for ingratitude!"

"Oh, no," protested Joel; "Mr. Quince has been a father to Dell and myself."

"Wait until I come back from Dodge, and I'll show you what a rustler I am," said Priest, arising to give his horse to the wrangler and issue directions in regard to camping.

The arrival of Dell and the cowmen prevented further converse between Priest and his protégé. For the time being a soldier's introduction sufficed between the Texans, but Dell came in for a rough caress. "What do you think of the range?" inquired the trail foreman, turning to the men, and going direct to the subject.

"It meets every requirement for ranching," replied the elder cowman, "and I'm going to make these boys a generous offer."

"This man will act for us," said Joel to the two cowmen, with a jerk of his thumb toward Priest.

"Well, that's good," said the older man, advancing to Priest. "My name is Allen, and this is my son Hugh."

"And my name is Priest, a trail foreman in the employ of Don Lovell," said the gray-haired man, shaking hands with the Texans.

"Mr. Lovell was expected in Dodge the day we left," remarked the younger man in greeting. "We had hopes of selling him our herd."

"What is your county?" inquired the trail boss, searching his pockets for a telegram.

"Comanche."

"And when did you leave Dodge?"

"Just ten days ago."

"Then you need no range – your cattle are sold," said Priest, handing the older man a telegram.

The two scanned the message carefully, and the trail foreman continued: "This year my herd was driven to fill a sub-contract, and we delivered it last week at old Camp Clark, on the North Platte. From there the main contractor will trail the beef herd up to the Yellowstone. Old man Don was present at the delivery, and when I got back to Ogalalla with the outfit, that message was awaiting me. I'm now on my way to Dodge to receive the cattle. They go to the old man's beef ranch on the Little Missouri. It says three thousand Comanche County two-year-olds, don't it?"

"It's our cattle," said the son to his father. "We have the only straight herd of Comanche County two-year-olds at Dodge City. That commission man said he would sell them before we got back."

The elder Texan turned to the boys with a smile. "I reckon we'll have to declare all negotiations off regarding this range. I had several good offers to make you, and I'm really sorry at this turn of events. I had figured out a leasing plan, whereby the rentals of this range would give you boys a fine schooling, and revert to you on the eldest attaining his majority. We could have pooled our cattle, and your interests would have been carried free."

"You needn't worry about these boys," remarked Priest, with an air of interest; "they have silent partners. As to schooling, I've known some mighty good men who never punched the eyes out of the owl in their old McGuffy spelling-book."

A distant cry of dinner was wafted up the creek. "That's a welcome call," said Priest, arising. "Come on, everybody. My cook has orders to tear his shirt in getting up a big dinner."

A short walk led to the camp. "This outfit looks good to me," said the elder cowman to Priest, "and you can count on my company to the railroad."

"You're just the man I'm looking for," replied the trail boss. "We're making forty miles a day, and you can have charge until we reach Dodge."

"But I only volunteered as far as the railroad," protested the genial Texan.

"Yes; but then I know you cowmen," contended Priest. "You have lived around a wagon so long and love cow horses so dearly, that you simply can't quit my outfit to ride on a train. Two o'clock is the hour for starting, and I'll overtake you before evening."

The outfit had been reduced to six men, the remainder having been excused and sent home from Ogalalla. The remuda was in fine condition, four changes of mounts a day was the rule, and on the hour named, the cavalcade moved out, leaving its foreman behind. "Angle across the plain and enter the trail on the divide, between here and the Prairie Dog," suggested Priest to his men. "We will want to touch here coming back, and the wagon track will point the way. Mr. Allen will act as segundo."

Left to themselves, the trio resolved itself into a ways and means committee. "I soldiered four years," said Priest to the boys, once the sunshade was reached, "and there's nothing that puts spirit and courage into the firing line like knowing that the reserves are strong. It's going to be no easy task to hold these cattle this winter, and now is the time to bring up the ammunition and provision the camp. The army can't march unless the mules are in condition, and you must be well mounted to handle cattle. Ample provision for your saddle stock is the first requirement."

"We're putting up a ton of hay a day," said Joel, "and we'll have two hundred shocks of fodder."

"That's all right for rough forage, but you must have corn for your saddle stock," urged the man. "Without grain for the mounts, cavalry is useless. I think the railroad supplies, to settlers along its line, coal, lumber, wire, and other staples at cost. I'll make inquiry to-morrow and let you know when we return. One hundred bushels of corn would make the forage reserves ample for the winter."

"We've got money enough to buy it," admitted Joel. "I didn't want to take it, but Mr. Quince said it would come in handy."

"That covers the question of forage, then," said Priest. "Now comes the question of corrals and branding."

"Going to brand the calves?" impulsively inquired Dell, jumping at conclusions.

"The calves need not be branded before next spring," replied the practical man, "but the herd must be branded this fall. If a blizzard struck the cattle on the open, they would drift twenty miles during a night. These through Texas cattle have been known to drift five hundred miles during the first winter. You must guard against a winter drift, and the only way is to hold your cattle under herd. If you boys let these cattle out of your hand, away from your control, they'll drift south to the Indian reservations and be lost. You must hold them in spite of storms, and you will need a big, roomy inclosure in which to corral the herd at night."

"There's the corn field," suggested Dell.

"It has no shelter," objected Priest. "Your corral must protect against the north and west winds."

"The big bend's the place," said Joel. "The creek makes a perfect horseshoe, with bluff banks almost twenty feet high on the north and northwest. One hundred yards of fencing would inclose five acres. Our cows used to shelter there. It's only a mile above the house."

"What's the soil, and how about water?" inquired the gray-haired foreman, arising.

"It's a sand-bar, with a ripple and two long pools in the circle of the creek," promptly replied Joel.

"Bring in the horses," said Priest, looking at his watch; "I'll have time to look it over before leaving."

While awaiting the horses, the practical cowman outlined to Joel certain alterations to the corral at the stable, which admitted of the addition of a branding chute. "You must cut and haul the necessary posts and timber before my return, and when we pass north, my outfit will build you a chute and brand your cattle the same day. Have the materials on the ground, and I'll bring any needful hardware from the railroad."

A short canter brought the committee to the big bend. The sand-bar was overgrown with weeds high as a man's shoulder on horseback, but the leader, followed by the boys, forced his mount through the tangle until the bend was circled. "It's an ideal winter shelter," said Priest, dismounting to step the entrance, as a preliminary measurement. "A hundred and ten yards," he announced, a few minutes later, "coon-skin measurement. You'll need twenty heavy posts and one hundred stays. I'll bring you a roll of wire. That water's everything; a thirsty cow chills easily. Given a dry bed and contented stomach, in this corral your herd can laugh at any storm. It's almost ready made, and there's nothing niggardly about its proportions."

"When will we put the cattle under herd?" inquired Dell as the trio rode homeward.

"Oh, about the second snowstorm," replied Priest. "After squaw winter's over, there's usually a month to six weeks of Indian summer. It might be as late as the first of December, but it's a good idea to loose-herd awhile; ride around them evening and morning, corral them and leave the gates open, teach them to seek a dry, cosy bed, at least a month before putting the cattle under close-herd. Teach them to drink in the corral, and then they'll want to come home. You boys will just about have to live with your little herd this winter."

"We wintered here once," modestly said Joel, "and I'm sure we can do it again. The storms are the only thing to dread, and we can weather them."

"Of course you can," assured the trail boss. "It's a ground-hog case; it's hold these cattle or the Indians will eat them for you. Lost during one storm, and your herd is lost for good."

"And about horses: will one apiece be enough?" queried Joel. "Mr. Quince thought two stabled ones would do the winter herding."

"One corn-fed pony will do the work of four grass horses," replied the cowman. "Herding is no work for horses, provided you spare them. If you must, miss your own dinner, but see that your horse gets his. Dismount and strip the bridle off at every chance, and if you guard against getting caught out in storms, one horse apiece is all you need."

On reaching the homestead, Priest shifted his saddle to a horse in waiting, and announced his regrets at being compelled to limit his visit. "It may be two weeks before I return," said he, leading his horse from the corral to the tent, "but we'll point in here and lend a hand in shaping you up for winter. Forrest is liable to have a herd of his own, and in that case, there will be two outfits of men. More than likely, we'll come through together."

Hurried as he professed to be, the trail foreman pottered around as if time was worthless, but finally mounted. "Now the commissary is provisioned," said he, in summing up the situation, "to stand a winter's siege, the forage is ample, the corral and branding chute is half done – well, I reckon we're the boys to hold a few cattle. Honest Injun, I hope it will storm enough this winter to try you out; just to see what kind of thoroughbreds you really are. And if any one else offers to buy an interest in this range," he called back, as a happy afterthought, "just tell them that you have all the partners you need."

CHAPTER VII
ALL IN THE DAY'S WORK

The brief visit of Priest proved a tonic to the boys. If a firing line of veteran soldiers can be heartened, surely the spirit and courage of orphan waifs needed fortifying against the coming winter. The elements have laughed at the hopes and ambitions of a conqueror, and an invincible army has trailed its banners in the snow, unable to cope with the rigors of the frost king. The lads bent anew to their tasks with a cheerfulness which made work mere play, sweetening their frugal fare, and bringing restful sleep. The tie which began in a mercenary agreement had seemingly broken its bonds, and in lieu, through the leaven of human love, a new covenant had been adopted.

"If it's a dry, open winter," said Dell at breakfast next morning, "holding these cattle will be nothing. The water holds them now without herding."

"Yes," replied Joel, "but we must plan to meet the worst possible winter. A blizzard gives little warning, and the only way to overcome one is to be fully prepared. That's what Mr. Paul means by bringing up the ammunition. We must provide so as to be able to withstand a winter siege."

"Well, what's lacking?" insisted Dell.

"Fuel. Take an axe with you this morning, and after riding around the cattle, cut and collect the dead and fallen timber in Hackberry Grove. Keep an eye open for posts and stays – I'll cut them while you're hauling wood. Remember we must have the materials on the ground when Mr. Paul returns, to build a corral and branding chute."

Axe and scythe were swung that morning with renewed energy. Within a week the required amount of hay was in stack, while the further supply of forage, promised in the stunted corn, was daily noted in its advancing growth.

Without delay the scene of activity shifted. The grove was levied on, a change of axe-men took place, while the team even felt a new impetus by making, instead of one, two round trips daily. The fuel supply grew, not to meet a winter's, but a year's requirements. Where strength was essential, only the best of timber was chosen, and well within the time limit the materials for corral and branding chute were at hand on the ground. One task met and mastered, all subsequent ones seemed easier.

"We're ahead of time," said Joel with a quiet air of triumph, as the last load of stays reached the corral site. "If we only knew the plans, we might dig the post-holes. The corn's still growing, and it won't do to cut until it begins to ripen – until the sugar rises in the stock. We can't turn another wheel until Mr. Paul returns."

Idleness was galling to Joel Wells. "We'll ride the range to-day," he announced the following morning. "From here to the ford doesn't matter, but all the upper tributaries ought to be known. We must learn the location of every natural shelter. If a storm ever cuts us off from the corrals, we must point the herd for some other port."

"The main Beaver forks only a few miles above Hackberry Grove," suggested Dell.

"Then we'll ride out the south fork to-day and come back through the sand hills. There must be some sheltered nooks in that range of dunes."

That the morning hour has gold in its mouth, an unknown maxim at the new ranch, mattered nothing. The young cowmen were up and away with the rising sun, riding among and counting the different bunches of cattle encountered, noting the cripples, and letting no details of the conditions of the herd, in their leisurely course up the creek, escape their vigilance.

The cattle tallied out to an animal, and were left undisturbed on their chosen range. Two hours' ride brought the boys to the forks of the Beaver, and by the middle of the forenoon the south branch of the creek was traced to its source among the sand dunes. If not inviting, the section proved interesting, with its scraggy plum brush, its unnumbered hills, and its many depressions, scalloped out of the sandy soil by the action of winds. Coveys of wild quail were encountered, prairie chicken took wing on every hand, and near the noon hour a monster gray wolf arose from a sunny siesta on the summit of a near-by dune, and sniffed the air in search of the cause of disturbance. Unseen, the boys reined in their horses, a windward breeze favored the view for a moment, when ten nearly full-grown cubs also arose and joined their mother in scenting the horsemen. It was a rare glimpse of wary beasts, and like a flash of light, once the human scent was detected, mother and whelps skulked and were lost to sight in an instant.

"They're an enemy of cattle," whispered Joel when the cubs appeared. "The young ones are not old enough yet to hunt alone, and are still following their mother. Their lair is in these hills, and if this proves a cold winter, hunger will make them attack our cattle before spring. We may have more than storms to fight. There they go."

"How are we to fight them?" timidly asked Dell. "We have neither dog nor gun."

"Mr. Paul will know," replied Joel with confidence. "They'll not bother us while they can get food elsewhere."

The shelter of a wolf-pack's lair was not an encouraging winter refuge to drifting cattle. The boys even shook out their horses for a short gallop in leaving the sand dunes, and breathed easier once the open of the plain was reached. Following a low watershed, the brothers made a wide detour from the Beaver, but on coming opposite the homestead, near the middle of the afternoon, they turned and rode directly for the ranch, where a welcome surprise greeted them.

Four men were at work on the branding chute. A single glance revealed both Priest and Forrest among the quartette. On riding up to the stable corral, in the rough reception which followed, the lads were fairly dragged from their saddles amid hearty greetings. "Well, here we are again, and as busy as cranberry merchants," said Priest, once order was restored.

"Where's your herd?" inquired Joel.

"He hasn't any," interrupted Forrest; "he's working for me. About this time to-morrow evening, I'll split this ranch wide open with two herds, each of thirty-five hundred two-year-old steers. I'm coming with some style this time. You simply can't keep a good man down."

"There were two herds instead of one to go to the old man's beef ranch," explained Priest. "We brought along a couple extra men and came through a day ahead. We can't halt our cattle, but we can have the chute and corrals nearly ready when the herds arrive. All we'll lack is the hardware, and the wagons will reach here early during the afternoon."

The homestead presented a busy scene for the remainder of the day. Every old tool on the ranch was brought into service, and by twilight the outlines of the branding chute had taken form. The stable corral was built out of heavy poles and posts, with a capacity of holding near one hundred cattle, and by a very slight alteration it could be enlarged, with branding conveniences added.

At this point it was deemed advisable to enlighten the boys regarding the title of stray cattle. Forrest and Priest had talked the matter over between themselves, and had decided that the simple truth concerning the facts was the only course to adopt. The older of the two men, by the consent of years, was delegated to instruct the lads, and when the question of brands to be adopted by the new ranch was under consideration, the chance presented itself.

"In starting this ranch," said the gray-haired foreman to the boys, as they all sat before the tent in the twilight, "we'll have to use two brands. Cattle are conveyed from one owner to another by bill-of-sale. In a big pastoral exodus like the present, it is simply impossible to keep strays out of moving herds. They come in at night, steal in while a herd is passing through thickets, while it is watering, and they may not be noticed for a month. Under all range customs, strays are recognized as flotsam. Title is impossible, and the best claim is due to the range that gives them sustenance. It has always been customary to brand the increase of strays to the range on which they are found, and that will entitle you to all calves born of stray mothers."

The brothers were intent listeners, and the man continued: "For fear of winter drifting, and that they may be identified, we will run all these strays into Two Bars on the left hip, which will be known as the 'Hospital' brand. For the present, that will give us an asylum for that branch of flotsam gathered, and as trustees and owners of the range, all increase will fall to Wells Brothers. However, in accepting this deputyship, you do so with the understanding that the brand is merely a tally-mark, and that in no way does it deprive the owner of coming forward to prove and take possession of his property. This method affords a refuge to all strays in your possession, and absolves you from any evil intent. All other cattle coming under your control, with the knowledge and consent of the owner or his agent, are yours in fee simple, and we will run them into any brand you wish to adopt."

"But suppose no one ever calls for these stray cows?" said Joel, meditating.

"Then let them live out their days in peace," advised Forrest. "The weeds grow rankly wherever a cow dies, and that was the way their ancestors went. One generation exempts you."

The discovery of wolves in that immediate vicinity was not mentioned until the following morning. The forces were divided between the tasks, and as Priest and Joel rode up the valley to the site of the new corral, the disclosure was made known.

"Wolves? Why, certainly," said Priest, answering his own query. "Wolves act as a barometer in forecasting the coming of storms. Their activity or presence will warn you of the approach of blizzards, and you want to take the hint and keep your weather eye open. When other food becomes scarce, they run in packs and will kill cattle. You are perfectly safe, as yours will be either under herd or in a corral. Wolves always single out an animal to attack; they wouldn't dare enter an inclosure. Taken advantage of in their hunger, they can be easily poisoned. A wolf dearly loves kidney suet or fresh tallow, and by mixing strychnine with either, they can be lured to their own destruction."

The post-holes were dug extra deep for the corral. The work was completed before noon, the gate being the only feature of interest. It was made double, fifty feet wide, and fastened in the centre to a strong post. The gate proper was made of wire, webbed together with stays, admitting of a pliability which served a double purpose. By sinking an extra post opposite each of the main ones, the flexibility of the gate also admitted of making a perfect wing, aiding in the entrance or exit of a herd. In fastening the gate in the centre short ropes were used, and the wire web drawn taut to the tension of a pliable fence. "You boys will find this short wing, when penning a herd, equal to an extra man," assured the old foreman.

The first round-up on the new ranch took place that afternoon. Forrest took the extra men and boys, and riding to the extreme upper limits of the range, threw out the drag-net of horsemen and turned homeward. The cattle ranged within a mile or two on either side of the creek, and by slowly closing in and drifting down the Beaver, the nucleus of the ranch was brought into a compact herd. There was no hurry, as ample time must be allowed for the arrival of the wagons and stretching of the wire, in finishing and making ready the upper corral for its first reception of cattle. There was a better reason for delay, which was held in reserve, as a surprise for the boys.

As expected, the wagons and remudas arrived at the new ranch hours in advance of the herds. The horse wranglers were detailed by Priest, and fitting an axle to the spool of wire, by the aid of ropes attached to the pommels of two saddles, it was rolled up to the scene of its use at an easy canter. The stretching of the wire was less than an hour's work, the slack being taken up by the wranglers, ever upholding Texas methods, from the pommels of saddles, while Priest clinched the strands with staples at the proper tension. The gates were merely a pliable extension of the fence, the flexible character requiring no hinges. "Now, when the stays are interwoven through the wire, and fastened in place with staples, there's a corral that will hold a thousand cattle," said one of the wranglers admiringly.

It was after sunset when the herd was penned. Forrest, after counting the round-up to his satisfaction, detailed Dell and Joel to graze the herd in a bend of the Beaver, out of sight and fully a mile above, and taking the extra men returned to the homestead. The trail herds had purposely arrived late, expecting to camp on the Beaver that night, and were met by their respective foremen while watering for the day. In receiving, at Dodge, two large herds of one-aged cattle, both foremen, but more particularly Forrest, in the extra time at his command, had levied on the flotsam of the herds from which his employer was buying, until he had accumulated over one hundred cattle. Priest had secured, among a few friends and the few herds with which he came in contact, scarcely half that number, and still the two contingents made a very material increase to the new ranch.

The addition of these extra cattle was the surprise in reserve. Joel and Dell had never dreamed of a further increase to the ranch stock, and Forrest had timed the corralling of the original and late contingents as the climax of the day's work. Detailing both of the boys on the point, as the upper herd was nearing the corral, it was suddenly confronted by another contingent, rounding a bend of the creek from the opposite quarter. Priest had purposely detailed strange men, coached to the point of blindness, in charge of the new addition, and when the two bunches threatened to mix, every horseman present except the boys seemed blind to the situation.

Dell and Joel struggled in vain – the cattle mixed. "Well, well," said Forrest, galloping up, "here's a nice come-off! Trust my own boys to point a little herd into a corral, and they let two bunches of cattle mix! Wouldn't that make a saint swear!"

"Those other fellows had no man in the lead or on the point," protested Dell dejectedly. "They were looking away off yonder, and their cattle walked into ours. Where were you?"

"One of my men was telling me about an old sweetheart of his down on the Trinity River, and it made me absent-minded. I forgot what we were doing. Well, it's too late in the day to separate them now. We'll pen them until morning."

The appearance of Priest and the readiness with which the strange men assisted in corralling the herd shortly revealed the situation to the crafty Joel. On the homeward canter, the gray-haired foreman managed to drop a word which lightened Dell's depression and cleared up the supposed error.

That was a great night on the Beaver. The two wagons camped together, the herds bedded on either side of the creek, and the outfits mingled around the same camp-fire. Rare stories were told, old songs were sung, the lusty chorus of which easily reached the night-herders, and was answered back like a distant refrain.

The next morning the herds moved out on their way without a wasted step. Two men were detailed from each outfit, and with the foremen and the boys, a branding crew stood ready for the task before them. The chute had been ironed and bolted the evening previous, and long before the early rays of the sun flooded the valley of the Beaver, the first contingent of cattle arrived from the upper corral.

The boys adopted Bar Y as their brand. The chute chambered ten grown cattle, and when clutched in a vise-like embrace, with bars fore and aft, the actual branding, at the hands of two trail foremen, was quickly over. The main herd was cut into half a dozen bunches, and before the noon hour arrived, the last hoof had passed under the running irons and bore the new owner's brand or tally-mark.

Only a short rest was allowed, as the herds were trailing the limit of travel, and must be overtaken by evening. When crossing the railroad a few days before, it was learned that Grinnell was the railroad depot for settlers' supplies, and the boys were advised to file their order for corn, and to advance a liberal payment to insure attention. All details of the ranch seemed well in hand, the cattle were in good condition to withstand a winter, and if spirit and confidence could be imparted, from age to youth, the sponsors of the venture would have felt little concern for the future. If a dry, open winter followed, success was assured; if the reverse, was it right to try out the very souls of these waifs in a wintry crucible?

The foremen and their men left early in the afternoon. On reaching a divide, which gave the party of horsemen a last glimpse of the Beaver, the cavalcade halted for a parting look.

"Isn't it a pretty range?" said Forrest, gazing far beyond the hazy valley. "I wish we knew if those boys can stick out the winter."

"Stick? We'll make them stick!" said Priest, in a tone as decisive as if his own flesh and blood had been insulted.

CHAPTER VIII
THE LINES OF INTRENCHMENT

The boys watched the cavalcade until it faded away in the swells of the plain. At each recurring departure of their friends, in spite of all bravado to the contrary, a pall of loneliness crept into the hearts of the waifs. Theirs had been a cheerless boyhood; shifted about from pillar to post, with poverty their one sure companion, they had tasted of the wormwood in advance of their years. Toys such as other lads played with for an hour and cast aside were unknown in their lives, and only the poor substitute for hoop, horse, or gun had been theirs. In the struggle for existence, human affection was almost denied them. A happy home they had never known, and the one memory of their childhood worthy of remembrance was the love of a mother, which arose like a lily in the mire of their lives, shedding its fragrance more fully as its loss was realized.

Joel was the more sensitive of the brothers. Forrest had fully discussed the coming winter with the older lad, and as an incentive to watchfulness had openly expressed doubt of the ability of the boys to battle with the elements. The conversation was depressing, and on the departure of the men, the boys resumed the discussion of the matter at issue.

"Mr. Quince thinks we can't hold these cattle," said Joel, watching the receding horsemen. "He's afraid a storm will catch us several miles out and cut us off from reaching the corral. Well, it will be my fault if it does."

Dell made a boastful remark, but the older boy only intensified his gaze at the fading cavalcade. A vision of his youthful sufferings flashed through his mind, and a mist, closely akin to tears, dimmed his eyes. He had learned the lesson that poverty teaches, unaware that the storm which rocks also roots the oak, but unable to make the comparison or draw the inference between surrounding nature and himself. For an instant the horsemen dipped from view, changing the scene, and a picture rose up, a vision of the future, of independence, of a day when he would take his place as a man among men. The past was beyond his control, its bridges burned, but the future was worth battling for; and as if encouraged by invisible helpers, the boy turned his face to the valley of the Beaver.

"We'll hold these cattle or starve," said he, unconsciously answering his gray-haired sponsor, fading from sight over the last divide. "Hold them. I can hold them alone."

"There's no danger of starving," commented Dell, following his brother into the tent. "We have provisions for a year."

"Then we'll hold the herd or freeze," answered Joel, almost hissing the words – words which became a slogan afterward.

The cattle drifted back to their chosen range. The late addition mixed and mingled with the others, now attached to the valley, with its abundance of grass and water. Nothing was said about the first four horses, from which the boys understood that they were, at least for the present, left in their charge. All told, sixteen horses, fully half of which were fit for saddle, were at the service of the ranch, ample in number in proportion to the cattle secured.

It was only the middle of August. An accident, and a little over two months' time, had changed the character of the Beaver valley. With no work pressing, the brothers rode the range, circling farther to the west and south, until any country liable to catch a winter drift became familiar to sight. Northward ho! the slogan of every drover had ceased, and the active trail of a month before had been deserted. The new ranch had no neighbors, the nearest habitation was on the railroad to the south, and the utter loneliness of the plain was only overcome by active work. To those who love them, cattle and horses are good company, and in their daily rides the lads became so familiar with the herd that in the absence of brands they could have readily identified every animal by flesh marks alone. Under almost constant contact with the boys, the cattle became extremely gentle, while the calves even grew so indifferent that they reluctantly arose from their beds to avoid a passing horseman.

The cutting, curing, and garnering home the field of corn was a welcome task. It augmented the forage supply, assuring sustenance to the saddle horses, an important feature in withstanding the coming winter siege. An ideal fall favored the ranch, the dry weather curing the buffalo grass on the divides, until it was the equal of hay, thus assuring the cattle of ample grazing until spring. The usual squaw winter passed in a swirl of snow, a single angry day, to be followed by a month of splendid Indian summer. Its coming warned the lads; the order for corn was placed; once a week the cattle were brought in and corralled, and the ranch was made snug against the wintry months.

The middle of November was as early as the railroad would agree to deliver the corn. It would take three days to go and come, and an equal number of round trips would be required to freight the grain from the railroad to the ranch. The corn had been shelled and sacked at elevator points, eastward in the State, and in encouraging emigration the railroad was glad to supply the grain at cost and freightage.

The hauling fell to Joel. He had placed the order, making a deposit, and identification was necessary with the agent. On the very first trip to Grinnell, a mere station on the plain, a surprise awaited the earnest boy. As if he were a citizen of the hamlet, and in his usual quiet way, Paul Priest greeted Joel on his arrival. The old foreman had secretly left a horse with the railroad agent at Buffalo, where the trail crossed, had kept in touch with the delivery of corn at stations westward, and had timed his affairs so as to meet and pay a final visit to his protégées.

"A battle is sometimes lost by a very slight oversight or accident," said the man to the boy. "The ammunition may get damaged, slippery ground might prevent the placing of a battery at an opportune moment, or the casting of a horse's shoe might delay a courier with an important order. I feel an interest in your little ranch, and when I know that everything is done that can be done to fortify against the coming winter, I'll go home feeling better. There is such a thing as killing the spirit of a soldier, and if I were to let you boys try and fail, it would affect your courage to face the future. That's the reason I've dropped off to take a last look at your lines of intrenchment. We've got to hold those cattle."

"Mr. Quince thinks we won't, but let the winter come as it may, we're going to hold the herd," simply said the boy.

There was a resolution, an earnestness, in the words of the lad that pleased the man. "Your Mr. Quince has seen some cold winters on the range," said the latter, "and that's the reason he fears the worst. But come as it will, if we do all in our power, put up the best fight in us, and fail, then we are blameless. But with my experience, if I let you fail, when you might have won, then I have done you an injury."

That was the platform on which men and boys stood, the outline on which their mutual venture must stand or fall, and admitted of no shirking on the part of any one. The most minute detail, down to a change of clean saddle blankets, for winter work, must be fully understood. The death of a horse in which reliance rested, at an unfortunate moment, might mean the loss of the herd, and a clean, warm blanket on a cold day was the merciful forethought of a man for his beast. No damp, frosty, or frozen blanket must be used on the Wells ranch.

On the return trip, an early start was made. A night camp was necessary, at the halfway point, the dread of which was robbed of its terrors by the presence of a veteran of the open. Before leaving the depot, Priest unearthed a number of bundles, "little things that might come in handy," among which was a sack of salt and two empty oak barrels. The latter provoked an inquiry from Joel, and an explanation was forced at the moment.

"Did you notice a big steer that came in with the last cattle, and which was overlooked in branding?" inquired Priest, meeting the boy's query with a question.

"A mottled beef, branded 7L?"

"That's the steer. Why do you reckon we overlooked branding him?"

"Dell and I thought it was an oversight."

"When you see what I'm going to do with that salt and these barrels, then you'll see that it was no neglect. That steer has undergone several Northern winters, has reached his prime, and the governor's cellar won't have any better corn beef this winter than the Wells ranch. Seven or eight hundred pounds of pickled beef is an important item in the winter intrenchments. In fact, it's an asset to any cow camp. There are so many little things that may come in handy."

The second morning out from the station, Priest bore off on a course that would land him well above the grove on the Beaver. He had never been over the range, and not wishing to waste a day with a loaded wagon, he angled away for the sand hills which formed the divide, sloping away to the branches of the main creek. Noon found him on the south fork; cattle were encountered near the juncture, and as he approached the grove, a horseman rode out as if to dispute the passage of an intruder. The old foreman noticed the boyish figure and delayed the meeting, reining in to critically examine cattle which he had branded some three months before. With diligent intent, the greeting was kept pending, the wayfarer riding away on a tangent and veering back on his general course, until Dell's suspicion was aroused. The return of Priest was so unexpected that the boy's eyes filled with tears, and the two rode along until the grove was reached, when they dismounted.

"If I had known that you were coming," said Dell, "I could have made coffee here. It was so lonesome at the ranch that I was spending the day among the cattle."

"A cowman expects to miss his dinner occasionally," admitted Priest; "that's why they all look so long and hungry. Where does that 7L steer range?"

"The big mottled fellow? – Why, down near the corral," replied the boy, repeating and answering the question.

"I want to look him over," simply said the old foreman.

The two remounted and continued down the valley. The noon hour had brought the herd in for its daily water, and no animal was overlooked on the homeward ride. The summer gloss had passed and the hairy, shaggy, winter coats of the cattle almost hid the brands, while three to six months' rest on a perfect range was reflected in the splendid condition of the general herd.

"That's one feature of the winter intrenchments that needn't worry us," said Priest; "the cattle have the tallow to withstand any ordinary winter."

"And the horses are all rolling fat," added Dell. "They range below the ranch; and there isn't a cripple or sore back among them. There's the mottled steer."

They were nearing the last contingent of cattle. Priest gave the finished animal a single glance, and smiled. "Outsiders say," said he, "that it's a maxim among us Texans never to eat your own beef. The adage is worth transplanting. We'll beef him. The lines of intrenchment are encouraging."

The latter remarks were not fully understood by Dell, but on the arrival of the wagon that evening, and a short confidence between the brothers, the horizon cleared. Aside from the salt and barrels, there were sheepskin-lined coats and mittens, boots of heavy felting, flannels over and under, as if the boys were being outfitted for a polar expedition. "It may all come in handy," said a fatherly voice, "and a soldier out on sentinel duty ought to be made comfortable. In holding cattle this winter, it's part of the intrenchments."

A cyclone cellar served as a storeroom for the sacked corn. Joel was away by early sun-up, on the second trip to the station, while those left behind busied themselves in strengthening the commissary. The barrels were made sweet and clean with scalding water, knives were ground, and a crude platform erected for cooling out meat. Dell, on the tip-toe of expectancy, danced attendance, wondering how this quiet man would accomplish his ends, and unable to wholly restrain his curiosity.

"Watch me closely," was the usual reply. "You will probably marry young, and every head of a family, on a ranch, ought to know how to cure corn beef. Give me a week of frosty nights, and the lesson is yours. Watch me closely."

The climax of the day was felling the beef. Near the middle of the afternoon, the two rode out, cut off a small contingent of cattle, including the animal wanted, and quietly drifted them down to the desired location. Dell's curiosity had given way to alertness, and when the old foreman shook out a rope, the boy instinctively knew that a moment of action was at hand. Without in the least alarming the other cattle, the cast was made, the loop opened in mid-air, settled around the horns, cut fast by a jerk of the rope, and the contest between man and animal began. It was over in a moment. The shade of a willow was the chosen spot, and as the cattle were freed, the steer turned, the horseman taking one side of the tree and the beef the other, wrapping several turns of the rope in circling on contrary courses. The instant the big fellow quieted, on its coming to a level, a pistol flashed, and the beef fell in his tracks. That was the programme – to make the kill in the shade of the willow. And it was so easily done.

"That's about all we can do on horseback," said the gray-haired Texan, dismounting. "You may bring the knives."

Every step in the lesson was of interest to Dell. Before dark the beef was cut into suitable pieces and spread on the platform to drain and cool. During the frosty night following, all trace of animal heat passed away, and before sunrise the meat was salted into barrels. Thereafter, or until it was drained of every animal impurity, the beef was spread on the platform nightly, the brine boiled and skimmed, until a perfect pickle was secured. It was a matter of a week's concern, adding to the commissary two barrels of prime corned beef, an item of no small value in the line of sustenance.

The roping of the beef had not been overlooked. "I can't see what made the loop open for you yesterday," said Dell the next morning; "it won't open for me."

Priest took the rope from the boy. "What the tail means to a kite, or the feather to an arrow," said he, running out an oval noose, "the same principle applies to open the loop of a rope. The oval must have a heavy side, which you get by letting the Hondo run almost halfway round the loop, or double on one side. Then when you make your cast, the light side will follow the heavy, and your loop will open. In other words, what the feather is to the arrow, the light side is to the heavy, and if you throw with force, the loop must open."

It seemed so easy. Like a healthy boy, Dell had an ambition to be a fearless rider and crack roper. During the week which followed, in the saddle or at leisure, the boy never tired of practicing with a rope, while the patient man called attention to several wrist movements which lent assistance in forming a perfect loop. The slightest success was repeated to perfection; unceasing devotion to a task masters it, and before the visit ended, the perfect oval poised in the air and the rope seemingly obeyed the hand of Dell Wells.

"It's all right to master these little details of the cattle business," said Priest to Dell, "but don't play them as lead cards. Keep them up your sleeve, as a private accomplishment, for your own personal use. These fancy riders and ropers are usually Sunday men. When I make up an outfit for the trail, I never insist on any special attainments. Just so he's good natured, and no danger of a rainy night dampening the twinkle in his eye, that's the boy for me. Then if he can think a little, act quick, clear, and to the point, I wouldn't care if he couldn't rope a cow in a month."

In considering the lines of resistance, the possibility of annoyance from wolves was not overlooked. There was an abundance of suet in the beef, several vials of strychnine had been provided, and a full gallon of poisoned tallow was prepared in event of its needs. While Joel was away after the last load of corn, several dozen wooden holders were prepared, two-inch auger holes being sunk to the depth of five or six inches, the length of a wolf's tongue, and the troughs charred and smoked of every trace of human scent.

That the boys might fully understand the many details, the final instructions were delayed until Joel's return. "Always bear in mind that a wolf is a wary beast," admonished Priest, "and match your cunning against his. Make no mistake, take no chances, for you're dealing with a crafty enemy. About the troughs on the ground, surrounding the bait, every trace of human scent must be avoided. For that reason, you must handle the holder with a spear or hay fork, and if you have occasion to dismount, to refill a trough, carry a board to alight on, remembering to lower and take it up by rope, untouched even by a gloved hand. The scent of a horse arouses no suspicion; in fact, it is an advantage, as it allays distrust."

In loading a bait, an object lesson was given, using unpoisoned suet. "After throwing off all suspicion," continued Priest, illustrating the process, "the next thing is to avoid an overdose. An overdose acts as an emetic, and makes a wise wolf. For that reason, you must pack the tallow in the auger hole, filling from a half to two thirds full. Force Mr. Wolf to lick it out, administer the poison slowly, and you are sure of his scalp. You will notice I have bored the hole in solid wood, to prevent gnawing, and you must pack the suet firmly, to prevent spilling, as a crafty wolf will roll a trough over and over to dislodge the bait. Keep your holders out in the open, exposed to the elements, scald the loading tools before using, and you have the upper hand of any wolves that may molest your cattle."

The trail foreman spent a pleasant two weeks at the Wells ranch. After the corn was in store, the trio rode the range and reviewed every possible line of defense. Since the winter could not be foreseen, the only safe course was to anticipate the worst, and barring the burning of the range from unseen sources, the new ranch stood prepared to withstand a winter siege. Everything to forefend against a day of stress or trial had been done, even to instilling courage into youthful hearts.

"There's only one thing further that comes to mind," said the practical man, as they rode homeward, "and that is to face an unexpected storm. If a change of weather threatens, point your herd to meet it, and then if you are caught out, you will have the storm in your back to drift the cattle home. Shepherds practice that rule, and the same applies to cattle under herd."

All horses were to be left at the new ranch for the winter. Dell volunteered to accompany their guest to the railroad and bring back the extra mount, thus leaving five of Lovell's horses in possession of the boys. On the day of departure, at breakfast, after a final summary of the lines of resistance, the trio dallied about the table, the trail foreman seemingly reluctant to leave.

"It's a common remark among us drovers," said Priest, toying with his coffee cup, "that a cowman is supposed to do his sleeping in the winter. But the next few months you boys must reverse that rule. Not that you need to deny yourselves abundant rest, but your vigilance should never sleep. Let your concern for the herd be the first and last thought of the day, and then I'll get my beauty sleep this winter. The unforeseen may happen; but I want you to remember that when storms howl the loudest, your Mr. Quince and I will be right around the bend of the creek, with our ear to the ground, the reserves, listening to the good fight you boys are making. Of course you could call the reserves, but you want the glory of the good fighting and the lust of victory, all to yourselves. That's the way I've got you sized up – die rather than show the white feather. Come on, Dell; we're sleeping in the summer."

CHAPTER IX
A WINTRY CRUCIBLE

The dreaded winter was at hand. Scarcely a day passed but the harbingers of air and sky sounded the warning approach of the forthcoming siege. Great flights of song and game birds, in their migration southward, lent an accent as they twittered by or honked in mid-air, while scurrying clouds and squally weather bore witness of approaching winter.

The tent was struck and stored away. The extra saddle stock was freed for the winter, and located around Hackberry Grove. The three best horses were given a ration of corn, and on Dell's return from the railroad, the cattle were put under herd. The most liberal freedom must be allowed; with the numbers on hand, the term *close* herding would imply grazing the cattle on a section of land, while *loose* herding would mean four or five times that acreage. New routes must be taken daily; the weather would govern the compactness and course of the herd, while a radius of five miles from the corral was a liberal range.

The brothers were somewhat familiar with winter on the plains. Cold was to be expected, but if accompanied by sunshine and a dry atmosphere, there was nothing to fear. A warm, fine day was usually the forerunner of a storm, the approach of which gave little warning, requiring a sleepless vigilance to avoid being taken unaware or at a disadvantage.

The day's work began at sunrise. Cattle are loath to leave a dry bed, and on throwing open the corral gates, it was often necessary to enter and arouse the herd. Thereafter, under normal conditions, it was a matter of pointing, keeping up the drag cattle, allowing the herd to spread and graze, and contracting and relaxing as occasion required. In handling, it was a decided advantage that the little nucleus had known herd restraint, in trailing overland from Texas, and were obedient, at a distance of fifty yards, to the slightest whistle or pressure of a herdsman. Under favorable conditions, the cattle could be depended on to graze until noon, when they were allowed an hour's rest, and the circle homeward was timed so as to reach the corral and water by sunset. The duties of each day were a repetition of the previous one, the moods of the old and younger cattle, sedate and frolicsome, affording the only variety to the monotony of the task.

"Holding these cattle is going to be no trouble at all," said Dell, as they rode homeward, at the end of the first day's herding. "My horse never wet a hair to-day."

"Don't shout before you're out of the woods," replied Joel. "The first of April will be soon enough to count our chickens. To-morrow is only the beginning of December."

"Last year we shucked corn up until Christmas."

"Husking corn is a burnt bridge with me. We're herding cattle this winter. Sit straight in your saddle."

A week of fine weather followed. The boys were kept busy, early and late, with the details of house and stable. A new route each day was taken with the herd, and after penning in the evening, it was a daily occurrence, before bedtime, to walk back to the corral and see that all was secure. Warning of approach and departure, on the part of the boys, either by whistling or singing, was always given the cattle, and the customary grunting of the herd answered for its own contentment. A parting look was given the horses, their forage replenished, and every comfort looked after to the satisfaction of their masters. By nature, horses are distant and slow of any expression of friendship; but an occasional lump of sugar, a biscuit at noon-time, with the present ration of grain, readily brought the winter mounts to a reliance, where they nickered at the approaching footsteps of their riders.

The trust of the boys, in their winter mounts, entitles the latter to a prominent place in the line of defense. Rowdy, Joel's favorite, was a veteran cow horse, dark brown in color, and, under the saddle, restless, with a knowledge of his work that bordered on the human. Dell favored Dog-toe, a chestnut in color, whose best point was a perfect rein, and from experience in roping could halt from any gait on the space of a blanket. The relay horse was named Coyote, a cinnamon-colored mount, Spanish marked in a black stripe down his back, whose limbs were triple-ringed above the knees, or where the body color merged with the black of his legs.

Their names had followed them from the trail, one of which was due to color marks, one to disposition, while that of Dell's chestnut was easily traceable, from black marks in his hoofs quartering into toes.

The first storm struck near the middle of December. It was preceded by an ideal day; like the promise of spring, a balmy south wind swept the range, while at night a halo encircled the moon.

"It will storm within three days," said Dell, as the boys strolled up to the corral for a last look at the sleeping cattle. "There are three stars inside the circle around the moon. That's one of Granny Metcalf's signs."

"Well, we'll not depend on signs," replied Joel. "These old granny omens may be all right to hatch chickens by, but not to hold cattle. All advice on that point seems to rely on corn-fed saddle horses and little sleep."

The brothers spent the customary hour at the corral. From the bluff bank which encircled the inclosure, the lads looked down on the contented herd, their possession and their promise; and the tie of man and his beast was accented anew in their youthful hearts.

"Mr. Paul was telling me on one of our rides," said Joel, gazing down on the sleeping herd, "that we know nothing of the human race in an age so remote that it owned no cattle. He says that when the pyramids of Egypt were being built, ours was then an ancient occupation. I love to hear Mr. Paul talk about cattle. Hark!"

The long howl of a wolf to the south was answered by a band to the westward, and echoed back from the north in a single voice, each apparently many miles distant. Animal instinct is usually unerring, and the boys readily recalled the statement of the old trail foreman, that the howling of wolves was an omen of a forthcoming storm.

"Let it come," said Joel, arising and starting homeward. "We'll meet it. Our course to-morrow will be northwest."

It came with little warning. Near the middle of the following afternoon, a noticeable lull in the wind occurred, followed by a leaden horizon on the west and north. The next breeze carried the icy breath of the northwest, and the cattle turned as a single animal. The alert horsemen acted on the instant, and began throwing the cattle into a compact herd. At the time they were fully three miles from the corral, and when less than halfway home, the storm broke in splendid fury. A swirl of snow accompanied the gale, blinding the boys for an instant, but each lad held a point of the herd and the raging elements could be depended on to bring up the rear.

It was no easy victory. The quarter from which the storm came had been anticipated to a fraction. The cattle drifted before its wrath, dropped into the valley just above the corral, where the boys doubled on the outside point, and by the aid of a wing-gate turned the wandering herd into the enclosure. The rear, lashed by the storm, instinctively followed the leaders, and the gates were closed and roped securely.

It was a close call. The lesson came vividly near to the boys. "Hereafter," said Joel, "all signs of a storm must be acted upon. We corraled these cattle by a scratch. Now I know what a winter drift means. A dozen men couldn't turn this herd from the course of to-day's storm. We must hold nearer the corral."

The boys swung into their saddles, and, trusting to their horses, safely reached the stable. A howling night followed; the wind banked the snow against every obstacle, or filled the depressions, even sifting through every crack and crevice in the dug-out. The boys and their mounts were snug within sod walls, the cattle were sheltered in a cove of the creek, and the storm wailed its dirges unheeded.

Dawn broke cold and clear. Sun-dogs flanked the day's harbinger and sunrise found the boys at the corral gate. The cattle lazily responded to their freedom, the course led to the nearest divide, wind-swept of snow, and which after an hour's sun afforded ample grazing for the day. The first storm of the winter had been met, and its one clear lesson lent a dread to any possible successors. The herd in the grip of a storm, cut off from the corral, had a new meaning to the embryo cowmen. The best advice is mere theory until applied, and experience in the practical things of life is not transferable.

The first storm was followed by ideal winter weather until Christmas day. The brothers had planned an extra supper on that occasion, expecting to excuse Dell during the early afternoon for the culinary task, and only requiring his services on corraling the herd at evening. The plan was feasible, the cattle were herd-broke, knew their bed and water, and on the homeward circle all that was required was to direct and time the grazing herd. The occasion had been looked forward to, partly because it was their very own, their first Christmas spread, and partly on account of some delicacies that their sponsor had forced on Dell on parting at the railroad, in anticipation of the day. The bounds of the supper approached a banquet, and the question of appetites to grace the occasion was settled.

The supper was delayed. Not from any fault in the planning, but the weather had not been consulted. The herd had been grazed out on a northwest course for the day, and an hour after noon, almost the time at which Dell was to have been excused, a haze obscured the sun and dropped like a curtain around the horizon. Scurrying clouds appeared, and before the herd could be thrown together and started, a hazy, leaden sky shot up, almost due west, heralding the quarter of the coming storm. The herd sensed the danger and responded to the efforts of the horsemen; but before a mile had been covered, it was enveloped in swirling snow and veering its march with the course of the storm. The eddying snow blinded the boys as to their direction; they supposed they were pointing the cattle into the valley, unaware that the herd had changed its course on the onslaught of the elements. Confidence gave way to uncertainty, and when sufficient time had elapsed to more than have reached the corral, conjecture as to their location became rife. From the moment the storm struck, both boys had bent every energy to point the herd into the valley, but when neither slope nor creek was encountered, the fact asserted itself that they were adrift and at the mercy of the elements.

"We've missed the corral," shouted Dell. "We're lost!"

"Not yet," answered Joel, amid the din of the howling storm. "The creek's to our right. Loosen your rope and we'll beat these leaders into the valley."

The plying of ropes, the shouting of boys, and the pressure of horses merely turned the foremost cattle, when a new contingent forged to the front, impelled onward by the fury of the storm. Again and again the boys plied the fear of ropes and the force of horses, but each effort was futile, as new leaders stepped into the track of the displaced ones, and the course of the herd was sullenly maintained.

The battle was on, and there were no reserves within call. In a crisis like the present, moments drag like hours, and the firing line needed heartening. A knowledge of the country was of no avail, a rod or two was the limit of vision, and the brothers dared not trust each other out of sight. Time moved forward unmeasured, yet amid all Joel Wells remained in possession of a stanch heart and an unbewildered mind. "The creek's to our right," was his battle cry. "Come on; let's turn these lead cattle once more."

Whether it was the forty-ninth or hundredth effort is not on record, but at some point in the good fight, the boys became aware that the cattle were descending a slope – the welcome, southern slope of the Beaver valley! Overhead the storm howled mercilessly, but the shelter of the hillside admitted of veering the herd on its course, until the valley was reached. No knowledge of their location was possible, and all the brothers could do was to cross to the opposite point, and direct the herd against the leeward bank of the creek. Every landmark was lost, with the herd drifting at will.

The first recognition was due to animal instinct. Joel's horse neighed, was answered by Dell's, and with slack rein, the two turned a few rods aside and halted at their stable door. Even then the boys could scarcely identify their home quarters, so enveloped was the dug-out in swirling snow.

"Get some matches," said Joel, refusing to dismount. "There's no halting these cattle short of the second cut-bank, below on the left. Come on; we must try and hold the herd."

The sullen cattle passed on. The halt was only for a moment, when the boys resumed their positions on the point and front. Allowing the cattle to move, assured a compact herd, as on every attempt to halt or turn it, the rear forged to the front and furnished new leaders, and in unity lay a hope of holding the drifting cattle.

The lay of the Beaver valley below headquarters was well known. The banks of the creek shifted from a valley on one side, to low, perpendicular bluffs on the other. It was in one of these meanderings of the stream that Joel saw a possible haven, the sheltering cut-bank that he hoped to reach, where refuge might be secured against the raging elements. It lay several miles below the homestead, and if the drifting herd reached the bend before darkness, there was a fighting chance to halt the cattle in a protected nook. The cove in mind was larger than the one in which the corral was built, and if a successful entrance could only be effected – but that was the point.

"This storm is quartering across the valley," said Joel, during a lull, "and if we make the entrance, we'll have to turn the herd on a direct angle from the course of the wind. If the storm veers to the north, it will sweep us out of the valley, with nothing to shelter the cattle this side of the Prairie Dog. It's make that entrance, or abandon the herd, and run the chance of overtaking it."

"We'll rush them," said Dell. "Remember how those men, the day we branded, rushed the cattle into the branding chute."

"They could do things that we wouldn't dare – those were trail men."

"The cattle are just as much afraid of a boy as of a man; they don't know any difference. You point them and I'll rush them. Remember that story Mr. Quince told about a Mexican boy throwing himself across a gateway, and letting a thousand range horses jump over him? You could do that, too, if you had the nerve. Watch me rush them."

It seemed an age before the cut-bank was reached. The meanderings of the creek were not even recognizable, and only an occasional willow could be identified, indicating the location of the present drift. Occasionally the storm thickened or lulled, rendering it impossible to measure the passing time, and the dread of nightfall was intensified. Under such stress, the human mind becomes intensely alert, and every word of warning, every line of advice, urged on the boys by their sponsors, came back in their hour of trial with an applied meaning. This was no dress parade, with the bands playing and horses dancing to the champing of their own bits; no huzzas of admiring throngs greeted this silent, marching column; no love-lit eyes watched their hero or soft hand waved lace or cambric from the border of this parade ground.

A lone hackberry tree was fortunately remembered as growing near the entrance to the bend which formed the pocket. When receiving the cattle from the trail, it was the landmark for dropping the cripples. The tree grew near the right bank of the creek, the wagon trail passed under it, making it a favorite halting place when freighting in supplies. Dell remembered its shade, and taking the lead, groped forward in search of the silent sentinel which stood guard at the gateway of the cove. It was their one hope, and by zigzagging from the creek to any semblance of a road, the entrance to the nook might be identified.

The march of the herd was slow and sullen. The smaller cattle sheltered in the lee of the larger, moving compactly, as if the density of the herd radiated a heat of its own. The saddle horses, southern bred and unacclimated, humped their backs and curled their heads to the knee, indicating, with the closing day, a falling temperature. Suddenly, and as clear as the crack of a rifle, the voice of Dell Wells was heard in the lead: –

"Come on, Joel; here's our hackberry! Here's where the fight is won or lost! Here's where you point them while I rush them! Come quick!"

The brothers shifted positions. It was the real fight of the day. Responding to spur and quirt, the horses sprang like hungry wolves at the cattle, and the gloomy column turned quartering into the eye of the storm. But as on every other attempt to turn or mill the drifting herd, new leaders forged to the front and threatened to carry the drift past the entrance to the pocket. The critical moment had arrived. Dismounting, with a coiled rope in hand, Dell rushed on the volunteer leaders, batting them over the heads, until they whirled into the angling column, awakened from their stupor and panic-stricken from the assault of a boy, who attacked with the ferocity of a fiend, hissing like an adder or crying in the eerie shrill of a hyena in the same breath. It worked like a charm! Its secret lay in the mastery of the human over all things created. Elated by his success, Dell stripped his coat, and with a harmless weapon in each hand, assaulted every contingent of new leaders, striking right and left, throwing his weight against their bodies, and by the magic of his mimic furies forcing them into obedience.

Meanwhile Joel had succeeded in holding the original leaders in line, and within a hundred yards from the turn, the shelter of the bend was reached. The domestic bovine lows for the comfort of his stable, and no sooner had the lead cattle entered the sheltering nook, than their voices arose in joyous lowing, which ran back through the column for the first time since the storm struck. Turning to the support of Dell, the older boy lent his assistance, forcing the angle, until the drag end of the column had passed into the sheltering haven. The fight was won, and to Dell's courage, in the decisive moment, all credit was due. The human is so wondrously constructed and so infinite in variety, that where one of these brothers was timid the other laughed at the storm, and where physical courage was required to assault a sullen herd, the daring of one amazed the other. Cattle are the emblem of innocence and strength, and yet a boy – in spite of all that has been written to the contrary – could dismount in the face of the wildest stampede, and by merely waving a handkerchief split in twain the frenzied onrush of three thousand beeves.

Dell recovered his horse, and the brothers rode back and forth across the mouth of the pocket. The cattle were milling in an endless merry-go-round, contented under the sheltering bluffs, lowing for mates and cronies, while above howled the elements with unrelenting fury.

"We'll have to guard this entrance until the cattle bed down for the night," remarked Joel, on surveying the situation. "I wonder if we could start a fire."

"I'll drop back to the hackberry and see if I can rustle some wood," said Dell, wheeling his horse and following the back trail of the cattle. He returned with an armful of dry twigs, and a fire was soon crackling under the cliff. A lodgment of old driftwood was found below the bend, and as darkness fell in earnest, a cosy fire threw its shadows over the nook.

A patrol was established and the night's vigil begun. The sentinel beat was paced in watches between the boys, the width of the gateway being about two hundred yards. There was no abatement of the storm, and it was hours before all the cattle bedded down. The welfare of the horses was the main concern, and the possibility of reaching home before morning was freely discussed. The instinct of the horses could be relied on to find the way to their stable, but return would be impossible before daybreak. The brothers were so elated over holding the cattle that any personal hardship was endurable, and after a seeming age, a lull in the elements was noticeable and a star shone forth. Joel mounted his horse and rode out of the cove, into the open valley, and on returning announced that the storm had broken and that an attempt to reach home was safe.

Quietly as Arabs, the boys stole away, leaving the cattle to sleep out the night. Once the hackberry was reached, the horses were given free rein, when restraint became necessary to avoid galloping home. The snow crunched underfoot, the mounts snorted their protest at hindrance, vagrant breezes and biting cold cut the riders to the marrow, but on approaching the homestead the reins were shaken out and the horses dashed up to the stable door.

"There's the morning star," observed Joel, as he dismounted.

"If we're going to be cowmen," remarked Dell, glancing at the star as he swung out of the saddle, "hereafter we'll eat our Christmas supper in October."

CHAPTER X
GOOD FIGHTING

Dawn found the boys in the saddle. A two hours' respite had freshened horses and riders. The morning was crimpy cold, but the horses warmed to the work, and covered the two miles to the bend before the sun even streaked the east. Joel rode a wide circle around the entrance to the cove, in search of cattle tracks in the snow, and on finding that none had offered to leave their shelter, joined his brother at the rekindled fire under the cliff. The cattle were resting contentedly, the fluffy snow underneath having melted from the warmth of their bodies, while the diversity of colors in the herd were blended into one in harmony with the surrounding scene. The cattle had bedded down rather compactly, and their breathing during the night had frosted one another like window glass in a humid atmosphere. It was a freak of the frost, sheening the furry coats with a silver nap, but otherwise inflicting no harm.

The cattle were allowed to rise of their own accord. In the interim of waiting for the sun to flood the cove, the boys were able to get an outline on the drift of the day previous. Both agreed that the herd was fully five miles from the corral when the storm struck, and as it dropped into the valley near the improvements (added to their present location), it had drifted fully eight miles in something like five hours.

"Lucky thing for us that it was a local storm," said Joel, as he hovered over the fire. "Had it struck out of the north we would be on the Prairie Dog this morning with nothing but snowballs for breakfast. Relying on signs did us a heap of good. It was a perfect day, and within thirty minutes we were drifting blindly. It's all easy to figure out in advance, but storms don't come by programme. The only way to hold cattle on these plains in the winter is to put your trust in corn-fed saddle horses, and do your sleeping in the summer."

"I wonder when the next storm will strike," meditated Dell.

"It will come when least expected, or threaten for days and days and never come at all," replied Joel. "There's no use sitting up at night to figure it out. Rouse out the cattle, and I'll point them up the divide."

The sunshine had crept into the bend, arousing the herd, but the cattle preferred its warmth to a frosty breakfast, and stood around in bunches until their joints limbered and urgent appetites sent them forth. In spite of the cold, the sun lent its aid, baring the divides and windswept places of snow; and before noon, the cattle fell to feeding so ravenously that the herdsmen relayed each other, and a dinner for boy and horse was enjoyed at headquarters. In the valley the snow lay in drifts, but by holding the cattle on divides and southern slopes, they were grazed to contentment and entered their own corral at the customary hour for penning. Old axes had been left at hand, and the first cutting of ice, to open the water for cattle, occupied the boys for fully an hour, after which they rode home to a well-earned rest.

Three days of zero weather followed. Sun-dogs, brilliant as rainbows and stately as sentinels, flanked the rising sun each morning, after which the cold gradually abated, and a week after, a general thaw and warm winds swept the drifts out of the valley. It was a welcome relief; the cattle recovered rapidly, the horses proved their mettle, while the boys came out more than victors. They were inuring rapidly to their new occupation; every experience was an asset in meeting the next one, while their general fibre was absorbing strength from the wintry trial on the immutable plain.

Only once during the late storm were wolves sighted. Near the evening of the second day, a band of three made its appearance, keeping in the distance, and following up the herd until it was corraled at the regular hour. While opening the ice, the boys had turned their horses loose among the cattle, and on leading them out of the corral, the trio of prowlers had crept up within a hundred yards. With a yell, the boys mounted and made a single dash at them, when the wolves turned, and in their hurried departure fairly threw up a cloud of snow.

"That's what Mr. Quince means by that expression of his, 'running like a scared wolf,'" said Joel, as he reined in old Rowdy.

"When will we put out the poison?" breathlessly inquired Dell, throwing his mount back on his haunches in halting.

"Just as soon as they begin to hang around. Remind me, and we'll look for tracks around the corral in the morning. My, but they were beauties! How I would like to have one of their hides for a foot-rug!"

"The first heavy snow that comes will bring them out of the sand hills," said Dell, as they rode home. "Mr. Paul said that hunger would make them attack cattle. Oh, if we could only poison all three!"

Dell rambled on until they reached the stable. He treated his mind to visions of wealth, and robes, and furry overcoats. The wolves had located the corral, the winter had barely begun, but the boys were aware of the presence of an enemy.

A complete circle of the corral was made the following morning. No tracks were visible, nor were any wolves sighted before thawing weather temporarily released the range from the present wintry grip. A fortnight of ideal winter followed, clear, crisp days and frosty nights, ushering in a general blizzard, which swept the plains from the British possessions to the Rio Grande, and left death and desolation in its pathway. Fortunately its harbingers threw its menace far in advance, affording the brothers ample time to reach the corral, which they did at a late evening hour. The day had been balmy and warm, the cattle came in, gorged from a wide circle over buffalo grass, the younger ones, as if instinctive of the coming storm and in gratitude of the shelter, even kicking up their heels on entering the gates. The boys had ample time to reach headquarters, much in doubt even then whether a storm would strike or pass away in blustering threats.

It began at darkness, with a heavy fall of soft snow. Fully a foot had fallen by bedtime, and at midnight the blizzard struck, howling as if all the demons of night and storm were holding high carnival. Towards morning a creeping cold penetrated the shack, something unknown before, and awoke the boys, shivering in their blankets. It was near their hour for rising, and once a roaring fire warmed up the interior of the room, Joel took a peep without, but closed the door with a shudder.

"It's blowing a hurricane," said he, shivering over the stove. "This is a regular blizzard – those others were only squalls. I doubt if we can reach the stable before daybreak. Those poor cattle – "

The horses were their first concern. As was their usual custom, well in advance of daybreak an attempt was made to reach and feed the saddle stock. It was Joel's task, and fortifying himself against the elements without, he announced himself as ready for the dash. It was less than a dozen rods between shack and stable, and setting a tallow dip in the window for a beacon, he threw open the door and sprang out. He possessed a courage which had heretofore laughed at storms, but within a few seconds after leaving the room, he burst open the door and fell on the bed.

"I'm blinded," he murmured. "Put out the light and throw a blanket over my head. The sifting snow cut my eyes like sand. I'll come around in a little while."

Daybreak revealed nothing worse from the driving snow than inflamed eyes and roughened cheeks, when another attempt was made to succor the horses. Both boys joined in the hazard, lashing themselves together with a long rope, and reached the stable in safety. On returning, Dell was thrown several times by the buffeting wind, but recovered his feet, and, following the rope, the dug-out was safely reached.

"That's what happened to me in the darkness," said Joel, once the shelter of the house was reached. "I got whipped off my feet, lost my bearings, and every time I looked for the light, my eyes filled with snow."

There was no abatement of the blizzard by noon. It was impossible to succor the cattle, but the boys were anxious to reach the corral, which was fully a mile from the shack. Every foot of the creek was known, and by hugging the leeward bank some little protection would be afforded and the stream would lead to the cattle. Near the middle of the afternoon, there was a noticeable abatement in the swirling snow, when the horses were blanketed to the limit and an effort made to reach the corral. By riding bareback it was believed any drifts could be forced, at least allowing a freedom to the mounts returning, in case the boys lost their course.

The blizzard blew directly from the north, and crossing the creek on a direct angle, Joel led the way, forcing drifts or dismounting and trampling them out until a pathway was made. Several times they were able to make a short dash between known points, and by hugging the sheltering bank of the creek, safely reached the corral. The cattle were slowly milling about, not from any excitement, the exercise being merely voluntary and affording warmth. The boys fell to opening up the water, the cattle crowding around each opening and drinking to their contentment. An immense comb of snow hung in a semicircle around the bend, in places thirty feet high and perpendicular, while in others it concaved away into recesses and vaults as fantastic as frosting on a window. It was formed from the early, softer snow, frozen into place, while the present shifting frost poured over the comb into the sheltered cove, misty as bride's veiling, and softening the grotesque background to a tint equaled only in the fluffy whiteness of swan's-down.

The corral met every requirement. Its protecting banks sheltered the herd from the raging blizzard; the season had inured the cattle, given them shaggy coats to withstand the cold, and only food was lacking in the present trial. After rendering every assistance possible, the boys remained at the corral, hoping the sun would burst forth at evening, only to meet disappointment, when their horses were given free rein and carried them home in a short, sure dash.

A skirmish for grazing ensued. During the next few days there was little or no sunshine to strip the divides of snow, but the cattle were taken out and given every possible chance. The first noticeable abatement of the storm was at evening of the third day, followed by a diminishing fourth, when for the first time the herd was grazed to surfeiting. The weather gradually faired off, the cattle were recovering their old form, when a freak of winter occurred. A week from the night the blizzard swept down from the north, soft winds crept up the valley, promising thawing weather as a relief to the recent wintry siege. But dawn came with a heavy snow, covering the range, ending in rain, followed by a freezing night, when the snow crusted to carry the weight of a man, and hill and valley lay in the grip of sleet and ice.

It was the unforeseen in the lines of intrenchment. The emergency admitted of no dallying. Cattle do not paw away obstacles as do horses and other animals to reach the grass, and relief must come in the form of human assistance. Even the horses were helpless, as the snow was too deep under the sleet, and any attempt to trample out pathways would have left the winter mounts bleeding and crippled. The emergency demanded men, but two boys came to the front in a resourceful manner. In their old home in Ohio, threshing flails were sometimes used, and within an hour after daybreak Joel Wells had fashioned two and was breaking a trail through the sleet to the corral.

The nearest divide lay fully a mile to the north. To reach it with the cattle, a trail, a rod or more in width, would have to be broken out. Leaving their horses at the corral, the brothers fell at the task as if it had been a threshing floor, and their flails rang out from contact with the icy sleet. By the time they had reached the divide it was high noon, and the boys were wearied by the morning task. The crusted snow lay fully six inches deep on an average, and if sustenance was rendered the cattle, whose hungry lowing reached equally hungry boys, the icy crust must be broken over the feeding grounds.

It looked like an impossible task. "Help me break out a few acres," said Joel, "and then you can go back and turn out the cattle. Point them up the broken-out trail, and bring my horse and come on ahead of the herd. If we can break out a hundred acres, even, the cattle can nose around and get down to the grass. It's our one hope."

The hungry cattle eagerly followed up the icy lane. By breaking out the shallow snow, the ground was made passably available to the feeding herd, which followed the boys as sheep follow a shepherd. Fortunately the weather was clear and cold, and if temporary assistance could be rendered the cattle, a few days' sunshine would bare the ground on southern slopes and around broken places, affording ample grazing. The flails rung until sunset, the sleet was shattered by acres, and the cattle led home, if not sufficiently grazed, at least with hunger stayed.

An inch of soft snow fell the following night, and it adhered where falling, thus protecting the sleet. On the boys reaching the corrals at an unusually early hour, a new menace threatened. The cattle were aroused, milling excitedly in a compact mass, while outside the inclosure the ground was fairly littered with wolf tracks. The herd, already weakened by the severity of the winter, had been held under a nervous strain for unknown hours, or until its assailants had departed with the dawn. The pendulum had swung to an evil extreme; the sleet afforded splendid footing to the wolves and denied the cattle their daily food.

"Shall we put out poison to-night?" inquired Dell, on summing up the situation.

"There's no open water," replied the older boy, "and to make a dose of poison effective, it requires a drink. The bait is to be placed near running water – those were the orders. We've got five hundred cattle here to succor first. Open the gates."

The second day's work in the sleet proved more effective. The sun scattered both snow and ice; southern slopes bared, trails were beaten out to every foot of open ground, and by the middle of the afternoon fully a thousand acres lay bare, inviting the herd to feast to its heart's content. But a night on their feet had tired out the cattle, and it was with difficulty that they were prevented from lying down in preference to grazing. On such occasions, the boys threw aside their flails, and, mounting their horses, aroused the exhausted animals, shifting them to better grazing and holding them on their feet.

"This is the first time I ever saw cattle too tired to eat," said Joel, as the corral gates were being roped shut. "Something must be done. Rest seems as needful as food. This is worse than any storm yet. Half of them are lying down already. We must build a bonfire to-night. Wolves are afraid of a fire."

Fully half the cattle refused to drink, preferring rest or having eaten snow to satisfy their thirst. The condition of the herd was alarming, not from want of food, but from the hungry prowlers of the night. Before leaving, the brothers built a little fire outside the gate, as best they could from the fuel at hand, expecting to return later and replenish the wood supply from headquarters.

The boys were apt in adopting Texas methods. Once the horses were fed and their own supper eaten, the lads fastened onto two dry logs, and from pommels dragged them up to the tiny blaze at the corral opening. It was early in the evening, the herd was at rest, and the light of the bonfire soon lit up the corral and threw fancy shadows on the combing snow which formed the upper rim. The night was crimping cold, and at a late hour the boys replenished the fire and returned home. But as they dismounted at the stable, the hunting cry of a wolf pack was wafted down the valley on the frosty air, and answered by a band far to the south in the sand hills.

"They're coming again," said Joel, breathlessly listening for the distant howling to repeat. "The fire ought to hold them at a distance until nearly morning. Let's feed the horses and turn in for the night."

Daybreak found the boys at the corral. No wolves were in sight, but on every hand abundant evidence of their presence during the night was to be seen. Nearly all the cattle were resting, while the remainder, principally mother cows, were arrayed in battle form, fronting one of the recesses under the combing rim of snow. On riding within the corral, the dread of the excited cows proved to be a monster wolf, crouching on a shelf of snow. He arose on his haunches and faced the horsemen, revealing his fangs, while his breast was covered with tiny icicles, caused by the driveling slaver during the night's run. His weight was responsible for his present plight, he having ventured out on the fragile comb of snow above, causing it to cave down; and in the bewilderment of the moment he had skurried to the safety of the ledge on which he then rested.

It was a moment of excitement. A steady fire of questions and answers passed between the younger and older brother. The wolf was in hand, the horns of a hundred angry cows held the enemy prisoner, and yet the boys were powerless to make the kill. The situation was tantalizing.

"Can't we poison him?" inquired Dell, in the extremity of the moment.

"Certainly. Hand it to him on a plate – with sugar on it."

"If Mr. Paul had only left us his pistol," meditated Dell, as a possibility.

"Yes, you could about hit that bank with a six-shooter. It's the risk of a man's life to wound that wolf. He's cornered. I wouldn't dismount within twenty feet of him for this herd."

"I could shoot him from Dog-toe. This is the horse from which Mr. Paul killed the beef. All trail horses are gun-proof."

"My, but you are full of happy ideas. We've got to let that wolf go – we can't make the kill."

"I have it!" shouted Dell, ignoring all rebuffs. "Dog-toe is a roping horse. Throw wide the gates. Give me a clear field, and I'll lasso that wolf and drag him to death, or wrap him to the centre gatepost and you can kill him with a fence-stay. Dog-toe, I'm going to rope a wolf from your back," added Dell, patting the horse's neck and turning back to the gate. "Show me the mettle of the State that bred you."

"You're crazy," said Joel, "but there's no harm in trying it. Whatever happens, stick to your saddle. Cut the rope if it comes to a pinch. I'll get a fence-stay."

Ever since the killing of the beef, Dell had diligently practiced with a rope. It responded to the cunning of his hand, and the danger of the present moment surely admitted of no false calculations. Dell dismounted with a splendid assurance, tightened the cinches, tied his rope good and firm to the fork of the saddle tree, mounted, and announced himself as ready. The cattle were drifted left and right, opening a lane across the corral, and Dell rode forward to study the situation. Joel took up a position at the gate, armed only with a heavy stay, and awaited the working out of the experiment.

The hazard savored more of inexperience than of courage. Dell rode carelessly back and forth, edging in nearer the ledge each time, whirling his loop in passing, at which the cowering animal arose in an attitude of defense. Nodding to Joel that the moment had come, as the horse advanced and the enemy came within reach, the singing noose shot out, the wolf arose as if to spring, and the next instant Dog-toe whirled under spur and quirt, leaving only a blur behind as he shot across the corral. Only his rider had seen the noose fall true, the taut rope bespoke its own burden, and there was no time to shout. For an instant, Joel held his breath, only catching a swerve in the oncoming horse, whose rider bore down on the centre post of the double gate, the deviation of course being calculated to entangle the rope's victim. The horse flashed through the gate, something snapped, the rope stood in air, and a dull thud was heard in the bewilderment of the moment. The blur passed in an instant, and a monster dog wolf lay at the gatepost, relaxing in a spasm of death.

Dell checked his horse and returned, lamenting the loss of a foot's length from his favorite rope. It had cut on the saddle tree, and thus saved horse and rider from an ugly fall.

"He lays right where I figured to kill him – against that post," said Dell, as he reined in and looked down on the dead wolf. "Do you want his hide, or can I have it?"

"Drag him aside," replied Joel, "while I rouse out the cattle. I'll have to sit up with you to-night."

CHAPTER XI
HOLDING THE FORT

The valley lay in the grasp of winter. On the hills and sunny slopes, the range was slowly opening to the sun. The creek, under cover of ice and snow, forced its way, only yielding to axes for the time being and closing over when not in use.

The cattle required no herding. The chief concern of the brothers was to open more grazing ground, and to that end every energy was bent. The range already opened lay to the north of the Beaver, and although double the distance, an effort was made to break out a trail to the divide on the south. The herd was turned up the lane for the day, and taking their flails, the boys began an attack on the sleet. It was no easy task, as it was fully two miles to the divide, a northern slope, and not affected by the sun before high noon.

The flails rang out merrily. From time to time the horses were brought forward, their weight shattering the broken sleet and assisting in breaking out a pathway. The trail was beaten ten feet in width on an average, and by early noon the divide was reached. Several thousand acres lay bare, and by breaking out all drifts and depressions running north and south across the watershed, new grazing grounds could be added daily.

A discovery was made on the return trip. The horses had been brought along to ride home on, but in testing the sleet on the divide, the sun had softened the crust until it would break under the weight of either of the boys. By walking well outside the trail, the sleet crushed to the extent of five or six feet, and by leading their horses, the pathway was easily doubled in width. Often the crust cracked to an unknown distance, easing from the frost, which the boys accepted as the forerunner of thawing weather.

"We'll put out poison to-night," said Dell. "It will hardly freeze a shoal, and I've found one below the corral."

"I'm just as anxious as you to put out the bait," replied Joel, "but we must take no chances of making our work sure. The moment the cattle quit drinking, the water holes freeze over. This is regular old Billy Winter."

"I'll show you the ripple and leave it to you," argued the younger boy. "Under this crust of sleet and snow, running water won't freeze."

"Along about sunset we can tell more about the weather for to-night," said Joel, with a finality which disposed of the matter for the present.

On reaching the corral, the older boy was delighted with the splendid trail broken out, but Dell rode in search of a known shallow in the creek. An old wood road crossed on the pebbly shoal, and forcing his horse to feel his way through the softened crust, a riplet was unearthed as it purled from under an earthen bank.

"Here's your running water," shouted Dell, dropping the reins and allowing Dog-toe to drink. "Here you are – come and see for yourself."

Joel was delighted with Dell's discovery. In fact, the water, after emerging from under a concave bank, within a few feet passed under another arch, its motion preventing freezing.

"Don't dismount," said Joel, emphasizing caution, "but let the horses break a narrow trail across the water. This is perfect. We'll build another fire to-night, and lay a half dozen baits around this open water."

The pelt of the dead wolf was taken, when the boys cantered in home. Time was barely allowed to bolt a meal, when the loading of the wooden troughs was begun. Every caution urged was observed; the basins were handled with a hay fork, sledded to the scene, and dropped from horseback, untouched by a human hand. To make sure that the poison would be found, a rope was noosed to the carcass and a scented trace was made from every quarter, converging at the open water and tempting baits.

"There," said Dell, on completing the spoor, "if that doesn't get a wolf, then our work wasn't cunningly done."

"Now, don't forget to throw that carcass back on the ledge, under the comb," added Joel. "Wolves have a reputation of licking each other's bones, and we must deny them everything eatable except poisoned suet."

The herd would not return of its own accord, and must be brought in to the corral. As the boys neared the divide and came in sight of the cattle, they presented a state of alarm. The presence of wolves was at once suspected, and dashing up at a free gallop, the lads arrived in time to save the life of a young steer. The animal had grazed beyond the limits of the herd, unconscious of the presence of a lurking band of wolves, until attacked by the hungry pack. Nothing but the energetic use of his horns saved his life, as he dared not run for fear of being dragged down, and could only stand and fight.

The first glimpse of the situation brought the boys to the steer's rescue. Shaking out their horses, with a shout and clatter of hoofs, they bore down on the struggle, when the wolves suddenly forsook their victim and slunk away. The band numbered eight by easy count, as they halted within two hundred yards and lay down, lolling their tongues as if they expected to return and renew the attack.

"Did you ever hear of anything like this?" exclaimed Dell, as the brothers reined in their horses to a halt. "Attacking in broad daylight!"

"They're starving," replied Joel. "This sleet makes it impossible to get food elsewhere. One of us must stay with the cattle hereafter."

"Well, we saved a steer and got a wolf to-day," boastfully said Dell. "That's not a bad beginning."

"Yes, but it's the end I dread. If this weather lasts a month longer, some of these cattle will feed the wolves."

There was prophecy in Joel's remark. The rescued animal was turned into the herd and the cattle started homeward. At a distance, the wolves followed, peeping over the divide as the herd turned down the pathway leading to the corral. Fuel had been sledded up, and after attending to the details of water and fire, the boys hurried home.

The weather was a constant topic. It became the first concern of the morning and the last observation of the night. The slightest change was noticeable and its portent dreaded. Following the blizzard, every moderation of the temperature brought more snow or sleet. Unless a general thaw came to the relief of the cattle, any change in the weather was undesirable.

A sleepless night followed. It was later than usual when the boys replenished the fire and left the corral. Dell's imagination covered the limits of all possibilities. He counted the victims of the poison for the night, estimated the number of wolves tributary to the Beaver, counted his bales of peltry, and awoke with a start. Day was breaking, the horses were already fed, and he was impatient for saddles and away.

"How many do you say?" insisted Dell, as they left the stable.

"One," answered Joel.

"Oh, we surely got seven out of those eight."

"There were only six baits. You had better scale down your estimate. Leave a few for luck."

Nothing but the cold facts could shake Dell's count of the chickens. Joel intentionally delayed the start, loitering between house and corral, and when no longer able to restrain his impulsive brother, together they reached the scene. Dell's heart failed him – not a dead wolf lay in sight. Every bait had been disturbed. Some of the troughs had been gnawed to splinters, every trace of the poisoned suet had been licked out of the auger holes, while the snow was littered with wolf tracks.

"Our cunning must be at fault," remarked Joel, as he surveyed the scene and empty basins.

Dell looked beaten. "My idea is that we had too few baits for the number of visitors. See the fur, where they fought over the tallow. That's it; there wasn't enough suet to leave a good taste in each one's mouth. From the looks of the ground, there might have been fifty wolves."

The boy reasoned well. Experience is a great school. The brothers awoke to the fact that in the best laid plans of mice and men the unforeseen is ever present. Their sponsors could only lay down the general rule, and the exceptions threw no foreshadows. No one could foresee that the grip of winter would concentrate and bring down on the little herd the hungry, roving wolf packs.

"Take out the herd to-day," said Dell, "and let me break out more running water. I'll take these basins in and refill them, make new ones, and to-night we'll put out fifty baits."

The cattle were pointed up the new trail to the southern divide. Joel took the herd, and Dell searched the creek for other shallows tributary to the corral. Three more were found within easy distance, when the troughs were gathered with fork and sled, and taken home to be refilled. It was Dell Wells's busy day. Cunning and caution were his helpers; slighting nothing, ever crafty on the side of safety, he cut, bored, and charred new basins, to double the original number. After loading, for fear of any human taint, he dipped the troughs in water and laid them in the shade to freeze. A second trip with the sled was required to transport the basins up to the corral, the day's work being barely finished in time for him to assist in penning the herd.

"How many baits have you?" was Joel's hail.

"Sixty odd."

"You'll need them. Three separate wolf packs lay in sight all the afternoon. Several times they crept up within one hundred yards of the cattle. One band numbered upwards of twenty."

"Let them come," defiantly said Dell. "The banquet is spread. Everything's done, except to drag the carcass, and I didn't want to do that until after the cattle were corraled."

The last detail of the day was to build a little fire, which would die out within an hour after darkness. It would allow the cattle time to bed down and the packs to gather. As usual, it was not the intention of the boys to return, and as they mounted their horses to leave, all the welled-up savage in Dell seemed to burst forth.

"Welcome, Mr. Wolf, welcome," said he, with mimic sarcasm and a gesture which swept the plain. "I've worked like a dog all day and the feast is ready. Mrs. Wolf, will you have a hackberry plate, or do you prefer the scent of cottonwood? You'll find the tender, juicy kidney suet in the ash platters. Each table seats sixteen, with fresh water right at hand. Now, have pallets and enjoy yourselves. Make a night of it. Eat, drink, and be merry, for to-morrow your pelts are mine."

"Don't count your chickens too soon," urged Joel.

"To-morrow you're mine!" repeated Dell, ignoring all advice. "I'll carpet the dug-out with your hides, or sell them to a tin peddler."

"You counted before they were hatched this morning," admonished his brother. "You're only entitled to one guess."

"Unless they got enough to sicken them last night," answered Dell with emphasis, "nothing short of range count will satisfy me."

A night of conjecture brought a morning with results. Breakfast was forgotten, saddles were dispensed with, while the horses, as they covered the mile at a gallop, seemed to catch the frenzy of expectation. Dell led the way, ignoring all counsel, until Dog-toe, on rounding a curve, shied at a dead wolf in the trail, almost unhorsing his rider.

"There's one!" shouted Dell, as he regained his poise. "I'll point them out and you count. There's another! There's two more!"

It was a ghastly revel. Like sheaves in a harvest field, dead wolves lay around every open water. Some barely turned from the creek and fell, others struggled for a moment, while a few blindly wandered away for short distances. The poison had worked to a nicety; when the victims were collected, by actual count they numbered twenty-eight. It was a victory to justify shouting, but the gruesome sight awed the brothers into silence. Hunger had driven the enemy to their own death, and the triumph of the moment at least touched one sensitive heart.

"This is more than we bargained for," remarked Joel in a subdued voice, after surveying the ravages of poison.

"Our task is to hold these cattle," replied Dell. "We're soldiering this winter, and our one duty is to hold the fort. What would Mr. Paul say if we let the wolves kill our cattle?"

After breakfast Joel again led the herd south for the day, leaving Dell at the corral. An examination of the basins was made, revealing the fact that every trace of the poisoned suet had been licked out of the holders. Of a necessity, no truce with the wolf became the slogan of the present campaign. No mushy sentiment was admissible – the fighting was not over, and the powder must be kept dry. The troughs were accordingly sledded into the corral, where any taint from the cattle would further disarm suspicion, and left for future use.

The taking of so many pelts looked like an impossible task for a boy. But Dell recalled, among the many experiences with which Forrest, when a cripple, regaled his nurses, was the skinning of winter-killed cattle with a team. The same principle applied in pelting a wolf, where by very little aid of a knife, about the head and legs, a horse could do the work of a dozen men. The corral fence afforded the ready snubbing-post, Dog-toe could pull his own weight on a rope from a saddle pommel, and theory, when reduced to the practical, is a welcome auxiliary. The head once bared, the carcass was snubbed to the centre gate post, when a gentle pull from a saddle horse, aided by a few strokes of a knife, a second pull, and the pelt was perfectly taken. It required steady mounting and dismounting, a gentle, easy pull, a few inches or a foot, and with the patience of a butcher's son, Dog-toe earned his corn and his master a bale of peltry.

Evening brought report of further annoyance of wolves. New packs had evidently joined forces with the remnants of the day before, as there was neither reduction in numbers nor lessening in approach or attitude.

"Ours are the only cattle between the Republican River in Nebraska and the Smoky River in this State," said Joel, in explanation. "Rabbits and other rodents are at home under this sleet, and what is there to live on but stock? You have to hold the cattle under the closest possible herd to avoid attack."

"That will made the fighting all the better," gloatingly declared Dell. "Dog-toe and I are in the fur business. Let the wolves lick the bones of their brethren to-night, and to-morrow I'll spread another banquet."

The few days' moderation in the weather brought a heavy snowfall that night. Fortunately the herd had enjoyed two days' grazing, but every additional storm had a tendency to weaken the cattle, until it appeared an open question whether they would fall a prey to the wolves or succumb to the elements. A week of cruel winter followed the local storm, during which three head of cattle, cripples which had not fully recuperated, in the daily march to the divides fell in the struggle for sustenance and fed the wintry scavengers. It was a repetition of the age-old struggle for existence – the clash between the forces of good and evil, with the wolf in the ascendant.

The first night which would admit of open water, thirty-one wolves fell in the grip of poison. It was give and take thereafter, not an eye for an eye, but in a ratio of ten to one. The dug-out looked like a trapper's cave, carpeted with peltry, while every trace of sentiment for the enemy, in the wintry trial which followed, died out in the hearts of the boys.

Week after week passed, with the elements allied with the wolves against the life of the herd. On the other hand, a sleepless vigilance and sullen resolve on the part of the besieged, aided by fire and poison, alone held the fighting line. To see their cattle fall to feed the wolves, helpless to relieve, was a bitter cup to the struggling boys.

A single incident broke the monotony of the daily grind. One morning near the end of the fifth week, when the boys rode to the corral at an early hour, in order to learn the result of poison, a light kill of wolves lay in sight around the open water. While they were attempting to make a rough count of the dead from horseback, a wolf, supposed to be poisoned, sprang fully six feet into the air, snapping left and right before falling to the ground. Nothing but the agility of Rowdy saved himself or rider, who was nearly unhorsed, from being maimed or killed from the vicious, instant assault.

The brothers withdrew to a point of safety. Joel was blanched to the color of the snow, his horse trembled in every muscle, but Dell shook out his rope.

"Hold on," urged Joel, gasping for breath. "Hold on. That's a mad wolf, or else it's dying."

"He's poisoned," replied Dell. "See how he lays his head back on his flank. It's the griping of the poison. Half of them die in just that position. I'm going to rope and drag him to death."

But the crunching of the horse's feet in the snow aroused the victim, and he again sprang wildly upward, snapping as before, and revealing fangs that bespoke danger. Struggling to its feet, the wolf ran aimlessly in a circle, gradually enlarging until it struck a strand of wire in the corral fence, the rebound of which threw the animal flat, when it again curled its head backward and lay quiet.

"Rope it," said Joel firmly, shaking out his own lasso. "If it gets into that corral it will kill a dozen cattle. That I've got a live horse under me this minute is because that wolf missed Rowdy's neck by a hand-breadth."

The trampled condition of the snow around the corral favored approach. Dell made a long but perfect throw, the wolf springing as the rope settled, closing with one foot through the loop. The rope was cautiously wrapped to the pommel, could be freed in an instant, and whirling Dog-toe, his rider reined the horse out over the lane leading to the herd's feeding ground to the south. The first quarter of a mile was an indistinct blur, out of which a horse might be seen, then a boy, or a wolf arose on wings and soared for an instant. Suddenly the horse doubled back over the lane, and as his rider shot past Joel, a fire of requests was vaguely heard, regarding "a noose that had settled foul," of "a rope that was being gnawed" and a general inability to strangle a wolf.

Joel saw the situation in an instant. The rope had tightened around the wolf's chest, leaving its breathing unaffected, while a few effectual snaps of those terrible teeth would sever any lasso. Shaking out a loop in his own rope, as Dell circled back over the other trail, Rowdy carried his rider within easy casting distance, the lasso hissed through the air, settled true, when two cow-horses threw their weight against each other, and the wolf's neck was broken as easily as a rotten thread.

"A little of this goes a long way with me," said Joel from the safety of his saddle.

"Oh, it's fine practice," protested Dell, as he dismounted and kicked the dead wolf. "Did you notice my throw? If it was an inch, it was thirty feet!"

In its severity, the winter of 1885-86 stands alone in range cattle history. It came rather early, but proved to be the pivotal trial in the lives of Dell and Joel Wells. Six weeks, plus three days, after the worst blizzard in the history of the range industry, the siege was lifted and the Beaver valley groaned in her gladness. Sleet cracks ran for miles, every pool in the creek threw off its icy gorge, and the plain again smiled within her own limits. Had the brothers been thorough plainsmen, they could have foretold the coming thaw, as three days before its harbingers reached them every lurking wolf, not from fear of poison, but instinctive of open country elsewhere, forsook the Beaver, not to return the remainder of the winter.

"That's another time you counted the chickens too soon," said Joel to his brother, when the usual number of baits failed to bring down a wolf.

"Very good," replied Dell. "The way accounts stand, we lost twelve cattle against one hundred and eighteen pelts taken. I'll play that game all winter."

CHAPTER XII
A WINTER DRIFT

The month of March was the last intrenchment in the wintry siege. If it could be weathered, victory would crown the first good fight of the boys, rewarding their courage in the present struggle and fortifying against future ones. The brothers had cast their lot with the plains, the occupation had almost forced itself on them, and having tasted the spice of battle, they buckled on their armor and rode forth. Without struggle or contest, the worthy pleasures of life lose their nectar.

The general thaw came as a welcome relief. The cattle had gradually weakened, a round dozen had fallen in sacrifice to the elements, and steps must be taken to recuperate the herd.

"We must loose-herd hereafter," said Joel, rejoicing in the thawing weather. "A few warm days and the corral will get miry. Unless the wolves return, we'll not pen the cattle again."

Dell was in high feather. "The winter's over," said he. "Listen to the creek talking to itself. No, we'll not have to corral the herd any longer. Wasn't we lucky not to have any more cattle winter-killed! Every day during the last month I felt that another week of winter would take half the herd. It was good fighting, and I feel like shouting."

"It was the long distance between the corral and the divides that weakened the cattle," said Joel. "Hereafter we'll give them all the range they need and only put them under close-herd at night. There may be squally weather yet, but little danger of a general storm. After this thaw, farmers on the Solomon will begin their spring ploughing."

A fortnight of fine weather followed. The herd was given almost absolute freedom, scattering for miles during the day, and only thrown together at nightfall. Even then, as the cattle grazed entirely by day, a mile square of dry slope was considered compact enough for the night. The extra horses, which had ranged for the winter around Hackberry Grove, were seen only occasionally and their condition noted. The winter had haired them like llamas, the sleet had worked no hardship, as a horse paws to the grass, and any concern for the outside saddle stock was needless.

The promise of spring almost disarmed the boys. Dell was anxious to know the value of the bales of peltry, and constantly urged his brother for permission to ride to the railroad and inquire.

"What's your hurry?" was Joel's rejoinder. "I haven't shouted yet. I'm not sure that we're out of the woods. Let's win for sure first."

"But we ought to write to Mr. Paul and Mr. Quince," urged the younger boy, by way of a double excuse. "There may be a letter from them at Grinnell now. Let's write to our friends in Texas and tell them that we've won the fight. The spring's here."

"You can go to the station later," replied Joel. "The fur will keep, and we may have quite a spell of winter yet. Don't you remember the old weather proverb, of March coming in like a lion and going out like a lamb? This one came in like a lamb, and we had better keep an eye on it for fear it goes out like a lion. You can go to the railroad in April."

There was wisdom in Joel's random advice. As yet there was no response in the earth to the sun's warmth. The grass was timid and refused to come forth, and only a few foolish crows had reached the shrub and willow along the Beaver, while the absence of other signs of spring carried a warning that the wintry elements might yet arise and roar like a young lion.

The one advantage of the passing days was the general improvement in the herd. The instinct of the cattle led them to the buffalo grass, which grew on the slopes and divides, and with three weeks of fair weather and full freedom the herd as a whole rounded into form, reflecting its tenacity of life and the able handling of its owners.

Within ten days of the close of the month, the weakened lines of intrenchment were again assaulted. The herd was grazing westward, along the first divide south of the Beaver, when a squall struck near the middle of the afternoon. It came without warning, and found the cattle scattered to the limits of loose herding, but under the eyes of two alert horsemen. Their mounts responded to the task, circling the herd on different sides, but before it could be thrown into mobile form and pointed into the Beaver valley, a swirl of soft snow enveloped horses and riders, cattle and landscape. The herd turned its back to the storm, and took up the steady, sullen march of a winter drift. Cut off from the corral by fully five miles, the emergency of the hour must be met, and the brothers rode to dispute the progress of the drifting cattle.

"Where can we turn them?" timidly inquired Dell.

"Unless the range of sand dunes catch us," replied Joel, "nothing short of the brakes of the Prairie Dog will check the cattle. We're out until this storm spends its force."

"Let's beat for the sand hills, then. They lay to our right, and the wolves are gone."

"The storm is from the northwest. If it holds from that quarter, we'll miss the sand dunes by several miles. Then it becomes a question of horseflesh."

"If we miss the sand hills, I'll go back and get a pack horse and overtake you to-morrow. It isn't cold, and Dog-toe can face the storm."

"That's our one hope," admitted Joel. "We've brought these cattle through a hard winter and now we mustn't lose them in a spring squall."

The wind blew a gale. Ten minutes after the storm struck and the cattle turned to drift with it, all knowledge of the quarter of the compass was lost. It was a reasonable allowance that the storm would hold a true course until its wrath was spent, and relying on that slender thread, the boys attempted to veer the herd for the sand hills. By nature cattle are none too gregarious, as only under fear will they flock compactly, and the danger of splitting the herd into wandering contingents must be avoided. On the march which lay before it, its compactness must be maintained, and to turn half the herd into the sand dunes and let the remainder wander adrift was out of the question.

"We'll have to try out the temper of the herd," said Joel. "The cattle are thin, have lost their tallow, and this wind seems to be cutting them to the quick. There's no use in turning the lead unless the swing cattle will follow. It's better to drift until the storm breaks than to split the herd into little bunches."

"Let's try for the sand hills, anyhow," urged Dell. "Turn the leaders ever so slightly, and I'll try and keep the swing cattle in line."

An effort to reach the shelter of the sand dunes was repeatedly made. But on each attempt the wind, at freezing temperature, cut the cattle to the bone, and as drifting was so much more merciful, the brothers chose to abandon the idea of reaching a haven in the sand hills.

"The cattle are too weak," admitted Joel, after repeated efforts. "Turn the leaders and they hump their backs and halt. An hour of this wind would drop them in their tracks. It's drift or die."

"I'll drop back and see how the drag cattle are coming on," suggested Dell, "and if they're in line I might as well start after a pack horse. We're only wearing out our horses in trying to turn this herd."

The efforts to veer the herd had enabled the drag end to easily keep in a compact line, and on Dell's return to the lead, he reported the drifting column less than a quarter mile in length.

"The spirit of the herd is killed," said he; "the cattle can barely hold their heads off the ground. Why, during that Christmas drift, they fought and gored each other at every chance, but to-day they act like lost sheep. They are half dead on their feet."

The herd had been adrift several hours, and as sustenance for man and horse was important, Dell was impatient to reach the Beaver before nightfall.

"If the storm has held true since it struck," said he, "I'll cut it quartering from here to headquarters. That good old corn that Dog-toe has been eating all winter has put the iron into his blood, until he just bows his neck and snorts defiance against this wind and snow."

"Now, don't be too sure," cautioned Joel. "You can't see one hundred yards in this storm, and if you get bewildered, all country looks alike. Trust your horse in any event, and if you strike above or below headquarters, if you keep your head on your shoulders you ought to recognize the creek. Give your horse free rein and he'll take you straight to the stable door. Bring half a sack of corn, some bread and meat, the tent-fly and blankets. Start an hour before daybreak, and you'll find me in the lead of the herd."

The brothers parted for the night. So long as he could ride in their lead, the necessity of holding the cattle was the lodestar that sustained Joel Wells during those lonely hours. There was always the hope that the storm would abate, when the tired cattle would gladly halt and bed down, which promise lightened the passing time. The work was easy to boy and horse; to retard the march of the leaders, that the rear might easily follow, was the task of the night or until relieved.

On the other hand, Dell's self-reliance lacked caution. Secure in his ability to ride a course, day or night, fair or foul weather, he had barely reached the southern slope of the Beaver when darkness fell. The horse was easily quartering the storm, but the pelting snow in the boy's face led him to rein his mount from a true course, with the result that several miles was ridden without reaching any recognizable landmark. A ravine or dry wash was finally encountered, when Dell dismounted. As a matter of precaution, he carried matches, and on striking one, confusion assumed the reign over all caution and advice. He was lost, but contentious to the last ditch. Several times he remounted and allowed his horse free rein, but each time Dog-toe turned into the eye of the storm, then the true course home, and was halted. Reason was abandoned and disorder reigned. An hour was lost, when the confident boy mounted his horse and took up his former course, almost crossing the line of storm on a right angle. A thousand visible forms, creatures of the night and storm, took shape in the bewildered mind of Dell Wells, and after dismounting and mounting unknown times, he floundered across Beaver Creek fully three miles below headquarters.

The hour was unknown. Still confused, Dell finally appealed to his horse, and within a few minutes Dog-toe was in a road and champing the bits against restraint. The boy dismounted, and a burning match revealed the outlines of a road under the soft snow. The horse was given rein again and took the road like a hound, finally sweeping under a tree, when another halt was made. It was the hackberry at the mouth of the cove, its broken twigs bespoke a fire which Dell had built, and yet the mute witness tree and impatient horse were doubted. And not until Dog-toe halted at the stable door was the boy convinced of his error.

"Dog-toe," said Dell, as he swung out of the saddle, "you forgot more than I ever knew. You told me that I was wrong, and you pled with me like a brother, and I wouldn't listen to you. I wonder if he'll forgive me?" meditated Dell, as he opened the stable door.

The horse hurriedly entered and nickered for his feed. "Yes, you shall have an extra ration of corn," answered his rider. "And if you'll just forgive me this once, the lesson you taught me to-night will never be forgotten."

It proved to be early in the evening – only eight o'clock. Even though the lesson was taught by a dumb animal, it was worth its cost. Before offering to sleep, Dell collected all the articles that were to make up the pack, foddered the horses, set the alarm forward an hour, and sought his blankets for a short rest. Several times the howling of the wind awoke him, and unable to sleep out the night, he arose and built a fire. The necessity of a pack saddle robbed him of his own, and, substituting a blanket, at the appointed hour before dawn he started, with three days' rations for man and horse. The snow had ceased falling, but a raw March wind blew from the northwest, and taking his course with it, he reached the divide at daybreak. A struggling sun gave him a bearing from time to time, the sand dunes were sighted, and angling across the course of the wind, the trail of the herd was picked up in the mushy snow. A bull was overtaken, resting comfortably in a buffalo wallow; three others were passed, feeding with the wind, and finally the sun burst forth, revealing the brakes of the Prairie Dog.

Where the cattle had drifted barely two miles an hour, sustenance was following at a five-mile gait. The trail freshened in the snow, narrowed and broadened, and near the middle of the forenoon the scattered herd was sighted. The long yell of warning was answered only by a tiny smoke-cloud, hanging low over the creek bed, and before Joel was aware of his presence, Dell rode up to the very bank under which the fire was burning.

"How do you like an all-night drift?" shouted Dell. "How do snowballs taste for breakfast?"

"Come under the cliff and unpack," soberly replied Joel. "I hope this is the last lesson in winter herding; I fail to see any romance in it."

The horses were unsaddled and fed. "Give an account of yourself," urged Dell, as the brothers returned to the fire. "How did you make out during the night?"

"I just humped my back like the other cattle and took my medicine," replied Joel. "An Indian dances to keep warm, and I sang. You have no idea how good company cattle are. One big steer laid his ear in Rowdy's flank to warm it. I took him by the horn any number of times and woke him up; he was just staggering along asleep. I talked to all the lead cattle, named them after boys we knew at school, and sometimes they would look up when I called to them. And the queerest thing happened! You remember old Redman, our teacher, back in Ohio. Well, I saw him last night. There was a black two-year-old steer among the lead cattle, and every time I looked at him, I saw old Redman, with his humped shoulder, his pug nose, and his half-shut eyes. It took the storm, the sullen drift, to put that expression in the black steer's face, but it was old Redman. During the two terms of school that he taught, he licked me a score of times, but I dared him to come out of that black steer's face and try it again. He must have heard me, for the little black steer dropped back and never came to the lead again."

"And had you any idea where you were?" inquired Dell, prompted by his own experience.

"I was right at home in the lead of the herd. The tepee might get lost, but I couldn't. I knew we must strike the Prairie Dog, and the cattle were within half a mile of it when day broke. Once I got my bearings, Rowdy and I turned on the herd and checked the drift."

A late breakfast fortified the boys for the day. It was fully twenty-five miles back to the Beaver, but with the cattle weakened, the horses worn, it was decided to rest a day before starting on the return. During the afternoon, Dell went back and threw in the stragglers, and towards evening all the cattle were put under loose herd and pointed north. The sun had stripped the snow, and a comfortable camp was made under the cliff. Wood was scarce on the Prairie Dog, but the dry, rank stalks of the wild sunflower made a good substitute for fuel, and night settled over human and animal in the full enjoyment of every comfort.

It was a two-days' trip returning. To Rowdy fell the duty of pack horse. He had led the outward march, and was entitled to an easy berth on retreat. The tarpaulin was folded the full length of the horse's body girth, both saddles being required elsewhere, and the corn and blankets laid within the pack and all lashed securely. The commissary supplies being light, saddle pockets and cantle strings were found sufficient for their transportation.

The start was made at sunrise. The cattle had grazed out several miles the evening before, and in their weakened condition it would require nursing to reach the Beaver. A mile an hour was the pace, nothing like a compact herd or driving was permissible, and the cattle were allowed to feed or rest at their will. Rowdy grazed along the flank, the boys walked as a relief, and near evening or on sighting the dunes, Dell took the pack horse and rode for their shelter, to locate a night camp. The herd never swerved from its course, and after sunset Joel rounded the cattle into compact form and bedded them down for the night. A beacon fire of plum brush led him to the chosen camp, in the sand hills, where supper awaited the brothers.

"Isn't it lucky," said Dell, as he snuggled under the blankets, "that the wolves are gone. Suppose they were here yet, and we had to build fires, or stand guard over the herd to-night, like trail men, could we do it?"

"Certainly. We met the wolves before and held the cattle. You seem to forget that we're not entitled to sleep any in the winter. Be grateful. Thank the wolf and go to sleep."

"See how the dunes loom up in the light of this camp-fire. I wish Mr. Paul could see it."

"More than likely he has camped in the dunes and enjoyed many rousing fires."

Dell's next remark was unanswered. The stars twinkled overhead, the sandman was abroad, curfew sounded through the dunes, and all was quiet.

"Here's where we burn the wagon," said Joel, as he aroused Dell at daybreak. "It's one of Mr. Quince's remarks, but this is the first time we've had a chance to use it. I'll divide the corn into three good feeds, and we'll make it in home for supper. Let's have the whole hummingbird for breakfast, so that when we ride out of this camp, all worth saving will be the coffee pot and frying pan. So long as we hold the cattle, who cares for expense."

The herd was in hand as it left the bed ground. An ideal spring day lent its aid to the snailing cattle. By the middle of the afternoon the watershed had been crossed, and the gradual slope down to the Beaver was begun. Rowdy forged to the lead, the flanks turned in, the rear pushed forward, and the home-hunger of the herd found expression in loud and continued lowing.

"I must have been mistaken about the spirit of this herd being killed," observed Dell. "When I left you the other day, to go after a pack horse, these cattle looked dead on their feet. I felt sure that we would lose a hundred head, and we haven't lost a hoof."

"We may have a lot to learn yet about cattle," admitted Joel. "I fully expected to see our back track strung with dead animals."

The origin of the herd, with its deeps and moods, is unknown and unwritten. The domesticity of cattle is dateless. As to when the ox first knew his master's crib, history and tradition are dumb. Little wonder that Joel and Dell Wells, with less than a year's experience, failed to fully understand their herd. An incident, similar to the one which provoked the observation of the brothers, may explain those placid depths, the deep tenacity and latent power of the herd.

After delivering its cargo at an army post, an extensive freighting outfit was returning to the supply point. Twelve hundred oxen were employed. On the outward trip, muddy roads were encountered, the wagons were loaded beyond the strength of the teams, and the oxen had arrived at the fort exhausted, spiritless, and faint to falling under their yokes. Many oxen had been abandoned as useless within one hundred miles of the post, thus doubling the work on the others. On the return trip, these scattered oxen, the lame and halt, were gathered to the number of several hundred, and were being driven along at the rear of the wagon train. Each day added to their numbers, until one fourth of all the oxen were being driven loose at the rear of the caravan. One day a boy blindfolded a cripple ox, which took fright and charged among his fellows, bellowing with fear. It was tinder to powder! The loose oxen broke from the herders, tore past the column of wagons, frenzied in voice and action. The drivers lost control of their teams, bedlam reigned, and the entire wagon train joined in the general stampede. Wagons were overturned and reduced to kindling in a moment of the wildest panic. The drivers were glad to escape with their lives and were left at the rear. A cloud of dust merely marked the direction which the oxen had taken. The teams, six to eight yoke each, wrenched their chains, broke the bows, and joined in the onrush. Many of the oxen, still under yoke, were found the next day fifteen miles distant from the scene of the incident, and unapproachable except on horseback. For a month previous to this demonstration of the latent power of cattle, the humane drivers of the wagon train were constantly lamenting that the spirit of their teams was killed.

When within a mile of the Beaver, the herd was turned westward and given its freedom. While drifting down the slope, Rowdy gradually crept far to the lead, and as the brothers left the cattle and bore off homeward, the horse took up a gentle trot, maintaining his lead until the stable was reached.

"Look at the dear old rascal," said Joel, beaming with pride. "That horse knows more than some folks."

"Yes, and if Dog-toe could talk," admitted Dell, stroking his horse's neck, "he could tell a good joke on me. I may tell it myself some day – some time when I want to feel perfectly ashamed of myself."

CHAPTER XIII
A WELCOME GUEST

The heralds of spring bespoke its early approach. April was ushered in to the songs of birds, the greening valley, and the pollen on the willow. The frost arose, the earth mellowed underfoot, and the creek purled and sang as it hastened along. The cattle played, calves were born, while the horses, in shedding their winter coats, matted the saddle blankets and threw off great tufts of hair where they rolled on the ground.

The marketing of the peltry fell to Joel. Dell met the wagon returning far out on the trail. "The fur market's booming," shouted Joel, on coming within speaking distance. "We'll not know the price for a few weeks. The station agent was only willing to ship them. The storekeeper was anxious to do the same, and advanced me a hundred dollars on the shipment. Wolf skins, prime, are quoted from two to two dollars and a half. And I have a letter from Forrest. The long winter's over! You can shout! G'long, mules!"

During the evening, Dell read Forrest's letter again and again. "Keep busy until the herds arrive," it read. "Enlarge your water supply and plan to acquire more cattle."

"That's our programme," said Joel. "We'll put in two dams between here and the trail. Mr. Quince has never advised us wrong, and he'll explain things when he comes. Once a week will be often enough to ride around the cattle."

An air of activity was at once noticeable around headquarters. The garden was ploughed and planting begun. The fence was repaired around the corn-field, the beaver dams were strengthened, and sites for two other reservoirs were selected. The flow of the creek was ample to fill large tanks, and if the water could be conserved for use during the dry summer months, the cattle-carrying capacity of the ranch could be greatly enlarged. The old beaver dams around headquarters had withstood every drouth, owing to the shade of the willows overhead, the roots of which matted and held the banks intact. Wagon loads of willow slips were accordingly cut for the new dams and the work begun in earnest.

"We'll take the tent and camp at the lower site," announced Joel. "It would waste too much time to go and come. When we build the upper one, we can work from home."

The two tanks were finished within a month. They were built several miles apart, where there was little or no fall in the creek, merely to hold still water in long, deep pools. The willow cuttings were planted along the borders and around the dams, the ends of which were riprapped with stone, and a spillway cut to accommodate any overflow during freshets.

The dams were finished none too soon, as a dry spring followed, and the reservoirs had barely filled when the creek ceased flowing. The unusual winter snowfall had left a season's moisture in the ground, and the grass came in abundance, matting slope and valley, while the garden grew like a rank weed. The corn crop of the year before had repaid well in forage, and was again planted. In the face of another drouthy summer, the brothers sowed as if they fully expected to reap. "Keep busy" was the slogan of the springtime.

The month of June arrived without a sign of life on the trail. Nearly one hundred calves were born to the herd on the Beaver, the peltry had commanded the highest quotation, and Wells Brothers swaggered in their saddles. But still the herds failed to come.

"Let's put up the tent," suggested Dell, "just as if we were expecting company. Mr. Paul or Mr. Quince will surely ride in some of these evenings. Either one will reach here a full day in the lead of his herd. Let's make out that we're looking for them."

Dell's suggestion was acted on. A week passed and not a trail man appeared. "There's something wrong," said Joel, at the end of the second week. "The Lovell herds go through, and there's sixteen of them on the trail."

"They're water-bound," said Dell, jumping at a conclusion.

"Waterbound, your foot! The men and horses and cattle can all swim. Don't you remember Mr. Quince telling about rafting his wagon across swimming rivers? Waterbound, your grandmother! High water is nothing to those trail men."

Dell was silenced. The middle of June came and the herds had not appeared. The brothers were beginning to get uneasy for fear of bad news, when near dark one evening a buckboard drove up. Its rumbling approach hurried the boys outside the tent, when without a word of hail, Quince Forrest sprang from the vehicle, grasped Dell, and the two rolled over and over on the grass.

"I just wanted to roll him in the dirt to make him grow," explained Forrest to an elderly man who accompanied him. "These are my boys. Look at that red-headed rascal – fat as a calf with two mothers. Boys, shake hands with Mr. Lovell."

The drover alighted and greeted the boys with fatherly kindness. He was a frail man, of medium height, nearly sixty years of age, with an energy that pulsed in every word and action. There was a careworn expression in his face, while an intensity of purpose blazed from hungry, deep-set eyes which swept every detail of the scene at a glance. That he was worried to the point of exhaustion was evident the moment that compliments were exchanged.

"Show me your water supply," said he to Joel; "old beaver ponds, if I am correctly informed. We must move fifty thousand cattle from Dodge to the Platte River within the next fortnight. One of the worst drouths in the history of the trail confronts us, and if you can water my cattle between the Prairie Dog and the Republican River, you can name your own price."

"Let's drive around," said Forrest, stepping into the blackboard, "before it gets too dark. Come on, boys, and show Mr. Lovell the water."

All four boarded the vehicle, the boys standing up behind the single seat, and drove away. In a mile's meanderings of the creek were five beaver ponds, over which in many places the willows interlapped. The pools stood bank full, and after sounding them, the quartette turned homeward, satisfied of the abundant water supply.

"There's water and to spare for the entire drive," said Forrest to his employer. "It isn't the amount drank, it's the absorption of the sun that gets away with water. Those willows will protect the pools until the cows come home. I felt sure of the Beaver."

"Now, if we can arrange to water my herds here – "

"That's all arranged," replied Forrest. "I'm a silent partner in this ranch. Anything that Wells Brothers owns is yours for the asking. Am I right, boys?"

"If Mr. Lovell needs the water, he is welcome to it," modestly replied Joel.

"That's my partner talking," said Forrest; "that was old man Joel Wells that just spoke. He's the senior member of the firm. Oh, these boys of mine are cowmen from who laid the rail. They're not out to rob a neighbor. Once you hear from the head of the Stinking Water, you can order the herds to pull out for the Platte."

"Yes," said Mr. Lovell, somewhat perplexed. "Yes, but let's get the water on the Beaver clear first. What does this mean? I offer a man his price to water my cattle, and he answers me that I'm welcome to it for nothing. I'm suspicious of the Greeks when they come bearing gifts. Are you three plotting against me?"

"That's it," replied Forrest. "You caught the gleam of my axe all right. In the worry of this drouth, you've overlooked the fact that you have five horses on this ranch. They were left here last fall, expecting to pick them up this spring. Two of them were cripples and three were good cow horses. Now, these boys of mine are just branching out into cattle, and they don't need money, but a few good horses are better than gold. That's about the plot. What would you say was the right thing to do?"

Mr. Lovell turned to the boys. "The five horses are yours. But I'm still in your debt. Is there anything else that you need?"

The question was repeated to Forrest. "By the time the herds reach here," said he, mildly observant, "there will be quite a number of tender-footed and fagged cattle. They could never make it through without rest, but by dropping them here, they would have a fighting chance to recuperate before winter. There won't be a cent in an abandoned steer for you, but these boys – "

"Trim the herds here on the Beaver," interrupted Mr. Lovell. "I'll give all my foremen orders to that effect. Cripples are worthless to me, but good as gold to these boys. What else?"

"Oh, just wish the boys good luck, and if it ever so happens, speak a good word for the Wells Brothers. I found them white, and I think you'll find them on the square."

"Well, this is a happy termination," said Mr. Lovell, as he alighted at the tent. "Our water expense between Dodge and Ogalalla will not exceed five thousand dollars. It cost me double that getting out of Texas."

Secure on the Beaver, the brothers were unaware of the outside drouth, which explained the failure of the herds to appear on the trail as in other years. It meant the delay of a fortnight, and the concentration of a year's drive into a more limited space of time. Unconscious of its value, the boys awoke to the fact that they controlled the only water between the Prairie Dog and the Republican River – sixty miles of the plain. Many of the herds were under contract and bond to cattle companies, individuals, army posts, and Indian agencies, and no excuse would be accepted for any failure to deliver. The drouth might prove an ill-wind to some, but the Beaver valley was not only exempt but could extend relief.

After supper, hosts and guests adjourned to the tent. Forrest had unearthed the winter struggle of his protégés, and gloating over the manner in which the boys had met and overcome the unforeseen, he assumed an observant attitude in addressing his employer.

"You must be working a sorry outfit up on the Little Missouri," said he, "to lose ten per cent of straight steer cattle. My boys, here on the Beaver, report a measly loss of twelve head, out of over five hundred cattle. And you must recollect that these were rag-tag and bob-tail, the flotsam of a hundred herds, forty per cent cripples, walking on crutches. Think of it! Two per cent loss, under herd, a sleet over the range for six weeks, against your ten per cent kill on an open range. You must have a slatterly, sore-thumbed lot of men on your beef ranch."

Mr. Lovell was discouraged over the outlook of his cattle interests. "That was a first report that you are quoting from," said he to Forrest. "It was more prophecy than statement. We must make allowances for young men. There is quite a difference between getting scared and being hurt. My beef outfit has orders to go three hundred miles south of our range and cover all round-ups northward. It was a severe winter, and the drift was heavy, but I'm not worrying any about that sore-fingered outfit. Promptly meeting government contracts is our work to-day. My cattle are two weeks behind time, and the beef herds must leave Dodge to-morrow. Help me figure it out: Can you put me on the railroad by noon?" he concluded, turning to Joel.

"Easily, or I can carry a message to-night."

"There's your programme," said Forrest, interceding. "One of these boys can take you to Grinnell in time for the eastbound train. Wire your beef herds to pull out for the Platte. You can trust the water to improve from here north."

"And you?" inquired the drover, addressing his foreman.

"I'll take the buckboard and go north until I meet Paul. That will cover the last link in the trail. We'll know our water then, and time our drives to help the cattle. It's as clear as mud."

"Just about," dubiously answered Mr. Lovell. "Unless I can get an extension of time on my beef contracts, the penalty under my bonds will amount to a fortune."

"The army is just as well aware of this drouth as you are," said Forrest, "and the War Department will make allowances. The government don't expect the impossible."

"Yes," answered the old drover with feeling. "Yes, but it exacts a bond, and stipulates the daily forfeiture, and if any one walks the plank, it's not your dear old Uncle Samuel. And it matters not how much sleep I lose, red tape never worries."

The boys made a movement as if to withdraw, and Forrest arose. "The programme for to-morrow, then, is understood," said the latter. "The horses will be ready at daybreak."

It was midnight when the trio sought their blankets. On the part of the brothers, there was a constant reference to their guest, the drover, and a desire, if in their power, to aid him in every way.

"I wanted you boys to meet and get acquainted with Mr. Lovell," said Forrest, as all were dozing off to sleep. "There is a cowman in a thousand, and his word carries weight in cattle matters. He's rather deep water, unless you cross or surprise him. I nagged him about the men on his beef ranch. He knew the cattle wouldn't winter kill when they could drift, and the round-up will catch every living hoof. He was too foxy to borrow any trouble there, and this long yell about the drouth interfering with delivery dates keeps the trail outfits against the bits. Admitting his figures, the water expense won't be a drop in the bucket. It affords good worrying and that keeps the old man in fighting form. I'm glad he came along; treat him fair and square, and his friendship means something to you, boys."

CHAPTER XIV
AN ILL WIND

The start to the station was made at four o'clock in the morning. Joel accompanied the drover, the two best horses being under saddle, easily capable of a road gait that would reach the railroad during the early forenoon. The direct course lay across country, and once the sun flooded the Beaver valley, the cowman swung around in the saddle and his practical eye swept the range. On sighting Hackberry Grove, the broken country beyond, including the sand hills, he turned to his guide.

"My boy," said Mr. Lovell, "you brothers have a great future before you. This is an ideal cattle range. The very grass under our horses' feet carries untold wealth. But you lack cattle. You have the range here for thousands where you are running hundreds. Buy young steers; pay any price; but get more cattle. The growth of young steers justifies any outlay. Come down to Dodge about the first of August. This drouth is liable to throw some bargains on that market. Be sure and come. I'll keep an eye open in your interest on any cattle for sale."

The old drover's words bewildered Joel. The ways and means were not entirely clear, but the confidence of the man in the future of the brothers was gratifying. Meanwhile, at the little ranch the team stood in waiting, and before the horseman had passed out of sight to the south the buckboard started on its northern errand. Dell accompanied it, protesting against his absence from home, but Forrest brushed aside every objection.

"Come on, come on," said he to Dell; "you have no saddle, and we may be back to-night. We're liable to meet Paul on the Republican. Turn your ranch loose and let it run itself. Come on; we ain't halfway through our figuring."

Joel returned after dark. Priest had left Ogalalla, to the north, the same day that Forrest and his employer started up the trail from the south, and at the expected point the two foremen met. The report showed water in abundance from the Republican River northward, confirming Forrest's assertion to his employer, and completing the chain of waters between Dodge and Ogalalla. Priest returned with the buckboard, which reached the Beaver after midnight, and aroused Joel out of heavy sleep.

"I just wanted to say," said Priest, sitting on the edge of Joel's bunk, "that I had my ear to the ground and heard the good fighting. Yes, I heard the sleet cracking. You never saw me, but I was with you the night you drifted to the Prairie Dog. Take it all along the line, wasn't it good fighting?"

"Has Dell told you everything?" inquired Joel, sitting up in his blankets.

"Everything, including the fact that he got lost the night of the March drift, while going home after a pack horse. Wouldn't trust poor old Dog-toe, but run on the rope himself! Landed down the creek here a few miles. News to you? Well, he admits that the horse forgot more than he himself ever knew. That's a hopeful sign. As long as a man hearkens to his horse, there is no danger of bad counsel being thrust on him."

The boys were catching, at first hand, an insight into the exacting nature of trail work. Their friends were up with the dawn, and while harnessing in the team, Forrest called Joel's attention to setting the ranch in order to water the passing herds.

"I was telling Dell yesterday," said he, "the danger of Texas fever among wintered cattle, and you must isolate your little herd until after frost falls. Graze your cattle up around Hackberry Grove, and keep a dead-line fully three miles wide between the wintered and through trail herds. Any new cattle that you pick up, cripples or strays, hold them down the creek – between here and the old trail crossing. For fear of losing them you can't even keep milk cows around the ranch, so turn out your calves. Don't ask me to explain Texas fever. It's one of the mysteries of the trail. The very cattle that impart it after a winter in the north catch the fever and die like sheep. It seems to exist, in a mild form, in through, healthy cattle, but once imparted to native or northern wintered stock, it becomes violent and is usually fatal. The sure, safe course is to fear and avoid it."

The two foremen were off at an early hour. Priest was again in charge of Lovell's lead herd, and leaving the horse that he had ridden to the Republican River in care of the boys, he loitered a moment at parting.

"If my herd left Dodge at noon yesterday," said he, mentally calculating, "I'll overtake it some time to-morrow night. Allowing ten days to reach here—"

He turned to the boys. "This is the sixteenth of June. Well, come out on the divide on the morning of the twenty-fifth and you will see a dust cloud in the south. The long distance between waters will put the herd through on schedule time. Come out and meet me."

The brothers waved the buckboard away. The dragging days were over. The herds were coming, and their own little ranch promised relief to the drover and his cattle.

"Mr. Quince says the usual price for watering trail herds is from one to three cents a head," said Dell, as their friends dipped from sight. "The government, so he says, allows three cents for watering cavalry horses and harness mules. He tells me that the new settlers, in control of the water on the trail, in northern Texas, fairly robbed the drovers this year. The pastoral Texan, he contends, shared his canteen with the wayfarer, and never refused to water cattle. He wants us to pattern after the Texans—to give our water and give it freely. When Mr. Lovell raised the question of arranging to water his herds from our beaver ponds, do you remember how Mr. Quince answered for us? I'm mighty glad money wasn't mentioned. No money could buy Dog-toe from me. And Mr. Lovell gave us three of our best horses."

"He offered me ten dollars for taking him to the railroad," said Joel, "but I looked him square in the eye and refused the money. He says we must buy more cattle. He wants me to come to Dodge in August, and I'm going."

Dell treated the idea of buying cattle with slight disdain. "You—going—to—buy—more—cattle?" said he, accenting each word. "Any one tell your fortune lately?"

"Yes," answered the older boy. "I'm having it told every day. One of those two men, the gray-haired one on that buckboard,—stand here and you can see them,—told me over a year ago that this range had a value, and that we ought to skirmish some cattle, some way, and stock it. What he saw clearly then, I see now, and what Mr. Lovell sees now, you may see a year hence. These men have proved their friendship, and why stand in our own light? Our ability to hold cattle was tested last winter, and if this range is an asset, there may be some way to buy more cattle. I'm going to Dodge in August."

Dell was silenced. There was ample time to set the ranch in order. Turning away from the old trail, on the divide, and angling in to headquarters, and thence northward, was but a slight elbow on the general course of the trail herds. The long distance across to the Republican would compel an early watering on the Beaver, that the cattle might reach the former river the following evening. The brothers knew to a fraction the grazing gait of a herd, the trailing pace, and could anticipate to an hour the time required to move a herd from the Prairie Dog to the Beaver.

The milk cows and calves were turned back into the general herd. The dead-line was drawn safely below Hackberry Grove, between imaginary landmarks on either slope, while on the creek, like a sentinel, stood a lone willow which seemed to say, "Thus far shalt thou go and no farther." The extra horses, now in the pink of condition, were brought home and located below the ranch, and the house stood in order.

The arrival of the first herd had been correctly calculated. The brothers rode out late on the morning designated, but did not reach the divide. The foremost herd was met within seven miles of the Beaver, the leaders coming on with the steady stride of thirsty cattle that had scented water. Priest was nowhere in sight, but the heavy beeves identified the herd, and when the boys hailed a point man, the situation cleared.

"Mr. Paul—our boss?" repeated the point man. "He's setting up a guide-board, back on the divide, where we turned off from the old trail. Say, does this dim wagon track we're following lead to Wells Brothers' ranch?"

"It does," answered Joel. "You can see the willows from the next swell of the prairie," added Dell, as the brothers passed on.

It was a select herd of heavy beeves. In spite of the drouth encountered, the cattle were in fine condition, and as the herd snailed forward at its steady march, the sweep of horn, the variety of color, the neat outline of each animal blended into a pastoral picture of strength and beauty.

The boys rode down the advancing column. A swing man on the opposite side of the herd waved his hand across to the brothers, and while the two were speculating as to who he might be, a swing lad on the left reined out and saluted the boys.

With hand extended, he smilingly inquired, "Don't you remember the day we branded your cattle? How did the Two Bars and the – – Y cows winter?"

"It's Billy Honeyman," said Dell, beaming. "Who is that man across the herd, waving at us?" he inquired, amid hearty greeting.

"That's Runt Pickett, the little fellow who helped us brand – the lad who rushed the cattle. The herd cuts him off from shaking hands. Turn your horses the other way and tell me how you like it out West."

Dell turned back, but Joel continued on. The column of beeves was fully a mile in length. After passing the drag end of the herd, the wagon and remuda were sighted, later met, with the foreman still at the rear. The dust cloud of yet another herd arose in the distance, and while Joel pondered on its location over the divide, a horseman emerged from a dip in the plain and came toward him in a slow gallop.

"There's no foreman with the next herd," explained Priest, slacking his horse into a walk, "and the segundo wasn't sure which swell was the real divide. We trailed two herds past your ranch last summer, but the frost has mellowed up the soil and the grass has overgrown the paths until every trace is gone. I planted a guide-post and marked it 'Lovell's Trail,' so the other foremen will know where to turn off. All the old man's herds are within three or four days' drive, and after that it's almost a solid column of cattle back to Dodge. Forrest is in charge of the rear herd, and will pick up any of our abandoned cattle."

The two shook out their mounts, passed the commissary and saddle stock, but halted a moment at the drag end of the herd. "We've been dropping our cripples," explained Priest, "but the other herds will bring them through. There's not over one or two here, but I'm going to saw off three horses on Wells Brothers. Good ones, too, that is, good for next year."

A halt was made at the lead of the herd, and some directions given the point man. It was still early in the forenoon, and once man and boy had fairly cleared the leaders in front, a signal was given and the cattle turned as a single animal and fell to grazing. The wagon and remuda never halted; on being joined by the two horsemen, they continued on into the Beaver. Eleven o'clock was the hour named to water the herd, and punctual to the moment the beeves, with a mile-wide front, were grazed up to the creek.

The cattle were held around the pools for an hour. Before dinner was over, the acting foreman of the second herd rode in, and in mimicking a trail boss, issued some drastic orders. The second herd was within sight, refused to graze, and his wagon was pulling in below the ranch for the noon camp.

Priest looked at his watch. "Start the herd," said he to his own men. "Hold a true northward course, and camp twelve miles out to-night. I may not be with you, but water in the Republican at six o'clock to-morrow evening. Bring in your herd, young fellow," he concluded, addressing the segundo.

The watering of a trail herd is important. Mere opportunity to quench thirst is not sufficient. The timid stand in awe of the strong, and the excited milling cattle intimidate the weak and thirsty. An hour is the minimum time, during which half the herd may drink and lie down, affording the others the chance to approach without fear and slake their thirst.

The acting foreman signaled in his herd. The beeves around the water were aroused, and reluctantly grazed out on their course, while the others came on with a sullen stride that thirst enforces. The previous scene of contentment gave way to frenzy. The heavy beeves, equally select with the vanguard, floundered into the pools, lowed in their joy, drank to gorging, fought their fellows, staggered out of the creek, and dropped to rest in the first dust or dry grass.

Priest trimmed his own beeves and remuda. A third herd appeared, when he and the acting foreman culled over both horses and cattle, and sent the second herd on its way. Each of the three advance herds must reach the Republican the following day, and it was scant two o'clock when the third one trailed out from the Beaver. With mature cattle there were few cripples, and the day ended with an addition to the little ranch of the promised horses and a few tender-footed beeves. There were two more herds of heavy beef cattle to follow, which would arrive during the next forenoon, and the old foreman remained over until the last cattle, intended for army delivery, had passed the ranch.

The herd never fails. Faith in cattle is always rewarded. From that far distant dawn when man and his ox started across the ages the one has ever sustained the other. The two rear beef herds promptly reached the Beaver the next morning, slaked their thirst, and passed on before noon.

"This lets me out as your guest," said Priest to the boys, when the last herd was trimmed. "Bob Quirk will now follow with six herds of contract cattle. He's the foreman of the second herd of beeves, but Mr. Lovell detailed him to oversee this next division across to the Platte. Forrest will follow Quirk with the last five herds of young steers, slated for the old man's beef ranch on the Little Missouri. That puts our cattle across the Beaver, but you'll have plenty of company for the next month. Mr. Lovell has made a good talk for you boys around Dodge, and if you'll give these trail drovers this water, it will all come back. As cowmen, there are two things that you want to remember – that it'll rain again, and that the cows will calve in the spring."

Priest had barely left the little ranch when Bob Quirk arrived. Before dismounting, he rode around the pools, signaled in a wagon and remuda, and returned to the tent.

"This is trailing cattle with a vengeance," said he, stripping his saddle from a tired horse. "There has been such a fight for water this year that every foreman seems to think that unless he reaches the river to-day it'll be dry to-morrow. Five miles apart was the limit agreed on before leaving Dodge, and here I am with six herds – twenty thousand cattle! – within twenty miles of the Beaver. For fear of a stampede last night, we threw the herds left and right, two miles off the trail. The Lord surely loves cattle or the earth would have shook from running herds!"

That afternoon and the next morning the second division of the Lovell herds crossed the Beaver. Forrest rode in and saluted the boys with his usual rough caress.

"Saddle up horses," said he, "and drop back and come through with the two rear herds. There's a heavy drag end on each one, and an extra man to nurse those tender cows over here, to home and friends, will be lending a hand to the needy. I'll run the ranch while you're gone. One of you to each, the fourth and fifth herds, remember. I'll meet you to-morrow morning, and we'll cut the cripples out and point them in to the new tanks below. Shake out your fat horses, sweat them up a little – you're needed at the rear of Lovell's main drive."

The boys saddled and rode away in a gallop. Three of the rear herds reached the Beaver that afternoon, watered, and passed on to safe camps beyond. One of Quirk's wagons had left a quarter of beef at headquarters, and Forrest spent the night amid peace and plenty where the year before he lay wounded.

The next morning saw the last of the Lovell herds arrive. The lead one yielded ninety cripples, and an hour later the rear guard disgorged a few over one hundred head. The two contingents were thrown together, the brothers nursed them in to the new tanks, where they were freed on a perfect range. A count of the cripples and fagged cattle, culled back at headquarters, brought the total discard of the sixteen herds up to two hundred and forty-odd, a riffraff of welcome flotsam, running from a young steer to a seven-year-old beef. The sweepings had paid the reckoning.

Several other trail foremen, scouting in advance of their herds, had reached the Beaver, or had been given assurance that water was to be had in abundance. A measurement of the water was awaited with interest, and once the rear herd grazed out from the beaver ponds, Forrest and the brothers rode around the pools to take soundings.

"I cut notches on willow roots, at each beaver dam, and the loss runs from four to six inches, the lower pools suffering the heaviest," said Joel, summing up the situation.

"They're holding like cisterns," exultingly said Forrest. "Fifty thousand cattle watered, and only lowered the pools on an average of five inches. The upper one's still taking water – that's the reason it's standing the drain. Write it in the sand or among the stars, but the water's here for this year's drive. Go back and tell those waiting foremen to bring on their cattle. Headquarters ranch will water every trail herd, or break a tug trying."

CHAPTER XV
WATER! WATER!

"Bring on your herds," said Joel, addressing a quartette of trail foremen resting under the sunshade. "Our water is holding out better than we expected. The Lovell cattle only lowered the ponds a trifle. From the present outlook, we can water the drive."

"That's a big contract," reluctantly admitted a "Running W" trail boss. "I had word on the railroad yesterday that the Arkansaw River at Dodge was only running at night."

"Water is reported plentiful around Ogalalla and beyond," doggedly said a pock-marked foreman.

"That'll tempt the herds to cross over," urged the Running W man. "The faraway hills are always green."

The conversation took a new tack. "Who knows the estimate on the total drive this year?" inquired a swarthy, sun-burned little man, addressing the pock-marked foreman.

"A rough estimate places the drive at six hundred and fifty thousand head," came the languid reply.

"There you are," smilingly said the Running W boss, turning to Joel. "Better revise your water estimate."

"Not now," answered Joel, meeting smile with smile. "Later on I may have to hedge, but for the present, bring on your cattle."

"That's to the point," languidly said a tall, blond Texan, arising. "My cattle must have water this evening."

The other trail foremen arose. "We all understand," remarked the pock-marked man to the others, "that this is the place where we drop our strays, fagged and crippled stuff. These are the boys that Mr. Lovell mentioned as worthy of any cattle that must be abandoned."

"At Wells Brothers' ranch, on the Beaver," assentingly said the little man.

"Our lead herds will not have many cripples," said the Running W foreman, turning to the boys. "A few days' rest is everything to a tender-footed steer, and what cattle the lead ones drop, the rear ones have orders to bring through to you."

"Thank you, sir," said Joel frankly. "We want to stock our range, and crippled cattle are as good as gold to us."

Spurs clanked as the men turned to their mounts. The boys followed, and Dell overtook the blond Texan. "If you need a hand on the drag end of your herd," said the boy to the tall foreman, "I'll get up a fresh horse and overtake you."

"Make it a horse apiece," said the young man, "and I'll sign your petition for the post office – when this country has one. I'm as good as afoot."

The other foremen mounted their horses. "I'll overtake you," said Joel to the trio, "as soon as I change mounts. Whoever has the lead herd, come in on the water above the field. The upper pools are the deepest, and let your cattle cover the water evenly."

"I'm in the lead," said the pock-marked man. "But we'll have to come up to the water in trailing formation. The cattle have suffered from thirst, and they break into a run at sight of water, if grazed up to it. You may take one point and I'll take the other."

The existing drouth promised a good schooling for the brothers. Among the old philosophies, contact was said to be educational. Wells Brothers were being thrown in contact with the most practical men that the occupation, in all pastoral ages, had produced. The novelty of trailing cattle vast distances had its origin with the Texans. Bred to the calling, they were masters of the craft. In the hands of an adept outfit of a dozen men, a trail herd of three thousand beeves had all the mobility of a brigade of cavalry. The crack of a whip was unheard on the trail. A whispered order, followed by a signal to the men, and the herd turned, grazed to its contentment, fell into column formation, and took up its march – a peaceful march that few armies have equaled. Contact with these men, the rank and file of that splendid cavalry which once patrolled the range industry of the West, was priceless to the boys.

The lead herd reached the Beaver valley at noon. When within a mile of the water, the point men gave way to the foremen and Joel Wells. But instead of dropping back, the dust-covered men rode on into the lead, the action being seemingly understood by every one except the new hand on the point. Joel was alert, felt the massive column of beeves yield to his slightest pressure, as a ship to the hand of the helmsman, as he veered the leaders out of the broken trails and guided the herd around the field to the upper pools. On nearing the water, the deposed point men deployed nearer the lead, when the object of their position explained itself. On sighting the ponds, the leaders broke into a run, but the four horsemen at hand checked the excited dash, and the herd was led up to the water in column formation. It was the mastery of man over the creature.

The herds arrived in hit-and-miss class. The destination of the pock-marked foreman's beeves was an army post in Dakota. The swarthy little man followed with a herd of cows for delivery at an Indian agency in Wyoming. The different Running W herds were under contract to different cattle companies, in adjoining states and territories. The tall foreman's herd was also under contract, but the point of delivery was at Ogalalla, on the Platte, where a ranch outfit would receive the cattle.

The latter herd arrived late at evening. The cattle were driven on speculation, there had been an oversight in mounting the outfit, and the men, including the foreman, were as good as afoot.

"This trip lets me out," said the young Texan to the brothers, "of walking up the trail and leading fagged-out saddle stock. A mount of six horses to the man may be all right on a ranch, but it won't do on the trail. Especially in a dry year, with delivery on the Platte. Actually, this afternoon is the first time I have felt a horse under me since we crossed Red River. Give me a sheet of paper, please. I want to give you a bill of sale for these six drag ponies that I'm sawing off on you. I carry written authority to give a bill of sale, and it will always protect your possession of the horses. They wouldn't bring a dollar a head in Ogalalla, but when they round into form again next summer, some brand ferret passing might want to claim them on you. Any cattle that I cull out here are abandoned, you understand, simply abandoned."

The boys were left alone for the first time in several nights. The rush of the past few days had kept them in the saddle during their waking hours. The dead-line had been neglected, the drifting of cripples to the new tanks below was pressing, and order must be established. The water in the pools was the main concern, a thing beyond human control, and a matter of constant watchfulness. A remark dropped during the day, of water flowing at night, was not lost on the attentive ear of Joel Wells.

"What did you mean?" he politely inquired of the Running W foreman, while the latter's herd was watering, "of a river only running at night?"

"All over this arid country moisture rises at night and sinks by day," replied the trail boss. "Under drouth, these sandy rivers of the plain, including the Platte and for a thousand miles to the south, only flow at night. It's their protection against the sun's absorption. Mark these pools at sunset and see if they don't rise an inch to-night. Try it and see."

Willow roots were notched on the water-line of each beaver dam. The extreme upper pool was still taking water from a sickly flow, a struggling rivulet, fed by the springs at its head. Doubt was indulged in and freely expressed.

"If the water only holds a week longer," ventured Dell, sleepless in his blankets, "it'll double our holding of cattle."

"It'll hold a month," said Joel, equally sleepless. "We've got to stand by these trail herds – there is no other water short of the Republican. I've figured it all out. When the Beaver ponds are gone, we'll round up the wintered cattle, drift them over to the south fork of the Republican, and get some one to hold them until frost falls. Then we'll ship the cripples up to Hackberry Grove, and that will free the new tanks – water enough for twenty trail herds. We have the horses, and these trail outfits will lend us any help we need. By shifting cattle around, I can see a month's supply. And there may be something in water rising at night. We'll know in the morning."

Sleep blotted out the night. Dawn revealed the fact that the trail foreman knew the secrets of the plain. "That trail boss knew," shouted Joel, rushing into the tent and awakening Dell. "The water rose in every pool. The lower one gained an inch and the upper one gained two. The creek is running freely. The water must be rising out of the ground. Let those Texans bring on their herds. We have oceans of water!"

The cattle came. The first week thirty herds passed the new ranch. It took riding. The dead-line was held, the flotsam cared for, and a hand was ever ready to point a herd or nurse the drag end. Open house was maintained. Every arriving foreman was tendered a horse, and left his benediction on the Beaver.

The ranch proved a haven to man and beast. One of the first foremen to arrive during the second week was Nat Straw. He drove up at sunset, with a chuck-wagon, halted at the tent, and in his usual easy manner inquired, "Where is the matron of this hospital?"

"Here she is," answered Dell, recognizing the man and surmising the situation. "One of your men hurt?"

"Not seriously," answered Straw, looking back into the wagon. "Just a little touch of the dengue. He's been drinking stagnant water, out of cow tracks, for the last few months, and that gets into the bones of the best of us. I'm not feeling very well myself."

Dell lifted the wagon-sheet and peered inside. "Let's get the poor fellow into the tent," urged the boy. "Can he walk, or can you and I carry him?"

"He's the long size Texan, and we'd better try and trail him in," answered Straw, alighting from the wagon. "Where's Dr. Joel Wells?"

"Riding the dead-line. He'll be in shortly. I'll fix a cot, and we'll bring the sick man in at once."

It was simple malaria, known in the Southwest as dengue fever. The unfortunate lad was made comfortable, and on Joel riding in, Straw had skirmished some corn, and was feeding his mules.

"As one of the founders of this hospital," said Straw, after greeting Joel, "this corn has my approval. It is my orders, as one of the trustees, that it be kept in stock hereafter. This team has to go back to the Prairie Dog to-night, and this corn will fortify them for the trip."

The situation was explained. "I only lost half a day," continued Straw, "by bringing the poor fellow over to you. He's one of the best men that ever worked for me, and a month's rest will put him on his feet again. Now, if one of you boys will take the team back to – "

"Certainly," answered Joel. "Anything a director of this hospital wants done – We're running a relief station now – watering the entire drive this year. Where's your outfit camped?"

"A mile above the trail crossing on the Prairie Dog. The wagon's empty. Leave here at two o'clock to-night, and you'll get there in time for breakfast."

"I'm your man. Going to the Prairie Dog at night, in the summer, is a horse that's easy curried."

The next evening Joel brought in Straw's herd. In the mean time the sick man had been cared for, and the passing wayfarer and his cattle made welcome and sped on their way. During the lay-over, Straw had lost his place in the overland march, two herds having passed him and crossed the Beaver.

"I'm corporal here to-day," said Straw to the two foremen, who arrived together in advance. "On this water, I'm the squatter that'll rob you right. You'll count your cattle to me and pay the bill in advance. This cool, shaded water in the Beaver is worth three cents a head, and I'll count you down to a toddling calf and your wagon mules. Your drafts are refused honor at the Beaver banks – nothing but the long green passes currency here. You varmints must show some regrets for taking advantage of a widow woman. I'll make you sorry for passing me."

"How I love to hear old Nat rattle his little song," said one of the foremen, shaking hands with Dell. "Remember the night you slept with me? How's the black cow I gave you last summer?"

Dell fairly clung to the grasped hand. "Pressnell's foreman!" said he, recalling both man and incident. "The cow has a roan calf. Sit down. Will you need a fresh horse to-day? Do you like lettuce?"

"I reckon, Nat," said the other foreman, an hour later, as the two mounted loaned horses, "I reckon your big talk goes up in smoke. You're not the only director in this cattle company. Dell, ransack both our wagons to-day, and see if you can't unearth some dainties for this sick lad. No use looking in Straw's commissary; he never has anything to eat; Injuns won't go near his wagon."

Straw spent a second night with the sick man. On leaving in the morning, he took the feverish hand of the lad and said: "Now, Jack, make yourself right at home. These boys have been tried before, and they're our people. I'm leaving you a saddle and a horse, and when you get on your feet, take your own bearings. You can always count on a job with me, and I'll see that you draw wages until my outfit is relieved. This fever will burn itself out in a week or ten days. I'll keep an eye over you until you are well. S'long, Jack."

The second week fell short only two herds of the previous one. There were fully as many cattle passed, and under the heat of advancing summer the pools suffered a thirsty levy. The resources of the ponds were a constant source of surprise, as an occasional heavy beef caved a foot into an old beaver warren, which poured its contents into the pools. At the end of the first fortnight, after watering fifty-eight herds, nearly half the original quantity of water was still in reserve.

A third week passed. There was a decided falling off in the arrival of herds, only twenty-two crossing the Beaver. The water reserves suffered freely, more from the sun's absorption than from cattle, until the supply became a matter of the most serious concern. The pools would not have averaged a foot in depth, the flow from the springs was a mere trickle, the beaver burrows sounded empty to a horse's footbeat, and there must be some limit to the amount the parched soil would yield.

The brothers found apt counsel in their guest. By the end of the second week, the fever had run its course, and the sick man, Jack Sargent, was up and observant of the situation. True to his calling, he felt for the cattle, and knew the importance of water on the Beaver to the passing drive.

"You must rest these beaver ponds," said Jack, in meeting the emergency. "Every time these pools lower an inch, it gives the sun an advantage. It's absorption that's swallowing up the ponds. You must deepen these pools, which will keep the water cooler. Rest these ponds a few days, or only water late at night. You have water for weeks yet, but don't let the sun rob you. These ponds are living springs compared to some of the water we used south of Red River. Meet the herds on the divide, and pilot the early ones to the tanks below, and the late ones in here. Shifting in your saddle rests a horse, and a little shifting will save your water."

The advice was acted on. While convalescent, Sargent was installed as host on the Beaver, and the brothers took to their saddles. The majority of the herds were met on the Prairie Dog, and after a consultation with the foremen their cattle were started so as to reach the tanks by day or the ranch at evening. The month rounded out with the arrival of eighteen herds, only six of which touched at headquarters, and the fourth week saw a distinct gain in the water supply at the beaver dams. The boys barely touched at home, to change horses, living with the trail wagons, piloting in herds, rich in the reward of relieving the wayfaring, and content with the crumbs that fell to their range.

The drouth of 1886 left a gruesome record in the pastoral history of the West. The southern end of the Texas and Montana cattle trail was marked by the bones of forty thousand cattle that fell, due to the want of water, during the months of travail on that long march. Some of this loss was due to man's inhumanity to the cattle of the fields, in withholding water, but no such charge rested on the owners of the little ranch on the Beaver.

A short month witnessed the beginning of the end of the year's drive. Only such herds as were compelled to, and those that had strength in reserve, dared the plain between the Arkansas and Platte Rivers. The fifth week only six herds arrived, all of which touched at the ranch; half of them had been purchased at Dodge, had neither a cripple nor a stray to bestow, but shared the welcome water and passed on.

One of the purchased herds brought a welcome letter to Joel. It was from Don Lovell, urgently accenting anew his previous invitation to come to Dodge and look over the market.

"After an absence of several weeks," wrote Mr. Lovell, "I have returned to Dodge. From a buyer's standpoint, the market is inviting. The boom prices which prevailed in '84 are cut in half. Any investment in cattle now is perfectly safe.

"I have ordered three of my outfits to return here. They will pass your ranch. Fall in with the first one that comes along. Bring a mount of horses, and report to me on arriving. Fully half this year's drive is here, unsold. Be sure and come."

"Are you going?" inquired Dell on reading the letter.

"I am," answered Joel with emphasis.

"That's the talk," said Sargent. "Whenever cattle get so cheap that no other man will look a cow in the face, that's the time to buy her. Folks are like sheep; the Bible says so; they all want to buy or all want to sell. I only know Mr. Lovell from what you boys have told me; but by ordering three outfits to return to Dodge, I can see that he's going to take advantage of that market and buy about ten thousand cattle. You've got the range. Buy this summer. I'll stay with Dell until you return. Buy a whole herd of steers, and I'll help you hold them this winter."

The scene shifted. Instead of looking to the south for a dust cloud, the slopes of the north were scanned for an approaching cavalcade. The last week admitted of taking an account of the cattle dropped at the new ranch. From the conserves of its owners, one hundred and four herds had watered, over three hundred thousand cattle, the sweepings of which amounted to a few over eleven hundred head, fully fifty of which, exhausted beyond recovery, died after reaching their new range.

By the end of July, only an occasional herd was arriving. August was ushered in with the appearance of Bob Quirk, one of the division foremen, on the upper march. He arrived early in the morning, in advance of his outfit barely an hour, and inquired for Joel. Dell answered for the brothers, the older one and Sargent being above at Hackberry Grove.

"I have orders to bring him to Dodge," said Quirk, dismounting. "Make haste and bring in the remuda. We'll cut him out a mount of six horses and throw them in with mine. Joel can follow on the seventh. My outfit will barely touch here in passing. We're due to receive cattle in Dodge on the 5th, and time is precious. Joel can overtake us before night. Make haste."

CHAPTER XVI
A PROTECTED CREDIT

The trail outfit swept past the ranch, leaving Dell on nettles. The importance of the message was urgent, and saddling up a horse, he started up the Beaver in search of Joel and Sargent. They were met returning, near the dead-line, and after listening to the breathless report, the trio gave free rein to their horses on the homeward ride.

"I'll use old Rowdy for my seventh horse," said Joel, swinging out of the saddle at the home corral. "Bring him in and give him a feed of corn. It may be late when I overtake the outfit. Mr. Quince says that that old horse has cow-sense to burn; that he can scent a camp at night, or trail a remuda like a hound."

An hour later Joel cantered up to the tent. "This may be a wild-goose chase," said he, "but I'm off. If my hopes fall dead, I can make a hand coming back. Sargent, if I do buy any cattle, your name goes on the pay-roll from to-day. I'll leave you in charge of the ranch, anyhow. There isn't much to do except to ride the dead-line twice a day. The wintered cattle are located; and the cripples below – the water and their condition will hold them. Keep open house, and amuse yourselves the best you can. That's about all I can think of just now."

Joel rode away in serious meditation. Although aged beyond his years, he was only seventeen. That he could ride into Dodge City, the far-famed trail-town of the West, and without visible resources buy cattle, was a fit subject for musing. There the drovers from Texas and the ranchmen from the north and west met and bartered for herds – where the drive of the year amounted to millions in value. Still the boy carried a pressing invitation from a leading drover to come, and neither slacking rein nor looking back, he was soon swallowed up in the heat-waves over the plain.

Sargent and Dell sought the shelter of the awning. "Well," said the latter, "that trip's a wild-goose chase. How he expects to buy cattle without money gets me."

"It may be easier than it seems," answered Sargent. "You secured a start in cattle last summer without money. Suppose you save a thousand head out of the cripples this year, what have they cost you?"

"That's different," protested Dell. "Dodge City is a market where buyers and sellers meet."

"True enough. And behind that are unseen conditions. The boom of two years ago in land and live stock bankrupted many people in Texas. Cattle companies were organized on the very summit of that craze. Then came the slump. Last year cattle had fallen in price nearly forty per cent. This year there is a further falling. I'm giving you Texas conditions. Half the herds at Dodge to-day are being handled by the receivers of cattle companies or by trustees for banks. That accounts for the big drive. Then this drouth came on, and the offerings at Dodge are unfit for any purpose, except to restock ranches. And those northern ranchmen know it. They'll buy the cattle at their own price and pay for them when they get good and ready."

Dell was contending for his view. "Do you claim that a northern cowman can buy cattle from a Texas drover without money?"

"Certainly. When one sheep jumps off the cliff and breaks his neck, all the rest jump off and break their necks. When money is pouring into cattle, as it was two years ago, range cattle were as good as gold. Now, when all that investment is trying to withdraw from cattle, they become a drag on the market. The Simple Simons ain't all dead yet. Joel will buy cattle."

"He may, but I don't see how."

"Buy them just as any other wide-awake cowman. You brothers are known in Dodge. This water that you have given the drovers, during the drouth, has made you friends. Mr. Lovell's word, in your behalf, is as good as money in the bank. Joel will come back with cattle. My only fear is, he won't strain his credit."

"Credit! Who would credit us?"

"Why not? There are not so many drovers at Dodge who had your showing at the same age. They have fought their way up and know who to credit. Your range and ability to hold cattle are your best assets. We must shape up the ranch, because Joel will come in with cattle."

"You're the foreman," said Dell assentingly. "And what's more, if Joel comes home with cattle, I'll hit the ground with my hat and shout as loud as any of you."

"That's the talk. I'm playing Joel to come back winner. Let's saddle up horses, and ride through the cripples this afternoon. I want to get the lay of the range, and the water, and a line on the cattle."

Joel overtook Bob Quirk midway between the Prairie Dog and the railroad. The outfit was drifting south at the rate of forty miles a day, traveling early and late to avoid the heat. On sighting the lone horseman in the rear, signals were exchanged, and the foreman halted until Joel overtook the travelers.

"This is the back track," said Quirk, "and we're expected to crowd three days into one. I don't know what the old man wants with you, but I had a wire to pick you up."

"Mr. Lovell has been urging me to stock our range – to buy more cattle," admitted Joel.

"That's what I thought. He's buying right and left. We're on our way now to receive cattle. That's it; the old man has a bunch of cattle in sight for you."

"Possibly. But what's worrying me is, how am I to buy them – if it takes any money!" dejectedly admitted the husky boy.

"Is that fretting you?" lightly inquired Quirk. "Let the old man do the worrying – that's his long suit. You can rest easy that he has everything all figured out. It might keep you and I guessing, but it's as clear as mud to that old man. We'll make Dodge in four days."

The ravages of the drouth were disheartening. A few hours after sunrise, a white haze settled over the dull, dead plain, the heat-waves rolled up to the cavalcade like a burning prairie, sweat and dust crusted over the horses under saddle, without variation of pace or course. Only three herds were met, feeling their way through the mirages, or loitering along the waters. Traveling by night was preferable, and timing the route into camps and marches, the cottonwood on the Arkansas River was sighted in advance of the schedule.

The outfit halted on a creek north of town. Cattle under herd had been sighted by the thousands, and before the camp was made snug, a conveyance drove up and Forrest and Don Lovell alighted.

"Well, Bob, you're a little ahead of time," said the latter, amid general greetings, "but I'm glad of it. I've closed trades on enough cattle to make up a herd, and the sellers are hurrying me to receive them. Pick up a full outfit of men to-night, and we'll receive to-morrow afternoon. Quince took the train at Cheyenne, but his outfit ought to reach here in a day or so. I've laid my tape on this market, and have all the cattle in sight that I want. Several deals are pending, awaiting the arrival of this boy. Come to town to-night. I'll take Joel under my wing right now."

Three horses were caught, Joel riding one and leading two, and the vehicle started. It was still early in the afternoon, and following down the creek, within an hour the party reached a trail wagon encamped. A number of men were about, including a foreman; and at the request of Mr. Lovell to look over their cattle and horses again the camp took on an air of activity. A small remuda was corralled within ropes, running from choice to common horses, all of which were looked over carefully by the trio, including the wagon team. A number of horses were under saddle, and led by the foreman, a quartette of men started in advance to bunch the herd.

Leaving Forrest at the camp, Mr. Lovell and Joel took the rig and leisurely followed the departing horsemen. "This is one of the best herds on the market," said the old drover to the boy, "and I've kept the deal pending, to see if you and I couldn't buy it together. It runs full thirty-five hundred cattle, twelve hundred threes and the remainder twos. I always buy straight two-year-olds for my beef ranch, because I double-winter all my steer cattle – it takes two winters in the north to finish these Texas steers right. Now, if you can handle the threes, the remnant of twos, and the saddle stock, we'll buy the herd, lock, stock, and barrel. The threes will all ship out as four-year-old beeves next fall, and you can double-winter the younger cattle. I can use two thousand of the two-year-olds, and if you care for the others, after we look them over, leave me to close the trade."

"Mr. Lovell, it has never been clear to me how I am to buy cattle without money," earnestly said Joel.

"Leave that to me – I have that all figured out. If we buy this herd together, you can ship out two thousand beef cattle next fall, and a ranch that has that many beeves to market a year hence, can buy, with or without money, any herd at Dodge to-day. If you like the cattle and want them, leave it all to me."

"But so many horses – We have forty horses already," protested Joel.

"A wide-awake cowman, in this upper country, always buys these southern horses a year in advance of when he needs them. Next year you'll be running a shipping outfit, mounting a dozen men, sending others on fall round-ups, and if you buy your horses now, you'll have them in the pink of condition then. It's a small remuda, a few under sixty horses, as fifty head were detailed out here to strengthen remudas that had to go to the Yellowstone. This foreman will tell you that he topped out twenty-five of the choice horses before the other trail bosses were allowed to pick. As the remuda stands, its make-up is tops and tailings. A year hence one will be as good as the other. You'll need the horses, and by buying down to the blanket, turning the owner foot-loose and free, it will help me to close the trade, in our mutual interest."

The cattle were some two miles distant, under close herd, and by quietly edging them in onto a few hundred acres, they could be easily looked over from the conveyance. On the arrival of the prospective buyers, the foreman had the cattle sufficiently compact, and the old man and the boy drove back and forth through the herd for fully an hour. They were thrifty, western Texas steers, had missed the drouth by coming into the trail at Camp Supply, and were all that could be desired in range cattle. The two agreed on the quality of the herd, and on driving out from among the cattle, the foreman was signaled up.

"One of my outfits arrived from the Platte this afternoon," said Mr. Lovell, "and we'll receive to-morrow. That leaves me free to pick up another herd. If Dud would try his best, he would come very near selling me these cattle. I've got a buyer in sight for the threes and remnant of twos, and if you price the horses right, we might leave you afoot. If you see Dudley before I do, tell him I looked over his cattle again."

"I'll see him to-night," said the foreman, calling after the vehicle.

Forrest was picked up, and they returned to town. The fame of wicked Dodge never interfered with the transaction of business, its iniquity catering largely to the rabble.

"I'll take Joel with me," said the drover to Forrest, "and you look after the horses and hang around the hotel. Dud Stoddard is almost sure to look me up, and if you meet him, admit that we looked over his cattle again. I want him to hound me into buying that herd."

Joel's taciturn manner stood him in good stead. He was alert to all that was passing and, except with Mr. Lovell, was reticent in the extreme. The two strolled about the streets during the evening hours, and on returning to the hotel rather late, Dudley Stoddard was awaiting the old drover. There was no prelude to the matter at issue, and after arranging with other sellers to receive the following day, Mr. Lovell led the way to his room.

"This is one of the Wells Brothers," said the old cowman, presenting Joel; "one of the boys who watered the drive on the Beaver this summer. I was up on his ranch about a month ago, and gave him a good scolding for not stocking his range somewhere near its carrying capacity. He's the buyer I had in view for your three-year-olds. You offered me the herd, on time, and at satisfactory prices. I can use two thousand of the twos, and Wells Brothers will take the remainder, and we'll turn you afoot. Say so, and your herd is sold."

"Well," said Mr. Stoddard, somewhat embarrassed, "I don't happen to know the Wells Brothers – and I usually know men when I extend them a credit. This boy – Well, I'm not in the habit of dealing with boys."

"You and I were boys once and had to make our start," testily replied Mr. Lovell, pacing the room. "The Wells Brothers are making the fight that you and I were making twenty years ago.

In our early struggles, had some one stood behind us, merely stood behind us, it might have been different with us to-day. And now when I don't need no help – Dud, it don't cost much to help others. These boys have proven themselves white, to yours and to my men and to yours and to my cattle. Is there nothing we can do?"

Mr. Stoddard turned to the old drover. "I'll renew my last offer to you. Take the herd and sell these boys the older cattle and remnants. You know the brothers – you know their resources."

"No!" came the answer like a rifle-shot.

"Then, will you stand sponsor – will you go their security?"

"No! These boys can't send home for money nor can't borrow any. Their only asset is their ability to hold and mature cattle. Last winter, the most severe one in the history of the West, they lost two per cent of their holdings. Neither you nor I can make as good a showing on any of our ranges. Dud, what I'm trying to do is to throw on this boy's shoulders the *responsibility* of *paying* for *any cattle he buys*. At his age it would be wrong to rob him of that important lesson. Let's you and I stand behind him, and let's see to it that he makes the right effort to protect his credit."

"That's different," admitted Mr. Stoddard. "Don, if you'll suggest the means to that end, I'll try and meet you halfway."

Mr. Lovell took a seat at the table and picked up a blank sheet of paper. "As mutual friends," said he, "let me draw up, from seller to buyer, an iron-clad bill of sale. Its first clause will be a vendor's lien for the cost of the cattle, horses, etc. Its second will be the appointment of a commission house, who will act as agent, hold this contract, and receive the beeves when ready for shipment to market. Its third clause will be your right, as creditor in a sale of chattel, to place a man of your own selection on Wells Brothers' ranch, under their pay and subject to their orders. As your representative, the privilege is granted of making a daily, weekly, or monthly report to you of the condition of the cattle and the general outlook of the buyers to meet this, their covenant with the seller, before November 1, 1887.

"I wouldn't enter into such a contract with you," continued Mr. Lovell, throwing down the sheet of paper, "but I want this boy to learn the value of a well-protected credit. At his time of life, it's an asset. I'll pay for my half when it's convenient, but I want him to meet his first obligation on or before the day of maturity. I can speak for the boy's willingness to make such a contract. What do you say?"

"Delivery here or elsewhere?" inquired Mr. Stoddard.

"My half here, within three days, the remainder on the Beaver, a seven days' drive. It won't cost you a cent more to send your outfit home from Grinnell than from Dodge. Ten days will end all your trouble. What do you say?"

"Don, let me talk the matter over with you privately," said Mr. Stoddard, arising. "The boy will excuse us. We'll give him a square deal."

The two old men left the room. Forrest arose from a couch and threw his arms around Joel. "It's a sale!" he whispered. "The cattle's yours! That old man of mine will ride Dud Stoddard all around the big corral and spur him in the flank at every jump, unless he comes to those terms. An iron-clad bill of sale is its own surety. You'll need the man, anyhow. I want to give the long yell."

Mr. Lovell returned after midnight, and alone. Forrest and Joel arose to meet him, inquiry and concern in every look and action.

"Take Joel and get out of here," said the old drover, whose twinkling eyes could not conceal the gloating within. "I've got to draw up that bill of sale. Just as if those steers wouldn't pay for themselves next fall. Get to bed, you rascals!"

"Would there be any harm if I went down to the bank of the river and gave the long yell?" inquired Forrest, as he halted in the doorway.

"Get to bed," urged the old drover. "I'll want you in the morning. We'll close a trade, the first thing, on fifteen hundred of those Womack twos. That'll give you a herd, and you can keep an eye over Joel's cattle until the Beaver's reached."

During the few days which followed, Joel Wells was thrown in contact with the many features of a range cattle market. In all the migrations of mankind, strictly cattle towns like Dodge City and Ogalalla are unknown. They were the product of all pastoral ages, reaching a climax on American soil, and not of record in any other country or time. Joel let little escape him. Here men bought and sold by the thousand head, in his day and generation, and he was a part of that epoch.

The necessary number of cattle to complete a herd for Forrest were purchased without leaving town. The afternoon was spent in receiving a herd, in which the veteran drover took a hand, assisted by two competent foremen. Every feature in the cattle, the why and wherefore, was pointed out by the trio, to the eager, earnest boy, so that the lesson sunk into Joel's every fibre. The beauty of the first herd received was in the uniform average of each animal, when ages, class, and build governed selection.

Forrest's outfit arrived that evening, and without even a day's rest arrangements were made to receive the two contingents the next morning. When it came to receive the Stoddard herd, the deftness with which the two outfits classified the cattle was only short of marvelous. The threes were cut out, and each age counted. The over-plus of the younger cattle were cut back, and the contingents were tendered on delivery. The papers were ready, executed on the ground, and the herds started, the smaller in the lead.

The drive to the Beaver was without incident. Forrest spent most of his time with the little herd, which used only eight men, counting Joel, who stood guard at night and made a hand. The herd numbered a few over fifteen hundred cattle, the remuda fifty-six horses, a team and wagon, the total contract price of which was a trifle under twenty-five thousand dollars. It looked like a serious obligation for two boys to assume, but practical men had sanctioned it, and it remained for the ability of Wells Brothers to meet it.

On nearing the Beaver, the lead herd under Bob Quirk took the new trail, which crossed at the ranch. On their leaving the valley, a remark was dropped, unnoticed by Dell, but significant to Jack Sargent. It resulted in the two riding out on the trail, only to meet the purchased cattle, Joel on one point and Forrest on the other, directing the herds to the tanks below. The action bespoke its intent, and on meeting Forrest, the latter jerked his thumb over his shoulder, remarking, "Drop back and pilot the wagon and remuda into the ranch. We're taking this passel of cattle into the new tanks, and will scatter them up and down the creek. Lovell's cattle? No. Old man Joel Wells bought these to stock his ranch. See how chesty it makes him – he won't even look this way. You boys may have to sit up with him a few nights at first, but he'll get over that. Pilot in the remuda. You two are slated to take this outfit to the railroad to-night. Trail along, my beauties; Wells Brothers are shaking out a right smart bit of sail these days."

CHAPTER XVII
"THE WAGON"

The little ranch had assumed a contract and must answer at the appointed time. If the brothers could meet their first commercial obligation, it would establish their standing, and to that end every energy must be directed. They were extremely fortunate in the advice and help of two young men bred to the occupation, and whose every interest lay in making a success of the ranch.

The trail outfit returned to the railroad that night. Everything was abandoned but their saddles – *burning the wagon* – while Joe Manly, one of their number, remained behind. Manly was not even the foreman, and on taking his departure the trail boss, in the presence of all, said to his man, "Now, Joe, turn yourself over to this ranch and make a useful hand. Drop old man Dudley a line whenever you have a chance. It's quite a little ride to the station, and we'll understand that no news is good news. And once you see that these cattle are going to winter safely, better raise the long yell and come home. You can drift back in the fall – during the beef-shipping season. I may write you when next summer's plans begin to unfold."

Accompanied by Dell and Sargent, and singing the home songs of the South, the outfit faded away into the night. Forrest's herd had watered during the evening, and moved out to a safe camp, leaving its foreman on the Beaver. He and Manly discussed the situation, paving the way in detail, up to the manner of holding the cattle during the coming winter. With numbers exceeding three thousand, close herd and corralling at night was impossible, and the riding of lines, with an extra camp, admitting of the widest freedom, was decided on as the most feasible method. The new camp must be located well above Hackberry Grove, and to provision it for man and horse was one of the many details outlined in meeting the coming winter. Joel was an attentive listener, and having held cattle by one system, he fully understood the necessity of adopting some other manner of restraint. In locating cattle, where there was danger of drifting from any cause, the method of riding lines was simple and easily understood – to patrol the line liable to assault from drifting cattle.

Forrest was elated over the outlook. On leaving the next morning, he turned his horse and rode back to the tent. "This may be the last time I'll come this way," said he to Joel, "as there is talk of the trail moving west. On account of fever, this State threatens to quarantine against Texas cattle. If it does, the trail will have to move over into Colorado or hunt a new route through unorganized counties on the western line of Kansas. In event of quarantine being enforced, it means a bigger range for Wells Brothers. Of course, this is only your second year in cattle, just getting a firm grip on the business, but I can see a big future for you boys. As cowmen, you're just in swaddling clothes yet, toddling around on your first legs, but the outlook is rosy. Hold these cattle this winter, protect your credit next fall, and it doesn't matter if I never come back. A year hence you'll have a bank account, be living on the sunny side of the creek, and as long as you stick to cows, through thick and thin, nothing can unhorse you."

The trail foreman rode away to overtake his herd, and Joel and Manly busied themselves in locating the new cattle. Dell and Sargent accompanied the last Lovell herd into the ranch that evening, and it proved to be the rear guard of trail cattle for that summer.

The ranch was set in order for the present. The dead-line was narrowed to a mile, which admitted of fully half the through cattle watering at the beaver ponds around headquarters. The new remuda, including all horses acquired that summer, to the number of eighty head, was moved up to Hackberry Grove and freed for the year. The wintered horses furnished ample saddle mounts for the present, there being little to do, as the water held the new cattle and no herding was required. The heat of summer was over, the water held in tanks and beaver dams, and the ranch settled down in pastoral security.

Under the new outline for the winter, an increased amount of forage must be provided, as in riding lines two grain-fed horses to the man was the lowest limit in mounting all line-riders. Machinery was available on the railroad, and taking a team, Joel returned with a new mowing machine, and the matter of providing abundant forage was easily met. Sufficient hay, from a few bends of the creek, in dead-line territory, supplied the home ranch, and a week's encampment above Hackberry Grove saw the site of the new line-camp equipped with winter forage.

While engaged on the latter task, a new feature was introduced on Wells Brothers' ranch. A movable commissary is a distinct aid to any pastoral occupation, and hence *the wagon* becomes a cowman's home and castle. From it he dispenses a rough hospitality, welcomes the wayfarer, and exchanges the chronicle of the range. The wagon, which had been acquired with the new herd and used on the above occasion, was well equipped with canvas cover, water barrels, and a convenient chuck-box at the rear. The latter was fitted with drawers and compartments as conveniently as a kitchen. When open, the lid of the box afforded a table; when closed, it protected the contents from the outer elements. The wagon thus becomes home to nomadic man and animal, the one equal with the other. Saddle horses, when frightened at night, will rush to the safety of a camp-fire and the protection of their masters, and therefore a closer bond exists between the men of the open and their mounts than under more refined surroundings.

Early in September a heavy rain fell in the west, extending down the Beaver, flushing the creek and providing an abundance of running water. It was followed by early frosts, lifting the dead-line and ushering in Indian summer. With forage secure, attention was turned to the cattle. The purchase of a mowing machine had exhausted the funds derived from the sale of peltry, and a shipment of cattle was decided on to provide the munitions for the coming winter. The wagon was accordingly provisioned for a week, the blankets stored in the commissary, and the quartette moved out to round up the wintered cattle. They had not been handled since the spring drift of March before, and when thrown into a compact herd, they presented a different appearance from the spiritless cattle of six months previous. A hundred calves, timid as fawns, shied from the horsemen, their mothers lowed in comforting concern, the beeves waddled about from carrying their own flesh, while the patriarchs of the herd bellowed in sullen defiance. Fifty of the heaviest beeves were cut out from the - - Y brand, flesh governing the selection, and the first shipment of cattle left the Beaver for eastern markets.

Four days were required to graze the heavy cattle down to the railroad. Dell drove the wagon, Sargent was intrusted with the remuda, the two others grazing the beeves, while each took his turn in standing guard at night. Water was plentiful, cars were in waiting, and on reaching the railroad, the cattle were corralled in the shipping pens.

Joel and Manly accompanied the shipment to Kansas City. The beeves were consigned to the firm mentioned in the bill of sale as factor in marketing and settlement of the herd which had recently passed from the possession of Mr. Stoddard to that of Wells Brothers. The two cars of cattle found a ready sale, the weights revealing a surprise, attracting the attention of packers and salesmen to the quality of beef from the Beaver valley.

"Give me the cattle from the short-grass country," said a salesman to a packer, as Wells Brothers' beeves were crossing the weighing scale. "You and I needn't worry about the question of range – the buffalo knew. Catch the weights of these cattle and compare it with range beef from the sedge-grass and mountain country. Tallow tells its own story – the buffalo knew the best range."

An acquaintance with the commission house was established on a mutual basis. The senior member of the firm, a practical old man, detained Joel and Manly in his private office for an hour.

"This market is alert to every new section having cattle to ship," said the old man to Joel, studying a sales statement. "The Solomon River country sent in some cattle last fall, but yours is the first shipment from the Beaver. Our salesman reports your consignment the fattest range beeves on to-day's market. And these weights confirm the statement. I don't understand it. What kind of a country have you out there?"

Joel gave Manly an appealing look. "It's the plains," answered the latter. "It's an old buffalo range. You can see their skulls by the thousand. It's a big country; it just swells, and dips, and rolls away."

It was the basis of a range which interested the senior member. "The grasses, the grasses?" he repeated. "What are your native grasses?"

"Oh, just plain, every-day buffalo grass," answered Manly. "Of course, here and there, in the bends of the Beaver, there's a little blue-stem, enough for winter forage for the saddle stock. The cattle won't touch it."

The last of many subjects discussed was the existing contract, of which the commission firm was the intermediary factor. The details were gone over carefully, the outlook for next year's shipments reviewed, and on taking their leave, the old man said to his guests: –

"Well, I'm pleased over the outlook. The firm have had letters from both Mr. Lovell and Mr. Stoddard, and now that I've gone over the situation, with the boys in the saddle, everything is clear and satisfactory. Next year's shipments will take care of the contract. Keep in touch with us, and we'll advise you from time to time. Ship your cattle in finished condition, and they'll make a market for themselves. We'll expect you early next summer."

"Our first shipment will be two hundred double-wintered cattle," modestly admitted Joel.

"They ought to be ready a full month in advance of your single-wintered beeves," said the old man, from his practical knowledge in maturing beef. "Ship them early. The bookkeeper has your account all ready."

Joel and Manly were detained at the business office only a moment. The beeves had netted thirty-five dollars a head, and except for current expenses, the funds were left on deposit with the commission house, as there were no banks near home; the account was subject to draft, and accepting a small advance in currency, the boys departed. A brief hour's shopping was indulged in, the principal purchases being two long-range rifles, cartridges and poison in abundance, when they hastened to the depot and caught a west-bound train. Horses had been left at Grinnell, and at evening the next day the two rode into headquarters on the Beaver.

Beyond question there are tides in the affairs of men. With the first shipment of cattle from the little ranch, poverty fled and an air of independence indicated the turn in the swing of the pendulum. Practical men, in every avenue of the occupation, had lent their indorsement to the venture of the brothers, the mettle of the pasture had been tested in the markets, and the future, with reasonable vigilance, rested on sure foundations.

The turn of the tide was noticeable at once. "I really think Uncle Dud would let me come home," said Manly to the others, at supper. "There's no occasion for my staying here this winter. Besides, I'm a tender plant; I'm as afraid of cold as a darky is of thunder. Wouldn't I like to get a letter from Uncle Dud saying, 'Come home, my little white chicken, come home!'"

"You can go in the spring," said Joel. "We're going to use four line-riders this winter, and there's every reason why you'll make a trusty one!"

"That's one of the owners talking," observed Sargent; "now listen to the foreman's orders: The next thing is to brand every hoof up to date. Then, at the upper line-camp, comes the building of a new dug-out and stabling for four horses. And lastly, freight in plenty of corn. After that, if we fail to hold the cattle, it's our own fault. No excuse will pass muster. Hold these cattle? It's a dead immortal cinch! Joseph dear, make yourself a useful guest for the winter."

A hopeful spirit lightened every task. The calves and their mothers were brought down to the home corral and branded in a single day. The Stoddard cattle, the title being conditional, were exempt, the Lazy H ranch brand fully protecting mutual interests. Only cripple, fagged, and stray cattle were branded, the latter numbering less than a hundred head, and were run into the Hospital brand, while the remainder bore the – Y of the ranch. The work was completed within a week, Dell making a hand which proved his nerve, either in the saddle or branding pen.

The first week in October was devoted to building the new dug-out and stable. The wagon was provisioned, every implement and tool on the ranch, from a hammer to a plough, was taken along, as well as the remuda, and the quartette sallied forth to the task as if it were a frolic. The site had been decided on during the haying, and on reaching the scene, the tent was set up, and the building of a shelter for man and horse was begun.

The dug-out of the West is built for comfort, – half cellar and the remainder sod walls. A southern slope was selected; an abrupt break or low bank was taken advantage of, admitting of four-foot cellar walls on three sides, the open end inclosed with massive sod walls and containing the door. The sod was broken by a team and plough, cut into lengths like brick, and the outside walls raised to the desired height. For roofing, a heavy ridge-pole was cut the length of the room, resting on stout upright posts. Lighter poles were split and laid compactly, like rafters, sheeted with hay, and covered with loose dirt to the depth of a foot. The floor was earthen; a half window east and west, supplemented by a door in the south, admitted light, making a cosy, comfortable shelter. A roomy stable was built on the same principle and from the same material.

The work was completed quickly, fuel for the winter gathered, when the quartette started homeward. "It looks like the halfway house at Land's End," said Manly, turning for a last look at the new improvements. "What are you going to call the new tepee?"

"Going to call it The Wagon," answered Sargent, he and Dell having accepted the new line-camp as their winter quarters, "and let the latch-string hang on the outside. Whenever you can, you must bring your knitting and come over."

CHAPTER XVIII
AN OPEN WINTER

An ideal Indian summer was enjoyed. Between the early and late fall frosts, the range matured into perfect winter pasturage. Light rains in September freshened the buffalo grass until it greened on the sunny slopes, cured into hay as the fall advanced, thus assuring abundant forage to the cattle.

Manly was the only one of the quartette not inured to a northern climate. A winter in Montana had made Sargent proof against any cold, while the brothers were native to that latitude if not to the plains. After building the line-camp and long before occupying it, the quartette paired off, Sargent and Dell claiming the new dug-out, while the other two were perfectly content with the old shack at headquarters. A healthy spirit of rivalry sprang up, extending from a division of the horses down to a fair assignment of the blankets.

Preparations for and a constant reference to the coming winter aroused a dread in Manly. "You remind me of our darky cook," said Sargent, "up on the Yellowstone a few years ago. Half the trail outfit were detailed until frost, to avoid fever and to locate the cattle, and of course the cook had to stay. A squall of snow caught us in camp, and that poor darky just pined away. 'Boss,' he used to say to the foreman, shivering over the fire, 'ah's got to go home. Ah's subjec' to de rheumatics. Mah fambly's a-gwine to be pow'ful uneasy 'bout me. Dis-a-yere country am no place fo' a po' ol' niggah.'"

Two teams were employed in freighting in the corn, four round trips being required, Joel and Manly assuming the work. Supplies for the winter were brought in at the same time, among the first of which were four sacks of salt; and the curing of two barrels of corned beef fell a pleasant task to Dell and his partner. There was nothing new in pickling the meat, and with the exception of felling the beeves, the incident passed as part of the day's work. Dell claimed the privilege of making the shots, which Sargent granted, but exercised sufficient caution to corral the beeves. Both fell in their tracks, and the novice gained confidence in his skill in the use of a rifle.

The first of December was agreed on to begin the riding of lines. That date found all the new cattle drifted above headquarters, and as it was some ten miles to the upper line-camp, an extremely liberal range was allowed the herd. Eight of the best wintered horses were stabled, and at first the line was maintained on the south bank of the Beaver. An outer line was agreed upon, five miles to the south; but until the season forced the cattle to the shelter of the valley, the inner one was kept under patrol. The outer was a purely imaginary line, extending in an immense half-circle, from headquarters to the new line-camp above. It followed the highest ground, and marked the utmost limit on the winter range on the south. Any sign or trace of cattle crossing it, drifting before a storm or grazing at leisure, must be turned back or trailed down.

The first and second weeks passed, the weather continuing fine. Many of the cattle ranged two and three miles north of the creek, not even coming in to water oftener than every other day. Several times the horsemen circled to the north; but as ranging wide was an advantage, the cattle were never disturbed. A light fall of soft snow even failed to bring the cattle into the valley.

Christmas week was ushered in with a display of animal instinct. The through and wintered cattle had mixed and mingled, the latter fat and furred, forging to the front in ranging northward, and instinctively leading their brethren to shelter in advance of the first storm. Between the morning and evening patrol of a perfect day, the herd, of its own accord, drifted into the valley, the leaders rioting in a wild frolic. Their appearance hastened the patrol of the inner line by an hour, every nook and shelter, including the old corral, being filled with frolicsome cattle. The calves were engaging each other in mimic fights, while the older cattle were scarring every exposed bank, or matting their foreheads in clay and soft dirt.

"What does it mean?" inquired Joel, hailing Sargent, when the line-riders met.

"It means that we'll ride the outside line in the morning," came the reply. "There's a storm coming within twelve hours. At least, the herd say so."

"What can we do?"

"Leave that to the cattle. They'll not quit the valley unless driven out by a storm. The instinct that teaches them of the coming storm also teaches them how to meet it. They'll bed in the blue-stem to-night, or hunt a cosy nook under some cut-bank."

A meeting point on the outer line, for the next morning, was agreed upon, when the horsemen separated for the evening. "Get out early, and keep your eyes open for any trace of cattle crossing the line," Sargent called back, as he reined homeward. "Dell and I will leave The Wagon at daybreak."

The storm struck between midnight and morning. Dawn revealed an angry horizon, accompanied by a raw, blue-cold, cutting wind from the north. On leaving their quarters, both patrols caught the storm on an angle, edging in to follow the circle, their mounts snorting defiance and warming to the work in resisting the bitter morning. The light advanced slowly, a sifting frost filled the air, obscuring the valley, and not until the slope to the south was reached was the situation known.

No cattle were in sight or adrift. Within an hour after leaving the line-camp, the experienced eye of Sargent detected a scattering trace where an unknown number of cattle had crossed the line. Both he and Dell dismounted, and after studying the trail, its approach and departure, the range-bred man was able to give a perfect summary of the situation.

"There's between fifty and a hundred head in this drift," remarked Sargent, as the two remounted. "They're through cattle; the storm must have caught them on the divide, north of the Beaver. They struck the creek in the flats and were driven out of the valley. The trail's not over two hours old. Ride the line until you meet the other boys, and I'll trail down these cattle. The sand dunes ought to catch them."

Dell and Sargent separated. Five miles to the eastward Joel was met. Manly was reported at the rear, the two having intercepted a contingent of cattle approaching the line, and was then drifting the stragglers back to the valley. On Dell's report, the brothers turned to the assistance of Sargent, retracing the western line, and finally bearing off for the sand hills. Several times the sun threatened to break through, lighting the valley, but without revealing any stir among the cattle in the shelter of the creek. In the short time since leaving their stables, the horses under saddle had whitened from the action of the frost on their sweaty coats, unheeded by their riders. There was no checking of mounts until the range of dunes was reached, when from the summit of a sand hill the stragglers were located in care of Sargent, and on the homeward drift. The cattle were so benumbed and bewildered from the cold that they had marched through the shelter of the dunes, and were overtaken adrift on the wind-swept plain.

The contingent numbered sixty-odd cattle, and with the help of the brothers were easily handled. Before recrossing the line, the sun burst forth, and on reaching the slope, the trio halted in parting. "A few hours of this sun," said Sargent, "and we've got the upper hand of this storm. The wind or sun must yield. If the wind lulls, we'll ride the inner line to-night and bed every hoof in the shelter of the creek. Pick up Manly, and we'll ride the valley line about the middle of the afternoon."

Joel turned homeward, scouting that portion of the line under patrol from headquarters. The drifting contingent was intrusted to Dell, leaving Sargent to retrace their division of the line, and before noon all had reached their quarters. From twenty to thirty miles had been covered that morning, in riding the line and recovering the lost, and at the agreed time, the relay horses were under saddle for the afternoon task. The sun had held sway, the wind had fallen, and as they followed up the valley, they encountered the cattle in large bunches, grazing to every quarter of the compass. They were not molested on the outward ride, but on the return trip, near evening, they were all turned back to the sheltering nooks and coves which the bends of the Beaver afforded. A crimpy night followed, but an early patrol in the morning found the cattle snug in the dry, rank grasses which grew in the first bottoms of the creek.

The first storm had been weathered. The third day, of their own accord, the cattle left the valley and grazed out on the northern divide. The line-riders relaxed their vigil, and in preparation for observing the Natal day, each camp put forth its best hunter to secure a venison. The absence of snow, during the storm, had held the antelope tributary to the Beaver, and locating game was an easy matter. To provide the roast, the spirit of rivalry was accented anew, and each camp fervently hoped for its own success.

A venison hung at headquarters before noon, Manly making a running shot at the leader of a band, which was surprised out of a morning siesta near the old trail crossing. If a quarry could only be found in the sand hills, a natural shelter for antelope, Sargent had flattered Dell into believing that his aim was equal to the occasion. The broken nature of the dune country admitted of stealthy approach, and its nearness to the upper camp recommended it as an inviting hunting ground. The disappointment of the first effort, due to moderated weather, was in finding the quarry far afield. A dozen bands were sighted from the protection of the sand hills, a mile out on the flat plain, but without shelter to screen a hunter. Sargent was equal to the occasion, and selecting a quarry, the two horses were unsaddled, the bridle reins lengthened by adding ropes, and crouching low, their mounts afforded the necessary screen as they grazed or were driven forward. By tacking right and left in a zigzag course they gained the wind, and a stealthy approach on the band was begun. The stabled horses grazed ravenously, sometimes together, then apart, affording a perfect screen for stalking.

After a seeming age to Dell, the required rifle range was reached, when the cronies flattened themselves in the short grass and allowed the horses to graze to their rope's end. Sargent indicated a sentinel buck, presenting the best shot; and using his elbow for a rest, the rifle was laid in the hollow of Dell's upraised hand and drawn firmly to his shoulder, and a prompt report followed. The shot went wild, throwing up a flash of dust before the band, which instantly whirled. The horses merely threw up their heads in surprise, attracting the startled quarry, which ran up within fifty yards of the repeating rifle. In the excitement of the moment instantly following the first shot, Dell had arisen to his knee, unmindful of the necessity of throwing another cartridge into the rifle barrel. "Shoot! Shoot!" whispered Sargent, as the band excitedly halted within pistol range. Dell fingered the trigger in vain. "Throw in a cartridge!" breathlessly suggested Sargent. The lever clicked, followed by a shot, which tore up the sod within a few feet of the muzzle of the rifle!

The antelope were away in a flash. Sargent rolled on the grass, laughing until the tears trickled down his cheeks, while Dell's chagrin left him standing like a simpleton.

"I don't believe this gun shoots true," he ventured at last, too mortified to realize the weakness of his excuse. "Besides, it's too easy on the trigger."

"No rifle shoots true during buck ague season," answered Sargent, not daring to raise his eyes. "When the grass comes next spring, those scars in the sod will grow over. Lucky that neither horse was killed. Honest, I'll never breathe it! Not for worlds!"

Sargent's irony was wasted. Dell, in a dazed way, recovered his horse, mounted, and aimlessly followed his bunkie. On reaching their saddles, the mental fog lifted, and as if awakening from a pleasant dream, the boy dismounted. "Did I have it? – the buck ague?" he earnestly inquired.

"You had symptoms of it," answered Sargent, resaddling his horse. "Whenever a hunter tries to shoot an empty gun, or discharges one into the ground at his feet, he ought to take something for his nerves. It's not fatal, and I have hopes of your recovery."

The two turned homeward. Several times Sargent gave vent to a peal of laughter that rang out like a rifle report, but Dell failed to appreciate the humor of the situation.

"Well," said the older one, as they dismounted at the stable, "if we have to fall back on corn beef for our Christmas dinner, I can grace it with a timely story. And if we have a saddle of venison, it will fit the occasion just as well."

The inner line was ridden at evening. The cattle were caring for themselves; but on meeting the lads from headquarters, an unusual amount of banter and repartee was exchanged.

"Killed an antelope two days before you needed it," remarked Sargent scathingly. "Well, well! You fellows certainly haven't much confidence in your skill as hunters."

"Venison improves with age," loftily observed Manly.

"That's a poor excuse. At best, antelope venison is dry meat. We located a band or two to-day, and if Dell don't care for the shot, I'll go out in the morning and bring in a fat yearling."

"Is that your prospect for a Christmas roast?" inquired Manly with refined sarcasm. "Dell, better air your Sunday shirt to-morrow and come down to headquarters for your Christmas dinner. We're going to have quite a spread."

Dell threw a glance at Sargent. "Come on," said the latter with polished contempt, reining his horse homeward. "Just as if we lived on beans at The Wagon! Just as if our porcelain-lined graniteware wasn't as good as their tin plates! Catch us accepting! Come on!"

Sargent was equal to his boast. He returned the next day before noon, a young doe lashed to his saddle cantle, and preparations were made for an extensive dinner. The practical range man is usually a competent cook, and from the stores of the winter camp a number of extra dishes were planned. In the way of a roast, on the plains, a saddle of venison was the possible extreme, and the occupants of the line-camp possessed a ruddy health which promised appetites to grace the occasion.

Christmas day dawned under ideal conditions. Soft winds swayed the dead weeds and leafless shrubs, the water trickled down the creek from pool to pool, reminding one of a lazy, spring day, with droning bees and flights of birds afield. Sargent rode the morning patrol alone, meeting Joel at the halfway point, when the two dismounted, whiling away several hours in considering future plans of the ranch.

It was high noon when the two returned to their respective quarters. Dell had volunteered to supervise the roasting of the venison, and on his crony's return, the two sat down to their Christmas dinner. What the repast lacked in linen and garnishment, it made up in stability, graced by a cheerfulness and contentment which made its partakers at peace with the world. Sargent was almost as resourceful in travel and story as Quince Forrest, and never at a loss for the fitting incident to grace any occasion.

Dell was a good listener. Any story, even at his own expense, was enjoyed. "Whether we had corn beef or venison," said he to Sargent, "you promised to tell a story at dinner to-day."

"The one that you reminded me of when you shot the rifle into the ground at your feet and scared the antelope away? No offense if I have to laugh; you looked like a simpleton."

"Tell your story; I'm young, I'll learn," urged Dell.

"You may learn to handle a gun, and make the same mistake again, but in a new way. It's live and learn. This man was old enough to be your father, but he looked just as witless as you did."

"Let's have the story," impatiently urged the boy.

"It happened on a camp hunt. Wild turkeys are very plentiful in certain sections of Texas, and one winter a number of us planned a week's shooting. In the party was a big, raw-boned ex-sheriff, known as one of the most fearless officers in the state. In size he simply towered above the rest of us.

"It was a small party, but we took along a commissary wagon, an ambulance, saddle horses, and plenty of Mexicans to do the clerking and coarse handwriting. It was quite a distance to the hunting grounds, and the first night out, we made a dry camp. A water keg and every jug on the ranch had been filled for the occasion, and were carried in the wagon.

"Before reaching the road camp, the big sheriff promised us a quail pot-pie for breakfast, and with that intent, during the afternoon, he killed two dozen partridges. The bird was very plentiful, and instead of picking them for a pot-pie, skinning such a number was much quicker. In the hurry and bustle of making the camp snug for the night, every one was busy, the sheriff in particular, in dressing his bag of quail. On finishing the task, he asked a Mexican to pour some water, and the horse wrangler reached into the wagon, at random, and emptied a small jug into the vessel containing the dressed birds.

"The big fellow adjourned to the rear and proceeded to wash and drain his quail. After some little time, he called to the cook: 'Ignacio, I smell kerosene. Look in the wagon, please, and see if the lantern isn't leaking.'

"'In a minute,' answered the cook, busy elsewhere.

"The sheriff went on washing the quail, and when about halfway through the task, he halted. 'Ignacio, I smell that kerosene again. See if the lantern isn't upset, or the oil jug leaking.'

"'Just in a minute,' came the answer as before. 'My hands are in the flour.'

"The big man went on, sniffing the air from time to time, nearly finishing his task, when he stopped again and pleadingly said: 'Ignacio, I surely smell kerosene. We're out for a week, and a lantern without oil puts us in a class with the foolish virgins. Drop your work and see what the trouble is. There's a leak somewhere.'

"The cook dusted the flour from his hands, clambered up on the wagon wheel, lifted the kerosene jug, pulled the stopper, smelt it, shook it, and lifted it above his head in search of a possible crack. The empty jug, the absence of any sign of leakage, gradually sifted through his mind, and he cast an inquiring glance at the big sheriff, just then finishing his task. Invoking heaven and all the saints to witness, he gasped, 'Mr. Charlie, you've washed the quail in the kerosene!'

"The witless, silly expression that came into that big man's face is only seen once in a lifetime," said Sargent in conclusion. "I've been fortunate, I've seen it twice; once on the face of a Texas sheriff, and again, when you shot a hole in the ground with your eye on an antelope. Whenever I feel blue and want to laugh, I conjure up the scene of a Mexican, standing on a wagon wheel, holding a jug, and a six-footer in the background, smelling the fingers of one hand and then the other."

CHAPTER XIX
AN INDIAN SCARE

The year closed with dry, open weather. The cattle scattered wide, ranging farther afield, unmolested except by shifting winds. The latter was a matter of hourly observation, affording its lesson to the brothers, and readily explained by the older and more practical men. For instance, a north or the dreaded east wind brought the herd into the valley, where it remained until the weather moderated, and then drifted out of its own free will. When a balmy south wind blew, the cattle grazed against it, and when it came from a western quarter, they turned their backs and the gregarious instinct to flock was noticeable. Under settled weather, even before dawn, by noting the quarter of the wind, it was an easy matter to foretell the movement of the herd for the coming day.

The daily tasks rested lightly. The line was ridden as usual, but more as a social event than as a matter of necessity. The occasional reports of Manly to his employer were flattering in the extreme. Any risk involved in the existing contract hinged on the present winter, and since it was all that could be desired, every fine day added to the advantage of Wells Brothers. So far their venture had been greeted with fair winds, and with not a cloud in the visible sky. Manly was even recalled by Mr. Stoddard early in February.

Month after month passed without incident. Spring came fully a fortnight earlier than the year before. By the middle of March, the willows were bent with pollen, the birds returned, and the greening slopes rolled away and were lost behind low horizons. The line-camp was abandoned, the cattle were scattered over the entire valley, and the instincts to garden were given free rein. The building of two additional tanks, one below the old trail crossing and the other near the new camp above, occupied a month's time to good advantage. It enlarged the range beyond present needs; but the brothers were wrestling with a rare opportunity, and theirs was strictly a policy of expansion.

An occasional trip to the railroad, for supplies or pressing errand, was usually rewarded with important news. During the winter just passed, Kansas had quarantined against Texas cattle, and the trail was barred from that state. Early in May information reached the ranch that the market interests of Dodge City had moved over the line into Colorado, and had established a town on the railroad, to be known as Trail City. A feasible route lay open to the south, across No-Man's-Land, into the Texas Panhandle, while scouting parties were out with the intent of locating a new trail to Ogalalla. It would cross the Republican River nearly due westward from headquarters, and in the neighborhood of one hundred miles distant.

"There you are," said Sargent, studying a railroad folder. "You must have water for the herds, so the new market will have a river and a railroad. It simply means that the trail has shifted from the east to the west of your range. As long as the country is open, you can buy cattle at Trail City, hold them on the Colorado line until frost, and cross to your own range with a few days' travel. It may prove an advantage after all."

The blessing of sunshine and shower rested on the new ranch. The beaver ponds filled, the spill-ways of every tank ran like a mill race, and the question of water for the summer was answered. The cattle early showed the benefits of the favorable winter, and by June the brands were readable at a glance. From time to time reports from the outside world reached the brothers, and among other friendly letters received was an occasional inquiry from the commission firm, the factors named under the existing contract. The house kept in touch with the range, was fully aware of the open winter, and could easily anticipate its effects in maturing cattle for early shipment.

The solicitors of the firm, graduates of the range, were sent out a month in advance of other years. Wells Brothers were advised of a promised visit by one of the traveling agents of the commission house, and during the first week in July he arrived at headquarters. He was a practical man, with little concern for comfort, as long as there were cattle to look over. Joel took him in tow, mounted him on the pick of saddle horses, and the two leisurely rode the range.

"What does he say?" inquired Dell, after a day's ride.

"Not a word," answered Joel. "He can't talk any more than I can. Put in all day just looking and thinking. He must like cattle that range wide, for we rode around every outside bunch. He *can* talk, because he admitted we have good horses."

Again the lesson that contact teaches was accented anew. At parting the following morning, in summing up the outlook, the solicitor surprised the brothers. "The situation is clear," said he quietly. "You must ship early. Your double-wintered beeves will reach their prime this month. You may ship them any day after the 25th. Your single-wintered ones can follow in three weeks. The firm may be able to advise you when to ship. It's only a fourteen-hour run to the yards, and if you work a beef-shipping outfit that's up to date, you can pick your day to reach the market. Get your outfit together, keep in touch with the house by wire, and market your beef in advance of the glut from the Platte country."

The solicitor lifted the lines over a livery team. "One moment," said Joel. "Advise Mr. Stoddard that we rely on him to furnish us two men during the beef-shipping season."

"Anything else?" inquired the man, a memorandum-book in hand.

"Where are the nearest ranches to ours?"

"On the Republican, both above and below the old trail crossing. There may be extra men over on the river," said the solicitor, fully anticipating the query.

"That's all," said Joel, extending his hand.

The stranger drove away. The brothers exchanged a puzzled glance, but Sargent smiled. "That old boy sabes cows some little," said the latter. "The chances are that he's forgotten more about cattle than some of these government experts ever knew. Anyway, he reads the sign without much effort. His survey of this range and the outlook are worth listening to. Better look up an outfit of men."

"We'll gather the remuda to-day," announced Joel. "While I'm gone to the Republican, you boys can trim up and gentle the horses."

The extra mounts, freed the fall before, had only been located on the range, and must be gathered and brought in to headquarters at once. They had ranged in scattering bunches during the winter, and a single day would be required to gather and corral the ranch remuda. It numbered, complete, ninety-six horses, all geldings, and the wisdom of buying the majority a year in advance of their needs reflected the foresight of a veteran cowman. Many of them were wild, impossible of approach, the call of the plain and the free life of their mustang ancestors pulsing with every heart-beat, and several days would be required to bring them under docile subjection. There were scraggy hoofs to trim, witches' bridles to disentangle, while long, bushy, matted tails must be thinned to a graceful sweep.

The beginning of work acted like a tonic. The boys sallied forth, mounted on their best horses, their spirits soaring among the clouds. During the spring rains, several small lakes had formed in the sand hills, at one of which a band of some thirty saddle horses was watering. The lagoon was on the extreme upper end of the range, fully fifteen miles from headquarters; and as all the saddle stock must be brought in, the day's work required riding a wide circle. Skirting the sand dunes, by early noon all the horses were in hand, save the band of thirty. There was no occasion for all hands to assist in bringing in the absent ones, and a consultation resulted in Joel and Dell volunteering for the task, while Sargent returned home with the horses already gathered.

The range of the band was well known, and within a few hours after parting with Sargent, the missing horses were in hand. The brothers knew every horse, and, rejoicing in their splendid condition, they started homeward, driving the loose mounts before them. The most direct course to headquarters was taken, which would carry the cavalcade past the springs and the upper winter quarters. The latter was situated in the brakes of the Beaver, several abrupt turns of the creek, until its near approach, shutting out a western view of the deserted dug-out. The cavalcade was drifting home at a gentle trot, but on approaching The Wagon, a band of ponies was sighted forward and in a bend of the creek. The boys veered their horses, taking to the western divide, and on gaining it, saw below them and at the distance of only a quarter-mile, around the springs, an Indian encampment of a dozen tepees and lean-tos.

Dell and Joel were struck dumb at the sight. To add to their surprise, all the dogs in the encampment set up a howling, the Indians came tumbling from their temporary shelters, many of them running for their ponies on picket, while an old, almost naked leader signaled to the brothers. It was a moment of bewilderment with the boys, who conversed in whispers, never halting on their course, and when the Indians reached their ponies, every brave dashed up to the encampment. A short parley followed, during which signaling was maintained by the old Indian, evidently a chief; but the boys kept edging away, and the old brave sprang on a pony and started in pursuit, followed by a number of his band.

The act was tinder to powder. The boys gave rowel to their mounts, shook out their ropes, raised the long yell, and started the loose horses in a mad dash for home. It was ten long miles to headquarters, and their mounts, already fagged by carrying heavy saddles and the day's work, were none too fresh, while the Indians rode bareback and were not encumbered by an ounce of extra clothing.

The boys led the race by fully five hundred yards. But instead of taking to the divide, the Indians bore down the valley, pursued and pursuers in plain sight of each other. For the first mile or so the loose horses were no handicap, showing clean heels and keeping clear of the whizzing ropes. But after the first wild dash, the remuda began to scatter, and the Indians gained on the cavalcade, coming fairly abreast and not over four hundred yards distant.

"They're riding to cut us off!" gasped Dell. "They'll cut us off from headquarters!"

"Our horses will outwind their ponies," shouted Joel, in reply. "Don't let these loose horses turn into the valley."

The divide was more difficult to follow than the creek. The meanderings of the latter were crossed and recrossed without halting, while the watershed zigzagged, or was broken and cut by dry washes and coulees, thus retarding the speed of the cavalcade. The race wore on with varying advantage, and when near halfway to headquarters, the Indians turned up the slope as if to verify Dell's forecast. At this juncture, a half-dozen of the loose horses cut off from the band and turned down the slope in plain sight of the pursuers.

"If it's horses they want, they can have those," shouted Joel. "Climbing that slope will fag their ponies. Come on; here's where we have the best of it."

The Indians were not to be pacified. Without a look they swept past the abandoned horses. The boys made a clear gain along a level stretch on the divide, maintaining their first lead, when the pursuers, baffled in cutting them off, turned again into the valley.

"It isn't horses they want," ventured Dell, with a backward glance.

"In the next dip, we'll throw the others down the western slope, and ride for our lives," answered Joel, convinced that a sacrifice of horses would not appease their pursuers.

The opportunity came shortly, when for a few minutes the brothers dipped from sight of the Indians. The act confused the latter, who scaled the divide, only to find the objects of their chase a full half-mile in the lead, but calling on the last reserve in their fagged horses. The pursuers gradually closed the intervening gap; but with the advantage of knowing every foot of the ground, the brothers took a tack which carried them into the valley at the old winter corral. From that point it was a straight stretch homeward, and, their horses proving their mettle, the boys dashed up to the stable, where Sargent was found at work among the other horses.

"Indians! Indians!" shouted Dell, who arrived in the lead. "Indians have been chasing us all afternoon. Run for your life, Jack!"

Joel swept past a moment later, accenting the situation, and as Sargent left the corral, he caught sight of the pursuing Indians, and showed splendid action in reaching the dug-out.

Breathless and gasping, Dell and Joel each grasped a repeating rifle, while Sargent, in the excitement of the moment, unable to unearth the story, buckled on a six-shooter. The first reconnoitre revealed the Indians halted some two hundred yards distant, and parleying among themselves. At a first glance, the latter seemed to be unarmed, and on Sargent stepping outside the shack, the leader, the old brave, simply held up his hand.

"They must be peaceful Indians," said Sargent to the boys, and signaled in the leader.

The old Indian jogged forward on his tired pony, leaving his followers behind, and on riding up, a smile was noticeable on his wrinkled visage. He dismounted, unearthing from his scanty breech-clout a greasy, grimy letter, and tendered it to Sargent.

The latter scanned the missive, and turning to the boys, who had ventured forth, broke into a fit of laughter.

"Why, this is Chief Lone Wolf," said Sargent, "from the Pine Ridge Agency, going down to see his kinsfolks in the Indian Territory. The agent at Pine Ridge says that Lone Wolf is a peaceful Indian, and has his permission to leave the reservation. He hopes that nothing but kindness will be shown the old chief in his travels, and bespeaks the confidence of any white settlers that he may meet on the way. You boys must have been scared out of your wits. Lone Wolf only wanted to show you this letter."

Sargent conversed with the old chief in Spanish, the others were signaled in, when a regular powwow ensued. Dell and Joel shook hands with all the Indians, Sargent shared his tobacco with Lone Wolf, and on returning to their encampment at evening, each visitor was burdened with pickled beef and such other staples as the cow-camp afforded.

CHAPTER XX
HARVEST ON THE RANGE

Joel set out for the Republican the next morning and was gone four days. The beef ranches along the river had no men to spare, but constant inquiry was rewarded by locating an outfit whose holdings consisted of stock cattle. Three men were secured, their services not being urgently required on the home ranch until the fall branding, leaving only a cook and horse wrangler to be secured. Inquiry at Culbertson located a homesteader and his boy, anxious for work, and the two were engaged.

"They're to report here on the 15th," said Joel, on his return. "It gives us six men in the saddle, and we can get out the first shipment with that number. The cook and wrangler may be a little green at first, but they're willing, and that masters any task. We'll have to be patient with them – we were all beginners once. Any man who ever wrestled with a homestead ought to be able to cook."

"Yes, indeed," admitted Sargent. "There's nothing develops a man like settling up a new country. It brings out every latent quality. In the West you can almost tell a man's native heath by his ability to use baling wire, hickory withes, or rawhide."

The instinct of cattle is reliable in selecting their own range. Within a week, depending on the degree of maturity, the herd, with unerring nutrient results, turns from one species of grass to another. The double-wintered cattle naturally returned to their former range; but in order to quicken the work, any beeves of that class found below were drifted above headquarters. It was a distinct advantage to leave the herd undisturbed, and with the first shipment drifted to one end of the range, a small round-up or two would catch all marketable beeves.

The engaged men arrived on the appointed date. The cook and wrangler were initiated into their respective duties at once. The wagon was equipped for the trail, vicious horses were gentled, and an ample mount allotted to the extra men. The latter were delighted over the saddle stock, and mounted to satisfy every desire, no task daunted their numbers. Sargent was recognized as foreman; but as the work was fully understood, the concerted efforts of all relieved him of any concern, except in arranging the details. The ranch had fallen heir to a complete camp kit, with the new wagon, and with a single day's preparations, the shipping outfit stood ready to move on an hour's notice.

It was no random statement, on the part of the solicitor, that Wells Brothers could choose the day on which to market their beef. Sargent had figured out the time, either forced or leisurely, to execute a shipment, and was rather impatient to try out the outfit in actual field work.

"Suppose we break in the outfit," he suggested, "by taking a little swing around the range. It will gentle the horses, instruct the cook and wrangler, and give us all a touch of the real thing."

Joel consulted a calendar. "We have four days before beginning to gather beeves," he announced. "Let's go somewhere and camp."

"We'll move to the old trail crossing at sun-up," announced Sargent. "Roll your blankets in the morning, boys."

A lusty shout greeted the declaration. It was the opening of the beef-shipping season, the harvest time of the year, and the boys were impatient to begin the work. But the best-laid plans are often interrupted. That evening a courier reached headquarters, bearing a message from the commission firm which read, "Have your double-wintered beeves on Saturday's market."

"That's better," said Sargent, glancing over the telegram. "The wagon and remuda will start for Hackberry Grove at sun-up. Have the messenger order ten cars for Friday morning. The shipment will be on Saturday's market."

Dawn found the outfit at attention. Every movement was made with alacrity. Two men assisted a husky boy to corral the remuda, others harnessed in a span of mules, and before the sun peeped over the horizon, the cavalcade moved out up the valley, the courier returning to the station. The drag-net from below would be thrown out from the old winter corral; but as an hour's sun on the cattle rendered them lazy, half the horsemen halted until the other sighted the grove above. As early as advisable, the gradual circle was begun, turning the cattle into the valley, concentrating, and by slowly edging in, the first round-up of the day was thrown together, numbering, range run, fully six hundred head. Two men were detailed to hold the round-up compactly, Dell volunteered to watch the cut (the beeves selected), leaving the other three to cut out the marketable cattle which would make up the shipment. A short hour's work followed, resulting in eighty-odd beeves being selected. Flesh, age, and the brand governed each selection, and when cut into a class by themselves, the mettle of the pasture was reflected in every beef.

The cut was grazed up to the second round-up, which contributed nearly double the former number. On finishing the work, a count of the beeves was made, which overran in numbers the necessary shipment. They were extremely heavy cattle, twenty head to the car was the limit, and it became necessary to trim or cull back to the desired number. Sargent and Joel passed on every rejected beef, uniform weight being desirable, until the shipment stood acceptable, in numbers, form, and finish.

The beeves were watered and grazed out on their course without delay. Three days and a half were allowed to reach the railroad, and a grazing pace would land the herd in the shipping pens in good season. The day's work consisted in merely pointing and drifting the cattle forward, requiring only a few men, leaving abundant help to initiate the cook and wrangler in their field duties. Joel had been a close observer of the apparent ease with which a cook discharged his duty, frequently halting his wagon on a moment's notice, and easily preparing a meal for an outfit of trail men within an hour. The main secret lay in the foresight, in keeping his work in advance, and Joel lent every assistance in coaching his cook to meet the emergency of any demand.

Sargent took the wrangler in hand. The different bunches of horses had seen service on the trail, were gentle to handle, and attention was called to observing each individual horse and the remuda as a whole. For instance, in summer, a horse grazes against the breeze, and if the remuda was freed intelligently, at darkness, the wind holding from the same quarter during the night, a practical wrangler would know where to find his horses at dawn. The quarter of the breeze was therefore always noted, any variation after darkness, as if subject to the whim of the wind, turning the course of the grazing remuda. As among men, there were leaders among horses, and by noting these and applying hobbles, any inclination to wander was restrained. Fortunately, the husky boy had no fear of a horse, his approach being as masterly as his leave-taking was gentle and kindly – a rare gift when unhobbling alone in the open.

"I'll make a horse wrangler out of this boy," said Sargent to the father, in the presence of Dell and Joel. "Before the summer ends, he'll know every crook and turn in the remuda. There's nothing like knowing your horses. Learn to trail down the lost; know their spirit, know them in health, lame and wounded. If a horse neighs at night, know why; if one's missing in the morning, name him like you would an absent boy at school."

The trip down to the railroad was largely a matter of patience. The beeves were given every advantage, and except the loss of sleep in night-herding, the work approached loafing against time. Three guards stood watch during the short summer nights, pushing the herd off its bed at dawn, grazing early and late, and resting through the noon hours.

An agreeable surprise awaited the original trio. The evening before loading out, the beeves must be penned, and Joel rode into the station in advance, to see that cars were in waiting and get the shipping details. As if sent on the same errand, Manly met him, having been ordered on from Trail City.

"I've been burning the wires all morning," said he to Joel, "for a special train for this shipment. The agent wanted us to take a local freight from here, but I showed him there were other train shipments to follow. A telegram to the commission firm and another one to my old man done the work. Those old boys know how to pull the strings. A special train has been ordered, and you can name your own hour for leaving in the morning. I have a man with me; send us in horses and we'll help you corral your beeves."

Joel remained only long enough to confirm Manly's foresight. Two horses were sent in by Dell, and the welcome addition of two extra men joined the herd, which was easily corralled at dusk of evening. An early hour was agreed upon to load out, the empty train came in promptly, and the first shipment of the year was cut into car lots and loaded out during a morning hour.

Before the departure of the train, an air of activity was noticeable around the bleak station. The train crew was insisting for a passenger schedule, there was billing to be done and contracts to execute, telegrams of notification to be sent the commission firm, and general instructions to the beef outfit. Joel and Sargent were to accompany the shipment, and on starting, while the engineer and conductor were comparing their running orders, Sargent called out from the rear of the caboose: –

"The best of friends must part," said he, pretending to weep. "Here's two bits; buy yourself some cheese and crackers, and take some candy home to the children. Manly, if I never come back, you can have my little red wagon. Dell, my dear old bunkie – well, you can have all my other playthings."

The cattle train faded from sight and the outfit turned homeward. Horses were left at the station for Joel and Sargent, and the remainder of the outfit reached headquarters the following day. Manly had been away from the ranch nearly six months, and he and Dell rode the range, pending the return of the absent. Under ideal range conditions, the cattle of marketable age proved a revelation, having rounded into form beyond belief.

"That's why I love cattle," said Manly to Dell, while riding the range; "they never disappoint. Cattle endure time and season, with a hardiness that no other animal possesses. Given a chance, they repay every debt. Why, one shipment from these Stoddard cattle will almost wipe the slate. Uncle Dudley thought this was a fool deal, but Mr. Lovell seemed so bent on making it that my old man simply gave in. And now you're going to make a fortune out of these Lazy H's. No wonder us fool Texans love a cow."

The absent ones returned promptly. "The Beaver valley not only topped the market for range cattle," loftily said Sargent, "but topped it in price and weight. The beeves barely netted fifty-two dollars a head!"

Early shipments were urged from every quarter. "Hereafter," said Joel, "the commission firm will order the trains and send us a practical shipper. There may rise a situation that we may have to rush our shipments, and we can't spare men to go to market. It pays to be on time. Those commission men are wide awake. Look at these railroad passes, good for the year, that they secured for us boys. If any one has to go to market, we can take a passenger train, and leave the cattle to follow."

The addition of two men to the shipping outfit was a welcome asset. The first consignment from the ranch gave the men a field-trial, and now that the actual shipping season was at hand, an allotment of horses was made. The numbers of the remuda admitted of mounting every man to the limit, and with their first shipment a success, the men rested impatiently awaiting orders.

The commission firm, with its wide knowledge of range and market conditions, was constantly alert. The second order, of ten days' later date, was a duplicate of the first, with one less for fulfillment. The outfit dropped down to the old trail crossing the evening before, and by noon two round-ups had yielded twenty car-loads of straight Lazy H beeves. When trimmed to their required numbers, twenty-two to the car, they reflected credit to breeder and present owner.

In grazing down to the railroad, every hour counted. There was no apparent rush, but an hour saved at noon, an equal economy at evening and morning, brought the herd within summons of the shipping yards on time. That the beeves might be favored, they were held outside for the night, three miles from the corral, but an early sun found them safely inside the shipping pens. Two hours later, the full train was en route to market, in care of a practical shipper.

On yarding the beeves the customary telegram had been sent to the commission firm. No reply was expected, but within half an hour after the train left, a message, asking Joel to accompany the shipment, was received from Mr. Stoddard.

"You must go," said Manly, scanning the telegram. "It isn't the last cattle that he sold you that's worrying my boss. He has two herds on the market this year, one at Trail City and the other at Ogalalla, and he may have his eye on you as a possible buyer. You have a pass; you can catch the eastern mail at noon, and overtake the cattle train in time to see the beeves unloaded."

"Which herd did you come up with?" inquired Joel, fumbling through his pockets for the forgotten pass.

"With the one at Ogalalla. It's full thirty-one hundred steers, single ranch brand, and will run about equally twos and threes. Same range, same stock, as your Lazy H's, and you are perfectly safe in buying them unseen. Just the same cattle that you bought last year, with the advantage of a better season on the trail. All you need to do is to agree on the prices and terms; the cattle are as honest as gold and twice as good."

"Leave me a horse and take the outfit home," said Joel with decision. "If an order comes for more beeves, cut the next train from the Lazy H's. I'll be back in a day or two."

Joel Wells was rapidly taking his degrees in the range school. At dusk he overtook the cattle train, which reached the market yards on schedule time. The shipper's duty ceased with the unloading of the cattle, which was easily completed before midnight, when he and his employer separated. The market would not open until a late morning hour, affording ample time to rest and refresh the beeves, and to look up acquaintances in the office.

Joel had almost learned to dispense with sleep. With the first stir of the morning, he was up and about. Before the clerks even arrived, he was hanging around the office of the commission firm. The expected shipment brought the salesmen and members of the firm much earlier than usual, and Joel was saved all further impatience. Mr. Stoddard was summoned, and the last barrier was lifted in the hearty greeting between the manly boy and a veteran of their mutual occupation.

The shipment sold early in the day. An hour before noon, an interested party left the commission office and sauntered forth to watch the beeves cross the scale. It was the parting look of breeder, owner, and factor, and when the average weight was announced, Mr. Stoddard turned to the others.

"Look here, Mr. Joel," said he, "are these the cattle I sold you last summer?"

"They carry your brand," modestly admitted Joel.

"So I notice," assentingly said the old cowman. "And still I can scarcely believe my eyes. Of course I'm proud of having bred these beeves, even if the lion's share of their value to-day goes to the boys who matured them. I must be an old fogy."

"You are," smilingly said the senior member of the commission house. "Every up-to-date Texas cowman has a northern beef ranch. To be sure, as long as you can raise a steer as cheap as another man can raise a frying chicken, you'll prosper in a way. Wells Brothers aren't afraid of a little cold, and you are. In that way only, the lion's share falls to them."

"One man to his own farm, another to his merchandise," genially quoted the old cowman, "and us poor Texans don't take very friendly to your northern winters. It's the making of cattle, but excuse your Uncle Dudley. Give me my own vine and fig tree."

"Then wish the boys who brave the storm success," urged the old factor.

"I do," snorted the grizzled ranchman. "These beeves are a story that is told. I'm here to sell young Wells another herd of cattle. He's my customer as much as yours. That's the reason I urged his presence to-day."

The atmosphere cleared. On the market and under the weight, each beef was paying the cost of three the year before; but it was the letter of the bond, and each party to the contract respected his obligation.

After returning to the office, on a petty pretext, Mr. Stoddard and Joel wandered away. They returned early in the afternoon, to find all accounts made up, and ready for their personal approval. The second shipment easily enabled Joel to take up his contract, and when the canceled document was handed him, Mr. Stoddard turned to the senior member of the firm.

"I've offered to duplicate that contract," said he, "on the same price and terms, and for double the number of cattle. This quarantine raises havoc with delivery."

"A liberal interpretation of the new law is in effect," remarked the senior member. "There's too many interests involved to insist on a rigid enforcement. The ban is already raised on any Panhandle cattle, and any north of certain latitudes can get a clean bill of health. If that's all that stands in the way of a trade, our firm will use its good offices."

"In that case," said Joel, nodding to Mr. Stoddard, "we'll take your herd at Ogalalla. Move it down to the old trail crossing on the Republican, just over the state line and north of our range. This firm is perfectly acceptable again as middlemen or factors," he concluded, turning to the member present.

"Thank you," said the old factor. "We'll try and merit any confidence reposed. This other matter will be taken up with the quarantine authorities at once. Show me your exact range," he requested, turning to a map and indicating the shipping station.

Wells Brothers' range lay in the northwest corner of the state. The Republican River, in Nebraska, ran well over the line to the north, with unknown neighbors on the west in Colorado.

"It's a clear field," observed the old factor. "Your own are the only cattle endangered, and since you are the applicant for the bill of health, you absolve the authorities from all concern. Hurry in your other shipments, and the railroad can use its influence – it'll want cattle to ship next year. The ranges must be restocked."

There was sound logic in the latter statement. A telegram was sent to Ogalalla, to start the through herd, and another to the beef outfit, to hurry forward the next shipment. Joel left for home that night, and the next evening met his outfit, ten miles out from the Beaver, with a perfect duplicate of the former consignment. It was early harvest on the cattle ranges, and those who were favored with marketable beef were eager to avoid the heavy rush of fall shipments.

The beef herd camped for the night on the divide. Joel's report provoked argument, and a buzz of friendly contention, as the men lounged around the tiny camp-fire, ran through the outfit.

"It may be the custom among you Texans," protested one of the lads from the Republican, "but I wouldn't buy a herd of cattle without seeing them. Buy three thousand head of cattle unseen? Not this one of old man Vivian's boys! Oh, no!"

"Link, that kind of talk shows your raising," replied Sargent. "Your view is narrow and illiberal. You haven't traveled far. Your tickets cost somewhere between four and six bits."

Manly lifted his head from a saddle, and turning on his side, gazed at the dying fire. "Vivian," said he, "it all depends on how your folks bring you up. Down home we buy and sell by ages. A cow is a cow, a steer is a steer, according to his age, and so on down to the end of the alphabet. The cattle never misrepresent and there's no occasion for seeing them. If you are laboring under the idea that my old man would use any deception to sell a herd, you have another guess coming. He'd rather lose his right hand than to misrepresent the color of a cow. He's as jealous of his cattle as a miller is of his flour. These boys are his customers, last fall, this summer, and possibly for years to come. If he wanted them, Joel did perfectly right to buy the cattle unseen."

The second train of Lazy H beeves reached the railroad on schedule time. The shipper was in waiting, cattle cars filled the side track, and an engine and crew could be summoned on a few hours' notice. If corralled the night before, passing trains were liable to excite the beeves, and thereafter it became the usual custom to hold outside and safely distant.

The importance of restocking the range hurried the shipping operations. Instead of allowing the wagon to reach the station, at sunrise on the morning of shipping, it and the remuda were started homeward.

"We'll gather beeves on the lower end of our range to-morrow," said Joel to the cook and wrangler, "and there's no need to touch at headquarters. Follow the trail to the old crossing, and make camp at the lower tank – same camp-ground as the first shipment of Lazy H's. The rest of the outfit will follow, once these cattle are loaded out. You might have a late supper awaiting us – about ten o'clock to-night."

The gates closed on the beeves without mishap. They were cut into car lots, from horseback, and on the arrival of the crew, the loading began. A short hour's work saw the cattle aboard, when the dusty horsemen mounted and clattered into the straggling hamlet.

The homeward trip was like a picnic. The outfit halted on the first running water, and saddle pockets disgorged a bountiful lunch. The horses rolled, grazed the noon hours through, and again took up their former road gait. An evening halt was made on the Prairie Dog, where an hour's grazing was again allowed, the time being wholly devoted to looking into the future.

"If we stock the range fully this fall," said Joel, in outlining his plans, "it is my intention to build an emergency camp on this creek, in case of winter drifts. Build a dug-out in some sheltered nook, cache a little provision and a few sacks of corn, and if the cattle break the line, we can ride out of snug quarters any morning and check them. It beats waiting for a wagon and giving the drift a twenty-mile start. We could lash our blankets on a pack horse and ride it night or day."

"What a long head!" approvingly said Sargent. "Joel, you could almost eat out of a churn. An emergency camp on the Prairie Dog is surely a meaty idea. But that's for next winter, and beef shipping's on in full blast right now. Let's ride; supper's waiting on the Beaver."

CHAPTER XXI
LIVING IN THE SADDLE

The glow of a smouldering camp-fire piloted the returning horsemen safely to their wagon. A good night's rest fitted them for the task of the day, which began at sunrise. The next shipment would come from the flotsam of the year before, many of which were heavy beeves, intended for army delivery, but had fallen footsore on the long, drouthy march. The past winter had favored the lame and halt, and after five months of summer, the bulk of them had matured into finished beef.

By shipping the different contingents separately, the brothers were enabled to know the situation at all times. No accounts were kept, but had occasion required, either Joel or Dell could have rendered a statement from memory of returns on the double and single wintered, as well as on the purchased cattle. Sale statements were furnished by the commission house, and by filing these, an account of the year's shipments, each brand separate, could be made up at the end of the season.

The early struggle of Wells Brothers, in stocking their range, was now happily over. Instead of accepting the crumbs which fell as their portion, their credit and resources enabled them to choose the class of cattle which promised growth and quick returns. The range had proven itself in maturing beef, and the ranch thereafter would carry only sufficient cows to quiet and pacify its holdings of cattle.

"If this was my ranch," said Sargent to the brothers at breakfast, "I'd stock it with two-year-old steers and double-winter every hoof. Look over those sale statements and you'll see what two winters mean. That first shipment of Lazy H's was as fat as mud, and yet they netted seven dollars a head less than those rag-tag, double-wintered ones. There's a waste that must be saved hereafter."

"That's our intention," said Joel. "We'll ship out every hoof that has the flesh this year. Nearly any beef will buy three two-year-old steers to take his place. It may take another year or two to shape up our cattle, but after that, every hoof must be double-wintered."

An hour after sunrise, the drag-net was drawing together the first round-up of the day. The importance of handling heavy beeves without any excitement was fully understood, and to gather a shipment without disturbing those remaining was a task that required patience and intelligence. Men on the outside circle merely turned the cattle on the extremes of the range; they were followed by inner horsemen, and the drag-net closed at a grazing pace, until the round-up halted on a few acres.

The first three shipments had tried out the remuda. The last course in the education of a cow-horse is cutting cattle out of a mixed round-up. On the present work, those horses which had proven apt were held in reserve, and while the first contingent of cattle was quieting down, the remuda was brought up and saddles shifted to four cutting horses. The average cow can dodge and turn quicker than the ordinary horse, and only a few of the latter ever combine action and intelligence to outwit the former. Cunning and ingenuity, combined with the required alertness, a perfect rein, coupled with years of actual work, produce that rarest of range mounts – the cutting horse.

Dell had been promised a trial in cutting out beeves. Sargent took him in hand, and mounted on two picked horses, they entered the herd. "Now, I'll pick the beeves," said the latter, "and you cut them out. All you need to do is to rein that horse down on your beef, and he'll take him out of the herd. Of course you'll help the horse some little; but if you let too many back, I'll call our wrangler and try him out. That horse knows the work just as well as you do. Now, go slow, and don't ride over your beef."

The work commenced. The beeves were lazy from flesh, inactive, and only a few offered any resistance to the will of the horsemen. Dell made a record of cutting out fifty beeves in less than an hour, and only letting one reënter the herd. The latter was a pony-built beef, and after sullenly leaving the herd, with the agility of a cat, he whirled right and left on the space of a blanket, and beat the horse back into the round-up. Sargent lent a hand on the second trial, and when the beef saw that resistance was useless, he kicked up his heels and trotted away to join those selected for shipment.

"He's laughing at you," said Sargent. "He only wanted to try you out. Just wanted to show you that no red-headed boy and flea-bit horse could turn him. And he showed you."

"This beats roping," admitted Dell, as the two returned to the herd, quite willing to change the subject. "Actually when a beef reaches the edge of the herd, this horse swells up and his eyes pop out like door-knobs. You can feel every muscle in him become as rigid as ropes, and he touches the ground as if he was walking on eggs. Look at him now; goes poking along as if he was half asleep."

"He's a cutting horse and doesn't wear himself out. Whenever you can strip the bridle off, while cutting out a beef, and handle your steer, that's the top rung a cow-horse can reach. He's a king pin – that's royalty."

A second round-up was required to complete the train-load of beeves. They were not uniform in weight or age, and would require reclassing before loading aboard the cars. Their flesh and finish were fully up to standard, but the manner in which they were acquired left them uneven, their ages varying from four to seven years.

"There's velvet in this shipment," said Sargent, when the beeves had been counted and trimmed. "These cattle can defy competition. Instead of five cents a head for watering last year's drive, this year's shipment from crumbs will net you double that amount. The first gathering of beef will square the account with every thirsty cow you watered last summer."

An extra day was allowed in which to reach the railroad. The shipment must pen the evening before, and halting the herd within half a mile of the railway corrals, the reclassing fell to Joel and Sargent. The contingent numbered four hundred and forty beeves, and in order to have them marketable, all rough, heavy cattle must be cut into a class by themselves, leaving the remainder neat and uniform. A careful hour's work resulted in seven car-loads of extra heavy beeves, which were corralled separately and in advance of the others, completing a long day in the saddle.

Important mail was awaiting Wells Brothers at the station. A permit from the state quarantine authorities had been secured, due to the influence of the commission house and others, admitting the through herd, then en route from Ogalalla. The grant required a messenger to meet the herd without delay, and Dell volunteered his services as courier. Darkness fell before supper was over and the messenger ready.

"One more shipment will clean up our beeves," said Joel to his brother, "and those through cattle can come in the day we gather our last train. We'll give them a clear field. If the herd hasn't reached the Republican, push ahead until you meet it."

A hundred-mile ride lay before Dell Wells. "You mean for the herd to follow the old trail," he inquired, "and turn off opposite our middle tank?"

"That's it; and hold the cattle under herd until we can count and receive them."

Dell led out his horse and mounted. "Dog-toe will take me safely home to-night," said he, "and we'll reach the Republican by noon to-morrow. If the herd's there, you haven't an hour to waste. We'll drop down on you in a day and a half."

The night received courier and horse. A clatter of caution and advice followed the retreating figure out of hearing, when the others threw themselves down around the camp-fire. Early morning found the outfit astir, and as on the previous occasion, the wagon and remuda were started home at daybreak. The loading and shipping instructions were merely a repetition of previous consignments, and the train had barely left the station when the cavalcade rode to overtake the commissary.

The wagon was found encamped on the Prairie Dog. An hour's rest was allowed, fresh horses were saddled, when Joel turned to the cook and wrangler: "Make camp to-night on the middle tank, below headquarters. We'll ride on ahead and drift all the cattle up the creek. Our only round-up to-morrow will be well above the old winter corral. It's our last gathering of beef, and we want to make a general round-up of the range. We'll drift cattle until dark, so that it'll be late when we reach camp."

The outfit of horsemen followed the old trail, and only sighted the Beaver late in the afternoon. The last new tank, built that spring, was less than a mile below the old crossing; and veering off there, the drag-net was thrown across the valley below it, and a general drift begun. An immense half-circle, covering the limits of the range, pointed the cattle into the valley, and by moving forward and converging as the evening advanced, a general drift was maintained. The pace was barely that of grazing, and as darkness approached, all cattle on the lower end of the range were grazed safely above the night camp and left adrift.

The wagon had arrived, and the men reached camp by twos and threes. There was little danger of the cattle returning to their favorite range during the night, but for fear of stragglers, at an early hour in the morning the drag-net was again thrown out from camp. Headquarters was passed before the horsemen began encountering any quantity of cattle, and after passing the old winter corral, the men on the points of the half-circle were sent to ride the extreme limits of the range. By the middle of the forenoon, everything was adrift, and as the cattle naturally turned into the valley for their daily drink, a few complete circles brought the total herd into a general round-up, numbering over fifteen hundred head of mixed cattle.

Meanwhile the wagon and remuda had followed up the drift, dinner was waiting, and after the mid-day meal had been bolted, orders rang out. "Right here's where all hands and the cook draw fresh horses," said Sargent, "and get into action. It's a bulky herd, and cutting out will be slow. The cook and wrangler must hold the beeves, and that will turn the rest of us free to watch the round-up and cut out."

By previous agreement, in order to shorten the work, Joel was to cut out the remnant of double-wintered beeves, Manly the Lazy H's, while Sargent and an assistant would confine their selections to the single-wintered ones in the – – Y brand. Each man would tally his own work, even car-loads were required, and a total would constitute the shipment. The cutting out began quietly; but after a nucleus of beeves were selected, their numbers gained at the rate of three to five a minute, while the sweat began to reek from the horses.

Joel cut two car-loads of prime beeves, and then tendered his services to Sargent. The cattle had quieted, and a fifth man was relieved from guarding the round-up, and sent to the assistance of Manly. A steady stream of beef poured out for an hour, when a comparison of figures was made. Manly was limited to one hundred and twenty head, completing an even thousand shipped from the brand, and lacking four, was allowed to complete his number. Sargent was without limit, the object being to trim the general herd of every heavy, rough beef, and a tally on numbers was all that was required. The work was renewed with tireless energy, and when the limit of twenty cars was reached, a general conference resulted in cutting two loads extra.

"That leaves the home cattle clean of rough stuff," said Sargent, as he dismounted and loosened the saddle on a tired horse. "Any aged steers left are clean thrifty cattle, and will pay their way to hold another year. Turn the round-up adrift."

After blowing their horses, a detail of men drifted the general herd up the creek. Others lent their assistance to the wrangler in corralling his remuda, and after relieving the cutting horses, the beeves were grazed down the valley. The outfit had not spent a night at headquarters in some time, the wagon serving as a substitute, and orders for evening freed all hands except two men on herd with the beeves.

The hurry of the day was over. On securing fresh horses, Joel and Sargent turned to the assistance of the detail, then drifting the main herd westward. The men were excused, to change mounts, and relieved from further duty until the guards, holding the beeves, were arranged for the night. The remnant of the herd was pushed up the creek and freed near Hackberry Grove, and on returning to overtake the beeves, the two horsemen crossed a spur of the tableland, jutting into the valley, affording a perfect view of the surrounding country.

With the first sweep of the horizon, their horses were reined to a halt. Fully fifteen miles to the northeast, and in a dip of the plain, hung an ominous dust cloud. Both horsemen read the sign at a glance.

Sargent was the first to speak. "Dell met the herd on the Republican," said he with decision. "It's the Stoddard cattle from Ogalalla. The pitch of their dust shows they're trailing south."

The sign in the sky was read correctly. The smoke from a running train and the dust from a trailing herd, when viewed from a distance, pitches upward from a horizon line, and the moving direction of train or herd is easily read by an observant plainsman. Sargent's summary was confirmed on reaching headquarters, where Dell and the trail foreman were found, the latter regaling Manly and others with the chronicle of the new trail.

The same foreman as the year before was in charge of the herd. He protested against any step tending to delivery for that day, even to looking the cattle over. "Uncle Dud wouldn't come," said he, "and it's up to me to make the delivery. I've been pioneering around all summer with this herd, and now that I'm my own boss, I'll take orders from no one. We made rather a forced drive from the Republican, and I want a good night's rest for both the herd and myself. Ten o'clock in the morning will be early enough to tender the cattle for delivery. In the mean time, our pilot, the red-headed clerk, will answer all questions. As for myself, I'm going to sleep in the new tent, and if any one calls or wakes me in the morning, I'll get up and wear him out. I've lost a right smart of sleep this summer, and I won't stand no trifling."

Joel fully understood that the object in delay was to have the herd in presentable condition, and offered no objection. The beeves were grazed up opposite headquarters, and the guards were arranged for the night, which passed without incident. Thereafter, as a matter of precaution, a dead-line must be maintained between the wintered and the through cattle; and as Manly was to remain another year, he and an assistant were detailed to stay at headquarters. A reduced mount of horses was allowed them, and starting the beeves at daybreak, the wagon and remuda followed several hours later.

The trail foreman was humored in his wishes. It was nearly noon when the through herd was reached, grazed and watered to surfeiting, and a single glance satisfied Joel Wells that the cattle fully met every requirement. The question of age was disposed of as easily as that of quality.

"We gathered this year's drive on our home ranges," said the foreman, "and each age was held separate until the herds were made up. I started with fifteen hundred threes and sixteen hundred twos, with ten head extra of each age, in case of loss on the trail. Our count on leaving Ogalalla showed a loss of twelve head. I'm willing to class or count them as they run. Manly knows the make-up of the herd."

Sargent and the brothers rode back and forth through the scattered cattle. It meant a big saving of time to accept them on a straight count, and on being rejoined by the foreman, Joel waived his intent to classify the cattle.

"I bought this herd on Mr. Stoddard's word," said he, "and I'm going to class it on yours. String out your cattle, and you and Manly count against Sargent and myself."

A correct count on a large herd is no easy task. In trailing formation, the cattle march between a line of horsemen, but in the open the difficulty is augmented. A noonday sun lent its assistance in quieting the herd, which was shaped into an immense oval, and the count attempted. The four men elected to make the count cut off a number of the leaders, and counting them, sent them adrift. Thereafter, the trail outfit fed the cattle between the quartette, who sat their horses in speechless intensity, as the column filed through at random. Each man used a string, containing ten knots, checking the hundreds by slipping the knots, and when the last hoof had passed in review, the quiet of a long hour was relieved by a general shout, when the trail outfit dashed up to know the result.

"How many strays have you?" inquired Sargent of the foreman, as the quartette rode together.

"That's so; there's a steer and a heifer; we'll throw them in for good measure. What's your count?"

"Minus the strays, mine repeats yours at Ogalalla," answered Sargent, turning to Joel.

"Thirty-one hundred and ten," said the boy.

The trail foreman gave vent to a fit of laughter. "Young fellow," said he, "I never allow no man to outdo me in politeness. If you bought these cattle on my old man's word, I want you to be safe in receiving them. We'll class them sixteen hundred twos, and fifteen hundred threes, and any overplus falls to the red-headed pilot. That's about what Uncle Dud would call a Texas count and classification. Shake out your horses; dinner's waiting."

There were a few details to arrange. Manly must have an assistant, and an extra man was needed with the shipment, both of whom volunteered from the through outfit. The foreman was invited to move up to headquarters and rest to his heart's content, but in his anxiety to report to his employer, the invitation was declined.

"We'll follow up to-morrow," said he, "and lay over on the railroad until you come in with our beeves. The next hard work I do is to get in touch with my Uncle Dudley."

"Look here – how about it – when may we expect you home?" sputtered Manly, as the others hurriedly made ready to overtake the beef herd.

"When you see us again," answered Joel, mounting his horse. "If this shipment strikes a good market, we may drop down to Trail City and pick up another herd. It largely depends on our bank account. Until you see or hear from us, hold the dead-line and locate your cattle."

CHAPTER XXII
INDEPENDENCE

The trail outfit reached the railroad a day in advance of the beeves. Shipping orders were sent to the station agent in advance, and on the arrival of the herd the two outfits made short shift in classifying it for market and corralling the different grades of cattle.

Mr. Stoddard had been located at Trail City. Once the shipment was safely within the corral, notice was wired the commission firm, affording time for reply before the shipment would leave in the morning. An early call at the station was rewarded by receipt of a wire from the west. "Read that," said the foreman, handing the telegram to Joel; "wants all three of us to come into the city."

"Of course," commented Joel, returning the message. "It's clear enough. There's an understanding between us. At the earliest convenience, after the delivery of the herd, we were to meet and draw up the final papers. We'll all go in with this shipment."

"And send the outfits across country to Trail City?"

"Throw the remudas together and let them start the moment the cattle train leaves. We can go back with Mr. Stoddard and meet the outfits at the new trail market."

"That's the ticket," said the trail boss. "I'm dead tired of riding horses and eating at a wagon. Give me the plush cushions and let me put my little feet under a table once more."

The heavy cattle train was promised a special schedule. The outfits received their orders, and at the usual hour in the morning, the shipment started to market. Weathered brown as a saddle, Dell was walking on clouds, lending a hand to the shipper in charge, riding on the engine, or hungering for the rare stories with which the trail foreman regaled the train crew. The day passed like a brief hour, the train threading its way past corn fields, country homes, and scorning to halt at the many straggling villages that dotted the route.

It was a red-letter day in the affairs of Wells Brothers. The present, their fifth shipment of the year, a total of over nineteen hundred beeves, was en route to market. Another day, and their operations in cattle, from a humble beginning to the present hour, could be condensed into a simple statement. The brothers could barely wait the intervening hours, and when the train reached the market and they had retired for the night, speculation ran rife in planning the future. And amid all their dreams and air castles, in the shadowy background stood two simple men whose names were never mentioned except in terms of loving endearment.

Among their many friends, Quince Forrest was Dell's hero. "They're all good fellows," he admitted, "but Mr. Quince is a prince. He gave us our start in cattle. Our debt to him – well, we can never pay it. And he never owned a hoof himself."

"We owe Mr. Paul just as much," protested Joel. "He showed us our chance. When pa died, the settlers on the Solomon talked of making bound boys of us. Mr. Paul was the one who saw us as we are to-day."

"I wish mother could have lived to see us now – shipping beeves by the train-load – and buying cattle by the thousand."

An eager market absorbed the beeves, and before noon they had crossed the scale. A conference, jubilant in its nature, took place during the afternoon, in the inner office of the commission firm. The execution of a new contract was a mere detail; but when the chief bookkeeper handed in a statement covering the shipments of this and the previous year, a lull in the gayety was followed by a moment of intense interest. The account showed a balance of sixty-odd thousand dollars in favor of Wells Brothers!

"Give them a letter of credit for their balance," said Mr. Stoddard, amid the general rejoicing. "And get us some passes; we're all going out to Trail City to-night. There's a few bargains on that market, and the boys want to stock their range fully."

"Yours obediently," said the old factor, beaming on his patrons. "And if the boys have any occasion to use any further funds, don't hesitate to draw on us. The manner in which they have protected their credit entitles them to our confidence. Our customers come first. Their prosperity is our best asset. A great future lies before you boys, and we want a chance to help you reach it. Keep in touch with us; we may hear of something to your advantage."

"In case we need it, can you get us another permit to bring Texas cattle into Kansas?" eagerly inquired Joel.

"Try us," answered the old man, with a knowing look. "We may not be able to, but in securing business, railroads look years ahead."

A jolly party of cowmen left for Trail City that night. Morning found their train creeping up the valley of the Arkansas. The old trail market of Dodge, deserted and forlorn-looking among the wild sunflower, was passed like a way station. The new market was only a mile over the state line, in Colorado, and on nearing their destination the party drew together.

"I've only got a remnant of a herd left," said Mr. Stoddard, "and I want you to understand that there's no obligation to even look at them. Mr. Lovell's at his beef ranch in Dakota, and his men have not been seen since the herds passed north in June. But I'll help you buy any cattle you want."

In behalf of the brothers, Joel accepted the offer. "These Texas cattle," he continued, "reach their maturity the summer following their fourth year. Hereafter, as fast as possible, we want to shape up our holdings so as to double-winter all our beef cattle. For that reason, we prefer to buy two-year-olds. We'll look at your remnant; there would be no occasion to rebrand, which is an advantage."

The train reached Trail City on time. The town was of mushroom growth – a straggling business street with fancy fronts, while the outer portions of the village were largely constructed of canvas. The Arkansas River passed to the south, numerous creeks put in to the main stream, affording abundant water to the herds on sale, while a bountiful range surrounded the market. Shipping pens, branding chutes, and every facility for handling cattle were complete.

The outfits were not expected in for another day. In the mean time, it became rumored about that the two boys who had returned with Mr. Stoddard and his trail foreman were buyers for a herd of cattle. The presence of the old cowman threw a barrier of protection around the brothers, except to his fellow drovers, who were made acquainted with his protégés and their errand freely discussed.

"These boys are customers of mine," announced Mr. Stoddard to a group of his friends. "I sold them a herd at Dodge last year, and another at Ogalalla this summer. Range on the Beaver, in northwest Kansas. Just shipped out their last train of beeves this week. Had them on yesterday's market. From what I gather, they can use about three thousand to thirty-five hundred head. At least their letter of credit is good for those numbers. Sorry I ain't got the cattle myself. They naturally look to me for advice, and I feel an interest in the boys. Their outfit ought to be in by to-morrow."

Mr. Stoddard's voucher placed the brothers on a firm footing, and every attention was shown the young cowmen. An afternoon and a morning's drive, and the offerings on the trail market had been carefully looked over, including the remnant of Mr. Stoddard. Only a few herds possessed their original numbers, none of which were acceptable to the buyers, while the smaller ones frequently contained the desired grade and age.

"Let me put you boys in possession of some facts," urged Mr. Stoddard, in confidence to the brothers. "Most of us drovers are tired out, disgusted with the slight demand for cattle, and if you'll buy out our little remnants and send us home – well, we'd almost let you name the price. Unless my herds are under contract, this is my last year on the trail."

The remnant of Mr. Stoddard's herd numbered around seven hundred head. They were largely twos, only a small portion of threes, and as an inducement their owner offered to class them at the lesser age, and priced them at the same figures as those delivered on the Beaver. On range markets, there was a difference in the selling value of the two ages, amounting to three dollars a head; and as one third of the cattle would have classed as threes, Joel waived his objection to their ages.

"We'll take your remnant on one condition," said he. "Start your outfits home, but you hang around until we make up our herd."

"That's my intention, anyhow," replied Mr. Stoddard. "My advice would be to pick up these other remnants. Two years on a steer makes them all alike. You have seen cripple and fagged cattle come out of the kinks, and you know the advantage of a few cows; keeps your cattle quiet and on the home range. You might keep an eye open for any bargains in she stuff."

"That's just what Jack Sargent says," said Dell; "that we ought to have a cow to every ten or fifteen steers."

"Sargent's our foreman," explained Joel. "He's a Texan, and knows cattle right down to the split in their hoof. With his and your judgment, we ought to make up a herd of cattle in a few days."

The two outfits came in on the evening of the fourth day. The next morning the accepted cattle were counted and received, the through outfits relieved, the remudas started overland under a detail, and the remainder of the men sent home by rail. In acquiring a nucleus, Wells Brothers fell heir to a temporary range and camp, which thereafter became their headquarters.

A single day was wasted in showing the different remnants to Sargent, and relieved of further concern, Mr. Stoddard lent his best efforts to bring buyer and seller together. Barter began in earnest, on the different fragments acceptable in age and quality. Prices on range cattle were nearly standard, at least established for the present, and any yielding on the part of drovers was in classing and conceding ages. Bargaining began on the smaller remnants, and once the buyers began to receive and brand, there was a flood of offerings, and the herd was made up the second day. The – – Y was run on the different remnants as fast as received, and when completed, the herd numbered a few over thirty-four hundred head. The suggestion to add cows to their holdings was not overlooked, and in making up the herd, two fragments, numbering nearly five hundred, were purchased.

"The herd will be a trifle unwieldy," admitted Sargent, "but we're only going to graze home. And unless we get a permit, we had better hold over the line in Colorado until after the first frost."

"Don't worry about the permit," admonished Mr. Stoddard; "it's sure."

"We'll provision the wagon for a month," said Joel, "and that will take us home, with or without a bill of health."

The commissary was stocked, three extra men were picked up, and the herd started northward over the new Ogalalla trail. A week later it crossed the Kansas Pacific Railroad, when Joel left the herd, returning to their local station. A haying outfit was engaged, placed under the direction of Manly, and after spending a few days at headquarters, the young cowman returned to the railroad.

The expected permit was awaiting him. There was some slight danger in using it, without first removing their wintered cattle; and after a conference with Manly, it was decided to scout out the country between their range and the Colorado line. The first herd of cattle had located nicely, one man being sufficient to hold the dead-line; and taking a pack horse, Joel and Manly started to explore the country between the upper tributaries of the Beaver and the Colorado line.

A rifle was taken along to insure venison. Near the evening of the first day, a band of wild horses was sighted, the trail of which was back-tracked to a large lake in the sand hills. On resuming their scout in the morning, sand dunes were scaled, admitting of an immense survey of country, but not until evening was water in any quantity encountered. The scouts were beginning to despair of finding water for the night, when an immense herd of antelope was sighted, crossing the plain at an easy gallop and disappearing among the dunes. Following up the game trail, a perfect chain of lakes, a mile in length, was found at sunset. A venison was shot and a fat camp for the night assured.

The glare of the plain required early observation. The white haze, heat waves, and mirages were on every hand, blotting out distinct objects during the day. On leaving the friendly sand hills, the horsemen bore directly for the timber on the Republican, which was sighted the third morning, and reached the river by noon.

No sign or trace of cattle was seen. The distance between the new and old trail was estimated at one hundred miles, and judging from their hours in the saddle, the scouts hoped to reach the new crossing on the river that evening. The mid-day glare prevented observations; and as they followed the high ground along the Republican, at early evening indistinct objects were made out on the border of a distant mirage.

The scouts halted their horses. On every hand might be seen the optical illusions of the plain. Beautiful lakes, placid and blue, forests and white-capped mountains, invited the horsemen to turn aside and rest. But the allurement of the mirage was an old story, and holding the objects in view, they jogged on, halting from time to time as the illusions lifted.

Mirages arise at evening. At last, in their normal proportions, the objects of concern moved to and fro. "They're cattle!" shouted Manly. "We're near a ranch, or it's the herd!"

"Yonder's a smoke-cloud!" excitedly said Joel. "See it! in the valley! above that motte of cotton-woods!"

"It's a camp! Come on!"

The herd had every appearance of being under control. As the scouts advanced, the outline of an immense loose herd was noticeable, and on a far, low horizon, a horseman was seen on duty. On reaching the cattle, a single glance was given, when the brands told the remainder of the story.

A detail of men was met leaving camp. Sargent was among them, and after hearty greetings were over, Joel outlined the programme: "After leaving the Republican," said he, "there's water between here and home in two places. None of them are over thirty miles apart – a day and a half's drive. I have a bill of health for these cattle, and turn the herd down the river in the morning."

The new trail crossing was only a few miles above on the river. The herd had arrived three days before, and finding grass and water in abundance, the outfit had gone into camp, awaiting word from home. There was no object in waiting any great distance from headquarters, and after a day's travel down the Republican, a tack was made for the sand hills.

A full day's rest was allowed the herd on the chain of lakes. By watering early, a long drive was made during the afternoon, followed by a dry camp, and the lagoon where the wild horses had been sighted was reached at evening the next day.

It was yet early in September, and for fear of fever, it was decided to isolate the herd until after the first frost. The camp was within easy touch of headquarters; and leaving Sargent and five men, the commissary, and half the remuda, the remainder returned to the Beaver valley. The water would hold the cattle, and even if a month elapsed before frost lifted the ban, the herd would enjoy every freedom.

The end of the summer's work was in sight. The men from the Republican were paid for their services, commended for their faithfulness, and went their way. Preparations for winter were the next concern; and while holding the dead-line, plans for two new line-camps were outlined, one below the old trail crossing and the other an emergency shelter on the Prairie Dog. Forage had been provided at both points, and in outlining the winter lines, Joel submitted his idea for Manly's approval.

"Sargent thinks we can hold the cattle on twenty miles of the Beaver valley," said he, sketching the range on the ground at his feet. "We'll have to ride lines again, and in case the cattle break through during a storm, we can work from our emergency camp on the Prairie Dog. In case that line is broken, we can drop down to the railroad and make another attempt to check any drift. And as a last resort, whether we hold the line or not, we'll send an outfit as far south as the Arkansas River, and attend the spring round-ups from there north to the Republican. We have the horses and men, and no one can throw out a wider drag-net than our outfit. Let the winter come as it will; we can ride to the lead when spring comes."

The future of Wells Brothers rested on sure foundations. Except in its new environment, their occupation was as old as the human race, our heroes being merely players in a dateless drama. They belonged to a period in the development of our common country, dating from a day when cattle were the corner-stone of one fourth of our national domain. They and their kind were our pioneers, our empire builders; for when a cowman pushed into some primal valley and possessed it with his herd, his ranch became an outpost on our frontier. The epoch was truly Western; their ranges were controlled without investment, their cattle roamed the virgin pastures of an unowned land.

Over twenty-five years have passed since an accident changed the course of the heroes of this story. Since that day of poverty and uncertain outlook, the brothers have been shaken by adversity, but have arisen triumphant over every storm. From their humble beginning, chronicled here, within two decades the brothers acquired no less than seven ranches in the Northwest, while their holdings of cattle often ran in excess of one hundred thousand head. The trail passed away within two years of the close of this narrative; but from their wide acquaintance with former drovers, cattle with which to restock their ranches were brought north by rail. Their operations covered a wide field, requiring trusty men; and with the passing of the trail, their first sponsors found ready employment with their former protégés. And to-day, in the many irrigation projects of the brothers, in reclaiming the arid regions, among the directors of their companies the names of J.Q. Forrest and John P. Priest may be found.

A new generation now occupies the Beaver valley. In the genesis of the West, the cowman, the successor of the buffalo and Indian, gave way to the home-loving instinct of man. The sturdy settler crept up the valley, was repulsed again and again by the plain, only to renew his assault until success crowned his efforts. It was then that the brothers saw their day and dominion passing into the hands of another. But instead of turning to new fields, they remained with the land that nurtured and rewarded them, an equally promising field opening in financing vast irrigation enterprises and in conserving the natural water supply.

Joel and Dell Wells live in the full enjoyment of fortunes wrested from the plain. They are still young men, in the prime of life, while the opportunities of a thrifty country invite their assistance and leadership on every hand. They are deeply interested in every development of their state, preferring those avenues where heroic endeavor calls forth their best exertion, save in the political arena.

Joel Wells was recently mentioned as an acceptable candidate for governor of his adopted state, but declined, owing to the pressure of personal interests. In urging his nomination, a prominent paper, famed for its support of state interests, in a leading editorial, paid one of our heroes the following tribute: –

"...What the state needs is a business man in the executive chair. We are all stockholders in common, yet the ship of state seems adrift, without chart or compass, pilot or captain. In casting about for a governor who would fully meet all requirements, one name stands alone. Joel Wells can give M – – a business administration. Educated in the rough school of experience, he has fought his way up from a poor boy on the plains to an enviable leadership in the many industries of the state. He could bring to the executive office every requirement of the successful business man, and impart to his administration that mastery which marks every enterprise of Wells Brothers...."

The golden age is always with us. If a moral were necessary to adorn this story, it would be that no poor boy need despair of his chance in life. The future holds as many prizes as the past. Material nature is prodigal in its bounty, and whether in the grass under our feet, or in harnessing the waterfall, we make or mar our success.